Three Complete Novels

KATHERINE STONE

Three Complete Novels

KATHERINE STONE

LOVE SONGS

BEL AIR

THE CARLTON CLUB

WINGS BOOKS
New York · Avenel, New Jersey

This omnibus was originally published in separate volumes under the titles:

This edition contains the complete and unabridged texts of the original editions. They have been completely reset for this volume.

This 1994 edition is published by Wings Books,
distributed by Random House Value Publishing, Inc.,
40 Engelhard Avenue, Avenel, New Jersey 07001,
by arrangement with Zebra Books, an imprint of Kensington
Publishing Corp.

Random House
New York • Toronto • London • Sydney • Auckland

Book Design by Kathryn W. Plosica

Printed and bound in the United States of America

Library of Congress Cataloging-in-Publication Data

Stone, Katherine M.
[Novels, Selections]
Katherine Stone : three complete novels.
p. cm.
Contents: Love songs—Bel Air—The Carlton club.
ISBN 0–517–10115–7
1. Man-woman relationships—United States—Fiction. 2. Women—United States—Fiction 3. Love stories, American. I. Title.
PS3569.T64134A6 1994
813′.54—dc20 93-42259
CIP

8 7 6 5 4 3 2 1

Contents

Love Songs

Part One

Chapter 1

SOUTHAMPTON, LONG ISLAND, NEW YORK
JUNE 1989

The appearance of Paige Spencer at the entrance of the Azalea Room halted conversations midsentence, drew admiring stares, and raised intriguing questions.

What was Paige doing in the elegant dining room of the Southampton Club on a Monday noon? On a Saturday evening, yes, of course, Paige would be here hostessing a celebrity dinner for charity, a black-tie gala for the Art Museum, or a lavish reception for the maestro of the Symphony. But on a weekday for luncheon?

What—who—was important enough to take Paige away from her busy schedule for a leisurely gourmet lunch?

Paige Barclay Spencer was a glittering symbol of the new generation of women, not just Southampton women—although Paige was one of them, and Southampton was proud to claim her—but all women. Paige so artfully balanced her roles of wife, mother, stylish society hostess, champion of worthy causes, patron of the arts, and successful Manhattan architect that the balance appeared effortless.

But everyone knew that to make such an intricate balancing act appear effortless took great effort and discipline—discipline that had not before, in the memory of the women in the Azalea Room, included leisurely weekday dining at the Club. Usually Paige spent the hours while Amanda was in school in the tranquil privacy of her study at Somerset, designing the buildings of exceptional elegance and taste that would become sublime counterpoints to the edifices of glitz and gilt that, too, were reshaping the skyline of Manhattan. Paige sketched the magnificent works of art and Chase Andrews transformed her visions into breathtaking reality.

Perhaps Paige was meeting Chase today. Perhaps she and Chase would begin their luncheon with a bottle of Krug champagne, gently touching crystal to crystal in a toast to the success of their next marvelous venture. Paige Spencer, architect extraordinaire, and Chase Andrews, stunningly successful and critically acclaimed real-estate developer, meeting for luncheon in the Azalea Room at the Southampton Club. How interesting. How *wonderful!* The scenario could get even more delicious . . . perhaps Chase's wife, the famous heart surgeon Diana Shepherd, would be joining them.

And even if Paige was dining alone, that was still intriguing, more insight into the remarkable woman. Maybe she simply felt like pampering herself with a gourmet luncheon elegantly served, a peaceful respite from her busy life, the talented artist drawing inspiration from the Club's luxuriant gardens and vistas of the wind-caressed sea. Perhaps she had swirled her honey-blond hair into a graceful chignon, artfully accented her sky-blue eyes, touched pale-pink gloss to her lips, and clothed her slim figure in soft folds of azure silk just for herself, a celebration of *Paige*.

Whatever the reason for her presence in the Azalea Room, it was fascinating . . . it was Paige.

Paige sensed the sudden hush that greeted her and saw the expressions of curiosity and surprise. She cast a brief glance toward the window table she had reserved to be certain that Julia had not yet arrived. Then, because the table was empty, she turned her attention to the women in the room, weaving among them slowly, greeting each by name, the gracious hostess always.

Once seated, Paige sipped a dry martini and gazed out of the window at the splendor of the June day. The gardens below the window bloomed in a bountiful pastel bouquet of azaleas, roses, and lilacs. In the distance, Peconic Bay shimmered beneath a cloudless pale-blue sky that was backlit in gold, a promise from the just-born summer sun that a warm summer lay ahead.

The day was perfect—soft, gentle, golden. A day to match the warmth and happiness Paige felt not just today but all days.

I'm content, Paige mused. *I'm forty-two years old, deliriously happy, euphorically content.*

A soft smile touched her lips as she remembered a time when "content" had been an enemy of dreams, a symbol of complacency. Paige was a veteran of the sixties, a foot soldier in the struggle for women to be whomever they wanted to be, to dream impossible dreams and then to live them. Paige began as a foot soldier, courageously and tirelessly engaging in the all-important battles, and now she was a general. Now, a conquering heroine, she was living her dreams, living more than she had ever dared to dream. Now "content" was a wonderful ally, a word gift-wrapped in happiness and joy.

"Content" had been an enemy once and so had "age." But forty-two was wonderful. Paige had never felt younger, more beautiful, or more creative.

Born in Southampton, a Barclay, Paige's blood was blue, her lineage impeccable, and there was and always would be vast wealth. At fifteen Paige had made the momentous decision to become an architect. Her ambition wasn't small. She was an artist, and she was going to sculpt elegant structures of stone that reached for the sky.

After graduation from Yale, Paige had moved to Manhattan. The first years were difficult, but her belief in her own talent was strong and relentless. Slowly but surely her stylish, elegant, tasteful designs began to make small statements and attract attention.

Paige's boldly traditional architectural style caught the attention of Edmund Spencer. Edmund was a bright, talented, uncompromisingly ethical Madison Avenue attorney. Edmund needed "something done" with his drafty loft. Paige transformed the cavernous space into a cozy, livable work of art. And sometime during the late-night hours when Paige and Edmund sat on cushions on the loft's hardwood floors, sipping wine and poring over her sketches, they fell in love.

Paige and Edmund were a perfect match. Armed with energy, talent, dreams, and now love, they set out together to conquer Manhattan. And conquer they did. As Spencer and Quinn became one of New York's most respected and prestigious law firms, Paige's magnificent architectural statements grew from delicate splashes of taste on the colorful easel of Manhattan to elegant strokes that redefined the city's skyline.

Then ten years ago Paige and Edmund left the vibrant energy of Manhattan for the tranquility of country estate life in Southampton. The decision to leave was trivial compared to the reason *why* they left. Paige and Edmund heard it at precisely the same moment: the soft chime of the biological clock. They wanted a baby. It was so simple, so easy, so amazing. Each believed that there could be no deeper or stronger love than what they felt for each other. And each learned with their precious Amanda new things about love. Priorities were set without hesitation. Amanda was the priority. The rest fell into place.

Edmund commuted into the city. Paige remained at Somerset, sketching still and being with Amanda. At home with Amanda, the fatiguing strain of battle, the persistent vigilance despite her remarkable success magically vanished, and Paige mellowed, like the finest of wines, better with age.

At ease, soldier.

Paige was at ease although her life was busier than ever before. She designed her magnificent buildings—more grand and celebrated every year—carefully selecting projects and finally choosing to work solely with Chase who shared her unwavering commitment to classic elegance and style. Paige was an architect, the talented sculptress she had dreamed she would be; and a loving and beloved wife; and a mother, the dream she had never even known to dream.

So very content. And so very lucky.

Paige was pulled from her thoughts by a sudden change in the Azalea Room. The soft hum of voices had stopped with a gasp, a sharp drawing of breath followed by breath-held silence as another impeccably dressed, beautiful woman appeared beneath the arched entrance. But this time the curious eyes didn't fill with admiration and the lips didn't curl into welcoming smiles as they had for Paige. And this time intriguing questions didn't dance and twirl. Instead, the questions thundered.

What was Julia Lawrence doing here? Who could she possibly be meeting? Jeffrey, of course. But Julia's stunningly handsome and powerful husband, the nation's leading network anchor, would be at the television studio in Manhattan preparing his evening newscast. Yet who in Southampton other than Jeffrey would choose to dine with *her?*

The answer came swiftly, shockingly, as Julia's lavender eyes found Paige and flickered briefly with relief. *Julia was meeting Paige.* The answer triggered another round of even more perplexing questions.

Why? Why in the world would Paige take time away from her busy schedule—her important work—to dine with Julia of all people?

True, there were reasons why Paige had to associate with Julia, reasons they all had to. Jeffrey Lawrence's name appeared at the top of every guest list for every party in Southampton. Jeffrey and Julia were always invited. And although the couple rarely attended, the number of invitations didn't diminish, because even a brief appearance by Jeffrey Lawrence virtually assured a party's success. Just as Julia's appearance could ruin it.

For Paige there were additional reasons to associate with Julia, other ties—the girls. Merry Lawrence and Amanda Spencer were best friends. Naturally, because of the friendship of the girls, Paige had to associate—*communicate*—with Julia. But plans for the daughters could be discussed over the phone. There was no need for Paige to meet with Julia for a leisurely luncheon at the Club, as if she approved of Julia, liked Julia, as if she and Julia were friends, too.

Was it possible?

No! But . . . but Paige was smiling, a fond, friendly smile—for Julia.

Paige was smiling, but inside she churned with anger at the unconcealed disapproval that greeted Julia as she wove between the tables as just moments before she herself had done. Her reception had been warm, appreciative,

admiring. And Julia's reception? Icy, silent, laced with contempt.

Julia wove gracefully, her lavender eyes slightly downcast as if she were Hester Prynne and her astonishing beauty and style were as shamefu as the scarlet letter A.

Julia was unwelcome in Southampton, *still.* Paige simply hadn't realized it. Paige was the hostess of the most splendid parties in Southampton, but her busy schedule kept her out of touch with the day-to-day socializing and the gossip. Paige hadn't heard the gossip, but she could guess the reasons why Julia caused such wariness. The reasons that weren't reasonable. The reasons that had nothing to do with reason, just emotion and passion and fear.

At the very heart was the chilling belief, apparently held by most of the women in the Azalea Room, that Julia Lawrence had the power to take everything away from them if she wanted to . . .

When Julia had arrived in Southampton six years before, she was only twenty. By then, by the time she moved into Belvedere with Jeffrey's grandmother, Meredith Cabot, twenty-year-old Julia had been married to thirty-year-old Jeffrey for almost three and a half years, and she was the mother of his three-year-old daughter. And by then, even before she arrived, there were those in Southampton who knew all about Julia and her crimes against their patrician sensibilities.

The crimes committed by the daughter-in-law she refused even to meet were relentlessly recited by Jeffrey's mother, Victoria Lawrence, from her Beacon Hill mansion in Boston. Victoria had lived in Boston for thirty years, but her wicked, influential tentacles still reached to her girlhood Southampton home.

Julia had no pedigree whatsoever, Victoria informed her Southampton friends. Julia's blood wasn't blue—it was red and hot and very, very *common.* Julia had seduced Jeffrey and forced the marriage because of the child. *The child,* Victoria whispered, as if speaking the words aloud might be lethal. Without providing reasons, Victoria strongly implied that Julia's trickery and deceit were even more scandalous because the child wasn't even Jeffrey's. Julia had deceived Jeffrey, then she had tricked Meredith Cabot, Southampton's revered and beloved Grandmère.

Julia and *the child* lived with Grandmère at Belvedere during the four years that Jeffrey was a correspondent in the Middle East. While Jeffrey risked his life in Beirut, Cairo, Damascus, and Tripoli, Julia had charmed Grandmère, somehow convincing the gracious and lovely dowager to teach her how to behave like a lady—the wife of an aristocrat like Jeffrey and the mistress of an estate as grand as Belvedere. The years in the Middle East were dangerous for Jeffrey, but he returned victorious having captured the coveted plum of network anchor. The years were triumphant for Julia, too. Her victory, the ultimate trophy, was Belvedere, because when Grandmère died she left the magnificent estate to Julia.

Victoria successfully convinced her friends that her daughter-in-law was an unscrupulous seductress. But Victoria's friends were of a generation, cloistered in an elite society of their own. Most of Southampton didn't even know of Julia's crimes against the Cabot family. They were left to form their own conclusions about Julia based on what they saw: Julia herself. She was so very different, and so very threatening.

Julia never wore fur. Her only jewels, worn always, were the elegant wedding band from Jeffrey and the delicate diamond-and-sapphire earrings from Grandmère. Julia's clothes had been modest—*homemade*—until Jeffrey returned from the Middle East. Then, when Julia needed a wardrobe to match Jeffrey's celebrity, her clothes were different still. Stylish, yes, but not always the creations of Dior, St. Laurent, Givenchy, or Chanel. Sometimes the splendid satin-and-sequin gowns she wore were Grandmère's, tastefully modernized by Julia.

And there was more. Julia redecorated Belvedere and made it a showcase without the help of de Santis or Buatta or Hadley. Julia cooked and gardened and cleaned. She never escaped to a spa for a day or a weekend or a week, never escaped at all, never needed to be away from her husband or her daughter. Julia simply stayed in Southampton and made a beautiful happy home for Jeffrey and Merry.

Was domesticity such an unforgivable crime? Was it unspeakable to depart at all from the traditions of wealth and leisure and privilege? Couldn't Julia Lawrence be a superwife and supermother without incurring glacial stares every time she entered a room?

Of course! If only . . .

If only she weren't so young—twenty-six!—and so astonishingly beautiful. If only the innocent lavender eyes and black velvet hair and rich creamy skin and lovely soft voice weren't magic to children and seduction to men.

All children were welcome always at Belvedere. Julia made the stately mansion a fairy-tale castle fragrant with baking cookies, warm with roaring fires, and enchanted because of the make-believe stories spun from Julia's remarkable imagination and told to the mesmerized children in her soft voice. The children flocked to Belvedere every afternoon, the moment school was out at Southampton Country Day, and they flourished at Belvedere with Julia. Shy children bravely joined in games, bullies relented under Julia's gentle wide-eyed gaze, and there was no conflict, only harmony and peace.

Fine, let her be the Pied Piper of Southampton!

But there was more, a threat greater even than the adoration of the children. The men, the husbands, wanted her.

Julia stirred something very primal, some essential ingredient in the lingering mysteries between men and women, something that all the legislation in the world would never change. Julia sent bewitching messages of sensuality and vulnerability, fragility and passion, the desperate need to be possessed, taken, and conquered by a man and then to join in the ecstasy of the conquest.

Men's eyes filled with hunger at the sight of Julia, and later in their beds with their wives the hunger lingered, painful, gnawing, unable to be satisfied by anyone but Julia.

Julia was a tigress. Her fangs and claws were hidden now, but when she decided, when she chose, she could devour the traditions of privilege and leisure, and the affections of the children, and finally, most treacherously, the passions of the husbands . . .

Not a tigress at all, Paige thought as Julia approached. Just a serious young woman who tirelessly devotes every moment of her life trying to make a happy home for the man she loves and for his precious child.

And succeeds? To the wary eyes of Southampton, Julia succeeded in spades and went on to conquer other children and other men. But Paige knew that Julia wasn't even confident of her success with Jeffrey and Merry. Julia struggled, an uncertain pilgrim, unwelcome and shy in the midst of the disapproving descendants of the *Mayflower.*

"Hello, Paige," Julia whispered softly when she finished the icy journey across the Azalea Room.

"Hi, Julia. Welcome." *Welcome!*

10 "I'm sorry I'm late."

"It's all right." Now Paige knew why Julia, who was never late for anything, not even fashionably, was late today. She hadn't wanted to arrive first.

Anger swept through Paige, familiar anger whenever she encountered something that was unfair. The foot soldier was within her still, ready and willing to bear arms to fight for a worthy cause. What worthier cause than her dear friend Julia who had been so misjudged from the very beginning?

Paige wanted to right the wrong. She would talk to every woman in the room, to every woman in Southampton if need be. Paige knew them, liked them, knew them to be nice, reasonable women.

Did you ever visit Julia at Belvedere when Grandmère was alive? Paige would ask. She knew they hadn't. No one had visited except her. Paige visited because Belvedere and Somerset were adjacent estates, because she had heard the stories and worried about Grandmère, because there was the little girl exactly Amanda's age, and because Paige, being Paige, had to see for herself. And what she had seen at once was that Victoria Lawrence's malicious accusations were simply untrue. There was great love at Belvedere, not treachery, not seduction, not deceit.

Paige could swiftly dispel the myth of the unscrupulous fortune huntress. The rest—who Julia really was—would be more difficult.

Have you ever seen Julia trying to seduce your husbands? Paige could query, knowing the answer would be no. Julia didn't *try* to seduce or enchant. She had no wish to be loved by any man but Jeffrey. At the parties where she caused such lingering hunger, Julia never left Jeffrey's side, and her lavender eyes sent intimate messages only to him. She didn't try to seduce but it happened anyway. When Julia entered a room there was magic. It was who she was, as much a part of her as her instinct to protect and nurture, and there was nothing she could do to change it.

No, they would admit truthfully, but it didn't lessen the hurt, or the fear, or the damage. Then, turning the tables, they might ask Paige pointed questions: *How would you feel, Paige, if Amanda preferred being with Julia to being with you? How would you feel, Paige, if Edmund wanted her?*

How would she feel if Amanda preferred her aunt Julia to herself? Or if Edmund's eyes filled with hunger for Julia? Whatever Edmund had felt when he first saw Julia—and surely he had felt something—he had suppressed it quickly and then vanquished it. What filled Edmund's kind eyes when he saw Julia now was warmth and fondness, never lust.

But what if Edmund *was* distracted by her? What if Amanda *was* happier at Belvedere? Wouldn't Paige's calm rationality evaporate, too? Wouldn't her sky-blue eyes view Julia warily? Wouldn't she become a tigress in return to protect her family?

She could tell herself, reasonably, that Julia wasn't trying to steal the children and husbands. Not a tigress, just a kitten—soft, innocent, defenseless. Somehow that image was little comfort. In the end, Julia's magic would still be there, menacing, threatening, beyond reason.

Paige could fight the fight for Julia. She might melt the iciness of the stares, but even a resounding victory would be hollow. No genuine friendships would emerge. And, Paige knew, Julia wasn't looking for more friends in Southampton. Her circle of love and friendship—Jeffrey, Merry, Paige, Edmund, and Amanda—was enough, bountiful. Julia wished for no more.

At ease, soldier. Don't force this war of principle on Julia. Julia doesn't care if she is liked or feared, welcomed or ostracized. She has other worries, other struggles.

"So, Julia, how many times were the words *riding lessons* spoken this morning before Merry left for school?" Paige asked, smiling fondly as she addressed the worry that loomed far larger in Julia's mind than her icy reception in the Azalea Room.

"A million trillion," Julia answered with one of Merry and Amanda's favorite numbers. She smiled softly at the memory of Merry cantering around the mansion before school. "The girls really want to learn how to ride this summer."

"I know. Beginning the second school is out. Five days and counting. What do you think, Julia?"

Paige and Julia needed to reach the same decision about the daughters who were best friends. Paige and Edmund had already decided. Of course Amanda could take riding lessons.

It worried Paige a little, naturally, as every new step in Amanda's life worried her. But Paige was willing to take the risks mothers needed to take. It seemed much more difficult for Julia to take the same risks, as if she had no right to take them, as if Merry wasn't really her daughter, just a precious child for whom she had been given the immense responsibility of caring until her real mother came to claim her.

With each new decision, Julia gathered all the data she could, then carefully weighed the knowns against the unknowns. For Julia there were mostly unknowns. Her own childhood had been so different from Merry's, without a glimmer of luxury or wealth. Swimming, sailing, ice-skating, riding were all foreign to Julia, foreign and somehow terrifying.

Every decision was a struggle for Julia, and the struggle was solitary because Jeffrey took no role in the daily decisions about his daughter. Paige tried to help, guiding gently and reassuring but never pushing. She never said, "Trust me, Julia. I'm sixteen years older than you. I know this will be fine." Paige had so very much more life experience than Julia, valuable lessons she could have shared, but as mothers of nine-year-old daughters, Paige and Julia were equals, equally experienced, equally inexperienced.

"We meet with the riding instructor at one-thirty?" Julia answered Paige's question with one of her own. She hadn't made a decision yet because there was more data to gather. The final piece was meeting with the man who would teach the girls. Then she would have to decide.

"One-thirty, yes. Julia, the Club manager is always very careful about who he hires and he says this man is an excellent instructor." Paige's calm reassurance didn't erase the worry in Julia's eyes. Paige would have liked to have had a nice relaxed luncheon with Julia in the Azalea Room for all to see, but she knew Julia couldn't relax until the decision was made. After a moment she suggested sympathetically, "Would you like to go to the stable now? Perhaps he's free. If not, we can look around until one-thirty."

"Do you mind, Paige?"

"No, not at all." And after, Julia, if you like, we can have lunch—sandwiches on the terrace—at Somerset.

Chapter 2

Their high heels clicked noisily on the cobblestones in the stable courtyard. The courtyard was empty on this Monday five days before school was out for the summer, but by next week it would be bustling with horses and their eager young riders. In the distance Paige and Julia heard soft whinnies, the splash of water, and the rustle of hay—signals that the grooms were busy caring for the large stable of valuable horses.

Paige and Julia crossed the empty courtyard to the stable office. The riding instructor was there, seated at the desk, reviewing the leather-bound lesson-schedule book. The sharp clicking of high heels, so-distinct from the familiar soft thud of leather riding boots, alerted him to their approach and he stood when they appeared.

This is the carefully selected and excellent riding instructor? Paige wondered the moment she saw him. Paige had expected, at the very least, neatly trimmed hair, spotless ivory jodphurs, a teal-blue turtleneck, and leather riding boots polished to a mirror shine. She had expected the image, or at least the comforting illusion, of a proper country gentleman, and she had imagined even more—a distinguished-looking man in his late fifties with a slight British accent.

This man was about thirty, Paige guessed. He wore a denim shirt rolled to his elbows, threadbare faded jeans, and battered cowboy boots. The sartorial look was rodeo, not fox hunt; bronco-busting, not dressage; dude-ranch chic, perhaps, but certainly not Southampton Club elegant.

His clothes were rugged, unrefined. And the man himself? He was handsome, very handsome, but there was a wildness about the coal-black hair, the fearless gray-green eyes, and the lean body that sent a strong yet graceful message of tightly controlled power. As if poised and ready to spring.

Like a panther, Paige decided. Wild, powerful, majestic. The panther eyes really were a blend of gray *and* green—granite and forest, emerald and steel . . . a violent winter storm tossing the Atlantic.

The panther eyes that met hers were polite, calm, and inscrutable, but Paige imagined he could will the eyes to seduce. She imagined that he, like Julia, could stir fiery passions and gnawing hungers. But, unlike Julia, this sleek panther surely was not oblivious to the effect of his sultry sexuality and his predatory gray-green eyes.

"Hello. How may I help you?"

His voice was another surprise. Hardly the voice of a cowboy! Accent-free, the voice was refined, aristocratic.

"We were looking for the riding instructor," Paige answered as she searched her memory for the name the Club manager had given her. Patrick, he had said. Patrick James. "Patrick?"

"I'm Patrick."

"I'm Mrs. Spencer, and this is Mrs. Lawrence. We have an appointment to meet with you at one-thirty."

"Yes, but now is fine, Mrs. Spencer."

After Patrick replied to Paige, he shifted his gaze to Julia in well-mannered acknowledgment of the introduction that Paige had made. Paige watched, wondering how the panther eyes would respond to Julia's magic. Would there be the silent recognition of predator meeting prey, conqueror meeting temptress, Adam meeting Eve?

But the gray-green eyes remained inscrutable, flickering no more than a polite hello and then returning calmly to Paige.

"You were interested in riding lessons, Mrs. Spencer?"

"For our daughters this summer. The girls, Merry and Amanda, are nine."

"Have they ridden before?"

"No."

"Did you want private lessons, or with a group?"

"Private—just the two of them, I should think."

Patrick nodded, then looked down at the lesson-schedule book. "I could give them a first lesson this Saturday morning at ten. After that I would like to schedule their lessons for midweek, if that's convenient for you. I should keep the weekend times open for adults who can't come on weekdays."

"That would be fine," Paige said.

As Patrick started to write "Merry and Amanda" in the lesson book at ten on Saturday, the decision made, a *fait accompli*, Paige realized Julia hadn't spoken, hadn't agreed.

"Julia?"

"Is it safe, Patrick?" Julia answered Paige's question with one for Patrick. "Is it safe for nine-year-olds to ride?"

Patrick turned to Julia, surprised by the softness of her voice and the worry in it. He wondered if the concern was false, a pretension, but the lavender eyes were serious and the astonishingly beautiful face frowned, losing none of its beauty with the frown but instead enhancing its fragility.

"It's safe, Mrs. Lawrence." That was the truth. It was all Patrick needed to say. But he revealed a little more about himself in the words he spoke and in the gentleness of his reassurance. "Horses are just big gentle creatures."

"Merry and Amanda are just little girls," Julia countered quietly.

"It's safe. Really. I will watch them very carefully."

"Would it be all right for us to watch, too, during the lessons?"

"Of course. If you like."

"Yes. Thank you."

As Paige and Julia walked from the stable back to the parking lot and lunch at Somerset instead of the Azalea Room, Paige asked Julia what she thought of Patrick.

"Oh," Julia replied absently, still preoccupied with the decision she had made and with the hope that it was right. "He seemed nice, didn't you think?"

"Yes." *I guess*, Paige amended silently. Nice, but a little menacing. What did Patrick do with the primal passions he stirred? Paige wondered. Did he satisfy the hungers? Or did he simply torment and tease and play with his prey? Did the panther prowl and devour? Or was he pure—provocative yet innocent—like Julia? Did he give his heart and his passion only to one true love, as Julia gave herself only, always, to Jeffrey?

Paige played with the questions briefly, then dismissed them. It mattered little to her whether Patrick James was an amoral panther, a noble savage, or an aristocratic cowboy. It didn't matter how he spent his private hours outside the riding ring. Even if he was this summer's seduction, as Paige imagined he would be, the season's most irresistible and intriguing sport for the ladies of Southampton, it didn't matter. All that mattered was that Patrick was a careful riding instructor. And she would be at the riding lessons, watching, making sure. And, because the first lesson was scheduled for Saturday, Edmund would be there, too.

"Maybe Jeffrey will be able to watch the lesson on Saturday," Paige suggested as they reached the parking lot.

"Oh." Julia's lavender eyes looked hopeful for a moment and then a little sad. "I don't know if he can."

"I hope he's not going to be out of town. Edmund and I are planning a small dinner party for Saturday evening."

14 "Paige and I are planning a small dinner party for Saturday evening." Edmund Spencer spoke the same words to Jeffrey Lawrence ten minutes later.

Edmund and Jeffrey were at Lutèce in midtown Manhattan for a business meeting over lunch. The business discussion had lasted almost the entire meal. At Jeffrey's request Edmund had reviewed the script for a soon-to-be-taped documentary on the Iran-Contra hearings. During lunch they had considered Edmund's questions and concerns point by point. Together they made small but critical changes in wording and added "alleged" in several places. Finally, as they drank coffee at the end of the meal, Edmund pronounced the script libel-free, not destined to be a repeat of the Westmoreland fiasco.

Business completed, the conversation shifted to other topics, personal ones, like dinner at Somerset on Saturday.

"I hope that you and Julia are free. I know you'll need to check with her," Edmund added with a smile. He and Paige had the same system—neither agreed to a social commitment without discussing it with the other and reaching a joint decision.

"That's the code, Edmund, but it hardly applies to seeing you and Paige. Julia and I always look forward to it."

"Thank you. Likewise."

"A small dinner party?" Jeffrey asked, curious. The Spencers and Lawrences had dinner together frequently, often at the last minute, casual get-togethers, not parties. The "parties" Paige and Edmund usually gave at Somerset or at the Southampton Club were always very grand and very elegant—black tie, satin and sequin gowns, hundreds of famous guests, silver fountains splashing vintage champagne. A *small* dinner party was unusual.

"It may be just the four of us and the newest member of my firm, a sensational trial attorney from California. This summer, while she studies for the New York Bar, she'll be living at our beach cottage."

"At SeaCliff?"

Jeffrey knew the small cottage perched on the cliffs very well. Somerset and Belvedere were adjacent estates, forested along their common border until the cliffs, where the forest opened to a spectacular panorama of sky and sea. As a boy, during the wonderful summers Jeffrey spent with his grandparents at Belvedere, he often made the long walk through the lush forest to the sea. When he reached the cliffs he would gaze at the vastness of the ocean and the sky, inhale the fresh salt air, and dream about the adventures that beckoned to him from beyond the azure horizon. Then he would scamper down the steep trail to the white sand beach and stand close enough to the water's edge to be splashed by the thundering waves.

Jeffrey never swam in the surf, never dove into the crashing waves, nor did battle with the powerful undertow. As a small boy he gave his grandparents a solemn promise that he never would. But later, when he was fifteen and won blue ribbons for the swim team at Exeter, he was very tempted. The surf was treacherous yet seductive, and he was such a strong swimmer! But Jeffrey resisted the temptation. He had given his word.

Jeffrey had boyhood memories of SeaCliff, and he had a more recent one, a mature one, the most wonderful memory of all . . . an afternoon in May three years ago making love to Julia in a meadow of wildflowers above the sea.

"SeaCliff," Edmund echoed. "I'd forgotten the cottage had a name."

Edmund had almost forgotten about the cottage itself. The beach and cottage were in a distant corner of the huge estate, a corner he and Paige avoided because of Amanda and the Iethal surf.

"Does she know about thesurf?" Jeffrey asked.

"Yes, and promises not to swim."

"Good. So, Edmund, who is this sensational import from California?"

"Casey English."

"I don't recognize the name. Should I?"

"Not yet. But you will."

"Sounds impressive."

"She is. Very." Edmund smiled and added, "Casey's been impressive all her life. Through high school she attended the Carlton Academy in Atherton, just south of San Francisco. Carlton's small school, very exclusive, academically rigorous, terribly expensive. But you've lived in the Bay Area, Jeffrey. Have you heard of it?"

"Yes. Some of my classmates at Stanford attended Carlton. As I recall, they did quite well."

"I imagine all graduates of Carlton do quite well. The academic requirements for admission are extremely rigid. No matter who you are, or how much money you have, you can't buy your way in. Because of the expense, most of the students are quite wealthy in addition to being exceptionally bright. But there are occasional scholarships for extremely gifted students who couldn't afford to attend otherwise."

"Like Casey?"

"What? Oh, no. Cost wasn't an issue for Casey, though I imagine she would have gotten a scholarship had she needed one. She graduated first in her class."

"The best of the best."

"Yes. She had similar academic success as an undergraduate at Berkeley and as a law student at Hastings. She clerked for our San Francisco office in the summer during law school. My San Francisco partners were dazzled, eager to keep her, but they assumed she'd join English and McElroy when she graduated."

"English?"

"Casey's father is Kirk Carroll English."

"A name I *have* heard of." Jeffrey smiled slightly at the understatement. Who hadn't heard of Kirk Carroll "K.C." English? The powerful high-profile attorney and his precedent-setting legal triumphs were legendary.

"Indeed. Anyway, Casey graduated first in her class from Hastings Law and surprised everyone by joining the San Francisco D.A.'s office."

"Altruism?"

"I'm not sure. I know she wanted rigorous trial experience. She felt what she'd learned in law school was a bit academic, more ivory tower than real world. But it may have been altruism, too. Casey is passionate about justice."

"Justice? Edmund, I thought justice was for judges and juries and the attorney's job was to . . ." Jeffrey searched for a tactful phrase.

"Win? No matter what?" Edmund smiled. "The euphemism, Jeffrey, is "to provide the best defense.' "

"Ah, yes."

"Well, while she was in the D.A.'s office, Casey managed to do it all—provide the best defense, get justice, and win. Her record was truly remarkable.

She won a number of very big cases, although none that could rival her final one. The defendant was a prominent and politically influential San Francisco attorney."

"That sounds tricky."

"Tricky and potential professional suicide. The D.A. assigned the case to Casey assuming, I imagine, that she would review the evidence, decide there was little hope of winning, and recommend that it not be pursued. Especially given the charge."

"Which was?"

"Rape. Not a middle-of-the-night assault on a stranger, where you at least have the hope of concrete evidence, but *acquaintance* rape. At best a million shades of gray and virtually impossible to push beyond reasonable doubt."

"But Casey decided to try it."

"She met with the plaintiff and was convinced by her story. And, as she made abundantly clear in her opening arguments, Casey English doesn't see shades of gray in rape. As she eloquently explained to the jury, sex in which both parties aren't wholly, *enthusiastically*, consenting is rape, pure and simple. Casey defogged the issue. All the jury had to decide was if the plaintiff was consenting or not."

"And Casey prevailed."

"Actually, justice prevailed. As the trial progressed, other women—other victims—came forward. Just before the closing arguments the defendant changed his plea to guilty."

"That must have been dramatic."

"Yes, and an immense victory for Casey. The perfect swan song. As soon as the trial was over, she decided to leave the D.A.'s office and made it known that she wanted to join an East Coast firm. The trial of the Nob Hill Rapist may not have made the evening network news, but in legal circles it was quite important. Casey English was suddenly in great demand."

"And you got her. And she gets to spend the summer in one of the most idyllic settings on Long Island."

"I do hope she finds it idyllic," Edmund said thoughtfully. "Although she won't admit it, I think the trial took a bit of a toll on her. Many attorneys—perhaps even K.C. English himself—criticized Casey for taking the case. She was in the spotlight for months, and it was a harsh, glaring spotlight that only softened into limelight at the end. I've assured Casey that she'll have complete privacy at the cottage. I hope she'll find it a peaceful break." Edmund smiled enigmatically and added, "I am also glad that she'll be stretching her long legs on our secluded beach rather than along Fifth Avenue where she might be spotted by Eileen Ford."

"What?" Edmund was afraid that Casey might be spotted by a top New York modeling agent?

"You'd begun to form a mental image of Casey English, hadn't you, Jeffrey?"

"Well . . ." Jeffrey replied sheepishly. He *had* formed an image. The Casey English he imagined was prim, no-nonsense, a smart, unglamorous woman who was a little tough and a little—maybe a lot—rigid. "Tell me."

"In addition to being a brilliant attorney who is passionate about justice, Casey English is also model beautiful. And very charming."

"I look forward to meeting her."

"As I said, you and Julia and Casey may be the only guests, but Paige is going to call Diana to see if she and Chase can join us. You still haven't met them, have you?"

It had become almost a joke. Over the past two years, despite careful scheduling and best intentions, Jeffrey and Julia and Diana and Chase had still not met. Invariably one of the two couples had been unable to attend whenever Edmund and Paige hosted one of their grand affairs at Somerset or the Club. And every dinner for six planned weeks in advance at Le Cirque, La Côte Basque, or Lutèce had faltered at the last moment. Jeffrey would have to fly to Chernobyl or Manila or Lockerbie, or have to be in the studio covering a fast-breaking catastrophe; Edmund would be in the midst of a trial, encounter a surprise twist, and need to work into the night to plan the new strategy; Diana would have to perform emergency heart surgery even though she wasn't on call; Chase would have a crisis with a hotel he was building—Chase and Paige; and when Merry had the measles, Julia didn't want to leave her—and four hours later, when tiny red spots appeared on Amanda's fair skin, too, Paige and Edmund were glad that the evening out had already been canceled.

"No, I still haven't met either one. I do, however, have an appointment with Diana at three this afternoon."

"An appointment? With Diana? Jeffrey, are you all right?"

"What? Oh, yes, of course. I guess I should have said I have an interview with her this afternoon. It doesn't feel like an interview because it's just the two of us, no lights, no camera, only fifteen minutes. She doesn't have time for anything more than that today, and today is when I need to see her."

"Because of the heart surgery she's doing tomorrow on the Soviet ambassador."

"Yes. Naturally it's big news. Very much in the spirit of détente and *glasnost*. I'll be doing live reports about the operation so I want to learn as much as I can about the Shepherd Heart and its creator before tomorrow. Which means, if even briefly, at last I will meet the famous Queen of Hearts."

"I don't think Diana likes being called the Queen of Hearts." Edmund frowned uncertainly and admitted, "Of course, she's never actually said so, not to me, but I get that impression."

"Really? It seems so apt."

"It is. And it makes wonderful headlines. Diana and Chase, the Queen of Hearts and the man who would be King. All of Manhattan could be their kingdom except for . . ."

"The Trump card."

"The Trump card," Edmund repeated quietly, solemnly acknowledging the monumental battle being waged by the two real-estate magnates. It was a battle of giants, stylistically so different yet each wanting to etch his signature, a permanent imprimatur, on the skyscape of Manhattan. It was a battle for Manhattan and a battle for immortality. "Anyway, since scheduling dinners together weeks in advance hasn't worked, we're trying the last-minute approach. Of course Diana may be on call Saturday and that will be that."

"This is quite a party you're planning, Edmund," Jeffrey said as he thought about the guest list. The men were impressive enough, but it was the women who truly dazzled—a famous heart surgeon, a brilliant trial attorney, a gifted architect . . . and Julia. Julia, who had left high school a month before graduation to marry him and have her daughter.

Would Julia feel uncomfortable—inadequate?—with these stunningly successful women? She wouldn't feel uncomfortable with Paige, of course, but with Diana and Casey . . . ? Jeffrey didn't know. He did know that his terribly bright wife, who *could* talk knowledgeably and insightfully on virtually any topic, would be silent as always. Would Julia spend the next few days dreading the evening? And when it arrived, would it be an ordeal for her? Jeffrey didn't know that, either.

He only knew that Julia wouldn't tell him.

"I'm particularly eager to have Casey meet Julia," Edmund said after a few moments of silence.

Jeffrey looked at him with surprise, wondering if kind and thoughtful Edmund had sensed his worry about Julia. But he was abviously quite serious.

"You want Casey to meet Julia?" Why? What could Casey and Julia have in common? Clearly they were both very bright and beautiful, but Casey's summer would be spent studying for the New York Bar so that she could dazzle New York as she had dazzled San Francisco. And Julia's summer would be devoted as always to Merry.

"Yes. I don't know how much free time Casey will have, or will allow herself to have. She's brilliant, passed the California Bar with ease, but doubtless will study compulsively anyway. If she does allow herself any leisure time, though, I thought she might enjoy spending it with Julia."

"With Julia? Why?"

"Well, they both grew up in northern California. And they are practically the same age."

"The same age?" Jeffrey had revised his image of Casey to include beautiful and charming, but the sensational trial attorney whom Edmund was so pleased to have joining his prestigious firm was only Julia's age?

"Practically. Casey is just a year older than Julia."

When Jeffrey returned to the television studio at two-fifteen he learned that Dr. Diana Shepherd's secretary had called to cancel the three o'clock interview.

"The message," the booker told him, "is that Dr. Shepherd is still in the operating room and will be until at least six."

"Terrific," Jeffrey muttered sarcastically.

That morning, after the booker had met with immovable resistance, Jeffrey had personally spent a great deal of time and patience talking to Diana's secretary. He had politely listened to how busy Dr. Shepherd was today, then countered with how flexible he was, that he could see her at any time except during his evening broadcast. Diana's secretary had been polite but firm. Jeffrey had been polite but even more firm. He didn't know if Diana was a silent participant in the negotiations—sending messages from the operating room—but finally he and her secretary had agreed to "fifteen or twenty minutes" beginning at three. And now . . .

"Her secretary said Dr. Shepherd would be willing to meet with you in her office after your broadcast, at eight, if you want."

"I want. Will you get a message to her that I'll be there?"

"Certainly."

"Good. Thanks."

Jeffrey walked into his office and pulled the door behind him. He noticed the folder on his desk—background information on Diana Shepherd M.D. assembled by his research team over the past few hours. Jeffrey now had plenty of time to carefully read the file before the eight o'clock interview—assuming it happened. Plenty of time to learn about Diana Shepherd and to prepare the evening newscast. Time to spare, time to call Julia.

Jeffrey called Julia often, if only for a few minutes, just to say hi, just to hear her voice.

"Hi, Julie."

"Jeffrey." Julia's soft voice filled with surprise and joy as it did every time he called. "How was your lunch with Edmund?"

"Very nice. Did Paige talk to you about a dinner party Saturday night?" *Does it terrify you?*

"Yes," Julia murmured, trying to recall what Paige had said, realizing that most of her thoughts had still been on the decision about Merry's riding lessons. "Something about a woman attorney who is joining Edmund's firm and will be
spending the summer at the beach cottage . . . Jeffrey?"

"Yes, darling?" He heard the soft worry in her voice. *Tell me, Julie. If you don't want to go to the party, it's fine with me.*

"I just arranged for Merry to take horseback riding lessons at the Club. Do you think that's all right?"

"Why wouldn't it be?" Jeffrey heard the sudden sharpness in his voice and felt a stab of pain in the part of his heart that was a raw open wound. The conversation had shifted from his gentle worry that Julia might feel uncomfortable at Paige and Edmund's party to a discussion of Merry.

Merry . . . Julia's precious daughter, the living symbol of Julia's greatest deception, the ever-present reminder that he could never really trust the woman he loved with all his heart.

"I just thought it might be dangerous," Julia answered softly as she fought tears and anger. The tears were old and familiar, but the anger was new. Julia knew anger of course, anger at herself, but recently she had felt the beginning of anger toward Jeffrey. Jeffrey, whom she loved so very much, but who refused still, after all these years, to love his daughter.

Jeffrey heard the hurt in Julia's voice and reminded himself of the promise he had made to her three weeks before on their tenth wedding anniversary: *All right, Julie, yes. If that's what you want. We will be a family.* And he reminded himself of the vow he had made to himself: *I will try.*

"It's probably not dangerous, darling," Jeffrey said gently. "Especially if she's taking lessons at the Club. When does she start?"

"Saturday morning at ten."

"Would you like me to go with you?"

"Would you, Jeffrey?"

"Of course."

"Thank you."

You're welcome, my Julie. I love you, and I made a promise to you. Jeffrey wanted the thought to stop there, but after all these years the taunting thought had a life of its own. It continued defiantly, *Just as you promised me—ten years ago!—that there would be no more lies.*

Jeffrey took a breath, banished the rogue thought, and returned to his loving worry about her.

"Julie? About the dinner party."

"Oh, yes." Julia frowned, searching her memory, trying to recall what Paige had said. She didn't remember Paige's words, but she remembered her enthusiasm. "I think we should go, don't you? I got the impression from Paige that Edmund is delighted to have her joining the firm."

"Yes. He is. Did Paige tell you that she's about your age?"

"No. Really? She must be very impressive."

"Yes." Jeffrey sighed softly. If it bothered Julia, even if it terrified her, he would never know.

She would keep her fear hidden, nestled beside the other secrets of her heart.

Chapter 3

The data assembled on Dr. Diana Shepherd by Jeffrey's research team included articles written about Diana, scientific articles written by Diana, and a copy of her curriculum vitae. Jeffrey read the articles with interest and made a surprising discovery when he read the C.V.

Diana Elizabeth Shepherd and Jeffrey Cabot Lawrence were born on exactly the same day thirty-six years before, she in Dallas, he in Boston. Who, Jeffrey wondered, had entered the world first on that distant November eleventh? And had the stars and moon and sun pulled with invisible strings on the just-born infants and mysteriously instilled similar traits in each?

Jeffrey Lawrence did not believe in astrology. "That proves you're a Scorpio!" Julia teased whenever he made the aloof pronouncement.

Jeffrey didn't believe in astrology, but his observant journalistic mind could not ignore the similarities between himself and Diana Shepherd.

Something deep inside had driven the two infants to set lofty goals, accomplish them, and then set new goals, loftier and more challenging, and accomplish *them*, too. Jeffrey knew the strength of his own ambition, and he saw the proof of Diana's in her impressive C.V. They both had abundant ambition and the other ingredients necessary to convert dreams and visions into reality: ability, determination, and drive.

Diana Shepherd was an achiever and so was he. Jeffrey guessed that, like him, she was demanding and perfectionistic, unused to failure and intolerant of it. *So*? So was almost every successful man or woman Jeffrey knew. Lofty ambitions, stunning successes, and intolerance of failure didn't make the celebrated Queen of Hearts his cosmic twin.

But there was the other similarity, the one in the photographs . . .

True, the rich sable-brown hair, intelligent oceanblue eyes, and classically sculpted features conspired differently in each—softly in beautiful Diana and powerfully in handsome Jeffrey. Different, yet somehow the same. As Jeffrey studied a photograph of Diana, he decided the similarity was in the eyes, a resemblance beyond the darkest shade of blue, a sameness in the direct yet appraising way they viewed the world.

Did her serious sapphire eyes ever sparkle? Jeffrey wondered. Was there warmth in the deep-blue depths? He knew that his relentless drive and demands for perfection were softened by humor and love. Was there softness in Diana Shepherd, too? Was there a private place in her heart for laughter and love, a core of gentleness at the center of the steel?

Jeffrey couldn't answer those questions by looking at Diana's photograph. He wondered if he would find out when he met her tonight.

Jeffrey's driver brought the limousine to a gentle stop at the main entrance of Memorial Hospital at seven-fifty. The limousine and driver were provided by the studio and would be waiting to take him home to Southampton after the interview.

Jeffrey entered the hospital against a stream of humanity as the day's visiting hours came to an end. Once the visitors vanished, the hospital could settle into its quiet nocturnal routine. Even as Jeffrey approached the bank of elevators, the lights dimmed—nights lights replacing bright lights—a signal that the hospital and its overnight guests were going to bed.

Diana's office was on the tenth floor of the Heart Institute. As Jeffrey walked along the dark, deserted corridor, his footsteps eerily loud, he wondered if she would be in her office and how he would find her in this vast shadowy maze if she weren't.

In the distance he saw a golden beam, a beacon of light guiding him through the darkness. The light came from Diana's office. The door was ajar to enable the bright light to illuminate the shadows. Jeffrey heard voices from within—no, not voices, just one voice, soft, with the faintest trace of a Southern drawl . . . a voice that was smiling.

Jeffrey knocked softly and moved so that she could see who was knocking. Diana was at her desk, talking on the phone. She smiled a warm hello and waved a hand for him to enter.

"Thank you again, Paige. It will happen sometime! Please give my best to Edmund and Amanda. Good-bye." Diana replaced the receiver, then looked at Jeffrey.

"Dr. Shepherd," Jeffrey greeted her formally.

"Mr. Lawrence," she replied, matching his tone and formality. This was a professional interview, after all, and they had never met. But that was almost a technicality. Only a series of flukes—their busy careers and the illness of a little girl—had prevented their meeting before. Diana's dark-blue eyes sparkled as she added, "We meet at last."

"At long last. Please call me Jeffrey."

"I'm Diana." The hand Diana extended to Jeffrey, her handshake hand, was jewelless. On her other hand she wore a gold wedding band crowned with a glittering four-carat diamond.

As Jeffrey shook her hand he marveled that it was the hand of a virtuoso, and he was touching the talent. Guided by her brilliant mind and resolute determination, Diana's graceful and agile fingers had carved great fame for her—top honors at Harvard Medical School, a surgical residency at Massachusetts General Hospital, the "Heart" Fellowship at Memorial Hospital, her extraordinary reputation as a cardiac surgeon. Over the years Diana's fingers had shared their magical gifts with countless patients, but that wasn't enough, the fingers couldn't rest. When Diana wasn't operating, her fingers were hard at work writing the scientific papers that had won her international acclaim.

And—the most astonishing accomplishment of all—Diana's remarkable vision, brilliant mind, and talented hands had created the Shepherd Heart. Her creation was a giant step beyond heart transplantation, beyond the Jarvik Seven, beyond what medical science had dreamed even for the next decade. The Shepherd Heart was a twenty-first-century invention created by a woman of the eighties.

"Will we see each other again on Saturday?" Jeffrey asked after they had shaken hands. From what he had overheard when he arrived, Jeffrey guessed the answer was no.

"I'm afraid not. I'm on call this weekend." *And my husband left me three weeks ago, to think, to decide.* Diana frowned briefly, then forced away the painful memory with the hopeful thoughts she had held ever since Chase left: *Chase will come back. He will decide to spend his life with you. Believe it.*

"Too bad."

"Yes." *Yes. Chase will come back.*

"Sometime . . ."

"Please excuse my attire," Diana said suddenly, shifting the topic and gesturing gracefully at her outfit.

The top layer, a crisply starched white coat with the words *Diana Shepherd*

M.D. embroidered in green, gave her the familiar professional appearance of a physician. But underneath the white coat Diana wore royal-blue surgical scrubs. The pajamalike cotton scrubs were loose-fitting except where she had cinched the drawstring of the trousers tightly around her slender waist. The Adidas running shoes she wore perfectly completed the image of fitness and energy and health. At a moment's notice, Jeffrey imagined, Diana could shed her white coat

and dash off for a three-mile jog, or teach a class in advanced aerobics, or expertly navigate a sailboat in a brisk breeze on Long Island Sound.

"You look fine."

"A little informal. I was in my civvies, all dressed up for our interview, until one of my colleagues started a very tough case and asked me to be available. I'm sort of on stand-by." After a moment she added, feigning worry, but in fact sending a challenge, "Oh, I said "case," didn't I?"

"Yes."

"A medical term made distasteful by the media."

"And it shouldn't be distasteful?" Jeffrey asked. Diana's dark-blue eyes smiled but gave deeper signals, little flickers of annoyance and impatience, turbulence beneath the calm. She was multilayered, complicated, *critical*—as was he.

"Perhaps."

"And perhaps not. Tell me. Educate me, Dr. Shepherd."

"There seems to be a perception that simply uttering the word "case" instantly depersonalizes the patient and thereby compromises his or her care. However, whether I refer to you as a "case', or even a very *tough* case"—a dark-blue sparkle told him she knew he could be tough—"or call you Jeffrey, I will always give you the best care I can possibly give."

"Maybe you're unique among physicians."

"I *know* that I'm not," Diana replied emphatically. Then, lightening her tone, she added with a slight smile, "However, media-bashing is just as bad as doctor-bashing, so that's the end of my minilecture."

"Except?" Jeffrey sensed there was more.

"Well, as long as I'm grinding an axe, and so far you don't seem too offended . . ." Diana tilted her head as she waited for confirmation.

"So far the sound isn't too grating. I'll let you know when I begin to feel steel splinters."

"OK. Speaking of depersonalization, the news media has made a "case" of the Soviet ambassador. Witness the fact that although I have been putting new hearts in people—nice, everyday folks—for almost six months, only when the patient happens to be a V.I.P. does the nation's leading anchor want to meet with me. The ambassador has been depersonalized completely into a symbol of détente."

"It's a very big story," Jeffrey murmured quietly. Diana was right, of course. Not that her observation was a newsflash for him. It was something he thought about, worried about, and tried to improve. Jeffrey knew well that the feelings of victims and their families were all too often sacrificed for the "story" and that dramatic and explicit pictures of bodies and carnage frequently filled the airwaves in living—dying—color long after the tragic event was over.

"Yes, well, the real story is that the ambassador is a fifty-six-year-old man who, like the fifty-six-year-old machinist I operated on last week, will die very soon without a new heart. The surgery may be an important step in Soviet-American relations—but for the ambassador it is a simple yet profound issue of mortality. Perhaps after tomorrow there will be more goodwill between Washington and Moscow. But all the ambassador cares about, and all *I* care about, is that perhaps after tomorrow he will have a chance to see his grandchildren."

"What can I say?" Jeffrey asked the intense sapphire eyes. "Point well taken, Doctor."

"Thank you . . . Anchor." Diana smiled. "Now, what would you like to know about tomorrow's surgery? I have a model of the Heart over here, fact sheets, brochures, visual aids. You're welcome to take everything, including the model, if it would be helpful for tomorrow's telecast. I do need the Heart back."

"Of course. That would be wonderful."

"Good." Diana closed the office door and led the way across her expansive office to a large oval oak table in front of a wall of windows that gave a panoramic view of Manhattan.

Jeffrey silently admired the magnificent view as they crossed the office, but when they reached the table his concentration focused entirely on the model of the Shepherd Heart. Diana's creation was made of clear plastic and was the size of four small clenched fists. Delicate wires were embedded in the plastic, webbing it with gossamer threads more fine than spun silk.

Jeffrey stared at the invention that was decades ahead of its time. It was so stark, so sterile, so clinical. What had he expected? Crimson plastic, heart-shaped, Diana's loving Valentine to the world? Filled with blood, of course, the Heart would become red. And, Jeffrey noticed, the wires connecting the model to the small boxes—the energy source and the tiny computer—were red and blue, small concessions to nature, wires the color of arteries and veins.

If his own heart failed would he want this webbed plastic placed inside him? Would he trust it to keep him alive? Could this stark, sterile creation beat with passion and love? Could it weep with pain and joy?

Jeffrey realized that Diana was waiting for him to ask questions. But the questions that filled his mind were philosophical, not technical.

"So, Dr. Shepherd, can you mend a broken heart?" he asked finally, frowning slightly, suddenly off guard, wondering if she would understand.

"No," she answered quietly. "It's a little scary, isn't it? A little nervy to remove a flesh-and-blood heart and replace it with a plastic one. I have to do that, though. I have to take out the entire native heart to make room for this one. I worried in the beginning about what I would be taking out with it."

"And?"

"The emotions and passions stay behind. All I do is replace a pump." Diana spoke softly, reverently, well aware of the profundity of what she did. "And I never call it an artificial heart. I call it a new heart. I call it . . . off the record, Anchor?"

"OK."

"I call it the Heart Nouveau."

"That's nice. Off the record, really?" Just like Queen of Hearts is off the record? The name was so perfect. Diana was so regal, even in her scrubs, her *royal*-blue scrubs.

"Really." Diana gazed at Jeffrey until he nodded agreement. Then she began to tell him how her Heart Nouveau worked, why it worked, all about the tiny computer in the wallet-size box that enabled the recipient to go anywhere, unencumbered by a machine, just like a normal human being—free. "The native heart responds to a complicated network of physiological impulses. It has been possible to simulate most of the physiological responses in the computer."

"Most, but not all? What's missing?"

"The mysteries beyond science. Like the inexplicable quickening of a heart as it falls in love. I don't know where that nerve synapse is. It's not programmed in a human being. How can I program it into a computer?"

They were interrupted by a knock at the door.

"Oh, dear," Diana apologized in advance. "That's probably someone from the O.R."

Jeffrey smiled. "They need help with the *case*."

"Yes. I'm afraid so."

"It's not a problem. I'm happy to wait."

Jeffrey watched as Diana crossed the office and opened the door. It was immediately obvious from her expression that it was not a messenger from the O.R. The intrusion was altogether different . . . and surprising. Jeffrey couldn't see the man, but he could hear his words as well as Diana's.

"Dr. Diana Shepherd?"

"Yes."

"Mrs. Chase Andrews?"

"Yes. Has something happened to Chase?" Diana's tone shifted swiftly from polite curiosity to sharp concern.

"This is for you, ma'am."

"What . . . ?" Diana took the envelope the man handed her. The engraved return address was a law firm on Park Avenue, not the familiar Madison Avenue address of Spencer and Quinn. Diana didn't finish the question because she already guessed its ominous answer; the clues were suddenly obvious and terribly painful.

"Divorce papers, Dr. . . . uh, Mrs. Andrews." The process server answered Diana's unfinished question anyway. His mission was accomplished: she had been served. His tone conveyed a mocking message. *How can you be surprised, Doctor? Here you are at eight o'clock at night working instead of being at home, and not even bothering to change your name.* "The papers will be filed with the court tomorrow morning."

The process server vanished quickly, leaving Diana with the envelope and its painful message. Chase had made his decision.

For a long, silent moment Diana's heart and mind were suspended between the new pain and an ancient one—when she hadn't been enough for a man she loved once before. Finally the disciplined part of her that helped her go on always, no matter how deep the anguish and loss, pulled her back to the present.

Diana slowly shut the office door and turned to Jeffrey.

"I guess you heard."

"Yes."

"I would appreciate it if you would keep this off the record."

"Once the papers are filed with the court it will be in the public domain." *And it will be a very big story.* "The court reporters are paid to check."

"I know. I'm just asking you not to mention it tomorrow in your coverage of the surgery."

"I'm not a tabloid journalist, Doctor." Didn't she know he wouldn't consider mentioning her private life—ever—in his newscast? Realizing that his tone had sounded harsh, Jeffrey added gently, "You have my word."

"Good. Thank you. Now, where were we?"

We were talking about the mysteries of the quickening of a heart as it falls in love, Jeffrey thought, but he said, "You were telling me about the programming of the physiological responses."

"Oh, yes."

Diana put the unopened envelope on her desk as she walked back to the oval table by the window. She resumed the explanation of her remarkable invention, but her eyes no longer sparkled and her voice was like the plastic heart—stark, sterile, clinical.

What is she feeling? Jeffrey wondered. *Does she want to scream with pain? What kind of heart beats inside the Queen of Hearts? A heart of ice? No heart at all?*

A wounded heart, Jeffrey decided as he listened to her mechanical words and glanced carefully into her cloudy sapphire eyes. A deeply wounded heart.

"I'm sorry," Jeffrey said quietly and sympathetically.

"It's . . ." Diana didn't finish the sentence, but her eyes communicated her thought, her warning, quite eloquently: *Stay away.*

Jeffrey understood the warning and the emotion behind it. Diana was reacting just as he would. Private grief, private rage, resentful of intrusion.

Just as he would react. That was what was so eerie. Before his eyes Diana was living the nightmare that haunted him, the secret fear that someday Julia might do this to him. *I'm leaving you, Jeffrey. It's over. There is someone else. There always has been.*

The scene would be just as it had been for Diana. One night, while he was still at the studio, a man would arrive with divorce papers. The blow would stun, but Jeffrey would recover quickly on the surface as Diana had. And in those anguished moments when the nightmare became a reality, he would not want the soft sympathetic voice of a stranger. He would want to be alone, face-to-face with the truth, face-to-face with his loss, his emptiness, his *failure*.

So leave Diana alone, Jeffrey told himself sensibly. But his heart had an emotional answer, an urge to help the bright, beautiful, wounded woman.

Besides, he reminded himself. *Who says Diana and I are really alike? The stars?*

"Chase could have picked a better time," Jeffrey offered very quietly.

"What do you mean?" Diana reflected on her own question for a moment and then finding an answer, she continued coolly, "Oh, I see, sometime when I had surgery scheduled on someone not so *important* as the Soviet ambassador? Just another *case* instead of a media event? You weren't listening to me earlier, were you?"

"Yes, I was. I meant that Chase could have picked a time when you would be able to have some privacy."

"You think I'm going to unravel, don't you?"

"No." Jeffrey hadn't even considered it. If he was presented with divorce papers ten hours before his newscast—or even ten minutes—he would be able to go on, a mechanical presentation, perhaps, but he would function. Of course Diana's situation was quite different. In ten hours she had to remove a dying heart and replace it with a new one. Could she really operate ten hours from now? *Should* she? If Jeffrey gave a lackluster and distracted telecast, he might get a few critical letters. More likely, the letters would be sympathetic. Had the nation's favorite anchorman been ill? The flu, perhaps? But a distracted performance in the operating room could be lethal. "Are you still . . ."

"Going to operate on the ambassador?" Diana finished Jeffrey's question and stared at him with eyes that were suddenly alive with anger.

"Yes," he replied quietly.

Diana fought to control her rage before speaking again. It was a legitimate question, of course, but not one she needed him to ask. She would ask herself that question, find her own private answer, and act accordingly, ethically.

"For the record, Mr. Lawrence," she whispered finally, a whisper of ice, "I would *never* jeopardize the welfare of my patient. If I am not prepared, for whatever reason, to give my very best, then I do not operate."

Jeffrey was about to apologize. He owed her an apology. He had assaulted her integrity. His attempt to help, to sympathize, had only offended. But the phone rang as he started to speak and Diana turned away to answer.

It was the operating room. She was needed.

"I have to go," she said flatly after she hung up. "The brochures and fact sheets should cover any areas I didn't discuss. Please close the door when you leave."

Then she was gone without a good-bye and before Jeffrey could offer either an apology or a thank-you.

As he put the brochures in his briefcase and the model of the Heart in its white cardboard box, he realized that Diana had been the first to leave, but he was the one who had been dismissed.

It was the Queen of Hearts who had decided when his audience with her was over.

The aching feeling that he had been the unwitting witness to a death—the death of a love—clung tenaciously to Jeffrey as the limousine made its way from Manhattan to Southampton. He guessed that Diana had been a little prepared; the divorce was something she feared even though she hoped it would never happen.

But even if Diana had been *completely* prepared, expecting it, the actual moment, like the moment of an expected death, was achingly somber, irrevocable, the end of hope—the empty forever end of all the joyous promises of love.

The eerie feeling clung and ominous thoughts taunted. Beautiful, successful, talented Diana had been unable to prevent the death of her marriage. Couldn't the same fate befall him? One night, perhaps tonight, he would return to Belvedere and Julia would be gone. She would leave a note, an apology: *Merry is not your daughter. She and I need to be with her father. I am so sorry, Jeffrey, please forgive me.*

Jeffrey fought the ominous thoughts with reason. The aching he felt was for Diana, *her* loss, *her* pain. What happened tonight wasn't a message from the stars, an astrological augur of things to come for him and Julia.

Still . . .

When Julia opened the mansion door Jeffrey felt his heart quicken—the wonderful and mysterious flutters of love that even the brilliant Queen of Hearts could not define.

"Julie," Jeffrey whispered softly, a joyful, relieved whisper of love.

"Hi." Her lavender eyes shimmered, happy to see him, relieved, too, as always, that Jeffrey had come home to her. "Is this the Heart?"

"Yes."

Jeffrey set his briefcase on the floor in the foyer and removed the plastic model from the cardboard box. He held the Heart for Julia and watched as her fingers delicately traced the webbed contours and her eyes became thoughtful and serious as her mind filled with the philosophical questions that he, too, had pondered.

"Will you tell me about it?" Julia asked. She hoped that even though Jeffrey was home later than usual they would sit in the great room as always—Jeffrey with a glass of Scotch and she curled against him—and talk. Like lovers resentful of any moments apart, they would share the events of their days, lovingly filling in the gaps of life when they couldn't be together.

"Yes, I will tell you about it . . ." Jeffrey hesitated, frowning slightly. He was home and she was here and her eyes glowed with love . . . but the fears still lingered.

"Jeffrey?"

"Just let me hold you a minute first." *Let me hold you and touch you and know that you are real and my fears are only imagined.*

Jeffrey put the model of the Heart on the marble table in the foyer. Then, not so confidently, he extended his arms to her.

Julia went to him swiftly, joyfully. *Just hold me always, Jeffrey. There is nowhere else I would rather be.*

The delicate, gentle hug became a strong, tight one, as close as they could be. Julia responded eagerly as his arms wrapped tighter, molding to him, her soft loveliness kissing his lean strength. Jeffrey's lips brushed the top of her silky black hair, caressing, nuzzling, whispering her name.

Julia looked up, saw the desire in his dark-blue eyes and felt a wave of trembling heat sweep through her. Smiling softly, she raised her lips to his.

Like the hug, the kiss began gently, softness touching softness, but, like the hug, the kiss gained strength and energy. Jeffrey was hungry for her and Julia was hungry for him. The kiss became warmer, deeper, closer, but it was still not enough.

"More?" Jeffrey whispered finally.

More was a word in the intimate vocabulary of their loving. From the very beginning of their love, a kiss had never been enough. They had always wanted more of each other, *all* of each other.

"More," Julia breathed.

They walked, hands entwined, up the sweeping circular staircase, beyond the room where Merry lay sleeping, to the master suite. The balmy night air floated gently through the open windows, carrying with it the fragrance of roses from the garden below. The perfume of a hundred roses came in through the windows and so, too, did the golden glow of the full summer moon.

Neither Jeffrey nor Julia moved to close the windows or drapes. Only the moon could see them, and neither wished for darkness while they loved.

Jeffrey made love to her slowly, a leisurely, sensual loving despite the powerful waves of desire that wanted all of her *now.* His hands explored gently, delicately caressing her graceful neck, her creamy shoulders, her soft, full breasts . . .

Jeffrey's gentle hands led the way, and his hungry lips followed. Hungry lips, talented lips. Rough and gentle, loving and teasing, whispering and probing, Jeffrey sensed her trembling desires and lovingly, expertly, answered them.

No part of Julia's naked loveliness was a secret to him. She gave all of herself to him, a joyous and unashamed gift of love and passion. No part was secret, no part forbidden. After ten years of loving, he knew her so well. And yet discovering her anew still held such mystery and such wonder.

Jeffrey made love to her and Julia made love to him. She knew his desires, too, and all the lovely ways to make him moan so softly. She loved to give him pleasure, loved to kiss brave, delicate, exquisite kisses until . . .

"Julie, darling." *I need you, all of you*, now.

"Jeffrey." *I need you, too.*

The wandering lips found each other, exploring there, deep and warm. And then they were together, where he belonged, where she wanted him to be. He stopped the kiss, but not the rhythm of their loving, to gaze into her moonlit eyes and whisper to her.

"I love you, Julie."

"I love you, too, Jeffrey."

They held the loving gaze as long as they could, until the crescendoing waves of desire took control, forcing their lips to join again and even their eyes to close. Then, swiftly, *swiftly* and together, they melted into a molten golden river of joy. And they were one, forged together by the fire of their passion and their love . . . so close that there was no room for secrets.

Julia fell asleep in Jeffrey's arms, nestled close, warm and lovely. She breathed softly, delicate whispers of contentment, and a gentle smile curled her lips. Jeffrey gazed at her and marveled at the perfection of this moment.

Sometimes—most of the time—their love was so perfect, like a brilliant diamond bathed in sunlight, a glittering kaleidoscope of color, ever-changing, ever-wondrous, always breathtakingly beautiful.

Perfect, glittering, and flawless—to the naked eye.

But their magnificent love, like all but the rarest of diamonds, wasn't free of flaws. What marriage, what love, was flawless?

None, of course. Jeffrey knew that. But their flaw, the tiny flaw in their almost perfect love, could be a fatal one.

The flaw was so tiny, so trivial compared to the immensity of his love, but, like the tiniest flaw in a beautiful diamond, it could destroy. The virtually indestructible stone could be shattered by a soft blow placed just so. The glittering gem could crumble into a million pieces, the wonder gone, the brilliance a mere memory, the rainbow of dazzling colors clouded to gray.

The flaw was Julia's lie to him about Merry. Jeffrey knew he wasn't Merry's father—he could not be—but Julia had told him, her lavender eyes so innocent, so bewildered, so unflickering, *You are her father, Jeffrey. There has never been anyone else.*

And all these years she had resolutely continued the charade, protecting the secret lover she defiantly claimed didn't exist. So many times she could have told him the truth! He encouraged her, gently, lovingly, and sometimes angrily, but Julia steadfastly maintained the ancient lie. Jeffrey didn't know the reason she kept her secret still, and that was what terrified him . . .

Because, from the very beginning, Julia had only deceived him about the important things.

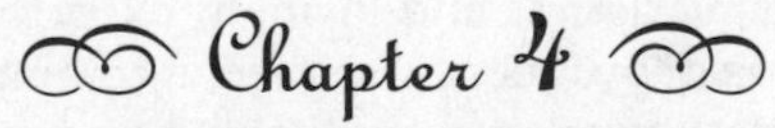

SAN FRANCISCO
FEBRUARY 1979

The day was perfect, the winter sun warm, the sea breeze invigorating, the sky bright blue and cloudless. As Jeffrey wandered through the Saturday-afternoon activity of Ghirardelli Square he was amazed by the rush of nostalgia that swept through him. It was his last day in San Francisco, and his last day, too, as a local reporter. Soon the camera crew would arrive and Jeffrey would tape his fond farewell to his loyal viewers. Then, once the taping was over, he would drive to Los Angeles and his new job as a network correspondent. He was eager to be on his way; the prospect was exhilarating, thrilling, but still . . .

He would always remember this elegant, stylish, sophisticated city. And he would remember this perfect day. He would etch today in his memory and recall its gentle sunny images on future days in distant cities ravaged by war; cities whose children didn't scamper across emerald-green lawns trailing silver-tailed kites but cowered instead on sunparched grass splattered red with blood; cities whose daytime sounds weren't laughter and music but rather the thunder of mortar and the anguished cries of death. He would recall the memory of this flawless day as a gentle antidote when the new visions of his life became too grim.

He crossed the park in front of Ghirardelli Square to the edge of the Bay and watched the sleek sailboats gliding swiftly across the sparkling whitecapped water, etching those graceful images, until a bell sounded, signalling the hour and drawing him from his reverie.

As Jeffrey turned to join the just-arrived camera crew, he saw her. She sat cross-legged on the grass, her long black hair dancing in the wind, her lavender eyes gazing serenely at the sea, and her full lips curled into a soft smile.

He added her image—a beautiful San Francisco woman—to the other images of the day. Not that he needed an image of a San Francisco woman. He had known many. But she was a perfect symbol of all the others he had known, so serene, so elegant, so beautiful.

As he was making a permanent memory of the lavender eyes, midnight-black hair, and sublime beauty, she turned her remarkable eyes from the sea to him. The lavender flickered with surprise, as if she had recognized him, then confusion, as she realized he was a stranger. Suddenly shy and embarrassed, she looked down, her long inky-black lashes delicately closing over her eyes like tiny fans.

Jeffrey felt surprise, and recognition, and confusion, too, but he didn't become embarrassed nor did he look away. Instead he stared at her, willing her to look at him again. When she obeyed his silent command, bravely lifting her magnificent lavender eyes to him, there was surprise, still, and recognition, again, but now the confusion was replaced by wonder.

She had recognized him, but it wasn't the familiar recognition—"Oh, you're Jeffrey Lawrence from Channel Four News!"—it was deeper, and he felt it, too.

It was a recognition of the heart.

Jeffrey suddenly felt the immense relief of being found, even though he had never known he was lost. And he suddenly felt full, a joyous, bountiful fullness, even though he had never for a moment in his splendid successful life felt empty. And he felt the triumph that accompanies the discovery of the missing piece in a puzzle, the piece that instantly makes the confusing picture crystal clear, even though he hadn't known there was a puzzle much less a missing piece.

For an astonished moment Jeffrey was lost in the wonderful-and-so-powerful feelings and lost, too, in her magnificent eyes and their seductive invitation: *Come be with me forever.*

The moment felt like an eternity, but in fact it was brief. Jeffrey's disciplined mind intervened, willing control over his racing heart and swirling thoughts, forcing a perfunctory spell-breaking smile on his lips, and commanding his legs to continue walking away from her and toward the crew and his future.

Jeffrey walked away, but he was shaken, and the inquisitive mind that had already won so many awards in investigative journalism sought answers.

You simply gift-wrapped her in your surprising nostalgia about leaving San Francisco, he told himself.

The explanation seemed sound. Emotion and sentiment had played very small roles in his life, cameo appearances, well scripted in advance. Today the sentimentality and emotions he felt about San Francisco had caught him by surprise. Those unfamiliar feelings, used to dormancy and suddenly awakened, had become rogues, awakening other fantastic feelings.

Fantastic feelings like falling in love? Of course not! His emotions had simply gone awry on this sentimental day. It had to do with him, not her.

Still, as Jeffrey taped his adieu to San Francisco, his gaze drifted to where she sat and he sent a silent command: *Don't leave*. As soon as the taping was over he would speak to her and prove that it was nothing to do with her, only his own surprising emotions, and he would be on his way to Los Angeles.

Don't leave, Jeffrey silently commanded the beautiful woman with lavender eyes. *Be there, so I can say hello and good-bye.*

Julia didn't leave. She was sitting on the grass still, even though the winter sun had set, taking the gentle warmth from the air and leaving in its golden wake an icy chill. As Jeffrey approached, closer than he had been before, he saw that she was even more beautiful, more bewitching, but less sophisticated. Her loose-fitting jeans bore no designer lable. Her pale-yellow cotton blouse was faded from many washings. Her V-neck blue sweater was threadbare and not cashmere. She didn't have an elegant purse fashioned by Gucci or Coach, in fact no purse at all, and no jacket. And on her lap, its title turned from his view, she held a book. The book was like her clothes, threadbare and tattered, its navy cloth cover frayed and showing cardboard.

"Hi. I'm Jeffrey."

"I'm Julia."

A gust of wind swept a strand of her long black hair into her eyes and across her lips. Julia's fingers trembled as she pulled the strand away.

"Are you cold?"

"A little, I guess," Julia admitted, although she had been trembling ever since she first met his dark-blue eyes, long before the sun fell into the sea.

"Would you like to go somewhere warm?" *Like to Southern California?* one of the frolicking rogues taunted. He reminded the frisky thought that he was only going to say hello and good-bye, to prove there was nothing. But there wasn't nothing. Her lovely eyes, her soft voice, her well-worn clothes had hold of his heart and wouldn't let go.

"Yes. Thank you."

"*Jane Eyre*." Jeffrey read the title of her tattered book as she stood. "A favorite?"

Julia nodded. She was proud to admit that the wonderful romance was a favorite. Proud and fond. Strong, patient Jane and handsome, troubled Rochester were beloved friends. Julia almost told Jeffrey that she hadn't damaged the book—she wouldn't do that to her friends!—despite the many times she had read it. Others had caused the damage, reading carelessly, but because of their carelessness the precious volume had found its way to a used bookstore and had been marked with a price just short of nothing, a price that Julia could afford.

"Here. Wear this," Jeffrey said as he draped his jacket around her slender shoulders. "So, shall we get a drink? Hot buttered rum? Irish coffee?"

He thinks I'm at least twenty-one, Julia realized with a tremble of excitement and fear.

"Just coffee would be fine."

"How about chowder? It's turned into that kind of day."

* * *

The Chowder House on Fisherman's Wharf was a warm sanctuary for others who sought escape from the sudden chill of the winter twilight. The popular restaurant was crowded and noisy, but Jeffrey and Julia were lost in their own world, in a wooden booth scarred by the initials of a hundred young lovers, enveloped by the warm scent of fresh-baked sourdough bread, the steaminess of the restaurant, and the magnificent feelings of being together.

"You're an actor," Julia said softly, stating it as fact even though she wasn't sure. It was what she had deduced from watching the stunningly hand-some man standing before camera crews and surrounded by admirers. He was probably a famous movie star. If she had had money to spend on movies, she might have known for certain.

"You really don't know who I am?" Jeffrey asked gently, not wanting to embarrass her and quite pleased that she wasn't a fan.

"No, I'm sorry, I don't."

"For the last four years I've been a reporter with Channel Four News. The segment we just taped was my final one. I begin work with the network in Los Angeles on Monday. How about you, do you live here?"

"I live in Berkeley." She added quietly, apologetically, "I don't watch television."

There was a television in the tiny house in Berkeley where Julia lived with her aunt Doreen, but it was in her aunt's bedroom and off limits to Julia.

You don't watch television and you must not read newspapers, either, Jeffrey mused. In the past few weeks all the Bay Area papers had run pieces about him, his summa cum laude graduation from Stanford, his extraordinary career at Channel Four, the excellence-in-journalism awards he had won, his promotion to the big leagues of network news, and his never-before-disclosed pedigree . . .

Jeffrey Cabot Lawrence was one of the truly wealthy. He wore his heritage of generations of wealth and privilege the way the forever wealthy do, quite casually, like a coat slung over the arm in case of rain. But close examination of the raincoat would reveal it was the best, perfectly tailored, just as close examination of Jeffrey revealed his perfect manners, his impeccable taste, and his love of the expensive and rare.

Jeffrey's appeal, his elegance and style, was suddenly explained. He was an aristocrat. It had to do with breeding, not money, although Jeffrey's personal fortune was already immense. Still, he worked for a living, worked very hard, and no blue-blooded strings had been pulled to get him the job at Channel Four or the important promotion to the network. Jeffrey Lawrence was a rich kid who could have done nothing, but chose to make hisown way and create his own success. The facts about Jeffrey made his devoted fans even more devoted.

Most of the Bay Area—the viewing and reading public—knew all about Jeffrey Lawrence.

But Julia did not.

"You are famous, aren't you?" she asked, remembering the crowd that had assembled to get his autograph after the taping.

"Not really. A little local fame."

"But you *will* be famous."

"Yes, I guess, if I accomplish what I hope to accomplish. The fame doesn't matter."

"Only the dreams."

"Yes," Jeffrey whispered, stunned by her choice of words. They *were* dreams, of course, and he thought of them that romantic way, but to others he had always referred to them as "career goals," not "dreams." Until now . . . "Only the dreams."

Jeffrey told Julia about his dreams. He used the words he always used when he talked about his plans, but Julia understood as no one ever had before.

"I love being at the heart of a news story as it unfolds, being an eyewitness and reporting what I see. So far I've just done local stories, but I hope to travel overseas and report from politically turbulent places."

That will give you a lot of camera time, won't it, if you're in the Middle

East or somewhere? the beautiful and sophisticated women who had been Jeffrey's lovers would ask when he told them. Then they would smile knowingly and add, *And you'll become famous and return as a network anchor.*

That all might happen, of course, but that wasn't Jeffrey's reason.

"That's very important," Julia replied quietly.

"I think so," Jeffrey answered even more quietly. That was his reason, because he believed it was important, not because it was a path to celebrity or fame. The planet was small, so small. Little political fires in distant places could spark destruction for all of mankind. That was Jeffrey's reason for his dream. The lovely intelligent lavender eyes knew his dream was important, but did they know why? Part of Jeffrey didn't want to ask, didn't want to hear Julia say, *It's important because you'll get a lot of camera time and then you can return as a network anchor.* But part of him, the part that was beginning to believe that unbeknownst to him his heart had been searching for her all his life, wanted to know. "Why do you think it's important, Julia?"

"Because the planet is so small."

As they curled their hands around the bowls of steaming chowder, feeling the warmth but not eating because their mouths had better things to do—talking and smiling and falling in love—Jeffrey softly told Julia, who already knew, the truth about his dreams.

Jeffrey told Julia the truth. Julia told Jeffrey some truths, too, and she told him some lies.

"You said you're from Berkeley. Are you a student?"

"Yes." Julia *was* from Berkeley and she *was* a student. But she knew that Jeffrey was asking if she was a student at the university and that with her Yes she was deceiving him.

"What year are you?"

"A senior." True, too, in a way. Julia was a senior in high school, even though she was only sixteen, a year, two years younger than most of her classmates.

"And what will you do when you graduate, Julia? Tell me your dreams." Jeffrey watched the lovely lavender eyes become confused. "Julia?"

"I . . . I don't know."

"When I first saw you today you were gazing out at the Bay and smiling. What were you thinking about then?"

"Just a make-believe story."

"A story about what?"

Julia looked at the wonderful, handsome man who made her feel so safe, magically luring her from her painful shyness, encouraging her to speak and welcoming her quiet words with a gentle smile.

"About love."

"Love," Jeffrey echoed softly. "Are you going to be a writer, Julia? A modern-day Charlotte Brontë?"

Julia considered his question, testing that dream, and finally said quietly, "I don't think so."

"What then?" Jeffrey pressed gently. "What is your dream?"

He thought she wouldn't answer. Her cheeks flushed pink and her eyes were confused again. He waited, smiling and sending silent messages: *Tell me, Julia. Trust me with your secret dreams.*

Julia had never dared to dream, but she had lovely wishes that lived in a part of her heart hidden even from her, a delicate, fragile place where hope and love lived still despite all the losses of her young life.

Jeffrey discovered that delicate, fragile, hopeful place.

"My dream is to make a happy life for someone I love," Julia whispered bravely. "It's not very important." *Compared to risking your life to save mankind.*

"Yes it is." Jeffrey spoke from a hidden place in his heart, a place of tenderness and love that Julia had discovered. "It is very important." *Nurturing a precious love may be the most important dream of all.*

"I love the sea," Jeffrey told her as they walked along the Wharf beneath the starry sky. The fishing boats creaked in their moorings, rocked by the brisk wintry wind and the whitecapped waves.

"It scares me."

"It does?" Jeffrey looked with surprise into the lavender eyes that hours earlier had gazed so serenely at the sea as she imagined stories of love.

"It's very beautiful when the sunshine glitters off it, but at night it seems so dark and cold." Julia could overcome her fear of the sea—she was teaching herself to overcome it, in the daylight, from a distance, by gazing at the sparkling blue and thinking about love. But at night, this close to the swirling water was terrifying. It would take longer to overcome the nighttime fears . . . because it was at night that the plane carrying her parents became a coffin of fire and fell into the dark cold depths. "And I don't know how to swim."

Julia's soft shrug became a tremble as an icy chill of fear swept through her. Jeffrey wrapped his arms around her, pulling her close, protecting her from the turbulent sea, wanting her never to be afraid.

And wanting more . . .

Her soft lips were cool at the surface because of the winter wind, but beneath, just beneath, there was fire and passion.

Julia had never kissed anyone before, but her lips discovered his instinctively with caresses that were timid and brave, gentle and ravenous. Timid and gentle with wonder. Brave and ravenous from a lifetime of hunger. Julia's hands explored instinctively, too, curling around his neck, weaving into his hair, and her body kissed his, pressing softly against him and trembling.

Jeffrey felt Julia's trembling and stopped his tender kisses to look at her. Her shivering was desire, not the winter wind, just as he trembled with desire for her.

"More?" he asked softly.

"More," she whispered, not knowing what she was agreeing to, but knowing that she couldn't say no.

Jeffrey got them a room at a motel on the Wharf. While he pulled the curtains and hung the jacket he had given her and turned the thermostat for heat and hooked the Do Not Disturb sign on the door handle, Julia searched for answers to the questions that swirled in her mind.

What was she supposed to do? What did he expect? She wanted to give him pleasure, but she had no experience. The romances she read were wonderful fantasies of love, not guide books of loving. But if she told Jeffrey the truth—how young she was and how innocent—the night would be over, wouldn't it?

His gentle blue eyes would darken with disappointment, or perhaps even anger, that she had deceived him, and he would tell her to leave.

And, oh, how she didn't want to leave him! The thought filled her with emptiness greater than all the losses of her young life. *I have to* act *experienced*, she told herself. But how?

With trembling fingers and a prayer that it was right, Julia began to undress.

By the time Jeffrey turned to devote his attention to her for the entire night, Julia had removed her threadbare sweater and pale-yellow cotton blouse and folded them neatly on a chair beside the bed. Julia had worn no bra that day, so with the removal of her blouse and sweater she was naked above the waist.

Naked and so beautiful, her skin rich and white, her full breasts high and proud. Julia stood before him, shy and brave, awaiting his appraisal and praying his eyes would fill with approval and desire.

"Julia. What are you doing?" Jeffrey asked gently as he moved toward her.

He had wondered if there had been a flicker of lavender uncertainty when he suggested a motel and had almost told her then that they could kiss all night, or talk, or sleep . . . but now she stood before him, half naked, the most beautiful woman he had ever seen.

"Oh." Julia frowned. Isn't this what I am supposed to do?

"You are so beautiful."

Jeffrey kissed the lovely frown away. Then his lips found hers and his gentle hands found her nakedness and Julia didn't have to worry about her inexperience because loving Jeffrey was as instinctive as kissing him had been. And for the first time in his years of expert, skillful lovemaking, loving was instinctive for Jeffrey, too. Always before, in the midst of pleasure, Jeffrey's mind was engaged, *Now I should do this*. His lovers proclaimed him *the best*, but that was simply Jeffrey, excelling at whatever he did.

He had made love many times before, with elegance and finesse, but never until Julia had he *loved*. Never, until Julia, had there been a purpose to the intimacy except pleasure. Now, beyond the exhilarating pleasure of touching her, was an urgent need to be as close to her as possible, to be part of her, to be one with her.

Jeffrey explored her exquisite, sensual body, touching hello, kissing hello, wanting to be all places at once. He was hungry for all of her, but he forced extraordinary control over his own desires, discovering her desires, savoring each new discovery, returning often to her eyes and her lips. Julia's perfect body responded without shame, arching to him, hiding nothing, keeping no secrets. She gave him all of her loveliness, a breathless trembling gift of joy.

Julia heard the lovely soft sighs of joy and realized with astonishment that they came from deep within her, carried from her heart to her lips on rushes of happiness. And she heard, too the wonderful soft deep sighs that came from him.

"Julia?" Jeffrey whispered finally when he could force control no longer, when he needed so desperately to be one with her.

"Jeffrey." She welcomed him and there wasn't any pain, not even a little, even though she was a virgin, because he had been so very gentle . . . as if he knew.

"My darling Julie."

"No one has ever called me Julie," she said quietly as she lay in his arms and his lips caressed the tangle of her silky black hair. No voice had ever before softened with affection for her. She had always been Julia, a serious name, not Julie, a tender loving one.

"Never?"

"Never."

"May I?"

"Oh, yes."

"Julie," Jeffrey whispered again.

He whispered her name over and over as he showed her his love. And sometime during their astonishing night of loving, Jeffrey embellished her name, speaking aloud what he already knew in his heart, a joyous, confident, wondrous knowledge . . . words he had never spoken before. "I love you, Julie. I love you."

Ten hours before he was to begin his new job with the network in Los Angeles, Jeffrey left Julia at the Telegraph Avenue entrance of the Berkeley campus. He left her reluctantly, missing her in advance, dreading already the twelve days until she could visit him in L.A.

As soon as his car was out of sight, Julia began the two-mile journey to the dilapidated house where she lived with her aunt Doreen. Her journey took her far away from the bright lights of Telegraph, but she was unafraid of the dangers that lurked in the remote dark streets of Berkeley. She had spent her life roaming streets filled with menacing strangers and she had survived.

And tonight, even if she had been afraid, her fears would have been vanquished by the magical words that echoed in her mind: *I love you, Julie.*

No one had ever loved Julia, not her parents, not her aunt, certainly never a man. Julia didn't know why she was unloved, only that she was. As a little girl she reached the only conclusion she could: something about her made her undeserving of love. Was it her shyness? Her seriousness? She didn't know. And she had no way of knowing that it had merely been her great misfortune to be born to parents who were too flawed and self-absorbed to love their daughter.

Julia's parents had been flower children. She was an accidental bud, a fragile blossom who should have been cherished but was only neglected. She became a wildflower, delicate but hardy, surviving the elements without protection. Until she was ten Julia and her parents lived in a commune in Haight-Ashbury. Her parents were two of the many would-be acid-rock musicians of the sixties. Her father was very talented and his star might have shined brighter than the rest, but he discovered he could make money more easily by selling drugs than by struggling for success.

Julia's parents were phantoms that floated in and out of her life, frequently away, erratic in the attention they paid her even when they were at home, unreliable, out of her reach—but so important to her!

She fought the loneliness of her life by creating wonderful fairy tales. In the lovely stories of her imagination, Julia was a princess, so very loved by her adoring parents. How they hated to be away from her! But they had to be away because they had to share the magic of their music with children less fortunate than she was.

There was no death in her fairy tales, or sadness or violence; and there were no villains, either, no wicked witches, evil sorcerers, or terrifying monsters. Julia's imaginary lands were populated by wonderful creatures like Puff—gentle magical pastel dragons that soared in the sky on gossamer wings and breathed soft mists of perfume, not swirls of fire.

Julia preferred her lovely happy fairy tales to the ones she read, but reading was still a wonderful escape. She taught herself to read, and one day someone emerged from a drug-fog long enough to realize that four-year-old Julia was intently reading an article from *Rolling Stone* magazine. That discovery precipitated a flurry of attention. How bright *was* she? How much knowledge was stored in the quiet, serious head? They discovered the truth about her—she was brilliant, gifted—and for a while she became a prized specimen. The interest in her remarkable intelligence eventually faded, but not before she was enrolled in kindergarten, the youngest student by over a year.

Julia's small heart pounded with joy at the sudden attention and ached when

the interest waned. It was more proof that there was something about her that couldn't hold love. A new pattern developed—joy and pain. Joy when there were flickers of interest from teachers and classmates because she was so very bright, and then pain as the interest died because she was so quiet and so shy.

When Julia was ten, her parents left for the last time. "'Bye, kid. Be good," they murmured as they left, although her imagination, as always, made it a loving farewell. Her parents never returned from whatever enchanted kingdom they were visiting because their small plane exploded in midair, a kiss of death from a fire-breathing dragon, and fell in a ball of flames into the cold, dark sea.

Julia never knew that her parents had been smuggling cocaine from Cartagena and that the fiery explosion had been caused by a bomb placed by a drug lord who resented intrusion in his not-so-enchanted kingdom. She never knew, either, that there was sixty thousand dollars of drug profit in her parents" bank account.

Her only living relative was her aunt Doreen, her father's sister. Doreen Phillips shared with her brother a genetic package of destruction—a compelling addiction to drugs and an associated addiction to finding the easiest way to survive even if it meant ignoring talent. Doreen didn't want Julia. A deep instinct had prevented her from having children of her own or even marrying. Doreen didn't want Julia, but the ten-year-old girl came with a sixty-thousand-dollar bank account.

Small compensation, Doreen decided, for the imposition of having to care for Julia. Not that Doreen cared for her more than anyone ever had. Long before she squandered all the drug money, Doreen told Julia that they were very poor and that Julia had to "earn her keep" by doing household chores in the neighborhood until she was old enough to get a real job.

The wonderful fairy tales that had sustained her during her lonely, loveless childhood died when her parents fell to the sea in flames. For two years following their death, Julia lived in constant pain, unnumbed by fantasies. When she was twelve, a little girl becoming a young woman, she read the romantic stories of Jane Austen, Louisa May Alcott, and the Brontës. The wonderful romances sparked her imagination and she began to invent her own stories of love.

As a little girl, by pretending that *she* was the beloved princess in her fairy tales, Julia had bravely convinced herself that one day her parents would love her. But the fantasy that her own life would be filled with such happiness had been brutally shattered when her parents died, and Julia vowed never to delude herself again. The heroines of her stories of love were other young women, women deserving of love, not her, never her . . . and she never allowed herself to dream that a man would ever say "I love you" to *her*.

I love you, Julie. She believed Jeffrey meant it for the moment, as others had shown flickers of interest in her before. But Julia, the terribly bright girl who had learned well the painful lessons of her young life, knew with absolute certainty that eventually he would lose interest in her. Jeffrey loved her beautiful body, her unashamed passion, *something* about her for now. But it wouldn't last.

It would be her fault, not Jeffrey's, when he left because it was she who could not hold on to love.

As Julia emerged from the last dark alley and walked up the creaking stairs to her aunt's tiny house, her heart whispered a gentle plea, *I love you, Jeffrey. Please love me for as long as you can.*

Chapter 5

LOS ANGELES
MAY 1979

Jeffrey knew he would love her forever, and he was restless to make definite plans for their life together. Restless, and a little afraid. Before he could ask Julia to spend her life with him, Jeffrey needed to tell her a very private truth about himself. He needed to tell his brilliant love, who could be anything she wanted but whose dream was simply to make a happy life for those she loved, that he could never give her children. It would just be the two of them. Was that—just him and all his love—enough for her? Or would he lose her?

Jeffrey's heart quickened as he neared his apartment on the first Friday evening in May, quickening with eager anticipation because Julia would be there, waiting for him, and quickening, too, with apprehension because this was the weekend he would tell her.

She was in the living room, gazing at the garden beneath the window, so lost in thought that she didn't hear him come in.

"Hello, darling."

Julia spun at the sound of his voice, and when she did, Jeffrey's loving smile faded to gentle worry. Her lovely lavender eyes were dark-circled and troubled, and she didn't rush eagerly into his arms.

"What's wrong?"

"I've come to say good-bye."

"*Good-bye?* Julie, why?"

"Because . . . there are things you don't know about me."

"Tell me," Jeffrey whispered calmly even though his heart raced with fear. *Tell me your secrets, my love, and I will tell you mine . . . and we will say hello forever, not good-bye.*

"I'm not a senior at Berkeley, Jeffrey. I don't live in a dormitory on campus. I live at home with my aunt. She's my guardian."

"Your guardian?"

"Yes. My parents were killed when I was ten. The small plane they were flying from Cartagena exploded in midair and fell into the sea."

"Oh, darling, I'm so sorry. Now I know why you are afraid of the sea."

"I'm not afraid when I'm with you," Julia replied swiftly, distracted from her confession by the concern and gentleness in his eyes. *Oh, Jeffrey, please look gentle still when you hear the truth.*

"I'm glad. You should never be afraid when you're with me." But she was afraid now, afraid of what she had to tell him, and he was afraid because she had come to say good-bye. Jeffrey urged gently, "So your aunt became your guardian after your parents died."

"Yes." Julia sighed softly. "Jeffrey, that was six years ago."

"*What?* You're telling me that you're only sixteen?"

"Yes. I know I should have told you. I'm sorry."

"*Sorry?*" he echoed harshly, stunned by the truth and angered by the lie. He had assumed, because she told him she was a senior in college, that she was twenty-one or twenty-two. But he had wondered if she was older, closer to his age, because of her insights, her serenity, and the maturity of her passion.

Sixteen? Sixteen-year-old girls had never appealed to Jeffrey, not when he was sixteen, or fifteen, or even fourteen. Even then the silly giggling, the pretense at sophistication, the false maturity had made him restless.

But Julia didn't giggle and her eyes didn't sparkle with the foolish expectation that life would glitter always with happiness. Julia's beautiful lavender eyes were serious, thoughtful, wise—eyes that knew about the sadness of life. Julia didn't giggle, but she smiled a smile that filled him with such desire. And her laugh was so soft . . . and when they made love it filled with wonder as if amazed that such joy could come from within her.

Julia wasn't sixteen, except in years.

She looked young now, younger than she had ever looked to him, as she bravely met his angry glare. Young, and so beautiful, and so lost, and so afraid. Jeffrey wanted her never to be lost or afraid! And, as that wish of love magically melted his fury, his spinning mind spun to an amazing conclusion: he could live with the truth—he loved her no matter what her age—and he could forgive the lie. It had been a necessary deception, hadn't it? Because if Julia had told him her age on that enchanted afternoon in Ghirardelli, he would have walked away, run away, wouldn't he? *Wouldn't he?*

Yes . . . maybe . . . *no*.

"So you're sixteen," he whispered gently with a soft loving smile. "It doesn't change the way I feel about you. I still love you, Julie."

Julia's lavender eyes shimmered with disbelieving joy. She had only come today because she believed she owed Jeffrey the truth. She knew he would be angry at first, but she prayed that their inevitable good-bye would be gentle. Yes, of course their relationship had to end now that he knew how young she was, he would say. But then maybe, her greatest wish, he would tell her gently that he *had* loved her. If only she could spend the rest of her life believing that for two and a half months she had truly been loved by this wonderful man . . .

That had been her wish, and it had seemed so foolish, such an impossible dream. She had never for a moment dared to dream Jeffrey would want her still. If she had imagined that, she might not have come at all, because there was the other secret, something she had never planned to tell him, the reason she had to stop seeing him now before he noticed the new softness of her sleek body.

"Julie?" Jeffrey asked gently. His anxious heart had calmed when he saw the joy in her eyes, but it raced again, suddenly worried, because now there was new lavender fear. "Another secret?"

"Yes." Julia frowned, hesitating, wishing she had a chance to think about this first. But the gentle eyes that had always been able to lure the innermost secrets of her heart urged her now and Julia heard herself say, "Jeffrey . . . I'm pregnant."

Her voice was soft, her words barely audible, but they echoed like thunder in his brain and plunged into his heart with excruciating pain as his mind filled with vivid images of Julia with another lover, a man whose loving had given her something he could never give.

As the images swirled and his heart screamed, Jeffrey's blue eyes darkened, emptying of all warmth and gentleness and filling with a stormy turbulence that was beyond anger. Julia watched the transformation and felt an icy chill as she read the dark and eloquent message.

Jeffrey didn't want their baby.

There was no room for children in Jeffrey's important dreams. If she'd had a chance to think she would have known. Now she knew and it caused such pain . . . new pain for the innocent life growing inside her, a tiny life she already loved so much, and old pain for another unwanted child, an unloved little girl with lavender eyes who had survived on fairy tales.

The little girl was a woman now. And for the past few months she had lived a fairy tale of love, an enchanted fairy tale that almost had a happy ending. Because Jeffrey loved her, wanted her . . . but he didn't want their baby.

"Jeffrey, I'm sorry," she whispered helplessly, hopelessly to his angry dark eyes.

The soft sound of her voice registered above the thunder in his brain, but as he focused on her apologetic eyes, another devastating revelation, perhaps the most devastating of all, swept through him . . . the real reason she had come to say good-bye.

"You're leaving me to be with the baby's father, aren't you?"

"No, Jeffrey, *you* are the father." Her eyes widened with astonishment that he could imagine she had ever had another lover. "The first night we were together I wasn't using any birth control."

"I can't be the baby's father, Julia."

"But you are," she countered softly. *I can see how much you don't want to be, but you are!* "Jeffrey, there has never been anyone else."

Her soft confession caused even more turbulence in his dark-blue eyes. How she wished she had known not to tell him about the baby! How she wished she could have had a gentle memory of their good-bye! But all gentleness had vanished from his eyes and voice, and Julia's breaking heart couldn't wait to see if it ever returned.

"I have to go. Good-bye, Jeffrey."

Let her go, reason urged as he watched her gather her tattered knapsack and begin to cross the room toward the door. *She is sixteen. She lies to you. She has lied from the beginning and is lying still. Let her go to her other lover! Your life can be yours again, your privacy, your freedom, your dreams*. To assume the responsibility of Julia and her lover's baby would be sheer insanity.

Jeffrey's heart made different pleas. *You love her. She is the other half of your heart. Can you really live your life without her?*

"Do you love me, Julie?" His voice stopped her, and when she turned and he held her lavender eyes, he added quietly, "Please tell me the truth."

"Oh, yes, Jeffrey, I love you."

"Then marry me."

"Marry?"

"Yes, marry. I love you, Julie. I want to spend my life with you."

"Jeffrey," she whispered softly, a whisper of hope and pain. "The baby."

Jeffrey fought the stabbing ache that swept through him and smiled a wobbly smile. "I want you, Julie, and I want your baby."

Your baby. Julia knew that the little life inside her had been created because of her lies, because she had deceived him into believing that she was experienced and prepared when in truth she had been so very innocent and so very desperate for his love, but it was still the precious child of *their* magnificent love. The part of Julia's bright mind that was firmly tethered to the lessons of her life warned her to flee to protect herself and her baby from further pain. But the defiant corner of her gifted mind that in gentle collaboration with her heart had imagined wonderful stories of love urged her to stay. Because not even her remarkable imagination had imagined a love as wonderful as Jeffrey.

Julia believed in Jeffrey. She believed in the kind, gentle, loving man to whom she had so joyfully given her heart. He had had every right to be angry that she had deceived him about her age and innocence, and of course he had been shocked and enraged to discover that those deceptions had created a little life

he might never have chosen to create. But someday Jeffrey would love his baby, wouldn't he? How desperately Julia needed to know the answer to that so important question. She couldn't know now, but stil her loving heart gave a confident reply, *Yes, he will. And until then, while Jeffrey follows his important dreams, you will love your precious baby.*

"Do you really want to marry me?"

"More than anything in the world."

Yes, Julia admitted softly, she had done well in school. But graduating from high school, or going on to college, didn't matter. What mattered, all she wanted, was to be with him as soon as possible. And that was what Jeffrey wanted, too.

As soon as possible was a week, they decided that weekend as they made joyful plans and gentle promises of love. They promised to love each other forever, and never to be afraid to tell each other the truth, and Julia whispered with glowing, hopeful lavender eyes, "No more lies, Jeffrey, I promise."

Julia promised no more lies, and she told him the secrets of her lonely, loveless childhood, shyly sharing those painful truths, and Jeffrey listened, holding her gently and loving her all the more, and waiting so patiently for her to confess to the words he knew to be untrue: *There has never been anyone else, Jeffrey.*

But Julia never confessed to that lie. She only met his expectant loving gaze, blushing finally because his blue eyes appraised her with such intensity. And Jeffrey didn't force her confession by telling her why the baby she carried could not be his because sometime during the weekend of joyful plans and promises of forever the most astonishing, most wonderful thought began to dance in his mind.

What if Julia was telling the truth? What if, in the past eleven years, everything had changed? What if the woman he loved so very much really was carrying his child?

"When I was fifteen I had mumps complicated by mumps orchitis," Jeffrey told the fertility specialist at UCLA five days before he and Julia were married. "My sperm count following the infection was extremely low, and the doctors said they didn't expect it to change."

"It hasn't," the specialist confirmed.

"Oh," Jeffrey said quietly. He had been so hopeful.

"I take it you have been unable to conceive?"

"I've never actually tried."

"So we don't know."

"We don't?" Eleven years before, despite occasional admonitions to practice birth control just in case, the solemnity of the specialists, the eloquently descriptive terms "sterile" and "infertile," and his mother's grim horror had sent a message that was abundantly clear: Jeffrey Cabot Lawrence was *never* going to pass his blue blood on to heirs. "Some of the doctors did recommend contraception unless pregnancy was desired, but frankly I thought that was because my mother tended to have a kill-the-messenger look every time we were given the prognosis."

"Perhaps it was," the doctor said with a wry smile. "As you know, although only a single sperm ultimately fertilizes the egg, the reality is that millions of sperm seem to be required to create an environment in which conception can occur. However, as long as any sperm are present, I, too, would advise contraception unless pregnancy is planned."

"You mean there actually *is* a chance?"

"A chance, yes, although it is vanishingly small."

"But not impossible." 41

"Doctors never say never. We believe in miracles like everyone else."

"So it would be a miracle."

"Approaching one. But, Jeffrey, your chance of fathering a child using the new technique of in vitro fertilization isn't vanishingly small. We once thought that test-tube babies would forever be a fantasy of science fiction, but just last year Louise Joy Brown was born in England."

Jeffrey knew, of course, about Louise Joy Brown and the remarkable advances in medical science . . . but what he needed now was a miracle.

And Jeffrey Lawrence didn't believe in miracles. At least, the journalist whose logical, disciplined mind was trained to deal with hard facts and incontrovertible data didn't believe in miracles. But wasn't that the same Jeffrey Lawrence who hadn't believed in falling in love—until it happened?

Jeffrey's heart had fallen swiftly, joyfully, confidently in love with Julia, and now that heart proclaimed with swift and joyful confidence: the miracle has already happened.

The fact that Julia's baby *could* be his was miracle enough, wasn't it? He simply had to accept it, to believe her baby was his and vow never to challenge that belief.

Simply . . . but it would be simple, as simple as falling in love with her, as joyous, as wonderful, as right.

Jeffrey and Julia spent the weekend before their wedding in romantic Carmel, making love in their charming room at the Pine Inn, strolling along Pebble Beach, laughing at the antics of the lively otters, and wandering through the quaint shops on Ocean Avenue.

Jeffrey had suggested Carmel because Julia had never been there. He knew she would love it, and he had memories of the unique gold jewelry crafted by talented local artisans. Julia had told him she didn't want a diamond, but her lovely eyes had filled with soft hope when he suggested a very special gold wedding band.

Jeffrey wanted something very special, a worthy symbol of their love; Julia was overwhelmed by just plain gold. Still, when she saw the matching rings, elegant swirls of white-and-yellow gold, her eyes filled with wonder. Delicate ribbons of the two golds had been woven together and then flamed by fire and melted together . . . forever . . . into one.

The smaller of the two rings was unusually small, as if specifically made for Julia's slender finger. When Jeffrey slipped it on her, it fit perfectly; and that was how it looked—perfect, elegant, designed precisely for her. And the larger matching ring fit Jeffrey's finger perfectly, too, as if it, too, had been designed precisely for him.

"You're going to wear a ring?" Julia asked as she watched him put the ring on his finger.

"Of course, darling," Jeffrey gently told her surprised and hopeful lavender eyes. "Don't you know how proud I will be for the world to know you are my wife?"

"No more presents, ever, Jeffrey," Julia said twenty minutes later. They were in a secluded park two blocks from Ocean Avenue. The magnificent wedding bands were in Jeffrey's coat pocket and his arms gently circled her waist as they stood beneath an arch of wisteria the color of her eyes. "We'll just give each other ourselves and our love."

"As your soon-to-be husband, I reserve the right to lavish you with presents." His eyes grew serious as he added softly, "But you never need to give me any because you are all I want. You are the greatest gift."

"*You* are."

"No, *you*." Jeffrey kissed her, and after a moment began to talk to her between kisses. "Someday I want to take you on a magnificent honeymoon. Maybe a three-week romantic meander through Europe?"

"Won't every day be a honeymoon?"

"Of course."

"So, we don't need to go to Europe."

"Julie?"

"I've never been on an airplane."

"And you're afraid to fly."

"Yes." Julia gave a soft shrug.

"We have a lifetime, darling. Someday, when you're ready, we'll fly together." Together, someday, they would conquer Julia's fear of the sky, but there was a more important fear to vanquish first—the lingering uncertainty he still saw in her lovely eyes when he told her of his love. As if she really didn't believe he would love her forever. "You're the romantic, but I've been thinking about the words to engrave on our rings anyway. On the ring I'm giving you, I thought, "'Julie, I will always love you, Jeffrey.' "

"You're the romantic."

"Because of you. So, what do you think?"

"I think that after you put the ring on my finger tomorrow I will never want to take it off."

"I will never want to take mine off, either. But that means they won't be engraved."

"It doesn't matter. I know the ring is from you. And besides," she added softly, "the words are engraved in our hearts."

Meredith Lawrence was born on September twelfth, twenty-four hours after Jeffrey left for a ten-day assignment in Vietnam. Merry had respiratory distress and her skin was jaundiced, but her tiny lungs matured quickly outside her mother's womb and the yellow of her pale skin responded nicely to the bili lights.

Eight days after she was born, the day before Jeffrey returned, Julia took her baby daughter home.

Her baby daughter. Julia had loved the little life from the moment she knew she was pregnant, but she was unprepared for the immense joy and wonder she felt when she first held Merry in her arms and greeted her small, beautiful face. And since that first moment the joy and wonder had only increased.

How eager she was for Jeffrey to see his daughter, this most astonishing of all gifts of love.

How excited she was to have him hold Merry and be swept away by this wondrous joy that was beyond all words . . .

* * *

The miracle had already happened, Jeffrey had decided when he learned that it was possible for him to be the father of Julia's baby. His heart accepted the miracle that day, a decision of love, and his mind had embraced it, too, with a vow simply to believe and never to challenge. But when he saw the infant curled in Julia's arms, the disciplined mind that was anchored to truth and reality could not be silent.

Because it was so obvious, so painfully obvious, that the golden-haired brown-eyed baby girl could not be his.

It wasn't, of course, the fact that the genes that colored eyes blue were strong on both sides of Jeffrey's family and Julia's baby had eyes the color of mink. That was the softest of science, easily dismissed. No, it was the hard science, his own except-for-a-miracle-infertility and the indisputable fact that this infant had surely been conceived before he and Julia even met.

When Jeffrey did his award-winning story on the Neonatal I.C.U. at Children's Hospital in San Francisco, he spent many hours in the I.C.U. gazing into incubators, looking at babies who were a month premature, and two, and even three, and learning about the prognosis of each group. Babies born two months prematurely *did* survive, but after weeks in the I.C.U., and Jeffrey had only been gone ten days and Julia's baby had been born and was already home.

"Here's your baby daughter, Jeffrey. I named her Meredith, after Grandmère. Oh, Jeffrey, she is such joy, such wonder." Julia stopped, was stopped, by the look of great sadness in his tired blue eyes. "Jeffrey?"

"All you all right, honey?"

"Yes, Jeffrey, I'm fine." Julia smiled lovingly, trying to erase the sadness that was surely because he had been away when the baby was born. "We're both fine. Would you like to hold her?"

But Jeffrey didn't reach for Merry. Instead he sat down across from Julia and gazed at her with sad and gentle eyes.

"Who is her father, Julie?" Jeffrey's heart, the heart that orchestrated the magnificent deception, the miracle that was now hopelessly shattered, had long since banished thoughts of Julia's other lover. The thought of one other man loving her and creating this precious little new life with her was almost too much to bear. And what if there had been many lovers? What if Julia had no idea who the father was? "Do you know?"

"You are her father, Jeffrey."

"No, darling, I'm not." Jeffrey sighed softly and smiled reassuringly at her. Of course Julia knew this baby could not be his. She had hidden her other lover, praying the baby would be Jeffrey's, or at least be born at a time when they could believe she was. Julia had been protecting him, just as Jeffrey had protected her by hiding his infertility. But now they needed to admit the truth, share the disappointment they felt, and swiftly go on together to share the wonderful joy of loving the little girl cradled so carefully in her mother's arms. Jeffrey said quietly, his voice apologetic because perhaps he should have told her before but . . . "When I was fifteen I had a mumps infection with complications that make it virtually impossible for me to father a child. I didn't tell you before because I didn't want to dampen your joy. I'm so sorry, Julie, but it would have been truly a miracle for her to be mine."

As Julia gazed at him with bewildered eyes, she tried to fight the ominous worry that Jeffrey's eyes first had filled with sadness, not wonder, when he saw his daughter, and that now he was searching for distant reasons why Merry couldn't even be his.

"But she *is* yours, Jeffrey," Julia whispered finally, quietly. She added softly, "And she *is* a miracle."

Jeffrey drew a soft breath and felt icy ripples of fear wash through him. *No more lies, Jeffrey, I promise*, Julia had vowed. But she was lying now!

"Julie, when was she due?" he pressed almost urgently. *Please don't lie to me!*

44 "You know that, Jeffrey. She was due on your birthday, November eleventh." How thrilled she had been when she told the obstetrician the date of the first time she and Jeffrey made love and he had calculated the due date.

"And she was born when?"

"September twelfth."

"And she's home already and healthy. That's not a baby born two months prematurely."

"We were very lucky, Jeffrey," Julia whispered softly.

Jeffrey stared at the woman he loved with all his heart and felt an immense sense of dread. He didn't believe her, the facts wouldn't allow him to, and Jeffrey knew Julia knew the truth, too. But she was maintaining the lie. She was going to protect the secret of her other lover. *Why?* Was she still not confident enough of his love to tell him the truth? Or was it something else, something worse . . .

Julia's lies had only been necessary ones, and she had only deceived him about the important things. Was this a necessary deception that was more important to her than their love?

Jeffrey stared at her with eyes that were stormy reflections of the turbulence in his heart. Julia returned his gaze, her lovely lavender eyes bewildered and innocent . . . so innocent, so unflickering, just as they had been when she had told him the other necessary and important lies.

"It's late, Julia," Jeffrey said finally, heavily. "I've been traveling for twenty-four hours and I'm exhausted. I have to be at the studio early tomorrow morning to begin editing the tapes. I'm going to bed."

Julia remained in the living room, nursing her hungry daughter and fighting the pain that swept through her. This summer she had begun to believe that Jeffrey wanted the baby. He had been so gentle, so loving, and he had taken such wonderful care of her. But he hadn't greeted his daughter with wonder and joy. In fact, he had searched for reasons that Merry couldn't be his, and when she had insisted that Merry was his, his eyes had darkened to the stormy turbulence beyond anger she had seen when she first told him of her pregnancy.

Jeffrey didn't want Merry. He didn't even want Merry to be his. Why? So that he could justify ignoring her? So he would feel less guilty about the career that already, because he was so talented, frequently took him away? So he wouldn't be torn between his dreams and the immense responsibility of a child he would never have chosen to have?

As Merry's tiny, eager lips nursed her full, creamy breast, Julia kissed gentle kisses on the silky blond head and silently renewed the vow she had made the day Jeffrey asked her to marry him. She would love her lovely little girl, as she already did, and she would ask nothing of Jeffrey, never pressure him, never make him feel torn or guilty. And someday . . .

Your daddy will love you, my little Merry, Julia promised with soft kisses. *But he is restless now, and has important dreams that he must follow. I believe in your daddy's important dreams, and someday he will believe in mine. You are the most important dream, my little love. Someday your daddy will know that.*

When Merry finished nursing, Julia carried her into the room where Jeffrey slept and put her in the cradle next to her side of the bed. As Julia crawled quietly into bed beside Jeffrey, she made more promises. *I love you, Jeffrey. I promise I will make this right. Merry and I will never interfere with your dreams.* And then because the confidence of their summer of loving had been so shaken and because there would always live within her the little girl who believed she could not hold love, she made a silent plea, *Oh, Jeffrey, please don't leave us.*

At three A.M. Merry awakened with a cry. The night before, on her first night home, Merry hadn't cried at all. Perhaps she would have cried if Julia hadn't been awake watching her sleep, watching her breathe, whispering soft reassurances to her whenever she stirred. But this night Julia wasn't keeping her vigil because fatigue had overcome her.

She quickly lifted Merry from the cradle, curled her into her arms, and walked out of the bedroom into the living room as Merry's cries became screams.

"Oh, Merry, please be quiet. Your daddy has to sleep. Be quiet, honey, please, please be quiet." Julia's soft tone wasn't comforting because Merry heard the panic in her mother's voice, and Julia's soft warm breast didn't calm her, either. Julia's hot tears spilled onto her infant daughter and her voice trembled, "Merry, Merry, please, Daddy has to sleep."

"Julia, what's—"

"I'm sorry, Jeffrey," she whispered as she looked up at his glowering eyes. "I'm so sorry."

Jeffrey's anger was intercepted by the fear on her lovely face. How could she be afraid of him? It was he who was afraid, afraid of losing her, afraid of the secret that was too important to reveal.

Don't be afraid of me, my lovely Julie! Jeffrey had vowed to vanquish all her fears, beginning with the most important one—her fragile uncertainty about his love. And he had almost succeeded during their magnificent summer of love, but now she trembled and looked as lost as she had looked on the evening he asked her to marry him.

He had known on that warm spring evening that she lied to him, that she was carrying another man's child, and that the secret of her other lover might remain hidden in her heart forever.

And he had chosen to marry her.

And now? Now the baby had been born, and his mind wouldn't allow his heart even to pretend the miracle had happened, and Julia was going to maintain her secret . . .

But nothing had changed. He loved her with all his heart.

Jeffrey carefully took Merry from Julia's arms and spoke very gently to the baby's crying face. "Merry, you're making your mommy cry. How come? Your mommy looks so tired."

Magically, Merry's screams became whimpers and then curious coos as her attention shifted to the deep voice and the strong arms that held her so securely.

"That's better," Jeffrey whispered. He looked from Merry to Julia. "Julie, did I hold you and kiss you and tell you how much I missed you and how I love you?"

"No."

"Why don't I do that after this little one falls asleep?"

"Is it all right that I named her after Grandmère?" Julia asked as the autumn sky began to lighten with the dawn. Merry was asleep now and they had been whispering gentle words of love between kisses.

"Of course," Jeffrey answered, his voice soft with love for Julia and for Grandmère. His beloved grandmother had been very lonely in the years since his grandfather's death, but Julia, loving Julia, had magically restored Grandmère's joyous laugh and youthful spirit. Their relationship had begun with letters, because Julia was so timid on the phone with the elegant voice she didn't know, but now there were frequent phone calls, and Grandmère, who had announced four years before that she was too old to travel, had come to visit for ten lively days in July. Julia loved Grandmère, and Grandmère loved Julia. And Grandmère was so excited about the birth of her first great-grandchild. "Grandmère will be thrilled. Why don't we call her right now? You tell her, Julie."

"Grandmère?" Julia asked moments later when a sprightly voice answered the phone a continent away.

"Julia? Are you all right?"

"Oh, yes. Jeffrey's home and we wanted you to know that our baby has been born. She's a beautiful little girl and we've named her Meredith."

"Meredith?" Grandmère's voice trembled.

"We call her Merry."

"Oh, my dear, there was a time, a lovely time a million years ago when Jeffrey's grandfather used to call me Merry."

Five hours later Jeffrey placed a call to Merry's doctor. It was a call he had to make, a call from a loving heart that was still searching for a miracle, and a call from a disciplined mind trained to double-check all the facts.

The doctor confirmed what Jeffrey already knew. Merry *was* premature, perhaps as much as four weeks, but certainly not almost nine, and she had done remarkably well for a baby born that early.

Merry wasn't his baby. Julia was going to maintain the lie. Those were the facts. In the middle of the night Jeffrey had told himself that nothing had changed. But it wasn't true. He loved her, yes, always, but now mixed in with the immense strength of his love were other powerful emotions—hurt, anger, fear. If he used the power of his love he could surely tranquilize the swirling emotions, couldn't he? But wouldn't they rage inside him still, in some hidden corner of his heart, burrowing deeper and deeper until they caused a festering wound that would contaminate all of their love?

Could he really simply forgive Julia's deception, and protect their love by living her lie, as he had once joyfully planned simply to accept the miracle?

Jeffrey didn't know. He only knew that he had to try.

But Julia didn't ask him to live her lie. As if in silent admission of the truth she could not speak aloud, she did not ask of him that he be a father to the daughter that was not his. During the increasingly infrequent times that Jeffrey was even home when Merry was awake, Julia very carefully kept her infant daughter far away from him.

Julia cared for the golden-haired little girl she loved so much, and she loved Jeffrey as joyously as she always had. And their magnificent love survived, flourished, because Julia, whose generous heart had lived for so long without love, had more than enough love for him and for his very precious daughter.

Chapter 6

Before Jeffrey fell in love with Julia, television viewers had been enchanted by his sincere, intelligent eyes, his aristocratic handsomeness, and his elegant charm. But after, there was something new, something more, something breathtaking.

No one could accurately pinpoint what the something was. It was very subtle, a subtext from the heart, a tender smile, a soft inflection, a gentle apology in the sensual blue eyes when there was tragic news to share. Jeffrey knew that his love for Julia lived inside him always, a magnificent fullness, a joyful warmth, but he had no idea that his joy overflowed from his heart to his face. It did, however, and whenever he spoke to the camera he was speaking to his love, and the viewing public became an unwitting yet willing recipient of the wondrous intimacy.

The viewers had ample opportunity to see Jeffrey. The extraordinary quality and impeccable honesty of his work advanced him with astonishing speed to the top of the very elite group of foreign correspondents. By Merry's third birthday Jeffrey had become the network's first choice to cover the most important news events throughout the world. A month later the network assigned him to the place it judged to be among the most critical to the survival of the planet . . . the Middle East.

It was an important assignment, one Jeffrey could not refuse, but one that was far too dangerous to have Julia and Merry to accompany him. So it was decided that he would go to Beirut and commute to New York by Concorde whenever he could and that Julia and Merry would live with Grandmère at Belvedere. Two weeks before he left for Beirut, Jeffrey drove Julia and Merry from Los Angeles to Southampton. He worried a little about being cooped up in the car with three-year-old Merry for the five-day drive. Julia worried even more because she didn't want Jeffrey to be annoyed by the chatter that to Julia was joy, a sparkling fountain of happiness from her bright little girl.

But the trip was wonderful.

Jeffrey drove, and Julia entertained Merry. Mother and daughter talked and played quiet games and watched the world speed by. And Julia told Merry the most magnificent fairy tales Jeffrey had ever heard.

"The beautiful little princess was so sleepy," Julia whispered lovingly to her daughter, who was in need of a nap but struggling to stay awake, "but she had to make a decision. Should she fall asleep on a soft cloud in the sky? Or on a gentle wave in the ocean?"

As Jeffrey listened he marveled that his lovely Julia, who was afraid of the sky and the sea, made them magical places for Merry. Julia wanted no fears for Merry and gave her daughter only gifts of happiness and love.

"Where do you think she wanted to fall asleep, Merry?"

"The sky. On a cloud. Daphne could take her there."

"Yes, she could," Julia answered softly. "So the little princess called to Daphne, and Daphne scooped her onto her back, and they flew to a cloud that was pink and so very soft. And Daphne stayed with the little princess, because Daphne was sleepy, too, and together they wished sweet dreams to the golden moon and fell asleep."

"Who's Daphne?" Jeffrey asked after Merry had fallen asleep.

"A dragon."

"And who are Robert and Cecily?"

"Twin sea serpents."

"And Andrew?"

"A unicorn."

"You made up these stories, Julie?"

"Yes."

"They're wonderful, darling." After a moment he said quietly, "You never

told me any of your stories of love. Will you tell me? Will you write them to me?"

They had promised to write, every night, during the hours when they should have been holding each other and loving each other and sharing the events of their days.

"I don't make up love stories anymore, Jeffrey. I don't need to because our love is more wonderful than anything I ever imagined."

"Oh, Julie. Will you write to me about our love then?"

"Every night. I promise."

"Moo cows, Mommy! Moo cows! Mommy! Mommy! Merry exclaimed with breathless glee the next afternoon as they sped past the animals she had only seen before in books.

Julia cast an apologetic glance at Jeffrey, but Jeffrey laughed softly at Merry's enthusiasm and asked, "Would she like a closer look, Julie? Should we stop?"

"If you don't mind."

"Of course not."

A mile later Jeffrey pulled to the side of the road beside a pasture where a herd of cows was grazing. Jeffrey held an excited Merry above the top of the wooden fence so she could see without obstruction, and when Julia moved beside him he whispered lovingly into her ear, "Moo cows, Mommy."

Julia's life at Belvedere with Grandmère and Merry was filled with great happiness. A perfect life, except she missed Jeffrey so much! He called often and came home to her whenever he could, but sometimes she didn't see him except on television for weeks, even months.

As promised, Jeffrey and Julia wrote to each other every day.

Jeffrey was an eyewitness to the important history of the world and he faithfully reported what he saw to a nation that increasingly relied on his vigilant eyes and intelligent mind. Jeffrey reported the news to the nation, and in the private words he wrote to Julia every night he shared his feelings about the tragedies he saw.

As Jeffrey was an eyewitness to the important history of the world, Julia was an eyewitness to the important history of Jeffrey's daughter. And in reporting the news of Merry's life, Julia was as good a journalist as he, reporting the events faithfully and without editorializing. Julia always wrote *Merry*, never *your daughter* or *our daughter*, because she had vowed not to pressure him . . . even though her heart cried restlessly, *Oh, Jeffrey, you are missing such joy, such wonder!*

Julia wrote about Merry and their happy life at Belvedere. And, in bold unashamed passages that were as magnificently intimate as their loving, she wrote bravely of her love, her passion, her desires, and her fantasies.

The daily letters and frequent phone calls prevented gaps in their love, their feelings, and their most private thoughts, but no number of intimate words of love could ease the pain of the physical separation. As weeks became months, the need to touch and to hold and to love—to be one—became almost desperate . . .

Between October 1985 and May 1986, Jeffrey was unable to return to Southampton at all. Beginning with the hijacking in October of the *Achille Lauro* the events were relentless—the fleeting but hopeful rumors of peace in Lebanon . . . the meeting of special envoy Terry Waite with the captors of four kidnapped Americans . . . the hijacking of the Egyptian airliner to Malta that ended in the death of fifty-seven passengers and crew as commandos stormed the plane . . . the simultaneous massacre of civilians in the Rome and Vienna airports at Christmas . . . the subsequent arrest warrant issued for Abu Nidal . . . the military police riots in Cairo . . . the clash of Libyan and U.S. forces over the Gulf of Sidra . . . the terrorist bombing of the TWA flight from Rome to Athens and the averting of a similar attempt at Heathrow . . . the United States” attack on Libya in retaliation for the bombing of La Belle Discotheque in West Berlin . . .

The events were relentless, and all the while, in a crescendo chorus, there was escalating violence in the civil war in Beirut.

Jeffrey could not leave. He had become almost as indispensable to the network and the viewers who trusted him as a general in a war. In a way he *was* indispensable. His fame, the common knowledge that his reports were respected, trusted, and viewed by a large segment of the free world, gave him access to places and people that other reporters did not have.

For over six months each planned trip to Southampton was postponed and ultimately canceled. Then, at last, Jeffrey came home. He called Julia from each milepost in his journey home to her, swiftly reassuring her, “I'm leaving Beirut.” Then, “I'm in Athens.” Then, “I'm at Charles de Gaulle. The plane is on time, darling. I will see you in four hours.”

He was like a wanderer too long in the desert and dying of thirst . . . and Julia was the oasis. He walked through the door of Customs and into her arms. They just held each other, without speaking, unable to speak, overcome by the immense relief of touching again and the wonderful feeling of life returning to their lonely bodies as they became whole.

“Oh, God, how I've missed you,” he whispered finally. “Shall we go home?”

Julia had told Grandmère they would be home by dinner and Merry was with Paige at Somerset. She had made the decision weeks ago that she wanted to be alone with him in a private place. Still, suddenly uncertain, she almost drove past the hotel where she had already booked a room. But when she pulled the car into a parking space near the room and removed the key from her purse, her uncertainty vanished because she saw such joy and desire in his eyes.

In the motel room at Fisherman's Wharf Julia had undressed herself, and her clothes had been threadbare, and she had worn no bra. Now Jeffrey undressed her, as he had always after that first time, and she wore expensive linen and silk, and beneath that elegance her lovely breasts were clothed in satin and lace.

Jeffrey's hands trembled as he undressed her and his mind filled with the brave words she had written about her fantasies. He knew how she dreamed of him undressing her so slowly, his tender, talented lips lingering and loving each newly revealed patch of her white, silky skin. Jeffrey had spent months dreaming about doing just that and much more, but . . .

“Oh, my lovely Julie,” he whispered against her naked breasts. “I need you too much.”

“Jeffrey . . . I need you too much, too.”

* * *

"What would you like to do today?" Jeffrey asked three days later when Julia rejoined him in bed after Merry had left for school and Grandmère had gone to visit a friend in East Hampton.

"Whatever you want."

"What would you do if I wasn't here?"

"I would miss you."

"What else?"

"Transplant the roses."

"Let's do that in a while."

Two hours later Julia led the way to a sundrenched island of rich dark earth and pointed to a cluster of six rose bushes.

"I think these are all ready to come out of the I.C.U."

"The I.C.U.?"

"This is the I.C.U. I put the plants that haven't done well over the winter here because it has the best sunlight. Once they're healthy, they can go over there, beneath our window."

Jeffrey smiled at her. She was such a nurturer, so loving, so gentle, giving intensive care always to those she loved.

Jeffrey first dug six holes in the ground beneath the window of their master suite. Then, very carefully, he began to remove the once frail but now healthy bushes from Julia's I.C.U.

"Oh, wait," Julia said as Jeffrey began to put one of the newly well roses beside an established bush. She looked at the metal tag on the bush. "That's Smoky. Smoky can't be next to Mister Lincoln because the colors will clash."

"What colors will Smoky and Mister Lincoln be?" Jeffrey's question was an innocent and interested one, but it caused his lovely Julia great pain, "Julie? What, honey?"

Julia shook her head. She had made a solemn vow never to interfere with his important dreams.

"Tell me." Julia was silent, so Jeffrey made a hopeful guess from his heart. "Is it because I won't be here when they bloom?"

Julia looked at him and nodded a soft apology. But it was an admission that filled Jeffrey with happiness.

"You always seem so calm when I leave."

"I cry after, Jeffrey. You're calm, too."

"But I cry, too, darling." That was the truth, and the other truth, what had been spinning in his mind, was that he couldn't do it anymore. He couldn't leave her knowing it might be seven months again. He *wouldn't*. "After we get these roses out of the I.C.U., let's go for a walk. I want to talk to you."

They walked along deer trails through the dense, lush forest that led to the bluff overlooking the sea. The bluff was an artist's palette of spring wildflowers, and in the distance was a charming cottage perched on a cliff. Jeffrey led her down the winding trail to the white sand beach. The surf was high and the waves crashed angrily on the sand. Jeffrey looked from the treacherous surf to the azure horizon and remembered the words his grandfather, Hollis Cabot, had spoken to him in this very place. *Always follow your dreams, Jeffrey, wherever they lead, no matter what anyone else says.*

Jeffrey had spent so many hours here dreaming about the adventures that lay beyond the horizon, loving the danger of the waves and the vastness of the sea, restless to follow the beckoning waves beyond the horizon to his dreams.

But now his dreams were here, beside him, and he looked into her lavender eyes and saw that the powerful waves frightened her a little even though he held her. Jeffrey drew her even closer, and after a few moments led her back up the cliff.

"I have to go back to Beirut, honey, until they find a replacement for me," he said when they reached the crest of the cliff and sat on a warm patch of grass in the meadow of wildflowers. "It shouldn't take very long. Then I'm coming home to see your roses."

"Oh, Jeffrey . . . but what will you do?"

"I thought I'd follow you around all day every day."

"You'll get bored and restless."

"I don't think so, but if you get tired of having me underfoot I could probably find a job as a reporter at a local station."

"Probably." Julia smiled, but her lips trembled and her eyes filled with tears of joy.

Jeffrey kissed the tears, and her trembling lips, and her tears again. And when the hunger of their kisses demanded more, he undressed her very slowly and tenderly caressed all the wonderful places of her lovely body with an exquisite gentleness that was beyond any fantasy Julia had ever imagined. Only the springtime sun watched as they loved in their fragrant ocean of wildflowers, and on that perfect day in May even the crashing surf in the distance became a soft splash, a gentle rhythm that matched their tender loving, a soft sigh in an endless afternoon of soft sighs of joy.

"Hello, Frank." Jeffrey smiled a warm greeting to the bureau chief on his return to Beirut three weeks later.

"Jeffrey. Welcome back. How was your month?"

"Very nice." Jeffrey took a soft breath. "Frank, there's something I need to discuss with you."

"I have something to discuss with you, too. Come on in." Frank opened the door to his office, but before either man could enter the room they were distracted by a commotion in the newsroom.

"Was anyone inside?"

"No."

"What happened?"

"An explosion in the school inside the diplomatic compound. Thank God school had already let out for the day."

"How the hell did they get inside the compound?"

"Who knows?"

Jeffrey quickly scanned the newsroom. He was the only reporter. He beckoned to a cameraman and said to Frank as they rushed out, "Drinks later, Frank?"

"You bet."

The diplomatic compound, the sanctuary for dependents and families from all foreign countries, was quite close to the bureau. A dark plume of smoke stretched into the sky above the flaming four-story building whose lower three floors served as a warehouse and whose top floor was a school.

A crowd had assembled in front of the burning building and watched helplessly as it was consumed by flames. At first the crowd was expectant, waiting to hear sirens pierce the fire-hot air, strident signals that help was on the way. But then they remembered. This was war-torn Beirut, not their homeland. No shiny red fire engine would arrive to douse the fire and send its long silver ladders up the scorched stucco walls.

It was so lucky that no one had been in the building.

Jeffrey interviewed several bystanders, quickly determined that no one had seen anything, then began his live report. As he spoke, he gestured at the flaming building, turning toward it and then freezing as he saw a glimpse of gold.

It was just a flame, wasn't it? Or the hot sun glinting off a pane of glass?

No, it was golden hair and it belonged to a little girl. She had gone to the classroom to get a book she had left and had cowered beneath a desk after the explosion until the flames and smoke drove her to the window.

No fire engines with long ladders would arrive, no hoses would douse the inferno, no nets would be held beneath the window so that she could jump to safety . . . it was too far to jump anyway.

Without a moment's hesitation Jeffrey ran into the blazing building. He made a few false turns but finally found the stairs and dashed up them, holding his breath and praying he could inhale something not so lethal as the dense smoke before he began the return trip with the little girl in his arms.

The golden-haired girl was about Merry's age. She was at the window, safe still, when Jeffrey reached the flaming classroom. He smiled a friendly hello before leaning out the window to take a much-needed gulp of air.

I need one of Julie's wonderful flying dragons, he thought as he gazed at the ground four stories below. *Daphne, where are you?* The silent question came with rush of emotion. *Julie*. And then confidence. *I am coming home to you, Julie*.

"Hi," Jeffrey said gently to the terrified little girl. "I'm going to take you out of here, OK? Put your arms around my neck. Good. Now hold very tight because we're going to be moving fast. When I say three take a deep breath from outside the window and then hold it until we're out of the building. OK? Ready? One. Two. Three."

Jeffrey couldn't see a thing because the smoke had become a heavy black veil. He moved in a direction that he believed was the opposite of the way he had come, a retracing of steps, and finally, gratefully, found the stairs. When they reached the second level there was a loud crash and a falling beam of fire. The beam struck Jeffrey, shattering his collarbone. As he gasped with pain he inhaled a lungful of smoke.

But their journey continued, and then they were outside, and the little golden-haired girl—who had held her breath and had been protected from the beam by his arms—was fine. Jeffrey was taken to the hospital.

"I just spoke to Julia," Frank told Jeffrey two hours later. "I told her that you're in good shape—broken collarbone and smoke inhalation notwithstanding. She wants to speak to you, naturally, so I've asked the staff to get some portable oxygen and arrange for a phone line. While we're waiting, I want to tell you about a call I got *before* you became a national hero. The network wants you to be the new anchor for the nightly news. The president of the news division called about an hour before you returned, looking for you, I assume, although it was a courtesy to let me know he was going to recruit you away."

"What did you tell him?"

"That I thought you'd been here long enough." Frank smiled wryly. "That it was dangerous for you here; although the willingness of all the factions to speak with you is wonderful for the network, your high visibility makes you a prime target for kidnapping. I told him I thought it was getting too risky for you to be here, and that was before I knew about your tendency to rush into blazing infernos to save little damsels in distress."

"I hadn't known about that one, either."

"Anyway, the network is looking for serious journalistic talent, like you, having at last decided to get rid of the celebrity anchor who has the misguided notion that *he's* the real news. They wanted you before you became a national hero, and were probably prepared then to offer you some editorial input. But now you can demand absolute editorial control, which, knowing you, you'll go crazy if you don't have."

Jeffrey had planned to come home and simply be with Julia, but he couldn't turn down the position of network anchor, and she didn't want him to.

And it was such a luxury to be close to her, to be able to call her a hundred times a day if he wanted, to hold her when he returned home late at night and as they shared the events of their days before going to bed.

Jeffrey began as the anchor for *The World This Evening* in August of 1986. By the following spring his newscast had gone from a distant third in the ratings war to a solid second. By October of 1987 the popularity of *The World This Evening* began to rival that of the number-one show, and long before the nation went to the polls in November 1988 and elected George Bush to the presidency, Jeffrey Lawrence had become the anchor from whom the majority of Americans chose to hear the news.

Christmas of 1988 was marred by two international tragedies—the devastating earthquake in Soviet Armenia and the terrorist bombing of Pan Am Flight 103 over Lockerbie. Six weeks after 1989 began, on a snowy night in February, Grandmère died. She had been a little tired that evening, nothing more, and Merry and Julia had taken turns reading one of Julia's fairy tales to her. Grandmère fell asleep with a soft smile on her face, and sometime in the night she died, very peacefully, smiling still.

"I don't want Merry to go to the funeral, Jeffrey."

"All right, darling." Jeffrey pulled Julia's tense body close to his and lifted her grief-stricken face to meet his eyes. He didn't need to know why Julia didn't want Merry to attend the funeral, but he needed Julia to talk to him. Grandmère's death had been devastating for Julia, but she hid her grief and focused her energy on her nine-year-old daughter. Julia was helping Merry, and Jeffrey wanted to help Julia. "Honey, tell me why."

"Because it's winter and the ground is so cold . . ."

The tears spilled then, finally, and her body began to shake. When she could speak she told Jeffrey about the horrible memory she had of her own parents" funeral. Then she sobbed softly and Jeffrey held her and kissed her and wished, as he often wished, that he could vanquish all the silent agonies of her heart.

"Julie. I don't want you to go to the funeral, either. Grandmère would understand why you weren't there. In spring, or whenever you want, we can take flowers to her grave."

Meredith Cabot's fortune was immense. Her will gave generous gifts to charity and to her loyal servants and equitably divided her liquid assets among her children and grandchildren. To Julia, she left Belvedere, a sum of fifteen million dollars, and the diamond-and-sapphire earrings that had been a gift from her late husband. And for Merry, her great-granddaughter and namesake, she left a trust fund of five million dollars.

Grandmère also left two very private letters, to be shared with no one else, not even each other, for Jeffrey and Julia.

Julia read the loving letter written to her as she knelt beside the grave where she had come alone to place a dozen winter roses and to say good-bye.

My beloved Julia,

Don't worry about me, my darling. I am in a heaven as wonderful as the enchanted kingdoms of your lovely imagination and I am happy because I am with my Hollis. My years on earth without him weren't so happy until you and your precious Merry came into my life. Since then there has been such *joy!*

Belvedere is yours, Julia, as it should be. Victoria will huff and puff, but Edmund has put in clever stipulations that will prevent her from even attempting to contest my will. Perhaps if I had been a mother like you, perhaps such stipulations would have been unnecessary. But I digress . . .

I know you would have worried about dismissing the servants—even though you could never have instructed them to serve you—so I have made them all millionaires! Belvedere is yours, and so are the earrings. They were a treasure from Hollis to me, and I want them now to be a gift from him to you. I left the rest of the jewels—of great value but none so precious as the earrings—to Victoria, since I know you would never wear them.

Wear my gowns, though, Julia. Plunge the necklines and raise the skirts! You are too timid to do this, I know, but you will make them enchanted as you do everything you touch.

Dearest Julia, I think you don't know how wonderful you are, how rare and precious are your gifts of love. You give so much, Julia, but you should take. My dearest grandson loves you more deeply than you will ever know. I knew the man Jeffrey was before he met you—a fine and magnificent man before, of course, but a little selfish. His love for you has changed him. He is so gentle now and so filled with love.

Believe in Jeffrey's love, my precious Julia, and believe in yourself.

Jeffrey read his letter in the privacy of the Manhattan apartment provided for him by the network. The apartment was two minutes from the studio, a place for the tailor-made suits, laundered shirts, and silk ties he wore on the air, and a place to sleep on snowbound nights or when a world crisis required that he stay in town.

Jeffrey rarely used the apartment for sleep, preferring to return to Julia no matter how late, but he used it now for privacy to read Grandmère's letter and privacy for the emotions he had kept tightly reined because of his worry about Julia. Jeffrey's dark-blue eyes had misted in the past few days, but he hadn't cried until now . . .

My darling Jeffrey,

Are you crying? Don't cry for me, Jeffrey, but be happy that you can cry. You never really knew about tears or laughter or love—Oh, yes, my darling, you did love your Grandmère!—until lovely Julia came into your life. She found a part of your heart that no one else could, the most wonderful part.

Forget about mumps and an army of doctors, Jeffrey, and let

Merry be yours. You thought your mother had spared me the details? No. I know that you cannot have children, Jeffrey, and I know that I greatly preferred an era when science wasn't so involved in our love. But do the genes really matter so very much?

Let yourself love that precious little girl, my darling, as much as you love her mother. Let yourself share that wonderful joy with Julia!

And there is something else, my dearest grandson. Sometimes when I look at Merry I see your grandfather. His eyes were dark brown, do you remember? And when she smiles in a certain way it is as if Hollis has returned from heaven.

I know Merry cannot be your daughter. But you can love her as your own as I have cherished her as my great-granddaughter.

The only obstacle, my darling Jeffrey, is in your heart.

Jeffrey held Grandmère's letter in his hands, his eyes blurred with fresh tears, his mind swirling with the loving wisdom from Grandmère. *You're right, Grandmère, it would be better not to know the truth. It would be better for me simply to believe that Merry was mine.* But Jeffrey knew the truth. He and Julia both did. And even though he had told Julia it would be virtually impossible for him to father a child, she was so careful with their birth control, not wanting to make a mistake, not wishing for any child except the lovely daughter she still kept so very far away from him.

Grandmère's letter caused rushes of pain—grief because Jeffrey loved Grandmère and would miss her terribly and other pains, ancient quiescent ones from a deep wound he believed had long since healed.

But as rushes of hurt and anger at Julia's deception swept through him, Jeffrey realized that the old wound wasn't healed at all. It had simply been bandaged by the thick, soft, protective covering of his love. Beneath the balm of love the wound was open still, unhealed and unhealing, raw, evergreen, and able still to cause great pain.

Until Julia trusted him with the secret of her heart the ancient wound would never heal. But until then, as he had done ever since Merry's birth, Jeffrey would gently and lovingly dress the gaping wound, covering it, hiding it, burying the pain far away.

And he and Julia would go on with their almost perfect love.

No more presents, ever, Julia had told him beneath a lavender arch of wisteria in Carmel moments after they had bought their perfect wedding rings. *We'll just give each other ourselves and our love.*

In memory of that spring day, the day before their marriage, Jeffrey and Julia never exchanged gifts—*things*—on their wedding anniversaries. Instead, they gave themselves and their love. Usually in response to the question, "What would you like for his anniversary?" each simply replied, "I only want your love."

But on their tenth wedding anniversary, in May, three months after Grandmère's death, each wanted other gifts of love.

"I'd like to take you on the honeymoon I promised you ten years ago," Jeffrey said quietly when Julia wished him Happy Anniversary and asked him what he wanted on this special day.

It was only the beginning of Jeffrey's wish. He wanted much more. He wanted Julia to accompany him when his work took him to safe, wonderful places. He wanted to show her the treasures of the greatest cities in the world, to see the beautiful places, marvel at them as he knew she would, and enjoy the luxurious surroundings of the fabulous hotels where he always stayed. Not that in all his travels Jeffrey had ever found a place as beautiful and luxurious as Julia's Belvedere, or rose gardens as lovingly tended and bountiful, or decor as tasteful and elegant, or suites as lovely and romantic, but still . . .

"It's time for me to outgrow my fear of flying, isn't it?"

"I think so, darling, with me to help you. You've made great headway. You used to seem frightened whenever I flew, and you don't anymore."

"I've just become a better actress." Julia sighed softly. She had tried not to let it show, part of her vow never to interfere, but Jeffrey had known anyway, so now she told him truthfully, "It terrifies me when you fly. I'm so afraid you won't come back."

"I will always come back to you, Julie." Jeffrey sealed the promise with a gentle kiss. "So, my love, will you think about it? Sometime in the next ten years, may I take you on a romantic honeymoon in Europe?"

"Yes."

"Good." Jeffrey decided not to push any further for now. He knew that Julia's fear of flying was far more than fear for herself. Her residual girlhood terror had another component, perhaps the greatest fear, the fear of orphaning her daughter as she had been orphaned. Jeffrey didn't push. Julia had heard his wish and he knew that she would try. He kissed her lips and whispered, "Now tell me what you want."

Jeffrey expected Julia's usual swift reply, "I only want your love," but her lavender eyes told him that she, too, had a special anniversary wish.

"Tell me," he whispered.

"I want us to be a family, Jeffrey." Julia's voice was soft, uncertain, laced with apology and hope.

He heard her hope and a rush of hope swept through him, too. At last she was going to tell him the truth and the ancient wound could finally heal.

"I know how busy you are, Jeffrey, but if there could be times when we could plan to do things together . . ." Julia's eyes grew timid under his intense gaze. Timid but resolute because it was time. Her lovely little girl needed her father. There were fathers far less busy than Jeffrey who ignored their children, Julia knew that, but that wasn't what she wanted for their daughter. Julia gave Merry all the love she could give, and it had been enough when Grandmère had been there, too, covering Merry in a downy comforter of love. But now Grandmère was gone, and Merry's best friend's very busy father always made time to be with his daughter, and Merry needed Jeffrey as much as Amanda needed Edmund. Julia asked softly, "Jeffrey, please?"

The hope that had filled Jeffrey's heart, the hope that the wound could finally heal, faded as the realization settled. Julia wanted to change the rules by which they had lived the last ten years of their lives, but she wasn't going to tell him the truth.

Now, after all these years, she was asking him to live the lie . . . and she was asking him to become a father to a little girl he didn't even know.

Jeffrey didn't know Merry, not the girl inside. He only knew the visual images his talented journalistic mind had made as he had observed from a distance the drama of a tiny baby becoming a little girl. Merry as an infant, cooing softly as she cuddled in Julia's arms . . . Merry as a sunny, lively toddler galloping on sturdy legs to Julia and laughing with glee . . . Merry as the little girl whose limbs had lengthened gracefully and whose white-blond hair had darkened into lustrous gold and whose soft voice, so very much like Julia's, spoke now in full, quiet sentences, not excited bursts of words.

Jeffrey knew from a distance the ever-changing cover of the lovely sunny book, but he didn't know *Merry.* He always had a warm smile and gentle hello for her, of course, and he wished happiness for the precious daughter of his precious love. When she was very young Merry had eyed him with obvious interest and curiosity, clinging to Julia but quite bold, peering at him and then erupting into gleeful laughter like a game of hide-and-seek. More recently, in the rare times that Jeffrey had even seen her since his return from Beirut, Merry's dark-brown stares ended with an embarrassed rush of pink in her cheeks when he caught her eyes and smiled at her.

When Merry called Jeffrey by a name she called him Daddy, and that had bothered him at first. But for almost ten years Daddy had just been a name without expectations . . . from Julia or from Merry.

Until now.

Now Julia expected him to embrace her lie.

On this tenth wedding anniversary, Jeffrey had asked of Julia that she conquer her fear of flying. And now she was asking of him that he conquer his fear of the ancient secret that was still to important to share.

Could he do it? Could he pretend to be the father of a little girl who wasn't his?

Jeffrey didn't know. But as he gazed at Julia's lovely, hopeful eyes he heard himself whisper quietly, "All right, Julie." *I promise I will try.*

When the old wound had been exposed by Grandmère's wise and loving letter, Jeffrey had quickly hidden it deep beneath thick, soft layers of love. Now the wound was exposed again, but this time it couldn't be so easily hidden because now they were living the painful lie.

Julia's wish that they become a family was a wish of love that promised forever. Jeffrey should have felt hope, and he did, but the old, unhealed wound came with old, unhealed emotions. The ancient emotions of hurt, anger, and betrayal surfaced from the depths, and now, after a decade of confident and joyous love, Jeffrey suddenly felt brittle, precarious, and raw.

It would take him a little time to conquer the ancient emotions, but he *would* conquer them.

The emotions were still swirling very near the surface three weeks later, however, when he returned to Belvedere after the interview with Dr. Diana Shepherd that had been disrupted by the arrival of her divorce papers. That night, ominous thoughts had taunted and he had been so relieved to find Julia waiting for him, so relieved to see the familiar love and joy in her eyes. After they made love, as she slept gently in his arms, Jeffrey thought about Julia's deception, the tiny flaw in the brilliance of their love. And as he drifted off to sleep, he wondered what flaw had shattered the love of Chase Andrews and his beautiful Queen of Hearts.

Part Two

Chapter 7

MANHATTAN
JUNE 1989

Diana stood on the balcony of the luxurious Park Avenue penthouse that she and Chase had shared for five years and watched with relief as the summer sun began to lighten the sky. Diana's night had been so dark, her sleep disrupted by nightmares and her wakefulness haunted by ghosts. Some of the ghosts were new—fresh, vivid phantoms of the marriage that had lived and died in the fabulous penthouse. But there were other ghosts, old ghosts—painful shadowy memories of Janie and Sam.

The night had been long and dark. With dawn came the promise of escape to the sanctuary of the hospital and the even safer haven of the operating room.

Are you still going to operate on the Soviet ambassador? Jeffrey Lawrence had asked her last night. The nation's leading anchor, excellent journalist that he was, posed the question evenly, without bias, but the question itself was a challenge to her ethics. Not that it wasn't a legitimate question . . . but Diana didn't need *him* to ask it for her.

Was it ethical for her to operate today? Her sleep had been fitful, her night long and tormented, but Diana was accustomed to sleepless nights and she knew from years of experience that her ability to concentrate in the operating room was absolute.

No ghosts were permitted in the O.R. No ghosts, no memories, no emotions. Diana was confident of her ability to keep the ghosts out. She had years of practice. When Diana operated, every corner of her brilliant mind was focused on the surgery. She was safe and so were her patients.

Safe and at peace.

Diana loved the peace of the operating room, its magnificent stillness interrupted only by the necessary sounds of surgery—the soft sighs of the ventilator, the rhythmic beeps of the cardiac monitor, the gentle whoosh of suction, the whispered snips of scissors clipping suture, the crisp snap of instruments, and the creak of rubber gloves moved by expert fingers.

Sometimes necessary words joined the other sounds, but most of the communications between Diana and the members of her team were silent. Diana didn't need to say "scalpel" or "clamp" or "sponge" or "forceps" to her scrub nurse because the highly trained nurse already knew. And she didn't need to ask the other heart surgeons who assisted her for "retraction" or "suction" or "cautery," nor did she need to tell them to hold the delicate leaflet of the mitral valve gently so that she could place a suture just so, because they knew that, too.

When Diana operated, the sounds were the necessary sounds of surgery only. She operated in absorbed and reverent silence, and because she was the leader of the team, her team members followed suit. There were no discussions about the weather, no light banter about politics, no mention of books or movies or the theater. Diana's team assumed, incorrectly, that she disapproved of casual conversation in the operating room. But she didn't disapprove. She knew perfectly well that surgeons could talk and operate at the same time.

Talk . . . or listen to music.

Talking wouldn't have distracted her, but *music* might have. Music might have permitted emotions that had no place in the operating room; it might have reminded her of the songs of love that had been written for her, and sung to her, and of a precious love that had died.

But music wasn't allowed when Diana operated and the ghosts stayed away and her talented hands worked their magic.

Would she operate today?

Yes. It was ethical.

Five minutes after leaving her Park Avenue penthouse Diana was in the surgical dressing room at Memorial Hospital. She hung her dress on a metal hook, exchanging mauve silk for royal-blue cotton scrubs, then reached for the four-carat diamond and the gold wedding band on her left ring finger. The gesture was reflexive, almost an instinct.

How many hundreds of times in the past five years had she removed the rings and secured them to her scrubs with the solid-gold safety pin Chase had given her for just that purpose? Surgeons couldn't wear rings when they operated—and Diana had doubts about wearing a flawless four-carat diamond ever—but the diamond was an Andrews family treasure and Chase wanted her to have it. And, he had asked lovingly, weren't her talented fingers skillful enough to remove and replace a priceless diamond without dropping it to the tile floor? Yes, she had replied with a sapphire sparkle, Of course.

Diana reached for the rings now, but her finger was already bare. She had removed them last night when she was called to the O.R., thankfully ending the interview with Jeffrey Lawrence, and after she couldn't force herself to wear the glittering symbols of the marriage that was over. Instead she had carried them curled in her hand as she walked back to her penthouse. Once there she had hidden them between layers of silk in her dresser drawer.

Diana sighed softly as she touched her already bare ring finger. She would have to teach herself to abandon the ritual of reaching for her wedding rings . . . just as she would have to learn about living her life alone again, perhaps this time forever.

"Good afternoon, I'm Jeffrey Lawrence. We are interrupting regularly scheduled programming to bring you this special report. The surgery to implant the Shepherd Heart in the Soviet ambassador has just been successfully completed. We expect to go to a live press conference at Memorial Hospital very soon. Although the eyes of the world are focused on this major advance in Soviet-American relations, one should not ignore the major advance represented by the Shepherd Heart itself. I would like to spend the next few minutes sharing with you what I learned in a conversation I had last evening with Dr. Diana Shepherd about her remarkable invention. This model was generously loaned to me by Dr. Shepherd for this telecast . . ."

Holding a model of the Heart to the camera, Jeffrey explained what he had learned from Diana and from the brochures she had given him. He had written the copy as he always did, and when he ran out of script, because the live press conference hadn't yet started, he embellished effortlessly until the producer signaled that they were ready to switch to the hospital.

Jeffrey watched the live press conference on the studio monitors. The conference room was crowded with radio, television, and newspaper journalists from around the world. Diana arrived with an entourage—her team of three nurses, two other cardiac surgeons, and an anesthesiologist. After introducing the members of her team, Diana gave a brief summary of the surgery and announced that the ambassador was recovering uneventfully in the I.C.U.

"The ambassador is in the I.C.U.," a reporter reiterated when Diana asked for questions. "What does that mean?"

"All patients who receive the Heart are "'recovered' in the I.C.U. It's quite standard."

The questions continued for twenty minutes, questions about the surgery, the Heart, the length of time on cardiopulmonary bypass, the ambassador's anticipated convalescence in the hospital, and his life expectancy. The reporters asked medical questions, and political ones. Did Dr. Shepherd expect a call from President Bush? From Gorbachev?

Diana listened to each question carefully, her intelligent blue eyes focused and thoughtful, and answered each appropriately—the medical ones seriously and the political ones with a slight twinkle.

The press conference could have gone on all afternoon. Diana had them captivated and was quite happy to answer their questions. But she brought the session to an abrupt close after a reporter from a local affiliate of Jeffrey's network asked a question that was neither medical nor political, simply private.

"Dr. Shepherd, was it more difficult for you to operate, to concentrate, in the wake of your personal news?"

"I beg your pardon?"

"The news that your husband, real-estate mogul Chase Andrews, has just filed for divorce."

Jeffrey couldn't hear Diana's answer. Whatever she whispered was lost in the hubbub that suddenly erupted in the conference room. But he saw her reaction. For an astonished moment she simply stared at the reporter with glacial disbelief. Then, quite elegantly, quite regally, the Queen of Hearts led her court from the room.

Jeffrey gave the nation a pleasant and eloquent recap of the special report, and then, as soon as he was off the air, he demanded with quiet rage, "I want to know *now* how that reporter knew about the divorce."

"Tough news, Diana."

Diana glanced up from the progress note she was writing. Dr. Thomas Chandler looked down at her, his face carefully composed to appear genuinely concerned.

"Has something happened to the ambassador, Tom?"

"I meant about Chase."

"Oh." Diana gave a frown that she hoped looked authentically confused. Then she said sweetly, resurrecting her Dallas drawl, reminding Tom that he might be a bigger-than-life Texan, but so was she, "It's not tough news, Tom, but thank you for your concern."

"You're good, Diana."

"You mean the surgery on the ambassador?"

"You know what I mean." That was Tom's parting line, his parting shot, and his voice hardened slightly as he delivered it.

Then he was gone and Diana was left to calm her racing heart and control the rushes of anger that pulsed through her.

In eight months Diana and Tom would be vying for the prestigious position of director of the Heart Institute at Memorial Hospital. They were both deserving candidates—heart surgeons of impeccable skill and extraordinary talent, capable administrators, academic scholars—and each wanted the appointment very much. It would be war, but the battle between the two had begun literally the moment they met. Diana was unused to enemies. Even when she had critical opinions of others she usually concealed her true feelings artfully beneath layers of gracious politeness. But the antipathy between Tom Chandler and Diana was so apparent and so mutual that it was pointless to pretend it didn't exist.

Tom looked like Tom Cruise, or, as admirers were fond of saying, Tom Chandler looked the way Tom Cruise *might* look at forty-one if the handsome young actor aged magnificently. Tom Chandler was indisputably handsome and fully expected that when he arrived at Memorial Hospital he would be Top Gun. Diana had been quite prepared to defer to the newly recruited cardiac surgeon, willingly admitting that Tom's experience and credentials should place him at a level above her, but the other surgeons at Memorial viewed Tom and Diana as equals. All of which simply aggravated the dislike at first sight.

"He's such a typical heart surgeon!" Diana had exclaimed to Chase.

"You're telling me that he's incredibly sexy, incredibly bright and has hypnotic sapphire-blue eyes?" Chase had countered lovingly to his heart surgeon wife.

"No," Diana had replied with a smile. "I'm telling you he is impossibly arrogant and egotistical."

Tom Chandler *was* impossibly arrogant and egotistical, but his talent in the operating room could not be denied. Not that Tom and Diana ever operated together—each had their own teams—but she knew of his work just as he knew of hers. Diana garnered attention and publicity for her Heart, but long before that remarkable invention she had been recognized nationally and internationally as a top pediatric heart surgeon. Tom achieved public notoriety for his research in heart transplantation, but like Diana he had long been recognized in the surgical community for the magic he worked on pediatric hearts.

Tom and Diana shared talent, dedication, and special expertise in cardiac surgery in children. They should have been respected colleagues, but instead they were engaged in a war of nerves, steel against steel, a war in which the strikes on the enemy camp were made with exquisite surgical precision and finesse.

Tom had a reason, of course, for being in the nurses" station on the pediatric ward tonight. He was making post-op rounds on his youngest patients just as Diana was. But he had no reason to engage in conversation with her except as a test to see how she was coping with the viewed-by-millions live announcement that her husband no longer wanted her.

Diana knew it was a test. She knew that Tom wanted to see if her rock-steady hands were trembling or if there were indications in her eyes or voice that she was shaken. *Tough news about Chase*. Tom's voice had implied that the news might be tougher than just the emotion of a failed marriage, as if her divorce from Chase might disqualify her as a candidate for the directorship. Because her happy marriage to extraordinarily wealthy and influential Chase was as important to the appointment as her own stunning credentials? Because with Chase, Diana could hostess phenomenally successful fund-raisers for the Institute?

Did Tom really think the announcement of her divorce might influence the board? Yes, obviously he did. And maybe it would. The board of Memorial Hospital was conservative, proper, and acutely aware of public image.

Diana sighed, finished the progress note she had been writing, and checked her watch to record the time in the chart. Seven P.M. All her patients were fine, stable, and in the more than capable hands of the on call doctors.

Time to go home.

Time to go home *after* the errand she had been planning ever since the end of the press conference.

Jeffrey was in his office, the evening broadcast just completed, preparing to leave when Diana appeared at his doorway. Jeffrey had no warning that she was coming. The studio's security guards recognized her from the special report and she mumbled something about needing to get the model of the Heart she had loaned the star anchor. Not that Jeffrey needed a warning. Had the guards called, he would have said, "Of course, send her right up," and he would have been waiting at the elevator to greet her. But no one called, and she was let in, and it was a security breach. "Crazies" tried to get into the studio and on the air all the time. Last year there had been a murder, live, at a station in D.C.

What if Dr. Diana Shepherd had been carrying a gun? The ice-blue eyes that met Jeffrey's looked as if they would be perfectly happy to kill him. Of course the Queen of Hearts didn't need a gun to assassinate. She had all the ammunition of medical science in her arsenal. Perhaps she had a syringe of curare or potassium concealed in the pockets of her stylish silk dress.

Diana's eyes blazed with sapphire rage. And, Jeffrey noticed in the few seconds between the time she appeared at his door and he spoke his greeting, there was another symbol of her iciness and perhaps her rage: Diana's left hand was ringless now, the dazzling crown jewel gone. Had the immensely skilled cardiac surgeon so swiftly excised Chase Andrews from her heart?

"Good evening, Doctor."

"You are really a bastard."

"Thank you. What have I done?" Jeffrey should have known not to feign innocence. He knew why Diana was angry. He was angry about it, too. Still, it annoyed him that she assumed he was the cause of the on-the-air revelation about her divorce.

"If I even intimated a confidential detail about a patient, I could be sued, censured, maybe lose my license. In medicine, it's called ethics, an essential inviolate code to protect privacy. But you journalists have that wonderful First Amendment. Anything goes, anything to increase the ratings. Let's see if we can get her to unravel on national television! Let's see if the Queen of Hearts is heartless after all! I don't need it, you bastard. I don't want it, and, dammit, I don't deserve it."

"I don't want it for you."

"Really? Then why did you do it?"

"I didn't."

"I don't believe you. The man was a reporter from your network."

"From a local affiliate, not this studio."

"How very convenient. Just far enough away from you to shift blame but close enough to boost the ratings!"

"Last night this journalism-bashing was tolerable, even intelligent, and your holier-than-thou attitude had a certain charm. But now, *Doctor*, you are questioning my integrity and that is not acceptable."

"Not *acceptable?* Your integrity is beyond question?"

"Just like your ethics. For the record, the divorce papers were filed first thing this morning. The court reporters from the local station made the discovery about ten."

"And you're telling me they weren't tipped?"

"Not by me."

"Perhaps by someone you know?"

Jeffrey had given Diana his word that his unwitting knowledge about her divorce would be off the record. Now was she actually accusing him of *planting* the tip? Yes, apparently she was.

"I am not responsible for your divorce, Dr. Shepherd," Jeffrey paused, his dark-blue eyes silently communicating the unspoken, *You are*. "Neither am I responsible for the information becoming available to the press. If the court reporters were tipped, and I have no reason to believe they were, perhaps it was by your husband or someone who is his friend."

The implication of "friend" was obvious. Jeffrey meant *mistress*.

Diana stared at him, her eyes shining with rage. Or was the shininess tears, a sign that the ice could melt? Jeffrey almost apologized, he should have, but . . .

"I repeat, Mr. Lawrence," Diana hissed softly. "You are a bastard."

With that she left his office. The box containing the model of the Heart remained on Jeffrey's desk. He would send it to her by courier. With a message? With a dozen red roses and an apology? There had been a veneer of ice tonight, but Jeffrey remembered the way Diana looked last night. She had been deeply hurt, and now that hurt would become public, the reasons for the decay of the marriage a matter of energetic and intriguing speculation. Were there other lovers? Was the iciness sexual, too?

Diana was wounded. She lashed out at Jeffrey from pain. Jeffrey understood it. But he resented it. Maybe someday, if she reflected at all, Diana would realize how insulting her remarks to him had been.

Jeffrey decided he would return the Heart without a message. He wasn't proud of what he had done—his lack of control and his cruelty—but his integrity meant as much to him as Diana's ethics meant to her.

Because we are so much alike?

No! the answer came swiftly. As Jeffrey began to search for differences—proof that he and Diana weren't alike at all—reason promptly intervened and called off the search.

It didn't matter. Very likely, hopefully, he would never see Diana Shepherd again. He already knew that she wouldn't be at the Spencer's small dinner party at Somerset on Saturday. He assumed that Chase wouldn't be there, either, and he imagined that because of Chase's work relationship with Paige it would be Chase, not Diana who received invitations to future galas hosted by Edmund and Paige.

Jeffrey would probably never see Diana again. And that was just fine because he had absolutely no desire to.

Chapter 8

"Grrrr."

"Grrrr?"

"My zipper's stuck. Would you zip it up for me?"

"You're asking me to dress you?" Jeffrey moved behind her and kissed her bare shoulders. "I would *undress* you in an instant, Julie, but aiding and abeting in concealing this body, I don't know."

Julia turned in his arms and tenderly kissed his lips, smiling as she did, so happy with the memories of this wonderful day. Jeffrey had been at Merry's first riding lesson, and he had watched, really watched, smiling encouragement to Merry and Amanda, not seeming the least bit restless or bored.

"Thank you for this morning, Jeffrey," Julia whispered as her soft lips caressed his. "It meant so much to Merry."

Julia didn't see the slight frown that clouded Jeffrey's handsome face, because he was returning her kiss. He had been at the stable for Julia, because it was what *she* wanted. Jeffrey couldn't imagine it mattered at all to the golden-haired little girl he didn't know. Merry had been shy and distant with him, as always.

"I'm glad, darling. So, do I get to undress you?"

"Not now. We're due at Paige and Edmund's in ten minutes."

"But later? If I zip you up now, do I get to unzip you the moment we get back?"

"Oh, yes."

"Welcome." Paige smiled warmly as she greeted the Lawrences ten minutes later. Focusing on Merry, who was spending the night at Somerset because the dinner party would probably not end before the girls" bedtime, she asked, "How is my favorite overnight guest?"

"I'm fine, Aunt Paige."

"Still pretty excited about your first riding lesson?"

Merry answered Paige's question with a vigorous nod of her blond head. In the hours since the riding lesson had ended, for Merry and Amanda their long golden hair had taken on new symbolism. No longer were they Alice in Wonderland or Goldilocks or Rapunzel. Now they were palominos with wonderful flowing manes.

"So is Amanda. She's in the day room."

Before cantering off to join Amanda, Merry said to Julia, " 'Bye, Mommy." And then lifting her face bravely to Jeffrey she whispered, " 'Bye, Daddy."

"I think we know where our girls are going to spend their summer," Paige said. "It's a full-time occupation, as I recall, helping the grooms with the endlessly intriguing tasks of raking hay, pouring oats, and cleaning stalls."

"Patrick may not want them there all the time."

Oh Julia, Paige thought fondly, marveling at her friend. Didn't she know that what Patrick wanted didn't matter? Patrick was a servant. He was paid, and probably not very much, to satisfy the whims of his employers—the wealthy mistresses of the great estates. All the whims, Paige mused. She had been struck again today by the alluring yet menacing sensuality of Patrick James and wondered about the whims that his mistresses would command him to satisfy.

Julia was one of the wealthiest mistresses of one of the greatest estates in Southampton . . . but because she was Julia, she considered Patrick's wishes not her whims and would never dream of making a command.

"I'm sure Patrick won't mind, Julia, but if you like we'll ask him. So, shall we go outside? Casey and Edmund are on the terrace."

En route to the terrace, Julia remembered the seventeenth-century Belgian tapestry Paige and Edmund had just acquired from Sotheby's. As Paige and Julia made a brief detour to the dining room to admire it, Jeffrey continued on to join Edmund and his dazzling new associate.

Casey English was looking forward to meeting Jeffrey Lawrence. Casey knew, of course, that Jeffrey was married. Although the private life of the nation's leading anchorman had eluded the pages of *People, Portrait*, and *Vanity Fair*, Casey, like most of America, had noticed the elegant wedding band he wore. Paige had told Casey that Jeffrey was *very married*, but the conversation had wandered to a new topic before Paige had had a chance to tell Casey about Julia.

Not that Casey was interested in details about Jeffrey's wife. Jeffrey was the one who appealed, as all handsome and powerful men appealed. Casey did not have affairs with married men—she did not need other women's husbands!—but she loved the provocative games, the innocent seductions, the way their eyes wanted *her*. She was very much looking forward to seeing flickers of appreciation and desire for her in the dark-blue eyes of the handsome and so sexy anchor.

"Oh, Jeffrey, here you are. I'd like you to meet Casey English. Casey, this is Jeffrey Lawrence."

"Hello, Edmund. Casey, how nice to meet you." *She really is model beautiful*, Jeffrey mused when he saw Casey's forget-me-not blue eyes, flawless smile, sleek, perfect figure, and dazzling golden-blond hair. Tonight the long spun-gold hair was even more magnificent because the setting sun caressed it with glittering flickers of red. No, Jeffrey realized after a moment, the streaks of fire were part of the spectacular hair, not reflected brilliance.

"I watch you every night," Casey purred. Her eyes told him with unashamed blue-violet candor that she watched *him*, not the news, and sent a playful-and-wistful message: *I know you are married, Jeffrey Lawrence. Too bad. We might have had fun, mightn't we?*

"I understand you are wonderful to watch in the courtroom," Jeffrey replied politely, marveling at her beauty, her confidence, and his lack of interest. Jeffrey was used to appreciative smiles from beautiful, confident women, although few as truly beautiful as Casey English, but his heart never quickened, never fluttered even for a moment. That mystery was reserved for only one woman, the most beautiful one of all, one who was not so confident . . .

One who appeared on the terrace now and whose lavender eyes quickly found his. Jeffrey smiled a loving welcome and said, "Casey, I'd like you to meet my wife."

"*Julia*," Casey whispered. It only lasted for a fraction of a second—the sun behind a cloud, the frown on the flawless face, the radiant confidence struck a staggering blow. Casey recovered quickly, although her voice was strained when she spoke again, and she barely heard her own words above the thundering pulse in her brain. "Julia Phillips."

"Casey. How lovely to see you. I had no idea." Had Paige mentioned Casey's name? If she had, she must have been so preoccupied with the decision to let Merry take riding lessons that it simply hadn't registered.

"You two know each other." Edmund stated the obvious.

"Julia and I were in high school together. How long has it been?" Casey asked casually, but of course she knew, knew exactly. "Ten years."

"Well, what a wonderful coincidence," Paige said. "Edmund, why don't you supply drinks while I get the hors d'oeuvres? Then we'll get acquainted and reacquainted."

"Let me help you, Paige."

"No, Julia. Stay here and catch up with Casey."

"We didn't really know each other very well," Julia said quietly, hoping that would end the discussion.

Julia saw the subtle shift in Jeffrey's eyes, the ominous darkening of the blue to the shade *beyond* anger she had seen only twice before . . . when she told him she was pregnant, and four months later when he first saw their baby girl. The darkness terrified her, a symbol of how much Jeffrey didn't want Merry. Was that why he was angry now? Because she and Casey had known each other in high school and that was a reminder of the time when their passion created a baby he didn't want then and didn't want still?

No, Julia reassured herself swiftly by filling her mind with images of today at the stable. Today was the beginning, the fragile beginning, of her dream. We are going to be a family . . . at last.

"No, we didn't really know each other very well," Casey agreed with matching quiet. She needed time to collect her swirling thoughts before she could delve into a discussion about that time. For years just the memory of Julia could summon the uneasy emotions. And now seeing Julia herself . . .

"It is lovely to see you, Casey," Julia repeated. Then, wanting to put the conversation clearly in the present, she added, "You've done so well."

So have you, Julia. You are married to the astonishing Jeffrey Lawrence, a man whose eyes fill with longing and desire simply at the sight of you. There had been no desire in Jeffrey's eyes, not even a flirtatious flicker, when Jeffrey met *her*, but when he turned to greet Julia, the love in the ocean blue had made Casey tremble. Casey's thought continued, bringing with it painful reminders, *You've done better than me, Julia . . . as always.*

While Edmund made drinks, Casey raved about SeaCliff—the magnificent views, the splendid privacy, the fresh layers of Laura Ashley wallpaper, the charm of the cottage.

She was buying time, dazzling as she could on automatic pilot while her mind spun and she tried to calm herself with bourbon. Every so often she would glance at Julia, hoping she was merely a mirage that would vanish as she had vanished once before.

Julia smiled shyly, an uneasy smile, her mind spinning, too, trying to convince herself that the conversation would stay away from the past. After all, she and Casey had barely known each other, she reminded herself. It was amazing that Casey even recognized her. Julia hoped the conversation wouldn't drift to the past, but the damage had already been done. Jeffrey was so angry. Why?

Jeffrey's mind filled with vivid memories of two conversations—a recent one with Edmund about Casey's impressive credentials, including her education at the exclusive and academically rigorous Carlton Academy, and a distant one when Julia told him, as they made their wedding plans, that graduating from high school and going on to college didn't matter, as if her schooling had been ordinary, unimportant, not exceptional.

But Julia had been at Carlton with Casey.

As Julia sat in bewildered silence and Jeffrey waited to learn more secrets about his wife, Casey dazzled and drank bourbon and tried to calm the unwelcome emotions that pulsed through her at the sight of Julia.

Julia . . . her nemesis, her archrival, her bitter enemy in a war Julia hadn't even known they were waging. *Julia . . .* who uncovered feelings, flaws, in her that Casey didn't want o know even existed.

Damn her! Damn Julia for making all those feelings come back to me!

Casey hated the feelings, hated Julia for causing them, and hated herself for being unable to conquer them despite her incredible will to be perfect.

Katherine Carole was Kirk Carroll English's first-born child. She was not the son her father wanted, and that terrible disappointment became permanent when the doctors told her parents that because of her difficult birth she was the only child they were destined to have.

Katherine Carole English was never "Kathy" or "Kitten" or "Katie." For a brief time she was "K.C. Junior," a whimsical name with an uneasy edge, and then finally, gratefully, she became Casey.

To Kirk Carroll English, worth was measured by achievement. Perfection was the standard. Winning was everything and second was no better than last. There were no rewards for success, only condemnation for failure. Casey dedicated her young life to trying to please her perfectionistic father. She never wholly succeeded, despite her remarkable accomplishments, because she could only be a daughter, not the son he wanted.

Casey was born with brains, beauty, and the legacy of generations of wealth and privilege. She fine tuned her gifts with unrelenting discipline. She earned all A's, never cheated on diets, and never procrastinated about her exercises. She studied the expressions of her beautiful face, mastering the alluring ones until they became instinctive and extinguishing the ones that weren't stunning, confident, or provocative.

Casey drove herself relentlessly, afraid of even the slightest blemish on her flawless record of success, and her hard work inevitably paid off. Something inside Casey, a renegade voice, sometimes balked at the hard work and urged her to relax her vigil just a little. It would be safe. She would still be the best.

But Casey never relaxed, and when Julia Phillips suddenly appeared at Carlton, an unwelcome and unexpected intrusion, she realized that everything that had gone before hadn't been hard work at all. Her successes had been deceptively easy.

It was so simple to be a gracious winner when all you did was win.

Julia was a scholarship student, an "extremely gifted" girl who had been discovered languishing in a public high school in Berkeley. Until Julia's arrival, Casey had been the brightest in her class, and the youngest. But Julia was brighter—better—and she was even a year younger than Casey.

Because of Julia, Casey discovered that her need to win was as essential to her life as her need to breathe. Without winning she would surely suffocate, wouldn't she? She would surely die a desperate, gasping death.

Casey *needed* to win. But no matter how hard she worked, she was no longer the best.

Julia was better. Julia was brighter and could even have been more beautiful had she understood the power of her intoxicating sensuality. But she was so shy, so naive, so unaware of her beauty—so unaware of everything!—that Casey easily retained her distinction as the most beautiful girl at Carlton. Had Julia been aware of her beauty, it would have been a bitter contest: Casey's radiant golden beauty against Julia's dark sultry allure.

Casey retained the distinction of being Carlton's most beautiful, but she lost the other all-important crown she had held for so long. She was no longer Carlton's brightest.

On every exam, every essay, every national test, Julia was better. Not a great deal better, a point, two points, but better. The margin was large at first—Julia was much better and the teachers in the school who had doted over Casey almost forgot about her—but Casey dug in, working harder, pushing herself beyond exhaustion, and gradually narrowing the gap. The scores became close, very close, but still Julia was always better.

And Julia, brilliant, otherwordly Julia, who spent the noon hours dreamily reading the romances of Charlotte Brontë and Jane Austen instead of flirting or making friends, didn't even know they were at war. What if Julia was the best and she wasn't even trying? What if Julia started to *try*?

The war Casey waged was a cold war, a war of spying, a war in which her mind toyed with sabotage, clever, devious ways to throw her opponent off track.

Perhaps a boyfriend for shy, naive, beautiful Julia. Wouldn't love be a distraction? Mightn't that affect her concentration?

The boys at Carlton would have done anything to win favor with Casey. Confident, dazzling, sexy Casey was the queen bee. She urged the boys to become involved with Julia, and they tried. But they couldn't "relate" to her. "She's from a different planet, Case!" they exclaimed, bewildered, disappointed that they had failed Casey. "Sorry, Casey, but she's really a space cadet." Julia was from somewhere else, an outer planet or a distant era of gallantry and romance.

Finally Casey decided to approach Julia herself, not to become a friend but as a way to spy behind enemy lines. She asked Julia to come to her mansion in San Francisco's prestigious Presidio Heights after school and to the beach parties on the weekends. Julia was startled by the invitations, and shyly grateful, but she declined, giving as her reason that she had to work after school and on the weekends.

To study? Casey demanded.

No, Julia repeated quietly, her lavender eyes so innocent, *to work*.

Casey didn't believe her. Julia didn't *work!* Surely she spent every second studying, never playing, rarely sleeping. That was how she won the war.

One afternoon Casey drove her BMW behind the car and driver hired by Carlton to chauffeur its star pupil between Berkeley and Atherton. If she could catch Julia in a lie, that would be a sort of victory, wouldn't it?

But Julia wasn't lying. Fifteen minutes after the car left Julia in front of a tiny, dilapidated house two miles from Telegraph Avenue, she reappeared wearing a brown-checked uniform and walked a mile to the hamburger stand where she worked, Casey learned, three evenings a week and every other weekend.

Unfamiliar, ugly, frightening emotions pulsed through Casey's beautiful body and horrible thoughts danced in her mind. The emotions were hatred and jealousy and frustration. And the thoughts . . .

Casey couldn't win by trying her hardest. She *was* trying, and Julia was still better.

Were there other ways to win? Other ways to defeat Julia? What if something happened to her? What if she got in an accident, went into coma, maybe even *died?*

Casey hated the thoughts! She hated herself for thinking them and sometimes even wishing them! And that made her hate Julia all the more. Casey never imagined a role for herself—she wouldn't allow her mind even to dabble with those thoughts—but she wished ruin for Julia, wished for some fate . . .

And then it happened. Casey won by default. During the spring of their senior year, Julia simply vanished. At first she was mysteriously absent from class every other Friday and Monday. Then, in May, she disappeared and never returned. Carlton's headmaster told the class that Julia left for "personal reasons." She had taken oral examinations before she left to satisfy graduation requirements. Although Julia would not be at graduation, she would receive credit, but not grades, for the coursework for that spring.

Which meant that Julia graduated *second* behind Casey. Casey was the valedictorian. Casey, not Julia, addressed her classmates—the brightest high school graduates in the country—and confidently told them of the great promise their futures held.

Casey won, but it was a bittersweet victory tainted with horrible truths she had learned about herself and her desperate need to win.

That summer, before she started her freshman year at Berkeley, she spent long hours trying to gain perspective and prepare herself for the next phase of her life. Never again would she allow herself to be consumed as she had been by the competition with Julia. *In college, and in law school, and in the practice of law, there will be other Julias*, Casey told herself. *Face it, Casey, you're not the best, not always. You won't always win, no matter how hard you try.*

She disciplined her mind to those truths and prepared herself to handle failures and to lose as graciously as she had always won. But it was all an exercise.

For the next ten years there were no more Julias—not a Julia or a Julian, not a woman or man who posed a threat to her success. She graduated first from Berkeley and first from Hastings Law. And she won a record number of cases during her three years with the D.A.'s office in San Francisco.

For ten years Casey's life was deceptively easy again. Julia was simply a disquieting memory, a phantom, a ghostly symbol of darkness in perfect golden Casey, a *flaw* that haunted still.

Gone, but not forgotten.

What had happened to Julia? Where was she? What was she doing? Writing? Of Julia's enormous talents her ability to write had seemed her greatest gift. *Please let her be a writer*, Casey prayed. *Please don't let her be a lawyer.*

Casey could imagine Julia doing both, writing and practicing law, because Julia could do anything—everything. What if Julia was at Harvard Law School? Casey compulsively looked for Julia's name on the staff of the Harvard Law Review and then on lists of graduates and practicing attorneys and was relieved, but not wholly comforted, when it wasn't there.

Julia was *somewhere*. What if Casey and Julia met again one day, battling on opposing sides in a court of law? Who would win?

Casey knew.

Julia would win.

And now, on a rose-fragrant terrace on a balmy June evening, Casey was face-to-face with Julia, her ancient enemy, and with the even greater enemy—whatever it was inside her that made her very survival dependent on winning. The uneasy emotions swirled, but Casey imposed reason on them, mind over emotion, fact over fantasy. Here was Julia and she was *not* a lawyer, *not* a threat.

On impulse, warmed by too much bourbon and the momentary victory of reason over emotion, Casey decided to end it forever. She would exorcise the dark demons by exposing them to the red-gold sunlight that filtered through the trees.

"There's something I need to admit to Julia," Casey said bravely. She looked from a worried Julia to an intrigued Edmund and teased softly, "Edmund, the way you mixed this drink! The bourbon is forcing me into a confession."

"When you ask for bourbon on the rocks, there isn't much mixing involved, Casey," Edmund countered lightly.

"Oh." Casey smiled. "Well, from here on, I'd better have Diet Seven Up all by itself."

"What's your confession about Julia, Casey?" Jeffrey asked evenly, his voice revealing nothing but casual interest to everyone but Julia. While he waited for Casey's answer, he poured himself a second large glass of Scotch.

"Casey . . ."

"Julia, it's nothing about you, nothing bad. How could it be? It's about me, and not a very big deal." Casey took a soft breath and then confessed to Julia's wary lavender eyes, "It's just, well, I really resented you in high school."

"Resented me? But you were always so nice to me."

Nice? Julia, couldn't you tell that that was a ruse? Couldn't you see how much I hated you?

"Well, I resented you, a silly schoolgirl rivalry, because you were so terribly bright."

The story was Julia's story, Julia's brilliance, more than Casey's jealousy. But in singing Julia's praises Casey was admitting, finally, graciously, that Julia was the best.

And it felt . . . wonderful. Casey's audience never guessed at the depth of the emotions behind the story. They heard only gracious praise for Julia, a fond reminiscence, not the retelling of a war.

A revisionist history, Casey realized. But wasn't history often mellowed by time and perspective? Wasn't it really in essence a girlhood rivalry, something to be outgrown, laughed about, and finally forgotten? Maybe she could even learn to like Julia. Maybe they could become friends.

Wouldn't *that* be a victory?

Edmund and Paige listened, smiling fondly, not the least bit surprised at this information about their shy and brilliant friend. In the middle of Casey's story, as she was regaling them with Julia's SAT scores—"rumored to be the highest in the country"—and Julia's offers of full scholarships to Harvard, Yale, Stanford—"You name the school, they wanted her!"—Jeffrey poured himself a third drink, walked to the edge of the terrace, and faced the sea.

"Everyone always thought you would be a writer, Julia. Are you writing?" Casey asked when her story was finished.

It took Julia a moment to realize the question had been directed to her. She drew her troubled eyes briefly from Jeffrey's taut body and answered distractedly, "Oh. No."

"*Yes*," Paige corrected with a smile. "For years Julia has been enchanting the children of Southampton with the most wonderful stories. Fortunately, she has written them down."

"For Merry and Amanda and the other children."

"They could—should—be for the world. All Julia needs to do is find an illustrator."

Jeffrey and Julia performed beautifully during dinner, even though her heart screamed *Why are you angry, Jeffrey?* and his heart felt as if a knife was in it, twisting with each beat, burrowing ever deeper.

"How long will you be at SeaCliff, Casey?" Julia asked politely.

"Until Labor Day. I'll spend the last week of August in my apartment in the city, moving in and taking the Bar, but I'll be back for the weekend and the party at the Club."

"The party," Paige clarified with a warm smile, "is in Casey's honor."

"And is very nice of you." Casey knew that the lavish party that Paige and Edmund were planning at the Southampton Club was more than niceness. It was good business, the proud introduction of the newest member of Edmund's prestigious law firm to the most powerful men and women of Southampton and Manhattan.

"When do you get the Bar results?"

"Early October."

"However, she starts work the day after Labor Day," Edmund added with a look that confirmed what they all knew: Casey would pass the New York Bar with ease. "Among other things, Casey's going to litigate Elliott Barnes versus the State."

"Really?" For the first time during dinner Jeffrey's interest was more than just forced politeness.

The State of New York versus Elliott Barnes was already headlines, a high-profile and an immensely controversial case. Elliott Barnes was an attorney who had successfully won a conviction against one of New York's most influential politicians on charges of bribery and racketeering. Barnes was a local hero for about a minute before the tables turned and suddenly he was facing allegations of tax evasion and fraud. Everyone expected the charges to be dismissed, obviously trumped up, but the District Attorney had decided to prosecute.

The firm of Spencer and Quinn, confident of Elliott Barnes's innocence, was going to provide his defense. And Casey English was going to do the all-important litigating for what was destined to be one of the city's most talked-about trials.

"Really," Edmund answered Jeffrey's question. "Big case."

"It certainly is." Jeffrey turned to Casey. "You've just spent three years working for the D.A.'s office in San Francisco, and now your first trial here will be against the Manhattan D.A."

"I may be sitting on a different side of the courtroom, Jeffrey," Casey said softly, and smiled a beautiful confident smile, "but I will be on the same side, the winning side, of the law."

"How many more secrets, Julia?"

They were in their romantic bedroom suite at Belvedere and it wasn't what it should have been. Jeffrey hadn't reached out to remove her dress the moment he walked in the door as he promised he would.

Everything had changed. His voice was quiet but terrifying.

"Secrets?"

"*Lies.*"

"Jeffrey, I don't understand."

"Really? Isn't that surprising for someone as bright as you?"

"Please tell me!"

"You had a full scholarship to one of the most competitive private schools in the country—*in the world*—and yet you told me that graduating from high school and going to college didn't matter."

"That wasn't a lie, Jeffrey! It didn't matter! I only went to Carlton because they offered me the scholarship."

"You were the top student in the class."

"I did my best. I owed them that because they were so nice to me."

"How did you graduate, Julia? By mail? Did you hide your diploma from me when it arrived?"

"Jeffrey, no! During the week before our wedding, they gave me oral examinations. They probably sent my diploma to my aunt. I never saw it."

"You never told me you graduated."

"You told me you didn't care! But you did, didn't you? You wish I was like Casey or Paige."

"*No*. No. All I have ever cared about was that you tell me the truth."

"That *is* the truth. Jeffrey, why can't you believe me?"

"Because of all the lies we have lived and are living still."

"What lies are we living still?"

"You tell me, Julia. They are your lies. Tell me!"

But she only stared at him, trembling at his rage, her lavender eyes so innocent and so bewildered. Jeffrey knew how innocent her lovely eyes could look even as they lied, and as he waited for her to speak, he suddenly felt the terrifying power of his anger and the even more terrifying wish to hurt as he had been hurt. He was like a wounded animal, strong and wild with pain, liable to attack even those he loved.

"Where are you going?" Julia asked, a whisper of despair, as Jeffrey grabbed his jeans and running shoes from the closet.

"I need to get away from you."

Jeffrey hurriedly changed his clothes in the oakpaneled library. Then he went outside and started to run. He had run for a mile through the dense forest before he realized he was heading toward the cliffs above the sea, to the place where he had sought answers as a boy and where he had found an answer three years ago . . . when he decided to come home to be with Julia because she was more important than all the other dreams.

His footsteps were guided by the moon that had watched their intimate loving four nights before, and last night, but the moon wasn't full anymore and there were dark shadows.

Just like the dark shadow that had fallen over their love. Tonight Jeffrey learned that there wasn't just the one flaw—the secret he knew Julia kept even though he didn't know why—there were other flaws, more secrets, more necessary deceptions and important lies.

Why was it necessary for her to hide Carlton from him?

When Jeffrey reached the bluff he saw the lights at SeaCliff. During dinner they had all promised Casey she would have absolute privacy. She could sunbathe nude as she studied in the hammock above the sea if she wished, or run naked on the white sand beach. No eyes would see her. Tonight she could be undressing with the curtains open to the moonlight . . .

But Casey had pulled the curtains and Jeffrey saw only shadows. It was just a minor invasion of her privacy, but for a fleeting, desperate moment Jeffrey felt an urge to invade even more.

Tell me, Casey, who did Julia love at Carlton? You saw Merry when she came to the dinner table to say good night to us. Does she look astonishingly like someone you have seen before? A teacher perhaps, whose career would have ended in scandal had his affair with the brilliant sixteen-year-old become public? Or the headmaster who granted Julia graduation after she completed private oral exams?

Did Casey English know the reason for Julia's deception?

Perhaps, but Jeffrey would involve no one else in their very private life.

He ran down the winding trail to the beach and along the sand until every cell in his body screamed from exhaustion and begged him to stop. But he didn't heed the agonized screams. He ran even farther and even faster.

Three hours later, long after the lights had been turned out in SeaCliff, Jeffrey returned to Belvedere and to Julia.

She was in their bed shivering beneath the satin comforter even though the summer night was balmy. She listened as Jeffrey showered and prayed that

the next sounds wouldn't be the sounds of him dressing again as he prepared to leave.

But Jeffrey didn't leave. He walked quietly to their bed.

Their marriage had no rules for fighting, no rituals to follow when they quarreled, because they didn't quarrel. And it didn't occur to Julia to pretend she was asleep, to turn her back to him, to pout or *play*, because Jeffrey was her heart, her love, her life. Instead of turning away, Julia faced him, bravely meeting his eyes, ready to try again to answer his confusing questions.

Jeffrey asked the same questions. And Julia gave the same answers, the only answers she could give, because they were the truth.

"Why didn't you tell me that you were a student at Carlton, Julia?"

"Because it didn't matter to me. All that mattered was for me to be with you."

"And to have Merry." Jeffrey's voice was quiet, controlled, but still the words sounded so accusatory.

"To be with you. And to have Merry. Yes." Julia paused, then asked softly, hesitantly, "Jeffrey?"

"Yes?" Tell me, Julia, please. Tell me the truth.

"Are you going to leave us?"

"Leave you?" Jeffrey echoed quietly, stunned by the question and the fear in her soft voice. Leave *you?* It was he who felt so vulnerable and so betrayed. Julia owned his heart, all of it, but he didn't own hers. "I will never leave you."

As he spoke the words Jeffrey wondered if now he had begun to lie to her.

Someday, for my own survival, my Julie, I may have to leave you. I can't trust your love and it's killing me.

They loved so carefully the next day, with soft caresses and gentle smiles. Each wanted love, only love, always love, and as they searched for ways to make their love strong and whole again, each remembered the promises of love they had made on their anniversary a month before.

"This is going to be a very busy summer," Jeffrey told her apologetically when he called from work on Monday afternoon. "I really must go to Europe to cover the President's visit to the Eastern Bloc countries, and the bicentennial of the Bastille, and the Economic Summit in Paris."

"Not to mention the nightly broadcasts, whatever else may happen, and special reports. I know, Jeffrey. I understand," Julia said softly, sadly. Jeffrey was telling her that he wasn't going to make time for them to be a family. Even though he had seemed to enjoy Merry's first riding lesson he really hadn't, not enough to make the effort.

"No, honey, you don't understand. This summer will be very busy, and it may be impossible for me to make definite plans, but I'm going to take a vacation during the second week of September. I just called Southampton Country Day and found out that Merry's classes don't resume until the eighteenth, so we'll have the week before school starts to be together." Jeffrey had tried to find a week before then, a time when he wouldn't be traveling with the President and someone else could anchor *The World This Evening*, but he couldn't. The *real* fathers had long since scheduled their vacations for July and August. "I'm all yours that week, Julie. Do with me what you will."

"Really?"

"Really."

"That means you'll be home for Merry's birthday. Oh, Jeffrey, thank you."

"You're welcome, darling."

"You owe me a honeymoon," Julia whispered softly after a few moments.

"You can collect any time."

"I applied for a passport today."

"Did you?"

"Yes. I thought, maybe in October or November, after Merry's been back in school for a while . . ." They were brave words, spoken from her heart, because she loved him so much and had made a loving promise to him to conquer her fears.

"Whenever you say, Julie, whenever you're ready," Jeffrey told her gently. "I love you."

Chapter 9

Casey spent the morning following the dinner party at Somerset planning her summer at Sea-Cliff. She made a comprehensive study schedule and compulsively outlined her other schedules as well—when she would exercise, when she would eat, *what* she would eat.

This was the disciplined way in which Casey lived her life, how she succeeded, how she was perfect. Every morning and every evening, no matter how early or late or how tired she was, Casey did the exercises that kept her thighs trim, her waist slender, her calves tapered, her arms taut, and her breasts high and proud. Casey only permitted the right foods, in small amounts, into her sleek and sexy body, and she carefully maintained a perfect tan. Sun in excess was bad, Casey knew, but she knew, too, that a slight golden hue accentuated her radiant red-gold hair and created the confident illusion that her successes were so effortless that she had endless hours to spend lazing in the sun.

Everything Casey did was carefully calculated for success . . . and it all paid off.

She calculated the words and inflections she would use in court, rehearsing and rehearsing until the meticulously scripted words flowed so naturally that even her legal opponents marveled at her gift of effortless, perfect speech. The words she spoke in the courtroom weren't left to chance and neither was the way she looked.

Casey's "look" changed from case to case depending on the crime, the judge, the jury, the opposing counsel, and the mood of the trial. The salary earned by young attorneys in the D.A.'s office was modest, but virtually everyone knew that Casey was an heiress whose monthly income from trust funds was far in excess of her yearly income from work. Casey didn't pretend to be impoverished. She wore designer clothes—Chanel, St. Jillian, Le Crillon, and Dior—with jewels by Tiffany and Shreve and watches by Ebel, Chopard, and Blancpain. Casey sometimes even wore "accessories" over her vision-perfect forget-me-not blue eyes, clear glass framed in tortoiseshell or wire-rim or the eyewear fashions of Anne Klein.

Her spectacular hair completed the look. She would pull the fire into a severe chignon, or loosely weave a thick red-gold braid, or let it fall free, a cascade of gold kissed by the sun, *depending* . . .

Before Casey stepped into the courtroom she spent tireless hours learning everything she could about the case, studying the applicable law and preparing the best defense. And she spent additional tireless hours preparing herself, her flawless flow of perfect words and the important message she conveyed by the way she looked.

Casey's decision to look beautiful—soft and feminine—for the Nob Hill Rapist trial was a decision that was closer to her heart than to her brain. She would wear chiffon and silk, she decided, in all the pastel shades of spring. And she would wear her dazzling spun-gold hair long and free.

Because the case was really about a freedom, wasn't it? she asked herself. Wasn't it really about woman's freedom to be beautiful, if she wanted, and soft, if she wanted, and feminine, if she wanted? Wasn't it really about a woman's freedom to be anything she wanted to be without fear?

Casey's summer in Southampton should have been easy. She simply had to follow her carefully calculated schedules for success. She had been given a promise of absolute privacy. There would be no intrusions, no distractions. So easy.

Except there *were* distractions and intrusions. Her privacy was invaded from within, from thoughts that swirled in her head and lured her into dangerous territory . . . *Julia.*

Why do I keep thinking about her? Casey wondered insistently. *Julia is ancient history, a demon purged.*

Julia was no longer a threat, except that Julia had won. Jeffrey Lawrence, who could have had any woman on earth, had chosen Julia. And it was so obvious how much he loved her! Casey had seen Jeffrey's love for Julia the second Julia appeared on the terrace. And Casey had watched his eyes throughout the evening and seen such love, such tenderness, and something else very deep, a desire so intense that it was almost pain.

To be loved that much! To be loved that much for who you were.

Julia's beauty and serenity had blossomed with Jeffrey's love, but she was simply a womanly version of the shy and brilliant girl who had unwittingly tormented Casey in high school. Julia hadn't changed. She had simply found a man, a remarkable man, who loved her deeply for exactly who she was.

Will I ever be loved for who I am?

Many men had fallen in love with her, of course. Rich, handsome, powerful men who were unafraid of her success, bewitched by her beauty, and seduced by the provocative words and alluring smiles that she rehearsed as compulsively as she practiced her performances in court.

But had those men really fallen in love with her or only with the talented actress whose every performance was flawless? And why did she never fall in love with them? And why, despite her triumphs, her successes, her letter-perfect performances, did she never feel a rush of joy, a tremble of desire, a quiver of happiness?

What if Casey and the talented actress were the same woman? What if that was really who she was? *All* she was? Just perfect, forever joyless, destined to live a passionless, disciplined life of schedules that were programmed for success, and permitted virtually no free time for Casey.

Free time? Time to be free?

Wasn't there perhaps—*please*—another Casey? the intruding thoughts wanted to know. Hadn't there once been a little girl who loved to run on the beach and play tag with the waves and chase the sun? Was that happy girl lost forever or was there still within her a Casey who could abandon her law books because the snow-white sand beckoned?

Yes, there was. The little girl existed still, and now she scampered down the winding trail to the beach, and the sand felt so soft and warm beneath her bare feet. Then she was running along the beach chasing the fiery beacon of the setting sun, half a mile, then a mile, not breathless, not aching, only buoyant . . . dancing . . . *free*.

Then the beach suddenly ended, abruptly, in a massive wall of steep cliffs. The beach was gone except for a delicate snowy ribbon of white sand that stretched into the sea. If she wanted to see the sun set—which she did—she would have to find a way up the steep cliffs. Or, perhaps, if she stood on the farthest reach of the snowy ribbon of sand there might be a view . . .

Casey chose the sandy peninsula. She stood at its very tip on a sea-slick boulder and strained to catch a glimpse of the falling sun. But the fireball was hidden behind the wall of cliffs. As she stood on the boulder, huge rolling waves kissed the rock, splashing her with a warm shower of salt.

Warm . . . *hot*.

But the wet heat on her face, mixed with the sea, was the salty hotness of her own tears.

Tears? Casey never cried. But she was crying now in this breathtaking place where she had come because a lovely distant memory, or perhaps a future dream, had urged her to chase the setting sun.

Were her tears because she had failed? Because the fiery star was setting out of her sight? Or were the tears because she was chasing something even more important and more elusive—herself, her happiness, her freedom—and that, too, was beyond her reach?

Patrick inhaled the warm salt air and experienced the exhilarating feeling of peace.

Peace was a rare but so welcome visitor in the turbulence of Patrick's life. Peace was an overnight guest, a bewitching and beguiling one-night stand, the deceptively tranquil calm at the center of the swirling storm.

There had been moments of peace before. Patrick had tried hard to preserve them forever, but they had always vanished. He hadn't expected peace again—ever. But here it was, a gift to treasure until the inevitable moment when he was once again forced to flee. He marveled at the gift that had come so unexpectedly, a glimmer of sunshine through a storm-gray sky, just three months before.

On that March day Patrick had been at a truck stop in New Jersey looking for work. He would find the driver of a moving van who needed a second driver for the transcontinental journey, or someone who had just arrived from the West Coast, a solitary worker who needed help unloading his van. This had been Patrick's life for almost five years, traversing the country, living from job to job, with a new name and without a home.

But, of course, Patrick had never had a home.

As he drank a cup of coffee he had glanced at a copy of *The New York Times*. On impulse he turned to the want ads. It was a small form of torture, a grim reminder of his destiny. He could never get a real job because that required an identity, an authentic name with a social security number and birth certificate to match. There had never been jobs that appealed, anyway, until now.

Riding instructor needed immediately. Southampton Club. Experience required. Call . . .

Patrick's heart raced as he read the ad. If he could ride again . . . It would be so very close to peace, almost like having a home.

Southampton Club. Patrick had never competed in a Grand Prix event held

in Southampton. But had he ever competed against a rider from the exclusive Club? No, he was quite certain that he never had. It was safe. No one would recognize him.

Experience required. Patrick had never taught riding, but he was a champion equestrian. He could lie about his experience, give false references, and hope that "immediately" meant that someone at the Southampton Club was desperate.

Someone—the manager—was desperate. Spring break—an event that used to be a week but now seemed to stretch from mid-March to mid-April—was about to begin. In a matter of days the children and grandchildren of Southampton would appear at the stable expecting lessons and trail rides and the man who was supposed to teach riding this year had just taken a position elsewhere.

Three hours after Patrick made the call to the number in the ad, he was in the manager's office at the Club. He tried to schedule the interview for the ollowing day so that he would have a chance to make himself presentable. He would spend all his hard-earned money—two hundred and twenty dollars—on an acceptable Ivy League haircut and proper country club clothes. Patrick knew the costumes and customs of the very wealthy. He could wear the elegantly tailored clothes beautifully and speak the polite language flawlessly. He had fitted in once, an elegant chameleon, adapting so convincingly that everyone assumed that he, too, had been born with wealth and privilege, attended prep school in the East, then Harvard or Yale, and vacationed in the usual playgrounds in Europe. He could do it again to get this job. But the manager at the Southampton Club didn't give him time to buy clothes at Brooks Brothers or even to trim his coal-black hair.

Besides, Patrick thought defiantly as a commuter train carried him swiftly from New Jersey to Southampton, the best riders in the world wore jeans, not jodphurs, when they practiced.

He knew about the wealthy because he had been among them once, cleverly disguised. And he knew about the best riders in the world because he had been one of them once, too.

"You've taught riding?" the Club's manager asked. He eyed Patrick skeptically but was obviously pleased that the voice had a refinement that was missing in the too-long hair and threadbare jeans.

"Yes."

"Where?"

"All over."

"The job is only for a month." The manager decided not to push for credentials. He needed someone beginning tomorrow. After spring break was over he would have two months to search for a more appropriate replacement before the summer season began.

"Will I be paid in cash?"

"If you like."

"Yes. And since the job's only for a month, I will need to stay here. I can sleep in the stable and shower in the members" dressing rooms before dawn."

"There's an apartment in the stable. It's small, but it has all the necessities. You can stay there."

The manager expected complaints about Patrick James—and prepared his retort, "only for a month"—but all he heard for the new riding instructor was praise. Patrick was a patient, tireless, excellent instructor. Even the threadbare jeans, denim work shirts, and battered boots met with approval. In fact Patrick's cowboy look became *fashion.* The expensive hand-knitted equestrian sweaters from Miller's, the linen jodhpurs and silk turtlenecks of Ralph Lauren, and the hunting boots by Beverly Feldman languished unworn in closets of the fabulous estates, forsaken for generic blue jeans, cotton shirts, and nondesigner boots. Even the "sporting" jewels—diamonds, sapphires, emeralds, and rubies set in equestrian motifs—remained in wall safes behind Impressionist paintings.

Patrick devoted tireless hours to teaching at the stable and, in his spare time, to earn additional money, he worked as the bartender for the lavish parties given at the Club.

At the end of spring break the manager asked Patrick if he would stay on indefinitely. Patrick accepted the offer and had no concern about its vagueness. He made his relationship with the Southampton Club even less binding by refusing a straight salary in favor of a percentage of each lesson he gave, paid in cash, every two weeks, and job-by-job payment for the bartending he did. He would live without charge in the studio apartment in the stable and his meals would be leftovers from the Club's gourmet kitchen.

Since he was not officially an employee of the Southampton Club, no paperwork was required. He never filled out a formal job application, never signed a contract, never provided names of references. The Club could fire him without notice and Patrick could leave without warning.

The manager hoped that neither would happen, but he wondered. Patrick was so different from the men he usually hired to supervise the summer sports—yachting and tennis and swimming—men who themselves frequently became intriguing summertime diversions. Patrick was handsome, very handsome, but despite his elegant speech, there was a wildness about him. The manager was quite certain that the rich and beautiful women of Southampton would want the wild and handsome riding instructor. But would Patrick be discreet? Would he respect the *rules*?

The women did want Patrick, as women always had wanted him. He had wanted women, too, some of them, the ones with whom he chose to share himself. Sex had always been a wonderful pleasure, a treasured freedom, a gift of intimacy, a solemn and joyful choice . . .

Until five years ago when Patrick chose to say no to a beautiful young heiress. He didn't want her, but she wanted him, and her rage at his refusal cost him everything—his freedom, his dreams, his chance for a lasting peace.

For five years Patrick had run. And now, because he had to ride again, he was back among the rich and powerful people he loathed. And the rich, beautiful women of Southampton, like the heiress who had cost him his dreams, wanted him—as a possession, a trophy, a plaything for their pleasure—when they chose, *because* they chose.

Once Patrick had chosen to say no and that choice had cost him everything. And now? Now he had nothing more to lose—except this precious peace. If he said no, he would have to be prepared to flee again.

And if he said yes? If he satisfied their whims? If he accepted their expensive gifts? He had nothing more to lose—except his self-respect and his fragile freedom to choose.

Patrick chose to say no to the women in Southampton who wanted him. To the petulant young heiress in Kentucky, his no had been gentle and kind, and still it had backfired. Now his no's were sullen, defiant, laced with contempt, and that backfired, too, because it made the seduction more challenging, the game more intriguing, the prize more valued. Patrick's contempt was alluring, his defiance seductive, his wildness appealing and erotic. The rich, beautiful women wanted to tame him.

Then, quite by accident, Patrick discovered the secret to his survival in Southampton.

"Patrick, do you give private lessons? At night?"

"No." Usually that was all he said, his voice hard and cold, his gray-green eyes disdainful, but on that night, perhaps because the woman was not so demanding as the others, he added gently, "I'm sorry. I really can't."

"Oh. Are you involved with someone?"

"Yes." He watched the transformation in her eyes at his lie. There was a softening, a little envy, a little admiration.

"And you are faithful to her?"

"Yes." That wasn't wholly a lie. Patrick knew that if he ever did fall in love he would be faithful.

He discovered then that fidelity was an ideal to these women who wanted him for their pleasure—the married women whose unfaithfulness sprung from unhappy marriages and the unmarried women who wished for love. He told them he had a lover to whom he was faithful and they left him alone. And he survived among the rich and privileged. More than survived . . . he found peace.

Peace. Peace among the people he hated. So strange to find peace here.

Patrick gazed at the crashing surf and long stretch of beach and felt the immense eager power of the black stallion beneath him. In a moment he would urge the magnificent horse to chase the setting sun, but first he wanted to etch the image of the scene in his mind. Tonight when he returned to his apartment at the stable he would begin to paint this breathtaking picture of sky and sand and sea.

Whenever he could, he came to this beautiful white sand beach at sunset, and he had discovered another idyllic place from which to greet the dawn. The owners of the estates had so much land, so many breathtaking vistas from their mansions, that the wonders at the edges were all but forgotten. Patrick discovered the wonderful remote places as he rode along the trails that connected the Club to the estates, trails that meandered through dense forests, along precipitous cliffs, and across vast expanses of fragrant meadow . . . and they became his private sanctuaries.

But today he was not alone. He made the surprising discovery as he approached the steep cliffs a mile beyond the vacant cottage. There was a woman standing at the tip of the peninsula.

The peninsula. Patrick had spent many evenings watching the ever-changing drama of the slender ribbon of sand. Its size, its shape, indeed its very *existence* were defined by the waves and the tide. At low tide the sand was an extension of the beach, a snow-white comma punctuating the sapphire sea. But as the sea began to flood, the rocky tip became divorced from the rest of the beach and the peninsula became an island encircled by water swirled by a lethal undertow. At the highest tides, the full-moon tides, the land disappeared completely, swallowed by the swollen sea.

The island could vanish quickly, like the sun into the sea, a gradual descent until the very last and then a free fall.

The tide was rising now and the woman, a stranger to Patrick and the treacherous peninsula, was probably lost in the magical beauty of the sea. Patrick rode across the river of water that had begun to divide the peninsula from the beach. The channel wasn't deep yet, and perhaps this evening's tide would not completely submerge the island, but she needed to be warned of the possible danger.

"Hello!" Patrick called as he neared.

Casey hadn't heard him approach. The pounding hoofbeats were muffled by the soft sand, the noise of the crashing surf, and the confusing thunder in her mind. But she heard the male voice above the other sounds. It would be Edmund or Jeffrey. And whichever handsome man it was, he would be smiling at her, an apologetic smile, because she had been promised absolute privacy.

She would be smiling, too, when she turned to greet him. Not that he would be able to tell she'd been crying, she realized with relief as her hands moved to wipe her tear-damp eyes and felt the sea-kissed wetness of her cheeks. The surprising tears, she discovered, were well camouflaged by the splashes of the sea.

The warm drops that had thankfully concealed her tears had, however, made her light cotton blouse quite transparent. The drenched fabric clung to her, revealing her provocative shape and the sensuous details of her breasts. Casey realized her nakedness before she turned and knew, too, that the mane of hair that tumbled down her back was dry still. She gave a gentle toss of her head as she turned, and the red-gold hair danced in the fading sunlight, fire lit by fire, until the silky strands fell in a luxurious cape over her round, damp breasts.

Like "The Birth of Venus," Patrick mused. The mane of red-gold hair modestly concealing a perfect body as it rose from the sea instantly recalled to his artistic mind the exquisite painting by Botticelli. Perhaps this barely clothed virtually-revealed vision *was* Venus being born in this enchanted spot on Long Island.

"Oh!" Casey's cheeks flushed pink.

Her embarrassed "Oh!" should have been a "Hello" softly purred. Casey had a soft purr, carefully practiced and trained to appear whenever she met a stunningly handsome man. But now, for this stunningly handsome stranger with gray-green eyes and coal-black hair, the purr wouldn't come.

Because the seductive purr belonged to the other Casey? *The other Casey?* Yes, you know, the Casey who doesn't cry. The Casey who would never have abandoned her schedule to chase the setting sun. The Casey who, had she decided to chase the setting sun, would never have let the fireball out of her sight, nor dashed to a dead end of sand, nor become sea-soaked, nor most assuredly *ever* have cried.

Whatever the reason tonight there was no softly purred "Hello," only flushed pink cheeks and an awkward "Oh!"

"What are you doing here?" she asked.

"Well, I guess I'm here to rescue you."

"Rescue me? From what?" *From myself? From the other Casey?*

"The tide."

"The tide?" Casey echoed. Was she dreaming? Was he really a knight in shining armor who had come to rescue her from a watery dragon? A knight, perhaps, yes, but he had forsaken his shining armor for a denim shirt opened to the warm ocean breeze.

"Come with me now," Patrick commanded solemnly.

Casey felt a tingling rush, so unfamiliar, so wonderful, and a sudden wish to be commanded by him, to make his solemn, seductive eyes glisten with pleasure, to play whatever game he wanted to play.

"All right."

"Do you ride?"

"Yes," Casey answered uncertainly. She had taken riding lessons at the Carlton Club in Atherton, but that had been years ago and she had never before ridden bareback. "Sort of."

"Climb on behind me and hold on."

"OK."

Patrick moved the horse beside the boulder and held the powerful black stallion perfectly still while Casey mounted.

"Hold on," Patrick repeated.

Casey obeyed by curling her arms loosely around his waist. When they reached the channel, deeper now and more turbulent, the stallion lurched as it high-stepped into the water. Casey felt the sudden tension in the animal's strong body and reflexively clung more tightly to Patrick, pressing against him, feeling his power, his tension, his strength.

The stallion crossed the channel in a burst of power. Once they reached the safety of the beach, Patrick calmed the horse quickly, then dismounted and circled his strong arms around Casey's waist as she slid to the sand.

"That wasn't a game," Casey whispered softly when she looked back and saw what was happening to the peninsula.

"No."

"The place where I was standing is almost gone." Had the enchanted moments of the gallant knight and mythical dragon really been life and death? Casey wondered. The question scared her because she had been so oblivious to the danger. What if he hadn't been riding by?

"Yes, but the higher ground may not sink tonight. The moon was last full ten days ago, so the tide isn't as high. You might just have been stranded until the sea began to ebb. If you're a strong swimmer you could have ridden a wave to shore." *Or if you're really Venus.*

Patrick couldn't swim. If he was caught on the peninsula on a full moon night, a night when every grain of sand dove into the sea, he would surely drown . . . unless, perhaps, it was a night when the sea was more laughing than angry and he could cling to a piece of wood and the friendly currents would carry him toward shore instead of dragging him below to the dark depths.

Casey could swim. She could have made it ashore without him, couldn't she?

"It wasn't a game," she repeated quietly, trembling as a sudden icy shiver of fear swept through her.

"I don't play games. Are you cold? Would you like my shirt?"

"No, thank you. I'm fine." The evening air was warm. The sheer cotton fabric she wore would dry quickly away from the ever-dampening spray of the sea and she would be concealed again. Not that his eyes were drifting to her breasts, her hips, her slender sea-wet thighs. The intense gray-green eyes remained focused on her face, smiling, curious, patient.

"OK."

"Who are you?" Casey asked, curious, too, and less patient than he. *Who are you that knows the phases of the moon and the secrets of the sea?*

"Patrick James. And you?"

"Casey English."

"So, Casey English. What are you doing on my beach?"

"I'm spending the summer at the cottage on the cliff."

"Oh. Only the summer?"

"Yes. Just before Labor Day I'll move into the city."

"To do what?"

To play games, Casey thought. *To be a magnificent actress who dazzles the world with brilliant performances, wonderful costumes, sharp legal acumen, and flawless rhetoric.*

Patrick said he didn't play games. What if, with him, she didn't play, either? What if she wasn't Casey English, heiress, attorney, grand master at playing games and winning? What if she was just the girl who had danced after the setting sun? What if she was just Casey, just herself, whoever that was?

"To work. I'm just a working girl." Casey realized she needed an explanation for why she was spending the summer at SeaCliff. She had never used the word "boss" before. She never thought of Edmund, or the D.A., or *anyone* as her boss. They were simply colleagues, more experienced than she. But now she said, "My boss owns the cottage. I can do the work I'm doing for him this summer there."

"That's very nice. You weren't working this evening."

"No." Casey hadn't told him the unimportant truths about herself—her immense wealth and her stunning successes—but if she really wasn't going to play she had to tell him the important things. "I was chasing the sun, but I lost it over the cliffs," she admitted softly.

Patrick hesitated only a moment. It was his private place, but he would happily share it with this woman who had come to the beach for the same reason as he. When her journey toward the sun had been blocked by the cliffs, she had turned fearlessly to the sea. But when the same thing had happened to him on a night in April, he had chosen to find a way up the cliffs because he belonged nowhere near the lethal waves.

"There's a path up the cliffs. It's steep, but it leads to a meadow where you can watch the sun until it falls into the trees. Would you like me to show you?"

"Yes. Please."

Patrick tied the stallion's reins to a branch at the base of the path, far from the waves, then led Casey through a lush green maze of ferns and forest to the meadow.

The enchanted meadow. Patrick's meadow was an ocean of wildflowers surrounded by towering pines and bathed in the fading rays of the golden sun. The sun danced above the pines, a fiery pirouette, twirling ever lower and finally disappearing into the green but leaving behind a magnificent farewell gift—a pastel sky of pink and gold.

Casey and Patrick watched the spectacular adieu of the summer sun in awed silence. There was nothing to say, no words to describe the beauty, the peace, the wonder.

No words, but Casey suddenly felt the heat of tears. *No!*

"What's wrong, Casey?"

"I don't know," she whispered the truth. Then she offered a lie. "Maybe a delayed reaction from what almost happened on the peninsula?"

But Patrick wouldn't allow the lie.

"You were crying before," he said gently.

"Yes." Casey started to apologize for her tears, but Patrick's expression stopped her. He looked concerned that she was crying, concerned about her, but not uncomfortable with the tears. Patrick's comfort with her inexplicable emotions made Casey feel wonderfully safe, wonderfully free. As if it was all right to cry. As if it was all right to be vulnerable and imperfect. "I didn't know why I was crying then, either."

"Do you always have all the answers?"

Yes, always. Always before . . .

"I guess not." Casey smiled a lovely soft smile, a smile she had never smiled before, a smile she had never practiced in front of the mirror until it was perfect. She had never seen this imperfect wobbly smile—and would have banished it if she had, even though in its vulnerability and softness it was more beautiful than all her flawless, confident smiles. "I would like to know this answer though."

"I'm sure you will in time. Tears aren't all bad, you know."

"No?" Casey asked hopefully. She *didn't* know. For twenty-seven years Kirk Carroll English's daughter had known only that tears were bad, always bad, an unacceptable sign of weakness and an intolerable flaw.

"Not to me. I think tears are like rain, sometimes unwelcome, sometimes nourishing." Patrick smiled and added, "It depends on whether you're a parade or a flower."

That brought a soft laugh. Earlier he had not permitted her to drown in the salty sea, and now he was not permitting her to drown in her salty tears. He spoke with a smile and a gentle tease, but the words were serious, too.

"So, which are you, Casey? A flower or a parade?"

The old Casey was a parade. And the new Casey? A fragile flower reaching bravely for the sun?

"I don't know," she whispered. *But I have to find out.*

"I need to get the stallion back to the stable before dark," Patrick said as the pastel sky faded to gray.

"The stable?"

"At the Southampton Club. Why don't I walk you back to the cottage?"

"Oh. Thank you."

Patrick led the way back down the trail from the meadow to the beach. They paused briefly when they reached the sand and gazed at the peninsula. It was an island still, a small mound of gray in the middle of the swirling sea. The sand was gray, not white, proof that it had been kissed by the tide, but it wasn't possible to tell now whether the kiss had been a gentle, chaste caress or a deep, consuming one.

"Thank you again for rescuing me," Casey said when they reached the trail to SeaCliff.

"You probably would have been fine."

"I'm sorry about the tears."

"You are?"

No, because there was something wonderfully purifying about my tears and the emotions that flowed with them . . . and there was something even more wonderful about the way they didn't bother you.

"No," Casey admitted softly.

"I'd better go. Without the moonlight the path through the forest will be very dark. Good night, Casey."

"Good night, Patrick."

She watched as he became a shadow in the twilight and then disappeared into the forest.

Who was he? she wondered. Who was this dark handsome stranger who knew the mysteries of the moon and the sea and was so wise about her tears? A poet? A writer? Or was he, perhaps, an attorney who was spending his summer studying for the Bar but permitted himself free time to gallop a prized stallion along a snowy beach?

Patrick belonged in Southampton, of course. He was a member of the Club and teased confidently about her being on *his* beach even though he surely knew the white sand belonged to Edmund and Jeffrey. When Casey had first heard his voice she had assumed he was Edmund or Jeffrey, but Patrick was only like them—rich, aristocratic, successful, powerful. Like Edmund and Jeffrey, and like her.

But Casey hadn't told Patrick those unimportant truths about herself. Instead she had told him the important things, and she had let him see her tears, and she had felt so safe with him and so free.

But now, as Patrick's shadow faded into the gray of the night, those wonderful fragile feelings faded too.

Patrick was going, *gone* . . . and he would not return.

She should have played! She should have dazzled and seduced and performed!

She shouldn't have shown Patrick her vulnerability, her confusion, her tears . . .

Chapter 10

"Hello, Diana."

"Chase."

Diana hadn't spoken to Chase for over five weeks, not since he left "to decide." In the two weeks since the divorce papers had been filed, they had been communicating through their attorneys. They had "his" and "her" attorneys—neither from Spencer and Quinn—although the entire divorce could have been handled by a single lawyer. The uncontested dissolution of the marriage of Diana Shepherd and Chase Andrews was quite simple, merely a matter of the equitable division of their immense fortune.

Quite simple, and going so smoothly one hardly realized it was being dissolved.

Dissolved.

How Diana wished the pain would be so easily dissolved!

She had hoped Chase would call. She needed to hear his voice. She needed to know if there was anger and bitterness. The loss of Chase's love was painful enough without the bitter legacy of anger.

Chase could have chosen a better time to let you know, Jeffrey Lawrence had observed that evening in her office. The celebrated anchor's tone hadn't mocked—not then—but the words had taunted nonetheless.

Had Chase really chosen the eve of the most high-profile surgery of her career to issue a less than subtle reminder that it was her dedication to her career that had destroyed their love?

It seemed so vituperative, so hostile, so unlike Chase. Admittedly he was unused to being thwarted. Yet, when he had been confronted by a situation in his private life, in his love, that he could neither control nor change, he had finally had to leave to decide—and there had been gentleness, a wistful sadness, not anger. And the dialogue through the attorneys had been civilized, amicable, without a whisper of bitterness. Chase wanted Diana to have the Park Avenue penthouse that was a safe five-minute walk to Memorial Hospital. And he didn't want any part of her Heart, at least not the plastic one . . .

"How are you, Diana?"

"I've been better, Chase. I'm going through a divorce. It's quite painful."

"I know," Chase agreed softly. "And it doesn't help to have the undivided attention of Manhattan's most malicious gossip columnists, does it?"

"No. They haven't really found much, have they?"

"There's nothing to find, Diana."

I know, Diana thought. The ravenous search for skeletons, the intense search for the *other woman* in Chase's life, would come up empty. Chase hadn't been unfaithful to her, nor she to him.

Or had she? Wasn't it her secret fidelity to a distant love that had destroyed their marriage?

"Is the settlement all right with you, Chase? You don't mind that I keep the penthouse?"

"The settlement's fine. I don't mind at all about the penthouse. I want you to be safe."

"Thank you."

"Diana, I was in Paris when the papers were filed. I met with the attorney before I left and we agreed he would file as soon as the documents were prepared. I didn't even know about the surgery on the Soviet ambassador until after I returned."

"I hoped there was something like that."

"I'm very sorry."

"It's OK. It was going to happen sometime. You've had your share of questions from the press."

"Yes, but I haven't been ambushed on live television."

"Well. It's over. I'm just glad the timing was accidental."

"I promise you it was." Chase paused, took a soft breath, and then continued, "Diana, I'd like to see you. I have something to give you."

"I have something to give you, too, Chase."

"Tonight? In an hour?"

"In an hour."

What did one wear to say a final good-bye to the man who was supposed to be her husband forever? Was there proper attire for such an occasion? Could even Emily Post provide guidance about the etiquette?

Chase had known and loved Diana in everything and nothing—the designer gowns she wore to the April in Paris Ball, the bright cheery dresses she wore under her white coat at the hospital, the wool skirts and cashmere sweaters she wore for their hideaway weekends in Maine, the silk negligees he removed so eagerly. Chase had known her and loved her in silk and denim, satin and tweed, lace and cotton, and, the way he loved her best, in nothing at all in the privacy of their bed.

Diana decided to look beautiful, as beautiful as the fatigue and strain of the past few weeks would allow. She chose a sapphire silk sheath, one of Chase's favorites, caught her dark-brown curls in a sapphire velvet ribbon, and chilled a bottle of Dom Pérignon. While she waited on the penthouse balcony, she gazed at the glitter of Manhattan and thought about the marriage that was over.

It should have lasted forever. That was what she and Chase had planned. They had been so sure of their love, so confident that their hearts beat in perfect harmony and always would. Chase loved the fact that Diana was a dedicated and brilliant surgeon. He was so proud of her and her remarkable career. And Diana loved Chase's magnificent buildings and was so proud of him, too, for his unwavering commitment to quality and beauty. They shared a passion for their careers, and they shared a breathless passion for each other.

There is nothing to find, Chase had said. Diana knew it was true. Chase needed no other woman to give him pleasure. And she had no need for anyone but Chase. Chase was the only man who had ever been able to make her forget about Sam.

Sam. For ten years after Sam left her, Diana's relationships, her attempts at love, had been tainted by his memory. In those years when the loneliness became too great, she had been like the mythologic Diana, goddess of the hunt, relentlessly searching for a new love in hopes of escaping the painful memories of the love she had lost. There had been men who wanted Diana and loved her. But she had been unable to return the love because Sam was there still, a twilight shadow, long and dark, preventing the sunny joy of a new love and making even the loving as desperate as it had always been with him.

Until five years ago when Chase Andrews entered her life, and her heart, and her bed. When Chase made love to her, his tender lips and gentle hands banished all thoughts, all memories, all pain, and she was lost—and found—in the magnificent and powerful commands of her own desires.

Chase wanted Diana, only Diana, always Diana. And she wanted Chase, the wonderful man who had rediscovered in her the softness and passion and laughter that had been hiding for so long in the shadows. They wanted each other, only each other, and they joyously made plans for forever.

Then Chase changed the plans.

No children, they had agreed, a solemn vow before they were married. Chase's buildings would be his children, his immortality, and Diana had her career, her hearts. They had talked about having children, about *not* having children, and Diana had been so sure that Chase's decision was firm. She would never have married him if it hadn't been, because she knew she would never have children . . . she would never have *another* child.

When Chase told her he wanted children, all the painful memories of Sam and Janie flooded back and began to shadow her love with Chase as they had shadowed other loves before.

Diana had never told Chase about Sam, and she had never told him, either, about Janie, Sam's gift of love, the beloved daughter who had died. Chase and Diana didn't tell each other about past loves, and there was no need to tell Chase about Janie, to share that sadness with him, because they weren't going to have children.

But six months ago Chase changed his mind, his heart, and they became entrenched on opposite sides of an abyss that grew and grew, darker and deeper, a giant wedge in their wonderful love.

Diana almost told him about Janie. But it wasn't fair to ask Chase to give up his dream of children because of her tragedy, was it? No, and that was certainly what Chase would do if he knew. Chase would stop pushing, but it wouldn't make his dream go away. And maybe, at some future time, the deep desires of his heart would urge him to start pushing her again.

You had a lovely daughter who died, Diana, he would say so gently. *But can't we have our own children? It wouldn't diminish your love for Janie or take away her precious memory.*

Then Diana would have to face the other truth. She loved Chase Andrews enough to spend her life with him. But she did not love him enough to have his children. She would not allow herself to love that much—as much as she had loved Sam—ever again.

So Diana only said, "No, Chase, no children," and he was left to assume that the reason was her career. They talked and pleaded and cried. And finally Chase simply had to decide. Life with Diana and without children? Or life without Diana and sometime, with someone new, life with children?

Chase had made his decision, as fifteen years ago Sam had made the same one: *I can live without you, Diana, and that is what I choose to do.*

Chase had dressed, too, to look especially handsome for her. He wore a charcoal suit, one of her favorites, the dark-gray exactly matching his smoky eyes.

"Hi." It was a small word, but Chase's eyes embellished it, giving it layers of meaning and emotion—happiness to see her because he had missed her . . . sadness when he remembered why, and that it would be forever . . . uncertainty because was he really sure? . . . and desire because she was so beautiful and he loved her still.

"Hi." Diana's greeting was a mirror of his, all the layers, all the emotions, all the desires. "Come in. Would you like champagne?"

"Sure."

They clinked crystal to crystal, a silent toast to whatever—a smooth dissolution, happiness sometime, sometime again.

"I'm sending you on a three-week trip to Europe," Chase said as he withdrew a thick envelope from his jacket pocket and handed it to her. "Beginning September eighth. I assume that with this much advance warning you can schedule the time away."

"Yes, but Chase . . ."

"You have to go, Diana. Everything's already booked and paid for."

"You're probably sending me first class, aren't you?"

"Every step of the way."

Diana smiled softly. Chase knew her so well! He knew that she would never book a luxury vacation for herself, even though she could easily afford it and he knew that she needed time away, time to think, time to heal. Where more lovely than Europe in autumn? By September she wouldn't be so raw, would she?

No. Diana knew from experience the salutary effects of time. Not that time necessarily healed . . . but it certainly numbed.

By September she would be a little numb, numb enough to face the thought that echoed in her mind, a relentless strident echo: *You have failed. You are not enough for the man you love . . . again.*

The thought demanded analysis. In September, in London and Paris and all the other wonderful places on her luxurious vacation, Diana would confront the thought and search for answers.

"Thank you."

"You're welcome."

What Chase had given her was a gift, and what Diana had for him was a gift from another time, from the beginning of his love, a gift which she now had to return.

"I thought you would want this back," she said quietly as she removed the four-carat diamond from the pocket of her silk dress.

"It's not necessary, Diana."

"But better, don't you think? Better if you have it back?"

Diana offered the diamond, a treasure that had been in his family forever, and finally Chase took it. He took the ring and he took the fingers that held it, the calm and talented fingers of steel that now were trembling. He gently drew her to him and even more gently began to kiss her.

Diana felt the familiar rushes of desire at his touch and wondered if they were really going to make love. Their minds had said good-bye and their hearts were learning to live with the death of their love, but did their bodies need to kiss a final breathless adieu, a lingering farewell to five years of uninhibited passion and desires fulfilled? Would that make it more real, more final, more dissolved? A last loving dissolve into molten gold?

The kiss deepened, but Diana couldn't lose herself in it. Wouldn't this be too painful, too great a torture? Tonight's loving wouldn't end in a joyous reconciliation, would it?

Diana pulled away and gazed into his eyes. She saw desire—and sadness—in the seductive smoke. Chase was saying good-bye and . . .

"I can't do this, Chase."

He gently held her face in his hands and gave a wistful smile that matched the sadness in his eyes. "I know." After a moment he added softly, "Diana, I am so sorry."

"I know."

Then Chase was gone forever. After he left, Diana stood above the glitter of Manhattan, quite alone, the bright lights below blurry from her tears.

July Fourth marked the tenth day since Patrick had rescued Casey and disappeared into the shadows of the night.

He's not coming back, Casey told herself. *Why would he?*

Casey had looked at herself in the mirror of her bedroom at SeaCliff after Patrick left and assessed the ravages of the sea and her tears. Very ravaged, she decided as she gazed at her wind-tangled hair, crumpled clothes, and oh-so-vulnerable blue eyes. She looked like a waif, alluring maybe in a wild sort of way.

But even if there had been an erotic appeal, it couldn't erase the inexplicable emotions. Even if Patrick had been drawn to the perfect body eloquently revealed beneath her scant sea-splashed clothes, he swiftly overcame the attraction with the memory of her uncertain words, her wobbly smile, and her far from dazzling tears.

Patrick James obviously wasn't interested.

But Casey didn't so easily abandon her new self. She studied compulsively, of course, and exercised, and ate almost nothing, but every day she ran on the beach and played tag with the waves and wished good evening to the sun as it disappeared behind the cliffs. Casey bid adieu to the fireball from the base of the cliffs, never following the fern-lined path to the meadow. The meadow was Patrick's enchanted place. He might be there, having taken an overland route through the forests to avoid her . . . and she had already driven him from "his" beach.

Casey felt more than thought. Answers didn't come, not in coherent phrases, but feelings began to surface from the depths of her soul, feelings she could not abandon and would not discipline away, unfamiliar but so welcome feelings of happiness and joy.

She was studying when Patrick knocked on the cottage door on the evening of the Fourth.

"Patrick."

"Hello, Casey. How are you?"

Patrick had his answer in her happy-to-see-him smile, but he asked the question to give himself time to adjust to seeing her again. He had been thinking about her, warning himself to stay away because she was soft and lovely and he could offer her nothing but remembering that loveliness and wanting desperately to be with her.

Casey had been in his thoughts, and he had begun making sketches of her, too, trying to capture the breathtaking look of awkward surprise and lovely vulnerability he had seen when she had turned from the sea to him. Patrick was a talented artist, and his artistic mind had made vivid images of that enchanted moment, but as he gazed at her now he realized that this time his immense talent had failed him. She was even more soft, more lovely than he had remembered.

"I'm fine, Patrick."

"I wondered if you would like to watch some fireworks with me."

"Yes. At the Club?"

"No. The real thing, in the meadow."

"I would like to very much."

They walked down the winding trail from the cottage to the sand, and when they reached the beach, Patrick retrieved a blanket he had set on a piece of driftwood.

"No horse?"

"The sunset is only the first act. I thought you might like to stay for the rest of the show."

"Oh, yes."

They watched the breathtaking fireworks of nature, the falling sun, the rising stars, the almost-full moon. And they listened to sounds of the summer night, the music of crickets, the songs of the nightbirds, and the gentle rustle of leaves as the balmy evening air wove through the maples.

"Such vastness," Casey whispered as she gazed at the inky sky glittering with an infinity of stars. "It makes me feel so insignificant." *It makes my dazzling accomplishments seem so trivial.*

"Really? I feel significant just being a part, however small, of the grandeur."

"Oh, Patrick. What makes you so wise?"

"I'm not wise, Casey."

"You seem to know what's important and what's not."

"Do I?"

"Yes." Casey smiled shyly and then asked softly, "What is the most important thing in the world to you?"

"My freedom," Patrick answered without hesitation.

Freedom, Casey thought. *Yes, Patrick, you are wise.* "Freedom to do what?"

"Freedom to watch the majesty of the stars and the sea, and ride on a white sand beach, and . . ." Patrick stopped abruptly because his thoughts, or perhaps his heart, had added a freedom that he had never even missed before. It was a magnificent privilege that had been taken away along with all the other privileges of freedom, and it hadn't mattered until now. But now it was the most precious freedom, the one he would miss more than all the rest put together.

"And?"

Patrick didn't answer. He only looked into her lovely blue eyes and smiled a gentle, wistful smile and thought, *And the freedom to love.*

* * *

Patrick kissed her good night. It was midnight, and they were at the door of her cottage. He had frowned slightly before the kiss, as if he wasn't sure, even though she saw desire in his eyes. It was a gentle kiss, a soft touching of lips, the most tender of hellos. As his lips greeted hers, Patrick wove his strong fingers through her silky red-gold hair, caressing with exquisite delicacy.

You don't have to be so careful with me, Patrick! Casey thought. *I'm experienced.*

But her experiences hadn't begun to prepare her for the unfamiliar and exciting sensations that swept through her at his touch. In fact, her experiences had only made her wary. She played the games of seduction magnificently, winning the hearts and desires of the most handsome and powerful of men. The rich and famous men wanted Casey, and she wanted them—until they touched her. Casey felt nothing when they kissed her and less than nothing when they made love to her—bewildered annoyance at their pleasure, smoldering anger that they expected her to be grateful as their hands and lips expertly urged her to sigh with ecstasy, and an immense sense of failure despite the triumph of her seduction. There was supposed to be more, wasn't there? Casey saw in their eyes that for them there was much more—joy and pleasure—but she felt nothing except a horrible feeling of imperfection and the even worse ominous belief that she was as cold as ice.

But Casey wasn't ice with Patrick.

He kissed her, and she kissed him, and she wanted more. She wanted to follow the commands of his gray-green eyes wherever they took her. But he stopped the kiss and gazed at her with eyes that told her so eloquently of their desire—and something else . . . a lingering worry.

Patrick, I'm not a virgin, Casey thought. *Or am I?*

What the hell am I doing? Patrick wondered. *She is so lovely, and I want her so much, but what right do I have to love her? What promises can I make to her? What certainties can I offer her? None, except the certainty that my life will be spent in hiding.*

"Patrick?" Casey's voice was suddenly apprehensive, as if she wasn't sure that he wanted her. Patrick saw the lovely vulnerability and knew that he couldn't say good-bye.

"May I see you again, Casey?"

"Yes."

"I have to work late tomorrow night, so the night after tomorrow? About nine?"

"All right. What work?"

"I teach riding at the Club."

"Oh, I see."

But Casey didn't see, and after Patrick left she lay awake trying to make sense of what he had said. Patrick told her he didn't play games, but he was playing now. Perhaps this summer he was teaching riding at the Club, as a lark, but surely his usual summers were spent yachting at the Cape, or lazing on the sun-kissed beaches of St. Tropez, or running his empire from his suite of offices in Manhattan.

Casey tried to make sense of it and when she did the realization came with a soft smile and a racing heart. She and Patrick were so very much alike. Each was rich, privileged, successful, but this summer each had chosen to cast off the cloak of wealth and success and simply *be* . . . simply be *free*.

This summer Patrick James was a riding instructor and Casey English was a working girl, and they were sharing the most important truths of all, truths about who they were, not what they achieved or controlled or owned or won.

This summer Casey and Patrick were sharing truths of the heart and kisses of fire and . . .

Casey shivered as she remembered Patrick's kiss and the promise in his sensuous eyes that when he returned in two nights their loving wouldn't stop

with a kiss. Casey's shiver was a tremble of desire and fear.

Desire because she wanted him so much. And fear because she was so afraid she would disappoint them both.

Casey ordered champagne from the Country Store. The delivery cost almost as much as the champagne because Casey told them it was a rush even though all she wanted was one bottle of their least expensive brand. She was a working girl, after all. The least expensive brand of champagne stocked at Southampton's small grocery still cost twenty dollars, a dusty bottle of Mumm's unceremoniously wedged between the Krug and Dom Pérignon.

Casey never offered Patrick the champagne. She only offered him herself, a trembling offer, a gift that he accepted and cherished and loved so gently.

Oh, Patrick, you have come to rescue me again, haven't you? Casey thought when his lips touched hers and ignited all the magnificent sensations. But what if she couldn't be rescued, not really? What if the trembling sensations faded, iced over? The flickers of desire that came alive at his touch were becoming flames, fanned by his tender lips and gentle hands, growing hotter and hotter, but what if they suddenly disappeared?

"Patrick, hurry."

"Casey?" Patrick saw the mixture of desire and fear on her lovely face and guessed at the cause of her uncertainty. "There's no need to hurry, Casey."

"Yes."

"No."

"No?"

"No."

Gently, lovingly, Patrick proved to Casey that her desires wouldn't vanish as magically and unexpectedly as they had appeared. The fire of their love wasn't a clever trick or a sleight of his talented hands. The fire was real, from the heart, magical but not magic.

The wonderful sensations didn't disappear. They only grew stronger and more demanding as his kisses deepened and expanded, covering all of her, kissing hello everywhere—her lips, her neck, her shoulders, her breasts, and then voyaging where she had never allowed anyone before, never wished it, but where she welcomed his exquisite tenderness.

Casey wasn't ice and the magnificent sensations weren't going to disappear, but when they became so strong, so powerful, she was swept with new fears.

"Oh, Casey," Patrick whispered gently as he gazed into her eyes. He had sensed that she was a virgin—not to sex but to love—and he had been so careful, but still he saw her fear. "Don't be afraid."

"Patrick, I . . ."

"It's OK, honey. It will be lovely. I'm with you, Casey."

Patrick *was* with her, holding her, smiling lovingly into her eyes, making her feel so safe . . .

Safe enough to allow the fire to explode without shame.

Safe enough to be free.

* * *

"Where are your eyes?" Patrick asked softly, finally, as their breathing became calm and their pounding hearts began to slow. Casey was curled against him, her red-gold head resting gently on his chest, but she hadn't spoken and he felt her trembling still, and then the wet heat of tears. "Casey?"

When Casey raised her head, Patrick delicately untangled the fire-gold silk until he could see her eyes.

"Hi."

"Hi." Casey smiled a brave and shy smile.

"Did I tell you that I've decided you're a flower?"

"Not a parade?"

"No, not a parade." Patrick gently touched the joyful, nourishing tears that fell from her forget-me-not-blue eyes. Patrick saw joy in the blue, and then a flicker of uncertainty, a whisper of disbelief, as if what had just happened could never happen again.

Patrick kissed her and held her very close.

And after a while he showed her over and over that it was the way their loving would be . . . always.

"What's in here?" Patrick asked as he lifted the knapsack Casey had packed.

The knapsack was heavier than usual, obviously carrying something more than just the blankets and sweaters they took for their nights in the meadow. For the past month Patrick and Casey had spent almost every night together, in the meadow if Patrick could get away before sunset and in the cottage or on the beach if the sky was already dark when he arrived.

"Champagne."

"Oh."

Casey knew Patrick's silences—the peaceful moments between their quiet conversations, the intimate silence when they held each other after they loved, the breath-held awe as they watched the sun fall into the trees and the stars light up the sky. Casey knew those lovely comfortable silences, but she didn't know the silence that traveled with them now as they walked along the beach to the meadow. She only knew that it was troubled, not peaceful, and that there had been a flicker of worry in Patrick's eyes when she told him she had packed champagne.

"Is the brand all right with you, Patrick?" she asked softly when they reached the meadow and he removed the bottle from the knapsack.

"Sure. I've never tasted champagne before."

"Oh! I guess I should have asked you. I could have gotten wine or bourbon or Scotch."

For the month they had been together Casey had never given Patrick anything but herself—no food, no liquor, not even coffee when he reluctantly left her bed at dawn. And Patrick had wanted nothing more. Tonight, on impulse, she packed the bottle of Mumm's that she had purchased before their first night of love.

"I've never tasted alcohol of any kind."

"Never?" Casey echoed with soft surprise. Surprise and gentle concern as she saw the sudden pain in his gray-green eyes and the solemn worry on his handsome face. There was obviously a reason Patrick had never tasted alcohol, a reason that caused him pain, and if she could help . . . After a moment she asked quietly, "Why not, Patrick?"

As he considered her question he wondered, as he had been wondering ever since they left SeaCliff, if this was the night he would tell her about himself . . .

about the crime for which he had been falsely accused and because of which it was his destiny to spend his life in hiding. Patrick had to tell her eventually, but once he did their relationship would irrevocably change—or end. He had planned to tell her just before she moved to the city. That way, if she didn't choose to share his destiny, she could leave gracefully, easily, murmuring softly how busy she would be with her work.

But now she was asking him why he had never tasted alcohol, and Patrick wondered if tonight he would tell her everything.

"There's never been a time in my life when I felt safe enough to drink, Casey."

Why not? she wanted to ask again, but didn't, because her wish was to help not intrude. She waited, smiling gently at the troubled eyes, and when the gray-green focused on her, away from whatever pain it was in the past and back to the present, she knew he would tell her sometime, but not tonight.

"How about now, Patrick? Do you feel safe?" she asked finally, softly, as her heart whispered a gentle plea, *Please feel safe with me! I feel so safe with you.*

"Very safe." Patrick smiled. "So, let's try this."

As he expertly opened the bottle, Patrick first saw confusion on her lovely face and then the worry. Worry that he had just lied to her.

"I do some bartending," he explained swiftly, wanting to reassure but shaken by a future worry of his own. *Oh, Casey, will you feel so terribly betrayed when I tell you the truth about myself?*

"But you've never tasted the drinks you make?"

"No. I've always wondered about champagne, though."

Patrick liked the taste of champagne, sipping it from the glasses Casey had packed, but the bubbly honey-colored liquid was even better mixed in a kiss with the intoxicating taste of Casey.

As Patrick drank the champagne and felt its effects, he knew he had been right to be wary of alcohol. Even in this idyllic place with the woman he loved, he felt the champagne insidiously stripping him of caution, making him bold and reckless. The effect was wonderful with Casey, a safe, warm, giddy joy. But in his boyhood home in the slums, where even the children were armed, the effect might have been lethal. Alcohol was lethal there—slowly lethal when it destroyed hearts and minds and hope, and instantly lethal when it caused a moment of carelessness, a loss of vigilance, in that concrete world of war.

The champagne didn't change their loving, because their passion was always uninhibited and free, but it did loosen the inhibitions of Patrick's heart, urging him to speak aloud the words that flowed through him in silent rivers of joy.

Patrick only told Casey one truth that night. It was the truth he had planned to reveal only after he had told her all the others . . . the most important truth.

"I love you, Casey. I love you."

"Oh, Patrick, I love you, too."

"When do you move into the city?" Patrick asked before he returned to the stable the following morning.

"My things arrive from California the last week in August. I'll go in that week to get settled." *To unpack my designer clothes and get my jewels from the safe-deposit box and make certain my Mercedes arrived without scratches and take the Bar exam*, Casey thought. She wasn't worried about telling Patrick the unimportant truths about herself, and she assumed he would have a similar confession, but she was in no rush to tell him. Even though they would be together still when they returned to their hectic lives of success and wealth, Casey was in no hurry to end this gentle and peaceful summer of love. "I don't actually start work until the day after Labor Day, so I'll come back out on Friday for the weekend. There's a party here that night that I have to attend." *A magnificent gala in my honor.* She gazed thoughtfully at his gray-green eyes and asked softly, "Could you come to the party with me Patrick?"

"The Friday of Labor Day weekend?"

"Yes."

"I'm afraid I can't."

"Are you sure?"

"Yes. I'm sorry. I have to work late. But why don't we plan something definite for the following night?"

"I'm free."

"Good. Let's plan on dinner then."

"A picnic in the meadow with more champagne?"

"Whatever you like."

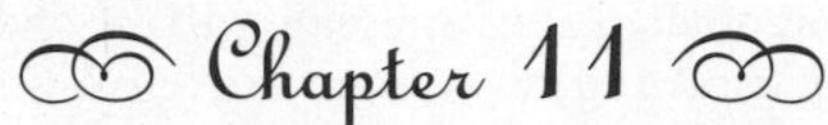

Chapter 11

SOUTHAMPTON, LONG ISLAND
AUGUST 1989

"Rained out?" Jeffrey asked with a smile when Julia appeared in the doorway of the library.

The day, the last Sunday in August, had begun with heat and humidity, but by midafternoon sheets of rain fell from the opaque skies. Merry was at a slumber party. Jeffrey and Julia had agreed that each would work, he in the library, she in her rose garden, until dinner.

"Rained out. I think I'll go to the grocery. Is there anything special you'd like?"

"You."

"For dinner."

"Same answer."

"You can have me after dinner."

"Promise?"

"Of course."

"Good. Then what I'd like for dinner is something we can eat very quickly."

"Daddy? Can I please talk to Mommy?"

"She's at the grocery, Merry."

"When will she be home?"

Jeffrey heard the edge of panic in the small voice on the telephone and thought, *Not soon enough*. He asked gently, "What's wrong, honey?"

"I need to come home. Could you ask Mommy to come get me, please?" The last word trembled.

"Yes, of course, but it may be a while."

"Maybe I should call Aunt Paige and Uncle Edmund."

"Why don't I come get you? Merry?"

"Oh. OK."

"I'll be there in"—Jeffrey thought about the distance from Belvedere to the Montgomery estate and decided he should be precise—"six minutes, OK?"

"OK."

Danielle Montgomery would not have walked Merry out to the car had the driver been Julia and she certainly wouldn't have offered even the hint of an apology. Merry was being overly sensitive, that was all. But the parent was Jeffrey, not Julia.

"Jeffrey, please accept my apologies. I should have checked with Julia, but of course we didn't expect rain. I thought we'd be at the pool all afternoon. Most nine-year-olds have seen it, anyway."

Jeffrey nodded absently to Danielle. His concern was Merry. Tears were threatening in her dark-brown eyes and she looked so small, so helpless, so afraid. And trying so hard to be brave.

The six-minute drive back to Belvedere was silent. Jeffrey kept glancing at her, smiling gently and sympathetically, but she couldn't speak. Her energy was focused on her fight against her tears; and, besides, she was obviously so very uneasy with him.

Why wouldn't Merry be uneasy with him? She didn't know him. As Jeffrey had driven to the Montgomery estate he realized that the brief phone call had been the first between them. And now as he drove cautiously on the rain-slick roads and glanced cautiously at the little girl who so valiantly battled her tears, he realized that he and Merry had never been alone together.

When they reached Belvedere, Merry dashed out of the car and into the mansion to find Julia. Her frantic search took her from room to room. Jeffrey followed the sounds of Merry's soft and desperate calls of "Mommy? Are you here?"

"Merry?" he asked gently of the trembling figure that looked so small in the great room, where the unsuccessful search had ended and the tears could be held back no longer.

Merry looked up at the sound of Jeffrey's voice. When he saw her face, Jeffrey drew a soft breath. Merry looked so lost, so fragile, so much like Julia had looked on the evening she confessed to him that she was only sixteen. And just as he had wanted to do with her mother ten years ago, Jeffrey felt a consuming wish to banish Merry's fears, to keep her safe and happy always.

"Tell me what happened, honey." Jeffrey knelt in front of her on the plush carpet.

"There was a movie. We watched it because it was raining, and it was so sad."

"What movie?"

"It was called *Old Yeller.*"

Old Yeller. In a rare motherly moment Victoria had dutifully taken nine-year-old Jeffrey to see *Old Yeller.* All children saw *Old Yeller*, Victoria had heard, and all children were supposed to love it. But it had made him so sad. Jeffrey never told anyone, not even his grandparents, and he had hidden his tears. But now the long-forgotten sadness swept through him.

Had he known Merry was going to be shown *Old Yeller*, Jeffrey—as Merry's father?—would have said No, just as Julia would certainly have said No had she known. Julia spent her life protecting her daughter, enveloping Merry in a warm, soft cloak of love, sheltering her from life's sadnesses as long as she could.

"When I was a little boy, Merry, just about your age, I saw *Old Yeller.*" Jeffrey spoke softly to the lovely, sad brown eyes. "And it made me very sad, too."

"It did?" she asked hopefully.

"Yes, it did."

"Why did he have to die, Daddy?" Merry demanded as Jeffrey's own nine-year-old heart had demanded twenty-seven years before. Her question trembled and new tears spilled.

"I don't know why he had to die, honey," Jeffrey answered gently. "Sad things sometimes happen in life."

Merry nodded thoughtfully. Then she looked bravely into his eyes and asked earnestly, "The news can be very sad, can't it? And then you have to tell people about the sad things that have happened. Does that make you cry sometimes?"

"Sometimes," Jeffrey admitted quietly. "Merry, how do you know about the news?"

"Because Mommy and I watch you every night."

A vivid collage of news events—events Merry should not have seen—flashed through Jeffrey's mind. The first was the indelible image of the Christmas massacre at the Rome airport when the daughter of a journalist had been murdered. That was three and a half years ago, never to be forgotten, but the news of the past four months had been filled with equally tragic horrors against children—the unspeakably evil rituals in Matamoros, the soccer-match disaster in Sheffield, the unimaginable act of the father in California who killed his young daughters, the ghastly aftermath of the Chinese students' stand for democracy in Tienamen Square.

In a matter of seconds Jeffrey thought of five tragedies he wouldn't want Merry to know about. He couldn't believe that she did know about them, that Julia would have allowed it.

"You watch the news with Mommy?"

"We watch you. Mommy always watches first and records the parts I can see. I used to be able to watch more, when I was little, but now I understand more so I get to watch less." Merry explained this paradox without confusion. It was obviously something she and Julia had discussed. "But I can watch all of your Special Reports when they are about politics or the economy."

Jeffrey smiled, but his emotions were suddenly very shaky and stunning questions suddenly swirled in his mind.

Merry watched the news to see *him?* Her *daddy?* It was Julia's wish that they become a family, but did this lovely, sensitive little girl have expectations of him, too? Did she need his love?

Jeffrey had assumed that Merry had no expectations of him. He knew that her life was filled, overflowing, with love. Merry had Julia's wonderful love and she had, too, the almost parental love of Edmund and Paige. This summer, on the few occasions when he had been home to join the frequent picnics at Somerset, Jeffrey had been so aware of the years of love and laughter and friendship and trust that bonded Merry and Julia with Edmund and Amanda and Paige. Jeffrey was peripheral to their circle of love; he always had been. Now, as he tried to join the circle, because he had given Julia a promise from his heart that he would try, he felt awkward, uncertain, and so out of place. He was welcomed, of course, but he was a stranger to the history of laughter and love that bonded them all, an outsider, and an imposter . . . because he did not belong at picnics with fathers and daughters.

But, over the summer, as he had watched the little girl with brown eyes who was so lively and laughing with Edmund and so silent and shy with him, how desperately he had wished that he did belong.

"Merry?"

"Mommy!" Merry's eyes lit at the sight of her mother and she dashed to greet her. "You're home!"

"Yes, darling." Julia knelt as Jeffrey had, to be at the same level as the dark-brown eyes. Julia tenderly stroked Merry's golden-blond hair and asked softly, "What happened?"

"They showed us a movie. It was called *Old Yeller.* It was very sad and I wanted to come home. Daddy came to get me. He saw it when he was little and it made him sad, too." Merry had been speaking to Julia, her trusting eyes focused on the mother who had been there always, a safe, gentle, loving haven, but then she turned, smiled shyly at Jeffrey, and added softly, "Daddy saved me just like he saved that little girl in Beirut."

"Thank you," Julia whispered softly to Jeffrey. Then she took Merry's hand. "Come help me in the kitchen, Merry, so Daddy can finish his work."

"I'm finished. Can I help, too?"

"Of course. You and Merry can set the table."

"I could show you how to make chocolate-chip cookies, Daddy, if you want," Merry offered quietly.

"I would like that very much, Merry."

Jeffrey's voice was quiet, too, but his heart was restless. He wanted to know this lovely little girl. He wanted Merry to know that she could trust him, too, as she trusted Julia and Edmund and Paige. He wanted her to know that she could count on him if she needed him.

Is that all you want? his racing heart demanded. *Or do you want even more? Don't you really want to become a family?*

Yes. That was what he wanted. He had promised Julia he would try and it had been a promise of love laced with uncertainty.

But now . . .

Jeffrey didn't know if Merry wanted him to be her daddy, if she needed more love in her life, but he would be there for her if she did, if she would allow it, if they could overcome their awkward shyness for each other.

As Jeffrey smiled at the dark-brown eyes that had bravely offered to teach him how to make chocolate-chip cookies and Merry smiled back, he suddenly believed that anything was possible.

I know Merry cannot be your daughter. But you can love her as your own as I have cherished her as my great-granddaughter. The only obstacle, my darling Jeffrey, is in your heart. As Jeffrey walked into the kitchen with Merry and Julia he remembered Grandmère's wise and loving words and thought, *You were right, Grandmère, because no truths have changed, but a great heaviness has been magically liftedfrom my heart. And where that leaden obstacle used to lie I now feel such joyous hope.*

"I'm going to miss you," Patrick whispered as his lips softly nuzzled Casey's neck. They were in the living room at SeaCliff watching the rain fall to the sea. Patrick stood behind her with his arms wrapped gently around her waist.

"I'm going to miss you, too. Five nights. You haven't changed your mind about Friday?"

"I really can't, Casey. I'm sorry. I wanted to talk to you about our dinner on Saturday. I thought maybe we should go to a restaurant instead of the meadow. There's a place in Southampton called Chez Claude."

Chez Claude. Paige had told her about the expensive and romantic French restaurant.

"Probably can't wear jeans or shorts there."

"We can eat somewhere else if you like."

"I have party dresses." *Just like you have tailor-made suits and silk tuxedos.* "And I'd love to have dinner with you at Chez Claude."

"I'll make a reservation then."

"Wonderful." Casey turned in his arms to look at his face. His voice had been so quiet, so solemn, and she wanted to see his eyes. They were solemn, too, so she asked softly, "Why do you look so grim about a candlelight and champagne dinner, Patrick?"

"Because we need to talk."

"About how we can see each other after I move into the city."

"Yes." Patrick kissed her lips, tenderly sealing that promise. *We will see each other after you move, my love, if you still want to see me once you know the truth.* "But, Casey, there are other things I need to tell you."

"There are things I need to tell you, too, Patrick."

Patrick feared what he had to tell her. Would Casey be terribly hurt that he hadn't told her sooner? Would she feel angry and betrayed? Would she want to escape from him? He wanted to make it very easy for Casey to say good-bye. That was why he had decided dinner at a restaurant—neutral territory in the real world—rather than in their enchanted meadow of love.

Casey didn't fear what she had to tell Patrick, nor did she fear what Patrick was going to tell her. They already knew the most important truths about each other. The details—their mutual confessions of lifelong wealth and successful careers—were trivial. Casey saw that Patrick was worried about what he had to tell her and guessed that his worry was because he had been playing games and felt a little guilty, as she did, that the confession hadn't come sooner. If that was what worried Patrick, it was something they would laugh about.

And if it was something else?

It still didn't worry her.

She loved Patrick, and she knew that he loved her, and nothing else mattered.

By three the following afternoon the movers were gone and Casey was left to unpack boxes and settle into her luxury apartment overlooking Central Park. She unpacked her law books first because they were old friends, though she had never realized it before. She had become an attorney to please K.C. English. But this summer, as she thought about the important and unimportant things in her life, Casey realized that she really believed in what she did. Being a good lawyer was important to her. She didn't have to be the best attorney on earth anymore. She had to be something even more important—she had to be the best attorney *she* could be.

The law books were familiar and welcome friends. So, too, were the expensive McGuire wickers with their pastel cushions because the light and elegant California-chic furniture reminded her of SeaCliff.

But Casey frowned as she hung her designer clothes in her spacious closets. The linens by Lauren and the silks by Dior and the chiffons by Chanel were so different from the light cottons she had worn all summer—the wonderful, simple outfits that Patrick removed with soft sighs and gentle, eager hands. The designer clothes belonged to the old Casey, the talented actress who performed flawlessly but without happiness or joy. When she clothed herself in the expensive fabrics would the new Casey suddenly disappear?

"No!" Casey said aloud, speaking to the gorgeous clothes and giving them fair warning. The new Casey would be there still beneath the elegant layers of satin and silk. *It will just take Patrick a little longer, lovely, delicious moments, to undress me.*

Casey smiled confidently at the beautiful clothes and finally selected two dresses that would return with her for her final weekend in Southampton. For the party in her honor at the Club, she chose Cassini sequins. The famous designer hadn't created the stunning cocktail dress expressly for Casey English,

but it was as if he had. The sequins were pale blue and soft violet—the precise pastels of her forget-me-not-blue eyes—and they shimmered against a background of sunlit gold lamé. Casey decided to wear the dazzling dress on Friday because that was the night she had to dazzle.

On Saturday, for the candlelight dinner with Patrick, she selected a dress by Laura Ashley. It was the color of rich cream, a soft romantic dress of ruffles and lace that looked like a country wedding dress from a different era. Casey had bought it in Union Square a week before she left San Francisco and had never worn it. It had been an impulsive, surprising purchase because the look wasn't her, but now she smiled at the beautiful dress and thought, *It is me. Maybe, even then, even before I left San Francisco, I knew there was another Casey.*

"May I help you?" the young woman asked with unconcealed disapproval when Patrick entered the exclusive Yankee Peddler men's clothing store in Southampton.

"I need some clothes."

Yes you do, the woman thought.

Patrick only really needed to buy something presentable for dinner Saturday night. He could come back, if Casey still wanted to see him after she knew all about him, to purchase additional slacks, shirts, and sweaters to wear when he visited her in Manhattan. Casey *would* want to see him still, wouldn't she? Didn't it make sense, and didn't it show confidence in their love, to buy an additional outfit or two right now?

Patrick had enough money. He had worked long hours over the summer, teaching riding lessons and bartending at the many parties at the club. Some nights the extra work had kept him away from her, as it would this Friday, but he knew that as soon as school started the riding lessons would diminish, and perhaps the parties would, too, so he had worked to earn enough to last all winter, enough to be able to travel into the city often to be with her.

There had once been a time when Patrick dressed as if he belonged among the rich and privileged. Now, with unerring instincts, he assembled outfits of impeccable taste and understated elegance, and when he emerged from the dressing room to view himself in a three-way mirror, the saleswoman gasped.

"I know who you are!"

"I doubt it," Patrick replied calmly, although his heart pounded anxiously. He knew that except for his long—for Southampton—coal-black hair, he looked as he had looked all those years when he blended in flawlessly at the posh country clubs that hosted the Grand Prix show jumping events. He had been quite well camouflaged in denim and cowboy boots, but what if this woman *did* recognize him?

"No, I'm sure." She smiled coyly and then announced triumphantly, "You're a model for Calvin Klein, aren't you? I know I saw you in a recent ad in *W*."

Casey looked at herself in the mirror as she dressed for the party in her honor at the Club. The dazzling Cassini was all wrong. The sleek sheath of sequins looked terrible against the paleness of her bare arms. Her once carefully golden-tanned skin was pale now, despite the sunny Southampton summer, because her days had been spent indoors studying so that her nights would be free to spend with Patrick. It had been a summer of moonlight, not sunlight, and how Patrick loved the whiteness of her pale skin as it was caressed by the moon!

Patrick would probably tell her the dress looked magnificent, a stunning contrast to the creaminess, and perhaps that was true.

It wasn't the dazzling dress that was the problem, she realized finally. It was the expectation that she had to dazzle. That was what was all wrong.

Tonight, amidst the most rich and powerful men and women of New York, Casey English was expected to charm and enchant, to speak perfect, clever, confident words, to bewitch and control. She would have to be on her toes, *point*, performing a graceful *pas de deux* in every conversation. But she didn't want to dazzle. She wasn't even certain that she could anymore.

Casey frowned at the dress that was a symbol of the dazzle that was no longer her and decided that on this night she needed other symbols, symbols of the new Casey, symbols of Patrick and their love.

She would wear her hair long, she decided, as she had worn it all summer. And she would weave wildflowers into the red-gold silk as Patrick had done so often in their meadow. Casey hadn't paid attention to how Patrick braided the flowers into her hair—her attention was distracted by the quivers of desire that pulsed through her at his touch—but she had seen what it looked like hours later, a spectacular tangle of hair and petals after a night of love.

Tonight she would wear wildflowers in her hair and it would be as if Patrick were with her.

But Casey couldn't get the flowers to stay in her silky hair. Somehow Patrick's strong and gentle fingers had woven works of art from wildflowers and hair, but her fingers were clumsy. The flowers slipped and fell, or showed more stems than petals, and even though Casey tried again and again, she failed.

And it was getting late, later. She was already late.

Finally, in frustration, Casey took her magnificent red-gold mane and with fingers that had been too clumsy and trembling to secure wildflowers in the fine silk expertly twisted it into a smooth, rich swirl on top of her head and secured the elegant crown with a barrette made of solid gold.

In those moments her fingers had belonged to the old Casey, and they had assumed control with swift and assured confidence. The old Casey hadn't returned in full force, however, and Casey didn't want her to. Still, as she drove her gold-tone Mercedes sport coupe toward the Club, speeding because she was almost an hour late, she wished for a few flickers of the old raidant confidence.

Just be yourself, she told her racing heart. *Your new self. Just be the Casey that you love and that Patrick loves.*

But what if I can only really be myself with Patrick?

Chapter 12

"Paige, I'm so sorry!" Casey exclaimed as she walked into the foyer at the Club. Paige was there, obviously waiting for her to arrive, her face more concerned than annoyed.

"Fashionably late, Casey," Paige reassured swiftly. "Is everything all right?"

"Oh, yes. It's just that I've spent the summer slipping into shorts and tops in under two seconds and my timing is off."

"Well, you look absolutely gorgeous."

"Thank you."

Edmund joined them. Like Paige, Edmund's smile graciously conveyed a message of welcome and no apologies necessary.

104 "How was the Bar exam, Casey? Passable?"

"They asked the right questions, Edmund."

"Just the few points of law you happened to review?"

"I guess." Casey laughed softly.

"So, are you ready to meet some people?"

"I guess," Casey repeated quietly, without a soft laugh this time because a rush of panic swept through her.

There weren't just *some* people mingling in the elegant rooms of the Southampton Club, there were well over two hundred. The bejeweled and coutured guests wandered from the lavish buffet in the Azalea Room to the garden terrace where a band played slow, sensual melodies of love and there was dancing beneath the moon.

These people will be your clients, Casey reminded her racing heart. *And you will do the best you can for them. That's all that is necessary. You don't have to perform and dazzle.*

Casey didn't perform, but she *did* dazzle with her unaffected loveliness, her polite smiles and soft murmurs of "Thank you" as she received compliments for her past accomplishments. With each new introduction, she began to feel a little more calm and a little more hopeful. *I can do this. I can be myself.*

Until she saw Patrick.

Strands of colorful lanterns had been festooned across the garden terrace. As the lanterns swayed in the balmy breeze, they cast light into distant corners of the terrace, illuminating the shadowy edges—including the place where the outdoor bar had been set up.

Casey knew Patrick in faded jeans and cowboy boots. And she knew his strong, lean body even better in nothing at all. Now he wore tight black pants and a red jacket, the generic uniform of a servant at a swank country club. Patrick was the bartender, a cut above the similarly dressed valets who parked cars and the waiters who circulated with silver platters of gourmet hors d'oeuvres and took orders for drinks. The waiters gave the drink orders to Patrick and he swiftly made the cocktails for the rich and famous men and women who had assembled to honor *her*.

Patrick was a servant at the party in her honor when he should have been her date!

I teach riding at the Club. I do some bartending. That was what Patrick had told her and it had been the truth.

And she had told him *I'm just a working girl*.

Just . . . Casey had said "just" as if in apology that she wasn't something better, but Patrick had never apologized for what he did. Patrick had never said "I *just* teach riding."

Casey had assumed he was something else. Something more? Something better? Because Casey English could never fall in love with *just* a riding instructor?

The old Casey couldn't have.

But the new Casey could and had.

It didn't matter what Patrick did!

Casey stared at him from across the terrace, willing his gray-green eyes to meet hers, but he was busy mixing drinks for her future important clients. Patrick was busy and so was she, graciously meeting the influential and powerful men and women even though she wished they would all vanish so that she could be alone with him.

She desperately wanted to go to him and tell him that it didn't matter, to reassure him, if he needed reassurance.

But it was Casey who needed reassurance. Casey whose heart raced with fear.

It didn't matter to her that she was Casey English, heiress-attorney, and he was Patrick James, riding instructor and sometime bartender . . . but she feared that it might matter very much to him.

Patrick knew the instant Casey walked onto the garden terrace. He sensed her presence even though he didn't look up to meet her gaze. He had been expecting her. By the time she arrived he had overheard enough conversations to know all about the Casey English the world knew, but who he didn't, the enchanting heiress, the sensational trial attorney, the dazzling golden girl who played magnificently and always won.

Patrick had always been so wary of the rich, beautiful women who wanted him for their pleasure, as a possession, a trophy, a plaything. Always so wary . . . and yet it had never occurred to him that Casey had been playing. But she had. The beautiful heiress-attorney and the riding instructor. Had he, and their starlit nights of loving, been merely a sensual reward for the long days spent studying in the cottage?

Oh, Casey, Patrick thought sadly. *I had no idea that you were playing with me. You played so well . . . and you won. Because I fell in love with you, Casey English, I really fell in love.*

"Champagne?" Patrick asked when Casey finally escaped the glitter of the party to join him in the shadows. "We don't have anything under a hundred dollars a bottle, I'm afraid. Or are you done playing Lady Chatterley?"

Casey had steeled her racing heart for anger in his gentle voice, but what she heard was even worse. Instead of the fire of anger, proof of emotion, proof that he cared, she heard only a detached coolness. Even the mocking question "Are you done playing Lady Chatterley?" was posed with the polite tone of a servant, as if there had never been anything between them, as if they were strangers. And when his eyes were illuminated for a moment by the light of a swaying lantern, the gray-green was mostly gray, a smoky veil that revealed nothing, a cloud that blocked her vision to his heart. The opaque gray eyes, like his terrifyingly calm voice, made him so very far away from her . . . and so very far away from the gentleness of their love.

"I wasn't playing Lady Chatterley, Patrick. And I thought that you . . ." Casey stopped, realizing that completing the thought, her belief that he was rich and successful, too, might push him farther away, if that was possible.

But Patrick finished the thought for her. "You thought *I* was slumming with *you?* The aristocrat and the working girl? No. Sorry to disappoint you, Casey."

"It doesn't disappoint me, Patrick. But I've disappointed you, haven't I?" she asked softly. *Oh, Patrick, I know I have hurt you! Please talk to me!*

"Let's just say that you were wrong about me and I was wrong about you."

"You weren't wrong about me."

"No? Well. It doesn't matter. Let's just say then that *you* were wrong about *me* and leave it at that."

"Leave it?" Casey echoed with rising fear. She fought the fear and continued hopefully. "Yes, of course, we can't really talk now. But, Patrick, could we meet later, after the party, so I can explain?"

"You don't need to explain."

"But I'd like to," she answered quietly. Then she added softly, a tentative whisper of hope and fear, "Tomorrow night at dinner."

"I don't think so, Casey."

A waiter appeared then, with drink orders, and Patrick returned to his task of mixing drinks for her guests, as if she weren't even there . . . and finally Casey withdrew from the silent shadows and returned to the party.

Patrick was angry, he had to be, and hurt, even though he had seemed terrifyingly calm, as if he had already made the decision that their love was over, a decision that wasn't even terribly difficult to make.

Was he never going to let her explain?

Yes, Casey assured herself with shaky confidence. *Of course he will. He needs a little time, and this isn't the place to talk anyway. We'll see each other again, later, won't we?*

Casey filled her heart with brave assurances and stole hopeful glances at him, searching for a flicker of warmth. Patrick resolutely avoided her hopeful gaze, but he was a powerful magnet still.

Finally, in a desperate act of survival, Casey turned her back to the shadowy corner and faced the area of the terrace where couples danced beneath the moonlight. As she turned, Casey's gaze fell on Jeffrey and Julia. She hadn't seen them until now, and now she watched as they danced, and Jeffrey's blue eyes caressed Julia with exquisite messages of love.

Julia. Tonight Julia wore her hair long and free, as Casey had wanted to but failed . . . and there was more. Artfully woven into the long strands of black silk were lovely delicate wildflowers . . .

Julia had been able to do what Casey had not.

Just as always. Julia was better.

I tried to be like you this summer, Julia, to be loved for who I really am inside. And I got so close, so very close to happiness and freedom, and now . . .

Now I have to get away.

Casey knew she couldn't escape to SeaCliff, not yet, but she desperately needed a little privacy, a little time, a few quiet moments in the roses away from Patrick, and away from Julia.

"Pardon me, Mr. Lawrence?" The valet sent to find the famous anchor spoke quietly and awkwardly. It would have been easier to interrupt Jeffrey Lawrence if he had been discussing the war being waged against the drug lords in Colombia, not dancing slowly with his beautiful wife.

"Yes?"

"You have a phone call from your exchange."

"Oh. Thank you." Jeffrey smiled reassuringly at the valet and then apologetically at Julia. Calls from his exchange almost always meant he would have to spring into action, go into town to anchor a special broadcast or even fly to the site of the tragedy. "I'll be back, darling."

After Jeffrey left, Julia was alone in a sea of faces that were familiar but not friendly unless Jeffrey was with her.

I really should talk to Casey, Julia thought.

Julia had had the same thought many times over the summer but hadn't acted on it. Of course Paige had reported that Casey was busy and seemed to be enjoying her solitude, but that wasn't the reason Julia hadn't called.

The reason was the uneasy memory of Jeffrey's bewildering anger after the dinner party in June. The anger had been prompted by Casey, an unwitting symbol of Julia's past, and since then Casey had become an unwitting symbol of that night, and Julia had made no effort to see her.

But it would be safe to see Casey now, because now that night was merely a blurry, bewildering memory, the tiniest ripple in the vast calm of their love, almost a mirage.

Jeffrey and Julia had survived that night. Their wonderful, joyous love was strong and whole again.

And in the past five days there had been magic.

The magic had begun on Sunday when she returned from the grocery and found Merry and Jeffrey in the great room. The three of them had spent the entire evening together. Merry had showed Jeffrey how to make chocolate-chip cookies, and during dinner her shy and sensitive daughter *talked* to him. Merry was a chatterbox with Julia, a fountain of words and insights and questions and thoughts, but she had always been too shy to speak her thoughts to Jeffrey.

But Sunday night Jeffrey had lured Merry from her shyness the same way that years before he had urged a shy Julia to speak by asking gentle, interested questions and welcoming her soft answers with a warm smile and loving blue eyes.

Sunday night had been magic, and the magic didn't vanish with the light of day. Each morning all week Jeffrey had left for work a little later than usual, lingering over breakfast, talking to Merry, and leaving reluctantly because it would be twenty-four hours before they would see each other again.

They hadn't made plans for this weekend, except that Jeffrey would be home. That might change because of the call from the studio, but even if the news of the world demanded that he be away this weekend, beginning next weekend and for an entire week they would be together. Already Julia and Merry had begun to make plans for the Vacation with Daddy. Merry, excited and shy, wanted to be so certain they made plans that Jeffrey would enjoy. The first three days of the vacation were going to be spent in Manhattan with the Spencers "doing" New York. "Will Daddy want to see the Statue of Liberty? Does Daddy like ballet? Mommy, are you sure?"

As Julia smiled at the recent memories, and the memory of their gentle summer of love, she knew that Casey could not be a threat to their happiness. It would be safe to talk to her now, safe for Jeffrey to find them together in the rose garden when he returned. Safe and polite, because Julia really did need to say good-bye to Casey and wish her well.

But Casey wasn't in the rose garden. When Julia reached the top of the stairs that led to the garden, she saw Casey disappearing in the distance past the pond toward the yacht basin. Julia didn't follow. Jeffrey would know to look for her in the rose garden but not beyond. Julia watched until Casey vanished from sight, then, as she turned to see if Jeffrey was returning yet, she saw a face in the shadows that was familiar and friendly.

"Good evening, Mrs. Lawrence," Patrick said when Julia approached. He smiled warmly at the beautiful young mother who watched her daughter's lessons so intently, her face a gentle blend of worry and pride.

"Good evening, Patrick. The girls are very excited about the show, I mean the *gymkhana*."

Gymkhana was Patrick's word. And it was a perfect word, the girls discovered when they found it in the dictionary—"a show for equestrians consisting of exhibitions of horsemanship and much pageantry." That was what they were planning, Merry and Amanda and Patrick, and the wonderful new word made their plans even more special and exciting. The pageantry and horsemanship was scheduled to take place the day after they returned from the long weekend in New York. All the parents would be watching because Jeffrey would be on vacation, and even though Edmund had to work he promised to be there by

four on that Tuesday, September twelfth, Merry's birthday. The girls' riding ability would be a surprise for Jeffrey and Edmund who hadn't seen them ride since the first lesson, but Merry and Amanda wanted the gymkhana to be a surprise for Paige and Julia, too. For the past week no mothers had been allowed to watch the rehearsals.

"I think you'll enjoy it. Merry and Amanda are both very good riders."

"They're jumping, aren't they?"

Merry and Amanda had made Patrick promise not to tell their mothers about the big surprise. Patrick had promised, but Julia looked so worried . . .

"Small jumps, Mrs. Lawrence. Very safe."

Julia gave a soft sigh.

"Really," Patrick repeated gently. "Very safe."

"Have you ever read *Gone with the Wind*, Patrick?"

"No. Why?"

Before Julia could answer, Jeffrey appeared.

"Here you are."

"Jeffrey, you remember Patrick, Merry's riding instructor."

"Yes. Of course," Jeffrey replied politely, acknowledging Patrick with a brief nod and a smile. "I have to get to the studio, Julie."

"Something in Medellin?" she asked softly as her heart whispered a silent prayer, Please don't tell me you have to fly to Cartagena.

"No. It's not Colombia, it's the Middle East. There's been a midair explosion of a commercial airliner over the Mediterranean."

"Explosion?"

"A bomb," Jeffrey answered solemnly. "Do you want to stay longer? I can have the limousine pick me up here."

"No, I'm ready to go."

Casey left the party at midnight. Some of the guests were still dancing beneath the stars but most had left and she had stayed fashionably long enough. *And*, she thought, *maybe if I leave, the party will end more quickly and Patrick will be free to come to me.*

When she arrived at SeaCliff, Casey removed the famous Cassini sequins as quickly as possible and changed into familiar shorts and blouse. She wrote a note to Patrick asking him to join her in their meadow of love and left the note on the cottage door.

Had he really decided, without allowing her a voice at all, that their love was over? Because she was rich and he was poor? Because she was a successful high-powered attorney and he had to tend bar to supplement the meager amount he earned teaching riding? Was it pride?

Or was it something more important, something she couldn't so easily reassure?

Perhaps what mattered most to Patrick was her deception. *I don't play games*, Patrick had told her that from the very beginning. And he hadn't been playing, but *she* had.

But hers had been such an important pretense! It was so important that

Patrick love her for *her*, who she really was, not for her dazzling successes, her immense wealth, her well-scripted flawless performances.

I don't play games. Patrick had told her that truth. And Patrick, who didn't play games, had told her something else, the most important truth . . . *I love you, Casey.*

As she gazed at the twinkling stars and listened to the sounds of the night, praying she would hear the rustle of ferns as he made his way to her, she let those hopeful words echo in her brain. *I love you, Casey.*

It was reckless, but he felt reckless. Nothing to lose, nothing *more* to lose.

It was torture, torture and joy, and he needed the joy.

Long before dawn, Patrick removed the jumps from the shed where they were stored behind the riding ring. He had used some of the jumps before, setting the rails no higher than three feet for the lessons he gave. Now he removed all the jumps to make tall fences and massive walls and he set the rails as high as they could go, high enough to challenge even a champion.

There were two champions living in the stable at the Southampton Club now—Patrick and Night Dancer. The coal-black stallion had arrived at the Club in July, a valuable show jumper recently retired from the Grand Prix show-jumping circuit and purchased for a twelve-year-old girl who wanted to learn to jump. Patrick recognized Night Dancer and knew from a month of teaching lessons to the horse's new owner that the once-champion could still leap over six foot walls.

It took Patrick two hours to set up the jumps and ten minutes to saddle and bridle the horse. And then there was joy for horse and rider, the exhilarating freedom of floating over jump after jump, the wondrous power of flying.

And there was torture, too, for Patrick, because jumping again reminded him of all he had lost and of a time when his life had held such promise.

James Patrick Jones's life had begun without promise. He had no father and his mother could not care for him. Although James spent most of his young life away from his mother, his vivid images of her—her auburn hair and emerald-green eyes—were bright threads woven into the colorless tapestry of the concrete slums of Chicago.

Sometimes the green eyes would be glazed with drugs and unseeing and James would be taken from her to live in an orphanage or foster home. In weeks or months she would reappear, her eyes clear and sparkling with tears as she was reunited with the son whom she would all too soon forget again and neglect.

When James was eleven, his mother vanished forever. He never knew if she died or if she simply lost her fragile interest in him, because her addictions to drugs and men and pleasure and pain were so much more compelling than her life with her young son.

James learned to survive with his mother, and without her. When he was with her, he committed the minor, necessary crimes of survival—stealing food when he was starving, and clothes or blankets when the icy Chicago winter threatened to kill. When he was without her, in the endless series of foster homes, James learned to survive, too, by being wary always, wary of violence, wary of peace, wary of love.

He lived in a dark-gray world of hopelessness, decadence, and violence, but his young mind saw lovely colors even in the gray and gentle images, even amidst the violence. His artistic mind saw the images and his talented hands made the visions real. While other children found escape in drugs and alcohol, James found private solace, private joy in his painting.

He survived through his art and by being very wary always.

When he was fourteen, James decided that there must be better places on earth. It was a valiant leap of faith, but he bravely promised himself that there *had* to be.

One night he simply ran away from the new "home" where he had lived for less than a month. Two days later he was in a heaven filled with radiant colors and immeasurable beauty—the luxuriant emerald hills of Kentucky. He found work in a stable. He had never been near horses before, but he felt an immediate love for the magnificent, gentle creatures. James rode one morning, bareback and without fear, and discovered a talent as wonderful and instinctive as his art.

His gift, his natural ability to ride, did not go unnoticed. Wealthy men and women paid him to jump their prize horses. James won ribbons, mostly blue, and trophies, mostly gold, and earned recognition in elite equestrian circles as one of the best riders in the world.

James's life in the slums of Chicago was far behind him, but it might come back to haunt him if the rich people for whom he showed the valuable horses ever knew his record of minor crimes. He decided that to survive among them he needed to become like them, adopting their patrician manners and refined speech and clothing himself in elegant clothes. James adapted beautifully, and although he avoided answering questions about his background, it was simply assumed that he was "East Coast"—Greenwich perhaps, St. Paul's probably, Yale or Harvard likely.

In January of 1984, Judge Frederick Barrington hired James to show his champion horses for the year the grande finale of which would be the Los Angeles Olympics. During that year, when he wasn't traveling to events on the Grand Prix show-jumping circuit, James lived in the gardener's cottage at Barrington Farm, the judge's bluegrass estate outside of Louisville.

James knew that the judge was a widower, but he didn't know that Frederick Barrington had a daughter until June when seventeen-year-old Pamela returned for the summer from the exclusive girls" school in Geneva where she had spent the year. Pamela was very beautiful, very spoiled, and very petulant when she didn't get precisely what she wanted when she wanted it. Pamela's petulance was usually short-lived because her demands were always promptly met and her whims were always swiftly gratified.

Seventeen-year-old Pamela wanted twenty-five-year-old James. But James didn't want her. She was much too young, much too spoiled, and it was much too dangerous. James would do nothing to jeopardize the first peace and happiness he had known in his entire life. Politely, gently, diplomatically, he resisted her advances.

But Pamela wouldn't take no for an answer. She had no experience with No and never planned to have any. And when it became clear that James would not accede to her wishes, her response was rage and revenge . . .

On that night in July, he was painting in the cottage when Pamela knocked on the door. Her long-nailed, exquisitely manicured fingers curled around a half-empty bottle of bourbon from which she had quite obviously been drinking.

She announced coyly that she had just made love with one of the many "boys"—the heirs her age who lounged by the pool at the mansion all day every day—but now she wanted a man. She wanted James.

He resisted her advances gently. But Pamela persisted, fueled by the confidence that she would get what she wanted, as she always had, annoyed that he would even dare to say No. When she tried to force the bottle of bourbon to his lips, James roughly pushed it away. And when she wove her fingers tightly, possessively around his neck and tiptoed to kiss his lips, he pulled away. As he freed himself, one of her long, sharp fingernails dug into his neck and left a deep scratch that bled.

Finally, her eyes blazing with anger, Pamela left the cottage. James was very sorry that he had caused anger but very relieved that she had gone away.

Ten minutes later he heard the shattering of glass followed by frantic screams. James rushed outside and followed the sound of the screams to the front porch of the mansion.

Pamela was on the porch, her clothes torn and dirty, gasping for breath as tears spilled from her frightened eyes. As James moved to help her, the judge appeared. Pamela fell into her father's arms and cried hysterically, "James raped me, Daddy! He *raped* me!"

James listened to Pamela's words with astonishment and then horror. Surely the judge, whom James respected very much, and who even sometimes called him "son," would realize . . .

But James saw the rage in the judge's eyes and knew that to survive he had to run.

As he fled, the still night air that already had been broken once by Pamela's cries was pierced again by shrillness, by the screams of police sirens and the frenzied barking of dogs—harsh, strident, ominous signals that they were frantically searching for him and that the peace in his life was shattered forever.

James fled with nothing except the clothes he was wearing. The rest of his clothes, the little money he had earned, the riders' trophies he had won, the documents—birth certificate, driver's license, passport—that were proof of who he was, and his paintings were all left behind in the cottage. James was forced to abandon his possessions. And he was forced to abandon something much more precious—his freedom and his dreams.

He knew he would never again soar over jumps, a champion rider on a champion horse, perhaps he would never even be able to ride. And never again would he be James Patrick Jones.

He would have to change his name, he knew, and spend the rest of his life in shadows. There was no doubt in his mind that if he was caught, his next home—the most permanent home of his life—would be prison. It would be the word of a man with a record of minor crimes in the jungle of Chicago against the word of the precious daughter of the revered judge.

James Patrick Jones became Patrick James. For five years he lived from job to job, always a different employer, crisscrossing the country, forming no relationships, and leaving no trail.

Then, last March, he answered the ad for a riding instructor in *The New York Times*. He rode again, and that brought such peace even among the heiresses who reminded him of Pamela Barrington. He rode, and he started to paint again, and just before sunset on an enchanted night in June, the greatest surprise of all, the greatest peace, he met Casey English and fell in love.

And tonight, over candlelight, he had planned to tell Casey everything.

What if he had told Casey his truth before she told him the truth about herself?

His Casey, the lovely, unpretentious, vulnerable woman he loved would believe him. She would protect his secret identity even though in so doing, in knowing the whereabouts of a wanted felon and concealing that information, she would jeopardize her entire legal career. *His* Casey would do that, and it would cause her great harm.

And what about the other Casey, the heiress who had been playing with him, the brilliant trial attorney whom he didn't know but whose most spectacular legal triumph to date was the conviction of the Nob Hill Rapist? Would *that* Casey believe the innocence of a man with a record of crimes of survival as a boy who had fled the scene of the "crime" and remained in hiding ever since? Or would that Casey call the police?

Patrick didn't know, and it didn't matter. Because, no matter which Casey were real, the love of Patrick James and Casey English was over.

It had to be.

Casey wandered through the maze of stalls looking for a door that might belong to the apartment where Patrick had told her he lived. The stable was quiet except for the scurrying of mice and the gentle whinnies of horses. Even the grooms had not yet arrived to begin their daily chores. As she walked through the stalls near the riding ring, she heard a new noise, the soft thud of hooves on sod. She followed the noise to the ring.

Patrick was there. Casey stood in the shadows and watched as he sailed over the mammoth jumps. As a teenager Casey had watched the best riders in the world compete at Grand Prix events held at the Carlton Club. Casey knew very little about show jumping, but she had been trained since childhood to recognize perfection, and it seemed to her that Patrick must surely belong to the most elite group of world-class equestrians.

She remained in the shadows until Patrick and the champion horse had finished flying over all the treacherous jumps and he had reined in the powerful animal and was whispering quiet words of praise as he patted the stallion's strong neck. Then she left the shadows and began the brave walk toward him.

"Casey." Patrick spoke with quiet calm even though the sight of her made his heart race.

Last night, when they spoke, the light of the lanterns had been behind her, illuminating the glittering sequins and the red-gold crown but not her lovely face. Last night, Casey's eyes had been hidden in shadows, and he had spoken to her as if she was someone he didn't know, a rich, beautiful woman who had used him for her pleasure, a woman who had played with him and for whom he could so easily feel contempt.

But now there were no shadows, and she was his lovely Casey, her long red-gold hair still damp from a shower, her blue eyes uncertain, vulnerable, needing his love.

As Patrick dismounted, he reminded himself sternly, *Your love can only harm her. And if she is not the lovely Casey to whom you gave your heart, she can only harm you.*

"Patrick, I'm so sorry I didn't tell you. I was going to tell you tonight. I didn't think it would matter."

"But it does."

"Why?"

"Many reasons." It had to be over, it had to be, but Patrick saw the exquisite pain in her lovely eyes, the bewildered sadness, and he wanted so much to hold her and make it gentle for her.

Casey saw the tenderness in his eyes, the familiar gentleness that hadn't been there last night, and her heart trembled with hope.

"Patrick, hold me, please."

"Oh, Casey, no." His voice was gentle, a soft but necessary protest. *If I hold you, lovely Casey, I won't be able to let you go. And I have to let you go.*

The softness in Patrick's voice gave Casey even more hope. Bravely, so bravely, she wove her trembling fingers around his neck and into his black hair and tiptoed so that her lips could touch his.

"Please, Patrick, make love to me."

"No."

"No?"

Patrick heard the surprise in her voice, as if he was not allowed to say no, and reminded himself that there might be a Casey he didn't know, a spoiled heiress who always got what she wanted, a Casey English who might be very like Pamela Barrington. *Make love to me, James*, Pamela had demanded as she wove her long fingers around his neck and tiptoed to touch his lips.

Pamela's long, painted fingers had woven tightly and possessively around his neck, leaving blood when he pulled free, and Casey's hands were delicate and tentative, but still she clung to him, even though he had told her no, and he filled his mind with images of Pamela and the memory of what she had done to him and all that she had taken away . . .

"I don't want you, Casey."

Casey pulled away then, with a soft gasp. Her delicate fingers didn't draw blood as they left his neck, and it was she who was wounded, so terribly wounded, by his words and the sudden harshness in his voice.

"Last Sunday you couldn't get enough of me, Patrick," she reminded him quietly, a soft, bewildered plea.

"I've had enough now."

"Patrick," Casey whispered, a whisper of pain, a whisper that made his heart ache. "We love each other."

"Love?" Patrick heard the cruelty in his voice, necessary cruelty. If he could make Casey hate him, perhaps it would be easier for her to forget his love.

"Yes, *love*. You said you loved me."

"I was drunk on cheap champagne."

"A little high, maybe, the first time. But you've told me over and over."

"It was what you wanted to hear. We had good sex, Casey, that was all."

His cruel words caused such pain! Patrick almost relented, almost whispered, *Of course I love you!* But as he fought the powerful urge, he saw a transformation in her blue eyes . . . and he knew that he had been right to be very wary of the Casey he didn't know. As he watched, the pain and hurt vanished and were replaced by icy determination and terrifying rage.

"Who are you, Patrick James?" Casey demanded as her cold blue eyes left his briefly to gaze meaningfully at the jumps.

"You know who I am, Casey."

"No, I don't. You played games, too, Patrick. There was something you were going to tell me about yourself tonight."

"Nothing important. You know all about me."

"I don't think so." Her angry eyes sent a final message, a warning. *But I will find out.*

After Casey left, as he dismantled the jumps, Patrick told himself over and over that there was no way that she could discover his true identity. He had covered his tracks so well and had been so very careful until the reckless indulgence of this morning. Casey had seen him jump and she had wondered if his talent was something special, something extraordinary.

But it was such a tiny clue, wasn't it?

Yes. Except that if anyone in the world was bright enough and determined enough to pursue his destruction, it was a spurned Casey English.

The instinct for survival that had driven him from the slums of Chicago in search of heaven and had later told him to flee that paradise for his life of shadows sent urgent warnings now. *You have to run now, today!*

Patrick sighed softly. He would run, he had to, but not yet, not quite yet. He was so tired of running.

Chapter 13

The crisis that had taken Jeffrey away from the party for Casey, the bombing of the commercial airliner over the Mediterranean, signaled the beginning of a week of terror. The unprecedented violence centered in the Middle East, but its energy and venom ricocheted, erupting in brutal acts of terrorism around the globe.

For forty-eight hours the entire planet was on alert.

Then suddenly there was calm. Was it the ominous calm before the next lethal storm? Or the stillness of death, a grim sign that there were no hearts left to fight? Or was it something else, something good?

The phoenix that arose from the ashes *was* good, a promise of peace, a hopeful beginning. Astonishingly, the ancestral enemies agreed to meet at a negotiating table with the leaders of the most powerful nations as arbiters. The ancient foes would talk and maybe, just maybe . . .

The historic peace conference was scheduled to begin in London on Monday.

On Friday night, moments after Jeffrey and Julia returned to Belvedere, the limousine had arrived to take Jeffrey into Manhattan and he did not return until ten-thirty Thursday night. For the six tense days and nights, Jeffrey had been in the city informing the anxious nation, talking to correspondents around the world, hoping like everyone else that this wasn't the beginning of the end. During those tense days and nights, in the rare moments when he could rest, Jeffrey went across the street to his seldom-used apartment.

Finally, as hopeful whispers of peace began to echo around the world, Jeffrey was able to return, however briefly, to Belvedere.

"Oh, I'm so glad you're home." Julia kissed his lips tenderly.

"I'm glad, too, darling." Jeffrey held her against him, wanting her close, needing closeness for what he had to tell her.

Julia heard the slight uncertainty in his voice and felt the tension of his lean body. *No, Jeffrey, please. Don't do this.*

"Jeffrey?"

"I have to go to London, darling. I'm booked on a flight in the morning. I'll be staying at the Dorchester."

"No."

"Julie?"

"Don't do this, Jeffrey."

"I have to, honey. I'm very sorry."

"*Sorry*? You promised to spend next week with us. Don't you remember?"

"Of course I remember. But darling, this may be the most important political event of our lifetime. I'm an expert on the Middle East. I'm the only journalist who will be able to get an interview with—"

"With *who*? A terrorist? An interview with a terrorist is more important than your promise to us?"

"No," Jeffrey answered very softly, soft words of truth from his heart. The vacation with Julia and Merry was much more important to him. In the past six days and nights he had missed Julia, as always, and he had missed Merry. The opportunity to cover the historic peace conference wasn't more important to Jeffrey personally, but he felt an obligation beyond his own wishes. "I really don't have a choice, Julie. I have to go."

Some rational corner of Julia's mind knew that Jeffrey had to go to London, but that whisper of reason was lost in the thunder of emotions that suddenly exploded inside her. Like Jeffrey, Julia had long lived with a deep wound. And, like Jeffrey, she had covered the painful wound with her immense love for him and the resolute belief that one day the wound would heal, because one day Jeffrey would love his daughter.

Julia had believed that day was so close! It had begun, two weeks ago, the most fragile of beginnings. Merry had waited so patiently for the father she loved from afar and needed so much. She had waited, living on promises from Julia—"Daddy loves you, darling, very much, but he is very busy. Someday, he'll have more time."—and in the past two weeks her sensitive brown eyes had filled with hope and excitement as she and Julia planned the wonderful vacation. *Are you really really positive that Daddy will want to go for a carriage ride, Mommy?*

And now Merry would be so terribly hurt, a hurt much greater than all the silent disappointments of the past when Jeffrey was home but still so far away, because this time Merry had begun to believe.

And now . . .

Now Julia was consumed with powerful and dangerous emotions that were beyond reason.

"Oh, Jeffrey, you are never going to forgive me, are you?"

"Forgive you for what?" Jeffrey asked, stunned by the question and the unfamiliar anger in her lavender eyes.

"For having Merry. Even now, after ten years, you wish Merry had never been born."

"That's not true."

"It *is* true! You wanted me to have an abortion, didn't you?"

"My God, Julia *no!* How can you even think that?"

"Because it's true. I saw it in your eyes when I told you I was pregnant."

"No you didn't," Jeffrey repeated firmly, urgently, truthfully. He knew what Julia had seen in his eyes—tormented anguish as his mind formed vivid images of her with another man, a wish that there had been no other lover, sadness that that secret love had given her a baby he never could give. In those swirling moments as he had tried to adjust to her devastating revelation, he had surely wished that her pregnancy was a lie, an innocent ploy to get him to marry her, but he had never wanted her not to have her baby. "I never wanted you to have an abortion. Julie, please, you must believe that."

Julia barely heard Jeffrey's gentle plea because her own angry words had taken her, too, to the memory of that evening, and now that memory turned Julia's anger inward, where it belonged, to herself.

Merry would be hurt because Jeffrey couldn't keep the lovely promises Julia had made to her, but the fault was hers, not Jeffrey's. On that evening in May, when the part of her mind that was tethered to the grim lessons of her loveless life warned her to run because his stormy eyes told her so eloquently that he didn't want his baby, Julia had listened instead to her heart. Her bright mind had told her to flee, to protect herself and her unborn child, but her heart had offered promises, *Someday Jeffrey will love his baby*, and she had listened to the confident wishes of her heart because she loved him so much.

Julia had believed the whispers of her heart, but it was such a selfish belief, fueled by her desire to spend her life with the man she loved . . . but at what

cost to her other precious love?

"Jeffrey." Julia spoke quietly now, her anger at him dissipated and even the anger toward herself lost in her immense sadness for Merry. "Please don't hurt Merry. It's not her fault that I became pregnant."

Jeffrey started to reply—"I would never hurt Merry!"—but Julia's other words almost stopped his heart.

"Whose fault is it, Julia?" Jeffrey paused then added very quietly, "Not mine."

"No, Jeffrey, not yours. It's my fault," Julia admitted softly, remembering the sixteen-year-old girl who had pretended to be experienced because the thought of him telling her to leave filled her with an emptiness greater than all the losses of her young life. "I'm to blame. I'm responsible."

"What else, Julie?" he asked gently of the beautiful eyes that had blazed with anger and now softened with bewildered sadness. Julia had just told him the beginning of the truth. At last she had admitted aloud that there had been another lover. Jeffrey needed to hear the rest. Then it would be over and the ancient wound could heal. "Tell me darling. The truth."

The world had just witnessed swift volleys of violence, an eruption of anger from ancient, painful wounds, and from the ashes of that bitter fury had arisen great hope.

Jeffrey's heart filled with hope now even though he still reeled from the words Julia had hurled at him and still ached as he thought of the silent anguish that had given her words such angry life. Had Julia really believed, all this time, that he had wanted her to have an abortion?

As he waited for Julia to speak, Jeffrey's heart raced with hope and he made a decision of love. He wouldn't go to London. He would spend the week with Julia and Merry, gently and tenderly healing the ancient wounds.

Tell me the rest of the truth, Julie, Jeffrey urged silently as he smiled at her troubled lavender eyes. *Tell me the truth so that our wonderful love can be at peace.*

When Julia finally spoke it was a whisper of sadness, an anguished truth that destroyed all hope for peace.

"I should never have married you." *I should have raised our lovely daughter by myself. I could have told her how wonderful her daddy was and she would have been spared all the hurt and disappointment.*

As Jeffrey stared at Julia in stunned disbelief, a thought taunted, *You always wanted her to tell you the truth and part of you always feared that when she did your heart would be shattered into a thousand pieces.*

His heart was in a thousand pieces now, each tiny piece bleeding and screaming with pain. A deep instinct for survival guided Jeffrey to the top drawer of the bureau in the foyer to remove the keys to his Jaguar. He had to get away *now.* His passport was in his briefcase and he had clothes and luggage in his apartment in town. Jeffrey thought there could be no more pain, but he remembered the last time he had gotten the keys to his car, ten days ago when he had answered the frantic call of the little girl who was not his.

"Jeffrey . . ."

He heard the soft whisper, but he didn't turn around before he left. He couldn't

"Where's Daddy?" Merry asked eagerly the next morning. She had gone to bed with the promise that Jeffrey would be home later that night and that she would see him in the morning before he left for a final day of work before his vacation.

"Oh, darling, Daddy had to go to London because of the peace conference. It made him so sad that he had to go, but there was nothing he could do."

"I understand, Mommy."

I know you do, my darling, Julia thought as she gazed at her terribly-disappointed-but-trying-to-be-brave little girl. Her very bright daughter *did* understand, rationally, despite her great sadness. How Julia wished that she had been so rational last night!

"Why don't I ask Patrick if we can videotape the gymkhana?" Julia suggested hopefully even though the suggestion made her own heart weep. Merry had spen her life seeing her father on videotape and now . . . "Then when Daddy gets home we'll show him the tape and tell him all about our weekend in New York."

When Daddy gets home. But what if Jeffrey wasn't coming back? He had been so angry when he left.

Of course Jeffrey had been angry! And of course he had left! What did she expect? In her own anger, anger at herself more than him, she had said such terrible things.

I must go to him and explain the emotions behind the terrible words. I will go, she vowed. *As soon as I can find a way I will go to London and talk to my love.*

Diana looked at her image in the mirror with unconcealed criticism. She was in the ladies" room of the first class lounge at JFK. Only her dark curls appeared unsubdued by the events of the past few months. Her hair was longer, rich and lustrous, a soft, luxuriant frame for the face that had become so thin since June. Her drawn face made her sapphire eyes even larger, and they looked haunted, mysterious, perhaps even intriguing. But Diana knew the truth behind the haunted, luminous, blue eyes; and there was no mystery, no intrigue, simply pain.

This morning, blue-black circles rimmed the saphire, a fresh layer, one layer deeper, because she had been called in at three A.M. to operate on a man with a gunshot wound to the chest. Diana hadn't been on call, not officially, not on the eve of her three-week vacation in Europe, but she had been unofficially on call almost constantly since the night she had received the divorce papers from Chase.

You haven't been taking very good care of yourself, she mused critically as she stared at her fatigued image in the mirror. The past few months had been filled—compulsively full—with work. There had been little food, little sleep, little privacy, and no time to think. *Hiding from something, Diana?*

The compassionate physician in Diana felt an instinctive urge to reassure the woman she saw in the mirror, *You should be nice to yourself, pamper yourself a little*.

Chase had booked a vacation to pamper, first-class, five-star, the best suites, a vacation that could be afforded by only the wealthiest in the world.

Diana's accommodations would be luxurious, befitting a queen, but the pampering would be an illusion. During the long nights in beds with silk sheets and feather pillows, Diana would be wakeful. Her brilliant mind, undistracted by the frantic pace—*escape*—of her work, would focus all its energy, compulsion, and curiosity on a thorough examination of *her.* Diana, the skillful physician, would take a detailed and probing history of her own life and do an intimate physical on the part she knew best . . . the heart.

Not *the* heart, her own heart.

Diana sighed as she swept a defiant curl away from her face with a gold barrette. *We'll be talking a lot*, she silently promised the face in the mirror.

 Heart-to-heart talks.

Diana had to discover how her cautious footing had led her not once but twice to a love that she believed would last forever but which had faltered and died.

There was still an hour before boarding would begin for her flight to London. She poured herself a cup of tea and found a comfortable chair in a corner of the first class lounge. From her vantage point she could watch the activity of planes on the tarmac and the activity of people in the lounge.

Diana sipped tea and succumbed to the fogginess of her sleepless night. When she was working, she could clear the fog, willing it away, but now she let the fogginess envelop her in a warm, comforting blanket.

Comforting, she admitted begrudgingly, *because you're letting your fatigue be an excuse not to think, not to begin the journey into your past.*

I will begin tomorrow, Diana vowed. *After a good night's sleep at the Dorchester I will begin the careful meticulous task of reviewing the signs and symptoms of my life that should have been clues to the diagnosis of what I have become: a stunning success professionally and a stunning failure in my private life.*

For now, the fogginess was just fine.

Except that Jeffrey Lawrence just walked in.

He was undoubtedly going to London for the peace conference, obviously flying first class, probably on her flight.

A strong and confident woman would walk over to him, stare calmly into his intense blue eyes, and apologetically confess to temporary hysteria in his office.

That was what a strong and confident woman would do, someone like who Diana would be in three weeks.

For now, she simply wanted to avoid him. She reached for a magazine that lay facedown on the coffee table beside her. She frowned slightly when she turned it over and saw the artist's flattering portrait of a beautiful and confident woman with huge sapphire eyes, a Mona Lisa smile, and unruly dark-brown hair curling sensuously from beneath the turquoise surgeon's mask . . . a portrait, ostensibly, of her.

The magazine was the September fourth issue of *Time* and she was the cover story. Diana hadn't yet read the words that accompanied the flattering image on the cover and didn't read them now. She folded the cover back, not that anyone would recognize her from the portrait, and flipped quickly through the pages about her. Pages and pages. Diana was amazed by the length of the article, a chronicle of her career, her immense success, her scientific stardom by age thirty-six. Most of the words, of course, were devoted to the Heart—which was why she had agreed to the article—complete with smiling photographs of many grateful recipients.

Diana flipped swiftly past the cover story and swiftly, too, past the news of the world. It was last week's news, before the unprecedented carnage began, but the world was filled with astonishing violence and tragedy even on a "quiet" week. She turned more pages in a determined journey toward the lighter stories to be found in Theater, Arts, Books, and People.

But en route to the lighter stories, Diana found her name in print once again, this time in Milestones. If only numbers of words were the measure of success, Diana mused, then the pages and pages of words in the cover story celebrating her immense success would surely offset the few pithy words that articulately documented her immense failure . . .

"Marriage Dissolved. Dr. Diana Shepherd, renowned heart surgeon and inventor of the Shepherd Heart (see Cover Story) and Chase Andrews, billionaire real-estate developer. After five years and no children."

No children. Diana stared at the words for several moments, then sighed softly and turned the page to People.

The People section would be safe, glamorous shots of celebrities, paragraphs about films wrapped, parties attended, intriguing couples, people she had heard of but didn't know.

But the People section wasn't safe—because Sam was there.

> *Sam Hunter returns home.* Last week, six-time Grammy award-winning songwriter and singer Sam Hunter moved from London, where he has lived for the past fifteen years, to California, where he has purchased a beachfront home in Malibu's exclusive Colony. The Dallas-born music superstar has just signed a three-album contract with Capitol Records, and although there are no firm plans for a U.S. tour, a spokesperson for Hunter did not exclude the possibility. When asked why the singer-songwriter decided to end his fifteen-year self-imposed exile, the spokesperson commented, "It was time." The extraordinary popularity of Hunter's poetic songs of love is reflected by his remarkable "crossover" success—a record ten of his titles have held number-one positions atop the hit parades of Pop, Rock, Country, and R&B. The most recent single, "Dance With Me," has been in top slots for the past ten weeks and his latest album, *Promises of Love*, has already gone platinum.

Diana read the short paragraph five times even though she knew its contents by heart after one reading. There was nothing more to be learned from the words on the page, but there were fifteen years of life between the lines.

Diana slowly closed the magazine and placed it on the coffee table. Her voyage into the past would begin today, this moment, because the voyage was, after all, about Sam Hunter.

Sam Hunter, who had entered her life on a sunny autumn day in Dallas in 1970.

Diana sat at one of the many tables in the foyer of Theodore Roosevelt High School. It was noon, and the foyer was crowded with students visiting with friends and wandering among the colorful tables piled high with items for sale—senior pins and school sweaters, dance tickets and book covers, cookies and fudge.

Diana sat at a table, selling nothing, waiting patiently for volunteers to sign up for the talent show she was planning. Talent shows weren't new to Roosevelt High School—the Revue was held every spring and was always successful—but Diana's show was to be held on the Wednesday evening before Thanksgiving. The proceeds would benefit Dallas's recently completed Children's Home, a much-needed safe haven for neglected and abused children. The autumn talent show was Diana's idea. She had already won the support of the faculty and student council. Now she simply had to hope that some of the many talented students at Roosevelt would donate their time to the project.

Diana had to hope, because it wasn't in her nature to arm twist or cajole. She sat quietly at her table, hoping not selling, wishing she had something to contribute beyond her ability to organize.

In her next life she was going to be able to sing! She loved the wonderful songs of the sixties. Music was a constant chorus to her happy life, a joyful, ever-present accompaniment even during the hours she spent studying to earn the A's that inevitably appeared on her report cards. Diana knew all the words to the wonderful songs, and sang them softly to herself, but she wasn't a singer. Her gifts lay elsewhere—in her bright mind, her boundless generosity, and her instinctive wish to share the joy and cheer of her life with others who needed joy.

Diana couldn't perform at her talent show, but she could make it a great success if enough talented students volunteered. So far, during this first noon hour spent at the table in the foyer, the response had already been better than she had dared to hope.

"Hi."

"Hi," Diana answered with surprise. Why was Sam Hunter, Roosevelt's star quarterback, stopping at her table? The sign she had painted clearly read "Talent Show Sign-Up'.

"I would like to volunteer for the talent show."

"Oh!" Diana knew Sam Hunter's talent—throwing touchdowns. For the past two years he had led Roosevelt's Roughriders to the state championship. He was a celebrity, not just at Roosevelt but in all of Dallas. His participation in the show would guarantee community interest. If Sam Hunter wanted to throw passes on stage, Diana decided, that would be fine. "OK. Great."

Sam looked at her for an expectant moment then finally said, "I sing."

Before Diana could reply, Sam's girlfriend appeared. Cheryl was a pretty, sexy cheerleader.

"Well, here you all are, darlin'."

"I'll be with you in a moment, Cheryl."

"I thought we were going for a drive." Cheryl's provocative pout sent a clear message that it was the parking not the driving that appealed.

"We are. As soon as I'm done here."

"Let's go now," Cheryl urged.

She added seductive emphasis to her suggestion with long, delicate fingers that played briefly with the buttons on Sam's shirt, then drifted meaningfully to his belt buckle. As Diana watched Cheryl's bold intimacy, her cheeks flushed pink with embarrassment and she wished that she could disappear.

Cheryl was not embarrassed, of course, and Diana couldn't interpret the look in Sam's dark-brown eyes. But he stopped the intimacy, gently but firmly. The strong fingers that curled over Cheryl's wrist were lean, as Sam was, not massive like the other players on the football team.

"I'll meet you outside in five minutes, Cheryl."

"I'll be waiting."

"So, . . ." Sam began after Cheryl left. "What do you need to know? My name is Sam Hunter."

Did he think she didn't know who he was? Admittedly Sam and Diana had never met before. It was more than just the size of Roosevelt, five hundred students per class, it was the fact that Diana Shepherd and Sam Hunter lived in completely different worlds.

The handsome star quarterback belonged to, perhaps led, the "in" crowd, the small, elite clique whose members, like Sam and Cheryl, were attractive, confident, and sexually sophisticated. Diana's group was academically sophisticated but socially naive. She and her friends won championships in debate and mathematics, not football and cheer-leading, were devotees of *The Hobbitt*, the Beatles, and Khalil Gibran, and scored among the nation's best on SAT's and National Merit exams. On weekends Diana and her friends assembled as a group, not in couples; and during the slumber parties the girls frequently held, they bemoaned their sexual naiveté but assured themselves with easy laughter that sex would happen, love would happen, everything would happen.

Diana and Sam had never met, but *of course* she knew who he was.

"Yes, I know. I'm Diana Shepherd."

"I know. I voted for you."

"You did?"

"Of course. You were the best candidate."

"Thank you."

Diana's opponent in last spring's election for student body president belonged to Sam's crowd, but apparently Sam had listened to the campaign speeches and decided, along with an overwhelming majority of the school, that Diana should be the first girl student body president in Roosevelt High's sixty-year history.

"You're welcome. So, what else do you need?"

"I need to have you audition." Of course even if Sam Hunter couldn't sing a note, even if his music "talent" matched hers, Diana would want him to participate, wouldn't she? "To know what you'll be singing, where it will fit in best."

"OK. When are the auditions?"

"After school next week. Oh, that conflicts with football, doesn't it?"

"Yes," Sam replied quietly. "Is there another time that would be possible for you?"

The talent show was Diana's brainchild, but the other student-body officers had agreed to attend all the auditions so that the final selections could be made by committee. Now Sam Hunter, star quarterback, school hero, probably the biggest draw for community attendance at the show, was asking if Diana could give him a special audition.

Sam Hunter *was* special, of course. Surely he knew that, even though his dark-brown eyes seemed more apologetic than arrogant.

"Sure. Any time. When would be good for you?"

"This week's game is Friday night, so Saturday morning or afternoon?"

Saturday evening was out, Diana assumed, because Sam and Cheryl would be celebrating the Friday-night victory at the dance in the gym.

"I work at the hospital Saturday afternoons, so I guess Saturday morning."

For the next three days Diana wondered anxiously what she would say to Sam Hunter during the short drive from her house, where he said he would pick her up at ten A.M., to Lincoln Park, where he suggested that the special audition take place. She and Sam had nothing in common, of course, and he probably viewed the happily innocent world of Diana and her friends, if he even knew about it, as hopelessly unsophisticated and perhaps even silly.

Diana searched for possible topics of conversation and found two: Cheryl and football. Football, she decided. She studied back issues of *Strenuous Life*,

Roosevelt’s weekly newspaper, and learned about Sam’s record-setting seasons. Then she rehearsed what she would say about his career, to sound knowledgeable and interested, and assuaged as much as possible her worries about awkward silences.

But there was another worry that was not so easily assuaged. How would she act impressed by Sam’s singing even if she wasn’t?

Diana rehearsed the words she would use to fill the uneasy silences, but on Saturday morning, before there had even been a silence, Sam asked her a question.

“The talent show is for the Children’s Home?”

“Yes.”

“I thought it was already built.”

“It is. It opened about six months ago. The funding is pretty good to cover the basics, but we can use the money made from the talent show for special events and outings.”

“We?”

“I’m a volunteer.”

“Is that what you’re doing this afternoon?”

“No. Today I work at Children’s Hospital. I spend Tuesdays after school at the Home.” Diana paused, and when Sam didn’t speak, she made a suggestion that bridged his interest in football and her interest in the children. “Maybe, sometime, an outing for the children could be to a Roughrider football game.”

Sam didn’t take his eyes from the road. He was, Diana had observed with surprise and relief, a very good and very cautious driver. His eyes remained on the road, but they became solemn at her suggestion.

“I can’t imagine that children who have been physically abused would enjoy watching something as violent as football.”

Diana searched for a polite reply—something that wouldn’t reveal her true lack of interest in the sport that was Sam’s future but which she too found to be violent—but before she found the right words they had reached Lincoln Park.

Diana hadn’t needed to rehearse the words she would say to Sam about football. And she hadn’t needed to worry about how she would act impressed even if Sam couldn’t sing.

She did need words—and never found the perfect ones—to tell Sam how she felt about his singing. He sang her favorite love songs more beautifully, more emotionally, than she had ever heard them sung before. Sam’s strong, talented fingers worked delicate magic on the guitar.

And his sensual dark eyes, and soft rich voice, and gentle smile worked magic on her heart.

Without even asking what she wanted to hear, Sam simply sang the love songs Diana loved the best—“Yesterday,” ‘Kathy’s Song,” ‘In My Life,” ‘April Come She Will,” ‘If I Fell,” ‘The Sound of Silence,” ‘Bridge Over Troubled Water,” ‘Something,” ‘It’s Only Love.”

“Why haven’t you been in the school’s talent show before, Sam? You’re so . . . you play so well.”

“This seemed like a worthy cause. Do you think you’ll be able to use me?”

“I think,” Diana bravely told the dark-brown eyes that flickered with uncertainty even though he was so special, “that I’d like to make it a one-man show.”

Chapter 14

Roosevelt High's Thanksgiving Revue wasn't a one-man show, but Sam Hunter definitely stole it, just as four days before he had stolen the state championship by passing a record-breaking last-second "long bomb" to the end zone.

The talent show was a stunning success, standing room only, a tribute to the worthiness of the cause and because the word was out that Sam Hunter was going to try his million-dollar hand at playing the guitar. It was quite obvious that no one, not even Cheryl, had known about Sam's talent. Except his parents, of course, but Diana wasn't able to identify them in the crowd that surrounded Sam in the punch-and-cookies reception that followed.

Then the show was over, and Sam still smiled his gentle, uncertain smile at her whenever they passed in the hallway, but they had no reason to stop, no reason to talk anymore about the order of the songs he would sing, or if he minded performing twice, opening the show and closing it, no reason to talk at all.

No reason not to return to their different worlds.

"Hello, Diana."

It was mid-December, three weeks after the talent show. She was in the student government office, *her* office, when he appeared in the doorway.

"Sam. Hello."

"How are you?"

"I'm fine."

"I wondered if you need other volunteers at the Children's Home. Now that football season is over I'm free on Tuesday afternoons."

"Oh! Wonderful. It doesn't have to be Tuesday. They can use help any day."

"Isn't Tuesday the day you go?"

"Yes."

"I'd like to go when you go. I thought you could show me the ropes."

"I'd be glad to. There aren't really any ropes. We just play with the kids and try to make them feel safe and loved."

That was candy-coating, of course, because there were some children who were painfully withdrawn and terribly mistrustful. But even those children made progress with time and the professional help of the counselors, psychologists, and doctors who worked at the Home, and their timid, grateful smiles made it all worthwhile.

"Will Cheryl be volunteering, too?"

"Cheryl? Oh. No."

At first Sam was very uncomfortable with the children. But they weren't uncomfortable with him. Even though he didn't think these children would be interested in football, Dallas was a football town and he was a folk hero. Football was Sam's entrée, but it was Sam himself, his gentle uncertain smile, the wonderful songs he sang, that melted the ice, swiftly and permanently.

In February, Diana found the courage to ask him something she had been thinking about for several weeks. Would he be willing to sing for the children who were inpatients at Children's Hospital? Diana rehearsed all the ways to make it easy for him to say no—he was so busy, he already so generously gave his time every Tuesday, she might not be able to arrange it anyway—but Sam instantly said Yes, of course, he would be happy to.

The evening of singing was scheduled for the second Thursday in March at seven P.M. in the hospital auditorium. The children from the Home would be there, too, because Sam was their friend.

Sam told Diana he would pick her up at six-fifteen. That would give him more than enough time to check the amplifiers in the auditorium and visit with the familiar small faces in the audience before seven.

As six-fifteen became six-twenty, Diana began to fight little worries. Five minutes late. *Only* five minutes!

Then ten. Then fifteen.

Diana found a listing for a Sam Hunter in the phone book with an address that was in the area for Roosevelt High.

He's trying to call me, she thought when she dialed the number and reached a busy signal. Diana quickly hung up and expected her phone to ring any second.

But Sam didn't call. At six-forty Diana dialed the number again, again busy, and then the hospital to say they would be late. She could go on to the hospital, of course, but she was just a spectator, someone in the audience who loved Sam's singing as much as the children did. Sam was the show, her one-man show starring Sam Hunter at last, but where was he?

Was he with Cheryl? Was she distracting him, bewitching him with charms that made him forget time and commitments to small children who were sick and sad and needed joy in their lives?

No, Diana thought. Sam wouldn't do that!

But how well did she really know him?

They talked, of course, on Tuesdays, as they drove together to and from the Home. But then it was Sam who asked the questions and Diana who gave the answers. She told him, because he asked, that she was going to be a pediatrician. Even though she knew it could be terribly sad to see the small, innocent faces bewildered by the harms that had befallen them—inexplicable sickness and even more inexplicable abuse—her own sadness was minor to the good she believed she could do. She wanted to ease their pain, to make them smile, to find the laughter that rang like crystal when it was filled with joy.

Diana hadn't asked Sam about his dreams—she hadn't yet summoned the courage—but there were other things, important things that she knew from what she had observed. She knew that he was very gentle with the children. Sometimes his smiles were as shy and as uncertain as theirs, but these children who had so little reason to trust felt very safe with him. He wouldn't disappoint them.

But then it was seven, then seven-fifteen, then seven-thirty. The line was still busy at the Sam Hunter number that might not even be his and Diana's own phone rang as the activities coordinator called to ask questions Diana couldn't answer.

Sam's show was supposed to last until eight-thirty. The children stayed until then, and sang anyway, and at eight forty-five the coordinator called a final time to see if Sam was going to reschedule. Diana said she had no idea, and the evening ended without explanations or promises.

But the evening wasn't over for Diana. Her anger had long since been replaced by concern. Something had happened to Sam. Even though he was a cautious driver perhaps there had been an accident . . .

Please let him be all right.

He finally called at ten P.M.

"Diana, I'm sorry."

"Where are you?"

"Home."

"What happened, Sam? Were you in an accident?"

"No. I just couldn't make it. I'm terribly sorry."

Once Diana knew Sam was safe, her anger returned and raged unopposed.

"How could you have done that to them?"

"I'm sorry."

"Have you any idea how disappointed they are? Did you think about the children who know you and are so proud of you?"

"Can we reschedule?"

"How do I know you won't do it again? What guarantee can you give me, and them, that something or *someone* more important won't come up next time? I don't think you have any idea of how damaging this was. These children trusted you, and trust is so fragile for them, and you've just shattered it!"

"I'm sorry, Diana."

"So am I, Sam."

Then there was nothing more to say, no reason to say a polite good night or good-bye, so sometime in the silence that followed, Diana hung up, not with a slam but with a sad, quiet disconnect.

Only after did she realize that Sam had offered no defense, no reason, no excuse. It was inexcusable, whatever the reason, of course. He must have known that.

Sam wasn't at school the next day. Diana learned from the records kept in the principal's office that the number she had been dialing was his. Had he and Cheryl had a lovers' quarrel and then a reconciliation over the phone that took the evening—*stole* the evening—from the children?

Diana spent the weekend fuming about what he had done and decided that she was going to find him on Monday and demand an explanation.

Sam found her first. He was in the hallway outside her home room when the bell sounded. Diana drew an astonished breath when she saw him, her anger suddenly stunned by worry. What was wrong? Sam looked quite ill, his skin very pale and his dark eyes clouded and distant.

"What's wrong, Sam?"

"Nothing. I just haven't slept well because of what happened. Diana, I really am terribly sorry. I would very much like to reschedule. I want you to know that you can trust me."

"Then help me understand why it happened."

"It just did."

"And it won't happen next time?"

"No."

Diana watched his cloudy eyes as he uttered the assurance and wasn't convinced. And, she decided, neither was he. Whatever mysterious thing had happened, he couldn't guarantee that it wouldn't happen again, even though he didn't want it to.

Sam didn't tell Diana what had happened. But it was no mystery. The entire school knew. Sam and Cheryl had broken up.

The concert was rescheduled for mid-April. Sam apologized to the children at the Home and solemnly promised he would be there next time.

During the three weeks before the concert, he and Diana spent Tuesdays at the Home, as always, and, as always, rode together in Sam's car. But for those three weeks they rode in awkward silence. Each was cheerful in the hours they spent with the children, but they had nothing to say to each other. Everything was on hold, waiting to see if Sam would disappoint the children again.

But Sam didn't disappoint. When he arrived to get her, five minutes early, on the night of the rescheduled concert, he smiled the first unencumbered smile of the past three weeks—as if he was relieved, too.

Sam was supposed to stop singing at eight-thirty, but the show continued for another magical hour. And then there was more magic because he didn't take her home right away. Instead he drove to Lincoln Park and they sat on the grass under the spring moon and he sang to her. That April night he sang all her favorite songs of love and one she had never heard before, one that was more beautiful than all the others, beautiful and sad, a bittersweet song of love and longing.

"What's it called?"

" 'Loving You.' "

"Who wrote it?"

"I did."

"Oh," Diana breathed. A beautiful and sad love song for Cheryl, the love Sam wanted but could not have. What if Cheryl had called tonight and wanted to reconcile? Diana shuddered. There might have been sadness again, not magic.

"I was going to sing it for you last time."

"Last time?"

"Three weeks ago."

"You wroteit before then?"

"I've been working on it since January."

"It's very beautiful."

"Loving You" was only one of the beautiful, original love songs Sam sang to her that spring. Every Tuesday after they said good-bye to the children at the Home, Sam and Diana went to the park.

He sang to her, and on a moonless night in May he kissed her. He kissed her on their Tuesday evenings after that, kissing between songs and then abandoning the songs and just kissing her, long, deep, warm kisses that made Diana forget everything except him.

No one knew about their love. Even though he kissed her and sang her songs of love, Sam and Diana never had an official date. But one starry night, in their private corner of the park, he asked her to the senior prom.

When Sam was five minutes late on prom night, Diana vowed simply not to look at the clock. When he was fifteen minutes late her heart began to ache and she prayed silent prayers, *No, not again* and *Please let him be all right*.

When he finally arrived, forty-five minutes late, she saw that he was not all right. Although they brightened when he saw her, his dark eyes were cloudy.

"Sam, what's wrong?"

"Nothing." *Nothing I can tell you about*. "I'm sorry I'm late. You look very beautiful."

"Thank you." *And you look so handsome and in such pain. Why, Sam? Do you wish you were taking Cheryl?* Diana crushed the thought quickly, helped by his gentle smile and the tender kiss he gave her after he pinned a corsage of white orchids on her dress.

* * *

She felt so wonderful in his arms as they swayed to the music they loved. Sam held her close to him, closer and tighter, but then suddenly he would stiffen and she could feel that he wasn't breathing and when she searched his face she saw that it had become ashen and tense as if in pain. After a few moments he would breathe again and smile a thin smile and pull her back very close to him.

Waves of nausea, Diana decided as she watched Sam's silent battle. He must have a stomach flu.

They left the prom early because they wanted only slow dances and the moonlit privacy of their own special place in Lincoln Park.

"Aren't you going to bring your guitar?" Diana asked as Sam began to lead her to their secluded spot without opening the trunk of his car.

"No. No singing tonight."

No singing. Diana's mind whirled. *Just kissing? Just loving? Just dancing to our own music of love under the moon?*

They danced, their bodies kissing as their lips did. Once, when her arms tightened around his chest, Sam winced and pulled away, just a little, but after a few moments he began a soft serious journey of kisses down her neck.

"Make love to me, Sam," Diana whispered bravely.

Diana had never made love. It was 1971, the era of free love. But Diana was uninfluenced by the mores of the time or the pressures of her peers. She had long ago decided that she would be a virgin until her wedding night. She would make love then with the man she loved, her husband and the father of the children she would have. Three children, Diana thought, maybe four, because she loved children so much and all the children she would care for at work wouldn't be enough.

She was uninfluenced by mores or peers. But Diana listened to the songs of her heart. And now those songs told her joyfully that it was right, wonderful, to make love with Sam.

"Oh, Diana," Sam answered softly. "I can't."

"Because of Cheryl?"

"Cheryl? God, no. Not because of anyone but you."

"Me?"

"Because you are so lovely and so precious and so beautiful." *Because your vision of life is joyous and pure and I don't want to cloud that magnificent vision with the truth*. "And so innocent."

"I don't want to be innocent."

Sam smiled a tender loving smile. Then, after a few moments, his handsome face grew solemn.

"Darling Diana, after tonight we'll never see each other again."

"Never?" Diana had known that after tonight it would be difficult for them to see each other. In two days she was flying to Bethesda for a summer research fellowship at the NIH. By the time she returned in late August, a brief visit before going to Boston, Sam would already be in Los Angeles practicing with the football team. They were going to colleges a continent apart—she to Radcliffe, he to Southern Cal—but they could write, couldn't they? And they could see each other at Christmas and spring break and summer. "You won't be in Dallas for Christmas?"

"No. My father just got a coaching job near Denver."

"Coaching?"

"He coaches college football."

"Oh." Diana hadn't known Sam's father was a coach, or anything about his mother, or if he had sisters and brothers. She really knew very little about Sam

Hunter except that the thought of never seeing him again filled her with sudden fear. *I could live the rest of my life and never again feel the way I feel with you—the happiness, the joy, the trembling desires that make me so brave.*

"Oh, Diana," Sam whispered gently when he saw the tears and sadness in the lovely sapphire. He kissed her tears and held her very close. "Don't cry."

"I'll miss you."

"And I'll miss you." *You have kept me alive. I wonder what will become of me without you.*

Chapter 15

CAMBRIDGE, MASSACHUSETTS
SEPTEMBER 1974

Diana left the desk where she was studying to turn the stack of records on her stereo. The records were old favorites, familiar study companions from high school that had endured during her three distinguished undergraduate years at Radcliffe and were with her still for her first year at Harvard Medical School.

As she walked back to her desk she paused at the window of her small Hilliard Place apartment, smiled at the large, wet drops that splashed against the pane, and thought, *Cozy.*

A cozy rainy night to spend studying the anatomy of the thorax, to the music of the Beatles.

When her telephone rang at eleven she assumed it would be a classmate frustrated by the spinning pace of today's lecture in biochemistry and wanting to borrow Diana's compulsive and comprehensive notes. A classmate—or Alan. Alan was a second-year law student whom she had dated for about a year, and with whom she had made love even though she knew he wasn't the man she was going to marry. Diana hadn't known that when they had first made love four months ago, but she knew it now and she needed to tell him directly.

If it's Alan, even though it's late and a school night, I'm going to invite him over and tell him, Diana vowed bravely as she walked to the phone. As she lifted the receiver she hoped very much that it would be a classmate calling about biochemistry.

"Diana? It's Sam Hunter."

"Sam."

"Remember me?"

"Oh, yes, I remember you." *And I never believed we wouldn't see each other again.* Not that this call meant they were going to see each other. Sam's voice sounded close, but Diana knew where he was—in Los Angeles preparing for the game against Washington State on Saturday. Diana knew the football schedule for the University of Southern California. She watched the games that were televised and read about the ones that weren't. She knew all the details of Sam's stunning career, and she knew the widely held prediction that this year he would lead his team to the national championship and in the process win the Heisman Trophy. "How are you?"

"Fine. Wet."

"Wet?" Her heart raced as she gazed at the rain pelting against her window.

It never rained in California, did it? "Where are you?"

"In a phone booth across from a place called the Coop."

"In Cambridge," she whispered. *Only four blocks away. Why?*

"Yes. I'd like to see you, Diana. Could we meet for coffee sometime, or breakfast or lunch or dinner?"

"Where are you staying?"

"I'm not sure yet."

Sam had just arrived. The final ride in his transcontinental hitchhike had let him off a soggy half mile away from Harvard Square. He knew Diana was still in Cambridge. He had checked before he left Los Angeles. From the undergraduate office he learned that she was in medical school, and from directory assistance he got her phone number.

Sam had money for a hotel—he had sold his car, his textbooks, everything but the clothes in his knapsack and his guitar—and should have called her once he found a room and changed into warm clothes. But he couldn't wait. He had to hear her voice.

Now that he had, he wanted desperately to see her. And she wanted to see him.

"Hi."

"Hi." His lips, slightly blue from cold, smiled his tender uncertain smile, and raindrops splashed from his hair onto his cheeks.

While Sam took a shower and changed into dry clothes, Diana made hot chocolate and turned the stack of her favorite records.

Then Sam was there, dancing with her, beginning where they had left off on a moonlit night in June. Beginning where they had left off and this time finishing their dance of love.

On that June night the rhythm of their dancing had been slow and graceful, a leisurely kissing of bodies. Now there was urgency, almost desperation, a reckless and furtive need to be together.

As if this was a stolen moment.

As if, even though their passion and desires were all-consuming, there could be an intrusion on their loving.

As if, even when they were melted together by the immense fire of their love, they could still be torn apart.

From the very beginning there was desperation in their loving, desperation for each other and desperation to hold onto the love. As if it wasn't real, couldn't last, wasn't meant to be . . . even though their hearts sang with joy.

"I just couldn't play football anymore," Sam told her three days after he arrived.

"You were supposed to win the Heisman Trophy this year."

"How do you know about that?"

"I know everything about your career. Test me. Ask me how many passes you completed last year and whose record that broke."

"How do you know?"

"Television. The sports page of the *Boston Globe*. *Sports Illustrated*."

"Really?"

"Of course." Diana smiled. Then, as her fingers delicately traced the jagged scars on his body and dipped gently into a concavity in the right side of his rib cage she added softly, "I'm glad you gave up football. Aside from how much more wonderful it will be to follow your singing career than your football stats, your body has had enough abuse."

"Enough abuse, yes. But it could take some more love."

"How many babies shall we have?" Diana asked one day in late October as they strolled in Boston Commons amidst the Saturday afternoon activity of children gleefully scampering through piles of fallen leaves.

"As many as you like. You'll be such a wonderful mother."

"And you'll be such a wonderful father." Diana smiled and asked, "Have you thought about names?"

"For our babies?"

"Yes."

"No, I haven't." Sam smiled lovingly at her. Then his dark eyes grew serious and he added, "I guess I would like to name one of our daughters after my mother. Her name was Jane."

"Was?" Diana echoed softly. They had spent hours talking about their love, the love songs he had written for her in high school, their dreams, their future, and Diana's loving family. But, even though she urged gently, Sam resisted talking about his family. "Your mother is no longer alive?"

"No."

"What was she like, Sam?"

"Very gentle. Very brave." Sam sighed softly and his eyes were far away. "She died in a car accident when I was six." *She died trying to save my life.*

Three weeks after Diana learned about Sam's mother, she learned about his father.

She was in the apartment studying and listening to one of the tapes Sam had made for her. The tapes were medleys of love songs, Diana's old favorites and the ones she loved even more—the breathtaking songs of love Sam had written for her. In the middle of one of the tapes of love was a twenty-minute instrumental called "The Chime Song." During his years in Los Angeles, Sam had spent many Sunday afternoons at the missions in Southern Californa listening to the chimes that rang from the bell towers. "The Chime Song" was a canon of all the beautiful chimes, tumbling one on top of the other, a breathtaking cascade of music and a triumph of Sam's talented fingers.

On that November night, Sam was at the Two Lanterns, the "in vogue" coffee house on Boylston where he waited tables and sang. When Diana's doorbell sounded at eleven she looked through the peephole before opening the door. Sam would be home soon, and at first glance she thought it was he having forgotten his key. But it was only someone who looked like Sam.

Diana smiled warmly as she opened the door. She was about to say, because they looked so alike, "You must be Sam's father. How nice of you to visit us." But her brain sent a surprising but forceful warning, Beware. The man looked like Sam, the dark handsomeness, the lean, taut body, the long-lashed brown eyes. No, the eyes were different. Sam's eyes were warm, gentle, loving, and this man's eyes were hard and cold. "May I help you?"

"I'm looking for Sam."

"Sam?"

"Are you Diana Shepherd?"

"Yes."

"Then you do know Sam Hunter."

Diana gave a brief frown, then smiled.

"Sam Hunter, yes, of course. We were at Roosevelt together in Dallas." She tilted her head and asked, "Are you his brother?"

"I'm his father."

"Oh! What can I do for you, Mr. Hunter?"

"You can tell me where Sam is."

Don't blush. Hold his gaze. Sound honest. Diana had no experience with lying, didn't believe in telling lies, but on this night the deepest of instincts made the lies come easily.

"I have no idea. I'm sorry."

"When was the last time you saw or heard from him?"

"Let me think. It must have been the night of the senior prom. We had never dated, but we knew each other. I didn't have a prom date and Sam was kind enough to take me. Mr. Hunter, is something wrong? Has something happened to Sam?"

Sam's father started to smile, and Diana relaxed just a little, but it was only a cruel trick to throw her off guard. As she was beginning to wonder if she had been all wrong to be wary of him, his smile became a mean sneer and the cold, hard eyes turned wild.

Diana felt a shiver of ice sweep through her, the terrifying realization of danger that comes with a frantic message to flee. Diana couldn't flee, and as her mind struggled to prepare for his next round of questions and her next round of lies, he grabbed her.

And all the waves of fear that had swept through her before were only tiny ripples compared to the terror she felt as his massive hands dug mercilessly into the delicate flesh of her arms.

"I don't believe you, missy," he hissed, a vicious sound that was more animal than man. "He's here, isn't he?"

"No! Let go of me! How *dare* you touch me!"

"How dare I?" He laughed an ugly laugh, then pulled her close to his snarling face and repeated meanly, "How *dare* I?"

Diana smelled the alcohol on his breath, and it triggered an important memory. During her undergraduate years at Radcliffe, she had worked as a volunteer in the emergency ward of Boston City Hospital. She had seen patients who were wild from alcohol or drugs and had marveled at the calm and reasoned way the doctors and nurses imposed control. She had only been a witness to the approach, never tried it herself, but . . .

"Mr. Hunter . . ." she began quietly, trying to make her voice calm and soothing, but having no idea if she succeeded because the sound was lost in the thunder of blood puling through her brain. "I honestly don't know where your son is. I do know that you are drunk and that you are hurting me, even though I'm sure you don't mean to. If you don't let go I will have to scream and my neighbors will instantly call the police. I'm sure you don't want that."

"Oh, you're sure I don't want that, are you?" he mocked with eyes that showed no fear.

Diana's threat was gently offered, and almost idle, because most of her neighbors in the solidly built apartment building were elderly and had long since gone to sleep behind their almost-sound-proof walls. But words were all Diana had against his immense strength, and now her mind sent even more frantic warnings, *"The Chime Song" is playing now, but in less than a minute it will be Sam's voice singing in the background, and in ten or fifteen minutes Sam will be home.*

"So, Mr. Hunter, do I call the police?"

"Be my guest. I'm leaving. I'm sure we'll have a chance to visit again sometime. I look forward to it."

His final words were a warning, painfully punctuated by his massive fingers that dug even deeper, almost to bone. Then he released her roughly, gazed insanely at her for an endless terrifying moment, then laughed an evil laugh and mercifully left.

As Diana closed the door, the trembling that had been a terrified quiver suddenly shook her entire body, and even though she took large gulps of air she felt as if she was suffocating. Trembling, suffocating, but still needing to be certain he was truly gone. Diana staggered to the window and watched with grateful relief as he got into his car and drove away with a squeal of tires and flagrant disregard of the stop sign on the corner.

The monster was gone . . . for now.

Without even grabbing a jacket before venturing into the icy November air, Diana started out the door of her apartment to run to the Two Lanterns to warn Sam. Earlier she had opened the door to an almost familiar stranger, and he had caused silent terror; now as she opened the door and saw a hauntingly familiar form through the blur of her tears, she screamed.

But it was Sam, not his father, and suddenly his strong, gentle arms were around her, holding her as she sobbed, and her terror was magically vanquished. She was with Sam, wrapped in the gentle wonder of their love, and she felt so safe.

"Diana, my darling, what's wrong?" Sam asked as her sobs quieted. He feared the answer; he had seen the bewildered terror in her lovely eyes. "Diana?"

"Your father was here."

That night Diana learned that not all the scars on Sam's body were from years of battle on the football field. Most were the result of another war, a lifetime spent living with a violent and irrational father. Sam's deepest scars, some visible, some not, were vestiges of unexpected and unpredictable outbursts of violence that were triggered by nothing except that in his father's warped mind Sam had done something deserving of punishment.

"For a very long time, Diana, I tried to figure out what I was doing wrong, what I had done to anger him and how to prevent his rage."

"But you weren't doing anything wrong."

"No. I did everything he wanted me to do. His dream was to be a great football star, but he never was, so he transferred the dream to me. And I fulfilled that dream for him, until now. Until now, until this act of defiance, I was a model son." *And still . . .*

"The night you were supposed to sing at the hospital the first time," Diana whispered softly. How well she remembered that night, her anger alternating with concern, Sam's apology without explanation and his cloudy eyes and face that looked like death even four days later.

"That night . . . I called you as soon as I could."

"Oh, Sam. But you insisted on rescheduling for three weeks later." *Even though you weren't certain the same inexplicable thing would happen again.*

"Why?"

"Because of you. And the children. And me. I have no idea why my fathr didn't want me to do the concert at the hospital the first time. Three weeks later he thought it was great. He was—is—completely irrational. He always has been. My mother tried to protect me from him when I was little, but she was a victim, too."

"Was he driving the car when she died?"

"No. *She* was. He was chasing us. I was six and I had done something, walked in the room or didn't, spoke or didn't . . . who knows? Anyway he went after me and she tried to intervene. He turned on her, but somehow she grabbed the car keys and me and we tried to escape." Sam sighed softly. "I remember that drive so well. It only lasted five or six minutes, but she kept telling me over and over that she loved me and that we weren't going back and that we would be together, away from him, forever. I knew we were going to crash and I wasn't afraid because I knew we would go to heaven, she and I, and we would never see him again. But only *she* went to heaven."

And you spent your life in a living hell, Diana thought as her heart filled with a new and powerful emotion: *rage*.

"Oh, Diana, how did he know about you?" Sam asked with obvious anguish. He had loved her in high school, and even though he never imagined a future with her—a future at all—Sam kept their precious love hidden, a secret and most wonderful part of his life that his father could never touch, never contaminate, never destroy. "He was never very interested in my social life, except for occasional vulgar locker-room teases about sex, but still I didn't want him to know anything about you. Even though I was in love with you that spring, I dated other girls and went to the parties with my crowd."

"But you took me to the prom."

"Yes. Our first and last date. I planned to tell him I was taking someone else, if he asked, but he never did. Until tonight I believed he knew nothing about you. But he must have found out afterward. He must have made a point of finding out."

Diana thought about the night of the prom, when Sam had arrived forty-five minutes late, and his body stiffened as if in great pain.

"He must have made a point of finding out because he sensed it was important to you, because you went out that night even though . . ." Diana fought the sudden emotion in her throat and finally whispered gently, "Tell me what happened."

"What happened, my beautiful Diana, was that I wanted to make love with you, but I couldn't." On that starry night Sam's ribs had been broken and every breath felt like a white-hot poker stabbing into his chest. Sam couldn't make love to Diana that night, but he had to see her, one last time, because she had been a beacon of happiness in the storm of his life.

But I can make love with you now, my darling, Sam thought. *And that's what I want . . . one final gentle night of love before I must leave you forever.*

Their loving that night was different, confident and not desperate, as if it had been the dark secret of Sam's father that had always made it so furtive. They loved slowly that night, so gently, so tenderly . . . the leisurely unhurried loving of a love that would last forever.

But in the morning, as dawn lightened the dark November sky, Sam held her and spoke the words he knew he must speak.

"I have to go, Diana."

"Go?" she echoed with soft surprise. Then, comprehending, she added quietly, "Oh, you're going to see him, aren't you? You're going to tell him that you will never return to football, no matter what he wants, and you're going to warn him that if he ever bothers us again we will call the police."

"Oh, my love, I wish it were so easy. My father is not afraid of the police."

"No, Sam, it was after I threatened to call them that he left."

Sam smiled lovingly at her. Diana's belief in goodness was so strong, her joyous heart so loving, that now she was choosing to deny what had really happened. She had told him every terrifying detail—including the way his father scoffed at her threat to call the police—but now she was softening her memory, as the memory of a frightening nightmare blurs with the light of day, because the evil of his violent father was such an aberration that she could not, or would not, believe it was real.

134 But even if lovely Diana chose to soften the memory—and Sam wished someday she would forget it altogether—he would never forget her terror, or her gasping sobs, or the disbelief in her lovely eyes as she stared at the ugly bruises on her arms where his father had so brutally held her.

Sam knew the true danger of his father. He knew that his search for the son who had finally defied him would be relentless. His father would be like an animal stalking his prey, but, unlike an animal, and far more menacing, once his father found him he would shadow his life, as he always had, appearing in the middle of the night to cause terror and deriving great pleasure from the power of the torment. The threat would be constant, punctuated by flurries of violence, and someday, as it had been for the loving mother who had believed they could escape, the violence might once again be lethal. Someday the father, whose fragile control on his rage became more tenuous as he got older, might arrive with the guns and knives that were his prized possessions.

Sam was not afraid of his father. There had been times in his life, many times, when the fear of life was far greater than the fear of death. If he could stay with Diana, live their love and have their children, and know that when his father returned he could simply give his own life to protect his love and their babies, he would have stayed.

But Sam knew that wasn't possible. He would not ask her to live a life clouded with fear, much less a life in which physical harm might come to her and their babies. He wanted only happiness and joy for lovely Diana. Which meant that as long as his father was alive, their love could never be.

"Darling Diana, my father left because he decided to leave," Sam told her gently. "Not because you threatened to call the police."

"So you're not going to see him?"

"No." *Because if I saw him now I might kill him*, Sam thought, hating the thought but fearing that the image of Diana's terror and her bruises might compel him to fight back as he never had before. It wasn't cowardice or fear of death that prevented him from greeting violence with violence. It was the fact that that would make him no better than his father, and it might be proof of what Sam feared the most, that some part of his father's madness, some trace of his poison, flowed in his veins.

"Then where are you going?"

"I'm not sure. I just need to get far away from you, and then call him, tell him where I am, and make him think that's where I've been ever since I left Los Angeles."

"Then you'll come back here."

"No, my precious love, I'm never coming back. I can't. Don't you see, darling? Our love isn't safe. You have to forget about me, Diana. You have to find a safe and joyous love and be happy."

"Sam, *you* are my love! Our love is stronger than your father! I'm willing to take the risk."

"But I'm not willing to take it for you."

Sam left, as he had left once before, with a sad and solemn vow that they would never see each other again. But, just as before, Diana didn't believe him.

She knew Sam would return to her and their love. She knew it even before the wonderful discovery that their final night of loving had created a new little life. Their baby, Sam's gift of love, was a memory and a promise. He would come back. He had left a part of him, a joyous living symbol of their love.

"We're very healthy and happy," Diana lovingly assured her parents for the hundredth time during their week-long visit to Boston in June. It was her hundredth reassurance because it was in response to her mother's ninety-ninth pronouncement that she and Diana's father, both eminent archaeologists, were not going on their long-planned dig in North Africa after all because Diana's baby was due in August and they weren't scheduled to be back until September. Diana added with a soft laugh, "Go!"

"It will be very difficult to reach us, Diana."

"I won't need to! Besides, Mother, first babies are often born late, aren't they? I'll probably still be quite pregnant when you return." Diana's voice softened as she spoke of the tiny life growing inside her. "This lively little one and I are going to have a very peaceful summer studying my second-year coursework so we'll have lots of time to play in the fall."

Diana named their daughter Jane, after Sam's mother, as she and Sam had joyfully planned on an autumn afternoon in the Boston Commons.

Janie arrived in early August, an easy delivery, a labor of love, a healthy, happy gift of life. She had Sam's dark-brown eyes and the dark-brown hair of both, and she was beautiful and smiling and soft and such a miracle . . .

"The defect is extremely rare, Diana," the pediatric cardiologist from Massachusetts General Hospital told her when Janie was three days old.

Only three days old, but the small lungs that had been fine at birth were suddenly struggling valiantly for air!

The doctor explained what was wrong with Janie's tiny heart and Diana understood perfectly because she had received honors grades in anatomy and physiology and embryology—in all her freshman classes at Harvard Medical School.

"So she'll need surgery," Diana said firmly.

"There's . . ." *Nothing we can do.* "There isn't a surgical procedure for this anomaly, Diana. I'm so sorry."

Diana understood those painful words perfectly, too. Her lovely Janie needed a new heart, and medical science could not give her one. Heart transplantation in adults was quite new, and quite disappointing, and even in the centers where transplants were still done, transplantation in a neonate was unheard of.

Medical science had nothing to offer Diana's infant daughter. The heart that she and Sam had given their precious child of love was broken and could not be fixed.

Janie spent the only month of her life in the small apartment on Hilliard where her mother and father had loved. There was still such love in that apartment! Diana held her little daughter, kissing her, loving her, whispering words of love.

"I love you my little Janie, oh my little girl, I love you so much."

Diana whispered soft, soothing words of love and she told Janie about her wonderful daddy and they listened to Sam's tapes over and over.

And Diana sang to her. And for that month of love Diana—who loved music but had never been able to carry a tune—sang with perfect pitch.

Janie died in Diana's arms, a peaceful death, a final breath and then no more.

Diana's parents arrived in Boston two days after their granddaughter's death. The happy letter Diana had written the day after Janie's birth reached their remote camp in Africa just before they began their journey home. Diana's parents gently, then urgently, tried to convince their beloved daughter to take time off from medical school and return to Dallas with them.

But Diana insisted that she was fine. She encircled her heart with a wall of steel, resumed her classes, and for the second year in a row received honors in all courses. She insisted that she was fine, even though the joy was gone from her sapphire eyes and her lovely face was taut, and so wary, ever vigilant, as if on guard for further pain. For the first year following Janie's death, Diana didn't allow herself to think, or grieve, or acknowledge the wish that was the only glimmer of hope in her dying heart—the desperate wish that Sam would return.

On the September night that marked the first anniversary of Janie's death, Diana sat in the darkness of the apartment where such great love had lived and died. The darkness was silent at first, but after an hour or two, without even thinking about what she was doing, Diana began to listen to one of the tapes of love Sam had made for her.

Then the darkness was no longer silent, and sometime later, the sound of love songs was interrupted by the ring of her telephone.

"Hello, Diana."

"Sam." She hadn't cried until now, hadn't allowed it, but the warmth and gentleness of his voice cradled her, as if he was there with her and she was safe in his arms, and he was rescuing her from the pain that had been too painful even to admit. Diana closed her eyes in the darkness and allowed herself to be enveloped by his gentle voice and the memory of the loving eyes. "Where are you?"

"In London. I've been here ever since I left Boston."

"Have you seen your father?"

"I've talked to him," Sam replied quietly.

He had called his father the moment he arrived in London, and, at first, as weeks passed and his father didn't appear, Sam's heart filled with the wonderful hope that it was over, that his father realized his son would no longer be his victim. But then the calls began, some threatening and crazy, some terrifyingly normal and almost fatherly. Those calls, the almost normal ones, were the ones that shattered all hope. Because as he listened to the questions about his personal life, his *women*, Sam knew that his father's madness had not abated, nor had his rage at his defiant son. His father was simply searching for other ways to punish Sam, a cowardly bully searching for more fragile victims.

His father's madness had not abated. In fact, Sam realized, it had become worse, more calculating, a time bomb still, ticking, ticking. Every sound, even the sounds of silence between calls, underscored the solitary life Sam was destined to lead, *must* lead.

But still he thought about Diana every day and night, missing her, loving her, fighting the powerful need just to hear her voice. For almost two years he had resisted—because what was the point in calling?—but tonight his heart had won the constant battle. Tonight he felt a strong, invisible tug, as if she needed him, too . . . but of course it was just his own need.

Perhaps he needed to hear that she was happy, that she had found a safe and joyous love. Perhaps if he knew that, he could stop dreaming about a time that could never be, a time when their love could live in more than dreams and memories and songs of love.

"Nothing has changed, Diana," Sam whispered finally, softly, his gentle voice filled with sadness.

"You're not coming back?"

"No. I just wanted to see how you are . . ." His words faded because they sounded so feeble, such a tiny corner of what he really wanted.

"I'm fine, Sam." Diana's voice was suddenly strong as she reflexively spoke the words she had spoken for the past year to anyone who dared be concerned about her.

"How is medical school?"

"It's good. I began my clinical clerkships early so I'll actually be graduating a year early."

"Just like college. Brilliant Diana," Sam whispered softly, so proud of the woman he loved. What a wonderful doctor Diana would be, what joy she would share, what good she would do with her bright mind and loving heart. How often he had wondered, in thoughts that were more dreams than reality, if he and Diana could live a hidden life of love. But she would have to give up so much, and even then there was no guarantee that his father wouldn't find them, and he wanted her to give up nothing.

Sam knew what he could offer Diana—his love, his heart, his life . . . and a lifetime of fear. He wished so much more for her! He knew, an aching knowledge, that there would be other men, safe loves, who would love her and give her all the happiness and joy she deserved.

"What about you, Sam?" Diana asked after several moments, her voice softening in response to his, and softening, too, because she loved him still, always, even though he wasn't coming back to her. "How are you?"

"I'm fine, too," he lied softly.

"Are you singing?"

"Yes. In pubs." Sam paused and then added quietly, with a trace of disbelief, "And a month ago I signed a two-album contract with BMI."

"Oh, Sam. That's wonderful." Diana smiled lovingly as she imagined the dark-brown eyes she loved so much, uncertain eyes, even though he was so special, because his lifetime of punishment had taught him that no matter how much he excelled or achieved, he was still flawed and unworthy.

"The first album will be released next summer."

"Will I be able to get a copy, a hundred copies?"

I'll send you one. I'll bring you one. Sam fought the wonderful thought. He knew this was the last time he could call her. She had been waiting for him, even though he had told her not to, because she remembered the last time he had said good-bye and then appeared three years later. Tonight, before they said good-bye, he needed to be sure that she understood there could be no future for their love.

"Yes, if you want to," Sam answered after a moment. "The album will be released simultaneously in North America and the U.K."

"They think it's going to do well, don't they?"

"That's what they think."

"And it will. I'll just have to get my copies before they sell out. I'm very proud of you, Sam."

"I'm very proud of you, too, Diana."

Diana's heart filled with new hope at the gentleness of his voice. For the past few moments they had been discussing their dreams. The last two years had vanished, and they were together again, dreaming together, sharing the greatest dream, their lifetime of love.

"Please come back to me, Sam."

"I can't, darling. I can't."

"You mean you don't want to," Diana whispered as the hope faded and anger rushed in to fill the sudden void.

"Oh, Diana, I want to. I love you so—"

"Love? You don't love me Sam, not really! When you love someone you don't leave them. You make plans to spend your life with them—you *do* spend your life with them—and nothing else matters." *If you had loved me you would have been with me, loving our baby with me, loving her and holding her, and then we would have held each other after she died . . .* "You don't tell someone you love them and then vanish for no reason."

For no reason. Sam ached at the words. He missed her desperately, every second of his life, but never, not even for a second, did he doubt his decision to leave her. Diana still didn't understand the true lethal danger of his father, and that meant she didn't understand, either, that he left her because he loved her so much—too much.

"My God, Diana," Sam whispered. "Please don't ever believe I don't love you with all my heart."

The anguished emotion in his voice stopped her anger, or perhaps it was time for the anger to stop. For the past year the steel wall around her heart had kept her emotions locked away. But tonight, the impenetrable fortress had come tumbling down, and the emotions had spilled out, a tumbling cascade over which she had so little control. The emotions spilled, falling one on top of the other—love . . . anger . . . sadness.

But Diana wanted control, just a little, because she wanted only love on this night with Sam. She would have a lifetime to live with sadness and anger . . . and the bitter truth that Sam didn't love her enough to find a way back to her. For now she clung to the softness of his voice, allowing herself to be wrapped for a final time in its warmth, feeling safe and loved. Because Sam *had* loved her—just not enough—and that wasn't his fault. She needed to live in his love now, whatever he could give her, for as long as it was there.

They talked for almost three hours, talking and sharing the silences, both knowing the good-bye would come, both wanting the gentleness to last forever. There was even laughter in the darkness, small bursts filled with surprise because it had been so long since either had laughed.

And then, when they knew it was almost time to say good-bye, there was such gentleness and Sam asked the question he had been wanting to ask ever since he realized that his lovely Diana doubted his love.

"Will you listen to my songs, Diana?" he asked, his voice soft and calm even though he desperately needed to hear her answer "Yes." Diana didn't understand the true danger his father posed, and he hadn't wanted to spend these precious hours giving her the details of horror that would convince even her lovely heart. But he wanted to convince her of his love, to make her believe how much she had been loved so that she could carry that confidence to her future loves. If she listened to his songs of love, songs that would always and only be written to her, then she would know.

"Yes, of course, Sam. You know I will."

Twenty minutes later they said a final good-bye. And then the warmth was suddenly gone, as if it had never been there, and she was alone in the cold darkness of her apartment and her unprotected heart screamed with pain as she confronted the harsh, bitter truth . . .

Sam had loved her, but not enough, and she was alone.

Sometime before the dawn lightened the autumn sky, Diana calmly removed the tape from the cassette player and gathered all the other tapes Sam had made for her. She didn't rip the once-precious tapes into a thousand pieces, because she felt sadness, not rage. Instead she simply put them in the trash in the basement of the apartment building. Then, as daylight broke, shattering the once-enveloping darkness and erasing even the shadowy memory of the gentle voice an ocean away, Diana put the wall of steel back around her heart . . . where it belonged.

"What a tragedy. This was going to be Sam Hunter's year to win the national championship."

"Something happened to Coach Hunter?"

"Yes. Haven't you heard? He was killed yesterday."

"Killed?"

The two male medical residents who were discussing the shocking news about the nation's top football coach turned in the direction of the soft female voice that had echoed *killed?*

All three were in the nurses" station on the Bullfinch Ward at Massachusetts General Hospital. Diana was in the fourth year of her surgical residency and had been asked to consult on a patient with possible cholecystitis on the general medical ward. It was late November, six years since Sam had left, and four years since the late-night call.

"Killed," one of the medical residents confirmed.

"Do they know who killed him?" Diana asked quietly. The death of Sam's father would not be a tragedy unless somehow *her* Sam was involved.

"Sure. It was one of his assistant coaches. I saw the poor guy interviewed this morning. He feels terrible, of course, but it was an accident."

"An accident?"

"They were all hunting together."

"Oh, I see," Diana whispered with relief, and not an ounce of guilt. She was a doctor, devoted to saving lives, committed by a solemn oath to life's sanctity, but she greeted the news of the death of the monster with hope that was almost joy.

Our love is safe now, Sam. If you love me, you will come back to me.

But Sam never returned. He could have found her easily because she remained in the apartment on Hilliard throughout her surgical residency at Mass General. Why did she stay in that place where so much had died? Was she waiting for Sam? Or was the effort of living her life, merely moving from day to day, already great enough that she simply didn't have the energy to find a new place to live?

Diana didn't analyze. She simply survived. She gave up her dream of being a pediatrician without thinking about why and set her brilliant mind to becoming a heart surgeon and inventing hearts that would save precious little lives without thinking about why, either.

Of course she would listen to his songs, Diana had told Sam in the darkness of night when she was wrapped in the warm gentleness of his voice. But it was a promise that could not survive the harsh light of day. Once Diana's heart had filled with joy at the sound of music. But now music, all music, triggered painful reminders of all she had loved . . . and all she had lost. And she listened no more.

The world heard Sam Hunter's magnificent songs of love, but Diana never did. If she had been listening, she would have known that he had loved her too much not to leave her, that he wished more for her than what his love might bring. Diana would have known of Sam's magnificent love, and, after his father died, she would have heard the most beautiful love songs of all, songs that called to her by name, in lyrics gift-wrapped in tender hope, gentle pleas for her to come to him if she loved him still.

If she loved him still. Most of Sam believed that in all the years they had been apart Diana had surely found a new love. He had wished love for her and had told her not to wait for the love that might never be. And that was why he reached out to her with his music, and not his loving arms, because it had been so many years, too many years, simply to appear on her doorstep, a confusing bittersweet memory from her past. If she loved him still, if by some miracle she had not found a new love, she would hear his songs and let him know. And whether she heard and no longer wanted him, or wasn't listening because she had found someone new, Diana's silence gave him his answer.

Eventually, as the hope faded in silence, the love songs written by Sam Hunter had a new theme, a sad theme, the poignant and poetic farewell to a great love that once had been but was no longer.

For a very long time Diana's heart was numb. Then it was ice. And finally, defiantly, her cold heart strained for a little warmth, even a few flickers. She allowed visitors into her heart, but she would not permit the visitors to find a home there.

Until Chase. Diana welcomed Chase into her heart. She even believed that she had given him all of it. Then Chase told her he wanted children, and Diana realized there was a part of her heart that she could not give. There was a part that would belong always and only to Sam and Janie. When Chase trespassed on that precious part, their love was over.

Diana's private life was filled with failure, but her professional life overflowed with great success. She invented a new heart, a magnificent creation that would save small lives—like the life of her precious daughter whom she had been unable to save—and the world sang her praises and crowned her the brilliant and beautiful Queen of Hearts.

As if hearts were her kingdom. As if she had some special knowledge about their mysteries and was an expert on love.

Queen of Hearts. How she hated the name! It was so wrong, so very wrong . . .

Because she had failed in her love with Sam and with Chase.

And because she had failed, the greatest failure of all, to save the life of her beloved Janie.

Part Three

Chapter 16

JOHN F. KENNEDY INTERNATIONAL AIRPORT
SEPTEMBER 1989

Something pulled Diana from the memories of Sam and Janie in time to catch her flight to London. As she rushed to the plane that would carry her to the luxurious three-week vacation in Europe Diana wondered why she was travelling at all. What was the point? The necessary journey was in her heart. She wouldn't even notice her splendid surroundings.

Diana's preassigned seat in first class was 2B, a nonsmoking seat on the aisle. Jeffrey Lawrence was in 2A.

"Doctor."

Jeffrey's greeting was polite, civil, without the trace of a taunt. Diana steeled herself for a haughty reminder of their last encounter and her "unacceptable" behavior, but his handsome face was solemn and nonjudgmental. And there was something else in the dark-blue eyes.

No doubt the famous anchor had seen grisly footage and heard grim reports that had not been shared with the world. Was it the vivid memory of those unspeakable horrors that darkened his eyes still, despite the hope for peace?

No, Diana decided. The turbulence in the ocean-blue depths was quite a different pain, quite a private pain.

Diana responded instinctively with a wish to help but not to intrude. She smiled a soft smile, a flicker of warmth, and said with a gentle lilt, "Hello, Anchor."

Diana would have said more, would have given Jeffrey the apology she owed him, but as she stowed her carry-on luggage beneath the seat and fastened her seat belt, he looked away, far away, out the window and beyond. And by the time the plane lifted off and Jeffrey withdrew his gaze from the sun-bright sky, Diana had retreated to her own private thoughts.

They didn't speak, but each held books opened in the middle and stared at the words as if riveted by the story even though neither read or even turned a page. Jeffrey drank Scotch, straight, more than one, and Diana sipped champagne. Both declined the gourmet lunch.

You have to apologize to him before you leave the plane, Diana told herself sternly.

As soon as the movie is over, she decided. The cabin would still be dark, nicely shadowed, and soon after, no matter how awkward their words, the plane would land at Heathrow and she would never see him again.

"Mr. Lawrence?"

"Yes?"

"I owe you an apology for what I said to you that evening in your office. It was inexcusable of me to accuse you of breaking your word. I'm very sorry."

"Don't be." After a moment Jeffrey added quietly, "You had a perfectly legitimate excuse."

"I did?"

"Yes, your heart . . ."

Jeffrey didn't finish his sentence because his attention was suddenly distracted by a flight attendant who was standing in the aisle behind Diana.

"Yes?" Jeffrey asked.

"I'm sorry to interrupt. I need to speak with Dr. Shepherd."

"Oh." Diana turned her attention from Jeffrey to the flight attendant. "Yes?"

"We have a medical emergency in the back of the plane. I can page for a doctor over the public address system if you'd rather not get involved. There probably are other doctors on the plane, but we have a passenger list for first class and I noticed your name so I thought . . ."

"It's no problem."

The "patient" was a five-year-old girl with frightened brown eyes and a terrible stomachache. Her name was Becky and she was traveling alone, an "unaccompanied minor" returning home to her mummy in London after spending a month in the States with her father.

"Hello, Becky." Diana knelt in the aisle beside the little girl and smiled reassuringly at the frightened eyes. "My name is Dr. Shepherd and I'm here to help you. OK?"

"OK," Becky agreed softly.

"Good. Your stomach hurts?"

Becky nodded.

"Can you show me where?"

It took Diana only a few minutes of quiet conversation and very gentle physical examination to make the most probable diagnosis.

"I need to speak with the pilot," Diana told the flight attendant when she was finished. "And could you arrange for me to sit beside Becky for the rest of the flight?"

"Of course. The plane's full, but I can work something out."

"Why don't you put her in my seat and I'll sit here?"

"Oh." Diana turned in the direction of his voice. She hadn't realized until then that Jeffrey had followed her to the back of the plane. "That would be very nice. Thank you."

"Should I carry her up front?" Jeffrey asked.

"Yes, please." Diana smiled and added softly, "Thank you, Jeffrey."

"Hi, Becky." Jeffrey knelt as Diana had so that he was level with the dark-brown eyes. Dark-brown eyes that bravely fought tears. Dark-brown eyes that reminded him of a little girl he didn't know but had wanted so very much to get to know. "Don't be afraid, honey. I know for a fact that Dr. Shepherd is one of the best doctors in the world. If I was sick I would want her to take care of me. I'm going to carry you to the front of the plane so she can keep an eye on you until we land. OK?"

Diana listened to the conversation and was impressed by Jeffrey's gentleness. She remembered the famous Beirut episode and guessed that he had an instinctive love for children, as she did. And there was something else they had in common, something in the depths of the dark-blue eyes, a ripple of excruciating sadness despite the smile for Becky.

There was something about little girls with dark-brown eyes that caused them both great pain.

Jeffrey and the flight attendant settled Becky in his seat and Jeffrey sat beside her until Diana returned from the cockpit. He vacated the seat as soon as Diana appeared and she walked with him as far as the galley that separated first class from coach.

"I think it's appendicitis," she explained to Jeffrey as moments before she had told the pilot. "The history is classic. Her abdomen is soft, which is a good sign. The appendix probably hasn't ruptured. There will be an ambulance waiting at Heathrow and a surgical team available at a nearby hospital when we arrive."

Diana sat beside Becky, talking softly and reassuring her as her experienced eyes and hands subtly monitored the girl's vital signs—the color and temperature of her skin, her respiratory rate, the radial pulse in her small wrist.

The ambulance was waiting when the plane landed and the medics and Becky's mother boarded as soon as the door was opened. Diana provided concise information to the medics, reassured Becky's anxious mother, and because the tiny veins had gone into hiding and Becky trusted her, Diana expertly inserted the necessary large-bore intravenous needle into her small forearm.

"Will you do the surgery, Dr. Shepherd?" Becky's mother asked.

"Oh! No . . ."

It wasn't just the red tape of licensure and the sticky politics of arriving at an unknown hospital and doing a cameo. Diana had operated, command performances, in operating rooms throughout the world. But those were heart surgeries and this was an appendix. Diana hadn't done abdominal surgery in years.

"You don't operate on children?"

"Only heart surgery. This surgery needs to be done by a general surgeon. It's much better for Becky."

By the time the IV was in and Becky was on the stretcher, the other passengers had long since disembarked. Except for Jeffrey. He had returned to the first class cabin to get his carry-on luggage but waited until Diana was ready to leave. Then he gathered her bag, too, and carried it for her as they walked to baggage claim and Customs.

"Where are you staying, Diana?"

"The Dorchester."

"So am I. Shall we share a cab into town?"

"Oh. Sure."

It was a silent cab ride. Both Jeffrey and Diana had been running on empty before all the worry about the little girl with dark-brown eyes. Both were exhausted, too tired to summon the energy to chatter gaily about the sights of London as they sped past them. They rode in silence, but unlike earlier, the silence now was almost comfortable, almost comfortable enough for Diana to break the peaceful stillness to ask Jeffrey to finish the sentence that had been interrupted by the flight attendant. Almost comfortable enough to ask, *What was my legitimate excuse, Jeffrey?*

But Diana didn't ask. She and Jeffrey were both very tired and there had been such sadness in his eyes before when he had started to tell her. Better to leave it alone. Better just to say good-bye to Jeffrey Lawrence with a final thank-you and a warm smile.

Jeffrey couldn't sleep. Perhaps he should not even have tried. It was early evening and the outside world was only just beginning to fade into darkness. But he had barely slept all week, and last night in his apartment in Manhattan he hadn't slept at all.

After a frustrating hour, he gave up. He showered, dressed, and began to review the notes he had brought for his reporting of the peace conference. Tomorrow he would spend the day at the network's London bureau going over a detailed plan for the coverage of the historic summit.

But he didn't need to review his notes. He knew precisely what he wanted—the maps, the graphics, the time-lines, the photographs of leaders and hostages—and he knew the history of the conflict. In the years he had lived in the center of the fire, and in the years since, he had spent long hours thinking about the eventual peace.

He put down his notes and poured himself a large glass of Scotch from a crystal decanter. The alcohol burned his empty stomach, a deep, sizzling sear.

Too much Scotch. Too little food. Too many nerves. Too much pain.

And nothing he could do to ease the pain.

I should never have married you. For over twenty-four hours the devastating words had echoed in his brain. Jeffrey couldn't banish Julia's words, the truth at last, from his memory. He would have to live with the harsh echoes and excruciating pain, a fragile creature without a shell, raw, exposed, hoping to heal swiftly but knowing it would take a very long time.

Jeffrey paced restlessly in his elegant suite and finally, on a sudden impulse, called the hospital where Becky had been taken. After that call, he made a second and even more impulsive call.

"Diana, it's Jeffrey. Are you awake?"

"Yes!" Diana laughed softly. "I'm too tired to sleep."

"I'm the same. I do have some good news. Becky is out of surgery and doing well. It was exactly what you predicte—appendicitis without rupture."

"Oh, good. Thank you for checking. I was just about to call myself."

"Are you in the mood for dinner?"

"Sure. I guess."

"Is that a definite no?"

"It's a definite yes. But you need to know that in addition to being too tired to sleep, I'm too hungry to eat."

"Would you like something to drink?" Jeffrey asked when they were seated beneath the mirrored ceiling in the Bar, the Dorchester's cheery blue-and-white-tiled restaurant.

"Just milk."

"Warm?"

"Maybe later."

Jeffrey ordered two milks. When the drinks arrived he raised his glass and she raised hers, and as the crystal touched in a gentle chime, it was Diana who whispered the toast.

"To peace." She tilted her head and embellished softly as she watched his eyes, "To world peace and to private peace."

"To world peace and to private peace."

Jeffrey held her gaze, smiled a wistful smile, and felt an astonishing impulse to tell her about Julia. Astonishing because his love was so very private.

Why would I be tempted to share the truths I have never told another soul with Diana who I don't even know? Is it because I was an unwitting witness to the death of her love and now fate has made her an unwitting witness to the death of mine? Is it because the sapphire eyes are sending a promise that they will be very gentle with the secrets of my heart? Or is it because on the same day in November thirty-six years ago . . .

It's probably because I'm so damned exhausted and maybe still a little drunk.

As Jeffrey fought the astonishing impulse to tell Diana everything, Diana waged a similar silent battle. Why on earth would she be tempted to tell stunningly successful Jeffrey Lawrence about the failures of her life?

Because I think he would understand. And because I think he would be gentle.

Jeffrey and Diana suppressed the remarkable impulses and spent the next thirty minutes discussing the historic peace conference and what Jeffrey thought and hoped it might mean. And then they shifted to her reason for being in London.

"Business or pleasure?" When Diana didn't answer right away and he saw sapphire confusion, Jeffrey pushed gently, "Doctor?"

"That's a surprisingly tough question, Anchor. Neither business nor pleasure, I guess."

"What then?"

"I'm here to spend the next three weeks trying to make sense of the first thirty-six years of my life."

"Oh, that."

"Yes." She laughed softly. "*That.*"

Diana didn't elaborate on her personal journey—even though the gentleness in his eyes and voice gave the carefully suppressed impulses sudden life and energy. Instead she gave him a detailed description of her luxury vacation, the cities she would visit and the fabulous hotels where she would stay—the Ritz in Paris, Loew's in Monte Carlo, the Lord Byron in Rome, the Excelsior in Florence, the Cipriani in Venice.

"And then, two weeks from Sunday, a five-day cruise through the Greek Isles."

"Wonderful," Jeffrey said quietly as Diana finished reciting the details of her itinerary. It *was* wonderful—almost precisely what he would have chosen for the honeymoon he had always promised Julia.

"What was my legitimate excuse for insulting you in your office that evening, Jeffrey?"

Dinner was over and they were almost done with the warm milk Jeffrey had ordered as a nightcap and Diana decided simply to ask. At first she wasn't sure he would answer. His dark-blue eyes deepened a shade, and the anguished pain she had seen earlier surfaced from the depths. Diana was about to withdraw the too private and too painful question when he spoke.

"Your heart was breaking." Jeffrey gave a shaky smile and added quietly, "Not that I'm an expert on broken hearts."

"No?"

"No. Only a novice. But what about you, Diana? Surely you've reviewed the world's literature on the subject. What do the great medical minds have to say?"

"They are strangely silent."

"But what do you think? Can a broken heart be mended?"

"I think it mends itself in time."

"As good as new? Or even better, like a broken bone? When I fractured my collarbone three years ago, the doctors said the healed bone would be stronger than before."

"I don't think a mended heart is ever as good as new because the scar never

goes away. But a mended heart may be tougher, more wary." Diana frowned slightly. "I'm not sure that being tougher is better for a heart."

"Except that it won't break again."

"Oh, but it will. Perhaps it won't break in exactly the same place, because the scar there is strong, but the heart is made of a thousand fragile places."

So, Jeffrey Lawrence, she thought, *when you finally heal from the anguish that is tormenting you now, and if you allow yourself to love again, the pain can happen all over.*

Diana knew they were dancing very close to the heart and that it was a dangerous dance for them both, but Jeffrey hadn't withdrawn and she took a chance with another very private question.

"Will you tell me, Jeffrey? I'm not an expert, but I am a little experienced."

"Will you have dinner with me tomorrow night?" Jeffrey answered Diana's question with a question even though the answer that had come to him without hesitation was, *Yes, I will tell you*. He hadn't spoken the words because he couldn't believe them. But the Scotch was long since gone from his body, even though the fatigue wasn't, and he still felt the astonishing impulse to tell her everything, to entrust his shattered heart to the Queen.

The following night as they dined at Tante Claire's, they shared the truths they had never shared before, anguished truths about lost loves and lost daughters.

"You don't really believe your marriage is over, do you, Jeffrey?" Diana asked quietly, after all the painful secrets had been shared and listened to.

"Julia said she should never have married me, Diana."

"She was hurt and angry. People say things in anger that they don't mean."

"Or *do* mean."

"Perhaps in that emotional moment Julia wished she hadn't married you. But ten years ago, Jeffrey, she chose to marry you. And," Diana added softly, "it sounds as though those ten years have been filled with great love."

"I thought so, Diana. I really believed our love was very strong despite Julia's secret."

"I believe that, too, from what you've told me." The words with which Jeffrey described his love were eloquent enough, but they were embellished even more by gentle longing in his eyes and tender pride in his voice. "You *are* going to talk to her, aren't you?"

"I have to. If only to hear everything, if she'll tell me. Maybe if I hear all the painful details I'll be able to hate her."

"I wouldn't count on it."

"You don't hate Sam."

"You mean Chase."

"No, I mean Sam."

"Sam is very ancient history, Jeffrey."

Just as Diana heard Jeffrey's great love for Julia, Jeffrey heard Diana's love still for Sam. Her heart was freshly broken by Chase, but that wound would heal with a scar that was strong and tough. From what Jeffrey had heard and from the way her sapphire eyes softened when she spoke of Sam, he didn't believe there was a scar in the place where Diana's heart had been broken by Sam. Her love for him lived in that place still, soft and gentle and evergreen.

"I somehow feel that the love between you and Sam isn't over."

"Has anyone ever accused you of being an incurable romantic, Jeffrey?"

"Only Julia."

"Sorry. Anyway, it *is* over with Sam. I admit that because of horrors I've seen in trauma rooms of hospitals and even on the nightly news I've come to understand that his father might truly have been dangerous. But even if Sam really did need to leave because of his father, the psychopath died ten years ago. Sam could have come back then, but he chose to stay away. End of story."

"But you don't hate Sam."

"I've tried to. But what was Sam's great crime? That he couldn't love me enough and forever? You know, don't you, Jeffrey Lawrence, where that argument logically ends?"

"Oh, yes." Of course he knew. Jeffrey knew because, like Diana, he was a perfectionist, critical and demanding. And like Diana, he placed the greatest demands and expectations on himself. Jeffrey didn't blame Julia for what had happened to their love, he blamed himself. It was *his* failure to win Julia's heart, not *her* failure to love him. "But, Diana . . ."

"Yes?"

Jeffrey hesitated. Tonight he and Diana had trusted each other with so much and been so gentle with that trust. He wanted her to believe that the words he was going to speak were because he cared very much, but he feared they might offend. Once before he had angered her with an offer of help.

But that was before they were bonded, as they were bonded now, by the secrets of their hearts.

"What, Jeffrey?"

"If you want to spend your life believing it was some failure in you that Sam couldn't love you enough—fine."

"OK." *I will.*

"But, please stop blaming yourself for Janie's death."

"Jeffrey . . ."

"It's time for you to forgive yourself, Diana."

"I think I'd better go home, darling," Julia told Merry at eight on Sunday morning.

They were in their suite adjacent to the Spencers" suite at the Plaza. The day before, the five of them had attended the matinee of Jerome Robbins's *Broadway* at the Imperial Theater and then had an early dinner at the Tavern on the Green. This morning, they were planning brunch in the Plaza's Garden Court and a carriage ride through Central Park before the ballet. Tomorrow they would do more touristy things—the World Trade Center and the Statue of Liberty and the Empire State Building—and return to Southampton in time for a good night's rest before the festivities of Tuesday—Merry's birthday and the gymkhana.

"I'll go home with you, Mommy."

"No, Merry. You stay here and enjoy the rest of the time with the Spencers. I'm just going to curl up in bed and sleep. I want to be completely well when you get home tomorrow afternoon."

I will be completely well because I will have seen Jeffrey and our love will be whole again.

Julia smiled lovingly at her daughter. Merry had been such a trouper yesterday, but Julia had seen occasional waves of unguarded sadness as Merry undoubtedly imagined how much more fun it would have been if only Daddy had been with them.

Daddy will be with us next time, darling, Julia vowed silently. *He has to be.*

"I'm sure it's just the flu, Paige," Julia said when she spoke with her fifteen minutes later.

"Were you ill yesterday, Julia? You didn't look quite right."

"I guess I was getting it yesterday. Today's worse. I'm going to Belvedere, disconnect the phone, and try to sleep it off. May I leave Merry with you?"

"Of course. But, Julia, maybe we should all go back."

"No. I'll be best on my own."

"Do you have nausea?"

"What? Oh, yes," Julia admitted truthfully, one of the few truths of the morning. She had eaten so little in the past few days that her stomach wished never to eat again.

"Julia, maybe you're pregnant."

"Oh, no, Paige. It's not that."

For sixteen years Julia's sleep had been tormented by the recurring nightmare of a fiery explosion in midair followed by a death spiral into the cold, dark sea. At first only her parents lived in the nightmare, but then Jeffrey did, and Merry.

The nightmare didn't vanish with dawn or wakefulness. It was always there, a dreadful fear, and every time Jeffrey flew, Julia fought the vivid lethal images.

Her fear had prevented her from traveling with him, even though he wanted her to, even though it might have made their love stronger.

As Julia boarded the overwater DC-10 she didn't think about the dream-shattering catastrophe above Cartagena sixteen years before, or her terrifying nightmares, or even about the recent tragedies that had befallen DC-10s in Sioux City or Tripoli. She did not remind herself that she was about to be enclosed in a coffin of fire.

Instead she boarded calmly and without fear.

Julia was no longer afraid of flying, because no fear was as great as the fear of losing Jeffrey.

"I figure you're either going to spend the entire afternoon studying the mummies or you couldn't care less."

"Couldn't care less. How about you? Either all day studying the Magna Carta or . . ."

"I thought I'd take a look at the Magna Carta and maybe the mummies." Jeffrey smiled in silent acknowledgment of the issue around which they were skirting. They had decided to spend Sunday afternoon exploring the wonders of the British Museum. That decision had been made together and easily. But each knew it wouldn't be easy to wander through the museum together since each had a different pace and different interests.

"So, Anchor, where should we meet?"

Jeffrey studied his guide book of the museum for a moment then suggested, "How about the Horological Room?"

"The Horological Room?"

"Clocks. Clocks, it says here, invented before and after the pendulum."

"That sounds quite comprehensive. And quite interesting."

"Good. So, clocks at five?"

"Perfect. Cheerio."

Jeffrey saw Diana from a distance at the Elgin Marbles and they peered together at the Rosetta Stone. But that was at three-thirty and he didn't see her again until their five o'clock rendezvous.

Diana arrived a few minutes early. As she wandered from clock to clock, she was enveloped by the ticking. It was so calm, so primal, perhaps like what a baby heard in its mother's womb, the comforting reassuring heartbeat.

At five, as all the clocks struck the hour at the same moment, the comforting ticking gave way to a symphony of sounds.

Chimes. And suddenly Diana was inside "The Chime Song." Each chime spilled onto the next, as Sam had made them do with his talented fingers, layer upon layer, a magnificent cascade of beautiful melodies.

Diana couldn't run. She was in the center of the room surrounded by an invisible wall of music that had become an inescapable prison of memories.

Jeffrey arrived just as the chiming began. He watched the transformation in Diana, her beautiful face losing its soft, bemused smile and freezing into a look of bewildered terror. It all happened very quickly. In a matter of moments the chiming was over and the clocks lapsed again into peaceful, rhythmic ticking. The frenzy was over, calm restored, but Diana was left ravaged.

Jeffrey put his arms around her and held her. After a few moments, he took her hand and led her silently out of the museum and into the late-afternoon sunshine.

"When Sam lived in California," Diana explained when she could finally speak, "he spent Sunday afternoons listening to the chimes in the bell towers of missions. He wrote a song, a canon of all the chimes, one on top of the other . . . it was just like being in the clock room."

"I'm sorry," Jeffrey said quietly.

"I used to play the tape of "'The Chime Song' for Janie when she needed to sleep. How she loved it! She always fell asleep with a look of such peace." Diana's words ended in a tremble and tears filled her sapphire eyes.

"Diana, I'm so sorry."

"It's not your fault. You didn't know. And it didn't occur to me even when I was in the room."

As the taxi turned onto Park Lane, nearing the Dorchester, Julia raised her eyes from the hands that were tightly clasped in her lap and looked out the window to the Sunday afternoon activity in Hyde Park. The sight of frolicking children, nannies pushing carriages, families enjoying the fading rays of the warm autumn sun, and young lovers strolling hand in hand reminded her of the distant Saturday afternoon in Ghirardelli Square that had been the beginning of the love between her and Jeffrey. Julia's heart filled with hope at the lovely memory. Perhaps later, after they talked and their love was whole again, she and Jeffrey could take a romantic walk in the park.

But Jeffrey already was taking a romantic walk in the park.

Jeffrey . . . and Diana Shepherd. Julia recognized the famous heart surgeon from the live press conference in June and from this week's *Time*. During the past week, in the late-night hours when she was alone and awake—missing Jeffrey and worrying about the events of the world—Julia had read the cover story. And she had marveled at the genius of Diana.

And now Jeffrey and Diana were among the Sunday crowd in Hyde Park and they were picture perfect, a stunningly attractive couple strolling together, his arm draped gently over her shoulders, their entire attention focused on each other, listening to the intimate words each whispered and smiling softly as the autumn sun cast their happiness in a golden glow.

As Julia watched, Diana stepped in front of Jeffrey, stopping him. Jeffrey's handsome face came into Julia's full view . . . and it was as if Jeffrey was looking at *her*, gazing at *her* with the gentle tenderness she knew so well and needed so desperately. But today Jeffrey's look of love was for Diana, not for her. And then

Jeffrey did something else that had always been, Julia believed, for her alone—very delicately he touched Diana's face and moved a strand of her dark-brown hair so that he could see her eyes more clearly.

If Julia had discovered Jeffrey making love to Diana, that scene would not have been as devastating to her heart and her love as this intimate scene of tenderness and affection. Julia knew that before she met him, Jeffrey had had many lovers. She knew that he had been able to enjoy the sensual pleasures of sex without the emotion of love. If he had angrily stormed away from Belvedere and into another woman's bed, a frenzied, irrational moment of lust in response to the frenzied, irrational words she had hurled at him, she would have been terribly hurt, but their love might have survived.

But what she witnessed now in Hyde Park wasn't lust. It was tenderness, affection, *love*. Julia knew the look and feel of Jeffrey's love, and now she saw him look at Diana and touch Diana the same gentle, loving way.

The love between Jeffrey and the talented and famous Queen of Hearts wasn't even a new love, Julia realized with anguished sadness. There was such familiarity in their intimacy.

How long had they been lovers? Was their affair the real reason that the dinners that Edmund and Paige so resolutely tried to arrange kept getting mysteriously canceled at the last minute? Was Jeffrey the reason that Diana's marriage to Chase had ended?

Julia remembered the night in June when Jeffrey had returned late after his interview with Diana. He had been troubled that night, a quiet uncertain despair, and he had needed her so urgently.

Had he, on the eve of the announcement of Diana's divorce, suddenly been torn between his two loves? Or had he and Diana truly just met on that night, but had he known immediately that there was something special between them, as ten years ago he had fallen so swiftly in love with *her?*

Ten years ago, Julia's lonely and innocent heart had made a gentle plea, *Please love me for as long as you can.* And over the years, urged by the gentleness of his eyes and his words and his touch and his smile—gentleness Julia now saw for Diana—she had believed in Jeffrey's love and in her own ability to hold it.

She had actually become confident of Jeffrey's wonderful love. Confident enough to believe that their bountiful love would overflow to their daughter. Confident enough to ask Jeffrey to take time from his important dream to begin to live her dream that they would be a family.

As she watched the tender intimacy between Jeffrey and Diana in Hyde Park, Julia felt her dreams die—all her dreams, her own dream of love with Jeffrey and her dream of his love for their daughter.

There was a time, before she knew she was pregnant, when she might have been willing to share Jeffrey's love with another woman. Perhaps even now, if hers was the only heart involved, she might have lived with Jeffrey's betrayal. Or perhaps not; because hadn't the unloved little girl become a woman who believed in herself and her own generous gifts of love?

It didn't matter what she might have done, because hers was not the only heart involved. Her lovely Merry had waited so patiently for her father's love.

Julia had believed with all her heart that someday Jeffrey would love his daughter. She had believed in him, and she had believed, too, that his great love for her would spill over to the child of their magnificent love.

But their love wasn't so magnificent, so bountiful, after all.

The dreams were over. Julia would not allow any more disappointment for the sensitive little girl who had waited so patiently for a father's love that would never be.

Hours before, she had boarded an airplane with resolute calm. Now, with the powerful determination of a mother bear driven by the deepest instincts of love to protect her precious cub from further harm, she quietly instructed the taxi driver not to stop at the Dorchester but to return to Heathrow instead.

Jeffrey had put his arm around Diana's shoulders because she had become very quiet again as she lapsed into painful memories of the infant girl who had loved the chimes. She had smiled a wobbly, grateful smile when Jeffrey touched her, and he kept her focused on the present with a question.

"Are you having dinner with me tonight?"

"You don't think it would be too much of a drag to appear in public with a teary woman?"

"Actually, I was thinking about dinner in my suite because I'll probably be getting calls from the bureau all evening. Thus," he continued with a soft tease, "begging the issue of being seen in public with a teary woman. Which, for the record, I wouldn't mind at all."

It was then that Diana had stepped in front of him, stopping him, and Jeffrey had gently moved a strand of tear-damp hair from beside her sad sapphire eyes.

"You're a very nice man, Jeffrey Lawrence."

"And you, Dr. Shepherd, are a very lovely lady."

The dinner in Jeffrey's suite was indeed interrupted by many phone calls from the bureau. But the calls didn't interrupt animated conversation, only thoughtful silence. Jeffrey and Diana were quiet, reflective, because they knew they were saying good-bye. Diana was flying to Paris in the morning and Jeffrey was beginning his coverage of the peace conference.

The surprising, wonderful interlude, the magical weekend suspended in time and untethered to the cautious rules that had guided their private lives, was coming to an end. But there were important legacies. Each felt more hopeful. The dark secrets had been exposed to the deep golden rays of the autumn sun and that gentle glow somehow made the secrets less menacing and less able to destroy.

Each would go on.

Diana would continue the journey into her past. And even though Jeffrey would no longer be there to guide her away from the consuming infernos of self-blame, he had taught her not to fall into those traps. Diana would remember his wise and gentle lessons and be kind to herself.

And Jeffrey would talk to Julia and try to save their precious love. Because of Diana's encouragement and hopefulness, Jeffrey believed there was a way to make his love strong and whole again. There was a way and he would find it.

When Jeffrey walked Diana back to her suite, he looked at her for a long time before he kissed her.

It was meant to be a good-bye kiss. But even though their hearts had greeted each other with such trust and such joy, Jeffrey and Diana had never even kissed hello. So the kiss became more hello than good-bye, warmer and deeper than either had planned, a tender greeting that came with powerful rushes of desire.

"Not what the doctor ordered?" Jeffrey asked softly when Diana pulled away.

"I don't know, Jeffrey, is it?" Diana had taken her lips from his, but she had not revoked her trust or her confidence that they would be honest with each other always.

"I've never been unfaithful to Julia."

"That doesn't surprise me. You love her very much."

"I've never even thought about being unfaithful before now."

"Despite innumerable opportunities?" she teased lightly. They weren't going to do this. She couldn't and neither could he, and they both knew it.

"Next life?"

"You have a date."

"Be good to yourself, Diana."

"Be good to yourself, too, Jeffrey."

Chapter 17

Jeffrey's fingers trembled and his heart raced as he dialed the number to Belvedere.

It was Tuesday evening. He was in his suite at the Dorchester preparing to write the copy for the broadcast that would go live to the East Coast at midnight.

Tuesday. September twelfth. Merry's tenth birthday.

Jeffrey wanted to wish her happy birthday and tell her how sorry he was that he would miss the gymkhana and promise to spend an afternoon, many afternoons, watching her ride when he returned.

Finally the overseas line connected to the Southampton exchange and Jeffrey heard the distinctive ring, so familiar and so welcoming. For over thirty years that ring had connected Jeffrey to a loving voice.

Please let her soft voice be loving now.

How many times had he called Julia, if only for a minute, just to say, "Hello, Julie, I love you'? How many times had he heard joy in her voice and her soft reply, "I love you, too, Jeffrey'?

What a luxury that had been! *Somehow* he would find a way back to that joyous love.

"Hello?"

Her voice was soft, but so very far away.

"It's me. How are you?"

"Fine."

"Julie, we need to talk." *We*, Jeffrey said gently, even though it was his desperate need, a need made more desperate by the sound of her soft voice. How he needed her. How he needed to love her. How he needed to see love and laughter again in her lavender eyes. "I should be home Saturday."

"I don't think we need to talk, Jeffrey."

"No?" Jeffrey's question was hopeful and wistful. Hopeful. *You mean we don't have to talk, we can just go on with our love?* And wistful. *Shouldn't we talk, darling, once and for all? Shouldn't we expose all the wounds and nurse them tenderly and allow them to heal?* The pain would be greatest for him, hearing about Julia's secret love, but what could be greater than the pain of losing her?

I never loved you, Jeffrey. Those words would cause a greater pain. But Julia would not speak those fateful words because she *had* loved him, *did* love him, didn't she? Their entire love had not been an illusion, had it?

"There's nothing to say, Jeffrey."

"Oh, honey, I think there's a lot to say."

"No, Jeffrey." *I'm not strong enough to hear your gentle, apologetic good-bye.* "It's over."

Julia's voice was small and soft, and their voices were carried into space before they reached each other, but Jeffrey heard the ominous message in her tone with terrifying clarity. It sounded as if she was saying good-bye.

"What's over, Julie?"

Jeffrey held his breath and almost asked the question again because the silence was so long. But finally she spoke, or the devastating words finally made it back from space, having languished longer there, as if they had sensed a home in that black emptiness.

"Our marriage."

"Our marriage? Julia, please tell me why."

"You know why, Jeffrey."

"Tell me." How quickly he had forgotten the lessons he had taught Diana! How quickly the gentle wisdom she had echoed to him when they said good-bye—"Be good to yourself"—had vanished! Now he was asking for more pain. Now he was asking to hear the words he had convinced himself Julia could not utter: *I never loved you, Jeffrey.* "Tell me."

Why was Jeffrey doing this? Julia wondered sadly. Was he testing to see if she knew about his new love? Why couldn't he just be relieved that she had so easily let him be free? Was he still torn, just a little, even though it had been so obvious to Julia that he had already made his choice?

"Julia?"

"Because there is someone else," she whispered finally, her voice hardening to fight her tears. She kept the fragile, icy control by remembering the image of Jeffrey and Diana in Hyde Park, and while she still had the strength of that dream-shattering memory, continued swiftly, "Will you come out on Saturday to get your things? It would be best if we weren't here, so if you could tell me when—"

"There's nothing I need." *Except what I can't have.* There were treasures at Belvedere, priceless treasures, but neither the woman nor the little girl belonged to him.

Sometime in the silence the phone line disconnected. Neither knew who had hung up first, or if the line, sensing the anguished silence, had severed on its own.

As Jeffrey felt the full effect, the staggering emptiness, he thought about the reasons he had called—to find a way back to their wonderful love and to wish Merry happy birthday. He had done neither, and he would never do either again.

He had lost the other half of his heart.

Julia knew her marriage was over the moment she saw Jeffrey with Diana. For the past two days she had prepared herself for the call she knew would come, rehearsing her words, emptying her heart, trying to force numbness where there was so much pain.

But she hadn't been prepared for the gentleness in his voice, the sadness, even though it was he who had found a new love, and it made the pain even worse.

Thirty minutes after the phone call ended, Julia forced herself to move. She had to get ready to go to the stable—the girls were already there—to watch the gymkhana and then birthday dinner at Somerset and then a lifetime of loving

her precious daughter and trying to make up for all the lies. *Daddy loves you, Merry. He is just so terribly busy. His work is very important.*

Fairy tales! Just like the fairy tales Julia had invented to numb the pain of her childhood because her own parents didn't love her. Julia had filled Merry's life and her heart and her hope with the same foolish fantasies. And now, in the years to come, Julia would have to explain gently, lovingly, to her daughter that she had been wrong, and that it was her fault, not Merry's, not Jeffrey's, *her* failure to hold Jeffrey's love.

Jeffrey stared at the wedding band that was a symbol of their love, the intertwined ribbons of white and yellow gold forged together forever by fire. Now the band was simply a glittering symbol of all that he had lost.

Once you put the ring on my finger I will never want to take it off, they had told each other the day before they were married.

Jeffrey never *had* taken it off, and he didn't want to now. But he had to. The pain of seeing it on his finger still would be greater than the pain of never seeing it again, wouldn't it?

Diana had taken her rings off so swiftly. At the time, because he didn't know her then, Jeffrey had decided it was a sign of iciness, the swift surgical excision of Chase from her heart. But Jeffrey knew Diana now and he realized, even though they hadn't discussed it, that she had taken off her rings for the same reason he had to: the rings were a shining, defiant symbol of her great failure to hold a love that meant so very much.

After Jeffrey removed the elegant wedding band, he stared at the nakedness of his ring finger. The skin that had been covered by the gold was so white, so long away from sunshine, a pristine symbol of the innocent and joyous hopes of a just-born love. The pure white skin was a painful symbol, a grim reminder of what he had lost, just as the gold had been.

And there was more, a reason that the pain might live forever. On that distant day, when it was too late to have the rings engraved before their wedding, Julia had whispered softly that the engraving in gold didn't matter, because the words were engraved in their hearts.

As Jeffrey put his wedding band in a dresser drawer in his luxurious suite he felt a deep twisting ache, a scream of pain as the words that had been so lovingly engraved now became open weeping wounds.

"Oh, Julie," he whispered, speaking the words aloud. "I will always love you."

Julia and Merry hadn't made specific plans for the Vacation With Daddy beyond the weekend in Manhattan, the gymkhana, and Merry's birthday dinner on Tuesday.

"Even though he's on vacation, he'll probably have to study," Merry had suggested solemnly.

"Probably," Julia had agreed softly. Her lovely, sensitive daughter was so shy and uncertain about the father she didn't know but who she needed and loved. For so long Jeffrey had been a phantom beyond her reach. And even though recently, in fragile, wonderful moments, he had begun to notice her, Merry was not bold enough to schedule every moment of his vacation to be with her. So they hadn't made special plans beyond Tuesday, and it was just as well because the disappointment of carrying out the special plans anyway, without him, was excruciating.

Wednesday was a relief, a day for which there had been no expectations. Julia suggested thinking of something special to do, just the two of them, or with Paige and Amanda, but Merry declined.

"You still have the flu, Mommy. Amanda and I can just go to the Club and ride and swim."

Wednesday, Thursday, and Friday were like all the other summer days, and on Saturday Paige gave the last slumber party before school for all the girls in Amanda's class at Southampton Country Day.

Normally Julia would have joined the party, enchanting the girls with her wonderful stories. Her stories had matured as the girls did, fairy tales still, not romances yet, but more sophisticated with each passing year.

But Julia didn't join the party on this Saturday.

"Does Jeffrey get home today?" Paige asked when Julia brought Merry to Somerset but declined Paige's offer to come in.

"What? Oh, yes."

"Well, assuming he doesn't whisk you to the hospital the instant he sees you, I'm going to take you to see a doctor on Monday."

"I'll be fine, Paige, really. I'm better every day."

"You don't look better."

"I am, though."

It wasn't true. Julia was worse, dying a little more each day, unable to stop the pain that gnawed at her heart.

She had to get control for Merry's sake.

After she returned to Belvedere, she paced from room to room searching for answers but finding only ghosts. It was a blustery autumn day, graying quickly with storm clouds. With every rush of wind, Julia's heart raced. Was it Jeffrey's car? Had he decided to come and get some of his things this afternoon after all? What if Diana was with him?

Julia couldn't be here.

She reached into a distant corner of her dresser drawer and found the jeans she had worn the day she et Jeffrey; jeans that had been there from the very beginning of their love; jeans that had been removed by him with expert hands and a soft laugh of desire after she had taken off her blouse and sweater.

Julia dressed in the old baggy jeans and a blouse, sweater, and tennis shoes. Then she went downstairs and outside through the French doors to the rose garden where Jeffrey had spent a spring morning transplanting roses and then had promised to return to see the magnificent summer blooms.

Face the ghosts, Julia told herself. *Go to all the magical places and exorcise the ghostly memories of love.*

On that lovely joyous day in May she and Jeffrey had walked through the dense forest to the cliffs above the sea. Julia followed that path now, staggering along the narrow deer paths, tripping over fallen logs, her eyes blinded by tears as she made the journey that had once been a journey of love. When she reached the cliffs, she gazed at the dramatic spectacle of the storm clouds over the Atlantic. The autumn sky was scowling, unhappy with what it saw on earth, and the sea was angry, too, gray-green and turbulent, boiling and fuming.

The meadow where Jeffrey and Julia had made love in a sea of wildflowers was barren now, the flowers past bloom and the grass brown from the hot summer. Brown, but slick from the huge rain-drops that fell from the gray-black sky. Julia stumbled down the steep trail that wound past SeaCliff to the beach and walked to the edge of the sea. The surf crashed, powerful and pounding, but Julia was mesmerized by the gray-green energy and strangely unafraid.

She had always been so afraid of the sky and the sea, but she had banished the ghost of the sky when she flew to London, and now she stared bravely at the turbulent sea and smiled a soft, dreamy smile.

Good-bye, ghost!

The place where she stood at the water's edge was as far as she had gone with Jeffrey on that springtime day of love. But now she looked down the beach to a white ribbon of sand that stretched into the ocean. The distant peninsula was surrounded by the swirling water, almost an island except that it was safely connected to shore by a snow-white isthmus of sand.

She decided to go to the peninsula, a place she had never been before, a place that might have terrified her even with Jeffrey at her side.

She would go there because it was a symbol of what her life would be from now on—going to new places without Jeffrey and conquering her fears.

When Julia reached the tip of the peninsula she stood on a boulder. Her slender body was tossed by the wind and pelted by the rain and the sea. She wavered a little in the powerful storm, weak from little sleep and less food, but she was determined to hold her ground against the gusting wind and swirling sea.

The sea that crashed and churned at her feet was a magnificent kaleidoscope of green and white. The sea had once been an enemy, a cause of fear, but now, even in its storm-tossed strength there was a friendliness. Hypnotic and beckoning, the foamy green whispered to her, urging her to journey to its emerald depths and promising a peaceful forever sleep.

It would be so easy to fall into the sea! The sea beckoned and the wind pushed and she was already enveloped in wetness, the sea, the rain, her own tears.

So easy.

When Patrick emerged from the forest onto the beach, he saw what had happened to the day since he left the cobblestone courtyard at the Club. The leafy ceiling of forest had shielded him from the rain, but during that protected journey the grayblack sky had opened. The rain spilled and the wind hissed and the sea roared.

The drama of the sky and the sea energized the powerful stallion beneath him and filled Patrick, too, with a sudden rush of energy. This evening he would paint this drama in green and gray. Patrick painted in the lonely nocturnal hours that used to be filled with love. Casey was still with him in those late-night hours, a tormenting memory, and he only made the torment worse by trying again to paint her portrait, to capture the breathtaking image of vulnerability and surprise as she turned from the sea and met his eyes. The image was as illusory as Casey had been—a mirage, a dream, something that had never really existed at all except in his imagination and his heart.

Patrick looked down the beach through the curtain of raindrops toward the peninsula where he and Casey had met. The peninsula would vanish today because the harvest moon was full and the sea was high and angry. The ocean would swallow the land soon and swiftly in a gigantic gulp, and he would watch that powerful drama from the safety of shore.

As his gaze fell on the farthest reach of the frail finger of sand, Patrick drew a sharp breath. It looked as if someone was standing on the lethal land.

Surely it was just a mirage, another illusion of the peninsula, a trick of his memory and his rainblurred eyes. Patrick strained for clarity through the rain, but clarity didn't come nor did the image fade. With a rising sense of panic he squeezed his strong legs against the belly of his horse. The stallion responded instantly, eagerly, pricking his ears to the wind and pounding his hooves on the rainfirm sand.

As Patrick neared his fear was confirmed. A woman stood precariously at the tip of the soon-to-vanish peninsula.

In June, Patrick had discovered another woman standing there but this wasn't *déj vu*. The sea had been friendly that evening, warm and calm, not swollen and angry, and then when he reached the peninsula there had been only a narrow ribbon of emerald water at its neck. Now the danger was real and imminent. Already there was a turbulent channel of water between the peninsula and the beach. The land would disappear today, swallowed whole, and even if the woman was a strong swimmer, the powerful undertow would pull her to the watery depths.

The land would disappear and so would she.

And, perhaps, so would he.

Perhaps? No, it was a certainty. Once he committed himself to trying to save her, either both would live or both would die.

Patrick did not hesitate. He could not watch her die.

The stallion balked the first time he approached the treacherous channel, sensing danger instinctively and veering violently away. Patrick gave a soft sigh. The woman would die, he would die, the horse would die. Or they all would survive.

"C'mon," he coaxed gently, his voice apologetic but firm. "C'mon."

As the water swirled and pitched, its soggy tentacles touched the stallion's withers and caused new panic. The horse lurched but maintained his footing, moving swiftly and powerfully to the temporary safety of the land across the channel—the peninsula that was now an island.

"Mrs. Lawrence!" Patrick called as he neared her and recognized her.

"Patrick?"

"You have to come with me now."

Patrick moved the horse beside the boulder where Julia balanced so precariously, then sat back on the withers of the stallion and extended his arms to her. Julia was confused but compliant. Patrick pulled her on—she was so light and so unresisting!—wedging her between his body and the strong neck of the horse. He gathered the reins, wrapping his arms around Julia, and curled his legs over hers to hold them both on the stallion's bare back.

"Wrap your fingers into the mane and don't let go," he instructed as he turned the horse with a pivot and cantered back toward the channel.

The stallion entered the now-familiar channel with only momentary hesitation, but even in the few minutes they had been on the island, everything had changed. The water was deeper now, deeper than the horse, and the currents had begun swirling around the island in a cyclone of water sucking down to the depths.

When the horse lost his footing, because the floor of the ocean had vanished, they all sank for a moment. Patrick's legs clamped over Julia's, but he still felt her slipping. He dropped the reins, wrapped one arm around her waist and curled the strong fingers of his other hand into the horse's mane.

It was a matter then only of whether the powerful stallion was stronger than the sea and whether its instinct for survival was greater than its terror. Patrick and Julia were simply passengers in a voyage of death or survival, their fate wholly dependent on the strength of the frightened animal and the grace of the sea.

At first, in the endless moments when the horse lost his footing, they were swept away from the sanctuary of the shore. Then, as the mighty legs began to pump, treading water, they were afloat, bobbing above the watery grave, but still voyaging toward the horizon and a smothering death.

"C'mon, boy," Patrick whispered gently to the creature who was fighting for its life and theirs. His whisper was laced with apology. Patrick knew he had no right to risk the gentle creature's life. "C'mon, *swim*. You can do it."

The horse responded, a long, slow battle, gaining a few feet and then being carried back, out to sea, but advancing again, and finally, miraculously, touching sand, finding footing, then lurching in the waves that crashed onto the shore and, at last, in a powerful rush, plunging onto the beach.

When they reached the safety of shore the horse stopped, its lungs gasping and its powerful heart pounding, just as the lungs and hearts of its riders gasped and pounded. After several moments Patrick reached to pat the horse's neck and reclaim the reins. As he leaned over, he touched Julia and felt her silent shivers. They were all chilled, but Julia was by far the most fragile. He had to get her to the warm safety of Belvedere.

Patrick knew well the trails that connected the estates of Southampton and chose the most direct route to the mansion, not the deer paths Julia had followed. As they rode, he held her securely in front of him, his chest touching her back, feeling her icecold shivers and sensing the tension of her silence. Julia didn't speak, didn't provide answers to the questions that danced in his mind.

What had she been doing on the peninsula? How could she have been so oblivious to the danger?

She looked ill, tired and haunted, worse even than she had looked at the gymkhana when Merry told him she had the flu. If she was ill, or even just recovering, why would she be here on this cold, stormy day?

Something else was wrong, something that made her shiver from a chill that was deeper and colder and more ominous than the residual chill of the ocean and rain and the near-brush with death.

Something even worse. *Something worse than death.*

Was it Merry? Patrick wondered as they neared Belvedere. There were no lights on in the elegant mansion and Patrick felt as if he was delivering her into the jaws of a dark monster, not the welcoming arms of a safe home. Her husband was probably in London still, but where was Merry on this stormy Saturday? If something had happened to Merry . . .

If something had happened to Merry, Julia Lawrence would look like this, Patrick knew, because he had watched Julia over the summer and had seen her immense love for her daughter, her motherly worries, and her gentle pride.

When they reached the cobblestone drive, Patrick dismounted, then circled Julia's waist and lowered her carefully onto the ground. She swayed a little when her feet touched the ground, but she recovered quickly and smiled a wobbly smile.

"Thank you, Patrick. You saved my life."

Patrick looked at her haunted lavender eyes and thought, *No, your life is still in jeopardy.* He wanted to offer to help, but she was withdrawing, backing away toward the mansion.

"Thank you," Julia said again before she turned and disappeared into the dark house.

Patrick was tempted to follow her, to ask what was wrong, but she obviously wanted to be alone, and he had a solemn responsibility to the animal that had saved them.

The heroic stallion was quite unscathed, not even chilled by the time they reached the warmth of the stable. Nonetheless Patrick carefully dried the rain and sea from the horse's coat before showering himself and changing into dry clothes.

He spent the evening in his small apartment. The outside world was quiet now, the storm's fury spent for the moment, but the silence didn't calm the worried memories that swirled in his brain. He couldn't forget Julia's haunted eyes, her icy chill, the dark mansion, the look of death.

Finally, at ten P.M., he opened the stable office, found the directory of Club members, wrote down the telephone number of Jeffrey and Julia Lawrence, and returned to his apartment to make the call.

Julia was in the master suite, in bed but not asleep, lying awake in the darkness and listening to the stillness of the night. The sound of the phone startled her. Her thoughts went swiftly to Merry but were calmed before she answered. Merry was with Paige, safe with Paige. If anything had happened to her this afternoon, if she had fallen into the sea, if Patrick hadn't saved her, Merry would still have been loved. Paige and Edmund, Merry's godparents, would care for Merry. Paige would be a loving mother and Edmund would be a loving father and Merry would even have a sister.

If she had fallen into the sea, Merry would have a mother, a father, and a sister—so much more than *she* had been able to provide.

When the phone rang Julia had been wondering if it might have been better for Merry if she was asleep now, forever, in the green depths of the sea.

"Hello?"

"Mrs. Lawrence? It's Patrick."

"Patrick."

"I just wanted to see if you're all right."

"Yes. I'm fine. Thank you. Thanks to you."

"Good."

"Yes. Thank you." Julia repeated the polite words, but despite repetition they didn't carry conviction.

"Is something . . . ? Has something happened to Merry?"

"What? No. Merry's fine."

"Oh. Good. Well. I just wanted to be sure you're all right."

"Yes. Fine. Thank you again."

"Well. Good night."

"Good night."

After he hung up, Patrick said aloud, "You are not all right."

And after she hung up, Julia whispered quietly, "Thank you for caring, Patrick."

"How do you feel, Mommy?" Merry asked when she arrived home from Somerset at noon the next day.

"I'm better, darling."

"Good! Is Daddy home yet?"

"Oh, Merry," Julia sighed softly. She tenderly stroked Merry's long golden hair and knelt so that she was close to her daughter's wide brown eyes. "Honey, Daddy isn't going to be living here anymore."

"He isn't? Why not?" Merry asked the question, but Julia saw almost instant comprehension in her very bright daughter's eyes. Comprehension that brought such sadness.

"We've decided it's best if he and I don't live together any longer."

"You and Daddy are getting a divorce?"

Julia hadn't even thought about the mechanics of what this meant. She had only been trying to live with what it meant to her heart.

"Yes. I guess so."

"It's because of me, isn't it?"

"Oh, Merry, no! Why would you even think that?"

"Because that's the reason with some of my friends."

"Oh, darling, it has nothing to do with you. Daddy loves you very much. He will always love you." Julia had to force confidence in her voice even though she had experience with this lie—it was the lie she had told Merry all her life. Julia had believed with all her heart that Jeffrey would be a loving father to his daughter. And even though she now knew it wasn't true, would never happen, Julia had to maintain the lie a little longer until she could control her own emotions enough to be strong for Merry.

"This is why you've been sick, isn't it?"

"Yes."

"Because it makes you so sad."

"You're a very smart girl." Julia smiled lovingly. *So smart, so sensitive.* "It makes me sad, but I'll be OK. *We'll* be OK. We can talk about it whenever you want, whenever you have any questions, all right?"

Merry nodded. She would have many questions, the same ones over and over. *Why? Why? Why?*

"So, darling, how was your party? Is everyone excited about beginning third grade tomorrow morning? We can have your class over tomorrow afternoon if you want."

"I would rather just be with you."

"OK," Julia answered softly as tears filled her eyes. "I love you so much, Merry."

"I love you, too, Mommy." Merry wrapped her arms around Julia and squeezed tight. When the hug ended, Julia gazed into Merry's eyes and saw flickers of worry, a signal that Merry had a question she wasn't sure she should ask.

"Ask me, darling," Julia urged, knowing that those questions, the ones her thoughtful daughter might hesitate to ask, were the most important ones.

"Will we still watch Daddy give the news?"

"Of course, if you like."

"I think we should, Mommy," Merry said solemnly, "because I'm sure Daddy's going to come back to us."

Julia and Merry spent Sunday playing card games in front of the fire, watching favorite movies, baking chocolate-chip cookies, and talking. The next morning, two hours after Merry had left for her first day of third grade, Julia put a dozen of the giant cookies in a hand-painted tin box and drove to the Club.

With school back in session and the lingering drizzle, the stable was as empty as the day in June when she and Paige had first met with Patrick. Julia retraced the steps of that day, familiar steps now, and found Patrick in the stable office.

Patrick didn't hear her approach because she wore tennis shoes, not high heels.

"Patrick?"

"Mrs. Lawrence. Hello." Patrick stood up from the desk and smiled. She looked a little better, he decided. *Still very fragile, but maybe a little stronger.*

"I just wanted to thank—" Julia interrupted her own thank-you because something he had said seemed so wrong. "You should call me by my first name."

It would cause horrified gasps throughout Southampton. It simply wasn't done. He was a servant and she was a lady. Not that anyone considered her a lady, Julia knew, and she knew, too, that it wouldn't be the first horrified gasp she would cause. How she hated the pretensions!

"All right. Do you prefer Julia or Julie?" Patrick asked, because he had heard her called both. Paige Spencer always called her Julia, but Patrick remembered clearly that Jeffrey had called her Julie the night of the party.

"Julia."

"OK," Patrick agreed softly, even though he preferred Julie. Julie was the right name for her, spoken the loving, gentle way Jeffrey spoke it, but now "Julie" seemed to make her sad lavender eyes even sadder. "Julia."

"I came to thank you again. And . . ." This time Julia stopped because she was suddenly embarrassed by the silliness of her impulsive gesture, such a trivial offering for saving her life.

"And?"

"I brought you some chocolate-chip cookies."

"Thank you," Patrick said softly as he took the hand-painted tin. He was very touched by her innocence and shyness. Such shyness that now, her mission completed, Julia was starting to withdraw. "Why don't we each have a cookie, Julia? With some coffee?"

"Oh." Julia hesitated, almost tempted.

But the temptation was because she knew what lay ahead of her after she left the stable. She knew the painful loneliness that awaited her at Belvedere. Once the silence of the huge mansion had been so peaceful, a lovely, expectant silence that would be joyfully punctuated by one of his many calls—"Hello, Julie, how is your day? I love you, Julie"—but now the silence was just an oppressive reminder of the dreams that had died.

Julia dreaded returning to the empty mansion and she dreaded, too, the stop she had to make first. She had to go to Somerset to tell Paige—if Paige didn't already know about the affair between Jeffrey and her good friend Diana.

"No, thank you, Patrick. I have some errands. I just wanted to thank you again."

"You're welcome. And Julia? You've thanked me enough, OK?"

"OK. Well, I guess I'll see you tomorrow at four for Merry's lesson."

"Good. I'll see you then. And . . . Julia?"

"Yes?"

"If you ever would like to talk, I'm here and not very busy now that school has started."

The lavender eyes didn't look offended, only shyly grateful, and she whispered again, "Thank you, Patrick."

"Oh, no, Julia. It can't be. You and Jeffrey . . ."

"It's over, Paige. You really didn't know?"

"I knew something was troubling you, but I never imagined it was your marriage."

"You didn't know that he was in love with someone else?"

"No, Julia. How would I know that? I don't believe it anyway."

"You'll see, Paige." *Paige would see. The world would see.* Jeffrey and Diana didn't need to be discreet any longer. Julia stood up, suddenly restless, even though her only destination was one of lonely pain. "I have to go."

"Why don't you and Merry have dinner with us tonight, Julia? Edmund is in Boston on business. It would be just us four girls."

"I'm not sure, Paige. Let me ask Merry."

Merry didn't want to have dinner with Paige and Amanda. She just wanted to be with Julia and watch Jeffrey's broadcast.

"Daddy looks sad, Mommy," Merry said quietly as they watched the Monday evening telecast of *The World This Evening*. "I'm very sure that he misses us."

It was agony for Julia to see Jeffrey, to know that he was back in the country, in Manhattan, only sixty miles away, but gone from her life. Julia didn't know if it was sadness she saw in his dark-blue eyes, but she agreed with Merry that Jeffrey looked different. Maybe it was simply that she saw him differently because of the pain in her heart and the tears that misted her eyes.

He is *different*, Julia reminded herself. *He is someone else's love.*

Even though I still love him with all my heart.

Chapter 18

"Is everything all right, Jeffrey?"

"Sure." Jeffrey turned his attention from the copy he was writing for Thursday evening's broadcast to the executive producer who had appeared at his office door. "Why do you ask?"

"The viewers are worried about you."

"Really," Jeffrey replied quietly. The *viewers?* Was his pain that obvious? Was he wearing his heart on his shirtsleeve? He, who was so famous for his objectivity that even his own political affiliation and personal stance on major issues were remarkably hidden beneath his unwavering commitment to the doctrine of journalistic impartiality? "What are the viewers saying?"

"That you seem a little flat. Last week, when you were in London, it seemed like a combination of jet lag and the exhaustion of covering the conference. But this week . . . They are concerned, you understand, not upset."

There had been many calls and letters of concern about the popular anchor. The change was quite noticeable although no one could precisely label what was different—just as it had defied diagnosis when it was there.

It . . . the subtext from the heart, the wonderful subliminal intimacy for Julia.

Now Julia was gone and so was the intimacy. The intimacy had always been subconscious, a direct connection from his heart to his face, an emotional path that bypassed his brain. It had been there when Julia lived in his heart. Now she was gone and Jeffrey's ocean-blue eyes no longer sparkled with joy and his voice no longer softened with loving tenderness.

Jeffrey knew how he felt inside, so raw, so empty, but he believed he had been performing well. Quite obviously he had not.

The viewers noticed something was different about their favorite anchor and contacted the network in hopes of learning the cause of the change. The executive producer, indeed the entire crew, had noticed the change in Jeffrey, too, but they had a major clue to its cause.

"Jeffrey, we've been keeping the camera off your hands all week."

"Off my hands?"

"Your wedding ring."

"You're telling me you think the viewers would notice that I'm no longer wearing a ring?"

"Instantly."

Jeffrey sighed. Not only had the viewers noticed a flatness, the crew had noticed that his wedding ring was gone and were covering for him, hiding his hands, forestalling the inevitable revelation that his marriage was over until he was ready to deal with the curiosity that such a revelation would ignite.

"Maybe I'll take next week off."

"Why not? You missed your vacation two weeks ago. I'm sure John can fill in."

After the broadcast, Jeffrey dialed a number that connected him to the once so familiar and welcoming ring of the Southampton exchange. The call was not to Belvedere, but to the adjacent estate.

"Hello, Edmund? It's Jeffrey."

"Jeffrey."

"Have you spoken to Julia?"

"Yes, both Paige and I have."

"So you know."

"Yes. We're terribly sorry."

"Thank you. Did Julia explain what happened?"

"She said that there is someone else."

"Yes." Jeffrey didn't ask Edmund if he knew the name of Julia's new love. It didn't matter. What mattered was that Julia had already told Edmund and Paige. It meant that she quite clearly had no second thoughts about her decision. "Edmund, has Julia asked you to file for a divorce?"

"No," Edmund answered truthfully. Julia hadn't asked that of him, but they had, at Edmund's gentle urging, at least discussed the issue. Edmund wanted to be very certain that she would come to him if there was going to be a divorce. He wanted to avoid for Julia, especially for Julia, the kind of excessive publicity that had befallen Chase and Diana because the attorney handling the case hadn't been sensitive enough to defer filing until after the surgery on the Soviet ambassador. The divorce itself would be terribly painful for Julia. Edmund wanted to avoid any additional anguish for her. "Julia hasn't asked me to file, Jeffrey. Are you asking me to?"

"Oh, no, Edmund. I'm not going to be the one who files."

"I see." Good, Edmund thought. Perhaps, then, he divorce would never happen, because that was precisely what Julia had said: *I'm not going to be the one who files for divorce, Edmund. I'm sure Jeffrey will be calling you.*

On Saturday morning Jeffrey took the Concorde from New York to Paris. At Charles de Gaulle he connected to a nonstop Alitalia flight to Venice's Marco Polo-Tessera Airport.

Diana was in Venice at the Cipriani. Tomorrow afternoon, if he was remembering her itinerary correctly, she would begin her five-day luxury cruise through the Greek Isles.

What am I doing? Jeffrey asked himself as the launch took him from the Piazza San Marco to the island of Giudecca and the lavish Cipriani. *Just flying halfway around the world to see if Diana is free for dinner tonight.*

And if Diana wasn't free? If she had met someone in her travels or if she was lost in her private journey and didn't want to be disturbed?

Jeffrey trusted the sapphire-blue eyes to tell him.

"*Sì, signore*," the concierge at the Cipriani replied when Jeffrey asked if Diana was registered.

"Could you ring her room for me?" Jeffrey asked as he moved to the ivory-and-gold telephone that sat on the marble counter.

"*Certo.*"

Diana wasn't in her suite then and still didn't answer when Jeffrey tried again an hour later after he had settled into his room and showered and changed. Refreshed and restless, he decided to explore Venice. Before leaving the hotel he made a reservation for dinner for two in the hotel's elegant dining room and left a note for her at the reception desk: "Diana, dinner here at eight tonight? Or next week in Manhattan? Jeffrey."

The launch from the hotel returned Jeffrey to the Piazza San Marco. He didn't climb the famous campanile or wander through the Doges" Palace or view the Byzantine mosaics in the Basilica. He had spent many hours marveling at the wonders of the City of Canals in the past, many hours during which he had wished Julia had been there to marvel with him.

Today he forsook the historic landmarks and just meandered through the maze of bridges and canals that was Venice. He followed no map but made clear decisions at each corner, turning left or right or continuing straight ahead as if there was a correct answer, a definite path to follow. But he was simply wandering, and his decisions, he assumed, were merely guided by whim—the appeal of an enchanting bridge, the coyness of a wily gargoyle on a distant building, the elegance of a statue by Verrocchio, or the lure of a fresh scent from a pizzeria. At least that is what he believed until his random meander led him to Diana.

Seated at a tiny sidewalk cafe far away from the tourist attractions of San Marco and the Grand Canal, Diana was sipping cappuccino and gazing across the cobblestone street to a bronze fountain of mermaids.

Jeffrey's gait slowed, suddenly uncertain, when he saw her. He was here because of his need, because he trusted her and needed to see her honest blue eyes and hear her honest words.

His need, her privacy.

But she greeted him with a soft smile of welcome, a smile that held gentle sadness, because she saw the emptiness in his dark-blue eyes and the left hand that looked so barren without the elegant ring, and a smile that held happiness, too, because she was so happy to see him. She had missed him.

"Hi."

"Hi. I . . . I came to wish you bon voyage."

"You look wonderful, Diana."

"It's the candlelight."

"It's more than that."

"Yes. I'm much better, Jeffrey, thanks to you." It had helped her so much to speak her secret pains and guilts aloud. Jeffrey had heard and understood, and he had told her what she needed to hear. *Forgive yourself, Diana*. She had heeded Jeffrey's wise advice and she was much better. "I'm not sure I would be so strong or so hopeful if I hadn't had you to talk to in London."

"You would be."

"I don't think so, Jeffrey." After a moment she asked quietly, "Are you going to tell me what happened with Julia?"

"When I called she told me our marriage was over. She has found someone else. I don't know who. It was a very brief transatlantic phone call."

"I'm sorry."

"So am I. But it's over." Jeffrey gave a soft shrug. "Tell me what you thought of the Uffizi."

"Are you going to tell me how you feel?"

"No. That's not why I'm here." Jeffrey paused. *I'm not really sure why I'm here, except it feels very right, but I am quite certain that I'm not here to talk to you about Julia.* He added quietly, "Besides, Diana, you know how I feel."

At midnight when Jeffrey kissed her at the door of her suite Diana didn't pull away as she had in London, except to pull him inside the elegant room. Because it was the next life, wasn't it?

Diana trembled at Jeffrey's touch and at her own fears. Was she strong enough for this? She was freshly strong, almost whole again, but still quite vulnerable. And Jeffrey was just-wounded and so very vulnerable, too.

And they were both so lonely.

Jeffrey held her beautiful face in his hands and looked into her eyes with an expression that gently reminded her what it was that was so special about them, how honest they were with each other, how much they trusted each other.

"What are you thinking, Diana?"

"That you're a lonely man and I'm a lonely lady."

"What else?"

"That this has disaster written all over it."

"It does? Even if we're very careful with each other?"

"Probably." Diana gave a soft laugh. "Probably."

The soft laugh came with a sudden rush that carried a light message. *Don't be so drearily serious and analytical about everything!*

"Are you any good at making love, Anchor?" she teased, suddenly playful, lightening the mood, causing a sparkle in his dark eyes.

"Do you want to find out, Doctor?"

"Yes!"

They began their loving, their discovery of the only parts of each other that they didn't already know, with smiling eyes and a soft chorus of laughter and gentle teasing whispers that cloaked their fears and awkwardness in a safe, warm cape.

"You're very beautiful, you know."

"I don't know, but thank you. You're very handsome. But, of course, you know."

"I do?"

"Don't you?"

"Don't *you*?"

Their loving began with smilesand teases and laughter. As they discovered each other and felt the hot rushes of desire, the smiling eyes smiled still but flickered with new messages and the whispers became more tender and less teasing and the soft laughs came from feelings of joy not from words. And their loving was warm still and not awkward, but it was no longer safe.

As the teases faded, because they had to, the emotions that replaced them were very dangerous. Because now when Jeffrey whispered, "So beautiful, Diana, so very beautiful," he wasn't whispering about her sapphire eyes or her sensuous lips or the surprising softness of her lovely body. Now when he told her she was beautiful, he was whispering about the way his heart felt about hers.

"You're invited, you know."

"Invited?"

"To float around the Mediterranean with me."

"I really just planned to wish you bon voyage."

"And you've done it magnificently." Diana started to add something but stopped.

"Speak."

"Well. You wouldn't be intruding at all, not at all, but I know that you may want to be alone, so . . ."

"So I accept your gracious invitation."

"You do? I'm so glad."

"May I help you?"

"Oh, yes, thank you. I was looking for Patrick."

"About halfway down this row of stalls there's a dark-green door on the left. He's probably in there."

"Thank you."

Julia had checked the stable office and riding ring and finally wandered into the stable itself where she found a helpful groom. She walked along the wide brick walkway between stalls and knocked when she found the dark-green door on the left halfway down.

"It's open!"

"Oh!" Julia exclaimed as she opened the door and realized that it opened not into another office, a tackroom, or an employees" lounge but into Patrick's private apartment.

"Julia." Patrick was as startled as she. He had expected one of the stablehands, perhaps the Club's manager, but not a Club member, not Julia. "Please come in."

The apartment was small and windowless. The door from the outside opened directly into the combination living room and kitchenette. The rest of the apartment, the bedroom and bath, was behind two closed doors.

The windowless apartment would have been dark and dreary, but it had been transformed into a painter's studio, a bright, cheerful clutter of pencils and brushes, watercolors and oils, sketches and paintings.

As soon as Julia was inside, Patrick moved to sweep a still-damp painting off the small couch and gestured for her to be seated. But Julia didn't sit. She stood awkwardly, suddenly very uncertain.

"How are you?" he asked. Patrick hadn't seen her for over two weeks, not since the day she brought the cookies. Amanda, but not Merry or Julia, had been at the lesson the following afternoon, and the next Tuesday Paige Spencer had called to cancel the girls" riding lessons indefinitely.

"Fine, thank you."

"Would you like some coffee?"

"No, well, yes, if it's easy."

"Very easy. Milk? Sugar?"

"A little milk."

While Patrick poured two mugs from a pot on the linoleum counter that separated the living room from the kitchen, Julia looked at the paintings.

"These are wonderful, Patrick."

"Thank you. Here's your coffee."

"Oh, thank you. Do you sell them?"

"No."

"What then?"

"When I run out of wall space I throw the oldest ones away."

Patrick kept no souvenirs of his life. He had kept souvenirs once, in a gardener's cottage in Kentucky, but he had been forced to leave those mementos behind and had kept none since. There hadn't been memories in the past five years that he had wanted to preserve anyway.

Except one. And on the easel in his bedroom Patrick was painstakingly painting her portrait, trying to, even though the one memory he chose to preserve was the most tormenting memory of all.

"Why do you paint?"

"It's very peaceful for me."

Julia answered with a wistful smile, as if she understood, as if she, too, had once known about peace.

"Do you think you could paint a pastel dragon, Patrick?"

"A pastel dragon?" Patrick echoed softly as he looked at her so-serious lavender eyes. Her startling question was obviously very important to her. "Maybe. What pastel?"

"Well, all shades, depending on her mood."

"Her?"

"Her name is Daphne." Julia's creamy cheeks flushed a lovely pastel, the palest of pinks.

"What does she look like aside from being a dragon of many colors?"

"I guess she looks friendly and gentle. She's a character in Merry's favorite stories and I thought it would be nice for Merry to have a picture of her. If that was something you would want to do? I'd pay you, of course."

"That wouldn't be necessary. You want me to make an enlargement from a picture in a book?"

"No. There aren't any pictures, just descriptions."

"I should read those then. Can you show them to me?"

"If you will allow me to pay you."

"I will allow you to pay me with chocolate-chip cookies." Patrick held up his hand to stop her protest. "I mean it. That's the deal."

"All right."

"Good. I guess I should read about Daphne."

"I could bring one of the stories by tomorrow. When is convenient for you?"

"This is a good time."

"Tomorrow, then, at ten?"

"That would be fine."

Julia left then as quietly and mysteriously as she had arrived and without ever touching her coffee or sitting on the couch or telling him why she had come.

She didn't come because she knew I was an artist. She came for another reason. Perhaps to talk? Patrick hoped that was the reason, that Julia had remembered his offer and decided to accept it.

She is like a fragile bird, Patrick mused after she left. *She knows I am extending my hand to her, offering her much-needed sustenance, but she is so wary, so afraid.*

It might take a very long time to earn Julia's trust, Patrick knew, but he was infinitely patient. *I will extend my hand to you, Julia, and I will hold it very still so that you will not be frightened.*

"Here is a description of Daphne," Julia told him the next morning. She had turned to page four of the first story she had written about Daphne. The story was printed in large bold letters—"Large enough for my old eyes to read to my great-grand-daughter," Grandmère had announced gaily when she bought the

word processor and printer for Julia—and bound in a pink notebook.

Patrick tried to read the passage Julia pointed out to him on the page, but it was impossible. He couldn't fully concentrate with her watching anxiously and, besides, there were questions he wanted to ask.

"What is this, Julia?"

"The story."

"Where did you get it?"

"I wrote it. It's one of Merry's favorites. She's almost too grown up for it now, but Daphne is an old friend." Julia thought sadly, *And Merry needs her old friends—the gentle dragons, the frolicking serpents, the magical unicorns, and the fairy princesses.*

"Could you leave the story with me overnight, Julia? I think it would be best for me to read all of it."

When Julia returned at ten the following morning Patrick was almost done with the sketch of Daphne. He had read Julia's wonderful story over and over, learning about Daphne and the other magical characters. Then he had taken a long walk and allowed his mind to fill with images of Julia's characters and of the enchanted land where they lived.

He had returned to his apartment after midnight and had then begun to put to paper the image his mind had seen of the shy but friendly and gentle dragon.

"Oh, Patrick. This is what Daphne looks like, isn't it?"

"I think so. I was just going to give her a little color. I think her expression is happy, so—daffodil yellow?"

"Yes. Should I come back later?"

"No. This won't take long. Pour yourself some coffee and pull up a chair."

"It won't bother you if I watch?"

"Not at all," Patrick answered confidently because he didn't want her to leave. But he didn't know. His painting had always been solitary and private.

But Julia Lawrence, the fragile sparrow, did not invade his privacy. Patrick painted and she watched, and finally it was Patrick who broke the peaceful silence.

"I wondered if you would like me to illustrate the entire story. I have in my mind what Andrew looks like, and Robert and Cecily and the castle. Of course I may be all wrong."

"You weren't wrong about Daphne."

"Well. We could work together. You could tell me if you agree with the images I've painted."

"That would be so much work for you."

"I told you, Julia. Painting is very peaceful for me. It's really not work. I loved your story. Are there others?"

"Stacks and stacks."

"I'd like to read those, too. Tomorrow, when you come, you can bring more. After I've illustrated this story, if you like the result, I can do others."

"Oh, Patrick, Merry will be so thrilled."

"How is Merry, Julia? Is she all right?"

Julia hesitated. Merry wasn't all right. Merry's optimism that Jeffrey would return had faded into quiet despair. The optimism had only survived a week because the next week, the week after Jeffrey returned from London but not to them, another network journalist gave the news on *The World This Evening* because the famous anchor was away on a well-deserved vacation. Jeffrey's vacation with Merry and Julia hadn't happened, but two weeks later he was on vacation without them.

"This is a difficult time for Merry, Patrick. Jeffrey and I aren't together anymore."

"A difficult time for both of you."

"Yes."

Chapter 19

"Edmund?"

"Oh, good morning, Casey. Please come in."

Casey walked across the plush carpeting of Edmund's office to the desk where he was working.

"Here is the brief on the Wright case."

Casey handed a thick legal-size folder to a surprised Edmund.

"Wright? I just gave you that case on Friday afternoon."

"Yes, but it wasn't difficult. The precedents were quite straightforward."

"Assuming you spent every second of the weekend working on it." Edmund smiled warmly at the brightest new star in New York legal circles. "I'm not complaining, of course, Casey, but sleep *is* permitted, and once in a while even a little free time."

"I know." Casey returned the smile and wished that it had been a confident smile of success and energy from the old Casey. But the old Casey had yet to reappear. Where was she? Where was the Casey who relished the challenging games and basked in the golden triumphs? Where was the perfectly disciplined actress whose every word, every smile, every move was calculated for dazzling success? Where was the Casey with the heart of ice? The abilities of the old Casey reappeared, of course, because they belonged to both Caseys, and even though it was only mid-October and she had received word that she passed the Bar just a week ago, Casey was known already among Spencer and Quinn's most valued clients. She was terribly successful, terribly busy, and terribly unhappy.

"Is everything going all right, Casey?"

"Everything's going just fine, Edmund, thank you. I thrive on being busy." *And I permitted myself a little free time once and the emptiness now is greater than had I never allowed it.*

"OK." Edmund wasn't confident that Casey was thriving, although she was succeeding beyond even his greatest expectations. She seemed tense and strained, but he had never actually worked with her before and perhaps this was usual. Besides, in the past few months Paige and Edmund, who had always believed themselves to be in touch with the emotions and sensitivities of others, especially their friends, had spent long, bewildered hours wondering how they had apparently witnessed the disintegration of two marriages, the marriages of their four closest friends, and been so unaware of the trouble in what appeared to have been paradise. Edmund's mind drifted to the most recent bewildering break-up, and, remembering that Casey and Julia had known each other since high school, asked, "Have you spoken to Julia, Casey?"

"To Julia? No."

"Neither have we. Not for weeks. Paige has tried, of course, but Julia has withdrawn completely and even Merry and Amanda only see each other at

school now."

"Edmund, I'm sorry. Obviously something has happened to Julia, but I don't know what it is."

"You have been working every second, haven't you?"

One had to make a concerted effort to avoid reading or hearing about the separation of Jeffrey and Julia Lawrence and the love affair between Jeffrey and Diana Shepherd. Such an effort necessarily included avoiding *W, Vanity Fair, People*, the society pages of *The New York Times*, the popular Manhattan insider's television show *Viveca's View*, and *The World This Evening*, because even the most unobservant of viewers could not help but notice the Mediterranean tan where once there had been elegant gold. The nation's leading newsman was news, and his alliance with the beautiful Queen of Hearts made it all the more titillating. Jeffrey and Diana avoided the limelight, but there were necessary appearances at charity dinners, and last weekend Manhattan's newest glittering couple had been together at the annual benefit for the Heart Institute.

Everyone knew about Jeffrey Lawrence and Diana Shepherd—except Casey. Her determined effort to be so absorbed in her work that she shut everything else out had clearly succeeded.

"Jeffrey and Julia are no longer together," Edmund clarified.

"What?"

"Apparently Jeffrey fell in love with Diana Shepherd."

"But he was so much in love with Julia!"

"Paige and I thought so, too."

"I can't believe it."

"But it's true." Edmund added quietly, "And, of course, Julia is devastated."

"Are they getting divorced?"

"I've spoken to both of them, and each seems to assume so, but neither has filed."

"Will it be a battle?"

"I can't imagine that it will. Belvedere already belongs to Julia so it would simply be a matter of dividing the remainder of the fortune and making custody and child-support provisions."

"Belvedere is Julia's?" Casey asked with surprise.

"Yes. The estate was left to her by Jeffrey's grandmother." Edmund paused, gave a soft sigh, and added solemnly, "I'm hoping it won't come to divorce. But if it does, for Julia's sake everything needs to be handled very quietly and very discreetly."

"By you."

"Or by you, Casey. It just needs to be done by someone who knows Julia and cares about her and will make absolutely certain that she doesn't get hurt any more than she already has been."

When Casey returned from Edmund's office to her own, she saw a familiar face waiting in the reception area.

"Mr. Tyler." Casey greeted him calmly even though her heart raced. John Tyler was a private detective. His services were used often by Spencer and Quinn.

Casey had already involved him in two of her cases, but she knew he was here today on a project for which he was billing her directly. "Please come in."

Find out everything you can about Patrick James, Casey had told John Tyler a week ago.

John had predicted it would take about a week, and now he was here, precisely a week later, to give her a detailed report of Patrick's life.

"I have nothing for you," John said when they were in Casey's office and the door was closed.

"I don't understand. You couldn't find a way to talk to the manager at the Club without revealing why?" That had been a stipulation. No one was to know the real reason for the inquiries.

"Sure I could. It was very simple. One phone call. I said I was double-checking a reference Patrick James had given for a line of credit. When I started to give the social security number he had allegedly given—mine, by the way—I was told they had no social security number for him. Apparently he's not a full-time employee. He just gets paid in cash for services rendered. I gather it's a fairly small amount of money, probably a yearly amount well below the poverty level. I asked for names of previous employers, again implying that I was simply double-checking what he had given me, and they have nothing."

"Did you research other sources?"

"Of course. I ran Patrick James and James Patrick through the usual lists and came up empty. It's probably a new name. Your man is in hiding, Ms. English, and may have been for a very long time."

"In hiding?"

"That would be my best guess."

"So, that's it? There's nothing more you can do?"

"Sure there's more, but I wanted to check with you first. The manager said that Patrick does some bartending. I have a tux for my more uppercrust under-cover work. I can make a two-minute appearance the next time Patrick is bartending and get a very nice set of prints from a crystal glass."

"Prints?"

"Admittedly a bit of a long shot. However, in the past few years there have been major attempts to get fingerprints of wanted criminals into centralized computer systems, so if he's committed a crime recently we may get lucky."

"A crime?"

"Well, I suppose he could have been printed—as I'm sure you were—when he became an assistant D.A. somewhere, but somehow I don't think that's likely."

"Let me think about it," Casey murmured, although it required no thought. Patrick was not a criminal!

"Sure. You know how to reach me."

After John Tyler left, Casey thought about what had prompted her investigation of Patrick. She could not believe that their love had been an illusion. It just couldn't have been! Patrick's cruelty that morning in the stable had been so unlike him . . . and so desperate.

The more Casey thought about it, the more she decided that Patrick had ended their love because of whatever it was he had been planning to tell her over candlelight and champagne at Chez Claude. Casey had known that whatever it was, it had worried him before he knew the truth about her. What if, once he learned that she was rich and successful, he had decided that his secret would matter too much to her?

Casey had wanted to discover his secret so that she could go to him and tell him she knew it and it didn't matter and that she loved him. Now she would never learn Patrick's secret unless he told her. But she would go to him still, because she had to, and tell him of her love.

I'll go to Southampton tomorrow, Casey decided. *I owe myself a little free time. I'll go to Southampton and see Patrick. And then, when Patrick and I are together again, and before I return to the city, I will visit Julia at Belvedere to see if there is anything I can do to help.*

"I didn't care if I fell into the sea that day, Patrick."

For a fraction of a second the paintbrush in Patrick's hand was suspended in midair, so startled was he by Julia's stunning admission, but he forced himself to continue painting calmly because he didn't want to drive her into hiding with his full attention.

Julia had been in his small apartment almost every weekday morning for the past three weeks. She watched him paint the magical characters from her wonderful fairy tales and at his gentle urging talked a little about her childhood. Julia told him the facts of her life, without the emotions, but Patrick heard enough to realize how alike they were.

He and Julia were both orphans. They had raised themselves, providing their own gentleness and nurturing. Patrick had survived his harsh childhood by filling his gray world with colorful visions, and Julia had survived hers by creating enchanted kingdoms populated by friendly serpents and kind dragons. Gentle images and lovely fantasies had sustained Patrick and Julia as children. Perhaps that was why, when they were older, they actually believed they could live their dreams.

But Patrick and Julia, refugees from a world of hopelessness and poverty, were imposters in the world of the very wealthy even though that wa where their dreams lived. And even though each had come so close to living the dreams, both had ultimately failed. The impertinent orphans had dared to reach for the fiery brilliance of their dreams . . . and each had been badly burned for the presumptuousness.

Julia had told Patrick the skeleton of her life, the bones without the heart, even though her silences and the anguish in her lavender eyes spoke eloquently of her deep sadness. And now the timid bird was trusting him with a most important truth.

"You didn't care, Julia?" Patrick echoed quietly, painting still.

"No. In a way I thought it would be better."

"For who?"

"For Merry."

"It wouldn't have been better for Merry, Julia." Patrick put down his paintbrush then and turned to her. He waited until she was looking into his eyes. "And it wouldn't have been better for me."

"Oh!" Julia's cheeks flushed. "Thank you, Patrick."

"You had to fight very hard to keep yourself from falling into the sea that day, Julia. If you had wanted to fall it would have been quite easy. Something made you hold your ground against the power of the wind and the lure of the sea."

"Something," Julia repeated quietly.

"I think you love Merry too much ever to leave her." Patrick paused. Then he took a chance, moving closer to her with his words, hoping she wouldn't back away. "And maybe you hope that Jeffrey will return."

Julia didn't retreat. She only smiled a lovely wistful smile.

"That will never happen."

"No?"

"No." Julia looked bravely into his eyes. "Have you ever been in love?"

"Yes. Once. The woman I fell in love with wasn't who I thought she was."

"I guess that's what happened to me, too."

"But you still love him, don't you, Julia? Despite what he has done."

"Yes." Julia tilted her head and asked softly, "Do you still love her, Patrick?"

"Yes. I still do."

Casey parked her Mercedes sport coupe in the visitors" parking lot at the Southampton Club. She knew the way to the stable through the forest from the sea, the path she had taken the morning after the party, and now she got directions from a gardener. When she reached the cobblestone courtyard, one of the grooms directed her to Patrick's apartment.

Casey was about to knock when she heard voices close to the door—Patrick's voice and a softer one. Casey withdrew into an empty stall a few feet away and waited. Her heart had been racing all morning and she had filled her mind with hope and confidence, but now she felt an ominous sense of dread.

Patrick had found someone new.

But you will remind him of your wonderful love, Casey told herself bravely. *And whoever she is, Patrick will still want to be with you.*

Whoever she is . . .

But *she* was Julia. Casey's ancient enemy. Julia with Patrick.

Had Julia lost Jeffrey? Or had she simply tossed him away because she found someone she wanted even more?

Yesterday, when Casey learned of the end of the love of Jeffrey and Julia, she had felt genuine sympathy and compassion for Julia's devastating loss.

But Julia had lost nothing.

As always, Julia had won.

And of all the things Casey English had wanted in her life, of all the things Julia had taken from her, Patrick's love was the only one that really mattered.

"I'll see you tomorrow, Julia." Patrick said the words every day, but today there was deeper meaning, a promise that from now on they could speak from their hearts, if they wanted to, as they had spoken today.

"Yes, Patrick," Julia echoed softly. "Tomorrow."

Casey overheard the gentle good-bye and the promise of tomorrow. And Casey saw the pale-pink flush of Julia's creamy cheeks and the innocent-yet-seductive lavender eyes as she gazed at Patrick.

Julia with Patrick. Did Patrick and Julia lie together under the stars in the meadow of love above the peninsula? It was Julia's meadow, after all, an enchanted corner of Belvedere. Patrick and Casey had loved in Julia's fragrant meadow of wildflowers, but they had been trespassing there.

And now Patrick was with the meadow's rightful owner. And what did Casey own? What was her legacy of love?

She owned only the feelings that churned within her now, the desperate feelings of imperfection, the flawed emotions that had first surfaced over a decade ago because of Julia. Emotions that had told her then, as they reminded her now, that somehow she had to win or she would surely die a gasping, tormented death.

Patrick watched as Julia disappeared along the brick walkway, and so did Casey. As soon as Julia turned the corner, Casey emerged from the stall.

"Hello, Patrick."

"Casey." Patrick's heart responded before his brain, a response of desire and longing, but his brain lagged only a second behind, hobbling his smile, filling eyes that wanted to smile with joy with wariness instead. "Hello, Casey."

"I've been trying to find out who you are."

"You know who I am."

"I know that Patrick James doesn't exist. Why is that, Patrick? An endless line of heiresses, perhaps, with the odd husband seeking revenge?"

"Leave it alone, Casey. Please."

I can't, Casey realized as she looked at the man she had loved as she had never loved before, the man for whom she would have forgiven anything, *anything*, if only he loved her, too.

But Patrick didn't love her, or perhaps he had for a while until someone better had come along.

Someone better, the best . . . Julia.

I can't leave it alone, Patrick. I can't fight the powerful feelings that are swirling inside me.

"I hope it is a secret that will destroy." Casey's whisper was a hiss of ice borne of her ancient but evergreen hatred for Julia and her sudden hatred for Patrick.

It is, Patrick thought heavily as he watched her leave. *It is a secret that will destroy, and if there is anyone in the world who can discover it, it is you, Casey. Brilliant, clever, vindictive Casey. My love, my greatest love, who is now my most bitter enemy.*

Patrick knew he should run. He had long overstayed his welcome in this peaceful haven. But now, because of Julia, he couldn't leave. Julia was so fragile, in such pain, and she needed him.

And Patrick needed Julia, too.

He needed her gentleness.

He needed her wonderful fairy tales.

Casey walked into the law offices of Spencer and Quinn at eleven.

"Casey!" Her secretary greeted her with obvious surprise. "I thought you weren't going to be in until this afternoon."

"I just couldn't stay away. Will you please reach John Tyler for me? Now?"

"Yes. Of course."

As Casey waited in her office she felt the return of the old Casey. The old Casey announced her dazzling arrival with the once-familiar rushes of power and control. The power to destroy. The control to vanquish the lingering whimpers of her broken heart.

By the time the private detective was on the line, Casey felt terrifyingly calm.

"Mr. Tyler? I want you to get the prints."

"Diana? It's Mark Hall."

"Hello, Mark." Diana looked at her bedside clock. It glowed 3:12. Three hours and twelve minutes of sleep wasn't terrible, she mused. She was the attending cardiac surgeon on call and the busy night had begun at four yesterday afternoon with an emergency case that lasted until eleven. By the time she had returned to her penthouse it had been almost midnight. Now Dr. Mark Hall, the chief resident in cardiac surgery, was calling, and that meant they needed her help with a new patient. "What do you have?"

"A knife wound to the heart."

"Still alive?"

"We cracked his chest in the E.R. and threw a few big stitches into the ventricle. He's in the O.R. now and should be on bypass soon."

"I'm on my way. And Mark . . . very impressive job."

"Thanks, Diana."

The emergency surgery on the man with the knife wound to the heart finished, successfully, at six. Diana had time to return to her penthouse for a refreshing shower and to dress for the day and still easily make the meeting of the executive committee of the Heart Institute at seven-thirty.

The shower and clean clothes gave the illusion of a morning that followed a good night's sleep. The illusion held until halfway through the meeting when Diana realized she would have to tap deep into her reserves to find the energy necessary to spar with Dr. Tom Chandler. She had to spar with Tom today, a legitimate battle, because they honestly disagreed about the staffing for Memorial's soon to be inaugurated helicopter transport service for emergency heart cases.

"Long night?" her secretary asked when Diana arrived at her office at nine.

"Not as long as the meeting." Diana gave a wry smile. "How is it so far today?"

"Quiet. Something did come up yesterday after you left for the O.R."

"Oh?"

"A man called from California to schedule an appointment with you. He wouldn't give me details except to say it was important and he wanted to see you as soon as possible. He'll be here at four today."

"OK. What's his name?"

"Sam Hunter."

"Sam Hunter?" Diana echoed softly.

"He said he was in high school with you in Dallas. Does that mean he's the same Sam Hunter who's the singer?"

"Yes," Diana answered quietly, marveling at the deceptive calm in her voice. Her heart wasn't calm—it had begun to race, an ancient reflex, when she heard his name—and unanswerable questions were already thundering in her mind. "He'll be here at four today?"

"Assuming his plane is on time."

Without another word Diana retreated to her office and privacy for her swirling thoughts.

Sam. Here. Today. *Why?* Had he read the cover story in *Time* and the notice in Milestones about her dissolved marriage? Was Sam coming to tell her, after all these years, that he should never have left her? The paragraph Diana had read about Sam in the same issue had mentioned no wife, no family, no personal details at all. What if Sam was free and was coming to see her because she was free now, too?

But Diana wasn't free. Jeffrey was in her life and in her heart. Jeffrey, her wonderful lover and friend. Jeffrey, with whom there was honesty and trust that had never existed before for either in their other loves. Jeffrey, with whom she had shared all her secrets, including the secret truth that Sam Hunter lived in her heart still and always would.

"Jeffrey Lawrence." Jeffrey answered the private line in his office on the third ring.

"Good morning."

"Hi." His voice softened. "How was your night?"

"A little busy."
"Meaning no sleep."
"No. I slept from midnight until three."
"Would you like to cancel dinner tonight?"
"Jeffrey, are you responsible for my four o'clock appointment?"
"What?"

"I'm scheduled to see Sam today at four."
"Sam? No, I'm not responsible, honey. Why is he coming to see you?"
"I don't know. He didn't give any details when he made the appointment."
"Are you OK?"
"I'm apprehensive. And," she sighed softly, "it would be nice to be facing this after a good night's sleep."
"You'll do fine."
"Whatever that is."
"I'm here, Diana."
"And you're willing to let the nation watch reruns of the news in case I need you just as you're about to broadcast?"
"I am absolutely willing to do that."

Chapter 20

His thick brown hair had a few threads of white at the temples and the years had put tiny wrinkles beside his eyes and age had made him even more handsome, but he was Sam. His dark eyes were sensitive still and no more confident than they had ever been despite his success. His smile was uncertain, too, as it always had been . . . and so gentle.

He was Sam and she loved him still.

He didn't want you! Diana reminded herself as she smiled bravely at his dark eyes. *He didn't want you and he isn't here today to tell you that he wants you now.* Diana saw warmth in Sam's dark eyes, a sparkle of friendship, but not the silent messages of love that had always made her tremble—as she was trembling now, even though the messages were no longer there. Diana hoped Sam couldn't tell and hoped that her eyes, like his, only sparkled with friendship and didn't betray her love.

Sam fought the powerful feelings of love that swept through him as bravely and as successfully as Diana did.

His precious Diana. When he had first met Diana, her sapphire eyes had glowed with happiness and the confident knowledge that life was good, wonderful, bountiful. The grim truths of his life had put bewildered sadness in the lovely sapphire, and he saw sadness still, as if there had been other sadnesses in Diana's life even though he had prayed there would be no more.

How he wanted to whisper words of love to her! But he had sung such words of love to her for years. And by the time he could sing songs that promised a safe forever for their love, it was too late for them. Perhaps she had heard, and felt a wistful sadness that it had happened after all, but too late . . . or perhaps by then she had stopped listening, because she had found another love and no longer cared. Whatever the reason, Diana's silence had given him his answer.

She didn't want you!

Sam would never have seen Diana again except that now something, someone, mattered more than his broken heart.

"Hello, Diana."

"Hello, Sam. Please come in."

Her heart raced as she led the way to the conversation area in her huge office overlooking Manhattan.

"How are you?" Sam asked as soon as they were seated.

"I'm good, Sam. How are you? Very successful, I know."

"So are you. I didn't realize . . . I imagined you in a pediatric practice in Texas. Then I saw the article in *Time*."

"Plans change." Diana shrugged. "Are you in town for a concert?"

"No, I'm here to see you."

"Oh?"

"Diana, my daughter needs heart surgery."

"Your daughter?" *You had a little girl, Sam, who needed heart surgery.*

"Yes." Sam removed several folders from the briefcase he had with him. "I brought all her medical records, Xrays, the cath report, and a copy of the cineangiogram. She's six months old. She was born with a ventricular septal defect. The doctors thought the VSD would get smaller as she grew and that it would only need to be corrected if it hadn't completely closed by the time she was six or seven. She was doing well until about three weeks ago. Now she's in congestive heart failure and the doctors at UCLA think she needs surgery very soon. Her heart surgeon there is Dr. Anthony Jones. He says he knows you."

Yes, I know Tony. He is one of the men I slept with in those years when I was desperately trying to forget about you. One of the men with whom the relationship might have been love, but it faltered because of memories of you, and I never even told him why.

"Tony is a superb pediatric heart surgeon. I'll be happy to provide a second opinion, Sam, but if Tony thinks she needs surgery soon, I imagine that I will agree."

"I'm not here for a second opinion, Diana. I'm here to ask you to do the surgery. There is no one on earth I trust more than you to take care of Janie."

Janie. Diana stood up abruptly and walked to the window. Her eyes filled with tears as she stared at the snarl of rush-hour traffic below. *I tried to take care of your other daughter, Sam—our Janie—but I couldn't save her.*

"Diana?"

Diana couldn't turn around, not yet. She shifted to a topic that would stop her tears, a reminder that Sam had chosen to make a life and have a baby with another woman.

"Does your wife want the surgery done here rather than in Los Angeles?" *Does your wife know about us? Or was it such ancient history, such insignificant history, that you didn't even share it? Perhaps Sam had simply said, "Diana and I knew each other in high school. She's very bright and she loves children."*

"I don't have a wife. Janie's mother was Roxanne."

"Roxanne?"

"The British rock star," Sam replied, a little surprised. Surely Diana, who knew and loved music, would know the songs and career of the famous Roxanne. "She and I were together for about a year. Our relationship was already falling apart when she became pregnant. Roxanne didn't want to have the baby—and wouldn't have wanted to even if everything was fine between us—but I insisted."

"Roxanne obviously agreed or she would have done something about it."

"I paid her to agree. I essentially bought my own baby. It's hard to imagine that money would have mattered to Roxanne, but her drug habit consumed every penny she earned. We agreed on ten million dollars to be paid after the baby was born, and I would get sole custody. The other stipulation, of course, was that she had to be drug-free for the balance of the pregnancy. For five and a half months, from the time I learned she was pregnant until Janie was born, Roxanne lived in an exclusive drug rehabilitation facility outside of London. I was there every day, and I always accompanied her when she went to the recording studio in London. I know she didn't use drugs during those months, except medications in the beginning that the doctors had to give her to treat the withdrawal, but I've wondered if the drugs she used in the first trimester might have caused Janie's septal defect."

Perhaps the drugs Roxanne had taken were responsible, or perhaps not. Perhaps, Diana thought sadly, it was simply Sam's destiny to have daughters with heart defects. Destiny, not genetics, because neither the anomaly in their precious Janie nor the septal defect that afflicted the little girl for whom Sam's voice filled with such love was hereditary. Both were fate, not genes, and there was a major difference between the two. The heart that had been given to the infant daughter of Sam and Diana was a heart that could not survive with what medical science could offer then. But the heart that had been created by Sam and Roxanne, if successfully corrected, would live to laugh and sing and fall in love.

After a moment Diana turned back to Sam, stronger now and tear-free, and said, "I don't know if it was the drugs, Sam. Septal defects just occur, often without any identifiable risk factors at all."

"That's what Tony said, too."

"Was Roxanne able to just give Janie up when she was born?"

"Without a backward glance."

"Is that why you left England, though? In case she changed her mind?"

"I guess that's partly the reason. I'd been thinking for quite a while about coming home."

"And now you're home with Janie and Roxanne hasn't followed you?"

Sam frowned briefly, a frown of surprise not of pain.

"Roxanne died of a drug overdose a month after Janie was born."

"Oh."

Janie has no mother. They both had the same thought at the same moment. The thought was filled with longing and pain and it brought those emotions close to the surface of their eyes as they looked at each other. Too close, too painful.

"Does Tony think Janie can travel safely?"

"On a nonstop flight, with oxygen available, yes."

"How soon was he planning to operate?"

"In three days, on Friday."

The more Diana heard, the more critical Janie sounded. Her condition was fragile, a delicate balance between the small heart that pumped valiantly but inefficiently and the medications she was being given. It meant that the surgery was riskier, the operative mortality even higher. Many septal repairs were almost elective—as they had hoped Janie's would be—but the surgery on a six-month-old in congestive heart failure was not elective. It was necessary and urgent, life-saving or life-ending.

"I need to review the records and speak with Tony."

"Of course." Sam stood up to leave. He didn't ask Diana when she would reach her decision—he didn't want to push her—but she saw the question in the dark eyes that obviously loved his infant daughter so much.

"Where are you staying, Sam?"

"Nowhere. I came directly from the airport. I was planning to fly back tonight unless . . ."

"Unless?"

"You need me."

Oh, Sam, how I have needed you.

"No. Why don't I call you tomorrow morning in Los Angeles? Eight o'clock your time?"

"That would be fine. Let me give you my telephone number at home."

Diana was in Jeffrey's office when he finished the evening broadcast. She sat on the couch, head bent, lost in thought.

"I've been worrying about you."

Diana looked up at the sound of his voice. "Jeffrey."

"Tell me." He closed his office door and sat beside her.

"Sam has a six-month-old daughter with a heart defect that needs almost immediate repair. Jeffrey, her name is Janie and Sam wants me to do the surgery."

"Oh, Diana. Do you know what you're going to do?" Jeffrey asked the question carefully, without prejudice, but he thought firmly, *You are not going to do this.*

"Not yet. I have to think about it. Can we do dinner another time?"

"Sure. Diana, I'm here to help if I can."

"You do help, Jeffrey."

Diana reached her decision at midnight. For hours her mind had spun with questions that had no answers.

Her brilliant mind could not arrive at the right answer. But her heart could. It was a confident answer and it came with a calm and clarity that matched the sparkling clear October sky.

It was the right answer, even her mind agreed, but her cautious mind offered a safety net, if he was willing.

"Hello, Diana. Do you have a case this morning?" Tom Chandler did not recall having seen her name on today's O.R. schedule, but it was six-thirty A.M. and she was in the surgeon's lounge.

"No. I came to talk to you. To ask a favor of yo."

"OK." The "OK" meant "OK, ask" not "OK, I'll do it whatever it is." Tom guessed it was something he would not want to do, a taunt of some sort, although he had never seen her sapphire eyes so serious or so unarmed.

"I'd like you to do a case with me, Tom. The patient is a six-month-old girl with a VSD. She's in failure, fairly well controlled for the moment with meds, but the surgery is semiemergent. I'd like to operate on Friday, but if that's not good for you we could schedule for the weekend or early next week."

"I can check, but I think Friday would be fine. Diana, what am I missing? Obviously I will review her records and examine her, but give me a clue. What's the worry?"

"It's not the surgery that worries me, Tom, it's the surgeon. I'm personally involved, enough involved that I can't say no but maybe too involved to really be objective about how I'll handle my emotions in the O.R."

"I didn't think you permitted emotions in the O.R., Diana."

"I try not to, Tom, just like you, but I may not be able to keep them out this time."

Tom stared at her in stunned silence. It was astonishing enough that Diana Shepherd was admitting to a possible chink in her magnificent armor, but to make such an admission to him was extraordinary.

"What would you like me to do, Diana?"

"Watch me. Take over if you think I'm not doing everything perfectly."

"You've done hundreds of septal repairs. You are regarded as one of the top pediatric heart surgeons in the world."

"So are you, Tom."

"Why me, Diana? You have a team of skilled surgeons."

"Because I know you won't cut me a millimeter of slack. And I'm counting on that."

Tom listened to her words and felt the effect of their meaning: *I'm counting on you, Tom. I'm trusting you.*

"OK, Diana," he agreed quietly. "Not a millimeter."

"You don't like the man, Diana, and I gather from what you've told me that he isn't crazy about you, either."

"But he's a wonderful surgeon, Jeffrey. He will not allow anything to happen to Janie. He may intervene too soon, but that's all right."

"You have a highly trained team of surgeons whom you trust and respect and work with every day. Why not have one of them watch you?"

"Because it's *my* team, Jeffrey. I'm the leader. I'm afraid they might hesitate to take over even if they thought I was making an error. Don't you see?"

"No, I don't."

"OK. Imagine that you had to do a live report, something so critical that even the slightest slip might cause your viewers to panic, and for whatever reason, you had doubts about your ability to find the right words. Who would you want to back you up? Correspondents from your own network who think you can do no wrong? Or an anchor from a rival network, someone like Dan?"

Jeffrey sighed softly. He couldn't fault the logic. His own "team" had taken over a week before gently suggesting that the viewers were a "little worried" about him and before almost apologetically informing him of their decision to keep the cameras off his ringless finger. Jeffrey's team had known he was in trouble, but they had covered for him, protecting him, not wanting to offend.

"The trouble is, Diana, that nothing I do, no matter what scenario you want to imagine, is ever life and death. And the surgery on Janie is."

"But with Tom as a backup . . . I may not like him, Jeffrey, but I have no doubts about his ability as a surgeon, his willingness to intervene if he doesn't like what I'm doing, and his commitment to do what is best for our patient."

"Why don't you just let Tom do the surgery, then?"

"Because I realize now that this is where my life has been leading me ever since my baby died. This is why I became a heart surgeon. And I'm good, Jeffrey, one of the best. I have to do this for Janie."

"For which Janie, darling?"

"For all the Janies in the world."

"Hello, little Janie. How are you tonight?" Diana whispered softly to the little girl in the crib in Memorial Hospital's I.C.U. The dark-brown eyes that belonged to Sam's infant daughter looked up at her and her beautiful face became a smile. "Is your breathing better? Yes? Good. Oh, you are so pretty, little one. Your daddy loves you so much. Do you know that? You do, don't you? So much. You're going to be fine, honey, just fine."

It was nine-thirty Thursday night. Janie had arrived at three. Her breathing was better now, quiet and calm, proof that the medications designed to remove excess fluid from her small lungs were working.

Sam was in his room across the street at the Clairmont Hotel. Diana had encouraged him to leave at eight, the end of visiting hours, even though hospital policy would have permitted him to stay with his daughter all night.

Sam needed a good night's rest. Sam did, and Janie did, and Diana did.

Diana had firmly encouraged Sam to go to the hotel. And there was someone who was going to make sure that she, too, went home to rest.

"Hi." Diana smiled when she saw Jeffrey in the corridor outside the I.C.U. He had gone to her penthouse after his broadcast, and after an hour of waiting decided to come find her.

"Hi. How is she?"

"Ready for surgery."

"How are you?"

"I'm ready, too, Jeffrey."

"After a good night's sleep."

"Are you really going to ply me with warm milk and then tuck me in and leave?" Her voice held a slight tease, but Diana wasn't trying to get Jeffrey to change his mind. For many reasons, tonight, like last night, she needed to sleep alone.

"That's exactly what I'm going to do."

Little Janie, little Janie, little Janie.

The words danced in her mind, defiant pirouettes in all the corners, twirling to the sound of cascading chimes. Diana's heart raced and her emotions would not be still, and today she could not keep her ghosts from the operating room.

The ancient ghosts had invaded her thoughts, but they did not banish the thoughts that were always with her—supposed to be with her!—when she operated. The ancient ghosts danced with the necessary thoughts in a dangerous and breathtaking *pas de deux*.

Diana tried to concentrate on the familiar wonder she always felt when she operated, and on the extraordinary wonder of operating on an infant heart. There was such purity and such innocence in the tiny organ, a pristine perfection, just as infants themselves were pristine and perfect and untainted. The hearts of adults always showed the ravages of their lives, diets that were less than ideal, and tobacco and alcohol and stress. But infant hearts were pure and clean, touched only by the hope and promise of their new lives.

Hope and promise.

Hope for Janie. A promise to Sam.

Little Janie, little Janie, little Janie. The words whirled and the music chimed, and even though part of her was able to concentrate, Diana felt that most of her was trembling—her heart, her emotions, and surely her *hands*.

Tom needed to take over. Any second he would, wouldn't he?

In the midst of all the swirling thoughts that made her heart tremble came one that suddenly made her heart stand still.

What if she was wrong about Tom? What if there was something so evil within him, a hatred so deep that the immense pleasure of watching her fail was worth the price of Janie's life?

"Tom?"

Diana's voice broke a silence that had lasted since the operation began. It was startling enough for Diana to speak, but the edge of panic in her voice startled him even more.

"What, Diana?"

"Why haven't you taken over?"

"Because you are doing brilliantly." Tom's answer was truthful and reverent. He had heard about Diana, the magic of her slender fingers—so delicate, so skillful, so sure—but all the words of praise had been inadequate to describe her true talent.

"Are you sure? I feel like my fingers are trembling and that I'm moving in slow motion."

"I'm very sure, Diana. Your fingers aren't trembling. You're not moving in slow motion. Really. I feel like I'm watching a most beautifully choreographed ballet."

A ballet. Like the ballet in her mind. Except the thoughts that twirled and danced and spun and leapt weren't beautifully choreographed. Each thought danced defiantly to the music of its own chime. Surely, eventually the frolicking thoughts would collide, tripping each other and causing a disastrous fall.

"If I stumble, Tom . . ."

"I will catch you."

But Diana didn't stumble. Despite her own trembling heart and wobbly emotions, the part of her that had spent the past fifteen years of her life training for this moment never faltered. With the confident, agile fingers of the highly trained seamstress that she was, Diana delicately embroidered the tiniest of stitches into Janie's heart, sewing the Dalcron to the small, pure tissue, sealing the hole that threatened her life, making it so that Sam's precious little Janie would have a life of hope and promise.

As the anesthesiologist got Janie ready to transport for routine post-op recovery in the I.C.U., Tom and Diana retreated to a corner of the O.R. to remove their sterile gloves and gowns.

"Tom, I don't know how to thank you."

"I did nothing."

"Yes—"

"*No.* Diana, you are really a helluva surgeon."

"I owe you, Tom."

"No you don't." Tom frowned briefly then heard himself say something almost as remarkable as the surgery he had witnessed. "Maybe we each owe each other a second opinion."

"OK." Diana smiled at the man who, in her opinion, had always been hopelessly arrogant and egotistical. Tom didn't look hopelessly arrogant and egotistical now, and Diana said quietly, "I like my second opinion much better."

When Diana walked into the surgery waiting room and saw Sam, all the emotions suddenly surfaced in her sapphire eyes.

"Diana?" he asked anxiously when he saw her tears.

"She's fine, Sam," Diana reassured swiftly. "Janie's going to be fine, a healthy little girl."

"Really?" Sam's dark eyes filled with tears of joy. He started to reach for her, to hold her, but he stopped and only whispered emotionally, "Thank you."

* * *

Janie convalesced quickly. Her young body responded robustly to the sudden increased flow of well-oxygenated blood and the disappearance of the fluid from her lungs. By the end of a week she was ready to return to her home in California. The wound in her chest was a perplexing discomfort but not an obstacle to soft squeals of joy whenever she saw her father and not an obstacle to being cuddled in Sam's loving arms.

Janie's dark-brown eyes lit with happiness whenever she saw Sam, or heard his voice, or sensed his presence. And, in that week, she learned to smile at the sapphire eyes and soft voice that came to see her so many times during each day and very early in the morning and late at night.

Diana saw Janie more often than she saw Sam, but she saw Sam frequently, too frequently. She had imagined that seeing him daily and maintaining the almost stiff distance between them would desensitize her to his effect. But it didn't happen. Her heart set a new pace every time she saw him. A new pace and a painful one.

Only once in the seven days before Janie was able to return to California did the words Sam and Diana speak to each other drift even a little into the past.

"You are such a wonderful father, Sam."

"I was never sure that I would be."

"Really?" Diana asked with surprise. So many times they had talked about the children they would have and Sam hadn't seemed uncertain at all.

"Yes. I worried that some legacy of my evil father might exist within me, some poisonous gene that had been lurking in darkness." *I knew I would be a wonderful father for our children, my love, because you would be there to protect me even if there was a darkness inside me. But on my own I wasn't sure and I was very afraid.*

"But there is no legacy of evil."

"No," Sam agreed softly. If a seed of evil or a trace of his father's poison lived within him, that darkness had been conquered by his immense love for his infant daughter. "No, there isn't."

That week their words only drifted once into the past, a brief allusion to Sam's violent father but not even a whisper about their gentle love. As if there had never been a love at all.

And then it was time to say good-bye.

"Good-bye, little Janie," Diana whispered softly to the smiling brown eyes that were snuggled so safely in Sam's arms. After a moment she looked up and said quietly, "Good-bye, Sam."

Then Sam was gone and Diana felt a great sense of loss but an almost greater sense of relief. Now, perhaps, the heart that Sam had owned for the past fifteen years would be hers again, hers to have and hers to give away.

In time, when they both were ready, Diana would give her heart to her wonderful Jeffrey.

Her wonderful Jeffrey. During the week that Sam and Janie were in New York, Jeffrey had stayed close enough to support her and love her and listen to her when she needed him, but he had stayed far enough away—not intruding and never demanding—to give Diana a chance to find love again with Sam if that was meant to be.

And if she and Sam had rediscovered their love?

Jeffrey would have been happy for her. Her wonderful friend and lover would have been saddened at the loss of their closeness and trust and love, but

Jeffrey would have been happy for her.

Just as, even though she would miss him terribly, Diana would be happy for Jeffrey if he could find a way back to his love with Julia.

Chapter 21

Casey discovered Patrick's true identity on Thanksgiving Day. John Tyler had gotten Patrick's fingerprints without difficulty—a brief tuxedoed appearance at a wedding reception at the Club in late October—but the prints were a "no match" with the hundreds of thousands on file.

But Casey didn't give up. Driven by the tireless energy of revenge against Patrick *and* Julia, she pursued the only other possible clue: Patrick's extraordinary ability to ride. Casey obtained old issues of *Horse, Show Jumping, Equestrian*, and *Grand Prix*, going back five years and then ten. Her luxury apartment was cluttered with stacks of the equestrian magazines and she spent countless hours going through each magazine, peering at small photographs of champion riders with faces frustratingly shadowed by caps.

Casey's countless, determined, disciplined hours finally paid off.

The photograph, taken eight years before when he had just been crowned Grand Prix Rookie of the Year, was shadowy, but it was definitely of Patrick.

Casey looked at the picture of the young champion and felt a rush of happiness for the obviously pleased and triumphant Patrick.

Happiness for Patrick's triumph? Not happiness at your own triumphant discovery? Now you know his real name and can find out his secret! Now you can destroy him!

Leave it alone, Casey. Please. It had been a quiet plea and there had been fear in his fearless gray-green eyes.

Casey hadn't left it alone, but now, as she held the key to Patrick's destruction, her heart made the same gentle plea. *Leave it alone*.

Casey heeded the whispers of her heart for ten days, but it was a battle that her heart ultimately could not win. Her need for revenge against Patrick *and* Julia was too powerful. The gentle whispers of her broken heart could not stop the inevitable course that had been set in motion the moment she saw her ancient enemy's innocent-but-so-seductive lavender eyes smiling at Patrick.

On December fourth Casey hired a new private detective, not John Tyler, and instructed him to find everything he could about James Patrick Jones.

"She is absolutely shameless," Addy Hamilton observed haughtily.

"A lady would be discreet," Danielle Montgomery concurred with matching disdain.

"No one has ever accused Julia Lawrence of being a lady."

"What are you saying about Julia?"

"Oh! Paige. I didn't realize you were here."

"Here" was Emily's, Southampton's charming and expensive gift shop. The shelves at Emily's were cluttered with the usual gifts of crystal, porcelain, and silver, but because it was almost Christmas, an elegant assortment of music boxes, wreaths, and ornaments had been added to the already bountiful shelves. Paige had been looking at an intricately embroidered tree skirt only one aisle away in the small store, but Addy and Danielle hadn't seen her beyond an expensive, imported, hand-carved crèche that was displayed on a top shelf.

Danielle and Addy withered a little under Paige's stern sky-blue gaze, although each had the same thought. Surely Paige and Julia, if they had ever been friends, were friends no more. The enchanted afternoons for the children of Southampton at Belvedere with Julia hadn't happened at all this school year,
and now Amanda spent her afternoons playing with their daughters, not with Merry.

"I overheard you saying something about Julia," Paige repeated finally.

"Well, Paige, you might as well know. Julia has been having a rather obvious affair with the riding instructor at the Club. He has a room, a *bed*, at the stable, and Julia spends almost every weekday morning there."

"Julia and Patrick?"

"It's true, Paige."

"Paige."

"Hello, Julia. May I come in?"

"Oh, yes, of course. Has something happened to Merry?" Julia asked anxiously, surprised by Paige's unannounced arrival at Belvedere and then concerned as she saw the sympathetic worry on her face. Julia had just returned from the stable. What if someone from Southampton Country Day had tried to reach her and called Paige when they couldn't find her?

"No, Julia," Paige reassured her quickly. "I just wanted to talk to you. How are you?"

"Fine."

"Good." Paige smiled warmly but she thought, *You don't look fine, Julia.* She looked fragile. Beautiful, of course, but very fragile. What if Patrick, the sensuous and menacing panther, was taking advantage of beautiful Julia's fragility and loneliness? "Julia, I heard today that you've been seeing Patrick."

It took Julia a moment to understand what Paige was saying. When she did, she was astonished. Paige, and apparently others in Southampton, believed she was having an affair with Patrick! Believed it and condemned it.

"Is there something wrong with Patrick, Paige?" Julia's eyes blazed with sudden anger. "I can't believe the small-mindedness of this place! It's wonderful, *lovely*, that Jeffrey Lawrence left me and his daughter for the magnificent Queen of Hearts! But when I become friends with the riding instructor—who, by the way, they all want—suddenly the patrician glowers begin. What Jeffrey did was wonderful and what Patrick and I are doing is . . . I don't believe Patrick James would leave his wife and child for another woman. It was Jeffrey who broke our wedding vows, Paige, not I. It was Jeffrey who broke our hearts."

"Oh, Julia."

"Do you think it's wonderful, too, Paige? Are you relieved that Jeffrey is with Diana?"

"How can you ask that?"

"Diana is your friend."

"*You* are my friend, Julia." *My dear friend whom I had always hoped to introduce to my other friend Diana because I thought you two would like each other very much.*

"Really? Did you think it was a gesture of friendship to tell me that Southampton is shocked that I spend every morning with the riding instructor? That I've *offended* the ladies? I have been hated here since the moment I arrived,

Paige. I couldn't care less what they're saying about me. Being with Patrick helps me get through the day."

"Couldn't I help, too, Julia? May I go outside and ring the doorbell again and start over? I came because I've missed you and I've worried about you and Merry. If you and Patrick are lovers, more power to you. I'm going outside right now, OK? If you don't answer the doorbell I'll be sorry, but I won't blame you."

Paige was halfway across the great room when Julia's voice stopped her.

"Paige, wait." Julia gave a soft, grateful smile. "I've missed you, too. I just haven't been able to see you."

"Because of Diana?"

"In part, I guess, yes. You've seen them together, haven't you?"

"We saw them at the benefit for the Heart Institute six weeks ago, but that's the only time. We haven't seen them socially, Julia, and we're not planning to."

"But you should if you want to, Paige. You and Edmund are Jeffrey's friends—and hers. You shouldn't feel caught in the middle of this."

"We don't feel the least bit caught in the middle! Don't you know that Edmund and I are completely on your side? Yes, we consider Jeffrey and Diana to be friends, but, Julia, you and Merry are part of our family."

"Thank you." Julia tilted her head and asked with soft amazement, "Do you really believe that Patrick and I are lovers, Paige?"

"It's none of my business."

"I can't imagine ever being with anyone but Jeffrey," Julia said quietly. *Someday*, some far away day, she would have to imagine it, wouldn't she? Or was she going to spend her entire life being faithful to a dream that had died? "Would you like to know what Patrick and I do every morning?"

"Only if you want to tell me."

"I'll show you." Julia crossed the great room to a mahogany bureau. From the bottom drawer, beneath a soft layer of linen placemats, she removed a stack of the original sketches Patrick had made of her fairy tale characters. The sketches were too large for the "books" Patrick was illustrating for Merry, but Julia was going to have them framed. "Patrick's an artist, Paige. He's illustrating some of my stories. We're trying to finish at least one by Christmas. I say "we," but it's really Patrick. He paints, and I watch, and we talk."

"My God," Paige breathed as she looked at the sketches. "This really is Daphne, isn't it? And Robert and Cecily and Andrew."

"I'm glad you think so. I hope Merry and Amanda will, too."

"Amanda?"

"I thought she might like one of the framed sketches. And the bookbinder I spoke to says he can make more than one copy of the stories."

"I know Amanda would love that, Julia. These are truly wonderful. You've found an artist whose talent matches the magic of your imagination."

"He really is talented, isn't he?"

"Yes. Have you talked to him about getting these published?"

"Oh, no."

"Why don't you? If Patrick agrees, I have a friend who I know would love to see them."

Julia had never cared about publishing her stories, but it would be an opportunity for Patrick to share his wonderful talent and supplement his meager income.

"I *will* ask him. Thank you, Paige."

"For coming over and telling you the ladies don't approve?"

"For coming over. For not leaving when I accused you of not being my friend."

"I *am* your friend, Julia. If there was any way I could help you and Jeffrey get back together . . ."

"There isn't, Paige. It's all over but the paperwork. I keep expecting Edmund to call and tell me Jeffrey has filed for divorce."

"Jeffrey hasn't filed. Isn't that a hopeful sign?"

"It just means he's been busy."

"Julia, your marriage isn't over in the eyes of the law and it isn't over in your heart."

"But it *is* over, Paige," Julia said firmly. "I'm just so very worried about Merry."

"Amanda misses her terribly."

"I don't think Merry is ready to be with Amanda yet. I've encouraged her to see Amanda, of course. But, Paige, how can I urge Merry to be with her best friend when I've withdrawn from you?"

"This all takes time, Julia. And Merry is with her very best friend because she's with you."

"Yes, my Merry and I are best friends. We've become even closer because of this, but I feel so helpless. She is in such pain and I can't make it better for her." Julia shook her head and added quietly, "Jeffrey never spent much ime with Merry, but he was so important to her. I had no idea this would be such a loss for her."

But I should have known because of how I felt when I lost my parents.

"Jeffrey hasn't seen Merry at all?"

"No." Tears misted Julia's sad lavender eyes. "I don't think he ever will."

"Oh, Julia. How can I help you? I could speak with Jeffrey, or Edmund could."

"No, Paige, please promise me that you won't."

"OK. I promise." Paige shifted tack as an idea came to her. "Julia, why don't you and Merry join us for Christmas? We're going to Maui. Amanda and I are leaving on the seventeenth and Edmund will be flying out on the twenty-third. We would love to have you and Merry come with us." Paige smiled a coy, conspiratorial smile and added lightly, "And Patrick, too, of course."

"Thank you, but I don't think Merry will want to. I'm afraid that part of the reason Merry can't see Amanda is because of Edmund, because Amanda has a daddy and Merry doesn't."

"Edmund loves Merry very much. Maybe it would be helpful for her to be with him. Anyway, think about it. It might be a good change."

"I'll talk to Merry."

"Good. And Patrick really is welcome to join us."

Merry didn't want to go to Maui for Christmas with the Spencers. She didn't offer a reason and Julia was torn between trying to get her sensitive daughter to talk and not suggesting ideas Merry hadn't considered.

Julia didn't ask, *Is it because you think Daddy might come home for Christmas?* She didn't want to plant that desperate hope. Not that Christmas held memories of Jeffrey. Christmas was a time of wonder and happiness and love because of Grand-mère and Amanda and Edmund and Paige. On Christmas, as with all events in Merry's life, Jeffrey had usually been uninvolved.

On December seventeenth, twelve hours after Paige and Amanda left for Maui, Patrick joined Merry and Julia for dinner at Belvedere. Merry hadn't seen

Patrick since September because she stopped her riding lessons—as she stopped all of her after-school activities—after Jeffrey left. Julia assured Merry that Patrick wasn't upset that she hadn't been riding and that he wanted to see her.

Merry wanted to see Patrick, too, but the evening was almost cancelled anyway because Merry had been very tired all week and on Sunday awakened with a stomachache. She felt better by late afternoon, she said, so Julia didn't call Patrick to cancel. After dinner, Julia and Patrick gave Merry an early Christmas present.

"Mommy!" Merry exclaimed as she opened the book and saw the title page. The title of her favorite story was printed in elegant script, and beneath the title was a colorful picture of a smiling, blushing-pink Daphne.

"Patrick did the paintings."

"Patrick, you did?" Merry's eyes grew wide.

"I did. It was easy because your mommy's descriptions are so good."

"I can't believe this! Wait until Amanda sees!"

Julia felt a rush of emotion, tears and happiness, as she watched Merry and heard her talk about Amanda again.

"We can make another book just like this one for Amanda if you want, Merry," Patrick told the glowing eyes.

"You can?"

"Sure."

"And we can mail it to her so she'll get it for Christmas," Julia added. "Or we could even take it to her."

As Merry considered the suggestion that they join the Spencers in Maui, Julia thought she saw a "maybe" in the sparkling dark-brown eyes.

"*Oh*." Merry's smile faded.

"Merry, darling?"

"My stomach still hurts."

"Would milk help? Maybe if I warmed it?" Julia cradled Merry gently as she spoke.

"I think if I just lie down and go to sleep."

"Do you want to settle here, on the couch, near us?"

Merry nodded. She didn't want to be too far away from her mother.

Julia got soft feather pillows and a down comforter and tucked Merry gently onto the couch.

"Patrick and I will be in the kitchen talking about doing more stories if you need us, darling."

"More stories?"

"More stories." Julia kissed her forehead. It was cool, not hot, not feverish. "Good night, my love."

"Where are you going to sleep, Mommy?"

"After Patrick leaves I'll get some blankets and curl up on the other couch. OK?"

"OK. 'Night, Mommy. 'Night, Patrick. Thank you."

"Coffee?"

"Sure. Shall we do dishes?"

"I'll do them in the morning. Oh, Patrick, Merry was so pleased! Thank you so much."

"You know it's been wonderful for me."

"But not profitable. Paige thinks we should show them to a publisher."

"I don't know, Julia."

"*Mommy!!!*"

Julia and Patrick rushed into the great room toward the scream of terror from Merry. She was sitting up, gazing at a dark stain on the down comforter.

Blood. Blood from the stomach that ached and gnawed.

"*Merry!*" As Julia wrapped her arms around Merry, her head touched her daughter's. The forehead that had been cool was now damp and clammy.

"Where's the nearest hospital?" Patrick asked as he leaned over to pick Merry up.

"In Southampton, about three miles."

"I'll carry Merry, Julia, and you drive."

"She has an ulcer," the doctor told Julia and Patrick several hours later.

Patrick and Julia had been given intermittent reports throughout the evening: *Her blood pressure is fine and her bleeding has slowed. We need to do some X rays of the stomach. If those don't give us the diagnosis, we'll have to look into her stomach with an endoscope. We'll be admitting her to the Intensive Care Unit so we can monitor her vital signs closely as soon as she's done in Radiology.*

The bulletins had been delivered with calm reassurance—Merry was stable and the diagnosis would soon be made—but punctuating the reassurances were troubling questions. Has Merry been taking a lot of aspirin? Has she been under stress? And then, questions that suddenly seemed very ominous, Has she had bleeding from her gums? Does she bleed excessively from minor cuts? Has she had an increase in infections? A decrease in energy?

"An ulcer," Julia echoed. That her precious daughter had a gnawing wound in her delicate stomach from the stress of how her life had changed filled Julia with great guilt. But the diagnosis of an ulcer seemed less frightening, something from which Merry would recover, than the diagnosis that might have prompted all the ominous questions about bleeding and infections and fatigue. To Julia that diagnosis sounded like leukemia.

"The ulcer is quite small, Mrs. Lawrence. There's no evidence that it has penetrated into adjacent organs and the bleeding has stopped. It should respond very well to medications and rest." The doctor's expression changed slightly as he continued, "It appears, however, that Merry has an additional problem . . ."

The additional problem was not leukemia, but the symptoms were similar for a similar reason: Merry's bone marrow was not making its necessary cells—the red cells, white cells, and platelets—as it should.

"It's called aplastic anemia. It means that for some reason the bone marrow has stopped production. Sometimes this is a suppression caused by a virus, or a drug, or exposure to a chemical, and sometimes, especially in girls Merry's age, it's idiopathic, meaning it happens without a cause that can be identified."

"Is emotional stress a cause of aplastic anemia?"

"Probably not by itself."

"How is the anemia cured?" Julia asked the question, knowing it was naive, hopeful, unrealistic.

"If the bone marrow is suppressed because of an external cause, like a virus or a drug, it may recover completely on its own. If the suppression is idiopathic, there is the potential for cure through bone marrow transplantation. Either way, for the moment we need to be prepared to support Merry's blood counts with transfusions."

"Transfusions?"

"We have very good screening tests, Mrs. Lawrence," the doctor swiftly assured the sudden, knowing look in Julia's intelligent eyes.

"Yes. I know." Last spring Jeffrey had done a special report entitled "How Safe is the Blood?" The report explored the safety of blood banks, the newest tests for antigens, the extraordinarily low risk of infection from screened volunteer blood. Julia knew all the data because she and Jeffrey had both read the articles and discussed the topic in detail, but still . . . "You could give her my

blood, couldn't you? I'm very sure that my blood is safe."

"I think mine would be safe, too," Patrick added quietly.

"Are you Merry's father?"

"No. I'm a friend."

"Does Merry have any siblings?"

"No, why?"

"I was thinking about the question of bone marrow transplantation. Related donor transplants have the best success rates. Siblings are ideal because there is a possibility of an identical match, but the immunologic match with parents can also be very good. Since you're a potential bone marrow donor for Merry, Mrs. Lawrence, we won't want to use your blood for transfusions."

"Because?"

"Because we don't want Merry to develop an immunological reaction to the components of your blood that aren't identical to her own. I'm actually ahead of myself, though, because I want to talk to you about transferring Merry to the Pediatric Hematology Center at Memorial Hospital in Manhattan. If she needs marrow transplantation, that's one of the best places in the country, and if she doesn't, if her marrow comes back, I still think you'd feel better having her watched closely by specialists."

"What about testing me to see if I can give her my marrow?"

"That should be done there."

"When did you want to transfer her?"

"First thing tomorrow morning."

"It's a good match, Mrs. Lawrence," Dr. Phil MacGregor told Julia late the following afternoon. "However, I would like to test Merry's father, too, in case his marrow is a better match."

"I see."

"Is that possible? Is he local? If not, if he lives near another major transplant center, we could have it done there."

Is it possible? Yes, it has to be, somehow I will make it possible. Is he local? Oh, yes . . .

"He lives in Manhattan." *He lives in Manhattan with one of Memorial Hospital's most famous doctors.*

"Why don't I talk to him, Julia? I am not one bit afraid of the great Jeffrey Lawrence." Patrick added quietly, "And you are."

"It's just that he has always been so angry about Merry."

"You're afraid he'll be angry with you for asking him to test his blood to save his daughter's life? You think he might say no? He can't be that much of a bastard."

"Patrick, he's—"

"I know. He's not a bastard at all despite what he's done to you and Merry. I know you love him still, Julia, which is yet another reason you shouldn't go see him."

Patrick was right, of course. If she went to see Jeffrey she might become emotional, perhaps even angry, and that wouldn't help Merry.

"I think I will ask Edmund to talk to Jeffrey. Jeffrey and Edmund are friends and I know Jeffrey has great respect for Edmund. Maybe there's even a legal way to ensure that he gets his blood tested."

"Julia, the Spencers are in Maui."

"Not Edmund, unless his plans have changed. Paige said he wouldn't be joining them until the twenty-third."

"Then I think it would be a very good idea to talk to Edmund," Patrick agreed quietly.

He had been thinking about calling Paige himself. He had urged Julia to call the number in Maui that Paige had left, in case she and Merry decided to join them, as soon as the diagnosis of aplastic anemia was made. But Julia had said no. Patrick hadn't pushed, even though he couldn't shake the ominous worry that there might soon come a time when Julia would need the support of all her friends.

Patrick had been with Julia since the moment Merry became ill. He had waited at Belvedere while she packed a suitcase for herself and her daughter, and she went with him to the stable while he packed the clothes he had bought last summer, the stylish clothes for visiting Casey in Manhattan. They both rode in the ambulance with Merry when she was transferred to Memorial Hospital. Patrick was with Julia and Merry all day at the hospital, and he was with Julia in her room at the Clairmont until very late at night. They would sit in her room, talking or not, and finally, when Julia was so exhausted that she would probably be able to sleep, he would walk down the hallway to his own room.

He wanted to be with her. And, if need be, he would hold her and protect her from the beckoning depths of the emerald sea. But Patrick wasn't sure that even his strong, determined grasp could save Julia if Merry died.

Julia had two loves and three friends. She had already lost one of her loves. If she lost the other, she would need the three friends she had on earth—Patrick and Edmund and Paige.

And still that might not be enough.

"James Patrick Jones is a rapist." The private detective punctuated the startling revelation by dropping the heavy envelope that contained his detailed report and copies of the Louisville police files on Casey's desk.

"A rapist?"

"Yet to be convicted because he has been on the lam ever since it happened. The victim, Pamela Barrington, is the daughter of a highly respected judge in Louisville. As you will see, the Louisville police file is quite thick. They've had leads from time to time over the past five years but nothing has panned out. They wanted to know why I was interested in the case. I told them, truthfully, that I didn't know and I protected your identity as my client, but—"

"I'm not about to jeopardize your career or mine by harboring a wanted felon," Casey interjected brusquely.

"I figured you wouldn't. Well. This will give you something to read for a while. James Patrick Jones had a record of nickel and dime juvenile offenses, stealing food and blankets, then seemed to be on the road for success as a champion equestrian. No one had any idea about his background until the rape."

"What physical evidence do the police have?"

"Pamela Barrington was a minor at the time. She was examined the following day by the family doctor—also a pillar of the community—who confirmed recent sexual intercourse but didn't collect samples."

"A good lawyer might get him off on that technicality."

"A better lawyer would convince the jury to believe the testimony of an innocent girl and the father who saw her terror moments after the event rather than the word of an ex-juvenile delinquent who made a career of concealing the truths about himself. Not to mention the fact that he ran and has been in hiding ever since."

After the detective left, Casey felt the full effect of the information he had given her. She had forced calm professionalism while he was in her office, but now, alone with the thick folder she would force herself to read tonight, her mind reeled.

Patrick, a rapist? Patrick, the perpetrator of the most vile crime against a woman? Patrick, who knew the secrets of the moon and the sea and the stars, and who made love so gently, so tenderly, so sensitively? Patrick, with whom she had felt so safe and so free and so loved.

And now so betrayed.

"Casey?"

Casey was pulled from her thoughts by the soft, hesitant voice, and when she looked up she saw her ancient enemy and the living symbol of Patrick's greatest betrayal. "Julia."

A distant corner of Casey's mind was struck by how fragile Julia looked, how thin, how anxious, and how her dark-circled lavender eyes were filled with sadness. But those images registered in a distant corner because mostly she saw the Julia she had always known, the enchanting seductress whose victories were so effortless.

"I'm sorry to bother you, Casey. I came to see Edmund, but he is in Washington for two days. His secretary suggested that perhaps you could help me."

"Help you?" Casey echoed in disbelief.

"Yes. I wondered if—"

"Julia." Casey raised her hand to stop Julia's words. She assumed Julia was ready to file for divorce. Edmund had said that he wanted to handle the divorce or have Casey handle it to ensure it was done with discretion and care so that there would be no more hurt for Julia. Edmund was away so now his secretary had sent Julia to her to begin the paperwork that would free her from Jeffrey and enable her to be with Patrick. "Don't waste your breath. I'm not going to help you."

"I realize you are very busy, Casey."

"You realize nothing, Julia. You have always lived in a dream world. But this dream is over. This time you are not going to win."

"I don't understand."

"Patrick will."

"Patrick?"

"Please tell Patrick—I mean *James*—that I know his secret." Casey's forget-me-not blue eyes flashed triumphantly at Julia. "He hasn't told you, has he?"

"Told me what?"

"Told you about James Patrick Jones and Pamela Barrington. No, of course he hasn't told you. But I think it's time he did. Why don't you go to him now, Julia, and ask him to tell you all about Pamela and James."

After a bewildered moment, a moment in which Casey finally took her eyes from Julia and turned her attention to the work she had on her desk, Julia quietly withdrew.

After Julia left, Casey thought about what she had done. She had acknowledged aloud her ten-year war with Julia and her intention to claim a victory at last. And she had sent a warning to Patrick.

Why? Casey wondered. So that Patrick could flee? Because she cared about him still, despite everything?

When Julia returned from the Madison Avenue offices of Spencer and Quinn to Merry's room at Memorial Hospital, Merry was asleep and Patrick was sitting in a corner reading and keeping vigil over Julia's sleeping daughter. Julia caught Patrick's eye and beckoned to him to join her in the hallway. They walked in silence to one of the waiting areas on the pediatric ward. The waiting area was empty, as most of the pediatric ward was, because any child that possibly could be home for Christmas was home.

"Did you talk to Edmund?"

"No. He was away. Patrick, was Casey English the woman you loved, the one who wasn't who you thought she was?"

"Yes. Why?"

Julia told Patrick about the bewildering conversation and Casey's warning to her and to Patrick.

"I didn't realize you knew her, Julia. You were at the party in her honor, of course, but so was all of Southampton."

"I don't really know her. We were in high school together. I've always thought she was very nice."

"*Nice?* Oh, Julia."

"Your name is really James Patrick Jones?"

"Yes."

"Who is Pamela Barrington?"

"Pamela is an heiress who says that I raped her."

"But you didn't," Julia replied swiftly and confidently.

"No." Patrick smiled slightly at Julia's instant and unquestioning support. "However, you're probably the only person on earth who would believe my word over hers. Casey obviously doesn't."

"Casey's going to call the police, isn't she?"

"Oh, yes. I guess it *was* nice of her to give me a little warning since there are a couple of things I would like to do before the police arrive. I need to go to the blood bank . . . and I need to talk to Jeffrey."

"No, Patrick. You should go to the police before Casey does. You should turn yourself in and tell them you didn't do anything!"

"Lovely Julia and your fairy tales. Whether I go to them or they come to me, I will be going to prison. There's no doubt about it. Since I have some very important things to do first, I'm going to let them come to me."

"I will hire the best lawyers for your defense."

"Thank you." Patrick smiled then added softly, "But there is no lawyer better than Casey, and I wouldn't be at all surprised if she decided to become involved with this case."

"Run then, Patrick! Leave now. When you get to a safe place, call me and I'll send you money."

"No. It's OK, Julia, I'm really very tired of running and hiding." *And there is no way I would leave you now.*

He would be leaving her soon, once the police found him, and then he would place the call that Julia had forbidden him to make. Even a criminal accused of a crime as heinous as the one they would accuse him of had the right to one phone call, didn't he? Patrick would make that call to Paige. In the meantime he would stay with Julia as long as he could and do whatever he could to help. "So, Julia, where to first? Blood bank or Jeffrey?"

"Blood bank," she answered without hesitation. Patrick's blood was safe and a very good match for transfusions for Merry. "I will talk to Jeffrey."

After Patrick left to donate more of his blood for Merry, Julia returned to her

daughter's room. Merry was still sleeping, and probably would be for a while because she was weakened and fatigued from her anemia. Julia placed a gentle kiss on Merry's pale cheeks and made a silent promise. *I'm going to go talk to your daddy, my darling, so you can be well.*

As Julia walked down the linoleum corridors toward the elevator that would take her to the lobby, she heard the overhead page. "Dr. Shepherd. Dr. Diana Shepherd."

Undoubtedly Diana Shepherd had been paged many times since Merry had been admitted, but Julia hadn't heard it until now.

Now she heard the name and it was a whispered suggestion.

Who would Jeffrey listen to? Who would he believe? Who would he trust?

Julia, whom he had always accused of secrets and lies? Julia, for whom his desire had waned? Julia, who had borne the child he never wanted? Julia, whom he had left? Or Diana, the woman he loved? Diana, the compassionate and dedicated physician whose surgical specialty was mending the broken hearts of children?

Julia knew that as emotionally difficult as it would be for her to see Jeffrey, it would be even more difficult to see Jeffrey's lover. But Julia didn't hesitate. Because Jeffrey would listen to Diana and that would help Merry.

Maybe, just maybe, Julia could find an ally in the Queen of Hearts.

Chapter 22

"I wondered if it would be possible for me to see Dr. Shepherd?"

"May I ask about what?"

"About my daughter. She's very ill."

"I'm Diana Shepherd." Diana had been near the door of her office and overheard the conversation. "Please come in."

"Thank you."

Diana led the way across her spacious office to the conversation area in front of the wall of windows that overlooked Manhattan.

"How may I help you?" Diana asked when they were seated. As she asked the question, Diana looked sympathetically at the beautiful young mother with the very ill daughter and made a silent vow. *I will help you however I can.*

"I'm Julia Lawrence."

Diana heard the words but did not instantly make the connection. In the months that she and Jeffrey had been together, Diana had formed a clear image of his wife. Her image of Julia was etched from Jeffrey's silent pain, not from anything Jeffrey said. Diana imagined a beautiful, self-absorbed, and calculating woman—a modern-day Cleopatra who had enchanted Jeffrey, stolen his heart, and cast him aside without a pang of remorse.

"Jeffrey and I . . ." Julia added after a moment, when it was obvious, so painfully obvious, that Diana didn't even know her *name*.

"Oh," Diana breathed. This shy and lovely woman was Jeffrey's Julia? Yes, Diana realized, because she was exactly who Jeffrey had so lovingly described the only time he had ever talked about her. That weekend in London there had been such gentleness in his voice, such love and such pride as he spoke of the brilliant and less-than-confident woman who was his wonderful love, and a wonderful and loving mother to her daughter. Until this moment, whenever she remembered Jeffrey's description of Julia, Diana had assumed it had merely been a deluded portrait of love. But now she saw that it had not. "How may I help you, Julia?"

"Has Jeffrey told you about our daughter Merry?"

"Yes." *Our daughter?* Diana's mind spun. Jeffrey had told her that Julia's innocent lavender eyes could lie without a flicker. There was innocence in the lavender, yes, but such pain and despair that Diana couldn't believe Julia was lying.

"Last Sunday Merry had bleeding from an ulcer. While they were treating the ulcer they discovered that she has aplastic anemia."

"I'm certain that Jeffrey has no idea."

"No. I wasn't going to tell him, but Merry needs a bone marrow transplant. Dr. MacGregor has already tested my blood as a potential donor. It's a fairly good match, but he would like to see if Jeffrey's might be better."

"I see," Diana replied quietly, although she didn't see. While she was deciding what to say next, her thoughts were interrupted by the ring of the private line in her office. The number to the private line was known to the O.R., her colleagues, and the nurses in the I.C.U. When it rang it usually was a question about one of her patients. "Excuse me. I have to answer that."

This time it was a call from the one person outside Memorial Hospital who knew the number.

"Hello, Doctor."

"Hi." Diana usually responded softly, "Hello, Anchor," but now her reply was stiff.

"I was thinking about last night."

"Yes." Last night. Something had happened last night, a new closeness, a melting of the vestiges of pain, a healing of the wounds in their hearts that kept their love a little distant despite their wonderful honesty and trust. Last night was the beginning of their forever. They both knew it. "I can't talk now."

"So I gather. I love you, Diana."

I love you, too, Jeffrey. "Same. I'll talk to you later."

As Diana walked back across the office to Julia she wondered if Julia knew who had been at the other end of the phone.

Julia's lavender eyes told her that she knew and that it caused her great pain.

You left Jeffrey, Julia, remember? Diana thought. *You hurt him terribly.* Yet it was Julia who looked terribly hurt, as if she didn't remember what had happened. Just as she apparently didn't know that Merry wasn't Jeffrey's daughter. Diana knew and Jeffrey knew. But Julia didn't know.

"What would you like me to do, Julia?"

"I thought if you explained to Jeffrey, maybe he would be willing to have his blood tested."

"Of course he'd be willing," Diana answered swiftly. Julia made her request quietly and calmly, but Diana felt her panic and fear. Diana knew the panic of a loving mother trying to save her dying child. She knew the desperation, had lived through it . . . although perhaps she had not really survived. "How could you possibly imagine that he wouldn't be?"

"I thought he would have told you. Jeffrey never wanted Merry."

That's not true! Diana thought instantly, remembering the sadness in his eyes as he talked about Merry, the distant wish for a miracle, and the more recent wish to be the father of the little girl who wasn't his but who had captured his heart.

"Jeffrey's blood will be tested today, Julia," Diana said calmly despite the swirling, bewildering thoughts. "I promise. Do I have your permission to speak with Dr. MacGregor about Merry?"

"Of course. Thank you."

Before Julia left, Diana almost gave her a gentle warning. *Jeffrey's blood may not be a good match with Merry's*. But she didn't because what Julia needed now was hope. And she didn't, either, because what if . . . ?

An hour later Diana appeared in Jeffrey's office carrying a small paper sack that contained needles, syringes, alcohol wipes, a tourniquet, and rubber-stopped glass tubes. Jeffrey greeted her with a surprised and loving smile that became quizzical as Diana removed the contents of the sack.

"May I have your arm, please?"

"You can have all of me. Diana?"

Diana didn't answer until after she had expertly rolled his shirtsleeve, applied the tourniquet, prepped the skin of his antecubital fossa, withdrawn the blood, and filled the tubes. Then she sat in a chair across from him and looked at him with thoughtful sapphire eyes.

"Julia came to my office this morning."

"Julia? Why?"

"Last Sunday Merry was admitted to Southampton Hospital with an acute GI bleed from an ulcer."

"Oh, no," Jeffrey breathed softly as rushes of emotion and concern swept through him. "How is she?"

"The bleeding has been controlled and the ulcer will heal without surgery, but there's a second more serious problem."

"*More* serious?"

"Merry has aplastic anemia."

"What does that mean?"

"It means that her blood counts are low and need to be supported by transfusions until either her marrow recovers or she gets a marrow transplant. I spoke with her doctor just before coming here. He thinks spontaneous marrow recovery is unlikely and is eager to proceed with transplantation as soon as possible. Since Merry has no siblings, the next best related donors are her mother and father. Julia is a good match, but there's a chance that the match with her father might be better."

Diana's sapphire eyes left Jeffrey's for a moment and drifted to the tubes of blood she had just drawn.

"Diana?"

"From everything you've told me, Jeffrey, it seems impossible for you to be Merry's father. But, darling, Julia truly believes that you are."

"She knows that I'm not."

"No, Jeffrey, she doesn't know that. Julia is a loving mother who is trying desperately to save the life of her dying child. She believes that you are Merry's father and hopes that your blood might be a better match than hers."

"But why did she go to you and not me?"

"I don't know. I can tell you it was very difficult for her to come to me. She was there when you called. She knew it was you and that obviously caused her great pain."

"Why? Julia left me."

"I know. I don't have any answers, Jeffrey. And there are very important questions that need answers. Julia truly believes that you are Merry's father and that you never wanted Merry."

"Never wanted Merry," Jeffrey repeated quietly even though the memory of Julia's words thundered in his brain. *You will never forgive me for having Merry! Even now, after ten years, you wish Merry had never been born. You wanted me to have an abortion, didn't you?*

Jeffrey started to protest—But that isn't true!—but he stopped. Diana didn't need to hear those words, because she knew the truth. The woman who needed to hear the words was Julia.

"What did Julia ask you to do, Diana?"

"To see if you would be willing to have your blood tested."

"Do you think she really believed that I might have refused?"

"I don't know. Maybe," Diana admitted softly, truthfully, to his anguished and disbelieving eyes.

"It was almost as if she was afraid to ask you herself."

"Afraid?" Jeffrey echoed quietly. How could Julia be afraid of him? But Jeffrey knew Julia had been afraid of him the few times that he had so angrily demanded that she tell him the truth about Merry. How he had hated the fear in her lovely, bewildered eyes! How he had wanted her only to be confident of his love! But her secrets, her lies, had caused him such pain. *Julia truly believes that you are Merry's father.* No wonder her eyes had been so innocent, so bewildered, so afraid . . .

"There are some very important questions that need answers," Diana said again. When his dark-blue eyes met hers, she added softly, "And there's something else you need to know, Jeffrey."

"Yes?"

"Julia may have left you for someone else, but she still wears the wedding ring you gave her."

At eight-thirty that night Diana called the immunology laboratory to get the results of the studies that had been done on Jeffrey's blood. She had earlier obtained the same data on the blood samples that had been run on Julia and Merry previously. Diana's experience with heart transplantation made her very familiar with tissue typing.

"Oh, Jeffrey," she whispered softly. "Merry is your daughter, darling."

"No." Jeffrey's eyes filled with tears and he couldn't speak. For a stunned moment everything was suspended in disbelief. Then, carried by thundering waves of pain, the horrible realizations began to crash down on him. *For ten years I have denied my own daughter. For ten years I have doubted the woman I love.* "Diana, are you sure?"

"Yes, Jeffrey, I'm very sure. The match is really astonishingly good, much better for transplantation than Julia's."

Diana's words pulled Jeffrey's thoughts away from the past and made him focus on the present and fuure.

"So I should be the donor."

"Yes. Shall I call Phil MacGregor? He gave me his home number."

* * *

Phil MacGregor used the word "remarkable" to define the match.

"You will be willing to donate your marrow, Mr. Lawrence?"

"Of course." *I would be willing to give my heart if Merry needed it.*

"Good. Let's plan to do the transplant the day after tomorrow. Why don't you come into the hospital tomorrow morning? We need to do a battery of routine pre-op tests. Has Diana explained the procedure to you?"

"No."

"I'll explain in full detail when I see you, but, essentially, I will harvest the bone marrow from your hip bone. The procedure is done under anesthesia. It's customary to remove quite a large sample of marrow, which means cracking little bits of bone. You'll have some discomfort after, like a small fracture, but—"

"Will it be painful for Merry?"

"No. The actual transplantation is basically an intravenous transfusion. The marrow cells enter the bloodstream and quickly migrate to the marrow."

"What are the chances of success?"

"With your marrow? I would say excellent."

"A cure?"

"We can hope for that. So if you could get fasting blood drawn at the lab first thing tomorrow morning—I'll call in the requests tonight—then go to Admitting and plan to come to my office at, say, eleven?"

"Fine. Have you told Julia?"

"Not yet. I'd like to tell her tonight, though."

"Of course."

"Did you want me to call her or would you like to?"

"Why don't you?" It would be a long time before Jeffrey could control his emotions and begin to find the words he needed to say to Julia.

A long time. And Julia needed to know about the plans for the transplantation now.

"What kind of man am I?" Jeffrey demanded aloud after the long, anguished silence that followed the conversation with Dr. MacGregor.

He stood at the living-room window of Diana's penthouse. Outside, snow was falling, blanketing Manhattan in a fleecy cloak that looked so virginal, so peaceful, so pure.

"You are a wonderful, loving man, Jeffrey Lawrence."

"*Wonderful? Loving*? Can you think of anything worse than denying your own child? Do you remember how we talked about Sam's and Julia's parents and what great harm they had done to their children?"

"They knew they were causing harm, Jeffrey. You had no idea that Merry was your daughter. You told me that for ten years Julia very carefully kept you and Merry apart."

"Because she thought I never wanted Merry! Julia was protecting Merry from the pain of a father who didn't want to love his daughter. Julia knew that pain so well because of the lovelessness of her own childhood. She kept us apart to protect Merry, but she must have believed that one day . . ." Jeffrey's words were stopped by emotion and the anguished realization that Julia had been waiting so patiently, so lovingly, so hopefully for him to claim his daughter. Finally, after almost ten years, when she could wait no longer, she had made a quiet, hopeful, almost apologetic request that he make a little time in his busy life for them to be a family. "You accused me of being a bastard once, Diana. You were absolutely right."

"I was absolutely *wrong*."

"No, *I* was absolutely wrong. God, I was so sure! Do you have any idea how many awards I have won for exceptional quality in journalism? I drive people crazy because I am so compulsive about accuracy and fairness. I have fired people for carelessness in gathering the facts. Did I ever tell you about the conversation I had with the reporter who asked you the infamous question at the press conference?"

"No, and I don't want you to tell me now. What I want is for you to remember that you did gather the facts, carefully and compulsively, and arrived at the only conclusion you could, even though you wished for something different. Jeffrey, you saw many specialists, including one a few months before Merry was born, and they all told you what?"

"That it would be virtually impossible for me to father a child. *Virtually*, not absolutely."

"But then Merry was born almost nine weeks prematurely. And even though you'd done an indepth report on neonatal I.C.U.'s the year before, you spoke with Merry's doctor and confirmed that she was premature—perhaps as much as four weeks—and that she had done incredibly well for a baby born that early."

"That was another miracle, Diana. Julia knew. She *told* me, so softly, her voice so full of wonder, that Merry was a miracle. And I didn't believe her. I didn't believe in the miracle even though I wanted to."

"Because the facts wouldn't allow you to, Jeffrey."

"I should have done more. I should have gotten blood tests then! I didn't even think about it because there was no doubt in my mind. And I call myself a journalist?"

"Jeffrey, darling, for the record, the kind of genetic detail done on your blood today wasn't available ten years ago. What you would have learned then was only that you and Merry shared some of the major blood group antigens—the most common ones, by the way. Until recently, blood testing has only been useful in *excluding* paternity, not in establishing it. You couldn't have known ten years ago what you know now. Now you know, beyond a shadow of a doubt, that the miracle really happened."

"Ten years too late!"

"It's never too late for love."

"You're not going to let me hate myself, are you?"

"I know you will hate yourself no matter how hard I try to stop you. I just hope you won't destroy yourself with hatred." Diana added softly, "A very wonderful and very loving man once told me to forgive myself."

"I told you to forgive yourself for the death of a daughter whom you loved so very much, and a death for which you were not to blame. But I have ignored my lovely daughter, Diana, and I *am* to blame." *And I will never forgive myself for what I have done.* "I have to . . ."

"Go. I know." Diana saw the torment in his dark-blue eyes and felt the power of his restlessness. For now Jeffrey needed privacy for his emotions. And later, sometime, he needed to be with Julia. Maybe he could find a way back to the love with his beloved Julia, who was the mother of his daughter, the woman who hadn't deceived him after all, and who still wore the wedding ring he had given her. Diana wished that happiness for him. She smiled a gentle smile and whispered softly, "Be good to yourself, Jeffrey."

* * *

Memorial Hospital was only five snowy minutes away from Diana's penthouse. Jeffrey went there first . . . To see his daughter.

Visiting hours were over and the hospital was very still but Jeffrey was used to roaming Memorial's halls after hours in search of Diana. He knew that visiting hours weren't strictly enforced, especially for parents of critically ill children. Critically ill children like Merry, and parents like Jeffrey . . . and Julia. Jeffrey slowed as he neared Merry's room, apprehensive about seeing the little girl he had denied for all her life, and suddenly apprehensive, too, about seeing Julia.

But perhaps Julia wouldn't be there. Perhaps Dr. MacGregor hadn't told Julia that she could stay beyond visitor's hours because he knew if he did that Julia would be at Merry's bedside every second and would never get the rest that she needed, too.

Most of the rooms on the pediatric ward were dark and empty for the holidays. As Jeffrey neared the open door to Merry's room he saw a soft beam of light coming from inside.

Merry was alone in her room. She sat on her bed, propped up against pillows, reading a book with a pale-pink cover. The light above the bed cast a soft glow, circling her golden head like a halo.

Jeffrey stood in the doorway and gazed at the little angel. Merry was so pale, her skin so white—except for the many bruises on her slender arms, large purple blotches caused by intravenous lines, venipunctures, and by tourniquets and blood pressure cuffs, because without enough platelets there was oozing of blood from the delicate capillaries.

Merry looked happily lost in the story she read, her dark-brown eyes earnest and a soft smile on her lovely face. She seemed quite absorbed with the story, and Jeffrey was content to watch her forever as he tried to control his swirling emotions, but suddenly she looked up and her eyes lit with radiant joy.

"Daddy!"

"Oh, Merry." Jeffrey walked to her then and sat beside her on the bed and gently touched her golden hair, her soft, pale cheeks, her frail shoulders. He wanted to pull her to him, but he was afraid he might hurt her.

"I knew you'd come back!"

"Merry, my darling . . ."

"Daddy, why are you crying? Don't cry!"

"I'm crying because I'm so happy to see you." Jeffrey held her lovely pale face in his trembling fingers and confessed to her smiling eyes, "And I'm crying because I haven't been a very good Daddy."

"Yes you have!"

"No."

"Yes! It's just that you've been very busy because your work is so important. You've had to be away from me, but that didn't mean you didn't love me . . ." Merry's words had begun confidently, an earnest recitation of the beliefs she had held most of her life, but the confidence faded as she made the bold pronouncement that Jeffrey loved her.

"I love you very much, Merry, so very much. How I have missed being your daddy!" *But how can you possibly love me?* "But why are you so wise?"

"Mommy always told me that you loved me. She said someday you would be able to spend more time with me. Mommy wouldn't lie."

"No. Mommy wouldn't lie." What a gift Julia had given him—his daughter's love even though Merry should have hated him!

"I was worried that you wouldn't come back, though," Merry continued quietly. "That's why I got the ulcer."

"Oh, darling . . ."

"I'm OK, Daddy. Really. As soon as I get my bone marrow transplant, I'll be fine."

"That will be the day after tomorrow, Merry. I'm going to be the donor."

"You are?"

"Yes, I am."

"And you're coming back to us, aren't you?"

"Oh, Merry," Jeffrey whispered. How he wished he could go back! "I'll be with you as much as I can, darling, but Mommy may not want me to come home."

"No, Daddy, she does want you to come home! She misses you. I know that Mommy cries, too, even though she doesn't want me to see."

"Does she?" Jeffrey asked hopefully as he felt the heat of fresh tears. He forced his eyes to leave Merry's lovely face for a moment to search for a distraction. He touched the book that she had been reading and asked, "Is this a good book?"

"Yes. It's one of the fairy tales Mommy used to tell me when I was little."

When I was little. Jeffrey's heart ached as he thought about all the years he hadn't known his little girl. Merry was a little girl still, but she was growing up, becoming a little lady.

"I remember Mommy telling you fairy tales, Merry. I remember a dragon named Daphne and sea serpents named Cecily and Robert." Emotion stopped his voice as he remembered the car trip from Los Angeles to New York and Julia's obvious apprehension that his bright, lively daughter might *bother* him. But he had loved the fairy tales, and he had loved Merry's obvious excitement as she pointed and exclaimed gleefully, "Moo cows, Mommy!"

"This is a picture of Daphne."

"That's a wonderful painting."

"Patrick did it."

"Patrick? The riding instructor at the Club?"

"Yes. He was having dinner with us the night I started to bleed. He carried me and held me while Mommy drove to the hospital. And that's his blood." Merry pointed to the plastic bag of rich red blood that hung on the intravenous pole beside her bed and was slowly dripping into her tiny veins, giving her strength, keeping her alive.

Jeffrey's mind filled with images of Patrick, the handsome man whose blood sustained his precious daughter. Did Patrick's lean, strong body sustain Julia, giving her pleasure, making her lavender eyes shine with desire and causing the soft sighs of joy that had filled Jeffrey with such immeasurable happiness?

"Daddy, what's wrong?"

"Nothing's wrong. Just a faraway thought. Would you like me to read to you until you fall asleep?"

"Yes."

Without hesitation, as if her daddy had read bedtime stories to her all her life, Merry moved over so that Jeffrey could sit beside her and then curled against him. Jeffrey gently wrapped his arm around her small shoulders, feeling her warmth and her softness and her lovely trust. *How much he had missed.*

"What if I just tell you a story, Merry?" Jeffrey asked finally, breaking a silence that had been so comfortable, so patient, so peaceful. Jeffrey looked from the book with the wonderful paintings by Patrick into her smiling brown eyes and suggested, "What if I tell you about the first time I ever saw you and held you?"

"OK," Merry agreed eagerly as she curled even closer to him. Her sparkling eyes became solemn, and she touched the dampness on his cheeks with her pale, delicate fingers. "But, Daddy, not if it's going to make you cry."

"These are happy tears, darling," Jeffrey whispered softly. "Besides, Merry Lawrence, you were crying the first time I ever held you."

"I was?"

"Yes. I guess you were upset because I hadn't held you until then."

"And I wanted you to hold me."

"I think so, because when I did, you stopped crying right away."

"I did?"

"Yes you did." Jeffrey gently kissed the top of her silky golden hair and searched his mind for other memories of him and Merry. There were so few, so painfully few. Jeffrey didn't have many memories of the two of them together, but he had memories of Merry, sunny, happy images his mind had recorded during all those years when he saw her from a distance. Jeffrey held Merry very gently and very close and lovingly began to tell her every scene he could remember.

Merry fell asleep in his arms, smiling happily, and for a long time Jeffrey just held her as tears spilled again. Finally, he pulled away and gently lay her head on the pillow and tucked the blankets around her and turned out the light.

"I love you, Merry," he whispered softly. Then he kissed her pale cheek and whispered again before he left, "I love you."

Chapter 23

Jeffrey paced around Manhattan only vaguely aware of the heavily falling snow, the ever-increasing chill, the festive Christmas decorations, and the joyous melodies of distant carols. He was lost in a snowstorm of memories, trapped inside a glass ball filled with snowflakes and a lovely Yuletide scene, his whole world turned upside down.

He wandered, almost oblivious to his surroundings, until he stepped off a curb without looking, and brakes screeched in the snow-slick street and a horn blared stridently, jarring him back to reality.

Reality. *Merry needs my marrow. I have to take care of myself. I have to stay alive for Merry.*

After that, Jeffrey walked in the snowstorm still, but now he walked cautiously and only in the safest areas, only amid the late-night shoppers beneath the twinkling lights of Fifth Avenue. The snow swirled, chilling him, and his thoughts swirled, chilling him, too, a deeper chill.

I have to stay alive for Merry. That was the first certainty that emerged from his stormy thoughts. As the hours passed another certainty surfaced. *I have to talk to Julia. I have to tell her.*

Merry's nurse had told Jeffrey that Julia was staying at the Clairmont Hotel across the street from the hospital. At midnight he walked into the warm lobby of the hotel, found a house phone, and asked the hotel operator to connect him to Julia's room.

Jeffrey had thought he could feel no greater pain—until a man's voice answered Julia's phone.

"Patrick?"

"Yes."

"This is Jeffrey Lawrence. May I speak with Julia?"

"Just a moment."

Would Julia take his call? Who could blame her if she refused?

But Julia didn't refuse.

"Jeffrey?"

"Hello, Julia. I wanted to be sure that Dr. MacGregor reached you."

"Yes. Jeffrey, thank you."

Don't thank me! his heart screamed. After a moment he assured quietly, "Dr. MacGregor is very optimistic. Merry's going to be fine, healthy."

"Yes," Julia replied softly. *Please.*

"Julia? May I see you? There's something I need to tell you."

"Oh."

Oh. It was only one word, and it was spoken so softly, but still Jeffrey heard her sudden apprehension. Oh, Julie, don't be afraid of me. "Please?" he asked gently. "It won't take long."

"All right."

"Tonight? I'm in the lobby of your hotel. There's a bar down here where we can meet."

"Why don't you come to my room?" Julia suggested quietly. She knew what Jeffrey was going to tell her and she knew that she would want privacy for her emotions when he did.

"OK. But I'd like to see you alone."

"We'll be alone."

"Hi." His heart quickened as always when he saw her and he smiled a shaky smile at the tired lavender eyes he loved so much and missed so much.

"Hi. Come in."

As he entered her small room, Jeffrey prepared his heart to see a room shared by Patrick and Julia. As Julia had promised, they were alone, but there were no signs that Patrick had even been there.

"Did Patrick go to the bar?"

"He went to his own room."

"Oh."

"There was something you wanted to tell me, Jeffrey?" Jeffrey didn't answer her question right away, but the message of his dark-blue eyes was so sad and so apologetic that it confirmed what Julia had already guessed. She continued softly, needing it to be over quickly because it was so difficult to see him. "Is it that you've filed for divorce?"

"No. It's not that," Jeffrey answered with matching softness. Then very gently, very quietly, very sadly, he said, "Julia, until tonight I believed with all my heart that Merry wasn't my daughter."

"Jeffrey," Julia whispered a gentle protest, as if she knew his words were going to bring a pain greater than all the other pains that had come before. "You were so angry with me for having her."

"*No*. I was never angry about Merry. I was hurt and angry about the secret I believed you were keeping—that she was the child of another love."

"But there was never anyone else, Jeffrey. I told you that!"

"I know you did, Julia," Jeffrey whispered softly. "I just didn't believe you."

"You would have wanted Merry? You would have loved her?"

"I do want Merry. I do love her."

Jeffrey watched Julia's beautiful eyes as the realization began to settle. He knew the layers and layers of pain that would follow, wave crashing upon wave as every memory was relived twice—the way it had been and then the way it might have been.

Jeffrey watched as the first waves of sadness washed through her. The waves were already huge, but they were merely the earliest warning of the devastating hurricane that loomed on the horizon. As he watched, a second emotion appeared in the stricken lavender . . . *fear.* Somehow he had caused fear again in the eyes he had only wanted to fill with confident happiness and joy! Why fear now?

"Julia?"

"Are you going to try to take Merry away from me, Jeffrey?" Julia added quietly, "I will fight you."

"Don't you know that I would never do that?" Jeffrey saw the answer in her eyes, *No, Jeffrey, I don't know that*, and after an anguished moment he whispered emotionally, "Oh, Julie."

Julie. His loving name for her spoken so gently now caused her such pain. And when she tilted her head because she had to look away and her hair curtained her eyes and his trembling fingers so delicately parted the black silk curtain, the pain was more than she could bear. She backed away from him and sat on the bed, her head bent, her body curled by an enormous invisible weight, her hands clasped tightly in her lap.

Her ringless hands.

Julia may have left you for someone else, but she still wears the wedding ring you gave her, Diana had told him just hours ago. The words had flickered in his brain, a fragile ray of sunlight in the blackness.

But Julia *wasn't* wearing her wedding ring. Her hands were so pale that there wasn't even a patch of greater whiteness where once the gold had been. There wasn't a patch of whiter whiteness, nor was there a depression in the delicate skin. If Julia had worn her wedding ring recently the fit would have been very loose because her fingers were much thinner now than the day they were married, thinner than he had ever seen them.

Jeffrey looked at his lovely Julia, already weighted down by the truths he had told her and bracing herself for even more pain, and wondered if he should just leave. But there were words she needed to hear, words he had rehearsed over and over as he wandered through the snow.

"Julia, I promise I will leave in just a few moments, but please let me tell you everything I came to say. OK?"

Julia nodded slightly, a resigned nod.

"I want you to know how sorry I am. I'm not asking you to forgive me because I know that what I've done is unforgivable." Jeffrey took a soft breath and continued shakily. "And yet, despite everything, because of who you are, you have given me the immense gift of Merry's love. When I saw her this evening she was happy—*happy*—to see me. I don't deserve Merry's love, Julia, but I am so very grateful that you have given it to me."

Julia looked up then. She gazed at him through a misty curtain of hair and tears and asked, "You saw Merry this evening?"

"Yes. I had to. I guess I should have checked first with you, but . . . I just had to see her. I'm sorry."

"Jeffrey, Merry is your daughter. She needs you. I want you to see her."

"Thank you."

Julia gave a shaky smile and then returned her gaze to the pale, ringless fingers in her lap, fingers that had become even more white because her unrelenting clench had not allowed blood to flow into them.

After a few moments Jeffrey continued with the words he needed to say.

"I would give anything to be able to undo the past. I loved you so much, Julia, and I believe that once you loved me, too, I guess I want you to know that deep down I really am the man you thought you married. I know now that you kept me and Merry apart because you believed I didn't want her. And you need to know that I never tried to claim her because I believed she wasn't mine. I never would have intentionally hurt Merry or you, although I know I have caused you both great pain." Jeffrey sighed softly. "That's all, Julia. Your dream was to make a happy life for the ones you loved, and you did that beautifully and lovingly for Merry and for me. I was so happy with you! You probably can't believe this, but my dream was to make you happy, too. I wanted so very much to give you all the happiness and joy that you deserved . . . but I failed miserably. I understand now why you needed to find someone new to love. I marvel that you stayed with me as long as you did. How you must have hated me for denying our lovely daughter."

Jeffrey might have said more, might have at least thanked her for listening to him, but emotion overcame him. As he gazed at her his emotions became even shakier, and finally he simply turned to leave. He had just touched the doorknob when Julia's voice stopped his hand and her words almost stopped his heart.

"I didn't find someone new to love, Jeffrey."

Jeffrey turned back to her and drew a startled breath when he saw her. Julia was sitting up now, straight and proud, the invisible weight suddenly cast away. She had parted the tangle of black silk so that she could see him clearly with eyes that were tear-free and no longer filled with sadness or fear or pain. The lavender gazed at him with hopeful wonder, as it had on a distant day in Ghirardelli when her eyes had been pulled from the sea by the silent call of his heart.

"Julie," Jeffrey whispered as a delicate tremble of hope began a brave search for even the most precarious footing in the emptiness. "You told me that our marriage was over because there was someone else."

"Yes. Because of Diana."

"Diana and I got together *after* you told me our marriage was over."

"I saw you with her in London."

"You came to London?"

"Yes. And I saw you with Diana in Hyde Park." Julia spoke with wonder, not anger. Wonder, because what if she had been wrong about what she had seen? On that autumn day, because no man except Jeffrey had ever touched her with affection and no eyes except his had ever smiled at her with gentleness, to Julia the tender intimacies she had winessed could only have been love. But in the past few months, and especially in the past few days, her dear friend Patrick had touched her and held her and smiled at her with such gentleness. "I saw the way you looked at her and the way you moved a strand of hair from beside her eyes."

"Is that why when I did that earlier it upset you so much?"

"Yes."

"Oh, my Julie," Jeffrey whispered, a whisper of hope and joy. "Diana was very sad and I was trying to help her. We were both very sad that weekend, both mourning losses of love. We became friends, honey, good friends but just friends. I spent the weekend telling Diana how much I loved you and how afraid I was that I had lost you. And Diana heard my love for you and kept assuring me that our love couldn't be over. Diana knew in London how much I loved you. And she knows how much I love you still. She told me that when she saw you in her office you were wearing your wedding ring. Were you?"

"Yes. I took it off after you called from the lobby. I thought you were coming to tell me that you were going to file for divorce."

"Did you wear it because you hoped we would get back together?"

"I didn't dare hope for that." Julia shrugged softly. "I just had to wear it."

"I just had to take mine off even though I never wanted to."

"Jeffrey?"

"Yes, my darling?"

"I never hated you. But how you must have hated me when you believed that I had deceived you about something so important."

"I never hated you. I only loved you. I will always love you." Jeffrey smiled gently, hopefully, and urged lovingly, "Julie, tell me what you want."

"I want what I have always wanted, Jeffrey. I want you to love me." Julia paused for just a moment and then spoke the other half of her dream, "And I want you to love our daughter."

"I love you both with all my heart."

Jeffrey held his arms out to her then, and Julia came to him joyfully as she always had, and they were together again at last, where they belonged. Jeffrey whispered her name over and over, his lips caressing her hair as he spoke, until finally he had to see her eyes.

"My lovely Julie," he whispered to the lavender that sparkled with such love and such happiness. Jeffrey cupped her face in his gentle and trembling hands and asked a question that he had tried to answer but couldn't, a question only Julia could answer. "In September you told me that you were responsible for our pregnancy. Why did you say that?"

"Because I *had* deceived you then, Jeffrey. I let you believe that I was older and experienced and in control when I was really just a virgin and completely unprepared."

"Oh, honey." Jeffrey kissed her lips softly, and after a few minutes told her truthfully, "If I had known you were only sixteen, I still would have made love to you if you'd wanted me to, or just held you if you didn't. And if I had known you were a virgin I would have been more gentle."

"You were very gentle, Jeffrey."

Julia kissed him, a gentle kiss that might have lasted forever, but suddenly she remembered something and pulled free.

"Julie?"

"Will you put my ring back on my finger?" she asked as she retrieved the elegant band from the pocket of her sweater.

"Yes, my love, in thirty minutes."

"Thirty minutes?"

"We can get married again, our own private ceremony, in thirty minutes, if you will have me."

"I will have you."

"Then I'm going to go to my apartment right now and get my ring."

"You still have it?"

"Of course I do. And I want it back on my finger, where it belongs, as soon as possible."

"Jeffrey, there's a snowstorm outside."

"Warm, lovely, beautiful snow." Jeffrey smiled. "I love you so much, Julie."

"I love you so much, too." As she gazed into his loving eyes, a slight frown crossed her face. "Jeffrey, while you're gone, I need to speak with Patrick. He's waiting for me. Patrick and I are friends, Jeffrey, not lovers. He has been very important to me since you left, and now he needs me."

"Why does he need you?"

"He has been accused of a crime he didn't commit."

"What crime?"

"I can't tell you. I need to talk to him first. I'm going to try to get him to leave, but if he won't he'll need my—our—help. OK?"

"OK." *I trust you, Julie. I'm going to spend the rest of my life trusting you.*

"Patrick, please."

"I won't be in prison forever. At least I don't think they can do that to me." Patrick frowned. Maybe *they*—under the dazzling direction of Casey English—could lock him up and throw away the key. "Then, when I'm out, I'll be free. I won't have to hide anymore."

"You will never go to prison, Patrick. I won't let anyone do that to you!"

"Please don't worry about me. Please spend every ounce of your energy on the life of love that lies ahead for you with Jeffrey and Merry. Forget about me, Julia. I dug this grave."

"You didn't!"

"Well. I'm choosing not to run or fight. I'm tired of running. First thing in the morning I'll go back to Southampton to ride and paint and take long walks on the snowy beach until they come get me. Don't worry about me, Julia, please. I'll be fine."

"Mommy!" Merry was wide-awake, bright-eyed, and eagerly waiting for Julia the following morning. "Daddy was here last night! Oh! Daddy's with you!"

"Daddy's with both of his girls forever," Jeffrey said lovingly as he kissed Merry good morning. "How are you today, Merry?"

"I'm *better!* My stomach doesn't hurt at all and I feel fine."

"I'm so glad, darling. I just wanted to wish you good morning and tell you that I'll be back. I have to go get admitted and arrange for someone to do the news for a while." Jeffrey shifted his loving gaze from his daughter to Julia as he left unspoken the other thing he had to do this morning.

I have to say good-bye to Diana, Julie. After I say good-bye I will never see her again. Jeffrey had told Julia that last night as they lay in bed, holding each other, gently sharing all the truths and all the fears, so that the ancient wounds could finally heal and their wonderful love could be at peace.

As Jeffrey silently reminded her now of the promise he had made about Diana, Julia smiled back, a loving, confident smile, so confident of his love *at last.*

Jeffrey was waiting in her office when she returned from rounds. One look at the dark-blue eyes she knew so well, eyes that would never lie to her, and Diana knew. She saw the gentle apology and the hope . . . apology for her and hope for his life and love with Julia and Merry.

"I'm happy for you, Jeffrey," she whispered truthfully. She would miss him very much, but she wasn't consumed by the feelings of failure she had felt when Sam and Chase had said good-bye.

"I would have spent my life with you, Diana."

"I know that." *And I know that Julia is a love that is greater than all loves. I know because your love for Julia is so very much like my love for Sam.*

Jeffrey put his arms around her and they held each other for a long time. Then, at the same moment, as if by silent signal, they both released their embrace and whispered a soft "Good-bye."

"Mr. Lawrence. Oh, Julia, I'm glad you're here, too," Dr. MacGregor said when they arrived at his office for Jeffrey's eleven A.M. appointment.

"Is something wrong? Has something happened?"

"Nothing's wrong, but maybe something has happened. The platelet and white blood cell counts done on Merry last evening and again this morning are up."

"She had a transfusion last night."

"Yes, but that would affect the red blood cell count—the hematocrit—not the white cells and platelets. Her red cell count before the transfusion hadn't fallen as much as I would have expected, but I elected to transfuse anyway because her hematocrit was very low. Even if her marrow is coming back I wanted to correct the anemia at least to a level that will give her a little reserve."

"Even if her marrow is coming back?"

"I've ordered repeat counts for this afternoon, but if they're still up I want to hold off on transplantation."

"You're saying that her marrow might recover?"

"Yes, if the aplasia was a temporary suppression from an external cause. From my review of her marrow aspirate I really didn't think that's what we were dealing with, but . . ."

"Doctors believe in miracles just like everyone else." Jeffrey quietly whispered the words that the specialist at UCLA had spoken to him four months before his miracle baby was born.

Chapter 24

"Hello, Judge Barrington. My name is Casey English. Thank you for taking my call. I am presently an associate with Spencer and Quinn in Manhattan. Before coming here I was with the D.A.'s office in San Francisco and was quite involved with the prosecution of rape cases."

"I see. What can I do for you, Ms. English?"

"I understand that your daughter Pamela was raped five years ago. I wondered if it would be possible for me to speak with her?"

"Why?"

"Because I am still very concerned about the issue of rape, Judge Barrington, and the impact of rape on its victims."

"It would be Pamela's decision."

"Of course."

"She just returned yesterday from Paris. She's spending the year abroad but is home for the holidays."

"I would be happy to fly to Louisville at any time. I think it might be helpful for Pamela to speak with me. I've really had a great deal of experience in talking with victims. Do you know if Pamela has fears that the man will return to rape her again?"

"I don't know. To be honest, we don't talk about it very much anymore."

"But the man has not been apprehended."

"That's correct."

"So she may be worried."

"I guess so. Let me talk with her this evening and give you a call tomorrow."

Casey wasn't sure what she would do if she couldn't meet with Pamela Barrington. She was supposed to have reported her knowledge concerning the whereabouts of a suspected felon to the police the moment she learned Patrick's true identity.

But she hadn't.

She had decided first to read all the documents the private detective had assembled for her. As she read about Patrick's boyhood, the details about the biological mother who alternately claimed and neglected him, the series of foster homes, the homelessness and hopelessness, Casey's heart ached.

Of course James Patrick Jones had become a criminal. Of course he hated the wealthy and privileged. Of course he felt rage and anger against women . . .

It all made sense, horrible, perfect sense. It was the classic portrait of a criminal—someone who had himself once been a victim and now left other victims in his wake of terror.

But, but, but . . .

Part of Casey, a place in her heart that wouldn't be silent, could not believe that Patrick had committed an act of such violence. Patrick was so gentle!

And there was something else in the Louisville police report . . .

According to Pamela Barrington, Patrick had found her that night sitting by the pond at the estate. She had always been a little afraid of him, she said, and that night he was even more terrifying because he was drunk, surly, menacingly powerful. He carried an almost-consumed fifth of bourbon, Pamela told the police. He offered her a swallow of the alcohol, and when she politely declined, he forced her to drink. Then he forced her to kiss him. As she tried to push him away she scratched his neck, drawing blood, and that enraged him all the more. He angrily threw the bottle against a boulder, shattering it, and then he raped her.

The judge's statement to the police confirmed the presence of a bleeding scratch on Patrick's neck. The judge didn't get close enough to Patrick to know whether he was drunk, but he recalled that Patrick's eyes were wild and the police found fragments of the bottle. There were fingerprints on the shattered glass, which, although the prints had never been entered into a centralized computer system, to Casey's untrained eyes exactly matched the prints John Tyler had obtained at the wedding reception in late October.

The deeply wounded woman within Casey wanted to punish Patrick for hurting her so much, for making her believe in his love then discarding her so cruelly and choosing Julia instead. And the dedicated attorney within Casey, the woman who believed in giving voice to the silent cries of victims and was truly passionate about justice, wanted to see justice done.

But the careful compulsive discipline that made Casey such an excellent attorney was very troubled by the testimony that Patrick had been drinking. On a moonlit evening in their romantic meadow of love, Patrick had told her that he had never tasted alcohol before because he had never felt safe enough to drink. And Casey had believed him because his voice was so quiet and his gray-green eyes flickered with pain and because she had witnessed his surprise when he felt the effects of the champagne.

I was drunk when I told you I loved you. Casey shuddered at the memory of those cruel words. But she needed to remember them, because Patrick hadn't been drunk that night, just a little high, a little giddy, but he didn't know the difference because alcohol was foreign to him.

And that was why she had to talk to Pamela Barrington. Casey had to watch Pamela's eyes as she asked the tough questions.

Casey told Judge Barrington the truth. She *did* care about the victims of

rape . . . even if the real victim of this rape had been Patrick.

Casey met with the judge and Pamela in the living room of the mansion at Barrington Farm on the afternoon of December twenty-second. The mansion reminded Casey of her home in San Francisco at Christmas, the huge tree decorated with expensive ornaments, the scent of pine, the crystal vases of holly, the mounds of elaborately wrapped presents. It wasn't a nostalgic memory—those grand Christmases hadn't been filled with joy—only an uneasy one. Casey's uneasiness grew when she met Pamela Barrington.

Because Pamela was so very much like her, a beautiful and privileged heiress who believed that life owed her everything her heart desired. Pamela's eyes clouded a little when she talked about Patrick, but there was no fear, no shame, no anguish that he had violated her. There was only anger and the intense desire for revenge. Pamela hadn't refused to meet with Casey—as a true victim might have, not wanting to relive the pain—she had welcomed the opportunity to re-create the drama. The talented, well-rehearsed actress was quite happy to give another performance.

"Did you see him drink, Pamela?"

"Yes. He had a bottle with him. He was drunk already, but he drank more in front of me and he forced me to drink, too."

"And it was bourbon?"

"Yes. Jim Beam. The police found the bottle shattered on a rock by the pond."

"Pamela, what if I told you that James Patrick Jones has a fatal allergic reaction to all types of alcohol including bourbon?"

The judge started to speak, but Casey held up her hand to stop him.

"Do you understand my question, Pamela?" Casey continued, clarifying her question as she would for a witness in the courtroom. "What if I told you that even a sip of alcohol would kill him in a matter of moments?"

Casey could tell that Pamela was searching her memory for proof that it wasn't true. But Pamela had never seen James Patrick Jones drink. It was she who had tried to force bourbon on him that night, part of her seduction, and he had shoved the bottle away, as if afraid even to have it near him, *as if it might be lethal.*

"Pamela?" the judge asked, hesitantly at first because he didn't want to believe . . . and then sternly, "*Pamela?*"

"Yes?" Pamela's eyes widened with surprise at the unfamiliar harshness of her father's tone.

"Did James rape you?"

"He didn't want me, Daddy," Pamela explained calmly, as if that was all the explanation that was necessary—the astonishing fact that James Patrick Jones had dared to say no to *her.* "You understand, don't you?"

"No. I don't understand, Pamela."

"He didn't want me!" Pamela repeated emphatically, annoyed and exasperated by the sudden obtuseness of her father. "He had to pay, Daddy, don't you see?"

"*Did he rape you?* Yes or no?"

"No! But—"

"Oh, Pamela," the judge sighed heavily, a sigh of shock and sadness for the wrongfully harmed James, and an almost greater sadness for the terribly spoiled daughter who was so unrepentant about what she had done. "All these years the police have been looking for him. And if they had found him, and if you had continued to lie, he would have gone to prison."

"I don't care! He *deserved* to go to prison!"

As Casey listened to the exchange between the defiant and remorseless Pamela and her horrified father, Casey, too, felt a deep horror.

Because she had been so much like Pamela.

Because she had wanted Patrick to pay for the unforgivable crime of not wanting her.

"Mr. Lawrence."

"For God's sake, call me Jeffrey."

"Jeffrey. Please come in." Patrick held open the door to the small apartment where he and Julia had spent so many hours. "Is Merry home? When I spoke with Julia last night she thought her blood counts might be high enough for her to be released from the hospital today."

"They were, and she's home."

"That's wonderful."

"We were very lucky," Jeffrey said quietly and with the same wonder that had filled Julia's voice years before when she had described their daughter's remarkable progress after her premature birth. "Patrick, I've come to thank you for all that you've done for Julia and for Merry, and to tell you that I will do everything possible to help you."

"I'm not a rapist, Jeffrey."

Jeffrey nodded. He didn't know that, but Julia did, and Jeffrey was going to spend the rest of his life believing her, trusting her, proving his trust and earning hers. *You'd better not be a rapist, Patrick.*

"Don't you think it would be better to turn yourself in?"

"I don't believe there's a chance in hell I can stay out of prison no matter what I do. This is Casey's show. I'm not going to spoil it for her. I'm quite sure she has a plan."

Patrick knew that Casey and the police would arrive soon. He was ready. He had spent the past few days soaring over jumps, walking along the beach to the meadow, and painting. Late last night he had finished the portrait that had tormented him for so long—the portrait of Casey, his wonderful Venus, the picture of an illusion. The magnificent portrait hung on the wall in his bedroom, a grim reminder of his folly.

"Julia and Merry and I would like you to come for dinner tomorrow night."

"For Christmas?"

"Yes."

Patrick shook his head in disbelief. Merry and Julia might want him to join them, but not Jeffrey.

"Yo will always be welcome in my home, Patrick." Jeffrey spoke truthfully to Patrick's obvious skepticism. "You saved my wife and my daughter. *There is no way I can ever repay you for that.*"

* * *

Twenty-four hours later, moments before Patrick was to leave for dinner at Belvedere, Casey knocked softly on the door to his apartment.

"I really underestimated you, Casey. I just didn't think you'd choose to do it on Christmas Day."

"May I come in?"

"Of course. Where are the police?"

In the moments before Casey answered, Patrick fought to calm his racing heart. It wasn't fear that caused his heart to pound. Patrick was unafraid of the police. He had accepted his fate. What caused his heart to gallop still, despite everything, was Casey. She wore a tailored navy-blue suit and her fire-gold hair was pulled tightly off her face and into a severe chignon. She looked like the consummate attorney, except for her eyes.

Her eyes were soft and vulnerable and uncertain, exactly like the eyes in the portrait that hung in the other room, a portrait that he had believed was the artist's deluded conception, the illusory memory of love.

Casey should have looked so triumphant. But instead she looked like the woman Patrick loved.

"No police, Patrick. Only this." Casey removed a large envelope from the briefcase she carried. Then she took a deep breath as her mind frantically searched for the words she had so carefully rehearsed. But the well-scripted eloquent flow of words, a brief yet complete explanation after which she could quickly leave, had vanished the moment she saw him and she fumbled as she tried to recall the important points. "This packet contains a copy of Pamela's statement recanting her accusation, the official notice from the Louisville police that all charges against you have been dropped, and a letter from Judge Barrington. I don't know what the letter says, but I do know that he liked you, Patrick, and respected you, and feels great remorse about what Pamela did. His letter should contain a check in the amount of five million dollars. It's obviously a great deal of money, but I think the judge truly believes it's small compared to the five years of your life that were taken from you and can never be replaced. The money is a gift from the judge to you, and it is not intended to dissuade you from filing a civil suit against Pamela. She's an adult now, with her own fortune, and the judge expects, and even supports, full legal recourse against her."

"Casey," Patrick said softly, interrupting the spill of words to which he had barely listened after the miraculous ones—*All charges against you have been dropped*—words that had been delivered to the briefcase where her vulnerable lovely eyes had been resolutely focused ever since leaving his. "How did this happen?"

"Oh. In her statement to the police Pamela said you had been drinking."

"But you knew that wasn't possible. And you got Pamela to admit that she lied. Is that right, Casey?" *Look at me!* "Is that what you did?"

"You were innocent, Patrick." Casey looked up then, into the gray-green eyes she loved so much. "You were the victim."

"You went to Louisville and confronted her?"

"Something like that."

"Casey . . ."

"Oh, your wallet and passport and birth certificate are in here, too. The clothes and riding trophies that were impounded by the police will be mailed to you. And there were some paintings . . ." As Casey spoke, her eyes drifted to the walls of Patrick's apartment that were covered with his wonderful art. Casey hadn't wanted to see the place where Patrick and Julia had loved but it was impossible to keep looking at him. “I didn’t know you were an artist.”

An artist, not a rapist! her heart cried. *Oh, Patrick, couldn’t you even have told me that?*

“I have to go, Patrick. I have a plane to catch.”

“Where are you going?”

“What? Oh, to Bermuda. I’ll be back in a week. Please let me know if you would like me or someone from our firm to handle the suit against Pamela.”

“I’m not going to file a suit against Pamela.”

“Oh, well, if you change your mind.”

“I won’t. I’m not interested in revenge.”

No, you wouldn’t be interested in revenge, Patrick, because you are so wise and you know what is important. Somehow you know the destructive power of revenge. Casey looked at him briefly, long enough to smile a wobbly smile, then turned to the door.

“Casey?”

“Yes?”

“Thank you.”

“You’re welcome,” she whispered softly.

Then she was gone, and he should have run after her. But she seemed so eager to get away from him. And he was still so very stunned by what had happened.

Eventually, a surprising flicker of reality surfaced from the stunning swirl of emotions and thoughts that consumed him . . . he was expected for dinner at Belvedere.

Patrick realized, after he left his small apartment, that he hadn’t looked at the documents, or read the letter from the judge, or even opened it to see if the check was inside.

None of that mattered. What mattered was that he was *free*. He was going to Christmas dinner at Belvedere as a free man.

Because of Casey.

Two days after Casey gave him his freedom, Patrick flew to Bermuda. He knew where she was staying, because he had called until he found the hotel where she was registered, and when he reached the hotel perched on a cliff above a white sand beach, his heart filled with hope. Had she chosen this place because it reminded her of a cottage above the sea where once there had been such love?

Casey wasn’t in her room. On impulse, or perhaps something much stronger, Patrick walked down the steep trail to the beach below. And in the distance, on the farthest reach of a rocky point, he saw her. She stood defiantly, facing the wind and the waves, her hair a red-gold beacon dancing in the muted rays of the winter sun.

“You’re just not afraid of the sea, are you?” Patrick asked softly when he stood on the rocky point a few feet behind her.

Casey hadn’t heard him approach; the wintry Atlantic was thundering, and the wind whistled and roared. But she heard his familiar, gentle voice above the wind and waves.

“Patrick,” Casey whispered to the sapphire waves. She spoke to the waves, instead of turning to him, because her eyes were filled with hot tears, just as they had been filled with tears on that June night when he had rescued her. “Why are you here?”

“Why won’t you look at me?”

Casey turned then, without drying her tears, because she had dried them on that distant balmy night, and Patrick had known anyway.

"You gave me my freedom, Casey. Do you have any idea what that feels like?"

"Yes, I do know, Patrick," she answered quietly. "Last summer with you, *I* felt free."

Casey had almost lost the gift Patrick had given her, *almost* drenched herself in hatred and revenge. But in giving Patrick his freedom, she had begun to believe again in the woman Patrick had discovered last summer, the lovely generous woman who she wanted to be. Her need to win wasn't as strong as her love for him. Now, perhaps, at last, she could be a gracious loser.

"Because of you, Casey, I'm free to ride again, and even compete if I choose, and I'm free to paint and even have my work published, and I'm free to travel to a foreign country and show my passport and have no fear that my real name will summon the police. Those are such wonderful freedoms, Casey, but there is another freedom that is more magnificent than all the rest."

"The one you didn't tell me about last summer."

"Yes. The most precious freedom of all, the freedom to love, the freedom to give your heart and know that your love won't cause harm. I can do that now, Casey. I can ask the woman I love if she will marry me. I thought, at least on the weekends, we could live in a cottage I'm going to build in a meadow of wildflowers."

"Julia's meadow. Now you are free to marry Julia," Casey whispered quietly, a gracious defeat, a generous wish for Patrick's happiness with her ancient enemy. "When she came to my office that day, wanting my help with her divorce, I guess, I was very rude. I need to apologize."

"It wasn't about a divorce. It was because Merry was ill."

"Oh. Patrick, I didn't know."

"I know and Julia knows, and it's OK. Everything's OK. Well, not everything, because I still haven't heard a yes to my marriage proposal."

"Patrick?" Casey asked softly as she looked into eyes that filled with such love, such desire for her.

"Casey, I don't want to marry Julia. I have never loved anyone but you. Will you marry me, my love?"

"Oh, Patrick. Have you come to rescue me again?"

"I have come, my lovely flower, to love you forever."

"Jeffrey?" Julia found him in the library at Belvedere at three A.M. on a snowy night in the middle of January. She had fallen asleep in his arms, but had awakened to find him gone. "What are you doing?"

"I'm reading the letters you wrote to me when I was in Beirut."

"Oh, Jeffrey." Julia moved behind him and rested her hands on his shoulders. She felt the tension in his muscles, a palpable sign of his despair as he read her loving descriptions of the daily events in the life of his little girl. "Please stop torturing yourself."

"I missed so much."

"But you're missing nothing now."

"Just all the hours of every day when I'm at work."

"While Merry's at school and with her friends. I miss her during those hours, too, Jeffrey, but she's a very happy, very healthy, and very loved little girl."

"Yes she is. Because of you. Because you wouldn't let her believe that her father didn't love her despite the evidence."

"And I was right." Julia tenderly kissed his lips. After a moment she pulled away and gazed at him with an expression that was thoughtful and a little worried.

"What, darling?"

"Merry is planning to have a father-daughter talk with you this weekend. I think you need to know in advance what she's going to propose."

"All right."

"Your daughter wants a baby brother or sister, perhaps one or two of each. She's very innocent still about babies and where they come from. I think she believes that if all three of us combine our wishes it will happen."

"Merry wants us to have another baby?"

As Jeffrey asked the question, so quietly, Julia saw the sadness in his eyes. She had worried that his reaction might be sadness not joy, sadness that the daughter he loved so much and who finally knew his wonderful love was ready so soon to share it.

"Jeffrey, Merry never *ever* talked about having brothers or sisters before. This is a sign of how confident she is of your love. She knows that nothing can diminish the bond between you, and she probably knows, too, that you have more than enough love for an infinite number of babies. Merry has always been a remarkably unspoiled and generous little girl."

"Like her mother." Jeffrey smiled, but the smile faded as a new sadness filled his eyes. "Julie, I don't deserve . . ."

"Yes you do, and your unborn babies deserve to have you as their father."

"Well, they deserve to have you as their mother. Do you want more children, honey?"

"I would love to have more children, Jeffrey."

"There are new techniques—in vitro fertilization—I suppose we could look into . . . What? Why are you smiling?"

"What's wrong with the old-fashioned way? We've practiced birth control ever since Merry was born. Couldn't we try without for a while?"

"Yes, but Julie, I think it was truly a miracle that Merry was conceived."

"I think, my love, that all babies are miracles."

"Yes," Jeffrey whispered softly. "Oh, Julie, have I ever told you how much I love you?"

"All the time, but I never tire of hearing it."

Julia tilted her head, and a strand of hair fell into her eyes. As Jeffrey very delicately moved the black silk, he saw a fleeting flicker of sadness in the lavender.

Jeffrey knew the cause, and even though Julia was more confident of their love than she had ever been, she couldn't erase the painful memories of his affair with Diana any more than he could erase the sadness he would always feel about the past he could not change.

The memories could never be erased, but they could be softened with love. Just as Julia gently commanded Jeffrey to stop torturing himself and then spent long, patient hours listening to his torment and helping him ease it, Jeffrey gently tried to stop the sadness in her eyes when her thoughts drifted to his affair by lovingly discussing the worries with her.

Now he saw a worry that lingered even after the fleeting flicker of sadness had vanished.

"What, honey? Tell me."

"Do you think about her?"

"Sometimes," Jeffrey admitted honestly. "Sometimes, when I feel so happy, so lucky, so overflowing with joy, I think about her. And what I think is that I wish she could have even a part of the happiness and love that we have. That's all, Julie. I just wish happiness for her."

Chapter 25

MANHATTAN
FEBRUARY 1990

"Happy Valentine's Eve." Jeffrey whispered the words between a tender kiss as he greeted Julia when he arrived home at ten P.M.

"Happy Valentine's Eve," Julia echoed softly.

"You're listening to music?"

"Yes. I bought a wonderful collection of love songs, most of my very favorite ones, released just in time for Valentine's Day." Julia smiled lovingly at Jeffrey, who was so very romantic in the intimate privacy of their own love, but who, she knew, never listened to other lovers' songs of love. "Let me go turn the stereo off so that we can go to bed."

This was their new pattern, to go to bed as soon as Jeffrey arrived home, and it was so much more wonderful than the old pattern they had followed for years. Because now, instead of talking for hours before going to bed, they went right to their master suite, pausing to gaze at their sleeping daughter on the way, and they awakened early so that the three of them could linger over breakfast together.

Jeffrey followed Julia across the great room to the stereo. As she reached for the record on the turntable, he glanced casually at the ivory-colored double album with elegant crimson script, and his eyes fell on two familiar crimson words: Sam Hunter. The discovery prompted more reading, and more discoveries. The album was called *Memories of Love*, and it featured a new love song entitled "Queen of Hearts'.

"Jeffrey?" Julia asked when she saw his obvious and surprising interest. And there was more, because, as she watched, his interested dark-blue eyes became confused, and gentle, and so thoughtful. "Jeffrey, darling, what is it?"

Jeffrey looked at her, his lovely Julie, and smiled a gentle smile. He would let it go, not mention Diana's name at all, not resurrect the still-painful memories. But Sam Hunter's newest song of love was entitled "Queen of Hearts," and Jeffrey needed to listen to it. He could come back to the great room in the middle of the night, when Julia was asleep, and listen to the song privately, and if it meant something tell Julia then . . . But there were no secrets in the love of Jeffrey and Julia anymore. There was only truth and trust and infinite faith in their magnificent love.

"It has to do with Diana, Julie . . ." Jeffrey began apologetically.

"OK."

"She was in love once, before her marriage to Chase, and for Diana, for her heart, that distant love was as strong and as forever as my love for you."

"And mine for you," Julia reminded him gently, reassuring him, knowing that he was only mentioning Diana because it was something important.

"Tell me."

"Her great love was Sam Hunter. They met in high school in Dallas."

"Oh," Julia whispered softly, with a slight frown because for some reason the revelation wasn't entirely a surprise. Julia knew well, and loved, the love songs written by Sam Hunter, especially the ones written a decade ago, which meant that although she had not known until now that Sam's Diana was Diana Shepherd, she had known for a very long time that Sam Hunter loved a woman named Diana. "Yes."

"Sam left her, and that caused great pain, and even though it was a long time ago, Diana has never really stopped loving him. Anyway, I noticed that his new love song is called "'Queen of Hearts,' and I wondered—"

"Sam had to leave her, Jeffrey," Julia interrupted gently but confidently. "He didn't want to, but he had to."

"What? How on earth do you know that?"

"Because it's in his songs. And all the songs are all here, Jeffrey, in this album, and there's a booklet with lyrics and dates when each song was written. We can look at them, or listen, but, darling, I'm really very sure that all his songs of love were written for Diana and that even though he loved her—I think *because* he loved her—he had to leave her."

"He sang to Diana by name?" Jeffrey asked softly.

"Not at first, but eventually. His most beautiful love song, until this new one, was "'Diana's Song.' It was released just before Lady Diana Spencer married Prince Charles. Sam lived in England at the time, and it would make sense that the most beautiful of all his songs of love was written for the most beautiful and enchanting royal bride, but I always believed "'Diana's Song' was written for the same woman to whom he had been singing all along. It seemed like the happy ending to the longing that had been in his songs until then, a joyous hope that they would finally be together." Julia paused, then added quietly, "But the ending wasn't happy. Sam sang to her, but she didn't come, and after that his songs were still beautiful, and very moving, but quite sad."

"Diana never heard his love songs, Julie."

"Oh, but she must have, if she listened to the radio at all."

"But she didn't. She couldn't."

"Why not?"

Jeffrey hesitated, but for only a moment, because he knew he had to tell Julia everything.

"When Sam left her—and you're right, my lovely Julie, it was because he had to—Diana was pregnant with his baby. Sam never knew about their daughter. Her name was Janie. She was born with a serious heart condition and died a month after she was born."

"Oh, no," Julia whispered softly as she remembered Diana's gentle concern and compassion when Julia asked for her help for Merry.

"Diana's life and love with Sam, and with Janie, had been filled with music. After Janie died, and when Diana believed that Sam didn't love her enough and would never return, she stopped listening to the music she once had loved. The memories of Sam, and the daughter who loved listening to tapes he had made, were just too painful. The day that you saw us in Hyde Park, honey, when Diana was so very sad, it was because she had heard a cascading of chimes that reminded her of a song Janie had loved."

"Oh, Jeffrey," Julia whispered after several moments. "Sam loved Diana so much."

"And Diana loved Sam. She would have gone to him if she had heard his songs. She still would."

"Sam loves her still, Jeffrey. That's why he wrote "'Queen of Hearts.' He must have seen her again."

"Yes. He did see her. In October he asked Diana to operate on his infant daughter . . . Janie. It was very emotional for Diana, but something she had to do, and the surgery was a complete success. Janie recovered quickly, and she and Sam returned to their home in California."

Jeffrey gazed at Julia's lovely eyes, tear-misted and thoughtful, and hoped that Diana would not be angry that he had revealed her secrets. Jeffrey had told Julia all the truths because he believed it was necessary because of what he had to ask of Julia.

But Jeffrey didn't have to ask.

"You have to tell her, Jeffrey. You have to go to Diana and tell her."

"For my Valentines," Jeffrey said at breakfast the following morning as he handed pink-and-white gift-wrapped boxes to Julia and Merry.

"Daddy!" Merry exclaimed as she removed the gold necklace with a pendant in the shape of a tiny, solid-gold, friendly dragon. "Mommy, it's Daphne."

"This is beautiful, Jeffrey," Julia said as she held the small and perfect re-creation of her fairytale character in her hand. "How did you do it?"

"I took one of the illustrated stories to a jeweler at Harry Winston."

"He did a magnificent job."

"He did, didn't he? See how you think he did with your present."

Julia's present was a necklace, too, a nacklace to match their elegant wedding bands, delicate ribbons of white and yellow gold, intertwined and then melted together by fire.

"Oh, Jeffrey."

"You like it." It wasn't a question, because Jeffrey saw the joy in her lavender eyes. "The other thing, before Merry has to rush off for school, is that I've scheduled time off for the same days that Merry is on spring vacation. Since that's only a month away I thought we should start making plans."

"You still might have to work, though, Daddy."

"No, Merry. I won't work on those days, no matter what."

"But if you had to, because it was something very important like the peace conference, that would be OK."

"It would be OK, wouldn't it?" Jeffrey gently asked his lovely daughter. Jeffrey knew the answer—"Yes, it would be OK"—because their love wasn't precarious any longer. "But it can't happen two vacations in a row, so I think we should start to make plans."

Five minutes after Merry left for school, Jeffrey and Julia walked to the foyer to watch for the limousine from the studio.

"I love the necklace, Jeffrey. And the vacation. We still haven't done our honeymoon, have we?"

"I was thinking we might have to postpone that until all our babies are grown. I can't imagine going on vacation without Merry, can you?"

"No, I can't."

Jeffrey kissed her for a long, tender moment. Then the limousine appeared on the cobblestone drive and he reluctantly pulled free and reached for the briefcase that contained Sam Hunter's *Memories of Love*.

"I love you, Julie."

"I want you to do this, Jeffrey." Julia smiled a loving smile, and there wasn't a flicker of uncertainty in her lavender eyes. Julia believed in Jeffrey's forever love. "I want happiness for Diana, too."

* * *

"Hello, Diana," Jeffrey said quietly when she answered the private line in her office at noon.

"Jeffrey."

"I need to see you. It's important."

"Jeffrey . . ."

"It's Julia's idea."

"Oh?"

"Are you free this evening?"

"No. In fact, I'm leaving at seven tonight for a week's vacation in Florida."

"Florida, not Malibu?"

"You know me so well. I actually had been having masochistic ideas, like dropping by for a post-op check on Janie. That's why I'm taking this vacation. I'm in need of a heart-to-heart talk with myself."

"Are there other topics?"

"Other than Sam? Well, yes, there's the directorship of the Institute. It's harder to convince myself that I *must* get the appointment now, for the good of the Institute, because Tom and I are no longer enemies. In fact, I think most of me wants Tom to get the job. I've been thinking about withdrawing my name from consideration."

"I just have a feeling that everything is going to work out."

"Really? What a remarkable prediction based on absolutely no facts, Anchor."

I do have the facts, Jeffrey thought.

"Can you see me before you leave, Diana?"

"You mean this afternoon?"

"Whenever you're free."

"I'm free anytime. I'm just doing paperwork."

"So, your penthouse in an hour?"

"OK."

"Hi." Jeffrey smiled warmly at the familiar sapphire eyes. He saw fatigue and strain, but Diana smiled a lovely, sparkling smile of welcome for him.

"Hi." Diana tilted her head and asked softly, "This was really Julia's idea?"

"It really was. Last night, together, we discovered something that you need to know. Julia knows how very important it is and made the suggestion that I see you before I even had a chance to ask." Jeffrey's solemn and gentle eyes left Diana's for a moment to glance at a far corner of the luxurious living room. "That wall of state-of-the art stereo equipment does work, doesn't it?"

"Yes. Chase used to listen to an occasional opera."

"Good. Although it hardly matters. There's a booklet inside the album with all the lyrics," Jeffrey explained as he removed Sam's album from his briefcase and handed it to Diana. Then, instead of waiting for her to make the slow, hopeful discoveries, wanting her to know *now*, he continued gently, "Sam loves you, honey. He always has."

"What?" Diana didn't even look at the album. She looked instead into the dark-blue eyes she trusted so much. Jeffrey knew of her love for Sam and would never hurt her. "How do you know?"

"Because it's all here in this just-released album of Sam's most beautiful songs of love. Sam sang his love to you, Diana. All the songs are here, all his messages of love, including his wish for you to be together again, if you loved him still, after his father died."

"He sang to me by name?" Diana asked softly.

"When it was safe to, after his father died, yes. And before that . . . well, darling, it's very obvious, beautifully, eloquently, lovingly obvious, that all his songs were always to you."

"All those years . . ." Diana whispered, a whisper of painful memories and immeasurable loss. "He loved me?"

"Yes, just as he loves you now, still. Sam's newest song, just written, is called "Queen of Hearts." I always thought that name was perfect for you, Diana, even though you believed it was so wrong. But Sam knows the name is perfect, too, and in this most beautiful love song he has proven that it is who you are." Jeffrey gently touched her cheek and gazed into her hopeful but still-disbelieving sapphire eyes. "I'm going to go now, darling. Don't get so lost in memories that you miss your plane."

"My plane's not until seven."

"No, Diana, it's at four." Jeffrey removed a United Airlines ticket from his jacket pocket. "It arrives in Los Angeles at eight-thirty. I decided to put you in Seat 2B."

"Jeffrey . . ."

Jeffrey smiled lovingly. "It's only a one-way ticket."

"I'm going to go see him, aren't I?"

"I hope so."

"Oh, Jeffrey, thank you." Diana smiled a lovely, hopeful smile and whispered softly, "And please thank her, thank Julia, for me."

"She asked me to do the same to you."

Diana still had the piece of paper on which Sam had written his unlisted home phone number. She had kept it, a loose scrap inside her address book, never transcribed to one of the pages but not discarded, either.

She dialed the number when she reached Los Angeles.

"Sam? It's Diana."

"Diana."

"Remember me?" Diana asked softly, suddenly swept to the memory of Sam asking the same question on a rainy night in Boston.

"Oh, yes, I remember you," Sam whispered gently, just as Diana had whispered the same words to him that soggy night. "Where are you?"

"At the airport."

"Are you coming to see us?"

"Yes."

"Let me get my healthy little girl bundled up and we'll be right there to get you."

"Is Janie asleep?"

"Yes, but she'll fall asleep again in the car."

"Why don't I just take a taxi? Wouldn't that be quicker?"

Sam was waiting on the porch near the front door so he could hear if Janie awakened, but *outside* so he could greet her as she arrived.

In October, both Sam and Diana had so carefully hidden the love they still felt. But now, in the sapphire eyes and in the dark-brown ones, the love was at the surface, radiant and hopeful and full of joy.

"Oh, Diana," he whispered softly. "How I have missed you."

"How I have missed you, too, Sam."

Sam gently touched her face, a tender caress of welcome and love, then he reached for her suitcase with one hand and her hand with the other and they walked into his beachfront bungalow and upstairs to his bedroom that overlooked the ocean. They stood for a moment and gazed at the rippling ribbon of gold cast by the moon on the inky black Pacific. Then Sam led her across the hall to the room where Janie lay sleeping so peacefully.

"Hello, little Janie," Diana whispered.

Janie didn't awaken, but her long dark lashes fluttered and her pink lips curled into a soft smile, as if she knew the familiar gentle voice had come to stay, as if she knew that from this moment on she would have a loving father *and* mother.

"She's so healthy, Diana. She can laugh forever because her lungs are so free." Sam smiled as he spoke, but his words caused sudden tears in her lovely eyes. "Diana?"

"Could we go back to your room and talk?"

"Of course."

They sat on Sam's bed, their faces illuminated by the moon. Sam gently cupped her sad, lovely face in his hands and tenderly kissed the tears that fell from the sapphire and waited in patient loving silence until at last she was able to speak.

"There are things I need to tell you," Diana whispered finally to his loving eyes. How sad he would be when he learned about the daughter whose small lungs had never had a chance to laugh forever. "Maybe tomorrow."

"All right."

"Tonight you need to know that I waited for you to return to me, but I never heard your songs of love. I know I told you that I would listen . . . but I didn't."

"I sang instead of coming to you, Diana, after my father died, because it had been so many years and I didn't want to intrude if you had a new love, or confuse you, and . . ."

"And because you knew that if I was waiting I would hear your songs."

"But you never did."

"No. I still haven't." Diana smiled a trembling smile. "I've only read the lyrics. Oh, Sam, such beautiful lyrics of love."

"For my most beautiful love." Sam gently kissed her trembling lips and whispered softly, "I will sing all the love songs to you, my Diana. I will spend my life singing songs of love to you . . . if that's what you want."

"Oh, yes, Sam, that's what I want."

"I love you, Diana. Oh, how I love you."

"And oh, how I love you, Sam."

Sam and Diana danced beneath the golden moon, as they had danced in their private corner of the park in Dallas, their lips and bodies gently kissing as they swayed to the music of love that lived within them, the joyous melodies of their hearts and souls.

And sometime during the moonlit night, their dance became a dance of love. And so slowly, so tenderly, in a rhythm of joy that promised forever, Sam made love to his beautiful Queen of Hearts.

Bel Air

Part One

Chapter 1

LOS ANGELES, CALIFORNIA
JUNE 1984

"Allison! I'm so glad you haven't left yet!"

"Hello, Meg." Allison smiled at the familiar drama in her friend's breathless voice. Virtually everything in Meg Montgomery's life was an "event'; it had always been that way. Of course, today actually qualified. Today Meg was getting married. Allison guessed calmly, "Is there a problem?"

"Yes! Jerome Cole just called. Apparently he is deathly—no, not deathly—*incapacitatingly* ill. Food poisoning or something."

Allison frowned slightly, a begrudging acknowledgement that this was at least a bit of a "situation." Jerome Cole was *the* wedding photographer for Los Angeles's wealthiest brides—brides like Meg and Allison. For the heiresses of Bel Air and Beverly Hills, a gold leaf album filled with photographs by Jerome Cole was as much a wedding staple as Mendelssohn's March, pearl-studded satin gowns, five-tiered cakes, and fountains of champagne.

There certainly are other perfectly good photographers in Los Angeles, Allison mused. But on this day, the third Saturday in June, all other good photographers would be booked. Not that the pictures mattered, not *really*, Allison thought. But Meg was so excited, so much in love, so hopeful that every detail of her fairy-tale wedding would be perfect. The pictures didn't matter, but, still, it was too bad . . .

"Jerome has an assistant," Meg continued while Allison was searching for a way to convince her friend that this was not, in fact, the end of the world. "And she is available."

"Oh! Good."

"Allison, I wondered if you could give her a ride? She doesn't have a car! And I don't want to worry about a cab getting lost."

"Of course I'll give her a ride, Meg."

"Great. Thanks. I think she lives quite near you. She has a basement apartment in a house on Montana and Twentieth in Santa Monica." Meg gave Allison the street address and asked, "Is that close?"

"Very. Only about five blocks away."

"Good. Her name is Emily Something-that-sounds-French. She doesn't sound French, though. I just talked to her. She'll be ready at three-twenty. Is that OK?"

"Absolutely. Meg, this is all going to be fine. It's such a perfect day for a wedding." Allison added, forcing enthusiasm, "I'm really looking forward to it."

I'm not really looking forward to it, Allison thought as she replaced the receiver.

Only a month ago, Allison had been planning her own wedding. Only a month ago, she had reconfirmed the Saturday afternoon date in September with Jerome, who would take the pictures; with Francois, who would provide the cut flowers, boutonniers, and corsages; with Wolfgang, who would prepare the rehearsal dinner at Spago; and with Martin, who promised that, as with Meg's wedding, the Bel Air Hunt Club would be Allison's for the entire day . . . the entire *night* if she wanted it.

Two weeks ago Allison had called them all, apologetically, to cancel. *Cancel*, not reschedule. The marriage of Allison Fitzgerald and Daniel Forester was not going to happen, not in September, not ever.

It was your decision, Allison reminded herself. *Your* decision. At the moment, the emotions and thoughts that had guided her with such apparent ease to the momentous decision were in hiding, taking with them the buoyant confidence Allison needed to counterbalance the sudden heavy weight of doubt.

Allison glanced at her watch. It was only three o'clock. She could leave at three-fifteen and still reach Emily's apartment before three-twenty. Allison could spend the next fifteen minutes thinking—stewing—about Dan, or she could call Winter, her best friend.

It was an easy choice.

"Meg must be in a tailspin!" Winter exclaimed after Allison told her about Jerome.

"Actually, she sounded surprisingly calm. This crisis probably distracted her from all the usual wedding day anxieties."

"There's still an hour left before the wedding. Plenty of time for a few more mini-dramas."

"True. I just hope everything goes all right."

"So do I. And it will. It should be a fabulous party, not to mention an interesting one." Winter elaborated merrily, "Connecticut's bluest-bloods and Wall Street's wiliest wizards mingling among the roses with Hollywood's glitziest and Rodeo's ultra-chic and—"

"Winter! I'm afraid the East Coast blue-bloods and financiers are going to be underrepresented, except for Cameron's family."

"*Daahling*," Winter whispered with mock horror and an elegant upper crust accent, "they don't approve of Meg Montgomery of Bel Air?"

"Of course they do, to the tune of many parties, galas, and receptions in honor of the newlyweds beginning the second they arrive in New York."

"Oh. So it will just be the usual group?" Winter sighed theatrically.

"I'm afraid so," Allison commiserated gaily. Just the usual group. Just four hundred of the richest and most famous men and women in Southern California.

"I've got to go," Winter said, suddenly realizing the time. "I'm not quite ready and Mark should be here in five minutes."

"Mark?"

"Mark. He's a third year medical student at UCLA. I met him in the Sculpture Garden Thursday evening, during my sentimental stroll around campus."

"And you're taking him to Meg's wedding?" *At the Club?*

"Why not? You'll sit with us at the ceremony, won't you?"

"Yes. Of course."

* * *

Mark looked at the street address he had hastily written in the margin of his neuroanatomy class notes, memorized it, and left his apartment on Manning Avenue five minutes before he was to pick her up. Holman Avenue was quite close and quite familiar. During his first year of medical school, Mark had dated a law student who lived in an apartment on Holman.

Mark knew Holman Avenue existed and was a plausible address for a student. But what about Winter Carlyle? Did the remarkable woman with the implausible name actually exist? Winter Carlyle was not listed in the phone book, and directory assistance either couldn't or *wouldn't* provide a number.

Winter Carlyle was a mirage, pure and simple, a vision of violet and velvet and ivory that had danced in his memory for the past two days, ever since she had vanished as mysteriously as she had appeared.

"Are you a neurosurgeon?" she had asked, startling him with the question, the surprising interruption, and *her*.

"I beg your pardon?"

"Are you a neurosurgeon?" She gestured gracefully to the *Textbook of Neurosurgery* that lay beside him on the grass.

Mark was studying. He had chosen a patch of grass in the Sculpture Garden on the UCLA campus, preferring the warmth and light of the early evening sun over the shadowy heat of his small apartment or the air-conditioned chilliness of the Health Sciences Library. The campus was virtually deserted during the recess before Summer Quarter. Until that moment, Mark had been alone amidst the silent bronze statues.

"No, I'm not a neurosurgeon."

"May I look at your book?"

"Sure."

"Thank you."

Before Mark could stand, Winter had floated gracefully onto the grass. She took the heavy textbook he handed to her, turned it facedown on her lap, and opened to the index. She scanned the medical terms, frowning as she searched, then smiling slightly when she found what she sought. She turned eagerly to the text, carefully reading the words; then she frowned again, not satisfied with what she read, returned to the index, and began the process anew.

Mark wtched in silent fascination, fascinated by her serious, purposeful search, but mostly fascinated by *her*.

She was stunningly beautiful. Shiny coal-black hair cascaded over her bare shoulders, a sensuous tumble of silky curls, and her skin was the color of rich cream. Her lovely eyes were black-lashed, hypnotic, *violet*, and even during her scholarly search her full, pink lips seduced.

Every movement—her slender arms, her tapered fingers, the thoughtful tilt of her head—was ballerina graceful, elegant, natural. If she was aware of Mark's appreciative gaze, it didn't bother her. Perhaps she expected it.

She is probably quite used to being admired, Mark decided.

So he simply admired her and waited. Finally, she closed the neurosurgery text, gave it a frown laced with disappointment, and sighed.

"Is there something I could help you with?" Mark offered quietly.

"Are you a doctor?"

"I'm a third year medical student. I'll get my degree in a year." Mark wondered if that credential would meet with approval or more disappointment.

"Are you taking a course in neurosurgery?"

"I'm doing a clerkship in Surgery. This month I'm on the Trauma Service.

We see quite a bit of emergency neurosurgery, so—"

"So you *do* know about subdural hematomas?"

"Yes." Of course. Subdural hematomas were standard third year medical student fare. But how did she know about them? Why were they so important to the remarkable violet eyes? Who *was* she? "What would you like to know?"

Winter considered Mark's question and finally answered, "Everything, I

guess. I have a friend . . ."

"Is he hospitalized at UCLA?" Mark interjected. If she wanted information about a patient, it would be best for her to speak directly with her friend's doctor. Mark could easily arrange that for her.

"He's a she, and she *was* hospitalized at UCLA three years ago. In fact, she was on the Trauma Service." Winter paused. She had very specific questions, but they didn't make sense out of context. "Could I tell you about her accident? Do you have time?"

"Sure."

"Thanks. Well, let's see. Her name is Allison. Until three years ago, what she did every moment she could was ride horses—ride and *jump*. She competed in show jumping—you know, six-foot-high brick walls, green and white railed fences covered with geraniums, that sort of thing. She was champion, really a champion. She was the youngest member of the 1980 U.S. Olympic Equestrian Team; but, of course, she didn't get to go to Moscow because of the boycott. This year was going to be her first chance to compete in the Olympics." Winter paused, sighed softly, and continued quietly, "Three years ago Allison had a terrible accident. It happened on the final fence during a jump-off. Something—a noise, a mouse, the wind, *something*—startled her horse when he was already in midair and she was hurled against the jump."

Winter shuddered at the memory. It should have been such a triumph for Allison; she had been seconds away from winning the Grand Prix of Los Angeles. But, instead, it was the end of her dreams and the beginning of a nightmare. Winter had been in the grandstand at the Bel Air Hunt Club proudly watching her friend fly over jump after jump. Allison looked so small and delicate on Tuxedo, her elegant champion horse, but her slender arms and legs were very strong. She expertly, invisibly, controlled Tuxedo's immense power, perfectly timing the gait, guiding him over the obstacles swiftly, flawlessly, *happily*.

Allison looked so happy when she rode! Even when she was competing, even when her concentration was intense, her eyes sparkled and her lips curled in a soft smile.

Allison smiled and Allison won. She loved show jumping and she was the best.

"Her horse was uninjured, but Allison . . . She was like a rag doll—limp, lifeless, broken. They rushed her to UCLA, to the Trauma Service, and they did emergency neurosurgery to remove a subdural hematoma. The doctors told us—Allison's parents and me—that a subdural hematoma is a blood clot pressing on the brain."

"That's what it is."

"Could you show me?"

Mark leafed through the neurosurgery text, to pages she had found but hadn't understood, and to new pages that might help her. He started with a colorful drawing of the anatomy of the brain. Mark explained it briefly, then turned to a drawing she had looked at before, one that showed a subdural hematoma and various neurosurgical approaches to its removal.

"Can we go back to the anatomy of the brain?"

When Mark found the page, Winter studied it in thoughtful silence, carefully reading the tiny foreign words and delicately tracing pathways of nerves and veins and arteries with her graceful fingers.

"Different parts of the brain control different things, like memory and vision and movement. Is that right?" she asked after she found a path that connected the back of the brain with the eyes.

"Yes." Mark was impressed that she had deduced that so quickly. He retraced
the path she had just discovered and elaborated, "For example, the occipital lobe controls . . ."

Over the next thirty minutes, Winter asked questions and Mark answered them, expanding detail with each answer, amazed at how swiftly she understood, how each question was more insightful and sophisticated than the last. He watched her eyes, serious, thoughtful, widening and narrowing with confusion, enlightenment, confusion again.

"The damage caused by the subdural hematoma would depend on which parts of the brain were compressed," she murmured.

Mark nodded solemnly.

"And on how promptly it was removed," he added, then hesitated, not wanting to ask. Over the last thirty minutes her sadness had vanished, replaced by wonder and curiosity. But now she was talking about damage, and they were back to specifics—the tragic story of her friend. "How is Allison?"

Mark's question didn't cause a cloud of sadness or a storm of pain; instead, it brought a surprised violet sparkle. She had forgotten he didn't know the story ended happily!

"She's *fine*," Winter answered emphatically. She qualified it a little, her voice softening sympathetically as she recalled her friend's shattered dreams, "She'll never jump again, of course. She'll never be an Olympic champion. It would be much too dangerous. Her depth perception is off, and she had other injuries—broken pelvic bones and crushed nerves—that make her less strong than she was."

Mark nodded solemnly. Allison was probably very lucky to be alive, much less *fine*.

"Her recovery was miraculous. For the first few weeks the doctors weren't even sure she would survive." Winter wondered how much of Allison's survival was medical science and how much was her friend's incredible will, alive and fighting inside her motionless body. "But she *did* survive, and then there were months and months of recovery. Allison was out of school for a year. She had to learn how to read again, and how to write, and how to walk and talk."

"But she can do those things now?"

"Oh, yes. She has a slight limp, because of the pelvic fracture. I sometimes wonder if she still has pain," Winter said quietly. Allison never mentioned it, but Allison wouldn't. Even during those long, frustrating months of recovery, when there must have been so much pain, Allison rarely spoke of it. Winter's thoughts drifted to that year, to the beginning, to the most frightening part of all. She whispered distantly, "For a while, when you told Allison something, she wouldn't remember it five minutes later."

"She couldn't make new memories," Mark said.

"Couldn't make new memories," Winter repeated thoughtfully. "Is that the medical description?"

"Yes."

What is she thinking? Mark wondered as he watched the lovely violet eyes grow even more serious. Is she thinking how awful it would be to forget each second of life as soon as it was over, to never make a new memory? Or is she thinking just the opposite, that it might be better to forget than remember?

"But now she can?" Mark asked after several silent moments. He hoped to retrieve a sparkle as they talked about Allison's miraculous recovery. "Now Allison can make new memories?"

"Yes. Now she's fine." Winter started to ask another question, but instead she caught her lower lip with her teeth, tugging softly, debating.

"Ask," Mark commanded gently. He guessed that they had come full circle, back to the beginning, to whatever had prompted the search. Back to the beginning with the question still unanswered.

She obviously hadn't been checking on a prognosis: Will my friend ever be all right? And she wasn't an attorney seeking information about the appropriateness of the medical care: Can my client sue? She knew those answers. Allison was *fine*.

It was something else.

"This is going to sound silly."

"That's OK."

"Before her accident, Allison had no sense of color or style or design. None." Winter paused, then gave Mark a gentle command. "Imagine Ireland. Happy images."

"All right."

"What do you see?"

"Green . . ."

"Good. Green eyes, fair skin, freckles, a long mane of auburn hair. That's Allison. Born in the USA, but roots that are pure Ireland. So, before her accident she would wear magenta or fuchsia or crimson or purple, and she had no idea that the colors clashed horribly with her own coloring."

Winter used the word *horribly*, but there was no horror, no cattiness, only fondness and warmth.

"Before her accident," Winter continued, "Allison's handwriting was round, *plump*, like when you're making the switch from printing to writing. And her doodles—Allison has always been a doodler—were primitive and childlike. You knew the doodles were horses because what else would Allison draw, but that was the only clue. If you didn't know Allison, you really couldn't tell."

"And now?"

"Now? Now her handwriting is elegant and beautiful. Her doodles are sketches she could probably sell. And she has an astonishing sense of color and style and design. In fact, she graduated from here two weeks ago with a major in Design and is going to be a designer at Elegance, *the* interior design store in Beverly Hills." Winter tugged at a blade of grass and asked quietly, "So what do you think? Is that medically possible? Something to do with the head injury? Or—"

"Or?"

"—or is it magic? Is the new incredible talent a divine gift to replace what was taken from her?"

Mark gazed at the lovely violet eyes so soft with hope. She wanted to believe it was magic. She wanted to believe in a divine wand that could swiftly convert tragedy to joy, wave away sadness, make wonderful new memories.

Mark wondered what magic she was awaiting in her own life, what pain or sadness needed to be transformed into happiness.

"It seems like magic," he replied quietly. Some magical, wondrous healing power of the brain that modern science had yet to discover.

Winter started to speak again but stopped at the sound of nearby bell tower chimes. She listened, counting silently as the gongs marked the hour. Her eyes widened as the realization settled.

"Eight o'clock! I've got to go."

Winter stood up quickly and so did Mark. She probably—*doubtless*—was late for a date, but Mark conjured up more enchanted images: stage coaches turning into pumpkins and white steeds turning into mice.

"Would you like to go out sometime?" he asked impulsively before she vanished forever.

"Oh!" The question caught Winter by surprise. It was so out of context! This wasn't the usual way dates happened, the way she *made* them happen. She hadn't flirted or teased or played. Her eyes hadn't seduced, her lips hadn't beckoned, her voice hadn't whispered provocative promises. There had been no games, no pretense, no acting at all.

There had only been serious, quiet conversation about brains and blood clots and magic.

"OK," she breathed finally, uncertainly. *I guess.*

"Saturday? Dinner? A movie?" Mark pressed swiftly, sensing her reluctance, not wanting her to change her mind.

"That would be fine." Winter's mind spun as she struggled to shift to the familiar role of temptress. It was a role she had mastered, with every performance flawless, effortless . . . until now. Now she searched for a soft purr, but the words came before the tone did. She heard herself ask him as seriously as she had asked about neurosurgery, "I have to go to a wedding on Saturday. Would you like to come with me?"

"Yes. What time shall I get you?"

"The wedding's at four, so three-fifteen." Winter gave him the address on Holman Avenue and Mark wrote it in the margin of his neuroanatomy notes. "Oh, it's a garden wedding."

"All right. My name is Mark, by the way. Mark Stephens."

"I'm Winter. Winter Carlyle."

Then she was gone and Mark was left with images. A graceful gazelle disappearing across a savannah . . . a soft pastel mirage in a harsh desert . . . serious violet eyes and a wish of magic . . . Cinderella at the stroke of midnight . . .

For two days Mark's mind had danced with the images. Now he was at the address she had given him on Holman.

The address—the glass slipper left by Cinderella before she dashed away. The address might or might not belong to Winter Carlyle, whoever she was, if she even existed.

Mark parked his car behind a powder-blue Mercedes Sports Coupe and felt a mixture of apprehension and anticipation as he walked to the entrance of the security building. He hoped she wasn't a phantom; but if she was, he didn't want the dream to end.

Mark scanned the names beside the intercom buttons and found W. Carlyle next to 317. As he pressed the button, anticipation vanquished apprehension, gaining strength as it pulsed unopposed through his body.

"Mark?"

"Hi."

"I'll be right down."

Winter took a final critical look in the mirror and wondered why she was so nervous. Because . . .

Because for the past two days her mind had replayed that summer twilight interlude again and again. She almost hadn't spoken to him at all. He had been so absorbed in his studying, concentrating intently, a slight smile on his lips. He had no idea she was there, watching him, envying his obvious joy at what he was doing. He was happy, like Allison had been happy when she was riding; doing what he wanted to do, concentrating, *loving* it.

Winter almost hadn't interrupted him, but when she had he had been so kind, so patient, and . . .

Whatever it was that made her heart race. Winter hadn't felt the full effect of him until after. Then she remembered the dark black curly hair and handsome face and strong, slender hands. Then she remembered the deep, seductive voice and sensuous smile and interested, curious pale blue eyes that made her ask about magic. Were his eyes really cornflower-blue? Were they really identical in shade to the most valued of sapphires, precisely the color of the magnificent sapphire earrings she wore now?

Or was her mind playing tricks?

Winter sighed. He's a man, she told her pounding heart as she rode the elevator to the first floor. Just like any other man. Completely in your control.

"Hello, Mark." It wasn't a trick of her mind. His eyes *were* cornflower-blue. She had remembered perfectly. But she had forgotten the intensity.

"Hello, Winter." She was even more beautiful than he had remembered; more violet, more ivory, more velvet.

Mark and Winter walked in silence to the curb.

"Where's the garden?" Mark asked as he opened the car door for her.

"The Bel Air Hunt Club."

"OK," Mark replied calmly, but his mind swirled.

The Bel Air Hunt Club. *That* garden was the most expensive, exclusive, well-tended garden in Southern California. What was Winter's connection to the Bel Air Hunt Club? Maybe none. Maybe the bride or the groom was a college friend who belonged there.

But what if Winter belonged there? What if the powder-blue Mercedes Sports Coupe belonged to her? What if the stunning gems adorning her ears were real sapphires? What if the sleek lavender dress she wore was pure silk?

Mark would find out soon enough. The Bel Air Hunt Club was only two miles away, in the heart of prestigious Bel Air.

Allison arrived at the address on Montana Avenue at exactly three-twenty. She decided to wait in the car. Emily knew she would be there and was doubtless frantically dressing and gathering her camera equipment for this sudden all-important assignment.

Allison noticed the young woman appear from behind the palmettos that framed the stucco house, but until her hesitant steps brought her to the open window on the passenger side of the car, it did not occur to Allison that she had been watching Emily.

"Are you Allison?"

"Yes. Emily? Hop in."

"Hi." Emily slid into the passenger seat and set her camera on the floor at her feet. "I'm Emily Rousseau."

"I'm Allison Fitzgerald. Hi." Allison smiled warmly, successfully suppressing her shock beneath layers of well-bred politeness and instinctive kindness.

Emily wore baggy bell-bottom jeans and a baggier denim work shirt. The shirt and jeans were clean, neatly pressed, but to the social event of the season?

To Bel Air's most lavish wedding?

Allison had noticed Emily the instant she appeared because her artistic eye had been drawn to the incongruity of what she saw. Emily's clothes were baggy and unstylish, as if designed to conceal, but her long golden hair glittered in the sunlight, a brilliant beacon that commanded attention.

Half-gold, half-denim; half-dazzle, half-drab.

And so anxious! Allison realized as Emily brushed a strand of gold off her face. Emily's hand trembled, her palegray eyes darting uncertainly toward Allison and back.

The same instinct that drove Allison to rescue and nurture wounded animals made her want to help Emily Rousseau. If it was just that Emily didn't have the proper outfit, the solution was easy. Allison had dresses, dozens of them, stylish, beautiful dresses, five blocks away. They would be big—long—on Emily, but . . .

It's not the clothes, Allison decided. Emily wasn't looking self-consciously from her unfashionable denim to Allison's elegant Mardik chiffon. Something else made her chew mercilessly at her lower lip.

"It's lucky you were available today," Allison offered cheerily as she turned off Twentieth onto San Vicente Boulevard.

"I hope so."

"Have you photographed a lot of weddings?" Allison asked hopefully, guessing at the answer, worrying alternately for the obviously anxious Emily and the always anxious Meg.

"None."

"Oh." *Meg, you and Cam will still be married. The pictures don't really matter, do they?* "But you work for Jerome Cole?"

"Yes," Emily answered swiftly, as if that made her qualified, as if Jerome's vast experience with celebrity weddings was contagious. "I've worked for him for three years, during my last two years at UCLA and for the past year since I graduated."

We're the same age, Allison thought. You, me, Winter. Allison and Winter would have graduated a year ago, like Emily, instead of two weeks ago, *if only* whatever it was hadn't caused Tuxedo to swerve with fright.

"So, you're a photographer."

Allison made it a simple statement of fact—firm, positive, indisputable. Two hours earlier, Jerome Cole had posed it as a frantic question: "You *are* a photographer, aren't you, Emily? You haven't bought my used cameras and darkroom equipment and chemicals for someone else, have you?"

The photography instructors at UCLA told Emily she was a photographer—a *talented* one—and Emily liked the pictures she developed in the makeshift darkroom in her windowless basement apartment, but . . .

"I'm a photographer, but I haven't really taken pictures of people." Emily's subjects were flowers and waves and the sun and the moon. She chose those subjects because they didn't mind if she took their pictures and they didn't get impatient if it took her an hour, or even two, to get exactly the image she wanted: the morning dew on a rosebud, the wind-caressed petals of a marigold, the fiery sun as it splashed into the sea, the just-born summer moon. "Most of my photographs have been of flowers."

"What do you do for Jerome?" Jerome Cole was a celebrity photographer. Flowers played a small role in celebrity photographs: a bridal bouquet, a suite at the Beverly Hills Hotel overflowing with roses on Oscar night, a fragrant colorful float in the New Year's Day parade, a mantle of carnations for the first thoroughbred to cross the finish line at Santa Anita.

"I work in the darkroom. I've developed almost all of the wedding sets in the past two years. I just haven't taken them."

"So you do know."

"I know what they're supposed to look like, yes." Emily frowned. "To me, they always seem so posed. Posed shots and shots of groups."

Allison wondered if Emily's frown was an artistic one—the *artiste* who didn't like the posed shots—or simply a worried one—the frown of a timid young woman anxious about assembling a group, asking them to follow her commands, urging them to look at the camera in unison and smile on cue. Especially *this* group, Hollywood's most dazzling, Bel Air's most rich and powerful, the Wall Street financiers and Greenwich aristocrats who had made the trip after all.

"I think the purpose is just to have a record of who celebrated the marriage. It's probably not essential to take group pictures." Allison found group photos uninteresting, too; but they were tradition in Bel Air and certainly in Greenwich. Allison could imagine Meg's horror and her own confession: *Well, yes, Meg, I did tell Emily that I didn't think group shots were essential. I didn't realize she wouldn't get a picture of your mother-in-law. Not one picture. I know, Meg, an unfortunate oversight.*

"I really appreciate the ride," Emily said suddenly, as if remembering something she had rehearsed, a politeness, and then forgotten.

"It's no problem. I'll give you a ride home, too. The reception will go on for hours, but I don't care how long I stay. We can leave whenever you're ready."

"The reception would be a good time to get pictures of everyone, wouldn't it?"

"Oh. Yes, I guess it would."

It was obvious that, despite her anxiety, Emily wanted to do a good job. Most photographers, *including* Jerome Cole, took the obligatory pictures—the jubilant wedding party, the satin gown raised demurely to reveal the garter, the bride and groom cutting the cake, the frosting-laced kiss, the "old, new, borrowed, blue," the bride's last dance with her father and first dance with her new husband—and left.

Emily was willing to stay for as long as was necessary. She wanted to give Meg the best wedding pictures she could.

Allison wondered if Emily's photographs would be good. She hoped for Emily's sake as well as for Meg's that they would be great.

Chapter 2

"Dearly beloved. We are gathered here . . ."

Here. Vanessa Gold smiled appreciatively at the fabulous setting, listened to the familiar words of the wedding ceremony, and thought about the descriptions she would use in Monday's column.

All the usual clichés and superlatives, she decided without worry. Clichés and superlatives were old friends—reliable, comfortable, time-tested. Vanessa's gaze drifted skyward, above the towering pines, and she made a mental note: *flawless azure sky*. To this she added: *caressing ocean breeze, the fragrance of a thousand perfect roses, solemn vows whispered above the cooing of distant doves and the soft splash of honey-gold champagne cascading from a silver fountain.*

On the spot—the lovely rose-scented spot in the fourth row on the bride's side—Vanessa decided to devote Monday's entire *All That Glitters* column to this wedding. It was Vanessa's decision to make. *All That Glitters* was hers, and had been for forty years.

"Do you Meg . . ."

Meg. Vanessa smiled lovingly at the bride, a mother's proud, gentle smile. Not a mother, Vanessa reminded herself. More like a *grandmother!*

By the time Meg Montgomery was born, Vanessa had already been well established as Hollywood's premier celebrity columnist. Vanessa was a celebrity herself, a feared and revered chronicler of the tumultuous and fabulous lives and loves of the rich and those who would be famous. Widowed by the War and childless, Vanessa had long since abandoned the idea of a family of her own. In the spring of 1960 she moved to Bel Air, to a "bungalow" on St. Cloud. Vanessa's new home was located an acre of lush gardens away from the Montgomery mansion and across the winding road from the Fitzgerald estate.

Vanessa was graciously welcomed by her new neighbors, Jane Montgomery and Patricia Fitzgerald. Fifteen years younger than Vanessa, Jane and Patricia had been best friends "forever" and very rich even longer. Both knew well the responsibilities of wealth and were relatively immune to the dangers that befell the newly rich and suddenly famous. Jane and Patricia were intrigued by Vanessa's provocative insider column and unafraid of exposés of their own lives.

A year after Vanessa moved to Bel Air, both younger women gave birth to baby girls. Meg Montgomery entered the world without drama, the third of five children; but Allison Fitzgerald's birth was a struggle. Sean and Patricia would be unable to have more children, the doctors said. Allison was their very precious only child.

Because of her friendship with Jane and Patricia, Vanessa Gold had the immense pleasure, the wonderful joy, of watching the lively little girls—Meg and Allison—become beautiful, lovely young women.

The bride, Marguerite "Meg" Montgomery, was stunning in an ivory gown of . . . Vanessa narrowed her eyes slightly, remembering Jane Montgomery's tease of yesterday afternoon. "Take a good look at the gown, Vanessa. I'm sure you'll recognize the designers!" Vanessa smiled. *Of course* she did. Meg's gown was undoubtedly designed by David and Elizabeth Emmanuel, the British couple who created the fairy-tale gown worn by Lady Diana Spencer the day she became the Princess of Wales. Wedding gowns for princesses . . . for Diana, for Meg.

Meg attended the exclusive Westlake School for Girls and graduated a year ago from Barnard College. While in New York, she met the groom, Cameron Elliott, of Greenwich, Connecticut. Cameron is vice-president of the Wall Street investment firm of Elliott and Lowe.

"For better, for worse . . ."

Worse. Meg and Cam would flourish in "better" and survive "worse," Vanessa decided. Meg and Cam were a splendid match. Meg had done well; she had found happiness and love.

Vanessa's gaze drifted from the bride to the other little girl whose life she had watched with such interest and care. Why had Allison broken her engagement to Daniel Forester? Theirs had all the makings of an ideal match, too; Bel Air and

Hillsborough, real estate heiress and newspaper heir, old money and old money, very nice young woman and very nice young man . . .

Vanessa was confident that Allison had her reasons. The willowy coltish girl had grown into a striking beauty, but she had probably not outgrown, never would, the strong will and determination that had made her a champion. Perhaps Allison was searching for something to replace her shattered dreams. Maybe she had discovered in time that it wasn't Daniel Forester.

"For richer, for poorer . . ."

Poorer. That wasn't an issue in this marriage or, for that matter, in the lavish lives of the assembled guests. Vanessa thought about the guests and played with the question of who among them was the wealthiest. It was unanswerable, of course, but an intriguing exercise nonetheless; and Vanessa kept coming up with the same surprising name . . . Winter Carlyle.

When Jacqueline Winter died five years ago, her eighteen-year-old daughter Winter inherited everything. *Everything* included thousands of carats of diamond, emerald, ruby, and sapphire jewelry designed by Tiffany and Winston and Cartier, gifts from enraptured lovers; and priceless works of art, more gifts; and the magnificent mansion on Bellagio; and the millions of dollars earned by Jacqueline but never spent because there were always rich and powerful men to provide for her; and whatever Lawrence Carlyle had left. No one really knew how great a fortune Jacqueline had accrued in her dazzling and tragic life, but it was immense and now it all belonged to Winter.

Vanessa sighed softly, wondering about the legacy of pain that accompanied Winter's vast fortune. Vanessa could predict with great confidence that life would be happy for the Meg Montgomerys and Allison Fitzgeralds of the world; tragedy might befall them, as it had befallen Allison, but the foundation of love created by their parents would right them again. Vanessa foresaw with equal confidence only unhappiness for Winter Carlyle. How could it be otherwise? As far as Vanessa could tell, the foundation of Winter's life had been as solid and enduring as quicksand.

"Forsaking all others . . ."

Others, and the inability or unwillingness to forsake them. That was the inevitable problem in this town. Meg and Cam wouldn't fall prey to that cycle of anger and betrayal and sadness, Vanessa decided. They had made their vows and would keep them. Vanessa hoped Meg and Cam would also keep their *avant-garde* plan to forsake the reception line. Tradition was one thing, but a warm June day, four hundred guests, and her seventy-year-old legs were another.

"You may kiss the bride."

Vanessa returned a wink to a beaming Meg as she and, her new husband walked happily down the satin-ribboned aisle.

"Meg, the ceremony was lovely." Allison gave Meg a brief hug. "You look absolutely beautiful. That gown!"

"Thank you! It did go well, didn't it? I was so afraid something would go wrong."

"Nothing did."

"No." Meg smiled happily at the shiny gold wedding band that snuggled against the three carat diamond on her ring finger. Her smile faded slightly, a tiny, *tiny* cloud on a vast horizon of euphoria, as her eye caught a glimpse of gold and denim.

"I don't know about this photographer, Allison."

Allison gave a reassuring smile, even though she didn't know either. Emily certainly was *trying*. She moved bravely through the rich and famous, taking many minutes with each photograph, waiting patiently until her eye saw the image she wanted. Emily didn't speak to the guests or smile. She just took her careful pictures, her gray eyes serious and intent. Emily's appearance drew an occasional arched eyebrow or disapproving frown—who was she? how *dare* she?—but was then promptly forgotten in the glittering glamour of the party.

"I think she's doing a good job," Allison offered hopefully, following Meg's gaze to Emily. "Who is that she's photographing now?"

"Rob Adamson. I'm amazed you don't know him, Allison. He owns *Portrait* magazine and moved here about a year ago from New York. He's with Elaina Kingsley, attorney for the stars."

Allison recognized Elaina. Elaina was a familiar face, a familiar *force* in the lives of celebrity Los Angeles. *A shark cleverly disguised as an ingenue*, Winter had quipped once, accurately. Elaina blended her innocent Southern belle looks and her soft River Oaks drawl to create an image that distracted and amazed as she successfully negotiated the toughest movie and television contracts in Hollywood.

Allison recognized Elaina. And there was something hauntingly familiar about Rob.

"I wonder if I could have met Rob once, a long time ago. He's from New York?"

"From Greenwich. He and Cam have known each other forever. They roomed together at Exeter and at Harvard."

If Rob and Cam were boyhood friends, that made Rob thirty, seven years older than Allison. In the fleeting spans of childhood and teenage and college, seven years was another generation. It seemed almost impossible that their paths had crossed.

Allison *had* lived in Greenwich, of course, but it was only for the school year when she was fifteen. That year she had attended Greenwich Academy for Girls, an exclusive private girls' school renowned for its academic and equestrian excellence. The show jumping coach at the Academy was very good, but the year away was miserable. Allison was homesick and her parents were daughter-sick. Even Tuxedo was stable-sick, Allison decided. Her sleek black and white champion horse missed the comforts of his posh stall at the Bel Air Hunt Club.

Technically, Allison had lived in Greenwich, but in reality she never saw anything beyond the oak and pine forested campus of the Academy. When she wasn't in class and didn't have to be in the dormitory because of curfew or study hours, Allison was at the stable. There were no boys at Greenwich Academy, no *men*, not even guests.

Wherever it was that Allison had seen Rob Adamson before, it was not in his hometown.

But it *was* somewhere. She was sure of it. Allison looked away for a moment, not wanting Rob to sense her stare and trying to prepare her mind for a fresh look. Then she turned back to the ocean-blue eyes and dark brown hair and high aristocratic cheekbones, and with the surprising clarity of the sun appearing from behind a dense dark cloud, her face brightened. She *knew*.

Rob was tall and strong and handsome, and *she* had been small and frail and pretty, but the resemblance was unmistakable.

"I knew his sister Sara. She was in grade twelve when I was in grade ten at Greenwich Academy. I wonder how she—"

"She's dead, Allison," Meg interjected.

"Dead? Oh, no." The memory, once rediscovered, had begun sending images

of Sara, and with the images came emotion, warmth . . .

Meg's words pierced the warmth with an ice-cold shiver.

"She was murdered." The characteristic drama vanished from Meg's voice, leaving its tone eerily flat, sinister, *dead*.

"Murdered?" Allison echoed softly.

"She married a fortune hunter. The Adamsons are convinced he killed her. I don't know the details, I don't even know if Cam does, but it was a murder that didn't look like a murder—a clever, perfect crime. There was no proof, no evidence."

"So he's not in prison?"

"No. There wasn't even a trial. There was no public scandal whatsoever. He's rich and free and he probably won't do it again because he's becoming even richer on Broadway."

"He's an actor?"

"No. Well, maybe he is. Maybe that's how he got her to marry him, playing a role, being charming and seducing her. Anyway, now apparently he writes and directs."

"What's his name?"

"I don't know. If Cam knows, he didn't tell me."

"But the Adamsons really believe he murdered Sara?"

"Yes," Meg replied somberly. "But apparently it wasn't something they could prove."

"It must be awful for them." Allison didn't look back at Rob, but she remembered his face and thought about the torment that must certainly swirl beneath the calm facade.

"Cam is pretty sure it's why Rob moved *Portrait* from New York to Los Angeles. He just couldn't stand being anywhere near the man."

"A grim topic for a happy day," Allison whispered apologetically.

"It's probably just as well you asked me, not Rob, about Sara."

"I guess so."

Allison and Meg stopped speaking, listened to the sounds of the day—the laughter of friends, the soft chimes of crystal touching crystal, the splash of champagne, the melody of love songs—and willed the happiness to wash away the sadness. It happened for Meg more quickly than for Allison.

"I should probably go find my husband. We're trying to mingle together, but we keep getting separated!" Meg stood on tiptoes and scanned the sea of rich and famous. "I don't even see him. But, speaking of gorgeous men whom I would *not* want to be separated from unless I was the proud wearer of a wedding ring, who is Winter with? Or, actually, at the moment, *without?*"

This time Winter had been swept away from him by two "old friends from Westlake" who had to "tell her something important." Winter had cast a beautiful apologetic smile and Mark had replied with an easy laugh.

Of course he wanted to be alone with her, but that would happen later, after the reception. And he was learning new things about her, watching her in her natural habitat among the rich, famous, and glamorous.

Winter belongs here, Mark decided within moments of their arrival at the Club. As the afternoon wore on, he wondered if she owned the place. Winter more than belonged, she *controlled*.

The serious young woman who had frowned thoughtfully at his neurosurgery text, posed intelligent, insightful questions, and asked shyly about magic had vanished. In her place was an alluring, confident vixen. Winter charmed them all, even the most celebrated and famous among them. Men flocked to her like moths to a brilliant flame, and women flocked, too, wanting to bask in Winter's golden rays but content even with her shadow. The men who noticed Mark assumed he was, like them, simply one in an endless series, captivated by the sensuous woman who beckoned like silk sheets to a canopied bed but made no promises.

Mark watched the seductive, provocative, bewitching Winter Carlyle and tried to reconcile this Cinderella with the serious, thoughtful one he had met at twilight in the Sculpture Garden.

It was really quite easy to reconcile the two *because she was so much like him.*

Mark, too, drew admiring stares. Even this afternoon he heard familiar stage whispers of "awesome" and "no wedding ring" and "those eyes." Mark could perform and charm and dazzle, too. He played the game magnificently, as she did; and, like Winter, Mark called the shots, playing, winning, beginning relationships and ending them, choosing when to begin and when to end.

They were both experts at a game that insured intimacy without emotion, sex without love, companionship without commitment; it was a game that was played a very safe distance from the heart, for whatever reasons.

Mark knew *his* reasons; he wondered about *hers*. Mark wondered who she was and why she belonged here and if *they* would play or if they were already way beyond that.

Whoever she was, she was looking at him now, sending a sparkling violet message of "Help." Mark lifted two full crystal champagne flutes from a silver tray and wove through the crowd toward her.

"Thanks," Winter whispered when Mark reached her. She turned to her "old friends from Westlake" and said, "I promised Mark a tour of the Club."

Winter cast *them* a beautiful apologetic smile and led Mark down a short flight of brick stairs away from the crowd.

"I brought champagne in case we run into any thirsty roses on our tour," Mark said when they were alone.

"Oh, you noticed."

Of course he had noticed. He had noticed and he had wondered. Winter sipped, or pretended to, from each of the four glasses of champagne she had held during the afternoon. But most of the expensive bubbly had been gracefully poured onto the base of a rosebush as she bent to admire the magnificent blossoms.

"I noticed." And I notice that it embarrasses you. Mark rescued her quickly, "So, where are we now?"

"We're on a sort-of-secluded terrace in the champagne-drenched rose garden."

"Ah. And where are the beagles?"

"No beagles, no foxes, no bugles, no red-coated riders galloping across a fog-misted moor."

"So what kind of Hunt Club is this?"

"The best kind—all the wonderful traditions without the hunt. The Club was founded by several British producers and directors who made their fame and fortunes in the Golden Age of Hollywood but still longed for Merry England—horses, country riding, royalty, champagne brunches, formal balls, Yorkshire pudding . . ." Winter paused for a breath.

"It's very nice." Mark smiled slightly at his understatement.

"I like the British flavor. Of course there have been concessions to California

chic. The guest rooms in the mansion are still pure Balmoral Castle—heavy forest-green drapes, carved armoires, four-poster beds—but the new bungalows beyond the pool and tennis courts are Malibu contemporary." Winter smiled wryly and added, with mock horror, "And now, on the same menu as beef Wellington, they offer platters of sprouts and yoghurt and fruit!"

"Oh, no." Mark laughed.

"Oh, yes!" Winter's eyes sparkled, met his, and held until the intensity became too great, until all she could think about was that she wanted him to touch her, hold her, kiss her, make love to her. She continued, breathless, flushed, barely able to concentrate, "I've always thought it would be nice to change the name to something even more traditional, like The Royal and Ancient Club of Bel Air . . ."

"Would you like to dance?" Mark spoke with a soft, seductive tone that told her he wanted what she wanted, all of it. They could start here, dancing in the rose-fragrant garden, their bodies swaying gently in a chaste hello.

A chaste hello, Mark mused as he set their champagne flutes on a white wrought iron table and extended his arms to welcome her. *Hello, Winter.*

They were already way beyond "hello." They had skipped a few chapters, beginning in the middle, in the enchanted part where there was magic and where they forgot all about playing and how important it was to keep a safe distance from the heart.

They danced in lovely sensual silence, saying that kind of hello, as the distant band played "Here, There and Everywhere."

Here, in this rose-scented heaven; there, in a four-poster bed in the mansion; everywhere . . .

Mark wanted to take her away *now*, but his logical scientific mind sought order. He forced himself to turn the pages back to Chapter One and fill in a few of the blanks.

Name? Winter Carlyle. Was that a real name or a stage name? *Blank*.

Age? *Blank*. But Mark had learned from Allison that she and Winter had both graduated from UCLA two weeks ago, so early twenties.

Family? *Blank*. Winter had made a point of introducing him to Allison and Allison's parents, and the introductions had been proud and fond, as if the Fitzgeralds were her parents and Allison was her sister. There were emotional links there but nothing genetic. The Fitzgeralds were red-haired and freckled and smiling and Irish. Winter's natural parents—whoever had given her the black velvet hair, violet eyes, ivory skin, and elegant sensuality—were absent.

Occupation? *Blank*. Winter was rich. Everyone here was rich. Mark knew a little about wealth, and he knew that for some it was a goal in itself, but for most it was a by-product; what they *had* not who they *were*. Who was Winter? What was Winter? Today, among some of Hollywood's greatest actors and actresses, Winter acted, and her performance was dazzling. Mark hadn't been to a movie in years. For all he knew . . .

"You're a famous actress, aren't you?" His lips brushed her silky hair as he spoke, a gentle caress.

Mark held her close, already learning about her lovely softness and the instinctive way their bodies moved together. At his words, Winter stiffened, just for an instant; but Mark felt it as if it had been he, not she, recoiling at the question.

Mark pulled away to look at her face and saw a brief but unmistakable flicker of pain before she conquered it.

"No."

"A not-so-famous actress?" he suggested carefully. Maybe Winter had tried and failed. Maybe, if he had seen a movie in the past few years, he would have known not to ask.

"Not an actress at all," Winter whispered softly. *Only an actress . . . always an actress . . . never an actress.*

Mark regretted causing even a second of sadness and searched for a topic with a happy ending, one that would bring a sparkle. "I like your friend Allison."

"Do you want to be with Allison?"

"No." *You know I don't.* "I want to be with you."

"Why don't we do that? Go be someplace together."

"Would you like to go to dinner first?"

Winter shook her head, ever so slightly, her eyes never leaving his.

"OK. Shouldn't we stay until the bride and groom leave?"

"No. We should go now."

Chapter 3

Too much sadness for a wedding day, Allison thought. She sat on a wrought iron loveseat in a secluded alcove of lacy white lilacs; sitting because her injured hip sent angry messages, and in the lovely fragrant sanctuary because tears threatened.

Allison had expected to feel a little sad and nostalgic today because of Dan. But now that sadness was just a frivolous, trivial indulgence compared to the real sadnesses of the afternoon—the demons that plagued Emily Rousseau and the unspeakable tragedy of Sara Adamson. Daniel Forester and Allison Fitzgerald weren't tormented by demons and their broken engagement was not a tragedy. It was too bad—perhaps something Allison would always regret—but it was a choice, a decision. It wasn't a lurking pain, nor was it a senseless twist of fate.

Allison watched Emily and tried in vain to convince herself that the photographer was fine—just a girl with a preference for jeans and a little understandable anxiety about the important assignment that had been thrust upon her. Until the accident, Allison herself had had a strong preference for jeans; she had lived in jeans or jodhpurs, and whatever colorful sweatshirt or turtleneck or blouse she happened to grab from her dresser as she dashed to the stable. And Allison, too, was anxious about the important assignments that would be hers at Elegance.

Maybe Emily's just like me, Allison told herself hopefully. But all the optimism in the world, all of Allison's unfailing ability to find the silver lining, could not force a troy ounce of similarity between them.

Emily's outfit was not a preference for jeans; it was a disguise, an obvious attempt to conceal. And Emily's anxiety was not just a simple case of "beginner's nerves"; it had depth and pain and fear woven through it.

Something troubled Emily, and it was surely much worse than the wedding-that-wasn't-to-be for rich and privileged Allison Fitzgerald; but even Emily's demons paled by comparison to the great tragedy of Sara Adamson.

Sara. Murdered. No.

Allison's mind filled with memories of Sara, clear, warm, vivid memories . . .

Allison could have spent the nine months at Greenwich Academy and never even met Sara Adamson. Sara was three years older, a senior when Allison was a sophomore. Sara didn't board at the Academy because her home was in Greenwich, and she didn't ride.

But Allison did meet Sara, and there had been a warm, quiet, special bond.

Sara was sitting on a wooden bench in the grandstand of the riding arena when Allison entered the ring at noon on her second day in Greenwich. Allison had studied the class schedule and study schedule and the required appearances at "gracious hours"—when they learned to be ladies—and decided that she would spend every noon hour at the stable, riding instead of eating. The pale, quiet girl who sat on the wooden bench had apparently made the same decision; except she *didn't* ride and she *did* eat lunch, slowly, gracefully eating food she removed from a pale pink cardboard box.

Sara and Allison exchanged awkward smiles the first day, and the second, and the third. On the fourth day, Sara introduced herself and asked shyly if Allison minded an audience. Allison introduced herself and replied gaily, "Of course not."

After that, there were days when Sara and Allison only smiled warmly, waved friendly waves, and uttered brief hellos. But there were other days when Allison spent more of the noon hour talking to Sara than riding. Allison explained to Sara about show jumping—the perfect arc, the oxers and verticals and walls, the carefully timed strides, the control of the horse's immense power—and Sara listend, fascinated.

Sara and Allison talked about riding and jumping and Allison's gold medal dreams; but when Allison asked Sara questions about her life, her dreams, the fragile older girl shrugged, smiled softly, and said little. Sara did tell Allison, apologetically but without elaboration, that she had to eat a special lunch and couldn't share it. Sara offered to have the cook at her estate prepare something for Allison, too. Allison always declined Sara's gracious offer for herself, but agreed, when Sara suggested it, that carrots and apples for Tuxedo would be nice.

"It looks like you're flying, Allison," Sara said one day as she watched Allison soar over jump after jump.

"It feels like that. Flying, floating . . ."

"Free."

"Yes, I guess. Free. Sara, I could teach you to ride, to jump if you want to."

"Oh." Sara's ocean-blue eyes sparkled for an uncertain moment and her pale cheeks flushed pink. She added quietly, "No. Thank you, Allison, but I can't."

Sara and Allison only saw each other at the riding stable. Their classes were held on different floors of the red brick building. A limousine dropped Sara at school each morning, minutes before the school day began, and was waiting when classes ended in the afternoon.

Allison was at the stable every day at noon. From September until late March, Sara only missed a few days. Sara was out of school for a week in November, and two other times she was gone for several days. Sara looked more pale and fragile when she returned after being away, Allison thought, as if she had been quite ill.

"I won't be here as much anymore," Sara told Allison on the first day of spring term. "Most days, I'll be spending the noon hour off campus."

Allison smiled at Sara's politeness. It was nice of Sara to let her know, but certainly not necessary. Allison *almost* asked Sara where she would be, not wanting to pry but because she saw such happiness in Sara's dark blue eyes. Allison didn't ask, but on a splendid warm day in May, she learned the reason for Sara's happiness.

Sara Adamson was in love! Allison didn't see the man's face, only his silhouette in the distance. But she saw Sara's face, her pale cheeks flushed pink and her eyes glowing as she walked toward him, carrying her special lunch, to join him inside a battered forest-green Volkswagen bug.

Allison saw Sara for the last time in early June, the day before the school year ended. Sara was at the stable at noon, waiting for Allison.

"Hi, Sara."

"Hi. I just wanted to say good-bye. I enjoyed watching you. Thank you for letting me."

She is so gracious, Allison thought for a stunned, silent moment.

"I enjoyed having you watch," Allison replied finally, truthfully. "I heard that you're going to Vassar."

"Yes." Sara smiled. "And you're going back to Los Angeles."

"It's home," Allison murmured, not wanting to offend. After all Greenwich, with its icy winters and rigid rules, was Sara's home.

"Good luck in the Olympics, Allison."

"Thanks! Good luck at Vassar, Sara."

"Good-bye."

"Good-bye." Be happy, Allison thought as she watched Sara leave. Be happy . . .

But Sara found something other than happiness, Allison thought sadly as she sat in the secluded alcove of lacy white lilacs. Sara fell into the arms of a murderous lover. Allison narrowed her eyes and tried to see the face of the man in the Volkswagen bug, the man to whom Sara had gone with such joy. Was that the man, or had that love faltered only to be replaced by the lethal one?

"Oh, sorry!"

Startled, Allison looked up into dark blue eyes that were so hauntingly like his sister's.

"Hi."

"Hello. I didn't mean to invade your privacy." Rob had escaped, seeking privacy, too. Of the four hundred rich and famous wedding guests, he had decided, fully half wanted more fame, more wealth, more celebrity; and those two hundred seemed to believe that a profile in *Portrait* magazine would help.

An article in Rob's magazine would help—it always did. But Rob and Rob alone made the decisions about whom to profile. He remained calmly yet firmly uninfluenced by praise or pleas from agents, by "anonymous" callers who claimed to be "friends" of the magazine-hopeful, and most certainly by attempts to impress and woo at a wedding reception. Even Elaina, with her infinite charms and the luscious intimacy of their relationship, couldn't influence his choices.

Rob had been a little flattered by the obvious hints of so many celebrities—it was high praise for *Portrait*—but eventually he felt annoyance creeping in. He left Elaina to cope with the not-so-subtle onslaught, many of whom were her clients, while he sought a brief respite in the lilacs.

Rob wasn't alone in the lilacs, but he looked at the serious jade-green eyes—

did they glisten with recent tears?—and her warm smile, and he instantly decided that this young woman would never try to convince him to put her in *Portrait*. Rob was quite safe here, but he gazed thoughtfully at the glistening eyes and realized that he had disturbed her.

"I'm just passing through, on my way to the next grove of lilacs," Rob said.

"No. Please. Stay. You're not invading my privacy." *I was thinking about*

your sister. Allison wanted to tell Rob that she had known Sara and how much she had liked her and how sorry she was. But if she told him now, she would cry. Maybe she would always cry. She *would* tell Rob sometime—some safe time in the future in another grove of lilacs on another summer day, or at the Club's legendary Autumn Ball, or at Meg and Cam's fifth wedding anniversary—some *other* time. "I'm Allison Fitzgerald."

"I'm Rob Adamson. Allison Fitzgerald. Let's see. Aren't you the interior designer *extraordinaire?*"

"You've been talking to my mother!"

"No, although I did meet your mother and father. It was actually Claire Roland who told me."

Claire Roland owned Elegance, *the* design store of Southern California. Claire was fifty-seven and could have retired years ago to her "best address" home on Mountain Drive in Beverly Hills, but she grew restless at the thought of even slowing down. Claire's mission was incomplete; there still existed houses in the Platinum Triangle—Beverly Hills, Holmby Hills, and Bel Air—that needed an infusion of taste and elegance and style. That would be her legacy to Los Angeles, Claire hoped, and to a generation of designers trained by her.

Claire was the first designer in Los Angeles to offer apprenticeships to students majoring in Design at UCLA. On paper the apprenticeship was for one quarter only, complete with grades and credit hours, but Claire made rare exceptions for students with great promise.

When Claire had first seen Allison Fitzgerald's name on the class list eighteen months before, she had worried. It was more than a little awkward. Claire had to give a grade and she was known for her toughness; but Sean and Patricia Fitzgerald were friends and everyone knew about Allison's tragic accident.

Claire worried, but within three weeks of her arrival at Elegance, she was speaking to Allison as a colleague, with the no-nonsense approach never seen by clients but which delighted the other designers. "Customers *can* be wrong, Allison, remember that," Claire would confide with a sly smile. "They can want mirrors over beds and trapezes and God knows what else, and that's *wrong*, so we politely suggest that they find another designer." Claire Roland was in the enviable but hard-earned position of being able to choose clients, as well as designers. Her designers were the best, and she wanted Allison to be one of them. "Taste and elegance, Allison. You have it. I have no idea why—you're so young, you were born and raised in California; it must be an instinct."

Allison knew that Claire's praise was genuine, but she knew from her riding that talent and instinct and natural ability had to be nurtured. Claire predicted a meteoric rise for Allison. In a year, maybe less, Claire announced confidently, Allison Fitzgerald would be *the* interior designer for the great homes of Southern California.

Three years ago everyone had predicted that Allison would be *the* equestrian Gold Medalist—she might even win three golds—of the 1984 Olympics. Allison feared predictions now. She had learned that crystal balls were very, very fragile.

"Claire gets a little carried away," Allison murmured un easily to Rob. Her uneasiness increased as Allison wondered what else Rob had been told about her. Did he know that she had almost died, too? Except her death would have been an accident, not murder. "I don't even begin at Elegance until mid-August, after the Olympics."

Allison watched Rob's reaction when she mentioned the Olympics. Did he know about her shattered Olympic dreams? Would his dark blue eyes soften with sympathy? Would they flicker with the concern of an older brother: Do you really want to watch the Olympic Equestrian Team, Allison? Wouldn't that be too painful for you?

Rob's expression didn't change. His handsome, untroubled aristocratic smile didn't waver. If Rob knew about her, he politely hid the knowledge, just as Allison hid her knowledge about Sara.

"Claire didn't seem carried away," Rob observed mildly. A thought teased from a corner of his mind. These jade green eyes would never *try* to get in *Portrait*, but if Claire's prediction about Allison's future was even close to accurate, Rob would be calling *her*. Profiles about people like Allison were what distinguished *Portrait* from the other celebrity magazines. Rob chose strong, interesting, intriguing people; people who succeeded against all odds; people, like Allison, who were champions at whatever they did.

"Well." Allison was eager to change the subject away from speculation about her future. Or her past. Or *his* past. That left the present. She was only here searching for her emotions among the lilacs, instead of in the sanctuary of her own apartment, because of Emily. Surely, Emily would be finished soon. "Do you know if Meg and Cam are about to leave?"

"Soon, I think. Are you planning to catch the bouquet?"

"*No.*" Allison softened her gasp with a slight smile. "I am planning to steer very clear of the bouquet. I'd like to wave good-bye, toss a little rice . . ." Go home.

"So," Winter whispered as she and Mark entered the living room of her apartment on Holman Avenue. Neither had spoken since leaving the rose terrace at the Club.

"So?" Mark's eyes and interest were on Winter, but he was aware of the modest furnishing in her nice-but-not-luxurious one-bedroom apartment; collegiate, not Hunt Club; Bruin chic, not Balmoral elegant.

"So, should I put on an album?"

"No. You should come here."

Winter obeyed. She had to. Her heart raced at the promise of Mark's touch; her body swirled with wonderful demanding sensations; and her mind had floated away, taking with it the vow she had made to herself to be in control . . . *always.*

Something else was in control now—her own desires.

And someone else was in control—Mark.

Winter stood in front of him, waiting in breath-held anticipation. But Mark reached for the gardenia in her hair, not for her. He removed the flower so gently, then unpinned the smooth, thick knot of hair until the black silk spilled loose and free down her back. Then, so delicately, he took the flawless sapphires from her ears.

"What are you doing?"

"I'm undressing you." Mark held the magnificent gems in his palm. "Where shall I put these?"

Anywhere. Just don't stop touching me. The gentle caresses as Mark's fingers brushed her hair and neck and shoulders sent warm—hot—tremors through her; dangerous tremors of desire, urgent, desperate . . .

"In the bedroom."

"Show me."

Winter led him to her bedroom. Mark set the earrings on the dresser, then joined her where she stood beside the bed. He reached for the zipper of her lavender silk dress.

"Hurry," she urged softly as his strong fingers touched her bare back.

"No," he answered with a gentleness that promised her it would happen—everything she wanted would happen—and it would be wonderful.

It would happen soon, because he wanted her so much, too. The exquisite pleasure of undressing her sent powerful rushes of desire through him. Her skin was so cool, so silky, and her violet eyes beckoned, and the soft sensuous curl of her lips . . .

Mark meant their first kiss to be a gentle hello, a soft whispered greeting, a tender promise. But there was too much passion, too much hunger, too much desire.

"Oh, Winter," he breathed as his lips touched hers.

"Mark."

They undressed each other quickly, kissing, touching, whispering, wanting.

When they were both naked, Mark pulled away. It was a monumental effort, defiance of a wonderful invisible magnetic force that willed their bodies to be together. Mark resisted the powerful force for a moment, knowing that soon and eagerly he would succumb to it, allowing it to win, marvelling in its strength. But now, in the soft summer twilight of her bedroom, he just wanted to look at her.

You are so lovely, Winter.

Winter trembled as his sensuous blue eyes caressed her, appraising, appreciative, full of desire.

Hurry, Mark.

Mark didn't hurry, even when they lay together between the cool sheets of her bed. He kissed a leisurely gentle path down her neck to the softness of her breasts, and slowly said hello *there*. And there were other gentle hellos, as his warm soft lips and his strong tender hands wandered, exploring, discovering, freeing ever-hidden desires.

Each new pulse of desire added to the last, crescendoing, hotter, stronger, wanting even more.

But how much more could there be?

More. Now her body was floating away! No, Mark held her and finally he put her exactly where he wanted her, exactly where she wanted to be. Her body floated up, just a little, as she welcomed him, all of him, at last.

At last, moving together in a rhythm of passion and desire. Hello, hello, *hello*.

And there was still *more*. Because, after it was over, Mark held her still—strong and gentle, close and tight. So close and so tight that there was no room left for the empty feelings of loneliness that were Winter's usual companions after making love.

"What are you thinking?" Mark spoke finally as he gently stroked her hair.

Winter moved her head slightly, a soft shake, a little shrug.

"Nothing?"

Winter raised up and gazed at him through a tangle of black silk. "No, I . . ."

Mark parted the tangle with amazing delicacy until he found her lovely violet eyes.

"You are wonderful," he told her.

"No." *I didn't do anything. You did.* "You are."

Mark tenderly traced a path around her eyes, down her cheeks, across her lips. His eyes were thoughtful as he studied her. Finally, he asked quietly, "Was that safe?"

Safe? Winter's mind reeled. No, it was dangerous, very, very dangerous. The danger was surfacing again as her skin responded to his touch, wanting more, and her desires willed her to follow whereever he led.

"Safe?" she whispered weakly.

"Are you on the pill?"

Oh. That kind of safe. Yes, of course. But there was nothing safe in the way Mark asked it! His voice was gentle and caring, assuming the responsibility if it wasn't safe, sharing that as they had shared everything else. There was nothing safe about Mark because he was so different from all the others.

"I have an IUD," Winter answered softly, marvelling that this discussion could feel so intimate, so tender, until he frowned. "Mark?"

"IUDs can cause problems, Winter."

I don't care! I'm never going to have children. The thought came to Winter swiftly—it had been part of her for so long—but the venom that usually came with it melted under Mark's gentle, worried gaze.

"Oh, well . . . Do they teach you this in medical school?"

"This?"

"How to ask intimate questions at intimate moments?"

Mark laughed softly. "They teach us how to take histories and do physicals."

"And you get A's in both."

"You think so?" Mark found her lips, starting the physical all over again.

"I know so."

Mark stopped the kiss with effort and whispered, "Would you like to go out with me sometime?"

"No." *I would like to stay in with you all the time.*

"How about dinner Monday night?" Mark ignored her words and read the message in her eyes.

"OK."

"I'll call you when I get home from the hospital, if you'll give me your unlisted number."

"I will." Winter made a move to get up.

"Where are you going?"

"To write down the number."

"There's no emergency."

"You're not about to leave?"

"No. I just wanted to get that settled before—"

"Before?"

"—before we make love again." And again. And again.

Chapter 4

Emily parted the heavy black curtains that divided her apartment into bedroom and darkroom and stared at the bedside clock. It glowed at her from the darkness of the windowless apartment that was barely lighter than the total inkiness of the dark-room: six-fifteen.

Six-fifteen. Was it A.M. Sunday morning, ten hours after Allison had driven her home from the reception? Or was it P.M., already Sunday evening? Or A.M. Monday morning, time to go to work?

Emily had no idea. The hours in the darkroom were timeless; enchanted, creative moments connected by a peace and joy that didn't belong to the rest of her life. Usually Emily set an alarm before she entered the darkroom, afraid to miss work, leaving reluctantly when the alarm sounded.

Emily opened the outside door and squinted at the fading rays of the summer sun. Sunday evening. Good. That meant she had more hours in the darkroom, with some hours to sleep, before work tomorrow.

Jerome would be pleased with the wedding photographs, wouldn't he?

Emily didn't know—she didn't have the confidence—but she liked the pictures. The bride and groom, caught in gazes of astonishment at what they had done and joy that they had done it; Allison, who had been so nice, so thoughtful, even though the day seemed to hold a special sadness for her; the stunning black haired-couple, violet eyes and sapphire ones, dancing amid the roses, falling in love; the confident sable-haired woman with the soft Southern accent and eyes that narrowed shrewdly if she wasn't on guard against that every moment; that *man* . . . that handsome man who watched her with smiling, curious dark blue eyes; and all the other celebrities whom Jerome would recognize and tell her about in intimate detail.

At first, Jerome simply stared at the photographs in stunned reverent silence. Finally, he murmured, "Uh, Emily, these are pretty good. Very good, really."

Spectacular, really, Jerome thought, staring at Emily as if seeing her for the first time. Jerome knew Emily worked magic in the darkroom, giving intriguing texture and imaginative richness to the photographs he took, but he had no idea . . .

"I'm glad you like them, Jerome."

"The Montgomerys will be very pleased."

Jerome studied the photographs for several more silent moments, his mind spinning as he realized the full measure of Emily's remarkable talent. Finally, he shifted his thoughts from the gifted photographer to her subjects, the celebrities whose lives fascinated him as much as they fascinated Vanessa Gold. Vanessa was a columnist, Jerome explained, but *he* was an unabashed gossip!

"My God, Emily! You got these two in the same picture? I thought they weren't speaking anymore. Do you remember what they were talking about?"

"No, I . . ."

"Think!"

"I really have no idea. I wasn't listening."

"Oh, well." Jerome moved on. "This is wonderful of Louis. He owns La Choix, you know. And look at Joan! Very flattering. She won the Oscar three years ago—or was it four—the sentimental favorite, of course."

"Who is this?" Emily pointed to a picture of the man with the smiling blue eyes.

"Oh! That's Rob Adamson. He owns *Portrait* magazine. Really a very nice shot, Emily. A masterful portrait of the master of *Portrait*."

"And is this his wife?"

"Elaina Kingsley? Not his wife yet, but it will happen. Someday soon, I'm sure, we'll be doing the photography for their magnificent wedding at the Bel Air Hunt Club."

"Oh."

Emily locked the door to her apartment and began the twenty-block walk to Mick's place. The day had gone well. Jerome had been pleased. If only tonight would go well, if only Mick wouldn't still be furious that she had agreed to do the Montgomery-Elliott wedding instead of going with him and his band for the two night "gig" on Santa Catalina Island.

Mick *would* be furious still, Emily knew it, but she knew, too, that by the time she reached his oceanside apartment, she would be able to handle his rage. The pill she had taken would be working its magic, numbing her, making anything possible.

The drug, a synthetic blend of mescaline and amphetamine, was already making the sky dance and the wind hum and the pastel hues of the summer evening pulse and glow and swirl. Cotton candy clouds floated close to the earth and streetlights were fine-cut diamonds scattering light like a thousand prisms. Houses stretched and melted and shrubs came to life, dancing and spinning and swaying in the balmy air.

Emily hallucinated easily. Her mind willingly embraced the drug-created monsters. The pulsing shapes and spinning colors and fantastic distortions didn't terrify her. They were old friends, soft, misty visions in a numb world, a welcome escape from the world she knew.

The mescaline let her hallucinate and the "speed" made her brave. She could appease Mick's anger. She could seduce him and recapture his love. Emily knew all the ways to give pleasure.

She had another pill in her pocket and Mick would give her cocaine if she needed it.

She could do it.

"Allison, *no*." Winter frowned sternly at the telephone as if her expression of disapproval could be transmitted through the telephone wires to her best friend.

"I'm only telling you because I promised I would, not because I want you to talk me out of it."

"I just don't understand why."

"Because when riders fall off horses, they get back on."

"You didn't exactly fall."

"Yes I did!"

"The doctors really said it was OK?" Winter already knew the answer. She knew the exact day, six weeks ago, when the doctors told Allison she *could* ride—ride, but never jump—f she wanted to, if she was *very careful*.

Winter remembered the day with vivid clarity, because it was the day Allison began to change. The change was subtle—a quiet determination. Allison was making plans, but her solemn jade-green eyes artfully disguised the magnitude of the decisions she was making.

Allison didn't ask for Winter's advice or discuss her thoughts until the decisions were made. Then she simply announced them, three monumental decisions, all in row.

I've told Dan I can't marry him.

I said yes to Claire. I'll start working at Elegance after the Olympics.

I'm going to ride again.

"You can't jump," Winter reminded Allison gently now, as she had reminded her six weeks ago. What if that were Allison's fourth monumental decision?

"I know that," Allison answered with a soft sigh.

"Then why?"

"Because I want to. I *need* to."

"And I want—*need* to be there when you do."

"I'm just going to sit on Ginger and ride around the ring. Very safe. Incredibly boring. *And* incredibly early."

"That's fine."

"We really should be there by seven." At that hour on a Tuesday morning, Allison was assured of having the outdoor ring at the Club all to herself.

"I'll pick you up at six-thirty."

"Are you sure?"

"Positive. It's no problem. I'll see you then."

It's no problem, Winter thought after she replaced the receiver. I'll be awake because Mark will have just left.

Mark had left Sunday morning at six, rushing to his apartment to shower and change in time for seven A.M. rounds at the hospital. Mark and Winter had been awake at six because they had never been asleep.

Tonight they would sleep. Mark *had* to sleep. Winter heard the fatigue in his voice when he telephoned, moments before Allison's call, to say he would be late, too late to go out for dinner, but, if she were still awake . . .

Winter would be awake, exhausted from her own sleeplessness but unable to sleep. Ever since Mark had left her bed yesterday—only yesterday?—Winter's heart had pounded restlessly, missing him, wanting him, needing him.

Rob jogged effortlessly up the incline of the palm-lined path at the crest of the Santa Monica palisades. The exercise felt good—an invigorating interlude between the demands and challenges of the day with *Portrait* and the pleasures and challenges of the night that lay ahead with Elaina. The Pacific Ocean sparkled below, deep blue in the summer twilight, lapping gently on the snowy white sand. Rob inhaled a plumeria-scented breeze and thought for the hundredth time, or maybe the thousandth, how right it had been for him to leave New York and move to Los Angeles.

There was a softness here, a warmth, a promise of new beginnings. Maybe it was the golden sun. Maybe it was the distance from the painful memories. Maybe, as the poets wrote, it was the healing passage of time.

Or maybe his heart had told him, finally, in agonal rebellion, that it couldn't survive on hatred alone; a heart needed other nourishment—a little love, a little laughter, a little hope.

Rob saw a glitter of gold ahead on the path, a brilliant torch lit by the setting sun, a confusing image of long golden hair and baggy denim, conflicting messages. . . .

She was the photographer from the wedding. Rob had noticed her then, of course, and wondered. At first he assumed the amorphous tent of denim was worn in hostile defiance; a clear condemnation of rich people who sipped expensive champagne and tasted rare caviar and glided through life in designer dresses, silk tuxedos, and dazzling jewels.

But as he had watched, Rob decided there was nothing defiant in her manner—just the opposite. She seemed meek, timid, uncertain, and so *serious* about her task.

The baggy denim clothes were not worn in defiance, Rob had concluded. They were worn to conceal. And the long golden hair that hid her face? Were there scars too horrible to expose to the world? he had wondered, sadly, sympathetically.

But as her head had tilted to take the wedding pictures, the golden curtain had parted, revealing delicate porcelain features carved on the palest of alabaster skin. Her eyes—such *serious* eyes—were the lightest of gray, the color of early morning mist.

Rob had been intrigued with the fragile, ethereal, beautiful young woman who sent such a clear message to stay away.

And now she stood on the bluff near his ocean-view pent-house, still half-gold, half-denim.

But now she was not alone. And she was not so fragile or so timid after all.

She was with a man, and they should have been young lovers lost in the raptures of their love, marvelling at the glorious summer sunset; soft, romantic, gentle. But *he* looked mean—angry energy in black leather—and *she* looked hard and wanton. He leaned, sultry, sexual, against a palm, and she leaned against him. His rough hands roamed all over her, claiming their territory for all to see.

She allowed the intimate exploration without resistance, her golden head tilted toward the pink clouds overhead.

Rob passed them swiftly, as far away as the narrow path would permit. As he passed, he saw her eyes. The pale morning mist was dense smoky fog and the serious clarity had vanished beneath a glassy glaze. Her gaze shifted slightly toward him, without recognition, as he passed. The glazed, foggy eyes looked at him, but what did they see? Was he a monster, his face contorted and grotesque? Was he a swirl of light and color? Or was he nothing, unseen to the sightless eyes, a faded image in a misty haze?

Rob passed them swiftly and wished he could just as swiftly banish her from his thoughts. The memory of the fragile ethereal young woman from the wedding had stayed with him until now. Now that bewitching memory was shattered, the delicacy harshly corrupted by what he saw.

The new sullied memory lingered, as the pleasant one had, but now there was an accompanying emotion: anger. Rob was angry at them both; at the man for his blatant disrespect of her, at the woman for allowing him to treat her that way, and at both of them for insinuating their decadence on this gentle summer evening.

"Sorry," Mark said when he finally got to Winter's apartment at eleven P.M.

"Is this what it's like to be a doctor?" Winter asked with a gentle tease and a radiant smile. She was so happy to see him!

"No," Mark answered flatly. "If I were a doctor, I wouldn't have made it at all." *When I am a doctor, there will be much longer nights than this.*

"Oh!" The surprising harshness of Mark's voice startled her, extinguishing her smile, putting doubt in her sparkling violet eyes.

Mark's tone reflected his fatigue and the incessant warnings that had bombarded his mind since the moment he left her bed. The warnings were simply reminders of the careful plans he had made for his life. *Do not get involved. Wait at least until residency is behind you. There will be no time for a love. It wouldn't be fair. You know too well what can happen.*

Mark had already dedicated the next four years to his career, just as he had dedicated the last three. It was not a sacrifice; it was a choice. Mark loved medical school and eagerly awaited the increased challenges and responsibilities of residency. He worked very hard, earned top grades, and his dream—a residency in internal medicine at Massachusetts General Hospital in Boston—was almost certainly going to come true.

There had been women, of course; a series of ideal relationships—sex without emotion, passion without commitment, laughter without tears, cancelled dates without regret.

Mark had made his choice, his plans; so far, it had been easy. Hard work, yes. Sleepless nights and exhaustion, of course. Dedication and resolve, always.

But Mark had expected that, planned on it.

Mark just hadn't planned on Winter Carlyle. He didn't even know he could feel this way. The warnings had bombarded his mind, but each missile had been intercepted—and exploded in midair—by the memory of Winter. She had already become a part of him; swiftly, confidently, she had found a home in his heart and in his mind.

And in his plans?

Mark gazed at the violet eyes that had been startled and hurt and confused by the harshness of his voice. He touched her cheek and whispered gently, "I missed you."

"I missed you, too," Winter murmured softly, but confusion and uncertainty lingered. She backed away slightly. "Are you hungry?"

"For you." Mark smiled, trying to reassure her.

"I went shopping after you called." It had been such fun, shopping in the gourmet stores of Brentwood and Santa Monica for Mark; and setting the small kitchen table with mauve stoneware plates and crystal champagne flutes and a vase blooming with daisies; and preparing platters of smoked salmon and sliced pears and apples and cheese and caviar. Such fun, but now . . . "You said you hadn't eaten."

"Winter." Mark's lips found hers, showing her his hunger for her, apologizing. It wasn't her fault that she had turned his world upside down. He repeated hoarsely, "I missed you."

Winter gently touched the dark circles under his blue eyes. She whispered softly, her confidence a little restored by his kiss, "You're hungry for food, too, aren't you?"

"Maybe." Yes, he was famished, but if he could only satisfy one hunger, he would choose her.

Winter caught one of his hands and led him into the kitchen.

"We have rose food," she teased, holding up a bottle of chilled champagne. "And cheese, crackers, salmon, pears, smoked oysters—"

"Do you think we need oysters?" Mark extended his arms to her. She had let go, to get the champagne, and he missed her already.

"No, we don't need oysters." Winter curled against him and kissed the angle of his jaw. She could stay here forever wrapped in his strength, but . . .

The memory of his words and their hidden warning still haunted her. Winter wanted Mark to know that she already understood about his dedication to medicine. She had seen it the moment she saw him on campus, absorbed in his studying, a slight smile on his handsome face. She respected his dedication, admired it, and she envied his obvious joy.

"Have you always known you were going to be a doctor?" she asked, pulling away, sitting down at the table and motioning to Mark to do the same.

"No." Mark paused and added seriously, "In fact, I spent most of my life knowing I wasn't going to be a doctor."

"Really? I wondered if you were older than most third year medical students."

"I am. I'm twenty-nine. How about you? A little older than the usual recent college graduate?"

"A year older. I'll be twenty-four in January."

Mark waited for Winter to tell him about the missing year, but she didn't.
He saw the soft seriousness in her eyes and realized she already had told him.

"You stayed out the year of Allison's accident, didn't you?" Mark asked.

"Her accident happened in September, just before Autumn Quarter of our junior year. Allison came out of the coma in the middle of October. I guess I had been in a coma, too, because I suddenly realized I'd been in the hospital, not in class, for the last six weeks."

Mark wondered why Winter couldn't simply say, I stayed out because Allison is my best friend, and she needed my help to learn to read again, and to write and walk and talk and make new memories.

"You took the year off to help Allison," Mark repeated gently.

"I guess so." Winter tilted her head thoughtfully. "We were talking about why you are so old."

Mark debated how much detail to give. His usual version of his unorthodox path to medical school was brief and unemotional; a sketchy outline of the chronology laced with humor at his apparent indecision and free of turmoil. Mark decided to tell Winter the truth. Someday—the day he said good-bye?—she might need to understand.

"My father is a successful—in fact, famous—heart surgeon. I was born while he was doing his residency in San Francisco. By the time I was six I had two younger sisters, a very unhappy mother, and an absentee father."

"Oh," Winter whispered softly. *A very unhappy mother. An absentee father. Just like me, Mark.*

What have I said that makes you so sad? Mark wondered, and waited. But Winter was silent and Mark continued his story.

"My father made his fame and fortune mending hearts, except at home, where he broke them. By the time he was established and could have spent time with us, the marriage was over and his children were angry and confused little strangers." Mark let the ancient emotions catch up with the words. "Home felt like war, a battle between my mother, who was good, and my father and medicine, who were the enemies."

Mark sighed as he remembered how everything had seemed so clear through his hurt young eyes.

"I graduated from Berkeley with a degree in business and joined the stampeding bull market as a broker with Merrill Lynch in San Francisco. It was lucrative, easy, pleasant, and—"

"Not who you are."

Mark nodded, marvelling that she understood. Usually when he recounted his journey from stocks and bonds to Hippocrates, the reaction was one of uncomprehending horror. *But . . . but . . . I thought that with HMOs and DRGs and malpractice insurance, medicine wasn't so . . . uh . . . attractive anymore. Couldn't you . . . don't really successful brokers make millions of dollars?*

"Not who I am," Mark agreed softly. "I returned to Berkeley, took the premed courses, and now I get the *New England Journal* instead of the one from Wall Street."

"And it feels right to be a doctor." Winter knew the answer.

"Yes. It feels very right." Mark reached for her hand, entwining his fingers with hers, and continued gently, "I just have to be so very careful not to—" He faltered, searching for the best words.

"Make the same mistakes your father did?"

"Put myself in a position where I can harm someone I care about. My father *did* make mistakes with his young family and the fragile feelings of his children,

but so much of the time he was away from us was beyond his control. As a doctor, especially during residency, your life is controlled by the whims of illness. Like this evening, just as I was leaving to take you to a candlelight dinner in Westwood, three people who had been involved in a bad car accident on the San Diego Freeway arrived in the E.R. The other trauma team was in the O.R., operating on a man who had been shot, so—"

"You had to stay. They needed you."

"Yes." *I wanted to stay. I wanted to help.* And something else, something that had made Mark's voice harsh when he saw her. For the first time ever, Mark had felt torn. He had wanted to stay *and* he had wanted to leave to be with her.

Mark had spent the next four hours with a twelve-year-old boy, the youngest victim. The boy had a severe open fracture of the femur. Mark stayed with him in the Emergency Room, during the emergency arteriogram in radiology, and until the orthopedic surgeons assumed his care. It was much more than baby-sitting; the blood loss had already been significant and the shattered thigh bone raised the ominous specter of fatty emboli to the lungs. Mark monitored the boy carefully, compulsively checking the measurable vital signs—the pulse, the blood pressure, the respiratory rate, the level of consciousness—and the immeasurable ones—the fright of an injured child. Will I live? Is my mother all right? Why can't I see her? Why does it hurt so much?

"There are the demands of long, unpredictable hours," Mark added quietly, "but the emotional demands can be even greater."

Winter nodded solemnly.

"I spent so many years blaming my father, as if he ignored us on purpose."

"And now?"

"I don't see him much. He's back in Houston, married to someone about your age." Mark smiled wryly. "We'll never be close, but the anger—my anger—is gone."

"And your mother?" Winter asked hesitantly, thinking about her own very unhappy mother.

"It's a happy ending. After the divorce and once my sisters and I were in our teens, my mother went back to school. For the past ten years, she has taught high school English and loves it. So—"

"So?"

"—now you know everything there is to know about me. What about you? Tell me about what you want to be and about your family."

Winter gazed for a thoughtful moment at their hands, Mark's strong fingers curled over hers. She felt safe now—almost safe enough to tell him her secrets and her dreams—but he had just finished telling her, so gently, that she couldn't count on him; he couldn't, wouldn't, always be there. Maybe he wouldn't even be there tomorrow.

Winter pulled her hand away, stood up, and began clearing the table. "It's late."

Mark joined her.

"OK. Your turn next time."

"Next time?"

"This weekend, if you're free. Starting Friday night, I'm on a break until after the Fourth."

"They give you vacation?"

"They give us a symbolic break between our junior and senior years. It's more than symbolism, though. They want us to have time to fill out our residency applications. Mine are almost done, because I'm spending next week in San Francisco. My sisters and mother and I haven't been under the same roof in years." Mark stood behind her, wrapped his arms around her waist, and kissed her neck as he spoke. "I don't have to leave until Monday morning. So I thought, if you're free, we could spend from Friday night until Monday together."

"I'm free."

"We could go somewhere."

"Yes." Winter turned to face him. "Or we could stay here."

"Or we could stay here."

Allison was strangely silent, Winter realized as she made the right turn off Bellagio between the brick pillars marking the entrance of the Club.

Allison had been cheerful and excited when Winter arrived promptly at six-thirty—eager to ride, confident of her decision—but as they drove from Santa Monica to Bel Air, her cheerful chatter stopped.

Allison's silence allowed Winter to drift—float—to her own thoughts, to the wonderful memories of last night and this morning. She and Mark had cleaned up the kitchen and gone to bed, to *sleep*. They hadn't made love. They had just kissed gentle kisses and curled close and fallen into necessary sleep and warm, lovely dreams. And then this morning, a half hour before the alarm would have sounded, they awoke together and made love, a tender good morning, a wish for a lovely day, a promise of next time. . . .

Winter parked her Mercedes in the nearly empty "members only" parking lot of the Bel Air Hunt Club. She heard the distant sound of tennis balls pinging off rackets and decided that the two other Mercedes, the Jag, and the Silver Cloud belonged to four of the Club's many tennis fanatics. Winter was about to make a comment about physical fitness addicts when she saw Allison's face.

The excited pink flush was gone. Allison's skin was tight and ashen around her bewildered jade-green eyes. She sat, stiff and frozen, her white-knuckled fists clenched in her lap.

"Allison?"

"I can't believe this," Allison whispered weakly. Her heart fluttered—a sparrow trying to flee her chest—her head swirled and her lungs gasped for precious air. *I'm afraid.*

No, Allison realized. It was more than fear, it was panic! She remembered learning about panic—and panic attacks—in the Introductory Psychology class she had taken to fulfill the social science requirement at UCLA. What if this was a panic attack? The symptoms fit: The panic came out of the blue, swift, powerful, without warning; her heart pounded; her world spun in dizzying fear; her breath was stolen; and she was consumed by a sense of doom.

No, Allison told herself. It's fear—panic *maybe*—but not a panic attack. *And whatever it is, I can control it.*

"You don't have to do this, you know," Winter said. "In fact, it's really a silly idea."

"No, Winter. I have to," Allison countered slowly. Speaking was such a struggle! Her brain was already completely consumed with the suddenly astonishingly difficult tasks of trying to breathe and trying to calm her heart. The additional task of searching for words and speaking them was almost impossible. "I have to."

I have to. I can't live my life with this fear. I can't never ride again because of *this!* Get in control, Allison told herself sternly. But how?

"You don't have to ride today, Allison."

"Yes I do," she breathed. Talking was a battle with her breathless lungs, a fight for the precious air. "Winter, I need you on my side."

"I am on your side, Allison, always. You know that."

"Yes." *Yes*. Winter's words reminded Allison of the other battles she had fought and won. Winter had been there, helping her, as she learned to speak again, and to read and write and walk.

This—this silly panic—was trivial compared to that, wasn't it? Trivial. Allison forced the word into her whirling mind, repeating it over and over, like a mantra. *Trivial. Trivial.* Miraculously, she felt a little more calm.

"I'm OK."

"Are you sure?"

"Yes." *Better, anyway.* "Let's go."

The miracle held. Her legs moved, unsteady, trembling, and she reined her heart in from a gallop to a canter.

Winter and Allison walked along the white marble chip path, lined with pale pink roses, toward the stable compound. As they neared the stable, the fragrance of roses faded in the smells of moist hay and polished leather and horses. The familiar once-beloved scents filled Allison with the memory of her dreams.

The dreams had died the day of her accident, but Allison hadn't known it, hadn't felt the emptiness, until much later. The long months of recovery were filled with their own goals, their own six-foot hurdles and conquests that felt like gold: reading, writng, talking, walking, remembering. Allison's heart and mind and strength and will were focused on being whole and healthy again.

Only after the bones mended as well as they were going to, and the crushed nerves only sent occasional angry messages of pain, and her auburn hair covered the scar on her skull and was a thick mane again, did the realization come. It was a feeling before it was a thought, an aching emptiness filling the place in her heart where her dreams had always lived.

The dreams were gone.

And then Dan was there. Dan, the kind, loving, gentle, young man who fell in love with her. Dan told her she was beautiful—yes, *beautiful*—and Allison laughed at his words with merry astonished eyes; but she had laughed again, at last. The empty aching retreated. *Yes, I will marry you Dan. Oh, well, they have design stores in Hillsborough, don't they? I'm not sure I'll even pursue a career as a designer. . . .*

It felt wonderful. Dan filled the emptiness. Dan became her new dream. Allison lost herself in Dan's love. *Lost herself*. That was the problem. Allison knew, from the aching that stayed in her heart after the horrible wounds had healed, who she *wasn't* anymore; but she had not yet discovered who she was, the new Allison.

She had to find out who she was, what she could do, what she wanted. Dan would help her, giving his proud, loving support, but it was his wonderful, generous love that gave Allison the confidence to be alone, to begin the journey to discover who she was all by herself.

I can't marry you Dan. I will always love you. You have given me so much.

Allison had said good-bye to Dan. In a month she would begin her career at Elegance, nurturing and challenging the incredible new talent that had risen like a phoenix out of the ashes of her shattered dreams.

And today she was going to ride. Allison had no illusions. She would never jump again, never compete, never win an Olympic gold medal, never spend her life riding and training and teaching others to ride.

Allison didn't want to resurrect the dream.

She only wanted to make peace with it.

Then she could go on.

When they reached the stable compound, Allison led the way to the tack room. Yesterday she had called to be sure that her key would still fit the tack room lock and that it was all right for her to ride one of the Club's horses. Of course, she had been told by a surprised voice. Why would the tack room locks have been changed? Why would the rules and privileges of the Club have been changed?

No reason, except that for Allison everything had changed.

"Hello, Ginger," Allison whispered ten minutes later, after she had taken a saddle and bridle from the tack room, signed the members" log, and walked along the rows of stalls to a once-familiar one. "Remember me?"

The horse whinnied and Allison smiled. Ginger's registered name was Bel Air's Ginger Lady. For years, Ginger and Allison—the flame-colored horse and the girl with the flame-colored hair—had been Bel Air's Ginger Ladies. Even after she got Tuxedo, and spent hours training, jumping, competing with him, it was Ginger who Allison still rode on the trails. Tuxedo dragged his champion thoroughbred heels at the prospect of a trail ride; Ginger always pricked up her ears, tossed her red-gold mane, and tensed with excitement.

Maybe today, Allison thought, she and Ginger could ride the trails after she rode in the ring.

After.

The panic came back in small, dizzying waves; each little wave carried the threatening promise that, if unchecked, it would swell into a monstrous one, crashing, consuming, destroying. Allison was on guard, fighting each wave.

Allison fought the panic and the memory of the sudden unexpected lurch of fright that could hurl her again into an immeasurable nightmare.

Ginger didn't lurch. She walked and trotted and cantered in amiable response to Allison's silent expert commands.

Winter watched from a distant corner of the outdoor ring, fingers crossed, breath held. After fifteen minutes, she relaxed a little, still vigilant but captivated by the grace and rhythm and elegance of horse and rider. Winter's eyes misted briefly, from sadness for Allison's shattered dreams, then from happiness as she saw her best friend's smile and sparkling eyes, despite the intense concentration. Allison's physical wounds had healed long ago. But, Winter realized, until this moment, Allison hadn't really fully recovered.

After thirty minutes, Allison brought Ginger to a halt in front of Winter.

"Wonderful." Winter smiled at her friend's flushed, happy face.

"Thanks. It felt good. In fact, I think Ginger and I are going for a ride on the Kensington trail."

The fabulous trails at the Club bore lovely British names: Kensington, Windsor, Knightsbridge, Covent Garden. Kensington was the sunrise trail, winding east through a forest of palmettos and ferns to a bluff overlooking the Los Angeles basin, the San Bernardino Mountains, the new dawn sun. Windsor was the sunset trail, meandering west to a breathtaking vista of the Pacific. The other trails criss-crossed like embroidery threads through a luxuriant tapestry of roses and lilacs and azaleas and rhododendrons.

Winter started to protest Allison's solitary journey, but stopped. Allison was fine, *better.*

"Shall I go have a cup of coffee at the Club and come back in an hour or two?"

"No. I'll call Mother when I'm done riding." Allison had spared her parents

advance warning of this momentous decision, but now she was eager to let them know. Sean Fitzgerald was a passionate horseman; her loving father would hug her tightly, his understanding outweighing his fear. Her mother's embrace would be tight, too; Patricia didn't share the passion for riding, but she shared with her husband the wish for Allison's happiness above all else.

"OK. How about a celebration dinner at the Chart House in Malibu tonight?"

"I'd like that. Winter? Thank you for being here."

Winter clutched the leather steering wheel of her Mercedes. She had been sitting like this, in the parking lot of the Club, for the past twenty minutes. Members were arriving—elegant breakfast meetings, tennis lessons, teenagers planning a day at the pool, riders—and she was beginning to draw concerned stares.

Allison had found peace. Allison had conquered her demons. Allison was going to find a new dream.

What about you, Winter?

I'm not strong like Allison.

But remember what Mark said? "Your turn next time?" What are you going tell him? You can't lie to him. His eyes won't let you.

I know!

The mansion on Bellagio—Winter's mansion—was only a half mile away. How many times had she driven by in the past five years, forcing her eyes not to drift, even slightly, toward the opening in the ten-foot wall of bougainvillea and the winding drive that led to her home?

Winter's demons lived there. Winter's dreams had died there.

It's been five years. Why go back now?

Because you have to. You have to find peace with the lonely, unloved, frightened little girl who lives inside you.

Winter sighed softly and turned the key in the ignition.

Only a half mile away . . .

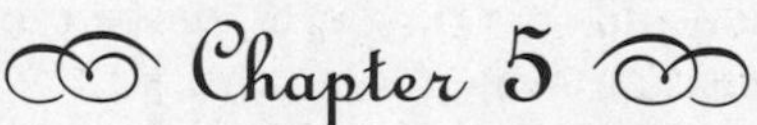

Chapter 5

LOS ANGELES, CALIFORNIA
JANUARY 1961

The birth of Winter Carlyle was news, and Vanessa Gold printed it in *All That Glitters* before anyone else in the world, scooping the celebrity columnists in Los Angeles and, to Vanessa's great delight, scooping even the columnists of Fleet Street. This baby, the love-child of American actress and Hollywood darling Jacqueline Winter and the distinguished and extraordinarily successful British director Lawrence Carlyle, would make headlines from Hollywood to London. The love-child was due, appropriately, on Valentine's Day.

But Vanessa received the call from one of her most reliable sources shortly after midnight on New Year's Eve, moments after the baby's birth, as "Auld Lang Syne" played in the background and confetti still floated to the floor and champagne-flavored kisses among the celebrity revellers grew deeper and longer.

Vanessa left the New Year's Eve gala at Cyrano's moments after receiving the call. She rushed first to the hospital—a worthwhile trip because she was able to speak with a beaming Lawrence Carlyle—then to her office, and finally to the printing presses of the paper where she stood her ground and watched as the obviously annoyed typesetter exchanged the new words for ones that had been typeset hours before.

Then Vanessa drove to her bungalow on St. Cloud and poured herself a glass of champagne. Before taking a sip, she raised the crystal champagne flute first to the south, toward the hospital where the infant girl lay, and then to the east, toward England and her soon-to-be envious competitors, the columnists of Fleet Street.

CELEBRATED LOVE-CHILD
ARRIVES WITH NEW YEAR!!

Moments after the stroke of midnight, as the old year took its final curtain call, Jacqueline Winter gave birth to a baby girl. Winter Elizabeth Carlyle's birth comes just five months after the much-publicized marriage of stunning American actress Jacqueline Winter and celebrated British producer/director Lawrence Carlyle. Although the already famous love-child was not expected until Valentine's Day, the new papa reports proudly, "She's small and delicate and doing just fine."

The actress and director met two years ago during the filming of *Marakesh*. A passionate but stormy on-location affair—in Casablanca, no less!—ended "badly." Jacqueline and Lawrence were reunited by the Academy Awards, which garnered statues of Oscar for each for *Marakesh*. By August, passion vanquished storm clouds, and the never-married-ever-loved pregnant actress and the never-married-ever-secretive father-to-be director were married.

Carlyle will keep Laurelhurst, his fifteen-hundred-acre estate in his native England, but the couple will reside in the Bel Air mansion previously owned by legendary studio tycoon Ben Samuels and purchased by Carlyle three months ago. Two-time Oscar-winner Carlyle has just wrapped his latest sure-to-be-a-blockbuster epic *Destiny*. The actress mother plans to resume her acting career in April with the lead role in *Fame and Fortune*.

Fourteen months later, Vanessa reported the divorce. The "forsaking all others" vow had cast another celebrity marriage asunder. At least, the rumor that was leaked—a huge, gushing leak—to all concerned was that Lawrence Carlyle had been unfaithful and Jacqueline Winter had thrown him out. Vanessa suspected a "dysinformation" campaign, but she was unable *ever* to uncover anything else and had to conclude, with the rest of Hollywood, that the reason for the divorce was "as advertised." Lawrence Carlyle returned to England where, nine months later, he married British author Margaret Reilly, the unassuming, talented, very successful writer of murder mysteries.

The marriage of Lawrence Carlyle and Jacqueline Winter became just another Hollywood statistic, another failed marriage that, on the face of it, seemed less messy in its dissolution than most. But Vanessa wondered. According to everyone, Lawrence never saw his child after the divorce, and that was surprising indeed. It seemed so unlike what Vanessa knew of Lawrence Carlyle. And it worried her, because it meant that the little girl's only parent was Jacque-

line Winter . . . and *that* meant the child had no parent at all.

It wasn't until she was four that Winter realized there was no one in her world whom she called Daddy. There was Mommy, of course. Mommy had flowing platinum hair and sapphire eyes, and she floated like a fairy princess, just beyond Winter's reach. Winter heard her mother's soft voice, but the softness was never for her, nor was Jacqueline's bewitching smile or her delicate touch. Jacqueline's smiles and softness were for her friends, the never-ending, ever-changing parade of handsome and powerful men who were there during the rare hours when Mommy was even at home.

There was Mommy—beautiful, fragrant, graceful, lovely . . . beyond Winter's desperate grasp.

But there was no Daddy. There were daddies on television and in books, and although Winter had no friends, she was mysteriously invited to birthday parties in Bel Air and Beverly Hills—her nannies would take her—and sometimes there were daddies there, too.

At age four, Winter made the discovery that her Daddy was missing, but she didn't have the courage to ask her mother, or anyone, about it until she was six.

Winter was much too shy to ask—much too shy and terribly lonely. Jacqueline paid people—nannies and governesses and housekeepers—a great deal of money to pay attention to the daughter she herself rarely saw or wanted to see. The hired help cared for Winter dutifully and without affection. It was so difficult—impossible!—to feel warmth for the quiet, serious little girl with the sorrowful, judgmental violet eyes. Winter resisted warmth, they decided, *spurned it*, preferring her own private world of make-believe.

Winter lived in a fantasy world rich with wonderful adventures and loving friends, with whom she shared the feelings she was too shy to speak aloud. *Why doesn't anyone like me? Why doesn't anyone touch me? Why doesn't Mommy ever play with me?* The pain screamed silently from her small, shy heart; but her fantasy friends had no answers. And there were fears, too—horrible fears—nestled in her heart beside the pain. *What if I die? What happens when I die? What if Mommy dies? Is death cold and dark?*

Winter knew no one liked her—*please* like me!—but she didn't know why. And she knew that she had no Daddy, and she didn't understand that, either.

Finally, Winter summoned six months of courage and asked her beautiful mother a question she had rehearsed a hundred times in her mind.

"Mommy, where is my Daddy? Everyone else . . ."

Jacqueline looked up from her first screwdriver of the day and gazed with surprise at her daughter. Despite her enormously successful career and an unending stream of famous and powerful men who wanted her, Jacqueline Winter was unhappy with her life. Of the many things that displeased her, one of the most annoying was her daughter. Winter's painful shyness was bad enough, an embarrassment, but add to that her looks . . .

Any daughter of Jacqueline Winter should have been at least pretty and adorable, and more likely enchanting and beguiling. But Winter was pale and gawky and her too-huge eyes stared critically at the world. Winter was,

Jacqueline decided, really and truly an ugly little girl.

Ugly and sullen and serious, and now Winter was asking about her Daddy!

"Your Daddy," Jacqueline sighed as the memory of her marriage crashed over her like an enormous unwelcome wave on a sandcastle. How she hated Lawrence Carlyle for leaving her! She should have let him have Winter, even though . . . But Lawrence had wanted Winter, and Jacqueline had been determined to punish him every way she could.

"Where is he?"

"In England."

"What's his name? What does he do?" Winter pressed with uncharacteristic bravery. She had a Daddy!

"His name is Lawrence Carlyle," Jacqueline answered, amazed at her own patience. She was a little lonely. She had just finished filming *Roses are Red* and, as far as she was concerned, had also just ended the affair with her on-screen lover. Jacqueline was feeling the familiar, unwelcome letdown of reentering the real world. Maybe it would be diverting to talk to her daughter for a while. Another screwdriver would help, too. "He makes movies."

"Like you?"

"No, he's a director and a producer."

Winter frowned at the unfamiliar and so important-sounding words. Jacqueline wasn't in the mood to explain, but she didn't want to be alone, either.

"I'll show you."

Jacqueline and Winter were in the breakfast nook of the mulberry, cream, and heather-gray country kitchen. Jacqueline stood up, hesitated a moment, then moved decisively to a remote drawer and removed a key. She refilled her glass with more gin than orange juice and gestured for Winter to follow. They crossed the living room to a back hallway that led to a room Winter knew but that had never held much interest for her. It was a cavernous room, with peach-colored walls and cushiony chairs and sofas arranged facing a mural on one wall. Winter had spent an afternoon gazing at the mural, a faded Italian fresco, but couldn't understand its appeal.

Jacqueline flicked a switch on the nearby wall and the mural parted, revealing a huge screen. Next, she opened a gray panel built into the wall, inserted the key, and turned it, inactivating the special security system Lawrence had installed to protect the irreplaceable library of films stored in the peach-colored cupboards that lined the walls.

A state-of-the-art security system wired the entire mansion, but extra protection was warranted in the screening room. Some of the reels of films were original prints, rare studio copies, some purchased, some bartered, some stolen. Lawrence had bought Ben Samuels's film library at the same time he had bought the mansion, in a transaction that was separate and very expensive.

Jacqueline had fallen in love with the mansion because of its magnificent views of Los Angeles and the ocean, its palatial rooms, its crystal chandeliers and marble floors. Lawrence had fallen in love with the secret hidden gardens, the tranquil pond filled with koi, and the rare treasures buried in the film library.

Ben Samuels's film collection was already the best in the world, but Lawrence made it even better. He added prints of all his own movies and all of Jacqueline's, and he purchased contemporary "classics" to complement the ones of the Golden Era. Lawrence offered Jacqueline an enormous price for the library at the time of the divorce, but she refused all his offers because she knew how much his precious prints meant to him. Jacqueline held all the cards; Lawrence was desperate to get away from her. Jacqueline's fury and Lawrence's desperation meant he gave her everything she wanted . . . everything but himself.

Jacqueline hadn't set foot in the screening room since Lawrence left. Now she walked along the once-familiar walls, opened a cabinet, and removed the reels of *Marakesh*, the Oscar-award-winning Jacqueline Winter-Lawrence Carlyle collaboration. Winter followed her mother to the projection booth and watched as, after a few false starts, Jacqueline wound the reel and started the projector.

Then she settled beside her mother in a cushiony chair in front of the huge screen.

When the first reel ended, Jacqueline briefly explained to Winter how to thread the next and disappeared to make another screwdriver. Winter's small hands threaded the projector quickly, then she scampered back to her chair and waited eagerly for Jacqueline to return so the magic could continue.

"You were wonderful, Mommy," Winter breathed when the last reel of *Marakesh* came to its end. "And my Daddy made that movie?"

Jacqueline nodded.

"Why is he in England?" *Where is England? Can we go there?* "When is he coming home?"

"He's never coming home."

"Why not? Doesn't he like us?" *Doesn't he like me? No one likes me, so why should Daddy?*

"No, Winter, he doesn't like us," Jacqueline said heavily, glowering at her empty glass as if it held the empty memories. Finally, she stood up. "Let's go."

"No! Can't we watch it again?"

"No."

"*Please!*"

"I said no."

"Are there other movies, Mommy?" She was being so brave, but she was so desperate. For the first time in her life Winter felt safe; in this enchanted place watching fantasy worlds come to life, she felt safe. And *happy.*

"Oh." Jacqueline shrugged. "I guess we could watch something else."

They spent the morning and afternoon watching Jacqueline's own girlhood favorites—*National Velvet, The Wizard of Oz, Gone With The Wind*. By the end of the day, Winter knew she was going to be an actress.

Until then, Winter had lived in the fantasies of her mind. Her imagination was vivid and creative, but this was even better.

Now Winter knew about Oz, and she could be Dorothy; and she knew about England—where Daddy was!—and she could be Velvet; and she knew about Tara, and she could be Scarlett.

Winter *was* Dorothy. She sang to the Japanese koi that swam lazily in the pond in a hidden garden beside the unused wing of the mansion. Winter joyfully serenaded the koi about places over the rainbow and the yellow brick road. The colorful, tranquil koi were her audience; Winter performed for them and talked to them, and they ate from her small hands. And she named them. The black one was Toto; the silver one, Tin Woodman; the white one, Belinda; the yellow one, Cowardly Lion; and the calico one, Scarecrow.

Winter was Dorothy and Velvet and Scarlett and a hundred other wonderful characters she discovered in the long, happy hours she spent in the screening room after she convinced Jacqueline to show her about the security system and promised to be *so* careful with the treasures.

Winter played all the roles to perfection. No one knew. No one watched her. If anyone had, if her audience had been other than the koi, they would have known what Winter knew: She was a gifted actress. Winter knew. She told no one because she was still shy and silent. Her shyness drove her deeper into the dreams that had become an obsession.

She was going to be an actress—she *was* an actress—but there was more! She was going to star in Daddy's movies and he was going to be so proud of her!

My Daddy will like me even though no one else does.

No one liked Winter. In the expensive private schools in Switzerland—in Geneva and Zurich—where she spent most of her life from the time she was eight, Winter finally learned why. The other girls stared at her and giggled and pointed. Their young eyes flashed with dislike and contempt and they hissed cruelly, "shy" and "weird" and "skinny" and "ugly" and "scaredy-cat" and "witch."

The vicious taunts stabbed Winter with excruciating pain. She stared at the other girls through tear-blurred eyes and wished she had the courage to say, But I'm Dorothy, I'm Scarlett, I'm Velvet! You like them, don't you? I can be them! I can be anyone you want me to be!!

Winter could, but no one gave her a chance because of the way she looked—so pale, so awkward, so serious. No one would listen, but it didn't matter because she didn't have the courage to speak.

Then everything changed.

Sometime between the time she flew from Los Angeles to Zurich shortly after her fourteenth birthday in January and the time she returned from the exclusive Swiss boarding school in May, Winter Elizabeth Carlyle became beautiful. Winter didn't know it. She never looked at herself in the mirror. And if the other girls at the school noticed, they were shocked into green-eyed silence.

Winter found out from a stranger on her way home. The stranger was a young man, although to Winter he seemed *so* mature. He stood beside her as she browsed through books in London's Heathrow Airport. Finally, he simply said, "You are the most beautiful creature I have ever seen."

He was handsome, and his eyes were brown and sincere, and he had a soft British accent, and he wanted nothing from her except for her to know that he thought she was beautiful. Winter smiled vaguely at his words. He returned the smile, then left. After a few moments, Winter went into the ladies' room and discovered that he was right.

The ugly duckling had become a swan; awkwardness had become grace; skinniness had become soft sensuality; pale, translucent skin had become rich cream; fine, stringy hair was black velvet; chapped, chewed lips were full and red; and the too-huge eyes were hypnotic, seductive, beckoning.

She was as beautiful as Scarlett O'Hara.

On the flight home, Winter thought a little about her beauty and a lot about the man in the London airport. What if he had been Daddy? Winter knew he wasn't, of course. She had made a study of Lawrence Carlyle, carefully filling scrapbooks with articles about him and photographs of him. Winter had seen all his movies, over and over and over. She read the murder mysteries written by his wife—her stepmother!—and spent hours analyzing a rare, precious photograph she had found in a magazine, a picture of Lawrence and his two young sons, her half brothers. Winter tried to see the family resemblance, but her father was so handsome, and her rosy-cheeked half brothers looked confident and happy.

The young man at Heathrow hadn't been Lawrence Carlyle, but he had been British, like Daddy. And he had told her she was beautiful. Maybe it was a wonderful omen.

Suddenly everyone liked her. Strangers smiled at her, and so did the ever-before-hostile housekeeper at the mansion, and so did her mother. Jacqueline was delighted in a bitter-sweet way. She was envious of Winter's youthful beauty but happy that at last her daughter looked the way she should. Jacqueline embraced the new Winter—spiritually, not physically—taking her on shopping sprees to Rodeo Drive and to lunch at the Bel Air Hunt Club, the Polo Lounge, Benito, and L'Ermitage.

No one seemed to care any longer that Winter was quiet and shy; she was beautiful, avishing, and that was enough. But Winter cared. She wanted to speak! She had been unheard for so long. Her shyness hadn't vanished, but her beauty gave her confidence.

At first her words were serious. She wanted to, tried to, share the pain and fears that had been imprisoned inside her for so long. She was like someone awakening from years of coma. What happened? Where am I? I've had the most horrible nightmares. . . .

Winter wanted to ask why, why, *why?* But when she did, Jacqueline and the housekeepers and the teenagers at the pool at the Club withdrew, suddenly uneasy, not liking her again.

Please like me!

Winter lapsed into thoughtful silence. When she spoke again, her voice was soft and purring, her words were charming and witty, and she was provocative and vivacious. Everyone loved Winter and it made her feel wonderful. The bright, clever words were hers, as much a part of her as the secret, hidden ones she couldn't utter, but for the dazzling delivery Winter borrowed liberally from the heroines she knew so well—the coquettishness of Scarlett, the dreaminess of Dorothy, the courage of Velvet, the passion of Lara, the boldness of Fanny, the will of Eliza, the soft loveliness of them all.

Winter was an actress. She created a magnificent, seductive, bewitching personality to match her stunning, provocative beauty. She wove a vivid tapestry of emotions and moods, but she was always confident, always golden, always in control.

It was better to be liked—much, much better—but Winter lived in fear that the lonely, frightened little girl who still dwelled in her heart would be discovered and she would be ostracized again. Winter didn't hate the little girl . . . it was who she was; but sometimes she ached desperately to tell someone about *her*, about how lonely and afraid she was, what wonderful dreams she had, how much she wanted to see her father.

By the time Winter was fifteen, her self-sufficiency and maturity had greatly surpassed that of her mother. She had long since abandoned hope that Jacqueline would love her, but as she realized the magnitude of her mother's despair, Winter's own anger began to melt into loving concern. It was a miracle that Jacqueline's career never wavered. She starred in major films every year, received four Best Actress nominations in addition to the one for *Marakesh*, and won one of them. Jacqueline Winter was a remarkable success. Her work earned her great wealth, but it paled by comparison to the fortune in jewels and other gifts lavished on her by the rich and powerful men who wanted her.

Jacqueline drank too much and too often, and she took pills. Her life between roles was barren and desperate. She never remarried, despite constant offers. Winter couldn't recall a genuine laugh, not a happy one, just the on-cue laughter of a gifted actress. Jacqueline added her brilliant dazzle to Hollywood's parties, but when she arrived home at dawn, she was often restless, unsettled, reluctant to be alone.

It was then, as the new day sun peered over the San Bernardino Mountains and cast a golden beam across the Los Angeles basin, that Jacqueline and Winter became "friends." They weren't mother and daughter; they were more like the only two girls still awake at the slumber party, determined not to succumb to sleep, talking honestly because they were too tired not to.

Jacqueline's motherly advice to Winter sprung from her own mistakes. She never told Winter she had made a mistake by ignoring her little girl, but Winter let herself believe she saw that regret, too, in her mother's alcohol-blurred eyes. Jacqueline focused on her mistakes with men and on her foolish belief that her own stunning beauty was immortal and required no care.

"Stay out of the sun, Winter. Oh, I see that you already know that," Jacqueline added with a smile, as if she had just made an important discovery. It was mid-August and Winter's skin was still the color of fresh cream.

For the first fourteen years of her life, Winter lived in the darkened worlds of the screening room at the mansion and movie theaters in Zurich and Geneva. She left those enchanted caves to re-create the fantasies in the tree-shaded garden by the pond or in her Spartan dormitory room in Switzerland. Until her life-changing fourteenth summer, Winter had never walked on the white sand beach a few miles from her home or spent frolicking, splashing, carefree afternoons by the pool at the Club.

During that memorable summer, when she was beautiful and had fashioned a personality to match, Winter spent most days at the pool at the Club. But by then she was Scarlett. She wore elegant broad-rimmed straw hats, sipped lemonade in the shade of a pink umbrella, batted her long, dark lashes, and purred in a soft Southern drawl that she needed to protect her delicate skin from the harshness of the summer sun. Winter held court in the shade by the pool, Scarlett entertaining the Confederate Army on the verandah at Tara. The young men were enthralled and the girls frantically tried to imitate. The imitations failed. Winter's rich white skin was seductive and elegant; without tans, the other girls simply looked pale, anemic, unhealthy.

"I do stay out of the sun, Mother."

"And don't smoke."

"I don't."

"And," Jacqueline smiled wryly as she toasted herself with a half-empty glass of gin, "you probably shouldn't drink."

I don't. I won't. And I won't take drugs. Winter had made those promises years ago as she watched her mother's drug and alcohol-ravaged life. She added quietly, "Neither should you."

"But I do." Jacqueline gave a wobbly smile and a shrug that said, It's too late. She continued softly, speaking from her heart, "Be careful with men, Winter. They will want you. Oh, how they will want you! Have them, enjoy them on your terms, but be in control always. And never let them get too close."

Winter nodded solemnly. She had already learned that, but it applied to everyone, not just men. *Everyone* wanted something from her. The men wanted *her* and the girls wanted to be close, basking in her golden brilliance, hoping she had something to spare, an ounce of fairy dust to sprinkle on them, a small touch of her magic. Everyone wanted. No one gave. And they only wanted her if she was dazzling and beautiful. No one wanted to hear about her fears or her secrets.

Winter wished she could tell Jacqueline she was going to be an actress—*like you Mother!*—and that it would reunite her with her father. Winter didn't know why Lawrence had left or why in all these years he had never tried to see her, but she heard the bitterness in Jacqueline's voice when she spoke of him and assumed—prayed—it was something between her mother and father, nothing to do with her. *He doesn't like us*, Jacqueline had told her. But Winter had been so young! Surely Lawrence didn't leave because of *her.* No, she told herself. Lawrence left because of Jacqueline. Winter could go to him now, but that would mean abandoning Jacqueline. Winter didn't even consider it.

She would find him someday—they would find each other—and her Daddy would love her . . . even when she told him about the shy, frightened little girl who lived inside her still.

It was her mother's idea that she stop going to school in Switzerland and Winter gratefully agreed. She spent her last two years of high school in Bel Air, living in the mansion, attending the Westlake School for Girls on North Faring.

Winter's appearance on the first day of fall semester at Westlake drew amazed and delighted breaths from her classmates. They knew her from the pool at the Club and the starlit summer dances and sailing trips to Catalina. Winter was their idol, their *ideal*; envy didn't even enter in because what Winter had was so far beyond their reach.

The other girls wanted something, a ray of her sunshine; *all* the other girls except Allison Fitzgerald. Winter and Allison had both lived in Bel Air since birth, but before the day Winter enrolled at Westlake they had never met. Until then, the lives of Allison Fitzgerald and Winter Carlyle had no common threads.

Winter had lived in a dark cocoon until she became a butterfly. Then, during the summer days while Winter lazed demurely in the shade by the pool at the Club, Allison rode. And at night, when Winter teased seductively in the summer moonlight, Allison slept, because she would ride again at dawn. And at the time when Winter decided to lose her virginity—*to give it away* when she was sixteen and he was twenty-two—Allison still blushed uneasily when boys approached her and was most happy cantering across rolling green hills, her long red-gold hair tossed by the wind.

Allison was warm and friendly to the new girl in the junior class. She had no desire to bask in Winter's dazzle, no need for reflected glory. Allison had her own golden aura, a halo of love and happiness spun from loving parents and golden dreams and a heart that beat confidently with hope and joy. Allison wanted nothing from Winter, but she welcomed Winter into her life, sharing her warm, loving parents and her own dreams without expecting anything in return.

Allison became Winter's friend, her best friend, her only friend. Winter didn't tell Allison her secrets, but she believed she could and that Allison would still be her friend.

On the eve of her eighteenth birthday—New Year's Eve—Jacqueline gave Winter the powder-blue Mercedes Sports Coupe and the flawless sapphire earrings.

"You need the car, and I want you to have these earrings. Lawrence gave them to me when I went into labor, just about eighteen years ago this minute. He said they were the exact color of my eyes." Jacqueline's voice was soft and distant, lost in a lovely memory.

"They are."

"I thought you would like to have them." Jacqueline shrugged uncertainly, as the moment came too close to love. "I never wear them. There's a necklace, too, in the safe."

"Thank you." *Mother, thank you!*

"Happy New Year and early Happy Birthday."

Jacqueline touched Winter briefly—a rare, gentle, almost loving touch—

before she left for a New Year's Eve Party. Winter was too stunned to touch back, and by the time she rushed to the door, to hug her, to thank her, to cry, Jacqueline was gone.

And Winter never saw her again. Just before dawn, Jacqueline's car plummeted over a cliff on Mulholland Drive and into eternity. Jacqueline's blood alcohol level was sky high. Her death was ruled an accident, but Winter wondered if her mother had known, if that was why she had given her the earrings, tacitly reestablishing the link with Lawrence after all these years of bitter silence. Winter wondered if Jacqueline had known she was saying good-bye.

"This is Jacqueline. I'm either not home or can't be bothered to answer. If you're calling about a role that has an Oscar attached—the statue, not just another nomination—leave a message. Otherwise . . ."

Winter listened to the tape in her mother's answering machine over and over. She had reels of Jacqueline's movies, but those were roles. The go-to-hell message on the answering machine was pure Jacqueline. Winter couldn't bear to erase it; but, finally, she stopped listening to it and put it, carefully wrapped, in the safe beside the boxes filled with jewels.

Allison and Patricia and Sean Fitzgerald wanted Winter to move in with them, to join their loving family, but Winter said no. She told all the live-in help to leave and resided alone at the mansion, grieving, waiting for her Daddy.

Winter expected Lawrence Carlyle to come to Jacqueline's funeral. All of Hollywood was there, all of Jacqueline lovers, all of Jacqueline lovers, all except Lawrence. It made Winter very sad, but in a perverse way it gave her hope. It was more proof that the reason Lawrence had stayed away all these years was because of whatever had happened with Jacqueline.

Three months after Jacqueline's death Winter sat in the living room of the mansion with Leo Stiles, the senior partner in the law firm handling the estate, and learned the staggering details of her enormous inheritance. The mansion, empty, was conservatively appraised at eight million. And then there were the five original Impressionist paintings, including two by Monet; the large bedroom safe filled with velvet boxes containing thousands of carats of precious jewels fashioned by Tiffany and Winston and Cartier; the priceless film library; Jacqueline's two Oscars; the millions of earned income shrewdly invested and never spent because there were always lovers who wanted to provide for her; the expensive furnishings; and Winter's trust fund provided by Lawrence Carlyle.

"Trust fund?" *From Daddy?*

"Yes. He has made substantial annual contributions since the divorce," Leo Stiles explained. "Since your mother was always able to provide for you, we just put the money in a special trust fund. The current value is about ten million."

"Is he still? . . ."

"Until you are twenty-one."

Winter bit her lower lip thoughtfully. It had been three months and each day she expected Lawrence to rescue her, his long-lost, long-loved daughter. What if he didn't even know about Jacqueline's death? Now there was a way to be sure.

"Do you know how to reach him?" Winter asked. She knew how. She knew the address of Laurelhurst and the address of Lawrence's film studio in London, and she even knew his phone number.

"Of course."

"Would you call him, speak to him directly, tell him that Mother died, and—" Winter paused. This was so important, sending a message to Daddy. "Thank him very much for all the money he has sent me, tell him how much it has meant to me, but tell him I don't need anymore." *I just need him.*

Two weeks later Winter called Leo Stiles to be certain the message had been conveyed.

"Yes. I spoke with him directly."

"What did he say?"

"He said fine and he thanked me for calling."

"Anything else?" *Anything about me?*

"No, that was all."

Winter waited for Lawrence Carlyle, aching with loneliness and fear, grieving her mother's death. But Lawrence Carlyle didn't come, and all the love and hope that had lived in Winter's heart turned into hatred.

The hatred tainted her dreams. She didn't want to be an actress anymore. How could she be? How could she find joy in something that had caused a life of despair for her mother and might lead a path to the door of the man she now hated with all her heart?

Winter abandoned her dreams, as she had been abandoned by the father she dreamed about. Lawrence Carlyle was no longer a part of her life. She would simply have to forget about him. Winter threw away the scrapbooks, and she made a solemn vow never to read about him again or to see another of his brilliant movies.

During the nine months between Jacqueline's death and the first day of her Freshman year at UCLA, Winter took a hard look at the lessons life had taught her.

It is better to be liked than disliked. Even though it meant hiding her deepest feelings, it was better.

It is dangerous to care. She had cared about Jacqueline, and just as they were finally finding something—fragile and gentle and maybe close to love—her mother was gone. She had cared about Daddy, and when she discovered he *didn't* care, something inside her died.

People leave you. Daddy, Jacqueline, *everyone*, unless she was sunny and charming and beautiful. The ones who knew her the best left her, as if there were something wrong with her, something impossible to love and easy to leave.

Three weeks before Freshman registration, Winter made an appointment to see Leo Stiles. It was about the mansion, she told his executive secretary.

Winter thought about living at the mansion during college. Allison—her best friend Allison, who was still her friend because she hadn't made the fatal discovery—was going to live at home. Allison was happy with her parents, close enough in Bel Air to the UCLA campus, and very close to the important place, the stable at the Bel Air Hunt Club. Again, Allison urged her friend to move into her parents" home, but Winter declined. She couldn't live with the Fitzgeralds—it wasn't her home—but she couldn't stay at the mansion, the magnificent house that had never really been a home, either.

Winter was afraid to stay at the mansion. It would be so easy to lapse into the fantasy days of her childhood, entombing herself in the dark screening room, isolating herself from the world, pretending the dreams hadn't died.

But the dreams *were* dead. Winter fought the self-destructive urge to stay in the mansion and die with them. She had to leave and find new dreams, something she wanted to do other than act. Surely there was something in the hundreds of courses offered at UCLA!

"Have you decided to sell the mansion?" Leo Stiles asked.

"No. Not yet. I assume it will just increase in value." Winter would sell it someday, when she found a new home for the priceless reels of film—celluloid dreams—and the Oscars, jewels, and paintings that were the only remaining symbols of Jacqueline's dazzling and tragic life. Until then . . . "I don't want to live there, but I want to have it maintained and safe. I have gardeners and a weekly cleaning service, but—"

"I don't remember offhand which services you have, but they probably are ones we recommended. If so, you don't have to worry about security. Anyway, I'll check if you like, and we can have the bills come through our office—we handle this for a number of the rarely inhabited homes in Bel Air—and send you quarterly statements."

"Yes. All right. Thank you." Winter paused. "There are fish—Japanese koi—in a pond in the garden. I had a man come out last week from a pet store in Brentwood. He says that there is enough natural food in the pond for them, but it's possible to set up reservoirs of food, just in case. I'd like to have him hired to come by once a month to check on them and set up the reservoirs. Here's his name and number."

"You'll be at UCLA?"

"Yes. I'm moving into an apartment on Holman Avenue in two weeks. I'll be sure you have the address and phone number."

Winter's hands trembled as she locked the front door of the mansion. Her childhood was inside, along with her dreams, and she was leaving them behind. Winter took very little with her from the mansion on Bellagio to her apartment on Holman Avenue two miles away, just the gifts from Jacqueline—the car and the earrings—and the lessons life had taught her.

Winter spent four of the next five years carefully following the lessons of her life, revealing little, dazzling, enchanting, controlling, and playing games that kept a very safe distance from the heart. Winter was *the* belle on a campus known for its belles and starlets; Winter outshined them all.

Winter played and performed with everyone but Allison. And one year Winter didn't play at all. Winter spent that year helping Allison fight her courageous battle, silently crying for her friend, tormenting herself.

It is dangerous to care. People leave you. The words haunted Winter as she watched Allison struggle to be whole again. She had brought her own bad luck to her best friend! But, no, Allison was protected by that halo of love. Allison survived, and then Allison flourished, falling in love with Dan, discovering wonderful new talents to replace the shattered dreams.

Winter returned to UCLA after the year away, hopeful that her own frustrating search for new dreams would be more fruitful than it had been during the first two years. She studied the undergraduate catalogue carefully, resolutely avoiding courses in Drama, Theater, and Fine Arts, but sampling classes in virtually every other major.

Nothing intrigued her, nothing challenged her, nothing quieted the incessant whispers of her heart that told her she was an actress, she had to act, no matter what. To hell with Lawrence Carlyle!

How can I be an actress?

How can you be anything else?

Winter was still searching for something else—or maybe she was searching for the strength to become an actress *anyway*—the evening she took the final sentimental journey around campus. She was searching for guidance from the hallowed halls, guidance that had eluded her for five years.

Winter's journey took her to the Sculpture Garden, to intense sapphire-blue eyes that made her forget to play and tease; eyes that made her talk about magic.

Sensuous sapphire eyes that told her, *Your turn next time.*

Winter sat in her car at the top of the circular driveway gazing at the mansion. She couldn't go in. The font door keys were in a desk in her apartment . . . but she would bring them with her next time.

Your turn next time.

She had to tell Mark everything—about the unloved little girl who still existed, about her sad mother, about the father she hated, about her dreams. She had to tell Mark everything, because he wouldn't settle for less. She had no choice.

And if everything was too much, if Mark didn't want to hear her secrets, if they made him dislike her, too . . .

Winter shuddered. *People leave you.*

Chapter 6

Mark arrived at eight P.M. Friday night. He kissed her hello, and from that moment until noon Sunday, he and Winter lived in a world of love and passion, an intimate world without boundaries, a sensual world without time.

At noon Sunday, Winter whispered seductively, kissing him as she spoke, "Residency applications."

"Ah, yes," Mark whispered in return. "Are you going to help me?"

"Of course. I *can* type."

While Mark arranged the still-to-be-completed applications on the kitchen table, Winter studied the brochures. Each program in internal medicine boasted excellent educational experiences, fine faculty, extensive research funding, state-of-the art clinical facilities; and each provided in fine print the details of the "on call" schedule, the number of months spent on each clinical service, meals provided "on call," and vacation time.

"This is a different kind of Club Med, isn't it?" Winter asked after several minutes of serious study.

"Yes." Mark smiled. The colorful brochures were filled with pictures of white-coated doctors and elaborate intensive care unit facilities, not pictures of sailboards skimming across white-capped waves, glittering seaside discos, and smiling vacationers sipping piña coladas.

"How do you decide which trip-of-a-lifetime package to take?" Winter asked, staying with the vacation theme, so far from the reality but amusing to Mark. "They all claim to be the best."

"These are the best," Mark admitted quietly. He was only applying to the most competitive residencies in the country.

"Oh." Winter smiled an appreciative smile. "Is there a best of the best?"

"That depends on who you talk to and what features you measure. Year after year, Massachusetts General Hospital seems to appear at the top of most unbiased lists."

"So that's where you're going? To Boston?"

"I'd like to. If they want me."

"They'll want you."

"Speaking of unbiased . . ."

"I admit it." Winter glanced through the ten brochures again, confirmed what she had already learned, and said, "You're only applying to East Coast programs."

"Yes." Mark had made that decision months ago, because he had never lived on the East Coast, because Mass General was the best, and because plans were so easy before Winter.

In the past few days, Mark had wondered about applying to UCLA, UCSF, Stanford, the University of Washington; but any top residency would be the same. The hours and emotions and responsibilities made it all-consuming; a journey to be travelled alone; a solitary voyage that was impossible to share and fraught with danger if one tried.

"I imagine Boston is wonderful. Charming, historic, misty salt air, the fragrance of clams and lobsters," Winter said.

"You've never been there?"

"No."

"I'm spending December and January in Boston," Mark said quietly, frowning slightly.

"Oh." It was bad enough that tomorrow Mark would be leaving for ten days. The thought of not seeing him for two months! *Too presumptuous, Winter*, she warned herself. It's not even July. By December . . .

"In December I'll be in the Intensive Care Unit at Mass General, and in January the Coronary Care Unit at Beth Israel."

"Busy."

"Very. The on-call schedule is every other night." Mark added quietly. "If you came to visit me, you might have to explore Boston on your own."

"That would be all right," Winter whispered as she gazed at the blue eyes that told her so eloquently, *I want you to come, Winter*. "I could visit at Christmas."

"That would be wonderful. But shouldn't you be with your family?"

Winter shook her head and gave a soft sigh. Mark hadn't asked her anything, not one question about *her* all weekend, but Winter knew he was waiting. And she was stalling, savoring every lovely moment they had together, fearing that when she told him, apologetically, that she hadn't always been beautiful or confident, and deep inside was still so shy and afraid, his eyes wouldn't fill with desire, and he wouldn't want to touch her and hold her and love her . . . because part of him would be touching a gawky, ugly little girl.

"Winter?"

As she looked at him, Winter felt tears in her eyes. *No!* She didn't cry, not with anyone watching, not since her huge eyes had filled with tears at the taunts of her childhood classmates and that weakness had made them tease her even more. Since then, the tears she shed for Jacqueline and for Daddy and for her dreams and for Allison had been private, hidden tears.

"Honey," Mark knelt beside her and cupped her face in his strong, gentle hands. Mark had sensed the pain and the secrets, hoping it would help if she told him, but not wanting to cause sadness. He started to wrap his arms around her, but Winter pulled away.

"After we're done with the residency applications, I have to take you somewhere," she said.

"Take me now, Winter."

Mark thought they might be driving to a cemetery, to a marble crypt that housed her beloved parents, but even before they left the apartment, as Winter retrieved a key ring from a far corner of a desk drawer, he revised his prediction. They were going somewhere else. And they were going in Winter's powder-blue Mercedes "because the Bel Air Patrol recognizes it."

Winter drove, following the same route they had taken last weekend, winding along Bellagio toward the Hunt Club. A half mile before the Club entrance, Winter turned through an opening in a wall of fuchsia and plum bougainvillea and onto a white pebble drive that led to a majestic mansion of stone.

Winter parked, got out, and led the way to the front door. Her hands trembled as she inserted the key. She knew what lurked on the other side . . . ghosts. Ghosts of her unhappy childhood and of her shattered dreams.

Winter opened the door and by reflex more than by thought moved swiftly to a gray steel panel in the foyer. She inserted a small key, turned it, and watched as a red light became a green one, a signal that the alarm had been disengaged. Winter paused for a moment, her eyes fixed on the green light, before turning to face the dark and sinister shadows of the house.

It had been so dark, an oppressive suffocating cave, in the months after Jacqueline's death, in those endless days and nights when she had waited for Lawrence. A huge dark monster waiting to devour.

Winter turned, and she realized that the dark monsters had been in her heart.

The foyer glistened with shining marble, and the pastel silks of the living room were light and cheery, and the summer sun streamed through the French doors, and a hundred roses bloomed brightly in the gardens beyond.

"Where are we?" Mark asked quietly, breaking the silence that had lasted since Winter had taken the keys from the desk drawer in her apartment. Mark had asked her such a question before; then they had been in the magnificent champagne-drenched rose garden at the Club. And now they were here, and this was even more splendid. But Winter's face was tense and troubled, and her ivory skin was rough with gooseflesh despite the summer heat.

"Home."

As she and Mark wandered from room to room, Winter told him her story. Her voice was soft and she spoke as if from a trance. Sometimes Mark wondered if she knew he was there. He tried to take her hand, but she wouldn't let him.

"I was ugly. See?" Winter showed him a rare photograph taken by a dutiful nanny—proof that she was doing her job—who had posed her in front of a birthday cake on her seventh birthday. It was one of the few pictures taken of Winter before her fourteenth summer. After that, there were hundreds of pictures, taken by admirers, given to Winter as gifts and carelessly tossed by her into dresser drawers.

"No, I don't see." Mark smiled at the little girl in the picture and her serious violet eyes peered back. He wanted to hold that little girl, to reassure her; and Mark wanted to hold the woman she had become and reassure her, too . . . but Winter wouldn't let him.

"No one liked me. I was very lonely, very afraid," Winter murmured as they walked along the plush carpet from her girlhood bedroom to Jacqueline's.

"Afraid of what?"

"What? Oh, everything. Of being alone, of being disliked, of dying, of my mother dying," Winter answered as they entered Jacqueline's bedroom. The bedroom ceiling was a skylight, now azure blue, but at night an ever-changing scene of moon and stars. The four-poster bed was dressed in lace and a thousand hand-painted wild-flowers bloomed on the walls. "This was her room."

Winter paused at a gray steel panel near the door, identical to the one in the foyer. She inserted another small key and inactivated the alarm. Then she walked to the Monet, a pastel portrait of springtime, and pulled gently on the right edge. The priceless painting moved, revealing the safe in the wall. Winter spun the dial on the safe, testing a distant memory, and, on the second try, opened it.

Winter removed a box from the middle of one of the many stacks of burgundy, midnight-blue, and purple velvet that filled the safe. She checked to the see that the contents of the box—a magnificent diamond necklace—had been undisturbed. She read the note inside, written in Jacqueline's lavish script, a notation of who had given her the necklace and when, then gently closed the velvet and returned the box to the safe. Winter checked two more boxes at random—a ruby and diamond bracelet and emerald earrings—then shut the safe and spun the dial.

"I have the only keys to this alarm system and one downstairs in the screening room," Winter explained. "I just wanted to check."

Mark nodded. Winter was checking her staggering fortune. Her wealth was staggering but valueless, a collection of gems and property and money without emotion. No, that wasn't true. There *was* emotion attached to the fortune. Winter had a staggering fortune of pain and unhappiness.

Winter stood in front of the marble fireplace, gently touched the two glittering Oscar statues, their mirrorlike shine proof that the cleaning service was doing its job, and frowned.

"She was a wonderful actress, but . . ."

Winter began Jacqueline's story, speaking in a soft monotone, as they left the bedroom and walked down the spiral staircase. In the sunny kitchen, Winter told Mark about Lawrence, how she had found out about her Daddy, how excited she had been. She led him slowly, reluctantly, to the screening room, idly checking the security system and opening the panels that concealed the priceless reels.

A soft, dreamy smile crossed Winter's face as she told Mark about the enchanted hours she had spent watching movies.

"Then," she said as their journey continued, "I would go outside and re-create what I had seen. We can go this way. It's a shortcut. This part of the mansion was never used, never even re-decorated."

The interior landscape changed dramatically as they entered the unused north wing. The rooms were open and airy, but the wallpaper fell in sheets from the plaster walls and the carpets were threadbare. Instead of vistas of Los Angeles stretching to the ocean, these rooms opened to secluded gardens shaded by weeping willows.

"I always liked this wing of the mansion the best," Winter told him softly. She liked it because it was near her private theater and the pond of koi; but she liked it, too, because her lively imagination had populated these rooms with brothers and sisters—her brothers and sisters, the ones she would have when Lawrence and Jacqueline were reunited, before she learned that her father had another family, a wife and rosy-cheeked sons whom he loved much more than her. "Especially this room."

This would have been her room, sandwiched between her siblings, surrounded by their laughter. On the outside wall, double French doors opened to the garden and the pond. Winter opened the doors and drew a soft breath as memories swept through her, memories of a little girl performing for her koi.

Even when she was beautiful and performed at the pool of the Club all day every day, even when her audience became enchanted men and admiring girls,

Winter still spent hours here. She didn't perform for the fish any longer. She told them, as she put pellets of food in their eager mouths, the secrets and fears she didn't dare share with any living soul—until she found Daddy.

Winter had thought about coming back here—just to this spot, never stepping inside the mansion—a thousand times in the past five years. But she hadn't. She had to stay away.

But she thought about the fish! And now her eyes filled with fresh tears as she approached the edge of the pond and she held her breath.

"Toto," she whispered as his black nose broke the surface, curious, ever-eager for food. "Toto."

Winter got a handful of pellets from the food reservoir that had been installed and maintained just as she had wanted, then sat on the edge of the pond. She fed the sudden swirl of orange and gold and white and black, identifying each one with relief as they took pellets from her ivory fingers. "And Belinda! And Lion, a pig as always. Hello, Scarecrow, here, it's your turn. Hi, Woodman."

"You know these guys," Mark whispered, fighting emotion that swept through him for the lonely, frightened, unloved little girl whose best friends had been these fish. *Oh, Winter.*

Winter turned to him with a happy smile. "I've known them all my life. Koi live for fifty years, sometimes a hundred." Her smile faded slightly. *Longer than my mother lived.*

"Only in this century has man outlived the goldfish. They taught us that the first day of med school."

Winter nodded solemnly, then returned to feeding the fish, speaking to them as she finished her story. Winter had told the fish this story before, how the ugly duckling became a swan, how if she behaved in a certain way everyone liked and wanted her, how she and her mother were just beginning to become close when Jacqueline died, how she waited for her father, how she gave up her dreams.

Then her story was over, and Mark knew everything—her fears, her secrets, who she really was. Winter stopped speaking and stared at the fish. They eyed her expectantly, waiting for food, and she waited for Mark to speak. Maybe he wouldn't. Maybe when she finally forced herself to look toward him, he would be gone.

He hadn't left yet. Winter felt his magnetic presence and the heat of his sensuous blue eyes staring at her. Mark moved behind her. Winter trembled as he gently touched her bare shoulders.

"I'm not who you thought I was, am I?"

"You're exactly who I thought you were." *Lovely and sensitive and vulnerable and warm and loving.* Mark leaned over and kissed a soft place on her neck beneath the fragrant silky strands of her hair. He whispered, "Exactly . . ."

Winter nuzzled against his lips, hoping, praying, but she stiffened as reality crashed and she heard the unspoken "except."

"Except," Mark continued swiftly, between kisses meant to reassure, "I want you to be happy."

"I am happy." *Now. With you. Never before.*

"And I want to be right."

"Right?"

"About your being a famous actress. I was so sure when I watched you at the wedding."

"Mark . . ."

"Darling." *We are so much alike.* "We have both been very strongly and very negatively influenced by our absentee fathers. I spent too much of my life not doing what I wanted because of him, and you're doing the same thing. You were an actress long before you even knew about Lawrence Carlyle. You created a wonderful fantasy and somehow *he* became the goal, not your acting. When the fantasy disintegrated, you threw everything away."

"Maybe," she breathed. *Maybe.*

"You wouldn't have to do movies, would you? You could do theater. Chances are you would never meet him."

"I want to do movies," Winter said swiftly, her heart racing. *I am an actress. I want to do movies.*

"Then do movies." Mark laughed softly. "But I thought the most legitimate was theater, and television and movies fell in somewhere behind."

"It's like your residencies, Mark. It depends on whom you talk to."

"So why are movies best?"

"Because a movie—a *motion picture*—is just that, a painting created by an artist, exactly the way he wants it. You don't drop by the Louvre to see if *Mona Lisa's* smile is a little more crooked or more demure or more sly than it was the last time you looked. You *know* her smile. I'm not explaining this well . . ."

"Yes, you are. Rhett *always* doesn't give a damn the same way, and Scarlett muses about tomorrow with that famous determined look every time."

"Yes."

"So."

"So?"

"So, it's movies."

"You really think? . . ."

"I do think. Movies it is." Mark wrapped his arms around her. "I have some other thoughts if you'd like to hear them."

"OK."

Mark sat beside her and gazed at her with serious, gentle eyes.

"I think the greatest loss was his. Lawrence Carlyle never had the joy of knowing you."

"Mark." Winter's eyes filled with tears again, but she didn't try to hide them. "Thank you."

"You're welcome." Mark smiled. "And I think, I *know*, I can't imagine spending the next ten days without you."

"But your mother and sisters . . . You have to go."

"Do I have to go by myself?"

"No."

A strand of long black hair clung to her tear-dampened cheek as she shook her head. Winter started to reach for it, but Mark stopped her, moving it gently himself.

"Didn't you ever take an infectious disease course in medical school?" he teased, glancing meaningfully at the delicate fingers that had been dabbling in pond water and mouths of hungry fish.

"Oh, Mark. Toto doesn't have germs!"

"I'm sure Toto doesn't, but still, we need to wash our hands, don't we, before we finish filling out residency applications and eat smoked oysters and . . ."

"Mark," Winter teased, giddy with the joy that had been building—*You're exactly who I thought you were . . . Then do movies . . . Do I have to go by myself?*—and now overflowed in a cascade of laughter and love. "Look at Toto's eyes. He doesn't believe you. Feed him, Mark. Show him!"

Mark never finished his list of thoughts. Maybe it was just as well. Mark's most important thought was one for which he couldn't predict a future, at least not a future brimming with the joy and love that pulsed through him now.

Winter Carlyle, I love you. For as long as we have together . . .

Until my dreams take me to Boston and your dreams keep you here.

Chapter 7

"I'm really going to do this, aren't I?" Winter asked quietly the next morning as she and Mark drove to San Francisco. Mark had started talking about her acting, encouraging her to make specific plans, as soon as they were north of the rush hour traffic of Los Angeles.

"Yes. If you want to."

"I want to."

"So?"

"So. I guess I should go back to UCLA and take all the drama classes I never took. I wonder if I can."

Mark pulled over at the next gas station.

"Why don't you find out? Call UCLA."

"Right now?"

"Why not?"

Ten minutes later Winter returned to the car with a sparkling smile.

"I told them I was a recent graduate in good standing! They said I could register for Autumn Quarter as a "'special' student."

"That sounds appropriate." Mark smiled. "What about auditioning for roles now?"

"I'm not in a rush anymore, Mark." Winter's desperate search for a new dream was over, and she felt so calm, so happy with the old familiar one. After a moment, she teased, "Why, do you think by the time I finally get in front of a camera they'll have to put a ski sock over the lens?"

"A ski sock?"

"They put gauze, or something a little more glamorous like silk stockings, over the camera lens to block out wrinkles. It works, and if it doesn't they can always do the close-ups a little out of focus so it's a romantic blur!" Winter smiled, then added thoughtfully, "I guess I *could* look at announcements of open casting calls."

"Unknown actresses do get cast, don't they?"

"Yes, it happens, but I think it's rare." *It happened to Vivien Leigh, didn't it? The other Scarlett.*

"It couldn't hurt to look at announcements."

"No, it couldn't."

So it was decided. Winter would take drama classes at UCLA in the fall. Over the summer she would look at casting calls in the paper and *maybe* even answer one. And she would spend time at the mansion. During the warm summer days when Mark was doing Orthopedic Surgery at Harbor General and Gastroenterology at Wadsworth, Winter would read Jacqueline's gilt-edged leather-bound scrips, watch movies, and practice by the pond.

After Winter's plans were decided, the couple lapsed into peaceful silence, holding hands, exchanging gentle smiles and loving glances as they drove through the hot San Joaquin Valley.

"Have you ever tried birth control pills?" Mark asked, breaking the peaceful silence with a worried thought.

"You. They made me sick." Winter didn't know how much was hormonal and how much was simply her aversion to pills of any kind. Jacqueline had taken so many drugs—pills and alcohol—and they had never helped. They had only slowly, relentlessly killed her.

Winter couldn't, or wouldn't, take birth control pills. She wanted a tubal ligation, but the doctor she saw refused to do the surgery. And, he told her, he expected any good doctor would refuse, too; she was young, healthy, and even though her eyes were so serious when she said she wasn't going to have children *ever*, she might change her mind.

Winter knew she would never change her mind. Her own childhood had been too sad. Winter was unwilling to risk such unhappiness for another life. Even if she was there to protect her baby from sadness, one day she might die, as Jacqueline had died, and her child would be alone, frightened, bewildered . . . as Winter had been.

"There really are problems with the IUD, Winter," Mark said seriously.

"Problems with fertility. I know, Mark." Winter had listened impatiently as the doctor had explained the risks. It didn't matter; she didn't want to be fertile! "I've only had the IUD for a year. Aren't problems related to having it for a long time?"

"The risks increase the longer you have it, yes, but—"

"Let's not talk about it now!"

"There are other things we can do, Winter."

"*Things*, doctor?"

Mark started to elaborte, but Winter stopped him.

"I know. Let me think about it, OK? Please?"

"OK."

Silence—not as peaceful as before—prevailed for five miles. This time Winter broke it with a worry of her own.

"Tell me about your family, Mark. What should I know before we get there?"

"You should know that they'll be *very* interested in you."

"Why? Don't you usually bring girls home with you?"

"No." Mark smiled at her. *Never.*

"Don't . . . if you wouldn't tell them who I am."

"I won't tell them about your parents if you don't want me to. But they'll know who you are, Winter, how wonderful you are, and they'll like you very much."

Mark's family *did* like Winter and she liked them, too. Mark's mother Roberta, and his sister Gayle, who was studying with the San Francisco Ballet, and his other sister Jean, who was a first year law student at Dartmouth, welcomed Winter with open arms and easy smiles. Roberta and Gayle and Jean *were* interested in the lovely young woman who obviously made Mark so happy, but their curiosity was gentle, not probing, and their laughter was frequent and merry.

They welcomed Winter, carefully explaining the "in" jokes and allusions that were part of their private family history—the history of four people who had weathered life's storms together and had survived, strong and close and loving.

"Joanne had twins, little girls, not identical," Roberta announced casually one evening over blueberry pie. Turning to Winter, Roberta added, "Joanne is my sister's daughter."

"Mother has grandbaby lust, Winter," Jean explained lightly.

"Grandbaby lust," Gayle agreed amiably. "That *may* have sounded like a perfectly innocent comment, simply updating us on the life of our cousin, but it is dripping with hidden meaning."

"Not at all!" Roberta laughed, but her twinkling blue eyes fell for a thoughtful moment on Mark, her oldest, the one for whom childhood had been the most difficult. What a wonderful father Mark would make!

Mark and Winter spent five days in San Francisco. They stayed in a motel because Mark insisted on their privacy, but they spent most waking hours with his family. Winter's eyes filled with tears as she said good-bye to Roberta and Gayle and Jean. She was eager to be alone with Mark, but the visit with them had been so nice.

The drive north from Los Angeles had taken five hours. The trip home took five days. Mark and Winter meandered along the Pacific Coast Highway, spending the nights in quaint hotels in Carmel, San Luis Obispo, and Santa Barbara, strolling at sunrise and sunset on white sand beaches, talking, laughing, touching, loving . . .

"You brought this blouse on purpose, didn't you?"

"My silk blouse with a thousand buttons?" Winter answered innocently. She loved the way Mark undressed her, *so slowly*, gently kissing each patch of bareness as he uncovered it, his talented lips making her tremble with desire that she knew would be fulfilled. "Yes."

On the third evening, Mark and Winter watched the summer sunset from the porch at Nepenthe as they drank champagne. Winter drank champagne now, enough to flavor their kisses, because she felt safe with Mark. Safe and warm and giddy.

But the wonderful, giddy, euphoric feeling wasn't the champagne, Winter realized. The euphoria was there *all the time* when she was with Mark . . . because of Mark.

"A penny for your thoughts," Winter whispered as she shifted her gaze from the red-orange sunset to his serious sapphire eyes.

"No. It's an irrational thought."

"OK. I'll give you ten million dollars."

"It's a worthless thought, Winter."

"Then it's a very highly leveraged one. Worthless, but I'm willing to pay ten million for it. I think you should take me up on it."

"How do you know about highly leveraged?" *Highly leveraged* was a term from Mark's previous career.

"I took courses in everything—except drama—in college," Winter answered. "I even did well in them."

"I'm sure you did."

"So, you're stalling. Ten million. I think it's a fair price, maybe even a steal for such a rarity. I didn't think you had irrational thoughts."

"I didn't used to." *Before you*. Mark smiled. Then he told her quietly, "I was thinking about your doing love scenes."

It was more than a thought, it was a vivid image. Mark imagined her lovely breasts artfully silhouetted but *revealed*, her graceful elegant body, her soft loving sighs, the desire in her violet eyes; and he imagined all the men who would watch her, and perhaps talk about her, and certainly *want* her.

"It's just acting."

"I wasn't thinking about you and the actor. I was thinking about all the people who would see you. I told you, completely irrational." *The irrational thoughts of a man very much in love.*

Winter smiled. She was so happy that Mark wanted their love, their intimacy, to be theirs alone.

"Why are you smiling?"

"Because that was definitely worth ten million." Winter's smile faded slightly. "Mark, what do you think about all my money?"

"What I think about money in general. It doesn't buy happiness, but it *can* buy freedom."

"Freedom?"

"Freedom to do what you want, be what you want, be *where* you want to be." Mark kissed her gently. "If I had all the money in the world, there is nowhere I'd rather be than right here, right now, with you."

"And in three days, there is nowhere else you'd rather be than doing Orthopedic Surgery at Harbor General, setting—what did you call the ones from the roller-skating accidents?—Colles' fractures?"

I want that, too, Mark thought. I want you and I want medicine. Mark wondered if it were really possible to have them both.

As soon as the first boarding call for PSA's July Fourth flight to Phoenix was called, Mick was on alert, eager to be on his way, restless, showing no regret that he would be away from her for the next two months. Mick's band was going on tour, playing at the many summertime rock concerts that dotted the country.

Mick curled his strong hand around Emily's fragile neck and pulled her to him for a final kiss—rough, possessive, without tenderness. He released her, smiled a mean smile, and removed a brown pill bottle from his tight jeans pocket.

"A little going-away present." Mick shoved the bottle containing an assortment of illegal hallucinogens and amphetamines into her hand.

"Thank you." Emily slid the bottle into her loose jeans and hoped she wouldn't need to take pills this summer. Maybe she wouldn't, with Mick gone.

"See you in September."

Emily nodded, but she thought, *I hope not.* She needed to find the courage to say a final no to Mick. *Good-bye, Mick. I want to be by myself. I feel better, more peaceful, when I'm alone.*

Emily would rehearse the words all summer, but if she was very lucky, she would never need to say them. If she was very lucky, Mick would find someone else and not want her anymore.

Lucky, Emily mused as she wove her way through the Fourth of July crowds at LAX. Had she ever been lucky? If there had ever been luck in her life, or joy or happiness or hope, Emily didn't remember it.

"Are you awake?" Winter asked when Allison answered her phone at seven-thirty A.M. on the fifth of July.

"Of course! Welcome back. Did you have a nice time?"

"Wonderful." Winter's voice softened with the memory. "Really wonderful."

"You liked Mark's family?"

"Yes. Very much."

"That's nice."

"Yes. Oh, and Allison?"

"Yes?"

"I made a career decision."

"Really?" Allison had watched Winter's frantic search for a career with sympathy and concern. Each quarter Winter enthusiastically declared a new major, but neither her boundless energy nor her fervent desire could urge the small flickers into flames. Nothing ignited her, nothing held her interest. Allison had heard the pronouncement—"I've made a career decision"—a hundred times.
 But now there was a new softness in Winter's voice. "What have you decided?"

"I'm going to be an actress."

"Good," Allison replied swiftly. *At last.*

"Good?"

"Well, I . . ." Allison faltered slightly. It had been so obvious in high school! Winter loved performing in the school plays, chattered constantly about movies, and by the beginning of senior year was already planning the Drama courses she would take at UCLA the next fall. But after Jacqueline's death . . . "You were so terrific in the plays at Westlake."

"Oh. I'd forgotten about those. Anyway, I'm going back to UCLA in the fall and begin with Drama 101." Winter smiled wryly. "Of course, Mark thinks I should start auditioning for parts now."

"Why not?"

"That's what he says."

"I could talke to Vanessa," Allison offered. "She always seems to know about casting calls."

"Thanks, but no. They're in the paper, anyway. I do plan to look, and if there is something, who knows?" *Who knows?* "Anyway, enough about me! How are you? Are you still being crazy?"

"Is that your incredibly subtle way of asking if I'm riding?"

"Perhaps."

"I am riding. I'm also reading mounds of novels and stacks of *Architectural Digest, Design, Arts and Antiques, Interior*, you get the idea." With each day Allison felt better, more confident of the decisions she had made, more eager for the challenges that lay ahead. "Oh, Meg called yesterday. She and Cam are back from their honeymoon. They leave for New York on Saturday, and Meg wants us to come over tonight to see the wedding pictures."

"You're kidding!" Winter's gasp crescendoed into a laugh. "To see the wedding pictures? Why in the world would we want to do that?"

"Meg thought we might want copies," Allison replied solemnly, suppressing a giggle with effort.

"No! Something in a poster, perhaps? Meg and Cameron saying their vows? I'm sure I'll want three or four for my apartment alone, not to mention the wonderful gifts they would make!"

"Stop!" Allison laughed. She continued thoughtfully, remembering Emily, happy for her, "Apparently, the pictures are wonderful. Not just of Cam and Meg, but of all of us. Besides, it's a chance to see the newlyweds before they move back East. Mark's invited, of course."

"He's on call," Winter sighed softly. The wonderful leisurely days were already a memory. Mark left for the hospital an hour ago. He would call her today if he had a chance and *hopefully* would see her tomorrow night.

"Do you want to go? Meg said about seven."

"Of course I want to go! Who knows, maybe they'll have a slide show of the honeymoon!"

* * *

Even before they reached the Montgomery estate on St. Cloud, Allison and Winter decided that the silver Jaguar they had been following since they turned off Sunset through the East Gate of Bel Air was also en route to view the wedding pictures.

"Rob Adamson and Elaina Kingsley," Winter murmured as Allison parked behind them.

"Oh." *Oh*. Allison had hoped to have a chance to talk to Meg, or even Cam, about Sara Adamson. Thoughts of Sara had been with Allison since the wedding, troublesome thoughts, sometimes weaving themselves into her dreams. The dreams usually vanished with dawn, vague disturbing memories without substance, but there was one recurrent dream that survived the light of day.

In the dream Sara was riding Tuxedo, her dark blue eyes glowing and happy. Then, as she jumped a green and white railed fence, Sara was hurled to her death. But it wasn't a tragic accident. It was *murder!* A man—a theatre-type, dressed as a Harlequin but *evil*—had sliced the leather girth of the saddle with a sharp bloody knife. The menacing Harlequin smiled wickedly as Sara fell, and he erupted into raucous laughter as she died.

As Allison felt more peaceful, and more eager about her own life, her own second chance, her thoughts drifted often to Sara . . . Sara who never had a second chance.

"It looks like Rob and Elaina are waiting for us," Allison said as she returned a friendly wave to Rob.

"Great. I never tire of talking to Elaina," Winter whispered through a sweet smile. Winter's dislike of Elaina was based on instinct and emotion, not experience. It was unfair, but she couldn't shake the image of a young Elaina Kingsley throwing taunts at a frightened Winter, leading the assault, laughing when Winter cried. It wasn't fair to Elaina; and it especially wasn't fair to Rob, who Winter liked and respected, but . . .

"Winter," Allison warned as they got out of the car.

"I'll be nice," Winter promised. Why not? She was in love, and somehow the mean little girls who had hissed at her, together with all the horrible sadness and fears of her childhood, had brought her to where she was now: in love . . . happy . . . with Mark.

"Hi, Allison." Rob smiled as Allison and Winter approached, "Hello, Winter. Do you both know Elaina?"

"Sure. It's nice to see you, Elaina."

Allison met Rob's warm, smiling eyes and thought, *I won't find out about Sara tonight.*

And why should she? Why should she ever find out about Sara? Why did Allison Fitzgerald need to know? What would she do with the knowledge? *Nothing*, but if she knew the facts, however horrible, she could deal with that reality and put an end to her own terrifying imaginings.

A selfish reason.

Allison looked at Rob and realized there was another reason, not selfish, just fantastic. Somewhere in her imagination—perhaps it was a dawn-vanquished dream—Allison had trapped the sinister Harlequin into a confession.

A silly reason.

"It looks like quite a crowd," Winter offered as they strolled toward the house. "Allison, at least your parents and Vanessa can just walk over."

"My parents are in Argentina."

"Oh, that's right! It's polo time."

"Polo?" Rob asked.

"It's really quite a group. Kings, crown princes, dukes . . . the whole monarch set," Winter explained merrily. During the summer between the junior and senior years of high school, Winter and Allison had gone with Sean and Patricia on the yearly pony-buying and polo-playing trip to Argentina. "And their *consorts*, too, of course."

"Fabulous," Elaina breathed.

"Yes, it is."

"Speaking of fabulous, Meg says the wedding pictures are fabulous," Allison said. Then, recalling Meg's exact word, a word Allison had never heard uttered by her famous-for-hyperbole friend, she added, "Actually, Meg called them *extra-ordinary.*"

"That's what she told me, too," Rob said with an uncomfortable twinge. As he had watched a fragile, timid, serious Emily Rousseau taking pictures at the wedding, Rob had hoped the photographs would be good; he sensed how important it was to her. But now, Rob's image of Emily was tainted and he hoped *what? Nothing*. Rob had no wish to cause her harm. Still, it made him strangely uneasy to hear that her photographs were extraordinary.

Extraordinary, Meg's word; dramatic Meg. Surely . . .

But the photographs *were* extraordinary. Meg and her mother had carefully displayed the photographs on tables and chairs and window sills and mantels throughout the first floor of the Montgomery estate. The displays were uncluttered, a few photographs in each location, because each shot deserved attention. The guests wandered from room to room with the hushed, reverent silence of museum-goers at the opening of a spectacular art exhibit.

"Meg," Winter whispered. "These are magnificent."

"Yes," Meg answered solemnly. She had been very moved by the photographs—a careful, loving, artistic celebration of her wedding. "As far as we can tell, Emily took at last one picture of each guest."

"One incredible picture of each guest."

"There are several breathtaking pictures of you, Winter, and Mark. That's his name, isn't it?"

"Yes, Mark," Winter answered. Breathtaking pictures of *Mark*, she thought, and a photograph of the two of them dancing on the "sort-of-secluded" terrace. Emily had invaded their privacy, but Winter didn't mind. To all other eyes, it would be a picture of Mark and Winter dancing; a lovely, graceful, melodic moment among the roses, but Winter knew better. Emily had captured the precise intimate moment when Winter had whispered, *We have to go now.* "There are breathtaking pictures of everyone, Meg. I'd like to have a copy of this one of you and Cam, and the one of Sean and Patricia by the ice sculpture, and the one of Allison . . ."

Allison admired the photograph for several moments before she realized she was admiring a picture of herself. The summer sun glittered off her long red-gold hair and her eyes were dark jade and her expression was thoughful and she looked almost beautiful. Emily had captured a look of serene beauty, yet Allison knew the thoughts behind her pensive expression had not been serene. At the moment Emily took the picture, Allison had been thinking about Sara.

"I know your parents would like a copy of this," Vanessa Gold said quietly as she moved beside Allison. "It's very lovely."

"Oh, thank you, Vanessa." Allison shrugged slightly. "Emily has really mastered the art of trick photography."

"Not at all." Rob overheard Allison's remark and joined them. He had already lingered many minutes admiring the photograph of Allison. He repeated firmly, "Not at all."

She's just mastered the art of portrait photography, Rob thought for the hundredth time that evening. Emily Rousseau *had* mastered it; her wonderful, talented, creative photography was the best Rob had ever seen—and he'd been looking.

Portrait was staffed by a talented group of writers who reliably created magnificent portraits in words; in-depth, honest, intriguing profiles of the people they interviewed. Each beautifully written article was accompanied by a photograph, a portrait that should have been as articulate as the words, but often wasn't. Rob used free-lance photographers because he had been unable to find a photographer he wanted to hire full-time, one whose talent matched the exceptional quality of the journalism.

Rob had been looking for a photographer for *Portrait,* and now he had found her. Emily Rousseau took the kind of portraits—unposed, insightful, honest, multilayered—Rob had always envisioned for the magazine.

Even the way Emily developed her photographs was creative, the texture and clarity a reflection of how she saw the mood, personality, and essence of each subject. Some portraits were sharp, clear, and glossy, as if reflecting unashamed ambition and power; Rob smiled as he noticed Emily had chosen to develop the photographs of Elaina that way. Other portraits—Meg and Cam, Winter dancing with Mark, and even the one of *him* taken while he was watching *her*—were soft, muted, romantic, like delicate pastel watercolors. Still others, including the beautiful, serious one of Allison, had great richness and texture, as if painted in oil.

Rob had been looking for a photographer for *Portrait,* and here she was.

Emily Rousseau. Drug addict, and whatever *else* made her look and bahave the way she did. Rob couldn't imagine sending Emily all over the world to homes, offices, studios of the rich and famous and powerful, except . . .

Except Rob had to imagine it, because he had to have Emily's incredible talent, her remarkable gift, for *Portrait.*

"These are the best photographs I've ever seen of these frequently photographed people," Vanessa said. "I assume Emily Rousseau will open her own studio. The minute word gets out, she'll be in constant demand."

Allison listened and decided she had better call Emily soon to arrange to have another portrait done. She didn't want to give her parents this one. Even if no one else saw the sadness in it, Allison did. If Emily could take another one, a happy one, it would make a wonderful present for Sean and Patricia's wedding anniversary in October.

Winter had already decided to schedule an appointment with Emily, too. She would need portraits for her portfolio. Even though Winter doubted she would answer a casting call this summer, or even next summer, there was no harm in being prepared.

Chapter 8

Vanessa spent a few minutes each day reading her *All That Glitters* column in the newspaper. She wasn't checking for accuracy—she did that on the galleys—and of course she knew what the column said; but Vanessa liked seeing and reading the words the way her readers did. The smudged newsprint, the bold-faced type, the plump exclamation points, and the italics gave her words life and character; so much more interesting than the same words in neat double-spaced lines on the pure white typing paper on which the column had been created.

Vanessa devoted her entire July sixteenth *All That Glitters* to *Love*, the "hottest property" in Hollywood. As she read the printed column at her desk overlooking Sunset Boulevard, Vanessa thought about the remarkable script and how smart Steve Gannon had been to have let her read it for herself in June, a full month before hundreds of copies floated around Hollywood, topping the teetering stacks on every agent's desk and lying beside the swimming pools and in the boudoirs of Hollywood's best young actresses.

Usually a producer presented Vanessa with an encapsulated version of his latest project. He would take her to a martini lunch at the Cafe Four Oaks or Ma Maison or Rebecca's and rave about the "incredible script" and the "dynamite director" and the "unbelievable cast" he was going to assemble; then he would expect Vanessa to begin the preproduction *hype* of his movie-to-be.

But Steve Gannon was an old friend and he knew the script was pure gold. The script had won Vanessa's enthusiasm, but she liked Steve's approach; she liked being included; she very much liked being allowed to arrive at her own conclusions. As soon as Steve gave her the firm dates for the open casting call, Vanessa ran the column she had written a month before, the moment she had finished reading the script.

PETER DALTON'S
ASTONISHING LOVE

Love, a screenplay by Pulitzer-Prize-winning playwright and three-time Tony-Award-winning director Peter Dalton, is a stunning exploration of the enomous treasures of the heart and the magnificent gifts of love. For a writer of lesser stature or lesser genius to give a script such a title would be an insufferable presumption. But the title is apt. Dalton has written a definitive work.

With *Love*, Dalton displays his six-octave talent. His previous work has proven his remarkable ability to plumb the depths of human despair, to venture into the caves of darkness in the soul, to rip apart the tender threads that seam the gossamers of sanity and madness. Now, with *Love*, Dalton's genius soars from murky darkness to the brilliant clarity and untainted splendors of love. The voyage is breathtaking and not without peril, but Dalton uncrosses the stars and delivers a happy ending.

At 32, Dalton is surely the brightest light in an impressive galaxy of talented young playwrights and screenwriters. His remarkable theater career began nine years ago, when his critically acclaimed one-act plays were first produced at La Mama's and the American Place Theater in New York. Since then, Dalton has garnered recognition for excellence in both writing and directing.

Merry Go Round, his first full-length work, was produced off Broadway in 1979 and won the New York Drama Critics Circle Award for best new play. The following year he won two Tony Awards—Best Director and Best Original Play—for *Storm Watch*.

In 1981, he won a third Tony—Best Original Play—for *Echoes*. In 1982, Peter Dalton entered the rarified world of literature with *Say Good-bye*, a chilling study of hopelessness and despair, for which he was awarded the Pulitzer Prize. An anthology of all Dalton's produced work, including *Say Good-bye*, was published earlier this year by Random House.

Now there is *Love*. One might logically assume the writer gave the world this gift in penance for *Say Good-bye*, but apparently *Love* was written before *Say Good-bye*. When Steve Gannon, President of Brentwood Productions and Executive Producer of the film, approached Dalton last January about making a movie of *Merry Go Round*, Dalton responded with a counter offer: first, *Love*—the manuscript for which lay in a remote corner of a desk drawer—then *Merry Go Round*. One can only wonder what other treasures Dalton has hidden away!!

Dalton will take time—a *little* time—away from his remarkable Broadway career to direct *Love*. He will move to Los Angeles in December to begin preproduction activities for the picture—over which he has "total artistic control." *Love* will be filmed entirely on location in LA between January and April. Dalton returns to New York in April to assume directorial responsibilities for his recently created company, Shakespeare on Broadway, which begins its inaugural season this summer, opening with *Hamlet* and showcasing the greatest stars of the New York and London stage.

Although the screenplay has already been circulated to Hollywood's best young actresses, Gannon says, "We are fully prepared to cast an unknown actress in the lead. Julia is a rare blend of innocence, courage, love, and magic; we will know her when we see her." The male lead will go to one of five top actors, already selected and waiting only to see which has the best chemistry with the lucky actress chosen to play Julia. So, aspiring actresses, if you believe in love and magic and the gifts of the heart, Gannon and Dalton want to see you during the first two weeks of August. Interested? Contact Brentwood Productions at . . .

Winter's heart raced, beating faster as she read *All That Glitters* the second time.

I believe in love and magic and gifts of the heart. I know about love. I'm living it.

Winter wondered what a camera—zooming in for a close-up of enraptured violet eyes—would have seen if she had tried to act "love" before she met Mark. How convincing could she have been? Not very, Winter thought, because even in her most romantic fantasies of love she had not imagined the feelings she felt now.

I wonder if I'm Julia? Winter decided to find out. She would type up a résumé—that would take no time—and attach one of the wonderful portraits Emily had done last week, then she would appear at the casting call to see if she was who Steve Gannon and Peter Dalton were looking for.

Winter had a very strong feeling that she was.

* * *

Emily saw the *All That Glitters* column from a too-far-away-to-read distance as she rode the bus along Wilshire Boulevard to the Beverly Hills office of *Portrait* magazine. She had an appointment with Rob Adamson . . . about a portrait, Emily assumed. His secretary, Fran Cummings, had been quite vague, except to say it had something to do with a job and he wanted to meet her in person. Fran had given her several options—lunch anywhere, a meeting at Jerome Cole's studio, dinner anywhere—but Emily selected a noon meeting in Rob's office.

Emily knew who Rob Adamson was now—Jerome had raved about the portrait she had taken of him at the wedding—and she couldn't very well ask *him* to come to the studio, nor could she dine with him. Emily was uneasy about seeing Rob again, remembering the curious dark blue eyes that had followed her at the wedding; but it was a *job*, a portrait of him, an engagement picture of him and Elaina Kingsley . . .

Emily noticed a clock inside a car dealership as the bus lumbered by. She was going to be on time. Good. She was lucky to have caught this bus. She had been late, but the bus was, too, delayed just long enough by a malfunctioning stop light.

Good . . . lucky, Emily mused. Those unfamiliar words again, but now they *almost* applied to her life. The past two weeks had been a busy, creative swirl—taking pictures, developing them the way she wanted, taking more pictures. If she could spend her life like this—taking beautiful pictures, too busy to think, lost in a timeless enchanted world of color and texture and images—then she might even be . . . another unfamiliar word . . . *happy.*

Emily reached the Beverly Hills offices of *Portrait* three minutes before her twelve-fifteen appointment.

"My name is Emily Rousseau," she told the receptionist. "I have an appointment with Mr. Adamson."

"Oh, yes," the receptionist barely concealed her skepticism. Why would Mr. Adamson have an appointment with *her?* The men and women who usually had appointments with Rob Adamson were of a type; they exuded confidence and power and success. This woman exuded *nothing*. No, that was wrong. She exuded the certain knowledge that she *was* nothing. "Mr. Adamson's secretary, Fran, is at lunch, but he is expecting you. His office is at the end of this hall. I'll let him know you're here."

Rob appeared in the doorway and smiled as Emily approached.

"Hello. I'm Rob Adamson." *I watched you at the wedding—you remember because you finally turned your camera on me. And I saw you another time—but you then were in a foggy, faraway world. I saw you—how well I remember—but I wonder if you saw me.*

"Hello. I'm Emily Rousseau."

"Please come in." Rob gestured to a conversation corner, a blue leather couch and matching chairs arranged around a glass top coffee table. Rob never met with anyone across the impersonal expanse of his carved oak desk.

"Thank you."

Rob thought about her voice. It was surprisingly soft and refined. Rob had expected—had prepared himself for—harsh, abrasive, street-tough, and life-wise. There was nothing harsh about Emily today. Her shiny golden hair swayed in silky waves as she walked, her gray eyes were clear, and her baggy denim jeans were topped with a billowy long-sleeved white cotton blouse.

Long-sleeved, despite the summer heat. Perhaps the long sleeves were necessary to cover knotted purple veins, scarred and damaged from years of intravenous drugs. Heroin? Cocaine?

Rob looked at the gray eyes beneath the strands of gold silk and forced the image away. Today Emily bore no resemblance to the glassy-eyed woman he had seen on the bluffs of Santa Monica; today she was the young woman at the wedding—fragile, timid, serious, ethereal.

Emily obviously didn't remember seeing him that balmy evening, and Rob wondered if it had all been a mirage.

Do you have an evil twin sister, Emily? Dr. Jekyll, do you happen to know a Ms. Hyde?

"Your secretary said you were interested in having me do some photographs?"

"More than some. I would like you to be the staff photographer for *Portrait* magazine."

"Oh!" Emily's surprise quickly became confusion. She didn't really know about the photographs that appeared in *Portrait*. She had seen the magazine in stores, of course, and she knew Rob owned it, but she had never opened a copy.

Rob correctly interpreted Emily's confusion. Why would she be familiar with *Portrait*? Rob guessed she had very little money. What money she has probably goes for drugs, he thought with an ache, not for clothes or food and *certainly* not for an expensive magazine like *Portrait*. Even as an aspiring portrait photographer, Emily wouldn't be lured to the pages of *Portrait* for inspiration; her work was already better than the best he had to offer.

Rob reached for the July issue of *Portrait* that lay on the coffee table.

"Each month we profile between ten and fifteen people, accomplished men and women in all fields—celebrities, leaders, innovators—talented people with vision and imagination. We explore who they are and why they are, what drives them, what motivates them." Rob explained the purpose of *Portrait* without trying to sell it to her. He didn't use any of the words the critics had been using since the first issue hit the newsstands two years before: "unique," "stunning," "exceptional," "intensely committed to quality journalism," "one of the best."

Rob handed the July issue to her. As Emily's fingers uncurled from the tight ball of white knuckles in her lap, Rob saw her bitten-short nails and her thin, pale fingers. He winced slightly—a wince of the heart, nothing Emily could detect.

Emily looked through the magazine, carefully examining the full-page color photographs that accompanied each article.

"The portraits don't match the quality of the journalism. That's why I need you," Rob said finally. Because you have the unique ability to peel away the veneer and find the essence, he thought, remembering how she had captured the graceful sensitivity of Allison Fitzgerald, the soft vulnerability of Winter Carlyle, the surprising toughness of Elaina Kingsley, and even his own unmenacing curiosity.

"You think I can take better pictures than these?" Emily asked weakly. She thought the portraits were excellent. He thought she could do better?

"These aren't terrible, I know that. I've got some of the best free-lance photographers in the world available to me. But, yes, I'm sure you can." Rob expected, hoped for, a slight smile—if smiling was something Emily Rousseau ever did—but saw only confusion and doubt. *Doubt?* "I realize you're probably about to open your own studio. . . ."

"My own studio?"

"I assume there has been a large demand for your work since the wedding."

"Well, yes, but . . ."

It obviously hadn't occurred to Emily to leave Jerome Cole. Why not? Rob wondered. Surely she knew that her place as photographer to the stars was secure. Was it lack of ambition? No, Rob decided, remembering the patient, careful pictures she had taken at the reception, staying longer, doing so much more than was expected. Lack of confidence? Yes, probably. *Why?*

"You may prefer to open your own studio," Rob said, firmly planting that idea in her mind, deciding if Emily said no to working for him, he would get

Elaina to help her set up her own business. Elaina had plenty of confidence to spare. "But let me tell you what I can offer, OK?"

"OK."

"An excellent salary. We can discuss the specifics of that now if you'd like." Rob was prepared to pay her a great deal, probably more than she would ever imagine.

Emily shook her head.

"All right. Let's see. You'd have quite a bit of creative freedom. Naturally, I have final approval on everything that goes into the magazine, but I saw the photographs you took for the Montgomery-Elliott wedding, and I obviously like your work or I wouldn't be offering you the job." His words only worsened her uncertainty. Smiling, Rob changed tack, "I guess I should define the job. Ideally, I would have you do all the portraits for every issue, but I know that is impossible. We profile people all around the world, important people with difficult schedules. I honestly don't know how many portraits any one photographer can do each month. We'll just have to see. Having told you it's an impossible job and you'll be frantically busy, I can also tell you there will be slow times. I'm sure five or six portraits a month, or even fifteen, won't be enough photography for you. So I have no objection to your doing outside work, as long as your top priority is the magazine."

"I wouldn't do outside work."

"There can be very slow times," Rob repeated, sensing interest in her eyes, not sure what it was he had said that was beginning to intrigue.

"There would be travel?" Emily asked softly.

"Of course. All first class, all around the world, fivestar hotels." The promise of luxury worried more than appealed, but traveling interested her. "As you can see, for the July issue we went to Rome, London, New York, Buenos Aires, Tokyo, and Paris."

"Paris." It was almost a whisper.

"Are you French?" Rob asked. *Rousseau* certainly was French, but her soft voice was unaccented.

"My father was French. I was born in Quebec."

"Is Paris a favorite city?"

"I've never been to Paris," Emily answered quietly. "But I've always thought I might live there someday."

It was then, when Emily spoke of living in Paris, that Rob learned she could smile. Her lips curved softly, just the beginning of a smile, and it came with a deep light in her gray eyes. *So beautiful.*

"I can promise you trips to Paris. And if you fall in love with the place, we can base you there."

Emily never officially said yes, but the soft glow in her gray eyes when Rob spoke of trips to Paris gave him his answer.

"When would you like to start, Emily?"

"We have so much work at the studio, at least until the middle of September. . . ."

So much work because of *you*, Rob thought. He knew Jerome Cole would make a great deal of money from Emily's work, but Rob guessed *she* would simply get whatever small salary she had always gotten.

"How about the beginning of October? That would give you a break between jobs." Rob wished Emily could start today. He doubted that Jerome Cole felt a sense of loyalty to her, but it was bad business to appear to be stealing her away.

"The middle of September is fine."

Rob walked to his desk and consulted his calendar. "September seventeenth?
That's a Monday."

Emily nodded.

"About your salary . . ."

"Whatever you think."

"OK." *I think I want to pay you a lot, but please don't spend it on drugs. Please spend it on something that makes you smile.*

Emily stood up and extended a small, thin hand. "I'll see you in September. Thank you, Mr.—"

"Rob," he interjected swiftly. "Thank *you*, Emily."

As Emily rode in the bus back to the photography studio, she thought about what she had just agreed to. Mostly it scared her. What if she couldn't take the kind of pictures Rob wanted? She had to try, that was all, because it was her escape to Paris.

Emily didn't know why Paris meant so much. It was something vague and distant in the past or in the future. Emily didn't remember a time in the past when she had been happy, when her heart had been full of laughter and trust and hope. She didn't *remember* that time, but it had existed, in the first ten years of her life, when she had lived in Quebec. She had been happy then . . . a happy, golden-haired French girl.

After Emily left his office, Rob glanced through the newspaper while he waited for Elaina to arrive for their one-thirty lunch date. The headlines of Vanessa Gold's *All That Glitters* column—Peter Dalton's Astonishing *Love*—caught his eye. After a few moments, Rob forced himself to read it.

As Rob read the column, his fists clenched into angry bloodless knots and his strong body braced for the full force of his fury. It was a horrible sinister joke, an evil sham. Peter Dalton knew *nothing* of love.

Except to betray it.

Peter Dalton. How Rob hated the man responsible for the death of his beloved little sister. . . .

Chapter 9

GREENWICH, CONNECTICUT
NOVEMBER 1954

Jeffrey and Sheila Adamson greeted the birth of their son, Robert Jeffrey, with relief, joy, and pride. A beautiful firstborn son! An heir!

Even before his birth, Rob's life as heir to the Adamson empire was destined to follow an inevitable path. It was a path paved with gold and lined with privilege, luxury, and success. The golden path led from boyhood in Greenwich, to prep school in New Hampshire, to college and business school at Harvard, and back to Greenwich and Wall Street. The path meandered, apparently shapeless and with no purpose beyond pleasure and privilege, but the shapelessness was an illusion. The path had a definite shape: it was a circle, beginning and ending in the same place. And it had a purpose: to prepare Rob to become the successor to the Adamson empire. And it had expectations: Rob had to be perfect.

For the first twenty-two years of his life, Rob followed the path without the slightest deviation, unaware that there was a path, effortlessly excelling in everything he did. Sheila and Jeffrey watched their brilliant, charming, handsome son with smug approval. They didn't have to worry about Rob, not ever. They could devote their worrying, their coddling, their protectiveness to Sara.

Sara Jane Adamson was born four years after Rob. At age six, as her family watched in horror, she went from consciousness to grogginess to coma in a matter of minutes and was rushed Code Three to Greenwich Hospital. The diagnosis was diabetic ketoacidosis.

Sara recovered quickly from her first episode of diabetic ketoacidosis and coma; but there would be other episodes, the doctors told Sheila and Jeffrey. Sara had "juvenile-onset diabetes." Her diabetes was "insulin-dependent" and "very brittle" and "very severe."

From the moment Sara returned home from Greenwich Hospital, she relinquished what little control she previously had over her own life. Sara had always been delicate and fragile and passive. She offered no resistance to the careful regimentation and supervision that greeted her when she arrived home, smiling bewildered reassurance at the sudden army of hand-wringing, ever-watchful nannies that surrounded her, napping when she was told, eating all of the prescribed food, no more, no less.

The doctors warned the Adamsons that Sara might rebel against the precision of her life. She was a child, after all, and it was quite normal—in fact *typical*—for young diabetics to test the rules by skipping meals or drinking sugary soft drinks. It was a logical defiance against the constraints placed on them by their disease. They wanted to play and eat and frolic like their friends.

But Sara didn't rebel. Sara was an angel. She lived like a precious, fragile bird in a gilded cage and never offered a peep of complaint. She wasn't allowed to have pets, because pets carried diseases and infections were dangerous for diabetics. She wasn't allowed to ride horses or ice skate or climb trees, because injuries, even minor ones, were dangerous, too.

Sara didn't have playmates, not children her own age, so she didn't really know what she was missing. When Sara played, she played with the army of kind, hovering nannies with the sympathetic worried smiles, or with her parents, or with Rob.

Even before Sara's diabetes was diagnosed, Rob protected his little sister. He instinctively sensed her fragility and amiably channeled his lively, healthy energy into quiet games he could play with her. Rob and Sara assembled jigsaw puzzles, played word and board games, made enchanted kingdoms out of blocks, and invented stories to go with the kingdoms. Rob roughhoused with his friends, Cam Elliott and the other young golden heirs, but he enjoyed, even more, the quiet times with bright, imaginative Sara.

When he was thirteen and Sara was nine, Rob was sent to Phillips Exeter Academy in New Hampshire. Rob *had* to go to Exeter; the golden path led there. Before Exeter, Rob attended Greenwich Country Day School and Sara was educated at home. Every evening, Rob and Sara would eagerly share what they had learned during the day.

But now, Rob was far away and Sara missed him terribly. Rob missed Sara, too, but he was caught up in the scholastic challenges of Exeter and the intriguing new feelings of a boy becoming a young man. When Rob saw his frail, lonely little sister at Thanks giving, tears of love and guilt filled his eyes. His life was so exciting, so exhilarating, so full of wonderful adventures. Sara's life was empty and lonely, and she looked to Rob for hope.

"Why doesn't Sara go to school?" Rob asked his parents one afternoon while his sister was resting. "She could go to Greenwich Country Day through Grade Six and then on to the Academy. I think she'd really enjoy it."

"It's too dangerous, Rob."

"I don't understand."

"Her diabetes." *We don't know how long Sara will live.* Jeffrey Adamson thought about saying those words to his bright thirteen-year-old son, but decided against it. Perhaps it was too much of a truth for a thirteen-year-old. Besides, it was a truth laced with unknowns.

All the doctors—all the specialists—agreed. Sara's life expectancy was upredictable. It depended on when the "complications" developed and how rapidly they progressed. The doctors talked about when, not if. Although the many specialists disagreed on several important aspects of Sara's diabetes—including, even, how "tightly controlled" she should be—they all recognized the severity of her disease. They gave the Adamsons gentle warnings, preparing them for the inevitable.

"Has something happened?"

"No." Jeffrey smiled thoughtfully. "Sara is doing very well."

No she's not! Can't you see how lonely she is? She's withering here, alone in her cage. Or maybe she's dying. Rob shivered at the thought. It was a private, secret worry. What if Sara weren't alive when he came home at Christmas? On impulse, Rob decided he wouldn't return to Exeter. But, he realized, that was precisely what everyone was doing to Sara—watching her, breath-held, waiting for her to die.

"Sara doesn't even have one of those bracelets," Rob murmured sadly.

"She doesn't need to. She's always with someone who knows about her diabetes," Sheila replied to Rob's seemingly out-of-the-blue observation.

"But that's wrong, don't you see?"

"I beg your pardon?" Sheila bristled.

Rob sighed. It was pointless to launch into a philosophical discussion. Pointless and dangerous. They were talking about Sara's freedom—he was—but Rob might start talking about his own freedom, about the dangerous feelings inside him that made him wonder if he really wanted to spend his life on Wall Street after all.

"The administrators and teachers at Country Day, and I'm sure at the Academy, are extremely responsible. They would watch Sara carefully. Her meals could be prepared here. Why don't you just ask her? Maybe I'm wrong. Maybe she wouldn't want to."

Sara cried, tears of joy, when Sheila and Jeffrey asked her if she wanted to go to Greenwich Country Day School. Sara's tears shocked them all. Sara

never cried, not ever, not even when needles poked her delicate skin.

"I expect letters from you," Rob told Sara the day before he returned to Exeter.

"About what?" she asked eagerly.

"The people you meet. I want to know all about the people, what they look like, who they are inside."

"You want portraits," she said quietly. "You want me to paint their portraits with words."

"Yes," Rob breathed, ever amazed by his brilliant little sister. "Portraits."

"Will you write to me, too, Rob?"

"Of course, Sara. I promise."

Rob kept his promise, and Sara kept hers. Rob loved the "portraits" from his sister. He learned about her teachers and classmates and the postman and her doctors. Sara gave wonderful descriptions, full of insight and humor and care. She defined the *essence* of the people she met. Rob felt as if he knew them, even though Sara never gave their names. *I agree with Juliet*, she wrote. *What's in a name?*

Sara never mentioned Allison Fitzgerald by name, but Rob learned a great deal about the magnificent fifteen-year-old rider with the flame-colored hair, the determined champion with the heart of gold. As Rob read the descriptions in his dormitory at Harvard he thought, *Thank you, whoever you are, for being so nice to my beloved little sister.*

Beginning in late March of Sara's final year at Greenwich Academy for Girls—Rob's senior year at Harvard—the frequent descriptions of the girl who flew over the jumps were replaced by descriptions of the new rose garden at the Adamson estate.

Mother is finally getting the rose garden she has wanted for the library courtyard, Sara wrote. *And I am helping the gardener select the flowers! Do you know about roses, Rob? Each has its own color and fragrance and the names are so lovely. Yes, yes, "What's in a name?" and "A rose by any other name . . ."—but Juliet can be wrong! My favorite rose is Pristine. She (!) is creamy white with delicate pale pink edges and so fragrant. We're planting one named Portrait (deep rich pink) and others—Smoky, Sterling Silver, Christian Dior, Summerwine, Blue Moon. . . . They'll bloom into a magnificent kaleidoscope of color and fragrance, every day a little different, every day a new miracle! You'll see, Rob, when come home in June.*

Sara wrote about the garden and the roses—the happiest letters she had ever sent—but she never sent a portrait of the gardener who was letting her help with the garden's colorful, fragrant design.

Rob assumed the gardener was Joseph Dalton. He was surprised that a portrait of the Eastern European immigrant who had designed gardens for the estates in Greenwich for years wouldn't intrigue Sara. Rob expected a sensitive, thoughtful, insightful portrait of the rugged white-haired gardener; the man whose blue-gray eyes had seen the ugliness and horrors of War, but who created lovely, exquisite kaleidoscopes of flowers. But Sara told Rob about the garden, not about the artist who created it.

In April, Sara wrote, *I've decided to go to Vassar instead of Radcliffe. I know we had planned to both be in Boston next year, Rob, but can we do one more year of portraits? Poughkeepsie is very close to New York City, so, the year after, when you're on Wall Street, I'll come visit you all the time!*

Sara punctuated her letter with frowning faces and smiling ones and never, Rob realized, offered an explanation for her last minute change in the plans they had talked about for years.

But plans changed. Rob knew it, and Sara's decision helped him make a decision of his own, one that had been teasing him, preventing sleep, for months. Rob wouldn't go to Harvard Business School . . . not this fall, anyway, and maybe *never.*

He didn't *have* to become President of Adamson and Witt, did he? Or President of the New York Stock Exchange? He didn't *have* to spend his life commuting between Greenwich and Wall Street, did he? Did he?

Rob told himself no. He could be whatever he wanted to be. He could pursue his interests in writing and literature and journalism. He could travel, meet new people, learn about the world that existed beyond the golden walls.

Long before Rob received the letter from Sara announcing her plans to attend Vassar, he had applied for the Hathaway Fellowship. The prestigious, highly competitive fellowship awarded three years of "advanced study of liberal arts" at Oxford University in England. What am I doing? Rob asked himself as he stayed up night after night carefully preparing the detailed application. What if I get accepted? Will I really go?

Yes.

Rob made the decision not to attend Harvard Business School before the Hathaway Fellowship recipients were announced in June. He told no one of his decision, not even Sara, but his heart quickened, restless and eager, as he thought about the infinite possibilities that lay ahead.

A week before Rob graduated summa cum laude from Harvard University, he received the letter from London. The trustees of the Hathaway Fellowship were pleased to announce . . . They particularly liked the clever, insightful collection of essays Rob had written about his trip to London the summer before, and they were intrigued by his proposal that he publish a collection of essays—his views of England—during his fellowship. In fact, members of the board had already spoken with the editor-in chief of *The London Times*. If the quality of Rob's future essays matched the quality of the essays they had already read, *The Times* would publish them as a series under the title Rob had proposed, "The Connecticut Yankee."

Rob wired a prompt acceptance to the Hathaway Foundation in London, informed Harvard Business School that he would not be attending in the fall after all, cancelled plans to spend July and August sailing the Caribbean with Cam Elliott, and couldn't wait to tell his parents and Sara the thrilling news.

As Rob drove between the imposing stone pillars of the Adamson estate in Greenwich, he faced the taunting worry that Sheila and Jeffrey Adamson might not greet his news with great pleasure. Rob decided to tell Sara first.

"I'm so proud of you, Rob! I expect frequent portraits!"

"You'll get them. Will I? From Vassar?"

"Of course. Rob, are they really going to publish what you write in *The London Times?*"

"That's what they say . . . assuming it's any good."

"It will be. It always is. And I love '"The Connecticut Yankee' as a title."

"That was a middle-of-the-night whimsy, and I inked it onto the application before I had time to reconsider."

"It's wonderful."

"Speaking of wonderful, Sara, I love your garden."

Rob and Sara were sitting on the warm grass in the courtyard, amid the fragrant, colorful collage of roses.

"Thank you. It's really Peter's garden."

"Peter?"

"Peter Dalton. Joseph Dalton's son."

"Oh."

"How often will you be home, Rob?" Sara kept the discussion on Rob's plans, not daring to mention hers.

"I'm not sure."

"I think I'll come visit you."

No, Rob thought, instinctively protecting her.

"I've always wanted to see Rome," Sara continued eagerly. "We could meet there."

Rob gradually became aware of another presence in the walled, private courtyard. A presence . . . a shadow . . . a long, dark, twilight shadow cast by a tall, dark stranger. Rob stood up and silently greeted the intruder's dark brown eyes with surprise, and then concern. The other man responded with matching surprise; then, sensing Rob's disapproval, the dark eyes sent an ice-cold message of defiance. The proud, defiant scowl for Rob became a gentle smile as the man turned to Sara.

"Sara, I'm sorry. I didn't mean to interrupt."

"It's fine, Peter. I want you to meet my brother. Rob, this is Peter Dalton. Peter, this is Rob."

Peter shifted a dark blue wire-bound notebook from his right hand to his left and extended a taut-muscled arm to Rob. The two men shook hands firmly, silently, appraising each other without smiles.

"I can come back later," Peter told Sara.

"No." Rob spoke to Sara, not to Peter. "It's time for me to tell Mother and Father about my plans."

"Let me know, Rob."

"I will. It will be fine." Rob smiled confidently at Sara and left the magnificent rose garden without looking at Peter Dalton again.

It wasn't fine. Sheila and Jeffrey sat in the elegant great room of the estate and stared at Rob with unconcealed horror.

Didn't their golden son know that the path-paved-in-gold had no detours, no intersections, no stop signs? Apparently not! They would have to make it clear.

"You have to go to Harvard Business School, Rob."

"I may, Mother, I probably *will*, but not this fall."

"This fall." *Not even a yield sign.*

"This fall I will be at Oxford." *This fall and two falls after that.*

"No."

"Yes. You don't understand," Rob whispered. He needed to give them more details. He needed to explain about his restlessness and his unhappiness when he thought about the life they planned for him. Surely . . .

"We do understand, son," Jeffrey countered solemnly.

Rob looked at his father hopefully, but the hope faded as his father continued.

"Perhaps you're worried that you won't make the grade at Harvard Business School."

"I'm not worried about that at all!"

"You don't have to be the top in your class in business school, too," Sheila murmured with obvious disappointment. Maybe Rob, perfect, confident Rob, was just feeling a little insecure. Sheila didn't like that sign of weakness—*any* sign of weakness in her strong handsome son—but it was better than the alternative, that Rob was rebelling. She added unconvincingly, "We don't expect you to be."

"But you do expect me to go Harvard Business School, join the firm, run the firm someday. . . ."

"Yes," Sheila and Jeffrey answered in unison.

Rob stared at their resolute faces and a series of realizations, each more shocking and more painful, pulsed through his body. They didn't understand and they weren't even going to try! They didn't care about his unhappiness or his restlessness. They only cared that he met their expectations. *Their* expectations, not his, as if they believed *they* had been the driving force behind his excellence all these years! Didn't they know that no one expected more of Rob than he himself did? Didn't they know that whatever he chose to become he would be the best he possibly could be?

The Hathaway Fellowship was very prestigious. There were far fewer Hathaway Fellows *ever* than there were students in one class at Harvard Business School. Couldn't they be proud of that accomplishment?

No. The realization pulsed through Rob and wrapped around him like a thick, golden rope, imprisoning him in his parents" expectations of what—*who*—he was to be.

"I've accepted the Fellowship and I'm going," Rob breathed finally, with great effort, as if the rope bound his chest, constricting his breathing, smothering him. "I'm leaving tomorrow."

"Don't you dare," Sheila whispered.

"Or what?" Rob demanded as he backed toward the door. He had to get away, fast, before he was doomed to a prison of wealth and luxury and despair.

"We cut you off," Jeffrey answered simply.

"Disown me? You would do that?" As Rob gazed at his parents, another realization swept through him, and it was the most painful of all. They were his parents, but he didn't know them and they didn't know him. All the years of proud smiles and loving praise were smiles and praise for themselves, for what they had created, not for him.

"We might."

"Then do it! You do what you have to do, and I'll do what I have to do."

Rob left the great room quickly. He had to get away! He dashed to his bedroom to get his passport. It was all he really needed. He could buy clothes in New York tomorrow, before he left, or in London after he arrived. What he needed was to leave.

But he had to say good-bye to Sara.

Sara was still in the rose garden and so was Peter, sitting beside her, reading to her from the dark blue notebook.

"Rob! What happened?"

"I think they're going to disown me," Rob whispered with disbelief.

"They won't. It's just an idle threat. They're afraid."

"And I'm not?" Rob hadn't been afraid—he had been only excited—until now. Now the rope had been cast off and he was adrift, following wherever the currents led, to a distant horizon and beyond.

Sara stood up, wrapped her pale, thin arms around her big, strong brother, and hugged him.

"They'll be fine and so will you, Rob. You are going still, aren't you?" Sara's tone was urgent, as if it were very important that Rob do what he wanted to do.

"Yes."

"Good." Sara smiled. "Being disowned really *is* an idle threat, you know. Unless you've somehow squandered the twelve million already!"

Rob and Sara had each inherited twelve million dollars on their eighteenth birthdays. Usually such trust funds established by grandparents for their destined-to-be-wealthy grandchildren came under the grandchild's sole control at age twenty-one, or even twenty-five. But, because of Sara's illness, the inheritance age for both Rob and Sara was eighteen; it seemed a young age to inherit such a fortune, yet no one knew if fragile Sara would even live to her eighteenth birthday. But she had. Rob had inherited his twelve million dollars just over four years ago, and Sara had inherited hers in February.

"No. I haven't touched it."

"Well, if you ever need more, let me know."

"Thanks." Rob gave her a brief kiss on the cheek and a final hug. "I'll send you my address as soon as I have one."

"OK. Rob?"

"What, honey?"

"I expect portraits!"

"So do I."

The following morning Rob flew to London. As the jet carried him swiftly to his destination, he forced the ugly scene with his parents from his mind, courageously replacing it with exciting visions of the life that lay ahead. Rob succeeded in suppressing the scene with Sheila and Jeffrey, but as it faded, another scene from the previous day came into clear, vivid, troubling focus.

The scene was of Sara and Peter in the secluded rose garden.

What the *hell* was Peter Dalton doing there?

Chapter 10

OXFORD UNIVERSITY, ENGLAND
DECEMBER 1976

Rob wrote long, enthusiastic letters to Sara at Vassar. He loved Oxford; he loved studying poetry and literature; he loved exploring England; he loved writing "The Connecticut Yankee" for *The London Times*; he had made the right decision. Sara sent enthusiastic letters in return, writing more about plays and poetry than about people. By Thanksgiving, the letters that flew frequently across the Atlantic were filled with intricate interpretations of *Finnegan's Wake*, reverence for the gifts of William Shakespeare, joy in the simplicity of Robert Frost, and critiques of plays they had seen in London and New York.

New York. Sara obviously spent a great deal of time in New York. It worried Rob to think about his sister in Manhattan, but her letters were so happy and full of joy that he suppressed his fear.

By Christmas, the anger that had driven Rob from the estate in Greenwich was a distant cloud on the vivid brilliance of his new life. He was safe, wandering an enchanted path that would lead to a career in journalism, *loving* it. Sarah knew how happy he was. Something made Rob want his parents to know, too.

Perhaps it was the Yuletide cheeriness of London, the Christmas Eve carollers at Harrod's, the enraptured rosy-cheeked children mesmerized by fairytale displays, and the scents of pine and bayberry. Or perhaps it was nostalgic memories of Christmas shopping in Boston and New York for just the right presents for Sara. Rob didn't know, but *something* compelled him to make the call.

Christmas had always been a time of joy and happiness at the Adamson estate, hadn't it? That was Rob's memory; but, of course, Christmas was also when he always returned home from school, the conquering hero, another perfect all-star semester at Exeter or Harvard behind him.

Even if his parents wouldn't talk to him, Rob was eager to talk to Sara, to *tease* her about the letters that had fallen victim, he assumed, to Reading Week and final examinations at Vassar. Sara's last letter had been postmarked from New York on the tenth of December.

"Mother?"

"Rob! Jeffrey, it's Rob. Are you coming home?"

She sounded so desperate, so uncertain, so unlike Sheila Adamson.

"No, Mother. Not yet."

Jeffrey picked up the extension in the library and asked the same question.

Silence prevailed for a few moments after Rob gave Jeffrey the same answer he had given Sheila. Finally Rob said, "I wanted to wish you all Merry Christmas. Is Sara there?"

"Sara is gone," Sheila whispered.

Gone? Rob's heart stopped and his mind screamed, *No!* Sara had the address of his flat at Oxford, but Sheila and Jeffrey didn't. If anything had happened to Sara . . .

"Gone?" *No, please*. Sara had looked so well that summer day in the garden, so beautiful and radiant, and she hadn't been hospitalized for two years.

"Sara doesn't live here anymore." The *either* was unspoken, but it was there, a heavy, sad sigh eloquently transmitted across the Atlantic.

Relief pulsed through Rob. Relief, elation, and finally curiosity.

"Where does she live?"

"Don't you know?" Jeffrey asked sarcastically. Jeffrey and Sheila assumed their two rebellious children would have been in touch, perhaps encouraging each other, ever strengthening the resolve that kept them away.

"No."

"She lives in New York City—in Greenwich Village—with her husband."

"*Husband?*"

"Peter Dalton, the gardener's son. They eloped two weeks ago."

"You couldn't stop it?" Rob asked, suddenly bonded to his parents in their protectiveness of Sara, forgetting that he was calling from London, the defiant son, the son *they* couldn't stop from *his* folly.

In a horrible, uneasy moment Rob wondered if he could have prevented Sara's marriage. If only he had spent the summer in Greenwich! If only he hadn't been blinded by his own selfishness!

He should have seen it that day in the rose garden—"Peter's garden"! Sara was so radiant, her voice so soft when she spoke Peter's name and her ocean-blue eyes so bright when they greeted the sensuous dark ones.

That summer day Rob had been consumed with his own desperate escape; but his subconscious mind had formed images of Peter and they came to him now, angry and menacing. There was a wildness about Peter Dalton, his strong, cougar-sleek body, his dark, defiant eyes, his sultry sexuality.

If only Rob had been home this summer *where he should have been!* He could have explained to his precious little sister, so carefully, so gently, so lovingly,

that Peter didn't love *her*; he only loved her money, her fortune, the twelve million dollars Sara and Rob had discussed so casually in front of him!

Rob had let Sara down. He should have known . . . he should have stayed home despite the storm that tossed inside him . . . he should have protected her!

"We couldn't stop her," Jeffrey replied heavily.

"Do you have her phone number?" Maybe it wasn't too late.

"Yes."

Sheila read the obviously unfamiliar number to Rob, then began awkwardly, "Rob . . ."

"Yes?"

Sheila sighed softly. It was something you didn't tell a brother about his sister—it was so private—but now it could be the difference between life and death.

"Mother?" Rob sensed that Sheila had an important message for her estranged daughter and that he was the messenger.

"Sara should never have children, Rob. Pregnancy would be too dangerous for her."

"Does she know?"

"Oh yes." The doctors had hinted about this to Jeffrey and Sheila from the very beginning, and they had told Sara when she was fourteen. Most women with diabetes could have children quite safely as long as they were carefully followed throughout the pregnancy, but Sara's diabetes was so "brittle" and there were already signs of "complications." The physiologic stress of pregnancy for Sara might be lethal. Sheila had watched as the doctors had very gently told her fourteen-year-old daughter about the dangers of pregnancy. Sara had nodded politely but her dark blue eyes were wide with amazement. She didn't have boyfriends! She couldn't imagine a time when she would. But now Sara was married to a man about whom the Adamsons knew virtually nothing, except that the relationship had been kept secret until it was much too late stop, until Peter had stolen their precious daughter from them. "Sara knows, but I don't know if he does."

"I'll discuss it with her, Mother," Rob promised uneasily.

"Thank you."

"I'm sorry," Rob told his parents before he said goodbye. For a moment, Rob wished he could rush to Heathrow, catch the first plane to JFK, and joyfully enroll in Harvard Business School. He couldn't do it, unless . . . *If I knew that if I returned home so would Sara, then maybe* . . . "I'm sorry."

Rob paced in his flat for five minutes before dialing the number in New York. He was searching for a gentle way to convince Sara to leave Peter *now.*

It's not too late, Sara! You're so young!

But I may never get old, Rob.

Finally, without really knowing what he was going to say, Rob took a deep breath and dialed.

Peter the gardener, Peter the fortune hunter, Peter the man with the dark, defiant eyes, Peter who Rob hated with an intensity that frightened him, answered. Rob identified himself and asked for Sara.

"Rob! Merry Christmas!"

Rob had steeled his heart for grief, regret, despair in her voice, but all he heard was joy—joy and happiness and love bubbling from the soul of is fragile sister.

"Merry Christmas, Sara. What the hell have you done?"

"I've out-rebelled you!" Sara laughed.

"I think you have." Rob laughed a little because Sara's merry laugh demanded it. "Although I was the first to be disowned."

"I'm sure they didn't disown you! I think they really *did* disown me."

"Sara . . ." Rob began gently, seriously.

"Rob . . ." Sara matched his serious tone briefly, then warned lightly, "No lectures, Rob. I'm sorry I didn't tell you. I almost did, the day you left."

"You knew then?"

"Yes. I wanted to tell you then. I wanted you to understand and approve, but—"

"But what?" *You knew I would try to stop you?*

"—you glowered at Peter that day."

"I did not."

"You did! Anyway, we're married now." Sara's voice softened. "We love each other, Rob. We're very happy."

"I'm glad," Rob replied without conviction. "What are you doing in New York?"

"Peter's a playwright and a director, and he's wonderful at both."

"Last spring Peter was a gardener," Rob murmured as evenly as he could, trying to banish images of *Lady Chatterley's Lover* from his mind.

"Is there something wrong with being a gardener?"

"No, of course not." Unless it was a ploy to meet an eighteen-year old heiress who had just inherited twelve million dollars. Wouldn't twelve million dollars be helpful in launching a Broadway career?

"Why is it so hard for you and Mother and Father to believe that Peter loves *me?*" The anger was gone and Sara's voice was so sad, so bewildered. *Can't I be loved for me?*

"Oh, Sara, no," Rob answered swiftly, his heart aching with guilt. He did assume Peter had married Sara for her fortune and, by telling her that, by even suggesting it, implied that she couldn't possibly be loved for who she was. Of course that wasn't true! "It's not hard to believe at all. We're just so used to protecting you, I guess."

"You don't need to protect me, not anymore, especially not from Peter. He's a wonderful man, Rob. I know you'll like him very much. He didn't marry me for my money. We're not even touching it, but we will if I have medical bills. We live in a cozy brownstone. I'm not going back to Vassar. Most of the books and poems and plays I wrote to you about were ones Peter and I read together or saw together, not ones from my courses anyway. Those are the answers to the usual questions. Do you have others?"

Lots, Rob mused, but he decided to focus on the most critical one.

"Does he know about your diabetes?"

"Of course he does! Before we were married, we met with Dr. Williams, the specialist I've been seeing in New York. Peter knows everything."

Rob hesitated, still aching from inadvertently hurting her in the name of caring, reluctant because it was so private, so intimate . . . but so important.

"Sara, does Peter know you shouldn't have children?"

"Yes," she answered softly, sadly, but without anger. "Peter knows I shouldn't have children. I take it Mother told you that?"

"Yes. She told me because she's worried about you. They miss you very much, Sara."

"Remember your delusion about them being excited about the Hathaway Fellowship? Peter and I had a similar fantasy that they might be happy for us, perhaps would even want to witness our marriage. Pure folly! They responded

to the news by first trying to pay Peter off and then by trying to demand a prenuptual agreement."

"As a wise sister once said to me, " 'They were afraid.' "

"You certainly are being magnanimous, Rob."

"It's Christmas, Sara. And I can afford to be, because I'm free."

"So am I, but it's much too soon."

"I thought I might send Mother and Father the odd postcard."

"Go ahead! Perhaps the Tower of London?"

"Very funny. Speaking of the odd postcard, you owe me a letter, Sara."

"I know. May I send you a portrait of Peter? I've been wanting to since last spring."

"Please do."

Peter Dalton was born on a bitter cold November night. Peter's humble birth in a small cottage in Danbury, Connecticut occurred exactly two years before Robert Jeffrey Adamson's golden birth in a magnificent estate in nearby Greenwich.

Peter's home was cold in the harsh, icy Connecticut winters, but he didn't even notice. His childhood was filled with the warmth of his loving parents. Peter's mother, Anne, taught him about the majesty of words. In her soft voice with its wonderful British accent, Anne read Peter her favorite poems and plays. Shakespeare, Brecht, Tennyson, O'Neill, Williams, Longfellow, Shaw. Anne joyously shared her great love of language and literature with her very bright young son.

From his well-educated mother, Peter learned to love the treasures of language. From his father, Joseph, Peter learned the mysterious secrets of flowers. As a little boy, Peter accompanied his father to the magnificent gardens of the Greenwich estates where Joseph worked. Peter helped Joseph plant bulbs in the warm, rich soil, and he listened in wide-eyed amazement as his father made promises about the fate of the small, bland bulbs. Joseph was a man of few words, but to Peter, that made each word his father uttered so important. Joseph spoke in broken English and his voice was very deep. The heavy accent and rich tone gave a mystical quality to the promises Joseph made.

"This one," Joseph would say, holding a taupe bulb that looked to Peter like all the rest, "will be bright blue, like a summer sky."

The flowers always blossomed *just as Joseph promised*. How did his father know the secrets of the flowers? Peter wondered. Was Joseph a wizard like Merlin? Or a gypsy with magical powers?

For six years, Peter lived in a world of beautiful words and beautiful flowers, a world of warmth and laughter and love. It didn't matter that the Daltons were poor and sometimes cold. Joseph designed the gardens of the great estates of Greenwich, creating colorful, fragrant works of art, but he made little money. Joseph designed only a few gardens each year; he was an artist, and his art took time and patience and loving care. Anne planned to teach as soon as Peter was in school. Until then, it was too important to be at home with her bright little boy, teaching him. The Daltons were poor and their cottage was sometimes cold in winter, but they were rich in love and happiness.

When Peter was six, everything changed.

Anne became ill and then, suddenly, in the dark of night, she died. Joseph fell into troubled, tormented silence, and the tiny cottage that had been filled with such laughter and joy became a dark, suffocating coffin.

Peter watched his father's anguish in bewildered silence and grieved the loss of his beloved mother in the privacy of his small bedroom. It was then, at the age of six, that Peter Dalton began to write. The eloquent, emotional words flowed like tears from his confused, lonely heart.

Two months after Anne's death, Peter was awakened by a noise—a cry in the darkness—and he found Joseph huddled, sobbing. Joseph's sobs pierced the agonizing silence that had lived in the cottage since Anne's death; for Joseph, the sobs were a final, desperate attempt to escape a silent madness that threatened to destroy him.

Peter wrapped his small arms around his father and listened in the icy darkness as Joseph told Peter the grim stories of his life.

Joseph had been forced to flee his home—his homeland, everything he loved—by the soldiers of the most horrible war of all time. Joseph had escaped with his young bride, his first wife, and they were *almost* free! But, as Joseph watched, helpless, screaming, the woman he loved was murdered before his eyes.

Joseph fled again, this time to England. He found work there, in the country gardens of Kent, and a new name, and a new love. Joseph met Anne in England, and after the war they sailed together to America. Joseph and Anne made a wonderful life, rich in happiness and joy and love, until Anne, too, was taken away.

Six-year-old Peter listened to the torments and horrors and loves of his father's life. After that, the bond of love between father and son became even stronger. Each was an artist, driven by silent passions and visions. Joseph poured his soul and emotion into the fragrant pastel gardens he so lovingly created. Peter eloquently translated the confusing, inexplicable tragedies of life into words. Peter helped Joseph create the wonderful gardens—never very many each year . . . just enough to keep them warm in winter—and in the long winters, Joseph proudly read the plays, stories, and poems written by his talented son.

Peter went to Yale University, on scholarship. After graduation, he moved to New York City. Peter lived in Greenwich Village, but he travelled frequently to the small cottage in Danbury to visit Joseph.

Eighteen months after Peter moved to New York, six months after *The Village Voice* raved about his first one-act play, his father was hospitalized with pneumonia. Joseph never fully recovered from the pneumonia, because there was cancer, too. Peter returned to Danbury to be with Joseph and to help him create the gardens he had promised for that spring. Sheila Adamson wanted a rose garden for her library courtyard. Peter and Sara gave her one, a beautiful one, one that Joseph would have loved.

Joseph never saw the rose garden Peter and Sara created. He was too ill to leave the cottage. Peter and Sara told him about it in the long hours they spent with him until his death. Peter and Sara were with Joseph when he died, and he died with a soft smile on his rugged face, a smile for Peter, a smile for Sara.

Sara knew the stories of Peter's life, and the stories of Joseph's life, too. In the portrait she wrote to Rob, Sara didn't give the details, just the essence of the father and son who were so alike, the proud, talented artists whose visions of the world had been shaped, sometimes brutally, by the inexplicable whims of fate.

Sara began her portrait of Peter the way William Shakespeare began *Romeo and Juliet:* "Two households, both alike in dignity . . ."

As Rob read Sara's portrait in his flat near Oxford, he searched between the lines and found more that worried than reassured.

The two households—the Adamsons and the Daltons—were alike in dignity, proud and strong, but weren't they also at war? Weren't the stars inevitably

crossed? Didn't the dark, talented, sensitive son of the proud, tormented father harbor resentment toward the wealthy and privileged Adamsons of the world?

Rob worried, even though Sara's letter brimmed with love and joy and happiness. Sara ended the ten page letter with: *And in case you don't know, Rob Adamson, in case you didn't notice while you were glowering at him, Peter Dalton is the most handsome man alive (relatives excluded from this analysis for obvious reasons!!!).*

The day after Rob received Sara's portrait of her husband, he received a short letter from Peter.

> *Rob,*
>
> *If Sara were my sister, I would doubtless feel the way you must. Please believe I know how special she is, how precious, how much I love her. I promise I will take care of Sara. I will love her with everything I have and give her everything I have to give.*
>
> *Peter*

Rob met Peter the following summer. Rob returned "to the Colonies" for a long Fourth of July weekend. Rob's visit had purpose: He hoped to begin mending fences with his parents, and he wanted to *really* meet Peter. Rob needed to see if the boundless joy Sara sent across the Atlantic in letters and over the telephone was real.

Sara's happiness *was* real. Sara was obviously very much in love with Peter. Although Sara's great joy was quiet and private as Sara always was, Rob could tell because he knew her so well. It was more difficult to tell about Peter, who Rob didn't know, and who was distant and wary with his brother-in-law. Peter's dark eyes always softened when they gazed at Sara, though, as they had that day in the rose garden. Rob decided, because his sister believed it and because he *wanted* to believe it, that Peter was very much in love with Sara, too.

Rob and Sara attended performances of two of Peter's one-act plays at La Mama's, and he saw for himself his brother-in-law's remarkable talent. Rob served as liaison between Sara and their parents, calmly reassuring Sheila and Jeffrey that their daughter was fine, happy, safe.

But was she safe? The question taunted Rob as he flew back to London on the eighth of July. *Was fragile Sara really safe with the dark, silent stranger who took her horseback riding in Central Park and ice-skating in Rockefeller Center and on wind-tossed rides on the Staten Island Ferry?*

Rob hoped so. Rob *prayed* so.

"Sara, what's that noise?" Rob asked when he called to wish her a happy twenty-first birthday. The noise sounded like a bark.

"That's Muffin. I think the phone startled her."

"Muffin?"

"Maybe the name is too preppie, but she really is a Muffin." Sara laughed. "Come here, honey, say hello to your Uncle Rob."

"Sara?"

"She's a blond cocker spaniel puppy, suddenly shy. She's curled in a wriggling ball of fur in Peter's lap."

"Sara . . ."

"Rob, there is no reason whatsoever that I can't have a puppy. Mother and Father were unbelievably paranoid about the lurking dangers."

"They just wanted you to be safe."

"I know," Sara replied with surprising softness.

"Have you spoken to them?" Rob asked hopefully.

"Yes. I used your ploy of sending them the odd postcard. I think it was the Statue of Liberty that did the trick. Not terribly hidden symbolism, but it worked. Mother and Father and I had lunch together last week. I think we've reached a cease-fire, if not a truce."

"That will happen. I've made it to the truce stage with them." After a moment, Rob added quietly, "I think we may be headed for peace."

"That would be nice," Sara said wistfully, knowing it was a long way off for her. Sheila and Jeffrey still harbored the unconcealed hope that Peter Dalton would disappear from their lives and Sara would return to Greenwich. When she spoke again, Sara's voice was filled with pride, "I just sent you the reviews for *Merry Go Round*. The critics loved it!"

For her twenty-first birthday, Sara got Muffin. For her twenty-second birthday, Sara travelled to Rome.

Sara sent the telegram to Rob in his office at *The London Times*, where he had worked full-time in the eight months since the Hathaway Fellowship ended.

Rome. On My Birthday. Be There. Sara.

Rob smiled as he read Sara's telegram. Then a slight frown crossed his face as he realized with amazement that he hadn't seen his sister for two and a half years. Rob felt so close to her—through frequent letters and phone calls—but he couldn't wait to see her. Rob had something to tell her, plans to discuss with Sara and Peter when he met them in Rome in two weeks.

But Peter wasn't in the lobby of the Lord Byron when Rob arrived. Only Sara was there.

Peter let Sara come alone! How could he? Rob's instant reaction was anger. If Peter loved Sara, how could he let her travel all that distance by herself? What if she became ill? What if the plane were delayed and she got behind on her meals? What if the plane were *hijacked?*

Rob's anger was swiftly subdued by Sara's words and the way she looked. His sister had never looked healthier, happier, more radiant, more beautiful.

"I don't know which of my strong, handsome men is the bigger worrywart—you or Peter!" Sara teased the horror from Rob's deep blue eyes. "As you can see, I'm fine!"

"I admit you look fine—no, you look wonderful."

"Peter wanted to come, of course, but he's in the middle of rehearsals for *As You Like It*. And, I waited to tell you this in person: *Storm Watch* is going to be produced on Broadway next fall! It's an incredible play, Rob, and Peter's going to direct as well."

"I can't wait to see it."

"You'll come?"

"For opening night." Rob smiled. "By then, I should be living in New York. I have a plan that I need to talk to you about."

"I need to talk to you, too," Sara said quietly. That was why she was here, alone, to see her brother.

Rob and Sara spent the week exploring Rome, visiting the happy sites—the sparkling fountains where wishes made are destined to come true, the Spanish steps, the Sistine Ceiling, the Borghese Gardens—and strolling along the Via Condetti and through the Vatican. Sara looked wonderful but she fatigued easily. "Too much fresh air," she exclaimed lightly. Sara napped between their morning and afternoon excursions, and they ate early dinners so she could be in bed before nine.

They explored, and they talked, and Rob told her about the idea that had been dancing in his mind for over two years.

"It's a magazine. I'm going to call it *Portrait.* We'll paint portraits with words, like you and I have always done, although there will be photographs as well."

"Rob, this is so exciting!"

"I'm glad you think so." Rob was excited about his magazine-to-be. It would take hard work and it would be risky, but if he insisted on quality—quality writers, quality photographers—and if he selected the right people to feature . . .

"Do you need my twelve million?"

"No! That's for you and Peter."

"We don't need it, Rob. We're happy."

"Well, I don't need your money, but thank you. I do, however, need you."

"Me?"

"I hoped you would be one of the writers."

"Really?" Sara's eyes widened and sparkled.

"Of course. I imagine there will be many interviews to be done in New York City. I don't plan to send you gallivanting all over the globe. I'm sure Peter wouldn't want that, either."

"No, he wouldn't."

"I thought a portrait of Peter, written by you, would be nice for the first issue."

Sara smiled lovingly at her older brother. "I know you will like Peter when you really get to know him, Rob. I know you're still a little skeptical about him."

"No."

"Yes!" She continued very softly, her eyes dreamy, "I want to know that you and Peter will be friends always, no matter what."

"Sara . . ." Rob wanted to stop the ominous tone of her voice. It was so incongruous with how she looked—healthy, robust, with flushed cheeks and sparkling eyes, as if she had never been ill in her life and would live forever.

"Promise me, Rob."

"I promise, Sara." Rob made the promise because he wanted an end to the sudden mood of gloom. He would like Peter, for Sara's sake. The three of them would become good friends. Together they would take New York City by storm.

Rob made the promise swiftly, easily, in good faith.

But it was a promise he could not keep.

Two months later Sara was dead. It happened too quickly for any of them—except Peter—to be with her. From the moment the bleeding began to the moment Sara died at Columbia Presbyterian Medical Center was less than one hour.

Dr. Williams, Sara's specialist in New York, made the call to the Adamson estate in Greenwich and to Rob's flat in London. "Bleeding, shock, overwhelming sepsis, uremia, renal failure," he explained to Jeffrey and Sheila, and again to Rob.

Why? Why? *Why?* they asked in disbelief.

Didn't they *know?* Weren't they prepared? Hadn't Sara told them?

Apparently not. Apparently, they didn't know that Sara was five months pregnant.

"How dare you come here!" Rob hissed when he opened the door of his parents" home and saw the gaunt, anguished face of Peter Dalton.

"I wanted to explain," Peter whispered.

"*Explain?* I know how women get pregnant, and I know that any man who loved Sara would never have allowed this to happen."

"Rob, I love Sara!"

"Love? Sara is dead, remember? You never loved her. You only loved her money."

"*No!* How can you say that? Please, Rob, let me explain!"

"Get the hell out of here." As Rob stared angrily into Peter's eyes, powerful, unfamiliar feelings swirled inside him. The strong, terrifying feelings were urging him to harm Peter.

Finally, because he was afraid of what he might do, what he *wanted* to do, Rob slammed the door.

Two weeks after Sara's death, Rob and Sheila and Jeffrey met with Dr. Williams. It was a desperate attempt to make sense of the senseless.

"Sara told me that she and Peter met with you before they were married and that Peter knew everything, including the dangers of pregnancy."

"That's right. I was quite blunt about the risks."

"So Peter couldn't have misunderstood."

"No. He understood. In fact, he decided to have a vasectomy. I told him—them—that they should think about it, but Peter was quite firm. Before they left my office that day I arranged an appointment for him with a colleague."

"The operation failed?" Was that what Peter Dalton had wanted to explain? Was it all a horrible, tragic accident?

"No. I checked last week. I assumed that Peter followed through with it—he seemed so definite—but he didn't. My colleague keeps his records for five years, so I had him check. The appointment was cancelled three days after it was made."

"And you never asked Peter about it again?"

"I didn't see Peter again until the night Sara died. She always came to see me by herself."

"Peter didn't come with her?" Sheila whispered. She had been with Sara, her precious daughter, for every appointment until the horrible announcement that Sara was getting married. If Peter cared about Sara at all, he would have been with her!

"No. I urged Sara to bring him with her." Dr. Williams frowned slightly. "In the past year her condition deteriorated quite rapidly. There were decisions to be made about hemodialysis and—"

"But she looked wonderful!" Sheila interjected. "She spent the weekend with us two months ago, just after she returned from Rome, and she looked so healthy." *So happy, so loving as she said good-bye.*

That was why Sara arranged to meet me in Rome, Rob realized. She knew that she was pregnant and how great a risk it was.

"Sara did look wonderful," Dr. Williams agreed. "But she wasn't." He added, because it was the truth, because it might help, "Sara was dying. Even with heroic interventions she wouldn't have lived much longer."

"But that made pregnancy even more dangerous!"

"Yes," Dr. Williams answered grimly.

"Sara knew?"

"Of course she knew. We tried very hard to convince her to terminate the pregnancy."

"We?"

"Sara's obstetrician and I."

"What about Peter? Where was Peter?"

"I don't know."

"Why didn't you call him? Or us?"

"I couldn't, not without Sara's permission. You know that."

But who was taking care of Sara? Who was protecting her?

Not Peter Dalton. Not the man who claimed he loved her.

After Dr. Williams left, Rob and Sheila and Jeffrey sat in the great room as twilight fell, darkening the room, forcing them deeper into their dark, unspeakable thoughts.

Finally, Sheila's voice broke the eerie stillness.

"He killed her. Peter killed her."

"Mother . . ." But it was what Rob had been thinking, too.

"Sheila," Jeffrey whispered weakly.

"He pretended to have the operation, and when she got pregnant, he probably pretended the surgery had failed. Peter knew Sara would never have an abortion." Sheila's voice broke. After a moment, she whispered, "And he knew what would happen if she didn't."

"Sheila, Dr. Williams told us that Sara was dying. She was going to die, dear, even if she hadn't been pregnant."

"But may be Peter didn't know! Sara looked wonderful. She looked as if she would live forever." Sheila's words ended in a soft sob.

Or maybe Peter did know, Rob thought grimly. Maybe he didn't want to waste any of his inheritance on costly heroic measures. *Either way . . .*

"Peter murdered Sara," Sheila whispered, finishing Rob's thought. *Peter murdered her as surely as if he had fired a bullet into her heart.*

Sheila Adamson believed Sara's death was cold-blooded, premeditated murder. The Adamsons' high-powered attorneys listened to Sheila's words, perhaps even shared the horrible belief, but knew that legally there was nothing to be done. It was pure supposition; not a shred of evidence; nothing that could be proved.

The attorneys strongly advised the family to mention "the theory" to no one. The accusations were libelous, and if Peter Dalton was the kind of man the Adamsons believed him to be, if he heard their accusations, it might be *very dangerous*.

Rob and Jeffrey heeded the attorneys' warnings, and Sheila did eventually, after she told Victoria Elliott, her closest friend.

The Adamsons mourned in dignified silence. The hatred lodged in their hearts, burrowing ever deeper, killing them slowly.

Rob moved to New York and created the astonishingly successful *Portrait* magazine. But it was a joyless triumph. *Portrait* glowed with stories of remarkable, talented, creative men and women; people like Peter Dalton, whose career was as dazzling and distinguished as Sara proudly predicted it would be. Peter was the toast of Manhattan, although he rarely heard the toasts himself, preferring private shadows to the brilliant glitter of Sardi's, Lutece, Le Cirque, or The Brook Club.

Rob watched Peter's success, heard the toasts, and pulsed with helpless rage. Rob answered the frequent query, "When is Peter Dalton going to appear in *Portrait?*" with stony silence and a private vow: *Never.* Not that that would hurt Peter. Nothing Rob could do would harm Peter. And what harm, what hurt, could begin to match what Peter had done to Sara?

Finally, because New York held neither joy nor peace, only powerless torment, Rob moved to Los Angeles.

Rob blamed Peter for Sara's death. As time passed, as emotion was tempered by rationality, Rob saw Peter's crime as the carelessness of a self-absorbed man, not cold-blooded murder. Rob couldn't believe such evil lived in a human heart. And, if such evil existed, Rob didn't *want* to believe that lovely, gentle Sara had been its victim.

Peter Dalton's crime was a careless betrayal of trust, not cold, calculated murder . . . but the result was the same.

Peter should have protected Sara. He *promised* he would.

Peter had broken that promise and Sara was dead.

And for that, Rob hated Peter Dalton with all his heart.

Chapter 11

LOS ANGELES, CALIFORNIA
AUGUST 1984

I don't belong here, Allison realized, finally diagnosing what was wrong. *Here* was the paddock on the first day of equestrian events at the 1984 Summer Olympics.

The paddock area was an excited, energized bustle of horses and riders. Allison had been sent a special pass by the United States Equestrian Show Jumping Team. They were her friends, the men and women who would have been her teammates.

The special paddock pass was a thoughtful gesture, and her riding friends had welcomed her so warmly—"Allison, you look wonderful!" But they wore jodhpurs; and she wore a light cotton dress. Their bodies were sleek and fit and strong; and she was slender, but not strong enough anymore, and damaged. Their hearts pounded with restless, eager energy as they neared their dreams; and her heart ached with the realization that she was now merely a visitor in a world that for so long had been her home.

And was that pity Allison saw in their eyes? Pity for her and surprise that she had actually come?

These ten days in August were going to be the final chapter in the story of Allison Fitzgerald, Champion Equestrian. Allison had spent the summer making peace with the dream. And she *did* feel at peace—at peace with what she had lost and hope for what lay ahead.

Allison believed that spending these days watching her friends—and Tuxedo—compete for gold and silver and bronze, being a small part of the energy and excitement one last time, would be the perfect ending to the story.

But she was wrong. The story—*her* story—had ended three years ago.

They belonged here. *She* didn't.

As Allison hurriedly left the paddock area, she expected to feel the heat of tears in her eyes. But there were no tears! Instead of emptiness, Allison felt relief.

And then the once-familiar, almost-forgotten rushes of determination and joy. Determination and joy were old friends. They had always accompanied Allison to the stable, and now they were with her as she left.

Determination and joy stayed with Allison, gaining strength and energy as she navigated the sluggish freeways across the Los Angeles Basin to Beverly Hills. By the time Allison eased her car into a parking space in the patrons" lot behind Elegance, her eyes sparkled and she was smiling.

"Allison!"

"Hello, Claire. I'm reporting for duty."

"Today? The Olympics just started."

"Today."

"Terrific. Except I haven't gotten your work area set up yet. The partitions have been ordered but haven't arrived. I'm planning to create a space over here." Claire wove among the colorful samples of carpeting, wallpaper, and fabric that perpetually cluttered the floors of Elegance. Elegance was a workshop, without pretense or glamour. Allison's "office" was going to be a cubicle created by partitions.

"See?" Claire extracted an ivory business card from a small box on the floor. In gold script, above the name, address, and telephone number of Elegance, were the words *Allison Fitzgerald, A.S.I.D*. "Proof positive that this will be your spot."

"It looks perfect!" Allison added seriously, "The work area isn't terribly important, Claire, but I would like some work."

"You've got it." Claire glanced at her watch. "Arriving in fifteen minutes."

"Really?"

"Yes. This has been your project from the very beginning. I've been filling in until you arrived."

"What is it?"

Claire gave a sly, knowing smile. "Bellemeade."

"Oh!"

Bellemeade was a landmark in Bel Air, an exquisite French Country cottage built in the late 1930's by movie producer Francois Revel for his paramour, the famous Celeste. Bellemeade was small by Bel Air mansion standards, a romantic, charming love nest with private views of dazzling golden sunsets over the sapphire-blue Pacific.

"Bellemeade was recently purchased by Steve Gannon. He's President of Brentwood Productions and also happens to be a very good friend. Steve bought Bellemeade as an investment—it's bound to appreciate—and he can write it off his taxes by using it to house the studio's imported talent in the meantime."

"Imported talent?"

"Actors, actresses, directors who need a place to stay while they're here filming or writing or accepting their Oscars. *Important* imported talent, of course. An elegant house in Bel Air is a giant step beyond even the best suite at the Beverly Hills Hotel."

"Mr. Gannon wants us to decorate Bellemeade?"

"He'll want you to call him Steve, and yes, he does. It's a beauty make-over, really. The house is structurally solid, but the interior is a fixer-upper. It was last decorated in the mid-fifties, so you can imagine, but an elegant face-lift and a tasteful amount of make-up will make it the showcase of Bel Air." Claire smiled.

"And it's all yours, my dear."

"Mine?"

"Steve has given you a very nice close-to-seven-figure budget—we'll go over that later—and total freedom, unless this Peter Dalton fellow has strong ideas."

"Peter Dalton?"

"He's the first imported talent who'll be living there. He's the one who wrote *Love* and is moving here for the winter to direct it. I'm sure, if you've spoken to Vanessa Gold recently, she has mentioned him."

Allison nodded. She had seen Vanessa at a welcome-home-from-Argentina dinner for her parents, and Vanessa *had* raved about the "astonishing" screenplay and its "incredibly gifted" author.

"Dalton is due to arrive December first, which means you will be very busy."

"That's fine." *That's good.* "What's happening today?"

"Dalton is in town because they're casting *Love* this week. Steve is going to bring him by, after he sees Bellemeade, to meet us—you—in case he has any preferences for the decorating style." Claire twinkled. "Steve knows there are things we *will not do*, but he thinks Peter Dalton will have very traditional tastes. Oh. Here they are now."

Claire led the way back through the maze of samples to the office foyer.

Steve Gannon looked like a movie producer—rich, powerful, energetic. Allison was instinctively comfortable with such men because they reminded her of her rich, powerful, energetic, and loving father. She smiled warmly at Steve as Claire made the introductions.

Then it was time to meet Peter Dalton.

"I'm Allison," she told the long-lashed, dark brown eyes.

"I'm Peter."

"Hi." Allison smiled, and Peter smiled, too, but she thought she saw flickers of sadness in the dark eyes. No, that *had* to be wrong. This very handsome man was the writer who was giving the world the definitive work on love *complete with a happy ending*. He wouldn't be sad.

"Hi."

"Allison will be the designer for Bellemeade," Claire explained. "Did you have a chance to see it?"

"We were just there," Steve answered. "I gave Peter a whirlwind tour of Bel Air and the Club and UCLA."

"Do you have ideas about how you would like it decorated, Peter?" Allison asked.

"No," Peter answered. After a moment, he added quietly, "I . . . I'm sure whatever you do will be very nice."

"I hope so."

The conversation faltered quickly. Claire murmured something about how talented Allison was, and Steve said something similar about Peter, and the "prized students" exchanged awkward smiles. After a few moments, Steve announced that he and Peter had to rush off to a meeting with the casting director for *Love*.

"Peter could have been a *little* more enthusiastic about Bellemeade, couldn't he?" Claire asked with obvious disapproval after Steve and Peter had left. "Admittedly, the interior is somewhat drab and oppressive at the moment, but he knows that will be fixed—for him!—and the setting itself is absolutely breathtaking."

"I'm sure Peter is quite preoccupied with the movie," Allison said.

"So is Steve, but that doesn't prevent *him* from being polite, does it? No, I imagine Peter Dalton is wondering why he's leaving his penthouse on Fifth Avenue and his estate in the Hamptons to spend four months in *déclassé* Bel Air in *déclassé* California. If Peter were our client, not Steve, I might suggest to the arrogant writer that he find another designer!"

"I didn't think Peter seemed arrogant," Allison countered softly. *He just seemed sad and lonely.*

"No? Well, aloof, at least. Anyway, Bellemeade is the project of a lifetime for you, Allison. It's just a shame that it has to be such a rush, especially since I'm not sure Peter Dalton will appreciate it no matter how fabulous it is. I wonder if I should just tell Steve that December first is impossible and let him put Dalton at the Beverly Hills Hotel like everyone else!"

"December first is fine, Claire."

"Well, there *is* the dog."

"The dog?"

"Dalton is bringing his dog with him. That's why he wants a house, not a hotel. The dog is probably a designer-eating Doberman!"

"Claire . . ." Allison began, then stopped. She was about to say, I think it's nice that Peter wants his dog with him. I'm sure he's a very nice man. *Sure?* You're the one who thinks his dark eyes are sad and lonely, not aloof and arrogant. Aloof and arrogant makes sense—"incredibly gifted" Peter Dalton has ample reason to be aloof and arrogant—but sad and lonely doesn't. "Do you have the keys to Bellemeade? I'd like to go take a look right now."

"I have the keys and the code for the alarm system, but I don't think you have enough time before your next appointment."

"My next appointment? Claire, I'm at the Olympics today!"

"I know, isn't this working out well?"

"Claire, it will be a miracle if I can finish Bellemeade by December first—and that's assuming I spend every single minute on it!"

"I know. Don't worry. Your next client doesn't want you to begin until December second."

"Who is my next client?"

"His name is Roger Towne. He owns the Chateau Hotels. You've heard of them—small luxury hotels, very elegant, very upscale, all around the world. The Chateau St. Moritz is the most famous, but perhaps it will be surpassed by the Chateau Bel Air, for which, hopefully, we are doing the interior design."

"Hopefully?"

"It depends on what Roger Towne thinks of your work. He lives in San Francisco, but he flew down for the Opening Ceremonies. We arranged that I would show him photographs of what you've done—the Doheny mansion, the March library, Fairchild House—and he could meet you on his next trip if he's interested."

"Why me?"

"He was specifically referred to you."

"Who referred him?" It had to be Dan. Dan lived in Hillsborough, just south of San Francisco.

"Rob Adamson." Claire talked as she walked, leading Allison toward her office. "The appointment is in ten minutes. Why don't you use my office? The notebook with the photographs is on my desk."

As Allison waited for Roger Towne she thought about Rob. Before Meg's wedding, Allison had never even seen Rob; now she saw him all the time!

Allison recalled how, as a little girl, she would learn a strange new word—"asylum," 'indigo," 'Serbia," 'requiem"—and suddenly everyone would be using it. Allison always wondered if the new word had been there all along and she had just been inattentive, or if it was a remarkable coincidence. Now the same thing was happening with Rob Adamson; once discovered, he was everywhere. But Allison knew she had never seen Rob Adamson before Meg's wedding; she knew he hadn't been there all along and she had simply been inattentive.

Rob hadn't been there before, and now he was, all the time, by remarkable coincidence.

Allison and Winter would be having Sunday brunch at the Club, and Rob and Elaina would appear on the path that led from the garden terrace to the tennis courts. "Elaina in Ellesse," Winter would whisper as she cast a cheery smile. Or Allison would be browsing at Giorgio or Chanel or Gucci on Rodeo, and she would look up and Rob would be there, browsing, too. One Monday night they had both been in the express lane, buying a six-pack of sugar-free soft drinks, at Ralph's in Santa Monica. And last Saturday Allison had seen him jogging on San Vicente.

On those frequent chance meetings, Allison and Rob would acknowledge each other, as well as the coincidence, more with twinkling eyes, warm smiles, and friendly waves than with words . . .

Just as it had been with Sara. Not many words, just a lovely warmth, a special bond.

And now Rob was sending her important clients, looking out for her, just like an older brother would. How thoughtful of him!

"Hello?" A deep, pleasant voice interrupted her reverie.

Allison looked up into pale blue eyes, sun-blond hair, an easy smile, and the unmistakable look of confidence worn by someone who has created his own empire through hard work and vision. Rob had the same confident look, and so did Steve Gannon, and Allison's father; and Dan would look this way, too. As Allison smiled at the pale blue eyes, her thoughts drifted briefly to a man who *should* have been on that list, but wasn't. Peter Dalton didn't wear the easy confidence of tremendous success. Peter searched the emotions of the heart and soul, and he wrote eloquently about that voyage, but his dark eyes didn't sparkle with confidence. Instead, they flickered with uneasy sadness at the visions they saw. *Didn't they?*

"Hello."

"I'm Roger Towne."

"I'm Allison Fitzgerald."

"You come highly recommended." Roger settled into a chair across from her.

"Rob doesn't have the foggiest idea about my work!" Allison exclaimed with a soft laugh.

"He actually doesn't claim to. It's *you* who comes highly recommended."

"Oh!"

"Rob says if even a tenth of who you are flows over into what you design, I will be delighted with the result." Roger delivered the compliment effortlessly.

"Oh." Allison felt the warmth rush to her cheeks, but she remained steady under the pale blue gaze, strangely comfortable, strangely bold. She tilted her head and asked, "Roger, have you known Rob long?"

"For about two years. We met at my hotel in New Orleans. Why?"

Allison's eyes widened and sparkled. "Rob's crazy, you know."

* * *

"We have the Chateau Bel Air," Allison told Claire an hour and a half later.

"You dazzled him. I could hear the coquettish laughter."

"We just hit it off. He's very nice, very funny." *Very nice*. Allison had decided that about Peter Dalton, too. Roger Towne and Peter Dalton, such different men. Both very nice? "Besides, I don't think I could really dazzle anyone with this mane, do you?"

Claire's silence told Allison what she already knew. It struck her as she caught her image in the Kentshire mirror that leaned against the wall in Claire's office. The long red-gold hair belonged in a paddock or galloping across field or floating over a jump—places she no longer belonged—but not here, not on the exciting young designer of Beverly Hills!

"I was in Rinaldi's today. Normally, they are booked every day from dawn until dusk, but the fear of Olympics gridlock has driven the regulars out of the city, so the place is empty. I'm sure you could call right now and get an immediate appointment."

"You'd let me off early?"

"I think you've done a fair day's work!"

Allison had planned to think about it for a day or two, but . . . why not?

"I guess I will then."

"Let me just give you the keys to Bellemeade and the instructions for the alarm, so you can stop by on your way in tomorrow morning. Take a long, leisurely look at Bellemeade and *maybe* you'll have an office by the time you return."

Allison had forgotten about the curls! They had been there as her hair grew out after the neurosurgery, but she had been so eager to feel the weight of her mane again that she had hardly noticed.

Allison smiled as she watched soft curls appear where before there had been a long, sleek wall. Curls, suddenly freed, bouncy, somehow hopeful.

You're not a filly any more, Allison thought. Good-bye Bel Air's Ginger Lady.

"You like it," the stylist murmured as he noticed Allison's smile.

"Oh!" Allison had been intrigued, mesmerized, by what was happening to the suddenly freed short curls. She hadn't thought at all about how the new cut made her look.

"I know women who would kill for these curls, this look!" the stylist continued. "Very soft, very feminine, but still so *chic*. And, of course, with your eyes . . ."

Allison gazed at her suddenly huge jade green eyes and the soft red-gold frame around her face, and she had a sense of déjà vu—a recent memory of looking at an image of herself, a beautiful image, and appreciating the image before she realized it was *her*. When was that?

Allison remembered—the beautiful but sad picture Emily had taken of her at Meg's wedding—and that memory recalled something else that she had entirely forgotten. Emily was coming to her apartment at seven-thirty tonight to do the portrait for her parents" anniversary—a happy, exhilarated portrait of Allison after her first day at the Olympics.

Allison had forgotten, and that scared her because of those horrible months after her accident when she couldn't remember *anything*. But Allison swiftly calmed her fear. *It's been an eventful day and you* did *remember.*

Allison smiled away the brief frown and replaced worries about the past with plans for the future. Bellemeade was her top priority. The Chateau Bel Air would come later, and working with Roger Towne would be easy and fun.

And Bellemeade? Easy and fun? Perhaps not . . . but, somehow, Bellemeade was terribly important.

The interior design Allison would do for Bellemeade would be French, of course, something light and cheery and floral, with wonderful wallcoverings and drapes by Charles Barone and pastel silk chaises and delicately carved blond woods and Lalique crystal. Perhaps Emily had some lovely photographs of roses or lilacs or wildflowers.

I want to make Bellemeade very beautiful and very happy, Allison thought. The thought continued before she could stop it.

I want to make Bellemeade very beautiful and very happy for Peter . . . for sad, lonely, nice Peter Dalton.

Chapter 12

"The Dynasty Room has excellent food," Steve told Peter when he stopped the car on Hilgard Avenue in front of the Westwood Marquis. "I assume you can have it served in your suite. Are you sure you don't want company?"

"No, thank you, Steve."

"All right. I'll pick you up at seven tomorrow morning."

"Fine. Good night."

As Steve drove from the Westwood Marquis to his home on Mountain Drive in Beverly Hills, he wondered again if he had made a big mistake when he decided to produce *Love*.

Everything about this project was different, beginning with the remarkable concessions he had already made to the very serious, very quiet Peter Dalton.

The very serious, very quiet, very *decisive* Peter Dalton. Peter knew precisely what he wanted—demanded it—and Steve agreed. Peter wanted to choose the principal cast, especially Julia, himself; Peter wanted an agreement in writing that he wouldn't give interviews or make promotional appearances; and Peter wanted absolute approval of the final product with power to block release if he wasn't happy with it.

Steve had made those phenomenal concessions to Peter Dalton because *Love* was the best script he had ever read. Before making the concessions, Steve had done some checking on Peter—beyond the impressive credentials of three Tony awards, a Pulitzer Prize, and nonstop successes on Broadway. Steve spoke with actors and actresses Peter had directed—famous ones and not-so-famous ones—and with producers. And Steve was more than reassured.

Peter Dalton was the best. The actors and producers made the pronouncement swiftly and with great respect. Peter was tireless and energetic, they told Steve. A perfectionist, of course; but Peter had a remarkable ability to gently lure the best out of everyone. He was always calm, they said, always serious, never temperamental.

The men and women with whom Peter worked on Broadway smiled when they spoke of him—warm, thoughtful smiles, but not smiles of close friendship. No one seemed to know about Peter's private life—except that when he wasn't *in* the theater he *had* to be somewhere writing, because the remarkable plays kept appearing despite his full-time directing commitments.

A private man, a private genius, *and* a man who knew precisely what he wanted. Even for this trip, to choose the cast, Peter requested a hotel near the UCLA campus rather than the usual suite at the Beverly Hills Hotel.

Everything will be different with *Love*, Steve thought as he turned into the drive of his home in Beverly Hills. I hope it's worth it.

Peter poured himself a glass of bourbon from the full decanter in his suite at the Westwood Marquis and took a large swallow. In moments, he felt the effect of the bourbon on his exhausted mind, loosening thoughts, freeing memories.

Peter *was* exhausted. He hadn't slept last night, driven as always into wakefulness by his nightmares. Usually Peter spent those dark, wakeful hours writing, but last night he read the words he had written four years before, for Sara, and hadn't read since. And after, as dawn had lightened the summer sky, Peter wandered around the UCLA campus, restless, wondering what the hell he was doing.

Keeping your promise to Sara, he reminded himself.

Peter sighed, drank more bourbon, and thought uneasily about the exhausting day that had followed the sleepless night.

Steve had been so polite, so gracious, but Peter didn't need to be treated like royalty! He didn't need—or want—guest privileges at the Bel Air Hunt Club. And he certainly didn't need a house as splendid as Bellemeade.

Peter chided himself for not acting more impressed, more appreciative, more gracious. His tired mind had been so consumed with his own memories.

If Steve found Peter's lack of enthusiasm rude, he probably dismissed it as artistic temperament, or maybe simply jet lag. Steve had only one concern . . . that Peter deliver the movie of the decade. That was the bottom line. Everything else—the creature comforts, the gracious pleasantries—were fluff.

Steve didn't care if Peter was effusive about the Club or Los Angeles or Bellemeade, not really, but someone else *had* cared. Peter narrowed his dark eyes, frowning at the uneasy memory, thinking it was the one scene of the day he would do over if he could.

It was the scene at Elegance. The designer, Allison, had seemed so nice, so enthusiastic, so eager to make Bellemeade something he would like. Allison, whose coloring reminded Peter of the richenss of autumn—luxuriant jade, sunlit red, radiant gold—and whose merry eyes and full lips sent a wonderful, healthy promise of a bountiful harvest. Peter had dampened that marvelous spirit, made uncertainty flicker in the remarkable jade eyes.

He *should* have been more positive about Bellemeade, more appreciative, more polite, but the words hadn't come.

Peter was sorry, but it didn't matter. Nothing mattered, not where he lived, or if he caused a moment of disappointment in lovely jade eyes, or if they all thought he was arrogant and rude.

Peter was in Los Angeles for one reason . . . to keep his promise to Sara.

Peter had made three promises to Sara. One—this one—he would keep. The second he would try *again* to keep. And the third he would never keep.

Promises to keep. It was a line from Sara's favorite poem by Robert Frost. *The woods are lovely dark and deep/ But I have promises to keep/ And miles to go before I sleep.*

Sara's favorite poem, and what Peter's life had been since Sara's death; a desperate wish to sleep—to find lovely dark woods and fall asleep forever—but there were miles and promises, because of Sara.

Sara, Sara . . .

There had always been girls in Peter's life. From the moment his young, healthy body wanted girls, they were there. In junior high and high school, in Danbury, there were girls like him, girls with little money whose parents worked for the wealthy, privileged inhabitants of Greenwich. Sex was a free pleasure, a wonderful pleasure, a desperate, frantic pleasure in lives that had little joy. At Yale there were girls, smart girls who were going to be doctors and lawyers and Supreme Court Justices and President. Sex with the smart girls wasn't so frantic or so desperate, or so uninhibited.

Then Peter moved to New York, and there were the uptown girls with the go-to-hell looks and the incredible confidence. They had never met anyone like Peter. They loved his wildness, the dark, restless part that could never be tamed. And they loved the passion—the passion of a tormented poet—in his sensuous dark eyes. The uptown girls tried to tame the modern-day Heathcliff, knowing it was impossible but loving the exciting, provocative game.

There had always been girls in Peter's life, but there had never been love.

Then Joseph became ill, and Peter returned to Connecticut because his father had promised Sheila Adamson a rose garden. Peter met Sara and fell deeply, astonishingly in love. Neither Peter nor Sara had expected love in her lives, certainly not then, maybe not ever. But they fell in love quietly, confidently, joyously.

"I have diabetes," Sara told Peter a month after they met, two weeks after they first whispered *I love you.*

"What does that mean?" Peter asked gently. His eyes told Sara the question was, really, *What does that matter?*

Sara told Peter what it meant, what it had meant for her: living in a glass cage, being watched so carefully, a precious specimen on display until it became extinct. And what it would mean for them: She might not live very long, she couldn't have children.

Peter listened, fighting tears, making silent vows that he would never make Sara feel trapped, feeling contempt and anger toward the family who had imprisoned her, a family he disliked *already* because of their wealth and privilege.

But even before Peter and Sara were married, Peter realized how difficult it would be for him to keep those vows. He wanted to protect Sara—Peter even felt a begrudging closeness to the family who had only wanted the same thing—but he had promised to let her be free.

"I don't want you to have the vasectomy, Peter."

"Sara, I want to."

"But, Peter, what happens when they find the cure?" Sara's dark blue eyes glistened with hope and love.

"All right," he whispered gently, holding her close. Peter blinked back tears and wondered if it had anything to do with a cure, or if Sara simply wanted *him* to be able to have children, somebody, after . . . "Sara."

Sara pulled away and looked at him with serious eyes.

"Peter, I've never had any control over my life. Let me be responsible for this, please."

"For our birth control?"

"Yes."

"All right. But, Sara, I want to go with you for your regular appointments with Dr. Williams."

"No, Peter. Diabetes is my disease. It's part of me—a friendly rival—but I don't want it to be part of *us*. I'll take good care of myself, Peter, I promise. But . . ."

"But?"

"Someday, there may be decisions to make. You have to trust me to make them, Peter."

"You have to trust me to help you."

"I will. If I need help."

Peter touched Sara lovingly on her pale cheek, and Sara took his strong hand in her small one and whispered, "Make love to me, Peter. I'm not that fragile."

Peter and Sara lived in a private world of love. Peter became a brilliant star in the glittering galaxy of stars who lived in Manhattan. Some of the stars sought the lime-light, the dazzling galas, the ever-flowing champagne, the attention of adoring, interested media and fans; other stars, like Peter, preferred quiet, anonymous solitude. In Manhattan, both life-styles were allowed, both were respected.

"Are you a happy man?" Sara asked Peter as they celebrated their second wedding anniversary in their made-cheery-by-Sara apartment in Greenwich Village.

"My God, Sara, don't you know how happy I am?"

"I know." Sara did know, and she knew that Peter's life before their love hadn't been happy, and that was why he wrote what he did. "It's just that your plays are so—"

"Grim? Tragic? *Real?*"

"—tormented, dark, heart-stabbing," Sara added with a loving smile.

"Van Gogh painted flowers and he was *not* a happy man."

"Van Gogh painted tormented flowers."

"Ah."

"Look at William Shakespeare. Tragedies, comedies."

"You're comparing me to Shakespeare? You are so good for me!" Peter laughed softly and gazed lovingly into her eyes. "OK, Sara Dalton, someday I'll write a happy play, just for you, hearts that aren't broken and flowers that aren't tormented. But I can't do it yet. It would destroy my image as the author of darkness. OK?"

"OK. I love you, Peter."

"Oh, Sara, I love you, too."

Peter loved Sara too much and he fought that silent battle within himself. He wanted desperately to protect her, but he had promised to let her be free. Sara wanted to ice-skate, so Peter took her to Rockefeller Center and hand-in-hand they skated around the rink. Then Sara told him about a girl she had known at Greenwich Academy, a champion rider, and how she floated over jumps, so happy, so free. Peter held his breath and prayed that Sara would be safe as, together, they learned to horseback ride in Central Park. Sara *was* safe, and her pale cheeks were rosy and her eyes glowed with such happiness.

Peter kept his promise, loving Sara, letting her be free; and Sara kept hers, taking good care of herself, living a delicate balance.

They were going to live and love forever. Peter began to believe there would be a cure—or that maybe their love was the cure . . .

Then Sara got sick. Peter noticed the change—weakness, fatigue, strain in her lovely eyes—immediately.

"Darling, how are you?"

"Fine." Sara forced a loving smile, but her ocean-blue eyes misted briefly.

Peter knew Sara was dying, and battling with the horrible choices that might prolong her life but cause great pain.

"I love you, Sara."

"I love you, Peter. I need—"

"You need what?" he asked gently. *Anything, darling. My life, if I could give it to you.*

"—I need to know that you trust me to make the right decision."

"I trust you, but can't I help you, please?"

"You do help me, Peter."

Two weeks later Peter wondered if it had all been a mirage. Sara looked better again, *fine*, in fact; but that only lasted a few weeks. A new pattern emerged—good times and bad times—subtle changes Peter pretended not to see because he knew how hard Sara was fighting. But they both knew, and they held each other even tighter and touched each other more often—*almost always*.

Then, four months before Sara died, everything changed again. Sara looked wonderful, glowing, healthy, happy. Her energy soared and her eyes sparkled with joy and hope. She insisted on going, alone, to Rome, and Peter held his breath. But she would be with her brother, and even though Peter sensed that Rob was uneasy about him, he felt a kinship with the brother-in-law who loved Sara, and who shared the conflicting instincts to protect her and allow her to be free.

Sara returned from Rome, safe and happy; and then she spent a weekend in Greenwich making peace with her parents; and then Sara came home to spend the rest of her life with him.

"We're going to have a baby, Peter."

"Sara?"

"I'm three months pregnant."

"Honey." *No*. He should have had the vasectomy! But Sara had wanted to be in charge of that intimate part of their lives, and Peter had let her, and something had gone wrong. Peter looked at Sara's glowing blue eyes and her proud smile, and he realized it wasn't a mistake. "You got pregnant on purpose."

"Yes."

"But, Sara." The doctor had told them it was a great risk three years ago, and now . . . *No*.

"I want to have our baby, Peter." *I want you to have our baby.*

"I only want you, Sara. This is too much of a risk."

"Peter." Sara fought tears. *You can't have me much longer anyway, my darling.*

"Sara." Peter held her close to him and kissed her hair as tears spilled from his eyes.

After a few moments, Sara pulled away and gently kissed his tears.

"Peter! I'm goint to be fine and the baby's going to be fine. Our only problem will be that this place is too small for the four of us!" Sara cast a loving glance at Muffin, who observed the entire somber episode with sad, knowing eyes and now wagged her tail at the familiar lilt in Sara's voice.

Pretend with me, Peter, please.

"Would you like to move to a penthouse on Park Avenue?" *I'll pretend, darling. We'll make these the happiest days of our life, our love.*

"Perhaps." Sara smiled, then curled up quietly against him.

The next day, Peter arrived home from the theater with an announcement.

"I've decided to take the next few months off."

"*As You Like It* opens in two weeks," Sara countered quietly, but it was a weak protest and it told Peter what he feared.

"That's not as important as what I'm going to be doing." *I'm going to be spending every second I can with my beloved Sara.* "I've decided, by popular demand, to write a love story."

"Peter! A happy ending and everything?"

"Everything."

Peter and Sara spent their last two months together in their brownstone in Greenwich Village, loving each other so gently, so tenderly, each knowing that they were saying good-bye, each pretending that Sara and the baby would be fine, both *believing* it because their love was so strong, so magical, so joyous.

Peter finished *Love* in six weeks. He gave it to Sara to read, but she gave it back and asked him to read it aloud to her. *Love* was Peter's lovesong to his beloved Sara, a loving, joyous celebration of what she meant to him and of their forever love.

"I'm not Julia," Sara said softly when Peter told her that *she* was the magnificent heroine. Did Peter really believe she was that lovely, that loving, that generous?

"Yes, you are, darling."

"I'm not, but thank you."

"You are, and you're welcome." Peter kissed her tenderly.

"What are you going to do with the play, Peter?" Sara asked after a few gentle, loving moments.

"Read it to you, over and over, and to our baby—our *babies*—and to our grandchildren. By then, you and I should be able to do the parts by heart."

"I think the whole world needs to hear the words."

"You do?" Peter had known Sara would want him to produce *Love*. That was why, even though it was Peter's lovesong to Sara, the story bore no resemblance to their own. Julia was Sara—Sara's loveliness and innocence and courage—but only the people who loved Sara—Peter and the Adamsons—would see her in Julia.

"Yes. Peter, you have people standing in subzero weather hoping to get last minute seats for your plays about tormented souls. Don't you think it would be lovely to share this?"

"Maybe."

Two nights later, Sara awakened Peter at midnight.

"Peter, we have to go to the hospital."

"Sara?" Her voice was so calm it terrified him. Sara had made peace with what was going to happen. Peter hadn't. *Please, no.* "What is it?"

"I guess it's labor. And I'm bleeding. I already called an ambulance."

Peter took Sara's hand and didn't let go until after she died. The doctors and nurses swirled around, working frantically and in vain to save Sara and her baby. Peter and Sara were in the eye of the storm, gazing lovingly, whispering, oblivious to the chaos, lost in their own private world for a final time.

"Peter, promise me that you and Rob will be friends. Go to him, become his friend, please."

"All right, darling. The *three* of us will become best friends. Rob will be living in New York, too, remember?"

"You and Rob, *please*."

"I promise."

"And Peter?"

"Darling?"

"Promise to make a movie of *Love*."

"A movie? You want to go to Hollywood?"

"A movie, just the way you wrote it. A happy ending, OK?"

"OK," Peter smiled through tears at the slight twinkle in her blue eyes.

"And Peter?"

"Yes?"

"Find someone else to love. Find someone lovely with whom you can share your life."

I'm sharing my life—my love—with you!

"Sara . . ."

"Thank you for letting me be free." *Thank you for allowing me to make this choice. It's what I wanted.*

"Sara . . ."

"And Peter, thank you for loving me."

"Oh, Sara, I love you so much." *Don't leave me, please. I can't live without you.*

Peter almost didn't live without Sara. He felt himself slipping into the silent madness that had possessed his father in the months after his mother's death.

Silent madness.

The oppressive stillness was pierced by the telephone two weeks after Sara's death. Sara's attorneys wanted to talk to Peter about his enormous inheritance. Peter didn't even want to hear about it. He told the attorneys to give everything to the Juvenile Diabetes Foundation. Peter didn't want Sara's money; he wanted Sara. Even though Peter hated the disease that had stolen his wife from him, he knew Sara didn't hate it. Sara had been calm about her fate—her lifelong battle with her friendly rival—not bitter. The bitterness and rage belonged to Peter.

It was probably Muffin who saved Peter. In mechanical silence, Peter cared for Muffin, feeding her, walking her, nothing else. Peter took care of Muffin in the same distracted, silent way that Joseph Dalton had cared for his six-year-old son in the months following Anne's death.

Then, one day, Peter *looked* at Muffin. Muffin, who Sara had loved. Muffin, who had been the baby Peter and Sara would never have. Muffin, whose tail hadn't wagged and who lived in the somber silence, curled up in a corner, quietly bewildered by how her world had changed.

Peter's sad dark eyes met Muffin's bewildered ones. The sudden attention—a *look* from Peter—caused a hopeful, uncertain tilt to Muffin's blond head.

"Muffin," Peter whispered. He had fed her and walked her, but he hadn't spoken to her for almost six weeks.

Muffin's small blond tail moved a little, a tentative wag.

"Come here, Muffin."

She bounded joyfully, gratefully, across the room and into Peter's lap.

"Oh, Muffin, you miss her, too, don't you?" Peter's words ended with a sob and he cried into Muffin's soft fur. "You miss her, too."

That evening, with Muffin curled up in his lap, Peter began to write again, carving anguished words from his soul. The first play he wrote after Sara's death was *Say Good-bye*, for which he won the Pulitzer. Peter's entire life became his work, writing, directing, writing more. Peter directed during the day, and in the long, lonely nights, when he was driven into wakefulness by the nightmares that were his constant companions, he wrote.

Two years after Sara's death, Peter and Muffin moved from the bright, cheerful apartment in Greenwich Village, where there had been such love, to a small flat in Chelsea. The flat was dark and barren, and Peter did nothing to decorate it, but it had a garden and was a short walk to the theater district.

Peter wrote, Peter directed, Peter succeeded.

Peter survived.

Even though part of his heart—most of it!—wanted to join his beloved Sara in the dark, lovely woods and a forever sleep.

Peter survived.

He had promises to keep.

Promises to keep. In his suite at the Westwood Marquis, Peter filled his glass with bourbon for the third time.

I will make the movie, Sara.

I will find Rob and try to become his friend—again. Peter had tried, two years before, when his brother-in-law was still in New York, but Rob had refused to take his calls.

But the third promise—*find someone else to love*—could never happen. Peter didn't even want it to.

That promise, darling Sara, I can never keep.

Chapter 13

"I really love your hair!" It was the third time Winter had made that pronouncement during the short drive from Holman Avenue to Bel Air. Winter had worried that she wouldn't like Allison's short hair. She remembered the red-gold curls that had appeared, finally, after Allison's operation, and the huge, bewildered jade-green eyes that had stared from beneath the curls. Allison had been so haunted then. Winter was afraid the short hair would recall that awful time.

But Allison's eyes weren't bewildered, and the whole look was beautiful and confident and full of hope. Allison's were the eyes of a champion again, envisioning new golden trophies and blue satin ribbons, something that made Allison look wonderful.

"Thank you," Allison laughed. "I like it, too."

"So, we're heading for Bel Air. Why?"

"We have to take a look at my first official project."

"You're doing a house in Bel Air? I'm impressed!"

"Not just a house, Winter, *Bellemeade*."

"You're kidding. How exciting!"

"How scarcy."

Allison turned off Perugia onto the cobblestone drive that swept to the French Country cottage.

"I've always loved this place." Winter smiled. "So romantic, so charming."

"Have you ever been inside?"

"No. I can't wait."

As Allison and Winter wandered from room to room in Bellemeade, Winter's enthusiasm waned and Allison's crescendoed.

"It's dark and dank and grim," Winter whispered.

"But the spaces are wonderful! And the cathedral ceilings and circular staircase and marble fireplaces and hardwood floors. And look at the windows,

Winter! Done right, Bellemeade can be very lovely." Allison frowned. "Done right *and* in record time. Everything has to be ready by November thirtieth."

When Allison finished explaining the reason for the rush, because Peter Dalton was arriving, Winter made a quiet confession.

"I wasn't going to tell you this until it was all over, Allison. I thought I'd just tell you *after* where I had placed—one hundredth runner-up, or one thousandth, whatever—but . . . I answered the casting call for *Love*."

"You did? And?"

"And I still don't know. I've been called back three times, and last Friday they did a screen test."

"That's terrific, isn't it?"

"I guess. I think I was the only unknown actress to get a screen test. The well-known actresses were screen-tested, too. Apparently, Peter Dalton doesn't spend a lot of time at the movies. He doesn't even know the big stars."

"So that gives you an equal chance."

"Maybe." Winter smiled. "Actually, I feel that I have an unfair advantage. When I read the scenes, I just pretend I'm talking to Mark."

"Is it really the love story of the decade?" Allison asked.

"Me and Mark?"

"I know you and Mark are. I meant *Love*."

"Probably. I've only read the parts of scenes they've given me, not the entire script. But the parts I've read are stunning, breathtakingly beautiful."

"When do you read the entire script?"

"I *could* read it now. There are plenty of copies floating around, but it seems presumptuous. If they're interested in me, they'll give me a copy of the script. Peter Dalton is supposed to be in town this week looking at the screen tests, so we'll see."

Allison didn't tell Winter she had met Peter. Winter would want to hear what Peter was like, and Allison really didn't know what to say.

Peter and Steve moved foreard in their chairs at the same moment, as if pulled by a powerful magnet. The magnet was on the screen, a lovely, bewitching woman with violet eyes and ivory skin and such softness when she spoke of love.

"My God," Steve whispered.

Peter simply nodded. At last they had found Julia.

It was Friday afternoon. Peter and Steve had spent the past four days viewing the screen tests. Now the search was over.

"Who is she?" Peter asked. He assumed she was a well-known star, unknown, as they all were, only to him.

"I have no idea."

Steve turned on the screening room lights from the control panel in the center of the room, looked through the stack of folders on the table, and removed the one with the number that corresponded to the number on the test. As Steve started to open it, reminded himself that *Peter* had absolute control over casting, suppressed his curiosity and handed the folder to Peter.

"It looks like no acting experience," Peter said as he scanned the standard bio sheet prepared by the casting staff. Under previous performances was written *None*.

Christ, Steve swore silently. It was really amteur night at the movies. The best goddamned script *ever*, perhaps Broadway's bes director, but theater was theater and film was film. A novice film director was worrisome enough, but an unknown inexperienced actress, too? "You mean no film experience."

"No. No acting experience. No, wait," Peter said as he turned to Winter's brief résumé attached to the bio sheet. Peter smiled. "Here she has written "a few plays in high school," followed by two exclamation points and a smiling face."

"A smiling face? Great. What's her name?"

"Winter Carlyle."

Steve's frown turned upside down. Winter Carlyle. Maybe she didn't have the acting experience, but she sure as hell had the genes.

Winter Carlyle. Steve's mind searched for a memory of her. He had a recent memory; a somber memory of black hair, a black dress, a black veil. Steve hadn't gotten close enough at Jacqueline's funeral to see the face beneath the veil. He had that recent memory, along with a distant one. How long ago had it been? Ten years . . . no, twelve, before he met his wife. He and Jacqueline were doing *The Last Time* together, she as actress, he as director; and they had made more than the movie. For three wonderful months they had been in . . . in *passion*, at least. Steve had seen Jacqueline's daughter only once, from a distance, but he remembered huge, shy violet eyes.

What a beautiful woman that little girl had become! Beautiful like her mother, with Jacqueline's incredible talent. Steve wondered what else Winter had inherited from her mother.

"She's the daughter of Jacqueline Winter and Lawrence Carlyle," Steve told Peter. Then Steve turned to the casting director, who sat in smug silence two rows back. Four days ago she had told Steve that there was a promising unknown, but he had insisted—logically—that they begin with the screen tests of Michelle and Madolyn and Paula and Rachel and all the other talented, established actresses who wanted to be Julia. "Did you know that? Did you know who she was?"

"No," the casting director replied. "She never said a word. She was quiet, serious, not the least bit pushy. I don't even think she has a copy of the script."

"Well, let's get one to her," Steve said. "And a contract to her agent. We should probably give them the weekend."

Steve looked at Peter. He knew Peter was eager to get back to New York. Peter had interrupted rehearsals of his new play, *Shadows of the Mind*, to cast *Love*.

"If you like, Peter, assuming we can get it set with Winter and her agent, we can meet for coffee at the Garden Terrace at the Marquis Monday morning, instead of for martinis at the Polo Lounge Monday afternoon." *Why not?* Steve thought. Everything was different about this project. Why not seal the deal over black coffee instead of dry martinis? "Then, if Winter's on board and you trust me to decide which of the five actors we've already lined up reads best with her, you'll be back in New Your Monday night."

"That would be fine." Peter looked again at Winter's résumé. "I don't see an agent's name listed."

"Really? Then we'll just send everything directly to Winter Carlyle."

Mark let himself into Winter's apartment at five-thirty Sunday afternoon. He had been on call Saturday night at the VA. Winter was expecting him, but she didn't hear him come in. Mark found her, sitting on her bed huddled over the script, crying.

"Darling." Mark kissed her lovely damp eyes. In the past two months there had been tears—sad tears and happy ones—flowing without shame from emotions that had been hidden for a lifetime. "This is what I call a sodden heap."

"Hi." Winter smiled through her tears. "This is at least the fifteenth time I've read this and it still makes me cry."

"Is it sad? I thought it was supposed to be happy."

"It is happy." *It reminds me of us.* "I don't know if I can even say these beautiful words without crying, much less say them the way they deserve to be said."

"That good?"

"Yes. This motion picture has to be painted with the most delicate brush in the world and every tiny stroke has to be perfect."

"But you want to try?"

"Yes, I want to try. I want to paint a perfect Julia if I can." Winter added quietly. "And if I don't have to do love scenes."

"Oh, Winter, I should never have mentioned that."

"Yes, you should have." Winter curled up close to Muffin and whispered softly, "I'm going to tell them, over coffee at the Marquis, no nudity."

Winter arrived at the Garden Terrace early, ordered black coffee, and waited. She spent the anxious moments before Steve and Peter were due to arrive rehearsing what she would say, wondering for the hundredth time if she should have asked attorney-agent-shark Elaina Kingsley to represent her, and hoping she would not be disappointed with Peter Dalton.

Winter hoped Peter Dalton wouldn't be wearing an open-collared, vivid print shirt, heavy gold chains, a smug sleazy-sexual smile, and dark glasses. Winter didn't want Peter Dalton to be a commercial love guru, a smooth savvy writer who wrote the beautiful words only to pluck heartstrings and put mega-dollars in his bank account.

Winter wanted Peter Dalton to look like . . .

. . . the dark, handsome, serious man who was approaching her table with a soft smile and sensitive dark brown eyes. Someone, like her, who knew about love.

"Winter? I'm Peter Dalton."

"Hi."

Steve Gannon was with Peter. Steve introduced himself, and he and Peter sat down. After they ordered coffee, Steve got right to business.

"Winter, have you read the script?"

"Yes." Winter smiled at Peter and said softly, "It's really wonderful. I would very much like the part."

"Then this is easy," Steve said. "We plan to start filming in early January, wrap by late March, and release by August. That's a tight schedule, lots of hard work, maybe seven days a week, long hours every day."

"*Love* will be filmed entirely in Los Angeles?" Winter asked. That was what she had read in Vanessa's column, but Winter wanted to be sure. She didn't want the part if it meant being away from Mark. They would be apart, because of his clerkships in Boston, but she would visit him at Christmas, as soon as her Autumn classes at UCLA were over. Then, in January, she would be so busy with *Love* that Mark's second month in Boston would go quickly.

"Yes, entirely in LA." Steve paused. "Are we waiting for your agent?"

"No."

"Did you take a look at the contract? It's all quite standard, of course, but I want to make sure that you understand."

"I did look at it." Winter had spent three hours Saturday afternoon at the mansion, carefully comparing the contract that had arrived by courier Friday afternoon with Jacqueline's, which were filed, alphabetically by movie title, in an oak cabinet in the library.

"And?"

"There are two problems." *Three*, Winter thought, if you count the fact that my heart is about to jump out of my chest. *Come on, Winter, let's see some acting here*.

"Oh?"

Winter smiled sweetly, as if the problems were very minor, before she spoke. "No nudity."

"*What?*"

"And no love scenes that are . . . suggestive. Kissing is all right, but nothing else."

"Winter, we don't want anything pornographic, but there have to be love scenes. There have to be bare breasts and—"

"Then I can't do it."

"Virtually every actress in Hollywood . . ." Steve started naming names.

"Then you sould ask one of them to be Julia."

Winter stared bravely at Steve, but she turned when she heard a soft laugh from Peter.

"It's all right, Steve," Peter said.

"What's all right?"

"There doesn't have to be nudity."

"Christ," Steve breathed, relenting because he had to, because Peter had artistic control. "I can just see this movie coming out with a G-rating."

"I don't have a problem with love being for general audiences," Peter said quietly.

"OK." Steve sighed heavily, for the record. "What's the other problem, Winter?"

"I would like a piece of the movie."

Steve gazed at Winter for a stunned moment, then laughed. "Just when I was wondering if you were really Jacqueline's daughter."

Jacqueline Winter had never had a problem with suggestive love scenes—on or off screen—or nudity, and she had always demanded a piece of the movie. Of course, that was a demand Jacqueline could make. As an established actress, it was standard for her to receive a percent of the profits. But for an unknown actress!

"Did you know my mother?"

"Of course." Steve saw the sudden sadness in Winter's eyes and said gently, honestly, "I was very sorry about her death."

"Do you know my father?"

"Yes. Not very well. I see him at Cannes every year or two. I *would* see him at the Academy Awards, except he never bothers to come to pick up his Oscars."

The issue of Lawrence Carlyle—if it was an issue—had worried Steve ever since he learned he was about to cast Winter in *Love*. Steve didn't know the real details of the swift divorce of Jacqueline Winter and Lawrence Carlyle—no one seemed to know; but, even years later when Steve and Jacqueline had had their affair, Jacqueline had still spoken of Lawrence with great bitterness. If Winter shared Jacqueline's bitterness, the press would go crazy, searching for skeletons, exploring the estrangement of the famous director father and his destined-to-be-famous actress daughter.

"Do *you* know him?" Steve asked Winter after a moment.

"No. He left when I was one. I don't remember him."

"And you haven't seen him since?"

"No."

"Do you want to?"

"No."

This was bad; very, *very* bad. The press would have a field day. If *Love* and Winter Carlyle were the sensations Steve expected them to be, the issue of Lawrence and Winter Carlyle would have to be dealt with, head-on, long before the Academy Award nominations were announced.

Of course, Steve thought wryly, without breasts or erotic love scenes, and with a novice actress and director, he probably had nothing to worry about . . . except having paid a huge amount of money for the flop of the year!

"We'll give you a piece of the movie," Steve sighed finally. *Why not?* "How much did you have in mind?"

Allison looked at the photographs on the desk of her recently completed cubicle at Elegance and thought, smiling, *Emily Rousseau, you are so talented!*

Emily had managed more trick photography with her—the portrait she took the night Allison had gotten her hair cut was wonderful, radiant, happy—and a week later, at Allison's request, Emily had provided her with a selection of magnificent photographs of flowers, sunsets, mons, and the sea.

Allison finally chose six of Emily's breathtaking nature shots to have enlarged, signed by Emily, and framed for the walls of Bellemeade. No matter what else, Peter Dalton would have six lovely, peaceful photographs to look at. No matter what else . . .

Allison rested her hand on the telephone on her desk before dialing. In the past three weeks she had gotten so good—so *bold*—at using the phone. Allison had called Rob Adamson to thank him for referring Roger, and that had felt easy and comfortable; and she had laughingly told Roger, when he called long distance with ideas for the Chateau Bel Air, that she couldn't think about his hotel *yet* because of Bellemeade; and she had firmly and decisively placed rush orders—insisting on guarantees of delivery much sooner than was their *usual* policy—with Lalique and Charles Barone and McGuire and Stiffel.

Allison was becoming an expert at using the phone.

So dial, she told herself.

"Brentwood Productions," a voice answered on the third ring.

"This is Allison Fitzgerald calling for Steve Gannon."

"Just one moment please."

Steve answered promptly and with a slight tease.

"Allison? You want more money after only three weeks on the job?"

"Hello, Steve. No, I just have a silly question."

"Shoot."

"Do you know what kind of dog Peter has? What size?"

"Are you building a dog Bellemeade to match?"

"Not exactly." Just pillows, cozy places to curl up, custom-made to match the bedspread in the master bedroom, the cheery curtains in the kitchen, the expensive sofa near the marble fireplace in the living room. Frivolous, elegant, silly.

"It's a cocker spaniel. I know that because my daughter wants one."

"Thank you." Not a Doberman, Claire, Allison thought with a smile. Just a nice, lovable cocker spaniel.

"Anything else, Allison? More money?"

"No, thank you, Steve. Not yet."

Chapter 14

Donald Alexander Fullerton died of leukemia on the seventh of September. Mark watched him die. Donald's death marked the end of a courageous battle; a war fought with everything medical science had to offer and the

gallant spiritual weapons of a dying young man.

Donald was twenty-nine, Mark's age. Donald's wife, Mary Anne, was twenty-seven and pregnant. Mark had been on the Hematology-Oncology inpatient service at UCLA for seven days. Donald had been Mark's patient. Mark had gotten to know Donald and Mary Anne very well.

And now it was over. A life ended after twenty-nine years. *Why?*

Mark held Mary Anne Fullerton for a long time after Donald died. Then Mary Anne's family led her away, to begin the rest of her life. Mark took care of the paperwork, the red tape of death, made rounds on his other patients, signed out to the on-call team, and walked out of the hospital into the glaring autumn sun. It was late afternoon, almost evening, but the sun was still too bright, too hot, too brilliant on a day that was filled with so much sadness.

Mark walked to his apartment on Manning and quickly changed into his jogging clothes.

He had to go to the beach and run, until the physical ache matched the emotional one, until the salty tears were dry, until the powerful urge to scream with helpless rage was exhausted.

Then Mark could go to Winter.

This was the solitary voyage of medicine; impossible to articulate, unfair to share.

Since July, Mark and Winter had virtually lived together in her apartment, but he kept his apartment for necessary sleep and necessary privacy.

Necessary sleep. Mark would call Winter just before he left the hospital, after he had been up all night and it was eleven the next night and he *had* to sleep because it would start again the next day.

"I'm going to my apartment to take a long hot shower and collapse into bed," he would say.

"OK."

"I'll call you tomorrow."

"OK."

Winter never pushed or pouted or sulked. Mark could have said good night then but he didn't want to, because he had been thinking about her, missing the soft promise of her voice, feeling warm and alive as memories of her came to him.

"How was your day, Winter?" he would ask, not wanting to say good night.

And they would talk. And thirty minutes later, still at the hospital, Mark would whisper reluctantly that he should go. And Winter would say, so softly, "You could take a shower here, Mark, and collapse."

Mark didn't use his apartment for necessary sleep. He slept, always, with Winter.

Necessary privacy. The past two and a half months had been amazingly free of the kind of tragedy that had befaller Donald and Mary Anne. Until today, Mark hadn't felt the need to stay away from Winter until his emotions were spent.

And now . . . It wasn't fair to take the sadness, or his troubled silence, home to her. *Was it?*

Mark drove down Westwood Boulevard to Wilshire. He *should* have turned right on Wilshire, toward the ocean. But Mark continued on Westwood and in a few blocks turned left onto Holman.

Mark let himself in the main security door but knocked when he reached Winter's third-floor apartment. He had a key, of course, but she wasn't expecting him.

"Hi. You didn't have to knock." Winter smiled and searched the troubled
blue eyes.

"Come jogging with me, Winter."

"Jogging? *Moi?*"

Winter never exercised, but her body was sleek and slim and her energy seemed limitless. She bounded up stairs without breathlessness, and her gait was gazelle-graceful and buoyant. Mark imagined the muscles beneath the beautiful skin, like coiled springs of a black panther, naturally strong and fit and healthy.

"Someday, Winter . . ."

"Someday, I will fall victim to the design flaws, just like every other woman on earth."

"Design flaws?"

"Breasts that can't forever defy the laws of gravity. Cellulite—the ultimate symbol of planned obsolescence!—appearing out of nowhere. Why are you smiling?" Winter was glad the blue eyes smiled a little, but they were still *so* troubled.

"You."

"I'm not impressed that jogging changes anything, and that's based on years of observing the results on the jogging path on San Vicente. However, I *will* go jogging to be with you."

Mark sat on the bed while Winter disappeared into her closet. When she reappeared, she was wearing a clinging gold tank top and peacock-blue nylon shorts—both emblazoned UCLA—and tennis shoes.

Winter twirled a model's twirl and asked, "How do I look?"

"I see no design flaws."

"I think I'd better braid my hair." Winter stood in front of the dresser mirror, her back to Mark. As she braided her long black hair, she caught glimpses of his thoughtful expression in the mirror.

Mark looked at Winter's perfect body and let his thoughts drift to a distant time . . . Winter with strands of white in her coal-black hair; Winter with wrinkles around her eyes from years of laughter; Winter with pink-white marbled lines on her abdomen from the children she had borne; Winter with breasts that fell from life and nursing.

It was a lovely image because Mark was there, sitting on their bed, watching her braid her black and silver hair, waiting for her sparkling violet eyes to look at him again. Mark was there, in that distant scene, and it meant that *they* had survived. They were together, and their magnificent love had history and age and wonderful, comfortable wrinkles.

Mark smiled, but it was a wobbly smile. His own happy vision was clouded by the memory of Donald and Mary Anne, whose forever love was over.

"Is there a price tag on that thought?" Winter asked gently as she turned.

"No. It's not for sale. The investment is much too speculative." Mark saw a flicker of hurt in Winter's eyes and added gently, "OK, for *free*, I will tell you I was thinking how lovely you will look with cellulite."

"Good, then that settles it. I will set a leisurely pace along the sand, possibly in the water, and you can jog in circles around me, or to the horizon and back if you want." Winter took a broad-rimmed straw hat from her dresser. "Shall we go?"

She led the way to the apartment door. Winter turned to face Mark before she opened it.

"Something terribly sad happened at the hospital today, didn't it, Mark?"

"Yes."

"Will you tell me?"

Mark wrapped his arms around her, held her close, and whispered softly, "Yes, darling, I will."

Allison was on the phone when Winter appeared in Elegance just before noon on the twelfth of September. She smiled and gestured for Winter to come into her cluttered cubicle.

"You are guaranteeing delivery by November fifteenth. Will you please confirm that in writing? Yes, I'm serious. Good. Fine. Thank you."

"You're beginning to sound like an attorney," Winter observed when the conversation ended.

"I have to. Who knows if it will make any difference? The furniture and chandeliers and drapes and rugs will arrive when they arrive."

"How is Bellemeade going?"

"*I'm* on schedule. I just hope everyone else is. How are you? Shopping, I see."

"I just wanted to see what the Rodeo Collection had for its fall line of campus casuals."

"They had some things." Allison smiled at the bulging sacks with designer labels that Winter had set on top of the stacks of sample books in her office.

"Some. I'm not sure what the well-dressed special student is wearing this fall. I guess I'll find out on Monday. So, can you *do lunch* today?"

"I'd better not."

"OK. I really stopped to say that Mark and I would like to take you to dinner Friday night."

"That's not necessary, Winter!"

"We were thinking Spago Friday night, and then you and I could have dinner—Mark's on call—at the Club Saturday."

"Winter." Allison smiled. "You and my parents. They suggested dinner both nights, too, although not at the actual sites of the rehearsal dinner and wedding that aren't to be."

"I thought that was a nice touch," Winter replied. "You're the one who believes in getting back on the horse no matter how hard the fall."

"Winter, I *chose* not to marry Dan and it was the right decision. I'm not going to spend this weekend moping around, wishing I was getting married."

"That's good, but Mark and I still would like to have dinner with you Friday."

"Why don't you and Mark have dinner with me and my parents?"

"We'd love it."

"I *am* selecting china, silver, crystal, and linens this week," Allison said after a moment.

"For what?"

"For Bellemeade. The china's easy—Minton's *Bellemeade*—but I haven't decided yet about the rest. I'm going to spend Saturday morning at Pratesi, Geary's, Neiman-Marcus. Would you like to help?"

"Sure. And shall we plan to have a memorial dinner at the Club Saturday night?"

"I'm having dinner with Emily."

Winter waited, trying to interpret Allison's hesitance. Finally, with a laugh, Winter asked, "So? May I join you?"

"Of course, Winter." Allison frowned slightly.

"But?"

"But Emily and I were planning to eat in Westwood—Alice's, The Old World, maybe the Acapulco. I'm not sure Emily has clothes that would be right for dinner at the Club. It might be awkward for her."

"Westwood's fine, jeans are fine," Winter replied swiftly, but her reassurance didn't erase the worry in Allison's eyes. "Now what?"

"Emily begins working at *Portrait* on Monday. On Tuesday, she leaves for her first assignment—in Hong Kong."

"So you and Emily were planning to see *Hong Kong*, Lawrence Carlyle's latest blockbuster."

"I'm sure Emily really doesn't care."

"No, Allison, I would like to see *Hong Kong*. I'll probably be required to see a number of the great Lawrence Carlyle's movies for my Contemporary Film seminar. It's fine, really."

"Are you sure?" Allison didn't know why Winter hated the father she had never known, but the bitterness had appeared in her friend's voice—where before there had been such pride—in the months after Jacqueline's death.

"I'm sure." Winter stood up to leave. "Jeans Saturday night, Allison, but I plan to be *very* dazzling for dinner Friday."

After Winter left, Allison thought about her best friend. She chided herself for hesitating, even for a moment, before telling Winter her concern that Emily might feel uncomfortable about dinner at the Bel Air Hunt Club. As if Allison didn't know that Winter's reaction would be one of sympathy and compassion!

Winter didn't cut a millimeter of slack for the Elaina Kingsleys of the world, but for someone like timid Emily Rousseau—someone who might be ridiculed for how she looked—Winter was as protective as a mother bear.

Allison smiled softly as she thought about Winter.

What a friend Winter had been when Allison needed her the most . . .

Winter talked to Allison—all day, every day—as her friend lay in a coma. Allison couldn't speak to answer, but she heard Winter's words and her mind and spirit answered, fighting even harder.

Sometimes Winter scolded her, and Allison heard Winter's heart-stopping fear, "Allison Fitzgerald, don't you *dare* die! Don't you dare. I will never forgive you if you die."

And sometimes Winter whispered softly, lovingly, and Allison heard the tears, "I love you, Allison. You're my best friend, my *sister*. Don't leave me, please."

When Allison finally awakened from her coma, it was still just the beginning of the nightmare. Now Allison could *see* the fear in the eyes of her beloved parents. Sean and Patricia's eyes would fill with fresh tears as they patiently gave their precious daughter words to remember and she couldn't. At first, Allison didn't understand the game, or her parents" incredible sadness when she couldn't play. But, as she improved, Allison *knew* that she couldn't remember, and she, too, was filled with bewildered terror.

When Sean and Patricia had to leave the room because they couldn't stop their tears, it was Winter who stayed, loving and scolding.

"Allison, it's almost Christmas. Do you know the most wonderful gift you could give your parents? Your memory. Now pay attention." Winter shook a slender ivory finger at her friend, just as she had waved a tiny finger at the greedy koi years before. "Pay attention and remember these three things, OK? Candy canes . . . tinsel . . . a partridge in a pear tree."

On Christmas Eve, three days later, Allison whispered, "Winter?"

"Yes?"

"Is this right? Candy canes . . . tinsel . . . a partridge . . ."

Winter was there, helping Allison fight to awaken from the coma, then helping her fight to remember. And Winter was there, too, during the long, painful months of recovery. Winter helped Allison learn to read again, and write, and talk and walk.

"Don't walk if it hurts, Allison."

It always hurts, Winter. It always will. If I let the pain become an obstacle, I will never walk. I have to get beyond the pain.

It was then that Allison explained to Winter how champion riders urged their horses, and themselves, over walls and fences that seemed too high and too wide and too dangerous to ever clear.

"If you focus on the jump that's right in front of you, Winter, you'll never get over it. So you think about what's *beyond* the jump, on the other side, and you make *that* a place you want to be. That way, when you jump, you're flying from where you are to where you want to be."

With the words she and her riding friends used when *they* talked about it, Allison explained to Winter how champions soared over the impossibly high jumps. Allison didn't tell Winter her own private wording: *You send your dreams over the jump first, then simply follow after them.*

Allison didn't know—and never would know—why on that fateful September day when she joyfully sent her dreams ahead of her over the green and white railed fence *she* had been unable to follow.

Now Allison had unwittingly put an imposing obstacle—*Hong Kong*—in front of her dear friend. Could Winter find a way to soar over this hazardous jump? Was there a place *beyond*, a place of dreams, where Winter wanted to be? Allison didn't know, and it worried her.

"Are you sure this is OK, Winter?" Allison asked as she, Winter, and Emily approached the brightly lighted marquee of the Odeon Theater on Lindbrook Avenue in Westwood on Saturday afternoon. Allison had asked the same question the evening before, at the wonderful dinner with her parents, Winter, and Mark, and earlier today as she and Winter looked at silver, crystal, and linens in the elegant shops of Beverly Hills.

"It's *fine*," Winter murmured. She smiled bravely, first at Allison, then at Emily. But Emily looked confused. Apparently, Allison hadn't told her about Winter's connection to *Hong Kong*.

By way of explanation, Winter silently led them to one of the huge glassed-in posters that advertised *Hong Kong*. The poster was a vivid collage of scenes from the movie: the Hong Kong skyline, quaint junks in the harbor, glittering statues of jade, the famous actor and actress entwined in a passionate embrace. The names of the stars were in large teal-blue letters, but one name was even larger, because he was even bigger box office: Lawrence Carlyle.

Winter tapped her finger on the glass over his name and whispered quietly, "Daddy." After a moment, she turned to Emily and embellished unnecessarily, "We're not very close."

"We don't have to see *Hong Kong*, Winter," Emily replied swiftly. "Why don't we see what's playing at the Bruin or the National or the Westwood Village?"

"No, Emily, really. I want to see *Hong Kong*. You just need to be aware of the situation in case I do something crazy."

"Such as?" Allison asked.

"I don't know." Winter laughed uneasily. "I might hurl Milk Duds at the screen, something embarrassing like that. Allison, don't worry! It's not as though the great Lawrence Carlyle himself is going to be in the theater."

Allison, Emily, and Winter had the Odeon Theater almost to themselves. They had chosen a matinee to be certain they could get seats, but this was Westwood on the Saturday before UCLA began its Autumn Quarter. The students had arrived and were busy patrolling the dormitories, meeting roommates, sharing the highlights of their life stories, *flirting*. Not even the best movie of 1984 could entice the undergraduates away from those provocative endeavors.

After they selected their seats, Emily disappeared without a word. When she returned, five minutes later, she was carrying three very large, very *expensive* boxes of Milk Duds.

Emily cast a questioning smile at Winter as she handed her one of the boxes. "I just want you to know, Winter, that if you want to throw Milk Duds, I'm with you all the way."

"Me, too," Allison agreed. "Hand me my ammunition, please."

"Thank you, Emily," Winter whispered softly, quite moved by Emily's shy, thoughtful support. "Thank you."

Ten minutes into *Hong Kong*, Winter announced quietly, "It's safe to eat your Milk Duds, ladies. I'm OK."

Winter wasn't OK, not really. She clutched her unopened box of Milk Duds tightly, squishing the candy inside.

Winter had been wrong when she'd said it wasn't as if the great Lawrence Carlyle himself would be in the theater! Lawrence Carlyle *was* here, in the only way Winter had ever known him, in the way she had grown to love him, through the sensitive genius of his movies. Lawrence Carlyle, the wonderful, talented artist who painted magnificent motion pictures.

Winter *felt* the movie more than she saw it, tossed by emotions and memories, finally calming the storm with a fantasy.

Someday—a million moments from now—she would meet Lawrence Carlyle. It might be on the white-sand-dotted-with-pink-umbrellas beach at Cannes, or in the Dorothy Chandler Pavilion on Academy Award night, or afterwards at Swifty Lazar's gala winner's party at Spago.

Mark would be there, and Allison, and even Emily. Winter smiled as she envisioned Emily's role in the fantasy. Emily would have her camera, of course, to capture Lawrence's bittersweet expression of great love for the daughter he had abandoned and deep regret for all the lost years. Emily would have her camera, but stuffed into the back pocket of her baggy jeans would be a huge box of Milk Duds just in case.

As Allison watched *Hong Kong*, she cast careful glances at Winter. Despite the brave announcement that she was fine, Allison sensed Winter's tension and saw the strain on her friend's beautiful face. Allison was just about to suggest—insist—that they leave, but when she glanced at Winter again, the tension had vanished. Winter's lips curled into a soft smile and her violet eyes gazed dreamily at a lovely distant vision.

Somehow, Allison realized with relief, Winter has found a way to get beyond this enormous hurdle.

After the movie, Allison, Winter, and Emily walked around the corner to the Acapulco Restaurant.

"Would you like margaritas?" the waitress asked.

"A Diet Pepsi for me, please," Winter said. Winter drank champagne now, a little, but only with Mark.

"That sounds good," Allison agreed. The sophisticated tests done at UCLA showed that Allison still had altered depth perception from the accident. That was why the doctors had told her it would be too dangerous for her to jump again, and that was why Allison never had anything to drink when she was driving.

"Diet Pepsi for me, too," Emily said. Emily hadn't had a drop of alcohol or any other drug since Mick had left on July Fourth; and it felt good, *better.* Mick had returned and that was good, too, because he had found someone new and didn't want Emily anymore.

When the Diet Pepsis arrived, Winter raised her glass and smiled.

"Here we are, each on the brink of our new careers, and it's exciting and scary, is it not?" Winter's violet eyes sparkled. More exciting than scary!

"Yes."

"Absolutely."

"So, we should make toasts to us and our tremendous success, shouldn't we?" Winter smiled and turned to Emily. "To Emily, and her great success with *Portrait.*"

"Thank you," Emily whispered as the three glasses clinked.

"To Allison," Winter continued, "and her great success with Bellemeade."

After the glasses clinked again, Winter gave a soft smile and looked at Allison. Allison had to make the toast to her best friend, but Winter didn't need to tell her what to say. There was that *one perfect word*, the word that described what Winter's life had become since Mark and the word that was the title of the magnificent movie in which she would star.

Allison knew what to say.

"And to Winter, and her great success with *Love.*"

Part Two

Chapter 15

BEL AIR, CALIFORNIA
NOVEMBER 1984

"Allison, this is unbelievable," Steve raved as he, Allison, and Claire walked from magnificent room to magnificent room. It was noon on the thirtieth of November. The new interior design for Bellemeade had been finished exactly on time. "Claire, you knew."

"Of course!" Claire beamed. She had steadfastly forbidden Steve see Bellemeade until everything was done. Claire knew Steve would be thrilled, and she knew, too, that the triumph was all Allison's. Claire had been there, the safety net beneath the high-wire, but Allison's pure gold instincts hadn't even wobbled. "A masterpiece."

"It really is," Steve agreed.

"I'm glad you like it, Steve," Allison murmured without much energy.

Allison was exhausted. How many visits had she made to Bellemeade, just to see if the morning sun—and afternoon and evening—caressed the pastel fabrics as she had imagined? How many times had she travelled up and down the elegant circular staircase that swept to the spectacular master suite? How many phone calls had she made, reminders, *threats?*

As Allison looked at the finished product now, her exhausted mind remembered the battles. The wallpaper in the kitchen hadn't been hung perfectly and Allison had insisted that it be done again. She had driven to the warehouse herself to help locate the mysteriously misplaced fabric for the dining room chairs. The first hand-painted trousseau trunk from France had been cracked and the replacement had arrived only yesterday.

Allison wasn't like a homeowner who had done the work herself and knew, uneasily, where the flaws were hidden. It was just the opposite: *Allison knew there were no flaws in Bellemeade.* Allison hadn't permitted flaws, even though the cost to her was high. Now her exhausted mind cried for sleep and her hip sent hot, angry, relentless messages of pain.

It was nice, at least, that Steve was pleased.

"I'm going to call Paige the second I get back to my office," Steve said.

"It does have *Architectural Digest* written all over it, doesn't it?" Claire smiled knowingly.

"I am also going to call my wife. She'll either want us to move in here after Peter leaves or—what Claire has been pushing for for years—she'll want our house completely redone. Allison, are you available?"

Allison replied silently with a smile that wavered a little because of a sharp pain in her hip.

"Allison has to turn her attention to the Chateau Bel Air," Claire told Steve. "First, however, she is taking a well-deserved week off, starting *now.*" Claire turned to Allison with a warm smile. "I'm serious, Allison. Then you will return, revitalized, to face the Chateau and the ever-expanding list of people who want you to do their homes."

"A list to which my name will be added?" Steve asked.

"Of course."

When Steve, Allison, and Claire reached the front door, about to leave, Steve said, "Shall I take the keys now?"

"I need to come back this afternoon," Allison answered. "A few finishing touches."

"What more can there be?"

Allison gave a slight shrug. She just wanted to fill the magnificent Lalique vases with fresh roses. Perhaps the beautiful French crystal vases filled with fresh pastel roses would become the signature on every home, every hotel, every penthouse she designed; Allison was thinking about it. But, no matter what, she wanted roses in the vases at Bellemeade, so it would be lovely and bright and fragrant tomorrow when Peter arrived.

"I'm going to put roses in the vases. I'll drop the keys by your Brentwood office after I'm done, Steve. Is that all right?"

"Of course, but there's no hurry, Allison. I have an extra set I can give Peter in the morning."

"I'll drop them off today. I don't need them."

Allison picked up the gold-foil boxes of roses at the florist in Beverly Hills, met Winter at the Westholme Avenue enrance to UCLA, and together they drove to Bellemeade.

"Allison, I can't believe this is the same dark, dungeony place. It feels like a springtime meadow. So romantic."

Romantic? Allison's weary mind spun. She wanted Bellemeade to be light and lovely and peaceful and happy, but romantic? Had she overdone?

"Allison, your hip is really bothering you, isn't it?" Winter asked bluntly when she returned from her tour of the house. Allison was in the kitchen arranging the roses. Winter saw the strain in her friend's eyes and was reminded of those long months of recovery when Allison had never complained as she fought a private, silent, determined battle against her pain.

Allison looked surprised at the bluntness of Winter's question. Then she answered honestly.

"It hurts."

"Can you rest?"

"Yes. Claire has given me next week off. I'm planning to soak in hot bubble baths and sleep and read." Last week, at a bookstore in Century City, Allison had bought the recently published collection of plays by Peter Dalton. The collection included all of Peter's produced works—his one-act plays and his full-length ones: *Merry Go Round, Storm Watch, Echoes, Depth Charge, Say Goodbye*, and three others. The book did not contain his just-produced-on-Broadway *Shadows of the Mind* or the soon-to-be-produced *Love.*

Allison planned to curl up in her bed, relaxed after a hot bath and with a cup of tea, and read the gifted words of the man she had met last August . . . the man for whom she had worked so hard to make Bellemeade lovely, happy, flawless.

“Good,” Winter said firmly. She tilted her head and asked, with a twinkle, “Do you think you’ll feel like making Christmas cookies on the fifteenth?”

“Sure. Why?”

“I told Mark I’d bring Christmas cookies with me to Boston.” *And I’ve never made Christmas cookies.* No one had taken the time to show painfully shy Winter Carlyle how to make Christmas cookies. No one had cared if Winter had that childhood joy. In fact, the cook at the mansion had never wanted to muss her kitchen for the quiet, gawky child. There were always Christmas cookies at the mansion, of course, exquisite delicacies that arrived in ornate boxes and hand-painted tins from the best bakeries around the world. “Do you realize that Mark has only been gone for six hours and I’m already counting the minutes until the sixteenth?”

“I realize that.”

Winter walked across the plush teal-blue living room carpet to the framed photograph of a new moon signed E. Rousseau. She gazed admiringly at the photograph for a moment, then asked, “Do you think Emily would like to help make Christmas cookies, assuming she’s not in Hong Kong or wherever?”

“I . . . we should ask her.”

“I’ll give her a call,” Winter said. “She is really talented, isn’t she?”

Emily gathered the just-developed portraits from the dark rooms in her Santa Monica apartment and carefully put them in folders. In a few moments, she would leave to catch the bus to Beverly Hills for her four o’clock meeting with Rob.

As she put the photographs in a manila folder, Emily’s gaze fell on her fingernails. They were long now, and gently tapered. For Emily, to have fingernails that were long and tapered, instead of bitten-short, was such an incredible accomplishment! Her fingernails looked presentable now and she didn’t wear jeans anymore. Emily wore *outfits*, identical to the stylish ones displayed on the mannequins at Bullock’s-Westwood. Emily bought her new outfits—slacks, blouses, sweaters, and sweater vests—in subdued colors, and in sizes that were loose and unrevealing. But still she was more stylish, wasn’t she?

Emily wondered if Rob noticed.

Of course not!

Rob Adamson *expected* women to have long, tapered fingernails, stylish, elegant clothes, and dazzling jewels. Rob expected women to be beautiful and confident. Rob would never notice *her*; but he liked her photographs and that meant so much to Emily.

As Emily stepped out of her night-dark apartment into the bright November sun, she thought about the women Rob did notice . . . beautiful, dazzling, confident women like Elaina Kingsley . . .

Emily had done a portrait of Elaina in early November—a “surprise” birthday present from Elaina to Rob. She had taken the photographs in Elaina’s luxury condominium on Roxbury in Beverly Hills—Elaina’s condominium, or Rob and Elaina’s?

Elaina had positioned herself on the couch in the elegantly decorated peach and cream living room, staring critically at Emily as she tested lenses and filters. Elaina’s critical gaze was unconcealed, as if Emily’s eyes became unseeing and her heart could feel no pain when she viewed the world through the lens of her camera. Maybe Elaina didn’t care if her critical stare caused Emily pain. Why *should* she care?

At first, Elaina had been impatient, restless, irritable with Emily's slowness. Elaina's phone rang incessantly, but the calls were answered by her machine. Emily and Elaina heard each message as it was recorded; high-powered messages from high-powered people for high-powered Elaina, the all-important, ever-shrewd negotiator. In the midst of the high-powered messages came a warm one, in a voice familiar to both women, Rob's voice. "Hi, kiddo. I've made dinner reservations for eight o'clock at the Bordeaux Room. I'll be by to get you at seven-thirty."

Eventually, Elaina's nervousness about the camera, along with her impatience with Emily's slowness, dissipated. Elaina relaxed, and like most people Emily had photographed, she began to talk—openly, honestly, without inhibition—to the camera . . . as if Emily wasn't even there. It was then, in those unposed, unguarded moments, that Emily took the magnificent, natural, revealing portraits.

Most people eventually relaxed and chattered to the camera, enjoying the release of nervous energy, unconcerned that Emily was a silent witness. But there were exceptions. Allison had talked to Emily, not to the camera. Allison had smiled warmly and asked Emily questions about *herself*. When Emily hadn't been forthcoming with answers, Allison had shifted cheerfully to a discussion of Emily's talent, and how much she would like to put her photographs in the beautiful homes she designed. Allison hadn't chattered about herself, and neither had Winter. Winter had sat patiently, without a trace of irritation or restlessness. Finally, when Emily asked if Winter knew what she wanted her portfolio portraits to look like, Winter had simply posed, quietly, perfectly.

Elaina chattered, a breathless outpouring on a number of subjects, including her relationship with Rob and how much they loved each other. "I hope you'll photograph our wedding, Emily. I know Rob would want you to." Elaina had frowned briefly, then admitted to the camera, "Of course, Rob hasn't proposed yet—not officially—but he will. We'll probably be married in June, at the Club."

Rob expected women to be beautiful, confident, dazzling, like Elaina, Emily reminded herself as the bus travelled along Wilshire from Santa Monica to Beverly Hills. Rob wouldn't even notice Emily's tapered fingernails or her sort-of-stylish clothes. The nails and clothes were Emily's own private badges of courage, small, brave signs that her life was better.

Better. So much better. Mick was with someone else and Emily spent her life taking beautiful pictures. And once a week, if she was lucky, she met with Rob. Emily felt better, happy, at peace. She didn't even think about moving to Paris anymore! It was too important to be here, taking beautiful pictures and meeting with Rob, seeing his smiling blue eyes, hearing his gentle voice tell her how much he liked her photographs.

A very nice way to end the afternoon, Rob thought with a smile as he waited for Emily to arrive for their four o'clock meeting. Meeting with Emily was completely unnecessary, but Rob enjoyed seeing her, looked forward to their meetings, regretted the weeks when his travel schedule or hers prevented them.

Rob didn't need to meet with Emily at all. She could—*did*—get all her assignments through Fran. And Rob certainly didn't need to tell Emily the kind of portrait he wanted her to take. He didn't even know what he wanted until he saw it—Emily's latest remarkable portrait.

Remarable . . . Emily took photographs of the world's most glamorous women without make-up, and they looked more alluring, more beautiful than ever. She captured a sparkle of laughter in the eyes of men who never smiled and thoughtful reflection on the faces of men who always laughed. Her magnificent portraits were glimpses—careful, gentle, loving glimpses—into the spirit and the soul.

Rob didn't need to meet with Emily before her assignments to tell her what kind of picture to take, nor after to select together which photograph should appear in the magazine. *That* was Rob's decision, but he always asked Emily and she always pointed to the one he had already selected.

There was no need for Rob to meet with Emily—ever—except that he wanted to.

So Rob and Emily would meet each week, if it could be arranged. They would talk about *Portrait* and her photographs. Quiet, serious, business conversations. Sometimes, Emily Rousseau would smile. Emily's soft, lovely smiles were rare, but her pale gray eyes were always clear. Rob wondered about drugs and about the man on the bluffs at Santa Monica. Rob hadn't seen Emily and her lover again, but he hadn't even wanted to run the risk. The day Emily had agreed to work for *Portrait* Rob had changed his jogging route entirely, following the well-worn grassy path along San Vicente Boulevard, avoiding the Santa Monica Palisades altogether.

Rob glanced at his watch. Emily would be here in five minutes, exactly on time as always, for their unnecessary—but for him somehow so necessary—meeting.

"Rob?" Emily appeared in his open doorway, a little flushed, a little late. "I'm sorry. There was a traffic accident."

"It's fine. Hi. Come in."

"I brought the photographs of the Prince."

"Oh, good." Rob had been tempted to tell Emily to come empty-handed. They could just talk, couldn't they? Rob wasn't sure. They used Emily's photographs as a focus—a crutch!—but the conversation never strayed far. Maybe, without the photographs, there would be nothing to say.

Nothing to say, but so many questions to ask.

Who are you, Emily Rousseau? May I do a portrait of you? May I try to discover who you are and why you are the way you are?

Rob admired the photographs Emily had taken of the Prince, told her which one he liked the best, and when that business was done, he said, "I promised you a trip to Paris."

"It's not . . . it doesn't matter."

"I've decided to profile four top fashion designers in Paris—LaCroix, Chanel, St. Laurent, Dior. How good is your French?"

"It's good."

"So, you can be my interpreter."

"You're going?"

"*We're* going. I'd like to do the interviews myself, with you as interpreter if necessary. And, of course, you have to take the photographs."

"When?"

"The third week in January, if it can be arranged. I have commitments the weeks before and after, but at this point that week is entirely clear. I thought you might like to stay in France for a while, maybe take a vacation? I need you back by mid-February, of course, by the time the Academy Award nominations are announced."

Now that *Portrait*'s home was Los Angeles, Rob had decided to establish an Academy Awards issue. This would be its inaugural year. Rob planned to profile fifteen people—the five nominees in the categories of Best Actress, Best Actor, and Best Director. The issue had to be on the stands before the Academy Award ceremony, which meant five frantic weeks from announcement of nominees to publication.

"Emily? Is there a problem about going to Paris?" Rob had thought Emily would be pleased. He had even hoped for a rare, beautiful smile. But her pale gray eyes were uncertain.

"No, Rob. It's fine."

Two weeks later, just before four o'clock on the fourteenth of December, Rob looked at Emily's name on his appointment calendar and frowned slightly. He and Emily *had* been scheduled to meet today at four, but Emily had been delayed in San Francisco.

"She's on your calendar for next Friday," Fran replied when Rob asked if they had set a new time when Emily had called to cancel. "It would be very tough to get her in before then."

"Oh. All right."

At four-thirty, Fran appeared at Rob's door, smiling coyly.

"Yes?" Rob asked, returning her smile, curious.

"Peter Dalton is on the line." Fran's smile flattened as she watched Rob's reaction . . . Rob's lack of reaction. Rob looked completely blank, almost stunned. "Rob, Peter Dalton. You know, the Broadway sensation who is here doing *Love*, the movie of the century. Rob? I put him on hold because I thought you would want to take the call. I mean, I assume he'll be in the Academy Award issue in '86, but that's over a year away, so . . . Rob?"

Fran screened all calls very politely, but she was a brick wall. She rarely even put an unsolicited caller on hold, usually just taking a message no matter what Rob was doing.

But *Peter Dalton*? Fran assumed Peter Dalton would be the exception to the rule, someone Rob would be happy to talk to, undeniably the type of talent he loved to feature in *Portrait*.

"I'll just take a message," Fran murmured finally.

"No. Put him through."

Rob closed his office door while Fran returned to her desk to transfer Peter's call. Then Rob waited, fists clenched, unable to stop the ancient emotions that swept through him.

"What do you want?"

"Hello, Rob."

Silence.

"I will be in Los Angeles for the next four months," Peter continued finally. "I thought—hoped—that sometime we might talk."

"About what?"

"About Sara. I promised her . . ."

"You promised *me* that you would take care of Sara, that you would protect her and love her." Rob paused. When he spoke again, his voice was ice, "I will make you a promise, Peter, and I will keep it if I can. I don't know if it's possible for you to love—to ever care about anyone but yourself—but if you do and I learn of it, I promise you I will do everything I can to take that love away from you."

"Rob . . ."

"If I can hurt you, Peter, if I can make you ache until you want to die because the loss is so great, I will do it. That is my promise to you."

Rob hung up then, quietly, gently, his rage more frightening in its control than if it had been violent. Rob's fury was ice-cold, strong, powerful. His hatred toward Peter hadn't lessened with the passage of time or distance or the golden warmth of the California sun. The hatred was evergreen, its roots strong and healthy, burrowing ever deeper into his heart.

Rob made the threat and meant it, but he knew its emptiness. If Peter ever found someone to love, Rob wouldn't even know it. Rob's rage had not become an obsession. He wouldn't allow it to be. He wasn't going to spend his life tracking Peter Dalton, hoping for a chance at revenge, because revenge—Peter Dalton's pain at the loss of a great love, even Peter Dalton's death—would be so empty, so joyless, so trivial compared to the irreplaceable life of beloved Sara.

Rob's eyes fell on his open appointment calendar. How he wished this hour had been spent with the lovely gray eyes and soft voice! Rob's thought continued. It was a surprising thought, but it brought such peace. . . .

How Rob wished Emily would walk into his office, even now. Perhaps Rob would tell her why his face was ashen, his body trembling, his eyes dark and stormy. Or perhaps he wouldn't tell her, but, still, just having Emily here, with him . . .

"Thanks for the ride." Winter grasped the passenger door handle and started to lift it as they neared the United terminal at Los Angeles International Airport.

"Winter! Sit and stay!" Allison commanded with a laugh. She had last tried that command on a recalcitrant Labrador retriever when she was nine and the puppy was a puppy. Winter looked at her friend with startled eyes that reminded Allison of the surprised-but-trying-hard-to-understand puppy. "I haven't stopped the car."

"Then stop it!" Winter laughed.

The laughter—the giggles—had begun last night, while Allison, Emily, and Winter made Christmas cookies. Allison's and Emily's were true masterpieces—*designer cookies*, Winter announced happily—and Winter's were simply culinary reflections of her restless euphoria about seeing Mark.

"We are two hours early for your flight. Of course, it may take that much time to find a place in the baggage compartment for your bulging suitcase," Allison teased. She knew what was in Winter's suitcase. Winter had popped in and out of Elegance almost daily for the past week to show Allison her purchases. Winter called the new wardrobe of luxurious cashmere sweaters and stylish wool skirts and slacks and a camel's hair coat her foul weather gear for snowy Boston.

"Do you think Mark will remember me?"

"After sixteen days?"

"Seventeen. Seventeen desolate days and nights."

"Daily and nightly phone calls notwithstanding, I think Mark *will* remember you." Allison gave her friend a brief hug before Winter opened the car door and hailed a porter. "Have a wonderful time. Merry Christmas. Happy Birthday. Give Mark my love."

"You, too. Thank you."

Allison carefully negotiated the traffic, impressive for seven-thirty Sunday morning nine days before Christmas. The sky awakened as she drove north on the San Diego Freeway and made plans for the day that lay ahead. The sky was becoming robin's egg blue, promising sun and an invigorating crispness.

A beautiful day for a trail ride, Allison thought. She hadn't ridden in months, not since before the Olympics, before Bellemeade. Allison's hip was better after the week of rest and so was she, eager again and energetic. The Chateau Bel Air was so well in hand that Allison was even working on additional projects.

You can relax, Allison told herself. Everything is under control. You can take a nice, long, peaceful trail ride.

The woods are lovely, dark, and deep. The words floated in Peter's mind as he rode along the Windsor Trail. From the stable compound, the trail wound through a dense, lush forest. After a mile, as the trail steepened, pale blue sky replaced the evergreen ceiling. At its crest, the trail opened to a panoramic view of the ocean.

Peter dismounted, tethered his horse to a nearby branch, and walked to the cliff edge.

So peaceful, except Peter's mood didn't match the tranquility of the setting.

I am trying to keep my promises to you, darling Sara.

Peter gazed at the ocean and the sheer cliff below—one step into eternity—and his dark eyes hardened angrily as he remembered Friday afternoon's conversation with Rob.

It hadn't been a conversation. Rob wouldn't give him a chance! Perhaps Peter didn't *deserve* a chance to explain. Peter blamed himself for Sara's death; he had loved her too much, allowed her to be free . . . too free? Peter blamed himself and always would. Rob obviously blamed him, too. Fine. Peter was willing to accept the blame. But couldn't he and Rob even *try* to get beyond the blame . . . for Sara's sake, for her memory, for the promises?

Apparently not, and Rob's unwillingness to try filled Peter with anger, frustration . . . and hatred.

Ginger whinnied at the sight of Peter's horse—a stablemate—and Allison started to smile as she recognized Peter. But her smile faded when she saw Peter's eyes—dark, turbulent—glaring at her without recognition and with a clear message that she had intruded.

"I'm sorry."

"Don't be. I was just about to leave."

"I can just ride on."

"It's not necessary." Peter unwrapped the reins of his horse and, without mounting, disappeared into the green maze of palmettos and ferns.

Allison watched in stunned, disappointed, *angry* silence. After Peter vanished into the lush forest, she dismounted and walked to the edge of the cliff.

You have no right to be angry! Allison reminded herself as the surprising and so unfamiliar emotion swept through her. *Peter Dalton didn't ask you to make a lovely, happy place for him to live. He never even pretended to care.*

Had Allison really expected to hear from Peter? After all, Steve was her client, not Peter. And Steve had been effusive in his praise of Bellemeade; but it would have been nice to hear from Peter, too . . . if he even liked his new home, if he even *noticed*.

Claire's instincts about Peter—aloof, arrogant, impossible to please—were obviously entirely accurate. And Allison's kinder instincts—sad, lonely, nice Peter—were obviously entirely wrong.

But, until this moment, Allison had been unwilling to revise her initial impressions. She had read Peter's plays, read them and cried, and had spent long, quiet hours thinking about the unhappy man who had written the beautiful, unhappy words. And now . . .

"Allison?"

The storm had vanished from his eyes, leaving just dark uncertainty.

"Hi, Peter."

"I didn't recognize you. I'm sorry."

"My hair." Allison ran a hand through her soft curls. *My hair and whatever it was you were thinking about when I arrived.*

"Yes." Peter smiled. "I feel like I'm living in a French Impressionist painting."

"I guess I overdid."

"*No*, not at all. Bellemeade is lovely . . . magnificent." Peter added quietly, "I should have let you know before this."

"It doesn't matter."

"Well, it does." Peter had been overwhelmed by Bellemeade, but his thoughts had been, *I don't need to live in this lovely place!* And now, as Peter looked at the thoughtful jadegreen eyes and pink-flushed cheeks, he realized he should have told her how wonderful it was. Perhaps he didn't deserve to liv there, but Allison Fitzgerald deserved to know. "It *does* matter and I apologize. So, belated thank you."

"You're welcome."

"Muffin loves her pillows. She's not used to such elegance."

Muffin? Peter Dalton, writer of such dark, tormented dramas as *Say Goodbye*, has a cocker spaniel named Muffin? *How nice.*

"Oh, well." Allison blushed. "I'm glad Muffin likes them."

The silence was filled by soft whinnies and uncertain smiles.

"I really do have to go," Peter said finally. "Steve and I have a few more locations to chose."

"It was nice seeing you again, Peter."

"It was nice seeing you, too, Allison."

"It must not have made the connection at O'Hare," the man at the lost baggage counter at Logan Airport told Winter and Mark. He had already told fifty other passengers the same thing, only two hours into his shift. "If you can fill this out, we'll have the bag delivered to your address in Boston as soon as it arrives."

"When will that be?"

"Probably first thing tomorrow morning."

Winter shrugged amiably, took the form, and moved to a counter to fill in the information. It didn't matter. Nothing mattered. She was with Mark and the desire in his blue eyes told her how much he had missed her.

"Could I borrow a shirt or something? My new silk negligees—wait until you see them!—are in Chicago."

"I like the idea of you without clothes," Mark whispered as he pulled her close and kissed her.

"I like that idea, too . . . soon."

Winter didn't need anything, just Mark, *except* . . .

Winter and Mark had agreed to *no Christmas presents*. Winter knew Mark would be too busy to shop in Boston and she didn't want him to spend precious time before he left—time *they* could be together—looking for gifts for her! No presents, they agreed, just each other.

So it wasn't a present, just a surprise, something to erase the worry she sometimes saw even though he hadn't mentioned it since that sunny morning in the San Joaquin Valley. *I had the IUD removed, Mark. Now I—we—have a diaphragm.*

But the diaphragm was in the suitcase in Chicago. Winter had simply, happily, unthinkingly tossed it in amidst the romantic silk negligees.

Winter thought now, as she curled up in Mark's arms as the taxi neared his apartment, *This is Mark. I need him. It will only be for one night of love, a night I wouldn't miss, not for anything in the world.*

Chapter 16

Mark's on-call schedule in the Intensive Care Unit at Massachusetts General Hospital was every other night. The first two weeks of December had been "quiet," the ICU beds virtually empty, as if a divine wand had waved, banishing sickness for the holidays.

The day after Winter arrived the pace at the hospital became frantic. The ICU beds swiftly filled with desperately ill patients. On the alternate nights when he *could* leave the hospital, Mark didn't return to the studio apartment until after midnight, exhausted, apologetic.

"Isn't it better to be busy?" Winter asked. "This way they really get to see how terrific you are."

"Yes, but what about you?"

"I'm fine. Boston is a charming, wonderfully historic city. I love the snow and I'm perfectly happy wandering around, rehearsing my lines, gazing at the MGH from across the Charles River and thinking of you inside saving lives."

Winter tried to reassure him. *Mark, I have been on my own all my life! Until now.*

Being this close to Mark, touching him for six hours out of forty-eight, seeing his sensuous blue eyes, was so much better than being a continent apart.

It was better for Mark, too . . . better and worse. Better, *wonderful* to know that he would hold her soon. And worse, because he felt guilty that he had so few hours to share with her.

I'm sorry were the two words Winter heard the most. Mark greeted her with "I'm sorry" when he called to say it would still be an hour or two; and when he arrived home four hours later, or five; and as he drifted off to necessary sleep before they made love because he was exhausted and in six hours it would begin again.

I'm sorry. The words echoed in Winter's mind as she roamed the romantic city of Jennifer and Oliver. Winter wanted to remind Mark gently, lovingly, "Love means never having to say . . ."

But Mark had never said "I love you," and Winter had never told him, either; and Jennifer and Oliver's was a different love story, one with a sadder ending than theirs would ever have. Besides, those were someone else's words of love. Winter had to find her own way of letting Mark know that she was happy—so happy—just to be near him.

"I'll be able to leave the hospital at noon on Christmas Eve—if I don't get any admissions that morning. We could plan on dinner somewhere that evening."

"A candlelight dinner right here would be nice." Winter smiled coyly.

"Smoked oysters?"

"Even better. You'll see." Winter had already been to the best restaurants in Boston, examined their menus for Christmas Eve dinner, and made arrangements with the chef at the Colonial Inn to prepare a feast *to go*, something she could reheat in the small oven in the apartment whenever Mark was free.

By ten-thirty Christmas Eve morning, Winter had gotten the food, set a festive holiday table, and heard from Mark that *so far* it looked like he would be able to leave at noon. On impulse, she decided to walk to the hospital to meet him as he left.

Mark had promised Winter a tour of "The General," but it hadn't happened yet. One day she had stood in the circular drive in front of the immense red brick building topped like a Christmas tree with the red neon letters MGH—Massachusetts General Hospital—but she hadn't ventured inside. It seemed too imposing.

But today, on Christmas Eve, as the light snow softened the morning chill and as she thought about the man she loved so much who was inside, "The General" seemed more like a home than a hospital.

A gigantic home with slick linoleum floors and pale yellow walls and fluorescent lights and colorful signs that attempted to decipher the intricate maze of corridors. Winter studied the signs for familiar words. She would avoid the Intensive Care Unit. Winter didn't want to disturb Mark. She would be waiting for him, at the Main Entrance, at noon.

Winter wandered to the Phillips House, the private hospital within the hospital. As she entered the Phillips House, the slick linoleum changed to plush carpeting and pale yellow plaster was covered by Laura Ashley wallpaper. It looked like something Allison might have decorated! Next, Winter went to the Bullfinch, the historic open ward with the lovely name. Winter expected cheeriness, the echoes of chirping birds, but the ward was desolate and disturbing, filled with men and women with vacant eyes and sallow skin.

At eleven forty-five, Winter followed signs—thinking, with a smile, that she should have left a trail of bread crumbs—back toward the Main Entrance and the Emergency Ward. Emergency *Ward* not Emergency *Room*, as it was called on the West Coast. As Winter walked along the corridor past the "E.W." and toward the Main Entrance, she saw Mark.

Mark was in the Emergency Ward with a patient, an admission that meant it would be hours before he could leave the hospital. Winter's immediate reaction was disappointment mixed with anger, frustration, and a strong feeling that it wasn't *fair;* but, as she watched, unnoticed by Mark who was wholly involved with his new patient, the ice in her emotions melted into love and pride.

The patient was an elderly woman with frightened eyes and gasping breath. *Someone's grandmother*, Winter thought as she remembered what Mark had told her the afternoon Donald Fullerton had died. Mark hadn't jogged at all that autumn day. Instead, he and Winter had walked along the white sand beach for hours, talking, touching. *If you treat every patient the way you would want someone to treat your mother or father or children or sisters or brothers or best friend—someone you love—then you'll always do your best. You can't give more than that, Winter, but you have to give that much, always.*

Mark's new patient was someone's grandmother, afraid, perhaps in pain, perhaps dying. Mark smiled at the woman with gentle, reassuring eyes, wrapped his strong fingers around her frail wrist, and appeared so calm as he studied the cardiac monitor that beeped irregularly over the stretcher and quietly gave medication orders to the E.W. nurse.

As Winter watched, a miracle happened. The woman's terror subsided and her breathing slowed. The intravenous medications were working their magic and Mark was working his. Mark's attention was entirely focused on his patient. There was no restlessness, nothing that told the woman if she had only chosen to come thirty minutes later, he would be on his way home. Mark's eyes and smile and calm voice sent only one message: He was here to help her.

If Mark's patient had only chosen to come to the hospital thirty minutes later, Winter thought, then analyzed her own thought. The woman hadn't *chosen* to be sick! On this day of all days, the woman would choose to be home, baking cookies, wrapping presents, surrounded by the love and laughter of lively grandchildren. The woman didn't choose to be sick or be here, not today, not ever.

But she was here, and she was so lucky that the sapphireblue eyes and gentle smile and strong hands and brilliant mind of Mark Stephens were caring for her. *Caring*, Winter mused. It was the right word. Mark cared. It was so obvious.

This—the chaos of the Emergency Ward, the drama of the hospital, the battle waged between doctors and disease—was Mark's natural habitat. Mark belonged here, was happy here, thrived, contributed.

Winter started to withdraw, afraid that Mark might sense her loving stare, but she stopped as she saw a young nurse move close to Mark—closer than was necessary!—and speak softly to him swaying slightly toward him, her admiring eyes searching his handsome, serious face. Mark answered the question, but his eyes kept their calm vigil of his patient, the cardiac monitor, and the carefully calibrated drops of lifesaving medication that dripped slowly into her veins.

Oh, Mark, Winter thought. This is where you belong, even though it takes you away from me for so many more hours than we can share and even though there are hazards—young, beautiful hazards—here, too.

Winter withdrew quickly. Outside the snow was falling heavily, a quiet, fleecy, enveloping fog. Winter didn't walk back to the small apartment. Instead, she walked toward Beacon Hill and its elegant, brightly lighted old houses. As she walked, her thoughts swirled like the snow.

She had actually begun to *resent* the unknown patients that kept Mark away from her! As if they were conspiring against her and her love. How selfish, how foolish. How natural, Mark would say quietly if she told him.

She had actually begun to *resent* the nameless, faceless patients. What was next? Resenting Mark? Believing that he stayed away later and longer than was really necessary? That was why doctors" marriages failed, wasn't it? That was why Mark's parents" marriage had failed.

But now she understood! As Winter trudged through the soft snow, she vowed that Mark's patients would never again be anonymous. They would be, as Mark had told her they had to be, someone's mother, someone's grandmother, someone's *love*.

Mark finally left the hospital at five o'clock that evening and arrived at the apartment six minutes later.

"Hi. Merry Christmas Eve," Winter said.

"Hi. I'm—"

Winter stopped the "sorry" with a long, hungry kiss. *Love means . . .*

"Don't be," she breathed finally.

"OK," Mark whispered as he pulled her back to him for more.

Mark showered and changed into jeans. Winter wore a provocative wine-red satin negligee that looked like an evening gown. Mark and Winter ate the gourmet Christmas Eve dinner by candlelight.

"What do you think, Mark? Is Mass General the best?" Winter asked when they finally finished the elegant meal. They had eaten very slowly, far more interested in loving gazes and long, deep champagne-flavored kisses than in gourmet food.

Mark considered Winter's question for a moment. Is MGH the best? Yes. Is it the best for me? Yes. Is it the best for us? *No*.

"I think you should do your residency here," Winter continued before Mark answered.

"You do? Why?"

"Because it's your dream."

So are you, darling Winter.

"Well. We'll see, Winter. Maybe they won't want me."

"They will," she whispered softly to the eyes that hadn't slept all last night and were so exhausted, but trying so hard to fight fatigue to be with her. So hard, too hard.

Winter fell silent, lost in thoughts that had been tormenting her since the scene in the Emergency Ward. It wasn't fair to Mark that she was here. It wasn't like Los Angeles, where the apartment was hers and Mark didn't feel responsible for her when he was away. Here, in Boston, Winter was a visitor, a *guest*, Mark's guest—at least in his gentle, tired mind. It wasn't fair to him. This all-important month in the ICU was Mark's audition for his dream, *his* casting call! And as much as Winter reassured him that she was quite happy wandering around Boston by herself, Mark still felt torn, compelled to be awake with her, even if it meant sacrificing necessary sleep.

Mark saw the worry in Winter's lovely eyes, as well as the sadness, and he wondered if this were the beginning of the end. Was she going to tell him she couldn't stand having so little of his life?

Winter's frown fell on their plates. Mechanically, she began clearing the table, still lost in thought.

"Winter?"

"I want to get the rest of the turkey in the refrigerator so we don't get salmonella," she answered distantly.

Mark smiled and moved behind her as she wrapped the leftover turkey in tinfoil. He wove his fingers through her long black hair and gave a soft tug. "Hey, Winter Elizabeth Carlyle, talk to me."

Winter turned and gazed into his eyes.

"I think I should go back to LA, Mark."

"OK." Mark couldn't object. He couldn't promise that tomorrow would be better.

"You think I'm leaving because I'm upset that I see so little of you, don't you?"

"That would make sense," Mark answered gently. *I don't blame you, Winter!*

"But that's not why!"

"No?"

"No. I was there today. I saw you in the E.W. and—"

"And?"

"—and this is so important for you, this month, and I think it's hard for you to have me here to worry about, even though you don't have to worry about me, but I know you do." Winter stopped, breathless, wishing she had rehearsed this, desperately wanting Mark to understand that it wasn't because she didn't care about him; it was the *opposite.*

Mark pulled her close until their lips almost touched, smiled into her glistening violet eyes, and asked quietly, "Did I ever tell you how much I love you?"

"No," Winter breathed.

"Well, I do. Very, very much."

"I love you, Mark."

"I have something for you."

Winter couldn't believe Mark left her then, but it was only for a moment, and he returned with a gold box tied with a violet velvet ribbon.

"No Christmas presents," she whispered, remembering her own Christmas surprise. Winter had told Mark about the diaphragm *after* they had made love her fourth night in Boston. He hadn't noticed—the doctors had promised her he wouldn't—and it hadn't occurred to him that it had been in her lost luggage, not her purse; and he had been so pleased that she'd given up the IUD.

"It isn't a Christmas present." Mark smiled. "It's for your birthday."

Winter's birthday present from Mark was a music box, a delicately carved quaint English cottage in a bright, lovely garden of roses. When Winter gently lifted the carved thatched roof, her wonderful music box played "Here, There and Everywhere."

"Mark."

"So?"

"So?"

"May I have this dance?"

Mark and Winter swayed gently to the music that recalled a rose-fragrant terrace and a June wedding and the enchanted beginning of their magical love. They kissed as they danced, kissed and whispered.

"How is the woman you admitted?" Winter's lips touched Mark's as she spoke.

"Better. I think she'll be fine."

"And the nurse?"

"The nurse?"

"The one with the fawn-eyes and too-small dress who kept brushing against you."

"I didn't even notice."

"Good. That's nice."

"This is nice."

"I still should leave, shouldn't I?"

Mark's blue eyes answered lovingly, *Yes, I guess, but I will miss you.*

"I'm leaving on one condition."

I don't want you to leave at all, Winter. Don't give me conditions!

"Yes?"

"When you call and wake me up in the middle of the night because you finally have a chance to call—and I want you to!—or when you haven't been able to call for two days, please don't begin with 'I'm sorry.' "

"OK."

"Please begin with 'I love you.' "

"That's very easy. I love you, Winter."

"I love you, Mark. I wonder if we could tell each other that when we make love."

"For me, it would just be a matter of whispering what I'm already thinking."

"For me, too."

"Shall we try? Right now?"

"Yes. Right now."

Allison loved the Club at Christmas! The twinkling lights and flickering candles and wreaths of holly and scents of pine and bayberry and nutmeg . . .

And the tree. As a little girl Allison had sat where she now stood, in front of the glittering tree, mesmerized by the lights and colors and exquisite enchanted ornaments from around the world. Allison wondered if her remarkable eye for color and design had always been there, simply jarred back to life by her fall, because the memories of the Christmas tree and the prisms of light were so vivid; sparkling memories of red and green and blue and gold; memories of color, of emotion, of little-girl wonder.

Allison gently spun a gold ball. As it twirled, it sent bursts of color, a tiny private display of fireworks. Allison was so glad she had stopped here on her way to Christmas Eve dinner with her parents and Vanessa. The red-orange fire crackled, soft carols filled the air, and in the distance, like delicate wind chimes, sterling silver gently touched fine bone china. How peaceful it was, how beautiful, and what a luxury to be alone in this lovely place. . . .

"Good evening."

Whoever he was, whoever owned the soft, low voice, he shared the same impulse to be in this enchanted place.

"Peter. Hello." Allison felt warmth in her cheeks as she turned and met his dark eyes.

"Hello, Allison. It's very beautiful, isn't it?"

"Yes. Very." Allison searched for more words to describe the lovely room, but for her it was a room of feelings, not words, a place of private memories, a page from her girlhood diary. Allison couldn't find words for those private feelings, but she found other words, happy words, to speak to Peter. "How's Muffin?"

"Muffin is terribly spoiled lounging around on her designer pillows."

"Good."

"And I'm terribly spoiled lounging around in my designer house." Peter smiled.

Good. Allison smiled, too.

"Have you selected all the location sites for *Love?*" she asked. "Winter says you start rehearsing right after the New Year."

"We have them pretty well lined up. You know Winter?"

"She's my best friend. She's very excited about the movie." Allison added softly, "Winter says the script is wonderful."

"Oh, well . . ."

The compliments had been exchanged—Bellemeade, Allison's triumph, and *Love*, Peter's triumph-to-be—and neither searched for more words. They smiled soft smiles and gazed at the twinkling lights of the magnificent tree and listened to the distant sounds of carollers and silver and china. Neither Allison nor Peter searched for more words, because neither was restless with silence in this beautiful, peaceful place.

Finally, because she was already late for dinner, Allison said quietly, "I have to go. Merry Christmas, Peter."

"Merry Christmas, Allison."

BEVERLY HILLS, CALIFORNIA
JANUARY 1985

Rob probably won't be in, Emily told herself. He'll be at lunch, but . . .

If he was here and not busy, she could show him the photographs she had just developed of Cecelia Fontaine. In the four months Emily had worked at *Portrait*, she had never "dropped in" on Rob. In fact, *she* never even made an appointment to see *him*.

Rob and Emily were leaving for Paris in the morning. If Rob wasn't in, she would just leave the photographs on his desk with a note, *I thought you might want to see the pictures of C.F. before Paris. Emily.* She might even add something bold like, *I'm looking forward to the trip*.

Rob's office door was open, and Emily heard a familiar, soft Southern drawl . . . Elaina.

"You'll be at the Ritz?"

"Yes, at the Ritz," Rob answered. There were more words, more deep tones, but they became indistinct, as if Rob had walked across the huge office, farther away from the door. Or maybe his words became muffled because his lips had found Elaina's. Emily put the envelope of photographs on Fran's desk and wrote a brief explanatory note: *Fran, Photos of Cecelia Fontaine, Emily.* She was turning to leave when she heard Elaina's next question.

"Is *she* staying there?"

Emily froze. Elaina was talking about her! And her voice held such contempt—contempt to match the criticism Emily had seen in her eyes the day she had done Elaina's portrait. Emily should have left—an instinct for self-preservation—but she didn't. She heard Elaina's diatribe, all of it, a scathing, breathless critique.

"She is? In those clothes? I admit, her new Annie Hall look *is* an improvement over the wilted flower child image, but *still*. She must embarrass you, Rob. No matter how wonderful her photographs are, you can't really want her to be an ambassador for the magazine! I don't understand why she doesn't do something about it. She may have been poor last summer, at the wedding, but you certainly are paying her more than enough to get decent clothes, do something with her hair. I could talk to her if you want."

There was a pause—silence. If Rob spoke, his voice was too low, or too distant, for Emily to hear.

Finally, Elaina continued, softly, seductively, "I know you're not looking forward to this trip, Rob, being with her. But, if I can't be with you, there is no woman in the world I'd rather have you be with than Emily. I won't have to spend one second feeling jealous!"

Tears streamed down Emily's cheeks as she pushed her way out the heavy front door of the office building and into the bright January sun.

Did Rob dread going to Paris with her? Was he embarrassed to be seen with her? Did he pay her all that money because he hoped that she would make herself look better and stop humiliating him and the magazine he loved?

Probably, Emily realized miserably. *Of course*.

Rob was dreading the trip to Paris and *she* had been unable to sleep because she was so excited. Emily practiced her French, the language of her childhood, reviewed French history, and studied guide books of Paris so that she might be knowledgeable if there were times when she and Rob were together other than the interviews with the couturiers. Emily had no expectations beyond the hope that Rob would smile at her and be pleased with how well she spoke French and how helpful she was. Emily didn't expect Rob to notice her, but she also neer expected that he would notice and hate what he saw.

But, of course he would!

Emily stood in the winter sunshine on Wilshire Boulevard. She was only a few blocks from Rodeo Drive and only a half block from Elegance. She had money, lots of Rob's money, in the bank. She could find Allison—Allison who was so stylish, so fashionable. She and Allison could go to Rodeo Drive, buy beautiful clothes, make Emily look . . .

But she was probably an embarrassment to Allison, too!

Allison and Rob were alike—impeccably bred, polite, kind—too polite and kind to let their real feelings show.

Emily didn't go to Elegance, and she didn't go to Rodeo Drive. Instead, she crossed the street to the bus stop to wait for the bus that would take her back to Santa Monica, to her lightless basement apartment and the bottle of drugs she hadn't opened—hadn't *needed*—since Mick left last summer.

There was no *point* in going shopping. All the money in the world, all the fabulous clothes on Rodeo Drive, couldn't make her worthy of Rob Adamson. Emily had no idea what was wrong with her, but there was *something* deep and painful; and it crashed like a lethal tidal wave over the fragile feelings—hope, joy, happiness—whenever they dared to find a home in her heart.

Emily hadn't even thought about packing the bottle of drugs in the small suitcase she would take to Paris. But as the bus rolled along Wilshire and dark, ugly feelings wiped away her excitement about the trip, Emily decided it was safer to bring the pills. In case the pain became too great.

"Rob, please don't be angry!"

Rob had listened to Elaina's tirade with a quiet fury that erupted—"Don't talk about Emily like that!"—just seconds after Emily left.

Elaina was stunned by Rob's reaction. Stunned and frightened.

"Rob, I wasn't being hurtful. I offered to talk to her, to help her, remember? I wasn't being critical of *her*, just of how she looks. Rob, please don't be angry!"

Rob looked at Elaina's confused, startled, *anxious* brown eyes and forced himself to examine his own anger. He was as angry with himself as he was with Elaina. Hadn't he, too, worried in the beginning about hiring Emily? Hadn't he conjured up images of drugs and denim and wantonness walking into the homes of celebrities around the world with the imprimatur of *Portrait?*

Yes. And now, Rob didn't *care* about Emily's clothes. He only noticed—and *cared*—that her gray eyes were clear and sometimes she smiled.

"I'm sorry, Elaina. I overreacted. But, for the record, Emily does not embarrass me. I'm proud to have her working for the magazine. I do *not* want you to talk to her."

And—something Rob didn't tell Elaina—*I am very much looking forward to Paris*.

A week later, Rob strolled along the Left Bank of the Seine and mentally measured the success of the trip to Paris.

From a *business* standpoint, it had been pure triumph. The interviews with the four top couturiers had gone beautifully, candid conversations laced with humour and insight and personality. The ease of the interviews had been because of Emily. She listened, attentive and smiling, quietly providing the correct translation when the designers' English faltered, speaking in soft, flawless French, unobtrusive and intriguing.

The designers *were* intrigued with Emily, with her perfect French, the physical delicacy so much like Parisian women, the dazzling sun-gold hair, the exquisite face. But the clothes . . .

Rob watched each designer react to the paradox of Emily, wondering if her meant-to-conceal clothes were an *avant-garde* fashion statement from some renegade Californian designer whose creations had yet to make the pages of

Vogue or the runways of New York and Paris. Rob watched as the Parisian designers discounted that possibility, frowning slightly, and how each, as the interview progressed, wanted nothing more than to dress Emily in his own magnificent silks, satins, and chiffons.

Rob's high school French was good enough to enable him to understand the designers" offers of gifts to her—"*Un petit cadeau, cherie, s'il vous plait. Une*

blouse, une robe elegante, les pantalons la mode"—and Emily's polite, quiet, *amazed* refusals.

Rob didn't know if Emily eventually relented, accepting a silk blouse or scarf or some token, because he left at the end of the interview and she stayed to take her famous portraits. Rob wouldn't see her again until the next morning, when they met in the lobby of the Ritz moments before they taxied together to the design studio.

From a business standpoint, the trip to Paris had been an immense triumph, but from a personal standpoint it had been a disaster.

Rob had hoped this trip would enable him and Emily to get to know each other, to feel comfortable outside the realm of work. But it hadn't happened. Even before they'd left Los Angeles—at four-thirty the day before they left—Emily had Fran rebook her airplane seats in Coach, not First Class with Rob, and cancel her reservations at the Ritz. Rob knew Emily never travelled First Class, never stayed at the Five-Star hotels he was happy to pay for, but he had thought that this trip, travelling with him, she would.

Perhaps her boyfriend, the menacing man from the bluffs of Santa Monica, was travelling with her, Rob decided when Fran told him. But at LAX the next morning, Emily was quite alone and quite uncomfortable with *him*.

Rob had hoped he and Emily would meet each morning for breakfast in the dining room at the Ritz. They would drink rich black coffee, and eat fresh-baked croissants frosted with sweet butter and orange marmalade, and talk at least about the day ahead. Perhaps they would even have a chance to stroll along the Champs-Elysées or through the Tuileries or the Jeu de Paume or the Louvre. And, in the evening after Emily returned from the afternoon photosessions, they could have dinner together in the Latin Quarter.

Rob had hoped that he and Emily would become friends.

But it had been a total failure. Emily appeared in the lobby at the Ritz each morning, just moments before their "work day" began; she sat through the interviews, making them a great success; then Rob left and she took the photographs; and that was all. Rob suggested dinner once. Emily looked surprised, confused, *troubled*, and finally she shook her head no. Rob spent the evenings in his suite at the Ritz, writing the profiles on the designers, sipping champagne, gazing at the City of Light, and wondering what she was doing, where she was hiding.

The operation was a success, Rob thought now as he strolled at twilight along the Seine, but the patient died.

Rob walked along the Boulevard Saint Michel into the heart of the Latin Quarter, its sidewalk cafés alive with students from the Sorbonne, laughing, talking. Discussing Sartre and romance, Rob mused hopefully. But, he thought, like youth everywhere, the students were probably actually discussing the stock market, money, fast cars, and good sex.

Years ago, Rob had spent a romantic evening here, in the shadow of the Sorbonne, discussing the existential dilemma. The girl had been beautiful, French, with wide, intelligent eyes and provocative lips. She and Rob had spent that spring night together, in a swirl of cheap wine and Gaulois cigarettes and profound, profound conversation about the meaning of life, or its meaninglessness. And it was probably all just flirtation, because afterward they made love, again and again, and that was Rob's most vivid memory.

As Rob turned off the Boulevard Saint Michel onto the Boulevard Saint Germain, he caught sight of Emily in a bookstore. She looked very French. Her loose pantaloons and shapeless smock were perfectly acceptable in the Latin Quarter. Rob hesitated a moment. Emily hadn't wanted to be with him. She had made that abundantly clear. They had said good-bye after the interview at Dior today. Rob was returning to Los Angeles tomorrow. Emily was remaining in France for another week.

Rob started to turn away, to leave the French girl alone in her city, but Emily looked up and saw him. Rob smiled uncertainly as he joined her.

"Hi."

"Hi."

"Did the photo session go well this afternoon?" Rob asked, knowing that business was safe ground.

"Oh, yes. Fine."

"I think all the interviews went very well, don't you?"

"Yes. I hope the photographs will be all right."

"They will be." Rob smiled, then commanded gently, not allowing her the option of saying no, "Come have a cup of cappuccino with me. I'd like to hear your thoughts about Paris."

Emily told him, as they drank cappuccino in the Café de Flore, how much she liked Paris, how strangely at home she felt here.

"Are you planning to move to Paris?" Rob asked. His emotions were mixed. He would miss seeing Emily—he would get her magnificent photographs by mail instead of in person—but that selfish reason was offset by the soft glow in her eyes. Emily did seem at home, relaxed here, relaxed at last even with him.

"I don't know." *Should I? Do I embarrass you, Rob?* Emily looked bravely into the smiling dark blue eyes—eyes that were too polite to reveal their disapproval—and repeated softly, "I don't know."

"How long are you planning to stay this trip?"

"I'll be back in Los Angeles on Saturday, a week from tomorrow."

"The whole time in Paris?"

"Paris, Versailles, the Loire Valley." Emily frowned slightly, debating. Finally, she added, "I'm doing some moonlighting."

"For the Chateau Bel Air. I know. It's perfectly fine with me, Emily. I told you that."

"Did Allison tell you?" Emily asked quietly. Had Allison checked with Rob to make sure he really didn't mind as long as her work for *Portrait* didn't suffer? Emily hoped not. She hoped that Rob and Allison didn't talk about her like Elaina and Rob did.

"No. Roger Towne told me. A euphoric, thrilled, *acquisitive* Roger Towne."

"Acquisitive?"

"I'm quite sure Roger would like to acquire your talent full-time for Chateaus all over the world."

"Oh, well . . ."

"I will more than match any offer Roger makes." Rob knew Roger wouldn't try to lure Emily away from *Portrait*, not that he wouldn't want her. It simply wasn't done, not among gentlemen, not among friends. It wouldn't happen, but pretending it might gave Rob a chance to remind Emily—because he wondered if she really heard his praise—how valuable she was to him.

"I wouldn't ever leave *Portrait.*" *You.*

"I hope not." Rob smiled. "So, this coming week isn't a real vacation."

Emily tilted her head and smiled shyly.

"What?" *What are you thinking, Emily?*

"I shouldn't tell you this, Rob."

"Tell me."

"Taking photographs isn't work." *Living the rest of my life is work. Taking beautiful pictures is escape, happiness. . . .*

Rob and Emily walked beside the Seine along Le Quai de la Tournelle. When they reached the Pont de la Tournelle, Emily stopped.

"Well, my hotel is this way. Thank you for the cappuccino, Rob."

"You're on L'Ile de Saint Louis?" On the *dark* L'Ile de St. Louis, Rob thought as he looked beyond the bridge Emily was planning to cross. The bright lights of the Latin Quarter were far away.

"Yes."

"Let me walk with you, Emily. It looks a little dark and deserted." *And I'm in no hurry to leave you. Are you in a rush to get away from me, as always?*

"Oh, all right. Thank you."

Across the Pont de la Tournelle, on L'Ile de Saint Louis, the streets became darker, shadowed by magnificent ancient buildings, classical majestic reminders of the grandeur of Old Paris.

"Here it is."

Emily's "hotel" was a house whose small, inexpensive rooms were rented to those—almost exclusively French—who knew to look there. The front door was opaque glass and it opened directly to a poorly lit, very steep flight of stairs.

Rob walked up the stairs with Emily. The hotel was probably safe, but . . .

Emily's room was at the top of the stairs on the right. It was a garret, austere, windowless. Broken springs protruded from beneath the small, narrow bed and it sagged in the middle. An unshaded lightbulb hung from the ceiling and provided the room with its only light. A crooked chair was shoved under a dilapidated table. Guide books anchored the corners of a map of Paris that lay open on the narrow bed.

"Vintage Paris," Emily whispered, suddenly embarrassed that Rob had seen the room. *I feel more comfortable here, Rob, than in a suite at the Ritz.*

Emily bent her head, sending a golden curtain of fine silk across her face, hiding her eyes. Rob wanted to find the gray eyes, smile at them, reassure them.

Very gently, and without giving it much thought because it felt so right, so natural, Rob moved the silky gold away from Emily's face.

At his touch Emily stiffened, and the gray eyes beneath the golden curtain were no longer simply shy and embarrassed . . . they were terrified.

"Please don't." Emily backed away, two steps. In another step she would reach the bed.

"Emily?"

"*Please.*"

"Emily, what's wrong?"

Rob took a step toward her and watched the terror crescendo. *You're afraid of me, Emily? Why?*

"Please go away, please go away, don't hurt me, please. . . ." Emily's voice was soft and distant, like a little child saying an incantation that no one would heed, a prayer that would be unanswered, a final weak plea not to be hurt.

"Emily." He was the cause of her fear! The more he pushed, the greater her fear. Finally, Rob whispered helplessly, bewildered, "All right. I'm leaving, Emily. I'm sorry."

Rob closed the door behind him as he left and Emily stared at it through a blur of tears. Then she began to tremble, shaken by the emotions that swept through her. *Relief . . . disappointment . . . pain.*

Relief, because Rob had left.

Disappointment, because she'd believed Rob was different—so different— and he wasn't. *Yes,* he was, just a little, because he had listened to her pleas. *No,* mostly he was the same, and there was no hope.

Pain, the screaming, unbearable pain deep inside her.

Emily reached into a corner of her small suitcase and removed the bottle of drugs Mick had given her. Her hands shook as she twisted off the cap and the pills spilled onto the narrow bed and the colorful map of Paris. Emily picked a gray pill with green speckles off Monmartre and swallowed it quickly. She put two other pills in her coat pocket for later, in case the first pill lost its magic before she was ready to return from her dark walk into the night.

Emily felt more calm now. She was going to escape. The pain would be numbed for a few precious hours. The pill was in her stomach. *Good.* In a few minutes she would begin to feel its effect. Emily made herself forget about Rob and think about the lights and colors of Paris, the shapes that were out there, the intriguing hallucinations that awaited her, the friendly monsters.

Calm, calm . . .

Rob stood on the Pont St. Louis glaring at the flying buttresses of Notre Dame—eerie forms in the darkness—trying to make sense of what had happened.

What the hell did Emily think he was going to do?

Please go away, don't hurt me! How could Emily possibly think he would hurt anyone, much less *her?*

Rob had left the tiny garret because that was what Emily wanted—her pleas had been desperate—but it couldn't end like this.

He strode quickly back toward the small hotel, climbed the stairs two at a time, and knocked on the splintered wooden door to her room.

"Emily, let me in."

No! Fear seized her at the sound of his voice and the sudden violence of the pounding. Fear and more disappointment: Rob wasn't any different at all. At least she had taken the pill. That would make it better, but still . . . *no.*

"Emily?"

Emily opened the door slowly, a reluctant acceptance of her destiny of pain. She tilted her delicate face up to him and her gray eyes met his, proud and defiant, but so wise, so painfully wise. *I know what you're going to do, Rob, and I will do it, whatever you want, because I have no choice.*

Rob gazed at her lovely face and the gray eyes that sent a proud message of hopelessness. *Hopelessness? Why?*

"Emily, please, tell me what happened."

Emily felt little rushes, evidence that the pill was beginning to work. *Please hurry!*

"Emily?"

"You know what happened."

"I don't."

"You wanted to"—Emily searched for a polite way to say it—"have sex with me."

"What? Emily, no." *Yes, if that's what you wanted. If your eyes had told me I could kiss you, I would have, but . . .* "You seemed embarrassed about the room. I pushed your hair off your face so I could see you while I convinced you not to be embarrassed. That's all.

Rob's thoughts drifted to that balmy summer evening on the Palisades in Santa Monica. Emily's lover's hands had roamed all over her delicate body—intimate, explicit, ugly—and she had allowed it . . . or the drugs had allowed it.

"Tell me, Emily."

"Tell you what?"

"Tell me why you thought I wanted to make love with you." *Tell me why you assumed I would force myself on you.*

"Make *love?*"

Such bitterness! Emily, talk to me.

The pill was beginning to work. *Good.* She was beginning to feel a little strong, a little brave.

"Make love," Rob repeated softly. Emily *might* have seen desire in his eyes, but to react to his gentle touch with such terror! "Why did you think that?"

"Because that's what all men want," Emily replied simply.

"Maybe your boyfriend, Emily . . ."

"My boyfriend?"

"I saw you with him last summer, a couple days after the wedding. You were on the Palisades in Santa Monica."

So you know all about me, Rob. Emily's heart ached. *You've always known.*

"Emily, maybe all *he* wants is sex, but—"

The drug was working now and her illusions—that Rob had been warm and kind because he saw something good in her that no one else had ever seen—were shattered. There was nothing more to lose. *Tell him everything, Emily. Why not?*

"Sex is all that any man has ever wanted from me." Then, because there was nothing more to lose, no more illusions to protect, she added defiantly, "There have been a lot of men, Rob. It goes way back."

"How far back?" Rob asked gently, fearing the answer.

Emily had never told anyone. Memories swirled, tossed by the drug, and she reembered the people who had asked her this before. There were the doctors when she had tried to kill herself. Is someone touching you, Emily? Is someone making you do things you don't want to do? Is someone making you feel bad? No, she had told them. He's touching me because he loves me, and I want to do these things, don't I, to earn his love? And I am bad, because if I weren't, he wouldn't want to do these things to me, would he?

Emily hadn't told the doctors or social workers or psychologists at the hospital or the teachers at school. They learned nothing from her about why she had taken the handful of pills that had almost killed her. But Emily learned something. She learned about pills. She learned that just before she was about to die there was a wonderful foggy floating feeling. If she could feel that way, again and again, without dying . . .

And if she took too many pills, if she died, it didn't really matter.

"Emily? How far back does it go?"

Emily had never told anyone and now she was going to tell Rob *of all people.* Rob, who she desperately wanted to believe was different. And maybe *he* was, but she wasn't, even with him.

"My stepfather."

Oh, Emily.

"Do you want to talk about it?" he asked quietly.

Rob looked for an answer in her eyes, but the clear gray had become cloudy. He looked beyond her to the pills scattered on the narrow bed. "Emily, what have you taken?"

"Something gray and green."

"You don't know?"

"Some specially designed hallucinogen." She smiled bravely, defiantly. It doesn't matter what it was, Rob! It's working.

Rob felt helpless, and very angry. He wa angry at the men who made Emily fearful of *him*, and angry at Emily for counting him among them, and angry at himself for ever leaving her.

Emily was leaving him now, escaping into another world.

"Let's go for a walk," Rob suggested. He wasn't going to leave her again. He was going to stay with her, protect her, until she was in control.

Maybe then she would want to talk—or maybe not—but if she did, it wouldn't happen in the tiny, poorly lit room with the bed covered with drugs. Rob would return to the glitter of Paris with her, to protect her from the demons of the night and, if he could, to protect her from the demons of her heart.

Rob could tell Emily was hallucinating. She would stop and stare, tilting her head, smiling softly, mesmerized by a light or a shape or a color. Then it would be gone. She would look confused for a moment, then she would walk on until she found something else.

Emily led and Rob followed. She was Alice in Wonderland admiring all the creatures. Rob wasn't sure Emily knew he was there. She would look at him, as if making a surprise discovery, and carefully study his face. Rob guessed she saw a kaleidoscope of a thousand faces in his own. He hoped the faces Emily saw in his were friendly ones. Rob hoped, too, that deep down, beneath the layers of drugs and the layers of pain, some part of Emily knew that he cared.

Finally, the drug-world began to fade. Emily gazed at him uneasily and they were back to what had started this all—a shy, embarrassed look, Rob's attempt to reassure, a gentle touch that recalled a lifetime of pain and fear.

Perhaps Emily Rousseau had never felt the gentle touch of a man who cared.

Rob and Emily sat in a remote corner of a café, still crowded and alive at two in the morning, and he ordered espresso for both of them. No wine, he thought. No more drugs. Talk to me, Emily.

"Do you want to talk about your stepfather?"

"There's not much to say."

Hours ago they had sat in a café, drinking cappuccino, and Emily had seemed so relaxed, so at home. Now her gray eyes were clear of drugs, and in that clarity Rob saw sadness and resignation.

I've already told you everything, Rob. You know the horrible truth of my life.

Wouldn't it help for Emily to talk about it? Rob wondered. He knew nothing about this! It was in the news, of course, out it was so much easier, so much more pleasant, to deny it existed. At the very least, it belonged to other people, women he didn't know, never would know. But now it belonged to this beautiful woman, and Rob was ill-equipped to help her, except that he cared.

"Emily, you can trust me. I'm your friend. I really am.I think it would help to talk about it."

"What do you want to know?"

"How odl were you?" Rob answered her question aloud. Silently, his mind gave another answer. *Nothing. I want to know nothing. I want it never to have happened to you.*

"I was ten and eleven and twelve."

"It happened more than once?"

"All the time." Emily added softly because she wanted Rob to know, "I tried to stop him, Rob. I pleaded with him."

"You couldn't stop him, Emily. How could you? He was a grown man and you were a little girl. It wasn't your fault."

"He made me believe it was," she whispered distantly.

"It *wasn't*. Hasn't anyone ever told you that before?"

"No one knows. No one knows but you. Please don't ever tell anyone." *Please don't tell Elaina . . . or Allison.*

"I won't. I promise." Rob smiled gently. He wanted to touch her, to hold her, but that would frighten her, a betrayal after all. "You never told the police . . . anyone?"

"No."

"But he stopped when you were twelve."

"He left." Her stepfather had vanished the day after Emily tried to kill herself. He simply disappeared, which had made her mother terribly unhappy, and Emily had felt even more guilt because that was her fault, too. "And I left four years later, right after I took the final exam of my senior year of high school."

"That was in Quebec?"

"No. We moved to a small town in northern California when my mother married my stepfather. My stepfather was—is—American. He adopted me. I changed my name back to my real father's name when I was eighteen. My real father was French . . . a fisherman. His boat capsized and he drowned when I was three."

"I'm sorry." Rob wondered how different Emily's life might have been—joyous and full of laughter—if a storm-angry wave hadn't crashed on a fragile fishing boat.

Emily smiled softly, wistfully. There was so much she couldn't change.

"You ran away from home?" Rob asked after a few silent moments. *He* had run away—sort of—with twelve million dollars in the bank and dreams of gold that were more wonderful than the luxurious promises life had held since the day he was born.

"No one tried to stop me, Rob." Emily shrugged. "I had been accepted at UCLA, but I needed more money for tuition and living expenses than I was able to save from the jobs I had during high school."

Rob held his breath, hoping Emily hadn't run away from a loveless home to the streets of Los Angeles. But she hadn't. She found work—working two or three jobs at a time—and a tiny basement apartment in Santa Monica that no one else wanted; and one day she saw a "Help Wanted" sign in the window of Jerome Cole's photography studio.

"And then, one Saturday in June, Jerome got food poisoning, and I got to take wedding pictures, and—" Emily smiled. *And then I got to work for you.* The smile faded, remembering that Rob knew everything about her—he always had—even though his eyes were still kind. "I don't see Mick anymore."

"Mick?"

"The man you saw me with."

Good. It was a start, but it wasn't enough.

"Emily, if you've never talked to anyone . . . don't you think it would help?

There are people who are trained—"

"You think there is something wrong with me." Emily stared at her espresso, looking for a shape or a color, some proof that the pill was still working. But there was none, no cushion for the pain.

"*No*," Rob answered swiftly, decisively. He gazed at her until she lifted her eyes and met his. "I know there is nothing wrong with you, Emily. You were an innocent victim." *And you still are.*

"I'm all right, Rob."

No you're not! Rob thought, remembering her reaction to his gentle touch: pick a drug, any drug, to escape.

It was three-thirty A.M. when Rob and Emily returned to her tiny room on L'Ile de Saint Louis. Rob stood a safe distance as Emily opened the door to the apartment and flipped the switch for the bare lightbulb that hung from the ceiling.

"Thank you, Rob."

Rob smiled as his mind searched for the right response. *You're welcome, Emily. I enjoyed the evening.* The polite response would have been a lie. His own helplessness, his inability to really help her, had tormented him all evening as he watched her cast about, adrift, alone, desperate. Rob hated that, but—*but being with her* . . . Rob didn't want *that* part to end.

"My flight back to LA leaves at four tomorrow afternoon. Would you like to have lunch with me?"

"Yes."

"Good. I'll be here at eleven."

"All right."

As he started to leave, Rob's eye caught sight of the map of Paris strewn with pills.

"Emily, promise me you'll throw the pills away."

Emily answered with a sad smile. *I can't promise you that, Rob.*

Chapter 18

"Are we still going to Aspen, Rob?" Elaina heard the soft plea in her own voice and wondered if Rob knew it wasn't a seductive pout, but rather ice-cold fear.

Elaina wasn't so tough when it came to Rob Adamson. Elaina had spent her entire life wanting it all and *getting* it all. And she had never wanted anything more than she wanted Rob. The blowup before Rob left for Paris—his surprising anger when she merely spoke the truth about Emily Rousseau—had terrified her. Rob's anger had abated quickly, but the next day he left for Paris and the memory of his inexplicable fury had lingered. When Rob called Elaina from Paris, his voice sounded pleasant, normal, but they needed to be together, touching, loving, passionately erasing the nagging vestiges of the angry words.

Elaina and Rob had been planning the week-long vacation in Aspen for months. They would leave the Friday following Rob's return from Paris and stay in a suite at the just-opened Chateau Aspen. It would be a perfect vacation, a wonderful week of passion and luxury in Roger Towne's newest Chateau.

When Rob returned from Paris, he was preoccupied and distant. It had nothing to do with her or them, Rob assured Elaina. But even in bed she felt the distance.

"Of course we're going to Aspen, Elaina. There are just some things I need to take care of before we go."

Then take care of them, please!

There weren't "things." There are just the one thing: How Rob could help

Emily. During the five evenings between Rob's return from Paris and the trip to Aspen, when he and Elaina could have been dining by candlelight at Adriano or the Cafe Four Oaks, Rob was in the Health Sciences Library at UCLA, reading. It was a painful, agonizing read—the story of Emily's life and thousands of others—but the search was worth it because there was hope and help.

And the help was nearby! Dr. Beverly Camden, a leading authority, herself a victim, had an office in Santa Monica two blocks from St. John's Hospital. Rob read both of Dr. Camden's books: *Little Girl Lost*, which revealed the tragedy, the betrayal, the loss of joy and trust and innocence; and *Little Girl Found*, which told of the hope.

Rob met with Dr. Camden on Wednesday, two days before he and Elaina were to leave for Aspen. Dr. Camden listened in silence as Rob told her about his "friend," carefully revealing nothing that would betray his promise to Emily that he would tell no one about her.

"I've read your books," Rob told Dr. Camden when he finished. "And I think she could be helped."

"I know she could. It sounds as though she has made great progress on her own."

"Does it?" Rob asked hopefully.

"Yes. For one thing, she told you about it."

"She told me because she had taken some kind of drug."

"No. Drug or no drug, Rob, she knew she was telling you. And there are other very positive signs: her clothes, her fingernails." Dr. Camden looked at the concerned dark blue eyes that had noticed what many others might have dismissed as trivial. The short-bitten fingernails that had been allowed to grow were an important symbol of his friend's desperate wish to rediscover the joy and happiness and confidence that had been so harshly, so inexplicably, stolen from her. "She's searching for a little pride, a little self-worth."

"She should have so much!"

"Of course she should. *Everyone* should. But she has none."

"As if she's to blame," Rob whispered. "She's just an innocent victim, like a little kitten playing in a storm who is suddenly struck by lightning."

"Not like a little kitten, Rob. A kitten would have known instinctively not to play in a storm, that there were dangers in doing so. There were no warnings for your friend, no instincts she could draw on. That makes it all the more devastating, because it was so *unexpected*, so contrary to everything her life had taught her. She probably was a trusting, happy child. She may have been thrilled that she was going to have a new daddy. And he was probably charming to her, told her how much he loved her, how much fun they would have."

"In therapy, does she have to go through all of that, what actually happened?" *So much pain, too much.*

"No, not necessarily. Only if it's helpful to her. Many women block out the abuse all together, remembering only years later, after multiple failed relationships or marriages. But your friend already remembers. What she needs to focus on is the little girl who played hopscotch on the playground and laughed with her friends and smiled at the golden sun and giggled at the thought of ice cream cones and soft puppies. I need to help her find that innocence again. I need to help her believe that the joy and hope and happiness she felt—and the *trust*—were real, and that what happened was a horrible fluke, a bolt of lightning that would never happen again."

"But I think it *has* happened to her again and again. She believes that all men will hurt her."

"You said she wears clothes that are unrevealing, *concealing*, and that she is very beautiful. She is obviously trying not to send a message of sexuality, but it's backfiring because it makes her look like a victim and that attracts cruel men."

"I never thought her clothes made her look like a victim," Rob murmured almost to himself. Vulnerable, *yes*. Precious and fragile, *yes*. But to want to *hurt* her?

"That's because you're not that kind of man." *You're the kind of man that your friend doesn't believe exists.*

"Why would she be with men like that?"

"She needs to be loved, Rob, just like everyone else in the world. I'm sure these men tell her they love her; I'm sure her stepfather told her that, too. For her, sex has always been an act of violence, not an act of tenderness and love. She's known nothing else. But now a deep instinct is telling her there *has* to be something better. She knows about real love—some fragile, resilient corner of her heart knows about it—but can she trust that knowledge?"

"Trust," Rob echoed softly. That was the central issue. How could Emily trust any man? Why *should* she? The first man she had trusted with her love and her innocence and her joy had brutally betrayed her.

"She trusts herself the very least," Dr. Camden said. "And she doesn't trust men. Does she have women friends?"

Rob considered the question for a moment. Allison Fitzgerald—warm, generous, kind Allison—was Emily's friend, wasn't she? Rob got the impression more from the way Allison spoke of Emily—pride in her talented friend and perhaps a sigh of concern—than when Emily spoke of Allison. Rob remembered the conversation in Paris about Emily moonlighting for the Chateau Bel Air. *Did Allison tell you?* Emily had asked. Rob remembered that there had been a flicker of disappointment in Emily's eyes, as if she were about to learn that she couldn't trust Allison, either.

"There are people who would like to be her friend," Rob said.

Dr. Camden nodded thoughtfully. It was quite obvious that Rob Adamson wanted to be the young woman's friend—*at least*—and Dr. Camden guessed there could be much more. She wondered if the woman knew it. Of course not, she thought. Even if Rob told his friend how much he cared, she wouldn't believe it because she had no confidence in herself. Dr. Camden looked at Rob and felt a sense of urgency about his friend. There was a wonderful life waiting out there for her.

"Will she come see me?"

"I don't know. I thought I could do a portrait of you." Rob paused, not wanting to reveal too much about Emily. Many people worked for him; it wasn't a betrayal. "She's with the magazine. I could arrange for you—"

"Don't trick her, Rob," Dr. Camden interrupted. "Don't ever give her a reason not to trust you."

"So I should—?"

"Tell her the truth. Tell her you read everything you could and met with me and that I would very much like to see her." Dr. Camden added a serious, quiet warning, "It may backfire, Rob. She may consider even this a betrayal. She may be very angry."

"I can't imagine her being angry."

"Oh, Rob, then you don't know about the rage of an innocent victim."

But Rob *did* know. The rage of innocence betrayed lived in his own heart because of Sara.

"I guess it's a risk I have to take," Rob said. "To help her."

"Yes."

"I'm serious about doing an article on you and your work for *Portrait*. It's something I should have done—should have known to do—a long time ago."

"Well, after she's fine, then I'd be delighted. I think that now it might muddy the waters, perhaps discourage her from coming to see me."

"All right." Rob stood to leave. "Thank you very much. I appreciate you taking the time to meet with me."

"You're welcome. And Rob? She's very lucky to have you as a friend."

"I haven't scheduled your next appointment with Emily," Fran told Rob when he returned to his office after seeing Dr. Camden. "She's due back from Europe the day after you leave for Aspen. You'll be in Aspen, then she'll be in New York. Oh, but that reminds me. Lawrence Carlyle is certainly going to get the Best Director nomination for *Hong Kong*. I checked with his studio in London. He's leaving in two weeks for a three-month shoot in Africa. Wouldn't it make sense for Emily to take his picture in London now? I know she'll call before she leaves Europe, to see what I have scheduled for her. I could arrange to have her stop in London on her way back."

"Lawrence Carlyle hasn't been nominated yet."

"But he will be! And then Emily—or whoever, although Emily would be the best because Lawrence Carlyle photographs are always so *unrevealing*—is going to tramp into the bush?"

"I guess. If need be." Rob had already decided—as much as he, too, would love to see what Emily Rousseau could do with Lawrence Carlyle—that Emily would just do portraits of the nominees who happened to be in Los Angeles. That way she could keep daily appointments with Dr. Camden. "So, when can I meet with Emily?"

Fran flipped the calendar two weeks ahead. It was Rob's calendar, but Fran made notations in the margins about the travel schedules of Emily and the staff journalists.

"You want to meet with her before the nominations are announced?"

"I want to meet with her as soon as a meeting can be scheduled."

"OK. Let's see. She'll be in New York and you'll be in San Francisco. The afternoon of the fourteenth looks OK." Fran tapped a tapered finger on the calendar, on a date around which she had drawn a large red heart. "Like at three?"

"All right. Make it three and block out the rest of the afternoon. What's the red heart?"

"God, you're such an incurable romantic! February fourteenth, Rob Adamson, is Valentine's Day."

"And you're such a skeptic," Rob countered lightly, reaching a quick decision. He wanted to talk to Emily alone, in private, without the possibility of interruption. "I think, as a Valentine to all the staff, I'll just close the office at three that day."

"You're kidding."

"No. Why don't you generate some cute little heart-shaped memo and send it around?"

"With pleasure. You still want to meet with Emily at three that day?"

"Yes."

Allison sat at the huge picture window in the plush dining room of the just-opened Chateau Aspen and watched the dawn awaken to a blizzard of snow.
She curled her hands around a mug of rich hot chocolte and smiled.

I probably look like a contented cat. Warm and cozy and completely happy to sit by a window and watch windy, snowy swirls.

Warm. That was the adjective Allison would apply to this moment, this weekend, every moment she spent with Roger Towne. It had been that way since hey first met—warmth, not fire, nothing dangerous, just wonderful comfortable feelings.

Just as it had been with Dan.

Warmth without fire, but maybe the warmth would become fire. Maybe the warm smiles and easy laughter were kindling that someday would explode into flames. Allison thought it might happen, but she was in no hurry. It was so nice this way, touching with smiles, eyes, and words, not hands and lips; happy together but not desperate apart; working harmoniously on the Chateau Bel Air.

Allison wondered if Roger's expectations differed from hers. If they did, *he* was respecting *her* wishes. When Allison arrived yesterday for a long weekend in Aspen, Roger showed her promptly to her own elegant suite, instantly assuaging any worry she might have had that he expected them to share a room.

After Allison was settled in her suite, Roger gave her a tour of the hotel, followed by a sleigh ride through Aspen, followed by a candlelight dinner and a nightcap in front of a roaring fire, complete with roasting chestnuts. Then Roger escorted Allison to her suite, caressed her only with his handsome smile, and wished her good night.

Allison awakened early, arrived in the dining room before the skiers—if *anyone* was going to ski today—and found a window seat from which to drink hot chocolate and gaze happily at the swirling blizzard.

"Good morning, Allison."

"Rob! Hi. You made it. Roger was worried."

"We got in late last night. There were long delays in Denver because of the storm, which, I see, has now arrived in Aspen."

"I feel like I'm inside one of those glass balls—a chalet scene—that someone has just turned upside down." Allison smiled. "I love it, but I guess the skiers won't be happy."

"It will probably pass through quickly, leaving blue sky and powder snow. You aren't a skier?"

"No."

"May I join you? Is Roger on his way down?"

"Yes, of course. I don't know about Roger." Allison frowned briefly. *Roger and I aren't lovers.* Rob wouldn't know that, and he would *assume.* Since New Year's Eve, Roger and Allison had had dinner with Rob and Elaina twice, and three days before Rob and Emily left for Paris, Allison, Roger, and Rob had had a leisurely lunch together at The Bistro. "Will Elaina be joining us?"

"I doubt it. I imagine Elaina won't be up for hours." Rob sat down across from Allison and told the waitress he would like a mug of hot chocolate, too. He leaned over to study Allison's almost-full mug and asked, "Have you already eaten the marshmallows?"

"There weren't any!"

"No? And Roger calls this a luxury hotel?"

"It *is* a luxury hotel. Except for the marshmallow problem—and those may be available on request—there are virtually no flaws."

"Virtually?"

"Well, I was just thinking that an overstuffed chair, suitable for curling one's

legs under while spending an entire day drinking hot chocolate, right here, would be nice."

"In the dining room."

"Yes! Do you think that's just too bold a design statement?"

"Not at all. Any other flaws?"

"I guess I would have a few photographs by our friend on the walls."

Our friend, Rob mused. How he wished Emily knew she had friends.

"Do you know her very well?" Rob asked, trying to sound casual but delighted to have an easy entrée into a discussion of Emily with Allison.

"Emily?"

"Yes."

Allison hesitated before answering.

"I think of Emily as a friend," Allison began after a few moments. "I like her very much, but I guess I really don't know her very well. She's quite private."

"And it's not your style to pry."

"No, I guess not." Allison wondered if she should say the next, but she saw the gentle concern in Rob's eyes and continued thoughtfully, "I've wondered if there was something—something very troubling—in Emily's past. That's just a feeling." Allison frowned slightly. "And, for as nice and as kind as Emily is, and as talented, she doesn't really have much confidence."

"No, she doesn't," Rob agreed quietly.

"I do know how much Emily enjoys working for *Portrait*," Allison said after a moment.

"Really?"

"Yes." Allison added something she believed to be true, although Emily had never actually said it, "I think it's really how much she enjoys working with you."

"Oh." *I hope so.*

Rob and Allison watched the snow swirl in silence for several minutes.

"Speaking of *Portrait*," Rob began as he turned from the stark whiteness of the blizzard to the smiling jade eyes, red-gold curls, and pink-flushed cheeks, "I would like to do a portrait of you. Interior designer *extraordinaire*."

"Me?"

"Of course. I'd like the article to appear after the Chateau Bel Air is open, perhaps the August or September issue?"

Bellemeade was going to be featured in *Architectural Digest* in June. That had been Claire and Steve's decision to make. The focus of the *Architectural Digest* article would be Bellemeade—its architecture, its history, its recent interior design . . . Bellemeade, not Allison. An article in *Portrait* would be quite different—*her* story, not the story of Bellemeade or the Chateau Bel Air.

"I'm very flattered, Rob."

"Is that a yes?"

"It's a no," Allison said softly. "It's too soon."

"You think you're a flash in the pan?"

"No . . ." *But I've learned not to count gold medals before I've won them.*

"Is it because of your accident?" Rob asked gently.

So Rob knew. He probably had known from the very beginning, from the day last June in the fragrant alcove of lilacs.

"It would be hard to do a very thorough article about you without mentioning your riding and your accident," he added truthfully.

"I know. That wouldn't be a problem as long as I wasn't portrayed—*portraited!*—as a courageous heroine."

"But it did take courage, Allison."

"No, Rob. I just did what I had to do to survive."

"So?"

"I guess I just want to keep a low profile for now."

"Fair enough. You probably won't give me a call when it's time, will you?"

"Probably not."

"I'll check back every six months or so, OK?"

"Sure." *Tell him, Allison. Tell him now, gently, that you knew Sara.* "Rob, there's something I've wanted to tell—"

At that moment, Roger appeared. For the next hour, Roger, Rob, and Allison talked, marvelled at the silent power of the snowstorm, and drank hot chocolate. Then Rob left.

Some other snowy morning, I'll tell Rob how much I liked Sara and how sorry I am, Allison thought after Rob was gone.

Or will I? Allison wondered as she analyzed her feelings, a mixture of relief and guilt. Relief, because it would be difficult, emotional, for both of them. And guilt. Why guilt? she asked herself. Was it really wrong not to want to recall Rob's pain? Was it really impolite not to want to see sadness in his dark blue eyes?

No, Allison decided. It wasn't wrong . . . it was right.

That snowy morning in Aspen, Allison decided that she would never tell Rob she had known Sara. Rob, who Allison would never want to hurt; Rob, who was her friend; Rob, with whom there had always been a special bond.

"Come to bed," Elaina whispered softly, hiding the plea as well as she could. Rob stood at the bedroom window gazing out at the snowstorm. He was just across the room, *but so far away.* And she wanted him, needed him so much! A day in bed—a day of breathless sex and daring intimacy—would bring Rob back to her, wouldn't it?

"It's nine A.M., Elaina. Time to get up."

"And do what, Rob? We're snowed in. Let's enjoy it. Bed and room service and long hot showers and more bed . . ."

"I told Roger and Allison we would meet them for cocktails at seven and dinner at eight."

"*Tonight!* Ten lovely sensual hours from now. We should be famished by then. Rob? . . ."

Rob barely heard Elaina's words. He was thinking about Emily, worrying about what he would say to her on the fourteenth. *Happy Valentine's Day, Emily. Oh, by the way, here are some books you should read because you don't know about love or valentines, just violence and betrayal. And here's the name of a doctor you should see.*

Rob worried about how he would say what he needed to say and how she would react, but his thoughts about Emily went way beyond that. Rob ached for her. He wanted her to be happy. He wanted so much to help her.

Rob wished Emily were here right now, in this elegant suite, warm and safe beside the fire, protected from the icy winter storm. Rob wished he could spend however long Emily needed with her, in these luxurious rooms, talking to her, listening to her, helping her purge the pain from her heart.

He and Emily could hide in this perfect place, and when they emerged, the blizzard outside would be over, and so would the blizzard within. And Emily's life would be golden and sunny *always*.

Fantasy, Rob told himself. Emily would feel so *trapped* here! Emily didn't believe she deserved beautiful things. She would want to run away from this beautiful, luxurious place.

Would you lock her in? Rob's mind demanded of the part of him that had created the wonderful fantasy. Would you *force* Emily to stay against her will? Wouldn't that make you one of *them*, the evil men who had harmed and imprisoned her?

And even, if by some miracle, Emily would agree to be here with him, words were only words, promises only promises. Emily had years of emotion and experience and pain—all *real*—that would eloquently refute anything Rob promised her about love. Rob knew Emily's healing couldn't happen overnight. It would be a long, painful process with many setbacks; a dream constructed from a lifetime of nightmares; a delicate belief that would take faith and nurturing and patience and time. *Time* and the feathery weight of new, wonderful experiences to counterbalance the oppressive weight of the old, horrible ones.

Rob wanted to make everything right and gentle for Emily *now*.

He wanted, he realized, to *show* Emily about love.

But it was Elaina, not Emily, who was here with him. Elaina, who was in his bed. There had been many women in Rob's life and in his bed. Making love had always been such an easy pleasure; a welcome sharing of ecstasy . . . effortless, exciting, *good*.

It had never been that way for Emily. For Emily, there had been only terror.

"I'm going for a walk," Rob said, finally answering Elaina's plea for him to join her in bed.

"Rob, there's a blizzard! It's very dangerous."

"I'll be back."

Rob trudged through the deep, fresh snow, whipped by the icy wind, acutely aware that the beacons that guided the path to safety were lost in a white fog of snow.

This is what Emily's life is like, Rob thought sadly. Every day of her life is like walking in a blizzard without beacons, a foggy, turbulent world of harm and danger.

Rob had always known about Emily's lovely fragility, but now he realized her remarkable strength. What courage it must take to venture into the world—a world of danger—day after day! What an effort to be always wary—to know there are no safe ports in the storm—and yet to go on, in a brave, solitary search for peace and beauty.

Oh, Emily. Let me help you. Let me show you about love.

"Why don't you go ahead, Elaina? I need to make some calls. Please tell Roger and Allison I'll be along soon."

"All right." Elaina didn't tease him—"It's Saturday night, Rob, forget the magazine!"—she just kissed him softly on the lips before leaving for Roger's suite.

That afternoon, after Rob returned from his long walk, had been . . .

Elaina had no words to describe the tenderness of their lovemaking. Rob had been so gentle, so careful, so loving. He had never made love to her like that before. It was as if . . .

Don't think it, Elaina warned herself. But it was impossible to suppress the horrible thought. *It was as if Rob were making love to someone else.*

After Elaina left to join Roger and Allison, Rob dialed the number he had memorized before he left Los Angeles. Emily's number was in Fran's Rolodex, of course, and E. Rousseau was also listed in the telephone book.

Rob just wanted to say hello—maybe more—if Emily was home. She was due back from France sometime today.

The first time he dialed, Rob let Emily's phone ring fifteen times. He waited ten minutes, redialed, and this time listened through thirty rings before hanging up.

Perhaps it was just as well. It was an impulse and it might have confused or worried her.

Just concentrate on what you're going to say to her when you see her, Rob told himself as he walked to Roger's suite. *Just be sure you have rehearsed, over and over, those so very important words.*

Chapter 19

By Valentine's Day, *Love* was ahead of even the optimistic filming schedule Steve and Peter had planned. Steve was on the set most days, watching without interfering, marvelling at the genius of Peter Dalton.

Peter was calm, serious, never temperamental or even the least impatient. And Peter's calm professionalism was contagious. The crew was calm and serious, the cast was calm and serious; they were all serious, dedicated professionals working harmoniously to create the movie of the decade.

Even Bruce Hunter. Bruce was a party boy. He was famous for off-screen romances with his costars and was the gold standard for egocentrism in Hollywood. Bruce had reason to be egocentric: He was *huge* box office. Bruce's enormous success was attributable to his Greek God looks, his stunning sexuality, and to the remarkable fact that, in addition to everything else, he could act! Bruce Hunter had been selected to play Sam, the male lead in *Love*, because his on-screen chemistry with Winter Carlyle was sensational.

Peter's style as a director was to allow the actor great freedom in defining and exploring the role. He provided guidance and direction as necessary. Peter's style presupposed that the actor had a serious interest in the character he was portraying. The actors and actresses with whom Peter usually worked—the *best* of the London and New York stage—had such a commitment.

Bruce Hunter did not. Bruce spent no time thinking about his character's motivation; he simply awaited direction. And like a gifted natural athlete—"What shall I do now, Coach? A long bomb into the end zone for a TD? OK, no problem."—Bruce could deliver.

"Give that last line with a little more sincerity, Bruce," Peter would say.

"More? All right. Like this?"

Bruce would deliver Peter's magnificently crafted lines exactly as the director told him to, every scene perfect, every scene bringing Bruce Hunter closer to an Academy Award.

"Look more loving, Bruce."

"More loving? What do you mean, Pete?"

"I mean," Peter answered softly, "you need to look at her as if you would give your life for her."

"Jesus!"

"Do it."

"OK, you got it."

Peter's working relationship with Bruce was easy but uninspired. His working relationship with Winter was what he preferred—a serious, analytical, artistic collaboration. Winter cared *so much* about Julia and about Peter's astonishing script. Winter wanted to speak every line as well as it could be spoken, to make every emotion exactly right. In the beginning Winter was obviously uncertain about her talent, but with Peter's calm support her confidence blossomed and her wonderful natural talent matured.

"Were you happy with that scene?" Peter would ask, joining Winter during a break, waiting patiently for her honest reply.

"Not completely," Winter would admit truthfully.

"What didn't you like?"

"I don't know, Peter. It just didn't feel right. What did you think?"

Peter and Winter would discuss it quietly, gifted actress to gifted director, and when they did the scene the next time, it would be better, and eventually, when Peter and Winter were both satisfied, the scene would be perfect.

"Cut," Peter said just before noon on Valentine's Day. "Let's break for lunch."

The crew dispersed. As usual, Bruce Hunter looked a little lost. On most sets, "breaks" were a time for flirtation, even sex in a costar's trailer, but not on this set. Bruce had imagined, assumed, that he would have an affair with the beautiful Winter Carlyle. But Winter was remote, interested only in her work. After a confused moment, Bruce shrugged and ambled off to have lunch with the crew.

Within two minutes of Peter's announcement of the break, the sound stage was empty, except for Winter, who hadn't moved from the sofa where she had sat during the scene, and Peter, who had joined her there.

"You're green."

"What?" Winter turned to look at Peter, moving her head slowly. Fast movement sent waves of dizziness and nausea.

"Green," Peter repeated with a gentle smile. "Even with filters, the camera is seeing green."

"Flu."

Peter nodded. "I'll drive you home."

"Peter, we're not done filming for the day."

"Yes we are."

Peter and Winter could have driven to the set together every day—Bellemeade and Holman Avenue were very close—but that would have changed their relationship. In those predawn and after-dusk hours, Peter and Winter might have easily drifted from discussions of the movie to more personal topics.

During the early morning and late evening commute, Peter *might* have asked Winter questions about her best friend, Allison.

Tell me all about Allison, Winter, Peter might have said. Then he might have even asked, *Does Allison have someone? Is Allison in love?*

Winter could have easily answered those questions, but she would have been unable to answer the most perplexing question that danced in Peter's mind about Allison Fitzgerald: *Why do I keep thinking about her?*

Peter and Winter didn't speak at all on their Valentine's Day drive from Burbank to Westwood. Peter could tell that Winter's energy was focused on her battle with nausea. He sent sympathetic smiles but didn't disturb her concentration by talking to her.

When they reached Holman Avenue, Peter walked with Winter to the door of her third-floor apartment.

"I noticed a Westward Ho a few blocks away. I'm going to buy some chicken noodle soup and ginger ale, and then I'll be right back."

Winter smiled a wobbly appreciative smile.

"I have soup here, Peter. I'm fine, really. Thank you."

"You sure?"

"Yes."

"OK. Steve and I agree we'll make this a three-day weekend. Call me Sunday and let me know how you feel about working Monday?"

"I'll feel like working Monday."

"Call me."

"OK."

Peter drove to Bellemeade, distractedly tossed a tennis ball for a lively Muffin, and thought about Allison Fitzgerald.

Answer your own question. Go see her.

"Allison?"

Allison looked up from the photographs she had just carefully spread out on her desk. Two hours ago she had moved the latest catalogues from Henredon, Clarence House, Baker, and Brunschwig and Fils onto the floor to make room for the twelve long-stemmed red roses that had arrived from Roger. An hour later, when Emily appeared with the photographs she had taken in France, Allison hastily removed everything else from the top of her usually cluttered desk.

Allison's desk had been transformed from the clutterof success to tranquil elegance, from catalogues, fabric samples, sketches, phone messages, and idea lists to fragrant long-stemmed roses arched over spectacular photographs of Paris, Versailles, and the Loire Valley.

"Peter," Allison breathed. What was *he* doing here? "Hi. No movie today?"

Try to speak in complete sentences, Allison told herself. Peter is a talented-writer, remember? But it was hard enough to speak *at all* to the sensuous dark brown eyes.

"Winter is ill. The camera crew tried every filter they had, but she still looked pale green."

"Oh!" Allison stood up. That was why Peter was here. Winter had sent him. "Did Winter want me to—"

"No, Winter's fine. It's the flu, or something she ate, or the fact that she's pushing too hard. I just gave her a ride to her apartment and extracted a promise that she would have some soup and take a nap." Peter continued, with a voice that didn't exude the confidence one would expect from the extraordinary man that he was, "I decided to drop by and see what you're doing."

"Oh." Good. *Why?*

"So, what are you doing?"

"I was just looking at these photographs, trying to decide which ones are the best."

Peter moved beside Allison to look at the photographs.

"They're all the best," Peter said after a moment. "All masterpieces."

"That's what I thought, too."

"These must have been taken by E. Rousseau, the photographer who did the pictures for Bellemeade."

"Emily Rousseau. Yes. You probably also recognize her work from *Portrait* magazine. Beginning with the December issue, Emily has taken most of the portraits." Allison looked at Peter for a smiling confirmation, an "ah, yes, of

course," but his handsome features were somber. "Don't you read *Portrait?*"

"No," Peter answered quietly. He looked from a magnificent photograph of Le Petit Trianon at Versailles to Allison's slightly puzzled but smiling jade-green eyes. Her smile encouraged him. Peter was here today, testing his instincts, not believing it was possible, and Allison was passing his test with flying colors. "I wondered if you would like to have dinner with me tonight."

"Oh!" *Yes.* "I . . . have plans."

"The red roses?"

"Yes, he's—" Just a client? Allison couldn't say that about Roger any longer. It wasn't true. "Yes."

Now Peter had the answers to his questions.

Why do I keep thinking about her? Because she is so lovely, so special.

Does she have someone in her life? Yes.

"I'd better go. It was nice seeing you, Allison. Good luck deciding about the photographs." *Good-bye.*

"Thank you," Allison whispered. "Good-bye."

Allison watched Peter weave through the maze of the office and out the door into the afternoon sunshine and the bustle of Wilshire Boulevard . . . gone.

But not forgotten. Now Allison would have this memory to play and replay in her mind, just as she replayed the three other times she had seen Peter Dalton. Allison replayed the scenes and she changed the endings. Before Peter, Allison had only wanted to change one scene in her life story, the dream-shattering scene of the jump with the green and white rails.

But now, because of Peter, there were other scenes she wanted to change. Why hadn't she ridden back to the stable with him that December morning? Why hadn't she asked him to join her family for Christmas Eve dinner? What if Peter had been alone, and lonely, on Christmas?

Allison tormented herself about the ways she could have—*should have*—changed the scenes with Peter. *And she imagined new scenes.* Just last night, at Von's in Santa Monica, Allison had seen a red-ribboned dog toy—for Valentine's Day—and had wondered if she should buy it for the famous Muffin.

Of course not! Reality had crashed swiftly. Pure silliness. You don't *know* Peter Dalton. Just because you keep thinking about him.

Allison looked at the vase of red roses from Roger. More reality, wonderful reality. On that snowbound weekend in Aspen, her relationship with Roger had become more than warm. There had been long, lovely kisses in front of fires and softer laughs and gentler gazes. And since Aspen, in nightly long-distance phone calls, Roger and Allison had talked about the two days they would have together, beginning to night. The two days, and nights, would start with a Valentine's Day dinner at Adriano with Rob and Elaina. Tomorrow would be spent looking at Emily's photographs, making those decisions and others for the Chateau Bel Air, and afterwards, beginning tomorrow night and ending with Roger's Saturday evening flight to Chicago, they would be together.

And tonight, or tomorrow night, or both nights and Saturday until he left, Allison and Roger would make love. And it would be gentle and warm and lovely and right, *wouldn't it?*

In a month, *Love* would wrap. Peter Dalton would return to New York. And Allison would never see him again.

But would she replay this scene—Peter's mysterious appearance at Elegance on Valentine's Day—over and over. Would she want to change its ending, too?

Yes! So change it now! The urgent command came from deep inside, from a place other than her brain. The message from Allison's brain was loud and clear and logical: *Roger is real, wonderful, right.* The illogical command came from somewhere else. Her heart, perhaps?

Allison didn't know and didn't analyze. She simply obeyed the powerful command.

By the time Allison walked out of Elegance into the February sun, Peter had almost reached the corner. He was about to turn, about to vanish.

"Peter!"

Somehow Peter heard her soft call above the harsh noises of Wilshire Boulevard. He turned just as Allison caught her heel in a grill in the sidewalk. Allison gasped silently as the twist sent a sharp stab of pain into her hip. She recovered her balance quickly and walked toward him, smiling as he approached.

"Are you all right?" Peter asked as he rushed to meet her. "You're limping."

"I'm fine." Allison frowned briefly. Peter had never even seen her walk enough steps to realize she had a limp! *You don't know Peter Dalton and he doesn't know you,* her brain reminded, *warned.* "I always limp."

"Oh." Peter smiled reassuringly. He was so happy to see her! In the moments since he had left her, Peter had felt such a loss. He had been just about to return to Elegance. "Did I forget something?"

"Yes." *Courage,* Allison told herself. When Rob had described her as courageous that snowy morning in Aspen, Allison had replied honestly, "I just did what I had to do to survive." Perhaps this was survival, too, something she *had* to do, something her heart knew more than her mind. So bravely, so softly, Allison told Peter, "You forgot to ask me if I wanted to go riding with you on Sunday."

"I did forget that, didn't I?" Peter replied gently. "Do you want to?"

"Yes." *Very much.*

Emily arrived thirty minutes early for her three o'clock appointment with Rob and waited in the lobby until it was time to take the elevator to the suite of offices. She sat quietly, almost immobile, but her heart pounded restlessly, anxiously, and terrifying thoughts paced back and forth across her mind.

What if Rob's memories of Paris were ugly? What if Rob's enduring images were of Emily's drug-glazed eyes and the horrible things she had told him about herself? What if Rob didn't want her to work for him anymore? What if he couldn't even look at her anymore?

Please, please, please, just let it be the same, Emily's heart cried. Emily didn't dare wish for more. She dreamed, though—lovely dreams—that the new concern and gentleness in Rob's voice would be there still, but, if not, just let it be the same as before.

At two-fifty-eight, Emily took the elevator to the sixth floor. Rob was there, near the elevator, when the door opened. He had been pacing between his office and the elevator as he waited for her to arrive.

"Hi." He smiled. *Hello, lovely Emily.* Rob took the armful of folders from her. "Here, let me take these."

"Hi. Thank you. I have the portraits of the Paris designers and the work I did this week in New York."

"Great."

The first thirty minutes of their meeting was like any other. Rob admired the magnificent photographs, Emily smiled shyly, and together they selected which portraits would appear in the magazine.

"I wanted to talk to you about the plans for the Academy Award issue," Rob said after they were done with the portraits from Paris and New York. He

was easing into the uncharted, dangerous, so important territory—Emily's *life,* Emily's *happiness*—through the familiar route of business.

"OK."

"I'd like you to just do the portraits of the people in town. For all I know, that will be all nominees except Lawrence Carlyle, who's already in Africa. If none of the nominees is in town, we'll have to adjust, but—"

"All right."

"All right?" Rob was about to deliver the next rehearsed lines, convincing her despite her reluctance, but Emily had said all right. She would be in LA. Good. That meant she could begin to see Dr. Camden right away.

"Yes. All right." *If I'm here and you're here, working on the Academy Award issue, we can meet every week. Everything can be the same as always.*

"Good." Rob smiled. That was easy. Now came the difficult part, the delicate part, the important part.

Rob walked to his desk, removed the two books from the locked side drawer, and returned to the chair beside her.

"I got these books for you, Emily."

Emily looked at the books Rob held in his hands: *Little Girl Lost,* the story of the destruction of young, innocent lives, and *Little Girl Found,* the story of hope for those victims. She read the words on the books. As the meaning of the words sank in, her reaction was instant—defensive, angry, hurt—a reflex from someone who had known only hurt and betrayal for so long.

"Emily, I read the books and I met with Dr. Camden who wrote them."

"You told her about me?" *You promised! Did you tell Elaina? Allison?*

"I told Dr. Camden that I had a friend—"

"A friend?"

"A very good friend. I told her nothing that would identify you in any way. Emily, she wants to see you. She's a victim herself. She understands. She can help you."

"Help me? Or help you? You're the one who's embarrassed to have me work for your precious magazine! You're the one who thinks there's something wrong with me, something that needs to be fixed!"

"There's nothing wrong with you, Emily. My God, how can you think I'm embarrassed because of you?"

"I know you are." Emily stood up, shaking, her fists clenched in tight balls.

"*No.* I care about you, Emily. Very much. There's nothing wrong with you. You've been harmed and you can be helped. You can be happy."

"*Happy?* Happy is for people like you, Rob, not me." Emily paused, and when she spoke again her voice was a soft hiss, a whisper of ice, cold and empty and dead. "I wanted to trust you, Rob." *So much.*

"You *can* trust me, Emily."

"No. I can't. But don't worry. You and Elaina don't have to endure another day of mortification. I don't work for you anymore. Good-bye, Rob."

Emily was almost to the door when Rob's voice stopped her, startling them both because it was suddenly full of his own rage.

Emily turned to face him. Her gray eyes flickered with fear and acceptance.

She knew he was going to hurt her, and she accepted it. The look in her eyes made Rob's rage even greater.

"Take these." Rob forced the books into Emily's hands. She took them but recoiled instinctively, as if even that were an act of violence and betrayal. Rob closed his eyes for a second, forcing control, preventing the instinct that made him want to hold her, to keep her with him until she understood, agreed, acquiesced. Rob's instinct was compassion, but to Emily it would only feel like more violence, more brutal intrusion on her will. Rob sighed heavily and breathed through gritted teeth, "Please, Emily. Take these and read them. Please think about seeing the doctor."

"I don't work here anymore. It doesn't matter."

"It matters, Emily," Rob whispered as he watched her *escape from him*. "It matters very much."

For two hours after Peter left, Winter sat in the living room of her apartment, fighting waves of nausea and fighting what she knew to be the cause. Both fights were losing battles, but Winter finally controlled the nausea enough to walk two blocks—a million twirling miles—to the pharmacy on Westwood Avenue.

Winter bought three different kits, for a second opinion and a third, not that any confirmation was necessary. Winter knew. She had known for at least a month.

Winter gazed at the deep purple color. "Definitely positive," the directions read. "Congratulations, you are pregnant!"

Now Winter had violet proof—the clear deep violet of her own eyes—and she wondered if her baby—their baby—would have violet eyes like hers or sapphire ones like Mark's.

Mark frowned as he parked in front of Winter's apartment five hours later. He didn't see Winter's car. She had expected to be home early. By six at the latest, she had said.

She's probably off buying heart-shaped chocolates, Mark decided lovingly as he removed the box of long-stemmed roses from his car.

Thinking about Winter buying Valentine's Day treats filled Mark with joy. Thinking about Winter *always* filled him with joy. Mark saw such sadness, such tragedy, such pathos at the hospital; it tore at his heart, making him weep, but his pain was always blunted by the lovely memory of Winter. Mark loved her so much. He felt so lucky.

Winter's apartment was as dark as the inky black February sky. An icy tremor of worry rippled through him. Where was she?

Making a movie, Mark answered his worry quickly, suddenly realizing how Winter must feel when he would call to say he'd be home in an hour, but by the time he checked the X-rays, wrote the orders, handled a few more details, it would really be two or three hours.

Winter had told Mark how quickly the hours passed on the set. She would think they had been working on a scene for an hour, but suddenly it would be time for the dinner break. Making a movie was like working in the hospital; time wasn't measured by minutes or hours, but by the tasks to be accomplished. A lumbar puncture, two blood cultures, a 14 gauge IV, the car scene, the beach scene, one more close-up . . .

Mark turned on the light in the kitchen, placed the Lalique vase—carved crystal partridges, Winter's birthday present from Allison—by the sink, and opened the goldfoil box of roses. When Mark's eyes fell on a saucepan filled with soup on the stove and the box of saltine crackers on the counter, he frowned. Winter *had* been home and she had left soup, uncovered, on the stove. Winter, who had made a teasing but serious show of refrigerating food promptly ever since he had explained to her about salmonella!

Mark left the kitchen in search of more clues to Winter's whereabouts, never expecting to find *her.* He flicked on the living room lights and saw her purse and coat tossed on a chair. Anxiety increasing, Mark walked to the bedroom. The bedroom door was open. The light from the living room cast a soft beam toward the bed, making a golden halo around the shiny black velvet hair on the pillow.

Mark walked quietly into the bedroom, not wanting to waken her yet worried, wondering why she was asleep. Worry won out. Mark knelt beside the bed and gently kissed her temple.

"Mark." Winter's violet eyes fluttered open and her mind sought anchors. The room—the outside world—was dark and Mark was home. She had just been planning to take a quick nap. Winter had felt so dizzy after her trip to the basement of the apartment building to put the sacks containing the pregnancy kits in the trash. She had decided on a brief nap, then soup, then *after* she would think about what she was going to do.

"Are you all right? Where's your car?"

"At the studio. Peter gave me a ride home."

"Are you sick?" Mark curled the fingers of one hand gently around her wrist, feeling her pulse, and touched her forehead with the other.

"Do I seem sick?"

"Your pulse is a little fast, but you don't feel warm."

That was the physical—heart pounding, because Mark was here, touching her, but no fever, not one that would register on any scale except an emotional one. Winter couldn't give Mark her history. *You see, doctor, I took a crazy chance. It was just one time! One wonderful night of passion with the man I love.*

"What are your symptoms?" Mark asked gently.

Winter looked at his loving, concerned blue eyes and remembered the pain in those same eyes when Mark had told her about his childhood without a father and how he had to be very careful not to make that same mistake.

You didn't make the mistake, Mark. *I* did.

"I'm just a little tired. I'll be fine." Winter made a move to get up, swirled, and smiled weakly.

"I'm going to make you some soup." He kissed the tip of her nose. "I'll go turn it on and be right back."

While Winter waited, listening to the distant noise of water running in the kitchen, her swirling thoughts suddenly crystallized; as if, while she had been sleeping, in dreams she didn't remember, her questions had all been answered.

In a month Mark will find out about his residency and he'll—we'll—have to make plans. If Mark's plans include me, if he wants me to be with him in Boston, then I'll tell him about our baby. If not, he will never know. I'll stop seeing him before he notices any changes.

It was so easy! If Mark didn't want her, he could still live his dream, unsullied, unharmed. Winter would never force Mark to repeat the mistake of *his* father. And she wouldn't allow herself to repeat the mistake of *her* mother.

Winter felt the new life inside her—a tiny, swirling hurricane, boldly and dramatically announcing its presence—and wondered what a similar small storm had done to the love of Lawrence Carlyle and Jacqueline Winter. Had Lawrence and Jacqueline been lovers, driven by passion, but not enough in love to marry? Had the creation of their "love-child" precipitated a marriage that should never have happened? Perhaps Jacqueline had loved Lawrence as desperately and as confidently as Winter loved Mark. Perhaps Jacqueline had believed, even though Lawrence didn't love her *enough*, that she could make it work.

But the marriage of Jacqueline Winter and Lawrence Carlyle hadn't worked.

He doesn't want us, Jacqueline had told a six-year-old Winter, bitterly, honestly.

Perhaps Winter had already repeated one of Jacqueline's mistakes—a careless night of passion—but she would make no more. And Winter wouldn't repeat Jacqueline's greatest mistake of all: No matter what, Winter would raise this new little life with love and gentleness and care. Her baby would *never* feel loneliness, rejection, or fear. Winter's baby might not have a daddy, just as she had never had one, but the swirling hurricane would have—already *did* have—a mother who loved her, or him, so very much.

If Mark doesn't want me, if he doesn't love me enough to take the risk, then . . .

But Mark does want me, doesn't he?

Winter's eyes filled with hot tears as Mark returned to the bedroom carrying the vase full of roses.

"Happy Valentine's Day."

"Mark . . ."

"Why are you crying?" Mark put the vase on the dresser, sat beside her on the bed, and snuggled her into his strong arms.

"I just don't want this to ever end."

Mark pulled Winter close but didn't answer. He didn't want their fairy-tale love to ever end, either. Mark would never stop loving Winter, but he couldn't promise that this bliss, this happiness, this *dream* would last forever.

Chapter 20

"Allison, it's Peter."

Allison had been expecting Peter's call ever since she had awakened at six A.M. to the sound of torretial rain assaulting her bedroom window. The rainstorm hadn't abated at all in the past three hours, despite the glowers Allison cast at the gray-black sky and despite the fact that she had ironed—ironed!—her jeans and had spent hours planning her outfit. Apparently, the soggy storm simply didn't care.

"Rain," Allison said with a soft sigh.

"Rain."

Allison waited, breath held, in the silence that followed.

"Would you like to go to brunch?" Peter asked.

"Yes."

"I guess the Bel Air Hunt Club has a Sunday brunch that's supposed to be good."

"It's supposed to be the best in Southern California!"

"Shall I still pick you up at ten?"

"Sure." *No, wait. I need time to plan my brunch outfit!*

* * *

It didn't matter what Allison wore—except for her smiles and her sparkling eyes—and it didn't matter that the Sunday brunch at the Bel Air Hunt Club was the best in Southern California. All Peter remembered about that gray rainy morning and afternoon were the eyes and the smiles; and her soft voice and joyous laughter; and the way she made him feel.

And Allison remembered the same things about Peter, except for the joyous laughter, which was hers, an old friend that had been lost since the accident. Because of Peter, Allison rediscovered her wonderful lost laugh and the feelings that came with it, sunny feelings of exuberant, boundless, untarnished joy.

And because of Peter, Allison discovered something new, something deep inside her that she had never even known existed.

Allison had felt its periphery—the lovely warmth at the edges, the easy, comfortable warmth she had felt with Dan and with Roger. But Allison hadn't known about its center until Peter. Because of Peter, because his sensuous, dark eyes and soft, seductive voice led her there, Allison discovered a place inside herself where there was fire, a magical place that swirled with hot, powerful, exhilarating feelings.

Peter felt the magnificent fire, too. But for Peter, the powerful, exhilarating feelings weren't new, because he had fallen in love once before. Still, as he gazed at Allison's sparkling eyes and felt his entire being respond with joy and desire, Peter's mind spun, astonished.

It wasn't possible! Peter had known—so surely, so confidently and without bitterness—that he would never fall in love again. Peter had lived his forever love; he would be content to live the rest of his life with the lovely memories of Sara.

But now he was falling in love *again*. Somehow the jade-green eyes and soft voice and joyous laugh had bravely, astonishingly, miraculously penetrated the fortress of memories that surrounded Peter's brain and traversed the treacherous moat of pain that encompassed his heart.

What did Peter and Allison talk about as they sipped vintage champagne and then hot chocolate as the brunch ended and the Club served its traditional Sunday tea? Nothing and everything. The endlessly fascinating raindrops that splashed on the bay window . . . and other things, important things.

"It's so hard to talk to you!" Allison's words were *so* important, and they would have worried Peter very much, except she made the pronouncement with merry eyes, smiling lips, and a voice that sang.

"Hard, Allison? Why?" *It's so easy to talk to you.*

"Because of what you write, the way you write. See? I can't even express my thoughts in complete sentences, much less clearly!"

"How do you know what I write, Allison? Has Winter shown you the screenplay for *Love?*"

"No. I read the book of your plays that was published last year."

"Oh." Peter wanted Allison to tell him what she thought about his plays, but first he had to convince her that it wasn't really hard to talk to him at all. He suggested, "Why don't we review the incredibly eloquent words I have spoken to you since we met last August? OK?"

"OK."

Allison listened, amazed, as Peter repeated their conversations—the August day at Elegance, the December morning on the Windsor trail, Christmas Eve at the Club, Valentine's Day at Elegance. Peter remembered every word, every scene, just as she did!

"You remember."

"Yes. I do," Peter answered quietly. And that was remarkable, astonishing, too. Peter hadn't remembered any other conversations, not the exact words, since Sara. Except, he thought, frowning briefly, the threatening promise made by Rob last December. Peter forced away that memory and smiled at Allison. "Do you remember?"

"Yes." Allison tilted her head. "I thought the line about living in a French Impressionist painting was clever."

"*No*," Peter replied with a smile. "But even if it was a brilliant line—which it wasn't—it glittered all by itself. Perhaps I write eloquent dialogue, Allison, but I certainly don't speak it. The French Impressionist comment *was* honest, though, and that's all that matters, isn't it?"

"I guess." Allison smiled and added honestly, "Yes."

"Good. So, Allison Fitzgerald, tell me honestly, in your own words, what you thought about my plays."

"All right," Allison answered softly. "I thought your plays were sad . . . and complicated . . . and lonely . . . and wonderful."

Sad, complicated, lonely, wonderful. All the things you are, sad, complicated, lonely, wonderful Peter Dalton.

Peter and Allison never left their window table at the Club to sample the lavish buffet. Champagne was served to them in crystal flutes, then hot chocolate in fine china, and at four, a red-coated waiter appeared with a platter of hot raspberry scones.

"It's four?" Peter looked at his watch. "I guess we've been here for a while." *For a wonderful while*. Peter didn't want it to end, ever, but . . . "I'm—Muffin and I—are having dinner at Steve's at six."

"Muffin, too?"

"Yes. Becky—Steve's nine-year-old daughter—and Muffin have become friends. Becky comes by every afternoon after school to feed Muffin and play with her. I actually think Muffin is a closet Californian. She seems quite at home lounging in the California sunshine, preferably in the kitchen on a designer pillow, and she loves scampering on the beach."

"But has she mastered frisbee-catching?"

"Becky is trying, but there's still a little New York, a little *decorum* left in Muffin."

Allison heard the surprising softness in Peter's voice when he talked about Muffin. Softness and fondness, like the fondness of good friends who had weathered storms together and survived.

"Have you had Muffin a long time?"

"Since she was a puppy." Peter's dark eyes darkened for a moment as he counted the years, drifting back in time to Sara's twenty-first birthday, a year before she died. "Five years." Peter added after a thoughtful moment, "Muffin is a good little dog."

Peter and Allison talked about Muffin, and about a puppy Allison had loved as a little girl, and then another hour was magically gone. Finally, reluctantly, Peter whispered that he should take her home.

Peter hadn't realized the depth of his loneliness! He hadn't allowed himself to realize it. Peter had made certain that his life was frantically busy. When he allowed his thoughts to drift to the past, which he did because he never wanted to forget *her*, Peter's memories were the lovely memories of Sara and of their love, not memories of his own grief at what he had lost.

Peter lived a life of discipline, creativity, and memories.

A life of loneliness.

As Peter drove away from Allison's apartment, the immense magnitude of his loneliness hit him, staggering him. *It was as if he had just lost Sara again.*

Peter drove away from Allison, but it was an act of great discipline. What he wanted—so desperately—was to turn around and ask her to be with him forever.

Allison hadn't even known about loneliness until Peter left. But, *then*, loneliness was there, a powerful new emotion mixed in with the other powerful new emotions of the day. Allison missed Peter, felt empty without him.

Allison wanted more of him, *all of him*.

Peter hadn't even mentioned seeing her again when he left, already late, to get Muffin and go to dinner at Steve's. But Peter *would* see her again, wouldn't he? Sometime, all the time, in the few weeks before he returned to New York?

Allison paced around her apartment—lonely, excited, restless—until her pacing caused angry tremors of pain in her hip. Allison hadn't even explained to Peter about her limp! She would explain next time . . .

Next time?

This magical time had just been a fluke, hadn't it? a distant corner of Allison's mind taunted. Because Winter was ill, and Peter had a free moment and happened to wander into Elegance. And if *she* hadn't rewritten the scene . . .

Quickly, too quickly, the enchanted hours with Peter became a misty dream. Allison gazed at the rain that still catapulted against her apartment windows. The plump raindrops had been part of the day. The raindrops were *real*, but what about all the rest? What about the fire and the magic?

At eight, Allison called Winter to see how she was feeling. Winter said she was better, but Allison heard a soft sigh of fatigue as her friend spoke. Allison hadn't told Winter about Peter—that she would be seeing him today—because . . . And Allison still didn't tell Winter—after she and Peter had spent the day together—because, because . . .

Because Allison didn't know what to say.

Allison paced restlessly again after her call to Winter. When her hip cried "Enough!" Allison telephoned Emily.

"Hello." Emily's voice was a whisper, small, tentative, almost afraid.

"Emily? It's Allison."

"Hi."

"Are you all right?"

"I'm fine."

"Roger loved the photographs."

"Oh. Good."

"We'll need large prints, larger than what I used for Bellemeade."

"Oh. OK. The ones I did for Bellemeade are as large as I can develop in my darkroom here."

"You told me there is a good photo lab in Century City?"

"Yes. We can have them done there."

"It's probably just as well. Roger wants to use more than we had planned—because they are all so wonderful—and if someone else is doing the enlargements, it won't cut into your time for *Portrait*." Allison waited, wondering if she had lost the connection, and finally asked, "Emily?"

"Yes. I don't work for *Portrait* anymore, Allison."

"What? Emily, since when?" The news was startling. The flatness in Emily's voice was almost terrifying.

"I told Rob on Thursday."

Was that why Rob and Elaina hadn't joined Allison and Roger for the Valentine's Day dinner at Adriano after all? Was Emily's decision to leave *Portrait* the reason for Rob and Elaina's surprising last minute cancellation of dinner plans they had all made in Aspen?

"Emily, what happened? Are you all right?"

"Nothing happened. It just wasn't working out at *Portrait*."

Since when? Allison wondered. In Aspen, Rob's voice had been so gentle when he spoke of Emily. And Emily's voice had been gentle, too—as it always was when she talked about Rob—on Valentine's Day when she had dropped off the photographs for the Chateau Bel Air at Elegance on her way to a meeting with Rob! A meeting at which, apparently, nothing had happened—except that Emily left *Portrait*, Rob and Elaina cancelled dinner plans, and now Emily's voice sounded so flat, so defeated.

"Emily, are you all right?" Allison asked again. "You sound a little—"

"I'm a little tired, but I'm fine, Allison, really."

"I'm sorry about *Portrait*."

"So am I," Emily whispered.

"Do you know what you're going to do?"

"No." Emily looked at the books—*Little Girl Lost* and *Little Girl Found*—that lay on her beside table. She had read them, over and over and over. That had taken courage, but the next step . . . "I don't know."

"Well, you know I can keep you very busy."

"I may be moving to Paris." Emily had almost flown to Paris Friday night. She had almost thrown the books—already slightly warped because they had been read and reread by Rob—away, gathered all her belongings—a ten-minute task if she did it slowly—and flown to Paris. Escaped to Paris, forever.

"Paris? Emily, do you feel like getting together now?" Allison asked impulsively, her worry about Emily increasing. "We could—"

"It's really not a good time, Allison." After a moment, Emily added softly, "Thank you."

"Let's have lunch sometime this week, or dinner, or a movie, OK?"

"OK." *Maybe.*

When the telephone rang at ten P.M. Allison knew it would be Peter. She had been staring at the phone, *willing* it to ring. Peter would be getting home from dinner at Steve's just about now.

"Hello." *Hello! Hello!*

But it wasn't Peter. It was Roger, calling from Chicago. Roger, with whom Allison had been uneasy and remote at their romantic Valentine's Day dinner; Roger, with whom Allison did not make love Thursday or Friday or Saturday; Roger, who wanted to know what had happened.

"Allison, did you actually meet someone else between our weekend in Aspen and Thursday night? No, I take that back, between the time we spoke Wednesday evening and when I saw you Thursday?"

No, I met him before I met you, Roger. The same day, moments before. And I've been thinking about him ever since.

"Roger . . ."

"*Is* there someone else, Allison?"

"I don't know. I'm not sure." *Yes, for me, Yes. And for Peter?*

"But maybe?"

"Maybe. Roger, I . . ." Allison didn't know what to say. No matter what happened with Peter, a love with Roger could never happen now, could it? Now Allison knew about fire, and even though the fire came with danger and uncertainty and loneliness, it ignited feelings within her—*life* within her—that would never again be content with warmth. "I'm sorry."

Peter and Steve watched the "dailies" from Monday's shoot in the screening

room at the studio in Burbank. It was nine P.M. For the rest of the cast and crew, the day had ended two hours ago.

"She's not a hundred percent," Peter said. "She's giving her usual one hundred and ten percent, but she's still ill."

The greenish tinge had left Winter's rich, creamy skin, but her violet eyes were cloudy and uncertain, trying to look deeply in love as she waged a private war against nausea.

"I think we'd better cancel tomorrow's shoot," Peter said.

Steve sighed. *Love* had been going so well! Ahead of schedule, harmony on the set, no ego problems, almost too good to be true, certainly too good to last. Steve knew from years of experience that once a movie started to fall apart, once the balance was disrupted by weather or tempers or rolls of film that mysteriously didn't print, it could unravel quickly and disastrously.

But Winter was ill. It was obvious. Winter wasn't a prima donna. She wasn't playing games. She probably wouldn't even want to cancel another day, but they really had no choice.

"I guess so," Steve agreed reluctantly. "I'll go set the telephone calls to the crew in motion. Do you want to call Winter and Bruce?"

"Sure." Winter and Bruce and Allison. Peter had almost called Allison last night when he'd gotten home from Steve's, but he didn't trust himself. He might have just told Allison Fitzgerald what was in his heart. *I miss you, Allison. I want to see you. Now.*

It was *his* desperation, not hers, *his* ears of loneliness erupting like lava from a long dormant volcano—hot, rushing, consuming. *He* was desperate and so confident of his feelings, and *she* was lovely and somehow so innocent and vulnerable. Peter wanted Allison, but he had to be so very careful not to rush her.

Peter called Winter and Bruce before he left the studio. He called Allison from Bellemeade after he finished taking Muffin for a quick, soggy walk.

"Is this too late to call?"

"No." *No time is too late, ever.*

"Winter is still sick, better but still a little wobbly, so we won't be filming at all tomorrow. Would you—?"

"Yes." *Yes to anything.*

"Yes?" Peter laughed softly. "Are you free all day?"

"No," Allison admitted. "But I can be free by mid-afternoon."

"Call me whenever and I'll come get you. I'll be here, making dinner for us, OK?"

"I can drive myself."

"Oh. All right. You don't even need to call first. I'll be here."

Dr. Camden looked at the frightened dark-circled gray eyes that stared at her in proud defiance at eleven Tuesday morning. It was such a familiar look! This pale young woman was here because an instinct deeper than the layers of pain told her to *try*, but she didn't really believe it would help. She believed she would try, and that would cause more pain, and then she would fail.

"You're Emily Rousseau?"

"Yes. I think you know about me. Rob Adamson . . ."

"Rob didn't tell me your name or anything that would identify you."

"Oh, well . . . I read your books. Rob thought—I thought—maybe you could help me."

"I *can* help you, Emily. I can help you find the little girl in you that was joyous and happy and able to trust and love. I can find her with your help. It's hard work, very hard, but it's so worth it."

Dr. Camden looked at the tormented gray eyes and knew the fear she saw wasn't the fear of hard work. Emily's fear was that she would fail—even though others like her had succeeded; and it was fear that she really was unworthy, really somehow to blame for what had happened to her.

Dr. Camden smiled and added confidently, truthfully, "You're going to make it, Emily. I know you are."

Chapter 21

Allison arrived at Bellemeade at two-thirty Tuesday afternoon. The February sky had been pearl-gray when she left Elegance and gray-black an hour later when she emerged from her apartment dressed in the outfit she had selected last night after Peter called. Allison's carefully selected outfit was an ivory silk blouse, a tailored camel skirt, cocoa-brown suede pumps, and delicate gold earrings.

Understated elegance, Allison hoped, and sophisticated, like the women of New York Peter Dalton must know so well. Sophisticated, modern women who would dress elegantly and drive confidently to his home without bothering to call in advance.

Allison stared at the ominous gray-black clouds as she left her apartment and silently warned, *Don't you dare!* She should have bought an umbrella this morning on Rodeo, but that would have taken time, and the day was already moving in slow motion.

Just as Allison reached Bellemeade the sky opened. As she dashed from the driveway to the front door, Allison was drenched by the incredible cloudburst, a soggy omen that answered, Don't *you* dare pretend to be sophisticated when you really aren't!

Peter was just finishing in the kitchen, the dinner made, the oven timers set, when Allison arrived. He had planned to spend the afternoon in the living room, in front of a fire, watching for her to arrive, greeting her when she did. He had even bought an umbrella in case it was raining.

And now she was here, drenched.

"Hi. Allison, I'm sorry. I was in the kitchen. I didn't see you."

"I'm earlier than I thought I'd be. I don't even own an umbrella. I should have—" As Allison shook her head, raindrops splashed from her red-gold curls to her already-damp and cold cheeks. She fought an ice-cold shiver.

The shivering had started last night, in the warmth of her apartment, moments after Peter called. Her heart had begun to gallop and she had recalled the sudden, unexpected panic that had swept through her just before she rode again. On *that* summer morning Allison had calmed the panic with a mantra, *Trivial, trivial.*

If she panicked now, that mantra wouldn't work, because there was nothing trivial about the powerful feelings that swirled inside her because of Peter.

But she wasn't panicking. She was only shivering and awkward and so aware of her wet hair and face.

And his dark brown eyes.

"Here. Let me take your coat."

"Thank you." Allison somehow unbuttoned the squeaky wet buttons of her unlined Burberry raincoat and searched for something to say.

The obvious topic, other than the weather, was Bellemeade. But Allison couldn't rave about the elegant marble foyer, the Lalique chandelier, the Kentshire antique mirror—no point even looking that way!—or the wallpaper that felt like spring. Allison couldn't say a word about this lovely romantic place, because it was her creation. Allison had made it lovely for Peter, and for all the other women he had brought here.

Say *something*, Allison told herself. And stop shivering. And don't even *think* about the fact that the ivory silk blouse is transparent from the rain, and the sexy romantic lace beneath is *much more* than a misty shadow. And beneath the lace, *completely revealed*, are your breasts, very cold, slightly shivering.

The handsome dark eyes have only to look.

"Where's Muffin?"

"She's asleep in the kitchen, on her designer pillow, recharging her batteries." Peter's eyes didn't leave Allison's, didn't drift at all. "Muffin's had a very busy day."

"Oh?"

"It started early this morning with a posh beauty parlor for dogs in Beverly Hills. Undoubtedly lots of fun. Then she had to be on the alert while I made the casserole, for obvious reasons."

"And she probably helped you put fresh roses in all the vases." From the marble foyer, Allison could see two Lalique vases, filled with beautiful roses artfully arranged by Peter.

"She did." Peter paused. This was silly. Allison was freezing and embarrassed and being a trouper and she really needed to get out of her clothes and into a hot bath. "Allison."

"Yes?"

"Let me get a towel for your hair." Peter disappeared into the powder room and returned with a plush pale pink towel chosen by Allison from the luxurious selections of Pratesi.

Peter didn't give Allison the towel. Instead, so gently, he towelled the sopping red-gold curls tangling her hair, *touching* her for the first time.

"Am I being too rough?"

"No." *No*. So gentle, so tender. Allison looked up at his dark eyes, gentle, sensuous eyes, filled with desire. "Peter."

Allison lifted her face to him, inviting his lips, sending a rich message of desire and welcome.

"Allison."

Her skin was cool from the rain, but just beneath the surface she was warm and soft and alive with passion. Peter felt Allison respond, eager, excited, with a soft laugh of joy, and he felt his own strong, powerful waves of desire.

He wanted her so much! But was he crushing her with the desperate demands of his desire? The tighter Peter held Allison's damp, warm body against his, the deeper his lips explored her mouth, the closer she moved, opening even more to him. But was he hurting her? Was he pushing her too fast?

Peter pulled away. He needed to know what Allison wanted, to know *her* desire, *her* pace, not his. It felt as if Allison wanted him too; now, desperately, all of him, but were his senses consumed by his own passion?

Peter looked at Allison's eyes, a little startled because the kiss had suddenly stopped, and her cheeks, flushed and radiant, and the soft, confident smile on her full lips.

"Allison, I . . ."

"Yes?"

"I don't want to push you."

"Peter," Allison whispered bravely. "I'm the one who arrived with clothes that need to come off."

"They do need to come off, don't they?"

"Yes." *Yes to anything*. "Yours do, too."

Peter was wet from holding her so tightly against him. He smiled, then led her by the hand up the circular staircase that swept to the master suite with its canopied bed, spring meadow walls, and crystal vases blooming with roses.

Peter couldn't make love to her slowly—he wanted her too much—and Allison wanted him, too. She wanted to become part of him, to melt her fire with his, to become one.

"Peter," she whispered to his passionate dark eyes.

"Oh, Allison, I want you."

"I want you, too."

Allison laughed softly as Peter undressed her, peeling away the wet clinging silk and the delicate lace until she was naked in front of him.

"You are so beautiful, Allison."

Dan had told her that—and she had dismissed it with a light laugh—and Roger had told her, too. But now, as Peter whispered the words and caressed her with his appraising, appreciative eyes, Allison at last believed it was true.

I am beautiful for you, Peter. You make me beautiful.

As Peter's eyes drifted to the scars on her lower abdomen, Allison's hands didn't move to hide the ugliness. Her hands had moved the first time, with Dan, even though he knew all about the accident; and her hands would have moved, too, with Roger.

But Allison stood, naked, unashamed, in front of Peter, feeling his desire, feeling so beautiful.

Then they were in bed, touching, whispering, exploring, marvelling in the wonderful discoveries, breathless in their wonder and desire and *need*.

Peter needed to be inside her, and Allison needed him to be. Where he belonged, where she belonged. Fire with fire, closer, hotter, deeper . . . *together.*

"I used to ride all the time." Allison spoke softly as she lay, safe and warm, in the gentle strength of Peter's arms. Her soft words were the first words spoken since the breathless whispers of their passion. "I had an accident during a show jumping event three and a half years ago. I broke my pelvis. The doctors operated a few times and the bones finally knit, although they're a little uneven. That's why I have the scars. That's why I have a limp."

"Does it hurt?"

"Yes, sometimes, when I overdo."

"Does it hurt when we make love?"

When we make love. Allison felt a rush of joy at Peter's words. They had just made love once, but Peter's question promised other times, many, many other times.

"No." *It will never hurt when we make love.*

"Does it mean you can't have children, Allison?" Peter asked gently after several silent moments.

"No, Peter. I can have children." Allison turned to reassure the gentle, dark eyes. But when her eyes found Peter's Allison wondered if she saw more worry than relief. "Peter . . ."

The bedside phone rang. It sounded with a muted romantic ring, a ring chosen by Allison because, she had decided, important imported talent, like Peter, should have only soft intrusions on their lives. The phone rang softly, but it was an intrusion nonetheless.

As Peter turned away from her to answer it, Allison moved away, too, to get out of the bed. She would wrap herself in a luxurious bath blanket—she knew where they were—and wander downstairs to give Peter privacy.

Peter caught her wrist. "Allison, don't leave."

"Oh. OK." Allison stopped but remained where she was, at the far edge of the bed, distant from him.

"Hello?" Peter answered.

"Hi, Peter. It's Winter."

"Hi, Winter. How are you feeling?"

"Definitely better, but if I could have one more day?"

Winter's nausea wasn't any less, but she was learning to handle it, to *act* through it. She had spent most of today, when she wasn't sleeping, practicing looking well in front of the mirror, training the waves of nausea not to leave ripples of discomfort in her violet eyes. Winter was getting better at concealing the symptom, but it took great effort. By tomorrow night she would have it mastered—for the movie and for Mark.

Winter *had* to learn to hide it from Mark. It would take no time for the top senior medical student at UCLA to correctly diagnose persistent nausea in a "woman of childbearing age."

"Of course you can. I'll call Steve."

"I already have. He says OK, too."

"Are you resting?"

"Yes! I'm doing all the right things."

"Let me know tomorrow how it looks for Thursday."

"I'm sure I'll be fine, but I'll call you."

As soon as Peter replaced the receiver, he turned to Allison and asked, "Why did you start to leave?"

"To give you privacy."

"Who did you think would be calling?"

Allison shrugged, embarrassed, except, *except* handsome, passionate Peter Dalton hadn't just arrived on the planet. Peter was nine years older than Allison, nine years more experienced. Allison wasn't the first woman in Peter's bed. Perhaps she wasn't even the first woman in Peter's bed this week.

"A girlfriend. A lover."

Peter's dark eyes narrowed slightly, amazed, concerned, a little sad. He couldn't believe Allison did this—breathless, intimate, joyous loving—every day, so why would she imagine he did? Didn't Allison know? Couldn't she *tell?*

Peter moved to her, to the far edge of the bed and gently held her face in his hands.

"There isn't anyone, Allison. There isn't anyone but you."

"Oh," she breathed softly.

"Why are you frowning? Does that worry you?"

"No." *No, it's what I want.*

"You're still frowning. Tell me."

"I was just thinking," Allison whispered. "What if Winter hadn't gotten sick?"

"I didn't just happen by Elegance because I suddenly had a free afternoon, Allison."

"You didn't?"

"No. I'd been thinking about you."

"But you left."

"I was just about to turn around when you appeared on Wilshire."

"Really?"

"Really. I was going to ask you if I stood a chance against the sender of red roses."

"I'd been thinking about you, too. I almost bought Muffin a dog toy for Valentine's Day."

Peter smiled and kissed Allison's soft lips.

"I bet Muffin's batteries are recharged by now," Allison whispered seductively between kisses.

"Just Muffin's batteries?"

"Mine, too."

"Allison?"

"Yes?"

"The sender of red roses . . ."

They had been talking between kisses, lips brushing and nibbling as they spoke, but now Allison pulled away and looked thoughtfully at his eyes.

"There isn't anyone but you, Peter." *There never has been.*

It was seven by the time Peter and Allison left the canopied bed and went to the kitchen, lured by the wine-scented casserole and thoughts of the stranded Muffin. Allison wore Peter's blue terry cloth robe, bulky, cozy, pulled tight around her slender waist, and a pair of his thick woolen socks.

Muffin bounded toward Peter when he opened the kitchen door, then stopped when she saw Allison. Her head tilted and she gazed up at Allison with half-curious, half-diffident brown eyes. Muffin's expression was apprehensive, but her small blond body wiggled with excitement.

Allison laughed softly and leaned over to talk to her.

"Hello, Muffin. This is pretty scary, isn't it? I don't blame you. I *do* look frightful. And you are so beautiful, all clean and shiny."

Muffin liked Allison's soft voice and bravely edged forward to Allison's extended hands. Finally, Allison touched the clean, soft fur and there was even more wiggling.

"See? This isn't so bad after all." Allison turned to Peter. "She really is pretty."

"You really are pretty," Peter whispered as he kissed Allison's tangled hair.

Peter patted Muffin, then opened the kitchen door to let her go for a run in the now-crisp, rain-free evening air. He wrapped his arms around Allison while they watched the golden fluff galloping in the yard.

"What are your plans for tomorrow?"

"To work very hard in the office until noon, and then go to my apartment and wait for you to come pick me up. So much for sophistication."

"Was that what that was all about?"

"A modern career woman ought to be able to get herself to a man's home—

especially if he's modern enough to be making dinner—without drowning in raindrops, shouldn't she?"

"I guess." Peter laughed. "But let's try it the other way tomorrow. I'm really pretty old-fashioned."

"So am I."

Peter picked Allison up at her apartment the following afternoon and returned her there at dawn the next day on his way to the studio.

After that, it wasn't a question of fashion—old or new—simply one of practicality. If Allison had her car in the garage at Bellemeade, she and Peter could stay in bed a little longer in the morning. They could have a cup of coffee together and kiss a leisurely good-bye. After Peter left, just as the sun was beginning to lighten the eastern sky, Allison could have a second cup of coffee and spend "quality" time with the playful cocker spaniel before getting ready for work.

It was better for Allison to have her own car at Bellemeade for *them*, for their new, wonderful, passionate love; and Bellemeade was also closer to Allison's work. The Chateau Bel Air was only a mile away, and she had two other projects in Bel Air—an estate on Sienna Way and a gatehouse on Stone Canyon Road.

Peter and Allison lived at Bellemeade in a private world of romance and passion and love. Each ventured, alone, into the world beyond Bellemeade, to their successful busy careers, and for the first three weeks they never made that journey together. Allison had dinner with her parents while Peter was viewing the "dailies" with Steve in Burbank, and although Sean and Patricia guessed that a wonderful love had happened in their daughter's life, they assumed it was Roger and waited patiently for Allison to tell them. Allison spoke to Winter on the phone, heard her friend's fond words about Peter, but still didn't tell Winter about *them*.

Peter and Allison's first trip outside Bellemeade, together, was for a trail ride at the Club. The winter rainstorm had long since vanished, but the sky still sparkled clear and bright and freshly washed. As Peter and Allison rode along the Kensington Trail, they were serenaded by a thousand singing birds, gently caressed by a balmy breeze, and enveloped by the fragrances of a just-born spring.

Allison and Peter rode through the lush fragrant paradise for almost three hours. When they returned to the paddock area, the outdoor ring, which had been empty earlier, was filled with colorful, treacherous jumps. Allison stared solemnly at the jumps as they rode past. After they returned their mounts to the stable, she led Peter back to the ring.

Peter watched Allison's eyes as she stared at the jump with the green and white rails. Thoughtful eyes, solemn eyes, determined eyes.

Allison had never told anyone—she didn't dare—but *she* had known for a very longtime.

"Someday, I am going to fly over that jump," Allison vowed quietly. As she turned to Peter—the man she loved, the man who made her believe that anything was possible—her eyes sparkled. "Will you be here when I conquer it, Peter? Will you watch me?"

Peter's response was swift and cold.

"No."

"No?" Allison echoed weakly.

"No." *I will not watch you die.*

Allison saw the once-familiar, now-almost-forgotten sadness in Peter's eyes.

For the past few weeks—their wonderful weeks of love—the dark sadness had almost disappeared. For the past few weeks, there had been great happiness in his eyes . . . almost always. Great happiness . . . and such love, such passion, such desire. There were times, flickering quiet moments, when Allison still saw the sadness, but mostly, Peter's dark eyes told her of his joy.

Mostly, Allison could make Peter happy.

And now her words caused him sadness. *Why?*

Peter and Allison walked in silence to the car and drove in silence to Bellemeade.

"I'm sorry," Peter whispered finally. "But it would be dangerous for you to jump again, wouldn't it?"

Allison had only mentioned her accident once, after she and Peter had first made love. It had been a brief explanation of her scars and her limp, nothing that would make Pter know how dangerous her plan to jump again really was.

"Have you been talking to Winter about me, Peter?"

"No, I haven't told Winter about us at all."

"About us," Allison echoed softly, distracted from the topic of her riding by the gentle way Peter spoke those words.

"Have you told her?"

"No, Peter. I wouldn't know what to say."

"You wouldn't?" *Didn't she know?*

"No."

"I'll give you the line, then." Peter smiled lovingly. "You would say, with feeling, 'Winter, Peter Dalton is very much in love with me.' "

"No, master playwright, I would say, honestly, joyfully, " "Winter, I am very much in love with Peter Dalton.' "

"I love you, Allison."

"Oh, Peter, I love you."

"How did you know it would be dangerous for me to jump again?" Allison asked two hours later as they lay in bed.

"Your eyes." *How dangerous and how important.*

"Oh." Allison curled up closer to him, remembering *his eyes*, wishing she could tell him she didn't mean it, that it wasn't important to her to conquer that jump. Perhaps Allison could tell Peter that someday. She had to think about it; she would think about it. But, for now, she wanted to shift to a more certain topic. "Did I ever tell you that Winter thinks you're wonderful?"

"No. Does she?" Peter was pleased. "I think Winter's wonderful, too. I assume she has someone."

"Why?" Allison teascd. "Are you interested?"

"No!" Peter kissed her. "I just get the impression there is someone important in her life."

"There is. His name is Mark."

Allison told Peter about Mark and Winter.

"I think I won't tell Winter about us," Allison's voice softened lovingly, "until after *Love* is over."

"Which should be Thursday. If you told Winter before then, what would happen?"

"Who knows? She might stop the filming, demand a 'cut and take three hours,' and quiz you about your intentions." Allison smiled, imagining a lively Winter doing that. Her smile faded with more recent memories—over the phone impressions—of her best friend. Winter sounded worried. Allison added thoughtfully, "This is a very important week for Winter. In addition to *Love* wrapping, Mark finds out about his residency."

"Will that be a problem?"

"He'll probably be going to Boston."

"And Winter won't be going with him?"

"I don't know," Allison whispered softly, thinking about Mark and Winter

and thinking about the other relationship that was about to be separated by a continent. Very soon, Peter would be returning to New York.

"Would *you* like to know my intentions?" Peter asked gently.

"Yes."

"I intend to come back here next November to make a movie of *Merry Go Round*. In the meantime, I intend to see you as much as I possibly can and to talk to you at least once every day." Peter sighed and added apologetically, "Shakespeare on Broadway is going to take a lot of time. We'll probably have to rehearse on Saturdays, which means there would be weekends—many weekends—when I couldn't come here. You could come to New York—any time, all the time. Allison? You have a say in this."

"I say yes." *I love you.*

Chapter 22

The dean of students at UCLA School of Medicine distributed the results of the residency match to the senior medical students at nine A.M. Wednesday morning. Mark took his unopened envelope, left the auditorium of the Health Sciences Building, and walked outside into the bright March sun. His agile fingers felt clumsy as they pried open the sealed flap, but then there it was: *Internal Medicine—Massachusetts General Hospital—Harvard Affiliated Programs*.

There it was, what he wanted, what he had wanted for four years, a dream come true.

But what about his other dream?

Winter wasn't even a dream. Mark had never dreamed about being so much in love. He had never believed he would need someone as much as he needed her, still, more, *more* every day.

For the past two days, *Love* had been filming on location at UCLA. As she had kissed Mark good-bye and good luck this morning, Winter had told him to come find her—a five-minute walk from the medical school—as soon as he knew his residency results. But Mark had seen the slight worry on her face when she had suggested it—as if he had suggested that she interrupt professor's rounds at the hospital—so he had told her he would arrive in time for the lunch break.

That gave Mark almost three hours, three more restless hours, in which he would ask himself again—as he had for months—if it was simply too selfish to ask Winter to come with him to Boston.

He had so little to offer her. *Just all his love and all his heart*. But Winter would see his love—see *him*—rarely; and he would be tired and distracted, as he had been at Christmas; and the joy would be mostly his—the warm memories of her sustaining him in the long hours in the hospital and the happiness of being with her in the precious moments when he was home.

But what was there for Winter in Boston? Long days and nights, patiently waiting for the rare moments, away from *her* dream—*I want movies, Mark, not theater*—in Hollywood.

Mark believed if he asked Winter to come with him, to marry him, she would say yes. He lay awake at night, holding her in his arms, thinking about the outcomes.

Yes, Mark, I will marry you. Mark's mind could stretch those words into a lifetime of happiness, a lifetime of sparkling violet and joyous laughter and gentle whispers and loving passion. Mark's wonderful visions magically bypassed the years of fatigue and disappointment and apologies. The visions weren't real, simply lovely images of his mind.

Fantasy. Cinderella *before* the stroke of midnight.

The *reality* was, at best, a constant struggle against disappointment; and, at worst, a disaster laced with bitterness, anger, and resentment. Mark and Winter could both try, could both want desperately to make it work, but still it could fail.

Mark was to meet Winter at noon. She wouldn't be looking for him until then. She wouldn't know Mark was one of the many spectators gathered near Pauley Pavilion to watch the filming of the next to last scene of *Love*.

Mark stood in the middle of the crowd. At first he was careful not to stare at her, afraid that his loving gaze might draw her attention. But Winter was totally absorbed in her work, patiently doing the scene over and over, smiling softly as she quietly discussed each take with the dark, handsome man who Mark assumed must be Peter. Winter looked so serious and so *happy*.

On a snowy Christmas Eve, Winter had watched Mark in the Emergency Ward at Massachusetts General Hospital and had realized that he was where he belonged, doing what he was destined to do, happy with his dream. And now, on this sunny day in California, Mark saw Winter living her dream, *loving* it.

And Mark knew what he had to do, just as Winter had known in Boston.

I have to leave her. Mark contrasted the scene he watched now—Winter, the actress, so happy—with a future scene he could imagine—Winter, his wife, alone in their apartment, waiting, fighting disappointment, *withering*.

The greatest loss was his, Mark had told Winter last summer about the father who had lost the great joy of knowing his lovely daughter. *The greatest loss will be mine, Winter*, Mark thought now.

Mark knew that lovely, loving Winter would find other loves, other happiness, other joy.

Mark wasn't sure that he ever would.

Love never broke for lunch because the day's filming was finished by one. Mark waited while Winter changed. Then they walked, hand in hand, across campus to the Sculpture Garden.

They sat on the same sunny patch of grass where the magic had begun nine months before.

Ask me to go with you, Mark. Trust me, trust us, trust our love.

I love you so much, Winter. Too much not to let you go.

"Winter," Mark began gently. "Next year, the next *two* years, will be like those days at Christmas."

"Snowy," she whispered hopefully. "Full of Christmas cookies and the ever-present threat of salmonella."

Mark smiled lovingly. *Marry me, Winter Carlyle.*

Winter's heart leapt as she saw the look in Mark's eyes. *You do love me, don't you, Mark? You do want me and our baby!*

Mark fought the powerful emotion that urged him to ask her to marry him with vivid images of Winter, trapped, lonely, not acting, waiting for him.

"It won't work, Winter."

Mark's eyes hardened as he spoke and his voice was harsh. Winter marvelled for a horrible stunned moment at what an actor *he* was. That loving look, so convincing for so long, but all an act.

"I know, Mark," Winter heard herself say. *She* could act, too. Her voice could be calm, even light and breezy, as if she didn't care at all! Mark wouldn't have the slightest clue her heart was breaking. She could give the performance of her life while her anguished heart cried, *He doesn't want you! Did you really believe that he would?*

Mark expected Winter to protest. If she had, could he have resisted? He would have tried—for *her*—but he might have told the suddenly hurt violet eyes the selfish truth: *I love you. I want you. Will you try with me?*

But Winter's lovely eyes weren't hurt, and now she was standing up, about to leave.

"I think it would be best if you moved your things out of my apartment today, Mark. I'll go to the mansion for a while to give you time. Good-bye."

Mark watched in stunned silence as Winter turned and walked away.

He *almost* ran after her. But what was the point? If she was being brave, as he was, because it was the *right* decision and they both knew it, then why spend long, tearful hours saying good-bye? And if she wasn't being brave, if she would have told him "No, I won't marry you, Mark," then so be it.

Perhaps Winter would have said no. In the seven weeks since Mark's return from Boston, their life had been so different than it had been last summer and fall. They were both so busy, and the rested moments together were vanishingly rare. Winter had seemed distant and preoccupied, but Mark had assumed logically that it was the emotional and physical strain of *Love*, and the added strain of her illness in February.

But maybe Winter had decided their love was over and had been only waiting to tell him until he found out about his residency at MGH, until he had a new dream to replace the lost one.

Mark sighed. It was over. It had to be. If it was what Winter really wanted, if it didn't cause her sadness, then that was even better.

Mark watched Winter disappear, vanishing as she had that magical evening last June. As he watched, her fading image became blurred by his tears, and he whispered, "Good-bye, my precious Cinderella."

Winter gave the second best performance of her life the following morning on the beach at Malibu, as they filmed *Love*'s final scene.

"*I will love you always*," Winter whispered, her violet eyes glistening with a promise of forever. Winter whispered the words over and over, her own heart screaming with pain, as she played Julia, whose heart overflowed with love and joy.

Finally, thankfully, Peter turned to Steve with a smile, "What is that movie expression, Steve? That's a wrap?"

"That's a wonderful wrap," Steve embellished. "Thank you all. Don't forget the party tonight at my house. We begin at six."

Winter didn't move. She sat on the sun-bleached piece of driftwood and gazed at the sea. The swirl of activity around her, the cast and crew preparing to leave, crescendoed, then faded.

Then Winter was alone.

No, Peter was there, sitting beside her as he had done so often in the past ten weeks. And, like all those other times, Peter seemed to be waiting patiently for her to speak.

But there was no scene to discuss. *Love* was over . . . wrapped . . . wonderful.

Finally, Winter turned to him, her eyes spilling tears she couldn't stop and revealing emotions she could no longer hide—pain, sadness, *anger.*

"She—I, Julia—should have died in the end, Peter. Or Sam should have left her. You may have won Tonys and the Pulitzer Prize for your brilliant, insightful writing, but you were *way off* with *Love*. Happy endings are Hollywood, not real life, Peter, don't you know that?"

"I know that, Winter."

Winter saw the sudden pain in his dark eyes. What was she doing lashing out at Peter? She admired Peter. They had worked so well together and he had so gently helped her make wonderful discoveries about her own talent.

She and Peter had had a wonderful professional relationship.

And now it was suddenly personal. And Winter was too raw, too emotional to speak. She needed to get away, to be alone.

"I'm sorry, Peter."

"Let's take a walk."

"No, Peter."

Peter stood, took her hand, and pulled gently, willing her to come with him. His hand was warm and strong, and his eyes were kind and sympathetic, and she had no resistance.

They walked for ten minutes in a silence broken only by the plaintive cries of seagulls overhead and the soft whispers of the sea.

"Something happened with Mark," Peter said finally.

"How do you know about Mark?"

"Allison told me."

Winter heard the softness in Peter's voice when he spoke Allison's name and the expression of love on his handsome face.

"You and Allison?"

"Yes. She was going to tell you tonight at the party."

"And I was planning to skip the party and see if Allison was free. I guess she won't be."

"I think we should all make a brief appearance, together, then if you want to see Allison by yourself . . ."

"I really don't have anything earth-shattering to tell her. Mark's going to Boston by himself and I'm going to stay here to pursue my brilliant career." Winter gave a weak smile. "Very eighties. Love takes a backseat to career."

"That's it?"

"That's it." Winter added softly, "Except my heart is broken. I guess it's your fault. Doing this movie actually had me convinced that it would all end happily, that life would imitate art, but it didn't."

They walked in silence for five minutes, then Peter asked, very quietly, very gently, "Winter, what about the baby?"

"The baby?" How did Peter know? No one else in the entire world knew. Winter hadn't even seen a doctor yet! She had gained a little weight but her sleek body concealed it well, especially in clothes, and even Mark hadn't noticed. Mark would have noticed in another week or two, but not yet. "What do you mean?"

"Aren't you pregnant?"

"How do you know?"

I know because you have a glow, a lovely womanliness, a radiance. I know because I saw those changes in Sara long before she told me, only then I had no idea what they meant.

"Pink cheeks, a higher wattage bulb backlighting your eyes, *green* skin a month ago," Peter murmured lightly. He added gently, "Fresh tears in your eyes now. Are you OK?"

"No," Winter admitted with a trembling smile. "But I will be—*we* will be. I just need a little time. Everything is so new right now. Peter, Mark can never know about the baby."

"Is that fair?"

"*Yes*. And please don't tell Allison."

"Do you think Allison would tell Mark?"

"No, of course not. But you know Allison. She would try to make it right. Allison believes in happy endings. Allison would try to convince me to tell Mark, and right now I am too susceptible to that suggestion."

"Maybe it's the right suggestion."

"No, Peter, it's not. Please. I just need a little time. Allison can't know, not yet."

Peter was already troubled by the secrets—*his* secrets—that he kept from Allison. Peter knew he had to tell Allison about Sara and he *would*, but it was still too soon. Their love was so new, so joyous. And Peter knew the tragic story of Sara would fill Allison's lovely jade eyes with tears and her generous loving heart with sadness. Peter hated keeping secrets—his own and now Winter's—from Allison.

"You *will* tell Allison, though, won't you, Winter?"

"Peter, I will have to tell her."

"Have a wonderful flight, Muffin," Allison whispered to the wiggling blond fur in the travel kennel at the airport. "See you late Friday night."

Allison stood up as the baggage handler carefully loaded Muffin's kennel onto a cart. She turned to Peter with tears in her eyes. Peter had stayed with her until the very last minute. In the morning, in New York, he would begin rehearsals of *Hamlet*.

It was Sunday afternoon and she would see him Friday night, but still it felt like a forever good-bye.

It *was* a forever good-bye to their private life of love in the romantic sanctuary of Bellemeade.

Allison and Peter's new life promised hours in airports and airplanes and taxis, and late night telephone calls with whispers of longing transmitted three thousand miles, and rare moments when they were together, trying to *love* a week's worth of loneliness into thirty-six precious hours. Allison tried to convince herself that their transcontinental love affair was glamorous and romantic—it was certainly sophisticated and modern—but she spent more time convincing herself *not* to quit her job and go with Peter *now*.

"Allison." Peter's dark eyes glistened, too. He didn't want to leave her, even for five days. Saying good-bye terrified him. He even thought of turning Shakespeare on Broadway over to someone else. But it was *his* incredible project, and he had cancelled his part in a production once before, to be with Sara, until . . . His life with Allison would last forever, Peter told himself. His fear was an ancient emotion, nothing to do with Allison, "This is going to be an adventure."

"It is?" Allison teased, but it helped her tears. "In what way?"

"I don't know. I was just trying to think of something redeeming about it."

"How about being incredibly productive because of unfulfilled passion?"

"I guess I will start writing again."

"Peter, you're going to New York to direct Shakespeare's greatest plays—in record time, with the most distinguished cast ever assembled. When are you planning to write?"

"At night, after I call you." *When I am awakened by nightmares*, Peter thought. But maybe the nightmares wouldn't return. With Allison in his arms, the nightmares had been driven away. Maybe with Allison in his heart, in his dreams, they would stay away still. "After I call you from my very small, very undecorated apartment."

"You don't have framed posters of your Broadway smashes hung on the walls, or the odd Tony casually displayed on a coffee table?"

"No." Peter frowned as he thought about his dark, barren, austere apartment. He wouldn't even have time, before Friday, to make it better. "Allison, it's really very minimal. I moved there because it was a close walk to the theater district, so I could go home during breaks totake care of Muffin. And it's very quiet for writing, but—"

"Peter! It doesn't matter." After a moment, she added, "It doesn't matter, but if you want me to, I can decorate it for you."

"You *will* decorate it by being there."

"Thank you," she whispered. "I *should* spend some time in the design stores and auction houses in Manhattan, anyway. Without a project, I might just spend every moment with you at your rehearsals."

"That would be fine with me."

"Peter, do you need both hands to direct?"

"What?" Peter laughed softly at the teasing sparkle in her eyes.

"If I could just have one hand, to hold, I would be very happy and very quiet."

Winter bought the copy of *Portrait* magazine's Academy Award issue in late March, but she didn't read it until the middle of April. Between the end of *Love* and the middle of April, Winter had been frantically busy, racing against a not-very-imaginary clock, fighting loneliness and the familiar pain of being left by someone she loved.

Think about your baby, Winter Carlyle, not about yourself.

Thoughts of her baby were wonderful antidotes for Winter's loneliness. She *wasn't* alone, and each day the new little life became more a part of her, a happy, joyful, hopeful part.

So happy, so joyful, that Winter decided it would be safe to read the *Portrait* article about Lawrence Carlyle. Winter studied the photograph first. Lawrence's face was shadowed by a safari hat, protection against the glaring equatorial sun, and he looked as if he had been typecast to play the role of an important director; a king surveying his kingdom. The portrait of Lawrence Carlyle revealed *nothing* of who he was. Emily Rousseau would not have taken such a portrait.

The accompanying article revealed little, too, nothing Winter didn't already know. The article revealed little, but it *concealed* one essential fact. It was a portrait of Winter's father *and she wasn't in it*. There was passing reference to Lawrence's "brief, tumultuous marriage to Jacqueline Winter," but no mention of the "love-child." Winter was an omission. She didn't exist!

Winter imagined a portrait of Dr. Mark Stephens—Chairman of the Department of Internal Medicine at Harvard—twenty years from now. There might be a passing reference to Mark's days at UCLA Medical School—"a charming playboy who nevertheless made top grades and never lost sight of his goals"—but no mention of Winter Carlyle or of their "love-child."

But that was because Mark would never know about his child, not because, like Lawrence, he would pretend his child didn't exist.

Winter closed the copy of *Portrait.* It was a mistake to have read the article, a mistake to have learned that, in the eyes of the great Lawrence Carlyle, *she* had never been born.

A mistake.

You're not a mistake, little one, Winter spoke silently to her unborn baby. I am so excited about you, so proud of you, so eager to get to know you better.

Winter *had* to conceal her baby's existence from Mark, but it was time to share the wonderful joy with her best friend.

"Did you have a nice weekened?" Winter asked when Allison answered her phone moments later. It was Monday night. Allison had just returned from her third weekend in New York.

"Very." *Nice, too short, I miss him already.* "Winter, how are you?"

"Allison, I need your help."

Good. At last. Allison hadn't even *seen* Winter for three weeks. Allison had tried, but Winter had said she was "too busy" and "right in the midst of something" each time. Winter didn't *sound* terrible over the phone and she never mentioned Mark, but she was a very talented actress.

"Anything, Winter," Allison answered quietly. Something in Winter's tone made Allison's thoughts drift to last summer, to the day she had ridden again for the first time. *I need you on my side, Winter,* Allison had told her best friend. And Winter had replied swiftly, *I am on your side, Allison, always.* "Anything."

"Could you come by tomorrow? I'm living at the mansion in Bel Air."

"The mansion? Since when?" *Why?*

"For the past two weeks. I was able to keep the same phone number I had at my apartment." *In case Mark calls.*

"I thought you were planning to sell the mansion, Winter," Allison said gently. *Why do you want to live in a place where the memories are so unhappy? Won't you feel lonely and isolated living there?*

"I was planning to, but for now I've decided to live here. So, can you come by tomorrow? Any time is fine."

"How about early?" *How about now?* "Like on my way to work? Seven-thirty? Eight?"

"Sure. Seven-thirty is fine."

Allison did a double take when she saw Winter's outfit. It was seven-thirty in the morning but Winter looked wide awake; and, Allison realized on closer inspection, it wasn't a bathrobe, anyway. Winter was wearing a silk caftan, elegant, expensive, and quite appropriate for lounging around a mansion in Bel Air, but definitely *not* her style. Winter's clothes always clung to her sleek body, accenting her flawless figure, sending provocative messages of beauty and grace. The silk caftan sent different messages—that it was concealing extra weight, that Winter didn't care.

Allison looked at her friend's face, at the slightly fuller cheeks beneath the beautiful violet eyes. Was Winter miserable and eating? Was she hiding her pain behind the walls of the mansion and her new extra pounds under layers of expensive silk?

"Allison, you're staring at me!"

"I'm sorry. I just . . . what can I do to help you?"

"Follow me."

Winter led the way across the living room, beyond the closed door of the screening room, to the unused wing of the mansion.

"I didn't even realize this was here," Allison said. In high school, on the rare occasions when they had spent time in Winter's eerily silent home instead of Allison's warm, cheery one, Allison and Winter were in the other wing, in the kitchen, by the pool, or in Winter's room.

"As you can see, this wing has been ignored for years, but I think it has potential, don't you? I couldn't see any hope for Bellemeade and look what you did, but even *I* can see new life for these rooms."

"You want me to redecorate for you?" Allison asked, amazed, disappointed. *That's the kind of help you meant, Winter? Professional? What about the emotional help of your best friend?*

"Yes. Allison, I know you're booked until about the year two thousand. I want the whole wing redone sometime, when you have time, but there are two rooms . . . if you could do them soon?"

"Of course." Allison was being *incredibly productive* during the days and nights away from Peter. And she would do whatever she could to help Winter.

"Here." Winter walked into the room with the French doors that opened onto the terrace with the pond of koi. It was the room that would have been hers in a different childhood, a happy childhood with brothers and sisters and love.

"This is lovely." Allison gazed appreciatively at the high ceilings and carved wood moldings and wall of windows.

"This will be my bedroom. I guess I'd like something flowery and cheerful. And I'll need a bed and dresser."

"OK. That's easy. We'll go over samples together." Allison walked toward a doorway, obviously very recently created, that connected the inner wall of Winter's bedroom to another room. "This is the other room?"

"Yes." Winter followed Allison into the smaller but still spacious room.

"What did you want here? Will it be your study?"

"He really hasn't told you, has he?"

"Who? Told me what?"

"Peter."

"Peter?" Worry pulsed through her. Allison knew Peter had secrets. He had told her *nothing* of his life before he met her, but Allison knew there had been great sadness. She had seen the sadness in his eyes, almost vanquished now by their joyous love, and she had read his tormented plays. She assumed the secret sadnesses of Peter's life belonged to an unhappy, perhaps tragic childhood. Allison hoped that someday Peter would tell her his secrets. She believed, *trusted* that he would.

And now Peter and Winter had a secret, shared by them, *kept* from her!

"This will be the baby's room," Winter said quietly.

"The baby?"

"She's—I think she's a she—due in September. I won't need furniture in here right away because I found my cradle."

Winter had been wandering in the mansion, exploring long-forgotten rooms, and had found her own cradle in a storage room. And in boxes nearby, Winter had found her baby clothes. Why had Jacqueline saved the cradle and carefully folded the tiny clothes? Was it loving sentiment? Or was it merely the same compulsion that had made Jacqueline save and carefully catalogue the magnificent jewels from all her lovers?

"Mark's baby," Allison whispered. *Peter's baby?*

"Yes. Mark's baby," Winter said softly. "Allison, Mark doesn't know. I don't

want him ever to know. When I need to, I will tell everyone, including her, that her daddy died."

"Winter . . ."

"Allison! Can't *I* be allowed to make unchallenged decisions, or does that only apply to *you?*"

"What?" Allison was stunned by the emotion—*anger?*—in Winter's voice.

"Sorry." Winter's eyes filled with tears. "I'm still very raw and there are rogue hormones swimming around in my bloodstream making things even harder."

Allison walked to Winter and gave her a hug. *I'm on your side, Winter, always.*

"Let's go down to the kitchen, have some tea or whatever's good for moms-to-be, and talk, OK?"

"OK. My moms-to-be books say tea, in moderation, is all right."

Allison watched as Winter put a kettle on the stove in the kitchen and took two Limoges teacups from a cup-board.

"What did you mean, Winter, about me being the only one allowed to make unchallenged decisions?"

"I meant that a year ago, when you decided not to marry Dan and to work for Claire and to ride again, you simply made the announcements. You didn't ask for help, even from the people who love you."

"Oh." Allison frowned. Winter was right, of course. Allison hadn't talked to Dan as she made the momentous decision about *their* marriage. And she hadn't talked to Winter, Patricia, or Sean—the people who were with her, loving her, helping her survive after the accident—about her decision to ride again. Was that selfish? What if Allison had asked their advice and they had said no? Now there was another momentous decision—to jump the green and white railed jump—and she had shared it with Peter, and he had said no. Jumping the jump was something Allison needed, for *herself*, but was her need more important than erasing the worry from the eyes of the man she loved?

"Allison, I didn't mean to hurt your feelings," Winter whispered softly, apologizing for her earlier harshness. She added, smiling, and without resentment, "Besides, so far your momentous decisions have been pure gold."

"And yours isn't?"

"My decision to keep her is," Winter answered quietly. *That* hadn't even been a decision. Winter felt as if she had been given a precious little gift to love, a precious little gift *of* love.

"Winter, what horrible thing would happen if you told Mark?"

"He would marry me."

"And that's horrible?"

"Allison," Winter's voice faltered and new tears dampened her eyes, "Mark didn't want me."

"I just can't believe that."

"It's what happened." Winter gave a wobbly smile. "So, here I am, in this mansion for the duration. You've heard of confinement?"

"You're not going out at all?"

"Only to see my doctor at Cedars, for which I will wear a large straw hat and a blond wig. As soon as the prerelease ads for *Love* start appearing, I will be recognized. Maybe it doesn't matter. By then Mark will be in Boston, completely involved in his residency, but I just can't take the risk of him finding out."

"What about food? Clothes?"

"I've spent the past few weeks—I've only just gotten really pregnant-looking—stocking up. I have canned goods and frozen food, all very healthy stuff, to last until about Christmas. I bought a few maternity dresses, which you and Peter will get to see. Nothing very glamorous."

Allison frowned at the mention of Peter's name.

"Why did you tell Peter, Winter, and not tell me?"

"I didn't tell him, Allison. He *guessed*. I have no idea how he knew. It was a month ago, the day we finished *Love*. You saw me that night. Did you think I looked pregnant?"

"No." Allison remembered that night very clearly. She had watched Winter closely, worrying about her. Winter had looked sad, exhausted, devastated, but not *pregnant*. "What did Peter say?"

"Something poetic about the color of my cheeks. I'm sorry I asked him to keep it from you, Allison. It wasn't fair to either of you. I just needed a little time. So now you both know and no one else needs to."

"Except my mother."

"No, Allison."

"She has to know, Winter, because I am not going off to New York every weekend unless I know you have someone to call if you need anything."

"I won't need anything."

"And there may be times that I can't be here to answer the door for the wallpaperers and painters and furniture deliveries."

"I was just planning to leave the front door unlocked. Allison, you don't have to be here."

"I *want* to be. And I want Mother to be able to be, too. She loves you, Winter. She's not going to be judgmental." Allison smiled. "She's an expert at not challenging momentous decisions. And she's getting very good at keeping secrets."

"Such as?"

"Me and Peter." Allison had told Sean and Patricia, finally, about Peter. Before Peter returned to New York, Sean and Patricia met and *liked* the man who had brought such great joy to their precious daughter.

"You and Peter are a secret?"

"Not *really*. It's just that we have so little time together that we're trying to keep it private. Mother hasn't told anyone, including Vanessa."

"Vanessa wouldn't print anything about you that you didn't want her to. With anyone else in this town, she wouldn't hesitate, but she cares about you."

"I'm sure you're right. But Vanessa's such a fan of Peter's work. She would think it was wonderful that Peter and I are together."

"It is wonderful."

"Yes." Allison smiled.

"Too wonderful to share."

"Except with you and my parents." Allison paused, then added, "And Emily knows. She just did five photographs—her best work ever—for Peter's apartment in New York."

"How is Emily?"

"Winter," Allison looked meaningfully at her friend. They had already strayed from the important topic and now Winter was meandering off on another path. "May I tell Mother, please?"

Winter hesitated a moment, then, with a grateful smile, whispered, "Yes."

"Good. And can she and I come over, like every day, with fresh fruit?"

"Yes," Winter answered softly. "Allison, thank you."

"Don't mention it! Now, would you like to hear about Emily? I don't really know very much. I'm not sure what work she's doing, if any, other than photographs for me. She's definitely moving to Paris in June."

"You still think something happened between Emily and Rob?"

"Something must have, although I have no idea what."

"Have you seen him?"

"No," Allison answered thoughtfully. She hadn't even seen Rob from a distance, not even a friendly wave in a check-out line at the grocery. She hadn't seen Rob, Allison realized, since that snowy weekend in Aspen. Since then, Allison and Peter had been living in their private world of love.

"Things change, don't they?" Winter asked, as if reading Allison's thoughts. "The other day, I was thinking about the Diet Pepsi toasts we made last fall at the Acapulco. Except for your success with Bellemeade, it didn't quite work out the way we planned, did it?" Winter sighed softly, sadly. "Something happened that made Emily leave *portrait*. And Mark and I—"

Winter's *love* without the capital *L*, the private love, the important love, had failed.

"But the movie, Winter. Peter said you were wonderful."

"Well, we'll see when *Love* is edited. Do you know when that will be? I assume Peter will be coming out to see it."

"Peter will be here for an entire week," Allison answered, smiling, "the first week of June."

Chapter 23

BURBANK, CALIFORNIA
JUNE 1985

Steve watched Peter as the final credits appeared on the edited, soundtracked, *completed* version of *Love*. To Steve's critical, experienced, savvy movie eyes, *Love* was a masterpiece, virtually flawless. But Steve still worried that Peter might not agree. Peter might have artistic differences, prejudices of style that could mire *Love* in the kind of conflict that so far had been remarkably absent.

But Peter didn't have artistic differences.

"It's everything I hoped it would be, Steve," he said quietly.

"Good."

"When will it be released?"

Steve arched an eyebrow, surprised by Peter's question. Peter had made it crystal clear from the beginning that his involvement would end with final approval of the movie. Steve and Peter had agreed, in writing, that Peter wouldn't make promotional appearances or grant interviews. But now Peter was asking about the commercial aspects of *Love* and his curiosity seemed more than idle.

"*Love* will open in theaters nationwide during the second weekend in August," Steve answered. "I've arranged private showings for the press and film critics in New York, Dallas, Chicago, San Francisco, and here in late July."

"What about the Los Angeles premiere?"

"That will be on August second. It's a Friday night. We have both the Westwood Village and Bruin theaters—they're across the street from each other—and Broxton Avenue will be ours, too, for the reception immediately following. Why, Peter? Are you thinking about coming?"

"I open *Romeo and Juliet* on Broadway the following night." Peter gave a wry smile. *Juliet* and *Julia*, heroines of two very different stories of love. "Would you like me to be at the premiere, Steve?"

"Of course I would like it, Peter, but it's not essential. Premieres are star and media events. Our celebrity guests will come to be *seen*, to be photographed by the paparazzi, and to offer their professional opinions about *Love*. The cameras and attention will be on our actor and actress guests, and, of course, on Winter and Bruce. You and I aren't nearly as interesting, Peter, although a show of solidarity is always nice."

"Where else do you plan to have Winter and Bruce appear?"

"Everywhere. *Good Morning America, The Today Show, The Morning Show*, Phil, Oprah, local talk shows in big cities. All the big shows are holding space for us already—everyone is very interested in *Love*—and now that I know you're happy with the finished version, I will contact Winter and Bruce and set firm dates."

"Steve, you and Winter and I need to meet."

"We do?"

"Yes, we do. Without Bruce. Is tomorrow afternoon convenient for you?"

"Sure," Steve answered, curious, worried, but sensing he would simply have to wait until tomorrow to find out why they needed to meet.

"Winter lives in Bel Air, in the house where she lived with her mother. Do you know it?"

"Oh, yes."

If there had been a rift between Winter and Bruce during the filming of *Love*, they had certainly kept it to themselves, Steve thought for the fiftieth time in the past twenty-four hours.

If this meeting was simply because Winter wanted to make appearances by herself, without her costar, that was fine. Separate appearances by Winter and Bruce would mean twice as much publicity for *Love*. Steve had considered calling her and telling her that—"You can fly solo on every show, Winter"—but perhaps Winter's battle was with Peter, not Bruce. In that case, Steve needed to be there to mediate. Besides, Steve was a little curious about visiting the mansion again after all these years.

Steve pressed the doorbell and let his thoughts travel to a time when the chimes were a melodic signal to Jacqueline that he had arrived. Steve was lost in that remote romantic memory when Winter opened the door. For a moment he was confused by the violet eyes, not Jacqueline's sapphire ones, and the black velvet hair, not Jacqueline's platinum blond.

Steve was pulled unceremoniousl to the present, however, when he realized he was looking at a very pregnant Winter Carlyle.

"*Terrific*."

"Thank you, Steve," Winter replied sweetly.

"This is why Winter and I thought it would be best for us to meet without Bruce," Peter explained as he and Steve and Winter moved to the living room.

"Is Bruce the father?"

"*No*," Peter and Winter responded in unison.

"Are you?" Steve asked Peter.

"No," Winter asked solemnly. "The baby's father is dead."

Steve tilted his head thoughtfully and said to Winter, "You're a helluva an actress—I think you have a very good shot at this year's Oscar—but that last line didn't convince me." Steve saw such worry in Winter's eyes—genuine, unscripted worry—that he added gently, "If he's really dead, I'm very sorry. If not, it doesn't matter, none of my business. But I am to assume that secrecy is important?"

"Yes. I can't appear publicly, Steve. After the baby's born, I can, but not before."

"And you're due, let me guess, the night of the premiere?"

"No, even worse. Early September," Winter smiled wryly. It meant she wouldn't be available for public appearances until at least six weeks after *Love* was released. "Steve, I'm sorry."

Steve shrugged and smiled. He liked Winter very much. She had been such a trouper, such a professional. Steve knew this couldn't be easy for her—not now, not a year from now.

"It's OK. Bruce thrives in limelight. I'm sure he'll be delighted to hear that you're involved in 'another project.' "

"I would be very happy to make appearances," Peter offered.

"Peter's going to win Best Screenplay and Best Director, of course, but he's going to get a special Oscar for being so nice." Winter smiled at the nice handsome man who she guessed *hated* the thought of public appearances—queries about why he wrote what he wrote, questions about his private life—but had offered anyway simply to help *her.*

"Bruce and I can make the rounds in August and September," Steve said. "*Love* isn't going to vanish by October. After your baby's born, Winter, and once you look the way you want to in front of a camera, perhaps you could appear on the morning network shows?"

"Yes, of course. That would be fine. I could do them from LA, couldn't I?"

"Sure." Steve turned to Peter. "I think we're all right for the television spots, Peter, but—"

"The premiere?" Peter guessed with a smile.

"I'm afraid so. Even though the press isn't nearly as interested in you or me as they are in the stars."

"The show of solidarity is suddenly a little more critical."

"Yes."

"I'll be there, Steve."

"And back in New York twenty-four hours later for *Romeo and Juliet?*"

"It won't be any problem."

As Steve stood up to leave, he had a vivid memory of young violet eyes peering around a corner, uncertain, afraid. Steve looked at the violet eyes now, at what they had become, and still saw uncertainty.

"When are you going to see the masterpiece, Winter?"

"When it comes to cable."

"Don't you want to see it?"

"I really don't know, Steve."

"Well, you're magnificent. I'm sure Peter told you."

Winter smiled softly and nodded. Peter *had* told her.

"You have a screening room here, don't you?" Steve asked.

"Yes."

"Then I'll get a print of *Love* for you, just in case, OK?"

"OK. Thank you."

As Steve stood to leave, he thought about Lawrence Carlyle, the ghost that haunted this mansion, the ghost that might haunt the film. The issue of Lawrence Carlyle could wait for another time, Steve decided. The estrangement of Lawrence and Winter *had* to be addressed and handled, but there was still time. Winter had other worries to deal with now.

"Winter, if there's anything you need. I'm here."

"Thank you, Steve."

After Steve left, Winter said to Peter, "That wasn't too bad, thanks to you."

"Steve's a reasonable man."

"Did I really say it would be *fine* to be at a television studio downtown at four A.M., trying to look bright-eyed and bushy-tailed for the wide-awake East Coast?"

"You did, Winter." Peter smiled. "Had I been directing the scene, I wouldn't have even asked you to do a second take. Your enthusiasm was really very convincing."

"I guess I was just relieved that—"

The phone rang, stopping Winter mid-sentence, The only people who ever called were Allison, Peter, and Patricia. Peter was here. Allison was on her way to take Emily to the airport. Perhaps it was Patricia, but . . .

It could be Mark. Tomorrow or the next day or the next, Mark would be leaving for Boston. Maybe he was calling to ask, *Do I have to go to Boston alone?*

"Hello?"

"Hi."

"Allison."

"Is Peter still there?"

"Yes. Sure." Winter handed the receiver to Peter and sat down on the sofa a little defeated, mostly annoyed at herself for still fantasizing.

"Hi. Are you at Emily's?"

"No. I'm on the Pasadena Freeway. Actually, I'm at a roadside café near the Pasadena Freeway."

"Are you all right?"

"I'm fine. A truck jacknifed somewhere between here and where I want to be. There's oil or honey—something gooey—all over the freeway and the road is now impassable and it's going to be at least an hour."

"And you're supposed to get Emily in"—Peter glanced at his watch—"twenty minutes."

"Yes. I tried to call her, but her phone has already been disconnected, so—"

"So give me her address."

"You don't mind?"

"Of course not. It will give me a chance to meet her even if it's only to wish her *au revoir*."

"Thank you." Allison gave Peter Emily's address. "I hate these freeways! So, how was the meeting with Steve?"

"It was fine. You and I are making an appearance at the premiere in August—more to give Winter the report than anything else, I think—and then how do you feel about doing some three A.M. babysitting in October?"

"Can't wait." Allison laughed. "Oh, speaking of waiting, there's a line forming at this phone booth."

"I should leave soon to get Emily anyway."

"Peter, I was going to give Emily the phone number and address of your apartment in New York."

"*Our* apartment."

"Our apartment," Allison echoed softly.

Emily sat on the narrow bed in her basement apartment on Montana Avenue. Allison would be here in ten minutes. Emily was ready.

The apartment looked exactly as it had when Emily had moved in six years ago—Spartan, sterile, dark. The dresser drawers and closets were empty, and the corner that had been Emily's darkroom was open again, the black curtains gone, the chemicals and pans discarded.

Emily was taking very little with her to Paris. Her camera, of course, and a small suitcase. The suitcase contained the picture she had taken of Robert Jeffrey Adamson—she didn't know his name then, only his gentle blue eyes—at Meg's wedding; the two very important books—*Little Girl Lost* and *Little Girl Found*—given to her by the man with the gentle blue eyes; a new soft cotton nightgown; a fluffy bathrobe; a change of lacy underclothes; and the letters.

The letters. One letter was written to the man Emily hated, and the other letter was written to the man she loved. Neither man would ever read the letters; but Emily had needed to write them, to give voice to the powerful emotions. She needed to *face* the hatred and to *admit* the love.

The letter to the man Emily hated, the evil man who had stolen her innocence and her trust and her hope, was a letter of rage, not forgiveness.

"Do you want to forgive him, Emily?" Dr. Camden had asked.

"No. He knew what he was doing, didn't he?"

"I think so," Beverly Camden had answered evenly, although her own feeling on the issue was strong. A man who would knowingly cause such harm to a defenseless child—a man who would steal trust and the hope of love *for a lifetime*—deserved no forgiveness, no pardon.

Emily told Dr. Camden she had written the letter of hatred and rage to her stepfather, but she never mentioned the letter written to the man she loved. If Emily had been stronger, she might have thanked Rob in person. Perhaps she might even have gone back to work at *Portrait*, met with Rob once a week, taken pictures at his wedding.

I hope you'll photograph our wedding, Emily. I know Rob would want you to, Elaina had said. *We'll probably be married in June, at the Club.*

If Emily had been stronger . . .

But maybe it was really a sign of *great strength*. Four months ago, Emily had been willing, *happy*, to spend her life meeting with Rob for an hour a week *if she was lucky*. Emily never imagined there could be more for her; she believed she didn't deserve more.

Emily was stronger now. She wanted *more* for herself and for her life. Emily wanted love. She had a right to love and be loved, *didn't she?* For now, Emily's belief was only a leap of faith. In time, if she was lucky, there would be new *good* experiences to counterbalance the bad. Emily already knew that Rob Adamson existed. There were other men like Rob, weren't there? Somewhere in the world? Maybe?

Finding love with a man was a very long way off. Emily was still learning to love herself, to believe in herself, to *trust* herself. But, someday, there would be love.

Emily's old clothes—cleaned and ironed and baggy—were going to the Goodwill. They were neatly folded in a cardboard box outside the basement door.

For her flight to Paris—for her *arrival* in her new home—Emily was wearing a new, brave look. Her outfit, purchased at Bullock's-Wilshire, was a little denim, but not at all drab. The ivory blouse was soft and silky and feminine. The calf-length skirt was designer denim, tight at her small waist, stylishly flared, not baggy. Emily wore lapis earrings, and they could be seen because her long golden hair was swept gently off her face with barrettes and braided into a thick, shiny rope.

The knock at the door startled her. Allison was early. Emily had planned to be at the curb, waiting.

"Allison, I—" But it wasn't Allison! It was a man, dark, handsome, smiling, curious.

Emily fought the instinct to reach for the barrettes that held her hair, leaving her face exposed, vulnerable, naked. *Courage*, Emily told herself. Besides, loosening the barrettes would accomplish nothing; the familiar, protective golden curtain was tightly woven into a long, silky braid.

"Hi, Emily? I'm Peter Dalton. Allison is stuck in traffic across town, so I get to drive you to the airport."

"Oh, that's not necessary. I can call a cab."

"*That's* not necessary. I want to give you a ride, Emily. I've wanted to meet you. I'm a great admirer of your work."

"Oh. Thank you."

"Is this all your luggage?" Peter asked as he reached for the small suitcase that stood beside her purse and her camera case.

"Yes." *I'm starting over, you see, in Paris. I'm just taking a photograph of the man I love, two very important letters, and the guide books for the rest of my life.*

Peter put Emily's suitcase in the trunk of the car and held the door open for her.

"Thank you."

"You're welcome." Peter smiled, a warm smile for a beautiful woman. Emily was quite different from what Peter had expected from Allison's gentle, concerned descriptions of her friend.

"Oh, before I forget." Peter removed a notecard from his shirt pocket. "Here's our address and phone number in New York. For the foreseeable future, that's where Allison and I will be on weekends."

"Thank you. I'll send my address and phone number as soon as I have them."

"Good. Allison says you'll be working for *Paris Match*."

"Just free-lance to begin with." When Emily contacted *Paris Match*, they had been eager to sign the already-famous photographer from *Portrait* to their full-time staff, but she had said no. It had more to do with *choice* than business—choice and control over her life. And the other thing, the haunting thing: Signing with another magazine seemed like a betrayal to Rob. Rob, who had never betrayed her, even though she had angrily accused him of it.

"I'm sure you'll be in great demand."

As they neared Los Angeles International Airport, Peter sensed Emily's tension. The pink-flush left her cheeks and her body stiffened beneath the soft folds of silk.

"I'll come in with you, Emily, if you don't mind. I'd like to see the new international terminal."

"Oh, all right."

Peter and Emily drew stares—the dark handsome man, the beautiful blond woman. The stares would have terrified Emily if she had been alone. But she wasn't alone. Peter was right beside her. After a while, Emily courageously met the stares of the men who passed her, *and they weren't menacing, only appreciative*.

Just as Peter's dark eyes smiled appreciatively at her. Appreciatively, gently,
 supportively, as if Peter somehow knew this was a huge step for her and he was here to make sure she didn't lose her fragile footing.

Emily's courage *might* have faltered without Peter. She might have forgotten the months of hard work, her new strength, her belief in herself. She might have unbraided her golden hair, pulled the silky blouse loose from the waistband, and gone into familiar, comfortable, *horrible* hiding.

But Peter *was* there, smiling and somehow wise. Emily made the giant, all-important step, and she would never forget Peter's kindness.

Now the balance of Emily's experience with men was shifted a little more to the good. Now she knew there were two kind, gentle men in the world: Rob Adamson and Peter Dalton.

"Please wish Allison good luck with the opening of the Chateau Bel Air," Emily said to Peter before she boarded the Air France flight to Paris.

"I will, but I know for a fact Allison thinks she could open with unpainted walls and bare floors littered with sawdust, and as long as your photographs were on display, it would still be a hit."

The private opening of the Chateau Bel Air was held on a Thursday evening in early July. The invited guests wore tuxedos, designer gowns and jewels, and expressions of obvious approval as they wandered through the elegant hotel during the champagne reception that preceded the gourmet dinner in the splendid Versailles Room. The invited guests were rich, powerful, famous, and discerning. They needed to know about the best hotels in Los Angeles, hotels with spacious conference rooms for hammering out multimillion dollar deals, and hotels with luxurious suites for intimate weekends of romance.

As the rich and powerful guests strolled through the magnificent Chateau Bel Air, they made vows to use this grand place—for business, *and* for those very special, very private, very discreet weekends of love.

"Rob, how nice of you to come!" Allison smiled at the ocean-blue eyes she hadn't seen since February in Aspen. She felt a moment of nostalgia, sorry that it had been so long, afraid that . . . No, the special bond, the special warmth, was still there.

"I wouldn't have missed it, Allison. This is an absolute masterpiece."

"Thank you, Rob. Of course, the photographs," Allison began automatically. It was the way Allison had answered every compliment throughout the evening: *Of course, the photographs by Emily Rousseau are what really make it work!*

"Is she here?" Rob asked.

"Emily? No. She moved to Paris a month ago."

"I see."

Allison saw sadness in Rob's eyes and strain on his handsome face. *Something happened between Rob and Emily. Something that left them both so sad.* Rob had come this evening to see Allison's triumph, but he had come, too, in hopes of seeing Emily.

"Did you see Emily before she left, Allison?"

"Yes."

"How was she?"

"She seemed sad—a little lost—after she left *Portrait*," Allison told the dark blue eyes that obviously cared so much.

"Lost," Rob echoed quietly. *Little Girl Lost.*

"But, then . . ."

"Then?"

"Then . . . I don't know. In a way that I can't really define—just a feeling, I guess—Emily seemed to get better."

"Better?"

"Yes. Better." Allison frowned slightly, wishing she could be more specific, wishing she had something to say that would erase the obvious concern and worry in Rob's eyes. Allison believed Emily was better, stronger, more confident, but it was just a *feeling*. "I've gotten a few postcards from her from Paris. She's busy—naturally—and I think she feels very much at home in Paris."

Rob and Allison were interrupted briefly by someone who wanted to congratulate Allison.

"Is Elaina with you?" Allison asked Rob when they were alone again.

"No. I'm here by myself. What about you? Roger, brokenhearted Roger, says there is someone new in your life. Is *he* here?"

"Roger's not brokenhearted! But he *is* right. There is someone. He couldn't be here tonight," Allison answered softly. Peter was in New York at the final dress rehearsal of *Hamlet*.

"He sounds very important to you," Rob said with a smile.

"Yes, he is very important to me," Allison answered quietly. She smiled into Rob's dark blue eyes. "I would like you to meet him, Rob. I know you would like him and he would like you."

"I would like to meet him, Allison. Will that ever happen?"

"Yes." Allison *knew* Rob and Peter would meet sometime. Peter would certainly be in *Portrait's* Academy Award issue, if not before. Allison and Peter's love was still very private, a lovely secret known only to a trusted few. Allison suddenly wanted to share her wonderful secret with Rob. "In fact, Rob . . ."

This time Rob and Allison's conversation was interrupted by someone who wanted to speak to Rob. Then someone, and someone else, and someone *else* wanted to speak to her. By the time Allson was free and she looked for Rob again, he was gone.

Allison was going to say, "In fact, Rob, you'll meet him next month at the premiere of *Love*."

Rob Adamson certainly would be among the celebrities who received engraved invitations to the gala premiere of *Love*. Rob would be there, and Allison would proudly, happily, *joyfully* introduce her dear friend Rob to her beloved Peter.

BEL AIR, CALIFORNIA
AUGUST 1985

Allison arrived at Winter's mansion at seven P.M. on the first of August, twenty-four hours before the Los Angeles premiere of *Love*.

"I bought you a dress for the premiere." Allison handed the pale blue box tied in a gold ribbon to her surprised friend. "Or at least for our private premiere after-party. I got it at a maternity boutique on Dayton, very upscale, for pregnant actresses and Hollywood wives, I guess. No one recognized me, of course, or seemed the least bit interested in why I was buying a glamorous maternity gown. I was actually a little disappointed because I had prepared about ten plausible reasons." Allison's eyes sparkled conspiratorially, "Anyway,

I *did* pay in cash and made sure I wasn't followed!"

"Allison," Winter whispered softly as she opened the pale blue box. Tears filled her eyes as she removed the lavender and ivory silk gown. The maternity clothes Winter had bought in March and early April, to last throughout her pregnancy, were uninspired, *something* to wear during the long months in the mansion. "It's beautiful."

"It is, isn't it?" Allison smiled.

"This is going to be such fun. What are you wearing?"

"For *Love*, I'm wearing pastel chiffon." *So romantic*, Allison had decided when she bought the dress last week at Gorgissima.

"And for *Romeo and Juliet?*"

"Gold lamé, very sleek, very Fifth Avenue. Peter has tuxedos rented on both coasts."

"Talk about a whirlwind weekend. *Love* in Westwood, *Romeo and Juliet* in Manhattan. Saturday night you'll be at the Tavern on the Green, drinking champagne till dawn, waiting to read the reviews."

"The part of the weekend Peter and I are looking forward to the most is dinner with you tomorrow night after the premiere. We'll stop by with the food about six."

"You two look so glamorous!" Winter exclaimed when Allison and Peter arrived the following evening. "Allison, that dress. Peter, gorgeous in a tuxedo."

"You look pretty glamorous yourself, Winter Carlyle," Peter said.

"I love my upscale maternity gown."

Allison and Winter followed Peter as he carried boxes of gourmet food, prepared at the Club, into the kitchen.

"Do you think we have enough food?" Winter laughed. "Just figuring out *what* we have will keep me busy until you return!"

"Why don't you wait, Winter?" Allison suggested. "Just leave everything in the refrigerator, and we'll set out plates and fire up the microwave when we get back."

"Allison, I may be almost eight months pregnant—God knows I look it—but I'm quite healthy."

"Just don't overdo."

"I won't."

"Are you going to watch the movie tonight?"

"I don't think so," Winter said. As promised, Steve had given her a print of *Love*. *Someday* she would settle into the cushiony chairs in the screening room and watch her performance as the heroine of the romantic film of the decade, but not yet.

"We'd better go, Allison," Peter said quietly.

"OK." Allison smiled thoughtfully at Winter. "I really hate leaving you alone, Winter."

"I'm not alone, Allison." *I have my lively little baby frolicking happily inside me.*

* * *

Allison didn't remember when it happened, or whether Peter withdrew his hand from hers or she from his, but she became aware that her hands were alone, clasped tightly in her lap. The unsettling realization that her fingers were no longer entwined with Peter's was just a tiny ripple in the storm-tossed sea of confusion and fear that raged inside her as she watched *Love*.

Who is Julia? The bewildering question came with a swift, confident answer: *Julia is the woman Peter loves.*

But where is Julia? No longer, apparently, in Peter's life, but still, *so obviously*, in Peter's heart.

Did Peter write Love *for Julia? Was* Love *Peter's gentle and so-eloquent plea to his beloved Julia to return to him?*

Yes. Of course. What other explanation could there be?

The devastating questions with their heart-stopping answers thundered in Allison's mind as she watched *Love*. They thundered still even after the movie ended and the theater fell silent.

The silence lasted for several moments. Every man and woman in the audience needed a little private time in the still-dark theater to reflect on the magnificence of what they had seen; time to brush tears from eyes and clear emotion from throats; time to wonder sadly how such a perfect love had eluded their lives; time to make vows to find such a love or to gently nurture a once-cherished-now-neglected one.

The reverent, reflective silence was finally broken by a single clap. The clap broke the silence and with it the magical spell that had been cast on them all. The audience had to leave the enchanted world of Julia and Sam, but they weren't leaving empty-handed. They left with the gifts Peter had given them, together with their own solemn vows to treasure and nurture whatever love existed in their lives.

The clapping became a roar and the audience stood. Allison stood, too, and somehow unclasped her numb hands to join the applause.

Allison didn't look at Peter—she *couldn't*—not during the seemingly endless applause and not when he leaned *so close* and whispered to her that he and Steve were leaving to have "a word with the press." After Peter and Steve disappeared, Allison moved with the river of rich and famous that flowed from the sanctuary of the dark theater into the bright lights of the gala reception, where champagne splashed and celebrities mingled and the only topic of conversation was astonished praise for *Love*.

"The script was brilliant, poetry really."

"Winter Carlyle, what a debut!"

"*Love* will sweep the Academy Awards."

"Vanessa Gold certainly was right about Peter Dalton. His is truly a six octave talent, from despair and hopelessness—did you ever see *Say Good-bye?*—to this! Absolutely amazing."

"What a gift!"

"What an imagination."

Imagination? Allison's reeling mind focused for a moment. Didn't they see it? Couldn't they tell *Love* was real? Apparently not! Maybe *she* was wrong. The thought came with a flickering hope, but it faded quickly.

Allison wove through the crowd to a far corner where the lights weren't so bright and where she would have to speak to no one. She spotted Vanessa in the distance, prayed that the columnist hadn't seen her sitting beside Peter, and was suddenly so glad that no one knew about *them*.

Because there was nothing to know. Peter and Allison weren't in love, not really, because, *because* Peter had another love.

Tears threatened. Allison wanted, needed, to escape, to find a private place where she could be alone with her swirling thoughts. Once before, Allison had escaped from a grand celebration because tears threatened and she needed privacy to think about shocking revelations. On that beautiful June day Allison had escaped to a fragrant alcove of lilacs, and she had been alone until a handsome

man with smiling blue eyes had found her.

Find me now, Rob. Help me get away from here.

From her vantage point in the shadows, Allison scanned the crowd for him, recalling sadly that this was the night she had planned to proudly, happily, *joyfully* introduce her good friend Rob to her beloved Peter. Allison searched for Rob, knowing that she wouldn't tell him anything or ask him to help her flee, but needing to see his kind eyes and hoping the warmth of his smile would melt the shivers of icy fear that pulsed through her.

But Rob Adamson was not in the celebrity crowd that had gathered to celebrate Peter Dalton's magnificent triumph.

Peter's magnificent triumph. Peter's and Winter's and Steve's and Bruce's.

And Julia's. Whoever Julia was, wherever she was.

On an August day, just a year ago, Allison had stood in a bustling paddock surrounded by haunting memories of her shattered dreams and had realized *I don't belong here.* Allison had rushed away from the paddock to Elegance, to explore her wonderful new talents and find wonderful new dreams. She had begun her new career that day. And, that day, she had met Peter.

Because of Peter, Allison had discovered the fire and passion and love that lived in her soul. And, because of Peter, Allison had discovered a dream she had never even known to dream.

And now Allison felt this dream—the dream of love—shattering, too, and the haunting words came to her again: *I don't belong here.*

"Allison. Here you are. Are you ready to leave?"

Allison couldn't meet Peter's dark eyes, but she felt them, staring at her, intense, curious, demanding.

"Yes," she whispered.

Peter and Allison didn't speak as he drove from Westwood to Bel Air, toward Winter's mansion and the festive late night dinner that was going to be such fun.

Peter didn't slow down as they neared the entrance to the mansion on Bellagio. He drove past, a half mile further, finally stopping the car in a distant corner of a parking lot at the Club. The remote corner would have been dark, but the full summer moon cast a soft, golden glow.

"Allison, what's wrong?"

"Please tell me, Peter."

"Tell you what, darling?"

"Tell me about Julia."

Allison spoke bravely to the dark eyes whose gaze she had avoided since the movie ended. Now Allison wanted, *needed*, to see Peter's eyes. Her jade eyes were illuminated by the moonlight, fully exposed, but the moon was behind Peter, casting shadows on his handsome face, concealing the message of his dark eyes. Allison couldn't see Peter's eyes, but she sensed the effect of her words on him, stunning him, as if she had inflicted a blow.

And Allison knew she had not been wrong . . . *Julia was real.*

Peter didn't answer right away, and in moments that seemed like forever, the summer night became eerily still, soundless, as if waiting in breath-held silence for his reply. Allison thought she heard a distant whinny, but maybe it was just her imagination. Or maybe it was a ghostly reminder of the *other* dream that had died.

"Allison." When Peter spoke at last, his voice was soft and gentle. "Julia is a fictional name and the story is fiction."

Peter paused, and in that new endless moment, Allison's heart cried, *Oh, Peter, please don't lie to me! Please don't pretend that the passion and emotion for Julia flowed from your brilliant, creative mind, not from your loving heart. I know it isn't true!*

Peter didn't lie to Allison.

"But," he continued very quietly, "she is based on a woman I knew."

"And loved." *And still love!*

"Yes." Peter reached for her hands, to hold her while he told her the rest, but Allison wouldn't let him have them. "Allison . . ."

"Please tell me, Peter. What woman?"

"My wife."

"Your wife?" Allison echoed weakly. Allison had prepared herself, *steeled* her trembling body as well as she could, to hear her beloved Peter confess to another love, a passionate affair that had ended badly and still lingered in his heart, its smoldering embers ever ready to burst into new flames. *She had not imagined a marriage.*

"We were married eight years ago. We were together for four years before she died."

"Died?" It was a whisper of pain.

"Yes. I wrote *Love* just before her death. She wanted me to write a happy love story. I promised her that I would make *Love* into a movie and that I wouldn't change the ending."

"Even though . . ."

"Even though."

Peter had given Allison the truth, the essential facts, as succinctly and unemotionally as he could, but the effect on her lovely eyes was still devastating. Peter helplessly watched the array of emotion—fear, surprise, sadness, confusion.

"Why didn't you tell me before, Peter?"

"Because of these." His hands trembled as he so gently touched the hot tears that fell onto her cheeks. "I didn't want to make you cry."

"Don't touch me!" Allison's words and the harshness of her voice startled them both. In the wonderful months of their love, Allison had longed for Peter's gentle touch, welcoming him always and with such joy. *And now Peter's gentle touch caused pain.* Bewildered, Allison added softly, "Please."

"All right, darling." Peter reluctantly withdrew his hands from her tear-damp cheeks. "Allison, I was going to tell you."

"You should have told me a long time ago." *Why didn't you tell me, Peter? Why did you hide something this important from me?*

"Yes, I guess I should have," Peter agreed softly. He had only wanted to protect his precious Allison from sadness, and instead he had hurt her so deeply. He needed to explain, to make her understand. He continued gently, "But when should I have told you, darling? In those few enchanted weeks we had together at Bellemeade, when the delicate roots of our new love needed joyous nurturing? Or in the past few months when we've had rare, desperate moments together and we have wanted to fill them only with happiness? I knew it would make you sad, Allison. I couldn't—didn't want to—do that to you."

"So you just let me be emotionally ambushed."

"I guess I foolishly hoped . . ." Peter couldn't finish the sentence, because suddenly the hope that Allison would see *Love* as the world would see it—a celebration of the gifts of love created by a gifted writer—was *so foolish*.

For the past few weeks, alone in his apartment in New York, Peter had been driven from sleep not by nightmares but by worry. Did he need to tell Allison about Sara before the premiere? he had asked himself over and over again in the darkness. No, he had decided finally. It wasn't necessary. He didn't have to
414 put sadness in the joyful heart of his lovely Allison—not yet.

Love was about Sara, not him, he reminded himself. *Love* was about Sara's loveliness, Sara's innocence, Sara's courage. Only the people who loved Sara—Peter, her parents, and Rob—would see Sara in Julia.

Love was about Sara. But *Love* was also Peter's lovesong to Sara. And Allison, the woman who loved him, would know the words flowed from his heart.

So foolish. He should have known. He should have told her. He should have caused her tears then instead of now, because now there was doubt in the jade-green eyes that before had glowed only with joyous, untarnished confidence in him and in his love. Doubt where there should be none, ever.

How much harm had he done in the name of love? Peter gazed at her hurt, bewildered eyes and had his grim answer: *So much*.

Peter desperately needed to undo the harm, to restore her radiant confidence, but Allison was so wounded, so wary, *so far away.*

"I was very wrong, Allison. I should have told you before." *I should have held you in my arms and told you and kissed your tears until they were vanquished. Let me hold you now! Let me kiss your tears!*

But Allison didn't want him to touch her.

"Yes, you should have." *How could you have kept something this important from me? What other monsters are lurking in the darkness, waiting to devour my heart and my dreams?* "What other secrets, Peter?"

"No other secrets, Allison. I promise you, darling, there never will be."

Allison started to speak, but she couldn't find coherent words for her swirling thoughts and emotions. Suddenly, she felt so tired, so defeated. Instead of speaking, she sighed softly and slowly shook her red-gold head.

"What, darling? What are you thinking? Tell me."

"I feel so lost, Peter," Allison answered finally. "I thought I knew about you and us." *I believe in us. I trusted us . . . you.*

"You do know about us, Allison. Please don't feel lost." *Lost*. That was how he had felt when Sara died, how he had felt until he found Allison. Peter didn't want Allison to feel lost, not ever; there was no reason. "Allison, don't you know how I feel about you?"

"Tell me how you feel about her."

"Allison . . ."

"Honest words, Peter, *please*."

"All right, darling," Peter agreed softly. *The truth*. "I loved her very much. After she died . . . That was a very difficult time for me, Allison."

"That was when you wrote *Say Good-bye*," Allison whispered quietly. She had read Peter's plays last December, before their love. She had wept at the sadness in the beautiful words and had wondered about the talented writer whose life had obviously not been so happy. *Say Good-bye* had been the most tormented and most magnificent of the plays she had read. *Now she knew why.* As with *Love*, the words and emotions in *Say Good-bye* had flowed from Peter's heart. *Love* was the joyous celebration of a forever love, and *Say Good-bye* was its dark twin, the anguished farewell to that forever love when it died.

"Yes. I started writing again and directing. I immersed myself in my work and planned to let it consume me for the rest of my life." Peter paused, then whispered gently, "But, one day, something incredible happened."

It was then that Peter realized Allison couldn't see him. Her lovely anguished face was illuminated by golden moonlight, but the moon was behind him, a halo he didn't deserve, casting shadows and doubt where he wanted none. Peter moved a little, not toward her, because Allison didn't want that, but enough so that she could see the love in his eyes.

Please see my love, Allison!

Peter gazed at her, waiting for even a slight acknowledgement of the *something incredible* that had happened, but Allison's confusion only seemed to deepen when she saw the familiar look of love and tenderness on his handsome face. Didn't she know?

"Allison," Peter whispered urgently, "the *something incredible* that happened was that I fell in love with you."

"Oh!"

"Yes," Peter lovingly told the startled eyes. "*Oh!* Allison, I always believed that love—if love even existed—would never touch my life. When I fell in love eight years ago, it was such an astonishing and unexpected gift. After she died, I knew I would never love again. I sealed myself off from the possibility. I was immune, impenetrable, surrounded by a wall of memories and without a breath of desire. I wasn't looking for a new love, but one day I innocently walked into Elegance, and . . . well, speaking of being emotionally ambushed . . ."

That brought a trembling smile to Allison's lips and a sudden mist of hope to Peter's eyes.

"I love you, Allison, with all my heart."

"I love you, too, Peter," Allison replied quietly. *I love you with all my heart, too. But this secret was so important. It terrifies me that you didn't tell me.* "But I need time. I have to think about what you have told me and I have to try to understand why you kept this secret from me."

"I told you why, Allison. I wanted to protect you from sadness and it backfired. I was very foolish and I am so sorry." *And so afraid.* "May I hold you, please, just for a moment?"

Allison listened to Peter's gentle apology and saw the love in his eyes and *wished* that his loving arms could protect her from the terrible hurt. But he had caused the hurt, and Allison had already learned—a horrible, bewildering discovery—that tonight Peter's gentle touch caused her even more pain.

Allison wished she could go to him, as she always had, so joyfully, so confidently. *But she couldn't.* It had been a night of truth and secrets, of golden moonlight and dark shadows, and she needed time to think about what she had learned, the *truth* about Peter's forever love and the *secret* he had kept from her in the name of love. Time to think, time to understand, time to forgive, time to *heal*.

"Peter, no. It's too soon."

Earlier, when Peter's face had been in shadows, Allison had only sensed the effect of her words—"Tell me about Julia"—on him. Now she saw the effect of what she had just told him—*I can't let you hold me, Peter, not even for a moment*—in his dark eyes. Another stunning blow, and such pain!

Allison didn't want to punish Peter, or herself, but she had no choice. She was too raw, too wounded, too shaken. A deep instinct warned her to stay away until she was stronger. She *would* be strong again. Their love would be strong again. It *had* to be.

"All right, darling," Peter whispered softly. Then he asked, a gentle, uncertain plea, "But will it—we—be all right?"

Allison looked at his worried, loving eyes and answered with a promise from her heart, "Yes, Peter, we will be all right. I just need a little time. Right now, we should go to Winter's. I'm sure she's wondering where we are."

"OK," Peter whispered quietly, aching with fear and churning with anger at himself for his foolishness. *Take all the time you need, my darling Allison, but please, don't let this hurt us. I love you so much.*

Chapter 25

"How was it?" Winter asked eagerly when Peter and Allison arrived at the mansion ten minutes later. Her smile faded as she saw their strained smiles and troubled eyes.

"Wonderful," Allison said. She added, to make it the truth, "You were wonderful, Winter, really sensational. *Everyone* raved about you."

"What's wrong?"

"Nothing," Allison aswered swiftly. That was the truth, too, wasn't it? *Yes*. She just needed time to believe it was true. Someday, when she was confident again of their love, Allison would ask Peter more about his wife, who she was and how she had died. Some faraway day Allison would ask Peter those questions.

"Peter?" Winter persisted.

"Nothing's wrong, Winter."

"I think we're still just a little stunned." Allison forced a smile for her friend. This wasn't fair to Winter! Winter had worked so hard, *Love* meant so much to her, and her performance had been magnificent. "The movie was stunning, *you* were stunning. You should really see it sometime."

"Sometime I will. So, we're not closing before we open?"

"No," Peter found a soft laugh. "Not at all. Speaking of opening, how about a little champagne? Or, for the pregnant star, chilled ginger ale?"

Winter had both champagne and ginger ale chilling in silver bowls in the living room. Peter opened the bottles and filled the crystal champagne flutes. When each held a glass of honey-colored liquid, they softly touched crystal to crystal, wordlessly toasting the magnificent movie.

"What time is your plane for New York?" Winter asked.

"Eight-thirty."

"That means we should start on the gourmet crab puffs I spent all day making, before we have the gourmet dinner I spent all day making!" Winter made a move toward the kitchen, but Allison stopped her.

"Winter!" This was Winter's night—or should have been—a night to celebrate with two people who loved her very much, a small oasis in her lonely, isolated life. Not that Winter ever gave a hint that she was lonely, or that she missed Mark desperately, or that she was so afraid of what lay ahead. Winter, the remarkable actress, hid it all. But Allison knew. "Peter and I can sleep on the plane. We're not in any hurry. Sit."

"And stay?" Winter's words took her back to the day in December, when it was Allison who had given the command: "Winter! Sit and stay!" That distant day, the night of love, the tiny new life created from that loving . . . Winter's eyes clouded briefly at the memory.

"I have a toast," Peter said quietly. "To Winter, who gave so much love and loveliness to the movie and will give so much of both to her baby."

"Peter. Thank you." Tears threatened. Winter smiled a wobbly smile, stood up, and announced firmly, "That's it. Time for crab puffs."

"Let me help you."

"No, Allison, you really have to banish the invalid concept from your mind. You sit and stay with Peter. I'll be right back."

Winter disappeared beyond the crystal and flowers on the dining room table through the door that swung into the kitchen. Allison sat on the edge of a chair across from Peter, eyes downcast, suddenly uncomfortable at being alone with him in lights that were brighter, more probing, than the soft gold of the August moon. Allison's thoughts drifted to Peter's wife—his *wife*—and to the love that had died four years ago but had been enough, Peter believed, to last him a lifetime.

"I have a toast for you, for us, too," Peter began. He saw the sad eyes as she looked up when he spoke and pleaded softly, "Allison, don't do this."

"I can't help it."

"I'm so sorry. I don't want you to be sad or worried *ever*. There is no reason for you to be."

"I can't just turn it off, Peter. I need to work through my feelings."

"We'll do that together, OK? This weekend, every night on the phone, next weekend."

Allison heard the edge of panic in Peter's voice and saw his fear. *Fear?* What did Peter fear? Was he afraid of losing her? Didn't he know that could never happen?

"Peter . . ." Allison stopped because suddenly Peter's gaze shifted beyond her and the fear in his eyes became terror.

Winter stood at the top of the stairs that led from the dining room to the living room. She leaned against he wall, her violet eyes bewildered.

"Winter!"

"Something's wrong," Winter whispered. "Something's happening."

Winter didn't feel pain. She just felt a strange emptiness—an eerie feeling of doom—followed by a hot dampness on her legs.

The hot dampness was blood. Winter didn't see the blood, but Allison and Peter did.

"Winter, it's time to go to the hospital," Peter said, moving swiftly beside her, uttering the ominous words Sara had spoken to him four years before.

"No," Winter said as Peter lifted her in his arms. "It's too soon. Peter, it's too soon!"

"It will be all right, honey," Peter murmured mechanically, shifted in time, reliving the most horrible night of his life, placed here again by some demonic force bent on his destruction and the destruction of those he loved. "Allison, you drive. The keys are in my right-hand pocket. Let's go."

The sound of her name jerked Allison into action. Until then she had stared, immobile, terrified by how Winter looked and even more terrified by Peter. His dark eyes had filled with hopelessness and a heart-stopping wisdom.

As if he knew what was going to happen. As if he had seen it all before.

And there was something else in Peter's stricken eyes . . . *blame.*

As if whatever horror was about to unfold was his fault.

Allison drove. Peter was in the backseat with Winter, cradling her, whispering reassurances to her. His voice was soft and low and gentle, but the promises he made to Winter—"You'll be fine, honey, and so will the baby"—sounded false, as if he were an actor who had perfectly memorized his lines but hadn't bothered to study his character's motivation.

Peter's reassurances lacked conviction, but his hopelessness seemed to give Winter strength. She countered defiantly, "I *am* all right, Peter! My baby *is* fine!"

They reached the Emergency Room at UCLA three minutes after leaving the mansion on Bellagio. Peter carried Winter inside. They were instantly surrounded by an ER staff that was stirred into prompt action by the sight of blood. In moments, Winter was on a stretcher being wheeled into a "trauma room" as one nurse took vital signs, another searched for veins, and a doctor asked a few pithy questions.

Allison and Peter followed the procession into the room, but once inside they were separated from Winter by a wall of doctors and nurses.

The doctor asked questions: "When are you due?" 'When did the bleeding start?" 'Is there pain?" 'Did your doctor do an ultrasound?" 'Have there been any problems with your pregnancy?"

And Winter answered, her voice still strong and defiant despite the blood loss and the chilling pallor of her face: "In September." '*What* bleeding?" 'No pain, just a queasiness, a little cramping like a period." 'No ultrasound, no problems. I'm fine, healthy, and so is my baby!"

The nurse announced the vital signs as the doctor took the history and felt Winter's abdomen: "Pressure eighty over fifty, pulse one twenty-eight."

"We need two lines," the doctor said. "Fourteen gauge. Type and cross for five units. The usual blood work plus a coag screen. Have you paged OB?"

"Stat-paged," the nurse answered, then turned her head slightly as she heard the distinctive sound of paper footsteps running on linoleum.

The OB team appeared, clothed in operating room attire, including once-sterile paper galoshes.

"You have some business for us?" the chief resident asked, quickly assessing the situation, relieved that Winter was conscious, frowning as he noticed the blood.

"Yes. She's about eight months, followed at Cedars, uncomplicated until now, developed painless bleeding fifteen minutes ago. Her blood pressure is dropping."

"Baby?"

"I hear heartbeats."

"Good. Sounds like a previa."

"I think so."

"OK. Lines in? Great. We'll take her upstairs right now. Call L&D and let them know we need a double setup. Thanks." The chief resident moved to the head of the stretcher, smiled at the most beautiful violet eyes he had ever seen, and said, "Hi. I'm Dr. Johnson. We think your placenta is blocking the outlet of your uterus and it's bleeding. I need to take a look, but if that's what you have, we'll need to do a Caesarean section."

Dr. Johnson talked as he and the OB team wheeled Winter's stretcher out of the ER to a waiting elevator. Allison and Peter started to follow but were stopped by a nurse.

"Are you family?" she asked, then, looking at Peter, she added, "Are you her husband or the baby's father?"

Allison watched Peter for a horrible breath-held moment. *No more secrets, Allison*, he had promised, but her confidence in him and their love was still shaken. From a deep instinct for self-preservation, more than from conscious thought, Allison steeled herself for another dark, destructive secret. She waited, fearing that Peter was going to say, "Yes, I'm the baby's father." He looked so confused by the nurse's question, so frantic that the stretcher was disappearing and he wasn't with Winter. After a long, bewildered silence, Peter finally whispered, "No. No to both."

"Then you'll need to wait in the Labor and Delivery Waiting Room. This elevator goes directly to the Delivery Room. You'll need to take another one. Just follow the blue line on the wall."

"I can't be with her?" Peter asked numbly.

"No."

Allison saw more confusion on his handsome face. Confusion, and such pain!

Once in the Waiting Room, Allison tried to erase Peter's pain. Winter is strong and healthy, she reminded him. And this was a hospital of miracles. Allison had been saved here. Winter would be saved, too. Winter will be fine, Allison gently assured Peter. And Winter's baby will be fine.

But Peter didn't seem to hear her reassurances. His dark eyes gazed beyond her to a horrible, distant memory.

Peter has been here before, Allison realized finally. *He is reliving a nightmare.*

Was this how Peter had lost his wife? And his unborn child? *Yes*, it must have been. This was why Peter had asked Allison if her accident meant that she couldn't have children, and why he had looked worried, not relieved, when Allison had said no. And this was why he was able to tell before anyone else that Winter was pregnant.

Oh, Peter, Allison thought as she helplessly watched his terrible torment.

The chief resident appeared, finally, an hour later. He was smiling.

"Winter is all right."

"And the baby?" Allison asked.

"She's fine, too. She's premature, so we've put her in the neonatal ICU to watch her carefully, but so far her lungs are strong and she's doing well."

"Winter's really OK?" Allison pressed.

"Yes. She had a placenta previa—that was why she was bleeding—so we did a Caesarean. She's in the Recovery Room now, groggy but awake." Dr. Johnson saw Allison's concern and relief and decided he was talking to a loving friend of the astonishing violet eyes. "Winter's going to be very weak for a while. She lost quite a bit of blood. In the old days, we would have given her transfusions, but now, if the blood count isn't dangerously low, we prefer to give iron and let the body rebuild its own blood supply."

"Because of AIDS," Allison said.

"Yes. Winter will be fine, but for the next few weeks she'll be quite weak and wobbly. Does she have someone who can help her?" The doctor guessed he was looking at that someone.

"Oh, yes." Allison smiled. Helping Winter until her boundless energy and exuberant health returned would be a tiny, *tiny* repayment for the long, patient months her friend had sat by Allison's bed and taught her how to read again, and write, and remember. A repayment you don't owe, Allison! Winter would exclaim, her violet eyes hurt by the suggestion. *But I want to help, Winter! Just like you wanted to help. I'm on your side, Winter, always.* "Can we see her and the baby?"

"Not now. The nurses are still getting them settled in. It's best not to disrupt that process." Dr. Johnson correctly interpreted the flicker of worry in Allison's eyes and added, "Really, both Mom and baby are fine. It's time for everybody to get some rest. Why don't you come back at eleven this morning, during visiting hours?"

"All right. Give her our love, though, OK?"

"OK."

After the doctor left, Allison turned to Peter. He hadn't spoken at all during

Allison's conversation with Dr. Johnson. In fact, Peter hadn't even moved from the corner of the room where he had stood, stiff, waiting, bracing himself for the inevitable news of the death of the mother and her child.

But Peter had heard the doctor's words. Allison saw it on his handsome face as he tried to reconcile this ending—a happy one—with the ending four years before, the one that had almost ended his life. Peter tried to find joy in the fact that Winter and her baby were fine, but part of him was lost in the grim memory of a woman and baby who had died.

Earlier in the evening, Peter's secret had caused a distance between them, and Allison had kept them apart because she needed time. When Peter had asked her so gently if he could touch her, hold her, *just for a moment*, she had said no. She had been too wounded, not strong enough or confident enough to forgive him swiftly and return to his loving arms.

But now Allison gazed at Peter's tormented face and his bloodied arms and clothes, and she suddenly felt very strong and very confident. She didn't need time. Allison and Peter didn't need to spend the next hours, days, and weeks of their love reliving his past and finding loving ways to reassure her. Allison didn't need to be reassured of Peter's love, and she *wouldn't* put him through the painful memories.

They wouldn't talk about it at all, unless *Peter* needed to.

Allison would just love him, as she already did, with all her heart.

Allison walked across the room to him. When she stood in front of Peter, she looked up into his dark eyes and smiled softly at him.

"I need a hug, Peter," she whispered gently. *You need a hug.*

Without speaking, Peter circled her with his strong arms and so tenderly, so gratefully, drew her to him. Allison felt the taut emotion that stiffened his body. And then she felt it flow out, a river of grief and pain.

In the few hours left before dawn, Peter and Allison showered together and lay together, awake, touching, loving. As the pale yellow of a new summer day crept into the bedroom window, Allison gently kissed a circle around his lips. *Goodbye kisses. Peter recognized them.*

"I'm not going, either," he said.

"It's opening night of the greatest production of *Romeo and Juliet* in history. Your production. You have to be there." Allison added softly, "And I have to be with Winter."

"I know that, darling. And I have to be with you."

Allison shook her head and gazed lovingly into his eyes. She was going to spend today, the weekend, next week, getting Winter's home ready for the baby. She and Winter hadn't done that yet—gotten baby supplies!—because there had still been time. They had laughed about doing it and had decided they would rely heavily on Allison's mother, whom they both loved, who had kept Winter's secret a secret, and for whom this baby would be like a grandchild. After Allison visited Winter this morning, she would go to her parents and tell them the wonderful news. Then she and her mother would go shopping.

Peter could be part of it—Allison didn't want him to leave!—but maybe he was an expert on baby supplies, and maybe it would tear him apart with sadness.

Allison wanted no more pain for Peter.

"I'll just get a phone at my table at the Tavern on the Green and we'll talk all night while we're waiting for the reviews."

"Good. But you'll call me before then, won't you? As soon as you arrive in New York?"

"And before I leave for the theater and during intermission," Peter teased gently. Then his eyes grew serious. "I hate to leave you now. I promised that we would talk and that I would help you understand."

"All I need to know is that you love me."

"I do love you, Allison, more than anything in the world."

"Then we've had our talk." Allison kissed him, pulling away reluctantly after a long, hungry moment. "You have to get ready or you'll miss your plane."

"I was thinking about next weekend," Peter said, reaching for the curve at the back of her neck, his strong fingers caressing.

"Oh." Allison bit her lip. She had planned to go to New York next weekend, but now she needed to be with Winter. She needed to be with Winter and she needed to be with Peter.

"I would like to spend four days—and four nights—in an elegant suite at a luxury hotel. I hear they have a very nice one nearby. The Chateau Bel Air, I believe it's called. Stunning interior design, conveniently located to Bellagio, and yet private, romantic." Peter smiled lovingly.

"You'll come back next weekend? You can get away?"

"I *will* get away. I don't know, Allison, but it seems that if you've just written and directed a movie that the movie critics *already* love, and directed a play that, modesty aside, the theater critics *will* love, at some point you can do what you want, play hooky, be with the woman you love. What do you think?"

"I love you."

"Winter!" Allison had approached Winter's hospital room with trepidation, preparing herself for a ghostly, fatigued version of her best friend, reminding herself what she must have looked like in those most critical days in the ICU after her accident.

Winter looked pale—her rich creamy skin was translucent—but she was sitting up, propped against pillows, her violet eyes clear and sparkling as she wrote on a notepad that lay on her lap.

"Hi!"

"You look wonderful, glamorous as always."

"I'm a little wobbly, but I'm fine." Winter's voice softened, "Thanks to you and Peter. You saved my life."

"No," Allison countered swiftly, but she wondered. Perhaps Peter *had* saved Winter's life. Perhaps the horror of the other time—when he had tried desperately and unsuccessfully to save a life—had made Peter act as quickly and as surely as he had last night.

"*Yes*. Thank you." Winter noticed Allison's frown and shifted happily to a wonderful topic. "Have you seen her?"

"Not yet."

"Oh, Allison, she is such a miracle! She has tiny delicate little hands and feet, and her mouth is so pink, and she is so soft."

"The nurses say she is beautiful," Allison said. The nurses had spontaneously offered that bit of information when Allison arrived on the ward looking for

Winter's room. "They say that most babies aren't really beautiful, and that premature babies never are, but she is."

"It doesn't matter," Winter murmured distantly. Part of her, she realized, had assumed that her baby would be like she had been—gawky, awkward, clumsy, *ugly.* Winter would atone for what had been done to her. She would love her little girl so much! Was she disappointed that her daughter was already beautiful?

No, of course not. Not if it would make her precious baby's life even easier.

"Have you decided about her name?" Allison asked after a few moments. Winter had been so certain that her baby would be a girl, but she had never mentioned a name.

"I've been working on it. Here." Winter handed Allison the notepad. "See what you think."

"OK." Allison read aloud from the top of the long list, "Marcia Lauren . . . Lauren Marcia . . . Marky . . . Laura . . ."

"I've decided against those," Winter interjected. *I've decided not to name her after the men who didn't want me.* "You can skip down past all the feminine forms of Lawrence or Mark."

"All right. Let's see. Autumn . . . Spring . . . Summer." Allison tilted her head thoughtfully. "Winter?"

"I think that's what's left of the anesthetic making me goofy. No seasons. Read on."

"Allison . . . Jacqueline . . . Patricia . . . Julia." Winter's best friend . . . Winter's tragic mother . . . Allison's loving mother . . . the role Winter played in Peter's movie, an imaginary role based on the woman Peter had loved and lost. Allison suppressed a frown. This was Winter's decision, not hers.

"It's none of those, either." Winter retrieved the notepad from Allison, turned to the next page, wrote three words, and handed the notepad back to Allison. "This is her name."

"Roberta Allison Carlyle."

"Roberta is Mark's mother," Winter said softly, remembering the kind woman whose children teased her about "grandbaby lust." Roberta Stephens would never see her granddaughter. Or would she? a mysterious voice within Winter asked. Was it a voice driven by anesthetic goofiness? Or was it the voice of a new mother who wondered if she could really hide this miracle from the man she loved?

"It's a beautiful name, Winter."

"Yes." Winter smiled. "I think we should call her Bobbi."

Part Three

Chapter 26

PARIS, FRANCE
SEPTEMBER 1985

Emily emerged from the darkroom of her spacious apartment on Rue de Bourgogne and glanced at her full-to-overflowing appointment calendar to confirm the time of her afternoon appointments. She frowned slightly as she realized the date: September seventeenth. One year ago today she had started to work for *Portrait*, for Rob. One year ago today . . .

Now Emily worked for herself. Now she cared about herself. Now she believed in joy and happiness and love.

Her new life, her new hope, had begun a year ago today *because of Rob*.

Emily looked up from the appointment calendar and saw her image in the mirror above her desk. It was one of many mirrors in her cheery apartment, mirrors that demanded Emily notice herself, demanded that she smile at her own image.

Emily smiled now, softly, thoughtfully, approving the cover of the book—her long golden hair swept off her face and twisted into a soft chignon, the cashmere heather-gray sweater, the mauve silk scarf—but knowing the real change, the real *beauty*, was deep inside.

The phone rang. Emily took the appointment calendar with her as she moved to answer it.

"Emily, love, it's Brian, calling from foggy London."

"Hello, Brian." Brian was a free-lance journalist. He and Emily had done five feature stories together, he writing, she photographing.

"Emily, I'm really in a jam. When are you taking the pictures of Monique LaCoste?"

"This afternoon."

"Great. Listen, I cannot get out of London, not by plane or boat. The entire country is shrouded in an impenetrable fog. Could you do the interview?"

"I'm not a journalist, Brian."

"I can tell you exactly what questions to ask. All you have to do is get the answers and I'll write the story. It's very easy, Emily, but don't tell anyone I said so. Monique LaCoste is a top movie star, so you just run down the usual movie star questions."

"The usual movie star questions?"

"Right. You ask who she's in love with now, and why she made her last picture—her *motivation*—and has she ever been raped or was she sexually abused as a child."

"What?" Emily asked softly.

"That's very *in* now, Emily. A few years ago it was bulimia and anorexia—all the big stars had one or the other—then alcoholism, then cocaine addiction. Now it's rape and—"

"I can't do it, Brian."

"Surely you establish rapport while you're taking those incredible portraits,"
 Brian pressed.

"I just can't do the interview, Brian."

There was still something about saying no that frightened her. For so much of Emily's life, her no's to men had been received with mean laughter, followed by force and violence. Now she said no, waited for the violence, and when it didn't come, her eyes misted with grateful tears of relief. Emily didn't date—it was much too soon—but she established professional relationships with men throughout Europe, repelled their occasional advances with fear and grace, and wondered what had happened to the kind of mean men who had terrorized her life for so many years. As Emily became stronger, they seemed to have vanished.

Still, Emily couldn't let down her guard. She had to be wary.

"That's a definite no, Emily?"

"It really is, Brian. Sorry."

"Well. You were my first choice. I'll give Bernard a call. I understand you are photographing the new Canadian Ambassador for *Dominion?*"

"Yes. On Friday."

"I did my interview with him when he was in London last week. Nice man. These interviews are such a wonderful—"

"No," Emily interjected sharply. She tried to soften it a little as she repeated, "No."

"OK. You have your reasons. Lunch next week if I ever get out of soupy England?"

"Sure." *Thank you.*

Before she left her apartment to meet Monique LaCoste at a portrait studio on Rue du Faubourg Saint-Honoré, Emily checked the movie theater schedules in *Le Journale. Love* had just opened in Paris and was playing on the Champs-Elysées. The theater lines would be long, but Emily didn't mind. She had been looking forward to seeing *Love* very much.

"This is the worst fog I've ever seen," Margaret Reilly Carlyle murmured quietly, ominously, as she and Lawrence drove slowly through the opaqued streets of London.

"A night for a good murder," Lawrence observed, trying to lighten the somber mood and the treachery of the drive.

"No doubt nights like this inspired Doyle, not to mention Jack the Ripper."

"And Margaret Carlyle?"

"I'm inspired to find the nearest hotel and hole up for the night."

"We're very near the theater."

"How do you know?"

"There," Lawrence announced with triumph and surprise as a brightly lit marquee appeared behind a veil of smoky fog.

"Luck!" Margaret exclaimed, laughing, relieved.

Margaret and Lawrence Carlyle were not alone in the theater. *Love* had lured many Londoners into the cold, somber, misty evening. A love story with a happy ending was a perfect counterbalance to the heaviness that enveloped London.

Lawrence Carlyle hadn't braved the fog in search of a love story with a happy ending. Or *had* he?

Lawrence realized, as he watched, that he *had* been hoping to see a happy ending, hoping to see that life was happy for the little girl with violet eyes. Lawrence watched Winter through a blur of tears, so happy for her, so sad for him.

The following afternoon, Nigel March, the press agent for Carlyle Productions, arrived at Laurelhurst with a face to match the grim grayness of the autumn fog. Margaret and Lawrence ushered him into the sitting room, cheerily lit and warmed by a crackling fire, and served him tea before addressing the issue at hand.

"Fleet Street is going crazy," Nigel said finally. "They are really going to have a go at us with this one, Lawrence."

"Did you get a copy of Vanessa Gold's column?"

"Of course. It's been reprinted in all the local rags. Which do you prefer?" Nigel asked as he opened his briefcase. "*The Sun? The Daily Mirror?*"

"Just give me a copy and Margaret a copy," Lawrence commanded irritably.

Lawrence's irritation increased as he read Vanessa Gold's *All That Glitters* column published three days before in Los Angeles.

> The recent release of *Empress*, Lawrence Carlyle's epic saga of the French Revolution, creates a real-life drama that surpasses even the glittering imaginings of Hollywood's best writers. There is no doubt that *Empress* will receive Academy Award nominations in the top categories: Best Picture, Best Original Screenplay, Best Director, Best Actress, and Best Actor. The main competition—indeed the only competition as far as this writer is concerned—is *Love*, which will compete, perhaps successfully, in every category.
>
> On the face of it, the match-up is between the incredible gifts of Lawrence Carlyle and those of Peter Dalton, but the real drama is an ancient one between father and daughter.
>
> Lawrence Carlyle vanished from his infant daughter's life over twenty years ago. Although the stunning star of *Love*, Winter Carlyle, has been unavailable for comment, she is scheduled to appear on *Good Morning America* and *The Today Show* early next week. Undoubtedly, the question of the estrangement of talented father and talented daughter will arise. One wonders how Winter, the abandoned child, will answer it. One wonders, even more, what Lawrence Carlyle will have to say.

"Jesus Christ," Lawrence whispered.

"*The Daily Mail* has a lovely portrait of you and Margaret and your sons, to which they have convincingly grafted a picture of Winter. Quite a family photo. It will appear in tomorrow's edition." Nigel March arched a critical eyebrow. Lawrence Carlyle should have told him about this months—years!—ago. Why hadn't he?

"Oh, no," Margaret breathed.

"Margaret, we need to call the school and get the boys home *now*. Nigel, you're going to have to keep Fleet Street at bay for a few days."

"What are you going to do, Lawrence?"

"I'm going to talk to her."

"To reconcile?" Nigel asked hopefully.

"Lawrence, can't you just let the attorneys handle it?" Margaret asked.

"If I find that she's doing it for publicity, I'll send an army of attorneys against her. But, Margaret, what if she doesn't know?" Lawrence cringed at his own question. *What if the little girl with the violet eyes had spent her life hating him?*

"But you told me you discussed it with Jacqueline on a number of occasions."

"I did, but remember what an actress she was. Nigel, please get Steve Gannon for me. He'll know where Winter is."

"I don't want to see him, Steve!"

"You have to, Winter."

"Sometime, I know. But not now, not yet." Winter's mind drifted to the fantasy she had created a year ago as she watched *Hong Kong* with Allison and Emily. In that lovely fantasy, when Winter finally met Lawrence Carlyle, Mark would be there, and Allison, and Emily armed with a camera and a box of Milk Duds. But that was a fantasy, and now Allison would be in New York with Peter, and Emily was in Paris, and Mark was gone.

Now Winter was alone.

No, Winter's heart corrected swiftly. She wasn't alone. Bobbi was with her.

"Winter, the press is going crazy with this now. It will only get worse. It's all they'll ask you about next week on the shows."

"He's planning to be here tomorrow?"

"Yes. Winter, I'll be right beside you the entire time."

"No, Steve." *Bobbi and I will manage.* "That's not necessary. Tell him to come here, to this house, at noon."

"I think I should be there."

"No. Thank you. He's not an axe-murderer, is he?"

"No," Steve said, then asked quietly, "Are you?"

"No." *I'm a mother who can't imagine how a father could ever leave his baby. I need to look him in the eye and ask him what kind of man he is to have done that to me.*

After Steve hung up, Winter held Bobbi close to her, nuzzling her dark black, silky hair, gently kissing her daughter's soft cheeks, silently renewing the promises she had made the moment she knew she was pregnant. *I will love you, precious little one, and protect you, always.*

It was such an easy promise to keep! Loving Bobbi was instinctive for Winter, effortless and strong and good, like the way she had loved Mark, like the way she had once loved her own father.

Winter barely slept that night. She wandered quietly, restlessly, around the mansion, reliving the pain and loneliness and fears of her childhood.

In the morning, Winter dressed in a beautiful pale blue silk sheath. She decided to wear the sapphire earrings that Lawrence had given Jacqueline hours before Winter's birth and that Jacqueline had given Winter hours before her death. Winter remembered that Jacqueline had mentioned a matching necklace. Winter decided she would wear that, too.

Winter went to Jacqueline's bedroom, in the wing of the mansion where she and Bobbi didn't live, and opened the velvet boxes of jewels in the safe until she found the one containing the long strand of flawless sapphires and a note, in Jacqueline's elegant script: *From Lawrence, December 31, 1960.*

At eleven-thirty, Winter gently put Bobbi in her cradle, wound the key to the music box Mark had given her, lifted the carved thatched roof, and softly sang the lyrics, as she always did when she watched her precious daughter fall asleep.

By eleven-forty-five, Winter was in the living room, waiting. She paced—despite dizziness from her sleepless night and a blood count that had still not returned to normal—during the fifteen-minute eternity. As she paced, Winter rehearsed her opening line.

Lawrence Carlyle arrived at precisely noon.

"Hello, Daddy." Winter's delivery was perfect—just as she had practiced—ice-cold, bitter, defiant. But, as she saw the living form of the man whose photographs had meant everything to her as a child, filling her scrapbooks and her dreams, Winter's eyes filled with sudden, surprising tears. Perhaps, if Emily Rousseau had ever taken a portrait of this man, Winter would have been prepared for the sensitive eyes, the quiet shyness, the *uncertainty* she had never imagined in the great Lawrence Carlyle.

"Winter." Lawrence had prepared his lines, too, an eloquent articulation of the rage he felt toward the young woman who was using him, just as her mother had used him. But Lawrence heard Winter whisper "Daddy," saw sad, brave, shimmering violet, and his own eyes became moist as he whispered hoarsely, "My God, you really don't know, do you?"

"Don't know what?" Winter asked, stunned by his emotion, worried by his words.

"May I come in?"

She stood aside and watched Lawrence enter with trepidation that reminded Winter of her own fear about returning to the mansion after five years. Hers had been the fear of the lurking monsters.

Were there dark monsters lurking here for Lawrence Carlyle, too?

"I don't know what?" Winter repeated weakly, sensing danger.

"You don't know that I'm not your father."

Winter swayed, unsteady, weak. Lawrence caught her and guided her to the living room, gently settling her into a chair, then sitting across from her, finding her eyes, not letting them go.

"I'm not your father, Winter."

"I don't understand."

"Jacqueline and I met during the filming of *Marakesh*. We had a brief affair, very stormy, very emotional. We weren't good for each other. When we saw each other again at the Academy Awards the following spring, we exchanged civil hellos, nothing more. Then, in May, while I was filming *Destiny* in Montana, Jacqueline simply appeared. Our affair resumed, and two months later Jacqueline told me she was pregnant with my child."

"With me."

"Yes, but you weren't mine. Jacqueline was already pregnant—and she knew it—when she came to Montana in May. She wanted me—or thought she did. Our marriage was a disaster. I was too quiet for her, too serious, not very exciting."

"So was I."

"Jacqueline knew our marriage wasn't working, but I was the one who made the move to get out and that infuriated her. She matched my desperation to get away with desperation not to let me, or to harm me if I wouldn't stay." Lawrence paused. He smiled gently as he continued, "My marriage was a disaster, but I had a lovely little daughter who was my life. When I told Jacqueline I wanted a divorce, I also told her I wanted custody of you. I had already discussed this with my attorneys and they thought we could prove that she wasn't—"

"—a terribly good mother."

"Yes, that she wasn't a terribly good mother. But Jacqueline had a trump card I knew nothing about until it was too late. She knew you weren't my child. I didn't believe it. I hated having them get blood from you, hurting you for even those few seconds, but we did all the blood tests, more than once. I wanted so badly to prove that you were mine, but the tests proved, quite conclusively, that you couldn't be. I brought all the documents, if you want to see them." Lawrence gestured to the briefcase he had dropped in the foyer when he'd caught Winter

as she swayed. "I tried to get custody of you, anyway, but it wasn't possible. The more I wanted you, the more Jacqueline was determined to punish me by preventing me from even seeing you. I fought it for a very long time, Winter, but I finally realized it would be worse for you to be caught between us, and the attorneys convinced me I would never win."

"But you paid child support."

"It wasn't child support and I wasn't required to pay it. I just wanted to be sure you had money in case something happened to Jacqueline. I had no rights and no obligations. I agreed never to contact you. Jacqueline agreed—*in writing, under oath*—to tell you, when you were old enough, that I was not your father. I saw her in Cannes when you were six. She told me all about telling you. She said she told you that your father had died, that I had married her as a favor, and that we had parted as friends. It was an elaborate story, very convincing. I had her repeat it to me each time I saw her over the next ten years, and it was always the same."

"She never told me. She just said you left because you didn't want us."

"I wanted you."

"You loved me?"

"I loved you very much, Winter."

"I never knew," Winter whispered. Then, very quietly, she added, "Maybe I did know. Maybe that's why I was so lonely, because there had been love and then it was gone."

"Oh, Winter, I am so sorry."

"I waited for you to come to me after she died."

"I would have come if I had known—even imagined—that you were waiting. But I believed you knew. I thought I was nothing at all to you, a face and a voice that you were too young to even remember."

"I missed you all those years."

"I missed you, too . . . all those years."

Winter heard the soft sound, a vibration that only a mother would hear, but when she looked up she realized Lawrence heard it, too.

"I have to—"

"May I come with you?"

"Yes." Winter led the way to the wing of the mansion where she and Bobbi lived in the wonderful rooms decorated by Allison.

"This was always my favorite part of the mansion," Lawrence said.

Winter stared at the serious, sensitive man who wasn't her father but was so much like her!

"Mine, too."

Bobbi was awake and cooing, wanting Winter, wondering at her mother's surprising absence.

"Oh," Lawrence breathed. He looked questioningly at Winter—May I pick her up?—then gently lifted the baby out of the cradle from which he had lifted Winter so many times. "Who are you?"

"She's Bobbi."

"Hello, Bobbi. You look just like your mother looked at your age."

"No. I was an ugly baby, an ugly child," Winter reminded him.

"You were? I don't remember that. I thought you were very beautiful." Lawrence's words were causing pain, fresh wounds for both of them, so he carried Bobbi to the French doors that opened onto the terrace surrounding the pond of koi. "We used to spend hours here, Winter, you and I. You loved watching the fish."

"I did?" No wonder this place had been her sanctuary! In this place, for the first year of her life, she had been safe and happy and *loved*.

"You laughed when they splashed and giggled when they ate out of your tiny hands."

Lawrence and Winter sat at the edge of the pond in the warm autumn air. Lawrence held Bobbi, gently, lovingly, as he must once have held Winter. Bobbi was intrigued with the deep voice and strong arms and warmth, but she was hungry, too.

"Are you starving?" Winter asked gently as she took her suddenly fussy daughter from Lawrece's arms. "I—I have to nurse her."

Lawrence stood up.

"I'll . . ."

"Don't go. I mean . . ."

"I'll wait downstairs. I won't leave, Winter. I don't want to leave. Take your time feeding this hungry little girl. I'll still be here."

Lawrence waited for Winter and Bobbi in the screening room. After thirty minutes, they joined him in the peach room with the cushiony chairs.

"I used to spend hours in this room watching the movies," Winter told him.

"So did I, with you on my lap."

"You cared about all these treasures more than she did, didn't you?"

"Yes," Lawrence answered softly and looked at Winter gently. *These treasures, and the greatest treasure . . . you.*

Winter smiled at him through fresh tears.

"Do you have a screening room at Laurelhurst?" she asked finally.

"Yes," Lawrence answered casually, not suspecting until he saw the sudden sparkle in the glistening violet. "Winter . . ."

"They belong to you. You should have taken them with you when you left." *Just like you should have taken me!*

"No, Winter."

"Yes!" Winter laughed. "I'm shipping them to you whether you like it or not! It will take me a little while to find the best movers and arrange for insurance."

"You have other things to do."

"Not really. Bobbi and I have lots of fun making telephone calls. She loves tugging on the cord! Really. It's settled."

"Thank you."

Winter, Bobbi, and Lawrence spent an hour in the screening room, then walked to the kitchen for tea.

"You haven't asked me about your real father, Winter."

"No, I . . ." *You are my real father!*

"I don't know who he is. I don't think Jacqueline knew, either."

Winter nodded solemnly.

"I loved her, even though she wasn't a terribly good mother," Winter whispered after a few moments.

"I loved her, too, Winter. I wished I could make life happy for her, but what I had to give wasn't enough for her. Jacqueline was always searching for something more—more magic, more enchantment, more love. I think she found it, in brief spurts, in the films she made, when she could be someone else for a while, but then the letdown of returning to her own life was devastating."

Lawrence held Bobbi while Winter made the tea.

"Tell me about Bobbi's father, Winter."

"He didn't want me. He didn't love me enough."

"You spent your life believing that about me and you were wrong. Are you sure about him?"

"Yes." *It is dangerous to care. People leave you*. Lawrence, Jacqueline, Mark. But she *had* been wrong about Lawrence! And Mark? Winter relived the scene—such a brief good-bye scene!—in the Sculpture Garden over and over. She was acting, pretending it didn't matter, rushing to get away from Mark before he saw that her heart was breaking. What if Mark had been acting, too?

"Winter?"

"Maybe I'm not sure," she whispered quietly.

Lawrence and Winter drank tea and played with Bobbi, and, in little bits, Winter told Lawrence the fears and secrets she had always planned to tell him when they were reunited.

"And I had a dream that I would be a wonderful actress and I would star in one of your films."

"In the briefcase, beneath all the legal documents, is a script for a movie I'm going to film on my estate in England next spring. When I saw you as Julia, I knew you were perfect for the lead. I was going to call you—thinking I'd need to remind you who I was—and then the *All That Glitters* column appeared."

"I'm not going to act for a while. I want to be with Bobbi."

"Bobbi is very lucky to have you as her mother," Lawrence said quietly. "If you wanted to be in the movie, Winter, Bobbi could be with you. I would want both of you to live with me and my family at Laurelhurst during the filming. My wife, Margaret, will love you and Bobbi. And my sons will be enchanted with you both. My twelve-year-old will demand more blood tests because he'll want you to be his sister. And my sixteen-year-old will demand them, too, to prove that you aren't, so he can marry you."

Winter laughed lightly, but Lawrence saw the soft hope in her eyes.

"I'm not your father, Winter," Lawrence reminded her gently, sadly. "The tests really are conclusive."

"But we are so much alike!"

"Yes. And we loved each other very much." Lawrence added softly, something he had never told anyone, "When Margaret was pregnant, I secretly hoped we wouldn't have a daughter. As far as I was concerned, you were my daughter. I didn't want to replace you."

Lawrence and Winter and Bobbi spent the afternoon together. As twilight began to fall over the autumn sky, Winter agreed that she and Bobbi would spend Christmas at Laurelhurst. She also decided to read the movie script Lawrence had brought with him.

"We will make other movies together, Winter," Lawrence assured her. "But take a look at this role and know that you wouldn't really be away from Bobbi during the filming."

"All right. Thank you." Winter frowned briefly. "What shall we do about the press?"

"I think we should tell them the truth."

"Do you want to give the story to Vanessa Gold, or are you angry with her?" Winter asked.

"I'm not angry anymore, are you? Vanessa's words were simply righteous indignation for an abandoned little girl. Did you know that she came to the hospital the night you were born?"

"No."

"Maybe that's why she was so surprised—and outraged—that I vanished from your life. When I talked to her that night, I'm sure she saw how much I loved you. It's fine with me to give Vanessa the story."

Winter made two phone calls. The first was to a thrilled and amazed Vanessa Gold. Winter gave Vanessa no details over the phone, saying simply that she and Lawrence would like to meet with her, to *explain*. Vanessa replied simply, "Fine. Wherever. Whenever."

Winter's second call was to Patricia Fitzgerald, because Allison was probably just landing in New York and because Bobbi was still a secret. Patricia said she would be delighted to babysit her surrogate granddaughter.

After she finished the two calls, Winter thought about Bobbi's real grandmothers: Roberta Stephens, whose merry eyes twinkled when she talked about grandbabies, and Jacqueline, who had had magic and love—Winter's love, Lawrence's love—but had frantically searched for more.

Lawrence watched Winter's beautiful face become very sad as she thought about Jacqueline.

"Winter?"

"I don't want Mother to seem like the villain in all this. Perhaps she *is*, but I did love her. Sometimes I think she was trying very hard."

Lawrence nodded thoughtfully.

"All right, Winter," Lawrence said quietly, marvelling at her lovely generosity despite the pain she had suffered because of Jacqueline. "I don't want that, either. We'll tell Vanessa it was a terrible misunderstanding."

"It *was* a terrible misunderstanding. And . . ." Emotion swept through Winter as she remembered the words, *Mark's words about Lawrence*. But she and Lawrence had another chance. She and Lawrence were the lucky ones. And Jacqueline?

"And?" Lawrence asked gently.

"The greatest loss was hers."

Chapter 27

"Hello, Muffin," Allison greeted the excited blond fluff as she let herself into Peter's apartment at ten P.M. Friday night. Peter was at the theater. Allison had taken a cab from LaGuardia into Manhattan. "How are you? Come help me unpack."

Unpacking was a quick process. Allison had clothes in New York, just as Peter had clothes in Los Angeles. Only six weeks until November, Allison thought with a smile. "In six weeks, Muffin, you'll be a California girl again. How does that sound?"

If wiggling were a measure, it sounded very good to Muffin.

"It sounds good to me, too." Allison laughed. "How about a cup of tea?"

After she made the tea, Allison sank down into a dark couch made soft and bright with plush pastel accent pillows. Muffin curled up at her feet, on her own pillow, and Allison turned on the television to watch the news while she waited for Peter.

"Terror struck in Paris today as seven armed men seized the Canadian Embassy. No group has yet claimed responsibility for the act of terrorism, however four hostages are being held at this time. Three of the hostages are Canadian, all members of the military. The fourth hostage, pictured here in a passport picture released to the press by the terrorists, is an American citizen. Emily Rousseau is a free-lance photographer living in Paris."

"Oh, no!" Allison gasped as she saw the photograph of Emily. "*Emily.*"

The news was sketchy. Allison checked all channels, but there were few details. Emily had been in the embassy doing a photograph of the new Canadian Ambassador to France. For unknown reasons, she had not been released with the embassy staff and the other women who were in the embassy at the time of the takeover. One newscast commented on this, wondering if it was because Emily was an American, a valuable prize, but noted that several American men *had* been released.

The information was frustratingly meager. Allison was seized with helplessness and an overwhelming need to do something, or find someone who *could.*

Rob could do something. Rob had journalistic connections, and he cared very much about Emily.

It was seven-thirty in Los Angeles. Allison called Directory Assistance. The number provided for Rob Adamson, Allison realized as she wrote it down, was his office number at *Portrait*. Rob's home phone number was unlisted.

But Elaina Kingsley was listed. Allison reached Elaina at home.

"Elaina. It's Allison Fitzgerald. Is Rob with you?"

"Rob? No." *Rob hasn't been with me for months*, Elaina thought sadly. She was still bewildered by what had happened. Elaina didn't *know* what had happened, why it had all just fizzled out. Rob had been quiet, apologetic, firm—"It's over, Elaina. I'm sorry"—but almost as bewildered as she.

"Are you expecting him?"

"No." *But every time the phone rings, I hope it will be him.*

"Elaina, I need to speak with Rob. Could you give me his home telephone number?"

Allison reached Rob's answering machine and left a message.

"Rob, this is Allison Fitzgerald. Would you please call me as soon as you get this message—no matter what time. I'm at a number in New York, area code 212 . . ."

Allison watched the twenty-four-hour news channel. The hostage situation at the Canadian Embassy in Paris was mentioned twice every thirty minutes, but each report was the same. The embassy was under siege, hostages had been taken, the authorities were awaiting demands from the terrorists.

Peter returned to the apartment from the theater at eleven-thirty.

"Peter!"

"Hello, darling. Allison, what's wrong?"

"Oh, Peter . . ."

The phone rang and Peter answered it.

"Hello?"

"Hello. This is Rob Adamson returning Allison Fitzgerald's call."

Peter's heart raced at Rob's *name*, at the sound of Rob's voice, and at the stunning fact that Rob was calling for Allison. Allison knew Rob? Allison knew

Rob and something was wrong and . . .

"It's Rob Adamson," Peter said quietly.

"Oh, good." Allison took the receiver and Peter held his breath "Rob?"

"Hi," Rob answered tentatively. Rob hadn't seen or spoken to her since the opening of the Chateau Bel Air. Allison's voice told him she wasn't calling out of the blue on a Friday night from New York to say merrily, The interior designer *extraordinaire* is ready to be in *Portrait*. "Allison, what's wrong?"

"I was calling about Emily, to see if you knew anything."

"What about Emily?" Rob asked anxiously.

"Oh, you don't know!"

"Know what, Allison?"

"Rob, Emily is being held hostage in the Canadian Embassy in Paris. It's on the news. I thought you would have heard."

"I just walked in," Rob murmured, stunned, seized with fear.

"I thought you might be able to find out more, or that you might know someone who could."

"Yes. I do. I will. I—I'll leave for Paris tonight." Rob was supposed to take the eleven P.M. Qantas flight to Australia. His bags were already packed. He had just been for a long run on the beach before getting ready to leave. He would go to Paris instead. "I'd better get going."

"Will you let me know, Rob? I'll be at this number until Sunday, then back in LA."

"Yes, I will."

Rob hung up without a good-bye or a thank-you. Allison returned the receiver to its cradle and fell into Peter's arms.

"Peter, I'm so afraid for her."

"She'll be all right, darling."

Peter's heart and mind were caught in the midst of two horrors: the horror of what was happening to Emily, and the horror of what *might* happen to his love. The angry promise Rob had made last December—the promise to destroy a love if Peter ever found one—thundered in his mind. *If I can hurt you, Peter, if I can make you ache until you want to die because the loss is so great, I will do it. That is my promise to you.*

"You called Rob Adamson, Allison," Peter whispered as calmly as he could, given that his mind screamed, *Why?* "He owns *Portrait* magazine, doesn't he?"

"Yes. Rob knows Emily, of course, and I thought he might have connections."

"Do you know him?" Maybe Allison didn't actually know Rob. Maybe she just knew his name and knew about him through Emily.

"What? Oh, yes."

"Is he—?" Peter paused. He needed to absorb this—*Allison knows Rob Adamson*—and to force control into a voice that threatened to betray his fear. Had Rob been Allison's lover? Was he the mysterious sender of red roses on Valentine's Day? *Oh, Allison, have you made love with this man who would happily destroy me and us?* "Did you date him?"

"What? Oh, no." Allison pulled away from the strong arms that held her so securely just enough to see his face. He looked so worried, so *afraid!* She found a trembling smile and whispered gently, "Peter, Rob is a friend."

"Oh." Peter pressed his lips against her red-gold curls and drew her close to him again.

No more secrets, he had promised her on that moonlit night last August. That night he learned that he had kept the secret of Sara for too long. His foolish hope to spare Allison sadness had backfired. The revelation that night had caused more than sadness; it had *threatened their love.*

Since that night, after Bobbi was born, Peter and Allison had so gently, so tenderly, so lovingly repaired the damage he had caused, restoring the trust and the joy and the love. Now their love was whole again, stronger even, and more confident.

And now there was a new secret that threatened to destroy.

Since that moonlit August night, Peter and Allison hadn't spoken of Sara, or of his past, again. Now Peter would have to journey back to that time, and he would have to take his lovely Allison on that painful voyage. He would have to cause her merry eyes to sadden with bewildered tears again.

Rob was Allison's friend, but she obviously hadn't told him about *them*, not yet, because in these months when she and Peter were mostly a continent apart, they had protected the rare moments together by keeping their love hidden. Peter knew Allison wouldn't tell Rob about their private love before November, when he and Allison would be together always, forever. Then Peter would tell Allison everything—how he blamed himself for Sara's death, just as Rob blamed him for causing it.

Peter wanted to be the one to tell Allison—he *would* be—but even if she heard the story from Rob, the truth would be the same no matter who spoke it.

The truth was the same, and Peter's only defense against Rob's rage, Rob's attempt to destroy their love, would be so painful for Allison to hear.

The truth was, simply, that Peter's great crime—his only crime—was that he had loved Sara Adamson Dalton *too much.*

I'll tell Allison everything in November, Peter decided. *I will hold her and love her and tell her the simple, painful truth.*

Peter would keep this final secret until November, only six weeks away. Only six weeks until their forever . . .

"Robert Jeffrey Adamson," the distinguished white-haired United States Ambassador to France read the name on Rob's passport. Rob presented the passport to the guard at the embassy entrance. Security had been increased in all embassies in Paris in the past twenty-four hours.

"Rob."

"And your relationship to Emily Rousseau, Rob, is what?"

"A friend."

"Do you know her family? The permanent address on her passport is a house in Santa Monica where she apparently rented a room for the past six years. The owners don't know how to reach her family, and despite the publicity no one has come forward."

"No one will. Emily left her family years ago."

"You are, I believe, the owner and publisher of *Portrait* magazine."

"I'm not here for a story. I'm here to help Emily."

"Help?"

"Whatever I can do."

"Frankly," the Ambassador said with a sigh, deciding the worried blue eyes and strained face really cared about the young woman hostage, "we're all feeling a little helpless. The French police and an international terrorist unit and a special team from the U.S. are working together, but I'm sure you've heard the demands—outrageous demands for release of so-called political prisoners."

"There are no plans to meet the demands?" Until this moment, Rob had firmly believed in the policy of not negotiating with terrorists, no concessions whatsoever. It made sense—reasonable, rational.

But this was emotional, this was *Emily.*

"No. Paris has become a war zone in the past few months—car bombings, hostage-taking, *plastique* exploding in cafeterias and department stores. It's a war that the French government has no intention of losing."

"So what are they doing to get her—them—out?"

"Talking. Plans beyond that, if there are any, are top secret."

"I see. You know, I might be a much more valuable hostage than Emily. I *would* be. I have a great deal of money, and even though we don't believe in concessions to hostages, from the terrorists" standpoint, I would be a good bargaining chip because there are many influential people who would put pressure on the authorities to get me released."

"You want to trade yourself for Emily?"

"Yes." Rob repeated quietly, firmly, "Yes."

"I don't think that's possible."

"Will you at least tell the negotiators, or let me tell them?"

"I will tell them. I think the terrorists might be happy to have you, too, but they wouldn't necessarily release Emily."

But at least I could be with her!

"Besides, it's very likely that Emily will be released anyway. Terrorists rarely hold women hostages for very long. It's a bit of a mystery why she is being held at all. She seems to have no political ties that would be of value to them, except that she is American, but there were American men in the embassy who were released. Do you have any idea?"

Rob had an idea, but it was unspeakable. It filled every corner of his heart and his mind, tormenting him, making his desperation to free her, or be with her, almost frantic.

Rob shook his head but his mind screamed, *Because evil men sense Emily's vulnerability and want to harm her!*

"You will tell them that I am offering myself in trade," Rob said, giving an order, barely maintaining control.

"I will."

"I'm staying at the Ritz. Will you call me if there is any news?" The command became a plea as the reality of his helplessness—the helplessness of all of them—settled in.

"Yes. I will call you."

The Ambassador called the next day to say that Rob's proposal had been rejected and to report that there was no news. For the next five days, the telephone in Rob's room was silent. Rob used the phone twice, shortly after he arrived, to leave messages on Fran's answering machine at his office and on Allison's machine in Santa Monica. He told Fran to reach the people he was supposed to meet in Sydney, Auckland, Bangkok, Hong Kong, and Tokyo, to cancel, and to say that he would be in touch. Rob didn't tell Fran where he was. Rob's message to Allison was that he was in Paris and he would call her if there was news.

For five days and nights after Rob arrived—six days and nights after Emily had been taken—the phone was silent and there were no messages for him when he returned from his daily pilgrimage to the cordoned-off area in front of the besieged Canadian Embassy on Avenue Montaigne.

Rob paced between the hotel and the embassy, restless to be away from either place too long, tormented by the silence of the room and by the ineffectual hubbub of the reporters and onlookers who hovered outside the embassy. A crowd kept vigil, waiting, expectant, hoping for drama.

The Canadian Embassy had become another tourist attraction in the City of Light, another place to spend part of a gorgeous autumn day. The September sun bathed Paris in unseasonable warmth and the city responded gaily, pulsing with laughter and energy, forgetting even the recent reigns of terror that had plagued its streets during the too-hot summer.

In most parts of Paris everything was sunny and vibrant. But on the Avenue

Montaigne was a small island of terror, a zone of war. Emily's girlhood home had probably been just like this. From the quiet street, Emily's house probably looked like any other house. Outside, children laughed and played, and there was an eerie illusion of normalcy. But inside, there had been terror, assaults on bright sunny days and moonlit nights, in defiance of all that was good and lovely.

The entire block around the Canadian Embassy, a majestic structure of once-white marble, was roped off. Helmeted, armed, uniformed guards were posted at frequent intervals. In the center of the empty street was a van, equipped with electronic equipment, which served as the command post for the small war that was being waged in the center of Paris.

Rob stared at the gray-white walls of the fortress—Emily's prison, her latest prison—and sent screaming messages from his heart.

I'm here, Emily. I'm here and I care so much. Please hear me, please know.

The call from the United States Ambassador came at eleven-twenty on Rob's sixth night in Paris. Rob stared for a moment at the phone, the strident noise piercing the darkness, and his mind took him unwillingly, horribly, to a late night call years before, the night Sara had died.

"An antiterrorist team stormed the embassy an hour ago. Emily is here."

Emily? Emily's body?

"She's alive?"

"Yes."

"How is she?"

Rob heard the hesitation in the Ambassador's voice, and then the grimness as he answered, "She's very bad. In shock, I think. She refused to go to the hospital, so the French police brought her here. So far, the press hasn't discovered she's not with the other hostages."

"I'm on my way." Rob started to add, *Please tell her I am on my way and I will help her*, but he didn't. He had tried to help Emily once before and all she had felt was betrayal.

The street in front of the United States Embassy was empty, a gray ribbon illuminated by streetlights and the full autumn moon. Rob asked the taxi driver to wait and dashed to the front door.

When he saw the Ambassador's grim face, Rob's heart wept. *No! Emily, you were supposed to wait. I was on my way.*

"She's alive," the Ambassador answered Rob's fear swiftly. "Barely."

"Where is she?"

"In my office."

Emily was curled up, a tiny embryo wishing she had never been born, on a huge leather couch. Her golden hair was snarled, her clothes dirty and torn. She didn't move; the slightest undulation of her chest was the only clue to life.

Rob knelt beside her.

"Emily," he whispered softly to the tangled gold, the incredible beacon that shone above the wreckage. "It's Rob. Honey . . ."

Rob could tell that Emily heard him. Something rustled beneath the gold, but he couldn't see her face. What if his voice, his name, caused more fear?

What if it was the lethal shock, the final betrayal?

"Emily, I won't hurt you. I want to help you. I know you may not believe that, but it's true. May I look at your face, Emily? May I move your hair so I can see your eyes?"

Rob held his breath, fearing more withdrawal.

But Emily nodded slightly, and, *so gently*, Rob parted the tangled hair until he saw her face. Her skin was deathly pale and her gray eyes were cloudy, beyond fear, beyond hope, almost beyond life.

"Rob?"

Rob's heart leapt as the gray flickered a little, a sign of life, not fear. *Good, darling, know that I care about you.*

"You're safe, Emily. I'm here. I will take care of you. Honey, I think you need to go to the hospital."

"No, please, Rob. Just take me away." Emily's eyes met his. Her plea tore at his already-weeping heart, but her voice gave him hope, a spirit not quite dead.

Going to the hospital might kill her, Rob realized. The intimate examination by strangers, studying her, poking, prodding, invading, might be too much. If Emily didn't go, she might die, too. She would die in his arms. Rob fought his own fear and said gently, "OK. No hospital. We'll go somewhere else. I'll carry you."

To Rob's amazement, Emily slowly pushed herself up.

"I can walk."

Rob put his tweed jacket over her frail shoulders, draping her torn clothes and protecting her against the coolness of the autumn night. He put his arm around her and was stunned by how light she was, how little there was of her, how gratefully the delicate, trembling body fell against his. Rob grabbed her camera and her purse from where they lay on the floor. Very slowly, Rob and Emily walked across the office to the door and toward the taxi that waited outside.

"Thank you," Rob murmured to the Ambassador. "One more favor. We'll be at the Ritz. If you need to talk to me or if the authorities need to talk to her, that's fine, but I would appreciate it if the press didn't know."

The Ambassador nodded, then frowned and whispered, "She needs to see a doctor."

"I know that, but she needs privacy even more."

Rob planned to leave Emily in the taxi in the circular drive at the Ritz while he arranged for a room, but as he moved to get out, Emily moved with him. Rob sheltered her with his arm and she turned her face against his chest.

"Monsieur Adamson. How may I be of help?" The concierge asked when Rob and Emily stopped at the reception desk.

"I need another room, a suite."

"*Mais oui.*" The concierge looked briefly at Emily and promptly deduced that she was an actress or a rock star, *certainly* on drugs. "You would like the bridal suite?"

"A two-bedroom suite."

"Yes, of course. And your other room?"

"I'll keep it, too, for a while."

"*Certainement*. Pierre will show you to the suite."

"If you'll just give me the keys," Rob said impatiently. He felt Emily slipping, her weightless body becoming heavy as she no longer had the strength even to resist the pull of gravity.

Emily stayed pressed against him, needing his strength.

When they entered the elegant suite, Rob guided her toward one of the bedrooms, talking to her, reassuring her, "You need to rest, Emily, to sleep, and you need food, and—"

"A shower."

"Are you strong enough for that?" *I can help you. I can remove your torn*
 clothes and bathe you, but I know that would terrify you.

He had to walk such a careful line! He wanted to take control, as he had wanted to take her to a snowbound suite in Aspen, lock the doors against all the outside storms, and talk to her, cry with her, hold her if she would let him, until the demons were purged and she believed in herself and happiness. But control and power and strength over her weakness were her greatest enemies, her greatest oppressors.

"I think I am."

"OK." Rob guided her to the bathroom door. "I'll be in the other room if you need me. Emily?"

"Yes?"

"Honey, you can trust me. I know you don't believe that, but it's true."

Emily gazed at him and her gray eyes softened with a faint happiness, a distant memory.

"I do know that. I do trust you, Rob."

Emily withdrew and closed the door, and Rob held his breath, praying she wouldn't throw the lock. She didn't. After a moment, Rob returned to the suite's living room and paced, worried, restless, *elated*—"I do trust you, Rob"—until finally the sound of water splashing against marble stopped and there was silence.

Silence, and it went on forever. Rob envisioned Emily on the shower floor, her fragile skull cracked as she fell. Finally, he returned to her bedroom.

"Emily?" he called softly, and when she didn't answer, he called more loudly, more urgently, "Emily?"

The bathroom door opened. Emily's face wasn't flushed from the heat of the shower, but more pale, more gray, more near death. The circles under her gray eyes were deep and black. She probably hadn't slept—or maybe there had been brief dreams between the nightmare she was living—much in the past seven days. Hadn't slept, hadn't eaten.

Rob wondered if he should just take her to the hospital. *Against her will?* No, never.

"Why don't you get into bed and I'll order some food."

"No food." Emily walked into the bedroom barefooted, wrapped in the plush terry cloth robe provided by the hotel, bulky and baggy against her small frame.

Her gait was unsteady and wobbly as she made her way to the bed. Rob pulled back the heavy covers, opened to the cool clean sheets, and Emily crawled in, carefully, modestly, in the bulkiness of the robe. When she was lying down, Rob tucked the covers over her and sat in a chair beside the bed.

"Shall I tell you a bedtime story?" he asked.

Rob thought he saw a faint, dreamy smile on her lips.

"OK. Once upon a time there was a beautiful princess. She had long golden hair and eyes the color of the morning mist . . ."

Emily fell asleep in moments, but Rob stayed beside her for another hour, watching the gentle rise and fall of the covers as she breathed. Finally, he went to his bedroom, but he couldn't sleep. He sat in the living room of the suite all night, every few minutes walking to the open door of her room, making sure the covers still rose and fell.

Chapter 28

Emily slept through the night and in the morning, when the bright autumn sun streamed through the bedroom curtains Rob had forgotten to close, he drew them quietly and she slept still.

Rob left the suite twice, leaving notes for Emily each time. The first trip was a brief one, to his other room in the Ritz, to get his things. The second trip, mid-morning, taken when Rob saw that she hadn't stirred and perhaps wouldn't awaken all day, was shopping at the *Bon Marché*.

Emily would need clothes when she awakened. Clean, fresh, new clothes that bore no memory of her ordeal of horror. Rob bought jeans, a cotton blouse, a V-neck sweater, and a warm jacket for her, and a casual outfit for himself, too, because all he had packed in the luggage for his trip to Australia and the Orient was formal.

Rob bought what he thought would be comfortable for Emily—a loose, concealing outfit in subdued colors—although he had a vague memory that the torn and dirty clothes she was wearing last night had been colorful.

Rob bought Emily a pale blue nightgown, too, made of soft flannel, with a ruffled collar and long sleeves, modest and innocent and warm.

When Rob returned to the suite after shopping, Emily was still asleep. He went to his bedroom, lay on the bed, fully clothed, with the door open, and fell asleep.

Five hours later, Rob was awakened by Emily's screams. The suite was dark, shadowy. The bedside clock told him it was eight o'clock. He rushed into Emily's room. She was sitting up in bed, gasping, sobbing.

"Emily!" Rob knelt beside her and saw confusion in her frightened eyes. Had Emily forgotten he was here? Was she so ill last night that she didn't even remember? Had she forgotten what she'd said? *I do trust you, Rob.*

"Rob," Emily whispered, and her gray eyes flickered with hope.

"This is going to be bright," Rob warned gently as he reached for the bedside lamp. He wanted to drive away the darkness and its demons as quickly as possible.

"Yes." Emily squinted, but her lips curled into a soft smile.

"I think you had a nightmare."

Emily nodded.

"Why don't I call room service and we'll have a nice dinner in the living room. OK?"

"Yes. OK."

"Oh, I got you some clothes. I'll be right back."

Rob returned in moments with the packages from the department store. Then he left to order dinner, while Emily dressed.

Tears filled Emily's eyes when she saw the baggy jeans, symbols of her old life, symbols of the only way Rob had ever known her.

The only way he will ever know me, Emily thought sadly. She *believed* she had made such progress! But those evil men had seen through her delicate facade of strength and courage. They knew she was a victim and always would be.

Emily had had such lovely fantasies of seeing Rob again. He would be in Paris, doing a portrait, and they would pass on the Champs-Elysées. Rob would do a double take, then whisper, his dark blue eyes smiling appreciatively, "Emily, is that you? You look wonderful!" And she would smile, a beautiful, confident smile, and answer softly, "I am wonderful, Rob. Thanks to you."

But now . . . Emily looked at the baggy jeans and tears spilled from her eyes.

Finally, she put on the lovely nightgown, under the bulky robe, and walked into the living room.

As they ate the gourmet dinner, Rob cast careful glances at Emily, trying to assess but not stare. His horrible fears that she might die in her sleep were eased. Emily still looked pale, ravaged, exhausted, but she was stronger. She would be even better with more sleep, if her nightmares didn't conspire to prevent the necessary rest.

Here, in the City of Light, on a dark night in January, Rob had urged Emily to talk about her demons, hoping that talking might help vanquish them. Would it help for Emily to talk now? If she could speak of the horrible ordeal in the embassy, would the nightmares be quieted?

"Emily?"

"Yes, Rob?"

Rob's heart ached. He didn't want to hear about it, but, for her, if it could help . . .

"Do you want to tell me what they did to you?" he asked gently.

Emily saw the worry in his blue eyes and smiled softly.

"They did nothing, Rob."

"Nothing?" Was Emily denying what had happened? Was the horrible memory banished to her dreams, a torment that would awaken her for years to come? Was she trying to spare *him*? "They didn't touch you?"

"No, Rob," Emily answered truthfully. "They were planning to, after it was over, as a reward." Emily frowned at the terrifying memory of their taunts, their wicked promises, their evil laughs, the pleasure they took in her fear. "They made threats, that was all."

Thank God, Rob thought. If they had touched her, if they had carried out their threats, he wondered if Emily would still be alive, or if she would have found a way to die.

The rich gourmet food and her week of sleepless terror made Emily's gray eyes grow weary long before the meal was over.

"Back to bed," Rob said gently.

"OK."

Rob followed Emily into her bedroom. She looked at him shyly but without fear as she removed the bulky bathrobe, revealing the modest nightgown, before crawling into bed. When she was in, Rob tucked the plush satin covers around her.

He was about to ask if she wanted to fall asleep to a bedtime story, when *she* asked a question.

"Why were you here, Rob? Why were you in Paris?" *Would I have seen you on the Champs-Elysées if this hadn't happened? Was I that close to my fantasy*?

"I was here because of what happened to you, Emily. I came as soon as I heard."

"You did?"

"Yes, of course," Rob told the astonished gray eyes.

"When was that? How long ago?" *How long was I in that hell*?

"A week ago."

"A week?" Emily whispered softly, sadly, "Then you need to go back soon."

"I do? Why?"

"Because of *Portrait.*" Emily frowned slightly. "And because of Elaina."

"*Portrait* will survive. And I don't see Elaina any more."

"You didn't marry Elaina?"

"Marry? No." Rob gently moved a strand of golden silk that had fallen into her eyes. Emily didn't stiffen at his touch, and Rob saw no fear. "I couldn't marry Elaina, because I am in love with someone else."

"Oh. Well, you need to get back to her then."

"Emily, I am with her. I am with the woman I love."

Rob watched her lovely gray eyes fill with tears as she understood the meaning of his words.

"I love you, Emily."

Emily's tears spilled, like a gentle, nourishing spring rain, without clouds, without doubt, without fear.

"I love you, too, Rob."

"You do?"

"Yes," she whispered. *I have loved you for a very long time.*

Emily wanted to gaze into his loving ocean-blue eyes forever and to lose herself in his gentle voice. But her exhausted-trying-to-heal body fought the lovely wishes of her heart, demanding sleep.

"Sleep now, darling Emily," Rob whispered as he watched her valiant struggle to stay awake, his own heart filled with immeasurable joy. "I'll be right here when you awaken. Tonight I think I'll tell you a story about a man—we'll pretend he's a prince—and how he fell very much in love with the golden-haired princess. It all began at a magnificent wedding in a rose garden . . ."

In the morning, while Emily was still sleeping, Rob made calls to Fran and Allison. Rob told Fran he would be away a little longer, perhaps much longer, and he would call her later with details.

Rob apologized to Allison for not calling the minute Emily was freed. He didn't explain the delay—"I was so afraid she was going to die, Allison"—and Allison just asked Rob to give Emily her love. Allison didn't tell Rob about the postcard she had received from Emily. It had been mailed from Paris two days before the embassy was seized and had arrived in Santa Monica while Emily was still being held hostage. Emily had written, *Dear Allison and Peter, I saw* Love *last night—twice!—at a theater on the Champs-Elysées.* Love *was wonderful, something to remember when the moments of one's life are not so joyous. Your movie is a gift, Peter, a generous loving gift.*

While Emily slept, Rob paced quietly in the suite, thinking, planning. At ten A.M. he wrote her a note—*I'll be back soon. I love you*—and walked out of the Ritz and across the Place Vendôme to Van Cleef and Arpels. Rob had decided to simply order the ring today, with a request—a demand—that it be rushed. But the ring was there, already set, a flawless two-carat emerald-cut diamond set between delicate rows of glittering baguettes. It was exactly what Rob wanted, beautiful and perfect, like Emily.

"Flawless, *oui monsieur,*" the jeweler assured. "Of course, it may need to be sized. This ring will only fit a very slender finger."

"If it needs to be sized, you can do that in less than a day, can't you?"

"*Mais oui.*"

* * *

Emily was awake, dressed in the baggy jeans, cotton blouse, and V-neck sweater, when Rob returned to the suite.

"Good morning."

"Hi." Emily smiled shyly. Last night would all have been a dream if she didn't have Rob's note. Last night, Rob had spoken the words and this morning he had written them, and now his blue eyes were telling her all oer again.

"I got something for you." Rob smiled and added uncertainly, "I hope you like it. If not, I can take it back."

Rob removed the small blue velvet box from his jacket pocket. His hands trembled as he handed it to her, and Emily's trembled as she opened it.

"Rob." Emotion stopped her words. After a moment, she whispered, "I don't understand."

"It's an engagement ring. Emily, will you marry me?"

"Why wouldn't I like it?" Emily asked, not answering his question, fearing his answer to her own.

"Because—" Rob answered gently, "because part of you believes you don't deserve beautiful things. Emily, if this makes you uncomfortable, we can have simple gold bands, or no bands at all. All I really care about is marrying you. I don't want you to change, darling. I only thought you could be happier."

I was happier, Rob! You never knew me the way I could be—strong and happy and full of hope.

Emily frowned as dark fear from the old Emily Rousseau—the Emily with no self-confidence, no belief in herself—taunted her. *What if Rob doesn't love the new Emily?*

No! He must. He will. Rob was the one who knew to search for the loving, beautiful part of you! He knew your life could be happier. He wanted that for you.

"Emily?" Rob saw her fear and uncertainly, fear and uncertainty caused by *him*. "Darling, I'm sorry. I'll take the ring back."

"No, Rob. Don't take it back, but give it to me later. Ask me again, later, to marry you." *If you still want me.* "Tonight, at dinner, at the Tour d'Argent. OK?"

"OK," Rob answered uneasily. His anxiety increased as Emily gathered her purse and the jacket he had bought for her. "Emily, where are you going?"

"I can't wear jeans to the Tour d'Argent, can I?"

"*Yes*. Emily, as far as I'm concerned, you can always wear jeans."

Emily wrote an address and phone number on a piece of paper and handed it to Rob.

"This is the address of my apartment. I'll be ready at seven-thirty."

"Emily, please don't go!"

"Rob, why not?"

"I'm afraid you won't come back."

Emily's surprised, lovely smile reassured him a little.

"With all the collateral you have?" she asked softly.

"What collateral?" *The ring, which you don't want? The cotton nightgown*? Rob asked sadly, "What? Are you leaving your camera?"

"No, Rob. I'm leaving my heart."

Emily did a portrait of the fashion designer at Givenchy soon after she'd arrived in Paris. The designer made Emily the same offer the designers at LaCroix, Dior, Chanel, and St. Laurent had made in January, an offer to clothe her in his finest silks and satins—the smooth, feminine Givenchy lines—as a gift. Although by June Emily Rousseau already looked more stylish, the designer knew he could make her look sensational.

Emily took a taxi from the Ritz to Givenchy.

"*Bonjour.*"

The designer gazed at the young woman with the brilliant flowing golden hair, baggy jeans, and bulky jacket without recognition. Emily swept her hair off her face. "*C'est moi.*"

"*Emily.* Are you all right?"

"*Oui. Merci.*" Emily smiled. She didn't want to talk about the ordeal in the embassy. "You told me once you could make me look beautiful."

"You are beautiful. But I can dress you in something that will make you look exquisite."

"Something soft and feminine? Something for being in love?"

"*Certainement.*"

The dress was chiffon, soft layers of pastel, like a spring garden. The designer told Emily to sweep her golden hair off her face and gave her pastel satin ribbons to weave in with the gold.

"Just a single strand, a ray of sunshine mixed in with the flowers," he suggested. "Then let the rest of your magnificent hair fall free, like a golden waterfall cascading down your back."

Emily arrived at her apartment building on Rue de Bourgogne at three o'clock. After reassuring her landlady that she was fine, Emily went to her bright, spacious apartment. Without hesitation—she had already decided—Emily removed the letter she had written to Rob last spring from a locked drawer in her desk. Emily didn't reread the letter. She knew its words—her love for Rob, her gratitude, the news that she had seen Dr. Camden and had worked very hard and was better. Emily didn't reread the letter. She just sent it to him, by messenger.

Rob's heart pounded anxiously when Emily's letter arrived. He recognized her handwriting immediately and feared what he had feared ever since she left . . . that she wasn't coming back, that he had frightened her away again.

Rob read the letter and tears spilled from his eyes. When he could speak, he dialed the telephone number Emily had left for him.

"I miss you, Emily."

"Did you get my letter?"

"Yes. I miss you. I love you. May I come over now?"

"Yes." Emily was ready—it would take only a moment to slip into the dress and do her hair—and she missed him, too. *Please let this be all right.*

Emily was so beautiful and so uncertain, as if she really didn't *believe* he would love her this way, too.

"Emily." Rob reached into his pocket as he walked toward her, removing the blue velvet box. "Will you marry me? I can't wait until our champagne dinner to ask you."

"Yes. I will marry you, Rob."

Rob slipped the diamond ring on her trembling finger. It fit perfectly.

"My nails . . ." The long, tapered nails had fallen victim, as she had, to the terror in the embassy.

"They'll grow back, Emily. While we're on our honeymoon."

"Our honeymoon?"

"Oh, Emily, this afternoon I was so afraid I would lose you again. I kept myself busy by making wonderful plans for us. I spoke to the U.S. Ambassador. He can arrange for us to be married—very soon—right here, if you want."

"I want."

"Then, if you want, we can wander around Europe for three or four weeks."

"I want that, too."

Rob stood in front of her, gently took her hands in his, and smiled.

"I love you, Emily."

"I love you, Rob."

Rob and Emily had never kissed. They had barely even *touched*. Rob would marry her, spend his life with her, even if they never could kiss, even if that was still too great a terror for her.

Emily saw the love and uncertainty in his dark blue eyes, and read his thoughts.

"Rob, I have never been kissed by a man who loves me."

Rob and Emily made love for the first time on their wedding night. They made love gently, tenderly, in the darkness. Emily didn't stiffen with fear as Rob worried she might, and he could feel her *relief*, but for Emily, there was no pleasure and no joy.

There was no pleasure for her the next night, or the next, or the next, even though it was Emily who wanted to make love, Emily who desperately wanted their love to be whole. Each night she would remove her modest nightgown and curl up quietly in bed beside him. They would make love in the darkness, silently, swiftly, joylessly.

Afterwards, Emily would put on her nightgown again and Rob would put on his pajamas, and, still silent, she would fall asleep.

Emily would fall asleep and Rob would lie awake rehearsing the gentle words he would speak to her lovely gray eyes in the daylight. "Darling, maybe it's too soon for you to make love," he would plan to say. But what if those gentle words caused her pain? What if her gray eyes became cloudy and she asked, hurt, worried, as she had asked once before when Rob had only wanted to find happiness for her, "You think there's something wrong with me, don't you, Rob?" Or, so softly, with tears in her eyes, "Don't you want to make love with me, Rob?"

Rob wanted to *make love* with Emily. He had wanted that for a very long time. His desire for her was so strong. Rob had to be so careful, so controlled, for fear that the power of his desire might feel, to Emily, like familiar violence. Rob wanted to *love* Emily, to share the wonderful pleasures of their love and their loving.

Rob hated the silent, joyless sex.

Rob rehearsed the words but he never spoke them, because, in the morning, Emily's lovely gray eyes would look at him with such hope. *Was I all right, Rob? Do you still love me*?

Rob didn't speak the words, because they would hurt her, and because the joy and love that filled their days was so magnificent. Rob loved Emily more—even *more*—every second of every day. Rob and Emily *touched* in the bright, sunny daylight—holding hands, sharing gentle caresses of affection and warmth, not sex—as they smiled and laughed and talked and loved.

Their days were perfect, golden crescendos of joy and love and happiness that should have led to nights of breathless passion.

But the nights were all the same . . . silent, dark, joyless. Rob knew that for Emily making love without terror, without the fortification of drugs, was a monumental triumph, a symbol of her great trust in him. In some ways, Emily was like a virgin, modest and shy. But, Rob realized sadly, Emily had the modesty and shyness of a virgin, but none of the wonder, none of the innocence, none of the *hope*.

Rob lay awake, rehearsing lines he never spoke, loving Emily with all his heart, hoping that one bright, sunny day they could talk about this without causing her pain.

Eleven days after Emily married Rob, she made an astonishing discovery about herself.

They were in Salzburg at the castle. Emily had left Rob to take a photograph of the valley and lake below. When she returned, she looked up as she approached him and suddenly stopped, stunned.

It was as if she were seeing Rob for the first time ever.

Rob leaned against the stone wall of the castle, his body lean and strong and taut, his handsome face lifted toward the autumn sun, his dark brown hair softly tousled by the breeze, a slight smile on his lips. Emily gazed at Rob—the man she loved with all her heart—and realized that she had *never really looked at him*.

To Emily, Rob was, had always been, *gentleness*. When she thought about him, she thought about his kind, smiling blue eyes, his gentle smile, his soft voice, and his loving heart. She never thought about his *looks*.

Rob's looks were sensational. He was a stunningly handsome man—handsome, sensual, *sexy*. Other women noticed, appreciated, and *wanted* Rob. But until now, Emily had never really noticed her beloved Rob's alluring sexuality, because for her sex had always meant violence, not gentleness, not love.

Until now . . .

Powerful, unfamiliar, *exciting* feelings pulsed through Emily as she stared at him. Rob Adamson, the handsome man who so proudly, so happily wore the gold wedding band she had given him. Rob Adamson, her *husband*, the wonderful, sensual man who loved her and wanted her. Rob Adamson, the man whom she loved, *the man whom she wanted*.

The powerful feelings—Emily's desire for Rob—brought with them a wonderful confidence and a soft, seductive smile.

"Hi, Rob."

"Hi." Rob returned Emily's smile with a look of surprise. Her beautiful pale gray eyes sent a bewitching message—bewitching, provocative, beckoning. He asked with a soft laugh, "What?"

"Come with me."

"All right. Where are we going?"

"Back to our room."

"Are you all right?"

"Yes." *Oh, yes.*

When Rob and Emily were inside their sunny, charming Austrian hotel, with its brocade chairs, lace doilies, and woodframe bed topped with a downy puff, Emily gazed bravely into his ocean-blue eyes and whispered, "I want you."

"You do?" Rob asked softly as his heart raced with joy. *You do, my beloved Emily?*

"Yes. Rob, show me how to make love."

Rob didn't show Emily how to make love . . . *they showed each other*, learning, discovering, marvelling together. As Emily learned about the wonder and beauty of her desire for Rob, he learned new things about the astonishing intensity of his love for her and new things about his own capacity for tenderness.

Rob and Emily made love in the gentle light of a golden autumn sun that filtered through lace curtains. They made love with open eyes and gentle hands and tender lips and loving words whispered softly.

"Rob? What are you doing?"

"I'm loving you, Emily. Let me love you. Trust me."

"I do trust you, Rob."

Emily showed him her trust. And Rob showed her the gentleness of his love.

"Emily, are you cold, darling?" Rob asked moments later as he felt her trembling beneath his lips.

"No."

"Are you afraid, honey?" *Please don't be afraid!*

"No, not afraid. Rob?"

"Yes?"

"Don't stop, please. Rob?"

"Yes, darling?"

"I need you. I need all of you."

"Oh, Emily," Rob whispered as she welcomed him and he smiled into her glowing gray eyes. "I love you so much."

"I love you so much, too."

Afterwards, they lay together, caressing gently, silently marvelling at the wonder of their love and of their loving. Rob pulled away, just a little, because he wanted to see her eyes. Tears spilled softly from the lovely gray, tears of happiness and joy.

As Rob gently kissed Emily's tears, he felt a sudden mist of emotion in his own eyes.

"My lovely Emily, why are you crying?"

Emily smiled a loving smile and gently touched the joyous tears that now fell from the dark ocean-blue.

"I don't know, my darling Rob," Emily whispered. "Why are you?"

Chapter 29

BEL AIR, CALIFORNIA
OCTOBER 1985

"Winter, are you OK?" Allison asked as soon as her friend answered the phone. Winter's voice was so flat.

"I have *something*—a virus of some sort. Actually, I'm a total mess. I'm just finishing my period. I have a virus. I can't even do my stupid sit-ups because, in addition to being tired, for some reason all my muscles ache. So, I'm a mess. How are you? How was your weekend in New York?"

"Short. Wonderful. Winter, why don't I come over and babysit my favorite baby in the world so you can get some rest?"

"No, Allison. Thank you. Bobbi senses that her mommy is under the weather so we're just playing quiet smiling games." The flatness in Winter's voice vanished as she spoke of her daughter. Winter loved Bobbi so much! "She is such a miracle, Allison. Every second of every day."

"I know. That's why I'd love to come see her."

"We're fine, really. Tell me about you and Peter. November is only two weeks away. T minus fourteen and counting."

"But who's counting?" Allison laughed.

"Are you still both planning to take off all of November?"

"That's the plan. Peter doesn't begin work on *Merry Go Round* until December. Steve's daughter is very eager to take care of Muffin, so Peter and I may even go away for a while."

"How nice. A love story with a happy ending."

Allison hesitated, thinking about another love story, one that *should* have ended happily.

"Have you thought any more about Mark?" Allison asked.

"I think about Mark all the time, Allison," Winter admitted softly, too tired even to deny it. "But I should never have told you I wondered if I could go a lifetime without telling him about Bobbi. Those words were said during my postpartum euphoria."

"You're still euphoric about Bobbi."

"Euphoric about Bobbi, realistic about Mark." *Realistic*, but . . . "Allison, I'd better go. Bobbi is napping and I should be, too."

"Are you sure I can't babysit?"

"Yes, I'm sure. Thank you. As soon as I'm well, would you like to come over and play with us?"

"I'd love to. Let me know if there's anything I can do."

"I will. Thanks, Allison."

When Allison's phone rang two minutes later, she assumed it would be Winter. It was too early for Peter's nightly call from New York, still only halfway through the second act of *Macbeth*.

"I'm on my way!"

"Allison? It's Meg."

"Meg! Hi. Are you in town?"

"No. I'm calling from Greenwich. Cam's at a board meeting in the city. I thought it would be nice to catch up."

Allison felt a twinge of guilt. In her many, many trips to New York in the past six months, she had never called Meg and Cam. A call to Meg and Cam would have meant dinner, at least, a waste of precious moments when she and Peter could be alone.

"How are you, Meg?"

"Fine . . . wonderful . . . *pregnant*."

"Congratulations."

"Thanks!"

"When are you due?"

"In February. We're very excited." Meg paused briefly, then asked, "Allison, how's Winter?"

"She's fine," Allison answered carefully. The question about Winter followed *too closely* on the heels of Meg's announcement about her own pregnancy. Bobbi was already two and a half months old, but her existence was known to just a trusted few.

Surely Meg didn't know about Bobbi, and yet her voice carried the promise of something dramatic, a delicious secret.

"Why?" Allison asked.

"Oh, I just hoped that Winter hadn't gotten involved with Peter Dalton."

Allison knew Meg and her love of drama, but still her heart began to race and icy shivers of fear pulsed through her.

"Peter Dalton directed *Love*, so of course Winter knew him," Allison said quietly, forcing calm, as if *her* calm would tranquilize Meg and her dramatic new. "Meg, why would you hope that he and Winter hadn't gotten involved?"

"Because Winter is Peter Dalton's type—a beautiful young heiress. Of course, Winter may not be *blue-blooded* enough for his taste. I don't really know about the branches of Winter's family tree. And she's probably not innocent enough, either." Meg took a breath, then confided ominously, "Actually, Allison, *you* are more Peter Dalton's type."

"Meg. What are you talking about?"

"I'm talking about Peter Dalton. Allison, he's the man I told you about at my wedding."

"What man?"

"The man who murdered Sara Adamson. Peter Dalton is the fortune hunter who committed the perfect crime." Meg paused, waited, then finally, taking the stunned silence to be a signal that Allison wanted to hear more, continued, "Sara's mother told Cam's mother. The attorneys told Sheila Adamson not to tell anyone, but she did. Cam's mother told me this weekend. She had to, of course, because I'd been talking about seeing *Love*, and she kept telling me not to without giving a reason. So, I paid careful attention because I knew you'd be interested, given that you knew Sara and know Winter. It's really an incredible coincidence, isn't it? Allison?"

"Yes?"

"Do you want to hear about it?"

"Yes." *No!*

Somehow Meg's breathless words registered above the thundering of the blood in Allison's brain and the screaming of her heart.

"Peter's family was very poor. He and his father hated the wealthy patricians of Greenwich. Maybe Peter wanted Sara's money, but *maybe* he just wanted to harm her for who she was—rich, privileged, born with a silver spoon. Just like us, Allison."

"But, Meg, you said Sara was dying." The words came from Allison's trembling heart, a defiant heart that refused to even *consider* that what Meg was telling her could be true.

"She *was* dying. It was just a matter of time—a very *short* time—before all her fortune would have been his, anyway. That shows how evil he really is, doesn't it? He was too greedy to spend even a penny of the money he would inherit on expensive medical techniques that might have kept her alive a little longer. Or, maybe, he just wanted privileged Sara Adamson to suffer."

No! It's not true! I don't, won't, can't believe it!

"Does Rob believe Peter murdered Sara?" Allison asked, finally breaking the silence that had fallen after Meg finished her devastating story.

"I imagine so. Apparently, there was an angry, almost *violent* scene between Rob and Peter. Peter actually had the nerve to show up at the Adamsons' estate a few days after Sara died."

"So Peter knows how Rob feels about him."

"Yes, of course. Well, Allison, I'd better go. I need extra sleep these days because of the baby. I just thought you'd want to know. I'm so glad Peter and Winter weren't involved."

Peter and Winter weren't involved, but there was another innocent young heiress . . .

* * *

In the three hours between the time the conversation with Meg ended and Peter made his nightly call, Allison replayed her friend's words a hundred times, a thousand times, and she replayed, too, every scene of her love with Peter. There were some scenes that Allison wanted to change, just a little, but this time the mind that had urged her, *warned* her, not to run after Peter on Valentine's Day—changing that scene and her life forever—wouldn't permit *any* changes.

Allison *wanted* to forget that Peter had kept the secret of Sara until he was *forced* to tell her because of *Love.*

She *wanted* to forget the horrible fear in Peter's dark eyes after Rob had called the night Emily had been taken hostage, when Peter had asked so innocently, "He owns *Portrait* magazine, doesn't he?" As if he didn't *know* Rob, as if they hadn't been *brothers-in-law* for four years.

She *wanted* to forget that Peter didn't read *Portrait* and that Rob hadn't been at the premiere of *Love.*

And she *wanted* to forget that Peter had promised *no more secrets.*

Allison wanted to forget all those moments, *but she couldn't.*

The greatest battle of Allison's life had been her fight to heal her injured brain so that she would be able to *make new memories.* Allison had fought that battle like a champion, with courage and determination and a spirit that wouldn't lose. She had fought . . . and she had won. Now her healthy mind faithfully recorded all the memories with Peter, every second of their enchanted love.

And now some of those memories threatened to destroy.

The autumn night was moonless. As darkness fell, Allison's apartment became a somber place of silent shadows. Allison sat, numb and immobile while a war raged inside her, a war between her heart and her mind.

There has to be a simple, logical explanation, her heart offered bravely, remembering Peter's reason for not having told her sooner about his wife and his marriage. Peter had wanted to protect her from the sadness. A simple, logical explanation . . . *a loving explanation.* Surely there would be a loving explanation this time!

Such as? came the taunt from her mind.

Well, maybe Sheila Adamson, devastated by the death of her daughter and wanting to place blame for the blameless, had gone a little crazy. Perhaps she made up stories because she couldn't face the tragic reality of Sara's fatal illness. And maybe Peter and Rob had really been like brothers when Sara was alive, but the sadness of her death had made it too painful for them to see each other. Maybe Peter didn't tell me he knew Rob because he wanted to talk to Rob first. Maybe . . .

Make-believe! You're rewriting endings again. Won't it be interesting to see what the master playwright has to say for himself?

Peter will tell me the truth. I know he will. I know that somehow, somehow, this will be all right.

You don't know that! You are scared to death that this ominous dark black cloud won't have a silver lining no matter how much you want it to.

The war raged inside her, confusing her, exhausting her. Allison wondered if she would have the strength to talk to Peter when he called. She prayed that swiftly, so swiftly, he would gently provide the answers—answers she couldn't even imagine—that would make their love safe.

"Hello?"

"Hello, darling. I have such a wonderful surprise for you." Peter's voice was so excited, so happy. "I hope you like it. Allison?"

"Please tell me about Sara Adamson, Peter."

A distant corner of Allison's mind—the corner that would remind her unmercilessly of this conversation—counted the agonizing seconds of silence before Peter spoke.

"I told you about Sara, Allison," Peter answered finally, quietly, as his mind swirled. Rob had gotten to her! But how? When? Peter had worried about waiting until November to tell Allison all the truths about Sara. He had considered telling her sooner, even though he wanted to wait until they had all the time and all the privacy in the world. Then he'd learned that Rob would be in Europe, on his honeymoon, until November, and he knew it was safe to wait. By the time Rob and Emily returned, he and Allison would be far away, on a white sand beach in the South Pacific or in a cozy cabin in the mountains. But Rob had gotten to her. *Damn him!* "Whatever Rob has told you—"

"I haven't spoken to Rob. It was someone else." Allison heard the anger, laced with fear, in Peter's voice, and she felt her hopes and dreams begin to die. Peter wasn't going to swiftly, tenderly, gently tell her about a mother-in-law whose grief had led to horrible falsehoods, or about a man who was like his brother until the pain of a shared loss made it easier for them not to see each other any longer. Peter wasn't going to make it right. He *couldn't*. Allison asked sadly, "Does it matter who told me, Peter?"

"It matters what you were told."

"I was told the truth. You were married to Sara, the sister of a man you knew to be my friend but whom you pretended not to know."

"I was going to tell you, Allison."

I was going to tell you, Allison. Peter had whispered those same words to her the night he was forced to reveal the secret of his marriage because of *Love*. Allison had believed those words then, and Peter's words of love, and Peter's promise that there would be *no more secrets*.

Now those words, *all Peter's words*, seemed so meaningless, so empty.

Empty. But as Allison felt her dreams of love shatter and die, she didn't feel the emptiness that had accompanied the death of her dreams of blue satin ribbons and Olympic gold. Allison was *full* now, not empty, *full* of powerful and unfamiliar emotions. The new, powerful emotions were terrifying in their strength. And they were beyond her control, *controlling her*.

When Allison finally spoke it was with a voice she didn't recognize, a voice that hurled accusations with a soft hiss, a voice fueled by the immense power of her shattering dreams. At first the voice startled her. The voice with which she had always spoken to Peter—a soft, loving voice laced with joy, a voice just for Peter—was gone. But so was Peter, *her* Peter. And this new voice, this voice of venom, would be understood by the *real* Peter, the evil Harlequin of Allison's nightmares, the man who cut the girth of Sara's saddle with a bloody knife and burst into raucous laughter as he watched fragile, innocent Sara die.

"When were you going to tell me, Peter?" the new voice demanded. "Certainly not *before* you encouraged me to jump the green and white railed fence. That was your plan, wasn't it, Peter? You even *pretended* that you didn't want me to jump again. But you were going to relent, weren't you, Peter? Yes, Allison, you would say. I will watch you. Go ahead, Allison, jump the jump, one last time! One last time, and then I would be dead, too, *just like Sara*. Another heiress whose blue blood you spilled with such joy."

"My God, Allison, what the hell are you talking about?"

"You told me your wife died, Peter. But you *forgot* a few tiny details. That's strange, isn't it? Peter Dalton is so famous for carving the finest point on a thought or an emotion. Yet, you forgot to tell me who she was. And you forgot to tell me why she died."

"Why she died?" *Why had Sara died*? Why couldn't Sara have lived a long, happy life of love? Why couldn't she have been blessed with children and grandchildren and the magnificent privilege of growing old? Why couldn't there have been no pain for lovely Sara? Why? Why? Why? Peter had no answer to such tormenting questions. That was why he wrote. Something deep inside drove him to search the mysterious questions of life. Peter explored the questions, but he had no answers. Peter said sadly, quietly, truthfully, "I don't know why Sara died, Allison."

"Oh, but you do know, Peter! Sara died because you *wanted* her to die."

"*What*?"

"She died because you killed her."

This time the silent seconds were measured by the anguished screams of loving hearts, betrayed, broken, dying.

"Is that what Rob believes?" Peter asked finally, his voice a whisper of despair.

"That's what the Adamsons believe."

"And what about you, Allison? Is that what *you* believe?" *Yes*, Peter realized, and with this staggering realization came the beginning of the horrible emptiness that would live with him for the rest of his life, the excruciating pain of the great loss of this love. The loss was even worse this time, because this time it was more than the tragic loss of a joyous, wondrous love. This time, there was the agonizing *betrayal* of that love.

Peter's pain would be everything Rob had promised.

Rob had won.

Allison never answered Peter's question. Sometime in the horrible silence that followed, her trembling hands returned the telephone's receiver to it cradle.

Allison wasn't numb anymore. She remembered the venom of her words and the emotion that gave life to her unspeakable thoughts. Allison had learned new emotions because of Peter Dalton. Because of Peter, Allison had learned about love and fire and passion.

And tonight, because of Peter, Allison learned about hate.

Allison's telephone rang again, four hours later, at one A.M. Allison was awake, sitting in the cold darkness. The harsh noise didn't even startle her. Allison had been surrounded with harshness for hours, the thundering sound of her heart, the piercing cries of her mind. *Peter murdered Sara. Peter is the evil Harlequin. Peter is the one you were going to trap into a confession.*

Had she trapped Peter into a confession? *No*. In fact, if Allison allowed herself to remember Peter's voice, there had been such despair, such hopelessness.

Peter is the evil Harlequin, she reminded herself.

The ringing phone was just another strident noise in the night.

Peter, leave me alone! I can't ever hear your voice ever again. I can't.

Strident, persistent. Allison knew Peter wouldn't hang up.

"Peter, leave me—"

"Allison, help me!"

"Winter?"

"Help me . . . please . . . so sick . . ." Winter's breath came in gasps.

"Winter, I'll call the medics and be right there, OK? Winter, honey, hang up the phone."

It took Winter a moment to respond. Then Allison heard the receiver hitting the phone, close to the cradle, missing it. Then, finally, silence.

The October night was filled with more strident noises—the ambulance sirens and the sound of the alarm at the mansion as the paramedics crashed through the front door. The Bel Air Patrol arrived just as Allison did and quickly silenced the alarm.

Allison rushed to Winter's bedroom. The medics were there, crouched over Winter who lay on the floor. The medics started IVs and oxygen. Their trained eyes reflected worry as they worked on the barely conscious woman who was gasping and in shock.

Allison caught a brief, terrifying glimpse of Winter. She didn't even look like Winter! Her rich creamy skin was angry red and her full pink lips were icy blue. Allison bundled an awake, but strangely quiet and subdued Bobbi in a soft blanket as the medics disappeared with Winter, sirens screaming. The Bel Air Patrol officer offered to drive Allison and Bobbi to the UCLA Emergency Room, Allison gratefully accepted the offer.

Déjà vu. The unsummoned thought settled in Allison's mind as she recalled the other middle-of-the-night rush to UCLA to save Winter's life. But this time Peter wasn't here, *directing a scene he had written so carefully, so evilly,* a scene in which the pregnant mother and her unborn child were destined to die. Allison recalled the terror in Peter's eyes that night. Had it been remembered terror, *remorse* for what he had done to Sara? Or had it simply been rage that he was being forced to face his crime again? Had Allison ever accurately read the messages of Peter's dark eyes? Had there been arrogance—icy contempt for her wealth and privilege—from the very beginning? Was the sadness just a facade, just the Harlequin's sinister disguise worn to lure *her* into his trap?

That August night Winter had fought Peter's fear, the assurances that sounded *false*—were false!—with strength and defiance. I'm fine, Peter! My baby is fine!

The night Bobbi was born, Peter could not will Winter to die, as he had willed Sara to die on another night.

But tonight, Winter was quiet. Tonight, Winter had no strength to fight.

Finally, thankfully, the Bel Air Patrol pulled to a stop at the brightly lighted Emergency Room entrance. Allison pulled herself gratefully from her dark thoughts and rushed inside to be with Winter. She cuddled Bobbi and told the senior on-call resident what she knew about her friend's illness, while a junior resident and two nurses were in a curtained room with Winter.

"She said it was a virus."

"What were her symptoms?"

"She didn't really say, except that she was tired and hadn't been doing sit-ups because her muscles ached."

"Aching muscles?"

"Yes."

"Anything else, Allison, anything at all?"

Allison tugged briefly at her lip. It seemed irrelevant, private. In fact, she was surprised Winter had even mentioned it to her.

"Winter said she was just finishing her period."

At that moment, the junior resident appeared from behind the curtain.

"Her shock is responding to fluids and pressors. The room air blood gasses are pending, but I put her back on oxygen because she was cyanotic."

"OK. Good. This is her friend."

The junior resident turned to Allison.

"Was she lying in the sun today?"

“I’m sure she wasn’t. Winter never lies in the sun.”

“Allison says Winter just finished her period.”

The two men looked at each other and exchanged knowing nods. Allison guessed that the answers she had given were simply the final pieces in a jigsaw puzzle for which the picture was already clear.

“You think it’s T.S.S.,” the senior resident said to the junior resident.

“It all fits.”

“T.S.S.?” Allison asked.

“Toxic Shock Syndrome,” the senior resident replied. “We’re going to take Winter upstairs now, Allison. She’ll be in the Medical ICU.”

The residents disappeared behind the curtain with Winter, where they needed to be. Allison remained in the corridor and was soon approached by the E.R. administrator, who needed her help to complete the paperwork. The administrator led Allison to a cubicle near the entrance of the Emergency Room.

“Who is to be listed as her Legal Next of Kin?”

In August, on the night Bobbi was born, Allison had provided that information without hesitation: Lawrence Carlyle.

But now?

Now Allison was *holding* Winter’s Legal Next of Kin in her arms. Allison kissed Bobbi’s silky black hair. *Oh, little Bobbi!*

After the paperwork was complete, Allison asked directions to the Medical ICU.

“The baby can’t go upstairs.”

“Oh! All right.”

Allison called her parents. In fifteen minutes, Sean and Patricia arrived at the Emergency Room parking lot to collect the quiet, precious bundle.

“How is Winter?”

“I haven’t been able to go upstairs. I’m really afraid—”

“She’ll be all right, Allison,” Patricia Fitzgerald interjected firmly. “We’ll get Bobbi tucked in, then one of us will be back.”

“OK. Mother, I think Bobbi only nurses.”

“Allison, your father and I can handle this.” Patricia smiled lovingly, remembering for a moment how much she and Sean had loved caring for their own infant daughter. Patricia looked into that beloved daughter’s jade-green eyes now and saw such heart-stopping worry, such strain, such confusion. She added gently, “One of us will be back to be with you, Allison. In the meantime, you should think about who needs to be called. Peter, of course. And maybe Lawrence?”

After her parents left with Bobbi, Allison went to the Medical ICU. The senior resident told her that Winter’s condition was guarded. He, too, asked ominously if there was anyone who should be notified.

Allison sat in the Waiting Room and considered the question. Who needed to know?

Peter? Peter, who cared about Winter. Peter, who had gently helped Winter discover her remarkable talent and had carefully kept the secret about her pregnancy and who, perhaps, had even saved her life. No, *that* Peter did not exist. He never had.

Lawrence? Winter had told Allison that Lawrence and Margaret and “the boys”—as Winter fondly called them—were in a remote corner of India making another block-buster. Allison didn’t have the energy to begin the long search for Lawrence tonight. Perhaps tomorrow. Perhaps—*yes!*—it wouldn’t be necessary to reach Lawrence at all, because Winter would be fine.

Mark? Mark needed to know. Allison didn't even question the decision. Tonight her own world of love had been brutally shattered. With every ounce of her being, with all of her heart, Allison had believed in her magical love with Peter, but now she knew she was wrong; it had all been merely a horrible illusion. Mark and Winter believed their magical love had ben just an illusion, but wasn't that *wrong*, too?

On a night when everything else was *so wrong* and *so evil*, calling Mark because of Winter felt *so right* and *so good.*

Allison dialed Directory Assistance in Boston. When Mark didn't answer his home phone number, she called the operator at Massachusetts General Hospital. Yes, Dr. Stephens was on call, in the Emergency Ward. She would connect the call.

Mark glanced at the institutional clock in the E.W. nurses" station. It was six A.M. His twenty-four-hour shift would end in one hour. The E.W. was quiet now, at last, and Mark had only one more chart to complete.

Mark sighed softly. He was very tired.

"Long night, Mark." Jill, one of the three night shift nurses, smiled and gently touched his shoulder.

Mark returned the smile but not the touch.

"Dr. Stephens, call on line one," a voice announced over the intercom that linked the nurses" station to the triage desk.

"Maybe the long night's not over yet," Mark said as he depressed the blinking button of the phone beside him. "This is Dr. Stephens."

"Mark, it's Allison Fitzgerald."

"Allison, what's wrong?"

"Winter was just admitted to UCLA. They think she has Toxic Shock Syndrome."

A thousand questions bombarded Mark's mind, instinctive medical questions, sophisticated clues to the severity of Winter's illness. What is her blood pressure? Her platelet count? Her BUN? Her arterial oxygen content? Her protime? Those were medical question Allison couldn't answer. But there was one question Allison could answer, and it would tell Mark what he needed to know.

"Did Winter ask you to call me?" *Please. Please have her be well enough to have asked!*

"No, Mark, she didn't. She's too sick."

"I'll be there, Allison. I'm on my way. Please tell her that. And, Allison, please tell her that I love her."

Chapter 30

Seven hours later, Mark told Winter himself. He whispered the words against her feverish temple as a chorus of beeps played in the background.

"I love you, Winter. I wanted to ask you to marry me last March, but it seemed so selfish and you seemed . . . But were you acting? Were you *playing* wit me the one time it really mattered not to play? Yes, I was playing, too, pretending it was best. But it *wasn't* best. At least, it hasn't been best for me."

Mark gazed at Winter's motionless body, her closed eyes and long black eyelashes that didn't even flicker. Could she hear him? *Please . . .*

"Would you like to hear my plan?" Mark asked hopefully. Winter's lifeless body gave no reply, but he continued as if she heard every loving word, "OK, here it is. I have survived the past few months by promising myself a wonderful reward on New Year's Day—a gift to me on your birthday. I was going to call you then—find you, wherever you were filming—and ask if we could spend my vacation, two weeks in February, together. If you said yes, I might have even asked you then and there—because I couldn't wait—if you would spend more than my vacation with me, if you would spend your life. Winter, darling, I can finish my residency here, in LA, and you can do your movies. I don't think my parents ever had as much love as we have. I don't think *anyone* ever has, do you? I know we can make it work, if it's what you want, too. So, you didn't have to get sick to get my attention, you've always had it. Oh, Winter, my darling Winter."

Winter's eyes fluttered. Her long dark lashes trembled and her violet eyes opened briefly.

"Mark. You need to know about Bobbi." Winter's whisper ended in a gasp, frantic gulps for air, and her pink lips quickly turned deep blue.

The residents and nurses rushed in, signalled by the heart rate monitor that started racing as Winter's breathing failed.

"It could be fluid overload."

"Or ARDS. She was hypoxemic on room air on admission, but her saturation has been fine on nasal prongs."

"It's not fine anymore. Whatever the cause, she needs to be intubated *now*."

Mark listened but didn't participate. He knew the words of his colleagues were correct and that their plan—to put a tube in Winter's throat and allow a ventilator to breathe for her—was necessary and appropriate.

All Mark could think was *Please help her. Please care for her as you would care for someone you love. She is who I love . . . so very much.*

Mark held Winter's hand during the intubation. Her hand was lifeless, because she had been given curare to paralyze her temporarily, so that she couldn't struggle as the cold steel blade of the laryngoscope pressed against the delicate tissues of her throat.

Don't hurt her! Mark watched in horror as the steel blade arched Winter's long, lovely neck to allow passage of the endotracheal tube into her larynx. The doctors were doing everything correctly, but *still*.

As Mark watched, he fought the facts that bombarded his brain, facts about Toxic Shock Syndrome, facts he had learned, memorized, always got *right* on the big tests. Young women—young *healthy* women—die of Toxic Shock. The ones who die are like Winter, ones whose illness was caught too late, after the lungs and kidneys and liver and bone marrow had been assaulted by the toxin for too long.

The hope—the only hope—was *aggressive* support. Aggressive . . . cold steel in her lovely throat, machines to control her breathing, needles in her veins dripping in medicines to keep her out of shock, all that modern medicine had to offer.

What could Mark offer?

Only his love.

When Mark left Winter's room to give the ICU nurses a chance to perform their many tasks, he found Allison in the waiting room.

"How is she, Mark?"

"She's on a ventilator, which is probably better for her. This way, she can get more rest, not expend energy struggling to breathe."

Allison nodded.

Mark and Allison were alone in the waiting room. Mark thought someone else, someone whose name Winter had made such an effort to speak, would be there, too.

"Where is Bob, Allison?" Mark asked finally.

"Bob?"

"Winter just spoke his name. I assume he is her new love." *I assume Winter heard my words of love and wanted to give me her answer: Mark, there is someone else.*

"Mark, what exactly did Winter say?"

"She said, '"You need to know about Bob—Bobby.' "

"You do need to know, Mark."

"Can you tell me?"

"I think you and Bobbi should meet. Come with me."

"I don't want to leave Winter."

"We won't be far, just at my parents" house in Bel Air. We can leave the number. It's important, Mark."

"Hello, Mark," Patricia Fitzgerald smiled warmly, trying to ease the heart-stopping worry in his tired eyes. "How is Winter?"

Patricia would have been at the hospital every minute with Winter, but she had a precious little life to care for here.

"Stable," Mark answered, instinctively trying to reassure. But his mind taunted, *Stable?* Not really. The emergency intubation was a huge setback.

"Mother, we're here to see Bobbi."

Good, Patricia thought.

"In your bedroom, sleeping."

Allison led the way. When they reached the open door, Allison stood aside to let Mark enter. Bobbi was lying on her stomach on the bed, in a soft cradle of feather pillows, sleeping peacefully, beautifully, her tiny delicate lips curled in a soft smile.

"Allison?" Tears filled Mark's eyes as he asked the question.

"We call her Bobbi, but her real name is Roberta, after her grandmother." Allison's voice broke as her own tears spilled.

Mark awakened Bobbi gently and held her close against his heaving chest. Bobbi cooed, intrigued with his warmth and his eyes, unconcerned about the hot tears that splashed on her head as he nuzzled against her.

Allison withdrew to give Mark privacy for his tears and joined her mother in the kitchen. When Mark finally reappeared, he was carrying Bobbi.

Patricia smiled and teased very gently, "Mark, it took me an hour to convince Bobbi to close her sapphire eyes."

"It's very nice of you to have taken care of her," Mark murmured. Bobbi was his daughter, his responsibility now. Mark needed to assume care of Bobbi, and he needed to be with Winter. His tired mind had not yet decided how he would manage both.

Patricia looked at Mark's exhausted, worried eyes.

"Mark, leave Bobbi with me. I love taking care of her. Why don't you plan to stay here, too?"

"I can call my mother."

"Fine. I would love to meet her. Please tell her that she'll stay here, too. That way, she and I can take turns watching Bobbi and visiting Winter, OK?" Patricia was planning to insist no matter what the fatigued sapphire eyes replied.

"Yes. Thank you," Mark whispered. "Thank you."

On the third day, Winter squeezed the strong hand that had held hers almost without pause; on the fourth day, her blood pressure maintained itself without medications; on the fifth day, the tube came out of her throat and she began to give Mark the answers to all his questions, to whisper to him all the loving words he had whispered to her, over and over, for the past five days.

"I love you, Mark."

"Do you know how angry I am with you?" Mark asked lovingly.

"Yes, you've been telling me." Winter smiled. Mark had scolded, as Winter had scolded Allison years before when she lay in the coma, loving; frightened scolding. *Don't you dare leave me, Winter! How could you imagine I didn't love you or want you? Were you ever going to tell me about Bobbi?* "I probably would have lasted until about my birthday, too. Then I would have called you. I thought about it all the time, wondering—"

Mark stopped her words with his lips, kissing her for a long, tender moment, showing her, then finally telling her, "Never wonder again."

"I won't."

"The residency director says they'll have a place for me here begining in July."

"Bobbi and I want to move to Boston."

"This is something we have to talk about."

"Yes." Winter smiled. "Will you call me the second you get to Boston?"

"Of course." Mark kissed her again, a good-bye kiss; he had a plane to catch. "You'll know it's me because the first words you hear will be I love you."

"Oh, Mark, I love you, too."

Winter was discharged from UCLA after eight days. She and Bobbi returned to the mansion; Roberta Stephens returned to San Francisco; and Winter and Mark made forever plans in soft whispers three thousand miles apart.

Three days after Winter returned home, she and Allison sat in the kitchen of the mansion on Bellagio.

"What's wrong with you and Peter, Allison?" Winter asked. "Don't say 'nothing,' because you look like death and Peter sounds like death."

"You've talked to him?"

"Not about what's wrong. Peter won't talk about it. He has called several times to see how I am. He won't talk about what's wrong, Allison, but he asks about you all the time."

"What do you tell him?"

"The truth. That you look terrible. Lost. Sad." Winter paused, then asked gently, "Allison, can't you tell me? Can't you let me help you?"

"No, Winter, I can't talk about it."

"Another famous momentous and unchallengable decision?"

"Winter—"

"I'm sorry," Winter whispered swiftly, softly, as she saw the sudden tears in Allison's haunted, uncertain eyes. The familiar look of serious determination—the look of a champion who made momentous, solid gold decisions—was gone. Allison looked bewildered, the way she had after the accident when she realized she had lost her dream. "Allison, I just can't imagine what could have happened between you and Peter. You two were—*are*—so much in love. I know it isn't someone else, because you both are suffering. Can't you tell me? Maybe, if you talk about it, it won't seem quite as bad."

"Winter, I can't," Allison whispered. *I can't tell you, because it is unimaginable.*

Unimaginable, except that now Allison could force her mind to imagine it. She could recall the vivid memory of the nightmare of the evil Harlequin, a memory that was new and fresh, renewed every night, tormenting, driving her to gasping wakefulness in the rare exhausted moments when she finally fell asleep.

Allison could imagine it—a surreal fantasy—but her defiant heart refused to *believe* it.

And yet, there it was, a huge, sinister wall, built with rock-solid incriminating bricks of facts . . .

Peter hid his marriage until he was forced to tell her because of Love.

Peter hid his relationship with Rob, even though he knew Rob and Allison were friends.

Peter promised no more secrets, and that had been a lie.

From the very beginning, Peter Dalton had kept dark secrets, hiding the truth, revealing little bits only when he was forced to.

Why? Allison demanded of the massive wall of incriminating facts.

Why else? the answer bounced back again and again, *Because he is guilty, because he is the evil Harlequin.*

Allison knew how champions flew over jumps that seemed impossibly high and impossibly dangerous: *You make the place beyond the jump a place you want to be.* And she knew how she had landed safely every time except one: *You send your dreams over first, then simply follow after them.*

Allison didn't know what lay beyond the monstrous wall. Was it where she wanted to be? Did her dream—her love with Peter—exist there?

Allison couldn't find the answers by herself, and she knew that Winter couldn't help her find them, either.

Only Peter could answer the unanswerable questions.

Allison needed to hear Peter's answers. She *would* hear them. She would go to New York, look into his dark eyes, and hear what he had to say. That was the only momentous decision Allison could make, and it wasn't even a decision because her heart gave her no choice. It wasn't a *decision*, Allison realized, but it was *momentous*, because . . .

Was she planning a rendezvous with a murderer?

Or a rendezvous with the man she loved?

As they walked, fingers entwined, beneath the lighted marquee of the Via Condetti Cinema in Rome, Emily slowed. *Love* was playing.

"Who did you see *Love* with, Rob?" Emily asked with a gentle tease. It didn't matter; Emily was so sure of Rob's wonderful love.

Emily expected a handsome, sheepish grin, but she saw something else, an unfamiliar expression, unfamiliar and uninterpretable.

"Rob?"

"I haven't seen *Love*."

"Really? Then let's see it together. Now." Emily tugged gently on his hand, but Rob didn't move and his eyes became stormy.

"No, Emily. I won't ever see *Love*."

"Rob? What's the matter? Please tell me."

Rob took her hand, and as they walked around Rome, retracing the steps he and Sara had taken the February before she died, he told Emily everything. He had already told Emily about his beloved sister who had died of diabetes, but it had been the story of Sara, of her life and of her loveliness, not of her death. That she had died so young was sad, tragic, enough. Emily didn't need to hear the tormenting truths of how, why Sara had died.

But now Rob told her everything.

"I don't believe Peter would have harmed her," Emily said when Rob finished.
Emily surprised herself with the confidence of her voice, and she surprised and worried Rob with the words.

"*Peter?*" Rob asked. "You *know* him?"

"Peter and Allison—"

"Oh my God."

"I don't know him, Rob, not really. I just have one memory of him. Peter drove me to the airport the day I moved to Paris. I was very frightened. I think Peter sensed my fear and wanted to help. He *did* help. He was very kind." Emily smiled lovingly. "Peter Dalton reminded me of you, Rob, and it gave me such hope."

Rob's mind swirled. Sara had told him how alike he and Peter were, but his sister had been horribly, *fatally* wrong! No two men on earth could have been more different.

"When I was in the embassy," Emily began quietly, "I had to find ways to convince myself to stay alive. I could have died so easily, Rob. I could have gotten them to turn their weapons on me. I thought about it."

"Emily . . ."

"But," Emily continued softly, "three days before I was taken hostage, I saw *Love*. I kept myself alive in the embassy by replaying *Love*, over and over in my mind, imagining that *we* were the lovers, Rob, you and I. Doing that, thinking about *Love* and about us, saved me. *Love* is Peter's movie, Peter's vision, Peter's gift. I just can't believe—"

"Peter Dalton is evil, Emily," Rob interjected flatly. He added gently, "You of all people should know about evil men."

"You really believe Peter murdered Sara?"

Rob considered Emily's question for several moments before answering.

"Just after Sara died, when I was so emotional and so angry, and my mother was so convinced, I did believe it," Rob answered finally. "As time passed, as rationality replaced emotion, I decided it hadn't been *intentional*, just negligent, the carelessness of a self-absorbed man. I *blamed* Peter for Sara's death, but I didn't believe he killed her. But now . . ."

"Because of me—" Emily whispered softly, "because of me you have learned new things about cruelty."

It was true. Knowing Emily—what had been done to Emily—had taught Rob about ugliness of the soul he had never imagined existed. But he had learned even more from his beloved Emily . . .

"Because of you, darling Emily, I have learned new things about love."

Rob and Emily sat in silence, surrounded by the noises of Rome at twilight, the harsh blare of horns in rush-hour traffic and the soft, peaceful splash of fountains where wishes made are destined to come true.

"Rob," Emily spoke finally, "I know about evil men. I don't believe Peter Dalton is one of them."

"He's very clever, very devious."

Emily thought for a long time before speaking again, and when she did, she spoke from a deep corner of her soul.

"Do you trust me, Rob?"

"Of course I do."

"I have trusted you with my life," Emily whispered. "Every part of me, nothing hidden."

"I know, darling."

Emily met his ocean-blue eyes.

"Come see *Love* with me, Rob."

"Emily . . ."

"Trust me, Rob." Trust *me*.

After seeing *Love*, Rob and Emily wandered the streets of Rome in wordless silence, she afraid, he tormented. On a January night not too long ago, Rob had followed Emily around Paris, feeling so helpless yet wanting so desperately to protect her from her demons.

And tonight, Emily had loosed Rob's demons, the years of hatred that gnawed destructively at his heart.

I'm sorry, Rob, Emily thought as she watched eyes that didn't seem to see her, tormented, confused, stormy eyes. *I thought it might help*.

When Rob spoke, finally, as dawn yellowed the autumn sky, his voice was soft and bewildered.

"Is it possible that Peter really did love her?" Rob had seen what Emily had only guessed. *Love* was intensely personal, and the lovely, loving, *loved* Julia was really Sara.

"Why isn't that possible, Rob?"

"Because, if Peter loved Sara so much, he would never have let her become pregnant."

"Maybe Sara wanted to be pregnant. Maybe it was *her* decision."

"Emily, you're saying Sara had a death wish."

"No, my darling," Emily answered softly. *She knew about the wish to live and the wish to die*. "Not a death wish, Rob, a *life* wish; a wish to be just like everybody else."

Chapter 31

It was raining when Allison arrived in New York. The rain reminded Allison of happier times . . . a joyous, loving champagne brunch on a soggy gray day . . . rain-soaked curls tenderly dried . . . wet silk and lace gently removed by strong hands trembling with desire.

The rain reminded Allison of love.

But it was cold tonight, and dark, and the love was lost somewhere in darkness.

Allison hadn't told Peter she was coming. When she arrived at his apartment in Chelsea at nine P.M., Allison saw no ribbon of light beneath the door. Where was he? At the theater, perhaps, although his role in Shakespeare on Broadway was virtually over. This was the week—the wonderful, happy week—when Peter should have been packing, tying up loose ends, and, in two days, moving to LA to be with her *forever*.

Allison knocked on the apartment door, not expecting an answer, wondering if she would let herself in if Peter weren't there.

But Peter was there, in the darkness.

"Allison. Come in."

Allison gazed into the darkness before entering. She saw shapes—partially packed boxes that would already have been shipped, if only . . . And she saw a small shadow—Muffin. But Muffin didn't wiggle with excitement or bound gleefully to Allison as usual. Muffin sensed the sadness. For the past eleven days, she had lived again in the once-familiar, long-forgotten silence of death.

As Allison walked inside, Peter turned on a small lamp, took her rain-wet coat, and looked at her damp red-gold curls.

"Would you like a towel for your hair?" he asked gently, sadly, remembering, as she did, the other time her rain-damp curls had needed to be dried and how those moments had flowed into wonderful loving and joyous love.

"No, thank you." Allison walked into the tiny living room and sat on the couch. She hadn't looked into Peter's dark eyes—she couldn't—but as he had taken her coat, Allison had seen the anguish on his strained, handsome face. Anguish, sleeplessness, pain. "Peter, please tell me what happened to Sara."

Peter sat in a chair across from her, staring at jade eyes that wouldn't meet his, and started the story from the very beginning.

"Did you have a forest-green Volkswagen bug?" Allison asked, interrupting him as he told her about the spring he and Sara met and fell in love while they created a rose garden.

"Yes. How did you know that, Allison?"

"I knew Sara, Peter. I was at Greenwich Academy that year, Sara's senior year. She used to watch me ride every day at noon, until spring." *Until she fell in love with you.* Allison remembered the joy on Sara's face, the soft pink radiance, the ocean-blue glow as Sara got into the battered VW with the man she loved.

"You knew Sara," Peter whispered with disbelief. Then, remembering too, he added quietly, "You were the girl with the flame-colored hair, the champion rider. Sara loved watching you ride. She said you looked so free, so happy as you floated over the jumps. It was because of you, Allison, that Sara and I took riding lessons in Central Park."

"Peter, please tell me what happened," Allison whispered after a moment. She heard such love in Peter's voice, a loving memory of Sara *and* love for the girl with the flame-colored hair. *Tell me, Peter, please. If there is a way to make this right . . .*

Allison listened in silence as quietly, softly, Peter told her *everything*. His deep, gentle voice took Allison on an emotional journey back in time, to a time when there had been great love and great joy . . . and then great sadness.

Peter told Allison of Sara's wish to be free, to have what little control she could have over the disease that would kill her; and of his promise to Sara to let her be free; and of his own fear and his own battles, as he kept that promise by fighting his own desperate desire to protect her and keep her safe, always.

Peter whispered, so softly, that he had almost believed Sara's diabetes was *cured*. But then, beginning in the last year of her life, Sara had looked very ill, as if she were dying. And then, two months before she went to Rome, as if by a miracle, it all changed again. Sara looked wonderful, radiant, healthy, happy. Her pregnancy—the pregnancy she had planned and wanted—gave her such energy and such hope.

Peter paused, then quietly he told Allison how Sara had died, quickly, peacefully, smiling as she lovingly asked him to make even *more* promises.

Peter stopped speaking, because Sara had died and his story was over.

"Sara *was* dying, Peter," Allison whispered finally, lost in the memories, vaguely aware that she knew parts of the story that Peter didn't. Hadn't Peter even known Sara was dying? Did he believe Sara might still be alive if only he had *protected* her? Did that add even more torment to the guilt he already felt?

Guilt. Allison heard the guilt and self-recrimination in his quiet voice. But now she knew the truth. And she knew that Peter Dalton was guilty of only one thing.

And it was not a crime.

"You loved Sara too much," Allison whispered. *You are only guilty of a generous, unselfish, limitless love.* Her jade eyes found his at last.

Peter's tired, anguished mind searched for words that would admit *that* crime—his only crime—and allow his love with Allison to survive and flourish still.

Peter's search was interrupted, the silence shattered, by the ringing of the telephone.

Allison was closest to the harsh intrusion. She answered it—Peter's apartment used to be a place where the phone rang for her, too—by reflex, and also to stop the ringing.

"Hello?"

"Allison? This is Rob."

"*Rob.*"

"Allison, I need to speak to Peter. It's a personal matter."

"I know about Sara, Rob. I knew her. I was at Greenwich Academy. I should have told you."

"You were at Greenwich?"

"Yes, for a year, Sara's senior year. Sara used to —"

"—watch you ride, at noon, in the stable," Rob whispered. *You are the lovely young girl who was so nice to my sister!*

"Yes. Rob, I know everything. I know what your family, and maybe you, believe happened. But Peter didn't harm Sara. He never would have harmed her." Allison's eyes filled with tears and her voice trembled. "Rob, Peter loved Sara very, very much."

"Is Peter there, Allison? May I speak with him?"

Allison placed her hand over the receiver and looked questioningly at Peter. "He wants to speak with you, Peter."

Peter didn't want to talk to Rob. Peter wanted, *needed*, to talk to Allison, only to Allison. Her soft words to Rob echoed in his mind—*Peter didn't harm Sara. Peter never would have harmed her*—and gave him such hope.

Peter didn't want to talk to Rob, but he had made a promise, and now Rob was calling him, and maybe lovely Allison had made a way for them to speak, to *talk*, at last.

Once, Allison had planned to proudly, happily, *joyfully* introduce her dear friend Rob to her beloved Peter. Now wasn't a time of great joy, but this was an introduction of sorts, a beginning, and Allison was the link, the connection, between these two strong men. Rob was her dear friend and Peter was her beloved, and she believed in them both.

Peter took the phone from Allison's hand and breathed without emotion, "Rob."

"Thank you for taking my call, Peter," Rob began, realizing it was more than *he* had been willing to do. And, when Rob finally had agreed to speak to Peter, he hadn't listened. He had only delivered a promise of a forever hatred.

"I will understand if you don't tell me. Perhaps I have no right to ask."

"Sara told me about her pregnancy after she returned from Rome, Rob," Peter quietly answered the question he knew Rob was going to ask. "She was thrilled about it. It was what she wanted, what she planned. I know you blame me, Rob. I blame myself."

"Sara wanted us to be friends, Peter," Rob's voice was shaky with emotion.

"Yes, she did."

In the long silence that followed, both men had the same thought: *I don't know if it is possible for us to be friends.* And both had the same remarkable feeling, the exhilarating feeling of hope as the deep strangling roots of hatred in their hearts began to die.

Two households, both alike in dignity . . .

Maybe it was impossible for these two proud, strong men to ever be friends—and maybe not; time would tell. But, at least, they would no longer be bitter enemies. It was a start, a beginning of the promise each had made to Sara.

"Sometime, Peter," Rob spoke finally, "Perhaps you and Allison would have dinner with us?"

"Yes . . . perhaps . . . sometime."

The call ended without specific plans, but for the first time, it ended without hatred and rage.

After he hung up, Peter stared at the phone for several moments, calming himself, recovering, feeling the immense unburdening as hatred retreated from his heart. Then he heard a soft sound and looked up.

Allison was getting her soggy raincoat from the closet.

Allison was leaving.

When Allison reached the door, about to leave, about to return to the rain and cold and darkness, Peter's voice broke the stillness.

Peter's voice . . . a bewildered whisper of despair.

"Allison, you don't believe me!"

Allison spun, startled. Her jade eyes gazed at him with confusion and surprise.

"What, Peter?"

"You told Rob that you believed I loved Sara and that I would never have harmed her. But you don't believe it." Peter whispered hoarsely, "You believe I murdered Sara."

"Peter, *no*. I don't believe that." *I believe you loved Sara so much . . . too much . . . forever.*

"Then why are you leaving, Allison?"

Because I don't belong here. Allison's thought came swiftly, confidently, filling her eyes with bewildered sadness.

Peter saw the sadness and the lost, bewildered look, and he realized what was happening.

Allison was leaving him so that he could be with Sara. Peter had taken Allison on the voyage into his past and she was still there, lost in *his* memories of love.

Make new memories with me, Allison!

Peter moved to her and took her hands in his. Then, so gently, he carefully began another journey with Allison, *their* journey, a journey into the present and the future. Peter spoke softly, lovingly, about *their* joyous forever love.

"Do you remember when I called you that night, Allison? Eleven nights ago? I told you I had a wonderful surprise. Would you like to hear about it now?"

"What? Oh. Yes."

"I bought Bellemeade. I bought Bellemeade for us, darling, so we can live and love in that enchanted romantic place forever. I'm moving to Los Angeles, to Bel Air, to be with you always. I will write screenplays—only happy ones if that's what you want. And I think I will begin a theater company—Shakespeare in Westwood, something like that. Muffin will get to be the California girl she really is."

Peter paused. Was Allison listening? Was she hearing his soft words of love? Muffin was listening. Muffin heard her name and Peter's gentle tone, and her blond head cocked, a small tilt of hope.

"Allison?"

Peter gazed into Allison's lovely jade eyes. She still wasn't completely with him; she was still a little lost in distant memories, but less lost, less bewildered. Allison was finding her way back to him, to their love, guided unerringly by his loving voice and by the fiery beacons of her own heart.

"Allison? Darling?" *Come with me, Allison. Be with me in our wonderful love.*

"Yes?" Allison's eyes began to focus. "Yes, Peter?"

"Do you know why I told you I wouldn't watch you jump the green and white railed jump?"

"No, Peter. Why?"

"Because I love you too much, Allison. Because I couldn't stand the thought of losing you. It's a selfish reason." Peter whispered quietly. "If you really want to jump again, I'll be there with you."

"I don't want to jump anymore, Peter. It isn't important," Allison answered swiftly. She smiled then, and the magnificent jade was suddenly clear and bright and sparkling with love. She asked softly, "Do you want to know why?"

"Yes, darling. Tell me."

"Because I love you too much, too."

The Carlton Club

Part One

Chapter 1

SAN FRANCISCO, CALIFORNIA
NOVEMBER 1980

Dr. Leslie Adams gazed out University Hospital's eleventh floor picture window mesmerized by the magnificence of San Francisco at daybreak. As she watched, the pearl-gray sky became pale yellow. It was the kind of pastel autumn dawn that promised a soft muted sun. It would be a gentle sun, just wrm enough to melt the thick layer of fog that covered San Francisco Bay like a plush down comforter.

Leslie knew the kind of fresh, crisp, exhilarating day it would be. A warm 471
sun. A cool, but not cold, breeze. A day for light woolen scarves and rosy-red cheeks and mugs of hot chocolate. Leslie loved days like this. She had memories, lovely distant memories, of such days . . . a walk in a secluded pine-scented meadow . . . a wind-tossed ferry boat ride across white-capped water . . .

Leslie thought about the rich taste of hot chocolate as she curled her hands around her barely warm cup of overbrewed black coffee and sighed. The sigh was a little nostalgic, because of the memories, and a little wistful, because she would love to be out there today, enjoying the autumn briskness. But mostly it was, simply, a sigh of fatigue.

It had been a long, busy sleepless night; but she had made it, and her patients had made it. Everyone had survived. Now, finally, as the night's cold darkness yielded to the warmth of the new-day sun, the hospital was silent. At peace. Sleeping.

Mark would tell her that, even if only for an hour, she should try to sleep.

Mark. He had hoped she would have an easy night. That was what he was really telling her ten hours ago . . .

"I have a feeling it is going to a quiet night," he said as he walked into the doctors' write-up area.

"Mark! Hi," she said looking up, a little startled, from the medical record she was reviewing. "What did—"

"I said I have a feeling it's going to be a quiet night," he repeated as he settled into a chair across from her. "Very quiet. No more admissions. No midnight fever work-ups or chest pain . . ."

"Dream on," she said, laughing.

"This is a very strong feeling," he countered lightly. Then he leveled his dark brown eyes at her and added seriously, "Which means that Dr. Leslie Adams, intern *extraordinaire*, can get some sleep."

Leslie's eyes met his for a brief awkward moment, then fell, unable to hold his gaze. They both knew that, even if the night was quiet, Leslie wouldn't sleep. She wouldn't even try. I can't really sleep at the hospital, Leslie explained easily to anyone who questioned her habit of staying up all night when she was on call.

It was true. It *was* difficult to sleep at the hospital. The interruptions were frequent, and the hours when it was even possible to sleep were few. It was true, but those weren't the real reasons. The real reason was too personal, too superstitious, too silly to tell anyone . . .

Leslie believed that if she stayed awake, alert, keeping vigil over the patients in her charge, nothing bad would happen to them. Somehow her wakeful presence would protect them against the unknown, unpredictable catastrophes that could and did occur.

So, Leslie didn't sleep. She simply patrolled. A quiet, serious sentry. A highly trained shepherd. Unobtrusive, but ever-present. It was illogical. *Silly.* But it was *working*. It felt right.

Doing what felt right was what Leslie had always done. At George Washington High School in Seattle, doing what felt right won her recognition as Most Inspirational and Most Likely To Succeed. Doing what felt right drew good-natured teasing from her friends about being *too* good, *too* perfect: predictable, reliable Leslie. They teased her at Radcliffe, too, when she chose biology over a Saturday night "mixer" or an organic chemistry experiment over the Harvard-Yale crew race.

The teasing was always gentle. They were her friends, after all. And no one begrudged Leslie her rules. She didn't try to impose them on anyone else, and she didn't expect anyone else to follow them. Her friends knew that Leslie's rules were just for Leslie, just the way Leslie had to do things.

Now, as an intern, she had to stay up all night, awake, alert, vigilant. It was the only way that felt right. It didn't make sense, she knew that, but it felt right.

Except when Mark teased her. Then she felt foolish. What if Mark guessed the real reason, her silly superstition? Mark was so rational, so logical. He would think it ridiculous. He would think *her* ridiculous. Mark, of all people –

"No plans to sleep?" Mark asked finally, interrupting the silence, sorry that he made her uncomfortable.

Leslie tossed the chestnut curls that fell into her sapphire-blue eyes and smiled bravely. "No plans to sleep. I have a feeling it's going to be busy."

Mark smiled. She could be so sensitive. And so proud.

"Any problems with your patients?" he asked.

"No. The patient I just admitted with acute asthma is already clearing. I'm just reviewing his old chart. Then I'll be all caught up," Leslie said, ready for the busy night to begin or for a long quiet night of patrolling.

"I think I'll go home, then," Mark said, standing up suddenly.

Go home. Mark's words caught Leslie by surprise. It was only seven. For the past month, because he no longer had a reason to leave—because he no longer had a *home*—Mark frequently spent extra hours at the hospital. Even when he could leave, when other residents were in charge, he often stayed to help Leslie with her patients or to review charts or to read journals.

It must be better than being alone, Leslie decided as she watched the new pattern emerge. It must be better for Mark to be here than to be alone with all the unanswerable questions that must be tormenting him. Not that the hospital really provided escape. Leslie saw the pain and sadness in his dark eyes, even though he tried to hide it. Even though he told no one, not even her.

She knew of course, because Janet was her friend. She and Janet talked about it all the time.

But Mark and Leslie never talked about it.

"Home," she echoed softly.

"If you don't need—"

"No," Leslie said quickly. "Everything's under control."

She sensed his restlessness as he leaned against the doorjamb waiting for her to say good-night. Restless, eager, full of anticipation, there was a glimmer of hope in the dark eyes where, recently, there had been none. Was Mark rushing off to see Janet?

No. Leslie would have known *that*.

Mark was leaving, eager, full of hope, to be with someone else, and just the thought of whoever she was made his eyes sparkle with life and happiness.

"Have a nice evening," Leslie said gaily, smiling above the ache that consumed her.

"You too." Mark smiled back. "Try to get some sleep."

He would have told her to try to sleep now, ten hours later, if even for an hour.

Had *he* slept, Leslie wondered as she took a swallow of lukewarm, bitter coffee. Where had he slept? And with whom . . .

Stop thinking about him, she told herself sternly, forcing her thoughts away from Mark and back to the glorious day that was unfolding before her. This time as she gazed out the window she focused on the thick layer of fog that lay beneath the pale yellow glow of the autumn dawn.

Fog. It wasn't supposed to be there. It was November. This kind of fog—thick, opaque, smothering—was a summer phenomenon. Leslie had learned about the notorious San Francisco summer fog, four months before, the day her internship began. Four months. It seemed so long ago.

The department chairman had told them, the internship class of 1980–81, how delighted he was to have them in his internal medicine program. He *was* delighted. He looked at the bright, healthy, eager young doctors assembled before him. He knew they were among the nation's best. The internship class that listened intently to the words of their department chairman that day in June was a select group. And carefully selected at that.

They had all graduated at the top of their medical school classes. They had all been elected to Alpha Omega Alpha, the medical school equivalent of Phi Beta Kappa. The only question, a question the most competitive among them might ask a colleague, was, When were you elected to AOA? junior year? autumn of senior year? or, perish the thought, *spring* of senior year?

They had all spent the month between medical school graduation and the beginning of their internship preparing for the year that lay ahead. Some simply rested, knowing but not really believing the rumors of the exhaustion that would beset them (not *them*). Some traveled. Some got married. Some read—*reread*—textbooks of medicine. Some studied the "how-to" manuals for interns.

All framed their recently earned Doctor of Medicine diplomas. *None* spent any time dreading the year to come. The University of California at San Francisco was the internship they wanted. It was the ultimate trophy, the reward for their hard work. It was the best.

They were the best.

That June day, the day the internship started, they were eager. *Ready*. The department chairman looked at them thoughtfully. He knew from years of experience that, as prepared as they were, as smart as they were, as eager and as confident as they were, they were *not* ready. They could not be adequately prepared for the year—the ordeal—that lay ahead.

He tried to tell them. He knew that they would hear his words, but they wouldn't understand. In a month he could repeat the speech, and they would look at him with their dark-circled eyes and gaunt faces and nod wisely. In a month they would understand. He wondered if any of them would remember that he had told them.

"Your internship is like our weather here in San Francisco," he said earnestly, his gray eyes serious.

They listened, politely, smiling. He was such a distinguished physician. They were so glad to be here!

"In the summer months we have fog. Oh, there are brief glimpses of sun and clarity, but mostly, it is foggy and gray and dismal at a time—summer!—when it should be just the opposite. That's what these summer months of your internship will be like. They will be foggy, confusing and grim."

The eager faces looked puzzled. Was he being funny?

"There will be questions you can't answer," he explained. "Problems you don't know how to handle. Patients you can't save. It is very different from, for example, National Boards. On National Boards there are clear questions with correct answers, and I know from your applications how well you all did on your Boards . . ."

A titter of relief. *Good, he knows how good we are. But what is he talking about?*

"But *doctors*," he continued, "take care of real patients and lots of foggy questions without clear answers. There will be days when the shades of gray, like the fog, seem relentless. It's difficult because it is so different from what you expect. In summer you expect sun not fog. When you start your internship, having graduated top in your class, you expect to continue to have all the right answers."

He looked at them, knowing what they were thinking: I *do* have the right answers. I *will* have. I always have had.

"But," he said pleasantly, "the fog of your internship will lift as predictably as the San Francisco summer fog vanishes. By mid-September the breezes will be fresh and cool, and the skies will be clear and blue. Your spirits will lift. Your confidence will be restored. You'll understand that shades of gray are part of medicine. Come September it will be smooth sailing."

It had been exactly as he predicted: a difficult, confusing, disillusioning adjustment. But it had also been just as he promised. By September, when the sun came out, the fog vanished and the skies were blue, they *were* adjusted. They knew they could and would make it. The exhaustion, the pressure, the energy required did not change.

But the fog had lifted.

Now, almost two months later, the fog had returned.

How would the department chairman explain it? A fog relapse. What could it mean? The interns have gotten too confident, too sure. Let the fog return! A *reminder.*

As Leslie toyed with the meaning, the *symbolism*, of the fog, she thought lovingly about her parents in Seattle. Her mother, a journalist, and her father, a professor of English at the University of Washington, could spend endless hours happily analyzing the symbols and metaphors and hidden meanings in their favorite books and poems. Leslie was their only child, the precious daughter who, despite the genes that should have made her a writer or a poet, was a scientist. Susan and Matthew Adams watched her grow up with proud loving amazement. How could *their* daughter prefer Galileo to Faulkner, volunteer work at the hospital to the Repertory's production of *Man and Superman*, science projects to novels and physics to poetry?

This November fog, Leslie decided finally, feeling truly the daughter of her literary parents, was *not* a professional fog. It was not a soupy signal that the lessons of shades of gray and uncertainty had been inadequately learned and needed remedial work. If it was a symbol at all, Leslie concluded, it was a symbol of personal fog.

In the distance Leslie heard the comforting sounds of the hospital waking up, preparing for the new day. The elevators, silent and immobile all night, now moved constantly as they shuttled the rested day shift to its wards and retrieved the tired night shift. Leslie heard the rattle of breakfast carts being wheeled from room to room, the clank of the bedside scales, the quiet chatter of nurses' reports and the almost soundless footfalls of the morning blood-draw team in their rubber-soled shoes.

Even though Leslie heard the familiar reassuring noises that undeniably heralded the close of another night on call, her thoughts were not tranquil. She was thinking about the fog. The surprising dense fog outside the window. And the fog inside—the personal fog that had settled, firmly, around her. Again.

Again. It had been there in summer, all summer. But, like the San Francisco fog, it had vanished—had been *banished* by her—in September. It was back now, an enveloping unsummoned presence, because everything had changed. Because maybe it wasn't impossible anymore. Because she could dare to think about it. About *him.*

It wasn't really very complicated. One didn't need a degree in English to decipher the meaning of the mysterious fog. Even a scientist could make the correct diagnosis, Leslie thought wryly. Even an *intern* . . .

The diagnosis was simple: Mark David Taylor, M.D.

Chapter 2

The alarm sounded noisily, a too harsh intrusion on a pleasant but unremembered dream. Mark groaned and in one motion rolled over and depressed the alarm silence button. As he awakened, Mark realized two things. The first was that he was unusually tired, fatigued beyond the chronic feeling of being sleep deprived. The second realization was even more unusual. Unusual and startling.

Mark realized that he wasn't unhappy. His first feeling, preceding consciousness by a few moments, was *not* the familiar aching sadness that had been with him for the past month.

For the past month. Ever since Janet had left him.

This morning's feeling was happy and eager and so energetic that it almost erased the fatigue. The feeling was new. Mark had never felt it before. Not even with Janet. Not even in the beginning. Not ever before.

As Mark's consciousness caught up with the vital feeling that had awakened the instant the alarm sounded, he remembered the cause of the feeling: Kathleen. And he knew why his chronic sleep deficit seemed more acute. Kathleen hadn't left until three. Only four hours ago she was still in his bed making him feel the way he still felt even after she was gone.

Kathleen. As he showered, Mark thought about her, remembering last night, astonished that he had only known her for a week.

As Mark recalled the events of the past week he resisted any attempt to put meaning to them. He was still reeling from Janet's angry words, still trying to make sense of Janet's condemnation of their marriage. Her condemnation of him. For the past month Mark lay awake at night, tired but unable to sleep, wondering how to save his marriage and what he would do if it wasn't salvageable.

For the past month Mark had taken his life one day at a time. In the few moments he had that weren't of necessity focused on his patients, he tried to make sense of what happened. He tried to understand the venom of Janet's words.

One day at a time.

And now there was Kathleen and the wonderful feeling that, for the moment, obliterated the anguish and turmoil about Janet.

One day at a time.

Kathleen.

One night at a time.

Mark met Kathleen on Halloween. Mark was on call on Halloween.

"You are always on call on Halloween," Janet might have said if they hadn't separated three weeks before.

Just as she said that he was *always* "on" on Thanksgiving or Christmas (which was also her birthday) or their anniversary or his birthday. It wasn't true of course. It was the luck of the schedule. He was *always* on call every third night, at least. Sometimes every other night. Sometimes those on call nights coincided with *real world* events like holidays and birthdays and anniversaries.

"Besides," he would have asked Janet, "what would we do if I was off on Halloween? Go to a party with my friends most of whom you detest?"

That—the way Janet felt about his friends, about medicine—was part of the news she had given him three weeks before.

"I hate your friends and I hate medicine," Janet had said. Then she added quietly, "And I think you do, too."

By Halloween there was no Janet, and Mark didn't care whether he was "on" or "off" on Halloween. Or any other time for that matter. Except that Halloween meant craziness. Halloween was like a full-moon night, only worse. But since Mark was on call for the critical care units at University Hospital, he would probably feel very little of the Halloween impact.

The emergency room, particularly at San Francisco General Hospital, would be hit the hardest by the Halloween phenomenon. There they would see lacerations that were unusually long and deep and old and dirty because of the blood alcohol level of the victim. They would see broken bones, the result of the inevitable conflicts as the traditional Gays' Halloween Parade made its way along Castro Street to the jeers and taunts of macho "straights." They would see the drug fall-out from parties: angel-dust (PCP) "freak-outs," cocaine-induced headaches and palpitations and the age-old marijuana death paranoia made worse by the ghoulish costumes on fellow party-goers.

Halloween in the ER was the stuff anecdotes were made of. Anecdotes to tell at parties. To your friends. Medical anecdotes to tell medical friends. Everything Janet hated.

Mark was quite content to be on call for the critical care units instead of the emergency room. His admissions would be legitimately sick, uncostumed, undrugged and uncrazed by the Halloween spirit.

Mark was paged to the emergency room at ten P.M. on Halloween.

"We have a fifty-six-year-old woman with substernal chest pain," the harried resident told him, "radiating to her left arm, lasting maybe five minutes. Responded to nitro. Has chronic angina but this lasted longer. No EKG changes. Pain-free now. Probably just angina, but I'd like to bring her in as a rule out. It's a soft hit . . ." the voice trailed off apologetically.

A hit was an admission, any admission. A night with no admissions was a no hitter. A soft hit ment it might be safe to send the patient home, but . . .

Soft hits were fine with Mark. He believed in erring on the side of the patient. It was safest to admit the woman. Just in case.

"Sounds appropriate to me. I'll be right down to get her. Is it a zoo down there?"

"An unbelievable zoo."

"Listen, after I get her tucked in, if it's quiet up here, I'll be happy to come help."

"Thanks, Mark. That would be great."

Mark found that his patient, although sick, sane and undrugged, *was* in costume. At least her head was. The rest of her was already clad in a bland, standard issue hospital gown. She wore a white wig with perfectly curled ringlets and a diamond tiara. Marie Antoinette, or someone, Mark thought idly, noticing at the same time how lovely, gracious and regal-looking she was. She extended a beautifully manicured and lavishly jeweled hand to him.

"Hello, Dr. Taylor," she said, as if meeting him at a party.

"Hello, Mrs. Jenkins. How are you feeling?"

"Fine, now. Really. No pain. I probably could go—" she stopped abruptly. It was obvious to Mark that his elegant, gracious patient felt uneasy about going home. The soft hit became a hard one. She was worried. She felt sicker than she looked. The pain must have been worse than she described. Admit. Admit.

"No, we want you to stay," Mark said firmly. "You're completely pain free now?"

She nodded and smiled. A voice reached them from behind.

"Mother, I just spoke to Father. Oh, hello! Sorry!" she exclaimed, startled as she opened the curtain surrounding her mother's monitored bed to find that her mother was not alone.

She was completely in costume. She wore a gray and mauve, floor-length velvet gown studded with tiny pearls and cut low in front, revealing her round, full breasts. Her dark black hair was piled on her head and draped with pearls. Her dark-lashed violet eyes sparkled with surprise and pleasure when she saw Mark.

"Kathleen, this is Dr. Taylor, the CCU doctor. Dr. Taylor, this is my daughter, Kathleen."

"Hi," Mark said. She is so beautiful, he thought.

"Hi," Kathleen said. She glanced at her mother and was relieved enough by how comfortable she looked to spend a moment noticing her mother's doctor.

The usual clichés, Kathleen thought: tall, dark, handsome. Clichés, she mused. *Tall.* That was easy, a statement of fact. Kathleen embellished it a little. Mark was a perfect height. *Dark*. Completely inadequate to describe the dark brown hair that curled sensuously over his ears and onto his neck or the intense, thoughtful, serious dark brown eyes made darker by the blue-black half-circles under them. *Handsome*. Unbelievably, indescribably handsome, Kathleen thought. The whole dark, earnest, strong, romantic package.

Tall, dark and handsome. It didn't begin to do him justice.

"How's Mother?" Kathleen asked after a moment.

"Fine," Mark and Virginia Jenkins answered in unison.

"No evidence of any damage, but we're going to admit her for two or three days, just to be certain," Mark explained.

"As a rule out," Virginia Jenkins explained to her daughter.

Mark looked from beautiful mother to beautiful daughter and arched an eyebrow. A rule out was medical jargon, short for rule out myocardial infarction, heart attack. At some centers such an admission was called a ROMI. During the daily morning report at such centers the resident would say, "We admitted two ROMIs last night." In San Francisco the resident would say, "We admitted two rule outs."

Clearly Virginia and Kathleen Jenkins had been to centers favoring the rule out jargon and were familiar with it.

"Dr. Taylor walked in just moments before you did, Kathleen, so I haven't had the chance to give him my past history. I do have legitimate coronary artery disease," she explained to Mark, "confirmed by angiogram. It's not severe enough to bypass. Yet. I'm followed at the Atherton Clinic by Dr. Brown. Occasionally my chronic stable angina acts up, and I get admitted as a rule out. Fortunately, I always *have* ruled out," she added firmly, a trace of worry in her voice.

Tonight's episode of pain was different, Mark thought. She's just not admitting it. Even to herself.

"You're an excellent historian, Mrs. Jenkins. I'll give Dr. Brown a call once we get you settled upstairs."

"We were at a ball at the Fairmont," Kathleen interjected. "We thought it best to come here rather than to drive all the way to Palo Alto. She usually gets admitted to Stanford Hospital." Kathleen was as polite and gracious as her mother. They didn't want to offend anyone, neither Virginia's usual physician nor Mark.

"You did exactly the right thing. We'll keep Dr. Brown posted and transfer you to Stanford Hospital in day or two if you like."

"If my enzymes are normal you'll just discharge me in two days anyway. So I might as well stay here."

Mark was a second-year resident. He was a year ahead of Leslie and was her supervising resident. As his intern, Leslie assumed primary care of all patients admitted by Mark on his on-call nights. Then they managed the patients together, Leslie as intern and Mark as supervisor.

The morning after Halloween, Leslie became Virginia Jenkins's intern. That afternoon the cardiac enzymes returned slightly elevated, and the electrocardiogram showed minor ST segment changes without Q waves.

"She's had a very small subendocardial MI. She probably had more than five minutes of discomfort even though she really insisted that was all. She was denying a little last night. I'm sure she'll give you the whole story, Leslie," Mark said to her. "No point pushing her because we have the diagnosis. But she needs to understand that whatever she felt and isn't telling us about is an important warning signal."

Virginia Jenkins did tell Leslie. It wasn't a confession. It was simply an amazed appreciation that the weakness she had felt all day long—weakness and heaviness without pain—was her heart.

Kathleen stayed in her mother's room as much as visiting hours would permit. Between visits she read in the waiting room. William Jenkins returned from New York at the news of his wife's hospitalization. He visited mostly in the evenings.

Mark decided that Kathleen looked even more beautiful in broad daylight, wearing soft silk blouses and tailored skirts and allowing her long black hair to fall free. Serene, understated, elegant beauty.

Mark and Kathleen saw each other several times every day. Sometimes they would just wave at each other, she sitting in the waiting room and he rushing off to rounds, the ER, the ICU or Radiology. Whenever he could, even for a moment, he would stop to talk. Each day Mark and Leslie met with Kathleen and her parents to discuss Virginia's progress and the plans. The Jenkinses took the news of Virginia's small heart attack calmly.

"It's a warning, Mother," Kathleen said, her voice a little shaky. "You push too hard."

It was decided that Virginia would remain in the CCU at University Hospital in San Francisco for several days. Then, if stable, she would be transferred to Stanford for the balance of her ten-day hospitalization.

During that time Mark and Kathleen learned few facts about each other, but they both knew that they felt good—happy—every time they waved, every time they talked, every time they even caught a glimpse of each other. The warm happy feeling persisted while they were apart, and it was renewed, strengthened, the next time they saw each other.

At eight o'clock the night before Virginia was to be transferred to Stanford, Mark found Kathleen in the visitors" waiting room. He was on call again but not very busy, not too busy to stop for a moment.

"Hi!" Kathleen smiled. Then a moment of worry flickered across her violet eyes. "Is Mother . . . ?"

"She's fine. Rock-stable. I just wanted to say hi. And good-bye. I may not see you in the morning."

"Oh," Kathleen said, frowning slightly. Then she added, "You certainly work hard. You're here all the time. It must be difficult for your wife."

Kathleen's eyes drifted toward Mark's wedding ring. It was a plain solid band of eighteen carat gold. Very traditional. Very married.

But he doesn't act very married, Kathleen thought.

Mark looked at his ring. He still wore it. His marriage wasn't *over*, just in trouble. Mark had no idea if he and Janet could ever recover from the angry words and the bitterness. It was too soon to know, too soon to predict. They were in a holding pattern. Since that afternoon in early October, he and Janet had spoken to each other, over the phone, a few times. Those conversations were slow, difficult and punctuated by painful silences and even more painful words. They agreed they needed time apart, time to let the anger and emotions cool, time to think. Then, maybe, they could try to work it out.

In Mark's mind the marriage wasn't over. He didn't even have a clear idea about what Janet thought was so wrong. Even though he had moved into a tiny apartment near the hospital, bought a new, albeit inexpensive, stereo and opened his own checking account, Mark had not removed his wedding ring. He hadn't even thought about removing it.

As he looked from Kathleen's sparkling violet eyes to the scuffed soft-gold ring given to him five years before by a woman he could barely speak to anymore,

Mark wondered why he still wore it.

"We—my wife and I—are separated," Mark told the violet eyes, watching them widen at the news. Kathleen was the first person he had told. Mark assumed Leslie knew because Leslie and Janet were friends. But Leslie didn't mention it to him because Leslie wouldn't. And no one else knew. Until now.

"Separated?" Kathleen echoed softly.

480 "For about a month."

"A trial separation?" Kathleen asked.

"I wonder what that means," Mark mused. Until he had spoken this word, separation, he hadn't even put a label on what was happening to him and Janet. To his marriage. "*Trial* separation. Meaning let's try it, and if we like it we'll get separated often. Or . . ."

Kathleen laughed. It was a light, lovely appreciative laugh.

Mark shrugged and smiled. He hadn't been appreciated for a while. Not for Mark the person. Mark the man. And recently from Janet not even appreciated for his one indisputable accomplishment: Mark, the doctor.

"Does it mean," Kathleen asked finally, after their smiling eyes had met for a moment, "that you could come to a party with me?"

"Oh!" Mark was surprised, pleased. Now that what he and Janet were doing had a label—separation—it needed a definition.

It only took him a moment, but in that moment Kathleen added quickly, "Or would that be unethical because of Mother?"

"No," he said firmly, "and yes. Sure. I'd love to."

Kathleen nodded, smiling.

"But I don't have anything that's very Henry the Eighth."

"Louis Quatorze!"

"Oh, right. I knew that. I had you pegged as Marie Antoinette."

"We were just generic Louis Quatorze. I don't even like to pretend to be someone who got guillotined!"

"No." Mark shuddered.

"Oh, dear," Kathleen said suddenly.

"What?" Is she thinking of a gracious way to retract the invitation, Mark wondered uneasily.

"Well, there's no special attire, *but*"—she wrinkled her nose—"it is an engagement party. For my best friend. Would that be hard for you?"

"No," Mark said, relieved that she wasn't withdrawing the invitation. But, he thought, it might be hard. I don't know. I'll find out. Then he remembered a real obstacle. "When is the party? I may be on call."

"You're not! At least not by my calculations. It's this Thursday night. Day after tomorrow, You're on tonight, so every third would put you on again Friday. Is that right? Can you come?"

"That's right. Yes, I can come," Mark said, flattered that she had bothered to learn even that little detail about his life.

Thursday night, Mark thought. A party on Thursday night. Thursday night was a *school* night, or it had been, for Mark, from kindergarten through medical school. For *twenty* years. Then, for the past two years, as an intern and resident, Thursday night was still a work night. Or the night before a long work day. Not a party night.

Who had parties—engagement parties—on Thursday night?

He would find out.

Kathleen gave him her parents' telephone number in Atherton, and they agreed over the phone the next night that she would meet him at his apartment at seven-thirty. The engagement party was in a private home near the Presidio at eight.

Thursday evening Mark left the hospital at seven, rushed to his apartment, showered, shaved and was knotting his tie when Kathleen arrived promptly at seven-thirty.

"Hi," he said, dazzled as always by her appearance. To-night she wore her black hair piled in soft curls on top of her head. Small tendrils escaped down her long ivory neck. Mark took her camel's-hair coat and silently admired the violet, silk cocktail dress.

"Hi. Am I early?"

"No, you're on time. I'm almost ready. I didn't get away from the hospital until seven."

"Was it OK for you to leave when you did?"

"Yes. Of course." Or I wouldn't have left, Mark thought. Janet knew that. Maybe Kathleen didn't. Except that Kathleen would, *should*, understand because her mother had been a patient. Kathleen would be outraged if a doctor left her mother, if her mother needed him, simply because the doctor had a date with *her.*

Kathleen caught the sharpness of Mark's tone and turned her attention to his apartment in an attempt to divert the conversation. The apartment was terrible. It was so tiny. The living room, dining room and kitchen were all one area. The limited floor space was cluttered with unpacked cardboard boxes. The apartment was clean but sterile. The only sign of life or personality was a stereo balanced on cinder blocks, two speakers and a stack of record albums.

Kathleen couldn't think of one positive thing to say about the apartment, and Mark had been edgy about her last question. Perhaps if she looked at the albums . . .

"It's pretty bad, isn't it?" he asked, his voice stopping her as she walked—it would only take a few steps—across the living room to the stereo.

Kathleen turned slowly and smiled at him. Her eyes met his.

"It really defines the concept of *trial*, doesn't it? she asked lightly, her eyes sparkling.

They both laughed.

Chapter 3

Janet would have loved the engagement party, Mark thought. He was the only doctor there. The others, Mark deduced, were an intriguing mixture of attorneys, stock-brokers, market analysts, advertising and corporate executives. *Beyond* YUPPIE, Mark decided. These people, Kathleen's friends, were not struggling to get to the top. Despite the fact that none was over thirty-five, it was clear that they were already there. They had power and wealth and confidence.

None of them cared that Mark was a doctor, but all of them cared that he was Kathleen's date. *That* interested them. The men eyed Mark with curiosity, the women with frank admiration.

"My God, Katie, where did you get *him?*" The beautiful women, Kathleen's friends, asked her in front of him.

And behind his back, he heard them say, "When you're through with him, *please* give him my number!" and, "Is he married?"

His wedding ring! He still wore it. He had planned to take it off, at least for the evening. Or, *beginning* with the evening. He wasn't sure. But she had arrived and he had forgotten. Inertia? Ambivalence? Or something less significant like an overworked preoccupied resident who just forgot?

 Mark listened with interest to the conversations of Kathleen's friends. They chatted about books and politics and theater and the stock market and sports and restauants and vacation spots and real estate. Mark had little to add. He hadn't seen a movie since *Star Wars*. He knew vaguely that the Forty Niners were finally having a good season. Since he and Janet had separated, he started watching the late night and early morning newscasts, as much for companionship as for information. At least he was current on current events. Of course he read a lot, but in the past year the only nonmedical reading he had done was written before the twentieth century.

It didn't matter that Mark said little. He fit in anyway. Because he smiled appropriately and he was a good listener. But mostly Mark fit in, was welcomed, because he was with Kathleen. Kathleen was the queen bee. This was her group. These were her friends. They loved her, deferred to her. They liked, maybe envied, her date.

Mark realized how little he knew about her.

How old was she? Meeting her as he had at the bedside of her ill but youthful mother, Mark assumed she was young. Maybe twenty. But now as she talked knowledgeably about *Joanna*, the new musical to be introduced by Union Square Theater, Kathleen seemed older. She could be twenty. Or thirty. Or older.

Kathleen's appearance gave no clue. Her wrinkle-free, animated face changed age with the mood of the moment. She was older when the conversation was serious, and younger when she laughed or teased the bride-to-be.

What did Kathleen do? If she was twenty she was probably a student. But these were her friends. They weren't twenty, and they weren't students. They had influential, responsible, demanding jobs. Mark knew she had something to do with Union Square Theater, but he got the impression that it wasn't a job.

Mark noticed that no one asked her, "How's work?"

No one asked Kathleen many personal questions, except, "How is your mother?" and, gesturing toward Mark, "Who is he?" and, whispering, "What ever happened to Bill? I thought . . ."

Kathleen's annoyance at being asked personal questions about Mark within his earshot was obvious. Her violet eyes scowled briefly at her inquisitive friends. They got the message. Mark was different. Kathleen cared about him. She brought him to the party because she wanted to be with him. It was a date, *their* date. He wasn't simply someone to show off to her friends.

Yes, they realized, Mark was very different.

As the evening wore on, fortified by champagne or Mark's smiles or both, Kathleen found the courage to touch him. Tentatively, she rested her slender, soft white hand with its delicate, purple veins on his arm, her perfectly manicured, tapered fingers wrapping lightly around his forearm.

Mark responded by putting his hand on top of hers. After a few moments he entwined his fingers with hers. Mark's large hand with its closely clipped fingernails—for percussion of chests and pain-free palpation of abdomens—dwarfed her delicate, exquisite one. Kathleen's hand was jewel-free, pure and white. Mark's hand, the hand that held hers and returned her squeeze, the hand that wanted to touch more of her, was not so pure. That hand was adorned with a band of gold.

"Let's go out to the terrace. It's cool but the view is so spectacular," Kathleen whispered to him after a while, after they had mingled with her curious friends long enough.

But there was no view. While they had been inside the fog had come. Dense, heavy, opaque fog. They couldn't even see across the terrace.

"Evening fog!" Kathleen exclaimed, "How unusual for November."

"Oh, well," Mark murmured, putting his arm around her. "Are you cold?"

"Not with your arm around me," she answered quietly, moving closer against him. "Do you want to leave? It's almost ten."

"Well, it is a . . ." Mark paused.

"School night?" Kathleen asked quickly.

"A school night. I hate to pull you away from your friends."

"This is the first of a million pre-nuptial 'do's for Betsey and Jeff. I needed to be here, of course, but we can leave now."

Mark wanted to leave, but it was not because he had to get some sleep. He just wanted to be alone with Kathleen. He was alone with her now on the terrace, and the moment, holding her against him, talking to her, was perfect. Too perfect to disrupt.

"Whose house is this?" Mark asked.

"Jeff's parents. We told them this party was for the kids only. They're spending the night at the Stanford Court. This party will go on until dawn."

Mark wondered if Kathleen would return here after she left him.

"These are your good friends, aren't they?" Mark asked, stating the obvious. He was working up to the tougher questions. How old are you? What do you do? Who are you?

"My best friends. My childhood girlfriends and boy—My very oldest, dearest friends. We've known each other since—"

"The Katie days?" Mark asked, wondering about the boyfriends. How many of these men had been Kathleen's boyfriends? How many had she slept with? Were any current boyfriends? Who was Bill?

Kathleen could have told him if he had asked. Six. Six had been boyfriends. Real boyfriends. Man friends. She could have told him. But she might not have.

Kathleen laughed, nodding.

"Since the Katie days, yes. The Katie days were good days. I had long, black braids and made a pretty good little Katie. Then came the preppie days. We all disbanded and regrouped for the holidays and vacations. Then I was Kit—and Kit-Kat," Kathleen hesitated, then said, "and *Kitzy!* Awful."

"You prefer Kathleen."

"I do."

"So do I," Mark said. Then he asked, "Disbanded from where?"

"What? Oh. From Atherton, mostly. Some, like Jeff, from San Francisco proper. We were—are—the Carlton Club Kids. The Carlton Club is a country club in Atherton. Terribly upper crust, you know," she said, giggling, with a British accent. "Anyway, we met there as Kids, spent our summers there, riding our horses, swimming, playing tennis, going to parties and dances. Some of us went to school together, but mostly we were scattered among private schools in the United States and Switzerland."

"Rich kids."

"Oh yes," Kathleen said gaily. "You'd recognize the last names of about half the people in the house. Most of them work for, in other words *manage*, companies of the same name. Some have broken away completely of course and established themselves from scratch. Some aren't doing anything."

Mark got the distinct impression that Kathleen fell into that group. But he asked, "Do you work for the company of the same name?"

"Do you know a company with Jenkins in its name?" she asked lightly, turning in his arms so that she faced him. She looked into his eyes, her own flashing, smiling. Teasing.

"No," he answered, wanting to kiss her.

"Would you like to know what my father does?" she asked, her face close to his.

"Sure," he sighed as he felt her body pressing closer to his.

"He's the CEO—Chief Executive Officer—of an international computer and business machine company that I bet you've heard of."

"Oh?" Mark didn't care. He would kiss her. The fog made it all right. And Janet had left *him*.

Kathleen told him the name of the company as their lips met. Mark heard the name. The full effect would register later.

All he cared about now were her soft, warm hungry lips. And his. And the lovely body that pressed, molding perfectly against his. And the soft, silky hair that fell down her back as they kissed. Mark held her and kissed her, intoxicated by the smoothness of her skin, the gentle touch of her hands on his neck, the warmth of her mouth . . .

Until she began to shiver.

Mark pulled back.

"Cold?" he asked. Of course she was cold, he thought, in her sheer silk dress in the mid-summer's November fog. Despite his warm kisses and his arms around her, she was cold.

"I don't know," she said. Cold or nervous, she thought. Nervous? *Anxious?*

"You're shivering."

"I must be cold."

"Let's go in."

"Let's go in and leave."

"OK."

They drove in silence to Mark's apartment. He held her hand, releasing it only to shift gears in his vintage Volkswagen Beetle. The protected foggy mood had been disrupted by the harsh brightness inside the house and by the knowing glances of Kathleen's best friends. Knowing, slightly envious glances at their beautiful friend with her hair flowing sensuously down her back and her cheeks flushed. They *knew* why Kathleen and her tall, dark, handsome date were leaving so early. And they were a little jealous.

Kathleen's friends knew because they knew Kathleen. They knew Kathleen always got her way. Effortlessly. And they knew how much men wanted Kathleen. Always.

But as Mark and Kathleen drove in silence, holding hands, Kathleen didn't know. And Mark didn't know.

He knew he wanted her. He knew he wanted to hold her naked body against his, to kiss her, to make love to her.

Janet's words roared in his ears. "You don't even want to make love anymore. Maybe you *can't*."

Mark wanted to make love with Kathleen. More than he had wanted anything for a long time.

And Kathleen wanted to make love with Mark, but it scared her. He scared her because he wasn't a Carlton Club Kid. He took everything so seriously. He spent his days and nights saving people's lives or watching them die. He wasn't ready to give up on his marriage, and she could get hurt.

She had never felt this way—not quite *this* way—about anyone ever before.

"Would you like to come in?" he asked as he parked his VW behind her BMW. She could easily get into her car and return to the party or home or wherever Carlton Club Kids go at ten-thirty at night when the workers are sleeping.

"Sure," she said, shivering inside her camel's hair coat.

Mark's apartment was on the second floor of an old Victorian house which had been converted into apartments. Its occupants were mostly interns and residents because it was only a five-minute, albeit uphill, walk to University Hospital.

Mark held her hand as he led her up the stairs. He hadn't made a decision except that he didn't want her to leave. He heard his phone ringing as they approached the apartment. It would be Janet. He hadn't heard from her for a week. Not once, he realized, since he had met Kathleen. It could only be Janet. Leslie was on call, but she wouldn't call him on his night off. There were senior residents in the hospital to help her. It could only be Janet. He could let it ring.

Mark slowed his pace and opened the door only after the ringing had stopped. Once inside Mark unplugged the phone and turned to look at Kathleen.

"Probably Janet," she said, because she couldn't think of anything else to say. Because Janet *was* the issue, phone call or not.

"Probably. She knows I often disconnect the phone when I'm not on call," he said. "Would you like something to drink?"

"No, thank you."

Mark lifted the stack of four records that lay on the stereo turntable up the stem until they rested, poised, ready to drop one by one. Then turned on the stereo.

Neither spoke or moved until the needle met the record and the music began. In those moments Kathleen tried to guess, What will it be? Jazz? Blues? Rock and Roll? Waylon Jennings or Neil Diamond? Barbra Streisand or Beverly Sills? Mozart or the Bee Gees?

Those four records, obvious favorites, played and replayed, would tell her something new, something *else* about him.

Mark listened to the first few bars, adjusting the volume, then looked at her quizzically.

"*Scheherazade,*" Kathleen said, smiling, gazing into his eyes.

"Very good," he said, walking toward her. "Do you want to take off your coat?"

Kathleen looked up at him and said softly, bravely, "I want you to take off my coat."

And my dress, she thought, shivering again.

Mark smiled. He kissed her as he unbuttoned the leather buttons of her coat. When he had it off he held her against him, kissing her, reaching carefully for the tiny silk-covred buttons of her dress. Patiently, he began to unbutton them with one hand, the other hand buried in her soft, tangled black hair, holding her head, pulling her mouth against his.

Finally his patience faltered.

"How many buttons?" he asked.

"Too many," she answered. "Chic but not practical."

"Maybe I'm hurrying too much?"

"I think we're both in a hurry," Kathleen said. "No time to think about it."

"I have thought about it," Mark said. He had made his decision.

"You have?"

"Yes. But, still, will you help me with these damned buttons?"

"With pleasure."

Mark's bed was a double-bed mattress without box springs that lay on the

floor. The sheets were a slightly rough, cotton blend and the pillows were lumpy.

It didn't matter.

He held her lovely naked body against his slender strong one, kissing her, tracing paths all over her with his tongue, touching her, moving her, moving with her to the rhythm of the music he loved, whispering her name.

"Kathleen."

"Mark."

They smiled at each other with open eyes and closed mouths until the desire they saw in each other's eyes made them close their eyes and open their mouths. They moved together lost in the warmth of their bodies and the mood of the music and the strength of the passion.

"Oh, Mark!" she whispered urgently when the wonderful sensations began to crescendo.

"Kathleen." He felt her quickening breaths, the pounding of her heart and the rhythm of her hips. The force of her desire was as demanding as his own, under the cool silkiness of her skin.

After they made love the first time, his breathing slowed and he reluctantly moved off her so that she could breathe without his weight.

Mark whispered, "*Kitzy.*"

"You'll pay for that!"

"Really? How?"

"I'll show you in a minute. After I recover." She rolled toward him and touched his hair. "Or should I go now? It's late."

"I don't want you to go." *Ever.*

"I have to go, sometime. My parents worry if I'm not home by dawn," she said, smiling into his thoughtful brown eyes. "OK, let's see how I did."

"You know how you did. Sensational."

"No. With name-that-tune. *Scheherazade*. Then *Sleeping Beauty.* Then *Swan Lake*. Then whatever's playing now. I recognize it, but I can't name it."

"*Giselle*. It's my ballet suite. Sort of the old standbys but my favorites," he paused, then he said, "I can't believe you were paying attention."

"Listening, yes. Subliminally. Paying attention, no. How could I? You had my undivided attention." *You still do. I want to do it all over again. And again.*

"If you promise that's true, I'll go turn the stack."

"It's true. The music is nice. Sensual." He could probably make the national anthem sensual, she thought as she watched him walk, naked, into the other room. Tall. Dark. Handsome. *Naked*. The missing necessary adjective. It completed the perfect picture.

When he returned, she said, "This is for Kitzy. Hold still and enjoy."

"What?"

"Sensory overload."

"This will be punishment."

"You'll see. You have to hold still, and you'll want to move. You'll want to touch me."

"And you won't let me?"

"No. Never. Not after Kitzy."

"OK."

Kathleen did what he had done to her, kissing his entire body, tracing little circles with her warm, moist tongue and her velvet, soft fingertips over his nipples, along his thighs, between his thighs. She kept her body away from his, but her silky hair caressed his face, his chest, his abdomen and his legs as she moved, slowly, lovingly. As she kissed him in places that Janet never had. In ways that Janet never had.

When he wanted her, her whole body next to his, part of him, Kathleen came to him, eagerly, willingly. Because she wanted him, too. She didn't want to play games. Not with him.

At three o'clock she said, "This time I really am leaving."

She had tried, halfheartedly, at one. And at two. Each time she had gotten as far as the stereo, flipped the stack and, at his urging, returned to his bed.

"I don't want you to."

"I don't want to, but I have to. Besides, you're on call tonight, right?"

"Uh-huh."

"So, I'm leaving."

"OK. Not really, but OK." As she dressed, he asked. "How old are you, Kathleen?"

"Twenty-seven. How about you?"

"Twenty-seven."

She kissed him, a long, deep good-bye kiss.

As she turned to leave, he asked, "What do you do?"

"What you mean? What do I get paid to do?"

"Yes."

"Nothing," she said. "Absolutely nothing."

Mark was suddenly aware that his shower water had turned ice-cold, rudely interrupting his reverie.

Damned apartment, he thought. Although, despite its many other drawbacks, ample hot water had never been a problem.

Mark shivered as he returned to his bedroom. He glanced at his clock and learned the reason for the cold water. He had been in the shower for thirty minutes, lost in the magnificent memory of Kathleen.

The ice-cold water, the still-disconnected phone, the fact that he would be late for rounds—something he didn't tolerate in others—brought Mark abruptly back to the reality of his life.

As he rushed to get ready he thought about Janet. Now he had been unfaithful to her—something to add to the list, *her* list, of things he had done to destroy their marriage.

He had never been unfaithful before. Until last night, he had never even made love with anyone but Janet. Mark had only kissed a few girls, and they had been girls. He was sixteen when he met Janet, and after he met her there had been no one else.

Until now. Now he had been unfaithful to her. But was infidelity really an issue during a trial separation? Was it really a violation of the same magnitude? More new terms and definitions. More confusion.

More *fog*, he thought as he ran through the unseasonal, still-thick fog that lay in his path while he made his way finally, late, from the apartment to University Hospital.

As he breezed through the revolving door into the hospital's main lobby, Mark forced himself to forget about Janet and Kathleen. He had trained himself to do this. It was necessary. At work, he had to focus, without distraction, on his job, on his patients. The personal problems had to be put aside, banished from his thoughts. It was something else Janet complained about, his ability to turn his emotions off and on. His cool objectivity.

But it was something else that made him good at what he did, at being a doctor. It allowed him to give his patients undivided attention. Mark was certain that Leslie Adams had the same ability to disassociate the personal from the professional. Leslie was always professional, and she was very good at what she did.

Leslie Adams was the one woman he *could* think about in the hospital. Thinking about Leslie made Mark smile. He smiled then, despite the fact that he was twenty minutes late, as he ran up the eleven flights of stairs two steps at a time. Mark never used the hospital elevators. He was impatient with their slowness and knew the exercise, the only exercise he got, was good for him. In a thirty-six hour, oncall period, Mark traveled repeatedly between the eleventh-floor ward, the seventh-floor intensive care unit, the ground floor ER, the basement level morgue, the fourth-floor lab and the third-floor radiology suite. It gave Mark ample exercise. It showed. He was in good shape.

Leslie Adams, M.D., Mark mused.

She was a terrific intern. The best. In any other profession Leslie might have been considered compulsive to a fault, but not in medicine. In medicine compulsion was the key—compulsion balanced by good judgment—the ability to focus on the important and de-emphasize, but never *ignore*, the apparently trivial.

Too many interns couldn't see the forest for the trees. But not Leslie. She saw the big picture, but she compulsively paid attention to the details.

If she didn't know what something meant, what to make of a slightly abnormal lab value or a patient complaint that didn't seem to fit, she asked for help. For another opinion. For Mark's opinion.

"Mark," she would say, her brilliant blue eyes frowning earnestly at the patient lab data sheet. "Mr. Rolf's LDH is still elevated. It doesn't make sense. He's not hemolyzing, and his other enzymes are normal. I've checked all his meds, and none of them can do this. In every other way, he's improving . . ."

"So what's your plan?" Mark would ask, knowing that Leslie had a plan. But knowing, too, as good as she was, as solid as her judgment and instincts were, she was unsure of herself. It was something else that made her good. She listened, she learned and she asked questions when she didn't know.

Leslie Adams wasn't afraid of saying those three words that had been *verboten* in medical school: I don't know.

Leslie would make mistakes. They all would and *did*. That was the trickiness and vagary of medicine. But Leslie would never make big mistakes, never careless ones. Her mistakes would be slight errors in judgment due to inexperience or because she was fooled or misled by a symptom or sign or lab value that didn't fit and turned out to be important. Leslie's mistakes would never cause harm to a patient. They would be little errors that would damage her confidence, make her examine herself even more critically and remind her, if she would admit it, that she was human after all.

Leslie's compulsive, careful attention to detail would probably protect her from making the kind of mistake that was so serious it would drive her away from medicine. Even if she alone knew about it.

As Mark reached the sixth floor, he slowed his pace a bit.

He was late, but everything would be under control. Leslie had been on call. Everyone would be safe and sound.

Mark shook his head slightly as he thought about her, the hospital watchdog, pacing the halls all night long, warding off trouble. He guessed that was the real reason for her sleeplessness, because she believed, somehow, it would help. She had to do it. It was part of her compulsion.

Mark also knew that Leslie's calm cheeriness, almost too much at times, was only a façade. It *had* to be. Inside she was a bundle of nerves, anxiety and fatigue just like the rest of them. She probably had the same critical opinions about her colleagues, the nursing staff, the call schedule and the soft hits that they all did. She just withheld comment. They were all critical, hypercritical, of themselves and of each other. They were all perfectionists at heart, suddenly confronted with the imperfect, imprecise, nonscientific realities of the practice of medicine.

Leslie and Janet were friends. Mark wondered what Leslie thought of him. Of course she knew what had happened between him and Janet. And why. Leslie probably had more insight into his marriage than he did. Did she think he was as despicable as Janet did? Probably. Compulsive, critical Leslie wouldn't be very tolerant of the sort of behavior Janet attributed to him.

But if Leslie felt only contempt for him as a human being it didn't show. In fact, in the past month, she had seemed almost sympathetic, as if she knew, understood, and didn't judge. Or was she just overcompensating because she felt guilty about her real *critical* feelings?

She probably doesn't think about it—me—at all, Mark decided. Leslie, the true professional.

As he rounded the corner onto the ward, Mark saw his team—two medical students and two interns, Leslie and Greg—circled around the chart rack. Mark saw Leslie before she saw him. She was looking at her watch and frowning, concerned but not annoyed.

Then Greg saw Mark and said, "Chief, ho!"

Leslie looked up quickly and smiled. Her sapphire-blue eyes sparkled with a look of relief above the dark circles, the tell-tale signs of her sleepness night.

Chapter 4

Janet Louise Wells was born at noon on Christmas Day, 1953. She was born in her parents' small, snowbound farmhouse five miles west of Kearney, Nebraska, and one hundred thirty miles west of Lincoln where six months earlier her future husband, Mark David Taylor, had been born on a hot humid day in July.

Janet was a perfect baby, then a perfect child, then a perfect teenager. Her cheerfulness and serenity were pervasive and genuine. Everyone liked her. It was impossible not to like the pretty girl with the spun-gold hair, clear, gray eyes and ready, flawless smile. Janet made friends easily because she smiled and was so pretty.

And because she shared her toys. Possessiveness was not in Janet's nature. Generosity was. She was noncompetitive. She threatened no one. Janet spent the first sixteen years of her life genuinely content with her life on the tiny farm, attending the small rural school, baking with her mother, sewing with her grandmother and playing with her friends.

And singing.

Janet loved to sing. No one knew how much she loved it. They heard her sing in the church choir and admired her clear, lovely voice. There were no music classes at her school, no choral groups, no band.

It didn't matter to Janet. She preferred to sing by herself anyway. She didn't need or care about an audience. In the late afternoon, after school and before dinner, she would run to the far corner of her father's cornfield, and she would sing.

Janet sang anything and everything. She learned the songs by listening to records and to the radio. She learned the tunes instantly and the lyrics after listening only a few times. Janet preferred musicals. She would sing every song in order. Telling the story. Living the story.

If Janet was possessive about anything it was her private time in the cornfields. Without it she would not have been so content. Or so generous. Or so happy.

On July 11, 1969, the day Mark David Taylor celebrated his sixteenth birthday, Harold Wells told his fifteen-and-a-half-year-old daughter and his twin thirteen-year-old sons that they were selling the farm, they had no choice, and were moving to Lincoln.

Janet entered Lincoln High School that fall as a junior. She left her class of sixteen students, her best friends in Kearney, and entered a class of three hundred students in which the groups and cliques had been firmly established since winter of the sophomore year.

Janet was an outsider because of timing and because of who she was: a country girl in a city.

Janet wouldn't have minded being alone, being an outsider, if she had been able to have privacy, but her new home was an apartment with no yard. She had no cornfields. She had no place to escape.

No place to sing.

Janet met Mark on the first day of school. If Mark hadn't been junior class president, and if he hadn't appointed himself in charge of orienting the new juniors, he and Janet would never have met. Mark's crowd, the achievement-oriented, scholar athletes and their aggressive, confident female companions would have been inaccessible, and probably unknown, to Janet.

There were twenty new entering juniors. Mark led them around the three-story, brick building through the cafeteria to the study halls, the gym, the student lounge and the library. Mark gave the tour cheerfully, enthusiastically, trying to make them all feel comfortable and welcome. But his mind was on Janet.

Mark had never seen eyes so clear or so big or so gray. Or hair quite so blond and silky. Or a smile so demure and beautiful.

"I'll show you to your home room," Mark said to her after the tour was over.

"Oh. OK. Thank you," she said quietly, her eyes meeting his directly without embarrassment.

Janet walked silently beside Mark, not fidgeting, not anxious, not even, apparently, trying to think of something to say. Mark found Janet's silence strangely peaceful.

Except that he wanted to find out about her.

"You're from Kearney?"

"Near Kearney."

"Do you like Lincoln?"

"No. Not really," she said calmly without breaking her stride.

Her words made Mark stop. Lincoln was his home. He *loved* Lincoln.

"You don't? Why not?"

Janet stopped when Mark stopped and looked up at him with her smoky gray eyes.

"No cornfields," she said. "I miss the cornfields."

"Lincoln is surrounded by cornfields!"

"I miss *our* cornfield," Janet replied simply.

Within two months, Mark had retrieved his class pin from Sara, a smart pretty cheerleader, and was dating Janet. Mark couldn't tell how Janet felt about him. He was used to girls flirting with him, teasing him and sending him clear, interpretable signals.

Janet sent no signals; but she always said yes when he asked her out, and she always seemed happy when they were together. Janet spoke little, smiled a lot and listened attentively when Mark spoke.

Being with Janet made Mark realize how hard he and his friends were trying. They were all trying to prove, beyond a doubt, that they were what they believed themselves to be: the best student, the best quarterback, the best actress, the best-looking or the best personality.

The Best.

Janet didn't try. She didn't care about being the best. Janet was Janet. And Mark loved being with her.

After a while he stopped trying to impress her. He didn't need to. She knew who he was, and she liked him.

Janet made things for him. He would find chocolate chip cookies in his locker. Or a hand-knit muffler. Or a hand-made card, cleverly decorated, a thank you for a special date. Mark loved Janet's presents. They were reminders of Janet, of the peace and happiness he felt when he was with her. That peace, the peacefulness of being with Janet, balanced the relentless pressure of the rest of his life.

Pressure. Pressure to be the best. Pressure to be a doctor—to be the *best* doctor. Pressure not to disappoint anyone, especially his father, and pressure to live up to his magnificent potential.

Janet's life, briefly filled with an unfamiliar turmoil of its own when her family moved to Lincoln, became peaceful because of Mark. And because of her music. Janet discovered that although she no longer had her own private stage, her father's cornfield, the big city offered intriguing new outlets for her singing.

There were music classes. Janet took as many as her schedule would allow. And choral groups—Janet joined them all. The music teachers instantly recognized her talent. Raw, untrained talent. They were intrigued by the pretty, blond girl with the lovely, haunting voice.

The other girls in the school who sang and acted and vied for solos in the choral groups and for leads in the school musical productions promptly recognized Janet as a foe. She was another competitor in an already overcrowded, competitive group, a group in which everyone wanted to be the best.

Janet didn't want to compete, but she wanted to sing. She was unruffled by audiences and unflattered by the praises of the teachers.

The strong loveliness of her voice—so rich, so sensuous, so moving—amazed Mark when he heard her sing, finally, in January. Always before, her singing engagements had conflicted with one of his many commitments.

Mark kissed her after the performance that night. It was their first kiss although they had been dating for almost four months. When Mark kissed her, Janet put her arms around his neck, stretched her fingers into his dark brown hair and pulled his mouth deep into hers.

After that they kissed often. Long, quiet, passionate kisses that filled Mark with great peace and made him forget, for a moment, the pressures of his life.

Mark wanted Janet to sing for him when they were alone.

"Find me a cornfield and I'll sing for you anytime."

Mark found a cornfield for them five miles outside of Lincoln. They found a private distant corner where they could lie together, holding each other, kissing each other, and where she coud sing just for him.

Mark's competitiveness, his need to be the best, was so inbred that he couldn't stand to see anyone bypass a chance for success. A chance to be the best. A star. So, it was *his* fault that Janet auditioned for the lead in Lincoln High School's production of *South Pacific* that spring. It was her fault, because of her talent, that she won the part. As Nellie, Janet got to "wash that man right outta my hair," to be as "corny as Kansas in August" and to sing a lovely, romantic, moving duet about "some enchanted evening."

Janet was a sensation. The standing ovations, the rave reviews in the Lincoln newspapers, the sell-out performances were all testimony to her marvelous, captivating talent.

But Janet's success made some people squirm. Who the hell does she think she is? the girls who dated Mark's friends, who considered Mark one of *theirs*, wondered. It was amazing enough that the quiet, country hick could seduce Mark into leaving lively, vivacious Sara. "She has to be putting out!" they hissed. And now Janet had virtually stolen the lead from another one of *them*.

It was too pushy. Too nervy. Didn't the country girl know her place?

Janet's success also made Mark's parents squirm. From the beginning they hoped this unfortunate *liaison* would pass, that Mark would outgrow Janet's country naiveté or get bored with her passivity. As the months passed, they were afraid he wouldn't. For the first time in his life, Mark countered their incessant plans for his future with plans of his own.

"Won't it be wonderful when you finish your residency and return to join your father in practice? You'll probably want to live nearby. In the country club, maybe."

Mark had been hearing plans like that for years. Usually he made no comment, silently acknowledging his parents' words with a taciturn nod. Now, because of Janet, he had plans of his own, and his parents didn't like what they heard.

"Janet and I are going to live outside of town. In the country. I won't mind commuting."

That made his parents squirm. As they watched their maybe-future-daughter-in-law prance around the stage in skimpy outfits, they squirmed even more. It was all so undignified. So improper.

Of course they hadn't minded watching Sara Johnston, daughter of Lincoln's best general surgeon, leading cheers at the football and basketball games. They wouldn't have minded having Sara as their daughter-in-law. In fact, that was what they had planned.

Janet detected the Taylors' disapproval of her almost immediately.

"Why don't your folks like me?" she asked. She did not say, "I don't think your folks like me," or, "I wonder if . . ." Janet asked, as a matter of fact, why they didn't like her.

"They had plans for me and Sara," Mark said. "Daughter of leading surgeon and son of leading internist, himself destined to be the leading internist. That sort of thing."

The best with the best, Janet mused.

Janet didn't like Mark's parents, either. She knew, although she and Mark never discussed it, that his father was the driving force behind Mark's obsession with success and achievement. Janet resented Dr. Taylor for it. She resented the pressure on Mark.

Mark loved Janet's performance in *South Pacific*. Janet loved it, too. She learned that she loved something more than just the singing. She loved performing. She loved the audience. She loved sharing her talent and her joy.

During the last month of their junior year in high school, Mark was elected student body president and give Janet his class pin and his letter sweater. And he kissed her breasts for the first time.

They lay in their cornfield on a balmy spring night, softly lighted by the vernal moon. They had kissed, without talking, for an hour. Slowly, Mark lowered his hand over her blouse, then gently slipped his fingers between the buttons, touching her soft skin. Then he carefully unbuttoned a button, trying to sense her reaction, hoping she wouldn't resist, knowing he would stop if she did.

Janet didn't resist. She moved closer to him. She helped him unbutton her blouse and unfasten her bra. Then she lay beneath him, her naked chest silhouetted in the spring moonlight.

Mark looked at her beautiful cream-colored breasts—young and fresh—waiting to be kissed, gently, roughly, every way, for hours and hours. Wordlessly Janet pulled his soft lips to her round, warm breasts.

A year later, after they had both been accepted to the University of Nebraska in Lincoln, after Mark had been named class valedictorian and after Janet had triumphed as Maria in the school production of *The Sound of Music*, they made love for the first time.

They had never discussed it. They had spent the past year holding each other and kissing each other. Bare chested. Nothing more. But that night, in their secluded cornfield under the same springtime moon that had shone on them a year before, Mark removed all her clothes. Then his. He watched the clear, gray eyes that squeezed tight for a brief moment as he entered her, then opened, smiling, as she wrapped her legs tightly around him and moved quietly, quickly with him.

"I love you," he told her afterwards. It was the first time he had told her that. He repeated joyfully, "I love you, Janet."

"I love you too, Mark."

During the four years at the University of Nebraska—home of the Cornhuskers—in Lincoln, Mark lived in the Phi Delta Theta fraternity. It was the same fraternity his father had pledged. Mark got A's in all his courses. He took the required pre-med courses: biology, physics, inorganic and organic chemistry and calculus. But he majored in English. Mark's favorite course was English literature.

Janet lived at home. She performed in all the University musical productions. She earned A's—and one A plus—in her music, dance and acting classes and B's and C's in her other classes. Janet took typing and secretarial skills classes because they seemed practical. Her favorite class was dance. The music courses added little, except exposure, to her natural singing talent, but the dance classes taught her something she didn't know, something she needed to know to win the roles she wanted. Janet was years behind the students who had started ballet at age five, but she had aptitude and energy.

Mark and Janet made love often, at least three or four times a week. Over eight hundred times before their wedding night, Janet calculated during a lecture on shorthand in the spring of her senior year. They didn't experiment in their lovemaking. They made love in the same way, the traditional way, quietly, passionately, every time. They never talked about it. There was nothing to discuss. It was completely satisfying for both of them.

Mark and Janet were married two weeks after graduation. Mark's parents paid for the entire wedding because it *had* to be held at the Riverwoods Country club, and they *had* to invite four hundred guests. Janet's parents didn't belong to Riverwoods, and they couldn't have afforded a wedding of any size.

Janet almost balked.

"What will we owe them, your parents, in return for this?" she asked. Mark had already told her he would not, could not, accept his father's offer to pay for his medical school tuition at any medical school in the country. Mark's father wanted Mark to attend Harvard Medical School, but Mark only applied to one medical school, the one with the lowest tuition because of his state residency, the University of Nebraska in Omaha. Mark refused his father's offer to pay for his medical education because what if he, *they*, decided not to return to Lincoln to practice after all?

"It will put us into debt, Janet, but I can work the first two summers," he said.

"And I'll be working. We'll manage. I don't want you to take the money from your father, either."

In response to Janet's question about the debt for their wedding, Mark said, "We're doing *them* the favor. They want this social event, and we're agreeing to participate. I just hope you don't mind too much. Or your parents."

"It's such a terrible waste of money, but if I stand in the way of it they'll dislike me even more. If that's possible. All I want is to marry you and leave Lincoln."

During the weeks before the wedding, Janet was unusually quiet in the presence of Mark's mother. She wanted to avoid any scenes or unpleasantness. They had already had a confrontation about the rings. Janet stood firm on few issues because all she really wanted was Mark. The whole process was simply a means to an end.

But Janet stood firm about the rings.

"I want eighteen-carat gold bands. Plain and simple," she explained to her future mother-in-law.

"Eighteen carat is so soft! It loses its shine."

"I know, Mrs. Taylor. That's why I like it. It ages, matures, with the marriage."

Janet's parents wore eighteen-carat gold bands. Their bands were scuffed and battered, but still golden like their marriage that had weathered the trials and joys of their twenty-five years together. Janet hoped her marriage to Mark would be as durable, as wonderful despite the hardships, as her parents'. Janet wanted bands like theirs. For luck.

Janet won that battle and secured her victory by quickly ordering the rings. They were engraved with their initials, the date and a single word: *Always*.

Mrs. Taylor persisted. An eighteen-carat gold band could be overlooked if the diamond was set properly.

"Have you and Mark chosen a diamond? You should probably get one of at least a carat."

"Diamonds are so expensive!" So frivolous, Janet thought, at a time when they knew they would be going into debt. Even if money wasn't an issue, Janet wouldn't have wanted one.

"We'll buy it for you. Or lend Mark the money to be repaid on your twentieth anniversary. Or"—Janet watched Mrs. Taylor almost choke on the next words—"you could have my mother's diamond. I'm sure she would have wanted Mark's wife to have it. It's almost two carats, emerald cut, flaw—"

"No, thank you. No diamond. Really, I'm just not the type."

Not the type is right, Mrs. Taylor thought. Not Mark's type. Not our type. And she won't let us make her better.

"With just the two plain gold bands," Mark's mother persevered, "it looks like a *shotgun* wedding. You know, dear, like you *have* to get married."

"We do have to get married, Mrs. Taylor," Janet said as she leveled her eyes, steel gray and serious, at her future mother-in-law's startled, blinking ones. Janet added, softly, carefully, "We have to get married because we love each other."

Chapter 5

During Mark's first two years of medical school, Janet worked as a secretary-receptionist in a neurosurgeon's office all day and had dinner ready for Mark when he got home from his afternoon classes. Mark spent most evenings at the library or in the anatomy lab, and Janet spent her evenings performing in community theater productions. She and Mark arrived home about midnight, made love and fell asleep.

During Mark's third and fourth years when he was on the wards, doing clerkships, being on call with his team, his schedule was erratic and unpredictable. If Janet was gone in the evenings, she might go for days without really seeing him. Janet decided to stop performing. It was an easy decision. She wanted to be with Mark whenever she could. Still, she missed it.

On March fifteenth of his fourth year, Mark learned that he matched for an internal medicine internship at the University of California in San Francisco. It was his first choice. Two months later, he learned that he would graduate from medical school with highest honors.

Two weeks before graduation, Mark's moodiness, the moodiness that would ultimately drive them apart, first surfaced.

Janet had seen glimpses of it in high school, when the pressure got too great, and his father talked about Mark hanging out his shingle below *his*, and when Mark told her how much he enjoyed his English classes.

But in high school and in college and until the final weeks of medical school, Mark's moodiness had been infrequent and curable. Janet could cure it. Mark would come to her, kiss her, hold her and make love to her. He would feel better.

The moodiness that began six weeks before his internship was different. It didn't go away so easily. It seemed more resistant to her love. For the sixteen months between the end of medical school and the day that Janet told him she had to get away from him, the moodiness increased until it became a dark constant presence. And it was aggravated by fatigue and pressure and his compulsion to be the best.

Mark immersed himself in medicine.

Even though he hates it, Janet decided, finally, after endless months of watching his torment.

She was convinced that Mark hated medicine, even though he did it well, even though he was the *best*. When she suggested to him, gently, carefully, that he didn't like what he was doing, Mark became incensed. He loved medicine, he answered swiftly. Didn't she know that?

No. She knew just the opposite.

So Janet hated medicine for him. She hated every part of it: the sick patients, the relentless call schedule, the arrogant, competitive residents (his *friends*), the compulsive personalities. Janet hated it for both of them. And, little by little, because Mark was on the other side, because he was one of *them*, because he defended *them* and *it*, Janet began to hate him, too.

It tore them apart because they both hated it, but Mark wouldn't admit it.

And because she couldn't comfort him, love him, out of his moods anymore.

Mark arrived home at four o'clock that Sunday afternoon, October fifth, fifteen months after his internship had started. He hadn't been on call. He had just been in the hospital since early morning making rounds with his team. He had slept eight hours the night before. Janet knew. She had watched him sleep as she lay awake, tormented, trying to decide what to do.

Talk, she decided. Talk to him when he was rested. She watched him sleep. He would be rested.

Janet paced, herself exhausted, until she heard him return.

"Hi," Mark said absently as he walked in the door and past her. Preoccupied, as usual.

"Mark?"

"What?" he snapped, startled.

Usually she just left him alone.

"We have to talk."

"About what?" he asked suspiciously.

He, they, had declared a moratorium on discussions about whether he really liked medicine. That had been six months ago. They hadn't discussed it since.

"Our marriage."

"Our *marriage?*"

That was a new topic. They had never discussed their marriage. What was there to discuss?

"OK," he said tentatively.

"It's in trouble, Mark," Janet said carefully. It's over, she thought. But, maybe, she was wrong. Maybe he could make her change the way she felt. If he really cared. If he really loved her.

"What do you mean?"

"I mean we don't have anything to do with each other anymore."

"Come on, Janet. We're together every second that I'm not at the hospital."

"We're in the same house. We're not together."

"This is ridiculous. I have no idea what you're talking about. I'm too tired—" Mark started to leave the room.

"Goddamn you!" Janet shouted.

"Janet!"

"Listen to me, Mark, *please*. I hate this. I hate our life. I hate that you never touch me anymore. I hate your friends and medicine. And I know that you do, too." Janet held up her hand to stop him from interrupting. "You just won't admit it. I cannot live like this."

"Like what?"

"Hating the man I married. Not knowing you. Not being able to touch you. Having you pull away when I try. Not being able to talk to you. Not being able to comfort you."

"*Comfort* me?"

"Oh, Mark," Janet said softly as tears filled her gray eyes. "You don't have any idea what I'm talking about, do you?"

"No," he said honestly, his voice tired, "I don't. I can't believe that you hate me, Janet."

"I do, Mark. I'm really afraid that I do," Janet said as the hot tears spilled onto her cheeks. "I love the man I married so much. But this other man, this man I don't know . . ."

"I love you, Janet," he said weakly, almost mechanically.

"Do you, Mark? When was the last time you touched me? I'm sure you don't know. It was four months ago. You used to want to make love with me all the time. Now all you care about—pretend to care about—is medicine. You don't even want to make love anymore. Maybe you *can't?*"

"Janet!" Mark's shock was quickly replaced by anger. "You knew this wouldn't be easy. You knew that these years would be hard, the hardest. That I would be tired. That I wouldn't feel like making love every night."

"Four months, Mark."

"But nothing else has changed—"

"Everything else has changed. I could live with you forever, never make love with you again, if I believed that I made a difference to you. That I was part of your life."

"You are. You do."

"No. I used to be. But not anymore. You've shut me out. You are moody and angry and unhappy, and you won't share it with me."

"I am not."

"You don't even know," Janet said sadly, defeated.

"I am tired. This is hard work. That is all."

"No."

"Yes," Mark sighed. "Janet, this is so classic. This is why doctors' marriages fall apart. This is what happens. Don't let it happen to us."

"I'm not complaining about your call schedule or that you fall asleep during dinner or that you work on Christmas. That isn't what this is all about."

"But you *do* complain about those things."

"I *note* those things. They are annoying, but they don't end marriages. At least they wouldn't end mine."

"*End?*"

"End, Mark. You are not listening. I don't believe that you love me anymore."

"I do."

Janet sighed. Mark hated medicine and said he loved it. What did it mean when he said he loved her? He probably didn't even know.

"I don't feel loved."

"That's your problem," he said coldly.

"Maybe it is. When you don't feel loved, when *I* don't feel loved, I begin to hate myself. Look at me, Mark. I'm fat. I've gained twenty pounds in the past six months."

Janet had always been slender, fit. When she danced, she had no fat on her sleek, trim body. Twenty pounds didn't make Janet less beautiful, but it made her feel terrible. She was enveloped in a heavy thickness which, more than anything, was an ever present symbol of how unhappy she was.

"You look fine." Mark's tone reflected annoyance. He was tired of this conversation. He had other things to worry about. What was Janet's problem?

"Mark," she said finally, standing in front of him, trembling with rage and frustration. "Listen to me, damn you. I am leaving you. I cannot stand being with you anymore. I cannot stand hating myself and hating you."

"I don't believe you."

"Believe me."

Janet went into the bedroom and returned almost immediately with two heavy, obviously packed, suitcases.

"Janet—" Mark stood up.

"I have to leave, Mark. I am suffocating."

"Where are you going?"

"I have reservations at a motel tonight. It's near. I can take a taxi. Tomorrow I'll find an apartment near the office or on a bus line. You need the car."

Their rented house on Twin Peaks was on a bus line. It was an easy commute for Janet to the real estate office where she worked as a receptionist.

"Janet, don't leave. Can't we talk about it?"

"We've just been talking about it, and it's obvious that we can't talk. We can't communicate. We can't even agree on what has happened to us."

"Nothing has happened to us," Mark said firmly.

"You see!" Janet yelled in frustration. "Nothing has happened except that I hate you and myself and I'm leaving."

They stared at each other, glowering, for a moment.

"I'll leave," Mark said finally, angrily.

"No, why?"

"Because this is your home. You fixed it up. I couldn't stand being here without you. And I couldn't stand being blamed for hurting you even more by displacing you from your home," he said acidly.

"*Our* home."

"Not anymore apparently. Will it ever be again, Janet?"

"I don't know, Mark. I hope so."

He tossed the car keys at her, too hard, too fast. They hit her hand then the floor.

"Get out of here for an hour, will you, so I can pack in peace? Then bring the car back and I'll leave."

Janet called Leslie later that night.

"He's gone, Les," Janet said, tears streaming down her cheeks.

"Gone?"

"I was going to leave but he insisted."

"Oh, Janet, I am so sorry."

"It's what I thought, what I was afraid, would happen."

"I know. But still . . ." Leslie hesitated. "Do you want me to come over, now?"

"Yes. If you're not too tired."

Leslie met Janet at the Department of Medicine party held in mid-July at the Yacht Club. By then, three weeks into her internship, Leslie had worked daily—twenty-four hours a day—with Mark. She had worked with him, talked to him, laughed with him, and already, she had *fallen in love* with him.

Leslie was curious to see the woman whom Mark had chosen to be his wife, the woman Mark loved. Leslie hadn't expected to like her, not *really*. But as she and Janet talked that night, and as they spent time together over the summer when Mark was on call, they became friends. Good friends, caring friends, friends in spite of the fact that Janet was Mark's wife . . . Because, despite her friendship with Janet, Leslie's feelings for Mark didn't change. They just remained hidden, deep in a part of her that no one would ever know, where they belonged.

"I love your house!" Leslie said the first time she visited Mark's and Janet's rental on Twin Peaks one evening while Mark was working.

From the outside the small house looked like every other little box on the block—square, bland, off-white stucco—but inside it was cheery and cozy and unique. Janet had made it that way, decorating it with quaint pretty pictures of country scenes and with colorful, intricate needlepoint pillows and hooked rugs that she had made.

"It's so homey," Leslie said, genuinely impressed. Mark must look forward to coming home, she thought. Leslie paused in each of the five rooms. She spent the most time in Mark's study, the second of two bedrooms. In it hung his diplomas, his Alpha Omega Alpha certificate, a huge red and white Nebraska Cornhuskers banner, their wedding picture and dozens of other photos of their life together arranged in a beautiful, colorful collage.

"Mark David Taylor, M.D.," Leslie observed, studying Mark's medical school diploma. "M.D.T., M.D. Kind of catchy. Mark never uses his middle initial."

"He probably doesn't want to be reminded," Janet said with surprising coldness. "I'm sure that Mark's father, Dr. Taylor, had M.D. on his mind the moment Mark was born and pronounced male."

"Oh!"

"He's not a nice man, Mark's father," Janet said distantly, wondering what role Mark's father was playing in Mark's moods and in the destruction of her marriage.

"Oh."

Leslie spent time, when she was off and Mark was on, exploring San Francisco with Janet. And she spent the time when she was on working, *being*, with Mark. Admiring him . . .

One night in August she said to him, quietly, almost under her breath, "You know so much. It's so wonderful."

She might as well have said, "You're so wonderful."

Mark laughed.

"Leslie Adams, you are suffering from the intern-on-resident crush syndrome!" he said amiably.

Leslie blushed. Then, as she thought about what she had said—What if he guesses how I feel about him?—she turned pale.

"Hey, Leslie, I'm flattered," Mark said quickly, sensing her uneasiness, unaware of its cause. "Not many people think I walk on water. It makes me feel good. I plan to enjoy it while it lasts. Next week when you start working with Adam Russell you'll have a crush on him—all the facts he knows—and forget all about me."

For a moment, Mark wanted to tousle her chestnut curls and erase the troubled look from her large, serious blue eyes. But, instead of touching her, he smiled. It worked. Leslie smiled back. A tentative, awkward smile. But a smile nonetheless.

Oh Mark, she thought, I don't have a crush on your medical know-how, even though it's spectacular. I have a crush on *you*. And it's not a crush.

Leslie quietly ached for Mark, wanting him, dreaming about him, knowing that he was happily married to the woman who was becoming her closest friend. Sometimes Leslie was tempted to tell Janet. They would laugh about it. Janet would say gaily that, as much as she liked her, Leslie couldn't have Mark. He was taken.

But Leslie didn't mention it. It wasn't something she could laugh about. Not yet.

Janet wouldn't have laughed, either. She was suffering, aching, too. She knew that her marriage—which had been decaying for over a year—was now, finally, in its death throes.

By the time the summer fog lifted, by mid-September, Leslie's mind was clear on the subject of Mark. Leslie had made it clear, had forced herself to admit the impossibility, the silliness, of her feelings for Mark. Mark was a wonderful man. He was married to, in love with, a wonderful woman.

It was clear. The fog was gone. Now maybe she could tell Janet about it. And they could laugh.

On September twelfth Janet made a cake—a fabulous cake decorated with evergreen trees and snow-capped mountains in honor of Leslie's home in Seattle—for Leslie's twenty-sixth birthday. As Leslie watched her, friend serve the almost-too-beautiful-to-eat cake, she was tempted to tell Janet about how she felt—how she *had* felt—about Mark.

But Janet spoke first. Janet told Leslie about her marriage to Mark. About the marriage that she believed was over.

Leslie listened, quietly, her heart pounding, her mind spinning. *Don't ask me for advice, Janet. I don't even know if I can be impartial. I care about him too much.*

Not that Mark showed a flicker of interest in *her.* He praised her. He told her she was an excellent intern, and he teased her, gently, about her compulsive behavior. Mark treated Leslie the way an older, wiser brother treats his little sister. Teasing, fond, a little protective.

Even if Mark was free, even if his marriage to Janet was doomed to fail, it didn't mean he would fall in love with Leslie.

Leslie shuddered. Janet *was* her friend. That was the reality. The rest was fantasy.

Leslie had to help Janet. She had to help her save her marriage. Leslie listened in amazement and disbelief to what Janet told her.

Janet told her that Mark hated medicine.

"Oh, no, Janet. Mark doesn't hate it. Not any more than we all do. We all hate being exhausted and cooped up and feeling our lives passing by. We all feel that we're missing something during all those hours we spend in the hospital. It's a natural feeling. It's something we talk about."

"I think he hates it more than the rest of you."

"I don't see it, Janet. I really don't. And I work with him. Mark's a wonderful doctor. The best."

The Best. The words hit Janet like a knife. Of course Mark was the best.

"He's so moody and irritable," Janet continued.

"Mark? Not at work. Oh, he gets annoyed like we all do when we get inappropriate admissions or when the blood-draw team says they can't find a vein or when the X ray misses the area of pathology altogether. Our work situation is full of frustrations."

"You don't think he's sullen or angry?"

"No. But I haven't actually worked with him, on the same team, since mid-August. Maybe something has happened—"

"No. It isn't new. It's just getting worse. It's been going on for over a year."

Janet started to cry. "Maybe it isn't medicine, after all. Maybe what he really hates is coming home to me."

"No, *Janet*. Mark talks about you all the time. Things like, 'Here are cookies Janet made for the team' or 'Janet says we all should read *Heartsounds*' or 'I told Janet I'd be home by eight. I'm going to try.' "

Janet shook her head, still crying. She knew what Mark was like when he got home. It didn't help to hear that he seemed all right at work. It made it worse.

"I can't live with him anymore, Leslie. Not feeling the way I do. Not living the way we do."

"*Talk* to him, Janet. Mark is a reasonable, gentle, kind man," Leslie said softly.

Janet's wet gray eyes opened wide.

"I admit it, Janet. I think Mark's terrific," Leslie said truthfully. Then she added, "I think you both are."

Two and a half weeks later after Janet and Mark had their talk and Mark had left, Leslie sat once again in her friend's kitchen.

"How did you leave it?"

"What? Oh. We think for a week. Then we talk again next Sunday night. Go from there."

"It will probably work out."

"Not unless he suddenly gets some insight. We're million miles apart. Or maybe I'm just crazy," Janet said grimly.

"You're not crazy. You're not inventing this unhappiness. It's real. I just hope you two can work it out," Leslie said, realizing how much she meant it.

Mark and Janet belonged together.

Chapter 6

The November fog lasted through the weekend, thick in the morning and evening, clearing during the day. It had resettled by the time Mark left the hospital at six Saturday evening. To him the outside world hadn't changed a bit since he'd rushed to work, late, thirty-four hours before.

The phone was ringing when he entered his apartment. It was Janet.

"Hi, Mark."

"Hi."

"I think we should meet and talk." It was the first time in their five week separation that Janet suggested they see each other.

"All right."

"Can you come to dinner tomorrow night?"

"Not dinner. After. At seven. OK?"

"OK."

After he hung up, Mark called Kathleen. Her father answered.

"Hello, Mr. Jenkins," C.E.O. of . . . unbelievable, Mark thought. "This is Mark Taylor. How is Mrs. Jenkins?"

"Very well, thank you. They're going to turn her loose, to use Kathleen's phrase, next Tuesday."

"Great. Uh, is Kathleen there?"

"No, sorry. She's away for the weekend. Due back Monday evening. How did you like the party Thursday?"

"Very much. A little out of my league, but everyone was very nice." The nicest part was making love to your daughter, Mark mused.

"The Carlton Club Kids are their own league. Kathleen said you really held your own."

"Oh, she did? Well . . ."

"Shall I tell her you called?"

"Please. Have her call me if she wants to."

"She'll want to."

"Give my best to Mrs. Jenkins."

"Sure will. Thanks, Mark."

He is such a nice, low key man, Mark thought. A nice, low key C.E.O. of one of the world's largest and most powerful corporations.

Mark arrived at Janet's, at his and Janet's house, promptly at seven.

He drew a sharp breath when he saw her. She looked exactly the way she had looked when they met eleven years before: thin, wide-eyed, young, trusting. In five weeks Janet had lost all the weight she had gained. Maybe more. Her slender face made her huge gray eyes seem even larger. Her gaunt cheeks gave her a haunted, haunting look.

"You look great," he said.

"Thanks." She smiled. "Come in."

"Thanks."

"Do you want some coffee?"

"Sure. Please."

How long can we keep this up? she wondered. The careful politeness.

They sat in the living room. It looked the same. Janet had done nothing to move him out. His possessions and her possessions. *Their* possessions. Mark noticed with surprise that Janet didn't wear her ring. Mark still wore his, although he might, *would*, have removed it before his date with Kathleen. If he had remembered.

Had Janet been dating? he wondered. Had she made love with someone else, too?

"You look just like you looked the day we met," Mark said finally, gently.

"Do I? I feel better now. About the way I look."

"How about everything else?"

"I don't know. How do you feel?"

"I still don't understand," he said slowly. "Maybe I have been more distant and preoccupied. I didn't realize we hadn't made love for four months."

"You were so moody at home. Leslie says you're not that way at work."

"Leslie? We shouldn't get her in the middle of this," Mark said with an edge to his voice.

"I know. I *agree*."

"I don't think I'm moody at work or at home."

"There are days when you come home and don't even speak to me. At all. And when I try to touch you, you pull away."

"Not many days."

"Many, many days. Day after day. Night after night."

They sat in silence for a long time, an eternity of thoughts and memories and questions without answers.

He could have walked over to her and held her and made love to her, but he didn't. He couldn't. He didn't know who she was. She was the woman who had yelled at him in a rage a month before, but she looked like the sixteen-year-old girl with girl with whom he had fallen in love eleven years ago. She was the woman, not the girl. He didn't know her.

He had to find the old Janet. To retrace the steps. Then he could go to her. He wanted to go to her. To Janet. To his Janet.

"Do you remember the first time we made love?" he asked without looking at her.

"Of course," she answered, tears flooding her eyes.

Mark looked at her then, his own eyes glistening.

"What were you thinking?"

"What?"

"What were you thinking when we made love? It was a big step and we never talked about it. What were you thinking?"

"I was thinking what I always thought when you touched me," she said very quietly. "I was thinking, I love you. I love you."

"*Janet*," he said emotionally. But still he couldn't move to her. He looked at his hand and the scuffed, eighteen carat gold band he had worn for the past five years. "Why aren't you wearing your ring?"

"Because the ring is a symbol of you, of us. It means we're together. I have to feel how it would be without you. To feel the loss."

"How does it feel?"

"Awful. Empty. Sad." A small part relief, she thought. She didn't want to think *that*, but it was there. In her mind. In her heart. A part of the way she felt.

"So we should try again."

Janet nodded, crying.

"No?" he asked, confused.

"Yes. But it's still too soon. We are here, crying because we can remember how much we loved each other eleven years ago, but we can't even touch each other now."

"But we both want to try, don't we? I do," Mark said.

"Yes."

"I have clinics in December."

"*Clinics?*"

"It's new. To give everyone a break. Nine to five on week-days. No night call. No weekends. No holidays. I'll be off for Christmas, for your birthday. Should I move back in then? In three weeks?" Mark asked carefully.

"OK," Janet said believing it would never work. Not now. Not in three weeks. Not ever. But they had to try. She had to try. Maybe she was wrong.

Kathleen called Tuesday night.

"I learned something about you," she began.

"Kathleen!"

"Yes."

"What did you learn?"

"You told me you went to the University of Nebraska in Lincoln, right?"

"Yes."

"Then, what I learned is that you're a cornhusk."

"Cornhusk*er!*"

"No, those are the other guys. You're a cornhusk. Or you have a corn—"

"Kathleen, it's not even close to what you think it is."

"I know, but it sounds like it should be, doesn't it?"

"I don't think you can discuss such things over public airways."

"Wireways."

"*Any*ways."

Silence.

"So, you rang?" she asked, finally.

"I did. To thank you for Thursday."

"You're welcome."

"And," Mark hesitated, "I was going to ask you out . . ."

"But?" she asked, disappointed.

"A new development in the trial separation."

"Oh."

"A trial reunion."

"Is she there?"

"No. We don't start until December first."

"Oh. *Strange*. In the meantime?"

"In the meantime, I just have to think about it." I can't see you Kathleen, Mark thought. I can't.

"What *do* you think?"

"I think it's an eleven-year relationship. We meant for better or worse when we said it five years ago. We have to give it every chance. That's what I think. What I want."

"Oh," Kathleen said quietly, her voice and confidence a little shaky. Damn. Mark's wife was so lucky to have him. "Well let me know."

"If you don't hear from me, you'll know."

By December fifteenth both Mark and Janet knew their marriage was over. They both knew they had tried, maybe too hard, to resuscitate something that was dead.

Neither really understood what happened. Each understood it from his or her standpoint, but they couldn't agree. They couldn't make sense of it. They tried to talk patiently, but hit impasse after impasse.

At first the frustration erupted into rage.

Later it was replaced by sadness and grieving.

They spent hours reminiscing, remembering the beginning, the happy times. As they talked the memories became vivid, but they could not force the remembered joy and love into the present.

They made love once. Afterward they held each other and wept. They cried for the love that somewhere, somehow, was lost forever.

"How could it have happened to us, Janet?" he asked, bewildered.

Janet just shook her head, but the lyrics of a song, the song that summarized it for her, taunted her. She wanted to sing it for him; but it would just make him angry because he didn't believe her interpretation of what had happened, and it would anger her that he didn't believe her.

But, it was how she felt, had always felt. Every lyric.

If I can make you smile . . .
If I can fill your eyes with pleasure just by holding you . . .
Ah, well, that's enough for me,
That's all the hero I need be . . .

It *had* been enough, she knew, because there had been a time when she could make him happy, when she could fill him with peace with a touch or a kiss. It had been enough for her; she would never have wanted more, but somehow she lost the ability to comfort him. Her presence didn't matter anymore.

Whether Mark loved her any less, or whether his own torment, the torment he still denied, had become greater than the power of her love, she would never know.

They were left with no feelings. No stir of love. Just a present numbness and an aching pain and sadness for the lovely memories of the past—memories of love and passion and feelings that were gone . . .

The second week, their last week together, they filed for divorce and started to divide their property. The actual process of dividing their possessions was too painful to do together. It brought back too many memories: their wedding pictures, the hand-knit mufflers, the quilt for their bed, the souvenirs of happy times.

Janet agreed to pack the boxes for both of them after he left, but she needed to know what he wanted.

"Do you want the fine china or the everyday?" The four-hundred-guest wedding had left them with complete sets of the china patterns that Mrs. Taylor had insisted they choose.

"I don't care."

"Stainless or silver?"

"I don't *care*," Mark snapped, then repeated gently, "I really don't care, Janet."

"Is there anything you do want?" she asked finally.

"The Cornhuskers banner," he said impulsively. Then he wondered, *am* I really thinking about Kathleen? Certainly not *consciously*. He had focused only on Janet, on *them*. He had tried so hard.

But something within him, something subconscious, made him want the banner. He didn't want it for himself. He wanted to show it to Kathleen.

It all made him very sad.

For the first Christmas in years that Mark could have celebrated his wife's birthday with her, Janet flew home, alone, to snowy Nebraska. They both knew that the well-greased wheels of uncontested divorce in California were moving efficiently, inevitably toward dissolution of the marriage of Janet Wells Taylor and Mark David Taylor.

Mark, alone in San Francisco on December twenty-third, decided to call Kathleen.

"It's Mark."

"I recognize your, er, husky voice," she said, barely able to breathe. If you don't hear from me, you'll know, he had said. And now she was hearing from him.

"Cute Kitzy."

"So?"

"We are getting a divorce."

"Are you OK?" He didn't sound OK.

"Yes. It's hard. Sad."

"Do you want to talk about it?"

"Not really. Nothing to say. It's over."

Good, Kathleen thought. She didn't want to nurse Mark through the recovery period of a failed marriage. She wasn't interested in an event by event rehash. She had seen friends be helpful and sympathetic only to have the finally rehabilitated ex-husband spread his newly strengthened wings and find someone new, someone who didn't know quite so much about his weaknesses and his past mistakes.

Kathleen also knew that recently divorced men usually needed affairs with a number of women—a sexual spree—before even considering a serious relationship. Kathleen had slept with enough recently freed husbands. They were a drearily manic bunch.

Kathleen almost told Mark to call her in six or eight months when he was ready for the serious relationship, but she couldn't. Maybe Mark would be different. He was already so different from all the others.

"Kathleen, are you there?"

"Yes. Was it my turn to speak?"

"Uh-huh."

"OK. Hi. There. Now it's your turn."

"I have something to show you."

"I know. It *is* something."

Silence.

"Sorry," Kathleen said. This wasn't really her usual style. She didn't like it. He didn't like it. Kathleen the perfect lady. But Mark made her silly and giddy. And sexy.

"When can I see you?"

"Anytime. Except it's the holidays, isn't it? Do you have plans for Christmas?"

"I can't do a family Christmas, Kathleen," Mark said quickly, apologetically. "It's very nice of you. How's your mother?"

"Well. A hundred percent. Taking it easy. I didn't really mean family Christmas, though you would be welcome. I meant the Carlton Club Kids Christmas Celebration."

"That's not Kathleen's Carlton Club Kids Christmas Celebration, is it?" Mark teased.

"You've heard of it!" Kathleen teased back.

"Of course. Who hasn't?" Mark sensed the feeling, the Kathleen feeling, pumping into his body. He wanted to see her. "What is it?"

"Well, around here, the Atherton Mansion Gang—"

"Atherton Mansion Gang?"

"That's the folks. They aren't as alliterative as the Kids. Anyway, the AMG celebrates Christmas on Christmas Eve with present opening early Christmas morning. The rest of the Christmas day and evening are boring. As kids we hated Christmas night. So, we invented the Celebration. It's our biggest party of the year. It has grown as we have. Now it's held on the top floor at the Fairmont."

"And you don't have a date?"

"Not if you say no."

"It's fancy, isn't it?"

"Yes," Kathleen admitted. "It really is. Black tie. Tuxedo. The whole bit."

"I haven't worn a tuxedo since—" Mark stopped.

"Your wedding."

"Right."

"You probably don't have time to go tuxedo renting, do you?"

"No . . . listen, Kathleen, maybe we could see each other—"

"No, please, Mark. I really want you to come. The Kids have been asking about you. What I was going to say was, if you give me your size I'll get the tux with all the trimmings and bring it to you."

"Nothing crazy, Kathleen."

"No! The Celebration is when we all try to out-gorgeous each other. It's lots of fun. Photographers snapping souvenir portraits. It usually makes the society page of *The Chronicle.*"

"No," Mark said firmly. *I don't want that.*

"OK. We can avoid the press." *Maybe just a private photograph? As a memento?*

"OK."

"When shall I come to your apartment? Are you working on Christmas?"

"No, the whole day off." It was nice that Kathleen understood that doctors worked on Christmas, and that the idea didn't seem to bother her.

"Oh. You don't want to come down here for lunch? My parents would love to see you."

"No. Thank you."

"Well. The dust begins to settle about noon. I could be there by two. I could bring turkey and cranberry sauce . . . Is that too early?"

"No." *Now would be fine. Can't you come now*? "That's great. When is the party? The . . . er . . . Celebration?"

"It starts at eight, but it's best not to arrive until at least nine-thirty."

After he hung up, Mark thought about how many times they could listen to his four ballet albums, in bed, between two and nine-thirty. He didn't give a damn about turkey.

After she hung up, Kathleen had a similar thought. *Scheherazade, Sleeping Beauty, Swan Lake, Giselle*. Then *Giselle, Swan Lake, Sleeping Beauty, Scheherazade*. Then . . .

Chapter 7

By mid-January Mark had collected the boxes Janet had carefully packed. His half of the memories. Mark didn't need, couldn't use, any of the furniture. The divorce was all but fact, simply waiting for the required number of days to elapse.

Kathleen saw Mark every third night. She always saw him on the night before he was on call. It was the night he was the most rested. It was also the night he needed the most sleep. On those nights Kathleen was always in his apartment when he arrived home, and she forced herself to leave his bed by two in the morning.

Sometimes if he wasn't too tired on the night following his on call night, if he got home in time, he would call her, and she would come to him.

"I think I should get an apartment in the city," Kathleen announced to her parents one morning at breakfast. At that moment Mark was running his second code of the day, trying to resuscitate a patient who had had a cardiac arrest.

"Are you moving in with him, dear?" her father asked bluntly.

"No." Because Mark hadn't asked her. It was too soon. Mark needed his privacy. His private time.

"Then why?"

"I want to be able to spend the night with him. All night," she said. *So I can fall asleep and wake up in his arms. So I don't have to leave him in the middle of the night.* "I don't want to have to worry about you worrying that

I've crashed somewhere between here and there."

Kathleen's morality was not an issue. Only her safety and her happiness. She was twenty-seven years old and lived in her girlhood room, in her own wing of the mansion, because it was more splendid than any apartment. And because she enjoyed being with her parents.

Kathleen had complete freedom, but she had never wanted to spend the night with her other men. Not all night every night. Mark was different.

"Just let us know where you'll be, dear. Leave Mark's number with us. We know you are safe with him."

Neither parent had seen Mark since Kathleen's mother's hospitalization, but their memories of him, of his kindness, were strong and clear and enduring.

By the end of January, with Mark's permission, Kathleen had purchased a box spring to put under the mattress, four feather pillows to replace the lumpy ones and two complete sets of Laura Ashley sheets with matching comforters. She bought five live plants for the living room and hung the red and white Cornhuskers banner over the bed, even though it clashed with the pretty, delicate Laura Ashley patterns.

Mark stored the boxes of memories in the attic of the building.

Little by little, guided by Kathleen's stylish eye, the apartment looked better. Better, bigger, comfortable. Theirs.

"It still needs a face lift," Kathleen said one night. "A coat of paint in the living room. Some pictures . . ."

"Who's going to paint it?"

"I am. If that's OK. Some day when you're on call, so it can air out. OK? Please?"

"Sure," Mark said, putting his arms around her. "If you want to."

At ten in the morning on February fifth, Janet climbed the stairs to Mark's apartment. She had never been there, but Mark had given her the address. She carried a small box that contained the last of the memories and mail that hadn't been forwarded. It was nothing of great value. She could leave the box outside his apartment door.

One last detail. Janet was moving out of the house—their house—in a week.

She didn't even call to tell him. She didn't want to speak to him. Too painful. Nothing to say. Janet chose a time, ten o'clock on a Thursday morning, when she knew he wouldn't be there. She knew he was working on the wards at San Francisco General Hospital with Leslie.

Janet was surprised to find the door to Mark's apartment wide open. She saw drop cloths and smelled paint. She assumed it was the landlord. She walked into the apartment. As long as the door was open she might as well leave the box inside.

"Hello?" she called.

"Hello!" answered a surprised female voice.

Janet walked farther in and almost collided with Kathleen. Kathleen had been expecting Betsey, who was coming to watch, *only*, the painting process.

"Oh! Hello," Kathleen said. She had no idea that she was looking at Mark's almost ex-wife.

But she recognized the face.

"I'm Janet. I have a box of things for Mark."

"Janet. I'm Kathleen. I'm a friend of Mark's. I offered to paint his apartment."

Kathleen recognized Janet's face immediately. How could she forget it? It was *her.* She hoped Janet wouldn't recognize her. There was a chance she wouldn't. Kathleen looked so different today, in her painting clothes, than she had the day before.

But Janet did recognize her.

"Aren't you? Didn't—"

"Yes."

The day before, the Board of Union Square Theater had auditioned the finalists for *Joanna.* The finalists had been selected after two grueling weeks of auditions in front of choreographers, directors, producers and cast members of other Union Square Theater productions. Kathleen was a member of the board, and the board had an advisory say in the final selection.

Joanna was such an important production. Such a risk. It was the first original musical Union Square Theater had done—a musical opening not in New York on Broadway but in San Francisco on Geary. It was a landmark event for the theater. They all knew that *Joanna* had potential, great potential.

But they had to choose exactly the right cast.

Janet was there as a finalist. She was the only amateur who had survived to the finals.

J. Wells. Kathleen remembered the name on the roster, the name of the woman with the haunting beauty and the lovely, clear, soulful voice.

It was Kathleen who had suggested that they audition J. Wells for the lead not just for the supporting cast. Janet had overhead the suggestion. She knew who made it. Now she knew more about the sophisticated young woman with the jet-black hair and violet eyes.

"You're Mark's wife?"

"His ex-wife. Almost. I guess you know."

"I didn't know who you were yesterday. Different—"

"I'm using my maiden name."

Different name. Different woman.

True, Mark had never told her anything about Janet, but Kathleen had allowed herself to imagine a large, unsophisticated farm girl. Pretty, plump, uninspired. It was a comforting image.

Kathleen had left the audition thinking about the remarkable walk-on who had mesmerized and captivated them and who they hoped would captivate audiences in San Francisco and maybe even in New York. Who was the intriguing, beautiful woman with incredible talent and the huge gray eyes? Kathleen had wondered.

Now she knew.

"You were wonderful," Kathleen said.

"Thank you."

"You've heard, haven't you? The decision?"

"No. They said they would call sometime today," Janet answered quickly, eager to leave. She couldn't stand seeing Kathleen in Mark's apartment. Kathleen obviously belonged there. Janet was the outsider. Janet had to leave. It was too painful.

But Kathleen had something to say to her.

"They were supposed to call you at nine. You got the lead, Janet. You stole it right away from all those seasoned professionals. You deserve it. You were the best."

The Best. How Janet hated those two words. But she wanted the part—*any* part—in the musical. She had to start singing and performing again. Her sanity depended on it.

Janet eyed Kathleen skeptically. The lead?

Her skepticism was well founded. It seemed highly unlikely that a complete unknown would be selected as the lead. The concept of introducing a new musical was innovative enough. But an unknown musical with an unknown lead? It was so risky. Too risky. Janet couldn't imagine that anyone would be willing to take the risk.

510 But Janet didn't know Ross MacMillan. Ross took risks and converted them into phenomenal successes. When Ross founded Union Square Theater in 1976, everyone said it would fail. San Francisco didn't *need* another theater. Now theatergoers rushed to get season tickets and eagerly awaited announcements of Union Square Theater's upcoming productions. They were never disappointed.

Ross MacMillan took risks. They really weren't risks with Ross at the creative helm; they were opportunities. He knew what was possible, and he took what was possible and made it into something spectacular.

Ross MacMillan was thirty-three years old and looked like he should be on stage rather than behind it. But as crowd-stopping as his looks were ("Wasn't that Robert Redford?"), his ability to mesmerize an audience through his genius as a director was even greater,

Ross MacMillan was a Carlton Club Kid.

And Ross MacMillan was ultimately responsible for the decision to cast Janet Wells as the lead in *Joanna*. The board was advisory. It was his decision.

"Where were they supposed to call you?" Kathleen asked Janet.

"At work. But I don't go in until noon on Thursdays."

"Call there. Right now. When I left the theater yesterday you had the part. I think it would be best for you to check before you leave . . ." *Because this is about the worst possible scenario.*

Kathleen gestured toward the phone, realizing too late that beside the phone, beautifully framed, was the stunning portrait taken of Mark and Kathleen at the Celebration. A magnificent, romantic picture. Their private memory.

Janet saw the picture, recoiled for a moment, then dialed her office. There was a message to call Ross MacMillan at Union Square Theater. Janet memorized the number and dialed the theater.

"Really? I won Joanna?" *The* role. The role that would make or break Union Square Theater's innovative experiment. Janet's heart pounded. "Yes, I'll be there at eight Monday morning. Yes. Thank you, Mr. MacMillan."

After she replaced the receiver, Janet paused for a moment to look at the photograph. When she turned to Kathleen, her usually calm, gray eyes were stormy with emotion. Janet tried to smile.

"It didn't take him long, did it? Or—" Janet stopped. Was she looking at the reason? The real reason? Was Kathleen the reason for Mark's moodiness and detachment? Was she why Mark didn't touch Janet? How long had they been together? A year? Fifteen months?

"Janet," Kathleen said, blinking back her own tears. She realized now what a great loss it had been for both of them. She knew now why all that Mark had said about his failed marriage to Janet was that it made him sad. Why he still, quietly, grieved. "Mark and I met *after—after* it was over—and it has taken him a long time. It will take him a long time. Believe me, Janet."

"I have to go," Janet said, walking toward the door. She stopped, just before she reached it, and turned, tears running down her face.

"Will I see you again? I mean, through the production?"

"There will be a few parties."

"Don't . . . could you please—does he have to come with you?"

"No. I'll come alone. Or not at all. It's *your* show. You're the star."

"Thanks," Janet sniffed. "I really thought I was doing better."

"I can't think of anything worse than what you're going through right now, can you?" Kathleen asked, hopefully.

"No," Janet smiled, barely. "Oh. Would you—could you see that he does see the show?"

"Of course he will," Kathleen said, her own violet eyes glistening.

Mark would be so proud of Janet.

After Janet left, Kathleen sat, numb, immobile, for an hour, wondering for the thousandth time if she should just leave him alone, let him recover. Leave him alone and then hope that Mark, once healed, would find her again.

Mark never even mentioned Janet. Or his grief. He barely let it show. Only when he thought Kathleen wasn't watching. But what about the times when she wasn't there? What about when he was alone? Kathleen wondered.

How would she tell Mark about today, about meeting Janet?

Betsey found Kathleen in a lump in the kitchen when she arrived. Kathleen didn't tell her what had happened. They spent the afternoon chattering about nothing and listening to records while Kathleen painted.

Mark didn't call the next night. He probably got home too late, Kathleen decided. But the questions thundered in her brain. What if Janet had called him and told him what had happened? What if it brought them back together?

Mark would let me know, Kathleen thought.

The next day, the every third night that was theirs, Kathleen arrived at the apartment carrying three framed pictures for the newly painted walls. Two pictures were unoriginal, but they were Kathleen's favorite scenic posters of San Francisco. The first, bright and fresh, was a sleek, shiny sailboat with a multicolored spinnaker gliding across the shimmering blue bay. The second, soft and romantic, was a twilight silhouette of the city with a spring moon and a single star. The third picture was original. Made just for Mark.

It was a photograph—enlarged to a top-quality two-by-three-foot print—of a brick mansion with white marble pillars surrounded by perfectly manicured, emerald-green lawns and brilliant, exquisitely tended gardens of roses and lilacs and azaleas. The mansion and its luxurious grounds made an undeniable statement about wealth, taste, heritage and privilege. Chiseled into the marble and brick near the entrance were the words: The Carlton Club.

Kathleen smiled as she hung the last picture. It was perfect. The picture, the matting, the frame.

She hoped he liked it.

She hoped he liked her. Still.

Mark called at six. He sounded tired but normal.

"ETA one hour, OK?"

"Sure. Bad day?"

"The usual. But things are slowing down. A sick GI bleeder, but Leslie's here tonight. She's got it under control," Mark said lightly.

Kathleen had the distinct impression that Leslie was within earshot of Mark. Kathleen liked Leslie. She had been so gentle with her mother. Just as Mark had been.

Mark appeared an hour later. He was obviously happy to see her.

"I want to take a shower before I touch you. And I want to touch you. So I'm taking my shower now, all right?"

"OK," Kathleen answered, kissing his lips briefly as he passed.

"You did a great job of painting," he said.

Kathleen followed him from the entry area to the bathroom door. It was a matter of a few feet.

"Thanks. Wait until you see today's improvements!"

"Can't wait. Do you want you join me in here? After I wash off a few layers of blood and germs . . ."

"No thank you," Kathleen said, watching him undress. "I have to keep an eye on dinner."

She looked at his white resident's pants, truly splattered with blood, and said, "You are careful, aren't you. Mark? About the blood. About hepatitis? And the new one, *AIDS*?"

Mark was a little surprised that Kathleen knew that hepatitis was transmitted by blood and even more surprised that she had heard about AIDS. AIDS, Acquired Immune Deficiency Syndrome, was new. It had only been recognized in North America recently. San Francisco had a substantial share of the cases, and the rumors were just beginning that spread might be through blood products as well as sexual contact.

"Blood splashes on clothes don't do any harm. It's needle sticks, splashes in the eyes, mucous membranes. We're careful about those." Mark was talking about the transmission of hepatitis.

"Have you—do you—take care of patients with AIDS?" she asked.

"Of course," he said. Mark had two patients with AIDS, both dying, on his service right now.

"Does it bother you? The pictures I've seen—it looks awful."

"It is awful." The worst, he thought. "It doesn't bother me to take care of them. What bothers me is that it's killing young men, men my age, and we don't know what causes it, how to treat it, how to stop it . . ." Mark's voice, through the sound of the shower water, was angry.

"But if you know so little about it, and it's so awful, doesn't it bother you that you might catch it?" Kathleen persisted.

"I'm a doctor, Kathleen," Mark said with an edge to his voice. "I take care of sick patients all day, every day. There is no reason to think that you can catch AIDS by taking care of patients. Not if you're careful. Not if you take the usual precautions. And I *am* careful."

"I have to go check on dinner," Kathleen said, suddenly, realizing that the tone of his voice, sharp and intense, made her uneasy.

After she left the bathroom, as he lathered himself with soap for the third time, Mark thought about his patients with AIDS. They were young men wasting away—fighting because they were so young, had been so healthy, had everything to live for—and inevitably dying of the lethal mysterious new disease. He wondered if there was a *best* way to die. A warm, peaceful, quiet death . . .

Mark didn't know what was the best, but he knew that AIDS was one of the worst. They all knew it. It was the disease they all didn't want to get.

They were very careful.

When Mark rejoined Kathleen after his long shower, he looked refreshed and untroubled. He wore khaki slacks and an oxford shirt, open at the collar, with sleeves rolled halfway up his pale but finely muscled forearms.

He noticed the pictures immediately.

"They are wonderful, Kathleen," he said. Then, moving closer to the picture of the brick mansion, he asked, "What's this?"

"Look closely. The pillar on the left."

Mark leaned forward and read aloud, "The Carlton Club."

"I had to get something to counterbalance the Cornhuskers" banner."

"Maybe we should put this above our bed. It goes much better with feather pillows and Laura whoever sheets."

Our bed, Kathleen thought, a rush of joy pulsing through her. She said softly, "Ashley."

She thought of saying, No, the Cornhuskers' banner captures the spirit of the—*our*—bed. But it wasn't true. Their lovemaking was everything, all moods, Cornhuskers to Laura Ashley, uninhibited sport to proper Carlton Club. Laughter and quiet tenderness. Lust and romance. Adventure and tradition. Everything.

During dinner Kathleen told him about her meeting with Janet.

"I assumed she left the box at the door and that you brought it in when you came to paint."

"No."

"Oh."

Silence.

"Mark, do you remember the woman I told you about? The amateur we auditioned on Wednesday for *Joanna*?"

"The one you thought was so sensational? The one who got the lead over all the pros? Sure. I remember. Why?" he asked idly.

"Janet," Kathleen said quietly.

"*Janet*?" Mark asked. Of course Janet, he thought. That's what she had done in high school and college—stolen the leading roles from the pros. Not because she cared about being the best. Just because she needed to sing.

Mark blinked back a sudden mist in his eyes. Then he said, his voice husky, "Good for her."

After a few moments, he asked, "Did you know that on Wednesday?"

"No. Not until I met her, here, yesterday. She used—is using—her . . ." Kathleen hesitated.

"Maiden name?"

"Yes."

"Was she thrilled?" he asked, knowing that she had to be but that it might not show.

Kathleen only remembered the tears and Janet's hurt, comprehending expression as she looked at the photograph of Kathleen and Mark.

"I'm sure she was," Kathleen said.

The conversation shifted. They talked about nothing of importance. They talked less than usual. Mark was quiet.

Later, as they got ready for bed, he asked, casually, "Will there be parties for the production? Ones you'll need to attend?"

"Yes. I told her you wouldn't be at any of them. I probably won't be, either. It's her show. OK?"

"Yes."

A few moments later, he said, "I want to see the show, though."

"I know. She wants you to."

That night they made love in a new way. In the oldest way. The most chaste way. First they kissed for a long time. Just kissing, just their mouths. Their hands and their lips didn't explore. Then he entered her and they moved, together, united, entwined. Slow, rhythmic, leisurely lovemaking. Wonderful romantic lovemaking.

Kathleen had no idea that was the way that Mark and Janet had made love. Only. Always. Hundreds and hundreds of times.

* * *

Over the next two weeks there were periods when Mark was distant and preoccupied. Kathleen didn't know the cause. It could have been because of Janet. That would make sense. Or it could have been because of the death of both the AIDS patients within hours of each other. Mark had been there. He had watched them die. Helpless. Unable to prevent the inevitable.

Perhaps it was the long telephone conversation with his father. Mark asked

Kathleen to wait in the bedroom, but she heard bits, angry tones she had never heard from Mark before. When she decided the conversation was over—when she heard only silence from the other room—Kathleen joined him. Mark didn't even acknowledge her presence. He had already retreated to a corner of the living room and was reading. *The Adventures of Sherlock Holmes*. Kathleen picked up the book that lay on the end table, *Ulysses* by James Joyce, and tried to read, too.

She couldn't read, couldn't concentrate. Finally, she gave up and simply watched Mark, absorbed in his book, oblivious to her stares.

"This isn't good," she whispered after over an hour of silence.

Mark looked up at the sound of her voice, startled, almost disoriented.

"What did you say?"

"I said, this isn't good."

"What isn't?"

"You shutting me out like this."

Shutting me out. Janet's words. Now Kathleen's words.

Mark put his book down and went to her side.

"What do you mean?" he asked gently, with concern in his voice.

"I mean you had a horrible conversation, I assume, with your father, after which you withdraw completely and behave as if I'm not here and never existed."

"I'm *sorry*. I didn't realize," Mark said. "What *should* I do?"

"I don't know. How about saying, 'My father is such a bastard. Kathleen, do you mind if I just escape into the streets of London with Holmes for a while?' "

"That sounds easy," Mark said with relief.

"Except I don't think you're even aware when you are doing it."

"Have there been other times?" Mark pulled her close to him, gently, worried.

"In the past two weeks, several. In the past two months, a few."

"I honestly wasn't aware."

"I know." Kathleen believed him. He would know if he paid attention. It was probably an old bad habit. Kathleen wondered how Janet had felt about it, assuming it wasn't all simply because of Janet.

"So what should I do?"

"*Pay* attention. I don't need to know what's bothering you, unless you want to tell me. I just need to know it's not me."

"It's not you, never you," he said, kissing her.

"Then do I have permission to point it out when you're doing it? In case you don't know?" So you'll learn, she thought.

"Yes! Kathleen. I don't want to shut you out."

"And you won't snarl?" she asked, kissing him back.

"I don't snarl," he said softly.

"Oh yes, you do."

The next week was better. Mark's need to retreat into a book or lose himself in dark troublesome thoughts was not less, but he good-humoredly announced his moods and his intentions. Kathleen respected his privacy and struggled with

Ulysses as she waited for the mood to pass. It always did. It was always gone before they went to bed.

"You probably understand *Ulysses*, don't you?" she teased one night as she lay beside him. "I didn't really get it when we studied it at Vassar, although I think I got an A on the paper I wrote about it! I still don't get it."

"It's one of my favorites. A masterpiece."

"Can we pick our way through it sometime? Word by word?"

"Sure. But not now," he said, nuzzling her soft round breast.

"No," she sighed, "not now."

By the third week in February, Kathleen realized that despite the new ground rules, which allowed her not to take his moodiness personally, Mark had too much on his mind. Too many things to resolve: Janet, his failed marriage, whatever it was with his father.

Mark couldn't build a new relationship until the residual feelings and emotions about his marriage were resolved. That would take time. And privacy.

Kathleen couldn't help him. He wasn't that kind of man, and she wasn't that kind of woman.

They could solve *their* problems—Mark and Kathleen problems—together, but she didn't want to help him with old problems. She didn't want the burden of Mark and Janet problems.

By the end of February Kathleen made her decision.

"Betsey and I have decided to take a trip."

"Without Jeff? Without the groom-to-be?"

"He'll survive."

"Where are you going?"

"Hawaii. The Mauna Kea Hotel on the big island. It's a favorite. Betsey and I go there every six or eight months—just the two of us—to talk, take stock of our lives and lie in the sun. We've been doing it for years."

"When do you leave?"

"Day after tomorrow."

"When do you return?"

"Betsey will be back in a week," Kathleen said. She hesitated a moment before saying. "And I'll be back in four months."

"Four months!"

"You're snarling."

"This is not a snarl. We've gone beyond snarl. What the hell are you doing, Kathleen?"

"I'm giving you, in the jargon of the day, *space*."

"Oh God. *Why*?"

"Because you need it."

"Really? You know what I need and I don't?"

"Don't get angry, Mark," Kathleen pleaded. "You're right. I don't know what you need. I know what I need and what I *think* you need."

"Which is?"

"I think you need time to resolve your feelings about your marriage."

"The marriage is over. Resolved," Mark said flatly. He looked into her violet eyes and repeated, gently, "It's over, Kathleen."

"You don't think about it? About what went wrong?"

"Yes, of course. But mostly in the context of not making, trying not to make, the same mistakes with you. With us."

Oh, Mark, Kathleen thought, I'll stay.

But her decision was firm.

"Besides," she said lightly, "you need to sow some wild oats."

"Sow some wild oats? You make me sound like a sixteen-year-old—"

"Cornhusk-*er*."

"Kathleen, I'm twenty-seven, chronically tired, completely, deliriously happy to be with you . . ." Mark paused, then asked. "Do you really want me to sleep with other women while you're gone?"

"Yes!" No, not really, Kathleen thought, an ache settling in the pit of her stomach. Was the risk worth it? Sleep with them, Mark, she thought, but don't fall in love with them. Learn how special *we* really are.

"This is ridiculous."

Kathleen shrugged. "When was the last time you slept with someone other than me or Janet?"

"Never."

"Oh *no*. I'll see you in a year. Or two."

"Kathleen, you are reducing me to a nonthinking, unfeeling animal with irrepressible, insatiable urges. It's only a little bit flattering. It's mostly insulting."

"Mark," she began. I love you, she thought. I want you. Forever. This is the only way it can happen. She said, "Four months is a short time."

"A lot can happen in four months," Mark said grimly, recalling the last four months of his own life. He had lost the woman with whom he had planned to spend his life. He had fallen in—cared deeply about another woman. That happened so quickly that he hadn't had time to think . . .

Kathleen is right, he realized. Four months is a short time, but it could make a big difference. It could give him, give them, time to be certain.

Mark held out his arms to her. Kathleen fell into them gratefully.

"Where will you be?" He pressed his lips against her shiny black hair.

"Lots of places. *Incommunicado*." Kathleen planned to be in Atherton between short trips like the one to Hawaii, but it was better if Mark didn't know that.

"Ah, Communicado. Lovely spot," he teased. Then he said seriously, "So the rules of this trial separation are that we don't communicate? And I make love with every woman I meet?"

"Something like that."

"When do you re-materialize?"

"After Wimbledon."

"Wimbledon? The tennis championships? You're going?"

"Of course," Kathleen said lightly in her best Carlton Club voice that implied, Isn't everyone? "I always do. My parents and I go. CEOs get wonderful center court seats."

"So you'll be back when?"

"A day or two after the finals. July eighth or ninth, I think."

"In time to be with me on my birthday?"

"Which is . . . ?"

"July eleventh."

"If you want me to."

"I want you to."

"What if you don't, by then?"

"Then I'll let you know."

Chapter 8

Jean Watson—Mrs. Watson—was admitted to Leslie's service at University Hospital on April fifteenth. Before Leslie saw her new patient, she learned the details of her complicated medical history from Mrs. Watson's physician, Dr. Jack Samuels, a hematology-oncology specialist.

"She's the nicest woman in the world, Leslie. With a lethal disease. This hospitalization will probably be her last. We diagnosed breast cancer a year ago, positive nodes, negative estrogen receptors. We gave her aggressive chemo and haven't documented mets. Anyway, she was doing very well until a month ago when she presented with fatigue and bleeding from her gums. I did a bone marrow . . . she's aplastic."

"Not a marrow full of tumor?" Leslie asked.

"No. An *aplastic* marrow. Completely empty."

"Maybe it will come back."

"Leslie, she has no cells. Her marrow is completely wiped out. We've been supporting her with red cells, white cells and platelets all month."

"How about a marrow transplant? Maybe you could kill her tumor at the same time. Cure everything."

"I would love to transplant her, but we're already almost unable to cross-match her for blood transfusions. She consumes platelets as quickly as we infuse them. Immunologically, she'd be a nightmare to transplant. She would never survive."

"So she has an auto-immune process going on as well? Breast cancer, an aplastic marrow *and* an auto-immune syndrome?"

"Uh-huh."

"Maybe the tumor is making something, secreting some substance that is suppressing her marrow and making the auto-antibodies . . ." Leslie mused.

Dr. Samuels looked at Leslie for a moment. He had heard about her. His colleagues raved about how bright she was. And pleasant. And compulsive. But he had never worked with her. He had noticed her, of course. It was hard not to notice the slender, drawn face framed in chestnut curls, the bright sapphire-blue eyes and the trim but voluptuous figure unsuccessfully concealed by her white coat. And the smile, sometimes tired, sometimes wan, was always there. Always retrievable.

They all noticed her, the entire faculty, and they talked about her, kindly wondering, Who is she? What does she do when she leaves the hospital? Does she have anyone waiting for her? Is she happy?

They hoped so. They liked her.

Now, talking with her, mesmerized by her fresh, natural beauty and her large, attentive, concerned blue eyes, Jack Samuels knew, felt, what they had been talking about.

Then Leslie suggested that the tumor might be secreting a substance . . . *That* was what he thought. It would be extremely unusual. Reportable. Most interns, or even residents, would never have considered it.

"That's what I've been wondering, to, Leslie," he said.

"Does that mean we will be giving her more chemotherapy?" she asked.

"Maybe. I haven't decided. It's awfully hard to give chemotherapy that destroys the marrow to someone whose marrow you are trying to stimulate. Not to mention the trouble with supporting her with blood products."

"But if it is all due to tumor and we don't treat it . . ." Leslie said quietly.

"I know. This is a tough one. Let's discuss it after you see her and review her records. Let me know what you think," he said, scarcely believing what he heard himself say. Jack Samuels had never, ever, asked for an intern's opinion on such an important decision. Of course, as a faculty member, he went through the usual rituals of involving the interns, engaging them in Socratic dialogue. He even listened to what they said.

But he had never before solicited an opinion.

Leslie simply nodded and said, "OK."

"I guess she's not on the floor yet. I was going to introduce you."

"I'll see her as soon as she arrives. Then shall I call you?"

"Yes."

"All right. Thank you, Dr. Samuels."

"Call me Jack, Leslie," he said, amazing himself again, but chuckling inwardly at how his wife, herself a physician, would diagnose what had happened. An acute, self-limited attack of middle age, she would say, laughing.

From Jack Samuels's description, Leslie formed a clear picture of what Mrs. Watson would look like: frail, exhausted, dying.

"Mrs. Watson?" Leslie asked with surprise when she saw the woman sitting in the bed assigned to Jean Watson.

Jean Watson sat cross-legged on the hospital bed. She wore a modest, fluffy, bright-yellow robe. Her hair was dark red, her face freckled, her eyes merry and twinkly and her smile broad. Her fifty-eight-year-old face, wrinkled and full of character, instantly sent the message that those fifty-eight years had been full, interesting, happy ones.

"Yes?" she chirped.

"Mrs. Watson, I'm Leslie Adams. I'm the intern who will be taking care of you."

Leslie usually introduced herself as Leslie Adams, intern, rather than Dr. Adams. It caused less distance.

Sometimes Leslie had to be firm about who she was and the authority she had. Then she was *Dr.* Adams. *The doctor.* Those times usually occurred in the San Francisco General Hospital emergency room with alcoholics, drug addicts and psychotic patients who were too drugged, confused or belligerent to pay attention to anything but her size, her fragile prettiness and her sex. Leslie had to tell them, clearly, directly, that she was their doctor. And that she was in charge.

But it wasn't necessary with Mrs. Watson.

"You're a doctor!"

"Well, yes," Leslie said patiently. "Interns are doctors."

"Dear, I know that. I was reacting to your age, not your rank. You look so young! I've been in hospitals enough in the past year that I know the entire hierarchy. I'm even up on the name change. Aren't you really an R-1?"

Leslie smiled. It was true. The term intern was officially being abandoned. They would all be residents—first year, R-1s; second year, like Mark, R-2s; and so on. The term intern might disappear, but the job description, the tradition of being an intern, the ordeal of the internship year, wouldn't change.

"A rose by any other name," Leslie said, laughing.

"Ah yes. I see."

It surprised Leslie that Mrs. Watson thought she looked young. Before her internship Leslie *had* looked young, but she felt she had aged so much in the past nine months. She felt older. She noticed little lines on her face, around her eyes, that she had never seen before. She knew she looked drawn and gaunt. She felt the tugging of her skin.

Mrs. Watson was the picture of health, of robust, genetically predetermined long life. Leslie learned, as she took Mrs. Watson's family history, that her parents had died at ages ninety-two and ninety-four.

"And never misheard a word or lost a thought in all those years," Jean Watson said proudly.

It wasn't until Jean Watson removed her fluffy yellow robe that the magnitude of her illness became apparent. Her body was ravaged—thin, wrinkled, missing one breast and blue-black with bruises because the low platelet count did not enable her blood to clot properly.

"I'm a mess, aren't I?" she asked, smiling wryly.

Leslie smiled back, unable to think of anything to say. She was taken aback by the deathlike body attached to the lively, happy woman she was beginning to know.

"I think you need a central line, to minimize the needle sticks," she said, finally.

"A Hickman? I've had a few. They don't last long; they clot off in spite of my low platelets!"

Great, Leslie thought. Jack Samuels had forgotten to mention that problem.

"OK. Well, then, you'll just have to help me find the veins," Leslie said lightly, knowing how hard it would be, how fragile the veins must be, how overused already.

"They're pretty bad," Jean Watson said.

"Well, I'm pretty good at starting lines in tricky, delicate veins," Leslie said cheerfully. She knew it would be tough—tough for Mrs. Watson—because it *hurt* to have needle sticks over and over, and because it was frustrating. It was a reminder of the body's betrayal. The body had betrayed the mind and the spirit. The body had gotten sick, weak. The body was going to die.

As Leslie watched Jean Watson's body die over the next few weeks, despite chemotherapy and plasmaphoresis and white cell, red cell and platelet transfusions, Leslie learned about the quick, lively, loving mind that did not want to die. Not yet. Not ever.

Leslie spent many hours with Jean, caring for her, talking to her. Each day she patiently and as gently as possible searched for veins. She started intravenous lines for the necessary transfusions and medications, and she withdrew blood to check the blood counts. Leslie watched the first few moments of each transfusion. Jean's immunologically primed body might have a serious allergic reaction to the blood products.

They talked. Occasionally about a possible vein to try, rarely about Jean's medical condition and mostly about their lives.

"Next time. Next life, I am going to have a daughter," Jean said one day.

"You have pretty wonderful sons," Leslie said, gently tapping a potential vein, trying to make it stand up.

"I do. I know. But five boys and no girls!" she laughed.

Leslie had met all five sons, all redheaded and frecklefaced, like their mother. All with merry eyes and smiles, like hers. After seeing the sons and their mother, Leslie expected that Mr. Watson would be redheaded, too.

But he wasn't. He had a full head of dark curly hair and dark eyes that had managed to skip his children's generation. Perhaps his redheaded sons would have curly-black-haired girls. Grandchildren, maybe granddaughters, that Jean Watson would never see.

Carl Watson was a kind, loving man. He and the "boys," as the Watsons fondly referred to their sons, visited Jean daily. The boys ranged in age from sixteen to thirty. During their visits, Leslie always heard laughter coming from Jean's room—light feminine laughs surrounded by a chorus of deep masculine ones.

Seeing the Watsons together, laughing, talking, loving, made Leslie think
520 about her own parents. The weekly calls to her parents in Seattle began to last a little longer. Sometimes she called them twice a week. It was so comforting to talk to them, to hear their voices, to have her mother quiz her about her weight and her health and men.

The Watsons were so like Leslie's family. Close and loving. Except our family is lucky. At least we have been lucky *so far*, Leslie thought, wondering superstitiously how to insure the luck forever. The Watsons had done nothing wrong. Jean's illness was simply a tragedy. Senseless. Painful. Nobody's fault. No way to prevent it.

Luck. Fate. Divine will. . . .

Mark looked at the envelope for a moment. His name and address were handwritten, but the return address was engraved in dark blue script. Union Square Theater. On Geary. The handwriting looked like Kathleen's.

Mark opened the envelope quickly. Kathleen had been gone for six weeks. It seemed much longer.

It was Kathleen's handwriting. The envelope contained a note dated February twenty-seventh, the day before she left for Hawaii, two theater tickets and an engraved invitation.

Mark read the note first:

> *Hi! This note is to be attached to two excellent opening night tickets to* Joanna*—yet to be printed—and an invitation to the dress rehearsal party—yet to be engraved—and sent to you in time for both events. Assuming all has gone as planned, do with them as you will.*
>
> *I am looking forward to your birthday.*
>
> *Aloha,*
> *Kathleen*

Mark smiled as he read her note. It was a gentle reminder of her energy and her humor. Not that he needed to be reminded. He thought about her constantly. Missed her. Wanted her.

But he knew that she was right about this time apart.

He did need the time and the privacy. He had to try to solve the issues—the ones he could solve—like his real feelings about losing Janet. Sadness. Regret. But no urge to try again, to try to go back. There was no place to go. That place—the place in time where the love of Janet and Mark had flourished—existed only in their minds, because they could remember, and in their hearts, aching hearts, that had lost the feeling.

Mark and Janet were over. Mark had to salvage the lessons and move on. He had to try not to make the same mistakes. Already with Kathleen he had repeated a mistake, but Kathleen had told him. In time.

Mark needed this time alone to think of the other mistakes he had made, could make again, could avoid. But what about the mistakes he didn't recognize? What if Kathleen didn't recognize them either, until, as with Janet, it was too late?

Mark knew there would always be the risk of mistakes, of alienating someone he loved, because of his moods and because of the other problem. The big, unresolved problem. The problem that Janet had recognized and he had denied, vehemently, angrily.

Only now, as he spent his nights alone and forced himself to think, did he realize that Janet had been right. Mark didn't like being a doctor. It was so simple and so complicated. It was what he had been destined to be. By his father. By his own inner drive. Something about being the best . . .

But Mark didn't like it. More than that, Janet was right, he *hated* it.

What was he going to do about it?

Mark didn't know. It was too hard to make decisions in the midst of a busy residency, he told himself. Maybe it would get better. That's what everyone said. It gets better.

So far it hadn't.

And it had already destroyed one marriage.

Mark looked at the engraved invitation to the dress rehearsal party and checked his pocket calendar. He couldn't go. He was on call. That meant he would be off the next night, opening night. He could go to the opening night performance.

Mark looked at the tickets. *Two* tickets.

Kathleen, he thought, smiling. She was reminding him to take a date.

Even about that, his need to see other women, Kathleen had been right.

Without her, knowing that she expected him to see other women, Mark stopped resisting the advances that had begun the day his wedding band came off.

All he could compare it to was high school. That was the last time he had dated. In a way it was similar. Except the signals were stronger, clearer, more specific now. These women wanted to sleep with him.

Apparently none of them viewed him as marriage material. Kathleen's firm knowledge that just-divorced men make terrible husbands but enthusiastic lovers was shared by the women who approached him.

They wanted to have fun. They wanted to show him all the things he had missed while he was married. They had no illusions about falling in love. The ones who did, the ones who had secretly admired Mark for two years and who knew what kind of man he was, stayed away. Maybe in a year. When he was emotionally ready to try again . . .

Mark fell into the game easily. It was so simple. The stakes weren't high. No one got hurt, and it didn't jeopardize his relationship with Kathleen; it strengthened it. When she returned, before she returned, he would quit. Without regret.

Until her return Mark would play the game. It was a welcome escape from the problems that plagued him, an interesting, exciting diversion when the pressures became too great and the questions too unanswerable.

Mark rarely dated anyone more than three times.

Except for Gail.

Gail had made bold clear advances toward him since the first day of his internship. She saw his eighteen-carat gold wedding band and didn't care. Gail knew the turnover rate in physician marriages was about fifty percent, and she wasn't even particular about the marital status.

As head nurse in the coronary care unit, Gail knew a lot about reading cardiograms, interpreting arrhythmias and administering cardiac medications. Gail had been doing it for ten years.

Two weeks after Kathleen left, Gail called to Mark from across the CCU nurses' station. She held a cardiogram tracing. Her green eyes frowned.

"Mark, can you come here a minute?"

"Sure, what's up?"

"Look at this tracing. PVCs or APCs? I'm not sure."

Mark looked at the tracing briefly—it only took a moment—then looked at her with surprise.

"APCs, Gail," he said. He couldn't believe Gail would have any trouble making that determination.

"That's what I thought. Thanks." Her green eyes didn't leave his. "How are you doing, Mark?"

"I'm OK."

"Just OK?"

"Better every day."

Gail moved close to him and touched the belt that held up his loose white pants.

"No one is feeding you," she purred, her hand lingering.

"Gail!" he said, removing her hand, but not leaving as he might have done *before*. He was a little intrigued. He had lost weight since Kathleen left. More weight. And he hadn't seen anyone.

"What?" she asked, eyes sparkling, feigning innocent surprise.

"What?"

"Why don't you come over for dinner?"

In Gail's bed later that night, before they made love for the second time, she said, "I knew they were APCs."

"What?"

"I just wanted to get your attention."

"Under false pretenses?"

"Any way. Besides, you wanted me to."

He answered her with a kiss.

Yes, he thought, I probably did.

Chapter 9

Mark decided he would go to the opening night performance by himself. It would be wrong to take anyone to see Janet's show. It would spoil it for him.

Mark also decided that he should let Janet know he would be there.

They hadn't spoken since early January when she called to tell him he couldcome to pick up his half of the carefully packed boxes of memories. Mark dialed their old number. It had been disconnected. A live operator provided him with the new number. It had a prefix Mark didn't recognize. It was a toll call. Janet had moved out of the city.

"Janet. It's Mark," he said quietly when she answered.

"Hello." Her voice sounded calm.

"How are you?"

"Fine. Good."

"Where are you living?"

"North of the city along the coast. I'm renting a small cottage. It's part of a large estate," she said with enthusiasm. She love her new home and its private acres.

"Sounds nice."

"It is."

"How is the show?"

"Great, I think," her voice softened. "It's been wonderful. I have learned so much."

"Different from Lincoln High and Omaha Community?"

"In every way."

"I'm planning to come to opening night . . ." his voice trailed off as if he intended to add, if that's all right with you?

"Good. Kathleen got tickets. I haven't seen her at all. I thought she might come to some rehearsals."

"She's away until July."

"Oh." *Oh!*

"I'm coming alone, but I have two tickets so you'll spot me instantly. I'll be sitting next to the only empty seat in the house."

"I don't think I can see the audience."

"Not Lincoln High, is it?"

Janet always found him in the audience. Sometimes she watched him while she performed as if performing just for him.

"No," she said idly, thinking. Then she said, "Are you really going alone?"

"Yes."

"Why don't you take Leslie? I really want her to see the show. I don't know if she'll go on her own."

"I'd be happy to take her," Mark said immediately. Leslie would not invade his privacy. She would be there for the same reason that he was. Because of Janet. *For* Janet.

"Why don't you call her now? I know she's home because we just spoke. I spent most of the time trying to convince her to go to opening night. I think she wants to."

"I'll call her. What's her number?"

Janet gave it to him.

Before he hung up, Janet said quickly, as if she had to say it quickly or not at all, "Why don't you and Leslie come backstage afterward? I'll leave your names with the stage manager."

At work, Mark and Leslie called each other, paged each other, spoke over the phone frequently:

"Mark, I'm in the ER. This man is a lot sicker than advertised. Can you come down?"

"Leslie, it's time for you to go home. I have to be here all night. Give me the rest of your scut list and leave."

"Mark, Mr. Simpson just died."

"Leslie, the team is making cafeteria rounds in five minutes. Meet us there."

At the hospital, any time day or night, Mark and Leslie talked on the phone. Effortlessly. At the hospital. But as Mark dialed Leslie's home phone number he felt strange. He didn't know a Leslie with a home phone number, a Leslie outside the hospital.

Leslie probably knew every detail of his failed marriage. She almost certainly knew about Janet's meeting with Kathleen. Leslie knew Kathleen because she had taken care of Kathleen's mother. There was little doubt that Leslie knew a great deal about Mark's personal life, but she never mentioned it.

With this phone call, a call suggested by Janet because of tickets arranged by Kathleen, Mark was admitting that Leslie knew all about him.

"Hello?"

"Leslie. It's Mark." He never identified himself when he called her at work. She knew his voice. But now he almost said, It's Mark Taylor.

"Hi."

"I just talked to Janet, and we decided that you and I should go to the opening night performance and then meet her backstage afterward." Mark stopped, a little out of breath. This was ridiculous! At work, he didn't run out of breath when he gave her much longer orders—"Leslie, draw two blood cultures, three if you can, Gram stain the urine and sputum, hang a sed rate, get cardiology to see him stat, then, as soon as that's cooking—*before*, if it starts to take too much time—let's start him on naf and gent . . ."

"You have tickets?" Leslie had just called the theater. The show was sold out.

"Good ones. Kathleen's away but she arranged for tickets," he said. Why not just admit to everything? They both knew Leslie knew about the audition, Kathleen, everything. It was easier. It just felt strange.

"I'd like to go. It's April thirtieth, isn't it?" Only a week away.

"Right. And the next day I leave San Francisco General and return to University Hospital. As your resident on the heme-onc service I think."

"Yes."

"How's the service?" he asked.

Leslie told him in great detail about Jean Watson. By the time they hung up, after a typical at work conversation, they were both surprised and a little disoriented to find themselves in their own apartments instead of in the hospital.

Mark and Leslie had dinner, a light pre-theater soup and sandwich at the restaurant designed precisely for such a meal, *Le Soucon*, located directly across from Union Square Theater on Geary.

"You look pretty dazzling," Mark said finally, in a proud older-brother tone.

Leslie wore a black dress with sheer sleeves, tapered waist and slightly flared skirt. It was looser than the last time she had worn it. Every part of her was thinner, *thin*. Except her breasts. They were still full and round and ample, a sharp contrast of softness against her boney ribcage.

Leslie had piled her chestnut curls on top of her head, secured, barely, with a large gold barrette. She accented her large blue eyes with mascara and a suggestion of blue eye shadow and touched her full lips with soft pink lipstick.

So do you look dazzling, Leslie thought. Mark in a dark suit.

"Well, it's a different look than all white with stethoscope bulges and iodine stains," she murmured.

"You look very nice," he repeated.

Over dinner, Leslie asked, "Are you excited about next year?"

"Next year?"

"Being an R-3! It should be much nicer."

The R-3 schedule was better. Consultant services, less night call, no scut work.

"Yes, it should be," Mark said, distantly, then fell silent.

Leslie was taken aback. She had never seen this before, but she recognized it because Janet had described it so well.

"Sorry," he said recovering quickly, recognizing what had happened. I'm trying, Kathleen, he thought. I'm learning.

"Mark," Leslie began slowly. "If someone told you right now that you could never be a doctor in the United States—you know, some legislative decision banning all Marks from practicing—what would you do?"

Leslie watched his reaction and knew that Janet had been right all the time. Mark didn't want to be a doctor. Just the hypothetical question—the thought of not practicing medicine—made him smile, transported him somewhere else, to a happier place.

"I'd go back to school. Get a graduate degree in English. Teach English. Write maybe."

Mark's answer came quickly, confidently. He had thought about it. He knew what he would do. He knew what he wanted to do.

"That's what my father does. Both my parents actually."

"Really?"

"Yes. My mother is a journalist. Always writing. My father is a professor of English at the University of Washington." Leslie watched Mark's face, then added seriously, carefully, "I know my father would accept you in a minute as a grad student in his department. I know he would."

Mark started to say something then stopped. His expression changed and he shrugged.

"Just a pipe dream, Leslie. Maybe next life."

"This is the only life you can count on having, Mark," she said swiftly, surprising both of them by her urgency.

He smiled. A brotherly smile. A little sad. Then he asked, "What would you do? If no more Leslies could practice?"

"I don't know," she answered. It was a lie. Leslie knew exactly what she would do. She would pull up stakes and move to the nearest country that allowed Leslies to practice. No matter where it was.

But she couldn't tell Mark that.

Oh Mark, she thought. Don't do this to yourself! It's hard enough if you want to be doing it. But if you don't even want it . . . the thought of going through an internship and residency, knowing that you didn't want to be a doctor, that your dreams lay somewhere else . . .

It made Leslie sad.

Now she knew that what Janet had said was true. It had probably destroyed his marriage, and it was probably, slowly, insidiously, destroying him. He hated what he was doing, and he wouldn't talk about it. He wouldn't even admit it.

Mark was the best doctor Leslie knew. *The best.* The words Janet hated. Mark hated what he was doing, but he was driven to continue and driven to be the best.

"*Hey* Leslie! What are you thinking?"

"I was thinking about you," she said honestly, looking into the dark eyes that made her tremble deep inside. "I was worrying about you."

"Don't worry about me," he said. "Come on, it's time to go to the theater."

Leslie and Mark watched *Joanna* from the best seats in the theater. The seats had been hand-picked by Kathleen who knew the acoustics, the lighting and the best view of the stage. Leslie didn't look at Mark. She didn't dare. She was afraid of the emotion she might see in his eyes—regret, pride, love, sadness—as he watched the magic and magnificence of Janet's performance.

Janet *was* magnificent. The entire production was magnificent, obviously destined to be the stunning success Ross MacMillan knew *Joanna* could be.

Mark and Leslie stood in the foyer of the theater during intermission. They were surrounded by the excited, enthusiastic chatter of the delighted theater patrons, but Mark was silent, somber in the midst of gaiety.

"Is this too hard for you, Mark? We could leave," Leslie said finally.

"The only hard part," he said honestly, "is thinking about the four years that she didn't perform—the years she gave it up because I needed to have her at home."

"It's where she wanted to be," Leslie said. Unlike you, she thought, you're not where you want to be.

"Except I wasn't there. Not the way I should have been. I wasted four years of her life. I deprived her of doing what she loves."

"I'm sure Janet doesn't resent it," Leslie knew that Janet didn't resent it.

"I resent it for her," Mark said. Then he stopped abruptly and frowned slightly.

Out of the corner of his eye, as the door to the theater personnel area opened and shut, Mark caught a fleeting glimpse of a woman who looked like Kathleen.

I'm ready for her to come back now, he thought, knowing they still had over two months left to go.

After the performance, after the standing ovations for Janet and then the entire company, Leslie and Mark went backstage.

They didn't stay long; Janet was surrounded. They couldn't get near her. Leslie waved, smiled and shrugged, indicating that it was impossible to traverse the crowded area. Mark smiled and held Janet's gaze for a brief, awkward moment.

Janet returned the smile, then looked away. She was happy he had come, and she was relieved when she saw him leave.

She couldn't see him, talk to him, without aching, and he couldn't see her either.

Mark and Leslie drove to Leslie's apartment in silence. Mark walked her to the door.

"Thanks, Mark," she said.

"You're welcome. See you at eight A.M. for rounds."

Kathleen *was* in the theater, but she had no idea that Mark might have seen her. She had been in and out of town, pacing between Hawaii and Atherton, Bermuda and Atherton, New York and Atherton. She was restless about being away too long even though nothing would happen—restless about being at home, waiting for the time to pass, not trusting herself not to call him.

Kathleen couldn't miss the opening night performance of *Joanna*. Ever since Ross MacMillan—her good friend and sometimes lover—had invited her to be on the Board of Union Square Theater, Kathleen had devoted long energetic hours to it.

Two years ago, Ross and Kathleen hatched the idea of opening a "Broadway" musical on Geary. They worked hard, convincing the board, finding backers, reading script after script until they found *Joanna* and, then, finally, assembling the perfect company.

Joanna was their baby.

Kathleen wasn't going to miss opening night.

Of course, she also wanted to see Mark. Even at a distance. And she wanted to see who occupied the seat next to his.

"This is all a little nuts, Katie," Ross said to her when she explained why she intended to watch the production hidden off stage.

"Maybe. But I am sticking to my plan. I just couldn't miss opening night."

Kathleen knew where Mark would be sitting. She had carefully selected the seats. Kathleen recognized Leslie and watched them both with increasing relief. Kathleen watched the way Mark and Leslie interacted—didn't interact—and knew that the relationship was platonic. Leslie was, simply, a friend of the family. The family that Mark and Janet used to be.

Kathleen relaxed and enjoyed the spectacular performance. Afterward she waited in the private theater lounge while Ross, who produced and directed *Joanna*, went backstage to congratulate his triumphant company. As he left, Kathleen asked him to notice if Mark was backstage and to observe his interactions with Janet if he was.

"You're not in third grade anymore, Katie," he said good-naturedly, smiling as he left.

Kathleen paced while she waited anxiously for Ross to return.

"*So?*" Kathleen asked the instant he reappeared forty-five minutes later.

"So everyone was absolutely ecstatic including the critics. It's a smash, Katie. We did it."

"So what about Mark? Was he there?"

"*Jesus!*"

"Ross," she pleaded.

"He was there for under two minutes. A curt nod at each other—Janet was swarmed, of course—from across the room. They looked uncomfortable. Not in love."

"Thanks."

"You're welcome. I'd be a little worried about the woman with Mark. She's gorgeous."

"I'm not worried."

"Good. C'mon, let's go to my place and celebrate."

"I *can't*," Kathleen said, knowing then that the reason she hadn't slept with anyone in the past two months was because she couldn't. Wouldn't. Didn't want to.

Kathleen's other lovers had never interfered with her sexual relationship with Ross.

"I wish you had given me a little advance warning about this," Ross said amiably. They were good friends.

"I didn't know until right now."

"You are nuts, Katie, really nuts."

Chapter 10

Jean Watson's condition deteriorated rapidly during the first week of May. Mark and Leslie and Jack Samuels discussed the options—new experimental protocols, different chemotherapy, transplantation—and came up empty. There was nothing more to do.

Jean's marrow showed no signs of recovery. It was almost impossible to transfuse her. She had started to have serious allergic reactions to blood and blood products. Because she had no platelets, she bled. Because she had few red blood cells, she was weak and anemic. Because she had no white blood cells in her bloodstream, no defense against invasion by bacteria, she had infections.

Still her mind and her spirit lived.

When Leslie made her seven A.M. rounds on May first, the morning following the opening night of *Joanna*, she found Jean propped up on her bed pouring over *The San Francisco Chronicle*.

"I've never seen reviews like these. Not from these critics. Your friend Janet! Well, they simply ran out of superlatives and space. I'm surprised they didn't spill over from the theater page to the front page—she's headline news!"

Leslie laughed.

"It was really marvelous. Janet truly *was* sensational. I wish—" Leslie stopped short.

"You wish I could see it. So do I, my dear," she said in a matter-of-fact tone. Jean refused to feel sorry for herself. "But you can tell me all about it."

"I will. Don't worry. How are you feeling?"

"Bacteremic," Jean said simply. She knew the medical terms. Bacteremia meant bacteria in the bloodstream. Bacteria in a place they shouldn't be, but were, because she had no white blood cells, no defenses. Jean could tell when her bloodstream was contaminated. She felt a certain, indescribable but recognizable way. She asked as lightly as she could, "Who's in my blood today?"

"*Klebsiella*."

"The *E.coli* are gone?"

"So far."

Five days later two different bacteria, *Serratia marcesans* and *Pseudomonas aeruginosa* and a fungus, *Candida albicans*, all grew from multiple cultures of Jean's blood. Despite antibiotics her blood pressure dropped. She was in shock because of the organisms in her bloodstream.

There was nothing they could do, except make her comfortable.

Mark and Leslie were both on call the night Jean went into shock. It was a new on-call system. The R-1 and R-2 from the same team were on call together instead of on alternate nights. It provided better continuity of care, the schedule makers claimed.

Leslie preferred the new system because, apart from simply being with Mark, seeing even more of him, she trusted him the most medically.

At six in the evening, Leslie went into Jean's room. Carl was at her bedside. The boys had come and gone. They all knew she would die that night. The boys had already said good-bye.

Carl Watson held his wife's frail purple hand.

Jean's eyes flickered open when Leslie entered the room.

"Leslie," she whispered, a slight smile.

"Hi," Leslie said and sat down.

Jean's eyes closed. After a few moments her breathing quickened. It was a physiologic response to the acidosis caused by shock.

Leslie and Carl watched Jean. Then Leslie turned to him.

"Are you OK?" she asked barely able to speak herself.

Carl's eyes glistened.

"I want to be with her, touching her, when she goes," he said, his voice shaky with emotion. "But I'm a little afraid."

"Do you want me to stay?" she asked.

"If you have time."

Time? Leslie thought. Do I have time to watch this lovely, beloved woman die?

Leslie switched her pager to the silent-vibratory mode. She would know if she was needed, but the beeper wouldn't sound.

Leslie took Jean's other hand. Was it her imagination or did she feel a squeeze as she took it?

Then they sat, silently, watching, waiting.

Leslie had never watched anyone die. She had *seen* patients die, but she had always been involved in trying to prevent the death. Even at the final moment.

She had never just watched.

After twenty minutes, Jean's breathing pattern changed again. Slow deep breaths. Final breaths.

It wouldn't be long.

Leslie took Carl's hand, the hand that didn't hold Jean's, and held it.

When she did, they formed a circle. Jean's hands were held by her beloved husband and her dear Leslie, her surrogate daughter. The circle was complete when Leslie reached for Carl's hand.

Jean looked peaceful when she died. She simply exhaled one breath and didn't take another. It took Leslie a moment to realize that it was over.

Leslie and Carl didn't move after Jean died. They continued to hold Jean's hands and each other's.

Leslie detected the warmth leaving Jean's hand. It made her feel terribly empty and sad.

She didn't want Carl to feel it. He needed to remember the warmth. It would be too much for him to feel the warmth, the final vestige of life, leaving his wife's hand.

"Mr. Watson," Leslie began, a little firm, a little urgent. It was too much for her, too.

Carl looked at her, his cheeks damp with tears.

"She's gone," Leslie whispered, controlling her own emotion with difficulty. "Shall we go?"

Leslie pulled gently at his hand, the one she still held. Carl moved with her without resistance.

The hallway lights were bright, too bright. Carl and Leslie squinted as they emerged from the dimly lit room. Leslie signaled silently to the head nurse to let her know that Jean Watson had died.

All the arrangements had been made. After, *only* after Carl Watson left, the efficient, impersonal mechanics of the paperwork and red tape that accompanied death would be put into action.

Leslie walked down the hall with Carl to the visitors" waiting room. The boys were there. Leslie had assumed they had gone.

But, of course, they wouldn't leave. They waited for their father. To be with him. To take him home.

Leslie withdrew quickly. Carl Watson was whee he needed to be. Five minutes before, her pager had vibrated. The telephone number indicated on the lighted dial was that of the emergency room.

Leslie dialed the number. Mark answered.

"Anything wrong?" he asked. Leslie usually answered pages immediately. Even this slight delay surprised Mark.

"Mrs. Watson just died. I was with Mr. Watson."

"Oh. Is everything OK?" Mark should have just asked the question that was really in his mind: Are you OK?

"Yes. Fine. What do we have?" Meaning, what does the admission you must be paging me about have wrong with him or her?

"We have a fifty-year-old man—Mr. Peterson—with liver cancer who has hepatic encephalophathy," Mark said. It was the hematology/oncology service after all.

"I'll be right down."

Six hours and two admissions later, at midnight, Mark found Leslie sitting huddled in the doctors' write-up area staring out the window into the blackness. Mark closed the door behind him as he entered the small room.

He had been worrying about her.

"Leslie?"

Leslie spun around, surprised. Her blue eyes glistened, brilliant blue, wet with tears.

"Why did she have to die, Mark?" Leslie asked weakly. Hot tears spilled onto her cheeks.

Mark was beside her in an instant. Without hesitation he put his arms around her and held her, rocking her gently, stroking her dark curls.

"It was so sad," Leslie said finally, talking into his chest. "It was so awful, just *watching* her die. Not being able to stop it."

Leslie shook her head and began to cry again. Mark blinked back his own tears and whispered, "I know, honey. I know."

As Mark spoke his lips brushed against her soft chestnut hair.

Toward the end of May, on their second to last night on call together, Mark found Leslie sitting by the picture window on the eleventh floor.

It was five A.M.

"So this is where the Night Stalker lurks," he said, startling her.

Leslie spun around and suppressed a gasp.

He is so handsome! she thought.

Mark stood in front of her, his dark hair tousled, his baggy white pants pulled tight at his slender waist with an old leather belt. Instead of his usual oxford shirt and necktie Mark wore a blue, surgical scrub shirt. The deep V-neck revealed a few dark, straight hairs on his bare, white chest. The short, loose sleeves showed his strong, sinewy, pale forearms. His white coat, his shirt and tie, his medical armamentarium, except for the pager which was clipped to his belt, were elsewhere—probably folded neatly in his on call room.

Mark stood in front of her, looking almost naked. Just Mark, a critical minimum of loose clothing and a pager. The bare essentials.

"Where she lurks when it's safe to stop stalking. When the sun comes up," Leslie said. Then she added a question, "Or do we have some business?"

"No. I just had six hours of uninterrupted sleep thanks to you. I'm wide awake. Rested. I decided to see if the rumors were true. If you really, in the eleventh month of your internship, still pace."

"This is why I do it, you know," Leslie answered a little coolly, her voice a little sharp. She gestured toward the view of sunrise over Golden Gate Park, the bay and the bridge. "It's so beautiful."

"I wasn't being critical, Leslie," Mark said quickly as he sat down across from her. His view was northeast toward Pacific Heights with its elegant condominium buildings shining in the new day sun.

"I'm a bit sensitive today, I guess," Leslie said.

"Why?"

"Because yesterday Greg signed out to me, at *noon*, to go jogging. His so-called stable service included two oozing GI bleeders and a leukemic with a temperature of one hundred four."

"Sounds like Greg," Mark murmured critically.

"Anyway, I nonverbally registered my annoyance," Leslie said, then hesitated. Maybe she didn't want to tell Mark about this after all.

Mark looked into her blue eyes. Eyes, he had learned over the past eleven months, that could deliver clear, specific messages. Eyes that could make direct blows. Remarkable dark blue eyes that weren't always so merry or cheerful. As the months passed, Leslie's always positive faade yielded occasionally to the pressures of fatigue and the realities, the frustrations and the lack of perfection she encountered. Leslie never said anything, never lost her temper, but her eyes effectively communicated annoyance, impatience, irritation and even censure.

Mark had never been on the receiving end of one of Leslie's glacial glances, but he had seen them delivered—ice cold, unyielding, uncompromising. Leslie could set her jaw and dig in with the best of them.

Mark hoped she would never look at him that way. He hoped that she would never have cause.

"I'm sure you did," he said. "So, what did Greg say?"

"He said," Leslie said slowly, looking out the window, embarrassed, "that I was strung so tight if he touched me I'd twang."

Mark started a laugh but suppressed it as he caught the shy, almost hurt expression in her eyes.

"It's sort of a cute remark, especially coming from an idiot like Greg."

"He's more than an idiot."

"How did his patients do?"

"Fine of course. By the time he jogged back two hours later, I had taken care of everything."

"So he's not such an idiot, is he?"

"I thought it was sort of an unfair remark," Leslie said.

"And untrue," Mark said, hesitating a moment. Then he added gently, carefully, "When I touched you, you didn't twang."

She had been so soft! A little wounded kitten cuddling into him for protection. As Mark held the boniness of her ribs, he felt the womanly fullness of her breasts, the soft warmth of her skin and the strong rapid pounding of her heart.

When you touched me, she thought as she stared at the shimmering sunlight on the azure bay, when you put your arms around me, I wanted to stay there forever.

Mark and Leslie sat in silence for many minutes, watching the new day begin.

At last Leslie decided to ask him. It was a risk. It could make him mad, but she remembered the closeness of that night, the night Jean Watson died, the night he held her. She knew how much she cared about him—about what happened to him—even if it had nothing to do with her.

"Have you decided?" she asked.

"Decided?"

"To quit medicine," she said quietly. There. She had said it.

"*Quit* medicine?" Mark repeated, surprised but not angry.

Quit was as charged a word as *best*. Quit, something you never did. Best, something you always were.

"Yes. Quit."

"What made you ask that?"

"You told me the night we saw *Joanna* that you didn't want to be a doctor," Leslie said flatly, as if it were fact. They both knew he hadn't said *that*.

"I never said I didn't want to be a doctor," he said, amazed, thoughtful, but still not angry.

"No. But that's what I heard."

"Oh. Well," he began then stopped. When he spoke again, the words came slowly, tentatively, as if their very utterance might cause disaster. "Maybe I don't want to be a doctor."

The words were spoken and nothing terrible happened. Leslie's eyes, smiling, not shocked, met his.

"Maybe I don't," Mark repeated, his voice stronger. "I've never said that out loud before, Leslie. It's only been in the past few months that I've ever begun to admit it to myself."

"So, are you going to get out?" she asked again.

"You make it sound so simple."

"It is simple. Hand me your pager. I'll turn it in for you."

"The mechanics might be simple, but the decision is not so easy . . . lots of complicating factors. I'm not even sure that I want out. There's a lot about medicine that I enjoy, that I would give up reluctantly. Would miss. Maybe I can find a niche that would allow me to practice medicine and . . ." Mark paused.

"And do what you really want to do?" Leslie added quickly.

"And give me time to read. Write maybe."

"But you are thinking that you *might* quit, someday, aren't you?" Leslie pushed. Mark had to be desensitized to the word *quit*. A lot of angry people would shout it at him.

"I'm just beginning to think about what I can do. What I should do."

"You *can* do anything. You *should* get out. Now," Leslie said decisively.

Her tone took Mark aback. He looked at her and smiled. In the past month, working with her, making decisions with her, taking care of patients with her and seeing her enthusiasm, Mark had thought very little about quitting. It had been so pleasant.

"Is that what those crystal-blue eyes see for me in the future?"

'I'm not predicting what you will do," she said. Probably chairman of the Department of Medicine at Harvard, she thought. *The Best*. "Only what, for the record, for whatever it matters, *I* think you should do."

"Because you know I'm no damned good at this doctor business?" he asked, half teasing. He couldn't understand why Leslie felt so strongly.

"You know what I think about you. You're—" Leslie paused. There was no other choice. He was, and she had to say it—"the best."

Three nights later, their last night on call together, Mark was already waiting for her at the eleventh floor window when she arrived at five-thirty in the morning.

"I thought you went to bed at eleven," she said, her heart pounding. Why was he here?

"I did. I'm well rested. I wanted to talk to you," he said as he slid over on the plastic, turquoise couch with the blond, wooden handles to make room for her.

Leslie sat down, instead, in the chair across from him.

"You could talk to me, any time, during the day," she said.

"Not really."

Leslie knew what he meant. It was impossible to *talk*—about anything but medicine—while they were working. But this time, this quiet dawn time when everything was under control, when most house staff would be asleep anyway, this time was, somehow, different.

Leslie waited.

"I just wanted to tell you what a good doctor I think you are," Mark said. It sounded awkward. "Around here no one ever tells you when you're doing a good job. They just tell you when you've screwed up. I know you know I've felt this way since the beginning of your internship, but I wanted to tell you again."

"It sounds like you're saying good-bye," Leslie said quietly.

"I'm not. In fact I saw the schedule. You and I will both be at San Francisco General in July."

"Oh! Well, then, thank you. It's been wonder—"

Mark held up his hand. "Enough! Neither of us is good at this."

Leslie smiled. Then she said earnestly but with a slight twinkle, "I know you liked working with me this month."

"Why?"

"Because you've gotten lots of sleep."

"True. But that's not why—"

"Which you need," Leslie continued, "because of your active social life. Which, judging from the nurses is . . . uh . . . something."

"Oh. They don't really talk about it do they?" Mark asked, genuinely surprised.

"Mark, it's become a part of their daily report!"

Mark frowned. He didn't like the idea of being dicussed.

"I'm not being critical at all!" Leslie said quickly. "No one is being critical. They all like you. Respect you."

"They *all*?" Mark asked soberly.

"Gail. Julie. *Gail*. Chris . . ."

"It doesn't seem right," he said. It was nobody's business. They shouldn't be talking about it. About his life and God knows what else.

"It's OK. Harmless. They probably discuss it around me more than anyone else."

"Why?"

"They assume, because I'm your shadow about every other month, that I know something. Which I don't of course," Leslie added.

"Know something like what?"

"Like, if you're using them."

"They're using me."

"They know that," Leslie said quietly. She had heard more than she wanted to about Mark in their beds. Leslie hated hearing about it, but they sought her out looking for information she didn't have. Leslie added, "They seem to sense that there's a Kathleen out there somewhere and that when she returns the party's over."

"They're right," Mark said simply, deciding that the party was over now.

"Oh."

"You like her, don't you? You saw her quite a bit when her mother was here."

"Sure. When is she returning? Janet said something about July."

Janet.

"Is this a fact-finding mission?" he asked.

"No!" Leslie bristled.

"She's coming back in July. By the eleventh," Mark said quickly, pleasantly, sorry that he had offended her. He was annoyed that they talked about him, annoyed that they involved Leslie and sorry that she knew about him and them.

"You think this is all pretty strange . . . sleazy . . . don't you?" he asked bluntly.

Leslie shook her head slowly. Her eyes, sad and thoughtful and blue, met his as she said evenly, "This has all been such a hard time for you. For you and for Janet. There's no right, or wrong, way to deal with it. You just have to get through it. Survive it."

Yes, she thought it was sleazy—not that he did as much as the fact that they talked about it.

"How is Janet?" he asked a few moments later.

"Busy with the show. We talk but I haven't seen her since opening night. She sounds all right."

Chapter 11

At nine o'clock on July ninth Mark dialed the telephone number to Kathleen's home in Atherton.

Kathleen answered.

"You're back."

"*Just*. An hour ago." In that hour, Kathleen had learned that there were no messages, no letters from him. Nothing to indicate that the plans had changed or to suggest that he didn't want to see her. "We decided not to stay for the wedding."

"The wedding?"

"Charles and Diana. You know. The king and queen to be. They aren't tying the royal knot until July twenty-ninth, and I had a birthday party to go to."

"You weren't really invited?"

"No," Kathleen admitted. "But of course we didn't try."

"So," he said gently, "How was it?"

Meaning the past few months. Kathleen knew what he meant, but she was euphoric. She could tell from his voice how much he wanted to see her. She could afford to tease him just a little.

"Fabulous! Did you watch any of it? The Connors-Borg semi-final was the best tennis ever. I'm sure that's why Borg lost to McEnroe in the final. He looked exhausted. McEnroe's great, of course. We'll probably be watching him for years to come. And Chris Evert Lloyd won—a major victory for twenty-seven-year-old women everywhere."

"Kathleen," he said sternly, knowing she was toying with him. "How was it?"

"The longest, loneliest four months of my life. How about you?"

"The same. But it was a good idea. You were right."

"About everything?"

"About everything."

"Hmm. Did you enjoy opening night?"

"How did—you were there, weren't you?"

"I couldn't miss it. You didn't see me . . ."

"A glimpse. But of course you said you'd be away for four months," Mark's tone sharpened.

"I was away from *you*. Mostly out of town. But not the whole time. No."

"*Spying* on me?" he pushed, sharply.

"*No*, Mark. I saw you opening night. Period. Betsey couldn't believe I didn't drive by your apartment—she knows about my insatiable curiosity—to look for strange cars. I told her that all the cars around there are strange," Kathleen said lightly. Then she added seriously, "But of course that's not the point. The point was your time and your privacy. I don't want to know what you did. Or with whom."

As long as you come back to me, she thought.

"Good," he said, still edgy.

Kathleen was silent, blinking back tears.

"Kitzy, are you there?" he asked, finally, his voice softer.

"Yes."

"So?"

"So can we take it from the top? Starting with the longest, loneliest four months part?"

"Sure. Maybe we should continue this in person?"

"Do I get to see you before your birthday?"

"I hope so. I'm on call on my birthday."

"No. Mark, didn't you get promoted to an R-3?" she teased.

"I made the cut; but we're still on every sixh, and July eleventh happens to be one of them."

"Every sixth. It has a beautiful ring to it," Kathleen purred.

"It's all better, Kathleen. Everything's better. I'm going to enjoy this year," he said. Then he added gently, "We're going to enjoy this year."

"Good," she breathed.

Kathleen arrived at Mark's apartment the following evening with her arms full of packages.

"What's this?" he asked as he took the packages, filling his arms with them instead of *her.*

"Birthday presents and birthday cake," she said as she followed him into the living room. She noticed the champagne chilling in a mixing bowl filled with ice and the tray of cheese and crackers.

Kathleen smiled. Mark was planning what she had planned: a mature refined reunion, champagne and hors d'oeuvres and quiet conversation. They would spend hours telling each other about the past four months. And only after that would they . . .

Mark put down the packages and turned to face her.

"Hi," he said gazing into her violet eyes. He wanted to talk to her, laugh with her, hold her and love her. All at once. He was greedy for her. For all of her.

"Hi," she sighed. *How I have missed you.*

"Would you like some champagne?"

"Sure," she whispered. *I don't care. I would like you please.*

"Not really?" he asked. He walked toward her, smiling lovingly.

Kathleen trembled as he approached. She had dreamed of this moment for so long. That Mark would want her still. Her heart raced as she saw the desire in his eyes.

So much for a mature refined reunion.

They kissed as they undressed each other urgently, needing to be as close as possible as quickly as possible. Needing to feel whole, complete, again.

"Hi," he whispered into her shiny black hair.

"Hi," she breathed into his strong pale chest.

"I've missed you. Too much."

"Too much?"

"I need you now." *Right now.*

"I need you now, too," she whispered as he laid her down on the couch. She welcomed him onto her and inside her. Where he belonged.

"Kathleen," he whispered. "Kathleen."

"Do you think our relationship is purely sexual?" she asked, exhausted, giggling.

"No," he said firmly. "I know it's not."

Mark knew, because he had several purely sexual relationships in the past four months. Kathleen knew the reason for Mark's confidence and was glad about it, but she didn't want to think about him with anyone else. Ever.

"Good."

"Are you going to move in with me? Live with me?" he asked her four hours after she had returned to his arms.

"Am I invited?"

"Yes."

"Then I will."

"Do we need a bigger apartment?" he asked, idly stroking her silky black hair as she nuzzled against his neck. "I mean your wardrobe alone . . ."

"I don't think I'll move all my worldly possessions," she said. Not yet. Maybe someday. She hoped. "Besides, Atherton is an easy commute. I have time to dash back and forth during the day. Visit my parents while you're working. This is a cozy place for us."

"You've made it cozy. What will you do all day, Kathleen? Won't you get bored?"

"After I run out of domestic things, I'll do what I do every day. Lots of different things. I won't be bored."

"What *do* you do every day?"

"Meetings, shopping, seeing friends, committees, projects. I keep very busy."

"You seem to. Oh, there's a party Saturday night at the Yacht Club. Not as fancy as the Celebration, or any Carlton Club Kids" function, but a Department of Medicine tradition. I have to go to it."

Kathleen waited, wondering.

"OK?" he asked, finally.

"Do I go too? With you?" she asked weakly, unsure if he meant they both would go.

"*Kathleen!* Of course. Of *course*."

"Your friend Leslie doesn't like me," Kathleen whispered in Mark's ear, licking it briefly at the same time. They were dancing, moving slowly together, their long lean bodies draped comfortably together, swaying rhythmically. Mark and Kathleen didn't cling to each other. They didn't need to. The leisurely rhythm of their bodies, although chaste, revealed their true intimacy to anyone who was watching. Their bodies knew each other well.

People *were* watching. Many people. Gail, Julie and Chris watched with great interest. So this dark lovely creature with the violet eyes and aristocratic grace was their competition?

Good-bye, Mark. *Adieu*.

Leslie watched them in brief glimpses, too. She didn't want to, but it was impossible not to.

"Of course she likes you," Mark whispered back.

"No, she's glowering at me. Not glowering, actually. That's too strong. Just shooting ice-blue icicles my way."

"You're over-reading," Mark said, but he wondered. The messages of Leslie's eyes were always clear, exquisite, articulate communiqués, and Kathleen was a good observer. Neither woman was likely to get her signals crossed. He added, "She has no reason to dislike you."

Kathleen said nothing. She knew she was right. As the evening wore on Kathleen thought she learned the reason for Leslie's iciness. It wasn't that Leslie disliked Kathleen. Not really. It was just that Leslie cared so very much about Mark.

Kathleen wondered if Mark even knew.

No, she decided as she watched Mark speak with Leslie briefly as the party ended. He doesn't know.

"I think I should get a job," Kathleen told Betsey during lunch ten days later. It was the last week in July. They had spent the morning in San Francisco, buying the final pieces of Betsey's trousseau, and had returned to Atherton for lunch at the Carlton Club.

Betsey, her wedding only three weeks and one dress size away, picked at her watercress sandwich while Kathleen ate a seafood crepe.

"A job!" Betsey gasped. "For heaven's sake, why?"

"I think it makes Mark nervous that I don't work."

"But you do work. You're on a zillion committees, boards, charities . . ."

"I know. But it all seems flighty to him. Frivolous."

"Kathleen, friend, you are flighty and frivolous. Except," Betsey added thoughtfully, "when it comes to Mark."

"I care about him," Kathleen said gently.

"I know. Does he know how rich you are? Does he know what your father does? Does he know your mother's maiden name? That would be an eye-opener: how many streets, buildings, squares, monuments and bridges in the Bay Area have the same name?"

"He doesn't know any of it. Except what Father does. Do you realize that I earn more in a month, from the trust from my grandparents, than Mark earns in *one year?*"

"You're kidding. I thought doctors—"

"Were rich? So did I. But I know for a fact that interns and residents get small salaries. Especially when you consider the number of hours they work. Doctors make good solid livings. Some surgeons, like neurosurgeons I think, make a lot, but they work *hard*. I can't believe how hard Mark and his friends work."

"So, not very many rich doctors? Just a myth?"

"No. Of course they make very good livings compared to other people who work for a living. But," Kathleen said soberly, "nothing compared to our wealth. I think doctors are targets because they're identifiable. High visibility. Nobody even knows about us. Our names, as a family, appear every year on the ten, twenty or thirty richest lists, but nobody really knows that those families are composed of kids, like us, who are multimillionaires. We're hidden. We would really be targets if anyone knew we existed."

Betsey and Kathleen and their friends had been trained to keep low profiles because wealth had some very high price tags: kidnappings, ransoms, swindlers, drug dealers, gold diggers. No one looking at Kathleen or Betsey could guess at the wealth they represented. They looked like two young working women having lunch.

Except that they were having lunch at the Carlton Club. That was a clue. But they were safe there. They were safe with each other. It was why they stayed together. Why the Carlton Club Kids were all, still, best friends.

"Do you want to get a job?"

"No. Of course not! I am completely happy, and I'm already too busy."

"What would you do if you weren't rich, if you didn't have enough money to live on?"

Kathleen played with her seafood crepe for a moment before answering. Then her violet eyes sparkled, "I don't know. I guess if I couldn't find someone like us, which I couldn't because I wouldn't know *we* existed, I'd just have to go out and find some rich doctor!"

Chapter 12

"Hi," Mark said as he walked into the small lab in the intensive care unit at San Francisco General Hospital.

Leslie spun around, startled.

Everyone was a little on edge, watchful. The ICU was housing a very important, and very ill, patient. He was a police informant. He hadn't yet been able to tell his story. The people who wanted him never to tell it had already made one—very nearly successful—attempt on his life.

Everyone who worked in the ICU was on alert. Even though the patient was heavily guarded, the police were fearful of another attempt on his life. The police told them all to be on the lookout for someone who looked out of place, who didn't belong. Someone whom they didn't recognize . . .

But it was July. Half the physician staff was new. There were the interns, their eager faces just beginning to show the inevitable signs of strain and fatigue, and there were new residents, ones who had transferred from other programs. Then, there were fellows who had completed residencies elsewhere and had come to San Francisco for subspecialty training.

Leslie met new people every day. On her way to the lab just now, she had seen yet another new face. He was a handsome man with stylish blond hair, intelligent blue eyes and a long white coat signifying his status as a fellow. Probably the new nephrology fellow, Leslie decided. She knew a patient had just been admitted to the ICU for emergency hemodialysis. He smiled at her as she passed him. She returned the smile but didn't stop. She was carrying the blood gas she had just drawn. She would meet him later.

"Mark! Hi," she breathed. Then, as her edginess vanished, she teased, "Is this one of your nights? A cameo appearance?"

"Just you wait. You'll be amazed how quickly every sixth night rolls around. This is my fifth night on call of the year, and it's only July thirtieth."

"Well, it's my *tenth*, but who's counting?" Leslie countered lightly. Then, looking at his slightly tanned, less gaunt face and his relaxed brown eyes, she added, "You look good. Rested."

Happy, she thought. She realized that he hadn't been happy before, but she hadn't known it. It was only obvious in retrospect.

"I am. This R-3 business is just fine."

"You're on the infectious disease consult service, aren't you? Is it a good elective?"

"Very good."

"Anything new on AIDS?"

"Just that the epidemic is continuing with dramatic doubling rates. Most people think it will turn out to be a virus. Transmission probably like hepatitis B."

"Sexual transmission we all know about. Blood, too?"

"Probably blood. That's the rumor. Cases in hemophiliacs are being recognized."

"Huh."

"Nobody's sure, of course, but it would be a good time not to get a blood transfusion in New York or LA. Or *here*."

"It's such an awful disease," Leslie said, then, focusing on the blood gas machine and the blood sample she had brought into the lab, she said, "Damn!"

"What?"

"I get so tired of people using this blood gas machine and not flushing it with heparin afterward!"

"Is it clotted?" Mark asked, moving beside her to inspect the decrepit machine and its slender plastic tubing.

"The clot can be worked out, but it's such a nuisance."

"Allow me, your friendly mellow R-3."

Leslie laughed.

"I'm a little snappy aren't I?" she asked.

"A little."

"Have you met my intern, Hal? Excuse me, *Dr.* Hal Rollins."

"OK, so Hal thinks he has a few answers," Mark said, laughing.

"A *few*?"

"All."

"You told me, almost precisely a year ago, that by this time this year I'd have an intern with a crush on me, padding obediently behind me, wagging his tail and drooling. Instead, I get Hal, who, by his own humble assessment, is God's gift to medicine."

"In a month he'll have a crush on you. When he learns how little he really knows."

"Grrr. This is his blood gas I'm running. His patient. Hal didn't think he needed a repeat gas, so . . ."

"So you're just quietly doing it? Not good, Leslie. You have to be tough."

"I have to make sure that the patients are OK, right? Top priority."

"Yeah. But you have to be tough with these little whippersnappers, too," Mark said firmly. "OK, give me the syringe. The clot's gone."

"My hero," Leslie said, still fuming at the thought of her intern. "Hal's the one who probably clogged it up."

"Oh," Mark said, looking at the label on the blood gas syringe that Leslie handed him. "This is from the fellow who turned state's evidence."

"*Tried* to," Leslie said. "Got shot before he gave them the key information."

"How's he doing?"

"I think he'll get another chance. Today he's much better."

"That's why the ICU is teeming with police."

"Uh-huh. What do they think, someone's going to walk in and shoot him again, in broad daylight, in the ICU?"

"That's *exactly* what they think."

"It could happen," Leslie said firmly. But it was what she and everyone else feared. It was why they were all so edgy, why they were all so watchful.

"It could. Anyone in a white coat could get in. Assuming he, or she, wasn't wearing army fatigues or carrying an illconcealed submachine gun instead of a stethoscope. They'd just have to select a non-thug-looking psychopath—"

"Even thug-looking. Even battle fatigues—"

"Leslie, you really are in a charming mood tonight. Modern medicine hasn't come to that. I haven't spotted one thug, or one battle-fatigue-wearing intern, in this year's group. Maybe in the early seventies . . . but we're in a conservative era. Even Hal."

"Especially Hal. Those bow ties," Leslie said, laughing at last, shaking her head. "Bow ties!"

"OK. Here are your results," Mark said, reading the dials on the machine. "The pH is seven point—"

Three shots rang out. Then screaming. Shouting. Running. More shots.

Mark and Leslie froze.

"Stay here," Mark said, moving toward the door.

Leslie grabbed his arm.

"You stay here, too, Mark."

The door crashed open. A blond man, wearing a long white coat and carrying a black gun, entered and pulled the door shut behind him.

Leslie and Mark retreated to the far corner of the tiny lab.

"Don't say a word," the man hissed as he faced them.

When Leslie saw his face she gasped. It was the same man—the one who she had decided was the new nephrology fellow—she had seen moments ago. The man who looked like a board certified internist, not a thug. The man with the intelligent blue eyes . . .

The eyes were transformed now. They were wild, darting, crazed. *Crazy.* They were also a little euphoric, manic, triumphant. He had probably successfully killed his target, Leslie's patient. Now he only had to escape.

He ws prepared to take hostages. Or to leave more victims.

He pressed his back against the door and leveled the gun at Mark and Leslie. He realized in an instant that there was no way out of the tiny lab except by the door through which he had entered.

The assassin grabbed Leslie's arm and pulled her beside him.

"C'mon, little nursey. You're comin" with me."

He jerked her toward him and held her, squeezing her arm until it ached. Then he put the gun to her head, pressing its cold barrel against her temple, and put his finger on the trigger.

"One peep and you're dead."

The room was silent except for the sound of their breathing. Outside, in the hallway, the shouting and footsteps had become distant. They were chasing the assassin out of the hospital.

But he was still in the ICU.

He's bleeding, Mark realized. The man had been shot in the leg. Large drops of blood splashed onto the linoleum floor.

Surely, Mark thought, he left a trail of blood leading to the lab.

Despite the silence from the other side of the door—too silent given the commotion that would be going on in the ICU in the aftermath—they must be out there. The police must know exactly where the murderer is.

They probably have the hallway sealed off, Mark decided. How many guns are pointed at the door? What if they decide to open fire, believing the man is alone in the lab? If they open fire, they will hit Leslie.

The man held Leslie in front of him, pressed against the door. The gun was still pointed at her head. His finger was on the trigger.

Mark couldn't let it happen. Ten more seconds of silence, he decided, hoping it wasn't too much.

He counted patiently, evenly.

Nine. Ten.

"HEY!" Mark yelled and lunged at the startled assassin, who spun, the barrel of the gun leaving Leslie's temple and ramming, as he pulled the trigger, into Mark's chest.

"*Mark*!" Leslie screamed, rushing past the man who bolted for the door, opened it and ran into a circle of police. Trapped, he became frantic and started shooting, wounding two officers before he died.

"Mark, Mark," Leslie said, over and over, as she knelt beside him.

The bullet had created a gaping hole in Mark's chest. He gasped for breath. Despite the pain, he lay still. Afraid. In shock.

Bright red blood spurted from the wound and onto Leslie's face and chest as she hovered over him. Bright red blood. *Arterial* blood. He was losing blood quickly. With each heartbeat—and his heart was beating rapidly—another large spurt of blood left Mark's body.

He would bleed out, die from acute blood loss, very quickly. His strong young heart would pump harder and harder. Each pump more and more lethal.

Unless and until the hole in the artery was closed.

Leslie reached into the wound in Mark's chest with her left hand. She felt the hot blood pulsing toward her. She tried to determine the direction with the sensitive tips of her fingers, praying she would be able to reach the severed artery.

What if she couldn't find it?

What if her fingers wouldn't reach?

As Leslie rammed her hand inside his chest, deeper and deeper, she felt his shattered ribs and the sharp points of the broken bone tearing her own skin. She felt the warmth of his body, his hot pulsing blood and his lacy delicate lung moving, gasping against her hand.

"Leslie, let's get him out of here. Down to the trauma room."

The hall outside the tiny lab was now crowded with police, nurses, house staff, camera crews and reporters. The lab was too small for more than one or two more people. They couldn't take care of Mark there. They needed to get him into a big room with equipment and a trained trauma team.

"I have to—" Leslie said as her fingers finally reached the artery that was allowing Mark's life to bleed away. She gave her hand one final shove, stretching her fingers to the area of pulsation. With all her strength she pressed her fingers over the hot, slippery vessel.

The bleeding slowed.

"C'mon, Les!" The people in the hallway were getting anxious. They had no idea why Leslie wouldn't get out of the lab. Why she wouldn't move to let them get to Mark so they could take him to the ER.

"I'm tamponading an arterial bleeder," she said. "I have it now, so we can move him. But I can't take my hand away."

Until then they had only seen her back, her body hunched over Mark feverishly doing something. She turned slightly as she spoke. They saw her face, drenched in Mark's blood, and the red wetness of her chest.

They knew instantly she was right. They could all see how much blood he had lost. If she had the bleeding stopped, the top priority for all of them as they transported him to the trauma room was to protect her hold on the artery.

"Can we clamp it here, Leslie?"

In time, as soon as possible, Leslie's finger would be replaced by a metal clamp. Properly positioned, it would hold the artery closed until they could get him to surgery.

"I don't know. Maybe. I really have a good hold right now." Once she had the bleeding slowed, she had repositioned her hand, wedging the palm against the sharp bones of his broken ribs. She had a good, firm grasp of Mark's chest wall and of the severed artery.

"Ok. Let's move him, then. He needs to be intubated as soon as possible."

The hole in Mark's chest did not allow him to breathe effectively. Each breath, each gasp sucked air in through the hole, putting pressure on the lung, preventing its normal expansion, making it collapse.

Mark was unconscious. He needed many things all at once. He needed an endotracheal tube, intravenous lines, blood, oxygen and surgery. One and a half minutes after they left the ICU lab, Mark was in the trauma room in the emergency room, intubated, with two intravenous lines. Blood work had been sent.

San Francisco General Hospital was one of the first and best trauma centers in the country. A team of trained doctors, each with a specific pre-assigned task, quickly and efficiently worked to give each trauma patient the best possible chance of survival.

The senior surgical resident was the trauma chief. During his six-month rotation as trauma chief, he never left the hospital. Dr. Ed Moore was already in the emergency room when Mark was shot, caring for a patient who had been stabbed in the thigh. Ed wanted to get the other patient stabilized so that he could devote his full attention to Mark when he reached the trauma room.

Ed Moore quickly moved beside Leslie.

"OK, Les," he said brusquely. Meaning, I've got him now.

Leslie looked at Ed and said calmly, firmly, "I've my finger on the severed artery."

Ed drew in a breath when he saw Leslie's bloodied face.

"Hold onto it, Les. I'll get a clamp."

Ed eased the long silver clamp beside Leslie's finger. They couldn't see anything. It had to be done by feel. Leslie had to direct Ed.

"There," she said when she felt the cold clamp near the tip of her finger.

Ed opened and closed the clamp, taking a blind bite at the artery.

"OK. Let go."

As soon as Leslie released the pressure exerted by her finger, the blood, Mark's blood, spurted out at them.

"Damn," Ed sputtered.

Quickly Leslie pressed her fingers against the artery again. It was getting harder to maintain the seal. Her fingers cramped. The pain from the cuts in her own hand, cuts from Mark's broken, shattered ribs, throbbed in her palm. The new hot burst of blood made the artery even more slippery, more difficult to compress.

They tried again.

And again.

On the fourth try the clamp closed over the artery. When Leslie removed her fingers, there was no bleeding.

"Operating room in two minutes," Ed barked. "Where's the blood? I want two units—in him!—before we operate. And we're operating in two minutes."

With the endotracheal tube, oxygen and an attentive anesthesiologist managing Mark's breathing for him, Mark had regained consciousness.

Leslie saw Mark beckon to Ed. She had withdrawn to a corner of the trauma room as soon as the artery was successfully clamped. The energy and emotion that had enabled Leslie to act as quickly as she had now gave way to exhaustion and fear. Now that she was no longer an active participant, preoccupied with her task, she had time to think. And worry.

But Mark was in good hands. The best.

And he was talking! Leslie stood up straight as she watched Mark. Awake, alert, trying to communicate with Ed. Mark couldn't speak because of the endotracheal tube, but he clearly had a message. Leslie saw him gesture, saw them give him a pen and paper and saw him write something which he handed to Ed.

Leslie watched Ed's expression as he read what Mark had written. She watched Ed frown, then scowl. He began to speak animatedly, then angrily, at Mark.

Leslie couldn't hear what they said. The room was too full of other noises. It was filled with the sound of nurses and doctors and technicians making certain that Mark was stable, finalizing arrangements for the imminent transfer to the operating room and calling out laboratory results done on Mark's blood.

"The pO2 on the last gas is 280."

"Thanks! What's the pH?" the anesthesiologist asked.

"Seven point four."

"Great."

"His crit is twenty-eight."

A brief silence ensued, a break in the general hubbub.

"Did you hear that, Mark? Your crit is twenty-eight. And that's before rehydration. You've lost a helluva lot of blood," Ed Moore shouted, his voice especially loud because of the momentary silence in the trauma room.

Ed looked across the room at Leslie, at her blood-stained face and clothes. It gave him a rough idea—a grim idea—of Mark's blood loss, and he hadn't even seen the pool of blood in the ICU laboratory.

Leslie saw Mark's head move slightly from side to side. A clear negative message.

"OK, Mark, old buddy, I'll give it may goddamned best shot."

Ed walked toward Leslie and snapped to whoever was listening, "Where's Dr. T?"

Everyone was listening. Everyone had overheard Ed's last remarks to Mark. Everyone was wondering what had happened.

"Scrubbing," the head nurse answered, remembering that Dr. Moore had just asked a rather specific question.

"Good."

Dr. T., as they fondly referred to Dr. Jon Thomas, was the attending trauma surgeon. Dr. T. didn't scrub in on every case. It wasn't necessary. His trauma chief and the other surgery residents were highly trained. But Dr. T. came in for the critical cases. For cases like Mark.

Leslie was glad he would be there.

Ed stopped when he reached Leslie.

"If he's not a Jehovah's Witness, what is he?" Ed demanded.

"What do you mean?" Leslie asked, worried.

Ed shoved the crumpled piece of paper he held in his hand at her.

It read: *No Blood Tx*. It meant: No blood transfusions. It was written by Mark.

"He says he's not a JW, so what's his problem with receiving blood?"

Leslie shrugged. Then she remembered.

"AIDS," she whispered, almost to herself.

"AIDS? *Christ*. What's the evidence for that?"

"Not much, but apparently data is beginning to accumulate."

"Typical internist worrying, what *if*-ing. I have plenty of *hard* data about the mortality of Mark's type of chest wound, even given optimal management, such as blood transfusions. Leslie, this could cost Mark his life."

"Why don't you transfuse him anyway?" Leslie asked anxiously, knowing the answer.

"Because we have this in writing. Clear evidence that Mark does not want blood. Mark is conscious and sane, *legally* anyway. If he had whispered it to me, I might have misunderstood, or not heard it at all. But in writing, lots of witnesses. No can do. You know that."

"I know," she said weakly. Then she asked, "Can I talk to him? I could offer to give him my blood. Our blood has already intermingled. If I have AIDS, or if he does, the exposure has already happened."

As she spoke, Leslie held up her hand with her palm facing Ed. He knew that she had already been exposed to Mark's blood; it was all over her, but he hadn't realized until then how Mark could have been exposed to her blood. Reflexively, Ed reached for Leslie's badly cut had and looked at it closely.

"These are bad lacerations, Leslie," he said quietly.

Leslie shrugged. She would worry about her cuts later.

"So, you see, Mark's gotten some of my blood already," she said. "So could I talk to him?"

"Be my guest. He seems determined. What a fool!"

"Ed," Leslie pleaded gently, "please don't be angry with him."

"Hey, whoa, Les. I'm angry as hell at the guy. I also happen to like him. He's a friend. We go back two years and a lot of long, hard, on call nights. I'll try my best to save him," Ed said. Then he added sternly, "Even if I'd never met the bastard I would try my best to save him."

"Now you're angry with me," Leslie said grimly, realizing she *had* insulted him.

"No. I'm just angry. But don't worry. Being angry just pumps me up. I do my best operating when I'm a little mad," Ed said, briefly touching her shoulder on a rare patch of her coat that was white not red. "Hey, haven't you ever seen John McEnroe play tennis when he's angry? He always wins."

You have to win this one, Ed, Leslie thought as she watched him leave to go to the OR to scrub. You have to.

Then she walked over to Mark. His eyes were closed.

"Mark?"

The brown eyes opened. So much *pain*.

"Mark, it's Leslie. You need blood."

Pain and *fear*. Mark shook his head slowly, definitively.

"Because of AIDS?"

A slight nod, eyes closed.

"Mark, that is nonsense!"

Eyes opened, a trace of anger. But, mostly, pain and determination.

"Mark, what if I give you my blood? We've already—"

Mark's head moved swiftly to the side. *No*.

Ed was right. Mark had made his decision.

It's as if he wants to be allowed to die, Leslie thought suddenly. Mark *had* lunged at the assassin and into the gun. Now he was refusing live-saving, essential blood. Stop it, she told herself. It was just her own morbid imagination at work.

"Mark," Leslie said gently. "Shall I call Kathleen?"

Mark's eyes brightened for a moment, then faded. Joy then worry. He nodded.

"And Janet?"

A slight nod.

"Your parents?"

A strong no. Almost as strong as his refusal of blood.

"Gotta go, Leslie. OR's ready," the anesthesiologist said.

"Oh. OK. See you soon, Mark," she said.

"Are you going to scrub in, Leslie?" someone asked.

"What? Uh . . . no," she said. *No.*

Chapter 13

Leslie followed Mark's stretcher out of the trauma room and into the glaring light of the television cameras. Leslie stared directly into the light, her blue eyes wide, blazing with anger and astonishment at the harsh intrusion. The rest of her face and her hair were covered with blood.

Beyond the cameras she saw her intern Hal. Leslie could not interpret the look on his face, but, remarkably, she felt a sudden closeness to him.

Leslie rushed past them all, down the hall, to the women's locker room. She removed all her clothes, her white jacket, her blue and white flowered shirt, her bra, her slip, her underpants and her nylons. All were stained red, redbrown, with Mark's blood. Leslie eyed the clothes helplessly. They were ruined, but she couldn't throw them away. Not yet. She couldn't throw away Mark's precious blood even though it was useless to him.

If only she could give him back some of his own blood!

Leslie couldn't throw away Mark's blood. She couldn't even rinse it out.

Slowly, carefully, Leslie folded the clothes and put them into her overnight bag.

Eventually she convinced herself that she had to wash Mark's blood off her body. It was even more morbid not to. She stood in the shower and let it wash off, her eyes closed shut so that she couldn't see how much of his precious blood was flowing down the drain. Leslie didn't scrub it off. She just let the water wash it away. Finally she dared to look at the water at her feet. It was clear.

Then Leslie got the soap and shampoo she had removed from her overnight bag and took a usual on call shower. It was a quick shower taken at a quiet time with the pager lying next to the shower stall on the tile floor.

The lacerations on Leslie's palm and fingers stung. As she washed they began to bleed. Her blood.

Momentarily mesmerized, Leslie watched her own blood swirl down the drain. Then she focused on the cuts themselves. Several were deep, but none extended down to tendon. The sensation and motor function in her hand seemed normal. They were probably too deep and narrow—true puncture wounds—to suture, but they needed attention. Sometime she would return to the ER, clean the wounds carefully with sterile solution, and ask one of the orthopedic surgeons to take a look.

Leslie had clean underpants, nylons and a blouse in her overnight bag, but she had no extra bra, no white coat, no skirt. She found a clean surgical scrub dress, a royal-blue, cotton dress with a deep V-neck and short sleeves. The dress was loose around her narrow hips and waist but snug over her bare breasts.

She would borrow someone's white coat or find an extra white coat somewhere to cover up her immodest outfit. Not that it mattered. Not that anything mattered except Mark.

Leslie walked out of the women's locker room and into the glare of the television cameras. They had followed her and waited.

"Dr. Adams," a reporter said. "Just a word, please."

Leslie stopped. She was too bewildered not to.

The cameras pointed at her. They focused on the damp chestnut hair combed hurriedly, before she left the locker room, with the trembling fingers of her uninjured hand. They focused on the brilliant blue eyes, and they focused on the ample, round breasts that strained against the too tight scrub dress.

She looks like an NCAA swimming champion, the reporter thought—damp, healthy, fit, excited—except her breasts are too large for a swimmer.

"Dr. Adams, could you please tell us what happened?"

Leslie opened her mouth to speak, too stunned not to, but the question unleashed the memories. And her priorities. Her only priority was to find out about Mark.

"No," she said flatly into the camera. She leveled her clear blue eyes at the red light on the camera because the glare was less there. "No, I can't."

The cameras continued to roll as she sped away. They didn't have many words from Dr. Leslie Adams, but they had sensational color footage, before and after: before, the blood-soaked face and clothes; after, the clean, damp young woman, erotic and sensual in the ill-fitting scrub dress. Common to both sequences, captured in vivid color, captured as they delivered clear, eloquent nonverbal messages of astonishment, sadness, worry and anger, were those huge sapphire-blue eyes.

Channel Five had the best footage, but all the local stations had good shots. Good enough. They all ran the story on the shootings—the murdered would-be informant, the assassin, the wounded police officers and the critically injured resident—featuring the dramatic pictures of Dr. Leslie Adams. The segment was featured on every newscast on every channel for a full thirty-six hours.

All stations received a record number of phone calls.

After escaping the reporters, Leslie rushed to the operating room and went directly to the nursing station. The San Francisco General Hospital operating room was an active place. Cases were done twenty-four hours a day, seven days a week.

At that moment, Mark was one of four cases.

"How is he?" Leslie asked the head nurse, Gwen. Despite the other cases, Mark was everyone's primary concern. He was the most critical.

"So far, so good. They just started," Gwen said. Then, looking at Leslie, Gwen reached for a long white coat that hung on a hook on the wall. "Here. I don't know who this belongs to. It's been hanging here for at least three weeks. Whoever it belongs to, you need it more."

"Thanks, Gwen."

"We cleared out one waiting room for you and his friends and family. Waiting room B."

"Thanks," Leslie breathed. "I guess I'd better make some phone calls."

It was ten-fifteen. Leslie decided she would call Janet after the show. Leslie got Kathleen's parents' telephone number from directory assistance.

"Yes, Dr. Adams. Of course I remember you," Virginia Jenkins said. "You took such good care of me."

"How are you, Mrs. Jenkins?"

"Fine. Very well. No more angina even. They say I finally just clipped off the part of the narrowed artery that was causing the pain. So, I'm even better."

"I'm glad. Uh . . . is Kathleen there?"

"Oh, no, dear. She lives in the city. With Mark Taylor. Do you need their number?"

"Yes, please." Lives in the city with Mark. Virginia Jenkins sounded calm about it. Who wouldn't be? Leslie didn't know Mark's home telephone number. The page operator would have it, but Virginia Jenkins provided the number from memory.

"Thank you," Leslie said.

"Hi, babe," Kathleen answered the phone on the second ring. It was the time that Mark always called if he could. Even if it was to say he couldn't talk.

"Kathleen, it's Leslie Adams."

"Oh, Leslie. Mark's not here."

"I know, Kathleen. Mark's had an accident." Leslie's voice broke. Hot tears began to track down her cheeks.

"*Leslie!*"

"Mark is in surgery, Kathleen. He's been injured."

"Injured?"

"Shot."

"Shot! No. *No!* He couldn't be shot. How is he? Is he—"

"He's in surgery. He was shot in the chest. He was conscious before surgery. Not paralyzed," Leslie said. She gave Kathleen all the positive information she could think of. She didn't tell her about the blood. She didn't tell Kathleen that if Mark lost one more drop of blood he could die. "Come to surgery, waiting room B, OK? Kathleen, take a taxi. It's much safer."

"Yes. I will. Leslie, are you with him? Will you be?"

"I'm here. Very near. In the OR."

Two hours later Mark was still in surgery, still alive. Janet, Leslie and Kathleen sat in waiting room B. It had taken the press no time to find the location. They had already established interest in the blue-eyed heroine who wouldn't speak to them. Then someone identified Janet, star of *Joanna*, San Francisco's hottest theater production, and their interest soared. No one recognized Kathleen or even asked her name. *That* was very lucky.

Leslie had to pass through the reporters to get into the OR to check on Mark. Each time it was an ordeal.

They all felt trapped. They sat, silently, each on one of the three couches arranged at right angles to each other against the pale yellow walls.

Aware of Leslie's problem with the eager reporters, Gwen began to deliver the reports so that Leslie did not have to leave the room. Still, it made Leslie restless. What if something happened and Gwen couldn't get away? *Because* something had happened.

"He hasn't bled at all," she said. "And they've ligated the artery. They had to remove his right lower lobe."

Kathleen and Janet gasped in unison.

"It's not a big deal," Leslie and Gwen reassured them.

"Why is he still in there?" Janet asked.

"Because there are lots of bone splinters. They are picking them out one by one. And because the wound was contaminated. They want to clean it thoroughly. They don't want to have to go back in. They're just being very careful. His vital signs have been rock-steady."

"What's his crit, Gwen?" Leslie asked finally, reluctantly.

"Eleven."

Oh my God, Leslie thought.

"What does that mean?" Kathleen asked, sensing Leslie's concern despite her effort to appear calm.

"It's low," Leslie admitted. She didn't add that it meant he couldn't afford to bleed. Not even a little. If only I had gotten to the artery sooner, she thought, tormented, aching. If only . . .

"The press is a nuisance, eh? They're even quizzing *me* since they can't get at you," Gwen said on her third visit to waiting room B. "I've tried to get them to leave, but they sense my lack of authority. And, I think we may be coming face to face with a little chauvinism, ladies."

"I'm afraid so," Leslie said. "What we need is a chief of medicine." Or someone who thinks he is, Leslie thought. "Gwen, I can't dial out on this phone, can I?"

"No."

"Can it ring in?"

"The operator can connect to it."

"Would you page Dr. Hal Rollins? Then have him connected through to this extension?"

"Sure. Shall I page him stat?"

"No. Hal's pretty good answering his pages right away. It's one of his strong points."

While Leslie waited she remembered Hal's expression when she emerged from the trauma room. What was it? Certainly nothing she had seen before.

The telephone in the waiting room rang in three minutes.

"Hi boss," Hal said.

"How are things going, Hal?"

"Fine. *Nothing* is happening. It's like everyone—the whole world—is worried about Mark. It's weird. Tomblike."

Tomblike. A nice happy medical term meaning quiet.

But not a good term to use tonight.

"Er . . . uh . . . quiet," Hal said quickly. "I heard that Mark's crit is eleven, and they can't transfuse him?"

"Uh-huh. Listen Hal, I need a favor."

"Shoo—" he began then caught himself. He had actually started to say "Shoot boss" like he always did, but he stopped himself, a little horrified. When he spoke it was in a voice that Leslie had never heard before, a voice to match the expression she had seen earlier.

"Anything, Leslie," Hal said seriously. Then, before Leslie spoke, he added what had been on his mind. "You were really amazing. You really saved his life. You knew exactly what to do and you did it."

Leslie swallowed hard. Hal was complimenting her. He admired her. It had been admiration in his eyes. Leslie smiled slightly.

"Thanks, Hal. Now here's what I need. I want you to come down to waiting room B. Identify yourself to the press as someone with authority. I don't even care if you lie to them. Just convince them to leave this area. Not the hospital, just this area. I don't want you to infringe on their First Amendment rights. Just get them away. OK?"

"Sure. *No* problem."

Leslie stood near the door, listening to Hal's speech, marveling at his confidence.

"Ladies and Gentlemen of the press. I am Dr. Hal Rollins. I represent the Department of Medicine. I am afraid we have a hospital policy about these waiting rooms, about who can be in this area. It's a conflict, First Amendment rights versus patient confidentiality, but I'm sure you'll understand that we have to protect our patients" rights. I assure you I will be the first to hear of any changes in Dr. Taylor's condition and will notify you immediately. If you would care to follow Dr. Rhodes to the cafeteria . . . It's closed to the public at this hour, but the Department of Medicine has provided special passes for all of you. So, please, follow Dr. Rhodes."

Miraculously, they did follow Dr. Rhodes, the third year medical student who was carrying a fistful of yellow passes. Meal tickets. Probably Hal's entire supply for the month.

I misjudged him, Leslie thought.

Hal lingered outside the door until the press was out of sight, then he entered waiting room B.

"How'd I do, boss?" he asked, his voice a little less confident than usual, wanting Leslie's approval as he never had before.

"Fabulous, Hal. Truly. I'll see that you get all those meal tickets back. That was very generous."

"No *problemo*. I can get more. I have an in with the Department of Medicine secretary." The department secretary was the keeper, a notoriously stingy keeper, of the meal tickets.

Of course you do, Leslie thought. Typical Hal. But, still, she'd seen another side of him. And he of her.

She was grateful for what he had done, and he admired her for what she had done.

Five minutes after the press left, Janet stood up.

"I'm going to go."

"Janet!"

Leslie followed her into the hallway.

"I don't belong here, Leslie. I'm not helping him, and I'm preventing Kathleen from talking. Call me, please, as soon as you hear anything."

"I will."

Janet was right. Kathleen needed to talk. She started talking as soon as Leslie returned, but her words caught Leslie by surprise.

"Listen, Leslie, I know you don't like me. I know how much you care about Mark. But, believe me, I love him with all my heart. I really do."

"Kathleen, I—"

"And he loves me, Leslie," Kathleen continued firmly.

"I know that," Leslie said honestly. She had learned it that night. At least, she had admitted it to herself that night. She had seen the look in Mark's eyes at the mention of Kathleen's name.

Then Kathleen began to cry.

"Oh God, I wish he would quit medicine."

"What?" Apparently Mark had told her, and she didn't care. *Good.* "You wish he would quit—"

"Yes. He never would, of course. He loves it. He's committed to it," Kathleen sighed.

So she didn't know. Maybe there was nothing to know anymore. Maybe Mark had made peace with his inner conflict. Leslie remembered how happy,
550 how relaxed he had looked tonight. Before . . .

"Why do you wish he would quit?" Leslie asked.

"Selfishness. So he would be safe. From the diseases. From getting shot. What is there about being a doctor that should put you at risk to get *shot?*" she demanded.

Leslie had no answer. Mark wasn't the first doctor to get shot. It happened. Angry patients, angry families, patients demanding narcotics, psychotic patients . . .

"I don't know, Kathleen," Leslie said. Then she asked, curious, "You don't care if Mark is a doctor?"

"No! I don't care if he is anything or nothing. I just want to be with him," Kathleen smiled through her wet violet eyes, seeing a past memory or a future happiness. "If he wasn't a doctor, we would have more time together. Selfish. I'm selfish."

Their conversation was interrupted by Gwen who announced that they were beginning to close. Mark would be going up to the ICU in about twenty minutes.

Leslie and Kathleen slipped past the press assembled in front of the ICU. Hal was giving them an update, promising them an interview with one of the trauma surgeons as soon as the surgeon was free to leave Mark.

Leslie briefly introduced Kathleen to Ed Moore who was writing Mark's post-op orders at the ICU nursing station.

"He's OK so far, Leslie," Ed said. "But he still can't bleed. He has absolutely no reserve. We've already given him a blast of iron by vein."

So he can start making, remaking, red blood cells.

"You are a hero, Ed!"

"No, but we all gave it our best. And our luck has held, so far." Then he reached for her hand. The cuts were still unbandaged. Leslie hadn't had a chance to go back to the ER. Ed said gently, "You are the hero, Leslie. You saved his life."

"No," Leslie said, embarrassed, uncomfortable that Kathleen overheard.

"*Yes.* Here's the proof," he said examining her hand. "In thirty minutes, after we get him squared away here, you meet me in the ER. These wounds need attention."

"OK. Thanks."

There was some concern about allowing Kathleen in to see Mark. She was not family.

Leslie intervened quickly.

"Kathleen is his family. He needs her. They just don't happen to have the piece of paper and the blood test," Leslie said. Not yet, she thought.

"You'd make a good attorney, Leslie. Persuasive," the head nurse said. But the nurse allowed it mainly because of Mark. Anything to help Mark.

"Thank you," Kathleen said quietly as they walked toward Mark's room in the ICU.

"We kept the anesthesia pretty light. He's still out, but he should wake up soon," the anesthesiologist said to Leslie.

Leslie and Kathleen stopped at the door to Mark's room. The nurses were organizing the machines, lines, monitors, ventilator hoses and settings.

Mark lay still, motionless. So pale. A hematocrit of eleven made his skin white. Blue-white.

Leslie held back, knowing to wait for the nurses to get everything in order, to finish their necessary tasks. Leslie also held back because, as many times as she had seen ICU patients with lines and tubes lying motionless, it was always startling and a bit overwhelming.

Now the patient was Mark.

Kathleen did not hold back. She did not hesitate to move quickly toward the horribly pale, horribly still marionette who was Mark.

Kathleen smiled graciously as she worked her way around the busy, surprised nurses, careful not to disturb anything, ducking under tubes, stepping over cords, but aiming unerringly for the head of the bed. She had to get to a place where she could touch him, speak to him.

When she reached him Kathleen placed her head gently against his, temple to temple, and whispered into his ear.

"I love you, Mark. I love you."

Mark's eyes fluttered, and his hand, apparently lifeless until that moment, lifted off the bed and reached for her.

Kathleen caught his hand and held it. She whispered again and again.

"I love you, Mark. I love you."

Leslie watched Mark and Kathleen for a moment, her eyes flooded with tears. Then she left to call Janet and to let Ed Moore take care of her hand. As she left, Leslie knew for the first time in the long emotional evening that Mark would make it. He had a reason to make it.

Kathleen was his reason.

Chapter 14

James Stevenson flipped on the television's power switch. When Lynne was away, James drank his morning cup of coffee and smoked his first cigarette of the day in front of the morning news programs.

"After murdering his intended victim, the assassin hid in a small laboratory where two residents from the University of California's Department of Medicine were working. One of the residents, Dr. Mark Taylor, was shot. The other resident, Dr. Leslie Adams, pictured here . . ."

James looked up instantly at the mention of Leslie's name, just in time to see the dramatic footage, artfully spliced. James moved closer to the television and turned up the volume. His pulse raced, and his mind spun as he watched the horrible, grotesque picture of her blood-coverered face fade miraculously into the one of her just after she had emerged from the shower. Fresh, beautiful, sensual.

Leslie.

So she was here. In San Francisco.

She looked the same. James had seen that startled, bewildered look before—a similar picture, but a different time and a different place. That spring day, years before, her hair was damp, her face fresh from a brisk swim in the lake and her royal-blue tank suit clung to her the way the blue scrub dress did.

Leslie's raw, natural beauty. She didn't even recognize it, at least not then, in high school, when her lovely face was framed by unruly chestnut curls and her soft voluptuous body was carefully hidden under cardigan sweaters and tailored blouses.

The silky unrestrained curls. The womanly figure. The blazing blue eyes. The full seductive lips.

Leslie.

How long had it been? James knew without thinking about it. Nine years almost to the day. It was that August, two months after graduation from high school, their accidental final meeting by the fountain at Seattle Center. Leslie, with her girlfriends, romping and giggling, because that's what they did in those carefree days. And James, holding Cheryl, kissing her, oblivious to Leslie's presence until Leslie, literally, ran into them.

"Oh! James!" Leslie had pulled up short, red with embarrassment, breathing quickly.

"Leslie. Hi," he had said, pulling away a little from Cheryl. But Cheryl didn't let go. "Uh, this is Cheryl. Cheryl this is Leslie. And Joanne. And Betty. And . . ."

A brief awkward final meeting. An uncomfortable ending to something that had never really begun.

Or had it?

A week later Leslie mailed a letter to him. It arrived with letters from Cheryl. For some reason James didn't notice it. Leslie's letter remained unopened and was stored in a shoebox with all the letters from Cheryl. Ten months later James discovered it. Opened it. Read it. It was too late for him and Leslie, but just in time for him. Just in time to change his life. Forever. For the better.

But Leslie didn't know. All she knew was that she had sent a letter, a letter that must have been terribly hard for her to send, that was never answered. Never acknowledged.

James hadn't seen her, talked to her, for nine years.

Now he knew where she was.

Dr. Leslie Adams. Department of Medicine. University of California at San Francisco.

James turned off the television, lit another cigarette and sat, without moving, except to light the next cigarette, and the next, for hours.

"Hey you, Dr. Night Stalker," Mark called as Leslie walked past his hospital room. His door was open. It was five in the morning.

"Hi!" she whispered, peering into his private room.

Mark sat up in bed. The light was on. He was reading.

He had been transferred from the ICU after a week's stay. This was his fourth morning on the ward.

"Are you busy or are you just prowling?"

"Prowling. There's no lovely view from this place, anyway. And it never feels peaceful."

"No calms between storms?"

"Just when you think you've hit a calm spot, you realize it's only an illusion. It's really the eye of another hurricane."

Mark smiled. Then he asked, "Where's Hal?"

Leslie sat down in the chair next to Mark's bed without answering.

"Leslie, where's Hal?"

"Asleep."

"Leslie, it was bad enough, but acceptable, for you to do this as an intern, but you do not stay up all night while your intern sleeps."

"I know," she said sheepishly. *But I do.*

"How *is* Prince Hal?"

"What have you been reading, *Henry IV*?"

"Very good."

"I was raised on this," Leslie said, gesturing to the stack of books, classics of English literature, next to Mark's bed. "At least, surrounded by it."

"Lucky," Mark mused. Then he asked again, "How is the crown prince?"

"Actually, he's better," Leslie said honestly, but understating the magnitude of improvement. Hal had gone overboard in the admiration department. She appreciated the quiet moments when Hal was asleep because then he wasn't trailing around behind her, admiring her. "Toning down. Asking questions. He even has a bit of a crush on me."

"Good, I—"

"Told me so. I know. You were right. How are you?"

"Doing well. Retic—ing like crazy."

Reticulocytes—retics—were young red blood cells. Their presence in blood meant new red blood cells were being produced.

"And your crit is . . . ?"

"Twenty-four," Mark said proudly. "They are going to turn me loose to finish recuperating at home when I hit twenty-seven."

Home. To Kathleen.

"It still doesn't give you much leeway," Leslie said, looking at his pale white skin.

"You mean if I get shot again in the next few days? The re-bleed risk period is over."

"You are so lucky. You had the most uneventful, uncomplicated recovery in history."

"The reason I'm lucky is because you were there. Or so they say."

"I was lucky that *you* were there." *You saved my life, Mark.*

"That's nonsense. Anyway, I remember nothing between lunging at the guy and waking up in the trauma room. Are you ever going to tell me what really happened?"

Mark had asked her before, but Leslie always resisted giving details. She hated remembering. It was so personal, so private. It was so *intimate* to put her hand inside of him, deep into his chest, and, at the same time, it was so *impersonal* and anatomic. Like an autopsy.

"I told you. I put pressure on a bleeder."

"With one little finger?" Mark asked, holding up his hand, gesturing to hers. He knew what she had done. He had seen her hand. He had seen the scars on her palm, thick and uneven. Scars that would always be there.

"And after I stopped the bleeding," Leslie continued, ignoring him, "you went crazy and refused blood transfusions."

"I don't believe that decision was crazy."

"We'll never know. It turned out all right."

"Maybe we will know, someday, that it was the right decision."

Mark's telephone rang. It was six A.M. Leslie stood up and said, "Kathleen. I'll go."

"Stay put, Leslie. It's not Kathleen. It's probably a wrong number. Trunk lines crossed or something."

It wasn't a wrong number. It was Mark's father calling at eight A.M. from his office in Lincoln.

"Mark!" his father roared.

"Father," Mark answered flatly.

"Why in hell didn't you tell us?"

"I didn't want to worry you," Mark said, grimacing at Leslie. "It's just a flesh wound. How did you find out?"

"Sam Hall was at a urology meeting in San Francisco. He saw it on the news. When I ran into him in the hospital yesterday, he asked how you were and was surprised that your mother and I weren't in San Francisco."

"Oh. Well. You saved yourself a trip."

"Still in the hospital after ten days? That doesn't sound like a flesh wound. I want you transferred here."

"I'm going home in a day or two."

"Can Janet take care of you? Wouldn't it be better if you were here?"

Leslie couldn't hear Mark's father's words, but she heard Mark's tone and sensed the general flavor of the conversation, guessed what questions Mark was being asked.

Mark looked at her. He was a little embarrassed. Leslie stood up to leave, but Mark shook his head, covered the receiver with his hand and whispered to her.

"You don't have to leave, Leslie. Unless you want to. It's just about to get pretty ugly."

Then why don't I leave? Leslie wondered. Because Mark seemed to want her to stay.

"Janet and I are not together anymore, Father."

Leslie drew in a breath. It had been ten months since Mark and Janet had separated. The divorce had been final for months.

Mark smiled weakly at her.

"Not together?"

"Divorced."

"When did that happen?"

"Recently."

"When were you going to let us know?"

If Mark didn't let them know, no one else would. Certainly not Janet's parents. The Taylors had had no contact with Janet's parents after the wedding.

"Sometime. It didn't seem like an emergency."

"Not an emergency? Don't you know how happy this will make your mother? Delirious. It has been so hard for her, for both of us, thinking about you being married to that poor, gold-digging hick."

"*Father.*"

"Mark, you know perfectly well she was beneath you. No good for you. It was so awkward. I'm just glad you came to your senses and left her."

"She left me. If it were possible, I would still be married to her. But it isn't."

"Well, however it happened, it's a blessing."

"It's a *shame*, Father."

"Your mother will be thrilled."

Mark closed his eyes and tilted his head back. The skin over his knuckles stretched tight as he gripped the phone. A vein stood out on his temple, and his jaw muscles rippled.

Leslie watched, horrified. So much pressure. So much rage. So much inner turmoil.

All he needs is an ulcer, she thought, a bleeding ulcer from the stress. It could kill him.

Leslie touched his shoulder with her hand. Mark looked at her, startled. Then he smiled, wanly, and patted her hand.

"I'm OK," he mouthed the words.

His father continued, "So, son, will you still finish up on time? On July first?"

"Yes. The residency director says I can be off for a month and still fulfill board requirements on schedule."

"Good. I think I'll have the shingle made up today. Maybe you would like to live at home now that Janet is gone?"

"Father," Mark said, staring into Leslie's blue eyes, gathering strength from their unquestioning support. "I'm going to do a cardiology fellowship starting July first. I'll be doing that for two or three years."

"When did you make that decision?" his father hissed.

"Recently."

"Mark, we don't need any more cardiologists in Lincoln. The town's teeming with them."

"Then, maybe, I'll just have to practice someplace else."

"You *wouldn't*!" It sounded like, You wouldn't *dare*. "After all our plans."

"All your plans, Father. I have to make my own plans."

"Your own plans? Goddammit, Mark, these are your plans. Have been for years."

"Then they've changed. A lot of things have changed."

"I can't believe it."

"Believe it."

"You little bastard. After all I've—"

White with rage, eyes clouded, muscles taut and skin damp, Mark slammed down the phone. Hung up on his father.

Leslie sat quietly, awkwardly, waiting for him to remember that she was there. She had taken her hand away from his shoulder. Mark was very far away.

Minutes later he looked over at her and smiled sheepishly.

"I'm getting some insight into the complications you mentioned," she said, remembering their early morning conversation three months before.

"Uh-huh."

"I think you made it pretty clear."

"Leslie, believe it or not, we've had conversations like this for years. He doesn't hear what I say, even when I say it like that. Until recently, one of these wonderful father-son yelling matches would be followed by a call from me, apologizing. Doing what he wanted me to do."

"Oh."

"But not anymore."

Good.

"When did you decide to do the cardiology fellowship?"

"Just in the last month. It's a little late to apply for next July."

"I know. I'm already starting on mine for the following July." Then Leslie added quietly, "Also in cardiology."

Mark smiled.

"We'll be seeing each other at cardiology meetings for years to come, won't we?"

"So where are you applying? They'd make a spot for you here I'm sure."

"I need to leave," Mark said flatly. They *had* offered to find a position for him, to create a place for him in their highly competitive cardiology program. "Peter Bent Brigham has an unexpected opening as the *New England Journal of*

Medicine ads say. How about you?"

"Stanford's my first choice at the moment."

"You'll get in wherever you want."

So will you, she thought. But how about English graduate school, she wondered, looking at the volumes of Shakespeare, Faulkner, Joyce and Shaw beside his bed.

Leslie's pager sounded. She glanced at her watch. Eight-fifteen.

"Quarter past eight, Leslie. It's probably Hal wondering why you're late for rounds."

"I'm not late for rounds."

"You're not?" Morning rounds were always at eight.

"No," she said quietly. "We start at eight-thirty on nights after we've been on call."

"So Hal can catch a few extra winks?"

"So Hal can have a leisurely second cup of coffee . . ."

"To wake himself up after the long night's sleep he gets because his resident had been up all night keeping watch?" Mark teased.

"Something like that. Really, Mark, Hal has improved dramatically. I'm whipping him into shape. In my own way. Anyway," Leslie said frowning at the digits on her pager, "it's the Department of Medicine office. May I use your phone?"

Leslie dialed the number without curiosity. Calls from the Department of Medicine office were common.

"Oh, yes, I do have a message for you," the secretary said. "Here it is. Ready?"

Leslie took a three by five inch index card and a pen from the left breast pocket of her white coat.

"Go ahead."

Leslie prepared to write but as she heard the message, her hand froze with the pen poised above the paper.

" . . . in his office all day," the secretary finished.

"I'm sorry. Could you repeat the number?" Leslie asked, her mind reeling.

James Stevenson would be in his office—an office with a local telephone number—all day. Would Dr. Adams please call?

"Huh," Leslie said after she hung up.

"What?" Mark asked.

"Oh. A voice from the distant, distant past. From high school. An old boy—an old friend," Leslie said, distractedly, before leaving to find Hal for rounds.

Friend. Boyfriend. What was James?

What *had* he been?

Part Two

Chapter 15

SEATTLE, WASHINGTON
SEPTEMBER 1969

George Washington High School, Seattle's largest public high school, drew its student body from two junior high schools, Benjamin Franklin and Thomas Edison. The merger of the students from the two junior high schools was not a blend. It was the creation of a stratified, two-class society: the haves and the have not; the intellectuals and the hoodlums; the virgins and the hussies; those who would succeed and those who were destined to fail.

There were no railroad tracks separating the neighborhood whose teenagers attended Franklin from the neighborhood that sent its students to Edison, but there might as well have been. The separation was that distinct. The students who attended Thomas Edison Junior High lived on the wrong side of the imaginary tracks.

The main distinction between the two student bodies was environmental. Environment, not genes, segregated the two groups. The parents of Franklin students were university faculty, lawyers, doctors, bankers and college graduates. They raised their children on expectations of excellence, confidence in the child's ability, praise for success and reward for accomplishment. They provided their children with an environment that encouraged talent, intellectual creativity and realization of potential.

The parents of the Edison students were no less intelligent than the parents of the Franklin students, but their goals were different: enough money to pay rent and buy food and clothes. They worked hard to survive, struggling to make ends meet. Their principal goal for their children was that the child graduate from high school without getting arrested, pregnant, addicted or killed. Their only hope was that the child would survive, relatively unscathed, to age eighteen, to adulthood, to the age of self-sufficiency.

The Franklin students were not intrinsically prejudiced against the Edison students. They were simply realistic. Likes attracted likes. Everyone was most comfortable, especially given the pressure of teenage society toward conformity, to be with his or her own kind.

But crossovers did occur. The faculty child, rebelling against his achievement-oriented parents, sought and found new friends in the beer-drinking, motorcycle-riding gangs from Edison. Occasionally a serious, thoughtful, academically motivated student from Edison would appear in the honors classes. He or she was welcome, a curiosity but a kindred spirit nonetheless, to join the Franklin group.

If the goals meshed, crossovers were permissible, even encouraged. The new blood in the group added interest and sometimes a new romance.

In this clearly stratified two-class system, James Stevenson found himself in No Man's Land. He had attended Edison, but because of his scores on the pre-entrance placement tests, James was assigned to the honors classes. Those classes were populated almost exclusively by the very best of the Franklin graduates.

James did not share the goals of those students, but he did as well as they did, better even, on tests. James was as smart as the faculty kids, as smart as the kids with environmental privilege.

As smart as Leslie Adams and her friends.

They would have welcomed James instantly into their group, except that it wasn't clear that he wanted to be with them. James looked different, with his old faded jeans, his threadbare madras shirts and his black leather jacket.

James smoked. And drank. And swore. James rode a motorcycle. There was even a rumor that he had a girlfriend, a fourteen-year-old still at Edison, whom he *slept* with!

"He is a hoodlum," Leslie's girlfriends hissed.

"Not really," the boys in her group countered. "James set the curve on the last math exam, and he offered to help with the cerebral palsy bottle drive."

Part hoodlum. Although the actual proof was lacking. There was no evidence that James had ever broken the law—no real laws. He did smoke and drink and perhaps even have sex with a minor, but he didn't steal hubcaps or stereo equipment. He apparently was not involved with the rash of typewriter thefts from the school's third-floor typing class.

Part do-gooder. James joined in the altruistic efforts of the Franklin group. With them, James donated his time to community service. He helped raise money—through car washes and bottle drives—for the poor and disadvantaged. He tutored other students and worked in hospitals and nursing homes.

Unlike any student before, James apparently belonged to both groups. He was never committed, not totally, not uniquely, not in three years, to either group, and despite the divided allegiance, neither group sought to expel him.

James's friends from Thomas Edison had been friends since grade school. Most had known him since the day, at age five, when he changed his name from Jimmy to James. It had been James ever since. He insisted on it. As they got older, they called themselves the James Gang. They were secretly pleased that James, one of *them*, had successfully infiltrated the most elite faction of the Franklin group.

The boys from Franklin, the boys he met in the honors classes, were intrigued by James. They had to admire his brains—a critical factor—but they also admired his wildness, his lack of concern for authority, his nonchalance about drinking and smoking. And his sexual success. They were all at the age when they needed to experiment, to see how far the rules would stretch before they snapped.

James didn't worry about the rules, and he set the curves on he math exams.

James didn't seem to worry about very much.

Unlike the boys who accepted James on his terms, the girls, except for Leslie, rejected him.

"He's coarse," Leslie's friends said, wrinkling their noses. "And he's so strange-looking. He gives me the creeps!"

"I think he's interesting," Leslie said thoughtfully.

"*Leslie!* You have to be kidding," they giggled.

"No, I really think he is interesting."

Leslie also thought that James was very handsome, but she didn't dare tell them *that*. It was a matter of taste, anyway. There was nothing classically handsome about James. Nothing terribly aristocratic. No sign of privilege, environmental or otherwise.

James looked, Leslie decided, like a cougar. His dark green eyes were set wide apart in his face—cold, appraising, watchful green eyes. James's cheekbones were high and prominent above the hollow of his cheeks. His lips were thin, set in neutral, occasionally curling into a half smile. The inevitable cigarette dangled casually, erotically, from his lips, moving when he spoke, as if a part of him.

A cougar. Wild. Free. Untamed. And untamable.

James's thick black hair fell into his green eyes and curled sensually over his ears and down his neck.

At first James made Leslie nervous. He would watch her, the green eyes with the long black lashes calmly observing, squinting slightly as the smoke from his cigarette drifted into them. James never looked *pleasant* like the other boys. They were all full of smiles and winks and flirtations, trying to look sexy and provocative. James didn't try to look sexy.

James didn't have to try. The look was natural.

After a while James began to speak to her. They didn't have conversations. They just had brief and unexpected communications. Usually there was a message, indirect, a little hidden.

"The Macho Men are playing at the dance this Saturday," James would say. It was an announcement, not an invitation, but Leslie learned it meant that he would be at the dance. And that he wanted her to be? She didn't know.

She would go with her friends, and he would be there, wandering between the James gang and the Franklin group, watching her from the corner of his cougarlike eyes. He wouldn't dance. Not until the end. The last dance. Then he would ask her to dance. The slow dance.

"*Rosemaiden?*" he whispered one day as he passed her in the hallway. Rosemaiden was the award given to the girl voted Most Inspirational by the female student body. It was a yearly award. Leslie won all three years. It was an unprecedented accomplishment.

"Yes," she said weakly to his back as he continued down the hall.

James was entirely unpredictable. He appeared at some Franklin group parties and not at others. He usually arrived late and left early. He always arrived by himself and left alone. At the parties, James talked and joked with the boys, and he taunted the girls, Leslie's friends, because he knew they dislike him.

James always said something to Leslie. He never taunted *her*. Sometimes he teased, but he never taunted.

By senior year, Leslie had had four relationships with boys from her group. Boring, groping, silly relationships that weren't love or sex or anything but chaste attempts at growing up.

And, by senior year, Leslie had danced ten slow dances with James, had spent an entire quarter of a football game standing beside him—he had found her—saying nothing, had washed cars with him at a charity car wash, had seen him daily in honors classes at school and, in small cryptic pieces, had exchanged about two hours of dialogue with him.

But she thought about him *constantly*. She always felt his presence. The feeling made her anxious and uncertain. And eager.

One day in September of senior year, James caught up with her after class. It was Friday afternoon.

"Done much deer hunting with bows and arrows?" he asked.

"No!" Then, curious, not wanting that to be the end of another unfinished, uninterpretable exchange, she asked, "Why?"

"Perfect weather for it. I'm going tomorrow."

"Oh." *Oh?*

"So, do you want to?"

"Yes," Leslie breathed, not certain about what he was asking or what she had agreed to.

"I'll pick you up at nine in the morning. I know where you live."

A date? With James? To hunt deer with bows and arrows?

Leslie and her parents waited for James to arrive. They waited in anxious silence, each preoccupied with specific worries about the date. Matthew Adams opposed hunting for sport. Period. It was not a debatable issue.

Susan Adams's finely tuned journalistic eyes and ears had deduced a great deal about the mysterious James. Over the past two years she had heard words like "wild" and "thug" and "scary" and "uncivilized" uttered contemptuously by Leslie's dearest friends. She had also heard her daughter's quiet protestations. Susan and Leslie were best friends. It was a friendship that had survived even the teenage "Oh *Mother!*" years.

Leslie had not told Susan about James. Not really. Susan had to guess, and she guessed that Leslie was intrigued with James because he was so different and that Leslie didn't, or couldn't, discuss her attraction because she herself didn't understand it.

Susan waited. A little worried. But mostly curious.

Leslie waited, too, her heart pounding, her mouth dry, *rehearsing* dialogue, planning topics. There weren't many topics. There wouldn't be much dialogue because James didn't talk. All she could think of quickly reduced to silly soliloquies on topics that wouldn't interest James. It was that or silence.

Maybe he wouldn't come after all.

At five minutes before nine they heard James arrive, his actual appearance heralded by the roar of his motorcycle.

Matthew Adams breathed a momentary sigh of relief. His original worries were allayed, but they were promptly replaced by much greater ones. They weren't really going hunting. Even though he noticed a single wooden bow, unstrung, carefully secured to the motorcycle, it was obvious the expedition was not serious. Hunters drove large station wagons, vans, trucks even. Large enough to carry the prey. Hunters did not go hunting with bows and arrows on motorcycles.

Motorcycles . . . the magnitude of the new worry rapidly surpassed the old one. Matthew did not want his daughter, his only child, riding on a motorcycle. It wasn't a rule. They had never even discussed it. There had been no need. None of Leslie's friends had motorcycles. *They* wouldn't.

Susan and Matthew prided themselves on being liberal, rational parents. Their relationship with Leslie was close and open. They both realized in the instant James arrived that all the previous parenting had been easy. Because Leslie had made no demands. She hadn't fallen in love, wanted to make love, wanted to stay out all night, wanted to drink or try drugs. Leslie hadn't wanted to do anything the least bit worrisome.

Susan and Matthew had discussed this day in the abstract. What they, as well-educated, intelligent, reasonable parents would do when their daughter began to explore, experiment, question. They would lie in bed at night calmly discussing what they would do. Issue by issue.

"What if she wants to try marijuana? Or LSD?"

"We discuss it with her. If she's really determined, we insist that she do it at home, so she's safe."

"What if she likes it?"

"Leslie is not an addict personality," Matthew said firmly.

"What about sex? Lots of teenagers have sex now. It's almost standard."

"Not with Leslie's group."

"Still . . ."

"If she did want to, which she won't, we'd talk to her about love and sex, and if she was determined, we'd make sure she knew how not to get pregnant."

"She knows that."

"What if she wants to live with someone?"

"In high school?"

"Eventually."

"When the time comes it might even be a good idea. But that's years from now."

It all sounded very easy, as they discussed it in the privacy of their own bedroom, with their virginal daughter safely sleeping two rooms away. They would be rational, they decided, confident that they could allow Leslie the freedom they knew she would need. When she needed it.

But now, looking at James's motorcycle, both were consumed by irrational emotion. A year before, Susan had done an exposé for the magazine section of Seattle's largest newspaper on the dangers of motorcycles. Susan explored the issues of helmets and the horrible, not quite lethal accidents . . .

"Mom. Dad," Leslie said sternly, looking at her parents, surprising herself and them.

"Why don't you take my car?" Matthew offered.

"No," Leslie said, starting for the door, planning to dash out to the curb, not noticing that James was already walking toward the house. "*Please!*"

It was a *please* that forced Matthew and Susan to look at the big picture, the picture of their daughter growing up and taking the risks necessary to mature without rebellion or repression. They glanced at each other and shrugged, weakly.

The doorbell rang. Leslie opened it.

"Hi, James," she said.

"Hi," he said, looking at her parents, expecting their disapproval.

"James, these are my parents."

"Dr. Adams," James said, extending his rough hand to Matthew.

How did James know to call him doctor? Matthew had a doctoral degree in English.

"Mrs. Adams," he said, nodding to her, but not shaking her hand.

In six months, Susan would complete her Ph.D. in journalism. Then she would be Dr. Adams, too. Leslie wondered if James would somehow learn about that, just as he had learned about her father.

Matthew was tongue-tied. The truly liberal, intellectual parent would say something like, "Great day for hunting" or "Nice bike" or "Have a nice *weekend*." All Matthew wanted to say was "No way. Not with my daughter."

Susan was tongue-tied for another reason. She saw, *felt*, instantly what it was that made her daughter so strangely silent about James. She realized, as soon as she saw him, that Leslie's attraction was more than intrigue. It was something much more powerful, more dangerous.

"It's a lovely autumn day," Susan sputtered, finally.

James frowned at Leslie for a moment, observing her light windbreaker and school-clothes quality blouse and V-neck sweater. At least she wore jeans.

"Do you have a warmer jacket, Leslie?" he asked.

"A ski parka."

"That would be better."

"OK."

All three members of the family turned to the closet, fortunately nearby, to get Leslie's parka. Susan laughed, lightening the tension a little.

James stood his ground, smiled awkwardly and considered Leslie's parents" reaction to him. A little disapproval, especially her father, but mostly just concern about their precious daughter.

I know she's precious, James thought. Don't you think I know that? Don't you know that I will be so careful with her?

James wondered, for a moment, if he should tell them that, to reassure them. He decided not to. It offended him a little that they didn't know.

"Have fun," Susan murmured reflexively as they left.

"Oh boy," Matthew said, as he watched them getting onto the motorcycle.

"We're about to be tested?" Susan asked.

"I hope not. Leslie can't really be interested in him," Matthew said, confidently.

"You don't see it, either," Susan said quietly. Matthew didn't see it. Neither did Leslie's friends.

"See what?"

"What James has."

"Nothing!"

"Oh, no, darling. He has everything," she said, watching as James handed Leslie a helmet.

"Wear this," James said.

"OK," she said, trying to remember the current state law about wearing helmets. The law changed from year to year. It was an individual rights issue. The individual should be allowed to have a severe head injury if he so chose. Occasionally the state intervened. The state had to pay for the years—most of the victims were healthy teenagers—of hospitalization and care for the badly damaged victim. It was all in Susan's article. Leslie noticed that James wore a helmet, too.

It was probably law.

He got on. She got on behind him after he showed her where to rest her feet.

"Ready?" he asked.

She nodded, half shrugging.

But she wasn't ready. Her arms were at her sides.

"Hold on, Leslie."

Leslie looked around.

"Where?" she asked, finally.

"Put your arms around my waist and hold on tight. We'll be on the freeway. So you really have to hold on. OK?"

Leslie nodded and carefully put her arms around his waist. As soon as they started to move, her grasp tightened. It had to. And eventually she had to press her body against his back.

As the wind whipped against her face and she felt the warmth and strength of James, Leslie remembered her rehearsed dialogue, her planned topics and smiled. It was impossible to talk above the roar of the motorcycle and the sound of the wind. Before they reached the freeway, when they stopped at stop lights, they spoke briefly.

"Are you OK?" he asked above the sputtering of the motorcycle.

"Yes."

"Cold?"

"No."

"Let me know."

"I will," she said. How? She should have said how much she was enjoying it already. Exhilarating. The crisp autumn air. Touching him. She should have said she loved it.

But she didn't before they got onto the interstate, and after that they rode in silence for an hour.

They traveled east over the Lake Washington Floating Bridge across Mercer Island past Lake Sammamish. Beyond Lake Sammamish, the scenery shifted from urban and suburban to rural. At first there were farms, acres of green grass surrounding red and white farmhouses and alive with cows, horses, dogs and tractors.

After they drove through the village of Issaquah with its Swiss chalet architecture and single main street, the scenery changed again. They ascended into the heavily wooded foothills of the Cascade Mountains, gaining altitude, losing civilization, flanking themselves with dense forest and towering mountain peaks.

They exited off Interstate 90 at Snoqualmie, then rode along rutted country roads and finally turned onto a dirt road blocked by a gate with a large No Trespassing sign on it. Without hesitation James drove along a narrow path around the gate. The dirt road led deep into the woods. After about a mile James stopped and turned off the motor. He and Leslie got off the motorcycle, and James removed the wooden bow and quiver of arrows.

Leslie watched in silence as he strung the bow, using considerable force to relax the bow and slide the string into the notch.

"Do you want to practice?" he asked. "That tree over there makes a good target."

"You've been here before?" Leslie asked. Of course James had been here before. One didn't simply drive past No Trespassing signs without a moment's hesitation unless he knew where he was going. Not even James.

"Sure. This,"—he gestured expansively—"is all company property. This is where I spend every summer. Logging."

James disappeared every summer to work. Until now, Leslie hadn't known where. A logging camp. For Washington State's largest lumber company. It was a perfect job for James, Leslie thought. Outdoors. Untamed. A man's job.

"Oh."

"Have you ever used a bow and arrow?"

"No."

"I'll show you."

Leslie watched as James shot arrow after arrow. All landed within inches of each other in the trunk of a huge pine tree. It looked effortless, a fluid motion that was silent, except for the swish of the arrow as it left the bow and the soft thud as it hit its mark. Beautiful. Primitive. Natural.

"Want to try?" he asked finally.

"Yes!"

Leslie followed James as he moved closer to the tree.

"You should start from here," he said, handing her the bow and an arrow.

Leslie clumsily hooked the arrow into the bow string, then tried to level it against the strip of leather wrapped around the bow. She tried to imitate what she had seen James do, but she couldn't. The arrow wavered. She pulled gently on the bow string and met surprising resistance.

After a few moments, she looked at him and started giggling.

"Show off! This is really hard!"

"Takes practice."

"And strength. And coordination. It looked so easy when you did it."

"We'll do it together," James said. He stood beside her and put his arms

around her. His left hand wrapped over hers and held the bow. With his right hand James steadied the arrow and pulled back.

Leslie felt his strength and his closeness as he took her through the fluid motion, as a passenger, with him.

The arrow found its mark in the tree trunk in the center of the other arrows. Then James released her and walked to the tree to retrieve all the arrows.

He put the arrows in the quiver then looked at her seriously for a moment, as if about to say something.

The moment passed in silence.

"Let's go," he said finally. "Let's go find some deer."

"James . . ."

"What?"

"Can I be the hunter?" Leslie felt the same way about hunting as her father. The deer would be safe if she carried the bow and arrow.

"Sure," he said, half smiling. Then he added firmly, "But I don't kill animals for sport, either, Leslie."

"Then what are we doing?"

"Hunting. I thought the daughter of an English professor would know the meaning of the word." James paused. Then he said, "It means seeking or finding. Not killing."

"Like hunting for Easter eggs?" Leslie teased as the relief swept through her.

"Uh-huh," he said, refusing to be amused. He turned and started walking toward a path between the trees. "C'mon. Let's go."

Leslie followed, wordlessly. Finally she started giggling. James spun around.

"What?"

"I've just never hunted Easter eggs with a bow and arrows."

"Very cute."

"Thank you. So?"

"So I like to shoot arrows into tree trunks when I go deer hunting. OK?" James's voice had a slight edge for the first time. Until then, the teasing had been easy and natural.

Leslie backed off immediately. She realized as she marched behind him through the dense underbrush that she had been teasing him as if she knew him. She had even wrapped her arms around his waist as if he were simply one of the other boys.

But he was *James*. As they walkedon, single file, in silence, Leslie wondered if she had angered him. Or if he just thought she was silly.

Of course he thinks I'm silly, Leslie thought glumly. Silly and trivial. Leslie's mind searched frantically for future topics of conversation and found none.

The narrow path finally opened into a huge meadow. James slowed his pace as they neared the clearing. He turned to Leslie and put his finger to his lips. Leslie nodded meaningfully.

James saw the deer first and gestured to Leslie. She didn't see them right away. They were lost in the backdrop of the green-brown underbrush. When she saw them finally, as they came into focus separate and dstinct from the background, Leslie gasped.

They were so beautiful. So free. There were three of them—two adults and a fawn—grazing peacefully, unperturbed, unaware, until the scent reached them, of the intrusion. . . .

The adults looked up in unison, alert to the danger, suddenly wary.

Leslie wanted to reassure them. We aren't here to hurt you! They stared at each other for a while, animals and humans, motionless. Then, almost in slow motion, the deer moved into the woods, disappearing into the brown-green maze.

"They are so beautiful! So graceful. So elegant. I like deer hunting," Leslie said. Thinking, after she said it, what a silly thing to say.

"It's beautiful even if you don't see any deer," James said as he sat down on a fallen tree trunk, laid down his bow and arrows and lit a cigarette.

"Yes," Leslie said, taking a deep breath of the delicately pine-scented autumn air. She gazed up at the perfectly formed pine trees towering above her and the pale blue sky beyond. In a few moments the pine scent blended with the smell of cigarette smoke.

"Does it taste good?" Leslie asked.

"It's more than taste. It's warmth. Especially out here. It's like having your own bonfire inside you."

"I admit it smells good. Better here than in town." Leslie looked at the cigarette hanging casually from the corner of his thin mouth. She watched as the smoke curled around his face. His green eyes narrowed slightly. Leslie had watched her friends trying to smoke cigarettes in a sexy way, inhaling the exhaled smoke back through their nostrils, puffing smoke rings, holding the cigarette casually between their lips, practicing in front of mirrors. Most failed to look sexy despite the practice.

Leslie was confident that James had never practiced smoking in front of a mirror. His relationship with the cigarette was natural. And sexy.

"Haven't you ever even tried a cigarette?" he asked.

Leslie shook her head. *Silly little goody-goody me.*

"Want to?"

"Sure," she said bravely.

James took the cigarette from his mouth and handed it to her.

"It's easier to start with one that's already lighted," he explained. "Just inhale. Slowly and not too deep a breath."

Leslie felt the warmth inside her—it felt good—then the irrepressible instinct to cough. Then a warm dizzy feeling.

"Oh. Oh. Wow."

"Light-headed?"

"Yes. It's passing now. It felt sort of nice. What's that from?"

"Your brain was deprived of oxygen."

"*No!*"

"No. I guess it's the nicotine."

"It feels good. Is that why you smoke?" Leslie asked, deciding to take a second puff on the cigarette she held, non-sexily, in her hand.

"No. I don't even feel that anymore. I just smoke because I smoke. Are you planning to keep my cigarette?"

"Uh-huh."

"Great," James said, lighting a new one for himself. "This will make your parents like me even more than they already do."

"They like you!"

"Yeah. About as much as your girlfriends do."

Probably more than my girlfriends do, Leslie thought. It angered her that her friends didn't even try to conceal their contempt. She had always hoped that James hadn't noticed; but of course, he had, and it bothered him.

"They just don't understand you," Leslie said finally, weakly. She wondered if she should add, Not that I do either, of course. She didn't want to sound presumptuous.

"They understand that I am not one of their special elite group."

"But you are!"

"As a token. I fit in under that one all-important category. I do very well on exams."

"You set the curve," Leslie said quietly. "You're very smart."

"There are a lot of very smart people who don't do well on exams. There are a lot of people who are smart in ways that exams never test, but to your friends exams are the gold standard, the only measurement of worth and success."

Leslie watched the smoke curl up from her cigarette. Her second and third puffs had given her the same dizzy rush. She still felt a little light-headed. Or was the dizziness because of being with James? she wondered as she listened to him talk in long, articulate sentences, not the short phrases he used at school. Which one was the real James, she mused. James, fearless leader of the James gang? Or James, the reluctant but legitimate member of her group? Or was either the real James?

"That's not the only measurement of worth and success," she protested finally, weakly, knowing that it was a minimum requirement. Any other accomplishments, and most of her friends had other accomplishments, were added to the firm, essential base of academic excellence.

"Let's say we all had no food, we were surrounded by deer and all we had were bows and arrows . . ."

"James, *I* don't use academic success as a measurement of worth!"

"I know. Emotionally, you may, a little, but rationally, you don't. But your friends do."

"They are your friends, too. The guys are. They envy you. They admire you. They can't believe how well you do without studying."

"I study," James said seriously, thinking about how he studied, or tried to study, in the afternoon between school and dinner. Before his father got home. Before the drinking and the fighting started. Before it became impossible to study. Then James would leave. Sometimes he would go to the library at the university to study in the silence there. Sometimes his parents" screams disturbed him too much to study. Then he would go find a party or a girl. Or drive ninety miles an hour on his motorcycle.

James studied when he could. It explained his late, unpredictable arrival at parties. Everyone assumed he had been with his other friends, *his* gang, but usually, he had been studying, somewhere. Or with a girl, somewhere. Or alone, somewhere.

James was aware that Leslie was watching him. He leveled his cougar eyes at her and said, "Anyway, your girlfriends are hypocrites. They prance around celebrating sweetness and light and goodness, but they cannot personally accept anyone who is the least bit different. They keep me away from you."

They keep me away from you. His words thundered in her slightly dizzy head and made her heart pound.

"Whaaaat?"

"Whenever I walk toward you, they close in around you. I feel like the *Titanic* heading into a field of icebergs."

Leslie giggled. "That's good. They'd love being called icebergs. But you're unsinkable, aren't you?" she asked, inwardly furious with her *friends*.

"No," James said, standing up. "Let's walk farther. Beyond the clearing, about a mile, there's a nice view of the mountains. Here, give me your cigarette butt."

Leslie handed the smashed cigarette butt to James. He put it, and his, in his pocket to dispose of somewhere else but not here.

"Smokey is my friend," James explained a little sheepishly.

Nice, Leslie thought. She was learning that tough wild James was really nice sensitive James, but she had always known that, hadn't she?

They walked for two miles. James led the way along the narrow fern-lined path through the woods. They stopped once to examine deer hoofprints.

"These are pretty fresh. A doe and a fawn. Probably heading toward the lake," he said.

Leslie nodded.

"Watch this," he said. He flexed the index and middle fingers of his hand and pressed them into the soft dirt, making an imprint that was almost identical to the deer prints. "Can you tell the difference?"

Leslie looked closely. There were subtle differences, but on casual inspection of the prints, the real and the fake looked the same.

"We make prints like these when we're hunting with people who think they have all the answers," James said, smiling wryly.

Like my friends, Leslie thought.

"We do? We trick them on purpose?"

"Yes we do."

Nice, James.

They reached another clearing, a large meadow with a close-enough-to-touch view of the Cascade Mountains, a range of jagged peaks of green, brown and granite, snow-capped in autumn just at the summit.

"Wow," Leslie said softly. Wow. Silly. It was so beautiful. Too beautiful for words.

She watched James light a cigarette and extended her hand toward him.

"You want another one?"

"Yes!" she said, watching as he extracted one for her. He eyed her skeptically. She interpreted his look as concern about her parents" disapproval and said, "My mother likes you."

"How do you know?"

"I can tell. And my father would like you if he knew you."

"Not if I turn his daughter into a chain smoker."

"You're a chain smoker."

"I know. It's a terrible habit," he said lightly. "Anyway, you're not the smoking type."

James held the match for Leslie as she inhaled, in puffs, imitating the way she had watched him light his cigarettes. The coughing followed immediately, along with the warmth and the dizziness. It made her feel a little bold.

"Does your girlfriend smoke?"

"My girlfriend?" James's surprise was genuine. "Who can you possibly mean?"

"Sophomore year. The rumor was that you had a girlfriend who was still at Edison," Leslie said carefully. *A fourteen-year-old whom you were sleeping with.*

"Oh. She wasn't my girlfriend," he said. Then he added, "I've never had a girlfriend."

"Never?"

"No."

"Are you going to, ever?"

"Maybe, I don't know. If I do it won't be a silly public event. Or a game."

Silly. That word again.

"Unlike the relationships I have? And my friends have? Is that what you mean?" She knew that was what he meant and that he was right, but it wasn't a major indictment. All they could be accused of was wanting to fall in love, and they changed partners frequently because they didn't fall in love. Because there was no magic. Because they were all just good friends.

They could only be accused of being silly. And of wanting something more.

"Who is your current boyfriend, Leslie?" James asked in an I-rest-my-case tone of voice.

"No one," she said defiantly, then inhaled clumsily on her cigarette. It was close to the truth. Her relationship with David had fizzled out quickly. They had nothing to say to each other and weren't, they discovered, sexually attracted to each other, either. But something was beginning with Alan. He was captain of the swim team and, of course, an honor student.

"Uh-huh."

"Why don't you want to have a girlfriend, James?"

"It's not necessary," he said automatically. He had no trouble finding girls when he wanted or needed them. James realized that he had shocked Leslie and regretted it. He added seriously, "It doesn't seem right to get involved with someone else, to involve them in your life, until you know yourself what you're going to do."

A long silence followed. Leslie watched the smoke curl slowly, gracefully out of her cigarette. She felt light-headed; but she was thinking clearly, and her thoughts made her dizzy.

All her boyfriends. She used them and they used her. They were all searching for something exciting. Taking not sharing. Wanting not giving. Greedy. Directed by their fine minds and not their hearts. They *knew* love was out there. They had heard about it, read about it, talked about it and never felt it.

Then there was James. He wasn't going to play the game, because it wasn't a game.

It wouldn't be a game, Leslie thought. Not with you and me.

James felt her stare and met her startled blue eyes with his cool green ones.

"What are you going to do?" Leslie asked, flustered, vaguely remembering what she had meant to ask before they had both fallen silent. "Where are you going to college?"

"Where?" he asked. His tone implied that a more pertinent question would have been, Are you going to college? "I have applied to the University of Washington. I'll get in because of my grade point average. So I'll go there if I decide to go. I'll go for sure if we're still in Vietnam. I don't want to get drafted. My brother's in Vietnam."

"Oh. I didn't know that."

"Not the place to be."

"No." Not for someone who hunts for deer the way he hunts for Easter eggs. Not for *anyone*, Leslie thought. "What if you don't have to go to college?"

"I'll probably come back here to the logging camp. I could work my way up to foreman. I'm pretty smart. I do well on exams," he said wryly.

"Forever? Would you be a foreman of a logging camp for the rest of your life?" Leslie asked, trying to conceal her alarm and to suppress the thought that roared in her brain: What a waste! Leslie tried to suppress the thought because it was exactly what James resented so much about all of them. They had only one way of measuring worth and success.

"Life could be worse than being a planter of pines," James said firmly. "To rework Robert Frost a little."

Leslie's eyes widened. A planter of pines. Not a cutter of pines. Not a killer of pines.

"Don't look so surprised. We read some Frost last spring in English—"

"We picked *Mending Wall* apart, stone by stone."

"So I did a little outside reading. I like Frost," James said almost defensively. Then quickly steering the conversation away from himself, he asked, "Where are you going to college?"

"Radcliffe, *if* I get in."

"You will."

"I don't know. It's awfully competitive."

"So are you. Did you tell them you were a Rosemaiden?"

"I haven't told them anything yet. I'm mentally working on my personal statement. I have to decide pretty soon, though, because the application deadline is in a few weeks."

"Do you tell them what you plan to be when you grow up?"

Leslie shrugged.

"What *do* you plan to be? An English professor?"

Leslie looked at him for a moment. She hadn't told anyone. Not even her mother. It was just the beginning of an idea, because she had always preferred science classes to English or history or art. She had been a volunteer, a candy-striper, at a local hospital for two years, and she loved it.

"A doctor," she said quietly.

"You'll be a good doctor," James said immediately.

"Thanks!" Leslie said, relieved, happy that James didn't seem disapproving or threatened. She added quietly, "I hope so."

Chapter 16

Leslie expected things to be different with James after their day of deer hunting—a stronger bond, a new closeness—but as the weeks of autumn quarter passed, Leslie realized that nothing had changed. Nothing noticeable. The only change was the way she felt inside. Each day she left for school eager to see him, hoping for even a cryptic exchange and dreaming that someday there would be more.

Leslie could not forget the feel of her body against his. Each time she saw him, the memory that was always with her—as a muted, hazy warmth—became vivid, urgent, demanding. Uncomfortable.

Leslie wondered if James knew. She wondered if she should tell him.

She wondered if she would be able to suppress the urge to ask him to take her for another ride on his motorcycle. She wanted to wrap her arms around him, press against him and feel his strength.

It made Leslie uneasy to think that she might actually ask him. What if she wasn't able to resist? What if she really did ask him for a date? Unthinkable.

Except she thought about it all the time.

That fall Leslie and James had the same study hall. James's assigned seat was behind hers, five rows back and three rows over. Still, Leslie managed to watch him in brief, surreptitious glances. Usually James spent study period staring out the window. Occasionally he flipped halfheartedly through his textbooks.

One day in November, James spent the entire hour working on a sheet of paper that lay on his desk. His concentration was intense. He didn't look up or pause. Leslie watched him work, watched him peer at the paper, writing quickly, frowning occasionally, erasingsomething, then writing again. Now she understood how he could get the best grades without apparently studying. He did study. He studied like this, in brief, intense, energetic spurts with absolute concentration.

Finally, shamed by her own staring—unnoticed by James but detected by several of her friends who arched skeptical eyebrows—and shamed by James's obvious deligence, Lesle began to work in earnest on an assignment for her honors French class.

When the bell sounded signaling the end of study hall, James and Leslie were both still working. The rest of the class had predictably stacked books and returned sheets of paper to inside pockets of folders a full three minutes before the bell was scheduled to sound. They wanted to waste no part of the five-minute break between classes with anything as mundane as reorganizing their school work.

Leslie was still neatly putting away her almost completed French assignment when James reached her desk.

"Here," he said. "This is for you."

He handed her a manila folder as he walked by her desk and out of the study hall.

He was gone before Leslie could recover from her surprise enough to say something. Not that she would know what to say until she saw the contents of the folder anyway.

Her hands trembled as she opened it.

James had not been writing an essay on the meaning of the moral wilderness in Hawthorne's *The Scarlet Letter.* Nor had he been solving an equation for the advanced mathematics class. Instead, James had been drawing a picture. For her.

It was a picture, a *perfect* picture, of the meadow he had shown her. Every detail was exactly as she remembered it: the tall pines, the long dew-covered grass, the fallen stump and the deer, across the meadow, looking startled and curious and regal. James had drawn it in pencil, in perfect, careful detail, perfect proportion and perfect shading. Even in black and white, the warmth of the autumn sun, the exquisite beauty of the deer and the towering majesty of the pines were eloquently, colorfully, conveyed.

James was an artist! Even through her untrained and prejudiced eyes, Leslie recognized James's talent.

He was a talented artist whose picture precisely captured a wonderful memory—*the* wonderful memory—that they had shared. James had preserved the memory for her.

James wanted her to remember.

Leslie's hands trembled even more as she carefully returned the picture to its folder and placed the folder inside her notebook. Then she rushed to her final class of the day.

Leslie did not hear one word of the lecture her history teacher gave on William Jennings Bryan although she feigned an expression of rapt attention.

She resisted the almost irresistible urge to open her notebook and look at the picture.

She appeared calm and serious, but her mind raced. Why had he given it to her? Did anyone else know that he could draw? How could she thank him? *When* could she thank him? She had swim team practice as soon as school was out. She couldn't even try to find James because Alan was meeting her after class and walking with her to the pool. If only she would see James first, she could ask him to give her a ride to practice on his motorcycle . . .

Leslie didn't have a chance to look at the picture again until she got home that evening, *after* swim practice and *after* agreeing to go to the Homecoming Dance with Alan. When she finally looked at it again, in the privacy of her own bedroom, it was even more beautiful and more perfect.

Leslie decided to show it to her mother, her best friend. Even though she hadn't discussed James with Susan—what was there to discuss?—since the day she and James had gone deer hunting, Leslie sensed that Susan understood about James. Not that there was anything to understand. James was there. A presence. Undefined but important to Leslie. Susan seemed to know that.

Susan was making garlic butter.

"Mother, look at this," Leslie said, carefully holding the picture so that her mother could see it but away from the butter.

Susan said nothing, but she quickly washed her hands in hot water and after they were clean and dry took the precious picture for closer scrutiny.

"This is very good, Leslie. What a beautiful scene. Even in black and white you feel the color and the life. Who did it?" Susan asked. She knew that Leslie hadn't drawn it but wondered who among her friends had this surprising talent.

"James," Leslie said softly. "It's where we went that day to look for deer. The three deer in the picture are the ones we saw."

Susan frowned slightly. She remembered how happy Leslie had been after the deer-hunting expedition and how, over the ensuing weeks, the happiness and excitement had begrudgingly faded. Susan knew that James hadn't called, that he hadn't asked Leslie out again. Leslie's disappointment was painfully obvious. It was obvious despite the fact that unlike all the other boys she had dated, had wanted to date, Leslie didn't talk about James.

Now her daughter's face was radiant again.

"Did he just give this to you?"

"Today. He drew it—or at least finished drawing it—in study hall. It is good, isn't it?" Leslie asked. Not that it mattered.

"Really very good."

"I thought I should frame it. To protect it."

"There's a good frame shop a mile from campus on University Avenue. We can take it there. I think a cream-colored mat with a forest green border might look good," Susan said, knowing that her own sense of color and art was excellent unlike Leslie's and that Leslie wanted her advice on this important project.

"Great. Maybe we could go there this evening? It's Thursday night. They might be open."

"We can't have it framed yet. There is something missing from the picture," Susan said shaking her head.

"What?"

"His signature."

"Oh," Leslie said quietly. "Do you think he will sign it?"

"Of course," Susan said confidently. He had better sign it, she thought. He had better not be playing games with my daughter's heart. Susan's brief glimpse of James made her understand Leslie's attraction. James was different. Complicated. Sensual.

Susan understood it, but it made her uneasy as she thought about her uncomplicated and naive daughter.

"Of course he will sign it," she repeated firmly.

 The next day Leslie found James during lunch period. He was leaning against the wall reading the school newspaper, *The Potomac*. During an almost sleepless night, Leslie had practiced a hundred ways to thank him and to ask him to sign the picture. No matter how she asked it he could always say no.

"James?"

"Hi, Leslie," he said folding the paper.

"It's beautiful!" she blurted out, completely forgetting all the carefully worded, sophisticated thank yous. She repeated, flustered, "Beautiful. Thank you."

"You're welcome," he said seriously. The green eyes looked pleased.

"I had no idea you could draw," she continued, frantically searching for lost lines, for a place in the carefully rehearsed script. But to no avail.

"It's a hobby."

"You're really good."

"Leslie, you're not really an art critic."

"I know," she admitted. Then, because she was still not thinking clearly, she said, "But my mother knows. She works with lots of commercial artists, collaborating on articles and so on—"

"You showed it to your mother?"

"Yes!" Leslie said a little defensively. "And she thinks it's very good."

Leslie's eyes iced over for a moment. James caught the glare, smiled, then shrugged his shoulders. The iciness melted into sparkling blue radiance.

"Here's what else my mother says," she began, watching James's reaction. He looked curious. "She says we can't frame it—and it *has* to be framed—until you sign it."

"You want me to sign it?"

"Yes. Please," Leslie said quietly.

"OK. Sure."

Leslie took the picture, still protected in its folder, out of her notebook and handed it to James. She followed him into a classroom where he sat at a desk. In the lower right hand corner of the picture he wrote: *James 1971*.

"Thank you," she whispered when he handed it back to her.

"You're welcome."

They walked back into the hall. Lunch period was almost over. The hall was getting crowded.

"Are you going to the Homecoming Dance?" James asked casually.

Leslie's heart stopped. The Homecoming Dance was the mid-year prom. It was not like dances in the gym to which boys and girls went with their own groups. The Homecoming Dance was for couples only, with reservations in advance. A formal date. Was James asking her to go with him? Or was he just checking to see if she was going?

Leslie nodded slowly.

"With Alan?"

"Yes," she whispered.

James nodded as if confirming his suspicion.

* * *

"Well, time for class. See ya, Leslie," he said.

The only thing wrong with Alan, Leslie decided, was that he wasn't James, and since James had withdrawn again in the weeks after he had given her the picture, Alan would have to do. It made Leslie angry with herself, and with James, to wait for him to call night after night. She was angry because she waited and because James didn't call.

It was better to be busy.

Alan had transferred to George Washington from Lake Forest, Seattle's exclusive boys' school, during spring quarter of junior year. He had transferred because the George Washington swim team was the best high school swim team in the state. He wanted the visibility for college recruiters. Alan fit in perfectly with Leslie's group because of his grades and accomplishments. He held the Pacific Northwest record in the two hundred-meter freestyle.

Like James, Alan brought interesting new blood to the group. But unlike James, all the girls wanted him. Alan dated most of them a few times. By fall of senior year, it was obvious to everyone that Alan was mainly interested in Leslie.

It was an inevitable match. In addition to the usual academic and environmental compatibilities—Alan's father was on the faculty in anthropology at the university—Leslie and Alan even looked alike. They both had chestnut brown curls and large blue eyes. They both smiled a lot and laughed easily. Because life was easy and happy. They both did what was expected of them. They *achieved*, they *accomplished*, and they did it cheerfully because it felt right.

Alan and James were friends, as much as James was anyone's friend. Alan had no idea about Leslie's feelings for James. It would never have occurred to him.

Leslie did not fall in love with Alan, but she liked being with him. It made her feel good that he cared so much about her. Alan told Leslie that he loved her. Leslie told him that they were too young to know what that even meant but that she *liked* him very much.

Leslie did like Alan very much. She liked everything about him: the way he looked, what he said, what he thought, the way he kissed her. Now, *finally*, after the gropping, inept, insincere kissing and touching of previous relationships, Leslie actually wanted to be held and touched.

Sometimes when Alan kissed her, she pretended he was James.

On a Friday afternoon in mid-February James caught up with Leslie after their English literature class.

"We have to leave right after school if we're going to be on the ferry before the sun sets."

"We do?" she asked.

"Uh-huh."

"Why?" she asked weakly, stalling for time, making decisions, thinking about repercussions.

"Why what?"

"Why are we going?" She had made that decision. Whatever it was, she was going. With James.

"Because it's mid-February and the sky is blue and the mountains look like ice cream cones and you cannot waste a day like this. Not in Seattle."

It *was* a beautiful day. A sunny oasis in a mild but gray and drizzly winter.

"When do we leave?"

"Three-ten. I keep my bike in the parking lot near the gym."

"Bike?"

"Motorcycle."

"Three-ten," Leslie said as she left, her mind reeling, to deal with the repercussions.

As usual, Alan met Leslie at her locker after school.

"I'm not going to practice tonight," Leslie said, looking into her locker instead of at Alan.

"What? Leslie, why?"

"I just . . ." Leslie paused, searching for something that was technically the truth, "don't feel like it."

"Are you ill?"

"No."

"Cramps?" he asked softly.

"Alan!" That was too personal.

"Leslie I am trying to understand. We have a meet tomorrow, you know."

"Of course I know. I'll be there. My performance won't be worse if I skip this one practice. In fact it will probably be better."

"OK. I'll call tonight to see if you're all right."

"No, don't. I'm all right, really," she said, feeling guilty, unable to look at him.

"I'll see you tomorrow, then," he said. He kissed her briefly on the cheek.

Leslie smiled weakly. As soon as Alan left, she grabbed her books and dashed toward the parking lot near the gym.

James was already there.

"I forgot that you always wear a skirt," he said, looking at Leslie's tartan plaid kilt. "I guess you can ride that way. Your legs may get cold."

"It's OK," Leslie said. *I'll press them against yours to keep warm.*

"What are these?" he asked, gesturing toward her armful of books.

"Homework!"

"Can't you leave them here?"

"For the weekend? James, you and I have a test on Monday in English lit," she said. Then she noticed that James had no books.

"Give them here, then," he said. He took her stack of books and balanced them in front of him on the motorcycle. Then he looked at her, handed her his helmet and said, "Hop on."

Leslie tucked the free folds of her skirt around her thighs, then wrapped her arms around James's chest.

James didn't take them in the direction of the ferry terminal in downtown Seattle. Instead he drove along side streets, finally stopping in front of a small dilapidated house with an untended garden and sagging roof. James turned off the engine.

"Home," he said simply. "I'll be right back."

James took Leslie's books and disappeared into the house. While she waited, Leslie studied James's neighborhood. The street was narrow, and the sidewalks and road were crisscrossed with grass-filled cracks. A battered car without a left front tire was parked across the street. The houses looked old and sad and forgotten. Leslie was deciding what it would take to fix up James's house—not that much, really, a little paint, a weekend of gardening, some weed-killer—when he returned. Her books were gone, and he carried a motorcycle helmet for himself.

Without speaking they got back onto the motorcycle and sped off. It was almost rush hour. James avoided the freeway, selecting the more scenic route over University Bridge and along the shore of Lake Union on Eastlake Avenue.

They traveled on Denny Way past the Space Needle to Elliot Way and the Puget Sound waterfront.

They drove past the wharf, the aquarium, Pike Place Market and several commercial piers before arriving at the ferry terminal. Their waterside route was lined by fishermen casting lines off the piers and by native Seattleites drawn to the typically summertime tourist attractions by the beauty of the February day. Kites floated above the blue waters of Elliot Bay, Ivar's sold more iced tea than clam chowder and the air was filled with sounds of laughing children and frolicking seagulls.

The ferry between downtown Seattle and Bainbridge Island arrived just as James and Leslie did. James pulled into the commuter parking lot which was mostly empty at that time of day on the Seattle side of the commuter route. He chained his motorcycle and the helmets to a metal post.

"Two one-way . . . er . . . round-trip tickets on the Bainbridge line," he told the ticket seller.

After the ticket taker collected two of the four orange-colored tickets from James as they walked onto the ferry, James handed the return-trip tickets to Leslie.

"Here. You can keep these as a souvenir. I bought them for you."

"We don't need them?"

"Not if we don't get off the ferry."

"Oh. So you're allowed to do that? Just ride back and forth on the ferry? Like sitting through multiple showings of the same movic at a theater. I've always wondered if that was allowed."

Jame looked at her with amazement and slowly shook his head.

"*Allowed* in a movie theater means that you can out-glower the sixteen-year-old usher assigned to check the theater between showings. In my case, it's usually someone I've gone to school with since kindergarten. I don't suppose any of your friends would ever work in a movie theater."

Leslie shrugged, embarrassed. Her naiveté was showing.

"In the case of ferries you are *supposed* to get off. Most people take ferries to get to the other side anyway, but there are plenty of places to hide during the check between runs."

"Hide?"

"If you want to get off and hand the ticket taker those two tickets, you may."

"No. I want to hide," Leslie said, thinking, We *have* paid for the return trip. If anyone caught us—"If I hadn't been with you, you just would have bought a one-way ticket, huh?"

"Uh-huh."

Nice, James. Nice James.

They stood on the front deck of the ferry as it crossed Elliot Bay to Bainbridge Island. Bainbridge was a fashionable residential area inhabited by people who worked in downtown Seattle. They commuted by ferry, not by ferry, not by car. It was a peaceful, beautiful commute. They could read the morning newspaper, drink coffee and enjoy the dramatic seasons of the land, the water, the mountains and the sky. Sometimes a ferry broke down, or the winds were too strong and the waves too high to permit passage. Then, if they were lucky, they were stranded on the island to weather the storm in their Pacific Northwest homes.

Leslie looked at the Cascade Mountains to the east, the Olympic Mountains to the west and Mount Rainier to the south. The pristine white mountains sparkled in the winter sun. The rugged treacherous peaks were softened by the pink haze that heralded the end of the day. Elliot Bay glittered a deep blue, reflecting the sky above. So many days in winter the water was gray and cloudy, but today the water were clear and blue, crested with feathery whitecaps caused by the gentle blamy breeze.

Draw me a picture of this, James, Leslie thought. Draw me a picture of the water and the islands and the mountains and the sky. Or a picture of the graceful strength of the Space Needle. Or of the delicate white arches of the Science Center. Or of the sunny-day activity on the waterfront. Or of the powerful majesty of Mount Rainier.

Even if James drew her no pictures. Leslie would remember this day always. The memories were carefully, *indelibly*, etched in her mind. Memories of this glorious day in the city she loved. With James. Leslie would never forget it.

James stood close beside her without speaking. He, too, was mesmerized by the spectacle of the sunny day and the blue water and the beauty that surrounded them.

Too soon they reached Bainbridge Island. The ferry bumped gently against the creosote wood pilings of the ferry dock. James and Leslie watched the dock crew pull the ferry snugly into its berth with heavy ropes. As soon as the first car left the ferry boat, James said, "We'd better go."

Leslie looked at the deck. Except for them, it was empty. Everyone else had long since returned to their cars, eager to complete their commute and return to their homes to enjoy the sunset that was imminent and promised to be memorable.

Leslie followed him, silently, stealthily through the body of the ferry boat to the stairway at the stern. The stairway led to the car deck two flights below. At the bottom of the first landing James swung under the staircase into a storage space for life jackets.

It was dark. A few rays of natural light filtered through the slits in the staircase that formed the roof of the storage area. And it was small, just big enough for both of them to stand pressed against the stacks of orange life jackets.

Leslie started to speak, a sentence that would have flowed from a giggle, but James touched her lips with his finger.

Then she heard what he heard: footsteps. Efficient, official footsteps coming down the stairs. She held her breath. Her heart pounded. The footsteps slowed as they reached the landing. Then they sped up again, their rhythm restored as they took the second flight of stairs.

"The purser," James whispered as the sound receded.

"Does he check for stowaways?" Leslie asked, excited by this game, this adventure, this flirtation with harmless danger.

James nodded in the darkness. Leslie's eyes were accommodating to the dimness. She could see his face, close to hers, looking at her seriously.

"Now, what do we do if they find us?" he asked sternly. "Do we give them the tickets?"

"No, Bond. And if we think we're about to be caught . . ." Leslie paused. Then she added, conspiratorially, "We swallow them."

Leslie saw James's mouth curl into a smile.

They lapsed into silence. They had to be quiet and attentive. After a few moments, they heard the sound of cars being loaded onto the ferry.

"When . . . ?" she began.

"As soon as we hear a car door shut, near this stairway, we go."

Leslie nodded.

They listened. They heard doors shut in the distance, at the bow of the boat.

Gradually the sounds got closer.

Then they heard the door that was their signal. Like the finely trained secret agents they pretended to be, they moved in unison out of the storage area onto the stairs and up to the deck.

When they reached the deck, Leslie said breathlessly, "That was fun!"

"Because you had the paid-for return tickets, which you never plan to use, in your pocket," James observed mildly as he reached in his pocket for a cigarette.

Leslie started to protest but considered what he said. It was probably true. She had had her fingers on the tickets in her pocket the entire time.

"A Rosemaiden to the core, I guess," she said with a sigh as she gestured toward his cigarette.

"It's not all that bad. You want a cigarette? Or have you quit smoking?"

"I keep trying," she said. They both knew that the only other cigarettes she had smoked had been that day months before in a meadow with him. "But it's gotten cold all of a sudden. I need a nice warm cigarette."

In the fifteen minutes it took to reload the ferry, while James and Leslie hid beneath the stairs, all signs of summer had disappeared. The sinking sun pulled its warmth with it and left behind a bitter, cold winter evening and a spectacular sunset. The sky glowed red and pink and yellow and orange. The skyline of the city twinkled in the foreground. The buildings reflected the sunset back toward the twilight sky from their huge plate-glass windows.

"Do you want to go inside?" James asked, handing her his lighted cigarette.

Leslie shook her head vigorously. Not for anything. It was too beautiful. She inhaled deeply, her lungs filling with warmth, then irritation from the unfamiliar smoke. She coughed and laughed.

Then she felt wonderfully dizzy and giddy. And a little unsteady. She held on to the painted green railing of the boat and closed her eyes for a moment against the chilling wind that had picked up force as the boat began to move.

She began to shiver.

Without hesitation James put his arms around her.

"You're freezing," he whispered. His cheek touched hers.

"Not if you hold me," she whispered into the wind, wondering if he would hear.

"I'll hold you," he whispered back. He released her for a moment to open his parka. Then he wrapped the parka around both of them, pulled her hands inside and folded his arms around her again.

Leslie felt his heart pounding, felt his lips brush her hair as the wind blew it into his face and felt his arms tighten around her as she pressed even closer. It was hard to breathe, but she didn't want him to loosen his grip.

The back of her head rested against his cheek. She was warm and secure. He made her that way.

But now he was cold. After a few minutes Leslie felt his jaw move. His teeth were chattering.

Leslie pulled free and turned toward him. She put her warm hands on his shivering, ice-cold cheeks.

"*James*," she whispered, feeling his cold skin, looking at his white and purple lips and cheeks. Looking into his eyes.

James wanted to kiss her then, but he couldn't. His lips were numb. He couldn't form words to speak. He couldn't even hold his cigarette with his lips.

Instead, he pulled her toward him, cradled her head against his chest and held her.

"Let's get some hot chocolate," he mumbled into her hair, his voice slurred.

"What?"

He put his arm around her and guided her toward the too bright lights of the ferry boat canteen. By the time the boat docked in Seattle, fortified by a mug of hot chocolate and a shared cigarette, they were warm again, ready for the cold ride home on James's motorcycle.

An old station wagon was parked in the driveway at James's house. James
580 stopped at the curb but didn't turn off the engine.

"Shall I get off?" Leslie asked.

What is he doing home so early? James wondered. His father usually started his Friday afternoon drinking in a bar and often didn't arrive home until midnight, but he was home now. That meant trouble.

James hesitated.

"Leslie, I have to go in by myself. So, maybe I should just bring your books to the party at Larry's tomorrow night?"

How will I explain that to Alan? Leslie wondered. Why couldn't she go into James's house?

"I don't mind waiting out here. I'm not cold," Leslie said easily. She *did* mind waiting. James's neighborhood scared her, and she *was* cold; but it would be best to get her books now.

"You sure?"

"Yes."

"I'll be right back."

James wasn't gone long. Leslie thought she heard shouting from inside the house. Then she heard a door slam. James appeared carrying her books and an extra parka.

"Is everything OK?"

"Sure," he said not looking at her. "Here, wear this."

It was twenty minutes by motorcycle with James driving from his house to hers. Twenty minutes from one world to another.

In the final twenty minutes of a confusing, exciting, wonderful afternoon, Leslie had one last chance to touch him, to talk to him, to be alone with him . . . until when? Twenty minutes to try to decide if he really had wanted to kiss her when she touched his face with her hands. His eyes said so, but he didn't. What made him change his mind? Could she make him change it back? Should she ask him who owned the old station wagon and why there was shouting? Was he angry that she had made him go in his house to get her books?

Did I do something wrong, James? When will I see you again? Kiss me, James.

By the time they reached her house, Leslie's mind was exhausted. She knew she couldn't, wouldn't, question him. She didn't even care about the answers. She just didn't want him to leave.

They walked in silence to her front door. James carried her books.

"Do you want to come in?" Leslie asked finally. Unlike his house, hers was safe for visitors. She hoped it didn't offend him.

James frowned, his expression thoughtful.

"I'd better not," he said.

"You would be welcome to stay for dinner," Leslie pressed gently, detecting his hesitancy. He was considering it.

"No . . ."

"At least come see the way I have framed the picture you gave me."

That was a mistake. James stiffened and withdrew a step.

"I can't stay, Leslie."

"OK," she said lightly, reaching for her books, handing him his parka, all the while aching inside.

Leslie clutched her books against her breasts and looked at the doorknob. All she had to do was touch it, and he would leave. She couldn't move.

"Hey," James said, touching her cheek with his finger, "Leslie."

"Yes?" Her eyes met his.

"Thank you for coming with me. I had a nice time," he said.

He kissed her, lightly, beside her mouth.

Then he left.

At the swim meet the next day, Leslie set personal and meet records in the one hundred meter individual medley and the fifty meter freestyle.

"I guess you're feeling better," Alan said after the meet.

"What? Oh. I feel fine."

"Good. I'll pick you up at seven-thirty tonight."

The party at Larry's—nominally a Valentine's Day party—was a typical gathering of Leslie's friends. It provided a Saturday night social function for everyone. Those without dates visited with friends, gossiped about school, speculated about the college acceptances that would be sent in two months and discussed movies and albums and, in occasional philosophical moments, life itself. The couples usually retreated to the darkest room of the house to dance, to kiss or to be alone.

New relationships formed and old ones dissolved at such a rate that the profile of each party was unique. For the past three months, Alan and Leslie alone emerged as the enduring, constant couple. They were so comfortable with their relationship that they usually spent as much time visiting with their unattached friends in the brightly lit living rooms as they did closeted with the new couples in the darkened dancing areas.

But that night, troubled by Leslie's mysterious behavior the day before, Alan pulled her away from the others early in the evening.

"Let's dance, Les."

James arrived at ten. At least Leslie first noticed him then, leaning against a wall in the dance room, smoking a cigarette and drinking beer from a can. He stared at her, his face eerily illuminated each time he inhaled.

Leslie stared back at James, her face resting against Alan's shoulder, her arms wrapped around him, swaying gently to the Beatles' "Hey Jude." Leslie's blue eyes didn't blink. They watched James with wide-eyed curiosity.

Do you want me, James?

James returned her stare, unblinking, unflinching, his eyes hidden in shadows between puffs of his cigarette.

Dance with me, James.

Halfway through the dance, Alan raised Leslie's chin with his hand and guided her mouth to his. They kissed, moving slowly to the music, for the rest of the song.

By the time they stopped dancing, James was gone.

Chapter 17

April fifteenth was the date on which all colleges notified applicants of their acceptance—or rejection—by the school. That year—their senior year—April fifteenth was a Saturday. A victory party was planned. The party would be held at Alan's parents" summer cabin at Sparrow Lake thirty miles north of Seattle. It was scheduled to begin after the day's mail had arrived in Seattle and continue until midnight. The girls had to be back in their homes in Seattle by one. The boys would spend the night at the cabin.

Alan and James arrived at the cabin at ten Saturday morning to set up. They put food and beer in the refrigerator, gas in the water ski boat, wood in the fireplace and coals in the barbeque. Alan and James didn't need to wait for the day's mail. They already knew their college plans. James had been accepted at the University of Washington and had decided to attend. Alan had been offered numerous athletic scholarships. He decided to go to the University of California at Los Angeles because of UCLA's recent record in NCAA swimming championships.

But Alan was anxious about the news that the mail would bring to Leslie. She had applied to two schools in California: Pomona, in the Los Angeles area, and Stanford, three hundred miles away. The distance between Los Angeles and Stanford was substantial, but it was still closer that Leslie's first choice: Radcliffe was a continent away. Alan assumed that Leslie would be accepted at all three schools. He desperately wanted her to choose one of the California schools. He wanted to be near her.

In the past few weeks, Leslie and Alan had frequently discussed the decision Leslie would make. Sometimes their discussions were careful and gentle. Too often they were bitter.

It was Leslie's decision. Still, if by some chance she wasn't accepted at Radcliffe . . .

Betty, Joanne and Robin arrived at Leslie's house one minute ahead of the mail truck. Betty's mail had arrived mid-morning bearing news of her acceptance to Smith, her first choice. She had picked up Joanne, who already knew she was staying in Seattle at the University, and Robin, who was rejected by Vassar but still had the luxury of choosing between Bryn Mawr and Swarthmore.

Susan and Leslie were already at the curb watching the mail truck's painfully slow trek up the street.

Finally the mail was in Leslie's hand. She extracted the envelopes from Stanford University, Pomona College, Radcliffe College, Antioch, University of Michigan and Cornell University. She selected the one postmarked Cambridge, Massachusetts.

It was thin. Too thin, Leslie thought, her hands trembling. She took a deep breath and opened it as Susan, Robin, Betty and Joanne watched.

Welcome to Radcliffe College . . .

"I'm in," she whispered. "I got into Radcliffe."

"Hurray!"

"Of course you did. Whoever doubted it?"

"Congratulations, darling."

"Leslie, are you ready to go?"

"Now I am," Leslie said, lifting the bag that contained her swim suit, towel and extra clothes and handing the six envelopes, unopened except for the acceptance from Radcliffe, to Susan. "Here, Mom."

"Don't you—" Susan began, thinking abut Alan.

"I guess I'd better take these two," Leslie said, selecting the envelopes from Stanford and Pomona. "I'll open them on the way to the lake."

Leslie didn't want to open them yet. She didn't want to think about anything but how happy she was to have gotten into Radcliffe. To be going to Radcliffe. She had made her decision as soon as she read the first word of the letter. *Welcome.*

The letters from Stanford and Pomona didn't matter. Except that she had to tell Alan. Maybe, if she was lucky, the letters from both would begin with *We are sorry to inform you . . .* or, *Unfortunately . . .*

Unfortunately, as Leslie discovered when she finally opened the letters five minutes before they reached the cabin, she was accepted by both.

Leslie, Betty, Joanne and Robin were among the last to arrive. Everyone else had shared their news, some jubilant, some disappointed, all adjusting as the afternoon wore on and they shared the joy and the disappointment with their friends.

Everyone knew how much Leslie wanted to go to Radcliffe.

"So, Leslie, are you going to be a Cliffie?" someone asked as soon as she entered the cabin.

"Yes," she said firmly, looking at Alan across the room. "Yes, I am."

For the next five minutes, Leslie learned about the fates, bad and good, of her friends. Eventually she worked her way over to Alan who had retreated to a far corner of the cabin and was staring at the lake.

"I'm going to Radcliffe, Alan," she said quietly.

"I heard."

"It's what I want. What I've been working for."

"I know," he said bitterly. It was what you were working for before you met me, he thought. And I haven't made a difference. He looked at her. "Did you get in to—"

"Yes. To both. Alan, you're being unfair. I didn't try to talk you out of going to UCLA, to get you to look at East Coast schools."

"I know. I wish you had. I wish you had cared enough to try."

"I'm not going to let you spoil this for me, Alan," Leslie said.

She grabbed her bag, crossed the living room and went outside to the shed across from the main cabin. They used the shed for the girls' dressing area during parties. Leslie bolted the door and changed into her old blue tank suit. She hadn't worn it for years but decided it would be fine to wear under a wet suit if she did any water skiing. The water was too cold in April to swim or water ski without a wet suit.

Leslie was going for a swim anyway, despite the cold. She pulled on the tank suit she had purchased in eighth grade. It still fit perfectly in the hips and waist, but it was tight, *too* tight, over her breasts.

It didn't matter. No one would see her, and she had to swim. She had to swim, as fast as she could, until she was exhausted. She had to burn off some of her energy—her *ecstasy*—from being accepted at Radcliffe. And some of her anger with Alan. Then, when she was calm again, she would rejoin the party.

Leslie threw her towel over her shoulders, unbolted the shed door and walked, barefooted, across the lawn and down the four cement stairs that led to the sandy beach. She left her towel at the water's edge and walked without hesitation into the lake.

As soon as the water was deep enough, Leslie flopped onto her stomach and began to swim. She did the stroke that required the most energy and concentration: the butterfly. The water was barely tolerable.

After twenty minutes of swimming as fast as she could in the frigid water, concentrating on nothing but the style and pace and rhythm of her stroke, Leslie was exhausted. She swam back toward shore. When the level was waist-deep, she stood and trudged, head down, through the cold heavy water toward the beach. She thought about the reason for her icy swim—her acceptance to Radcliffe—and smiled. It still felt so good.

"A little cold, isn't it?"

Leslie looked up, startled. James sat on a piece of driftwood smoking a cigarette, staring at her. At all of her.

Her wet shivering body was covered with goose bumps as she hastily pushed her dripping wet chestnut hair off her face. James stared at the startled sapphire blue eyes and the full lips with the half smile that faded when she saw him. Her boyish hips and legs and her round firm breasts that pressed for freedom against the sheer fabric of the too small blue tank suit were subject to his gaze.

Leslie felt naked. She *was* naked except for the flimsy suit that became almost transparent when she was wet and her body was rigid from the cold.

James was staring at her, smiling, holding her towel.

"James," she breathed unable to move.

James stood up and walked toward her. He draped the towel around her like a cape. Leslie gratefully pulled the edges of the towel together. She was clothed again. Modest. Hidden from his inquisitive, penetrating eyes.

"Did you work it all off?" he asked.

"What?"

"Your fight with Alan."

"We didn't have a fight."

"Oh."

"He's annoyed because I'm going to Radcliffe instead of somewhere close to him."

"He's hurt."

"Hurt?"

"You'd rather go to a city where you know no one and take the chance of making new friends than be with him. It speaks for itself. Of course he's hurt."

"You think I should follow Alan to Los Angeles?"

"I think you should do what you want to do."

"I think I'm a little young to give up my life and my dreams for someone else, don't you?"

James shrugged. He stared at the water and avoided her eyes.

"If Alan were the right person for you, you could make the commitment," he said distantly.

I could stay at the University of Washington, James, if you wanted me to. I *would* stay, she thought, amazed at the realization. Or if you wanted to spend your life working at the logging camp . . . maybe I could be the cook. For the right person I could make the commitment.

"Leslie! James! We're going to water ski now. Leslie, you've already been in?"

Leslie and James were joined on the beach by the others. Alan continued to keep a cool distance from Leslie despite her attempts to approach him.

They water skied, played volleyball, barbequed hamburgers and roasted marshmallows. When the sun set, they turned down the lights and turned on the music. Leslie watched Alan dance with Betty, Joanne and Robin. He was showing her that he could have a good time without her.

It won't work, Alan, Leslie thought. I won't feel jealous or sorry. I won't apologize, and I won't change my mind.

Leslie glanced at her watch. Eleven. They had to leave by midnight. Maybe someone would like to leave now, but it didn't look like it. From her vantage point in the corner of an overstuffed sofa, no ne was ready for the party to end.

"Let's go," he whispered in her ear.

James. She hadn't seen him for a while. She assumed he had left.

Without saying anything, Leslie followed him. James went to the kitchen for a can of beer, then he led the way outside toward the woods that surrounded the cabin. After five minutes, James found a fallen tree. He leaned against the stump and lit a cigarette.

"Leslie?" he asked offering her a cigarette.

"No, thank you. I've quit."

"That's good. Terrible habit. Would you like some beer?" he asked, raising the can of beer toward her. She could have some of his.

"No, I—"

"Don't drink. That's right. Too young. Against the law."

"It is," Leslie protested weakly.

"What's going to happen to you next year at Radcliffe? Everyone will drink or at least know how to drink. You may even be old enough to drink legally in Massachusetts."

"Nothing's going to happen to me."

"And what about dope?"

Leslie looked at him blankly.

"Marijuana," James said.

"I don't need it."

"Natural high?" James asked, his eyes mocking her.

Why was James acting this way? Did he resent the fact that she was going to Radcliffe, too? If he did, why didn't he tell her?

Leslie sighed and sat down on the log six feet away from James.

"I think you should at least know what it tastes like," he said quietly after a few silent moments.

"What what tastes like?"

"Beer."

"Oh."

"I have a way for you to taste beer without drinking it," he said.

James took a large swallow of his beer and walked toward her.

"Leslie," James said gently, carefully lacing his strong fingers through her fine chestnut hair. "Come here."

He pulled her mouth to his and kissed her, a deep warm passionate kiss that tasted, at first, like beer. Then, as the kiss became longer and deeper, it tasted like James.

The moment James's soft persuasive lips touched hers, Leslie knew what had been tormenting her, confusing her, exciting her for almost three years. It was desire for James. The need to have his lips on hers. The need to touch him and feel *him* touch *her*.

James, she thought as she curled her fingers through his black hair and felt her body pressing closer to his. Naturally. Instinctively. *James*.

His hands held her face as he kissed her. Leslie lost herself in the feel of him, the taste of him, the warmth and strength and touch of him. She heard—*felt*—a soft deep moan. It was a moan of pleasure and desire and need. Did the moan come from James? Or did it come from deep within *her*?

They kissed with mouths joined and bodies straining through layers of shirts and sweaters and coats until, breathless, James pulled away. He still held her face in his rough but gentle hands.

"You like it," he said staring at her, his intense serious eyes glazed with desire. Desire and a trace of worry.

Can I stop? he wondered. I have to.

586 "I like—" Leslie began, confused by his words and the power of his eyes and the feelings that pulsed through her body. *I like you, James, I like it when you kiss me.*

"Beer," he said. His voice was husky. It would be impossible to stop now. Impossible to lighten the mood. It wasn't what either of them wanted.

Leslie traced his lips with her fingers and felt her body sway toward his as if James's body were a powerful seductive magnet.

"I want to be closer to you," he whispered. He unzipped her ski jacket, then his. As he kissed her again, James removed her jacket and her navy blue V-neck sweater until all she had against the cold, April night air was a cotton blouse, a pair of blue jeans and the warmth of James's body. He murmured against her hair as he pulled her tight against him, "Too cold?"

"No," she whispered, cuddling against him, feeling her body fit into his.

He kissed her mouth, her hair and her long ivory neck. His hands felt the soft fullness of her breasts under the light cotton blouse. Leslie moved closer, her breasts welcoming his hands, wanting their touch, her hips pressing rhythmically against his. James unbuttoned her blouse and found the velvety warmth of her breasts and the strong pounding of her young athletic heart.

Without thinking, without urging from James, because it felt right, and she wanted to, Leslie took her hand from the cool damp skin of his back to his belt buckle. Then, confidently, she loosened his belt and unbuttoned the top button of his jeans.

"Leslie! Where are you?"

James and Leslie froze.

It was midnight. Betty, Joanne and Robin were ready to leave. The party was over.

"I have to go," Leslie whispered, pulling away from him, buttoning her blouse.

"I'll give you a ride home," James said calmly.

"Now?"

"In a while. I'll get you home on time," he said staring at her. *Don't leave, Leslie, not yet.*

"Leslie! Come on!" The voices were getting closer.

The spell was broken. The privacy invaded. Leslie couldn't hold James's gaze. She couldn't look in his eyes and tell him that she didn't want to stay.

"I have to go, James," she said, bending down to pick up her sweater and her jacket.

James shrugged. Then he casually rebuttoned his jeans and rebuckled his belt. He swung his jacket over his shoulder and took a swallow of beer.

"OK, Leslie, let's go," he said and began walking toward the cabin.

"*There* you are," Joanne said as she spotted James and Leslie emerging from the shadows of the woods.

"Time to go?" Leslie asked. What was she doing? She wanted to go back in the woods with James. Was he angry with her? He acted like it didn't matter, but he *had* asked her to stay.

Leslie noticed Alan leaning, sulkily, against the cabin door. She stared at him for a moment. *I don't owe you an apology, Alan. Not for anything*, her blue eyes blazed defiantly.

Leslie knew that they were all watching her, wondering what she had been doing with James in the woods and what was happening with Alan.

Leave me alone, Leslie wanted to scream. Leave me alone with James.

She turned, expecting to find James still beside her, but he had withdrawn. He leaned against his motorcycle, slowly dragging on a cigarette, watching her.

Without a word, Leslie got into the back seat of Betty's station wagon.

Two weeks later James telephoned Leslie. Susan answered.

"Dr. Adams, this is James. May I speak to Leslie, please?"

Susan found her daughter.

"Leslie, it's James. Did you tell him I got my Ph.D?"

"*James!* What? No. You just got it a week ago. I may have told him you would get it this spring," Leslie said as she rushed past Susan to the phone.

"James?"

"Hi, Leslie."

She had never spoken to him over the telephone. Leslie sat down, then stood up, then twisted the cord in her hands.

"Hi."

"Do you want to go to the Senior Prom with me?"

"*Yes*," she breathed. *Yes! Yes!* Then she said quietly, "But I can't."

"Oh. Oh?"

"Alan already asked me."

"Alan," James said flatly. Then he asked, "Are you still going to Radcliffe?"

"Yes. Of course," Leslie answered distractedly as she tried to decide if she could cancel her date with Alan and go with James. She knew that she couldn't. It would be too rude. She explained, "Alan realizes that he and I don't have a future, but he thought we should go to the Prom together anyway. For old times" sake."

"Great."

"I already said yes," Leslie said brusquely, angry with Alan for asking her so soon and angry with James for not asking her sooner.

"Well, have a nice time," James said.

"James," Leslie began.

"What?"

"Thank you for asking me." Ask me to do something else. *Anything* else, she thought.

"Sure," he said. Then, just before he hung up, he added, "See ya, Leslie."

James *didn't* see Leslie except from a distance. Six weeks later they graduated from George Washington High School. Leslie graduated first in the class. She was given the Rosemaiden award for the third time and received a special award for service and a scholarship from a local society. Leslie was voted the girl Most Likely to Succeed.

James graduated in the middle of the class. Despite his ability, his overall performance had been erratic. James received no awards. He had been nominated Most Likely To Get Arrested, Most Likely To Get Someone Pregnant and Most Likely To Die Of Lung Cancer. Leslie assumed the nominations had been submitted by some of her friends. Since she was on the Senior Class Graduating Committee, Leslie was able to intercept—and discard—the nominations for James before they were placed on the ballot.

In August, two months after graduation, Leslie saw James for the last time.

Leslie, Joanne, Robin and Betty were at the Seattle Center. It was a beautiful balmy summer evening, a perfect evening to go to the center and watch the fabulous light show at the water fountain. It was one of the few evenings they had left before disbanding for college, one last chance to celebrate their friendship, reminisce about high school and forecast the unknown, exciting future that lay ahead.

The serious conversations between Leslie and her girlfriends usually degenerated into irrepressible giggling. Or singing. Or dancing. They were happy; their lives were good and full of promise.

Usually their exuberant behavior was unwitnessed, except by each other, and confined to the privacy of a slumber party or a remote stretch of sandy beach, but that August night they were too happy, too eager, too full of anticipation. They sang and danced unselfconsciously around the colorfully illuminated water fountain.

Leslie did a pirouette without watching where the spin was taking her and pulled up abruptly just before colliding with James.

James. James had his arms around a girl, no, a woman. She was a pretty woman, dressed up, who clung to James and eyed Leslie and the others with curious non-threatened amusement.

"James!" Leslie gasped, breathlessly.

"Leslie," he said, pulling away slightly from the woman. Enough, at least, to take a deep breath.

"Leslie, this is Cheryl. Cheryl, this is Leslie. And Joanne. And Betty. And Robin."

Leslie's friends viewed James with new curiosity. He wore slacks and a sport coat. He almost looked presentable. And Cheryl, older and sophisticated, was clearly intrigued with James.

Leslie could not speak. Her face was already flushed from exercise and exuberance. Now the warmth became hot and the color deepened for other reasons: embarrassment and mortification.

And something else. An emotion washed through Leslie that she didn't recognize. It was new to her and *strong*, whatever it was.

"You're not logging this summer?" Leslie blurted out. Why did I ask that, she wondered. Because I want *her* to know that I know James. That I know about James. That he is mine . . . The emotion was slowly, painfully, coming into focus.

"Yes, I am. I just came into town for the weekend."

To spend the weekend with Cheryl.

"Oh, well. Nice to see you, James. Nice to meet you, Cheryl," Leslie said with finality. She was suddenly desperate to get away.

"Good-bye, Leslie."

The feeling—the new emotion—stayed with Leslie, demanding definition, for two days. It was a gnawing, uneasy feeling. When she finally realized what it was and that she could only purge it by admitting it to *him*, Leslie wrote the letter:

Dear James,

It is jealousy, I realize, after fighting with it ever since I saw you with Cheryl. I am so jealous of her for being with you! For having you. For being your girlfriend.

I always wanted to be your girlfriend. I even thought I would be, when and if you decided to have a girlfriend. Silly, huh? Well, I'll survive, but it feels better to admit it. Even though you may be laughing.

As long as I've gone this far, since I'll probably never see you again, I might as well tell all. I think you're wonderful (I know you know this). So sensitive and talented. I enjoyed being with you so much (I am so jealous of Cheryl!).

I wish . . . I wish a lot of things . . . a lot of what ifs . . .

But, mostly, I wish you happiness.

Always,
Leslie

Leslie mailed the letter to James at the logging company in Snoqualmie, Washington. Leslie didn't reread it. She might not have mailed it if she had.

She wanted James to know her feelings for him had been real. Not silly. Not whimsical. It was important for her to tell him.

She decided that it didn't matter if James never acknowledged the letter. It didn't require an answer. But in the two weeks between the time she mailed it and the time she boarded the plane for Boston, a part of Leslie waited. Her heart pounded when the phone rang or the mail arrived or the doorbell rang.

But she didn't hear from James.

Not then. Not at all for nine years.

Not until that day in August when she was paged by the Department of Medicine secretary with a message to call Mr. James Stevenson.

Chapter 18

Ross MacMillan watched Janet out of the corner of his eye, eager to see her reaction to mid-week, mid-morning Manhattan. Their limousine moved stealthily along the narrow, crowded side streets, smoothly dodging cars and pedestrians.

She has to think this is fabulous, Ross thought. His own heart pumped more swiftly, energized and stimulated by the activity that surrounded him: the fast, purposeful pace of the streets of Manhattan. Ross loved New York City. Even in mid-August, even in the midst of the worst heat wave in recent memory, he loved it.

Usually Ross took August off. It was the only natural break between the theater seasons. *Usually* he spent August in Carmel, leading a slow-paced, *no*-paced existence. *Usually* that month of enforced rest was a necessary break.

But this was not a usual year. This was the year of *Joanna*. This year there was too much to do. There was no time to take a break.

Just a week ago they closed *Joanna* in San Francisco. The show had already been held over twelve weeks. Every performance had been sold out. There were still many theatergoers on the West Coast who wanted to see *Joanna*, but they had to end the run. They were taking the show to Broadway.

Ross and Janet had arrived in New York City the night before. *Joanna* was scheduled to open on Broadway in November. Ross was co-producing the New York production with Arthur Watts. Ross's maximum involvement would be in the preproduction phases, in the next three weeks, since he had to return to San Francisco by mid-September to give his undivided attention to the fall season at his own theater.

With two minor exceptions, all members of the original San Francisco company agreed to move to New York. No arm twisting was required. It was the chance of a lifetime to play on Broadway in an already critically acclaimed and box-office proven musical. The two company members that could not leave San Francisco "indefinitely" agonized for weeks over their decision.

It made life easier for Arthur and Ross that they would have the original company. It made it possible to close in San Francisco and open in New York in such a short period of time. The preproduction activity would focus on logistic, not artistic considerations.

They also both knew that the only cast member who was truly critical to the success of the smooth transcontinental move was Janet. It was her show. It was Janet's talent and energy and her unflagging professionalism that inspired tireless excellence from the rest of the cast. Janet was the unassuming and masterful leader. She quietly set a standard which they all, out of love or respect or pure role modeling, followed.

Janet was critical to the successful move, and Janet had not yet signed the contract. She had not yet agreed to star in the Broadway production of her show. She told Ross that she had never been to New York and that she was happy in San Francisco. She would have to see New York before deciding.

So Janet and Ross flew to New York in mid-August to see New York.

Ross watched her wide gray eyes calmly surveying the Manhattan scene through the tinted glass of the limousine.

Despite the fact that he had spent the past eight months working with Janet, Ross could not tell what thoughts lurked behind the gray. He was the director, and she was the star; *together* they had created a masterpiece. Their professional relationship was intense, intimate and creative, but he knew nothing—except the brief bits Kathleen had told him because of Mark—about her personal life. About who she *was*.

And the clear gray eyes provided no clue.

Until yesterday, on the flight from San Francisco to New York, Ross had never been alone with Janet outside the theater. Ross looked forward to the five-hour flight, sitting next to her in the first-class cabin. It would give him a chance to talk to her, to get to know her. But Janet started to read as soon as the plane took off from San Francisco International Airport.

Ross watched Janet read. She was completely absorbed in the book.

"Is that good?" he asked finally, gesturing to her book, Ken Follett's *Eye of the Needle*.

"Very good, she said.

"I wouldn't think spy novels would be your thing."

"It's not just a spy novel. In fact, it's more about relationships between men and women. Desires, needs—" Janet stopped abruptly and looked back at her book.

"Are you looking forward to seeing New York?" Ross pushed, pressing his advantage. She was a little off guard.

"I'm mostly nervous."

"Nervous?" he asked with amazement. He didn't think Janet had nerves. Just cool, steely calm and limitless energy.

"Of course."

"Why?"

"Because I'm afraid that I won't like it. That I won't be able to do the show there. And that will make you and Arthur angry with me."

Ross stared at her. He realized that she was being honest, and he realized for the first time that her decision about New York was not simply a matter of choice. Janet was not simply a star being stubborn. It *had* seemed out of character for her to behave like a prima donna. It wasn't her style. Her resistance to moving with the company to New York seemed inexplicable. As far as Ross could tell, Janet had no ties in San Francisco. Her injured but recovering ex-husband was in love with Kathleen.

Ross realized that Janet's reluctance about committing herself to the move to New York, sight unseen, was not a matter of whimsy. It was a matter of ability. Janet would move to New York if she *could*. If she could stand it. But why wouldn't she?

Now as he watched Janet watch Manhattan, Ross wondered what she was thinking. Did she like it? How *couldn't* she like it?

As they rode toward the theater where *Joanna* would play, Janet said nothing, and her expression didn't change.

They were met at the theater by Arthur, the director, the choreographer, the stage manager and the costume designer.

Arthur kissed Janet on the cheek.

"Hello, darling," he said brushing her cheeks lightly with his lips. "You look lovely."

"Hello, Arthur. Thank you," she said, smiling.

She likes Arthur, Ross observed. Maybe that will help. Ross wasn't convinced that Janet liked *him*, but of course he couldn't tell. There were no clues.

Janet walked around the theater an paced slowly on the stage.

"It's deeper than the one in San Francisco," she said, finally. "And not as wide. You'll have to restage at least two numbers."

"That's no problem."

She nodded.

"Janet, I want to hear the acoustics," Ross said. "Arthur claims they're the best in New York."

"OK. Do you want—"

"Sing *Dreaming*, OK? While I walk all around."

Without answering Janet began to sing. *Dreaming* was the song that had made her famous in San Francisco. It was a haunting love song. Ross ad heard her sing it hundreds of times, but still, even now, even as he paced from one extreme of the theater to the other, it moved him, sending a tingling shiver through him.

"God, she's good," Arthur whispered to Ross.

"The best."

"Is she going to come?"

"I have no idea."

"What can we do to convince her?"

"Probably nothing we do will make a difference. She'll just decide. But what have you planned?" Ross asked, half listening to Janet sing, knowing that she would turn them down, wondering why.

"After an elegant lunch, I thought we could look at places to live. The theater has options on several penthouses earmarked precisely for imported talent like Janet. They are all spectacular. The best in New York. I don't think she'll be able to resist."

Ross shrugged. He had heard rumors that Janet lived in a small cottage in the country. Maybe they should drive to Connecticut.

"Then we could take a look at Fifth Avenue. That's pretty dazzling."

Ross didn't know what, if anything, dazzled Janet. Certainly not her own fame. It seemed to please her, but it didn't seem to *matter* to her. Janet didn't wear expensive clothes or jewelry, even though, because of *Joanna*, she could easily afford them. And the salary she was being offered to star in the New York production could make her a regular buyer at any boutique in the world.

They visited the penthouses, shopped on Fifth Avenue, went to the top of the World Trade Center and saw the Statue of Liberty. Janet wasn't dazzled, but she was wide-eyed and smiling and polite.

"Magnificent," she murmured appreciatively at the sight of the Statue of Liberty.

They dined at Manhattan's trendiest restaurant. They were seated immediately because Arthur was recognized and Arthur was powerful. They were seated ahead of other less prominent, but substantial, clients, many of whom had reservation times before Arthur's. That was the way the restaurant operated. Clients were seated, or not, at the discretion of the maitre d'. Reservations, even ones made months in advance, were a minor consideration. Arthur usually appeared without reservations and was always seated promptly.

Arthur, Ross and Janet were joined by three other theater principals—two women and a man—all of whom were committed to wooing the reluctant Janet to New York. If they expected a woman who simply needed an extra dose of flattery or the unending reassurances that many superstars required, they were surprised. Janet had none of the usual airs. She wasn't playing games. In fact, had they not known who she was, they would barely have recognized the quiet young woman studying the menu, artfully concealing her horror at the prices, as the romantic captivating star of *Joanna*.

The subject of Janet's decision was not discussed, but they eagerly discussed the upcoming production as if Janet would be in it. Ross watched her gray eyes carefully. He couldn't tell.

Early in the evening Janet seemed intrigued with observing the people around her, New York's wealthiest, in designer dresses, perfectly coiffed, bejewelled and elegant on this Wednesday evening in August. Janet did not recognize many faces. She didn't recognize their faces; but she instantly appreciated their wealth and power, and she would have recognized the names of the companies they owned and the people they controlled.

As the evening wore on and the conversation fortified by fine wine and gourmet food became more animated, Janet withdrew. Fifteen people had stopped by the table to speak with Arthur and to meet Janet. She smiled graciously, nodded pleasantly at their compliments—many had flown to San Francisco expressly to see her in *Joanna*—and then grew progressively quiet as each successive wellwisher left.

By the time the cream of asparagus soup was served, Ross's attention had been commandeered away from Janet by Stacy, one of the two women who had joined them for dinner. Stacy decided early on that she would have little impact on Janet's decision—*of course* Janet would decide to move anyway—and turned her full attention to Ross.

By the time the china plates, empty except for Janet's, were being expertly and unobtrusively removed from the table, Stacy's hand equally expertly massaged Ross's inner thigh.

It was only when Arthur suggested that they go to his club for dessert and dancing that Ross forced his attention away from Stacy to Janet. They would go to Arthur's club if Janet wanted to.

Ross looked across the table, expecting to see Janet's placid smile, and did a double take. Janet wasn't smiling, although she seemed to be trying to. Her full lips were quivering, and her always calm and serene eyes were turbulent. Stormy. Troubled.

Ross stood up abruptly, dislodging Stacy's hand, and walked around the table to Janet's chair. He casually rested his hand on her shoulder.

"I think Janet and I will pass on the rest of the festivities. It's been a long day. We both have a little jet lag," he said, gently lifting Janet up as he spoke. She came willingly.

Ross guided her quickly to the coat room and into a waiting cab that took them speedily to the Plaza.

It was midnight. The streets of Manhattan were still crowded, full of activity, full of the life and energy that Ross loved—the life and energy that, somehow, were too much for Janet. If that was the problem. Ross waited for her to tell him, watching her cower, trembling in the far corner of the cab, her head bent down, her eyes staring at her hands.

Janet said nothing.

They rode in silence on the elevator to the floor of suites at the Plaza. They had adjacent suites. Janet's hand trembled as she aimed her key at the keyhole. Ross took the key and opened her door for her. Then he followed her inside her suite.

"So?" he asked finally.

"So I can't do it, Ross. I'm sorry," she said, tears spilling from her opaque gray eyes like raindrops from a thunder cloud. Her eyes were dark, ominous.

"Why?" he asked helplessly, not expecting an answer.

"I can't live here. I am so out of place."

"You aren't at all out of place. You are special."

"I can't breathe here. I can't rest or relax. Everything, everyone moves so fast. Expects so much."

I know, Ross thought, that's what I love about New York: being part of that activity, feeling the pace, keeping up with the pace.

"People expect a lot in San Francisco."

"It's different," she said. "And you know it."

"I know. It's a difference that I love."

"And I don't. I would suffocate here, Ross. I would be afraid to leave my glamorous penthouse apartment, and I would feel like a trapped bird if I didn't leave. I could never call a taxi or order a dinner at a restaurant."

"Everything would be provided for you, Janet. You wouldn't have to do anything," he said, watching the fear in her face. He had never seen fear before. Only calm and confidence and serenity.

I don't want you to be afraid, Janet, he thought.

"That's not living, Ross. I would hate it. I don't want to be a fragile creature shuttled from one gilded cage to the other. Of course it could be done, but I would hate it. I would suffocate."

"Janet, you are a strong successful woman," Ross said, trying a new tactic. He didn't want her to be afraid, but he wanted her to move to New York.

"I can't live here," Janet repeated firmly.

"Is it because of Mark?" Ross asked, knowing that he had no right to.

"*Mark?* No," Janet said softly. "I told you. You just can't transplant a Nebraska country girl to New York City. At least not this one."

"Janet, you will win the Tony if you do this show on Broadway. Don't you want that?"

Janet shrugged.

"Don't you want everyone to know that you're the best?" he asked.

"The best . . ." she said almost to herself. "No. Being the best has never mattered to me. I sing because I love to sing. I want you and Arthur to win the

Tony, but you can do that without me."

"I don't understand you. You knock yourself out for each performance. You work like a maniac. You're a perfectionist whether you admit it or not, and now you say you don't want to be the best. After all that hard work, you throw away a career opportunity that most other women would kill for?"

Ross was almost shouting. It was so frustrating. He didn't understand her, and he wanted to. Needed to. She was making such a critical decision—a *wrong* decision—and he didn't know why.

Janet retreated to a blue silk chair in the corner of the suite. She said nothing, but the tears began anew, and the look of fear returned.

Ross stared at her helplessly, realizing again how little he knew about Janet. He knew her better as Joanna. Strong, beautiful, fearless Joanna. Ross was enchanted by Joanna, by the way Janet played Joanna. Ross was a little in love with Joanna.

But Joanna didn't exist. Only Janet. A woman he didn't know. She had the most beautiful voice he had ever heard and remarkable eyes that told him nothing. Her sensuous mouth smiled easily. She could own New York but wouldn't even give it a chance.

Janet, a woman who had been in love once. Ross had seen it in her eyes when she saw Mark after the performance on opening night. Ross had seen the love and sadness in her eyes. And in Mark's. Ross hadn't told Kathleen about *that*. There was no point. Ross had seen something else in their eyes: It was over—for both of them—but there were memories.

Who are you? Ross wondered. Joanna. Janet. Mark's ex-love. No one's lover.

"You're staring at me," Janet whispered finally.

"I'm trying to figure you out. What makes you tick."

"Music," Janet answered quickly, preferring conversation to Ross's probing stare.

"Not enough to stay here."

"If New York was the only place in the world that I could sing, I would stay," she said slowly.

"What if Arthur and I put the word out? Blackball you."

Janet frowned briefly then smiled.

"You wouldn't do that," she said simply.

"I wouldn't?" he asked.

"No. You are a fair man."

How do you know? he wondered, pleased. Of course he would do nothing to hurt her, whoever she was.

"What are you going to do?"

"I can see what community theaters are doing in the Bay Area. I don't even need to be paid for a while. You gave me so much money . . ." she said quietly.

Gave is right, Ross thought. She refused to get an agent, to negotiate. She told him to pay her whatever seemed fair. He paid her a lot. It was fair.

"I don't suppose you'd want to hire me?" she asked carefully.

"For what?"

"For whatever you're doing this season. What *are* you doing?" she asked.

She had been so involved with *Joanna* and so worried about the move to New York that she hadn't even asked.

"*Peter Pan*. The world is ready for a revival."

"With a female lead?"

"No. I *might* have considered you, but I've already cast Peter." Ross had cast the lead before he left for New York. Auditions for the other parts would take place during his absence. He would return to select, from the pre-auditioned finalists, in September. "He's a little older than the traditional Peter. He'll play Peter as a young adult. Beautiful tenor."

Janet nodded.

"Have you cast the entire company?"

"Janet. You are a major star. There are no major female roles in *Peter Pan*. I can't really see you performing in the company, can you?"

"*Yes*. Ross, I don't have to be the star."

"Do you want a drink?" he asked, walking to the fully stocked bar in the suite, stalling for time, his imaginative, innovative mind beginning to whir. How could he use Janet in *Peter Pan?* It would have to be a whole new production. Probably contemporary. He had already cast a slightly older Peter. Maybe a real love story? A romance?

"No, thank you. Ross, have you already cast—"

"Wendy," Ross said. Janet could play Wendy. Wendy and Peter could *really* fall in love. They could write a few new songs for Wendy. Love duets for Wendy and Peter. It could work. It would be risky, but it could be done. He had taken chances with *Joanna*, and it had paid off.

Largely because of Janet. And she had been the biggest risk.

Janet could play Wendy. Janet could create a lovely, romantic Wendy.

"Ross?"

"No, Janet, I haven't cast Wendy yet."

"Do you mind if I audition?"

Ross stared at her.

"Audition?" he repeated blankly. He was already thinking of ideas for the production.

"For Wendy. May I audition for Wendy?"

"Do you want Wendy? Even if she's a new modern Wendy who falls in love with Peter?"

"*Yes!*"

"OK."

"OK? I can audition?"

"OK. You're Wendy. I'll call Jack in San Francisco right now. We'll meet there a week from today," Ross said, almost talking to himself. He was mentally planning major productions in two cities. Because of Janet, the one in New York had just become more complicated, and because of her, the one in San Francisco had just become more exciting. "I have to stay here and start the search for a new Joanna. Janet, let's have lunch together tomorrow. To discuss Wendy."

"Oh. All right," she said hesitantly.

"Something wrong?"

"No. *No*. I . . . it's just that—"

"What?"

"I was going to leave first thing in the morning to visit my family in Lincoln."

"Don't you want to stay in New York as a tourist now that pressure is off?"

"No."

"Will you have breakfast with me? Before you go? I just need to make sure this all makes sense in the morning? OK? Eight o'clock? You can catch a noon flight."

"Yes, fine," Janet said, standing up as she noticed that Ross was moving toward the door. "I'll see you then. And Ross . . ."

"Yes?"

"Thank you," she said softly.

"Don't mention it," he said as he left. He had to make some phone calls. He had to let Arthur know the bad news and to let Jack know what, the more Ross thought about it, might just be the best news of the season.

Chapter 19

Leslie didn't reach James until the day after he called. The first night she called too late. She left a message on the answering machine. The next evening he was still in his office when she called. He answered the phone.

"Hello."

"James?"

"Leslie."

"I was afraid I'd get your answering machine again."

"I'm expecting some calls. I haven't switched it over."

"What's O'Keefe, Tucker and Stevenson?"

"Architectural firm."

"You're an architect?"

"Uh-huh. And you're a doctor. And a television . . . uh . . . star."

"Oh, that's—"

"How I knew where you were."

"Oh," Leslie said and then fell silent. The memories of James flooded back at the sound of his voice. Why was he calling her after all these years?

"How is he?" James asked.

"Who?"

"The other resident. The one who was shot."

"Fine. He's fine," she said. After a moment of silence she asked. "How are you?"

"I'm fine. You?"

"Fine."

"Leslie, I'd like to see you. Explain to you about the letter—"

"The letter?"

"The one you wrote to me a million years ago. I didn't read it right away. I didn't even realize that you had sent it until ten months later. It's a little late to thank you for it but—"

"You're welcome."

"Can you have lunch with me? Or dinner? Or . . . ?"

"Lunch is hard. I can't get away. Dinner would be nice," Leslie said. Nice? A *nice* dinner with James? Dinner with *nice* James? Leslie's mind whirled.

"When?"

"It would be safest to plan for September, after I leave San Francisco General Hospital and go to University Hospital. Anything can happen here. Sometimes I don't get away until late. It's a little more predictable at University."

"Do you have your schedule?"

"Yes," Leslie said, looking at the pocket calendar provided by a pharmaceutical company. She had circled the on call days in red.

"Better make it after Labor Day," James said.

Leslie got the impression James was consulting his own calendar.

"OK. Let's see. I'm on call on the tenth so that's out. On the eleventh I'll be recovering from the tenth. How about the twelfth?" Leslie asked idly, trying to think why she had written the number twenty-seven on the twelfth.

"That's your birthday," he said quietly, wondering what he was doing. Leslie didn't have plans for her birthday. She must be uninvolved. But he wasn't.

"You're right," she said laughing. That's what the twenty-seven meant.

"So, are you free?"

"Yes," she said. There was something in his voice that made her ask, "Are you?"

"That night, yes," he said, hesitant. "My wife is working that night. She's a flight attendant."

"Cheryl?" Leslie asked quickly.

"Who? *No*," he said remembering. "No. No one you know. You aren't married?"

"No."

"So, I'll pick you up at seven," James said quickly before he changed his mind.

Leslie gave him her address and telephone number.

"You know the shot of you with your hair damp wearing that blue, V-necked scrub dress . . . ?"

"I never saw the pictures."

"Well, you looked exactly the way you looked at the lake that day. After you'd gone swimming in the ice-cold water. Remember?"

"I remember," Leslie said. How could I ever forget that day? Or that night?

"I don't think either of us should go," Kathleen said, gently touching his pale white temples with her barely tan fingers.

Usually by this time in August, her skin was golden brown, but not this year. She had spent every daylight minute of the past three weeks at the hospital with Mark, and now, finally, he was home. His hematocrit was twenty-seven, just over half of its normal value, and he was pale and weak; but he was home. She could take care of him all day and all night.

He caught her hand with his and pulled it to his lips.

"You're the maid of honor," he said as he kissed her hand and smiled at her. "And I want to go."

Mark didn't care about going to Betsey's and Jeff's wedding. In fact, he worried about his ability to do it. He was so *weak*. Just walking around his tiny apartment—it was so much bigger than his hospital room—left him breathless and damp and wobbly.

He didn't care about the wedding, but he wanted to be with Kathleen.

"You—we both—can change our minds anytime," she said firmly. Betsey could get married perfectly well without her. She wouldn't leave Mark home alone.

"Anytime in the next few hours?" he teased.

"It *is* only four hours from now, isn't it?" Kathleen gasped, glancing at her watch. "I wonder how Betsey is doing . . ."

"She's probably worried that you won't be there. So, call her and tell her that we're coming."

"You're sure?"

"I'm positive," Mark said confidently. It would be good for him to get out. He could—*would*—make it. Besides, weddings were happy, joyous occasions . . .

"Dearly beloved . . ."

The congregation remained seated during the vows. Mark was relieved. He wouldn't have to worry so much about his weakness. He could concentrate on the ceremony and watch Kathleen and listen to the vows.

"Do you, Jeff, take Betsey . . ."

Do you, Mark, take Janet . . .

Janet. Emotion swept through him as he remembered her gray eyes, brimming with love and joy and happiness, on their wedding day. She—*they*—had been so sure, so confident, as they had made those promises of forever.

"For better or worse . . ."

Or worse. He and Janet hadn't made it through that, and it was his fault. He hadn't let her help him. He hadn't shared the worst with her, even though he had made the pledge. He hadn't *known*. She had known. She had seen his torment. She had tried to tell him, to help him, to love him. But he hadn't believed her.

He had broken the pledge. And now—somehow, miraculously—it was *he* who had been given the second chance.

Kathleen. She stood a few feet away from Betsey and Jeff, smiling thoughtfully as she watched her dear friends exchange the vows. Mark gazed at her lovely profile, his mind spinning. Could he avoid the mistakes he had made with Janet? Could he, *would* he, share everything with her? Could they live and love through the best and the worst?

As Mark stared at her, lost in thought, wondering, hoping, remembering, Kathleen turned her head to find him. Her glistening violet eyes—emotional, full of love—met his. Her lips curled into a soft smile for him.

As if giving him an answer.

Yes. We can do it. For better or worse.

"And forsaking all others as long as you both shall live . . ."

I do.

I do.

Janet called Leslie three days before her birthday.

"Do you have plans for your birthday, Leslie?"

"I'm having dinner with a, uh, friend from high school."

"Oh."

"How's *Peter Pan*?" Leslie asked, quickly changing the subject. She did not want to dwell on her date with James. More than once in the past few weeks, she had picked up the phone to cancel it, but she hadn't been able to dial.

"Fantastic. The man who plays Peter, whose name *is* Peter by the way, is terrific. The new Wendy is going to be a wonderful part for me. We're still in the brainstorming phase. Ross keeps coming up with something even better, more innovative. He is so talented."

"You like him," Leslie observed. Since her return from New York and Lincoln, Janet spoke of Ross often. Her voice softened a little when she did.

"I respect him, Leslie. He's very talented. He was so generous about my decision not to go to New York," she said thoughtfully. "I made such a fool of myself—in front of him—when we were there."

"Without missing a beat he hired you to play Wendy," Leslie observed.

"I'm good box office, Les. In addition to being a creative talent, Ross is also a very shrewed businessman. Our relationship is strictly business," Janet said emphatically. Because it was true.

"As you like it!" Leslie teased.

"Cute. Listen, do you want to do a late birthday celebration next week? Dinner somewhere?

"Sure. Let's."

James arrived promptly at seven.

"Hi," Leslie whispered, barely able to breathe.

James looked different. Older. *More* handsome. His green eyes seemed wiser, and his dark black hair was laced with a few strands of white. Older. Wiser. Even better than her memories.

"Leslie. You haven't changed," he said. Beautiful, sensual, naive Leslie.

Leslie smiled a soft confident smile.

But she *has* changed, James thought. Inside. She has become a woman with womanly desires and knowledge and confidence.

Leslie was older and wiser, too.

"You look good, James," Leslie said. Very, very good.

"So do you."

James took her to a popular Italian restaurant in North Beach with notoriously excellent food and slow service. They both ordered iced tea instead of cocktails.

"Happy Birthday," James said as he raised his glass of iced tea.

"This is a nice way to spend it. It's nice to see you," Leslie said. *Nice. Except that you are married.* She needed to hear about it. She needed to put an end to the fantasies once and for all. "Tell me everything. From that mortifying night—for me anyway—at the Seattle Center to O'Keefe, Tucker and Stevenson, architects."

"How about you telling me? From frolicking teenager to doctor and heroine. You go first."

"OK. It's quick and easy. I did just what everyone expected me to do: four years at Radcliffe; then back to Seattle to the University of Washington School of Medicine for four years; then to San Francisco as an intern and now a resident." Leslie paused. Then she smiled and said, "Your turn."

"Never married?"

"Very close once. But fortunately we realized the impending mistake in time. We were in medical school together. Classmates. We thought we loved each other until it came time to apply for our residencies. He wanted to do surgery at Harvard, and I wanted to come here. Neither of us cared enough to compromise. Scary, huh?"

"An old theme," James said. She had chosen what she wanted to do over someone to be with once before. "*Then* you said it was because you were too young."

"And you said that if it was the right person I would make the commitment no matter how young I was."

"I said that?"

"Something wise like that. And . . ." Leslie paused. Why not tell him? "When you said it, I knew that I could have made the commitment for you. I could have given up Radcliffe." *For you.*

James looked at his iced tea and frowned. Then he looked at her.

"Really?"

Leslie nodded.

"It wouldn't have worked," he said flatly.

Leslie smiled and shrugged her shoulders. "I'm just telling you how I felt. *Then.*"

600 James reached in his pocket for a cigarette and lit it. Leslie watched the smoke swirl in his eyes as the cigarette hung casually from his lips.

Sometimes when she was particularly tired or annoyed, Leslie would actually level her glacial blue eyes at a smoker and send a clear message of righteous indignation and censure.

Now she looked at James and thought, He is so handsome, so sexy when he smokes.

She shook her head, smiling. James noticed.

"What?"

"Oh, just a little internal paradox I'm trying to resolve."

"About my smoking?"

"Yup."

"I won't," he said, starting to stamp out his cigarette.

"No. That's OK. Here's the paradox. I spend a lot of my life taking care of people who have irreversibly damaged—not to mention *killed*—themselves with cigarettes. Occasionally I even rant and rave about it. I've seen autopsies, specimens of blackened lungs and lung cancer—"

"I'm putting out my cigarette," James said pleasantly as he pressed it into the ashtray.

"But here's the rub. You look so good when you smoke. Most people don't, but you do. You always have. I like to watch you smoke."

"You want me to light up?"

"No," she said softly, seriously. "Because it's *my* indulgence and *your* lungs. And your life. The non-selfish part of me, the part that cares about you and not the thrill of watching you smoke, wishes you'd never smoke another cigarette."

James looked at her for a long moment. Finally the intensity of his gaze was too great. Leslie looked away.

"So, tell me about you. Starting with Cheryl."

"Cheryl," James mused. "Cheryl was the wife of my older brother's best friend. They were both in 'Nam, and Cheryl was lonely. It wasn't a meaningful relationship, Leslie."

"But a lively one?"

"It kept me busy that summer. Her husband and my brother returned from 'Nam in September. Physically whole but emotionally scathed," James said bitterly. "Anyway, Cheryl went back to him. Which is what we had planned."

"It looked like you liked her," Leslie said, remembering that balmy August night.

"Of course I liked her, but it didn't mean anything to either of us. It was just a hedge against loneliness."

Leslie shook her head.

"Leslie, what I had with Cheryl was no different than what you had with Alan. You knew it wasn't true love, but it felt good."

"But neither of us was married," Leslie said. Then she added thoughtfully, "And we never slept together."

"I didn't know that. I just assumed," James said, frowning, remembering. He had wanted to make love to Leslie that night at the lake. And a hundred other times. He had no idea it would have been her first time. No wonder she left.

"I was very naive in high school, James. You knew that. I grew up at Radcliffe."

James nodded. He wondered what other assumptions he had made that were wrong.

"So, I wrote you that silly letter," Leslie said. 601

"Not silly. A letter that saved my life."

"What?"

"It must have arrived at the logging camp with some letters from Cheryl. We only got mail twice a week, and Cheryl wrote every day. So it must have arrived with the other letters, and I didn't notice it. I usually only glanced at Cheryl's letters; they were all pretty similar. But I kept them all, including the unopened one from you.

"That fall I started school at the University of Washington as planned. The draft issue was still unresolved, and I had decided to give college a shot anyway. My enthusiasm for college lasted about two weeks," James said. He sighed and added heavily, "It was replaced by enthusiasm for drugs."

"Drugs?"

"Anything. Any form of escape," James said harshly, the memories bitter. "I'd been drinking alcohol for years of course. And a little dope . . . marijuana. But suddenly I had access to acid and amphetamines and mescaline. You name it."

"Why?" Leslie asked.

"Curiosity at first. Drugs were so available. They must have been available in Boston. You must have at least tried marijuana?"

"No," Leslie said remembering her own scorn for the students who used drugs, who *needed* to use drugs. Leslie's curiosity was satisfied by other things: the interesting people she met, her pre-med classes, campus activities, lectures. Her only experimentation had been sexual, and that hadn't come until her junior year and then only with someone she thought she loved.

"No? Well, I found they provided a perfect escape; I could make it through the day with pills. I saw lights and colors that weren't there, and I didn't see the things that were there, the real things, the things I would rather forget. I felt good about myself for once."

"Escape? Forget? Feel good about yourself? I don't understand."

"In high school," James explained slowly, "you always thought I was in control, knew what I wanted, was able to make choices. Right?"

"Right. You seemed so calm. Yes, controlled. And you were the only person in history who could choose to be with our group one day and your own gang the next. You bridged the gap effortlessly. Nothing seemed to bother you," Leslie said.

"It was all an illusion. I was a frightened little boy struggling to find a place where I could fit. I had no confidence that I could ever find such a place. Or that I would be accepted."

"But you were so talented, so capable!"

"I had no self-esteem. I didn't believe in myself. I only believed that ultimately I would fail."

"Why would you believe that?" Leslie asked, amazed.

"Because that was what I had been told," James said somberly. "Over and over by my alcoholic father."

"Oh!" Leslie gasped. Then she said softly, "The child of an alcoholic parent."

"Parents," James interjected. "Did they teach you about them—*us*—in medical school?"

Leslie nodded slowly, remembering.

"The alcoholic parent has no self-esteem and transfers his own self-hate to his children. The children are often over-achievers because they try to get parental love and approval; but the parent isn't capable of giving them that reassurance,

so the child, externally successful, always feels like a failure. Doomed to fail no matter what," Leslie said, summarizing what she had learned about the recently recognized syndrome.

"That's right. Of course, as a child I didn't understand that it was his problem, not mine. I only knew that I kept letting him down. So, then, it became my problem. I kept letting myself down. People with self-esteem don't have affairs with the wife of their brother's best friend, and they don't take drugs all day every day. People with self-esteem don't try to destroy themselves."

"Children of alcoholic parents become alcoholics," Leslie said. She saw the pain in James's eyes. She knew that, somehow, he had survived, but she wondered about the torment he had endured and the damage that might have been done.

"I was well on the way. I drank to escape. Then I turned to drugs. I was, *literally*, continually stoned for the first three quarters of college. For a solid nine months I had some drug, often more than one, in my system at all times."

"How did you afford them?"

James smiled weakly.

"Leslie, even though you were there on college campus in the early seventies, you seem to have missed the flavor. It was the era of free love, free drugs, brotherhood, escape. Turn on. Tune in. Drop out. Remember?"

"Vaguely," Leslie said, a little embarrassed.

"Anyway, the expensive drugs, like cocaine, weren't popular then. Most of the acid—LSD—was made after hours in the organic chemistry labs on campus. I got drugs from my friends. I had a series of girlfriends. I slept in fifty different beds, living a day or a week in one place, then moving on. For nine months my life was a hazy dream, a fog that never cleared. It wasn't all that unpleasant."

"It *wasn't?*"

"No, Leslie. In many ways it was very pleasant. I couldn't fail because I wasn't trying to succeed. I forgot about the ugly fights with my father. I was protected by a warm mist of drugs and sex and music. A lot of the time I felt good."

Leslie knew it was the alcoholic—the potential alcoholic—in him that was talking. A part of him environmentally, or genetically, yearned for escape from the painful reality of life. James had been badly bruised as a child. Sometimes the pain was still too great.

"Did you go to class?" Leslie asked. She did not want to hear more about the decadent drug life James had lived. And *enjoyed*.

"No." He smiled. "But I took the exams. I studied just enough to pass the courses. Just enough to stay in college and out of the draft."

"You could study while taking the drugs?"

"Sure," he said.

Just like the successful alcoholics, Leslie thought. The doctors and lawyers and other professionals who were alcoholic but still performed. *Excelled*.

"What happened?" Leslie whispered. She knew something had happened. She knew from the iced tea that James ordered without hesitation that he didn't drink. She knew from looking at him—at the clear green eyes that smiled at her—that somehow he had escaped the lifelong ravages. Somehow James had found a place where he fit.

"One night toward the end of the first year of college, I went to my parents" home. I still had a room in the house. I even stayed there sometimes during the year. That night my father threw one of his rages, berating me, calling me a worthless drug addict." James paused then smiled wryly. "It was true. For once my father was right. I had taken the second hit of LSD an hour before going home. I needed the extra fortification."

Leslie cringed at his words. *Oh, James, how difficult this must have been.* It was difficult to even hear about, to watch him as he told her. I was so sheltered, Leslie thought. Maybe I still am.

"Anyway, he told me to clear out of his house for good. He gave me until morning to take my belongings or he would throw them away. He was drunk and I was stoned. It was very ugly. I locked myself in my room and began going through my worldly possessions such as they were. I found the shoebox with the letters from Cheryl and tossed it angrily across the room."

James stopped. His eyes softened and he smiled affectionately at her. He was remembering naive, innocent eighteen-year-old Leslie.

"You don't know this, but when you're stoned colors can appear more vivid. Cheryl's stationery was cream colored. Your letter was written on pale yellow paper. When the envelopes scattered, yours caught my eye. It didn't look pale yellow. It looked bright yellow, and it *glowed*."

"James," Leslie said.

"Drugs and mysticism, Leslie, go hand in hand. The experience was mystical. *Something* caused me to notice that letter."

Leslie shook her head.

"Well, I read it, and I spent all night thinking about you and about the faith you had in me. You were the only one. You did, didn't you?" James asked gently. The painful memories were replaced by happy ones. By memories of Leslie.

"I thought you were wonderful," she said quietly. "I didn't know anything about you. I didn't need to. It wouldn't have mattered anyway. I knew how you made me feel."

"The only time I felt peaceful was with you."

"So why—" Leslie began.

"Weren't we together? I told you that once. That I had to find out about myself first. About who and what I could be. My father really had a stranglehold on my sanity. I was pretty convinced that I could never do or be anything. Except when I was with you."

"You were restless then. I sensed it but I didn't know why. Now you don't seem restless."

"I was lucky. My luck changed with your letter. That night, as stoned as I was, I made a resolve to become the James that you believed in. To stop the self-destruction. At least to try. The next morning I took all my clothes and your letter and left my parents" home, my home, for good. I spent the summer at the logging camp, detoxifying myself, strengthening my resolve and planning to see you. Those were the hardest three months of my life. The drugs didn't want to let go. Most of me didn't want to face the harsh realities of life."

"But you made it."

"I did. I returned to Seattle one day after you had flown back to Boston for your sophomore year. I telephoned your house. I don't think your father recognized my voice. I didn't leave a message."

"Why didn't you write?"

"It was still too soon. I had just made it through the summer. The real test was about to begin: returning to college, making choices and decisions. By Christmas break, I was ready to see you, but I heard from Robin that you were bringing a boyfriend from Harvard home for the holidays."

Leslie shook her head and grimaced. "It would take me a few minutes even to remember his name."

Oh, James, how different it could have been for us!

"Anyway, I decided that you had your life. And thanks to you, I was beginning to have mine. I wanted to let you know. I always hoped that someday I would have the chance."

This is the someday. On my twenty-seventh birthday, Leslie thought. Happy Birthday, Leslie.

"You became an architect."

"I got my degree in Seattle. Then I worked in New York City for a while. I joined the firm here eighteen months ago."

"And already have your name on the letterhead."

"I've done well. The luck has continued."

It's not luck, James. It's *you*, Leslie thought. Talent and hard work and the decision to make it. Not *luck*. Leslie realized that he still had doubts about his own worth. There were still vestiges—deep scars—of the damage done by his father.

"And you like it?"

"I love it," James said enthusiastically.

"Do you do houses?"

"For the past six months I've been working with an international land development company. The company has both residential and commercial holdings so, yes, I do houses. And buildings. And shopping malls. And resorts. You name it."

"Sounds exciting and creative."

"It's both. I couldn't ask for a better job."

Leslie looked at her plate of barely touched veal parmigiana. As they talked, the waiters had—at carefully spaced leisurely intervals—served and cleared antipasto and bread, then salad, then pasta, then the entree. Leslie paid little attention to the food. She nibbled idly and focused on James. Leslie looked at James's plate of barely touched food and smiled.

"This is supposed to be one of San Francisco's best restaurants. We're not really giving it our undivided attention," she said.

"Do you want to?"

"No," she said. Then, pushing her food around her plate, she forced herself to say what she had been dreading. "Tell me about your wife."

"Lynne," James said quickly. "We met two years ago. I was flying from New York to San Francisco to interview for the job with O'Keefe and Tucker. She was—is—a flight attendant. She noticed that I was drawing a picture and came over to look at it. It was like the picture I drew for you of the meadow. Drawing is relaxing for me. Anyway, Lynne asked me if I would draw her a picture of a calico cat named Monica. I thought she was kidding; but she carefully described Monica's personality to me, and I spent the rest of the flight drawing the picture. I handed it to her as I was leaving the plane. She ran after me and asked if I would consider doing the illustrations for her book." James paused as he remembered how excited Lynne had been about the drawing.

"Was there really a book?" Leslie asked after a few moments.

"Oh, yes. Lynne writes children's books in her spare time. She had just completed the first book, *Where's Monica?* She was looking for an illustrator. *Not* a husband."

"And she got both."

"Uh-huh. We've done two books since *Where's Monica?* They also feature Monica the cat and are actually pretty successful."

"How long have you been married?"

"We got married the day I moved here. Eighteen months ago."

"Tell me about Lynne."

"Lynne. Well," James's voice softened as he thought about how to describe the woman who was so much a part of his life and of the happiness he had found. "Lynne has been through a lot. She's strong and independent. She's three years older than I am. She's still a flight attendant because she enjoys it although eventually she may quit to write full time. She's . . . I'm not really describing her, am I?"

"It's hard," Leslie said. The words don't matter, Leslie thought. I can tell from the tone of your voice how much you love her.

"It is."

"Do you have children?"

"No," James said slowly. "And we won't. Lynne can't."

"Oh."

"It's OK. She can't and I shouldn't anyway. Neither of us should. We both had dismal childhoods, hated our fathers and barely survived the early seventies. Lynne was at Berkeley at the height of the "flower child" era. She did her share of drugs and sex. The doctors have said that because of damage to her tubes from infections it would be almost impossible for her to get pregnant. Besides, while I was poaching my brains with drugs, I was probably damaging my chromosomes, too," James added seriously.

"I think there are enough normal offspring from hippies and flower children that the chromosome damage theory is out. So you aren't even going to try?" Leslie asked. A man as sensitive as James and a woman who writes children's books would make wonderful parents, she thought.

"Lynne has never used birth control, and she's never gotten pregnant. I think the doctors are right. Anyway, we're quite happy with Monica and all my buildings as our surrogate children."

"I can tell that you are happy, James. I'm glad," Leslie said honestly. But part of her wished that things had worked out differently. That *she* had had a chance to make him happy.

"A lot of it is because of you, Leslie," James said seriously.

"No."

"Yes. Believe me. I know what a difference it made to me that you were my friend."

"My pleasure." Leslie smiled, blushing. *It made a difference to me, too. I haven't been able to find anyone to replace you.*

James walked her to the door of her apartment. It was almost midnight.

"Thank you, James," Leslie said.

"It was wonderful to see you again."

"It was wonderful to see you," she whispered and retreated quickly inside the door. "Good-bye, James."

As she heard his car drive away, Leslie began to cry.

Why was she crying? Because James had struggled against all odds and made it? Because James was happy? She was glad he was happy, but he could have been happy with her. It could have happened. It *should* have happened.

I expected it to happen, Leslie finally admitted to herself.

During all those years she had fantasized about seeing James again. It didn't consume her. She went for long periods of time without thinking about him at all. Then she would look at the picture he had drawn—the picture that had hung in her dormitory at Radcliffe and in her room in Seattle and in her apartment in San Francisco—and start to think about him again.

She had known that someday she would see him again. And now she had.

Leslie thought about the facts of their reunion. If someone had submitted it as a script for a Hollywood movie, it would have been rejected outright.

Forget it, Joe. The audience would never buy it. He sees her on television, blood dripping down her face because she's just saved some guy whom she also loves, who doesn't know it, by putting her finger inside his chest on his artery? He sees her and remembers the letter that changed his life, that got misplaced until he discovers it one night between acid-induced hallucinations? Then he tells her how he overcame incipient alcoholism and drug abuse to become a successful architect? And illustrator of children's books? No way, Joe. The public has to have a little reality sprinkled in. This is pure fantasy.

Besides, Leslie mused. It doesn't have a happy ending. The heros, Leslie and James, don't end up together. They don't fall breathlessly into each other's arms.

Leslie sighed. How often had she wondered where he was and what he was doing? Now she knew. He was very near. With Lynne. Happy. And the fantasy was over.

As he drove away from her apartment, James reached into his pocket for a cigarette. He pulled it out of the package with his lips and reached for a match.

Then he paused. His hand rested for a long moment on the matchbook in his pocket. Finally he took the unlit cigarette from his mouth and returned it to the package. Then he crushed the entire package in his hand and threw it across the front seat of his car.

Chapter 20

"How about dinner tomorrow night?" Ross asked Janet toward the end of September. They had just finished a long day of script rewrites for *Peter Pan*. "I'm leaving for New York the day after tomorrow."

"Oh? Sure," Janet answered absently. She assumed that Ross wanted to discuss some aspect of *Peter Pan* or *Joanna* with her before he left.

"What time would be good?"

"Why don't we just go somewhere nearby after we're done here tomorrow," she suggested.

Ross nodded. Janet didn't notice the look of surprise on his face.

At six-thirty the next evening, they walked two blocks to a French restaurant on Stuart Street.

"What did you want to discuss?" Janet asked after they had ordered dinner and been served drinks.

"Nothing."

"Nothing?"

"No, I just wanted to have dinner with you."

"This isn't business?" Janet asked weakly.

"No. It's a date."

"I thought you wanted to talk about the shows. If I'd known it was a date, I would have—" Janet stopped abruptly.

Gotten dressed up, Ross mused. Taken the day off to get ready?

"Would have what?" he asked, curious.

"I would have said no," she said flatly.

Ross's eyes narrowed. "What?"

"I'm not dating," she said carefully. His eyes were angry.

Ross took a swallow of his scotch.

"I hope you're not waiting for your ex-husband to come back to you, Janet," he said acidly. "Because I happen to know that he is very much in love with someone else."

Janet looked at him, her gray eyes foggy.

"I know that," she said quietly.

They finished their drinks in silence and forced themselves to exchange pleasantries with the ebullient waiter who served the elegantly prepared salad of butter lettuce and shrimp and finely sliced egg whites.

"I had no right to say that to you," Ross said flatly. "I'm sorry."

Janet shrugged, blinking back tears.

"Why didn't you throw your drink at me? Or just leave? Why did you stay?" he asked.

Ross had invited Janet to dinner because he genuinely wanted to know *her*. To know Janet Wells. Whoever she was. Janet had captivated him as Joanna. Vital, courageous, energetic and beautiful. Now Joanna was gone, replaced by Wendy, and the enchantment was starting anew. Wendy—Janet's Wendy—was a wholesome, naive and charming seductress, and she was seducing Ross.

But who was *Janet?* Were there parts of Joanna and Wendy in Janet? Or was Janet Wells different still? All Ross knew was the shell. All he knew was the quiet professional with the limitless energy and unbounded talent.

"I stayed because we work together. If I had left, angry, we would have had to discuss it later. You're leaving tomorrow. It might have meant weeks of tension."

"So this is pragmatic? In the best interest of the show?"

"Ross, I know that Mark is in love with another woman. Let's be specific—he's in love with Kathleen. My relationship with Mark ended a long time ago, but I learned something from our failed marriage. I learned that letting anger fester, not talking about things when they happen, is terribly destructive."

"So you sat here, through the insult and the silence that followed, waiting for me to apologize."

"No. Waiting to see if we could talk about it. Trying to decide if I should apologize. You asked me out for dinner. I accepted thinking it was business. When I found out differently . . . well, I insulted you, too."

"You are really amazing," Ross said, not understanding her, but wanting to. Liking her. Smiling at her. "Why don't you date?"

"Something else I learned from the marriage that didn't work," Janet said calmly, tilting her head slightly. "I gave up my career for the marriage. Now I am discovering how much all this means to me. I enjoy it. I'm *consumed* by it. It's my whole life right now."

"No time for anyone else?"

"No energy. And no courage. It's much too soon for me. Even a casual dinner date. It disrupts the balance."

"A delicate balance?" he asked gently. She exuded such confidence and strength. And such tranquillity. But Ross remembered the fear in her eyes in New York. He had to believe her. He had seen her fear.

"I guess so. Getting stronger," she said.

"I am so sorry I said that to you about Mark. I was angry."

"It's OK."

It's *not* OK, he thought. It's not me. I can't believe I said that to her.

"How's the production going in New York?" Janet asked.

Ross smiled. They could make it a business dinner. Then they would both be comfortable.

"I can't tell. Arthur sounds funny. That's why I'm going back tomorrow."

"How long will you be gone?"

"Depends on the situation. I hate to be away from here. I'm so excited about the show here, but . . ."

"We'll call you if we make any substantive changes," Janet said.

"Please do."

"Will you be staying at the Plaza?"

"Uh, no. I'll be staying with Stacy. You met her that night . . ."

"The one with her hand on your thigh," Janet murmured.

Ross raised an eyebrow. Janet shrugged.

"Stacy's father is a major backer for the New York production," Ross said, wondering why he was explaining about Stacy. "Stacy's a model."

"A cover girl, isn't she? At least I thought I saw her picture on *Vogue* a few weeks ago."

"You're very observant," Ross said. Starting with the hand on the thigh observation. "Anyway, I gave Jack the number. No surprises all right?"

"No surprises."

On September thirtieth James called the Department of Medicine office and asked the secretary to have Leslie call him.

Leslie was in the radiology department, waiting for an angiogram to be completed on her patient. It would be at least fifteen minutes. She returned James's call from the radiology department office.

"This is Dr. Adams returning Mr. Stevenson's call."

"Yes, Doctor. He is expecting your call."

"Leslie?"

"Hi," She whispered, her heart pounding. She had been thinking about him, *constantly*, for the past two weeks, from the moment he had left her apartment. She knew it was over. The story—their story—had ended. She knew it rationally, but she didn't feel it.

She simply felt restless.

"Can I see you?" he asked quietly.

"Yes," she breathed.

"Tonight? We'll go for a walk?"

"Yes. I'll see you at seven-thirty," she said, silencing the voice in her mind, in her conscience, that thundered No, No, *No*.

Yes. I will see you. I will be with you.

Leslie dressed carefully. *For a walk* James had said. Leslie remembered the last time she had gone for a walk with James. It was that April night at Sparrow Lake, nine and a half years before. Then she had worn blue jeans, a light cotton blouse and a blue V-neck sweater.

She would wear the same outfit tonight. The blouse and sweater were new. The jeans, her favorite pair, now faded and soft and threadbare, were the same. They had gone with her from high school to college to medical school to residency.

Comfortable old friends, she thought as she pulled them over her hips, noticing that they were looser now than they had been in high school. Leslie tucked the pale yellow, cotton blouse into her jeans and pulled the V-neck sweater over her just-washed hair.

What am I doing? she wondered as she looked at herself in the mirror. Trying to turn the clock back nine and a half years?

It was folly to think that they could start where they had left off. James's life had changed too much. James had responsibilities and commitments.

But James had called. James was on his way over to her apartment.

Leslie opened the door and stepped back, allowing him to enter, unable to look in his eyes.

James had dressed, as she had, in commemoration of the night at the lake. He wore jeans, an oxford shirt with sleeves rolled casually to mid-forearm and a khaki Windbreaker.

James pulled the door behind him.

"Hi," he whispered, covering her mouth with his before she was able to answer.

Leslie answered with her mouth and her arms and her body. The years vanished. They were back at the lake, controlled by passion and allowing the passion to control them.

"James," Leslie whispered, pulling away to breathe for a moment. And to whisper his name.

"Leslie."

James kissed her as he had that night at the lake. Gentle kisses on her face, her lips, her neck. He began to undress her, not the way a sexually experienced man undresses a woman, but the way a teenage boy discovers the wonderful forbidden secrets of a teenage girl.

James reached under her sweater and unbuttoned her blouse. He touched the soft fullness of her breasts under her clothes. Leslie slid her hands beneath his shirt and felt the strength of his back, strong and cool. She reached for his belt buckle just as she had years before. A remote corner of her mind expected to hear the voices of her friends calling to her because it was time to leave.

But not tonight. Tonight there were no curfews, no interruptions, no uncertainties.

They made love on the coarse rug, partially clothed, like teenagers desperate to be together but afraid of being caught. A stolen moment of teenage passion. It could have happened in a car or in the living room at her parents' home or on a bed of pine needles in the woods by the lake.

They made love eagerly, like curious teenagers full of wonder and passion. Afterward they lay on the floor exhausted, tangled in each other's clothes, holding each other.

Leslie closed her eyes and pressed against him, against his strong warm body, the body that had wanted her so much. She could lie here forever. With James.

Her mind spun. What had she done? Gone back to high school? No, the responsible adult in her chided. You *pretended* to go back to high school to justify making love with another woman's husband.

But she hadn't made love with James, Lynne's husband. Or with James the talented, successful architect. Leslie had made love with James the teenager, the loner, the deer hunter. He was the sensitive boy whom she loved and wanted. The only James she knew. James the boy.

Leslie felt James's face close to hers and the force of his eyes willing hers to open. When she opened them, who would *she* be? Leslie the doctor? Leslie the woman? Or Leslie the girl who had just been accepted at Radcliffe? She didn't know.

"Leslie," he whispered, his voice husky. A man's voice.

Leslie opened her eyes, afraid to look into his, but unable to resist. James's eyes told her of his passion, a man's passion for her. For Leslie the woman.

"You are so beautiful," he said, as he began to remove her clothes. this time there wasn't the awkward eagerness of a teenage boy. This time there was only the graceful ease of a sexually experienced man.

James removed all of Leslie's clothes and his, slowly, almost effortlessly as he kissed her. When they were both naked, he pulled her to her feet and led her into her bedroom.

They made love again, slowly, purposefully, carefully exploring each other and learning what gave pleasure, learning the rhythm and desire of the other. They had made love, with others, before. They were experienced, knowledgeable . . .

But still not in control. As James kissed her, as he explored her with his sensitive hands, his warm tongue and his soft lips, Leslie's body responded as it never had before, willing her to move, to touch him, to become part of him. As James felt Leslie's velvety skin, her round soft breasts, the rhythm of her body and the demands of her passion, his own control vanished and was replaced by a need to possess her. All of her. The need was urgent and powerful. It was a need to make their bodies one.

Leslie. His Leslie. At last.

Afterward, James held her, pressed against him, until her heart no longer pounded against his chest and her hands released their grip and rested softly on his back stroking him gently.

"What are you thinking?" he asked, finally, gently caressing the damp tendrils of her chestnut hair.

That earlier I made love with James the boy, she thought. *My* James. And now I have made love with James the man. Whose James? Mine? No. *Lynne's*.

Leslie shrugged. She didn't want to talk about it. Or even think about it. How could she make herself not think about it?

"Leslie?" he pushed, concerned, gentle, caring.

"That was wonderful, James," she said honestly. "Both ways were wonderful."

"You are wonderful."

"I wish . . ."

"You wish?"

"I wish we had done this a long time ago—that night at the lake—so we could have known how we felt."

"It would never have worked then," he said, kissing her forehead.

It won't work now, Leslie thought. In high school it was too soon. Now it is too late. Leslie remembered the love in James's voice when he told her about Lynne. She would never forget it.

But James was here, now, with her. He wasn't talking about Lynne; he was talking about her, holding her, loving her. Leslie wouldn't let herself think about Lynne. She wouldn't think about tomorrow. She wouldn't think about all the tomorrows without James. Not until she had to.

Leslie touched his temples with her fingertips, then moved her mouth against his, into his, seducing his body back into hers, needing him again, already, quickly. She needed James to make love to her, and she felt, as he responded to her touch, that his need was as great as hers. His desire was as strong and his passion as insatiable.

"Leslie!" he laughed softly, surprised, elated by her passion and by her willingness to show him.

"Is something wrong?" she asked, suddenly shy.

"No, my darling Leslie. Everything is perfect."

They lay in each other's arms, exhausted, unwilling to pull away.

"It's ten-thirty," James said, noticing the bedside clock.

Leslie stiffened, waiting for him to say, It's late. I'd better go. Good-bye, Leslie.

"We didn't go for our walk," he continued, kissing her ear, reassuring her.

"Disappointed?"

"No. Are you?"

"No. But I've always enjoyed our walks: evergreen-lined meadows, decks of ferry boats, woods by lakes. Very romantic."

James smiled and murmured gently, "Unlike this?"

Leslie smiled, turning to look into his eyes. "*Not* unlike this."

"We'll go for a walk next time."

Next time. Leslie's heart raced at the words. Next time. Nine years from now? Next life? When, she wondered.

"Next time," she repeated quietly.

"Will you see me again?" he asked in a tone heavy with meaning. It said, I have made a decision to see you, to be unfaithful to my wife, but you have to decide, too.

Leslie, the Rosemaiden, the most inspirational, the girl voted Most Likely To Succeed, would have answered with a resounding, indignant, self-righteous *No!* But that Leslie no longer existed. She had disappeared over the years, slowly, gracefully recognizing that life wasn't so simple and the answers weren't so clear, after all. The distinction between right and wrong was sometimes hazy, blurred by love and emotion and passion. Extenuating circumstances.

Leslie the Rosemaiden, the girl, had grown into the woman who lay in bed with James. Leslie had already made her decision. All that was wrong—knowing that James was married, sensing with absolute certainty that he loved Lynne, fearing that this would ultimately be painful for all of them—was offset, in Leslie's mind and heart, by what she knew was right. She loved James. She had always loved him.

Lying in his arms, making love to him and talking quietly to him *felt* right. Doing what felt right, that was what she had always done. She would do it now. For however long. Whatever the consequences.

"Yes, James, I will see you again," she said seriously in a voice that matched his. They both understood the significance of what they were doing.

"When again?" he asked. He held her even closer in silent acknowledgment of what she said. Of what it meant.

"Well, this month I'm on call every third night. I'm on call tomorrow, the first. So the first, the fourth, the seventh—"

"Then," James said slowly, obviously visualizing another schedule, Lynne's schedule, "how about this Saturday, the third? Are you free?"

Free, Leslie mused. Yes, James, I am free. You're the one who is not free.

"In the evening?" she asked, trying to learn the ground rules.

"For any part of the day or night that you can spend with me."

"I have to make rounds in the morning. If the patients are stable, I should be home by noon. If not—"

"I'll be working in my office. Just call whenever."

"OK," Leslie said, sitting up, assuming that James was about to leave. They had made plans to see each other again. That usually signaled the end of a date.

"Do you want me to leave?"

"Oh! I thought—" she stopped, embarrassed.

"If you don't want me to stay, to spend the night—"

"I want you to stay," Leslie said. Then she added lightly, "But as long as I'm up, can I get you anything? A cigarette?"

"I don't smoke anymore."

"Really?" Leslie whispered.

"Really. I quit smoking as soon as I knew that I had to see you again."

"When was that?"

"The minute I left you that night. On your birthday," he said, pulling her back into bed beside him.

He knew it then, but he waited two weeks before calling her. He spent those weeks thinking about it. He had to be certain of his decision, to be sure that it was more right than wrong. He realized, finally, after careful logical thought, that he really had no choice anyway.

He had to be with her.

Janet watched the red-orange autumn sun as it fell slowly over the rolling green hills and into the shimmering blue ocean. Her late afternoon walk had taken her, as it often did, beyond the vineyard, through the eucalyptus grove and up the gently sloping grass hills. From the top of the hills, she had a commanding view of the Pacific.

Her private hills, her private view, her private ocean!

How lucky I am to have found this place, Janet thought as she sat cross-legged on the grass watching the magnificent fiery sunset.

It had been a fluke. Or fate. Almost as if she were meant to find it.

It had been during one of her long drives last winter. Mark was gone, and all that was left of their marriage was the legal paperwork. Janet needed to escape the dreariness of the house that had been hers and Mark's. She bought an inexpensive used car and began to take drives, driving until she found an isolated beach or woods, or a meadow—where she could sing.

Janet's drives took her south to Carmel and Big Sur and north to the wine country, to Napa and Sonoma valleys. One afternoon in late January as she was driving back to San Francisco from the northern border of the wine country, she impulsively decided to return along Highway One, the Pacific Coast Highway, instead of the inland route.

Near Sonoma Coast Beach she saw a small cottage, barely visible from the road. She turned into the gravel drive that led to the cottage, wondering how she would explain herself to its inhabitants, but the cottage was uninhabited. She tiptoed up the red brick stairs to the wooden porch with a white railing. The door was padlocked. Janet peered in the windows.

She saw beautifully finished hardwood floors, a brick fireplace and a fresh yellow and white kitchen with lace curtains. And no furniture.

A beautiful, uninhabited cottage.

The next house Janet saw was a mile south of the cottage. Surrounded by a perfectly manicured lawn with box-wood hedges, the house itself was red brick with a cedar shake roof and white shutters. A car was parked in the circular brick driveway.

Janet drove in, parked, walked briskly to the front door and pressed the doorbell without allowing herself to reconsider.

A pleasant white-haired man, her grandfather's age, opened the door. Janet introduced herself and bravely began to ask questions.

Yes, it was his cottage.

"Would you be interested in renting it to me?" Janet asked, her heart thumping, her mouth dry.

"Renting?" he asked.

"Who is it, dear?" They were joined by his wife.

"This young woman would like to rent the cottage," he explained.

"I would take good care of it," Janet said quickly.

They smiled at her. She looked like a wonderful young woman, but every day they read or heard about horrible things being done by nice-looking people and about strangers taking advantage of the elderly.

"Well," the man began.

Janet sensed their reluctance and its reason.

"Why don't I give you my name, the telephone number where I work and some references? If you decide you would like to rent it, you could check up on me and call me with your decision."

Three days later they called her. Two weeks after that, Janet moved into the cottage that had been inhabited over the years by housekeepers, gardeners, grandchildren, and most recently a divorced but now remarried daughter.

The Browns had lived there for fifty years, raising their family and working the land. In the past ten years, they had begun to lease portions of the huge estate. The soil and gently sloping hills were ideal for growing grapes. Two of the largest vineyards substantially supplemented their yearly production by leasing from the Browns.

The revenue from the leased land was more than adequate. The value of the land itself was immense. The Browns had always lived modestly, and they loved their country home; but someday soon they would decide to live closer to their grown children and their growing grandchildren. The sale of the estate would make them very wealthy.

After Janet moved in, the Browns showed her a map of the property. It extended several miles north and south. And west, to the ocean.

"Of course, dear, you are welcome to go for walks on the property. Nothing is off limits."

Janet sighed, glancing at her watch in the autumn twilight. She had to start back soon, before it was too dark. Janet noticed the date on the face of her watch.

October second. It had been almost a year since she told Mark that they needed to separate. For a while. Forever.

As she walked back to the cottage, Janet's mind measured the sadness and the happiness of the past year. Was the great sadness of losing Mark and of their failed marriage balanced at all by the joy of singing and performing again? By her triumph as Joanna? And now by the challenge of the avant garde production of *Peter Pan?*

Her new life was satisfying and peaceful. The torment of the last year of her marriage was a vague, uneasy memory. She had handled small threats on her new-found peace and privacy—the threat of the move to New York and the date with Ross—honestly and directly. Little by little Janet was finding that she had control over her life. And over her own happiness.

Happiness? The word clawed at her. Was she happy? No. Not compared with the only happiness she had ever known, the happiness of falling in love with Mark, of being in love with Mark. Happiness was a word reserved for distant

memories. A life lived years ago.

But she was content. Peaceful. Alone but not lonely.

She felt so much better than she had felt one year ago, or even six months ago. Every day she got a little stronger.

Janet heard the telephone in her cottage ringing as she walked up the brick steps. She rushed through the unlocked front door into the dark room, instinctively weaving around furniture toward the phone.

"Hello?" she answered breathlessly, simultaneously switching on the lamp.

"Janet, it's Ross."

"Hi. Are you in New York?" It was a good connection. He sounded close.

"Yes. Still here."

"Everything's fine here. I haven't called because there haven't been any problems," Janet explained.

"I know," he said. He didn't add that he spoke with Jack at least once a day. "This isn't a *Peter Pan* call. It's a call about *Joanna*."

"Oh," she said tentatively.

"I need your help, Janet."

"I can't move to New York," she said instantly. So much for artfully handling small threats, she thought.

"Don't worry. I don't want you to. You're Wendy this season. Not Joanna."

"Good."

"So," he said carefully, "you know the it's-a-nice-place-to-visit-but-I-wouldn't-want-to-live-there idea?"

Janet didn't answer. She wished she could trust Ross. She didn't know if she could. He wanted too much from her. He expected her to be stronger than she was.

"Janet, the show's in trouble. I have spent the past few days trying to figure out what's wrong, but I can't put my finger on it."

"It's the same company except me," Janet said acidly. He is trying to get me to do the show no matter what he says.

"I don't want you here as Joanna. I want you here, just for a day or two, as a critic. You have such a good eye, Janet. You can find the weak spots. I would like—I need—your opinion," Ross said with an edge. *Why doesn't she trust me? Why is she so cold?*

"One or two days?" Janet asked, skeptically.

"That's all."

"When?"

"If you could come Sunday evening. The same flight we took in August—"

"OK."

"Great. The tickets will be at the airport. Do you want to stay at the Plaza?"

"That would be fine. Ross, I'm not even sure about the nice place to visit part," Janet said, underscoring the fact that she had no intention of staying very long in New York.

"I get the message," he said coolly.

Chapter 21

Janet dialed Leslie's number as soon as Ross had hung up.

"Hi, Les. How about dinner tomorrow night?"

"Love to but I can't." I have to be with James, Leslie thought, her heart beating swiftly, remembering. Anticipating.

"OK."

Janet didn't pry. It wasn't her style. Privacy was important to her. Her privacy and everyone else's. It didn't mean that she wasn't interested or didn't care.

Even though Janet was her best friend, Leslie couldn't tell her about James, but that was nothing new. Leslie had never been able to tell her friends about James. Her friends in high school hadn't understood about James.

And Leslie wasn't sure that Janet would understand, either. Not if she knew everything.

"I'm going to New York on Sunday."

"Really? Why?"

"Ross wants me to look at the show. Tell him what's wrong."

"Do you think it's a ruse to get you there?"

"I hope not, Les." *I hope Ross wouldn't do that.*

"You don't have to do anything you don't want to."

"I know. Speaking of that," Janet said soberly, "have you seen Mark? Is he back at work?"

"He is back. On consults at the VA. I saw him at Grand Rounds last week. He looks all right," Leslie said. All right, she thought, but not fully recovered. Still a little weak and a little pale.

"Do you know if he's leaving in July? Did he get the fellowship in Boston?"

"He said he wouldn't hear until mid-October. I'm sure he'll get it. And I think he'll go," Leslie said, lost for a moment in her own thoughts. A month ago, even knowing how Mark felt about Kathleen, Leslie would have been saddened at the thought of him leaving. Now, because of James, because her heart and body and mind were consumed by him, the thought of Mark leaving didn't affect her. *That*—the whimsy and the strength of her own emotions—troubled her.

Except there was nothing whimsical about her relationship with James.

"Oh," Janet said thoughtfully.

"Does it matter, Janet?" Leslie asked carefully.

"No. Well, yes. It would be better if Mark left," she said firmly. As long as Mark and Kathleen were together, as long as Kathleen was involved with Union Square Theater and as long as Ross and Kathleen and Mark all saw each other socially, it would be awkward. It meant that Janet might see Mark.

It would be best if Mark—and Kathleen—moved to Boston.

"You're probably right," Leslie said, speaking of them all.

Leslie dialed James's office number as soon as she returned to her apartment at two-thirty Saturday afternoon.

The phone rang ten times. Then twenty.

What if he had changed his mind? What if he had decided, as she had decided a hundred times in the past two days, that it was wrong, that they should stop now? Leslie had made the decision a hundred times and reversed it a hundred and one.

Leslie hung up and re-dialed. Maybe Lynne was home. Maybe a flight had been cancelled. But James would have called her at the hospital. Except he always called the Department of Medicine office, and it was closed on Saturday.

What if he had been in a car accident?

What if—"

"Hello?"

"James?"

"Hi," he said softly, happy to hear her voice.

"The phone rang so many times." She breathed with relief as she pulled her mind away from the horrors of the what ifs and into the gentle promise of his voice.

"I didn't realize that the ring was disconnected. I caught the blinking light out of the corner of my eye. Have you been trying to reach me for a while?" he asked, hoping not to hear that she had been home for hours, that they had wasted precious time.

"No, just for the past few minutes."

"When will you be home?"

"I'm home."

"Oh," he said. More precious moments. He could have been there when she arrived. He added gently, "I need a key."

"You have a key," Leslie said quietly. The night before as she was having the key made for him, she chided herself. Silly. Presumptuous. But James wanted a key. Not so silly after all.

"Thank you. You have a calendar."

"A calendar?"

"Of October only. I didn't know if your schedule for November was the same."

"No, it changes to every fourth night." Leslie's mind spun. James wanted to know when she would be free in November. "In November I'll be at the Veterans" Hospital. Tell me about the calendar."

"It's just all the times that we can—could—be together. Red circles around the days. The odd drawing."

Nice, James.

"Are we going for a walk today?" Leslie asked.

"Sure."

"Where?"

"The beach. The wharf. Golden Gate Park."

"Then what?"

"Dinner. Wherever you want."

"Then what?"

"You know what."

"Good."

"Why are we talking on the phone instead of in person?"

"Because you have to hang up in order to come over," Leslie began then stopped. Silly. She didn't want to let go of him, even for a few minutes, even for the minutes it took for him to come to her. Just hearing his voice, talking to him, was such a luxury.

How could she explain that to him?

"I need a car phone, don't I?" he asked. He understood completely. He didn't want to hang up either.

"Yes," she whispered.

"I'll get one. But right now I just want to see you. Leslie?"

"James?"

"Do you care about the beach?"

"No."

"The wharf or the park?"

"Not at all."

"Dinner?"

"I have food here. If we get hungry."

"Janet!"

Janet stopped, confused. Had she heard her name above the hubbub of the Sunday evening crowd of travelers at LaGuardia Airport?

"Janet," Ross repeated, reaching her side, touching her arm.

"Ross!"

"You sound surprised."

"I didn't know you were going to meet me," Janet said. She wished she had known. She had spent the last two hours of the flight worrying about the logistics of getting her luggage and finding a taxi. Then she worried further about how much to tip and what to do if the driver overcharged her or took her the long way because she looked so gullible.

"What did you think I would do?" Ross asked as mildly as he could. Did she really expect he would have let her find her own way to a hotel?

"I don't know. I was planning to take a cab," Janet said confidently, now that she didn't *have* to.

I should have let you, Ross thought, like millions of businesswomen do every day in this city and others. Janet asked to be left alone. Demanded it. So why had he bothered to meet her? Was he just being polite?

No, Ross decided, remembering the look of fear on her face the last time she was in New York. I met her because behind that cool independent faade is a fragile, vulnerable woman.

Janet's gratitude for his thoughtfulness was so deeply hidden behind those calm gray eyes that Ross was almost tempted to tell her to take the damned taxi cab.

It might be good for her.

They didn't speak during the twenty-five minute limousine ride from LaGuardia to the Plaza. Ross had planned to suggest that they have dinner. He could think of enough business to discuss to legitimize it as a non-date. In fact, he had told Stacy not to join them because they would be discussing business.

But he abandoned the idea. It wasn't essential that they discuss the show before she saw it herself. Maybe it was better if they didn't. He didn't want to influence her. He was counting on her honest, professional opinion.

Ross went inside the Plaza with her and stayed long enough to make certain that her room was ready.

"The limo will be here tomorrow at noon to take you to the theater."

"OK."

"Oh, Janet. I haven't told any of the company that you're coming. I don't want them to know until after you've seen the rehearsal."

Janet nodded. The only way she could see the production that Ross saw, the production that worried him so much, was if they didn't know she was there.

"I won't make any phone calls," she said before he left. It hadn't occurred to her to call members of the company.

It *should* have occurred to me, she thought, later, as she soaked in a bubble bath in her suite. They were my friends, my colleagues. I should have wanted to talk to them.

Why hadn't she wanted to? Because she knew that some of them resented her for not moving to New York to do the show? No. They understood her reasons. Because she didn't really like them? No. She liked them very much. The bond had been close and genuine.

Because it is easier not to get involved, Janet admitted to herself as she wrapped a large, pale pink bath towel around her, knotting it over her breasts.

Easier. Safer. More peaceful to be alone. Caring was too painful. It was too painful to care about anyone else. It was hard enough to care about yourself.

Janet awakened early the next morning. By eight she had dressed, breakfasted on croissants and coffee in her room and read *The New York Times*. As she drank the last cup of coffee from the china coffee pot, she allowed her gaze to drift away from her safe, elegant suite through the bay window framed in pink silk curtains to the outside world. To New York.

New York. The city she had met once, briefly, and hated.

This morning the city didn't look so menacing. A soft wind breathed gently through the brilliant red, orange and yellow leaves of the maples in Central Park. Carriages drawn by horses moved slowly, leisurely, through the park. Joggers, in colorful outfits of green, turquoise, burgundy and crimson, trotted through the cool autumn air.

The realization came to Janet slowly, not fully formed until she finished buttoning her coat: I want to be out there. I am going out there. By myself. For a walk in New York City.

Instead of walking across the street from the lobby of the Plaza to Central Park, Janet turned right, swept by the flow of people walking toward the business and shopping sections of Manhattan. Janet found herself in a sea of vigorous men and women. A sea of tweed jackets, Burberry raincoats, three-piece suits and leather briefcases. A sea of purpose and direction and magnetic energy.

I'm not drowning, Janet realized with a surprising rush of joy. I'm swimming, keeping pace, *enjoying* the activity and vitality of Monday morning Manhattan.

Janet felt like laughing. Or singing. Instead, she just smiled and kept walking, feeling part of it.

After a while, as her confidence grew, she realized that she could set her own pace. She could walk more slowly. She could stand at a corner and watch the crowd swirl past her. She could stand still, and she wouldn't sink. She could window shop at Tiffany and Gucci and Dior and Chanel.

By the time the stores opened, after she had walked for blocks and blocks, feeling the pulse, loving the feel, Janet was eager to do some shopping. Twice she had lingered in front of a designer boutique on Fifth Avenue, intrigued by a mauve, pale gray and cream colored silk dress in the window. The dress was feminine but not frilly. Elegant but soft. Womanly.

Janet had never owned a dress like that. She wore attractive, modestly priced clothes. Until recently, she never had money to spend on clothes, and even if she had, she would have selected conservative, neat, traditional clothing. Nothing with flair. Nothing that made a statement or would have so clearly been selected to draw attention to her stunning gray eyes and her sleek figure.

Janet had seen herself look dazzling, seductive and beautiful as Joanna, but that was make-believe. The clothes were costumes. Joanna was someone else—someone who didn't exist.

The mauve, gray and cream silk dress wasn't a costume, and the saleswoman was not acting when she told Janet how lovely it looked on her and that it was made for her.

Janet knew how it looked, and she knew how it made her feel: wonderful, full of energy and vitality. Like this city.

Janet bought the dress, a soft, cream-colored mohair coat, pale gray leather shoes and a matching purse.

Before returning to her suite to get ready to go to the theater, Janet stopped at the gift shop in the Plaza. She bought a coffee mug, bumper sticker and a key ring. All three were emblazoned with the logo: I love (a deep red heart) New York.

Why am I doing this? she wondered as she carefully applied eyeliner, mascara, eye shadow and pale pink lipstick. A little more than usual. A little stronger statement. A statement to whom? To what?

To New York. To vitality. To style. To feeling good.

Janet brushed her shoulder-length blond hair away from her face, teasing it slightly to add shape. As Joanna, she wore it swept softly off her face held by gold barrettes. Joanna had flair. That hairstyle suited Joanna; maybe, it would suit Janet.

Ross waited in the lobby. He smiled appreciatively at the striking blond woman with the gray shoes, the mohair coat and the dancing gray eyes. He noticed her from a distance, doing a double take because the look demanded it. And because there was something familiar . . .

"Janet," he whispered as she approached him. Joanna.

"Good morning," she said, her voice soft like his.

"You look . . ." Ross paused, searching for a word that wouldn't seem too personal, too private. Something that wouldn't offend her. He rejected wonderful, gorgeous, beautiful and sensational. He settled on a word that fit, an adjective he would never have used to describe her before. He said, "Happy."

"Happy," Janet repeated quietly. *Maybe I am. At least, I feel something. Something that feels good.* "Maybe that's it. I had a nice morning."

"In New York?" Ross teased.

"I'm hooked. At least, it's a nice place to visit."

Ross and Janet slipped into the theater unobserved. The company had already assembled and was just about to begin a full rehearsal. They met Arthur in the executive offices.

"You look fabulous, Janet," Arthur said without hesitation as he helped her with her coat. "What a dress."

"Thank you, Arthur," Janet said comfortably, obviously pleased.

Ross marveled at the effortlessness of Janet's and Arthur's exchange. If he had said the same words, Janet might have bristled, iced over. Arthur barely knew Janet. Maybe that was why he could be so relaxed with her. And she with him. Arthur treated Janet as if she were any other attractive woman.

Maybe she was. Maybe it was Ross who was trying to read between lines that weren't there, to find nonexistent depth beneath the still waters. Maybe Janet's iciness toward him was, simply, that she didn't like him. At least not personally.

Professionally, Ross worked with Janet more harmoniously than he had ever worked with an actress, much less a star. He respected her carefully considered opinions and her limitless talent. He listened to her, and she listened to him. When they disagreed—artistic differences—they talked about it. Janet's serious gray eyes would consider their disagreement thoughtfully, and they would sparkle when it was resolved.

So why couldn't he tell her that she looked fabulous?

Because she wouldn't let him.

"Let's go into the theater. They should be starting soon," Ross said.

"Janet, do you need a note pad? Something to write on?" Arthur asked.

Ross knew how Janet would answer. She never took notes. It was all in her head: every word, every scene, every flaw noted and not forgotten.

Janet smiled and shook her head.

Ross knew her very well, professionally.

620 They sat in the balcony, unnoticed. Watching. Not speaking. Occasionally Arthur would glance at Ross and grimace, or Ross would shift his position slightly, uncomfortable with something he had seen on stage. Janet watched intently, motionlessly, oblivious to Ross and Arthur.

They returned to Arthur's office during intermission.

"So?" Arthur asked as soon as he shut the door, looking to Janet for the answer.

She laughed. "So what?"

"So what's wrong with the show?"

Janet didn't answer but looked inquisitively at Ross.

"You know, don't you? You're just seeing if we come up with the same conclusion." It was so obvious. Ross couldn't miss it.

"I don't know, Janet. I honestly don't. Tell us."

"Let me wait until it's over. To be sure."

"That's fair," Arthur said. "But, Janet, give us a clue. Is it fixable?"

"Very."

"Are you going to want to talk to the company?"

"Do you *want* me to?"

"It depends on what the problem is, doesn't it?" Ross asked, annoyed that she wouldn't tell them, knowing that she was right to wait until the end.

"I think," Janet said slowly, weighing the pros and cons in her mind, "it would be helpful for me to talk to them."

"Today?"

"Sure," Janet said. She glanced at her watch. "Arthur, may I use your phone? I want to reach Peter in San Francisco before he leaves for the theater."

"Help yourself. I'm going backstage to tell them we'll do an hour dinner break at the end of rehearsal followed by uh . . . er . . . lengthy scene-by-scene critique. Sound reasonable? I mean, I don't want to pry."

"It's only your show, right, Arthur?" Janet answered lightly. "Sounds reasonable."

"Why are you calling Peter?" Ross asked mildly. "Or is it personal? Should I leave?"

"No! I just need to let him know that I'm here. I couldn't reach either Peter or Jack before I left. This looks like a very state-of-the-art phone that Arthur has," Janet added as she looked for the telephone receiver.

"It's a speaker phone," Ross said. "No hands required. That box on his desk is a receiver and an amplifier."

"Oh."

They both heard the telephone ringing, a familiar San Francisco city-proper ring. Peter answered.

"Hi," Janet said without identifying herself.

"Wendy, my beloved. How are you? I spent the weekend in Carmel brooding about our love scene in the second act. I think I've come up with a solution. It's pretty racy."

"Great. I'm with Ross now. I'm sure he'll be pleased."

"Ross is back? Wonderful."

"No, Peter. He's not back. I'm in New York."

"Terrific. Maybe we should just open *Peter Pan* in the Big Apple. As long as the company has moved there." The annoyance in Peter's voice broadcast flawlessly from the box on Arthur's desk. Peter was unaware that Ross could hear him.

"Peter," Janet said quickly. "I'll be back tomorrow. Or Wednesday at the latest. I'll call you as soon as I get in. I can't wait to hear about the second act.
I actually had an idea today, too. I think Ross will be back soon . . ."

Janet glanced over at Ross. He was scowling.

"I hope so. OK, love. See you soon," Peter said and hung up.

"We haven't accomplished much in your absence," she explained, shrugging. "We're still at an impasse with that scene in the second act."

Arthur returned before Ross could answer.

"Let's go, kids. Show time."

Ross, Arthur and Janet ate Chinese food in Arthur's office during the dinner break. They didn't discuss Janet's analysis of the problems with *Joanna*. Arthur announced that he was quite content to hear it fresh when she told the company as a whole.

Janet, Ross and Arthur joined the company on stage. Janet's entrance was greeted with gasps, curiosity and anticipation. What was she doing here? Was she joining them in New York after all?

Only Beth, the new Joanna, shuddered.

"Janet! You look great!"

"What are you doing here?"

"What a dress!"

"How long will you be here?"

Janet was surrounded. Her gray eyes dampened for a moment at the reception. They were her friends. Friends she had made no effort to see.

"Janet is here," Arthur said finally, "because, as you all know, the show's not quite right. Ross and I wanted her opinion."

The stage fell quiet. Had Janet just arrived or had she been there all day? Had she seen the rehearsal? What did she think?

Beth closed her eyes and sat down, exhausted, defeated.

"Hi, everyone," Janet began, trying to lessen the tension, knowing what they all didn't know, that her news was good, that the show could be fixed.

Janet walked over to Beth and offered her hand. Beth stood up and shook Janet's hand with her own cold, clammy one. Beth knew that she was shaking hands with the enemy, the woman that the company expected her to be, who she couldn't be, no matter how hard she tried. She felt their resentment. It was all because she wasn't Janet.

"You're terrific," Janet said to Beth. Then Janet turned to the assembled company and repeated what she had said. "Beth is a terrific Joanna."

Janet saw the skepticism, then confusion, on their faces. They trusted Janet. Janet wouldn't whitewash. Janet didn't say things that she didn't believe.

"Beth is a terrific Joanna. She's a *different* Joanna than I was. She gives Joanna a different personality that I did, but it's a perfectly legitimate interpretation. It's a valid, creative way to play Joanna. You never saw me do the show did you, Beth?" Janet asked.

"No," she answered almost apologetically.

"I think that's good. The problem is that everyone else here . . ." Janet said, looking for the first time at Ross. He was smiling, nodding. Maybe he hadn't known, but he knew now. He agreed. He knew that Janet was right. Janet smiled back at him and continued, "Everyone else here *has* seen me play Joanna. The entire company is still performing as if I were playing Joanna. But Beth's Joanna is different. Everybody has to change accordingly. You all have to adapt to Beth, the way you all adapted to me."

"How?" someone breathed. The "why?" that many of them felt was left unasked.

"First you have to decide that what Beth is doing with Joanna is valid. As I watched her do the first scene, so differently than I did, I thought, what is she doing? How dare she? Then I made myself watch, as an audience would watch, to see if her Joanna had life and appeal. And Beth's Joanna does, despite . . ." Janet paused. This company knew her. They knew she could be tough and direct. They expected her to be. She continued sternly, "Despite the lack of support Beth has gotten from the rest of the cast."

No one spoke. Beth wiped tears from her eyes, hoping no one would see her.

You're absolutely right, Janet, Ross thought. But how do you fix this kind of polarity?

"I am not coming back. I may never play Joanna again. If you all do this show right, the way you can, then Beth's Joanna, not mine, will become the gold standard."

"How, Janet?" someone else repeated.

"If everyone's willing, we should start now. First, Beth needs to tell us who her Joanna is. I'm sure you've done this already, but no one was really listening because you all knew Joanna. Right?"

A few reluctant defiant nods. Janet was right of course. Not that they were *trying* to undermine the show . . .

"So Beth tells us about Joanna. Then I'd like to just tell you, scene by scene, where I saw the weaknesses, where you weren't supporting *her* way and how I think you can change. The changes are minor, subtle but necessary, adjustments. If you don't make them, the show will flop. If you do make them, you might as well move here permanently."

Nervous, relieved laughter.

Janet looked at the director. He was new to the company, too. He had no idea, until then, what the real problem was. He had probably said the same words to them, trying in vain to get them to support Beth. Janet had invaded his territory, but he didn't look angry. He looked relieved. For the first time he sensed that they all might try.

As the evening wore on, as they played and replayed the awkward scenes, as they listened to Janet and to Beth and as they talked instead of arguing, they began to realize that it *was* possible. Exciting even. They weren't merely copying the San Francisco production; they were creating a new production with its own character and power. Everything was possible.

They worked until two in the morning. No one noticed the time. No one wanted to leave. Only Stacy—who arrived at seven and sat next to Ross in the front row for four hours—left before they were through.

Ross and Janet rode together in a taxi to the Plaza. Ross paid the driver and walked into the hotel with Janet.

"You're not staying here," Janet said as they rode up the elevator. "I'd forgotten."

"No. I thought I would see you safely to your room. It's late."

"Thank you."

Janet hesitated at the door of her suite. He had been so quiet. He hadn't even told her what he thought.

"Did you think it went all right tonight?" she asked. She held the key in her hand, but had turned, facing him with her back to the door.

"All right? Janet, you're a genius. Everyone managed to save face. Everyone felt so good. We're going to have a solid gold production. Yeah, it went all right," he said. Didn't she know?

"Sometimes you're hard to read. You were so quiet."

"I didn't want to meddle. It was your show," he said. It wasn't entirely true. He was quiet because he was thinking about her. "It always will be your show. I agree Beth has a good, valid Joanna, but I prefer the way you played her."

"I do, too," Janet said, frowning a little.

"What was that frown for?" Ross asked, as if Janet was just like everyone else. Ross didn't usually let frowns pass without comment.

"That was an ego frown," Janet said, shaking her head. "It matters to me, a little, that my Joanna not be forgotten."

"A little?"

"A little. A tiny frown. But it shouldn't matter at all. That sort of thing usually doesn't matter to me." But today, tonight, it mattered. Because of today. Because of feeling alive, vital, beautiful and proud. And happy?

"I'll never forget the way you played Joanna."

Janet looked up at him. Her gray eyes smiled appreciatively.

Ross would have kissed any other woman in the world who looked at him like that. Especially one that he had been wanting to kiss all night.

But, he didn't and the moment passed.

"I'd better go," Janet said as she turned to put the key in the lock.

"Are you leaving today?"

"Yes."

"What time? I'll send a limo."

"I'm not sure when I'll leave. But don't worry about me. I can get myself to the airport," she said confidently.

"OK. I'll see you Friday in San Francisco. Or maybe Thursday. Thank you again for what you did tonight."

"It was good for me," she said softly to his back as he left.

Chapter 22

Kathleen looked at her Cartier watch and frowned.

"It's exactly five minutes later than the last time you looked, right?" Betsey asked.

"Right. But it's aready three-thirty in Boston. They should have called him by now," Kathleen said, stabbing a piece of butter lettuce with a silver salad fork, then, uninterested in eating, laying the fork back down on her plate.

"Mark knows we're at the Club. He'll call. I don't understand why you are so anxious about this!"

"Because it may mean that Mark is moving to Boston in eight months."

"That you *both* are moving to Boston."

"I'm not sure of that, Betsey. I don't know if Mark will want me to go with him."

"Kathleen, he is so much in love with you. It's so obvious. We're all a little jealous," Betsey said, looking at her own two-month-old wedding band.

"Well I'm a little jealous of you. You and Jeff know each other so well. You know how much you love each other. You know that it's right to spend the rest of your lives together."

"Don't you know that about Mark?"

"I know it. I think I know it. It's just that our relationship is so new—"

"So exciting, so wonderfully romantic," Betsey added dreamily.

"But not real. Think about it, Betsey. I met him as his marriage was falling apart. We spent four months apart to give him time to get over it. The separation made us desperate to be together. Then, just as we were starting to see what it could be like, being together every day, Mark was shot—" Kathleen's voice broke. The memory was still too frightening.

"But each of these crises brought you closer together," Betsey said.

"But life isn't a series of crises. It's living every day. It's being able to renew your love from within, not because a crisis reminds you. Even now, this Boston thing is forcing the issue."

"So you're not sure?"

"I'm sure, but I don't think Mark is. And he is so cautious."

"What do you want?" Betsey asked.

"Six months. OK, that's greedy. *One* month," Kathleen said, her violet eyes seeing a happy image. "One month in which our only crisis is that we are getting low on milk."

"I just spent a month like that," Betsey said. "It was a little boring!"

Kathleen laughed, shaking her head slightly. She stopped abruptly as she saw the waiter coming toward their table with a telephone.

"A call for you, Ms. Jenkins," he said, connecting the phone to a plug near the table.

"Mark?"

"Hi."

"You got the fellowship!" Kathleen could tell by his voice, by the way he said the one syllable word.

"Yes," he breathed, excited.

"Congratulations. The guys at Peter Bent Brigam don't know how lucky they are."

"Maybe," Mark began.

"You accepted, didn't you?"

"I told them I'd let them know tomorrow."

"Why?"

"Because I want to discuss it with you."

"Oh," she said quietly. *Oh*.

Mark waited, expecting Kathleen to say something else. She didn't.

"So, lady, how about dinner tonight? At Gerard's?"

It was Kathleen's favorite restaurant because it was so romantic.

"Sure," she said slowly, wondering what it meant, what there was to discuss. "Shall I make reservations?"

"I've made reservations. For eight o'clock. I should be home by six-thirty."

"I'll see you then," Kathleen said softly, thoughtfully as she replaced the telephone receiver in its cradle.

He wanted to discuss *it*—something about his move to Boston—with her. Or maybe he just wanted to tell her what he had decided and why. Maybe he was just going to explain why it was best for him to go by himself.

He had chosen her favorite place, but it was a public place. Was that good or bad? He knew that she would not make a scene in public. He should have known that she wouldn't make a scene in private, either. She would accept what he told her because she knew that he would have thought about it carefully.

His voice was so eager, so excited, so loving and gentle, she reminded herself repeatedly throughout the long afternoon. She reminded herself, but still her stomach churned, and waves of apprehension washed through her.

Mark had reserved *their* table at Gerard's. It was the most romantic, situated in its own secluded corner. Kathleen wondered when Mark had made the reservation. They would not have gotten that table if he had only called today.

Kathleen watched the candlelight sparkling through the golden bubbles of champagne. She couldn't look at him, even though she felt his eyes on her.

"So . . ." he began quietly.

"So," she echoed, still gazing at the shimmering bubbles, her heart fluttering. Please don't tell me it's been a great few months, but . . . or that you want to move to Boston by yourself *at first* . . . Just tell me that you know it's too soon to be certain and why don't we see how we feel in spring . . .

"So, will you marry me, Kathleen?"

"*Marry* you?" she asked weakly, looking up then, needing to find his eyes.

"You seem so surprised."

"I am," she said softly. Her violet eyes were moist with joy. "Are you sure?"

"I'm sure. But you're not," he said, concerned.

"No. I am sure. Yes, Mark, I will marry you," she said, looking into his eyes, searching for doubt or hesitation and finding none. Mark's dark brown eyes were steady, full of love, happy. "Of course I will marry you."

"When?"

"Whenever. Whenever you want," Kathleen said, her mind spinning in a whirl of disbelief and joy. "How about mid-June? Just before we move to Boston."

"Kathleen, we don't have to move to Boston. Your family is here—"

"I want to. I love Boston. It's so charming and traditional, so steeped in history. Besides," Kathleen said, twinkling, "I can't wait to tell everyone that my husband—my *husband*—the cornhusk will be doing his cardiology fellowship at the Bent Peter!"

"Who told you . . . ?"

"Hal, of course. Leslie's cute little preppie intern. One day when you were still in the ICU, Hal regaled me with, as he called them, the academic sobriquets of Boston. Let's see, Massachusetts General Hospital is The General. Beth Israel is The House of God. And Peter Bent Brigham is The Bent Peter. I like the medical community in Boston already."

"You're terrific."

"So are you. You want to go to Boston, don't you?"

Mark nodded. Then he said seriously, "What I want most is to marry you. If we move to Boston that's icing on the cake."

"Oh, Mark. I love you."

"I love you, Kathleen."

They held hands across the table, fingers entwined, gazes locked in a look of love and confidence. After a few moments, Kathleen frowned slightly.

"What's wrong?" Mark asked instantly.

"I need to tell you about my financial situation," she said. He had to know before he married her.

"OK. Why, am I marrying into some debts?"

"No. Not debts, but responsibilities. Liabilities even."

"I'm intrigued. Tell me," Mark said lightly, unconcerned. He knew what Kathleen's father did. He knew that Kathleen was used to doing whatever she wanted, going wherever she wanted, buying anything she liked, but Mark believed that it wasn't essential to Kathleen's happiness to spend money.

They had been so happy in his tiny apartment, the apartment Kathleen had

painted herself. One day Mark would be able to support a more affluent life style for her. Kathleen seemed to know it would be a while and she never pushed. In fact, until now, she had never discussed money with him at all.

As if it didn't matter to her.

Kathleen told Mark then, in their quiet secluded corner, at the table with the pale pink table cloth and white roses, about her money. About her trust funds and her income. About her virtually limitless wealth.

"Your trust funds earn more money than I will ever make. More money in one year than I could make in ten," Mark said quietly.

Kathleen nodded, her violet eyes narrowed, trying to read the thoughts behind his serious brown eyes.

"I really had no idea," he said.

"I know. And we—my family—don't advertise it. That's the liability part. My wealth could make us and our children targets. Which doesn't mean we shouldn't enjoy it. The interest alone is far more than we could spend in a year even if we tried, and of course you would never have to pick up another stethoscope in your life," Kathleen said flippantly, then stopped, startled by the expression on Mark's face. It looked like relief. Like peace. But why? Mark loved medicine. He would never give it up, would he?

The expression passed quickly, leaving Kathleen a little confused.

"I think your family, your family lawyers, will insist on a pre-nuptial agreement," Mark said calmly.

"No! Don't be silly," Kathleen said, knowing they would strongly advise it. But it was her choice. Her money. Her marriage.

"I wouldn't object to signing one. I'm not marrying you for your money. I plan to stay married to you forever anyway," Mark said, smiling as he reached across the table to touch her face. He added soberly, "If anything did happen, I wouldn't want your money. You have my verbal prenuptial agreement."

"I don't want it because nothing is going to happen. I want you to promise that you will use the money. To buy a house if we want one. To take wonderful trips. To set up your office with its own cath lab. We don't need to struggle to make ends meet just because we don't want to touch my money."

"Just because . . . ?"

"Well, we can struggle to make ends meet if we *want* to, if it makes us feel like true newlyweds, but not because of any chauvinism about who should be the breadwinner. OK?"

Mark laughed.

"Kathleen, I really don't feel threatened by your money," he said truthfully. "Only amazed."

"And tempted to spend it?"

"Sure. For *us*. For a house that you love. For a trip we want to take. For things that make you happy."

"You make me happy."

"You make *me* happy."

* * *

"James, it's Eric. I think we've successfully negotiated for the additional property." Eric Lansdale sounded pleased.

"Great."

"Charlie's still hammering out the details, but it all looks very good."

"Charlie?"

"Charlie Winter. She's the corporate attorney. I'm sure you've spoken with her."

"*Ms*. Charlotte D. Winter? Of course. We've spent hours on the phone discussing easements and utility accesses. I've never met her. Somehow Charlie doesn't fit."

"It will when you meet her. Which may be soon. The three of us should go to Maui in the next week assuming this is all wrapped up. Will you be able to get away?"

"Sure."

"Good. Will you be at home this weekend? I may need to reach you if there are any problems. There has been some rumbling about sub-platting and not selling us the whole property. I'd want your input on what plats we must have. You have a copy of the plats, don't you?"

"Yes. Do you have my home number?"

"Yes. Let me check that it is correct."

James half-listened as Eric read the number. He had to give Eric Leslie's number. He had no choice. It was where he would be.

"That's right. But let me give you another number."

Eric wrote the number James gave him on a slip of paper and put it in his briefcase.

Eric smiled. He didn't know James Stevenson well, but he liked him. James was a tremendous discovery for Eric's company, InterLand. He was the most creative architect Eric had ever known. Creative and non-tempermental. And nice. James was a nice man—hard-working, professional, talented—and apparently not married but involved. It was nice that James had someone.

"James," Eric said still thinking about James's personal life. "You are welcome to bring someone with you to Maui. It won't be all business. We'll take the company jet. Plenty of room."

"Oh. Thank you."

"If I don't speak with you this weekened, we'll talk Monday," Eric said with finality. Charlie had just walked into his office.

"Fine. Have a nice weekend, Eric."

Charlie spoke as soon as Eric replaced the receiver.

"Those guys were tough," she breathed flopping with a sigh onto the cream-colored couch in Eric's office.

"Were?"

"I think so. Hope so. They may come back with a face-saving counter offer. They may want to keep a little of the land, but I think we've got them."

"Good attorneys?"

"Good," Charlie said smiling. "But not *great*."

"You're not an attorney, Charlie. You're a shark. *Ms*. Charlotte D. Winter," Eric said, his light blue eyes smiling at her, appraising her.

Charlie did look menacing in her attorney-at-law outfit with her attorney-at-law hairdo. Charlie wore a perfectly tailored, tweed suit with a silk blouse and a sensible, but expensive, Longines wrist watch. Her long, golden hair was pulled tight off her face into a secure chignon. Her soft, seductive brown eyes were hidden beneath a studied look of no nonsense efficiency.

"*Ms?* Who said that? Why are you laughing?"

"James said that. You have him completely terrorized. And Charlie, he's on our side. He's a good guy. And I'm laughing because you really can look ominous."

"Effective."

"Effective and efficient," Eric agreed, extending his hands to her, urging her

to come to him.

"James is so serious. He answers my questions so carefully, so cautiously," Charlie said, shaking her head, refusing to walk toward Eric until he stopped mocking her.

"I think it's nice that someone who works for me takes spending millions and millions of my dollars seriously. I like a little caution," Eric said, slightly sternly. He gave Charlie almost free reign in negotiations like the ones today. Charlie was shrewd, but she wasn't afraid to spend money. The money she spent always returned many times over. Charlie had uncanny instincts. Eric added, "You and James need to meet. Face to face. On the beach."

"I picture a boring, unattractive egghead."

"I think that's the same picture he has of you."

"Are you trying to set us up?"

"No! He's not your type. Not that I have any idea what your type is. Anyway he's involved with someone."

"I thought you were my type," Charlie said softly. It was a statement deep with meaning that spanned almost twenty years and a gamut of emotion and passion and pain. A statement that they both knew wasn't entirely true. Or entirely false.

"Parts of me are your type," Eric said, moving toward her.

Charlie stood up. In two quick motions, she removed the pins from her tightly knotted hair. The silky, blond strands fell down her back and into her face. Her brown eyes softened and beckoned.

"I know," she whispered as his lips met hers. "Those are the parts that I like the best."

"*Ms.* Charlotte D. Winter," Eric murmured as he gently kissed her long lovely neck.

Part Three

Chapter 23

PHILADELPHIA, PENNSYLVANIA
NOVEMBER 1945

"Charlotte D. Winter," Mary repeated firmly to the nurse on that snowy morning in Philadelphia, November 11, 1945. Her daughter was five hours old.

"Named after you, then?"

"Yes."

"What does the "D" stand for, ma'am?"

"Nothing."

The nurse arched an eyebrow but entered the mother's name and the baby's name as Charlotte D. Winter.

"Father's name?" she asked.

"Max D. Winter," Mary said softly, hoping that the nurse wouldn't recognize that name, wouldn't accuse her, accurately, of making up all three names.

The nurse didn't blink. The only thing that mattered was the horrible war that had killed so many people—so many fathers who would never see their infant daughters—was all but over. Nothing else mattered. Something tugged at the back of her mind. Maybe it was just the hope that Max D. Winter would return from Europe, or wherever he was, to see his daughter Charlotte.

Mary knew that her baby's father would never see his tiny daughter. He would never even know of her existence. There was no Max D. Winter. Only John, with no last name, a private in the Army that she had met on Valentine's Day nine months before.

It was on Wednesday, February 14, 1945 that John visited the North Philadelphia Library, Mary's library, one of the few libraries in the city that remained open during the war. It remained open because of Mary, because Mary refused to close the door on her books and because Mary was willing to work for almost no money. Mary's best friends, her only friends, were the characters in the books. She knew them so well. She lived their lives and their loves. Mary wasn't greedy. She wanted to share her friends with others.

So in spite of the war and because of Mary, the library remained open. It was a refuge for Mary and people like her, providing an escape to other worlds and to happier times.

Mary was sitting at her desk when John walked in. He wore an Army uniform with a single chevron on the jacket sleeve. Mary smiled at him, her large brown eyes conveying a message of sympathy and an offer of help. He looked so young, so bewildered and trapped, like they all were, in an inexplicable horror of hatred and murder.

He had come to her library to find an escape, a little peace, if only for a moment.

"May I help you?" Mary asked.

John shrugged. "I don't know. I had a few hours. Sail tomorrow for Europe. I was just walking around, and I saw the library. I used to like to read a lot."

"What do you like to read?"

"Anything," he said. Then he added hesitantly, "Except war stories."

"What's your favorite?"

"I don't know. When I was a kid, I used to read *The Wizard of Oz*. I read it a few times," he said, his voice distant, as if remembering those happy trouble-free days. Or, was he imply thinking about the land over the rainbow?

"Have you read the other Oz books? *The Scarecrow of Oz? Return to Oz?*"

"No ma'am."

Mary found *The Scarecrow of Oz* for him. John settled into a chair in the far corner of the library. He didn't move, except for the eager turning of pages, for four hours. By then it was dark and already an hour past closing time.

"John," Mary said gently, startling him out of the Emerald City and back to Philadelphia, the cold dark library and the war.

"Yes?" he asked, focusing slowly, reluctantly.

"I have to close the library now."

"Oh. OK," he said, handing the precious volume to her.

"John, I can lend it to you if you want," Mary said, as she had said to so many young soldiers over the past four years, knowing she would never see the books again. Most of the books she gave away were from her own collection. They were her closest friends. But Mary was willing to share.

"Really? I will return it. I promise," Jhn said as they all did.

Mary smiled. She didn't make them promise. She didn't want their minds cluttered with guilt. She wanted every part of the book to bring them happiness. She knew that some of the young soldiers would never return. It mattered so little—in contrast to *that*—whether or not they returned her books.

John asked her to have dinner with him. They ate in a small diner near the library. Afterward John walked Mary to her house on Elm Street.

"Would you like some coffee?" Mary asked as they stood on the porch of her house.

"Coffee? Yes, ma'am!"

Mary served coffee and fruitcake.

"What's your favorite book, ma'am . . . er . . . Mary?"

"*Rebecca*," Mary said without hesitation.

"I've never heard of it."

"It was published just before the war in Europe. The author is Daphne du Maurier."

"It's a love story, isn't it?" John asked, the gentleness of his voice surprising them both.

"A love story. And a mystery."

"Do you have a copy here?"

"No. I took my copy to the library. I lent it out and haven't gotten it back yet," Mary said, remembering that she had given it, over a year ago, to a young woman whose husband had just been killed in the South Pacific. Mary had given it to the woman because, to Mary, *Rebecca* was a story of hope. Mary didn't expect to get it back. It didn't matter. Mary knew that book, like all her books, by heart. She didn't need to read the words. She knew the words and the characters and the scenes. "I haven't been able to find another copy. After the war . . ."

"Tell me the story," John said.

Mary told him about Rebecca, and about Max de Winter, and the woman Max married after Rebecca's death, a shy unassuming woman capable of great love and deep passion. A woman without a first name, the second Mrs. de Winter, was a woman like Mary. Mary had given her a name: Charlotte. Charlotte de Winter. Mary had named her after Charlotte Bronte.

As Mary talked, her eyes softened with love, and she became Charlotte de Winter while John became Max, the intense, secretive, powerful husband. Max, the wonderful romantic lover.

That snowy Valentine's night in February, Max made love to his precious bride Charlotte. John—Max—held Mary in his strong young arms until dawn. Then he left. He never knew that she had been a virgin. Or that they had conceived a child. Or that Mary was forty-two years old, exactly twice his age.

John knew only that Mary was a wonderful woman. He would never forget her, and he would return her book to her.

Eight months later, a month before Charlotte was born, Mary received a package at the library. It had been postmarked in London two months before. It contained *The Scarecrow of Oz*, and a beautiful leather-bound copy of *Rebecca* with an inscription that read: To Charlotte, All my love, Max.

Two weeks later, Mary received a letter postmarked a month before in London.

Dear Mary,

I hope that the books arrived. I found the copy of Rebecca in a bookshop in London that had been closed during the war but reopened a month after VE Day. I read it before sending it to you. I think Charlotte is a perfect name for the second Ms. de Winter. You are very like her, and she is a wonderful person.

I have met a girl here—in London—and we will be married next spring. I enjoy England and look forward to making my home here. Maybe someday I'll even find a Manderley.

Love,

John

By the time Charlotte was one month old, Mary realized that she wouldn't have the courage to tell her daughter the truth. Mary didn't even know John's last name. Neither the letter nor the package had a return address. The war was over. Morality was rapidly returning. There were lots of fatherless children, but their parents had been married. Those children could hold their heads high.

Charlotte couldn't. Not if the truth were known.

No one had noticed Mary's pregnancy because no one noticed Mary. She had no friends, at least not flesh and blood ones. She hid her pregnancy under smocks, and convinced the city to hire an assistant librarian who managed the library for the eight weeks of Mary's mysterious absence.

When Mary returned to work, carrying the infant with her, she told the few people who asked that the child was her niece and had been orphaned when Mary's sister and brother-in-law had been killed in an automobile accident two weeks after the child's birth.

By the time Charlotte was old enough to need an explanation about why she had an "Auntie Mary" instead of a mommy and daddy, Mary had modified the story so that it conformed more closely to *Rebecca*.

Her parents, Mary told Charlotte, were killed in a sailing accident when Charlotte was one year old. Shortly after that, true to the fate of Manderley, their beautiful home mysteriously burned down. That was why Mary had no pictures of Charlotte's parents. All she had was the leather-bound copy of the book, *Rebecca*, that Max had given to Charlotte shortly before the birth of their daughter.

It was a book, Mary knew, that Charlotte should never read.

Charlotte accepted the story dispassionately and without a sense of loss. She had never known her parents. Her interest was curiosity not emotion, and Charlotte loved her Auntie Mary very much.

Mary devoted herself to her precious golden-haired daughter. Eagerly, lovingly, Mary introduced the little girl to her friends, the wonderful books that were her world. Charlotte loved the stories because she loved sitting on Mary's lap and watching Mary's huge brown eyes—Charlotte's eyes—twinkle and soften and glisten as she read.

As Charlotte grew older, she had a need for real friends, not imagined ones. She made friends at school. Charlotte preferred spending time with them to rushing home to hear about Jane Eyre or Amy, Meg, Beth and Jo or Scarlett O'Hara. Charlotte grew impatient with Mary's imaginary world and imaginary friends.

But she didn't grow impatient with Mary. She loved her. She worried about her friendless frail aunt, the lonely, aging woman who, as the years passed, seemed to retreat even farther into a world of make-believe.

Three days after Charlotte's sixteenth birthday, Mary knocked on Charlotte's bedroom door.

"Charlotte?"

"Yes, Aunt Mary? Come in."

Mary sat on her daughter's bed wringing her hands.

"Charlotte, darling. I am not well. I'm fifty-nine years old. I'm not going to live forever," Mary said slowly, hesitantly, not telling Charlotte the complete truth: *I am going to die. Soon.*

"Auntie! Fifty-nine is young! Maybe you shouldn't work so hard," Charlotte said, rushing to her side, putting her strong healthy arms around Mary's boney shoulders.

"Nevertheless, you and I must decide what will happen to you if I die before you turn eighteen. While you are still a minor."

"But you won't!"

"You and I have no relatives," Mary continued. "Your parents were both only children. I really have no friends who could take care of you."

I have friends, Charlotte thought. Parents of my school friends could take care of me.

"I couldn't bear the thought of you going to a foster home. So," Mary said firmly, her eyes seeing something far away, a far away make-believe friend, "I have created an aunt for you. I have told my attorneys that she exists, that she is my sister and that she lives with us now. She will take care of you if anything happens to me. She is a kind, lovely woman."

"Auntie—" Charlotte began then stopped. Her aunt was out of touch with reality. Charlotte knew it. She had learned it in little bits over the years. The only reality for Mary was her love for Charlotte. Even now this fantasy aunt was invented to save Charlotte from what could happen to an orphaned, underaged child.

So she has invented someone—a kind, lovely woman—to live with me, Charlotte thought, watching Mary's loving eyes. But there is no lovely woman, no kind aunt. There is no one. If anything did happen to Aunt Mary, I would *really* be all alone; but she doesn't know it, Charlotte thought sadly, and I can't tell her. She wouldn't understand.

"What is her name, Aunt Mary?" Charlotte asked gently.

"She is your Aunt Louise. Louise M. Alcott," Mary announced proudly.

So out of touch, Charlotte thought, tears filling her own eyes.

Two months later, Mary died in her sleep. Charlotte found her in the morning and held her small cold body for a long time before calling the police.

"Yes, Aunt Louise is living with me," Charlotte assured the appropriate authorities a week later. "She is a kind, lovely woman just like Aunt Mary. She'd be happy to meet with you. Of course Aunt Mary's attorneys know her very well."

Everyone accepted the fact of Louise Alcott's existence. Everyone assumed that someone had met her. Certainly someone must have witnessed the signatures granting Louise Alcott power of attorney until Charlotte's eighteenth birthday. Surely someone had witnessed the signing of the guardianship papers, but of course no one had. The legal documents had all been signed by Charlotte, in a script quite distinct from her own unfrilly style, and had been returned to the attorneys by Mary.

Charlotte had signed the papers and discussed the logistics of creating Aunt Louise simply to humor Mary. Over the years, Mary had involved Charlotte, a knowing, willing, loving accomplice, in other delusions. They had all passed without harm. This death delusion was morbid but, Charlotte decided, just as unreal even though Mary pursued it in a greater detail than any of the others. . . .

Mary carefully, patiently told Charlotte about her bank account—a checking account—and showed her how to write checks, repeatedly reminding her that these would need to be written in Louise Alcott's handwriting. Mary also showed her the shoeboxes full of money—Mary didn't really trust banks, but the checking account was convenient for paying bills—hidden beneath blankets in her bedroom closet. The money in the shoeboxes was Mary's life's savings, the accumulation of years of hard work and frugality. Charlotte was amazed that there was so much money—it looked like so much—because Mary had never hesitated to spend money on *her*.

Then Mary died, and it was not just a morbid delusion. Mary was really gone, and Charlotte was really alone, frightened and confused.

Why had she died? Charlotte's mind screamed. Sometimes in the quiet emptiness of the house she would scream aloud, "WHY? Why, Aunt Mary? *Why?*"

"Your aunt was very ill," the doctor had said. Charlotte didn't think to ask, Ill from what?

Despite Charlotte's anguish and grief, she was able to appear calm at the requisite meetings with the attorneys, the authorities and the doctor. She *had* to. She didn't want anyone to find out that she was alone. If they did, they would take her away from the house. It was all that she had left.

Charlotte arranged the funeral. It was a *real* detail that Mary had neglected entirely. Mary's funeral was surprisingly well attended. Charlotte's classmates and their parents came, as did Mary's co-workers from the library. Many other people who Charlotte did not recognize also attended. Mary had no friends. Who were they?

They were people who had visited Mary's library and found solace there. Most of them had visited during the war: grieving widows, lonely soldiers, restless wives and girlfriends. They remembered Mary's generosity and the gentle loving care she had given each of them as she helped them find a book that would be a comfort to them. They remembered Mary, even though many of them hadn't seen her for years, even though none of them was her friend. And they came to her funeral.

For three weeks, Charlotte grieved silently, fighting anger, loneliness, betrayal and loss.

She waited, Charlotte realized with horror on the twenty-first day after Mary's death, for Aunt Louise to come and comfort her.

"There is no Aunt Louise!" Charlotte yelled at the silent walls in the living room of Aunt Mary's house, *her* house. "No Aunt Louise. No Aunt Mary. No one."

The tears came then, at last. Charlotte cried and sobbed, the pain and grief and anger spilling in hot, wet drops down her young face. After several hours, exhausted, her emotions purged, the tears stopped.

I am by myself, she thought. I have my life to live. Aunt Mary has given me so much love. Even in her death, knowing how much I would hate having to live somewhere else, she has allowed me to stay here, in her house, in the house that I love.

The following day Charlotte returned to school, to her friends and real life. She told them politely, sparing details, that she and her Aunt Louise were doing "as well as could be expected."

Three weeks later, Charlotte was contacted by her attorneys. Mary had left a letter for Charlotte, with instructions that it be delivered six weeks after her death.

The letter began, *My darling daughter . . .*

In it, Mary explained about that Valentine's Day in 1945, about John (Max), and about her fear that people wouldn't understand and that Charlotte might be ostracized. The theme of the letter, a letter laced with guilt and doubt, was love. The deep irrefutable love that Mary felt for her daughter.

"Oh, Mother," Charlotte whispered softly, tears streaming down her face as she held Mary's letter in her trembling hands, "I love you."

Chapter 24

James arrived at Leslie's apartment two hours after he spoke with Eric.

"Hi," Leslie said, opening the door before he put his key in the lock. She had been watching for him. "What have you got?"

"Work," James answered, raising the hand that held a large black portfolio.

The other hand held his briefcase and an overnight bag. James was spending the weekened with her. Leslie's on call schedule at the Veterans" Hospital was every fourth night. It meant that once a month she had an entire weekend without night call, although she still made rounds each weekend day.

"Work?" she asked, laughing.

"Yes. I work, too. Even on weekends like you. I thought I'd work while you're making morning rounds. Or all-day rounds," he added, smiling, knowing that rounds could take a while. "How's your service?"

Leslie smiled back. James had picked up the medical jargon instantly. He was interested in what Leslie did. She told him about her patients. The happy outcomes and the sad ones. Sometimes she cried when she told him, and he held her, stroking her soft chestnut hair.

"My service," she answered, telling him about her medical service, her group of patients in the hospital, "is pretty sick. We had four very sick patients admitted last night."

"So I may get a lot of work done?"

"Uh-huh."

"Actually, that's OK. Just before I left, I got a call about the project I'm working on. They've just doubled the amount of acreage, so I have a lot of work to do."

"What is it?"

"A resort. In Maui."

"Really? May I see?"

"Of course," James said, moving to the table in the kitchen. They had never really discussed his work in detail. He had never brought any work with him before. "Until today we thought it would just be the main hotel. Which will look like this."

Leslie stared at the sketch that he handed her. It wasn't just a hotel; it was a work of art that blended elegantly, gracefully, *naturally* into the beautiful tropical setting. Leslie had never seen anything like it.

"James! This is so beautiful. This is yours?"

"It's my design, my project. I have tremendous creative freedom because the president of the company who commissioned it believes in quality above all. He doesn't limit me by the usual constraints of cost."

"It's wonderful," Leslie mused, still gazing at the sketch. "I've never been to Hawaii."

"Neither had I until last summer. I made the initial sketches over there. I have to go back this week now that we have more land."

"You'll still build this hotel, won't you?"

"Sure. In fact, construction is scheduled to begin next month. But now we can make an entire resort community," James said eagerly. It was obvious how much he enjoyed his work. "Now we have room for condominiums. Houses even. I'll make sample sketches of units this weekend, but I can't really do more until I go back and see the additional property."

"When do you go?" Leslie asked casually, even though she knew it might mean they wouldn't see each other as scheduled.

"I'm not sure. Next week sometime. The deal wasn't completely signed, sealed and delivered. In fact, they may need to reach me this weekend. I gave them your number. I hope you don't mind."

"Of course I don't," Leslie said, putting down the sketch and turning toward him, sensing what they both sensed, that something was missing.

As his lips found hers, kissing her hungrily, Leslie realized what had been missing: the kiss, the touching. Their minds had said hello, but their bodies hadn't, until then.

"Hi," he whispered, kissing her neck, wrapping his arms around her, molding her body against his. "I've missed you."

"I've missed you, too," Leslie whispered back. She led him into the bedroom.

Leslie closed her eyes, her head swirling with images, her body trembling with sensations as James touched her. The images were lovely: an alpine meadow, a red-orange sunset, sparking blue water, sailboats with colorful spinnakers, sandy beaches, snow-capped mountains, a muted autumn sun. The images—warm, colorful and sensual—formed a collage of all the wonderful moments with James. It was a collage that would, one day, include this moment: the wonder of James in her bed, making love to her.

As he touched her, as the warmth and rhythm of their bodies moving together became totally consuming, the images melted into a yellow-gold glow.

"James," she breathed from a voice deep in her soul.

"Leslie."

It was three o'clock Saturday afternoon by the time Leslie finished her rounds. As she drove along the Great Highway beside the Pacific Ocean, green-gray under the November clouds, Leslie thought about James. About James and Leslie. And James and Lynne.

The thoughts weren't new. They were with her whenever she had a moment to think, whenever she was away from the hospital *and* away from James. Leslie couldn't think, not rationally or analytically, when she was with him. His presence was too powerful, too demanding, too wonderful to tarnish with the thoughts that plagued her when they were apart.

It had been six weeks. In those six weeks they saw each other whenever it was possible.

It should never have started. That was a given. Once it had started, once they realized they had to, finally, acknowledge the unspoken feelings they had shared in high school, it should have ended quickly.

They should have made love once, like groping teenagers, finishing the scene that had been interrupted at the lake so many years before.

That would have been an appropriate ending. Almost understandable. Almost forgivable.

But they made love again and again. As adults. As a man and a woman full of passion and desire.

They should have ended it after they had replayed every moment they had shared in high school, after they had asked each other what they had been feeling then, all those years before.

"Why did you leave the party that night when Alan kissed me?"

"Why do you think? I couldn't stand it. I wanted you so much."

"Why didn't you tell me?"

"You know why."

"Why didn't you kiss me on the ferry boat?"

"I wanted to. My lips were too numb from the cold."

Oh. *No*. What if he had?

"Why would you just dance one dance with me? Or say something to me in the halls and then leave? Or come stand beside me for a quarter of a football game?"

"Because when you spoke to me, when I touched you, when I even just stood beside you, it reminded me that no matter how bad everything was in my life, you existed. You were real, and you seemed to like me."

"*Seemed* to? It must have been so obvious. I couldn't even be clever and coy. Not with you. But why just one dance? One monosyllabic phrase?"

"Those brief moments made me feel so good, but the feeling was almost too strong, too good. It reminded me of who I really was—how I had no right to be with you. I had no self-esteem, remember. Of course I didn't know why. I only made it through those years because I was driven by an instinct to survive and by feelings that drew me to you."

They should have ended it after they had relieved those high school days, after they had shared all the distant feelings and memories.

But they didn't. They began to share the rest of their lives. By the middle of November, Leslie and James were living entirely in the present, as lovers, as friends, as a man and woman who had met, learned about each other and chosen to be together.

Leslie knew it, but she sensed that James didn't. Somehow James had rationalized his relationship with Leslie so that it didn't jeopardize his marriage. Somehow the relationship with Leslie was still a relationship in the past. *Of* the past. It was not really happening in the present.

James had created his own private time warp. His relationship with Leslie should have happened years ago. It might have except for a misplaced letter. And it was happening now because it was destined—it had always been destined—to happen.

Leslie knew that as soon as James realized the folly of his logic it would be over. Leslie was a girl he had loved in his past, and she was a woman he *could* have lved in the present; but James had already chosen to spend his life with someone else. Lynne was his present and his future.

Leslie and James never discussed Lynne, but Leslie had seen his eyes that night, at her birthday dinner, when he told her about Lynne. James's life was with Lynne. The rest of his life.

There was no point in even thinking about what would have happened if James had not been married. Would this wonderful, passionate relationship they had now continue forever? Or was it stoked by the knowledge that it was fleeting, a nostalgic moment kindled by the unfulfilled desires of youth?

There is no point in thinking about *that*, Leslie thought as she parked in front of her apartment building, pulling into a space in front of James's car. No point in thinking at all, she decided, as she felt her heart quicken in anticipation of seeing him.

James was on the telephone.

"Monday morning?"

"I know it's short notice, but since we've got every square inch of the land, I thought the sooner we—you—saw it, the better."

"Monday's fine."

"We'll take the corporate jet. Plan to leave at eight-thirty. That will get us into our hotel by early afternoon. We'll just settle in on Monday. Then we'll go to the site and meet with the local contractors on Tuesday and Wednesday and fly back Thursday morning. Will you be bringing anyone?"

James looked at his pocket calendar. Lynne's schedule was written on it, and the days he could see Leslie were marked by a small blu dot. Lynne would return late Monday afternoon and fly again on Thursday. Unless she could join him in Maui, which was unlikely, he wouldn't see her for over a week. He wouldn't miss any time with Leslie. They would be able to see each other Thursday night, as scheduled.

"I don't think I will be bringing anyone."

"You're welcome to. You don't even need to let me know."

Before hanging up, Eric gave James directions to the private jet terminal at San Francisco International Airport.

"You're going Monday?" Leslie asked after James replaced the receiver.

James modded, frowning slightly.

"James?"

"Sorry. I . . . uh . . . need to let Lynne know. She's"—he continued glancing at his watch—"probably in her hotel in New York by now."

"I'll go take a shower. Give you a little privacy," Leslie said, leaving the room.

640 James caught her hand as she passed.

"Hey," he said gently, holding her hand. "I'm sorry."

"James," Leslie said carefully. Maybe today would be the day it was over. "I'm the intruder. Not Lynne."

After Leslie left, James dialed the number in New York that was provided on the computer-generated schedule he kept in his briefcase. It gave all the specifics of Lynne's itinerary, including flight times and hotel locations and telephone numbers. James carried the detailed itinerary with him, but he rarely referred to it. They had decided early on not to call each other, as a routine, when Lynne was traveling. They made the decision then because James was just getting started, they had substantial mortgage payments and they couldn't justify the expense. Now they could easily afford it, but the habit not to call was well established.

Lynne answered the phone on the second ring.

"Lynne?"

"James! Is something . . . ? Is it Mother . . . ?" Or, Lynne thought, remembering the manila folder she had handed to him as she left the day before, have you read it? Lynne's heart pounded as she waited.

"No, Lynne. It's nothing. Nothing has happened. I have to go to Maui on Monday. Eric was able to purchase the adjacent land, so we're going over to take a look."

"Oh."

"Do you want to come?"

"I don't get back until Monday afternoon."

"I know that's your schedule. Maybe you could change it. We're taking the company jet. We'll be back Thursday."

No, I can't change it," Lynne said flatly, wondering if she was his first or second choice, wondering where he was calling from and hating herself for calling their empty house all last night. Why did she need to prove it to herself over and over again? She knew. Without ever having made a call, without ever checking to see if he was gone all night, she would have known. She had known from the very beginning, the moment she saw him on September thirteenth.

She knew. That was why she had written the "Monica" chapter for him to read. She had to do something to make him talk to her about it.

"Have you read the chapter?" she asked quietly, knowing the answer. He wouldn't have read it last night. He wasn't home. He was with whomever it was who had taken him away from her.

"No, not yet. I'll read it before I go."

"No," Lynne said quickly, suddenly tired, too tired to deal with it. Too tired. She had been that way for the past four weeks: tired and weak and nauseated. She was too tired to argue or fight, or even to deal with the fact that she had lost her husband.

Tired. Defeated.

"You sure?"

"Yes. It isn't very good. I need to think about it a little more."

"OK. Are you feeling any better?"

"Not really. Each morning I hope that I'll wake up feeling normal. But . . . it's just the flu. Everyone has had it. Mine's just lasting a little longer," she said. *Because I can't really sleep, and I lie awake at night hating my husband for being unfaithful to me. I don't have the strength to deal with it. I have to leave him, but I don't have the energy.*

"Maybe you should see a doctor this week. You'll be home Tuesday and Wednesday. It might be a good idea."

"I know what's wrong with me. I have a bad virus, and there's a lot going on," she added icily.

"What?" *What did she mean?*

"Anyway, I am going to take some time off the following week. I'm going to spend Thanksgiving in Denver with Mother. I'll be gone from Tuesday until Sunday."

James looked at his pocket calendar.

"That means that the only time we'll see each other in the next two and a half weeks is the Monday before Thanksgiving."

"I guess so."

Neither spoke for several moments.

"Why don't I join you in Denver? At least for a few days?" James asked finally.

"No. I want to spend the time with Mother by myself."

"Lynne, are you all right?"

"No. I'm not all right. I don't feel well."

"That's all? Nothing else is wrong?"

"No," Lynne said, exhausted, but encouraged by the concern in his voice. Maybe she was wrong. Maybe it was over. Maybe . . . "No James, nothing else."

"I'll leave the name and number of the hotel in Maui on the refrigerator. And Lynne, please see a doctor."

Leslie finished her shower just before James hung up. She heard him tell Lynne to see a doctor.

"Is Lynne ill?" Leslie asked. *Why am I doing this? Why am I talking about Lynne? Am I trying to end it?*

"Oh. She's had the flu for four weeks."

The flu, whatever that is, doesn't usually last for four weeks, Leslie thought.

"What are her symptoms?" Leslie asked.

"Leslie, I don't want to talk about Lynne."

"Maybe we should. About Lynne. Or about us. About what's wrong."

"What's wrong with Lynne is she's got the flu and she hasn't been able to shake it because, as usual, she pushes herself too hard," James said firmly. Then he added more gently, "There is nothing wrong with us."

"No?" Leslie asked, weakening under his gaze, staring into the intense green eyes that said so much and made her want to believe this folly was possible forever.

"No."

"Oh."

"One thing wrong. One thing we should have done."

"What?" Leslie breathed.

"We should have made love on that ferry boat. Remember? Under the stairs."

"I remember."

"So, let's go find a ferry boat and make love. If we don't find one, we'll come back here to make love. We'll do that anyway. I just need to get out, get blown around by the wind for a while, OK?"

"You want me to come?"

"You're the one I plan to make love with."

Lynne felt unusually tired and ill as she boarded the nine-thirty flight from LaGuardia to O'Hare Monday morning. She had slept fitfully the past two nights. On Saturday night, after speaking with James, she tossed and turned, wondering if she could be wrong, hoping desperately that she was.

Finally at six A.M., three A.M., in San Francisco, she dialed their home phone number. She let it ring. Twenty rings. Thirty. Each unanswered ring harshly reminded her that she was right.

Lynne thought about the "Monica" chapter that she had left for James to read. It was so foolish. It was a *gentle* way of telling James that she knew, how hurt she was and how they had to talk about it. It began, *Large tears splashed from Monica's cornflower-blue eyes onto her soft fur. Monica was desolate. She had lost her best friend, Thomas . . .*

Thomas was Monica's best friend, and he was her boyfriend. Thomas was a regular in the Monica books. The chapter, written just for James, described Monica's suspicion that Thomas had found someone else and her bewilderment that it had happened. She had been so sure of their friendship and their love!

Lynne was glad that James hadn't read it after all. It made her seem pathetic and hurt. As she listened to the phone ring, unanswered because her husband was in someone else's bed, Lynne's true feelings crystallized. *Anger.*

Her inevitable confrontation with James would not be through an imaginary calico cat. It would be direct. She was leaving him as soon as she regained her strength.

On Sunday, Lynne worked, flying from New York to Atlanta to Orlando and back to New York. Sunday night she didn't sleep well, either, but this time she didn't call to check on James. She knew.

It was a short flight from New York's LaGuardia Airport to O'Hare Field in Chicago, but it was breakfast time and a meal was scheduled. It meant that the flight attendants had to move quickly and efficiently.

As senior flight attendant, Lynne worked the first-class cabin. Despite the short flight, two entrees were offered: Belgian waffle with sausage links or cheese omelette and fruit. Lynne had taken drink and entree orders before takeoff. Even before the seat belt sign was turned off, she was in the galley preparing the meal service.

As Lynne reached for the hot coffee pot, the feeling hit her. The galley swirled, her head swirled and her world swirled. She was vaguely aware that she was falling, but she couldn't prevent it. Something very hot touched her thigh, accompanied by grayness and swirling and nausea. A sickening thud echoed and re-echoed in her head.

The passenger in the first row witnessed the episode but couldn't unfasten his seat belt quickly enough to break her fall. He was at her side, calling for help, within seconds.

A crowd—the other first-class passengers, another flight attendant and the co-pilot—huddled in the small galley watching Lynne struggling with consciousness. Her face was white-green. Her blond hair was matted with blood over the right temple where she had struck her head as she fell.

A passenger who was a doctor arrived, instinctively reached for her radial pulse and asked for a damp cloth to put on her forehead.

Lynne could hear his voice. She understood that he was speaking to her, but she couldn't answer him right away. The nausea and the whirling still swept through her in overwhelming unexpected waves. She tried to focus, but the faces were blurred.

"Something hot on my leg," she said finally.

Lynne had spilled the pot of hot coffee when she fell. The doctor examined her legs, as much as was possible given constraints of the crowd and her privacy. He could see enough to tell that most of the burns were first degree, painful but not terribly serious. Fortunately the coffee had not been boiling.

"Please get some towels soaked in cold water for her legs. As soon as we can get her up, we'll need to remove her skirt and nylons and bundle her up in a blanket," he said to the other flight attendant. "What's her first name?"

Lynne's badge said Mrs. L. Stevenson.

"Lynne."

"Lynne? Can you hear me?"

Lynne nodded slightly. The cold towel on her forehead and the cold towels on her legs helped. So did lying very still on the floor.

"How do you feel?"

"Sick. Whirling," Lynne whispered. "Better."

"She's been sick for weeks, Doctor. The flu. But she's kept working."

"Lynne, open your eyes. Good. Follow my finger."

Lynne's eyes moved from side to side.

"Does that make you feel worse?"

"No."

She doesn't have nystagmus, he thought. He said aloud, "I thought it might be an inner ear infection—labyrinthitis—that sometimes follows a viral syndrome, but there's no evidence of it. Has this ever happened before?"

"No."

"Do you remember your heart pounding or fluttering before you fell?" Her pulse had been steady, but a little weak, since he had been feeling it.

"No."

"Did you eat any food that seemed bad to you?"

"Airline food you mean?" Lynne answered, her strength returning. And with it, relief. And a little humor. "No, nothing that seemed bad."

"Are you pregnant?"

"No, not me," Lynne said a little wistfully.

"Ulcers? Stomach pain? Bleeding?"

"No."

"Have you been eating normally?"

"No. This flu has made me sick. I've lost weight."

"Maybe it's only a virus with dehydration, but, young lady, you need to be checked. For now, I see a little pink in your cheeks where the green used to be. Want to try sitting up?"

One of the other flight attendants, Carol, helped Lynne into the bathroom, out of her coffee-drenched clothes and into a dress that Lynne had packed in her overnight bag.

"How are you doing?" Carol called through the door.

"OK. Wobbly. I may need to lie down again."

There were empty seats in the first-class cabin. Lynne lay across two seats, curled up, until she had to sit up for the landing. By the time they landed at ten A.M Chicago time, Lynne felt a little better.

"I'll take you to the crew lounge. We'll call James and then arrange to have you dead-headed back to San Francisco," Carol said as soon as all the passengers had deplaned. "They're bringing a wheelchair for you. Maybe you should go to a hospital here."

"No, I'd like to go home. I feel better. I can make it as long as I can just curl up. Oh, I forgot. James is going to Maui today. He's probably leaving about now. I have no idea how to reach him. He has to go on this trip anyway. Carol, can you see if I can get on something to Denver?"

I can really go home, Lynne thought. Home to Mother.

Chapter 25

James arrived at the private terminal at the San Francisco International Airport at seven-forty-five. His identification was carefully checked before he was permitted into the waiting lounge. Yes, his name *was* on the list, but would he mind providing proof of his identity?

As soon as James entered the private lounge, he understood the need for special precautions. People who flew on their own jets were a different breed. They expected excellence and quality. And they expected security. They were targets: targets for kidnapping and targets for terrorism. They expected protection.

Once in their secure private lounge, they could behave like anyone else, drinking coffee, reading *The San Francisco Chronicle* and *The Wall Street Journal* and watching the morning news shows. They behaved like anyone else, but they didn't *look* like anyone else. They looked powerful.

They looked, James realized, like Eric Lansdale. Eric was a nice very powerful and extremely demanding man. Eric expected perfection, just like everyone else in this exclusive lounge.

James looked for Eric in the lounge, but he didn't see him. James only saw men who reminded him of Eric. Many men. And one woman.

She stood at the large window of the lounge, gazing out at the fleet of unmarked corporate jets. Their jets were unmarked for the same reason that the men in the lounge didn't advertise who they were. The jets were identified by numbers only. No names, no logos, no publicity.

The woman wore a yellow and white cotton print dress. Her dazzling golden hair fell to her waist, casually swept off her face by a pair of sunglasses that rested on top of her head. She turned toward James, aware of a new presence in the lounge, as if she were expecting someone.

Her huge brown eyes registered surprise. He was not who she was expecting, but he was interesting. Handsome. She smiled briefly, appreciatively, before returning her gaze to the airfield.

A minute later, Eric entered the lounge. Eric was with a man whose resemblance to Eric was so striking that James assumed he was Eric's older brother. As Eric and the other man approached James, James saw the beautiful blond woman begin to cross the lounge, smiling.

"Hello, James," Eric said. "This is my father, Robert. He has just arrived on the red-eye from Philadelphia."

"James, I am so pleased to meet you. Eric has sent me the sketches of course. Truly brilliant."

"Thank you, sir."

The blond woman joined them.

"Good morning, Robert," she said warmly. "You look rested even though you must be exhausted." Charlie meant that he looked wonderful. Robust, youthful. Too young to be Eric's father.

"Hello," Robert said, returning her warmth, kissing her briefly on the cheek. Then he sighed and added, "I am tired. I don't sleep on planes. At least not on other people's planes. I plan to sleep all the way to Maui if you won't consider me too antisocial."

"Not at all. Eric, who's this? Not the ever dour James?" Charlie asked, deducing that the handsome, sexy man with the green eyes, black hair and seductive smile must be James.

"You're not—" James began as amazed by her as she was by him.

"*Ms*. Charlotte D. Winter," Eric said.

"I'm Charlie," she said, extending a long, graceful hand to James.

"I'm James."

The interior of the plane was like a home, beautifully decorated and impeccably maintained. It contained a large, comfortable living room, a formal conference room, a kitchen and dining area, two large bathrooms with showersand four bedrooms. As soon as the captain announced that it was safe to remove their seat belts, Robert withdrew to a bedroom.

"See you all in Maui. Eric, I plan to be so rested that I'll be ready for a game of tennis in the late afternoon."

"You're on."

During the five-hour flight, James and Charlie and Eric studied James's recent sketches, talked, read, drank coffee and ate the croissants and fruit that had been boarded moments before the plane left San Francisco.

"I didn't have them board a lunch. We'll be at the hotel in Maui by two. So—" Eric began.

"Basically, James, Eric didn't have them board a lunch because Eric never eats lunch," Charlie interjected, narrowing her brown eyes at Eric, taunting him.

"Who does?" James asked.

"Just me, I guess," Charlie said, reaching for another croissant.

"Charlie is actually capable of eating continuously without gaining a pound. She's always been that way," Eric observed.

Always, James thought. I wonder how long they have known each other. A long time, he decided. The three of them—Charlie, Eric and Robert—seemed like a family. Eric and Charlie seemed like a little more than a family. Something more than siblings.

Lynne can eat constantly, James thought, and she is thin. But her energy level is so high—at least until recently—that she needs the calories to keep up with the energy output.

"My wife—" James began, then stopped. Charlie and Eric were off on another topic. They didn't hear him.

After settling in his elegant suite with the panoramic ocean view, James took a nap. He had left Leslie's bed at five, returning home to pack and to leave the name of the hotel on the refrigerator for Lynne. He noticed the manila folder with the "Monica" chapter. He had time to read it, but Lynne had said no. She was sensitive about him reading her work if she wasn't happy with it. James left the manila folder, untouched, on the kitchen counter.

Rested and refreshed after his short nap, James decided to sit by the pool and read in the fading rays of the late afternoon sun. They had agreed to meet at six in Eric's suite. He had time.

"I hope you have sunscreen on."

James looked up at the sound of her voice behind him. She moved in front of him, blocking the sun. Her face was lost in shadows, but her hair shone brilliant gold as the sun's rays filtered through it.

"Number six."

"That's probably all right especially since it's almost sunset. You look like you've been under glass all your life," she observed uncritically.

James's skin was pale, but creamy, rich and smooth. He looks like a marble statue of a Greek god, Charlie thought. Even at rest, lying on the chaise longue, James's muscles were well-defined, delicately laced with blue-purple veins. Gorgeous, she thought.

"Not all my life. I used to spend summers working in a logging camp, sweating with the guys under the summer sun," James said.

"May I join you?" Charlie asked, still standing in front of him.

"Of course."

James watched her gracefully lower her lovely tan body onto the adjacent chaise longue. She wore a brown one-piece bathing suit. Modest but revealing.

"Eric and Robert are playing tennis."

"This is better."

"I think so," she said, smiling contentedly, stretching. She tossed the mane of spun gold behind her.

"Eric says you have a girlfriend," Charlie said casually, looking at him.

Charlie watched as a cloud of worry flickered across his eyes.

"*Boyfriend?*" she asked.

"What? No. I'm married."

"Oh. Well, he did say he thought you were *involved*. I assumed girlfriend. I guess marriage also falls into the involved category."

"I guess," he said, sitting up, looking at her. "Why?"

"Why am I asking you about your personal life?" Charlie paused, considering her own question. Then she said, "Why not?"

James laughed. "That's fair. What about you? Boyfriend? Girlfriend? Husband?"

"Attorneys prefer to ask questions, not answer them," Charlie said amiably. "But, fair is fair. None of the above. Not involved."

"Never married?"

"No," she answered immediately. Then she said, laughing lightly, "Yes I was. I'd forgotten."

"No," James said, aghast.

"It was a very forgettable marriage. And it was a long time ago."

"Why did you get married?"

"Because I was angry," Charlie said slowly, her eyes closed, her body arched elegantly toward the tropical sun.

"Angry?"

"With someone else. Not the poor groom-to-be. I married him to get even with someone else."

"Someone you loved?"

Charlie nodded her head slowly. Then she turned to look at James and said firmly, "Let's talk about you."

"You're more interesting."

"We don't know that."

"I do."

"You're just a happily married guy with no problems?" she asked, her tone implying that she knew differently. She had seen his eyes when she asked about his girlfriend.

"Boring," James said carefully.

They sat in silence for several moments.

"Tell me about your girlfriend, James," Charlie said, finally.

James sighed. It might be nice to tell someone about it. Maybe. It would at least be nice to have some time to think about it. He could do that on this trip. He could do it now if Charlie wasn't sitting next to him asking him.

Something about Charlie—something about her curiosity that was neither idle nor malicious—made him decide to tell her. Maybe it was because she reminded him of Lynne: blond, strong, independent, energetic; but also fragile, easily hurt. He could imagine Lynne marrying someone out of anger.

"Girlfriend isn't a good term," he began carefully.

"Lover?" Charlie offered.

"Let's just call her Leslie."

James told her about Leslie—and the relationship that never quite started—or ended—in high school. James didn't tell Charlie about his father, and he skipped the sordid details of his first year of college; but he told her that Leslie sent him a letter that changed his life, and that he saw her again, after nine years, on television in August.

"I saw her, too! I guess everyone did. The entire city," Charlie said. She vividly remembered the blood-stained face and the remarkable blue eyes that flashed with concern and astonishment and rage. "It made me want to meet her."

"It made me want to see her again," James said. "I wanted her to know, finally, how I felt about her. I—we—needed to finish what we began in high school."

"Finish? Is it finished?"

"No."

"What about your wife?"

"It doesn't have anything to do with Lynne."

"*What?*" Charlie sat bolt upright and stared at him. "What?"

"It started before I met Lynne. Leslie had already happened in my life. I wasn't carrying a torch. If I had been, I would have tried harder to find her, wouldn't I? And I wouldn't have fallen in love with Lynne," James said seriously. "Leslie is my past. Lynne is present, my future."

"That's complete nonsense!" Charlie exclaimed. "Leslie *is* in the present. When did you last make love with Leslie?"

James stared at her, but he answered.

"Last night."

"And Lynne?"

James narrowed his eyes as he tried to remember. When? Before Lynne had gotten sick. How much before? Before Leslie? Since Leslie?

"Lynne has been ill."

"This gets worse and worse."

"Not that ill. A bad virus. Enough to make her not interested in making love."

"That's pretty bad. Unless of course, the whole illness is just that she knows about Leslie."

"She doesn't," James said swiftly, confidently.

"What if she did?"

"I would never forgive myself," James said honestly. It would destroy her. She would never understand. Understand what? Why somehow it was permissible for him to have an affair with Leslie? Why he wasn't really breaking any rules? Not violating any trust?

"She knows, James. She has to know."

"No."

"Who are you going to spend your life with?"

"*Lynne*. I told you that. I *am* spending my life with her."

"Does Leslie know that?"

"Yes."

"So it's really perfect, isn't it?" Charlie asked with more than a trace of sarcasm. "Except that your wife is ill and you can't remember when you last made love to her."

James was silent. Lynne can't know, he thought. I would know if she knew. She would tell me. She would get angry. Lynne would do what Charlie would do.

"What would you do if you were Lynne and you found out?" James asked.

"Is she like me?"

"I think so." It's probably why I feel comfortable talking to you, he thought.

"I would let you know what I thought of you and your silly rationalization. Then I would leave you. In my younger days, I might have married someone else as quickly as possible." Charlie watched James, the frown on his face, the concern in his eyes. "James, I believe that you love them both. But you've promised your life and your dreams to Lynne. I think you would be devastated if you lost her. You're playing with a hot, dangerous fire."

James looked into Charlie's soft brown eyes.

"You're a wise woman, Charlotte D. Winter," he said.

"No, James. I am experienced, and some of my most important experiences were painful ones."

"Do you think you'll get married again?" James asked. He was ready to shift the conversation away from himself. He had heard what Charlie said. They were words he should have said to himself. Everything she said was true. Still, Lynne didn't know. It would never hurt her because she would never know.

He and Leslie knew, although they didn't discuss it, that they couldn't—wouldn't—continue much longer.

It was wrong. But when he was with Leslie it was good and right because she was good and she would never harm anyone. She didn't want to hurt Lynne any more than he did.

"Maybe. Probably. But will I ever fall in love again? I don't know. I may be too old."

"Really! How old are you, Charlie?"

"I'm a year younger than Eric. To the day. We were both conceived on Valentine's Day, the result of a special Valentine from our mothers to their soldier lovers. Eric was born on November eleventh, 1944. I was born exactly a year later."

"Is Robert really Eric's father?"

"Yes. Robert was just eighteen on that Valentine's Day in 1944. Eric's mother was a quite attractive and very wealthy twenty-three-year-old debutante. Robert didn't know her very well, but they got together that night. The next morning Robert went to the war in Europe. Two months later when the families—both steeped in wealth and blue-bloodedness—discovered that she was pregnant, they orchestrated a retroactive marriage between the two. So Eric wouldn't be a bastard. But, of course," Charlie said smiling but with a slight sharpness in her voice, "Eric *is* a bastard. So am I."

"Not so you'd notice," James said quickly. "Was Robert surprised when he returned?"

"I think the mail caught up with him before he returned two years later. He liked his wife well enough to have another child with her. They remained married for almost thirty years," Charlie said factually. Then her voice softened, and she said gently, "And, of course, Robert adored his little toddler son with the light brown hair and pale blue eyes just like his."

"They do look like brothers. And they seem so close," James said as he thought about his own father for the first time in years. James tried to remember a time when they were close. He couldn't. All he could remember was hatred and disappointment.

"The closest. They are best friends. They care so much about each other."

"And Eric's mother?"

"She and Robert were divorced six or seven years ago."

"That's too bad."

"Not really. Robert is much happier. He seems younger and freer."

"You've know them a long time, haven't you?"

"A long time," Charlie repeated distantly. So many memories. "I met Eric when I was sixteen."

Six months after the death of my mother, she thought but didn't say.

Chapter 26

Somehow Charlotte survived the months after her mother's death. She paid the bills—carefully writing the checks in Louise Alcott's elaborate script—and bought what food she ate with the money from the shoeboxes. She kept her clothes clean and ironed, went to school, maintained her excellent grades and pretended to her friends and teachers that she and her Aunt Louise were managing quite well.

Charlotte survived without help from anyone because she steadfastly refused to feel the pain. The pain of loneliness and loss and grief and even betrayal was replaced by numbness, an absence of feelings. Charlotte felt neither pain nor joy. She simply existed, plodding from day to day without thought or reflection.

For a week after receiving Mary's letter, Charlotte allowed herself a wonderful fantasy. She would find her father. He would be handsome and loving and oh so happy to see his daughter. Maybe she would even have a half brother or sister. She would move to England. She would have a family.

She would run an ad in the London papers. *Looking for John (Max), who made love to Mary (Charlotte) on Valentine's Day 1945 in Philadelphia. You have a daughter.*

Reality crashed down around her before Charlotte ran the ad. His name probably wasn't really John. He probably didn't live in London, or even England, anymore. Why would he read an ad in the personal section, anyway? He might not *want* to have an illegitimate daughter. He might be a horrible man. A rapist. A murderer. Mary had thought he was wonderful, but Mary lived in a dream world, a world of fantasy.

This is fantasy, Charlotte realized one day with horror. I am creating a fantasy about my father. I am beginning to believe it, to believe in a world that doesn't exist.

Don't do it, her mind screamed. Don't become like your mother. Don't lose touch with what is real.

Charlotte forced herself to forget about John just as she forced herself to feel no pain.

 That summer Charlotte got a job as a lifeguard at the Oak Brook Country Club. Located in Philadelphia's most elegant residential area, the club boasted an exclusive membership. All help, including lifeguards, was hired from outside the membership. Even though the teenage children of club members would have competed enthusiastically for the lifeguarding jobs, it simply wasn't done. Children of club members didn't work. At least, not at the club.

Charlotte Winter had a healthy wholesome look, the personnel manager at the club decided. Clearly not aristocratic—she wouldn't compete with the members" daughters—but quite acceptable. He hired her. He had hired the five lifeguards every summer for the past ten years. This was the first time he had hired a girl.

The Oak Brook Country Club was five miles from Charlotte's house on Elm Street. She rode her bicycle to and from work, pedaling fast in the coolness of the early summer morning and pedaling more slowly in the humid evening heat.

There were four of them. They arrived together during Charlotte's third week at the club. She watched them arrive, immediately struck by the casual, buoyant way they walked. Their nonchalant, self-assured, easy gaits sent clear messages of confidence and control. And why not? The world was theirs—a sumptuous buffet of experiences and pleasures. All they had to do was choose.

As they approached the pool area, the teenage girls who had been relaxed and giggly for the past weeks came to attention.

This is who they've been waiting for, Charlotte thought. She watched the four young men—four healthy, handsome fashion plates in light cotton slacks and designer polo shirts—survey their territory, smiling appreciatively at the girls. The girls smiled back with coy, carefully studied smiles and perfectly posed bodies. It was a ritual, Charlotte realized. It marked the beginning of summer at the Oak Brook Country Club.

One of the young men grabbed one of the girls and threw her, squealing with delight, into the pool.

Charlotte immediately, reflexively, stood up and blew her whistle. At first no one heard it above the laughing, giggling, squealing and splashing that followed as all the girls were thrown, willingly, into the aquamarine water.

Charlotte blew her whistle again and again.

Finally the pool area fell silent. Then all eyes were on her. Startled, amused eyes. One pair of pale blue eyes approached her.

"Is something wrong, lifeguard?" he asked smiling.

"Pushing, shoving, throwing people into the pool. It's not allowed," Charlotte said looking down at him from her perch.

"Since when?" he asked mildly.

"Since always."

"It's never been enforced. Not here."

"It will be enforced this summer. It's too dangerous," Charlotte said firmly, her heart pounding, her face suddenly warm.

"How will it be enforced?"

"I have the authority to prohibit people who break the rules from coming into the pool area. It's all written down in the club's policy manual," Charlotte said, feeling the dampness of her palms and a cold wave of fear washing through her body.

He sensed her fear. And relented.

"OK. You're the boss. It looks like we have one tough cookie on the lifeguard tower this year," he said to the still-mute group. Then he looked up at Charlotte. "I guess we're going to have our fun somewhere else."

Everyone laughed. Uneasy laughter. Then eager laughter. Maybe it would be *more* fun. Maybe they would have to save their touching for more private places. Maybe the sexual tension created at poolside would find a more intimate release.

The pale blue eyes looked back up at Charlotte, trying to learn a little about her. Charlotte's golden-blond hair was tucked, completely hidden, under the too large safari hat, and her enormous brown eyes were lost in the shadow of its brim. All he could see were her full lips and her flawless body in the emerald-green tank suit issued by the club.

"What's your name?" he asked.

"Charlotte. What's yours?"

"Eric. And this is . . ." Eric introduced the assembled group. Charlotte had been there three weeks. In that time, only the mothers with young children had introduced themselves. They asked if she would be giving swimming lessons and made certain that she would watch the wading-pool area carefully. No one Charlotte's age had made any attempt to speak to her.

Now Eric, even after their awkward initial exchange, was making introductions. Because, Charlotte realized gratefully, he is so well bred. His politeness is instinctive. He *could* treat her like a servant, like everyone else at the club did, but he didn't.

By the time the introductions were over, the chatter and laughter in the pool area had returned. When Eric spoke to her again, no one else heard.

"Charlotte, huh?" he asked, peering up at her, trying unsuccessfully to see her face.

"Charlotte," she repeated tentatively.

"I think I'm going to have to call you Charlie," he said finally. Without waiting for her reply, Eric headed toward the men's locker room to change into his swim trunks.

Over the next week, Eric and Charlie didn't speak, but he waved pleasantly from his chaise longue by the pool. Sometimes, grinning at her, he pretended that he was about to toss someone in the water. But he didn't.

Charlie learned a little about him that week. She learned that Eric and his three friends had just graduated from a prep school in New Hampshire and that Eric would be attending Harvard in the fall. Charlie decided that he didn't have a steady girlfriend, that he was immensely charming and that his life had been unencumbered by even a moment of sadness or denial. Eric had everything, and he was probably even kind.

Charlie ran into him in the parking lot one evening as she was leaving.

"Hi, Eric," she said smiling.

"Hi," he answered politely, a little confused by the beautiful girl with the flowing blond hair, and huge brown eyes and the vaguely familiar voice and lips. "Charlie?"

"Charlie. Without the safari hat."

"Wow," he said effortlessly. It was part of his charm. He made people feel wonderful.

"Well," Charlie said shrugging, suddenly uncomfortable. "See ya."

"Wait. Charlie. Do you want to go have a Coke or something?" he asked, gesturing toward the club.

"Oh. Thanks. It's getting dark and the light on my bicycle is broken. I should get going," she said truthfully. She had stayed late after work for a lifeguards" meeting. It was already dusk.

"Your bicycle? How far do you live?"

"About five miles," she answered, uneasy at the tone in his voice when she mentioned her bicycle. He probably didn't know anyone who didn't have a car. Mary had never owned a car. She had never learned to drive.

"Even if you leave now, it's going to be dark by the time you get home."

"I know. I'd better go."

"Wait. Why don't we put your bicycle in my car? I'll drive you home. We can have dinner if you haven't eaten."

Eric put Charlie's bicycle into the trunk of his car, a cream-colored Mercedes with blue leather interior.

As they ate pizza and drank Coke, Eric entertained her with stories about prep school, previous club lifeguards and his friends. Charlie listened appreciatively, her huge brown eyes focused, intent, smiling. Her laugh flowed easily from deep within her, swept by a rush of joy she hadn't felt for months. If ever. With Eric, Charlie felt alive again, no longer numb or empty.

When Eric asked her about her life, her family, Charlie just encouraged him to tell her more about himself.

Eric had never known anyone like Charlie. She was so natural, so unpretentious. She didn't even know that with every gesture, every glance, every laugh, she was seducing him, making him fall in love with her.

It had never happened to Eric before.

It had never happened to either one of them.

At eleven-thirty, Eric suddenly became aware of the almost empty pizza parlor.

"Charlie, it's eleven-thirty. I hope you won't be in trouble."

"No. I won't be."

At midnight, Eric parked in front of the tiny pale-green house on Elm Street. He noticed immediately that the house was dark.

"I'm afraid they may be mad at you," Eric said. "They didn't even leave any lights on."

"There is no one there," Charlie said reluctantly.

"No one home? They leave you alone?" Eric asked incredulously as they walked up the walk toward the dark front porch.

Suddenly Charlie froze. She was unable to force herself to walk a step closer to the dark empty house. She had to be numb to do that, and tonight, with Eric, she no longer felt numb. She felt alive and happy.

Now, seeing the house and unprotected by the armor of numbness the emotions that Charlie had denied since Mary died rushed into her, consuming her with dread and pain and loneliness. *They leave you alone?* Eric's words thundered in her brain.

"Charlie?" Eric turned toward her, wondering why she had stopped.

The emotions erupted into a sob. Charlie couldn't control the sob or the trembling that accompanied it. She covered her face with her hands and shook her head, unable to move, unable to stop crying, unable to even understand what had happened.

"Charlie!" Eric's arms were around her. "What's wrong?"

"There is no one," she sobbed softly into his chest. "I live here by myself."

"No one? Charlie, I don't understand. Charlie. Tell me," he urged, holding her tighter, trying to move her toward the house.

"I'm afraid to go in there," she whispered almost frantically.

"OK. Let's go sit in the car. Charlie, you need to tell me what's wrong."

She did tell him. Slowly and painfully, over the next hour, she told him everything.

"Why don't you come home with me? We have plenty of room," Eric said finally, holding her against him, not wanting to let her go.

"No. I feel better. It helps to have talked about it. I haven't told this to anyone. I'm sorry. It" not fair to have done this to you."

"I'm glad you told me. It makes me feel closer to you, and I want to be as close to you as I can," Eric whispered, pressing his lips against her silky golden hair.

"I should go in now," Charlie said with bravado.

"I'll go with you," Eric said, half dreading seeing the inside of the house himself.

But with the lights on, the house was cheerful, not oppressive. It had once been a happy place to live, filled with Mary's love for her daughter.

"You should go," Charlie said.

"I can stay a little longer. I need to call my parents, though, anyway. Do you have a phone?" he asked.

Charlie nodded. She didn't need a phone. Her school friends didn't call often anymore. She never used it, but a phone was a lifeline to reality. She was afraid to sever it.

Robert answered the phone on the second ring. It was one in the morning. He was working, reviewing a brief, in his study.

"Father, I know it's late."

"Are you all right?" Robert had been worried.

"Yes. I'm fine. I'm with a friend who needs me. I still won't be home for a while."

"Is there something I can do?"

"No. Not now. But my friend may need your help. Will you be home for dinner tonight?"

"Sure."

"Great. Will you tell Mother that I'm bringing a friend home for dinner, then?"

"OK. Eric, does your friend have a name?"

"Charlie."

After Eric hung up, Charlie stared at him, her eyes full of doubt.

"Eric, I don't want your father to know."

"I won't tell him, but I want you to think about telling him yourself. He's a lawyer, and he's a wonderful man," Eric said proudly. "Charlie, I'm just afraid that this could all backfire legally. I just want to be sure that you're not in trouble."

"What if I don't want to tell him?"

"Then no one knows but you and me."

She watched him in silence for several moments, her eyes full of sorrow. She wanted to turn the clock back, back to dinner and to the wonderful feeling of laughter and joy.

Eric walked toward her, disturbed by the look, by the sadness.

"What are you thinking?"

"That I never wanted you to feel sorry for me," she said.

"I don't. I feel sorry about what has happened to you."

"But, going to dinner at your house—"

"I decided to ask you before any of this happened. I decided while we were eating pizza."

"Really?" Charlie asked, brightening a little.

"Really," Eric said, folding his arms around her.

"Who's Charlie?" June roared at the breakfast table the next morning. June was three years younger than Eric. She wrinkled her freckled nose. "Probably some yucky preppie friend of his."

"I don't know," Robert said.

"I've never heard him mention a Charlie," Florence, Eric's mother, said a little skeptically. "When did Eric get home last night?"

"Late," Robert said. "But he did call."

Florence Lansdale's skepticism increased the moment she saw Charlie. Charlie didn't look like one of *them*. Her skepticism was instantly confirmed when June gleefully recognized Charlie as Charlotte, the lifeguard at the club. Charlotte was teaching June and her friends water ballet.

Robert Lansdale quietly admired his son's taste, wondered about Charlie's problem and made a vow to help her in any way that he could.

As soon as she met him, Charlie decided that she could trust Robert. He was a slightly older—old enough to be Eric's *father?*—version of Eric. He had the same kind blue eyes. Unlike his son's, Robert's eyes had seen sadness and pain—they had been to war—but still they were unafraid, full of life and hope. And something else. Something that Charlie didn't recognize, something she had never seen before. Robert Lansdale's pale blue eyes had the calm confidence of power.

Someday Eric would look exactly like Robert. His youthful good looks would mature into the strong handsomeness of his father. It made Charlie tremble a little in the way she had trembled when Eric kissed her last night.

After dinner, much to June's and Florence's annoyance, Robert, Eric and Charlie retreated into Robert's study. Robert listened without obvious emotion as Charlie told him her story.

Inside, Robert's stomach was churning with anger. How could a loving mother have done this? How could *anyone* do such a thing to this lovely, innocent, sensitive child? Charlie was so vulnerable, and this crazy scheme only made her more vulnerable.

"What do you think, Father?" Eric asked after Charlie was done.

"Charlie, I need to see all the papers. Your . . . uh . . . mother's will, the trust agreement, the guardianship documents. Everything. Can you get those?"

"Yes."

"Bring them all to me. And any other documents you have. I'll need to see them before I can decide what's best to do," Robert said firmly, concealing his own anxiety. Many laws had been broken. Mary's attorneys were probably innocent victims just as Charlie herself was, but they *were* victims. It all had to be handled carefully and discreetly, with a minimum of damage.

It was lucky that Robert Lansdale was one of the best attorneys in Philadelphia. And one of the city's most powerful men.

Over the next few weeks, while Robert studied the documents, made phone calls, persuaded various officials to find unorthodox solutions for their unorthodox dilemma, Charlie and Eric fell in love.

By summer's end when it was time for Eric to leave for his freshman year at Harvard, a few momentous decisions had been made. Robert decided that, despite Florence's protests, he would become Charlie's legal guardian.

"She's a waif, Robert. Her mother—Well! There were stories about her when she kept the library open during the war," Florence hissed.

If pressed, Florence would have been forced to admit that the stories weren't bad. Mary was known as a strange, but kind and generous woman. But Robert didn't press her because during the past two months he had learned things about Mary that troubled him deeply. Things that Charlie didn't know, that she should never know.

Florence did not win the guardianship argument, but she successfully drew the line at allowing Charlie to move into *her* home. Robert only relented because Charlie herself insisted on staying in her tiny house on Elm Street.

"I am comfortable there, Mr. Lansdale. It's a safe neighborhood. I'm established at the high school. I would prefer to stay there," Charlie said, convincingly, sensing how Florence felt about her.

"We have to maintain close contact, Charlie," Robert said.

"We will, Father," Eric said. "I'll be home every weekend to see Charlie."

"Not every weekend," Robert said mildly. Weekly commuting would be too disruptive to Eric's studies.

"Maybe not. On the weekends that I'm not home, Charlie can meet you for lunch downtown. Something official like that."

Then there was another momentous decision: Eric would see Charlie as often as he could, and she would apply to Radcliffe so she could be with him next year, as soon as she graduated from high school.

Charlie made a decision of her own too. She decided to be a lawyer, like Robert. In the hours she spent with him that summer, carefully going over all the papers, listening to his explanations of the law, of how the law could be applied and interpreted, Charlie felt happy. Law was real, tangible. It required thought and reason. It was open to interpretation but free of fantasy. It was a game of intellect. It stimulated her, and it couldn't get her into trouble. As a lawyer she would be unlikely to lapse into a world of delusion.

Charlie was so *afraid* of becoming like Mary.

She told Robert about her decision at lunch on Saturday the following spring. Eric was in his dormitory room at Harvard, studying for mid-term examinations. Charlie had just received her acceptance from Radcliffe.

"I've decided what I'm going to be when I grow up, Mr. Lansdale."

"What, Charlie?"

"A lawyer. Like you."

"You think you'd like to do what I do?" Robert asked, obviously pleased.

"I think so."

"You'd make a wonderful attorney, Charlie. You have the right kind of mind," Robert said.

"Thank you, Mr. Lansdale."

"Can't you call me Robert?"

"No," Charlie said smiling shyly, "I can't."

"Maybe someday? Maybe when we're working on a case together?" he asked.

"Maybe then."

Eric's and Charlie's first year together in Boston was blissful. By the second year, they began to have arguments. The arguments were bitter and damaging. Eric and Charlie had only two issues on which they disagreed . . . but they were major ones. The first was sex. The second was Charlie's career.

Charlie would not make love. She had promised herself that she would be a virgin until her wedding night. It was a promise she made the day she read Mary's letter, a letter from an unwed mother who was too ashamed to admit the truth to her daughter until after her own death. Charlie would not make the mistakes her mother had made. She would not live in a world of make-believe.

And she would not make love before she was married.

"Charlie," Eric would say, sometimes gently, sometimes in a rage of frustration. "I want to marry you. I *plan* to marry you. We could get married now."

"And I could give up my virginity and my career in one simple step?"

"Charlie, we have been more intimate than most married couples ever are."

It was true. Charlie was sexually uninhibited, eager, curious, loving. They had a perfect sexual relationship except . . . they didn't do *It*.

"So? Isn't that enough for now?" Charlie asked.

"It's just that it's so silly. Saving your so-called *ultimate closeness* after all the other things we've done."

"It's just the way I feel, Eric. You know it. I don't see why you can't respect it."

"I *am* respecting it, Charlie. But it is getting damned hard."

At the beginning of Eric's senior year—Charlie's junior year—the issue of Charlie's career became a source of friction. Eric told her that he planned to return to Philadelphia when he graduated from Harvard to get his Master's in Business Administration. That way he could spend his spare time at InterLand, Robert's company, while he was getting his degree. Robert decided that as soon as Eric completed graduate school he would assume the presidency of InterLand. That would permit Robert to devote more time to his true love, the practice of law.

"Why don't we get married in June right after I graduate from Harvard? We can spend the summer in Europe and get back to Philly in time to settle in before school starts."

"Eric, what about me?"

"What do you mean?"

"I want to go to law school."

"That's fine, Charlie."

"I want to graduate from Radcliffe and go to Harvard Law School. You're asking, no, you're *telling* me to transfer from Radcliffe at the end of my junior year, spend a year in school in Philadelphia and apply to law school there."

"Is there anything wrong with going to school in Philadelphia? I'm getting my MBA there, remember? Besides, InterLand, which happens to be the company that I am going to own and run, is in Philadelphia. Charlie, that's where we're going to live. That's where you're going to practice law. That is, if you plan to marry me."

Charlie did plan to marry him. She loved him deeply, passionately, and he loved her; but on these two issues they made each other very angry.

"InterLand could be headquartered in Boston," Charlie said sullenly.

Eric glowered at her. She was right of course.

"Is that what you want? You're right. I can have Father move the whole company to Boston. I can get my MBA here. But what do we do if Charlie doesn't get into Harvard Law School after all?"

"I'll get into Harvard Law School."

"So, shall I tell Father that my first official act as president will be to move the company?"

"Yes!" she yelled. Then she said, "No. Eric, I don't know. It's just that you never even considered what I wanted in all this. Never even asked me."

"I thought you wanted to marry me. I thought you wanted to spend your life with me."

"I thought you wanted to marry *me*, spend your life with *me*, too."

By the middle of autumn quarter of Eric's senior year, the arguments became almost constant. Although she agreed to get married in June *and* to move to Philadelphia, Charlie still fought it. Fought *something*.

They would argue bitterly about her career. Then they would collapse, finally, in each other's arms, needing love and comfort. But Charlie's determination not to make love would propel them almost immediately into another bitter argument.

By November, they argued more than they laughed, glowered more than they smiled and pushed each other away more than they held each other.

"We've reached an impasse, Charlie," Eric said one night, exhausted, defeated. "I don't know what's really wrong, but I know that this is no good."

"I agree," Charlie answered hotly.

"Let's spend some time apart. A few weeks to cool off."

"Fine," she said, leaving his dormitory room, slamming the door behind her, tears flowing from her eyes.

I don't know what's really wrong either, she thought as she stumbled across Harvard Square in the darkness. Except that it's something wrong with me, not him.

Chapter 27

Eric had known Victoria Hancock for years, from the pool at the Oak Brook Country Club, from dances and debutante balls, from dinners arranged by her mother and his. Victoria was the closest to a real girlfriend that Eric had had until he met Charlie.

That November when Eric returned to Philadelphia for a long weekend, to escape from Harvard and Charlie, he called Victoria. He needed someone to talk to; someone to laugh with; someone who knew him well enough that he didn't have to try; someone who would remind him of those carefree summer days at the pool—like those summer days when he met Charlie.

Eric had no intention of making love to Victoria when he called her. But it happened. It happened that weekend. And again at Thanksgiving. And again at Christmas.

Eric tried to reconcile with Charlie in early December. It worked for two weeks. Charlie was soft and loving. They talked about their wedding and their honeymoon. Eric didn't try to make love with her.

"Why aren't you pressing me to make love with you?" she asked, teasing, one night.

"I thought we were saving the *ultimate closeness* until June," he answered quickly. Too quickly.

"I am," Charlie said quietly, "but are you?"

Eric didn't answer her. His silence was answer enough.

"You made love to someone else?"

"Yes, Charlie. When we weren't together."

"I spent those weeks agonizing about what I had done wrong, how I could change to make our relationship better, and you were sleeping with someone else?"

"Charlie, it meant nothing. Besides, you're the one who has reservations about our relationship, not me. I agonized, hoping you would find out what was

really wrong."

"You didn't agonize. You played. You had sex with someone else!"

"It meant nothing. I missed you."

"So you found a surrogate? Is that what's going to happen every time we have a fight for the next fifty years?"

"Christ, Charlie. Don't be irrational."

"I hate you, Eric," she yelled. Irrational. Mary was irrational. "Get away from me."

Eric spent Christmas in Philadelphia with his family. Charlie refused to speak to him, except to admit, angrily, that she was planning to spend Christmas in the mountains. Eric decided that there was no way he could force her to spend the holidays in Philadelphia with him, but it worried him to think about her being alone at Christmas. Whatever was wrong—whatever made her so afraid of getting married—wouldn't be solved by her spending Christmas alone in the mountains hating him.

Victoria called Eric on December twenty-seventh, chiding him gently for not calling *her*. She had heard that he was home alone. She convinced him to go skiing with her the next day.

Charlie did not spend the Christmas holidays in the mountains. She spent them in Philadelphia in the little green house on Elm Street. She had decided to sell the house. She spent the cold days of Christmas week filling boxes with the bittersweet memories of her childhood. Most of the boxes—most of the memories—would be thrown away. Charlie kept all of Mary's books, including the leather-bound copy of *Rebecca* and the photograph album of Charlie's childhood that Mary had carefully, lovingly, maintained. Charlie kept the album because it contained a few rare photographs of her mother.

Charlie met with real estate agents and put the ouse on the market at a below-market value. Charlie wanted to sell it quickly. She might need the money for tuition at Harvard Law School.

On December twenty-seventh, Charlie met with Mary's doctor. Maybe he could give her the answers she was looking for.

"Doctor, after she died, you told me that she was very ill. What did she have?"

"I don't have a name for what she had. She was very troubled. She lived in a world of make-believe. She was delusional, sometimes even paranoid. She had periods of profound depression. Medications didn't help. She didn't fit into any specific psychiatric diagnosis. She took wonderful care of you. She was dysfunctional in many ways, but she cared for you. And for her library," the doctor said, his voice gentle as he remembered troubled, loving, frightened Mary.

"But why did she die, Doctor? What killed her?"

"Nothing killed her," he said carefully, watching Mary's daughter. Everything killed her, he thought. Life killed her. "She killed herself."

"Oh *no*."

As Charlie spent the evening thinking about her mother, she was filled with a strange sense of peace. Finally she had her answer. Finally she knew what was wrong, what it was that made her fight her marriage to Eric, fight making love, fight anything that might cause her to have children or a family.

She had to let Eric know. She had to set him free, to let him know that she had found out in time.

She dialed Eric's home number early the next morning.

Florence and Robert were eating breakfast. Eric and Victoria had already left to go skiing.

"No, Charlie, Eric is away for the day," Florence said. At the mention of Charlie's name, Robert moved quickly beside Florence. He had watched Eric's suffering as he worried about Charlie. Robert worried about her, too.

"Let me speak with her," Robert said reaching for the phone. Florence handed it to him. "Charlie, it's Robert. Where are you?"

"At the house," she said. Her voice was flat, lifeless. Its tone worried Robert very much.

"Charlie, I need to see you."

"Why?"

"Business. Minor details from the trust."

"Oh. All right. I'll tell you what I needed to tell Eric since he's away."

"Are you leaving?"

"Yes. This evening."

"I'm coming over to the house right now, Charlie," Robert said firmly and hung up.

"What's wrong?" Florence asked.

"I don't know. She sounds strange," Robert said as he rushed past Florence and out of the house. Maybe Charlie has found out, he thought, depressing the accelerator a little more.

As soon as he saw her, Robert knew. Her brown eyes were clouded with hopelessness and resignation.

"Hello, Mr. Lansdale," she said quickly.

Robert, he thought.

"Hello, Charlie. You look as if you've had some bad news."

"It's bad and good. It's good for Eric and you. And your wife."

"What is it?" Robert asked gently, already knowing all of it.

"I've been struggling—I'm sure you know this—about the marriage. I made my career, and even sex, seem like obstacles. Eric and I couldn't make sense of it, but it had nothing to do with Eric. It was all inside me, and now I know what it was."

"What do you know?"

"That something inside me knew that I shoudn't marry him."

"Why not?" he asked carefully.

"Because my mother was crazy. She killed herself," Charlie said simply, without emotion. Then she sighed and added, "And I am my mother's daughter."

"NO!" Robert said with such energy that Charlie jumped. "No, Charlie. You aren't crazy. You can't inherit what your mother had."

"How do you know what my mother had?"

"I know, honey. Maybe I should have told you. I would have if I'd known how much it worried you. I spoke with her doctors. And I spoke with teachers, school counselors and doctors who knew you. They all agreed that you are fine. Healthy. Normal. You're not at all like her. You never will be."

What Robert said was mostly true. They all agreed that Charlie was a remarkably well-adjusted, mentally healthy child. But no one could *guarantee* that what Mary had wasn't hereditary. How could they? They didn't know what it was.

Still, they all believed that Charlie was—would always be—perfectly healthy.

"You knew she killed herself?" Charlie asked, amazed, "Does Eric know?"

"No."

"Sometimes I feel crazy," she said urgently. She wanted to believe what Robert had told her. But . . . "I've felt crazy these past few months."

"You can make yourself *feel* crazy. Anyone can. Everyone does at some time.

But you're *not* crazy," Robert said emphatically. He continued gently, "You've just been troubled by some understandably troublesome questions. And now that you have the answers, you should feel relieved."

"I *was* relieved, in the opposite way. Because I could set Eric free."

"Don't you dare. It was *fair* for you to be angry about giving up your dream of Harvard Law School. That wasn't crazy. My son needs to be reminded of his egocentrism at times. He talked to me about moving InterLand to Boston. We can do it, Charlie. We *will* do it."

"You really think I'm not crazy?" she asked, still wanting to be sure, wanting to believe him, barely hearing anything else he said.

"I *know* you're not crazy."

"And you want me for a daughter-in-law?"

"Desperately. And a law partner. Even if it means I have to take the Massachusetts Bar," Robert said laughing, relieved to see the clarity and sparkle begin to return to her eyes.

"I don't mind moving here. Penn has turned out some pretty fine attorneys," she said, teasing him about his own alma mater.

"Are you really leaving tonight?" Robert asked, noticing the almost empty house for the first time. All his attention had been focused on her.

"No. I guess I should see Eric. When is he returning?"

"This evening. He's gone skiing for the day. Why don't you spend the day with me? See what being an attorney's really like," Robert suggested.

He didn't want her to be alone today. Not in this house after what she'd been through. A fine guardian he'd turned out to be. He should have insisted that she see a counselor, someone to help her after her mother's death. He should have anticipated her anxieties. Maybe he should have simply told her what he knew about Mary.

He had planned to, eventually, when she was older. But it was the fragile, sensitive little girl who had needed to know the truth and had suffered needlessly because she didn't know.

As Robert waited for her to finish packing, he hoped that Charlie's suffering was finally over and that she and Eric could have the happy life they deserved. And Robert hoped that his son wouldn't bring Victoria home with him that evening.

When Eric returned at nine, exhausted from a day spent in bed at Victoria's parents" ski cabin, he was alone. Charlie greeted him at the door with a smile that made him wish he had never seen Victoria in his life. Charlie told him what had happened, what she had learned and how Robert had helped her. She believed—as she thought about it more carefully, gently and patiently guided by Robert—that she really was fine. She had just been so scared. She had almost been a victim of a self-fulfilling prophecy.

"I inherited a lively imagination from my mother," she said sadly, "But maybe, hopefully, that is all."

Except I hope I inherited her boundless capacity to love and to give and to understand, Charlie thought as Eric held her. She knew he had spent the day with that girl, whoever she was. I have to try to understand it, she thought, succeeding a little, *enough*. She could see the regret and guilt in Eric's eyes.

"I love you so much, Charlie," he whispered.

"I love you, Eric. Make love to me."

"No."

"Yes. Tonight. Tomorrow night. Every night."

"No. On our wedding night. The reason I wanted to make love to you so desperately was because I was trying to get even closer to you, to find out what was really wrong. Now we know. Now I can wait. You really do want to wait, don't you?"

"Yes."

In the middle of February, Victoria telephoned Eric's room in Cambridge. Charlie was there with Eric. She saw the horror on his face and heard his words.

"How could you let this happen? . . . I thought you *were* protected . . . Why didn't you tell me? . . . Are you sure it's . . . What do you want me to do about it?"

Victoria told him that she was pregnant. Almost three months. It must have happened at Thanksgiving. The baby was definitely his.

For the next two weeks, Eric and Charlie talked about it, cried about it and tried to find a way to make it right.

There was only one way.

"The baby has to have its father," Charlie said from a belief rooted deep in her soul. She hadn't had a father. Babies needed their fathers.

"All I know, Eric, is that the joy of watching your child grow is the greatest joy in life," Robert said, aching for Eric and Charlie but remembering his own joy when he saw his tiny son for the first time. Even now as his beloved son's life was altered—exactly as his own life had been altered—by a senseless moment of lust, Robert believed that the pain would give way to pleasure as soon as the baby was born.

Eric would be happy. Victoria would be happy. The baby would be happy.

Florence was *already* ecstatic. Eric and Victoria were meant to be together. Charlie had been all wrong for Eric.

Eventually they would all be happy.

Except Charlie. Charlie would suffer, as she had before, an innocent fragile victim. Charlie might never recover. Robert lay awake at night worrying about Charlie. He would call her often, he decided. He would see her when he could. He would try to help her through this great loss. This *other* loss.

As Eric and Victoria were exchanging wedding vows in front of their families in the middle of March, Charlie was experiencing the *ultimate closeness* with a first-year law student she had met three days before.

Two days later, she sat in the Dean's Office at the Harvard Law School. The dean had received her letter, and he had called her in.

"You want to start law school this fall? After only three years of college?"

"Yes."

"That's why you took your LSATs last fall?"

"Yes."

"Why did you wait until now to apply? The deadline for applications was months ago."

"I thought I would be moving to Philadelphia. I was planning to be married. But not anymore."

"And that won't change."

"No. He married someone else." Charlie had waited until after the wedding.

Until the end, she had hoped that it wouldn't happen. Even though she knew it had to.

"Well, your grades are exceptional. As are your LSATs. As is your letter of recommendation."

"What letter?" she asked anxiously.

"From Robert Lansdale."

"I didn't ask him to write a letter. I wanted to do this on my own," Charlie said weakly.

"You did it on your own. I made up my mind before I asked you to come see me. Mr. Lansdale's letter just arrived today. He offers to pay for your entire education."

"It's not necessary."

"That's between you and Mr. Lansdale. Anyway, Charlotte, I am happy to offer you a position in next fall's entering class at Harvard Law School."

On the way back to her dormitory, Charlie met Eric. It wasn't an accident. He was waiting for her. She noticed his shiny gold wedding band immediately.

"Eric, I can't stand seeing you," she said, desperately trying to get past him, away from him. Eric stood his ground, blocking her path, forcing her to look at him. "I know you have to finish your classes up here this quarter, but let's try to avoid seeing each other. *Please*."

"Charlie, I just wanted to tell you—"

"What?" she asked helplessly. *Leave me alone*.

"That I love you."

"Well don't. Don't say it or think it or feel it. Another woman needs your love now, Eric. Give it to her," Charlie said. Tears streamed down her face as she ran away from the man she loved.

Charlie married the first-year law student a few months later. The marriage lasted six months.

During her three years of law school, Charlie spoke to Robert every few months. If he didn't call her, she called him.

"Listen to this torts problem, Mr. Lansdale," she said one day over the phone, her voice lilting, her love of law school obvious.

"Call me Robert."

"Maybe after I graduate."

They talked about Eric only once, two years after the baby, a son, was born.

"How's Eric?" Charlie asked softly. She didn't hate him anymore. She was happy in law school. She hadn't found anyone to love, but she was happy. She missed him only when she allowed herself to think about him, but she didn't allow herself to often. *No fantasies*.

"He's good, Charlie. He's a much better president for InterLand than I ever was."

"You really wanted to practice law full time," she said.

"Yes. But Eric has a knack for business. He loves buying land and building beautiful buildings. Which is, after all, what InterLand is all about. He's opening corporate offices in Dallas, Chicago and San Francisco. He's already taken over some smaller development companies in those areas," Robert said proudly. InterLand was flourishing under Eric's able management.

"How's the baby?"

"Bobby? He's wonderful. Eric loves him very much. He's Eric's life, really. Eric's work keeps him busy, but Bobby is his life," Robert said gently as he thought about his son and his grandson, his namesake. Eric had the kind of relationship with Bobby that Robert had with Eric. It was what Robert had hoped for his son.

And Eric loved Victoria, the way he, Robert, loved Florence, as a friend, companion and the mother of his precious child.

Robert attended Charlie's graduation from law school. He visited her once at her office with one of Boston's most prestigious law firms. They didn't talk as often after her graduation. Robert knew that she was doing well. He could hear it in her voice. And as much as he liked talking to *her*, Robert worried that his voice only reminded her of Eric. And all that unhappiness.

Robert and Charlie hadn't spoken for almost six months when he called her. It was late on an autumn night, five and a half years after Eric married Victoria.

"Charlie, it's Robert."

"Robert!" Charlie exclaimed, calling him Robert for the first time, without even thinking about it or realizing it because there was something so personal, so emotional, in his voice.

"Eric needs you, Charlie. Please come to him," Robert said.

Chapter 28

James let the phone ring twenty times. Then he hung up and re-dialed. After twenty more unanswered rings, he telephoned the airline. Lynne's flight had arrived, on schedule, six hours before. Then James phoned their neighbor. No, she hadn't seen Lynne's car. Only the living room light was on. James had turned it on before he left.

James looked at his watch. Ten minutes before six. He had to meet the others in Eric's suite in ten minutes.

Where *was* she?

James dialed Lynne's mother's number in Denver. He didn't want to alarm her, but he was alarmed, and she might know.

Lynne answered the phone. It was beside her bed.

"Lynne!"

"James? How did you know I was here?"

"I didn't. You weren't at home. I thought your mother might know where you were. Why are you there?"

Lynne told him about what had happened that morning on the flight from LaGuardia to O'Hare.

"Have you seen a doctor?"

"I have an appointment for nine tomorrow morning. I feel better now after resting all day."

"But you'll keep the appointment," James said emphatically.

"Do you think my mother would let me miss it?" she asked lightly, forgetting for a moment that she was talking to the new James, the James she hated, the James she had to leave. He sounded like the old James, her caring, loving James. "Why did you call home?"

"Because I wanted to see how you were feeling. And because I wanted to talk to you about Thanksgiving." And because he had spent the afternoon with a woman who reminded him of Lynne, who reminded him how much he loved

Lynne. What he and Charlie talked about had scared him.

"The plans for Thanksgiving will have to change anyway. I'll probably take this week off instead. I guess I'll be working Thanksgiving week."

"If you're well."

"I will be. How's—" Lynne stopped. She started to ask him about his trip to Maui. It was a question she would have asked the old James.

"What?"

"Nothing."

"I'll call you tomorrow to see what the doctor said. It may be this late or later. We're spending the day at the construction site."

The family practitioner who Lynne saw at nine the next morning made the diagnosis almost immediately. He confirmed it by running a blood test that returned within an hour. He referred Lynne to a specialist in Denver. Lynne met with her that afternoon. She confirmed the diagnosis, performed several additional tests and provided Lynne with the name of a specialist in San Francisco.

When James called that night, Lynne told him, truthfully, that the doctors told her she had nothing serious. She would be fine.

She didn't tell him that she had to be checked again in a month. Then, if the diagnosis still held, she would have to leave him, quickly, before he found out. She only hoped that her strength would return in time.

The doctors said it would. But she had to eat. And rest.

Peter Pan opened on Thanksgiving Day. James and Leslie sat four rows away from Kathleen and Mark who sat next to Ross and Stacy. Eric and Charlie sat in the first patrons' box, theater left.

When the final curtain fell, the audience was silent, stunned, not wanting it to be over. Ever. *Not* wanting to leave. *Wanting* to hear the love duets again. Wanting it all to begin again.

Wanting to stay in Never Never Land with Peter and Wendy.

Finally, a single clap broke the silence. Then another. Then the sound, a faint rustling of the entire audience standing up almost in unison, was heard. Then, with the roar of clapping and shouts of "Bravo," the spell was broken. It had to be. Unlike Peter, they had to grow up. They had a real world to face.

After the final curtain call, the audience filed out, strangely silent. The theatergoers were lost in thought, knowing they had witnessed a most remarkable theater event. They had been part of it, and now it was part of them.

"Wouldn't it be wonderful to be so young and so talented?" Charlie asked Eric as they drove to his penthouse in Pacific Heights. "I can't believe she's the same person who played Joanna. Two unforgettable roles. I wonder what she's like."

"I want to go backstage for a minute, Stacy," Ross said begrudgingly, giving way to the reality that the show was over. He had seen it in rehearsal a hundred times, but tonight it moved him as it never had. Wendy moved him. He wanted to see her.

Ross forgot for a moment that he would be seeing Janet, not Wendy.

"To congratulate the Ice Maiden?" Stacy asked, a little annoyed.

Ross frowned at her, but it *did* make him remember that it would be Janet backstage.

"Does it bother you to see her, Mark?" Kathleen asked. It bothered *her.* Janet's—Wendy's—allure, her sensuality and her loveliness were irresistible. Even Kathleen felt it.

"No, Kathleen," Mark said firmly.

Leslie hadn't seen James for ten days, not since before he left for Maui. Lynne had been at home recuperating. She was better now, James said. She was flying again.

James held Leslie's hand as they left the theater and in the car on the way home. They didn't speak. Both were deep in thought. Because of *Peter Pan*.

I'm living in Never Never Land, James thought, squeezing Leslie's hand, not wanting to let go, knowing that, like Peter, he would have to. Someday. Someday soon.

Oh, James, Leslie thought. We are saying good-bye, aren't we?

Each time Leslie and James made love—that night and the other nights in the three weeks until it was over—it was as if they would never touch each other again. It seemed they were both trying to remember every part of it because soon they would only have the memory. In those weeks, Leslie and James gave each other the indelible memory of a love that had to stop but would never really end.

James was waiting in the apartment when Leslie arrived home on December fifteenth. He stood up when she came in, but he didn't move toward her. Leslie saw the key, the still-shiny key that she had given him ten weeks before, lying on the coffee table.

Leslie knew this day was coming. She was prepared for it. Still, the hot tears splashed down her cheeks. At the sight of her tears, James's eyes filled, and he broke the vow he had made.

He put his arms around her, holding her, rocking her.

"Leslie. Don't cry. Please."

"I'm sorry, James. I will miss you so much."

"Leslie," he whispered, unable to speak.

They had both planned for this moment. They had rehearsed the mature, sensitive, brave things they would say. They both believed it had to be this way. It was best. They were lucky to have had the time together. They would always care. . . .

But neither could speak. The emotion was too strong.

They just held each other tightly. Finally, moving at the same moment, they pulled away.

"Good-bye, darling Leslie," he whispered hoarsely.

"Good-bye, James," she whispered through her tears.

James returned to his empty house. Lynne was in Chicago. She would be back in the morning.

Lynne. Her energy had returned, but she seemed different. Preoccupied. Almost compulsively busy. She spent every evening, long after he had gone to bed, writing. She had created her own deadline—*soon*—for her next Monica book, but she hadn't asked him to start illustrating it.

Lynne was pleasant, efficient and energetic. *Impersonal.*

They still hadn't made love.

James decided that Lynne was simply rebounding from her illness. Now that her energy had returned, she was making up for lost time.

Lynne's behavior was different, but it was not how she would behave if she knew about Leslie. She would confront him with it.

Still, they needed to talk. Now that *she* was well and *he* had said good-bye to Leslie.

James realized how little he and Lynne had said to each other in the past three months. He wanted to get close to her again. He wanted to fall in love with her again and to renew the promises—promises of love and friendship and trust—they had made to each other.

Lynne had the repeat test on December fourteenth. It confirmed the diagnosis. It meant she had to talk to James soon, as soon as she returned from Chicago. She called him at his office when she returned on the sixteenth.

"Lynne? Is everything all right?" James asked. She never called him at work.

"Yes. Fine. I just got in. James, we need to talk," she said tentatively. *How can I confront him with this? I know I'm right, but I don't want to hear about it. I don't want to see his face*. She decided, then, impulsively, to tell him over the phone. "James, I know that you're having an affair. I know it started September twelfth. I haven't had the energy to deal with it until now. But now I do. I want a divorce, James. I can't live with you anymore. I *can't*."

Lynne stopped abruptly, breathless, her heart pounding, her stomach aching.

"It's *over*, Lynne," James said quietly, shaken.

"Does it matter?" she asked sharply as her anger returned. He had admitted it. It was all true. A tiny part of her had held on to the hope that there was, that there could be, some other explanation.

"I love you."

"No," she said swiftly. "Not if you did this to me. To us."

"Lynne, we have all the time in the world to end our marriage. Let me talk to you. *Please*."

"It's pointless. And painful. I just want out, James. Please don't make it hard for me. It's not fair. It's been hard enough."

He could hear the pain—pain from months of suffering—in her voice. She had known for a long time. For the entire time.

"I'm coming home now. Wait for me. Please."

On the way home, James's mind spun as he tried to remember why it happened, how he could have let it happen. How could he have believed she wouldn't know? How could he have done this to Lynne? To Lynne, of all people . . .

It was what Lynne's father had done to Lynne's mother. Over and over. They stayed together because of their baby girl, because of Lynne, but it harmed Lynne much more than growing up without a father would have harmed her. She watched her mother suffer with each of his affairs. She learned to hate her father.

And she learned to distrust all men. When she grew up, Lynne played with men, toying with their feelings, hurting them the way her father had hurt her mother. And her.

Lynne hated men, distrusted them all. Until she met James.

Slowly, carefully, they had learned to trust each other.

How could I have done this to her? James's mind screamed at him as he drove home. It had all been so easy to rationalize because the proviso had always been, *Lynne will never know.*

Lynne was in the living room curled into the far corner of the overstuffed sofa. When she saw James, she pushed herself deeper into the cushions.

"Lynne, I am so sorry," he said moving toward her, seeing in her eyes that she didn't want him near her. He stood at the opposite end of the sofa.

"You know what's funny?" she asked, her voice bitter. "I really believed we had something. I believed that we had defied the odds. I didn't even have a clue that we were in trouble. Then—*overnight*—everything was different. How could you fall in love with someone else overnight?"

"I didn't, Lynne. She was someone I knew before I met you. I hadn't seen her for nine years. I saw her again by accident. I felt, I *convinced* myself, that I was doing something I should have done nine years ago. I even convinced myself, somehow, that it—our affair—was happening in the past."

James shrugged, realizing the emptiness of his words and how foolish they sounded.

Helplessly, he watched Lynne cry. He watched her pain and felt his own. Pain and regret.

"Talk to me, Lynne."

"Why? Do you want to hear about how much I hate you? About how much I hurt inside?"

"I want you to tell me how we can make it through this," James said firmly, evenly.

"We can't."

"You won't even try?"

"No. Why should I?"

"Because I love you."

"James. I've heard those words before. My father always told my mother that. For years she even believed him."

"Your father never felt this way about your mother. You know that."

"I do? From here it looks like, feels like, you're exactly the same kind of man."

James sighed. Why should she believe him? He hadn't given her any reason to.

"I stopped seeing her because I didn't wat to take the risk that you would find out. I didn't want to risk losing you."

"That's why you ended it," Lynne said slowly. "But why did you start it?"

"It seemed different, Lynne. Something that was very important to me personally. It was a way to make sense of what had happened in high school. It had nothing to do with you and me. Really. I don't know how to make you understand that. It didn't have anything to do with us. I didn't look for her because I was unhappy with us. I wasn't. I'm not. I want to spend my life with you. I didn't look for her at all. It just happened. It could never have happened with anyone else. It could never happen again."

Lynne's tears stopped as she listened. Her brown eyes stared at him with curiosity. She knew James so well. She knew that James—the James she had loved and trusted—didn't lie.

"I almost believe you, James," she said softly. "*Somehow* you honestly thought this didn't break the rules, that it transcended the rules."

James waited, barely breathing. Lynne was talking to him now, not as the little girl hurt by the father she hated but as Lynne, the woman he loved, the woman with whom he had created a union of love and trust.

But Lynne didn't say any more. She just stared at him, loving him, hating him and wanting him. Wishing it all was different.

"Will you give it a chance, Lynne?"

"I don't know." *Yes*.

"We can't lose more than we've lost if you leave now."

"Oh yes we can," she said instantly, without thinking.

"What?"

"We can lose it again," Lynne explained, flustered for a moment. "We can get it back and lose it again. It's already happened once."

"It won't happen again, Lynne. It won't. It can't."

Lynne sighed. It was a great risk. Maybe too great. She could only give it a month. She couldn't let him find out. Not unless she was sure of him and of his love. How would she know?

She would know. *But* she had known before. She had known, confidently, that he loved her. Until one day he changed.

Now he was back.

"James, I am so afraid," she whispered.

He moved to her then, carefully holding her hands, gently touching her tear-damp cheeks.

"I'm afraid, too, Lynne. I'm afraid of losing you."

Shreve and Company, one of San Francisco's oldest jewelry stores, located two blocks off Union Square near Gump's and Abercrombie and Fitch, was cluttered with shoppers. It was Christmas Eve. Decisions *had* to be made. A gold necklace for a girlfriend, diamond and sapphire earrings for a lover, an eternity ring for a wife, gold cuff-links—they could be engraved later—for a husband or a boyfriend.

Mark was there to pick up Kathleen's engagement ring. The store manager had promised that, despite the Christmas rush, the flawless, two-and-a-half-carat brilliant cut diamond would be in the six-pronged Tiffany setting by Christmas Eve. The diamond wasn't a family heirloom. It was simply a perfect diamond that Kathleen's father had purchased years before as an investment.

It had already quadrupled in value and was now worth at least a quarter of a million dollars. But when William Jenkins saw the look in Kathleen's eyes when he offered it to her—as long as Mark didn't object—it became priceless. And valueless. Because it would never be sold.

Mark didn't object. He was genuinely unthreatened by Kathleen's vast wealth.

Janet was in Shreve and Company on Christmas Eve to buy a pair of pearl earrings. It was a combination Christmas and birthday present to herself. Since her shopping spree in New York in October, Janet paid more attention to her appearance and to things that made her feel good. She had been thinking about buying a nice pair of pearl earrings for two weeks.

But not today, Janet decided after a few moments in the store, after gazing over the sea of anxious, indecisive shoppers. She shook her head slightly and turned to leave. Janet met Mark at the revolving door as he was leaving, the purple velvet box with Kathleen's ring tucked safely in an inside pocket.

"Janet!"

"Hello, Mark," she said, then almost immediately was swept out the door by the press of the crowd.

Mark was behind her, but he paused to let several women enter the revolving door ahead of him.

Janet stood outside, uncertain whether to leave, to lose herself in the crowded sidewalk, or to wait. Why wait for him? Why not?

Mark smiled when he saw her, obviously pleased that she had decided to wait.

"Hi. It's pretty crowded, isn't it?"

"Too crowded," she said, suddenly wanting to escape from the crowds. And from him? No. Seeing him didn't make her hurt. Not yet.

"Would you like to go for a cup of coffee? A hot buttered rum?"

In Omaha, at Christmas, they would drink hot buttered rum in front of a roaring fire. In Omaha, at Christmas, they had snow. In San Francisco, at Christmas, it was fifty degrees and the sun was shining.

"Sure," Janet said, glancing at her watch. She had time before the evening show. "Coffee would be nice."

The Christmas Eve crowds were in the stores, at the cash registers and cluttering the sidewalks, but the restaurants were empty. It was the last minute. The frenzied shoppers could not stop to eat. No more procrastination.

Janet and Mark found an almost empty bakery with a small dining area decorated with white wrought iron chairs and tables with green and mauve linen. Homey. Quaint.

"This is nice," Janet said, referring to the bakery. Maybe referring to seeing him.

"It's nice to see you," Mark said, meaning it, aching a little. "How's the show?"

"We've added five matinees for this week alone!"

"It's an incredible show. You are incredible."

"Oh, you've seen it?"

"Opening night."

"What did Kathleen think?" Janet asked, amazed at how easily she said Kathleen's name. "I got the impression from Ross that she and some of the other board members opposed the changes we made. Too iconoclastic."

"Kathleen was raised on *Peter Pan* in all its innocence."

"We all were."

"Anyway, all her doubts were erased when she saw it. In fact, she's seen it about five times. It's what she does when I'm on call."

"Have you seen it again?"

"No," Mark said, looking down at his coffee, away from her wide gray eyes. He could see it once, see her once, but after that it would be too hard.

"Leslie says you're moving to Boston."

"Yes. To do a cardiology fellowship. And . . ." Mark paused. Leslie had probably told her the rest.

"You're getting married," Janet said.

He looked at her quizzically. He was talking to Janet about his marriage to Kathleen. It felt strange. Wrong.

"Mark," Janet said, suddenly smiling, suddenly feeling better than she had felt in a long time, "I'm happy for you. I honestly am. We had our chance. It didn't work. It doesn't mean we shouldn't have other chances."

Janet stopped, amazed by her own words, amazed by the hope in what she said. Hope for his happiness. And for her own.

"Are you involved with someone?" Mark asked carefully.

"No," she said tossing her blond hair, a little embarrassed. Then she said, seriously, honestly, "Not yet."

But someday. Maybe.

After she left Mark, kissing him lightly on the cheek, wishing him only happiness, Janet walked back to the theater. Her spirits soared. She had seen him and it hadn't hurt. Not *too* much. Seeing Mark made her remember the possibility of love, the hope of love. Not with him. But, maybe, sometime with someone else.

Janet felt free, happy, almost whole again as she turned into the front door of Union Square Theater and into Ross.

"Oh! Ross. Sorry!" Janet giggled.

"It's OK," he said surprised, intrigued. What was going on? Where was the famous off-stage reserve? "You seem a little up."

Janet shrugged amiably. The glow didn't fade.

"I guess I am," she said as she breezed through the foyer toward her dressing room.

After ten feet, she stopped and spun around.

"Ross?"

"Yes?"

She walked back toward him, her heart pounding.

"I wondered if you would like to come over for dinner."

"Sure," he said calmly, carefully. "When?"

"Umm," Janet hadn't thought it out. She hadn't thought at all. It was an impulse. "Some night when we don't have a show."

"That's almost never. At least in the near term."

They were running the show every night—except Christmas—throughout the holidays. Maybe longer. The demand was that great, and so far the cast was willing.

"Tomorrow night," she said suddenly.

Christmas. It was the only night they weren't performing.

"It's Christmas!" Ross said immediately, before the meaning of her suggestion registered. It meant that Janet had no plans for Christmas.

Ross planned to meet Stacy's flight from New York at seven in the evening and take her to the Carlton Club Kids Christmas Celebration. Expendable plans, he thought, looking at Janet. Except that he couldn't really cancel his plans with Stacy at this late date.

"I know," Janet said, shrugging, suddenly feeling foolish, the glow a little dimmer. "It's just a night when we don't have a show."

"I have plans for the evening but none for the day. How about breakfast or brunch or lunch?"

"Brunch. At my cottage. It's a bit of a drive."

"That's OK. Now what's wrong?" he asked. Janet was giggling.

"I don't have any food! The stores are going to be closed tomorrow morning, aren't they? I don't really have time to go out now, not before the show," she said shaking her head, smiling.

"This is a great invitation," Ross teased.

"It seemed like a good idea at the time. Maybe we should do it some other time?"

"No," Ross said lightly but firmly. "Let's go into the office right now so you can make me a shopping list and draw me a map. I'll go to the store while you're in makeup. We can put the groceries in your car after the show."

Janet followed him into the theater administrative offices. She still felt good. *This* felt good.

"Let's see. Eggs. Milk. Cheese. Butter."

"Pretty low cholesterol so far."

"Oh! What do you want to eat?"

"No, I'm teasing. It's fine."

"All right. Chocolate cake mix. Double fudge frosting mix—"

"Whoa."

"It's my birthday."

"Christmas?"

Janet nodded.

"In that case," Ross said, "we'd better add champagne to this list."

* * *

Long before Ross arrived at the cottage at eleven Christmas morning, Janet regretted her impulsive invitation.

I don't know him. I have nothing to say to him. Nothing personal. We can talk about the show. Then what? I wish I hadn't . . . what? Seen Mark? Felt so good?

Janet didn't know except that the good feelings were replaced by anxiety as she waited for Ross. 671

But Janet's worry about conversation was unnecessary. Ross had a lot to say and many questions to ask as he poked around her cozy cottage while she made omelettes.

"Who owns this?"

"The people in the big house down the road. They're away for the holidays."

"How did you find it?"

"I was on a drive."

"Way up here?"

"I used to go for a lot of long drives after Mark and I separated," she said, then blushed.

"Is there anything between you and the ocean except those hills?" Ross asked, swiftly changing the subject. He didn't want her to retreat.

"No." She smiled, relieved, appreciative that he didn't press her about Mark. Even though she felt better—good—she didn't want to talk about Mark. "Just very pretty land that all comes with the rent. We can take a walk, later, if you have time. It's so beautiful."

Ross studied the photographs of her from *South Pacific* and the productions she did at the University of Nebraska and in community theater in Omaha.

"This was really all you'd done before you showed up for the audition last year?"

"I guess it was enough. I think I learned a lot from those amateur groups. No one was a prima donna. No one was a star. Especially in the community theater in Omaha. We were a family."

"Plenty of prima donnas started in community theater. You just don't have the prima donna personality."

He asked her about her childhood. She told him, briefly, pleasantly. Then she asked him about his. Ross told her, expansively, because his anecdotes made her laugh. He kept talking because of the soft interested look in her serious gray eyes as she listened. And because of the way her eyes sparkled when she laughed.

They walked all the way to the ocean. Janet showed him her favorite spots. She led him along her favorite path through the lane of eucalyptus trees.

"This is where I practice," she said, spreading her arms toward the green rolling hills and the blue ocean beyond. "And no one can hear me except the seagulls and the rabbits and the deer."

"Sing something for me," Ross said lightly.

Janet frowned, her eyes squeezed shut. The pain of a memory had hit her, unexpected, surprising, unsettling.

"I can't," she said finally, opening her eyes. She sang all day every day for Ross at the theater, but this was different. Private. Intimate. It was what she used to do for Mark. It wasn't something she could do again. Not yet.

Ross smiled, sorry he had said something to upset her, but relieved that it had passed quickly.

They walked along the beach, the cold wind blowing their hair and putting color in their cheeks. They didn't try to talk above the wind. Ross realized, as the afternoon wore on, that Janet didn't need to talk. She was comfortable with silences. She was comfortable to walk beside him, enjoying the beauty, without speaking.

Janet was peaceful. It made him feel peaceful to be with her.

She walked out to his car with him when he left at five. He had already stayed too long. He would have to drive directly to the airport.

"Thank you," he said. "Happy birthday."

Janet smiled at him, swaying almost imperceptibly closer to him.

His lips found hers, soft, warm and eager for his. He folded his arms around her and felt her softness press against him. Willing, sensual, passionate. They kissed for a long, soft, warm moment.

"I don't want to leave you," he whispered into her ear.

She looked up at him, her eyes glowing, her cheeks pink. She touched his lips lightly with her finger.

He didn't want to leave, and she didn't want him to.

But he had to.

"I'll see you tomorrow," he whispered hoarsely as he got into his car. And the next day. And the next, he thought, forgetting for a moment that Stacy was arriving for the week.

Stacy. Everything had changed. Plans were expendable, after all.

Chapter 29

Slowly, with painstaking care, James and Lynne fell in love again. Most days, because they were trying so hard, because they wanted it so much, they made some progress; but some days, they seemed to lose all that they had gained, and it seemed hopeless.

They spent the evenings they had together talking quietly, sitting together, holding hands. James called her from work when she was at home during the day, and he called her when she was away, every time she was away, talking for hours long distance.

James called her on Christmas night in her hotel room in Dallas.

"What's wrong, Lynne?"

Her voice was flat, defeated.

"You know what I thought about all day?" she asked weakly.

"No. Tell me," James urged, knowing that it had to be something—something painful—about Leslie. But knowing, too, that they had to talk about it.

"You quit smoking for *her*, didn't you?"

"Lynne," James began. It was something Lynne had tried gently, without nagging and without success, to get him to do. Now he had done it, quit for good, because of Leslie. But he had done it for Lynne, too. For the rest of their lives together.

"Well, I know you did. I've spent the whole day thinking about it, hating both of you, torn apart by anger. I can't get rid of the feeling. In the past nine days, I thought we made progress, but today, tonight, I'm back where I was," she said. Wanting to leave, she thought. Needing to get away from you.

"I tear myself apart with anger, too, Lynne. But the difference is that I know it will never happen again. I know what it meant. I know how I feel about you.

I know that you can trust *me*, but I can only tell you that. I can't make you feel it or believe it."

"I want to believe it." I am just going to have to decide, she thought. By mid-January at the latest. So much depends on it: my life, James's life, and another life, an innocent life that could be damaged, either way, if I make the wrong decision. Lynne sighed heavily, weighted by the burden of the decision that was hers to make. "James, talk to me about something that has nothing to do with us. I'm wallowing and I'm getting nowhere."

They spent hours talking about the news, books, politics and the weather. Anything to keep communication open. Something drove them both to try to make it work, but they couldn't force it. It had to happen. They had to give it every chance.

By the end of the third week, they had begun working together on Lynne's new Monica book. They spent the evenings talking about the illustrations that Lynne wanted. Sometimes it felt almost normal. Almost good.

James called her at home one afternoon. He had an idea for an illustration. She sounded distracted. She had been writing.

"Hi, am I interrupting something?" he asked as soon as he heard her voice.

"No," she said. "Yes, you are, James. I'm having an affair with a guy I've known since kindergarten."

They were both silent, shocked for a moment. Then she laughed. And he laughed. And he told her he was on his way home to put an end to it.

They made love that afternoon and that night, for the first time since September eleventh, the night before James took Leslie out for her birthday dinner. The next day Lynne hated him again, remembering what he had done, but the anger only lasted for an hour. It disappeared before she had a chance to tell him about it.

A week later Lynne returned at seven in the evening. She had been gone for two days. She found James sitting in the living room. The curtains were drawn, blocking the view of the South Bay and preventing anyone from seeing in. They usually didn't need such privacy in the living room.

Lynne's heartbeat quickened and her entire body tingled with anticipation. When she saw his eyes, she knew.

"Take off your clothes, Lynne," he said softly, seductively, not moving.

She closed her eyes for a moment. James.

It was *her* fantasy. One of the sexual fantasies she had trusted him enough to tell him. She had told him all of them. They were similar. They allowed him to control her as she had never allowed any man to control her. She was excited by his sexual power and by his desire for her.

James would interrupt whatever she was doing, quietly taking the pen out of her hand if she was writing, firmly turning off the stove if she was preparing dinner . . . It didn't matter what she was doing. That was part of the fantasy: When he wanted her, nothing else mattered. She never said no.

James would tell her to undress, and he would watch, his eyes appreciative, passionate and full of desire for her. Then she would stand in front of him naked, proud of her perfect body, feeling him wanting her, feeling her body respond to his gaze.

Sometimes the pleasure would be only for her. James would kiss her, warm gentle kisses until she lay exhausted and satisfied, and he would still be dressed. Sometimes he would undress, too, and make love to her slowly, forcing her to wait, not allowing her to be impatient. Sometimes they would make love quickly because just the sight of each other from across the room made them ready, desperate to be together.

They did whatever James wanted. It was part of the fantasy—her fantasy. James was in control. Because she trusted him. She never said no.

"Take off your clothes," he repeated.

"James, no," she said weakly. She wasn't ready for this. He was forcing her to prove that she trusted him again and that she would allow him to control her. No, her mind screamed. But her body trembled. *Yes, I want this. I want* *him. I need to be wanted this way again. By him.*

But what about . . . ? her mind screamed back.

He won't notice. It's barely noticeable, her body argued, pulsing with excitement.

"Yes, Lynne," he said. He commanded.

Lynne watched him as she removed her uniform: the tailored jacket, the checked blouse, the straight skirt. Their eyes locked, eloquently transmitting the feelings and desires of their bodies across the room. She moved closer until she stood almost in front of him. Then she took off the rest of her clothes.

When she was naked, he pulled his eyes away from hers, as he always did, to look at her. To caress her body with his eyes. She felt his eyes on her neck, her breasts, her stomach and between her thighs. She shuddered as waves of desire swept through her.

Then suddenly, he frowned and looked at her.

"Lynne?" he asked, his voice husky, but the mood suddenly, inexplicably shattered.

"What?" *What's wrong? Don't do this to me! I am trying to trust you.*

"Come here," he said tentatively.

"What, James?" *No, he can't tell. I can't even tell.*

He put his hand carefully on the lower part of her abdomen. The bulge was almost imperceptible, but it was there.

"Lynne?" he asked softly, looking up at her face.

Tears streamed out of her sad brown eyes. She cried silently.

"You're pregnant?"

Lynne nodded slowly, soberly. It was too soon. She still wasn't sure. And now it was too late. Now he knew.

James pulled her onto his lap, gently wrapping his arms around her trembling, naked body.

"Really?" he asked softly. She nodded again, looking at him. She had never seen such happiness in his eyes.

"Really," she said, wiping her tears.

"When?"

"When else? The last time we were together. September eleventh. The baby's just four months old."

"And it's OK?" he asked, the realization sweeping through him in waves of elation.

"So far. It's where it should be. In the uterus. Growing normally despite the scar tissue from the infections."

"This is what made you ill?"

"Yes. I wouldn't have felt so ill—so frustrated at being ill—if I'd had any idea. The G.P. I saw in Denver diagnosed it immediately even though I told him it wasn't possibe. I guess even the whirlies, like I had on the plane, aren't uncommon."

James held her face with his hands, looking into her eyes, making her look at him.

"Were you going to tell me?"

"Not if we got divorced. No."

"I had a right to know," James said sharply.

"You gave up that right the night after the baby was conceived," Lynne answered with a sharpness matching his.

Lynne watched the effect of her words register as pain in his eyes. The eyes that had been so happy a few moments before. *Am I ever going to stop punishing him? Or myself?*

Lynne curled her arms around his head and kissed his forehead.

"I'm sorry, James. Since I've known, all I have thought about was how to give this baby the best possible chance. I want the baby so much. I want it to feel safe and happy. I don't want it to have the kind of childhood I had."

"Or I had," James murmured.

"We're not likely candidates for parents of the year, are we?"

"Maybe we are, Lynne. At least we know how not to do it. And we both want the baby so much."

"You do? I didn't know."

"Neither did I. I guess we had rationalized it all pretty well since we didn't think we could have children. But when you told me, I felt something I've never felt before. I want our baby, Lynne. Just like I want our baby's mother."

James kissed her until she trembled against him and her body moved in a rhythm of love and desire.

"Is it all right to make love?" he asked, lowering her beneath him on the sofa, taking off his clothes.

"Yes, James. Mothers-to-be have their fantasies, too," she said, knotting her fingers in his black hair, breathlessly anticipating the feel of his naked flesh against hrs.

"I love you so much, Lynne," James whispered. And as they moved together, he said over and over, "So much. So much."

The next day, James called her from work.

"I want you to stop flying. We don't need the money. You can write your books and be at home with me. I want you at home. I want both of you at home."

"All right, James," Lynne said laughing. "I'll quit."

"Really?"

"That easy."

The next week he arrived home with his black portfolio full of sketches.

"I want to show you something."

"Maui?" Lynne asked, interested. He had been working so hard on the resort project. Days, nights, weekends. He would make love to her, tuck her into bed and then return to the kitchen table to work into the night.

"No, you've seen all the Maui sketches."

"All the *sensational* Maui sketches."

"Thanks," he said. Eric and Charlie raved about the Maui project every time James saw them, but it was nice to hear it from Lynne. "No, this isn't Maui. It's Monica Manor."

"What?"

"It's a new addition for the house. A room for Monica. A study for you. A study for me. It's principally for Monica, but I threw in some rooms for us, too."

"James, we don't know that the baby is Monica. The baby *could* be James junior."

"The baby will *never* be James junior, but we both think she's a she, don't we?"

"Yes, we think that. But we don't care, do we?"

"No. Not a bit."

James called Lynne in the middle of the afternoon on Friday, two days before Valentine's Day. He knew she had spent the morning supervising the first day of construction of the new addition.

"Hi. How are you?"

"Good. Do you really think these guys are going to pay any attention to all those intricate little lines you drew?"

"I really think they'd better. How's Monica? And Monica?"

"Monica the cat has gotten herself in an almost insoluble dilemma. I'm having a cup of tea hoping she'll be better by the time I return. And," her voice softened a little, choked with emotion, "Monica, the baby, *moved*."

"She did? Really? Why didn't you call me?"

"I called the doctor. It was a funny fluttering feeling. I wanted to be sure everything was OK, but that's what it feels like, and this is when it's supposed to start, in the fifth month. I didn't call you because I didn't think I should bother you." She had almost called him. She had been so excited.

"Call me."

"I will."

"What do you want to do for Valentine's Day?"

"You know."

"So," Mark said, walking up behind Leslie in the tenth floor nursing station, "this is a pretty miserable way for two off call residents to be spending the evening."

"Mark! I just thought I'd check a few charts before I left."

"On your rock-steady patients?" Mark teased. "At eight o'clock on Friday night?"

Leslie smiled at Mark, noticing, as always, how handsome he was. But her heart didn't pound and she didn't tremble.

I've outgrown whatever it was I felt for him, she thought comfortably. Love? *In* love? Now he is a good friend. A dear, good friend.

"I can understand what a single, unattached woman such as myself is doing hiding in the hospital," Leslie said. "But I can't figure out what you're doing here."

"Kathleen's in Hawaii plotting the wedding. She and her friend Betsey did this last year when they planned Betsey's wedding. I'm on my own for a week. So, what about drinks at the Cliff House?"

"You're on."

Their arrival was perfectly timed. The pre-dinner cocktail crowd was just leaving; the after dinner crowd hadn't arrived. They were seated at a window table. The pale yellow moon cast a long shimmering beam across the Pacific Ocean. The waves glowed in the darkness as they crested before crashing onto the rocks and beach below.

"Did you get the invitation to our engagement party?"

"The *engraved* invitation? Yes. Thank you. I'm planning to be there," Leslie said. She had decided she should go. It would be interesting if nothing else. It was in three weeks. She already knew that she wouldn't be on call.

"You can bring a date of course."

"I would if I had one to bring," she said lightly.

"What about the man you were with at *Peter Pan*?"

"Oh. You noticed."

"Naturally," Mark said. Actually, Kathleen had noticed them first, initially simply admiring James and then realizing that he was with Leslie.

Leslie looked at Mark. She hadn't told anyone about any of it.

"He was married. He *is* married. It's a long complicated story, but basically, that's the bottom line."

"Did you think he was going to leave her for you?"

"No, I never thought that. I never even wanted it," Leslie said truthfully. In the months since James left, she had realized that. Even though she missed him all day—every day, every night—she would not have wanted him to leave Lynne because of her. "But it was nice while it lasted."

"I wonder who the right man for you will be," Mark said thoughtfully, considering his own question. "You're such a superwoman. Bright, strong, independent—"

"You make me sound awful!"

"No, Leslie, you're incredible."

Leslie shook her head and held up her hand, signaling him to stop.

"I'm serious, Les," Mark continued, calmly ignoring her protestations. "You're beautiful and gracious. You know exactly what you want to do, and you're doing it. You don't have obvious needs. You'll have to find a man who's as capable and secure as you are."

"I thought you were Mr. Right," Leslie interjected, fortified by the scotch she drank too quickly as she listened to Mark. It made her feel warm and courageous.

"*Me?*" he asked, genuinely surprised, obviously flattered.

"Yes. I had such a crush—not an intern on resident crush like you thought—on you."

"Why didn't I know that?" He could tell from the serious blue eyes that she meant it. That it—he—had been very important to her.

"Because you weren't interested. But it's polite of you to pretend that you might have been."

"I'm not being polite," Mark said seriously, frowning slightly. Why hadn't he known? Because that was his specialty: not knowing the important things that affected himself and the people he cared about.

"Anyway, I had a crush on you while you were falling deeply, irrevocably in love with Kathleen," Leslie said lightly.

"I am deeply, irrevocably in love with her," Mark said gently, his voice becoming tender at the thought of her. Still . . .

"When's the wedding?" Leslie asked suddenly, focusing on what was real, not fantasy.

"June eleventh. I think those invitations are still at the engraver. I hope you can come. It will be at the Carlton Club. It should be nice."

"I'm in University Hospital emergency room in June. If I'm lucky, I'll be off on the eleventh," she said politely, not knowing if she really meant it.

They sat in silence for a while, watching the glittering waves and the winter moon.

"I saw Janet a few months ago," Mark said finally.

"I know. She told me. I think it did her a lot of good to see you."

"Really?"

"Yes. She just seems a lot more relaxed. More comfortable."

"She needs to find someone."

"I think she will," Leslie said. I think she already has, she thought. But there was no point in telling Mark about Ross. Ross, Kathleen's friend.

Their world was already too small.

"I can't go to Mark's and Kathleen's engagement party, Ross."

"You can. It's on Sunday evening. There's no show that night. Only the matinee."

"I don't want to go."

"I thought you said you were over him."

"I *am*."

"So?"

"It doesn't mean that I want to go to his engagement party."

"Why not?"

Janet sighed. Why was he pushing her? Why couldn't he just put his arms around her and tell her that he understood?

"Why not?" he repeated.

"Ross, Mark and I did something very sad and painful to each other. We made promises that we couldn't keep. We turned our hope into anger and bitterness. We're not angry and bitter any longer, but what happened still makes us sad. I think it makes Mark a little sad, a little wistful to see me. I feel the same way about him. There's just no point."

"You think Mark would care if you came to the party?" Ross asked, incredulous. He had seen Kathleen and Mark together. Nothing, no one, could put even the tiniest dent in their obvious joy.

"Yes. I think he would." Janet looked at him, her gray eyes sorrowful. She didn't want to argue with him.

He scowled at her. He didn't want to fight with her. He just wanted to hold her, to walk beside her on the beach, to hear her laugh, to hear her sing and to talk quietly to her.

He wanted to make love with her, but he was waiting for her to let him know when it was time. He was waiting for her to make the next move. He wondered if she would. She was so passionate. And so shy.

He scowled at her, wanting her, angry with her for throwing up this ridiculous obstacle.

He stood up to leave.

"It hurts my feelings, you know, Janet. *I* care about *you*, but *you* won't go to a party with *me* because it might make your ex-husband a little sad. Where does that put me in the list of people that you care about?"

"I'm sorry," Janet whispered to his back as Ross left, slamming the door behind himself.

"Katie?"

"Ross! Hi."

"Katie, do you think Mark would care if Janet came to the engagement party?"

"With you?" Kathleen asked. Then she added coyly, "Ross, are you going out with Janet?"

"Would Mark care if Janet came with anyone," he repeated flatly, avoiding Kathleen's question.

"No, of course he wouldn't care."

"Will you ask him?"

"Why?"

"Just to humor me."

"Sure. *Are* you coming to the party?"

"I don't know. I'd like to. Let me know what Mark says beforehand, though. OK?"

"Sure. I'll call you in a couple of days."

Kathleen didn't call Ross back until the night before the party.

"Here's what he said: 'Of course she can come . . .' "

"Ah-ha," Ross said. It didn't really matter. He had already made up his mind.

"No, wait, that's not all. He said, 'Of course she can come, but it might make us both a little sad.' "

"Oh," Ross murmured. "Does that bother you?"

"No. He's just being honest. I'd be sad if I tried to make a life with someone like Mark, or Janet, and it didn't work out. You make a lot of promises when you get married," Kathleen said.

If Ross came to any of her performances in the five nights following their argument about the engagement party, Janet didn't know it. She didn't see him at the Sunday afternoon matinee, either. She didn't see him, and she didn't talk to him.

By the time she got to her cottage Sunday evening, it was almost dusk. She changed into jeans, found a flashlight and headed toward the ocean.

Ross arrived an hour later and found the cottage empty. He took the flashlight from his car and began to walk toward the eucalyptus lane that by now had become familiar to him.

At first, Ross thought the noise was wind, or a seagull, except that it was night. Finally, as he drew closer, he recognized the haunting, seductive notes of *Dreaming*, Joanna's love song.

Ross stopped. He was invading her very private territory. He had asked her to sing for him once, out here, in her lovely, natural theater, and she had refused.

He waited until the song was over. Then, in the silence and darkness of the moonless spring night, he called to her.

"Ross?" she answered, her voice distant. She was much farther away than he had imagined. Or maybe she was just speaking softly.

He saw a light in the distance.

"Hi," he called, waving his flashlight.

"Hi." Her voice was barely audible.

"May I join you?"

"I'll meet you."

They moved toward each other, guided by the beams of their flashlights and their knowledge of the terrain.

When they reached each other, Ross extended his arms to her, folding them around her as she fell, gratefully, against him.

"You drive me crazy, you know," he said.

"You didn't go to the party."

"I realized," he said kissing the top of her head, "that the only reason I wanted to go to the party with you was to be with you. And you're here. So I'm here."

Janet pulled her arms free from his grasp, put her hands gently on his cold cheeks and guided his lips to hers. They kissed until all they felt was the warmth of their mouths and their bodies and forgot the cold ocean wind.

"Janet, Janet," he whispered to her.

"What?"

"What am I going to do with you?" he asked gently. "You drive me crazy."

"Make love to me, Ross," she said so quietly that he wasn't certain he had heard her correctly.

But as they lay on the dew-covered grass, as he made love to her in her own private theater, as he felt her body respond, instinctively, to his, he knew it was what he had heard. He knew that she wanted him.

Chapter 30

The June dawn filtered through the powder blue curtains in Janet's bedroom, its pale yellow rays awakening her gently, with warmth and light. Janet got out of bed, careful not to disturb Ross.

As quietly as possible, she started a pot of coffee in the kitchen then tiptoed onto the back porch while the coffee brewed. She curled into a painted cedar chair, closed her eyes and sighed with pleasure. She felt the warmth of the new morning sun on her face and the gentle breath of the soft ocean breeze finding her flesh under her modest cotton nightgown. She heard the quiet whispers of the eucalyptus leaves and the early morning songs of the gulls.

It was a perfect day. It felt like she felt: fresh, clean, full of hope and promise.

Janet sighed. She was so lucky.

"Good morning," he said, carrying two mugs of hot coffee. He was naked except for a pair of khaki trousers. He smiled as he handed her a mug and sat down opposite her, leaning casually on the porch railing.

"Good morning. Thank you. I didn't mean to waken you."

"This is too beautiful a day to waste in bed. By myself, anyway. What shall we do with this glorious day?" Ross asked, gazing out at the emerald-green hills toward the sapphire-blue ocean and avoiding looking at her as he asked the question.

It was Saturday. June eleventh. They both knew that it had special significance. It was a perfect day for a wedding.

Janet didn't answer.

"How about a picnic at the beach with long walks on either side?" Ross asked.

"How about an early picnic lunch so that you'll have time to make it to Atherton for the wedding?" Janet asked lightly.

"I'm not going to the wedding," Ross said. He had told her that six weeks ago. They hadn't talked about it since.

"Kathleen is one of your closest friends."

Ross turned and looked at her, then reached tenderly for a golden strand of hair that covered her eyes. He wanted to see them.

"*You* are one of my closest friends."

"Ross, it won't bother me if you go. I think you should. It's just that I can't."

"I know. I don't even know why we're discussing it. So, may I change the topic?"

"Sure."

"Arthur called me yesterday."

"Oh? How's Arthur? Still in seventh heaven about his Tony for *Joanna?*"

"The eight Tonys. All of which should have been yours for saving the show . . ."

"Ross," she began, shaking her head slightly.

He didn't know why it made her so uncomfortable to be complimented, to be told how good she was, how talented she was, how beautiful she was. She would have to get used to it. He wasn't going to stop telling her the truth.

"Anyway, guess *who* Arthur wants to have bring *what* show *where?*"

"You to take *Peter Pan* to Broadway. *When?*"

"To open in late September. Only he doesn't want me. He wants you. Although he's pretending that he wants both of us."

"Arthur has his own wonderful local talent. After all, Beth won the Tony for *Joanna*."

"Another of your Tonys. So," Ross said slowly, "how about it? We get a beautiful penthouse overlooking Central Park and do a four-month run in the Big Apple?"

"No," she said simply, pressing herself deeper against the chair as if to say, I won't leave here, this spot, ever. "No New York."

"Janet, you are drinking coffee out of a mug that says 'I love New York'!"

"You brought it to me!"

"It's your favorite mug!"

"It is," Janet answered, nodding her head, giggling. "I admit it's my favorite mug, but I don't want to move to New York."

"OK," Ross agreed quickly.

"OK?" Janet asked, surprised. He wasn't going to push her?

"Yes. I told Arthur you wouldn't want to, but I promised to ask you anyway. Besides, I have a much better way for you to spend your fall."

"What?" she asked, a trace of uneasiness in her voice.

"Harper and Peterson, the ones who wrote *Joanna*, have written a new musical. I just got it this week. It's called *San Francisco*. I think they wrote it precisely for you to perform in this city. I'd like you to take a look at it. If you like it, we'll open it this fall. If not, we'll find something else."

"*San Francisco?* Is it gold rush or earthquake or—" Janet asked eagerly. Not that it mattered.

"Contemporary. Flower children and little cable cars . . ."

"Where is it?" Janet asked, unable to breathe, unable to conceal her excitement.

Ross smiled. He loved to see the enthusiasm in her eyes just like he loved to see the desire in them when they made love.

"It's somewhere near."

"You tease!" Janet stood up. "Where?"

"In the trunk of my car. Sit back down. Let's take it with us for our picnic at the beach. We can spend this entire day reading the script and watching the waves. How does that sound?"

"Wonderful. Let's go."

"Janet." Ross's voice became serious. Janet sat down in her chair and looked at him carefully.

"What?"

"What about the other part? You said no New York but . . ." he paused. He'd given this a lot of thought. It was what he wanted. He had no idea how she would react. "How about the we'll get a penthouse part?"

In the months since that moonless March evening when they had made love for the first time in the hills behind the cottage, they had spent almost every weekend together there, in Janet's tiny house. But they were apart during the week. Ross had to be at the theater early every weekday. *Peter Pan* was only one of his productions.

Janet worked late every night. By the time she left the theater, it was usually midnight. If she drove straight home, it was almost two by the time she got to the cottage, and she didn't always go straight home. Sometimes Ross saw her leave with Peter.

One Wednesday night, Ross took Janet home with him to his fabulous condominium located ten minutes from the theater. They watched the twinkling lights of the city below, drank champagne, made love and fell asleep in each other's arms, but in the morning, Janet was restless to leave, pacing like a trapped, displaced animal, uncertain of her role or what she was doing in *his* home at seven in the morning.

They had never discussed it, but a pattern evolved. They spent two nights together and five nights apart. It wasn't enough for him, but he had no idea how she felt. He needed to know.

Now, in response to his question, Janet wasn't saying anything. She just looke at him, a little confused, a little surprised, a little worried and a little excited.

"Do you think it's wrong for people to live together?" he asked. We could get married, he thought. But it was much too soon for that.

"No. I think it's a good idea," she said honestly.

"In general, or for us?"

"In general," she said, then smiled coyly. "Maybe for us."

"I thought we could spend weeknights in the city at my place. I think if you brought some of your things, made it your home, too, you would feel comfortable there. And we could spend weekends here. More time when we're between productions. All of August."

"The Browns are planning to put the entire estate on the market," she said suddenly, remembering the disquieting news she had learned the day before. She sighed, "So I may be looking for a new place anyway. I'm sure that this property will sell quickly, even at the huge asking price, because it's a natural for residential development. I'm going to hate to leave."

"We'll find you another place. One with lots of property and a house big enough for script rewriting sessions by the sea and a piano and your clothes and my clothes and your books and my books and your albums and my albums. This cottage is cozy but awfully small."

Ross's observations about the size of the cottage were intentionally long-winded. He was giving her time. He could see that her serious gray eyes were considering his question, weighing it carefully, cautiously.

Finally she reached for his face with her hand, softly parting his tousled white-blond hair, tracing the lines at the corners of his eyes and touching his lips.

"Sometimes," she said, "you get angry, annoyed with me. I'm not always sure why."

"Because sometimes you seem to withdraw, get quiet," he said seriously. It worried him. Less and less each day, but still . . .

"I don't get quiet, Ross. I *am* quiet."

"I know," he said, reaching for her hand, kissing it. "I'm learning that. But sometimes you do put up walls. Your gray eyes cloud over and you hide."

"Maybe sometimes I do."

He pulled her head against his warm bare chest, cradling her for a moment, gently untangling her uncombed silken hair.

"So what do you think?" he whispered, holding her tight.

"I think we could try," she said slowly. Then she pulled herself free, her eyes flashing, "But what about Stacy?"

"*Stacy?* I haven't seen her since Christmas."

"Oh. Good."

"What about Peter?"

"Peter?"

"You know. Your leading man. The guy you leave the theater with when you don't leave with me. The guy who calls you all sorts of terms of endearment off stage as well as on. That Peter."

"Are you jealous?" she asked, laughing.

"Maybe."

"Peter's my friend. Sometimes we go for dinner after the show because we're starving and we like to rehash the performance. Are you really jealous?"

"This isn't very much fun."

"Ross," she said, kissing him playfully on the lips. Then she said, "Ross. Peter's gay."

"Oh," he said, kissing her seriously. "Oh."

"I, Mark, take you Kathleen . . ."

They stood beneath an arch of white lilacs and soft pink roses, eyes locked, hands joined, as they made their promises of forever in the lovely fragrant south garden at the Carlton Club.

Her glistening violet eyes told him much more than the words ever could. His moist, brown loving eyes answered back, eloquently.

I love you, Mark, with all my heart.

"For better or worse . . ."

I promise, Kathleen. I want you so much.

" . . . as long as we both shall live."

Afterward, as they stood in the reception line, greeting their many guests, Mark felt Kathleen's hand tighten around his forearm and heard the uncharacteristic strain in her gracious, lilting voice. He covered her hand with his, and she responded instantly, almost desperately, by intertwining her fingers with his.

As soon as the last guest had wished them well, Virginia Jenkins urged them toward the elaborate multi-tiered wedding cake.

"I need a private moment with my wife, Virginia," Mark said pleasantly but firmly. "Just a moment."

Mark led Kathleen across the perfectly manicured, emerald-green lawn to a private, secluded alcove behind a pink and lavender hedge of rhododendrons.

"Darling?" he asked when they were alone and away from view.

Tears spilled from the violet eyes. Kathleen couldn't stop the tears, and she couldn't speak.

"Second thoughts?" Mark asked easily. He knew that wasn't it, but it would draw her out.

"Oh, *no*, Mark, no," she answered quickly, touching his face with her trembling hands. She gazed into his eyes. "It's just . . . I just want to make your—our—life perfect. *Always*. I want it so much it scares me . . ."

I'm afraid, too, Mark thought as he wrapped his arms around her and pulled her tight against him, but my fears are real. I've made mistakes before. What if . . .

"You do make my life perfect," he whispered, kissing her black silky hair. "You don't even have to try."

"Did you go to the wedding, Leslie?" the head nurse in University Hospital emergency room asked when Leslie arrived for work that evening.

"No. The ceremony was supposed to start at four. I couldn't have made it back here on time," she said, glancing at the large institutional clock that read five-thirty-five.

Leslie's shift started at six P.M. and lasted until eight A.M. They called it the Lindbergh shift: a long, lonely, solo flight into the night.

"It's too bad you missed it. You and Mark are such good friends."

"It's just the luck of the draw," Leslie said flatly. She was glad she was working. She didn't really want to go to the wedding after all. "So, where's Dave? I might as well begin now, send him home a little early."

Eric answered the phone on the fifth ring.

"Hi," Charlie said. "Did I interrupt something?"

"No. I cut my damned hand. I was just trying to put another bandage on it."

Charlie recoiled at the anger and frustration in his voice.

"Another bandage? When did you cut it?"

"What time is it now? Seven? I cut it about one. I was washing those Saint Louis crystal highball glasses we used last night."

"Six hours ago? It's still bleeding?"

Eric didn't answer. He was staring at the huge gash on the palm of his hand and at the blood that flowed freely from the gaping wound. He put a cloth over it as he had repeatedly for the past six hours and clenched his fist. He could make the bleeding slow but it wouldn't stop.

"Eric?"

"I'm here."

"It sounds like you need to go to the hospital."

"It will stop."

"I know you don't want to go," Charlie said. It made her sad to think of him having to walk into a hospital. "But you may have to. I'll come over. If the bleeding hasn't stopped, we'll go. I'll go with you."

"*That* isn't necessary."

"I want to."

They arrived at the triage area of University Hospital emergency room at eight. The triage nurse examined Eric's hand and took him immediately into one of the acute trauma rooms. Charlie sat in the waiting area. For a while she stared at the prototypic emergency room posters on the gray-yellow walls. One was a compelling call for blood from the American Red Cross, another, the A, B, C's of basic life support from the American Heart Association and a third, a message about smoking from the American Cancer Society.

Some enlightened soul, probably in defiance of hospital policy, had hung a poster of two puppies curled in a wicker basket with a small fluffy kitten.

Charlie studied the posters for a while. Then she thumbed through the women's and sports magazines that lay on the tables, idly turning page after page, absorbing nothing. Finally, she put down the magazines, closed her eyes and succumbed to the memories.

She needed to remember because she knew that Eric was remembering. They were *his* horrible, painful memories, but she had to be there, then, to help him.

She was here to help him now. The memories flooded her with thoughts of that interminable, senseless nightmare. Memories that started with a late-night phone call from Robert ten years before.

"Charlie, it's Robert."

"Robert!"

"Eric needs you, Charlie. Please come to him."

"Robert, what is it?"

"Bobby—" he began, then was forced to stop because of the emotion in his throat. In a few moments he said the rest, hating the words, almost unable to speak them. "Bobby is dead."

"No, Robert, *No*."

"Please come, Charlie."

It started as a simple case of chicken pox. Bobby wasn't even very ill, his charming pleasant personality only slightly dampened by the common childhood virus. He stayed in bed, coloring and playing games with Victoria and Eric, while he watched TV, drank Seven-Up and took the children's aspirin that Victoria gave him for his fever.

It all seemed like a very routine case of chicken pox. Then Bobby started vomiting, becoming a bit confused and irritable. Quickly, almost in front of their eyes, he became comatose.

"It's called Reye Syndrome," the pediatrician said, the graveness in his voice giving them their first clue to Bobby's prognosis.

They stood outside the pediatric intensive care unit. Inside, a team of specialists hovered over their precious five-year-old boy. The team had already learned from laboratory studies that Bobby had liver failure, a low serum glucose and cerebral edema. They learned from his parents that he had had chicken pox and that he had been given aspirin.

"Reye Syndrome?" Eric asked.

"It's a newly recognized syndrome. It usually follows influenza or chicken pox. We don't know what causes it. It affects the liver and the brain."

"What about the aspirin? Why did they ask us about aspirin?" Victoria interjected. The doctor was about to tell them Bobby's prognosis. She didn't want to hear it. She knew. They both knew.

"There has been an anecdotal association made between aspirin and chicken pox and Reye Syndrome. It's just an observation at this point. It needs to be looked at scientifically," he said.

Still, as Eric and Victoria tried to deal with the senseless but inevitable death of their child, they had to find blame. They blamed the aspirin. And Eric blamed Victoria for giving it to Bobby, for killing their son.

"Why did you give it to him, Victoria?" Eric asked angrily, emotionally.

"We always give him aspirin when he's sick," she pleaded.

"If you hadn't given it to him—He wasn't that sick."

"Eric, don't you remember? That night you were reading to him?" she asked desperately. "You felt his forehead and told me to give him some."

"You had already given it to him. The day before."

The marriage ended the day they buried Bobby. Eric and Victoria left the funeral in separate cars with their own parents. They couldn't grieve together. There was too much anger and blame. They didn't have enough love to help each other. All their love had been for their child. He was the only reason they were together.

Without Bobby they had nothing. Nothing but pain and anger and hatred.

Charlie arrived at Eric's family home three hours after the funeral. She hadn't seen Eric since the day she was accepted to law school, two days after his marriage to Victoria five and a half years before. She hardly recognized the thin, sad man with the dark circles surrounding his lifeless, pale blue eyes, the light brown hair that should have been cut a month before and the hopelessness carved, deep, in his handsome face. Bobby had lived for five weeks. Eric had been with him every minute.

Without a word, Charlie walked past Robert and Florence and June. She put her arms around Eric and held him as he cried.

No one else had been able to touch him, to even begin to console him. Not even Robert.

In all those weeks, Eric hadn't cried, not until Charlie held him.

Charlie took a leave of absence from her law firm. Over the ensuing weeks, she listened to Eric's stories about his little boy. She learned to love the little boy that she had never known. She grieved for Eric, and she grieved with him.

They took long walks. They held each other. They spent entire days together without speaking and sometimes stayed up talking until dawn. They stayed in Robert's and Florence's home in separate bedrooms. Robert and Florence left them alone.

At the end of two months Eric said, "Charlie, you have a life to live."

"So do you," she observed gently. Then she asked, wondering if he knew, "What are you going to do?"

"Move InterLand to San Francisco," Eric said. He had just decided. "We have a corporate office there. I'm going to turn it into our headquarters. Want a job?"

"No, thank you," she said, hesitating a moment. Then she added firmly, "I have a job in Boston."

"Still?" he asked. He held her hand and gazed into her eyes. "I would never have made it through this without you. I haven't made it yet. But I'm healing. I will make it."

"I know you will, Eric." *I hope you will.*

Two years later, succumbing to pressure from Eric and ready for a change in job and geography, Charlie moved to San Francisco. She became InterLand's principal attorney, indispensible to the company and to its president.

Charlie and Eric made love to each other for the first time six months after she moved to San Francisco. Charlie finally experienced the *ultimate closeness* with the man she had loved so desperately years before. Their lovemaking was sensitive and intense, pleasurable and emotional, careful and caring.

But it was not the eager limitless passion of a man and a woman in love and full of hope for their love. Eric and Charlie weren't in love anymore. Too much had happened.

They weren't *in love*, but they loved each other. Deeply. The love grew even stronger as the years passed, as she worked beside him every day, as they laughed and talked and argued and teased. They made love often and traveled together whenever they could. They knew each other so well. They cared about each other so much.

Sometimes, sparked by a smile or a touch or a kiss, the magic of their past love would reappear, suddenly, in a warm, surprising, breathtaking rush, and they would be reminded, for a moment, of the wonder of that love and of the great joy they had once shared. . . .

* * *

Charlie sighed, opening her eyes to the too bright lights of the emergency-room waiting area.

She hoped this wouldn't be too hard for him. Her best friend. Her wonderful lover. Her beloved Eric.

But she knew it would be.

Chapter 31

"The fellow in Room One has a bad hand lac, Leslie," the triage nurse said, emerging from the room after obtaining Eric's vital signs. "I've got a tourniquet around his forearm. He's got an arterial pumper."

"Think it's an ortho case?"

"At least to stop the bleeding. He says the sensation in his fingers is fine."

"Good. I'll go take a look. Would you order an X-ray and page orthopedics? By the time they call back, I'll know if I need them. It sounds like I will. What's his name?"

"Lansdale, I think. His chart's still being made up. I just brought him right back."

Leslie walked into room One and looked at the man lying on the stretcher. He wasn't aware of her presence at first. He lay very still with his eyes closed.

In pain? Leslie wondered. In shock? No, his vital signs were fine. His cheeks looked pink, not white, under his tan.

"Mr. Lansdale?"

The eyes opened. Pale, pale blue, startled eyes.

"I'm sorry if I startled you. I'm Leslie Adams, the resident on call. What happened?"

"Crystal highball glass. I was washing it."

"Oh. Let me take a look," Leslie said as she sat on the stool next to him and carefully removed the sterile saline-soaked gauze dressing that the nurse had placed over his palm.

The wound was long, straight and deep. It looked almost surgical, as if cut with a sharp precise blade. Glass could do that. He had probably grabbed the already broken glass, forcing the razor-sharp edge into his palm.

It wasn't bleeding now. The tourniquet on his forearm occluded the arterial flow. Watching the wound, Leslie reached for the tourniquet and slowly released it. The white hand turned pink. Blood oozed into the wound and spilled, overflowing onto his hand. At one end of the wound, Leslie saw a rhythmic movement beneath the blood, causing a turbulence in the surface, like water just about to boil. He had a small arterial pumper. It would have to be clamped and tied, after his hand was anesthetized and after the wound was cleaned.

Leslie tightened the tourniquet again. The bleeding stopped.

"How long ago did this happen?"

"At one."

"Seven and a half hours ago?" As she had been examining the wound, she had been observing him, too. Despite his reserve, he seemed very much in control. *In charge*, even though his hand was bleeding without control. He was impeccably dressed, polite, handsome.

He did not look like the kind of man who would allow his hand to bleed uncontrollably for seven and a half hours. He did not appear to be intoxicated or drugged. He just seemed a little remote and preoccupied.

"Has it been bleeding like this for seven and a half hours?" Leslie asked the question again.

"Off and on."

"We'd better check your blood count. You may have lost a lot of blood."

"Is that necessary?"

"Yes," she said firmly. She had to be in control. "Let me first test the sensation in your hand and fingers. If that's OK, I'll put in a nerve block at the wrist to anesthetize your hand. Then we can clean it well—it needs extra cleaning because it's been open for so many hours—and sew it up."

"No anesthetic," Eric interjected. He wasn't specifically thinking, No one gave Bobby an anesthetic before they stuck needles and tubes in his small sick body. He wasn't thinking at all. He was just feeling. The aching, empty feeling from deep inside him made him say, again, more forcefully, "No anesthetic."

"Oh! Are you allergic?"

"No."

Leslie looked at his eyes and decided not to press the point. Patients with minor lacerations, patients who prided themselves on being impervious to pain and patients who dabbled in self-hypnosis occasionally opted for no anesthetic.

But this wound was not minor. It had to be extremely painful. The wound cleaning and repair that she had to do would cause even more pain. It would make her task more difficult, even if he didn't let her know how much it hurt, because she would know she was hurting him.

Leslie didn't argue. She knew, from his eyes, that she wouldn't win.

A woman dressed in surgical scrubs covered by a white coat entered the room.

"What have you got, Les?" she asked, nodding curtly, pleasantly at Eric.

"Sue, hi. I didn't realize I'd get the *chief*. Mr. Lansdale, this is Dr. Susan Miller, the chief resident in orthopedic surgery. I want her to look at the wound as well since it's such a deep cut to the hand."

Eric nodded silently. A specialist. He had met a lot of specialists. None of them had been able to help his son.

"It's a glass—crystal—cut. Seven and a half hours old. Sensory and motor are intact. He has an arterial pumper that needs to be ligated and a small tendon lac that's not through and through but may be suturable."

Together, Susan and Leslie cleaned and examined the wound. Susan had no idea that Eric's hand had not been anesthetized. She probed deep in the wound, looking for glass, for tendon lacerations, for foreign material. The careful exploration was necessary. Eric never flinched.

Susan tied off the small severed artery and put two sutures into the tendon. Then she left to join the rest of her team in the operating room to put a steel pin in the hip of a patient with an intertrochanteric hip fracture.

"I'd give him prophylactic antibiotics, Les. No data, of course, but a hand wound that deep and that old . . ." she said as she took off her mask and blood-covered gloves before she left.

"I agree. A cephalosporin?"

"Sounds good. Take care, Mr. Lansdale. Bye, Leslie."

"Thanks, Sue," Leslie said, settling onto the stool that Susan had vacated. Leslie put on a new pair of sterile gloves before suturing the wound closed. It would take a while to pull the edges of skin back together, stitch by stitch. As she selected the appropriate gauge suture material, a needle holder and a pair of smooth forceps, Leslie said to Eric, "She's a very good orthopedic surgeon."

Eric nodded.

"Would you like me to inject some local anesthetic before I close the wound?"

"No," Eric answered swiftly. Then he added, looking at the concerned blue eyes staring at him over the aquamarine surgical mask, "Thank you."

It took Leslie thirty minutes to close the wound. The skin came together well. If it healed without infection, the scar would, in time, be simply a thin white line.

During the thirty minutes, neither spoke. Leslie concentrated on her suturing, and he, she noticed when she looked away from the wound to get more suture or reach for a sterile saline-soaked cloth to clean the field, was concentrating, too. Not on her, or his wound, or the pain but on something else. Somewhere else.

Usually patients were garrulous while their lacerations were being sutured. Usually the fear that entered the emergency room with them abated once the anesthetic took hold. The fear subsided and the relief pulsed through them making them euphoric, ebullient, talkative.

The light banter that normally accompanied suturing a laceration made the experience enjoyable for Leslie and her patients. It eased the tension and distracted them both away from the intimacy of what was really happening. The intimacy of touching. The *invasive* intimacy of forcing needle and thread into another person's flesh.

With Mr. Lansdale there was no light banter. Leslie knew he felt every touch. She knew that he felt the touch of her warm hands and the sharpness of the needle as she pushed it through his skin and the pull of the thread as she brought the raw edges together.

I'm sorry, Leslie thought, with each thrust of the needle. I'm sorry that I'm hurting you.

Finally it was over. Gratefully Leslie replaced the instruments and removed her gloves and mask.

"All done," she said, startling him.

"Great," he said absently, not even looking at the wound. Not asking, as most patients asked so they could tell their friends, how many sutures she had placed. Not teasing her, as most did, about what a great seamstress she was.

He should look, Leslie thought. It's one of my best suturing jobs.

"The nurse will come in and bandage it while I go write your instructions and get your antibiotics," she said, leaving the room.

When Leslie returned five minutes later, Eric was sitting in a chair, calmly resting his bandaged hand on his lap. He smiled politely when Leslie entered.

It always amazed her how different people looked when they were sitting up than they looked lying down on stretchers. Leslie had decided, as she observed his profile on the stretcher, that he was a handsome man. Now she saw the full measure of his looks, the pale blue eyes in the aristocratic face and the controlled body that sent a message of strength and power.

"Here are the wound care instructions," she said, suddenly feeling uncomfortable, remembering that she had touched this man, put needles and thread in his skin, questioned him about his delay in coming to the hospital. She continued with effort, "Someone should look at the wound in four days—sooner if there is any problem—just to make certain it's healing well. Your own physician can do that."

"I don't have a physician."

"You're welcome to come back here. Just stop by at your convenience. Any of the doctors can look at it."

"Wouldn't it be best to come when you're here?" Eric asked.

Of course it would. Leslie always tried to schedule the patients she sutured to come back for wound checks while she was on duty. It was best for them. It gave her feedback. Why was she treating him differently? Why was she *encouraging* him to see another doctor?

690 "Yes," she breathed.

"So, what shift will you be doing in four days?"

"This shift. Six in the evening until eight in the morning."

"What would be the best time to come?"

"It's unpredictable. If we get busy . . . if someone comes in who's critically ill . . . it could be a wait," she said, looking at him, thinking he was not a man who was used to waiting.

He didn't look disturbed at the possibility of a wait, but Leslie had already learned something about his politeness and his control.

"Would five-forty-five Wednesday evening be convenient for you?" she asked.

"Sure. But you won't be here," Eric said pleasantly.

"I'll be here. I always get here early. I'll see you right before my shift starts." *So you won't have to wait. So I won't have to worry about you waiting.*

"That's very nice of you."

"No problem."

Leslie didn't watch him walk down the corridor toward the waiting room. She didn't see the beautiful woman with the long blond hair and the concerned brown eyes touch his face tenderly, thoughtfully. Leslie didn't see them hold each other, tightly, for a few moments before leaving the emergency room.

Leslie didn't see any of it because she was already in another room talking to a young woman with a urinary tract infection.

Four hours later, at one-thirty Sunday morning, the emergency room was finally quiet. Leslie had seen all the patients. They had all gone home—their throats cultured, their fractures set, their infections treated, their corneal abrasions patched and their lacerations closed—or been admitted.

Leslie sat in the triage area at the entrance of the emergency room beside a stack of patient charts that awaited her record of the patient's visit to the emergency room.

Leslie sat at the triage desk so that she would know immediately if any new patients arrived.

The red trauma phone rang. It was a direct line used only by ambulances and medic units. The triage nurse answered the phone and listened a moment while Leslie watched, curious. Then she shook her head at Leslie and wrote on a pad of paper L and D.

Labor and Delivery. It wasn't for the emergency room. They received calls from all ambulances coming to the hospital even if the patient was being directly admitted to a specific patient care floor. The ambulances all came to the emergency room entrance no matter where the patient was going.

After the triage nurse forwarded the call to labor and delivery, she said, "A little Gemini about to be born."

"Gemini? Is that good or bad?" Leslie asked idly.

"Neither. It's just what he, or she, is. It may begin to matter when he or she begins to socialize."

"Do you really believe that?" she asked, a little curious.

"I don't live by it, but I think it's interesting. We talk about *chemistry* between people. That's about as mystical as astrology!"

Leslie laughed. "I'm a Virgo, what does that mean?"

"It means you're strong and perfectionistic. Critical of others to some extent, but, mostly, you place demands on yourself."

"Sounds awful," Leslie said seriously. *It sounds accurate. It sounds like what Mark said that night at the Cliff House.* "Who am I supposed to be compatible with? If anyone!"

"Someone even stronger. A Scorpio, for example. They are very strong. Powerful," she said. "You need someone like that."

Mark had said that, too, Leslie mused, returning to the stack of unfinished charts.

The ambulance arrived five minutes later. The drivers waved at Leslie and the triage nurse as they wheeled the stretcher carrying the pregnant woman toward the elevator.

Ten minutes later the automatic sliding glass doors to the emergency room opened again. Leslie looked up when she heard the noise.

"James!" she gasped.

"Leslie," he breathed.

"What—"

"Lynne is about to deliver. She should have just arrived."

"She did. She should be up in labor and delivery by now. I'll show you how to get there," Leslie said, looking at him, her heart racing, her physician's mind wondering what Lynne was doing at University Hospital. It was a referral hospital for complicated pregnancies.

Her worry increased as she looked carefully at James. There was fear in the fearless green eyes.

"What's wrong, James?" she asked as they walked toward the bank of elevators.

"They aren't sure. She was fine until tonight. She suddenly had severe, tearing pain and bleeding. They think part of the placenta has torn away. They're transferring her here so they can monitor the baby. They think they'll have to do a Caesarean section."

Leslie nodded. Lynne probably had had an abruption of the placenta. Perhaps it was related to the uterine scarring that James had said would prevent them from ever having children.

James. Lynne. Lynne pregnant with James's child. James almost frantic with worry.

Leslie walked with him to the elevator that would take him to labor and delivery.

"I'll be here all night, James," she said. *If you need me.*

When James returned to the emergency room two hours later Leslie had just completed the meticulous notes she wrote on each patient's medical record. Another time, eight months ago, she might have shown him the picture she had drawn of the hand on the record of E. R. Lansdale, and James would have laughed at the sketch with its stubby fingers and poor proportions.

But tonight was a different time, Leslie thought, looking at his exhausted, worried face. At least the fear in his eyes was a little less.

"How is she?"

"Sleeping. They have her sedated and they've given her medications to stop labor. The baby is being monitored. They say she seems fine."

"She?"

"Or he. We just have assumed she will be a she," James said. Despite his fatigue and worry there was a trace of excitement and pride in his voice.

"What are the plans?" Leslie asked carefully. She knew that if Lynne had a partial abruption it was simply a matter of time before more placenta tore away. When it did, if they couldn't intervene quickly enough, the baby could die from lack of oxygenated blood, and Lynne could die from uncontrollable blood loss. What were they waiting for?

"To keep her stable overnight and do a Caesarean section first thing in the morning. If there's a problem, they'll do it sooner, as an emergency."

She's stable now, Leslie thought. Why wait until it becomes an emergency? She knew the obstetricians at University Hospital. They didn't wait to do necessary surgery for luxuries such as daylight or a newly rested team. They operated when it was necessary, *whenever* it was necessary. When they were tired, adrenaline and pure skill got them through.

A piece was missing. Something James didn't know.

"You should get some rest," Leslie said, almost reaching to touch his face, to move the black lock of hair that fell into his troubled eyes.

"I'm going to. I just wanted to tell you what was happening. There's a waiting room upstairs full of expectant fathers."

"There's an empty apartment five minutes from here," Leslie said removing her apartment key from her key chain. "Lynne's sleeping, gathering strength. You should do the same thing. Give the L and D nurses my number; they won't recognize it."

"When will you be home?" he asked, taking the key. He wondered what she had done with his key.

"Eight-fifteen. You'll have to let me in."

"I will," he said, smiling weakly, resisting the urge to touch her flushed cheek. "Thank you."

After James left, Leslie called the labor and delivery nursing station.

"Hi, this is Leslie Adams. What resident is taking care of Lynne Stevenson?" she asked. I shouldn't be doing this, she thought as she waited.

"Michael Leary."

Leslie hesitated. Michael Leary. One of the best residents in the Ob-Gyn program. And a fine man. He was the first man Leslie dated after James left, a man who might have meant a great deal to Leslie at another time. But then, in December and January, all that Leslie knew was that Michael Leary was not James. It had ended awkwardly with Michael. Leslie never really explained to him what happened.

"Is he around?" she asked finally.

"Right here. Michael. Leslie Adams is on line two."

"Leslie?" Michael answered.

"Hi."

"Hi."

"Michael, I don't want you to give me any specific information since I don't have her permission, but . . ." Leslie hesitated. She had no business knowing anything about Lynne's condition. James could tell her but Michael couldn't because Leslie wasn't medically involved with the case.

"What, Leslie?"

"Lynne Stevenson's husband is an old friend. He's pretty worried, but I don't know if he really understands how serious it could be. Maybe it isn't that serious. I'm just guessing based on what he's told me. Anyway, Michael, if anything happens to her, if James needs someone, will you call me?"

"Sure, Leslie. Thank you for letting me know," Michael said. He hesitated a moment, took a deep breath, and began, "Leslie, as long as I have you on the line, let me tell you about a patient we have up here. I want you to know about her, in case we get in trouble. I may need your help."

"OK," Leslie said.

As Michael spoke, as he told her about his patient, Leslie realized that he was telling her about Lynne, involving her medically so that she would know how serious it was. So that she could help James. Or Lynne.

"She's a time bomb, Leslie, but I can't operate on her until I have blood for her. She's already anemic. The blood bank is having trouble cross matching her. The bank is low on blood anyway. They haven't recovered from Memorial Day weekened. Nobody's donating because of the AIDS business—"

"Not *donating* because of it? That doesn't make sense."

"I know. But people are afraid they might get AIDS by giving blood as well as receiving it. I'm not transfusing anybody these days who doesn't need it. The patient I'm telling you about may not need it, but I can't begin the operation without blood available because if she starts to bleed we may not be able to stop her. On top of everything, she has a minor bleeding disorder. The hematologists are in now trying to figure out what it is."

So Leslie had her answer. They were waiting because they had to. They were waiting until they had blood in case they needed it and until they could figure out a way to make her stop bleeding if she started again.

"How's the baby?" Leslie asked.

"Baby's fine. But that could change quickly, too."

"Let me know if you need my help."

"Thanks, Leslie, I will."

By eight-fifteen, when Leslie arrived at her apartment, James had showered and dressed. Leslie could tell that he hadn't slept much.

"The hospital just called," he said. "They are going to operate at nine-thirty. Apparently they were waiting to get blood for her and to run some sophisticated coagulation tests."

Good, Leslie thought, Michael is telling him more. That was good. James could handle it. He needed to be a little prepared.

"They said I can be with her from nine to nine-thirty. But," James said, his voice heavy with worry, "they won't let me be in the operating room. We had planned that I would be there for the delivery. I thought they usually let fathers in the delivery room even if it was a Caesarean."

They probably do, James, Leslie thought grimly. But not in this case. Not when it may be a blood bath. They don't want you to watch your wife and baby die. Oh James!

"They said they may need to do a hysterectomy," he continued distractedly. "They said that the scar tissue may bleed so much that they may have to remove Lynne's uterus."

"That doesn't matter, does it?" Leslie asked gently. If the only casualty of the operation was Lynne's uterus, they would be very lucky.

"No. I guess not. I don't know. I just want it to be over. For Lynne and the baby to be safe," James said emotionally.

He knows, Leslie thought, wanting to hold him. He knows.

"I'd better go," James said.

"Do you—" Leslie began, then stopped. Want me to go with you? she had almost asked. "Will you call me? Let me know?"

"Yes."

After James left, Leslie took a shower and got into bed. The bed where James had slept. The bed where she and James had slept. She fell asleep, thinking about him, praying for him and Lynne and their baby.

At first the loud noise was part of the dream, an ambulance's siren, an ambulance rushing the dying mother and her infant to the hospital. But gradually the noise

pulled Leslie out of her nightmare, ringing relentlessly, rhythmically.

Not a siren at all. A telephone. Ringing.

Leslie glanced at her bedside clock. Twelve-thirty. It was light out. Half past noon. She had been asleep for three hours. In five and a half hours she had to be back to work. Who could be calling? Why hadn't she disconnected the phone as she usually did?

The fog of her deep, troubled sleep suddenly cleared as she remembered. *James.*

"Hello?"

"Leslie?" It was James, his voice faint, full of emotion.

Oh no, James.

"Yes," she said softly.

A long silence.

"They're OK," he said finally. The emotion was joy not grief, but it still left him speechless.

"They're OK?" Leslie asked, her own voice weak with emotion.

"Yes," he repeated, his voice a little stronger. "They are both fine."

"Oh, James. Thank God," Leslie breathed, her eyes brimming with tears. "Lynne's fine?"

"Yes. They did remove her uterus to stop the bleeding. They didn't give her any blood, though," James said thoughtfully. He knew a little about AIDS. He and Leslie had talked about it, about Mark's refusal to accept blood transfusions. James was glad that they hadn't had to transfuse Lynne. "She'll be anemic for a while, but . . . I just saw her. She looks fine."

"And the baby?"

"It's a boy," James said proudly, incredulously.

"A boy? James, you have a son," Leslie said softly, curling under the covers of her bed. "What's his name?"

"I don't know. We never talked about boy names," James said slowly, Leslie's words still echoing in his mind. You have a son. A son. James thought of his father. James's son would have a different kind of father. "Do you want to see him, Leslie?"

"Yes," she said. *No. I don't know.* She wasn't part of their life. James and Lynne and their baby boy. "If you want me to."

Leslie met James outside the nursery at five. They stared through the glass at the tiny boy, James's son, wriggling energetically in his crib. Lynne was asleep—not that Leslie would have met Lynne—but it meant that she and James could go for a cup of coffee in the cafeteria before her shift began.

"He's beautiful, James," she said.

"Oh, we have a name. Michael."

"After Michael Leary?"

"Uh-huh."

"That's nice. He's a nice man. It's a nice name." *Nice James.*

They drank coffee in silence.

"She probably got pregnant the night before your birthday," he said.

"Oh." *That was why she was ill.*

"She knew about us from the very beginning."

"Oh, no," she said, looking at the pain in James's eyes.

"She had planned to leave me, never tell me about the baby."

"How did you find out?" *When did you find out? Is that why we stopped seeing each other?*

James hesitated. He couldn't tell Leslie how he found out, while he and Lynne were acting out one of Lynne's sexual fantasies.

"I just did."

"And now?"

"Now," James said slowly. "Now we have a perfect little boy. It was a struggle, Leslie, trying to put our marriage back together. But we did. We are very lucky."

"You just love each other very much," Leslie said quietly, looking at James, knowing it was true.

They looked at each other for a long moment.

Finally Leslie noticed the time.

"I have to go. Do you want to stay at the apartment tonight?"

"No. Thank you. I'll go home," he said gently.

Home. Where he belonged.

Chapter 32

Eric Lansdale was already in the emergency room when Leslie arrived at five-thirty Wednesday afternoon.

"Hi, Mr. Lansdale. You're early."

"So are you."

"I always am," Leslie said lightly. She had come in early to say good-bye to James. Lynne and Michael were scheduled to go home in the morning. It had been a quick good-bye. They had said good-bye before. There wasn't much left to say. "How is your hand?"

Leslie sat on a stool in front of him and carefully removed the bandage. Without speaking, she squeezed the tips of his fingers with her hand, testing their strength and warmth, traced the suture line with her finger and examined his forearm for signs of ascending infection.

"Any pain?" she asked, wondering if he would even tell her.

"None. No pain or fever or drainage. I think it's healing well."

"So do I," she said, still holding his large hand in both of hers, naturally, as she would do with any patiet. Then she looked at him and released his hand, suddenly uneasy. Too intimate. Much too intimate.

"Good," he said, smiling slightly. "When do the stitches come out?"

"In six days."

"Will you be here?"

Leslie looked at her pocket calendar. "Yes. I'll be working the day shift that day. From eight in the morning until six at night."

"I'll be here at five-forty-five. If that's all right."

"That's fine."

After he left, one of the nurses said to Leslie, "Who was that?"

"Mr. E.R. Lansdale," Leslie answered quickly, concretely, still confused about her discomfort at examining his hand.

"He is gorgeous! I wonder what he does for a living. He looks rich."

He looks *something*, Leslie thought as she picked up the chart of her next patient, a third-year medical student with a sore throat.

696 It took less than five minutes for Leslie to remove the twenty-seven stitches she had so carefully sewn into Eric Lansdale's palm. The wound had healed beautifully.

"There," she said when she was done. "You're a free man."

"Are you free?" he asked casually.

"What?"

"Are you free for dinner? Tonight?"

He could tell by looking at her that she was and that she was reluctant and tempted at the same time.

"I made reservations at The Blue Fox, one of my favorites, for eight o'clock," Eric continued, calmly, insistently, sensing that she was considering it. "I'm already dressed. So why don't I just go with you to your place? I'll make myself a drink while you change. All right?"

Leslie did not remember agreeing, but ten minutes later they were on their way to her apartment.

"This certainly is a convenient location for you," he said as he parked his jade-green Jaguar in front of her apartment building two minutes after they left the emergency room patient parking area.

"A short walk to University Hospital. But I also work at San Francisco General Hospital and the VA. I bet a Jaguar has never been parked on this street before," she added, suddenly giggling.

"What's so funny?" he asked, his own eyes laughing.

"Nothing. Everything. This is so strange. I don't even know you," she said. *But I feel like I've known you forever, and I can either giggle or become mute because you make me feel wonderful and terrified. I have never felt this giddy, anxious, euphoric feeling before. This is so easy and so hard.*

"You're not afraid of me, are you?"

"No!" Leslie said lightly. *Yes. A little. A lot. Afraid of the way you make me feel.*

While Leslie took a shower and got dressed Eric poured himself a bourbon on the rocks, idly admired the framed etching of a meadow signed *James 1971*, and finally sat on the sofa in the small living room. He glanced at the stack of medical journals that lay on the coffee table, but he didn't reach for any of them. Then he noticed the thick book that lay on the end table beside him.

When Leslie returned to the living room, she found Eric reading *Moby Dick*. She wore a pale pink cocktail dress and pearls. As soon as he saw her, Eric stood up.

"And I thought a white coat stuffed with a stethoscope, tongue blades and pens looked fabulous on you," he said, obviously admiring her surprising softness.

Leslie blushed. "I don't get a chance to wear civvies very often," she said, shrugging.

"Too bad," Eric said. "Can I make you a drink? We don't need to leave for half an hour."

"I don't—" Leslie began then stopped. She had started to say, I don't usually dink. It was true. Even before last fall, even before James, she drank very little.

Alcohol made her sleepy, and since the beginning of her internship, she was always a little behind on sleep anyway. But she kept a supply of liquor so that she could offer drinks to her rare visitors. "Sure, thank you. I'll have whatever you're having."

"Bourbon on the rocks," he said, pouring her a drink, then handing it to her.

"Thanks. Were you reading *Moby Dick?*"

"I was just looking at it, wondering if I had ever really read it."

"I know I hadn't. Not really. Not with any appreciation. It is so powerful, so beautifully written. Like poetry," Leslie said.

Last summer as she watched Mark's pleasure—despite the pain of the bullet hole in his chest, his broken ribs and his weakness due to anemia—as he read the classics, Leslie felt a pang of conscience. She had read them all once as required reading in high school and college, but she had read them quickly, dutifully, without enjoyment or appreciation.

Watching Mark, Leslie wondered what she had missed. In the long lonely nights after James left, after she realized that it was useless to date anyone else for a while, Leslie discovered why Mark and her parents jealously guarded the hours they set aside to read the books they loved so much.

"Sometimes I read aloud to myself. Melville writes with such rhythm. It feels like the ebb and flow of the sea," Leslie said, feeling warm from a too large swallow of bourbon.

"*Call me Ishmael*," Eric began, reading the first line of the leather-bound volume.

"Ishmael," Leslie said softly.

"Eric," he said, realizing that she had never called him anything but Mr. Lansdale.

"Eric. That's what the E stands for."

"You didn't know my first name?"

"No. All our records have you as E.R. Lansdale."

"I guess the friend I was with the first night did that," Eric said absently. Charlie protected Eric's anonymity. And her own. Not that Leslie had ever heard of Eric Robert Lansdale. Eric doubted that Leslie had the time or interest, between the stack of medical journals and *Moby Dick*, to read the social or financial pages of *The San Francisco Chronicle*.

Eric read aloud the first paragraph of the book. Then the second. Leslie curled into her favorite chair, across from him, listening to his voice, watching his eyes and his mouth, feeling warm and secure. And anxious. She wanted the moment never to end.

"This is wonderful," Eric said after he read the first two pages to her. He looked at her and made a vow to himself, I am going to read this entire book to you. This book and a hundred others.

I don't even know you, he thought. But I am so sure.

They learned a little about the facts of each other's lives that night. They discovered that Eric had graduated from Harvard six years before Leslie entered Radcliffe. Leslie told Eric that she loved being a doctor. Eric told Leslie that he loved building beautiful buildings.

They learned a little about each other, but they learned a lot about how it felt to be falling in love.

They only touched once that night. Eric noticed the scar on her palm and reached for her hand.

"What happened?" he asked, tracing the edges of the large, irregular puckered scar left by Mark's shattered bone piercing her skin.

Leslie told him, briefly, wondering if he would remember seeing her on the news. If he had seen her, he would remember. He didn't.

"Not the kind of sewing job I'm used to," he said, looking at his own, thin, even scar.

Leslie smiled.

"They didn't even try to close my wound," she said. "It would have gotten infected." If you had come in any later, we might not have been able to close yours either, she thought. Why did you wait so long? she wondered but didn't ask. Maybe someday she would ask. Maybe someday he would tell her what he was thinking about that night, why he refused the anesthetic. . . .

It was midnight when he walked her to the door of her apartment.

"When can I see you again?" he asked.

"Whenever," Leslie said effortlessly, meaning it.

"I have a business dinner tomorrow night. How about Thursday?"

"Thursday's fine."

"Good," he said. Then he drew a deep breath and frowned.

"Eric? What's the matter?"

"I forgot all about a trip I'm taking at the end of the week. I leave Friday morning for Tokyo and Hong Kong," he said soberly.

"That sounds wonderful," Leslie said enthusiastically, but wondering, anxiously, how long he would be gone. "Does that mean Thursday night is no good?"

"No. That means I definitely have to see you Thursday night. Do you think it sounds wonderful, really?"

"Yes. Aren't you looking forward to it?"

"It's business. I go to those cities at least twice a year," Eric said. How jaded am I? he wondered. Do I look forward to anything? The pleasures in his life—a successful business transaction, a spectacular new building, making love with Charlie—seemed insignificant now, compared to the importance of being with Leslie. He was looking forward to Thursday night, and he was looking forward to returning from his trip. Unless . . . "Could you come with me?"

"To Tokyo and Hong Kong?" Leslie asked, incredulous.

"Yes. It's a ten day trip. It *would* be wonderful if you could come."

"I can't. Even if I had vacation time left, which I don't, I couldn't leave on such short notice."

"Because they need you?" *I need you.*

"Because they need warm bodies in all the acute medical units."

"I'll be here at seven Thursday night, then," he said. "Good-night, Leslie."

They didn't kiss. They would kiss next time. Or the time after. All their lives.

"Good-night, Eric."

At ten the next morning, the chief medical resident notified Leslie that, because another resident had just been diagnosed with serum hepatitis, she would have to fill in on the inpatient medicine service at San Francisco General Hospital.

"Who's covering here?" she asked.

"The consult residents will take turns."

"The new interns start today!" Leslie exclaimed, the magnitude of her new assignment setting in: the toughest ward service, the sickest patients and brand new interns. "Do I get some special compensation for this?"

"Isn't it enough that you were hand-picked because you're the best?"

"*That* worked last June. Can't I just ease into being an R-3 like everybody else?"

"It's only for nine days."

Nine days. It would keep her very busy while Eric was away. The time would pass quickly.

"OK."

"OK?"

"You mean I had a choice?" she teased, laughing. "Really, it's fine."

It was fine until she discovered that her first on call night was Thursday. She wouldn't be able to see Eric before he left.

Leslie found no listing for Eric Lansdale, or E. Lansdale, in the directory, but she found a listing for InterLand. He had said something about a company named InterLand.

Leslie spoke with three secretaries before she was finally connected with Eric's personal secretary.

"Mr. Lansdale's office, may I help you?"

"This is Leslie Adams calling for Mr. Lansdale. Is he available?"

"I'm sorry Ms. Adams, he is in a meeting. May I take a message?"

"Let's see. Tell him that I've just been transferred to San Francisco General Hospital and I'm on call Thursday night."

"All right. And that's Ms. Adams?"

"Well, it's Dr., but it doesn't matter. He'll know."

"I apologize Dr. Adams."

"It's fine, really."

"Thank you. Is there anything else I should tell him?"

"No. Yes. Tell him, *Sayonara*."

Eric got Leslie's message at three in the afternoon. It helped him make a decision he had been toying with all day. At five minutes past three he called Robert in Philadelphia, and at four-fifteen he walked down the private corridor that connected his office with Charlie's.

There was room, in the innermost part of the executive suite, for a third person. Eric had been looking for someone with whom he and Charlie could work creatively and effectively and compatibly. Now Eric had found him. James Stevenson. By mid-July the private corridor would provide undisturbed access between his office and Charlie's and James's. After the month he was spending with his wife and infant son was over, James would not return to his office at O'Keefe, Tucker and Stevenson on California Street. Instead, he would move to the executive suite on the fortieth floor of the InterLand building in an office with a panoramic view of San Francisco Bay.

The door to Charlie's inner office was open. She didn't hear Eric's footsteps on the thick wool carpet, nor did she immediately sense his presence. She was absorbed with the work that lay in front of her on the carved oak desk.

Eric smiled, watching her. When Charlie was working, she was so serious! She always has been, he thought, remembering the strong-willed lifeguard with her spungold hair hidden inside an over-large safari hat. He looked at her hair now, its golden brilliance knotted severely on top of her head. Her attorney look. It was very much like her lifeguard at the Oak Brook Country Club look. So serious.

"Hi," he said finally.

"Eric! Hi," she said, pushing the papers she had been reading away from her. "I will be so glad to leave this all for ten days. It will be a nice change, don't you think?"

Eric was silent, steeling himself against her brown eyes, now soft, radiant and eager about their trip to the Orient. They were closest when they traveled together. It was the closest they came to recapturing the magic—*their magic*—of being young and in love.

"We have the Empress suite at the Akasaka Prince in Tokyo. It's a three-bedroom suite. One for each night, I guess. Then, in Hong Kong, we're staying at—"

700 "I'm not going," Eric said flatly.

"The trip's off?"

"No. *I* am not going. The trip's still on. The meetings we have scheduled are necessary, especially the negotiations in Tokyo."

"I know that. That's why you have to be there."

"You're my negotiator."

"We do it together. Besides, Eric, it's the Orient. They won't negotiate with an unescorted woman. It's just not done."

"True, even though you do it all, a male figurehead is necessary. So I've arranged for the best, the very best figurehead for InterLand, not to mention a rather skilled negotiator and attorney. Just in case you need help."

"Robert?" Charlie asked weakly.

"Yes. I just spoke with him. He'll fly out tomorrow so you can leave, as scheduled, on Friday. He sounded excited about doing this, Charlie. It's been a while since he's been on the front lines negotiating. He's looking forward to it."

"Robert," Charlie repeated almost to herself. She couldn't travel with Robert, be with him constantly for ten days. What would she say to him? How would she and Robert fill the hours that she and Eric would have filled with quiet conversation, holding hands and making love? What would she and Robert do during the hours between meetings? What would they find to say at breakfast, lunch and dinner every day? She added weakly, "I don't know Robert."

"Of course you know him."

"I won't feel comfortable traveling with him," she mused. "We have to change all the hotel accommodations."

"Not really. A three-bedroom suite should give you both enough privacy. Charlie, why are you acting nervous about this? You travel with other attorneys all the time. All over the world. And you've known Father for twenty years."

"I don't know," she said honestly. It just feels strange, she thought. Charlie looked at Eric then and asked the question that he had been waiting for, worrying about. "Why aren't you going?"

"Because," he said slowly, watching her eyes, "I have met someone. I just met her. I don't want to be away right now."

Charlie took a quick breath. Over the years, Eric had met many women. He had had relationships with them just as Charlie had had relationships with other men. But Eric had never met anyone who could make him cancel a business trip, even a trivial one, and certainly not one this important.

In all those years, Eric had never met a woman who would make him cancel his plans to travel with Charlie. No matter what else, who else, was happening in their lives, Eric and Charlie would always travel together, rediscovering each other and the bits of magic that still were theirs.

Now, thirty-six hours before they were scheduled to leave on a trip that they had planned for months, Eric was telling her he couldn't go because he had just met someone.

"Who is she?" Charlie whispered.

"Someone. No one you know," he said carefully. He saw the hurt in her eyes. And the love. They had talked about this. That one day they might, if they were lucky, fall in love with someone new. They wished it for each other: to find a love untarnished by pain and hurt; a love they could protect and treasure; a love like theirs had been, once. Before all the pain.

Charlie doubted it would happen. Certainly not to her. And probably not to Eric. But now it *had* happened . . .

"Tell me about her," Charlie said, her surprise giving way to curiosity. And to excitement for Eric. If I'm hurt by this, it's my own fault, she told herself 701
sternly.

"There's nothing to tell," he answered, relaxing a little as he heard the teasing lilt in her voice. She would be happy for him in time. "I barely know her."

But I want to be with her, he thought. More than anything else. And I don't want to talk about her, share her, with anyone else. Not even the people I love. Not yet.

"Did you tell Robert?" Charlie asked.

"Yes! But he doesn't know any more about her than you do," Eric teased lightly. He remembered that Robert had been hesitant, at first, about making the trip, but when Eric told him the reason, Robert suddenly seemed eager to go.

"At least this will give Robert and me something to talk about," Charlie said slowly, her voice reflecting her uncertainty about traveling with Robert.

Eric telephoned Leslie's apartment hourly during his dinner business meeting. The prefix and the quality of the ring seemed vaguely familiar, but he had never dated anyone who lived near Parnassus Avenue. Throughout the evening, there was no answer at Leslie's apartment. At eleven, when he returned to his penthouse in Pacific Heights, he tried again.

"Hello?" she answered breathlessly.

"Leslie, it's Eric. Did I wake you?"

"No. I just got home. I heard the phone ringing as I was fumbling with my keys. I thought it might be one of my interns," she said. *I'm glad it's not. I'm glad it's you.*

"Are you expecting them to call?"

"Not really. I just left them fifteen minutes ago. But, it's the first day of the internship. Total chaos," she said laughing, tired, falling into the overstuffed chair. "What a day!"

"Tell me," Eric said carefully. *Just don't tell me about sick little boys.*

"OK. Just the highlights. Let's see. One intern decided to quit because another resident yelled at her. She isn't used to being yelled at, only praised," Leslie said, a little sympathetically and a little annoyed.

"Did she do something that wrong?"

"No. I actually have a low tolerance for the resident who yelled at her—for residents that yell at other residents in general—so I dried her tears and convinced her that this is all part of the magnificent learning experience of being an intern."

"She bought that?"

"I think so. I'll find out at eight o'clock tomorrow morning. My *other* intern decided to quit because one of our endocarditis patients threatened him with a scalpel."

"*What?*" Eric asked, suddenly concerned.

"The patient is an intravenous drug user—heroin mostly—which is why he has endocarditis. My intern needed to draw some blood from him, to monitor for toxicity due to the antibiotics we're using. The patient did not want a novice intern quote messin" with my veins end quote. He had a scalpel, complete with a very sharp blade, hidden under his pillow. He underscored how little he wanted the intern touching him by waving the scalpel at him."

"So, you had the man arrested," Eric said flatly.

"No!" Leslie said lightly, smiling at Eric's concern. It made her feel warm. His voice made her feel warm. Warm and eager. "I had a talk with the patient."

"*You* saw the patient?"

"He's my patient, too. I've actually taken care of him a few times. Anyway, I told him that he would let the intern try to draw the blood—one try, then I'd do it—or he could sign out against medical advice, which would probably kill him. I also told him that I was considering calling the police about the scalpel. That was a bit of a bluff."

"What happened?"

"He gave me the scalpel—not that he can't get another—and let the intern try. Miraculously, the intern hit the vein immediately and got the blood. He, too, will hopefully be there at eight o'clock tomorrow morning."

"I don't think you should work there," Eric said firmly. "I don't like it."

"It's safe, really," she said, loving the sound of his voice and his gentle concern. Safe, she mused, thinking about Mark, thinking about another resident who had been held at knife-point three months before. She added, a bit uncertainly, "You just have to be careful, sensible."

"You must be tired," he said.

"A little," she said. Exhausted. Physically and emotionally drained. Of course, if he wanted to see her . . . No, she had to sleep. She was on call beginning in nine hours. She added begrudgingly, "A lot. Did you get my message?"

"I'm not going away after all."

"Really?" *Really?*

"So. How about dinner Friday night?"

"I doubt if I'll be able to leave by dinner time," she said tentatively. And I'll have been up all night Thursday night, she thought, frustrated that she had agreed to cover at San Francisco General.

"Do you want to call me when you get off?"

"It may be late."

"It doesn't matter."

Eric gave her the unlisted phone number at his pent-house and the number to the private direct line in his office. He told her to call him whenever she had the chance. She wouldn't be interrupting anything.

Leslie didn't call him until ten o'clock Friday night. She called him from the intensive care unit.

"Eric, it's Leslie. I'm sorry, this is the first chance I've had to call."

"How are your interns?" he asked, relieved to hear from her. He had been thinking about scalpels hidden under pillows.

"The *kids?* They're fine. They've learned a lot in the past three days."

"Still not independent?"

"Aaah. No," she said wistfully. It was why she had to stay late: to double-check their orders, to discuss every aspect of their patients with them. It was what she was there for.

"On your way home?" he asked.

"In five minutes, I think."

"Do you have to go in tomorrow?" Saturday. Eric knew the answer.

"Oh, yes. Just to make rounds. But that may take all day," she said. *I want to see you.*

"Sunday?"

"I'm on call again Sunday."

"Are you too tired tonight? I could come over, read you a page or two of *Moby Dick*, watch you fall asleep . . ."

"That would be lovely."

What am I doing? Leslie thought as she towel dried her chestnut hair. She looked at herself in the bathroom mirrow. She wore a long, modest cotton nightgown under a light-blue terry cloth robe. Very modest. Very decent. Except that she was getting ready for bed while a man she barely knew waited in her living room.

She parted and combed her dark hair that, wet, fell below her shoulders. She looked at the dark circles around her blue eyes and sighed. I look tired. I *am* tired. Too tired to speak, or think, or analyze what I am doing.

"You look like a freshly scrubbed little girl ready for a bedtime story," Eric said gently when she wandered, awkwardly, into the living room. "A little girl up way past her bedtime."

"I am tired," Leslie said, enervated by the hot bath, too tired to think of what else to say.

"Come on, little one," Eric said, taking her hand, leading her into her bedroom and pulling down the bedcovers. "Crawl in."

Leslie slid out of her robe and under the covers. She smiled sleepily at Eric.

"May I join you?" he asked.

Leslie nodded, closing her eyes, succumbing to the cool softness of the bed and the warmth of his voice.

By the time Eric locked the door, turned out the lights, undressed and joined Leslie in her bed, she was almost asleep. She curled against him, her slightly damp, clean hair falling across his chest. He circled his arms around her, pulling her body, modestly covered by her nightgown, against his.

"You're a warm, snuggly kitten," he whispered, brushing his lips lightly on her head.

"Mmmmm," she murmured.

"Mmmmm," he answered, pulling her even closer.

In a few moments, he felt her breathing pattern change to slow, deep, peaceful breaths. She was asleep, peaceful in his arms.

"Precious little kitten," he whispered.

Leslie awakened promptly at six-twenty-five, her internal alarm reliably signalling to her five minutes before her alarm clock did. His arms were around her, gentle but secure. Carefully, Leslie pulled away, watching him, amazed at the wonderful, handsome stranger who was in her bed. Whom she wanted in her bed. Who *belonged* in her bed.

Quietly, without waking him, Leslie made coffee, showered and dressed.

I won't wake him, she decided. I'll just leave him a note.

It wasn't easy to write a note. What should she say? What *could* she say?

Dear Eric, Sorry about last night. Maybe tonight? No.

Eric, There's coffee in the coffee maker . . . Of course there is. He doesn't need to be told.

Eric, Here's a key to the apartment. . . . Too pushy.

Dear Eric, You are cordially invited for dinner tonight. . . . Assuming I get home on time.

"Good morning," he said. He was fully dressed, but unshaven, his hair hand combed. "What are you doing?"

Leslie looked at the crumpled sheets of paper on the table. And the still-shiny extra key. James's key.

"Good morning. I was writing you a note. Trying to," she said, smiling at him, so glad to see him, so happy about the way he looked at her.

"It's hard to write me a note?" he asked, moving beside her, resting his hand on her shoulder.

704 "It is. I don't really know you," she said.

"You know I want to see you tonight."

Leslie reached for his hand, their fingers interlocking instinctively.

"Why don't I drive you to work? I have to go to my place to clean up anyway."

"You'd have to pick me up," she said, her heart pounding. It would be nice to have him drive her to work. It meant they could be together a little longer.

"I don't have anything else to do all day. Except maybe make my famous chicken cacciatore," he said, amazed at what he heard himself say. Eric couldn't remember a weekend when he hadn't worked most of each day. At least, not since Bobby. . . . He hadn't *really* cooked for months . . . years, but today all he wanted to do was putter around her apartment, cooking for her, waiting for her to call.

Eric smiled. He was looking forward to the day. It made him feel full of hope.

Leslie gave him the extra key to her apartment. She giggled as they got into his Jaguar. She held his hand as they drove to the hospital.

"Just pull in here," she said, pointing to the emergency room entrance. It was the safest entrance. It was guarded by police officers.

"I'll be back at your apartment in about three hours," Eric said.

"I'll be here for at least six."

Eric smiled, leaned toward her and kissed her on the lips. His lips were soft, smooth and warm, surrounded by the roughness of his early-morning beard. It was meant to be a brief, good-bye kiss. But it was their first kiss. It lingered, until, suddenly, Leslie remembered where they were.

She pulled away then, gently, reluctantly. She looked into his eyes and trembled as she saw his desire. She whispered softly, "I'd better go."

"Have a nice day," he said, like a husband to a wife. It was the comfortable good-bye of a long-standing relationship, a relationship that had a history and would last forever.

It felt wonderful.

"Is that your famous chicken cacciatore?" Leslie asked, inhaling deeply as they walked into her apartment at six that evening.

"It needs a little more time. Do you want a drink?"

Leslie smiled. He was so at home in her apartment.

"Sure. Thanks. I'm just going to change out of my work clothes."

Leslie returned in ten minutes.

"You made the bed!" she exclaimed.

"I've had a wonderfully domestic day," Eric said as he handed her a drink. I've never had a day like this, he thought. And it's even better now. Perfect now. Because you're here. "I know your apartment very well."

"A little uninspired, isn't it?" she asked, knowing that it didn't matter to him, that he understood how busy she was. He knew she spent most of her life at the hospital, not in the small, bland apartment.

"Who is James?" Eric asked.

"James?" she repeated, her heart stopping for a moment.

"*James 1971*. The drawing."

"Oh!" Relief pulsed through her. Eric had simply noticed the one *inspired* item in her apartment: James's drawing of the deer in the meadow. "Someone I knew in high school."

"It's very good."

"Yes," Leslie agreed. Then she added with finality, eager to leave the subject of James squarely in the past, "He was a talented boy."

"My place is uninspired," Eric said, realizing for the first time that although his penthouse was stylishly and expensively decorated it lacked personality. It was a sterile showcase not a home.

"Not really," Leslie began. It was hard to imagine.

"Really. You'll see. It's all on a grand scale. The top floor of a condominium building in Pacific Heights. State of the art *Architectural Digest*. But," he said slowly, "it's just a place to sleep."

"This is just a place to sleep, too," Leslie said. *Unless you're here. Then it transforms.*

"No. This is a place to make chicken cacciatore and read *Moby Dick* and laugh and—" Eric stopped, distracted by her bright blue eyes, wondering how much he should say.

"And?" she asked innocently. She had no idea what he had been about to say; but she wanted to hear it. She wanted to hear all his thoughts. She wanted to know everything about him.

"And," Eric continued, honestly, gazing at her, "fall in love."

"Oh!" she said, startled, unable for a moment to hold his gaze. Then she looked at him again and murmured meaningfully, quietly, "Oh."

"Oh?" he repeated gently.

The kiss began then, in the small kitchen in Leslie's apartment. It was a long, deep warm kiss that made her mind swirl and her whole being tremble. The kiss continued, in leisurely sensuous moments, as they ate dinner, becoming wine flavored as they drank the Robert Mondavi chablis. It continued after dinner, gaining intensity and urgency, as they washed the dishes, whispering, laughing softly, touching.

"Shall we go to bed?" Leslie asked finally, sighing softly.

"I don't want to push you, Leslie."

"You're not pushing me," she said seriously to his concerned, passionate, pale blue eyes.

"Without even asking I've just—" Eric began.

"Made yourself at home? It's OK. Wonderful. You belong here," Leslie whispered, knowing it was true. *Whoever you are.*

"Where have you been all my life, darling Leslie?"

They made love slowly, discovering each other, lingering over each new discovery. It was a slow, leisurely lovemaking that celebrated the beginning of forever, *their* forever. There was no need to rush—until the sensations became too demanding, too intense, too undeniable—no reason not to savor this, the first of an infinite number of moments of pleasure. A lifetime of pleasure and love lay ahead for them.

They both knew it as their lips, their eyes, their hands and their flesh affirmed the knowledge quietly, passionately.

Over and over.

Chapter 33

"What are you thinking about?" Robert asked.

Charlie stiffened a little at the sound of his voice and continued to gaze out the window at the Pacific Ocean five miles below. In an hour they would land in San Francisco. Tomorrow Robert would return to Philadelphia, and she would return to work and report the tremendous success of the trip of Eric.

These past ten days would be a memory, a dream that had seemed so real at the time but faded quickly under daylight's scrutiny. In an hour she would wake up and return to the bright, harsh lights of reality. It would be over.

She was thinking, when Robert asked, how easy it had been to be with him. They had had so much fun touring the palaces and shrines and museums, walking for hours through fabulous gardens, dining at the finest restaurants in the Orient, while laughing, talking and learning about the culture. Learning about each other. She was thinking how wonderful he had been during the negotiations. She was in charge, but he was there, watchful, supportive, communicating with her through his eyes.

Charlie was thinking, when he asked, how much she would miss him.

"What, Robert?" she asked, turning to him.

"You've been staring out the window for the past hour, *thinking*, I assume, since your mind is never idle. I wondered what you were thinking about."

"Everything," Charlie said.

"That's what I thought," he teased. Then he continued seriously, "Were you thinking about the mystery lady?"

Charlie smiled. She hadn't really been thinking about Eric or the woman that had caused him to cancel the trip. Charlie hadn't thought about either of them for days.

"I wasn't, really. But we will know more, soon, won't we?"

"Maybe. Although I expect Eric will be very cautious. This time," Robert added carefully.

"This time? As opposed to—"

"The only other time he fell in love. With you."

"He wasn't cautious then?" Charlie asked, knowing the answer. Neither of them had been cautious.

"No. He didn't know it. None of us did. You were so young, so much had happened to you, so many unresolved questions. You were grieving for your mother, trying, by yourself, to understand her inexplicable death. And her inexplicable life. We all underestimated the emotional toll that it was taking on you. You hid it so well. None of us had really experienced a tragedy . . ." Robert's voice faded.

Until Bobby, Charlie thought.

"So I wasn't emotionally equipped to fall in love?" she asked after a moment. She wanted to know what Robert meant.

"Equipped, of course. Probably better equipped than most sixteen-year-olds. You had learned a lot about love from your mother. Prepared, no. Ready, no. Not until you got the answers that you needed."

"Which I did, finally, four years later at Christmas. Do you think," Charlie asked slowly, "that Eric and I could have made it then?"

If Victoria hadn't gotten pregnant.

"I think so, don't you?" he asked, looking carefully into her thoughtful brown eyes.

"I think so, too. It felt different—I felt different—for the two months that we had after that Christmas." Until the call from Victoria that changed everything. Charlie stared out the window, her eyes unfocused, seeing something that wasn't there. Something that used to be there but was no longer. "But now, as close as we are, as much as we care about each other—"

"So much has happened. Too much."

"But we didn't intentionally hurt each other."

"But you were hurt. You both were," Robert said. He looked at Charlie then asked a question he had wanted to ask for the past ten days. "Will you be all right if Eric falls in love?"

"I think he already has. I seem all right, don't I?" she asked lightly, uneasily. I've been all right for the past ten days, she thought. How will I be tomorrow? How will I be when this dream is over?

"You are a survivor, Charlie. You always have been."

"What about Florence?" Charlie asked quickly, wanting to change the subject.

"*Florence?*" Robert repeated, surprised.

Victoria and Eric had not been the only Lansdale couple to get divorced following Bobby's death. Robert's and Florence's marriage, already having outlived its viability and held together in large part by their love for their grandson, crumbled quickly.

"Will it bother you if she falls in love with someone else?"

"No! It would make me happy, assuage a little of my guilt."

"Guilt?"

"I was never in love with Florence. We got married because of Eric. We stayed together because of Eric and June. It wasn't unpleasant. Florence was—is—a loving, protective mother."

"A mamma bear protecting her cubs!" Charlie interjected.

"She wasn't very nice to you," Robert began, his brow furrowed, wondering if Florence had done any damage to the confused, tormented sixteen-year-old orphan.

"Robert, Florence was never unkind to me," Charlie said emphatically. "A little indifferent, but never unkind. I know I made her nervous."

"You did. Your effect on Eric did."

"Do you know my most vivid memory of Florence?" Charlie asked, nodding to the stewardess who was checking to be sure that seat belts were fastened for the imminent landing in San Francisco.

"No, what?"

"She threw pennies away," Charlie said seriously, still bewildered by the memory. "I watched her clean a kitchen drawer once. She just tossed the pennies in the garbage. So wasteful. So terribly wasteful."

"I used to be afraid of Orion," Janet said, looking up at the stars that glittered above the cottage. It was a balmy August night. The black, moonless sky sparkled with stars, brighter and more plentiful because there were no city lights to compete with their brilliance.

"Afraid of Orion?" Ross asked.

"I didn't know that *he* was a constellation. I just knew that he was out there, up in the sky, a huge, ominous hunter. I was afraid he would come after me. I used to hide under the covers when I knew he was out," she said thoughtfully.

It was a silly memory, but it recalled the fright—her fright—of a four-year-old child.

"I keep forgetting how timid you are," he said gently, kissing her hand.

"Timid," she mused.

"Personally timid, professionally bold. It's a beguiling combination."

"Have I beguiled you?" she asked, holding his hand against her lips.

"You know you have."

"Timid, Nebraska country girl and sophisticated city playboy—"

"*Playboy?*"

"That's what they say."

"*They* don't say that anymore, do they?"

Ross and Janet had been living together for two months. *They* knew it.

"No."

"So, playboys grow up. At least," he said, pulling her gently, leading her off the porch toward the bedroom, "this one has. Come with me. I'll protect you from Orion."

They began to make love the way they had made love since that first night in March. The only way that Janet knew how to make love: traditional, exciting, timid.

That night Ross did something different. He moved down her body, kissing her breasts, then the hollow of her stomach beneath her ribcage, then her navel, then the firmness of her lower abdomen, then –

Janet's body stiffened. She curled her fingers in Ross's blond hair, stopping him.

"Ross, please."

Ross sat up slowly, heavily. He had found another obstacle. Another hidden secret that she hadn't, wouldn't, tell him. Something that pushed them apart just when he had been feeling so close to her.

It was something to do with Mark—an intimacy between Mark and Janet—not to be shared with him.

"What, Janet?"

"I don't—" I don't know what you're doing, she thought. I don't know what I'm supposed to do. She saw the anger in his eyes. Why was he angry?

"You don't want me to make love to you?" he asked bitterly.

"Yes! It's just—"

"That some things are off limits? Reserved for someone else? Like your feelings?"

"Ross, *no*. What are you saying?"

"I'm saying," he said with carefully controlled rage as he dressed, "that you can't just give little parts of yourself. We're in much too deep for that. I'm in much too deep. Maybe you aren't in this relationship at all."

"Ross, where are you going?" The fright in her voice almost stopped him. Maybe it was something else. Maybe it wasn't Mark, a memory of Mark.

"I'm leaving. I'm going to *my* place in the city," he said, emphasizing his use of my. In the past months he had called his condominium in the city *our* place, but tonight they weren't sharing. They were separate. Again.

"Ross," she whispered to his back, tears of confusion spilling from her eyes. "I'm sorry."

"This every-sixth-night call is almost livable," Eric said.

Leslie curled against him on the sofa. The past six weeks, since she had simultaneously left San Francisco General Hospital and become an R-3, had been wonderful. They spent five of every six nights together. Even when she got home late, after her on-call night, he was there to tuck her into bed, to crawl in with her and to make love with her when she awakened in the middle of the night or in the morning.

Even on the nights when Leslie was rested they stayed home. They preferred to cook dinner together, alone, than to share each other with the world. They read *Moby Dick* aloud and talked and went to bed early.

"Mmmmm. Livable. But not the real world," Leslie said.

"Aaah. The work issue," he said, kissing her hair. They had discussed this before.

"Now, if you would alternate reading chapters about our friend the great white whale with reading selections from my stack of the unread *New England Journal, Annals of Internal Medicine* and *American Journal*, I would be a happy and well-read resident," she said, frowning at the stack of ever accumulating literature that needed her attention.

"And what will you do while I'm studying contracts, financial reports, land surveys, blueprints . . . ?"

"I'll take a nap or a bubble bath. Or I'll just watch you."

"Very helpful," he teased. Then he said seriously, "Do you think we can work effectively under the same roof? Or are we going to have to enforce time apart?"

Leslie knew that before he met her Eric often spent his nights and weekends working. He had to. He had that kind of job. And that kind of personality. So did she. They both had careers that came home with them, went to sleep with them and woke them up in the middle of the night. They always would.

"We have to be able to work under the same roof," she answered seriously. It had to become part of the life they were building together, part of making it livable, part of making a forever.

"I know, darling. And we can. Workaholics can conquer all obstacles, even passion. We start this weekend."

"Right. Let's discuss the ground rules. Can we touch while we're studying?"

"*Touch?*"

"Just feet, maybe?"

"Maybe."

"Good," she said, kissing him. "Why don't we start the weekend after next?"

The telephone interrupted what might have led them into the bedroom for the night.

"Who could that be?" Leslie asked, pulling away.

"Anybody. It's only seven-thirty for the rest of the world. Even though it's our bedtime."

"Hello?" she answered, laughing.

"Hi, Les, it's Janet. Am I interrupting?"

"Janet, you sound upset," Leslie said quickly. She hadn't heard such flatness in Janet's voice since the October night that Mark left. "What's wrong?"

"Ross and I had a fight. Two nights ago. He left. I haven't spoken to him since."

"A fight about what?"

"Oh, Leslie, I don't know. I think the specifics triggered some bigger issue. But I don't know."

"Well, what were the specifics?"

"Oh, Uh, I can't really even talk about it," Janet said. *I wish could. I wish I could just ask Leslie.*

"Janet, why don't you come over? We'll talk," she said, looking at Eric, smiling at him, feeling warm and generous and so lucky.

"No. Leslie, I don't even know why I called . . . If I talk to anyone, it should be Ross."

"You've had misunderstandings before. Things that weren't even really conflicts once you discussed them. You two tend to get your signals crossed," Leslie said buoyantly, trying to encourage Janet, feeling on shaky ground since she didn't know the issue. Still, it was true Ross and Janet had a history of misinterpreting each other. They needed to talk.

"I do need to talk to him. I'm just trying to build up the courage." Timid Janet.

"Why don't you come over?"

"No. It's not over, anyway. I'm two hours away."

"I'll be here."

"Thanks. How are you? How's Eric, whoever he is?"

"I'm fine and he's fine. Let me know, OK? Keep in touch."

Leslie put down the receiver and sighed.

"That was Janet," Leslie explained to Eric.

"The one who got divorced and is—*was?*—involved with someone who you think is good for her." Eric smiled wryly. Leslie and Eric spent almost no time discussing each other's friends. He accurately summarized the brief description Leslie had given him of Janet a month ago. "Right? Is she a resident?"

"Janet? No," Leslie said, realizing that she hadn't even told him Janet's last name. He would know Janet. Leslie was certain that Eric would have seen *Joanna* and *Peter Pan*. He would be surprised. She smiled, "No, Janet's an actr—"

The telephone rang again.

"I guess you'll get to meet her," Leslie said, assuming it was Janet having decided to come over after all. Leslie answered the phone on the second ring. "Hi. We'll see you in two hours!"

"Leslie?" the voice echoed a little. It was a familiar but distant voice.

"Mark?"

"Greetings from Boston."

"Hi! Is Kathleen on the line, too?"

"No, she's at a bridal shower for a classmate from Vassar. It turns out that she has about as many friends in Boston as she does in San Francisco. She didn't even know it until we got here."

"That's nice for her, since you're probably busy."

"We're both busy. Kathleen's already joined the major committees and boards, including the repertory theater and the history society!"

He's so proud of Kathleen, Leslie thought, detecting the love and pride in his voice. She is so good for him.

"How's your fellowship?"

"Great. The best. Very busy. Very stimulating. How are you?"

"I'm fine, Mark," she said looking at Eric, shrugging slightly. "Oh, a friend has been reading *Moby Dick* to me. Out loud. It's wonderful."

"A friend? Anyone I know?"

"No."

"Tell me about him. Or is he right there?"

"He's right here. Looking at me. Wondering who you are."

"This sounds serious."

"It is."

"Well, then, you are both invited to dinner at the Carlton Club in October.

We're flying in for the weekend—the Jenkinses' anniversary—and Kathleen's planning a dinner party at the club."

"The Carlton Club. Maybe I'll see it yet. Of course, I'm in the intensive care unit at San Francisco General in October."

"I hope you can come. I'd like to see you. Kathleen will let you know the specifics. *Moby Dick*, huh? Sounds nice," he said a little wistfully.

What sounds nice, Leslie wondered. Having someone read it to you? Having
time to read it? Anything but medicine?

No, she thought, Mark sounds happy.

"I hope we can come, too, Mark. Give my best to Kathleen," Leslie said before hanging up. As she slowly replaced the receiver she mused, I wonder why he called. . . .

"That," she explained to Eric, "was Janet's ex-husband. How strange for them both to call."

"Does he belong to the Carlton Club?"

"You've heard of the Carlton Club?"

"I am a member of the Carlton Club?"

"I thought it was just very old, very wealthy Atherton with some San Francisco proper thrown in."

"*Very* proper. It is. But there's reciprocity with the very old, very wealthy Oak Brook Country Club in Philadelphia. I don't spend much time at the Carlton Club, but if your friend's a member, I may know him."

"His new wife is a member. Kathleen Jenkins was her maiden name."

"Kathleen. I know Kathleen. We were on the Union Square Theater Board together for about four years."

"She's beautiful," Leslie said, her heart sinking. Has Eric been with Kathleen? Did Kathleen have *Mark* and *Eric?*

"Yes, she is. Bright, too," he said idly, holding his arms out to Leslie, wondering why she wasn't coming to him. "Leslie?"

"Did you date Kathleen?"

"What? Would you come to me?" Eric waited until he held her in his arms. "I never dated Kathleen Jenkins. I never even considered it."

"Really?"

"Really."

"I don't ever want to meet anyone that you dated," Leslie said thoughtfully.

"No?" he asked gently, realizing that he felt the same way.

"No."

Eric was silent. He couldn't agree to it. Someday, Leslie would met Charlie.

"Oh," Leslie continued, wondering. "were you on the board when they auditioned for *Joanna?*"

"That was my last year. I was just too busy, even though I enjoyed it. I go to all the productions. I even invest in a few."

"I hope your investing in *San Francisco*, the new one."

"I am, but how do you know about it? They're playing it pretty close to the chest, planning a big surprise."

"Janet is—"

"Janet Wells," Eric said, searching his memory. He had heard some rumors. Charlie kept him informed, even though he had very little interest in the lives and loves of people he barely knew. *Charlie*, he mused, frowning slightly. Then he said, "Let's see, I even head a rumor that she was dating Ross MacMillan."

"Was. Is. That's the question. Do you know him?"

"Sure . . . I think he cares a lot about Janet," Eric added, surprising himself, realizing that was not information from Charlie. It was his own observation. He remembered the way Ross talked about Janet—the tone of his voice—when he and Eric discussed Eric's investment in *San Francisco*.

"I hope he does," Leslie said. She pressed close to Eric. "This is nice. You already know my friends. Or at least my friends' friends."

"So, I don't have to meet them? Good. That's one less venture into the real world that we have to make."

"Do you think we'll always be this antisocial?"

"We're very social. We're just limiting our socializing to each other. We'll make the requisite forays, just like we'll start working at home, together. Besides, you don't know my friends. They are already bursting with curiosity."

"Are there lots of them?"

"Only three. My father and the two people that I work with most closely." Charlie, he thought, whom I loved and almost married. Would have married. And James, who has become my friend.

"When do I meet them?" Leslie asked, curious but not eager. They had so little time together.

"In November if not before. We're planning a trip to Maui. It's at the same time as my birthday, but it's not a birthday celebration. It's just a celebration. Can you get away?"

"I think so. I'll be ready for a celebration in early November. I spend October in the intensive care unit at San Francisco General. For part of the month I'll be on call every other night."

"Every *other* night?"

"It won't be a good month for us," she said apologetically.

"We'll manage. We'll just keep thinking about Maui."

"Maybe I should meet your friends before November. Will they be annoyed?"

"One will." *Charlie. The one you don't want to meet.* "But I'm not going to share you until I have to. And I have to in November."

"They're your friends."

"They'll be your friends, too," he said, knowing how much Robert and James would like her, how they would understand why he had just wanted to be alone with her.

And Charlie? How could he ask Charlie to hide *their* past to protect Leslie? Did he have any right to ask that of Charlie?

He would have to think about it. He would have to think about all the things that he should tell Leslie, all the things he *needed* to tell her.

He had until November. At least.

Janet arrived at Ross's security condominium building on Sacramento Street at eleven P.M. She used her coded card to activate the locked garage entrance.

I should park on the street, she thought. I should go in the front door and have the doorman announce me.

But then the doorman would know that she and Ross were having problems. For all of July she had lived there with Ross. In July she had belonged there.

And now? What if she asked the doorman to announce her and Ross refused to let her come up?

Janet parked her car in the space—her space—next to Ross's car. At least he was home. She took a second coded card and activated the elevator.

Her hands trembled.

What am I doing here? she wondered as waves of panic swept through her.

Three and a half hours before, she had left the cottage with a vague plan to visit Leslie after all. She had driven down the coast highway, across the Golden Gate Bridge and into the city. But instead of driving toward Leslie's apartment on Parnassus Avenue, Janet had driven, without apparent aim, around the city. Without apparent aim except that the drive had ended in Ross's garage. Was that her subconscious plan all along?

"Hello," she said when he opened the door. She looked at him briefly, noticing immediately how tired he looked. Then, she looked away, avoiding his eyes, afraid of seeing the anger.

"Hello. Come in," he said seriously.

The living room was cluttered with pages of script and musical score for *San Francisco*. Ross had been working on the staging for her show.

"You've been working."

"Trying to."

"August is your vacation month."

"I didn't feel like playing," he said flatly, wondering if she was going to talk to him, if they were going to talk to each other.

Wondering if they were even going to look at each other.

"Ross . . . I—" Janet began.

"You what?"

"I'm sorry. I don't know what happened."

"What do you *think* happened?" he asked hotly.

"I think," she said carefully, looking at her hands, "that I was, uh, uncomfortable about what you were doing, and it suddenly became a big issue. A bigger issue."

"What's the bigger issue?" he asked, moving closer to her, trying to make her look at him.

Janet shook her head then whispered, "I don't know."

"Sure you do."

"I *don't*," she said, her eyes, turbulent gray thunder clouds, meeting his, finally. "I don't know."

"OK," he said, barely controlling his anger and frustration. "Try this. I am tired of coming in second behind Mark. I'm tired of losing to Mark, to the *memory* of Mark. I can't do it. I won't do it anymore."

"*Mark?* What do you mean?"

"Remember Mark's and Kathleen's engagement party? Remember their wedding? No, of course you don't," he said bitterly. "You didn't go. We didn't go."

"I thought you understood. You said that you didn't resent it at the time," she pleaded. *You said, then, that you just wanted to be with me.*

"I've reconsidered it in light of the present situation."

"That's not fair."

"All's fair, isn't it?" Ross asked casually, knowing that it wasn't fair. He *had* understood why she couldn't see Mark and Kathleen. He hadn't resented it once he understood, but there were other examples. "You wouldn't sing to me, remember? That was because of Mark, wasn't it?"

"It was partly because of Mark, I guess, but it was mostly because I didn't really know you," she said thoughtfully. She added quietly, "I sing for you now."

"And now this," Ross said quickly. Janet did sing for him now. Privately. Whenever he asked.

"This?"

"I can only make love to you in a certain way. Part of you still belongs to Mark," he said bitterly.

"No," she said, tears spilling from her stormy eyes as relief began to sweep through her. Had he simply misinterpreted? Could they find a way out of this after all? Maybe. Maybe.

"No?" he asked, confused, encouraged by the half smile on her lips despite the tears.

"*No*, Ross. Mark never touched me there. No one has," she said, embarrassed, almost apologetic until she saw the look in his eyes as the meaning of

her words settled. Ross looked happy. Happy. And amazed. And concerned.

"Then why? Why did you stop me?" he asked gently.

"I didn't know what you were doing. What I was supposed to do," she said quietly, shrugging slightly.

Ross held her then, kissing her tears, blinking away his own. He had almost lost her because of a foolish misunderstanding that was rooted in his own ill-founded jealousy of Mark. Ross had never been jealous of anyone in his life. And, maybe, he needn't be jealous of Mark.

It was just that he wanted her so much.

"Oh, Janet," he whispered. Lovely, timid, naive Janet.

Part Four

Chapter 34

SAN FRANCISCO, CALIFORNIA
SEPTEMBER 1982

James glanced idly at the leather appointment calendar on his desk, then paused, staring at the date written in script at the top of the page: September Twelfth.

September twelfth. Leslie's birthday. One year ago today he had taken her to dinner.

James smiled. He could smile now, again, when he thought about Leslie. He hoped that she was happy, as he was. He hoped that she would find someone to love as much as he loved Lynne. And that, someday, she would have a child.

A child. James thought about Michael, his beloved son. He felt so lucky. He had Michael, and he had Lynne. His life was full—*overflowing*—with love and joy.

It would be safe to call Leslie, to wish her Happy Birthday and happiness.

A knock at his door interrupted James's reverie.

"Yes?"

"May I come in?" It was Charlie, looking like a corporate attorney but smiling a soft, womanly smile for James.

"Of course. What's up?"

"Nothing. Not true. *Everything*. But nothing that involves you. I'm just seeking refuge in your office."

"Be my guest," James said, smiling, gesturing to the burgundy leather couch that got no use by him but looked so comfortable.

"Thanks," she said, slipping off her heels and sinking into the couch. "I am so glad you're here. I used to be able to escape into Eric's office—"

"But?"

"He's no fun anymore. All business."

"You're all business, too. Except you're more efficient than me or Eric so you can indulge in these little breaks."

"Eric used to like the breaks."

"He's preoccupied," James said, defending Eric. James had never had a friend like Eric. James had never met a man he liked, respected or trusted as much.

"Yes," Charlie agreed.

"He's in love. He wants to get as much work done here as possible, so he'll be able to be with her. Is that so bad?" James asked. It was what James did, too, so that he would have as much time as possible to be with Michael and Lynne.

Still, he usually had to work in the evenings, after they put Michael to bed. He knew that Eric *and* Charlie worked at home in the evenings and on weekends. They all did. They all had to.

"No," Charlie said wistfully. "It's not bad at all."

"Charlie, what's really bothering you?" he asked suddenly.

"I miss him, James. Not just the little breaks," she said wryly. "I miss the evenings and the nights and the weekends and the trips."

"Oh," James said slowly. "I didn't know. I knew you were close . . ."

So Eric hasn't told him about us, Charlie thought. How could he? The story of Eric and Charlie wasn't complete without the part about the little boy who had died. And neither Eric nor Charlie would tell James, whose life had been made perfect by the birth of his son, about Bobby.

"We've known each other, cared about each other, for a long time," Charlie said thoughtfully. Then she added something she had never told Eric. Something she had admitted to herself only recently because she had to. "I thought we might even get married someday, after all, if neither of us found someone else. Sort of by default."

"*Default?*" James gasped. He couldn't imagine either Eric or Charlie doing anything by default. They were both so confident, so competent, so controlled. Controlled and in control. They didn't make mistakes. They didn't run their lives by default. But Charlie was serious.

"Long story," she said shrugging, smiling slightly. "Anyway, it's a moot point now. I think he's really in love, don't you?"

"I think so," James said gently, wondering how much the fact of Eric being in love hurt her. He couldn't tell.

"Do you know anything about her?"

"Not even her name. He told me that she is coming to the opening of the resort on Maui in November."

"I didn't know that," Charlie said softly, her stomach aching slightly. She would meet Eric's love, get to know her and probably like her. It would be nice to have it behind her. In two months it would be behind her. "Are Lynne and Michael coming?"

"Sure."

"I'm looking forward to meeting Lynne. And Michael," Charlie said truthfully. "I guess everything worked out just like you said it would."

"It worked out, Charlie, but not the way I thought it would. You were right. Lynne knew about it. She knew from the beginning."

"She knew about Leslie?"

"I can't believe you remember her name!" James exclaimed. "She knew there was someone. She didn't—she still doesn't—know who it was, except that she was someone I knew from high school. Anyway, it's a long story, too. But, fortunately, we survived it."

"More than survived. You seem very happy."

"I am. Listen, Charlie, I'd really like you to meet Lynne—and Michael—before November. Why don't you come over for dinner?"

"James, you are so nice. I'm OK, really."

"I know you're OK, but I *really* want you to meet my family. This Friday, how's that?"

"That's fine, James, thank you. I'm looking forward to it," she said. She put on her shoes and got ready to leave, the break over. She paused at the door. "I really am looking forward to meeting them."

After Charlie left, James reached for the phone to call Lynne, to let her know that he had invited Charlie for dinner. As he dialed the phone, he thought again about calling Leslie.

He wouldn't do it. It was safe—like their affair was safe—unless Lynne found out. It wasn't worth it. James wouldn't do anything that could jeopardize his life with Lynne and Michael.

"This is déjà vu," he said. 719

Leslie spun around. She was in the small lab near the intensive care unit at the San Francisco General Hospital running a blood gas. It was three o'clock in the afternoon on Saturday, October sixteenth.

"Mark!"

"Hi."

"Hi. Please withhold your déjà vu comments until after I've done the gas and we can get out of here," Leslie said, shivering involuntarily as she remembered the last time she and Mark were here together. The day he was shot. "How are you? You look good."

Mark looked handsome, his dark handsomeness enhanced by the fatigue in his eyes and the strain on his face, but he did not, really, look *good*.

Something is wrong, Leslie thought. Something that would make him spend part of his brief visit to Atherton for Kathleen's parents' anniversary at the hospital on Saturday afternoon with her.

"I'm fine. We're sorry that you can't come to the party tonight."

"But this is really the mountain coming to Mohammed."

"I wanted to see you," he said.

"That's really nice," Leslie said. Why? she wondered. She looked at his serious brown eyes and knew that he was going to tell her.

"You really love this, don't you?" he asked. It was more of a statement than a question. An uncomprehending, wistful statement of fact.

"And you really don't," she said, looking at him. That was what he wanted to talk about. *Finally.*

I like parts of it," he said swiftly.

He's still trying to convince himself, Leslie thought, still not allowing himself to quit.

"What parts don't you like?"

Mark hesitated. Then he said carefully, "I don't like the sadness. I don't like to see people who are sick, who are dying."

Who does? Leslie thought. I'm not a doctor because I *like* to see sickness and death. I'm a doctor because I want to help. But this isn't about why I'm a doctor. It's about helping Mark decide not to be one.

"What bothers you about it?" she asked, curious.

"It makes me feel sad. It makes me feel like I'm dying. It affects my whole life," he said. *It makes my life seem hopeless.*

"Then let it go, Mark. Get out of it," Leslie said emphatically. *Get out before it destroys you and Kathleen. Or before you destroy yourself.* She had wondered once before, in this tiny lab, if Mark had a death wish. Now she worried that he might see no way out but by his own death. What if he joined forces with the death and sadness that consumed him? What if, instead of fighting it, like she did, he gave in to it?

What if . . .

"I'm worried about you," she said seriously.

"Don't be, Leslie. I'm all right," he said unconvincingly. "I go for weeks at a time really enjoying my fellowship—"

"And then?"

"And then I go through periods of doubt. Don't you?" he asked hopefully.

That's why he's here, Leslie thought. To have me tell him that it's normal to feel the way he feels. To have me convince him not to quit.

"I feel the sadness. You know that. And sometimes I think it would be easier, emotionally easier, to be doing something else. But," she said firmly, "I don't feel
720 consumed by the sadness or the death. Mark, what about your interest in English? In writing?"

"I think about it a lot."

"*Do* it," Leslie said urgently. "What does Kathleen think?"

"I haven't discussed it with her. I don't know what she'd think."

"Well, you know for a fact that she didn't marry you because you're a doctor," Leslie said, remembering the conversation that she and Kathleen had had the night Mark was shot. She married him in *spite* of the fact.

"I do know that?" Mark asked, surprised.

"You should know that. If I know it, and I do, you should. Mark, you really should involve Kathleen in this," Leslie said carefully. She didn't want to offend him. Was he making the same mistakes with Kathleen that he had made with Janet? Was he shutting her out? "Kathleen must notice that you are worrying about something."

"Oh, I don't know. I don't think so. I just wanted to discuss it with you, as long as I was in town," Mark said lightly. "So, tell me about Eric. Kathleen thinks he's terrific . . ."

Kathleen's fingers trembled as she dialed the number. This was a desperate idea, but she was desperate.

Ross answered on the fourth ring.

"Ross, it's Kathleen."

"Hi, welcome home. Sorry I won't see you this trip, but—"

"I know, I understand. Maybe I'll come back for opening night of *San Francisco* next month. In fact, that's sort of what I called about. Is Janet there?" she asked.

"She's gone for a walk on the beach. Why?"

There was a long silence. When Kathleen spoke again, Ross heard the emotion in her voice.

"I just wanted to talk to her," Kathleen said shakily.

"To Janet? Katie, honey, what's wrong?"

"I don't know what's wrong. Something's wrong with Mark."

"What's wrong with him?"

"He's moody. Sometimes he's fine, sometimes he withdraws from me. I thought he might be depressed. I read his textbooks. He doesn't have the classic symptoms of depression. He was like this a little before we got married. I thought he was just getting over his divorce. I don't know, Ross. Sometimes I think he regrets that he married me—" Kathleen was crying.

"Katie. No one would ever regret marrying you."

"Thanks," she sniffed. "But Ross, Mark is unhappy and he's married to me. Those are the facts."

"Why do you want to talk to Janet?" he asked uneasily.

"I just wanted to know if he was like this with her. Do you know?"

"I don't know. We don't really talk about her marriage to Mark," he said. *And I don't want to.*

"Will you ask her if she'll talk to *me* about it?"

"Katie . . ."

"Ross, please. If she won't, she won't."

"If you want me to I will," he said hesitantly. Who was he protecting? Janet? Their relationship? Everything had been so perfect since August. "Where is Mark now, anyway? Isn't he with you?"

"He's in the city visiting Leslie at the hospital."

Leslie, Ross thought. Mark's friend. Janet's friend. Eric Lansdale's love. 721

"Why don't you talk to Leslie? Maybe she knows what's wrong with Mark," he suggested.

"I can't talk to Leslie about this. Really, Ross. She thought I was wrong for Mark from the beginning."

"*What?*" Ross asked, amazed. "How could you be wrong for Mark? For anyone?"

"I don't know. I just got the feeling Leslie thought I was a gold digger."

"You're the *gold.*"

"Well, an emotional gold digger, then: too trivial for Mark, not sincere enough. I don't know. I just know that Leslie doesn't approve of me. I can't talk to her," Kathleen said then paused. What am I doing? she wondered. She added slowly, "And I can't talk to Janet, either. It was a dumb, impulsive idea."

"Katie, I will ask her if you want me to. If it might help," Ross said.

"It won't help. Not really. This is my problem. I guess I just wanted to tell someone. *You.*" Kathleen tried to sound positive.

"I'm sorry about this, honey."

"I know you are, Ross. Thank you. I've got to go," Kathleen said suddenly, fighting back tears.

"Keep in touch, Katie."

Ross hung up the phone just as Janet walked in the door, smiling, her cheeks rosy from her brisk walk and the cool October ocean breeze.

"Who was that?" she asked, smiling, kissing him on the lips.

"It was Kathleen."

"Oh! How's she?"

"All right, I guess," Ross said unconvincingly, obviously concerned. He was not sure that he wanted to tell Janet, but he was unable to forget the pain in Kathleen's voice.

"What's wrong?"

"Something about Mark being moody and withdrawn," Ross said with a sigh.

"Oh," Janet said sympathetically. "That's too bad. I know how she feels."

"Do you know why he acts that way?" Ross asked. Maybe Janet would tell him something that would help Kathleen. Something *he* could tell Kathleen.

"I have a theory," Janet said slowly, thoughtfully, remembering. "I think Mark doesn't really want to be a doctor. And I think it torments him."

"If he doesn't want to be a doctor, why doesn't he just quit?" Ross asked, a little impatiently. Ross didn't do things that he didn't want to do. Not without a very good reason. He didn't really want to live in Janet's too tiny, country cottage, but he did because Janet was a very good reason.

"It's not that easy."

"Sure it is," Ross interjected firmly.

Janet smiled thoughtfully at him. "You see things so clearly," she said, teasing him gently.

"I just don't have much tolerance for indecisive adults."

"I know. I don't think it's a question of indecision, because there weren't any choices. From the moment Mark was born, he was destined to be the *best*," Janet said, smiling sadly.

"The best," Ross mused quietly, wondering if this had anything to do with Janet's insistence that being the best—even though she was—didn't matter to her.

"Mark was—is—the best at everything he does. He was raised to be and

now it is part of him. The compulsion and the drive and the expectations are within him."

"I have no argument with people wanting to be the best," Ross said irritably, his impatience surfacing again. "But why doesn't he quit medicine and become the best at something he likes?"

"I think Mark actually believes that being a doctor *is* the best. He has spent all of his life—*all of it!*—preparing to be a doctor, the best doctor. Now he's there and he hates it. It's a tremendous failure, and Mark doesn't fail," Janet said, frowning.

He failed you, Ross thought without venom. Ross had met Mark a few times. He liked him, respected him. Ross cared deeply about both the women who had fallen in love with Mark. As he listened to Janet, Ross became more sympathetic.

A failed marriage. A career—the *only* career—that had failed somehow. It quickly added up to a failed life. Mark *had* to start making choices.

"He's not a good doctor?" Ross asked.

"Leslie says he's a wonderful doctor. The best. He just hates it and it torments him."

"He has to get out," Ross said emphatically, surprised by his own sudden concern. *He has to get out for Kathleen's sake. And for his own.*

"I know. It's so easy for us to see that. It seems so obvious. I don't think we have any idea how difficult it would be for Mark to quit. Maybe impossible. It's hard to give up something you've believed in all your life," Janet said thoughtfully, carefully. "Something that *is* your life, part of who you are. It's like giving up on yourself."

I know how hard I tried to convince myself that my marriage could work, she thought. Even long after I knew it was over. I know how much I was willing to suffer before, finally, giving up on us. Giving up on Mark . . .

Ross and Janet sat in silence for a few moments.

"Does Leslie know?" Ross asked finally.

"Ross, when I left Mark, *he* didn't know. It was just my theory. But," she added, "I think that Leslie does know. Now."

Janet sighed and reached for Ross's hand.

"We are so lucky," Janet said.

Ross pulled her close to him and stroked her silky hair.

"So lucky," she repeated as she curled against him. "Until the new owner decides to stop renting the cottage!"

"He'll probably never decide that," Ross said. "This place is too small anyway."

"Do you think so?" she teased, feigning surprise. Ross complained almost daily about the tiny cottage. He needed floor space to spread his scripts; he needed his piano; he needed his stereo system. "Maybe someday we could buy a bigger place in the country."

"Buy a place together?" he asked.

"Yes," she said softly, realizing what she had just told him.

"Would you do that with someone if you weren't married to him?"

"No," she whispered, her cheeks flushed, her eyes glistening. It was what she wanted. It didn't scare her. It made her happy. If only he wanted it, too.

"Janet?" he asked carefully.

"What?" she asked, smiling, radiant.

"Will you marry me?"

"Yes," she breathed. "Yes, of course."

"Really?"

"Really."

"I love you."

"I love you."

Then Ross began to laugh.

"Ross!" she exclaimed, then started giggling. "Why are we laughing?"

"Because, in your—*our*—musicals at this point you sing a lovely song and wander off to bed with whomever."

"That sounds wonderful, as long as whomever is *you*."

"But we have something much more important to do," he said very seriously.

"We do? What?"

"We have to move. Into a bigger house with a bigger bedroom. Right now. Come on," he said, pushing her gently off his lap.

"Where?" she asked. Was it possible?

"Just a mile down the road."

"Ross. Really? *You* bought—" she stopped, unable to speak, tears filling her eyes.

"I did. It cost a pretty penny, too. And since the prettiest of my pennies are paying the salary of one beautiful, talented—"

"Are you marrying me for my money?" Janet asked with innocent, glistening, gray eyes.

"You bet. For your half of the mortgage."

" 'For your half of the mortgage.' What a wonderful title for a love song," she said dreamily as she followed him toward the door. "The house is furnished?"

Ross stopped, spun around and shook his head, smiling sheepishly.

"Maybe we should move in tomorrow, then," Janet teased gently, lovingly.

"Promise?"

"I promise."

"Let's go back to the traditional wandering off to bed with whomever, then," he said, taking her with him.

"To the tiniest bedroom in the world? With the man I love?" she asked seriously, kissing his lips hungrily.

"I love you, Janet."

Two hours after Mark left San Francisco General Hospital to return to Atherton, Leslie was paged to the pediatric intensive care unit.

"Hi, Leslie, this is Bruce Franklin. We just had a seven-year-old boy admitted with profound hypoglycemia and coma. It will probably turn out to be Reye Syndrome, but there are some atypical features. Do you have time to stop by? We could use your input."

"Sure. I'm a long way away from my last pediatrics rotation—"

"I know, but this may be an adult illness appearing in a child. We could really use your opinion."

"I'll be right there."

The boy lay motionless in the bed. He could have been asleep. His eyes were closed, but his long dark lashes didn't flutter. He wasn't asleep. He was in a coma, his breathing supported by a mechanical ventilator, his blood pressure maintained by medications that dripped in carefully measured, carefully timed drops into his tiny blue veins.

"It could be Reye Syndrome, Les, except that he was apparently completely well until today. No antecedent illness at all. And his liver enzymes are normal. His mother tried to wake him from a nap this afternoon, but he didn't wake up. His serum glucose was twelve. His spinal tap, except for the low sugar, is normal."

Leslie approached the boy, closely examining his face. Then, lifting the covers, she examined his small body. The pediatricians watched in silence, witnessing her blue eyes change from professional, thoughtful concern to horror.

"He wasn't well yesterday, Bruce," she said flatly. "He's cachectic. He has no fat and very little muscle mass. He's severely malnourished, don't you think? He *must* have a chronic illness."

"We agree, Leslie," Bruce said carefully. "He doesn't look like a healthy little boy, but his mother says he was outside playing, as usual, yesterday."

"Is she reliable?"

"Seems very concerned. Anything else?"

"Well, he has abrasions on his wrists and ankles," she said. As she spoke, Leslie lifted his frail, thin arms to look at the abrasions on both wrists. Without realizing the implication of what she was doing, she crossed the wrists, laying one on top of the other. The abrasions, abrasions that could have been caused by rubbing, met at the point where the bones of the forearms crossed each other. Leslie put the arms down quickly and looked at the ankles. The pattern of the abrasions was the same, caused by rubbing at the point where the bones crossed.

"Oh my God, Bruce," she whispered.

Bruce nodded.

"He was tied up, wasn't he?" Leslie asked in horror, realizing that Bruce and the others suspected it, too. She was their independent observer, their second opinion. "And starved—"

"And murdered," one of the residents said.

"Can't you save him?" Leslie asked.

"We're trying, Leslie. He's on maximal pressors and his pressure is still low. He has renal failure. He probably has hepatic failure, even though his enzymes are normal. He just doesn't have any viable hepatocytes left. We're giving him everything we've got," Bruce said, the emotion now evident in his voice.

"Do you think it's the mother?" Leslie asked, incredulous. Child abuse was a disease the pediatricians saw. Internists saw the ravages of self-abuse—drugs, tobacco, alcohol, obesity—but they rarely saw innocent victims. How could it be this little boy's mother?

"It almost has to be. When the medics arrived, he was in a bed looking like a child taking a nap, and she's the one who insists that he was outside playing yesterday. We know that can't be true."

"The father?"

"Apparently they're divorced. She has custody and a boyfriend who also seems very concerned."

"So what do you do?"

"We try to save his life. And we call the police. They may want to talk to you, Leslie."

"That's fine. Bruce, have you ever seen anything like this before?"

"We see it a lot, Leslie."

* * *

As Leslie drove to Eric's penthouse in Pacific Heights at four-thirty the next afternoon, she thought about what had happened. She was interviewed by the police. She saw the mother and her boyfriend, well-dressed, well-groomed, in tears as the police interviewed them. She watched the little boy die depite heroic resuscitative efforts. She thought about what Mark had said, about spending your life dealing with sadness and death and tragedy, about being consumed by it.

She was consumed by the horror of what she had witnessed last night. She had spent the night trying to understand how a human being could do that to another human being, how a *mother* could do that to her child. It was impossible for her to imagine, but it was real. The memory, the feeling in her stomach and her heart, would never leave her.

"You look exhausted, darling," Eric said, holding his arms out to her as she entered the penthouse.

Usually, despite her fatigue, Leslie was able to smile for Eric, to feel the rush of excitement at being with him again, but today there was no joy as she fell into his arms. Today she felt relief to be with him, to feel his warmth, his love, but she felt no joy.

The abused little boy was still with her. Her heart was full of him.

Leslie began to cry, silently, burying her head against Eric's chest.

"Leslie? What's wrong?"

She shook her head.

"Tell me, darling," he said warily, kissing the top of her head, catching strands of chestnut hair in his mouth.

Leslie hesitated. She knew that Eric didn't like to hear about her patients. They never discussed it, but he always seemed a little distant when she told him specific details about a patient. It didn't matter if the story was sad or happy. He was always polite; but he didn't ask questions, and he didn't seem interested. He always changed the subject as soon as possible.

It was something they needed to discuss sometime when they were both rested. In Hawaii, Leslie had already decided. She needed to know why Eric didn't want to hear about her work. It wasn't a small issue. Medicine was a part of her life, part of her. What if someday something so horrible happened that she needed to talk to him? Needed his support?

And now it had happened. She needed to tell him—to tell *someone*—and he was the man she loved. She was too tired and too upset to discuss the *issue* first.

"I have to tell you, Eric," she said, almost apologetically. She heard the apprehension in his voice. And the love.

"Tell me."

"Last night they admitted a little boy to the pediatric intensive care unit. At first they thought he had what's called Reye Syndrome—" Leslie stopped abruptly. Eric's body stiffened, and he lifted his lips away from her head. "Eric?"

"I'm listening," he said hoarsely, pulling away from her. "I made some coffee, shall I get you some?"

"No, I just need to go to sleep," she said, following him into the gourmet kitchen with the view of the Presidio. "Anyway, they thought he had what's called Reye Syndrome. It usually follows chicken pox or—"

"I know what it is," he said flatly.

"You do?"

"Yes. But that isn't what he had, right?" he added quickly. "He was a victim of child abuse. It was in this morning's newspaper."

"The media doesn't miss a trick," she said idly, remembering that there had been reporters. Fortunately, she hadn't been who they wanted this time.

"No. It must have been awful, Leslie," Eric said. His voice sounded stilted, uneasy. "Why don't you take a shower and a nap?"

Why won't you talk to me, Eric? I don't want to tell you the facts. I want to tell you how I feel. Why can't you let me? she wondered.

It would have made her angry, except that she saw a look of pain, almost of fear, in his eyes.

He wants to help me, but he can't, she thought. For some reason he can't.

Tears spilled out her blue eyes. Eric came to her quickly, put his arms around her and kissed her wet eyes.

"Leslie, I'm sorry. Don't be said. I love you so much."

"I love you, too, Eric." *I do love you. But we need to talk about this. Sometime. Some other time.*

Chapter 35

Eric met her at eight-thirty in the morning at the main entrance of the Veteran's Administration Hospital. Their non-stop flight to Maui was scheduled to leave at ten. Eric had decided against taking the corporate jet since they were all traveling at different times. Charlie and James were already there. Leslie couldn't leave until now, thirty minutes after her on-call night had ended.

"Good morning," she said, smiling, kissing him lightly on the lips.

"You look ravishing," he said.

Leslie had showered and changed into her travel clothes at the hospital. Her white coat and skirt and last night's colorful blouse were folded neatly in her overnight bag.

"I just look different than every other time you pick me up. No stethoscope, no rumpled white coat, no iodine stains. I also probably look happy. All last night I kept thinking, at the end of this tunnel is five days in Hawaii with Eric."

"All last night?" he asked as they drove out of the circular drive toward the coast highway and San Francisco International Airport.

"I'm afraid so," she said. In little bits, since meeting Eric, Leslie had abandoned her practice of staying up all night. If it wasn't busy she would try to sleep. "We were very busy. I was up all night, but I'm not the least bit tired. I'm not going to waste a second of the next five days sleeping!"

"Part of the next five days is for you to rest. You still haven't recovered from your month in the ICU."

"You need to rest, too."

"I plan to be right beside you the whole time."

"That makes it a lot more palatable."

They drove in silence for a while, holding hands.

"Oh, Janet called last night. I'm supposed to be sure that you don't think that she's upset that we're missing her wedding," he grimaced. "I think that was the message."

"Her wedding *and* the opening of *San Francisco*. These are five of the most eventful days of Janet's life," Leslie said thoughtfully, remembering how excited Janet had been when she called to tell Leslie that they had three weeks to plan her wedding. Her parents were coming out from Lincoln for opening night of

San Francisco. Janet wanted to get married during their visit.

The guest list was small but important: loving friends and family; Janet's parents and Ross's parents; and a few friends like Leslie and Eric. After the ceremony they would all have dinner at the Carlton Club. The next night they would go to opening night of *San Francisco* starring Janet *MacMillan*.

Leslie remembered Janet's excitement. And she remembered her disappointment when Leslie told her that she and Eric would be in Maui.

"You're upset," Eric said.

"No. It's just too bad. I would like to have been there. She's a dear friend. But," Leslie said smiling, "she knows how happy we are for them. I have squandered yet another chance to see the Carlton Club, however."

"Is that a burning desire of yours?"

"No. Just a burning curiosity. My friends keep choosing it as the place to celebrate their weddings."

"Maybe we—" he began, then stopped. Maybe we should get married, he almost said. It would have been so easy to say. It was what he wanted to say. But first, they had to talk. He had to tell her about Bobby. And Charlie. She must learn why it was so hard for him to hear about her patients and how he wasn't sure that he could have another child, that he could risk the pain, again.

They had to rest in Maui. And they had to talk.

"Maybe we?" she asked, curious, her blue eyes sparkling. She knew what he had almost said. And that he was saving that question for another time.

"Maybe we should have dinner there sometime," he said, smiling, not looking at her.

She would marry him now. And he would marry her. Even if they didn't talk about the obstacles they both knew were there, they would go into it blindly because they believed their love could overcome anything.

"Maybe we should!" she answered, laughing. *Take your time, Eric.*

Leslie had one glass of champagne and orange juice—a mimosa—once the plane reached a cruising altitude and slept, curled against Eric, for the remainder of the flight. She awakened, refreshed, as the wheels touched the landing strip of Kahalui Airport on Maui.

"What a warm, lovely fragrance!" she exclaimed as they walked, outside, from the plane to the baggage claim area.

"Welcome to the tropics, darling," he said, squeezing her. "It's a blend of plumeria and coconut and sugar cane."

"I love it."

They drove across the island along the Mokulele Highway toward Wailea. They drove through green fields of sugar cane blown by the warm tropical wind toward the bright blue Pacific, white-capped and sparkling in the distance.

"Who else will be here?" Leslie asked. It was time to learn about Eric's friends. They hadn't even discussed them.

"My two right hands. My attorney, Charlie, and my architect, James."

My architect, James. The words thundered in Leslie's head.

James. How many architects named James were there in San Francisco? Hundreds. *Hundreds*. Still she didn't have the courage to ask his last name. It *couldn't* be.

"Do they work for you or do they have their own firms?" she asked carefully, her heart pounding.

"Charlie and James are both corporate officers with the company. They don't work for anyone else."

Good. That ruled out James Stevenson of O'Keefe, Tucker and Stevenson.

Leslie's heart calmed slightly. Still, James had been working on a project in Hawaii. In *Maui*.

"This isn't a birthday celebration, but it's your birthday. . . ." Leslie began slowly, remembering what Eric had said in August. She needed more information. Even though she might not want it.

"Mine *and* Charlie's. No, we're celebrating the opening of a resort we built. It actually opened last week. We thought it would be good to see if it's really as sensational as advertised, as *we* advertise it."

"It's your resort?" Leslie asked, her uneasiness crescen-doing.

"Yes." *Mine. And yours.* "We're almost there."

Three minutes later they reached the entrance. A large sign read: Ocean Palms—An InterLand Resort.

InterLand. Eric's company. James had never mentioned that name. Or Eric's. It couldn't be. It *can't* be.

But as soon as Leslie saw the hotel, the beautiful, real-life creation of the wonderful sketches James had proudly shown her, she knew. She realized vaguely, as her mind reeled, that Eric was watching her.

"Well?"

"Oh, Eric, it's spectacular," she said truthfully, her heart pounding.

It *was* spectacular. A lush, lovely tropical paradise. The elegant white marble hotel harmonized perfectly, naturally, with the magnificent tropical setting. But that was James's special talent: his ability to translate his love of nature, his reverence for its grace and beauty, into the buildings he created.

Leslie stood in the breathtaking lobby of the hotel, waiting for Eric to register, eager to retreat to their room, wondering how—if—she could tell him. The lobby itself was a colorful fragrant garden of white, yellow and mauve plumeria trees, red and pink antherium and jade-green palms. Priceless oriental rugs lay on the white marble floors. A turquoise-blue waterway filled with red and gold and white koi flowed peacefully through the lobby. Beyond the tall, slender white pillars that supported the huge but seemingly weightless structure, Leslie could see the sapphire-blue ocean.

Leslie noticed the woman because even in the midst of the awesome splendor of James's creation *she* was striking. Her golden blond hair fell, free, to her waist, swaying rhythmically as she walked. She wore a white sun dress, cool, elegant against her golden tan. Her huge brown eyes softened as she saw Eric, then widened as Eric moved toward Leslie.

"Eric," she said smoothly, stretching a beautifully manicured hand toward him, smiling awkwardly at Leslie. It *can't* be her, Charlie thought. But those eyes. Those startled blue eyes. Charlie had seen those eyes before.

"Charlie. Hi. Charlie, I'd like you to meet Leslie Adams. Leslie, this is Charlie Winter."

Charlie and Leslie smiled at each other, both uncomfortable, both trying to appear unruffled.

"Hi, Charlie. I guess it's fair to say I had a different image," Leslie said lightly. Too many surprises, she thought, her heart racing.

You're not who, or what, I expected either, Charlie thought. She had been pacing back and forth in the lobby for an hour, waiting for them, preparing herself to meet the woman Eric loved, forming images of what that woman would be like. She had settled on someone young and dependent and naive. Someone, Charlie realized, like she had been once, before she had been forced to become tough and independent.

But that wasn't Leslie Adams. Charlie knew Leslie Adams. She knew *about*

Leslie Adams. She knew that Leslie could save the life of a colleague and be outraged that the media wanted to hear about her heroism. Charlie knew that Leslie could make a man like James put his belief in traditional morality on hold because he couldn't resist her.

Charlie knew that she would never like the woman that Eric had chosen to love; but now that woman was Leslie Adams, and Charlie already liked Leslie Adams. She had liked her the instant she saw her blood-stained face on television sixteen months before.

Charlie looked at Leslie. "I had a different image of you, too," she said pleasantly. Then she looked at Eric, frowned and asked, "Where's Robert?"

"He's not coming. It was a last minute decision. He couldn't get away."

"Oh," Charlie said, surprised by her own disappointment. She had been looking forward to seeing him. She hadn't seen him since their trip to the Orient in June. It would have been easier with Robert here. He made everything easier. He would know what to do about Leslie and James.

But Robert wasn't here. It was up to her.

"Eric, may I borrow Leslie for about twenty minutes?" Charlie asked suddenly.

"Now? Charlie, we haven't even gone to the room," Eric said, surprised but pleased that Charlie wasn't planning to ignore Leslie. Eric hadn't been sure how Charlie would react.

"I know. The owner of the pearl shop wants to give each of us, me, Leslie and Lynne . . ." Charlie paused as she watched Leslie drop her eyelids at the mention of Lynne's name. She knows, Charlie thought, but she just found out, too. She continued, "A special black pearl. It's a little mystical. She has to meet each of us, then she'll select the right black pearl. It's really very nice. The pearls are beautiful."

"This is an emergency?" Eric asked amiably.

"A true emergency," Charlie said, nodding solemnly but smiling. I have to talk to her, Charlie thought. A true emergency.

"Do you mind, Leslie?" he asked.

"Of course not!" *It will give me time to find James.*

"Good. I'll bring her to your room when we're through. It may be more than twenty minutes, if we get carried away."

"OK. What are the plans for this evening?" Eric asked. Then he explained to Leslie, "I'm sure that Charlie has something arranged."

"Cocktails and dinners here—at Jacques—at seven. *Birthday* dinner tomorrow at James's and Lynne's condo. Lynne's making a chocolate fudge and macadamia nut birthday cake," Charlie added without joy. When she and Lynne had planned it the day before, it had seemed like such a good idea. It would be a chance for them all to get to know Eric's love. An informal dinner among friends.

Oh my God, Charlie thought.

"It sounds very nice," Eric said, unable to interpret the look in Charlie's eyes. Or the look in Leslie's eyes. Maybe the next twenty minutes would help. Eric squeezed Leslie's hand before letting go and said, "See you soon."

Charlie waited until Eric was out of earshot.

"I assume you'd like to talk to James," she said flatly.

"Yes," Leslie breathed. How do you know? she wondered. "Does he know I'm coming?"

"No. James doesn't know it's you. Eric doesn't know about you and James, does he?"

"No, of course not." *How do you know?*

"Let's go to my suite."

Leslie watched as Charlie dialed the number to James's condo and heard her tell him lightly that she needed to see him about a business matter. Could he come to her suite? Yes. Now.

While they waited, Leslie noticed the suite, silently admiring the understated expensive decor: top-quality wicker furniture with pastel cushions, plush mauve, blue and cream area rugs on the white marble floor, silk curtains, eighteenth century French impressionist paintings and crystal vases overflowing with fragrant tropical flowers. The suite was like the entire hotel, a spectacular celebration of the natural beauty of the Hawaiian Islands.

Charlie's suite was cluttered with sundresses, belts and sandals strewn haphazardly in the living room. It looked as if Charlie had been trying to select the perfect outfit and had been wracked with indecision.

But who had Charlie been dressing for? Leslie wondered. For *her*, to make an impression on Eric's new friend? Charlie didn't have to try to make an impression. Her natural radiant beauty was irrepressible and unconcealable.

Or was Charlie trying to impress Eric? Or Robert? Leslie wondered, remembering the flicker of disappointment in Charlie's eyes at the news that Robert hadn't come.

Charlie offered no explanation or apology for the clutter. But, while they waited for James, Charlie wordlessly picked up the dresses and shoes and returned them neatly to the spacious closet in the bedroom.

"A business matter?" James asked, laughing softly as Charlie opened the door.

"No, James," Charlie said, standing aside so that he could see Leslie. "Something much more important."

"Leslie!"

"Hello, James."

"She's here with Eric," Charlie said.

"Oh," James said softly, smiling at her, trying to erase the worry from her troubled blue eyes. Good for you, Leslie, he thought. Good for you and Eric. "That's very nice, for both of you."

"Thank you," Leslie said gratefully.

"I think the three of us think it's wonderful," Charlie said impatiently, "but—"

"Lynne doesn't know your name, or that you're a doctor. She only knows that we knew each other in high school."

"Eric doesn't know that you even existed," she said, quickly explaining. "We haven't talked to each other about who we were involved with before we met."

James resisted looking at Charlie. This must be difficult for her, he thought. Difficult for everyone.

"Then, they don't need to know, right?" Charlie asked. "Lynne doesn't need to know, and Eric doesn't need to know. You can just pretend that you're meeting for the first time this evening."

Charlie only cares about protecting Eric, James thought. As difficult as this is for her, she doesn't want him to be hurt.

Leslie nodded slowly. She didn't want Lynne to know. There was no point, but she wasn't certain that she should hide it from Eric. She would have to think about it. It was her decision. Hers alone.

* * *

Three hours later Leslie heard herself being introduced to James. It was as if she were watching someone else.

"Nice to meet you, James," she heard a voice, her voice, say.

"Hello, Lynne."

Lynne. Leslie watched her with interest. She was softer, prettier than Leslie had expected. The hardness of Lynne's life—her troubled childhood, the toughness she was forced to develop in self-defense, the ravages of her years as a flower child, her husband's *affair*—was concealed deeply behind her soft brown eyes and easy smile. Lynne was happy. Just as James was happy.

Lynne raved about the resort, about Maui, about the tropical climate that, magically, made Michael sleep all night in the spite of his afternoon nap.

"I love it here. I'm coming back," Lynne said, smiling at James.

"She's already plotting an adventure for Monica in Maui," James added proudly. "And *insisting* on on-location writing."

"Lynne writes children's books," Charlie explained quickly to Leslie, remembering that Leslie *shouldn't* know about the Monica books. "And James illustrates them."

"How wonderful," Leslie said, looking at Lynne, wondering how deep beneath the surface the toughness lay. How would Lynne behave if she knew who Leslie really was?

During dinner Leslie sat very close to Eric. They touched only occasionally and then only briefly: a gentle squeeze of hands, a finger on a cheek. But they looked at each other often—loving, intimate glances—and smiled.

The topics of dinner conversation were neutral, orchestrated by Charlie. They talked about the resort, the wonderful gourmet food they were eating, books, movies and theater. They talked about Union Square Theater's production of *Peter Pan*. They had all seen it, which meant that James had seen it twice. Once, on opening night, with Leslie. And once again with his pregnant wife.

They talked about everything but Leslie for almost the entire meal, but just as dessert was being served, Lynne eyed Leslie for a long moment and said, "There is something so familiar about you, Leslie. Your name and what you look like. I know I've seen you before."

Leslie shook her head slowly. *No Lynne, you don't know me. You just know about me. I'm the one who almost ruined your marriage.*

"You were on television once, weren't you, Leslie?" Charlie asked, as if she had just realized it herself. "You saved another doctor's life."

Leslie smiled gratefully at Charlie.

"That's right," Lynne said, nodding. "When was that?"

Charlie cast a meaningful glance at Leslie. *You have to answer that, Leslie. Before James does.*

"A year ago August," Leslie said quietly.

"I think I saw it after that," Lynne said. "As part of a documentary on photojournalism. It *was* dramatic. Did you see it, James?"

"Yes," James said, looking at Leslie. "I guess I did. Did you, Eric?"

"No," Eric said with finality. He gently touched Leslie's hand—the hand with the ugly puckered scar—sensing that the discussion made her uncomfortable. He asked lightly, rescuing her, "So, how is the caramel custard?"

Their words forced Leslie to remember that horrible night in August sixteen months before. How it—those few moments of terror and its aftermath—had changed her life!

That night she had reached into the bleeding, dying chest of the man she believed she loved. *Dear* Mark.

Then the vivid photographs of her blood-stained face had reunited her with a boy she had loved, and he became the man that she loved as much, more, than the boy. *Dearer* James.

Now Leslie wished that none of it had happened. Now she was—because she hadn't yet had time to think about it—concealing the significance of that night from the man who mattered the very most. *Dearest* Eric.

She hadn't had time to think about it.

But it didn't feel right.

Later that night, Lynne said to James, "Eric and Leslie seem very much in love, don't they?"

"We're very much in love."

"I know. And so are they. But," Lynne said, narrowing her eyes, "something was wrong. Everyone seemed a little tense. When I'm the most vivacious person at a dinner party, something's wrong."

"You were great."

"I really dredged up my best coffee-tea-or-milk flight attendant manners, didn't I? I felt foolish, but I kept thinking there might be awkward silences. I wonder why."

"I told you about Eric and Charlie," James offered quickly.

"Maybe that's it. Maybe Leslie knows about Eric and Charlie. It was *Leslie* who seemed the most tense. Like she was hiding something."

You don't miss a trick, James thought. Please don't figure this out, Lynne.

"I'd better set the alarm," James said.

"You three are unbelievable. Is it really necessary to look at the property at seven in the morning?"

"Eric promised no business this trip," James said mildly, thinking about his friend. "Which means, business early in the morning only, so the rest of the day is free."

Eric kissed her as soon as they returned to their suite.

"That's too many hours to go without kissing you," he said.

"The price of socializing," Leslie said, kissing him eagerly, grateful to have his arms around her. "I guess we're not the public display of affection types."

"I never have been."

"No," Leslie said thoughtfully. Or was it because of James? Because he was sitting beside her, too? No, she decided. Then she added, truthfully, "Neither have I."

"Are you all right? You were awfully quiet," Eric said, frowning slightly, remembering the evening, troubled by it.

"I'm fine. Overwhelmed. Tired," she said. Then she added, almost as an afterthought, "I like your friends."

"Do you?"

"Yes. Very much." *One of them I have liked too much.*

Leslie lay awake long after Eric fell asleep, thinking, agonizing, weighing the impact of the truth against the discomfort she felt at the subterfuge and Eric's eventual reaction when, if, he ever found out.

I have to tell him, Leslie decided finally. I cannot hide this from Eric. Our relationship—our trust—is too important. I will tell him in the morning. As soon as he returns.

* * *

"Happy Birthday, darling," Leslie whispered to Eric's back. He was dressing quietly, trying not to wake her. It was six-thirty.

"Good morning," he said, sitting on the bed beside her, kissing her.

"I can't believe you're doing this."

"That comment brought to me by the lady who is on call as often as every other night?"

"You're right. It's your job," she said smiling sleepily. "I guess. But you *are* the boss."

"Tomorrow we sleep until noon."

"I may do that today. Or, at least, until you get back."

"It shouldn't be too long. We just need to decide if we want to purchase more land down the road for additional condos."

"Maybe you'll come back to bed?"

"Count on it."

"So what the hell is going on?" Eric demanded as soon as Charlie and James were in the car.

"What do you mean?"

"For months you've been teasing me for information about Leslie, counting the days until the unveiling, and now, nothing. Even if you didn't like her, you would have pretended to. You would have told me how much you like her. But neither of you has said a word about her."

"We like her very much, Eric. She's beautiful and smart. She's wonderful," Charlie said unconvincingly, looking anxiously at James. *Don't tell him.*

"At dinner last night," Eric continued, his anger beginning to surface, "no one asked her any of the usual questions. Where are you from, Leslie? How do you like being a doctor, Leslie? How did you meet Eric, Leslie?"

"I have to tell him, Charlie," James said with a sigh.

"Tell me what?"

James took a deep breath. "Leslie and I have known each other for a long time. Since high school."

"*James 1971*," Eric said with sudden comprehension. "So you were lovers in high school?"

"No. More recently than that," James said, then stopped.

Eric frowned, then said slowly, "It was her number you gave me a year ago, wasn't it?" That's why the prefix seemed vaguely familiar.

James nodded.

"When did it end?" Eric asked.

"Last December."

"Because Lynne was pregnant," Eric said flatly.

"I didn't know Lynne was pregnant. It ended because it had to end."

James waited. Charlie waited.

"Christ," Eric whispered finally.

They drove in silence for fifteen minutes, finally reaching the land that Eric was considering purchasing. Eric parked the car.

"OK, if we buy this, we can put the resort condo design in this area. But, James, what can you come up with to put over there?" Eric asked as he pointed to the green sloping hillside in the distance.

Eric's voice was unstrained, natural, as if he had never learned that the woman he loved had had an affair with his close, trusted friend.

Chapter 36

Eric returned to the suite at ten. Leslie held her arms out to him, inviting him to join her in bed. Eric stood across the bedroom. He didn't move toward her. Leslie let her arms fall to her sides and sat upright in bed.

"Eric?"

"I know about you and James."

"It was over long before we met."

"I know. It still—" Eric stopped. Still what? he wondered. He needed time to think about it. He needed to understand why it bothered him so much. "I'm going to go for a swim."

Leslie watched silently, helplessly, as he changed into his swim suit and left the suite.

She watched him from the balcony. She had no idea he was such a strong swimmer. Eric swam out into the ocean, against the waves, against the current. He swam as fast as he could, as hard as he could.

Leslie had done that once, years before, the day she had been accepted to Radcliffe. She had swum as hard and as fast as she could, hoping to clear her mind as she forced her way through the cold waters of Sparrow Lake. And that day, when she returned to the shore, exhausted, he was waiting for her with a bemused look in his green cougar eyes.

James.

Eric. Come back to me, Eric. Don't let this hurt us. It isn't about us.

Leslie watched him swim for a while, as he tried to purge himself of the secret—her secret—that troubled him so much. Finally it was too painful to watch.

Leslie decided to shower and dress. She would wear the sundress she had bought especially because she knew how much Eric would like it. The dress was blue and white and feminine. The blue matched her eyes.

Maybe she would be on the beach, waiting for him, when he returned to shore. Like James had been waiting on the beach for her once.

Eric swam with his eyes open, even though the salt water burned. When he closed his eyes, he saw images: Leslie laughing with James, Leslie kissing James, Leslie in bed with James, Leslie loving James, Leslie *wanting* James.

With his eyes open, he could force himself to think.

You have been with many women, Eric, he told himself. You have laughed with them, kissed them, made love to them and wanted them. They all came before you knew Leslie, before you knew there would, could, be a Leslie for you in your life.

How would Leslie feel if she met any one of them?

How would Leslie feel if she knew about the one that mattered most? How would she feel if she knew about Charlie?

She would feel awful, he decided. Just as he felt awful knowing about James. Even though James was his friend. *Especially* because James was his friend. Because he could imagine Leslie and James together, knowing each other, caring about each other, loving each other.

I will never tell her about Charlie, he resolved. I won't do this to her. Somehow I will tell her what she needs to know—about Bobby—without telling her about Charlie.

Eric swam until he was exhausted, too tired to think anymore. Then he just wanted to be with Leslie. He wanted to make the images of Leslie with James go away.

Eric looked toward the shore, amazed and worried by the distance. He had swum straight out to sea, hard and fast. He was already exhausted. Already chilled. The tropical waters lost their warmth as they deepened, as the turquoise-blue water that caressed the white sand beach became blue-black. Deep. Ominous. Cold. All he wanted was to be with Leslie.

James closed the heavy bedroom curtains. Lynne looked at him with surprise.

"I thought we could take a nap while Michael is napping," he said.

"A nap?"

"No," he said, sliding his hand under the halter top that she wore, pulling her against him.

"No," she repeated, reaching for the button of his shorts, finding his lips with hers.

"Tell me about the fantasies of a new mother," he whispered as he kissed her. He removed her top, revealing her breasts, still large from her recent pregnancy and full because she was nursing Michael. James began to kiss her breasts, slowly circling her nipples with his tongue.

He kissed her nipples. Then gently, carefully he began to suck.

"James," she whispered, breathlessly. *I don't need to tell you my fantasies. You already know them.*

"Leslie?"

"*Hi*," she breathed, startled, her heart pounding. She was still in the shower. She waited.

"May I join you? I'm cold and salty," he said.

"Yes. I'm warm and clean."

Leslie opened the shower door and extended her arms to him. They held each other tight for a long moment, immersed in the warmth and steam of the shower. Then they kissed, a deep, tender, needful kiss.

"You are salty," Leslie whispered softly, her lips touching his.

"And you are squeaky clean."

"Not really," she said. She could always defend, at least to herself, a relationship with a man she cared about. It was harder to defend an affair with a married man, even to herself, even with James. She had wondered, as she waited for Eric to return, how much that bothered him. What if it made him think less of her?

"Oh, Leslie," he said, holding her close. "I thought I was a rational man. I *was* until I met you."

"It doesn't have anything to do with us."

"I know that, rationally. But—"

"But what?"

"When I think of the two of you, together, I don't feel rational. I just *feel*."

"I've never been with anyone the way I've been with you. I've never felt the way I feel with you. I torment myself with images, too."

"Of?"

"Of you and all the unknown women. I wouldn't want to know any of them."

You won't, Eric thought. Not if I can help it.

"You know what I want to do today?" he asked.

"What?" she asked. Go back to San Francisco? Maybe they could go to Janet and Ross's wedding after all.

"Pull the curtains, get room service to bring us some supplies—"

"And hide out in our room?"

"Preferably under the covers."

"All day and all night?" Leslie asked enthusiastically.

"Well, no. We are committed for cocktails and dinner at, uh, James's and Lynne's at six."

"That's right, I'd forgotten. Your birthday dinner," Leslie said slowly. Happy

Birthday, Eric. Then she added brightly, trying to cheer them both, "And to see Michael."

As she spoke Leslie watched Eric's eyes. At the mention of Michael's name, they clouded for a moment. Why? she wondered. It was on the list of whys that she had planned to talk to him about during their five carefree days in Hawaii. But not now. Not this trip.

"So we spend from now until then making memories that will erase all other images once and for all?" she asked, kissing his lips hungrily.

"That's exactly what we do," Eric said as he returned her kiss, deeply, passionately.

Charlie pulled the curtains in the bedroom of her suite, darkening the room against the midday Maui sun. It would be easier to talk to him in the dark. Besides, it was already evening where he was, in Philadelphia.

Why am I calling him? she wondered as she dialed the number that was written in her address book, his home phone number, a number she had never used. I just am, she decided. For no reason.

"Robert? It's Charlie."

"Charlie! Is everything all right?"

"Everyone's all right, Robert. Every*thing* is a mess."

"It is hard for you, seeing them together?"

"Why didn't you come?" she asked, not answering his question.

Because I don't want to be your father, or your guardian, anymore. You have to get over my son on your own. Then . . .

"Did you want me to come?"

"Of course, Robert," Charlie said. "I thought you wanted to meet her."

"Meet Leslie?"

"Oh! *Have* you met her?"

"No. But I'm joining Eric and Leslie in Seattle—where her parents live—for Christmas."

"Oh," Charlie said. Christmas. Without Eric or Robert. For the past ten years she had spent every Christmas with Eric. Sometimes she spent it with both of them. Time to grow up, Charlotte D. Winter. The fantasy is over. "Did you know she's a doctor, Robert? Eric met her when he cut his hand last June."

"I didn't know that," he said, the concern in his voice obvious despite the six thousand miles that separated them. "Has he told her?"

"About Bobby? I don't think so. He hasn't told her about me. And I don't think he will."

Charlie told Robert about James and Leslie, and how Eric's reaction—a reaction she sensed despite his outward control—made her wonder if Eric would tell Leslie about her. Or Victoria. Or Bobby.

"He has to tell her about Bobby," Robert said. Then he added softly, "And he should tell her about you."

"I don't think he will ever tell her about either of us."

"He *has* to tell her about Bobby," Robert repeated.

Robert and Charlie talked for three hours. After a few initial moments of awkwardness, their conversation assumed the easy, free-form style of their ten days in the Orient.

"What are you doing for Christmas?" Robert asked, just before he hung up.

"I haven't made any plans yet," she said.

"We'll only be in Seattle for a few days. Leslie has to get back to work, er, the hospital, I guess. I thought about going home by way of San Francisco."

"Oh," Charlie said. She waited, her stomach fluttering.

"Actually, I thought about spending the week between Christmas and New Year's at the Pebble Beach Lodge in Carmel. Going for brisk blustery walks on the beach, warming up with cappucino in front of the fire, reading a few good books."

"Sounds wonderful," she said carefully.

"So, will you join me? I've reserved a two bedroom suite. I thought Eric and Leslie might be coming down, but they won't be. I can probably get the management to find a room for you."

"The suite is fine, Robert."

They walked at sunset from the hotel to James's condominium. The white rock path that ran beside the ocean was lined on one side with fragrant colorful hedges of plumeria, hibiscus and bougainvillea and on the other by white sand and azure sea. The sky glowed pink and gold. The huge, white fleecy clouds turned pink then red then black as the tropical sun fell below the horizon. A warm breeze caressed them gently as they strolled, hands together, fingers entwined.

They were whole again, one again. They had spent the afternoon cloistered, talking, understanding, loving. Nothing, no one could separate them. Nothing could threaten the security and confidence of their love.

Still, as they approached James's condominium, Leslie's heart began to pound, a restless, anxious, uneasy presence in her chest. Don't let this evening upset Eric, she thought. It would be so senseless. I love him with all my heart. Him alone. More than anyone. Ever.

"If we could just hold hands like this—" she began.

"All evening?" he asked.

Leslie nodded. "Is that too much of a public display?"

"I don't think so, do you?"

"No."

"Then I won't let go of you for anything." *Ever.*

But Eric did let go, once, early in the evening.

"Let's go see Michael. He's in the kitchen with Lynne," Leslie said, pulling his hand gently, meeting unexpected resistance, then release.

"You go. I want to talk to . . ." Eric began lamely.

Talk to who, Eric? *James?* No, of course not, Leslie thought. He just doesn't want to see Michael. Or is it Lynne? Why not, Eric?

Michael was a beautiful, smiling, happy baby with rosy cheeks and white blond hair and clear green eyes.

"He has James's eyes," Leslie said softly.

Lynne looked at her with surprise.

"Doesn't he? Doesn't James have green eyes?" Leslie added quickly, innocently, her heart racing, uncomfortable with the deception. . . .

But *this* deception—with Lynne—is necessary, she told herself firmly. If we are all going to be friends for the rest of our lives.

"Would you mind taking him to his daddy, Leslie?" Lynne asked, smiling lovingly at her lively, animated son. "He's not a big help in the kitchen."

"I'd love to. Then I'll be back to help you."

"Oh. Thanks, but don't bother. Without the distraction of Michael I'll be through here in no time."

Leslie carried Michael into the living room, his velvet-smooth, white dimpled arms clinging to her chest, his green eyes sparkling, curious.

"Look who I have," Leslie said as she joined Eric with James. They were discussing the condominium and the changes that James wanted to make in the new ones.

Michael began to wriggle with delight when he saw James. Leslie started to hand Michael to Eric to give him the wonderful pleasure of holding the happy, lovely child, but then she saw Eric's eyes. The pale blue had become dark, opaque and troubled.

He doesn't want to hold Michael, she realized. Why not?

As Leslie handed Michael to his daddy, she saw the limitless joy and pride in James's eyes. And the inexplicable pain in Eric's.

Leslie took Eric's hand. She would not let go again.

Chapter 37

"Shall we go for a walk?"

"During half-time?" Charlie teased lightly.

"Charlie, my dear," Robert said soberly. "We're late in the fourth quarter. Even a miracle won't save them now. I'm afraid the national championship has already been decided."

"And the bad guys won?"

"The bad guys won."

"Then, let's go for a walk."

Charlie loved their walks along the cliff-edges of the Pebble Beach golf course, down the steep trails—when he held her hand to guide her—to the white sand dunes, blown by the crisp, invigorating, salty sea breeze.

Charlie loved their long walks on the beautiful beach, but, then, Charlie loved everything about the past six days with Robert. They talked, they laughed and they drank cappucino and hot chocolate and scotch in front of the pine-scented fire in their suite. They browsed in the quaint shops in Carmel and watched the sea otters frolic off Point Lobos. They had the famous Ramos Fizz brunch at the Highlands Inn and dined on abalone steak near Cannery Row. They drove along the Seventeen Mile Drive and south, along winding roads that hugged the rugged coastline, toward Big Sur. They watched the low, pale winter sun set from the porch at Nepenthe. And they watched it rise from Monterey Bay.

Six perfect days.

Tomorrow it would be over.

"It's pretty windy," Robert observed as he opened the door.

"In that case let me do something with my hair," Charlie said. "I've spent too much time untangling it this week. I'm going to braid it. It will only take a minute."

"Braid it?" Robert asked. "I haven't braided anything since—"

"Your boy scout days?"

"The war," Robert said calmly, remembering. It had been something to do during the long hours in camp or in the bunkers. They braided grass or string or strips of leather. It kept their hands busy, a welcome, if small, release for their anxious energy. Something to do other than simply wait. Or think.

"So?" she asked, turning her back to him, showing him the golden mane of pure silk that fell to her waist.

Robert's strong hands became gentle as he carefully divided the silk into three strands, his fingers brushing lightly against her temples and her neck. Unsummoned, surprising sensations—pleasurable and frightening—pulsed through her body again and again as his fingers touched her as he gently wove the gold into a long, thick rope down her back.

"How do I fasten it?" he asked, holding the loose end.

"Here," she said weakly, willing her hands not to tremble as she handed him a barrette.

"OK," he said as he closed the barrette over her hair. Then he touched hershoulders, turning her to face him. He studied the new hair style and said, "I like it this way."

I like it all ways, he thought.

Why did I feel that way when you touched me, Robert? she wondered.

That evening they sat in front of the marble fireplace in the suite warmed by the roaring red-orange flames.

"Did you make a New Year's wish, Charlie?" Robert asked.

"A wish? Not a resolution?"

"Resolutions are just stepping stones to wishes. Just ways to make things the way you wish they would be. I prefer pure, undisguised wishes."

Charlie smiled. How like Robert. Robert believed that all things were possible. He made things possible. Robert was the most shrewd, powerful and sophisticated man that Charlie had ever known.

And, still, Robert made wishes.

"What do you wish, Charlie?" he pressed.

"I wish," she began slowly. I don't make wishes, she thought. Wishes are too close to fantasies. My mother believed in wishes and fantasies. I don't.

"You wish," Robert urged.

Charlie sighed. *If* I allowed myself a wish, what would it be? For a long moment she was silent. When she spoke, finally, the slow, careful words came from her heart, not her mind.

"I wish," she said simply, "that I knew where I belong."

"What does that mean?" he asked gently, knowing what it meant.

"It means," she began slowly. "It means that I didn't know I was where I belonged—with my mother—until after she died. And I didn't believe that I belonged with Eric until it was too late. Then he belonged with Victoria. And now—"

"Now he belongs with Leslie," Robert said firmly, watching the brown eyes under the golden hair.

"He does, doesn't he?" Charlie asked, realizing then that she hadn't even asked Robert about Christmas in Seattle with Eric and Leslie and Leslie's parents.

"Yes." Robert said. "He does. Does it bother you?"

"No," Charlie answered truthfully. "It did at first. I felt adrift. Again. Maybe I still do, given my wish, but I'm doing all right."

"I know you are. You always do," he said, gazing thoughtfully at the beautiful woman who was forced to be her own island, forced to be strong, forced to take care of herself. Even as a little girl she was alone, independent. No one had ever taken care of her. Not even the people who loved her. Not Mary. Or Eric. Or . . .

None of them had underestimated her strength, but they had all underestimated her needs.

740 "I'm just a survivor, I guess," Charlie admitted a little wistfully.

Just, Robert mused. Your life should be more than just survival.

They left Carmel early the following morning. Robert's direct flight to Philadelphia was scheduled to leave from San Francisco International Airport at ten.

"Are you all right?" Robert asked, breaking a silence that had lasted for twenty miles, from Santa Cruz to Santa Clara.

"Yes," she answered quickly, startled. "Why?"

"You're driving about twenty miles an hour below the speed limit."

"Am I?" Charlie asked, glancing at the speedometer. Robert was right. Charlie depressed the accelerator, shrugged and added sheepishly, "I guess it's the vehicular equivalent of dragging my heels."

"Why?"

"This has been so nice."

"It's been wonderful," Robert said and paused, watching her reaction to his words. He couldn't tell. Then he asked, "You don't mind going back to work, do you?"

"No. Not really. No." *I just don't want you to leave.*

"Sounds a little unconvincing, counselor. I thought you liked your job." Was it just because of Eric? Or was there more to Charlie's uncertainty? *Talk to me, Charlie.*

"It's a good job." *But it's not where I belong. Not anymore. Where do I belong?*

They drove in silence for five minutes. Charlie needed to constantly remind herself to maintain the car's speed. Her inclination was to let it slow down. She had to fight it.

"I wonder if you could pass the Pennsylvania Bar," Robert said mildly. A comment, not a question. Charlie didn't have to answer.

"The Pennsylvania Bar? Of course I could!" she exclaimed confidently. "*Why?*"

"Because any time you get disenchanted with this job, you're welcome to join me," Robert said, taking care to sound casual. Casual but sincere. He added, "Any time."

Charlie didn't answer. She just gnawed thoughtfully at her lower lip as they approached the airport.

The departing passenger area was tangled with cars and buses and taxis filled with holiday travelers returning home. Charlie stopped the car in front of the United terminal. Without warning, her eyes filled with tears.

"Charlie?" Robert asked, gazing at her sad, wet brown eyes, touching her chin gently with his finger.

"I don't want you to go."

"You don't?" he murmured softly, moving beside her, kissing her damp eyes, her flushed cheeks and, finally, her warm full lips.

It wasn't the kiss of a father. Or a guardian. Or even a dear friend.

It was the deep, probing, passionate kiss of a man who wanted her. A man who had wanted her for a very long time.

"I don't have to leave now, Charlie. Not this minute. Why don't we go somewhere?" Robert whispered, suddenly aware of the crush of cars and humanity that surrounded them. They had no privacy, and they needed privacy.

Trembling, her heart racing, Charlie shifted the car into gear. She wove through the traffic with difficulty, trying to concentrate on driving but wholly distracted by Robert's presence and the memory of his kiss. And by her reaction, by how much she wanted him. 741

Miraculously, Charlie negotiated the airport traffic in the departure area. As she drove away from the main terminal, she began to shake deep inside. What was she doing? What were *they* doing? Where was she taking them? She knew with certainty that she couldn't drive all the way into the city to her apartment. It was much too far.

Without making a conscious decision, Charlie turned into the driveway of a motel. They were still on the airport grounds. She parked the car near the motel lobby.

She smiled weakly at Robert, her eyes obscured by a curtain of gold that fell across her face as she bent her head. She would wait in the car while he registered.

Robert returned five minutes later with a room key. He opened the car door for Charlie and held her hand as they walked to the room. Once inside the room he held her, feeling her tremble at his touch. He held her tighter.

Then he kissed her. Charlie returned his kiss eagerly, hungrily.

Desperately, Robert thought. Sensing her tension, he pulled away and looked into her eyes: beautiful brown eyes, fawn eyes, passionate, sensual eyes, worried eyes.

"Do you want to do this?" he asked quietly. He didn't want to push her. It was too important.

"Yes," she breathed, finding his lips with hers. She began to unbutton her blouse as she kissed him.

"Charlie," he said, placing his strong hands over her trembling fingers, stopping them. "There's no hurry."

"Yes . . ."

"Why?"

"I'm afraid."

"*Afraid?*" he asked, suddenly concerned. Maybe it was too soon.

"I want this so much. I want it to be all right."

"I want it, too. I've wanted it for a long time. It will be all right. I would never do anything to hurt you. Don't you know that?"

"Robert?"

"Let me love you," he said, pulling her hands to his lips, kissing their ivory softness.

"Love me, Robert," she whispered.

At first, Robert controlled the pace of their lovemaking—a leisurely, sensual exploration—as he controlled her body, discovering desires and feelings that had been suppressed for so long. She responded to his touch instinctively, without thought or inhibition. Her natural sensuality escaped, freed by his careful sensitive fingers and his warm soft mouth. As her desire blossomed and she needed him urgently, he joined her, moving to her rhythm, her pace, meeting her passion with his own.

This is the ultimate closeness, she thought as they lay together, their bodies one. What I always knew—*believed*—it could be. Not a fantasy.

Just a wish come true.

"You wanted this for a long time?" she asked, remembering his words.

"A very long time. I remember a sixteen-year-old girl—"

"No," she whispered.

"No," he said, stroking her spun-gold hair. "But I was enchanted by you even then."

"I was enchanted by you," she said, realizing that it was true, that it had

always been true. There had always been something so special about being with Robert, even in the beginning. "You wanted me to be with Eric, didn't you?"

"Of course. I wanted it because it was what you, both of you, wanted. Because it made you both so happy." *In the beginning.*

"And then?" Charlie asked, knowing the answer. And then Eric fell in love with Leslie.

"And then our trip to the Orient."

"You thought about us . . . *this* . . . last June?"

"You're not paying attention," he said gently, kissing her.

"How can I?" she whispered into his mouth, lost for a moment in the warmth. She wanted to stay there forever, but she wanted to hear what Robert had to say even more. "Tell me."

"I thought about us long before last June, but you and Eric were still trying to make it work."

"Sometimes. If I had known—"

"A father doesn't compete with his son. I wouldn't do anything that could threaten Eric's happiness. And you would not have been receptive. You would never have left Eric."

Maybe not, Charlie thought, wondering what bound her so tenaciously to Eric for all those years. Of course she loved him. She always would. But they would never be in love again. Being with Eric seemed to be where she belonged. Or where she had once belonged. But maybe that was just because she didn't belong anywhere else.

"Why didn't you come to Maui in November?" she asked suddenly. Robert must have chosen to stay away for a reason. Something to do with her . . . *them.*

"You had to make peace with the reality of Eric and Leslie."

"And you didn't want to help me? To be there?" *You didn't want to be my father or my guardian. . . .*

"No," Robert said simply.

"Oh," she said, hungrily kissing his lips because she couldn't resist, because of what he had told her. He wanted to be her lover. Nothing else. Nothing less.

Robert answered Charlie's kiss by making love to her again. It was what she wanted, what her body demanded, what her heart needed. It was what they both wanted and needed, and as they made love again, they told each other of that need, that passion, that consuming desire. . . .

Afterward she lay with her head on his chest. After several silent moments Robert felt the dampness.

"Charlie?" he asked, lifting her head so that he could see her face. And her tears.

"I never cry," she sniffed.

"Until today. These don't look like tears of joy."

"I miss you already. *Again.* I missed you after our trip in June. Last time we said good-bye we didn't see each other for six months."

"You needed those six months," Robert said firmly.

To get over Eric, Charlie thought. To be ready for this. For Robert. Yes, I needed the time. But not anymore.

"It won't be another six months. I thought maybe just six days."

"Six days," Charlie repeated happily.

"There aren't any good transcontinental flights after about mid-afternoon. So, if we plan to work all day Friday, we should meet at some point midway: Dallas, Kansas City, Chicago."

"Chicago," Charlie said. "Or anywhere."

"We'll do Chicago this weekend. We can stay at the Drake and watch the snow fall on Lake Michigan. And, if we leave our room, we can see the Impressionist Exhibit at the Art Institute. OK?"

"Sounds wonderful," she purred. It all sounded wonderful, but the two words that sounded the best, the words that echoed in her brain, were *this weekend*. It meant there would be another weekend. Next weekend. And the next.

Four hours after Charlie's initial attempt to drop Robert off at the airport, they sat again in front of the United terminal.

"I'll call you when I get to Philadelphia," he said.

"It will be two in the morning your time."

"Is eleven too late to call you here?"

"No." *No time is too late. Or too early.*

"I'll call you, then." Robert leaned over to kiss her before he left the car.

"Don't make the mistake of kissing me like you did last time," she whispered, kissing him back. "Or you'll never get home."

"Was that a mistake?"

"You know it wasn't." *It was the best thing that ever happened to me.*

After Robert disappeared through the automatic doors, Charlie drove to her apartment. She was filled with a wonderful sense of peace.

Maybe it's because I finally know where I belong, she thought as warm tears splashed onto her cheeks for the third time that day.

Chapter 38

Wednesday, January nineteenth marked the end of a week of unseasonably warm San Francisco weather. Leslie awakened to the sound of rain pounding against her window. The large, wet drops were hurled against the pane by a bitter winter wind. Leslie smiled as she gazed at the gray-black clouds and the rivulets of rain water swirling down the street below.

It reminded Leslie of Seattle. Gray, enveloping, cozy.

Besides, her spirits that rainy morning were pure sun. Eric was returning from New York after a three day—three *night*—business trip. It was their longest separation. And it was too long despite the phone calls. Work permitting, she would be at his penthouse to welcome him home when he arrived at seven.

The cold, mercilessly soggy day resulted in cancellations of the late afternoon appointments in Leslie's internal medicine clinic. Could they possibly reschedule with Dr. Adams next week? Her patients wondered. It was so cold, and the roads were so slick. . . .

It meant that Leslie was at Eric's penthouse by dusk. She made herself a mug of hot chocolate and watched the gray mistiness of the day yield to the black emptiness of the winter night. The transition was breathtaking, somber but serene. By five-thirty the ominous darkness of night was dotted with the bright city lights, a galaxy of yellow-white stars in the blackness.

Cozy.

It took Leslie a minute to identify the harsh noise that intruded her silent night. An alarm? No. It was the buzzer for the intercom that connected the penthouse with the security guard in the building's lobby. Leslie had seen Eric

use it once when Charlie dropped by with some contracts.

Leslie depressed the black button.

"Yes?" she asked.

"Mrs. Lansdale is here. She says that Mr. Lansdale is expecting her," the guard said.

"Oh. Yes, of course. Please send her up," Leslie said.

Eric's mother was expected *next* month. Was this a surprise visit? From everything that Eric had told Leslie about Florence Lansdale it would be very unlike her to make a surprise visit.

Slightly flustered, her peace suddenly disrupted, Leslie hastily turned on the lights in the dark living room. The room was immaculate as usual. Leslie glanced at the Tiffany clock on the mantel. Five-forty.

I guess I can entertain Eric's mother for an hour and twenty minutes, she thought uneasily. Unless she has already decided not to like me.

Leslie stood by the door and opened it promptly as the doorbell chimed.

"Hello," said the young woman with dark-red hair and inquisitive eyes who extended a ringless hand to Leslie.

"I'm Victoria Lansdale. You must be Leslie."

"Yes," Leslie breathed. *Who is Victoria Lansdale? How does she know about me?* "Come in."

"Eric isn't expecting me until tomorrow. You probably know that. Anyway, when the rains hit Palm Springs this morning, I decided to come a day early. Where is Eric?"

"On his way back from New York. He should be here about seven."

"Oh. Well, ths way I get to meet you," Victoria said cheerfully. "Eric said you would be working, uh, on call tomorrow night."

"Yes, Leslie aid. *That's right. Who are you?* "Let me take your coat. Would you like something to drink?"

"Thank you. Sure. Are you having something?"

"Hot chocolate," Leslie admitted.

"That sounds perfect. And just about strong enough. I need my wits about me when I see Eric."

Leslie frowned.

"Because I haven't seen him for almost eleven years," Victoria explained, responding to Leslie's perplexed expression.

"Oh, I see," Leslie said slowly as if Victoria's explanation helped. But of course it didn't. Nothing was clarified.

"Not," Victoria continued, her airy voice suddenly somber. "Not since Bobby—"

Victoria stopped abruptly and covered her mouth with her hand. Her eyes widened, then narrowed.

"Oh, my God," she whispered. Her voice was barely audible through her hand. "You don't have any idea who I am, do?"

Leslie shook her head apologetically as she handed Victoria a mug of hot chocolate.

"I'm afraid I don't."

Victoria's calm friendliness vanished, replaced suddenly by agitation and worry. She put the mug on the coffee table and started to move toward the closet to retrieve her coat.

"I'd better leave."

"Victoria, wait! I don't understand."

"Of course you don't. Eric hasn't told you a damned thing."

"Why don't *you* tell me?" Leslie urged uneasily. There was something she need to know. Some hidden knowledge. Would she *want* the knowledge after she had it?

"Oh, no. If Eric hasn't told you yet, it's for a reason. I don't want to make him angry. You know Eric's temper."

Eric's temper? No, I don't know Eric's temper, Leslie thought. Just like I don't know about you. Or Bobby.

"Victoria. Please. You're here now. He knew you were coming."

"Tomorrow. When you would be working."

"Victoria," Leslie persisted firmly. "Who is Bobby?"

Victoria stared at her, *beyond* her to a distant memory, her eyes sad and thoughtful as she remembered her beloved son. Eric couldn't deny Bobby's memory. He shouldn't deny that Bobby existed.

"You have a right to know," Victoria said finally, shuddering inside. Eric would be furious, but it was her story, too. She had every right to tell Leslie.

Victoria returned slowly to the living room. She sat down on the cream-colored couch, wrapped her fingers around the warm mug of hot chocolate and sighed heavily.

Then, with great effort and emotion, she told Leslie the whole story. Beginning with Charlie and Eric. Victoria knew the details of Charlie's background and of her sometimes joyous, sometimes troubled relationship with Eric. Victoria told Leslie that it was during one of those troubled times that she, Victoria, became pregnant with Eric's child. With tears in her eyes Victoria told Leslie about their wonderful son. And about how they lost him.

As Leslie listened, waves of emotion swept through her: bewilderment, grief, anger. Some of Victoria's words echoed and re-echoed in her head.

Charlie was Eric's fiancée. Charlie loved Eric. Eric loved Charlie. Did they still love each other?

Bobby had Reye Syndrome. Now she knew why Eric had resisted coming to the hospital with his hand laceration. Why he had refused an anesthetic. Why he was reluctant to hear about the details of her work and his eyes filled with pain when she told him about the abused little boy. Why he couldn't hold Michael.

Charlie. Victoria. Bobby. Beloved by Eric. Part of Eric then and part of Eric now. Part of Eric's relationship with Leslie. It explained so much.

And he had never told her.

"I always wondered if Eric and Charlie would get together eventually," Victoria said quietly. "But—"

"*Victoria!*"

At the sound of his voice, Victoria stopped abruptly and looked up. He stood at the far side of the room.

"Eric," Victoria whispered, recoiling slightly. How long had he been there? Certainly long enough.

Leslie stood up to face Eric. She saw the anger—rage—in his eyes as he glowered at his ex-wife. It was the temper that Victoria knew and that Leslie had never seen.

After a moment, Eric shifted his gaze from Victoria to Leslie. His expression changed. The anger dissolved and was replaced by anxious concern.

"Leslie," he began helplessly. The ice-cold stare in her eyes—a look *he* had never seen—deepened his concern. How much damage had been done?

"I have to go," Leslie said urgently, suddenly feeling claustrophobic. *I have to get out of here. I have to think about what I have learned. I have to try to make sense of it.*

"Leslie, let me explain." Eric followed her to the foyer.

"Victoria already explained. I *appreciate* that she told me. I needed to know, Eric," Leslie said flatly, her voice as cold and lifeless as her eyes.

"Leslie, *we* need to talk about this."

"We *needed* to talk about it a long time ago."

"We need to talk now."

"I can't," Leslie whispered, her voice breaking slightly. *I love you. I hate you. Why did you do this to us? Why didn't you trust us?*

"I'll come over later," Eric suggested hopefully.

"No, Eric. Just leave me alone for a while. *Please.*"

After Leslie left, Eric returned to the living room. He sat heavily on the couch with his head in his hands. He was lost in his own thoughts, his own turmoil. He had forgotten about Victoria. After several minutes, he became aware of her, standing across the room, stiff and erect. She was steeling herself for his fury.

Eric looked at her with surprise, his eyes defeated not enraged.

"Don't blame me for this, Eric," Victoria warned, the strength of her warning undermined by the shakiness of her voice.

"Victoria," he sighed. It was an effort to speak. Impossible to be polite. And he didn't want to argue.

"I have finally, after all these years, convinced myself that I am not to blame for Bobby's death. You blamed me for his birth. And for his death. I believed you when you told me it was my fault. I always believed what you told me," Victoria said, her voice gaining strength. I believed you because you had such power over me, she thought. "But you were wrong to make me feel guilty, to accuse me of killing my own son."

Victoria paused. Her heart pounded with emotion. This was the reason she had decided to see Eric again after all these years. She wanted him to admit that he was wrong. Or did she only want him to forgive her?

As she watched his eyes, the surprise, the pain, the self-recrimination, her own anger subsided. Eric had suffered, too. He was still suffering.

"I never believed that Bobby's death was your fault. Not really," Eric said quietly, remembering the bitter accusations he had hurled at a time when he needed to blame someone. He hadn't meant them. He had no idea that Victoria had suffered even more because of what he had said in a moment of emotion and grief. If he had known, he would have told her. "I had no idea. I'm so sorry."

Victoria frowned. It wasn't what she had expected. There had been no battle. Eric had changed. Sometime in the past eleven years, his rage at the death of his son had abated. She saw sadness in his eyes. And pain. And wisdom. And love. Who had helped him make the transition? Charlie? Leslie?

Leslie, Victoria thought as she saw the sadness in his pale blue eyes.

"And I don't blame you for what happened with Leslie, either," Eric continued with great effort. He sighed heavily. "I have no one to blame but myself."

He stared at the half empty mugs of hot chocolate. How typically Leslie!

What he would give to be sitting with her now, drinking hot chocolate, telling her how much he had missed her, holding her. Loving her.

Apparently Mark hadn't heard the telephone ring. He usually heard it, even when he was in his study with the door shut. Kathleen waited a few moments. When he didn't emerge from his study she went to the closed door and tapped lightly. No response. Finally, her heart fluttering inexplicably, she turned the knob and looked in.

"Mark?"

Mark spun around in his swivel desk chair.

"Kathleen! I didn't hear you," he said breathlessly.

"Absorbed in your work as usual," Kathleen said brightly. But she wondered, Why does he act so alarmed? What are those papers on his desk? Is he really trying to prevent me from seeing them? "You didn't hear the phone, either. It's for you. It's the hospital."

"Oh. Could you tell them to hold for another minute? I'll take it in the bedroom," he said.

"Sure." As Kathleen retreated her heart ached. He was obviously waiting for her to leave the room. *Why?*

Ten minutes later Mark appeared in the kitchen.

"It's an angioplasty," he said. "I'll be back in four hours."

The grandfather clock in the living room struck nine as Mark kissed her briefly on the cheek.

"Drive carefully, Mark. It's beginning to snow."

After Mark left, Kathleen sat by the kitchen window of their Beacon Hill home and watched the flakes of snow. They fell silently, gracefully, illuminated briefly by the archaic street lamps before disappearing into the blackness. A fleeting moment of brilliance. Then darkness. Death.

I have to do something, she thought. It was the same thought she had every day. Over and over. But what could she do? She didn't know what was wrong.

She could hope that everything would—miraculously—be better again. That was what had happened after their trip to Atherton in October. It had been so unexpected. So welcome. In those few blissfully happy weeks, they had fallen in love again.

Ross called her during that time, only a week after her desperate phone call to him in October.

"How are you, Katie?" His voice conveyed his concern for his friend.

"I'm fine," Kathleen said buoyantly. "I'm sorry about last week. I was such a goose."

"A *goose?* That's cute British phraseology. Massachusetts is no longer a colony, you know," he teased, already relieved by the lilt in her voice.

"I'm just a little giddy. That's all."

"Things are better with Mark?"

"Wonderful. Starting about five minutes after I spoke with you." As soon as Mark returned from his visit with Leslie, Kathleen thought, pushing the thought away as soon as it surfaced. *Leslie.* "A little touch of hysteria, I guess."

Ross had never known Kathleen to be hysterical. Her despair had been genuine and deep-seated. He was glad that the storm had passed but decided to tell Kathleen what Janet had said anyway.

"Mark doesn't like medicine?" Kathleen's voice registered amazement and disbelief. How could Janet think that? "No Ross, I am sure that Janet is wrong. Mark loves medicine. It's his life."

"If he was torn—ambivalent—it would explain his moodiness, wouldn't it?" Ross pushed. Janet had convinced *him*.

"It could. Except that he's not moody anymore. And he loves medicine!" Kathleen exclaimed. But even as she spoke, a trace of doubt flickered across her mind. What was it? A distant memory . . . the look of peace in Mark's eyes when she had told him about her wealth and had teased him about never having to pick up another stethoscope.

"Well. I just thought I would pass it along. Janet thinks that Leslie believes it, too."

Leslie, Kathleen thought. Leslie knows something. Leslie made Mark feel better.

By the end of four weeks, Mark had lapsed back into moodiness. He retreated to his study every evening, closed the door and came to bed long after Kathleen had fallen asleep. Long after Kathleen had cried herself to sleep.

There were brief respites in the moods. Mark would unexpectedly emerge from his preoccupation and discover her again, almost surprised by her presence and her loveliness. His passion would leave her breathless and confused. She wanted to tell him, but in the moments when they *could* talk, when they held each other and loved each other, the words she planned to say sounded foolish. Because, then, there was nothing wrong.

When the bad periods came, as they did more and more often as the weeks passed, she couldn't talk to him because then he didn't hear her.

I have to do something, she thought again as she watched the snowflakes glitter and die. That cold snowy January night Kathleen made a decision.

It was wrong. It was an invasion of his privacy, but she had to know. Maybe it would give her the answer. Quickly, before she lost her courage, Kathleen went to Mark's study.

She looked at the desk in dismay. Mark had straightened it before leaving for the hospital. The top of the carved oak desk was bare. The mysterious papers had vanished. Mark had carefully put them away—hidden them—before he left, so that she wouldn't see them.

I have to do this, she told herself, fighting her own guilt. She closed her eyes and tried to visualize what had been on the desk.

A book. Large. Blue. Kathleen searched the bookshelves. It was on the lower shelf. A textbook of cardiology. Kathleen's fingers trembled as she flipped through the pages of scientific text interspersed with electrocardiographic tracings.

It has to be here, she thought. Whatever it is that Mark is hiding from me.

The twenty sheets of lined paper filled with Mark's meticulous, distinctly non-medical handwriting fell to the floor from the middle of the textbook. The top sheet was a list. The heading at the top of the page was *To Do*. Kathleen scanned the list briefly. The items seemed routine. Some were crossed out.

Kathleen drew a breath when she saw the last item on the list. Not routine. Not an item. A name.

Leslie.

Kathleen quickly turned to the other pages. It was a story.

Kathleen fell weakly into the overstuffed chair in Mark's study and began to read.

Leslie didn't drive straight home. Her apartment wasn't home anyway. Not without Eric. It was only a place to sleep, and she was exhausted but not sleepy. Instead, she drove west toward the ocean, finding her way through the blur of the blinding rain and her own tears. It was a route she knew by heart, the same route she took from Eric's penthouse to the Veterans" Hospital in Lincoln Park. She drove from Broadway to Divisadero to California to Park Presidio to Geary Boulevard and to Point Lobos Avenue. Her winding path brought her finally to the Great Highway and the beach.

Leslie parked her car and walked through the heavy, wet sand to the water's edge. The storm-tossed waves crashed violently at her feet splashing her face with wet salty drops. Huge cold rain drops, propelled by the brisk icy wind, pelted against her. Amidst the chilling dampness of the ocean and the rain. Leslie felt a surprising warmth on her numb cheeks. Tears, she realized. Her own hot tears.

At another time, in a different climate, she would have trudged into the ocean. She would have swum until the turmoil inside her had been purged, thrashed out of her heart and her mind as she thrashed through the pounding waves.

But this was no night for a swim. It was too dangerous, too cold, too sinister. And this problem would not be solved by one swim or a thousand. It could not be so easily purged. It would thrash back at her heart and her mind.

Why didn't he tell me? her mind thundered loudly as if competing with the roar of the waves and the hiss of the wind. Why didn't he make me part of his life? Why did he hide it from me? Why? Why? Why?

The answers didn't come. Just the questions, as cold and relentless and punishing as the winter storm. Finally the numbness of her cheeks and the trembling of her body forced her back to her car. The route to her apartment was familiar: Lincoln to Seventh to Parnassus. But tonight the rain-slick streets were hostile, treacherous. Leslie drove carefully and slowly. There was no hurry. No one was waiting for her.

Two minutes after Leslie entered her pitch-black apartment, the phone rang.

Eric, she thought as she subconsciously counted the rings. If I don't answer it, he will just call back.

Ten rings.

If I never answer he will come over.

Fifteen.

He will worry if I don't answer.

Twenty.

I don't want him to worry.

"Hello?"

"Leslie! It's Kathleen."

"Kathleen." Leslie shifted quickly into a different frame of reference, a different anxiety. Kathleen sounded frightened. It was midnight in Boston. *Mark*. "Kathleen, what's wrong?"

"It's—"

"Has something happened to Mark?" No, please, *no*. Without summoning the memory, Leslie recalled the night she told Kathleen about Mark being shot.

"No. He's all right," Kathleen began. Not really, she thought. I don't know.

It had taken Kathleen an hour to decide to call Leslie. After she read and re-read Mark's story. After she studied to *To Do* list with Leslie's name on it. In the end it wasn't a decision. She had no choice. She needed Leslie's help. She was desperate.

"Oh. Good," Leslie said, relieved only a little. Something was wrong. Something to do with Mark.

Slowly, disjointedly, Kathleen told Leslie about the story and the list. It was clear that if Kathleen knew their meaning she wasn't going to say it out loud. One of the possibilities was unspeakable.

From what Kathleen told her, Leslie concluded that Mark had decided to quit medicine. But what else had he decided to quit? All of it? His life? From what Kathleen told her, Leslie couldn't tell. And Kathleen couldn't tell.

Maybe Mark didn't even know.

"Kathleen," Leslie interrupted a long silence. "Let me call you back in five or ten minutes, OK?"

"OK. Mark won't be home for at least half an hour."

Leslie made three phone calls—one to another R-3, one to the chief resident and the third to an airline—and called Kathleen back.

"Kathleen, I'm going to fly to Boston early tomorrow morning," Leslie said definitively.

"Thank you," Kathleen whispered gratefully. She hadn't expected it, but she wouldn't protest. She needed help.

They didn't say the words, but the emotion and tension in their voices articulated fear. Leslie wondered what Kathleen feared. Was it simply fear of losing Mark? Or was it the bone-chilling fear that Leslie felt? The fear that Mark was planning something more than quitting medicine.

She feared that he was carefully, meticulously planning to kill himself. The *best* planned suicide ever. Planned to look like an accident.

"What shall I tell Mark?" Kathleen asked helplessly. She couldn't think of a plausible reason to explain Leslie's sudden visit.

Leslie thought for a moment. Then she sighed.

"Tell him that I need to get out of San Francisco for a few days because I just broke up with Eric," Leslie said slowly, with great effort. Her words made her ache deep inside, but her words were, simply, the truth.

Chapter 39

"Thank you for coming to meet me," Leslie said to a gaunt, strained Kathleen. Her healthy vivaciousness was gone. She looked sallow and weary. It wasn't a change that had taken place overnight. It represented weeks and weeks of constant worry and sleeplessness.

Mark must have noticed, Leslie thought. If he hadn't, it was a grim barometer of his own internal turmoil.

"Thank you for coming, Leslie. I'm sorry about Eric."

"So am I," Leslie said with finality. She didn't want to talk about it. She needed time, private, uncluttered time, to think about it. Since Kathleen's call last night, her thoughts and her restless, tormented dreams had darted at random between Eric and Mark.

She had to focus on one at a time, and she had come to Boston because of Mark.

"We have a cab waiting. We had a lot of snow last night. I'm not comfortable driving in it," Kathleen explained apologetically.

She isreally defeated, Leslie thought. The Kathleen that Leslie had known was the Kathleen who had confidently found her way through the maze of tubes and lines and cords and amazed ICU nurses to be with Mark. The only Kathleen Leslie had ever seen was unafraid. She would have been unafraid of driving in the snow.

"I could have taken the subway," Leslie said. "I know Boston. I went to college here."

"To Radcliffe?"

"Yes."

"I didn't know that. Well. I wanted to meet you."

Kathleen had almost brought the list and the short story with her. She wanted Leslie to read them as soon as possible. She wanted to be reassured that nothing was wrong.

As she watched Leslie's face as she studied the list and read the short story an hour later, Kathleen knew that Leslie couldn't reassure her.

First Leslie looked at the list labeled *To Do*. It was, generically, like the scut list that she and Mark and every other resident made every day. At work the list included lab results to check, social workers to contact, consults to call, X rays to order and articles to read. One by one each item on the scut list was crossed off. When every item had been crossed off, it was time to go home. One didn't let scut spill over to the next day because each day had its own long list. It couldn't be allowed to accumulate.

Leslie studied Mark's list. It was a personal scut list.

Journal subscriptions (crossed out). Had he cancelled them or renewed them? Cancelled, Leslie decided as she read the other items on the list. *Grant application* (crossed out). *Textbooks—to medical school library? Instruments. Summary of Patients* (crossed out). He wants his patients to be well taken care of, Leslie thought sadly. Only the best.

At the bottom of the list, Leslie saw her name. Underlined but not crossed out. He was going to talk to her, or write to her or leave something for her.

What does Mark get to do when all the items on his scut list are crossed out? Leslie wondered grimly. Does he get to go home?

Then Leslie read the story.

It's so beautifully written, Leslie thought as she began to read. He is so talented.

After a few pages, Leslie could no longer be objective about the writing style. She focused only on the words carved from the soul of a man about whom she cared very much.

It was written in the third person, but it was Mark's story. It was a story about a man driven by himself and others to be something he didn't want to be. A man driven to be the best. A man who was not allowed to fail. A man who was deeply in love with a woman.

It was a story of triumph. Toward the end, the man makes the courageous tormented decision to quit the life he hates and to find, *make*, something better. He has the support and love of the woman. Together they can find happiness. No matter what.

But the story didn't end there. There was a brief epilogue. The man and the woman went for a boat ride.

He held her hand. It made him strong. They stood by the railing, gazing at each other, lost in their love and oblivious to the roughness of the sea. The boat lurched suddenly. The jolt tore them apart and hurled him over the side into the dark emptiness.

Where all is forgiven.

Leslie said nothing for several moments after she finished the story. She couldn't be sure. He had made the decision to quit medicine. He was systematically cancelling journals and compulsively leaving no loose ends. He even finished a grant application for research he would never do. It all seemed logical and rational. Typical, compulsive Mark.

The story was a thoughtful, insightful look at himself. It was almost a celebration of the difficult decision that he made.

Almost.

"I don't understand the ending," Leslie said. Kathleen had told her about the story last night and its ambiguous ending, but Kathleen hadn't been able to interpret it. Now, even after reading it herself, neither could Leslie. "The rest of the story is clearly about Mark."

"That's about Mark, too," Kathleen said. "He likes to go on the harbor cruises. He had mentioned how easy it would be to be tossed over the railing."

"So you swim to shore," Leslie said simply. "Or wait until someone tosses a lifebuoy."

"Leslie, Mark doesn't know how to swim," Kathleen whispered, her voice laced with fear. "Not even how to tread water."

"Oh," Leslie said quietly. She realized then that Kathleen *did* know. She just couldn't, wouldn't, say it.

The *best*-planned suicide.

But it was a story, not a plan. Fact-based but fictional. A fantasy. One of many possible outcomes.

Mark's intention to quit medicine was real. The list proved it. The rest was . . .

"He loves you very much," Leslie said suddenly.

"Do you think that's me?" Kathleen asked weakly. It had been the only part that had given her hope.

"Of course it's you. He describes you—your energy, your vitality, your loveliness—perfectly," Leslie said. She saw the hope and the doubt in Kathleen's violet eyes, the eyes that used to sparkle. Suddenly Leslie realized that she had something to do with the doubt. Leslie smiled and said gently, compassionately, truthfully, "It's you, Kathleen. It's not Janet. *And* it's not me."

"Your name is on the list."

"He loves *you.*" *He held her hand. It made him strong*. Leslie remembered the words from Mark's story. And she remembered Mark's remarkable recovery from the gunshot wound. Against all odds. With Kathleen by his side.

Kathleen was what he lived for.

"Yes, she's here, Mark. She's OK," Kathleen said when Mark called at five-thirty that evening. "I'll be leaving in ten minutes to go to dinner and a movie with Sally. I'll be back at about eleven. There's food here if you don't go out."

It was what Kathleen and Leslie had decided. Leslie would talk to Mark alone. She would try to find out what he was planning *without* telling him that they had read his story. But if it was necessary to tell him that they had invaded his privacy, she would.

Kathleen and Leslie were both willing to accept the consequences of his anger at their betrayal.

He looks fine, Leslie thought when he walked in the front door twenty minutes after Kathleen left. Handsome, focused, smiling.

But Mark looked different, too. The change was subtle. What was it?

He looks calm, Leslie decided. At peace. At peace with his plan. Whatever it is . . .

"Leslie, I'm so sorry," Mark said walking toward her.

Sorry? Leslie wondered. Then she remembered. Mark thought she had come because of Eric. *Eric.* All day she had shoved him away from her thoughts, but she had felt a terrible emptiness in her heart. Because of him. A constant, subliminal, mournful presence.

Now as Mark approached her, his brown eyes full of compassion and concern for her, Leslie began to cry.

Mark wrapped his arms around her as he had done the night Jean Watson died. For a moment, Leslie succumbed to the comforting warmth and strength of him. She pressed her face against his chest as he gently stroked her hair. She felt so safe, so secure. But it was an illusion.

After a few moments, Leslie pulled away.

"Tell me what happened," Mark said gently.

"I didn't really come here because of Eric," Leslie said softly. "I came here because of you."

"Me?"

"Kathleen called me last night. She's very worried about you. She thinks you are planning something."

Leslie watched his reaction carefully. He looked surprised and a little embarrassed that they were so worried about him. But he was not angry or defensive. Not as if he had anything to hide.

"I am planning something," he said calmly. "I am planning to quit medicine."

"When?"

"*Tomorrow*, actually. I have an appointment with the cardiology fellowship director at ten. I was planning to call you tonight to tell you."

"What about Kathleen? When were you going to tell her?"

Mark looked confused for a moment, as if he had already told her. He *had* told her in the story, but not in real life.

"Tomorrow night. After it was over. I had no idea she was so worried," he said quietly, frowning, concerned.

"When was the last time you really looked at her, Mark?" Leslie asked forcefully, remembering how Kathleen had looked as she left for the movie. Remembering how Janet had looked in the months before her marriage to Mark ended.

Mark's frown deepened.

"I know that these past few months have been hard for her. They've been hard for both of us. I'm not as oblivious as you think. I needed time and privacy. I had to work it out myself. Maybe that was too selfish. I thought I was protecting her."

"You were excluding her," Leslie said gently, relieved that at least he knew.

"Not from my plans," Mark said quickly. *Not from my life.*

"What *are* your plans, Mark?" Leslie asked. It was the key question. So far his explanation had seemed honest and logical. He wasn't hiding anything.

"English grad school," he answered. He seemed a little surprised that she asked. That was what he—they—had always talked about. "What's going on, Leslie? I thought you would be happy about this."

"I am happy, Mark. I know it's right. It's just—"

"Just what?"

"Kathleen was so worried. Imagine what it took for her to call me," Leslie said gently.

"And she obviously transmitted the worry to you. That's why you came," he said sheepishly. "That was really nice of you, Leslie. I'm a little embarrassed. There's nothing to worry about."

Isn't there? Leslie wondered. What about the ending of the story, Mark? In your story the prince and the princess don't live happily ever after.

Leslie retreated to the guest bedroom long before Kathleen was due to return. She was emotionally and physically exhausted, too tired to think. Even about Eric. But the ache was with her, and the ache didn't fall asleep even though she did. The ache surfaced in her dreams. She dreamed—horrible vivid dreams—about Eric and Mark and Bobby and Michael. She dreamed about little boys who fell over boat railings into black cold water. She tried in vain to save them. Eric and Mark tried to save the little boys, too, but they couldn't. Instead, they were consumed by the terrible depthless sea.

In all the dreams, as desperately as she tried, Leslie couldn't save any of them.

Mark stood by the window waiting for Kathleen. When he saw her he went outside into the snowy, cold January night without coat or gloves. He put his arm around her and guided her through the slippery packed snow into the house.

He held her for a moment before speaking. Then he gazed at her, at her dark circles, frightened eyes and pale skin. Leslie was right. He *hadn't* looked at her for a while. Not really. He had been so preoccupied with his decision, *his* plan. It was for both of them, but he had *shut her out*.

"Oh, Kathleen," he whispered, pulling her close to him. "I am so sorry. I didn't want you to worry."

"Mark—" she began then stopped.

"There is nothing to worry about, darling. I had to make a very tough decision, a decision about which I had to be absolutely certain. That's all."

"Why couldn't I help you with it?" she asked weakly.

"Maybe I should have asked you to," Mark murmured uneasily. *For better or worse*. The words, the promises, echoed in his brain. He should have shared it with her. He continued, a little shaken, "I believed that you would support my decision—"

"Of course I would support it. Will support it. What have you decided?"

"I'm going to quit medicine, Kathleen," Mark said slowly, carefully, watching her reaction.

"Good," she said instantly.

"Good? You're not surprised, are you? I guess Leslie probably told you."

Leslie. And Janet through Ross. And your private papers . . .

Kathleen shrugged.

"It's good because it's what you want, and because you'll be safe and happy," she said as she touched his cheek gently. *I love you so much, Mark. Please don't leave me. Please be safe and happy.*

"I want to show you something," Mark said impulsively. He led her by the hand into his study. He took the heavy blue textbook off the shelf where Kathleen had carefully returned it with the papers inside.

Mark removed the top and bottom sheets—the *To Do* list and the epilogue—and handed the rest to her.

"I want you to read this," he said. *I want to share this with you.*

"I've read it, Mark," she whispered, her violet eyes full of apprehension. She gestured to the two sheets of paper that remained in his hand, the sheets he hadn't given to her. "I've read all of it."

She must have read it last night, Mark realized. After he had written the epilogue. No *wonder* she was so worried.

"And Leslie read it?" he asked. Now he understood Leslie's guarded enthusiasm about his decision.

Kathleen nodded slowly, watching him.

"Mark, I'm sorry," she said. "I was desperate. I didn't know what was happening. I know it was wrong."

"No. It's all right," he said unconvincingly. He wished Leslie hadn't read it, but it was his fault that he had isolated Kathleen to the point of desperation. He had to accept the consequences of his decisions. Beginning with his meeting with the fellowship director tomorrow, there would be many consequences.

"I'm sorry, Mark," she said, shivering involuntarily.

"It's OK," he repeated. This time his voice was convincing.

Mark set down the sheets of paper and took both of her hands, holding them, cupped, between his.

"What does it mean, Mark?" she asked.

"What?"

"The ending. The epilogue," Kathleen said as tears moistened her violet eyes. *The part you didn't want me to read.*

"It means," he said slowly, his voice breaking slightly, "that I am afraid."

"I love you so much, Mark." *Don't be afraid.*

"I love you, too." *More than anything.*

None of them slept well. Leslie awakened frequently, driven into gasping consciousness by the horror of her dreams. Mark and Kathleen lay awake holding each other. They knew they needed to rest. The hard part was just about to begin. But they couldn't sleep. They were both worried about what lay ahead.

They all tried to be cheerful at breakfast, but it was useless. The tension was palpable. Kathleen and Leslie knew how difficult the day would be for Mark. He had made the decision, he had put it on paper, but now he had to say the words out loud to people who didn't love him the way Kathleen and Leslie did. He had to say them to people who wouldn't understand. To people who might make him feel guilty. To people who might tell him—yell at him—that he had failed.

Today was just the beginning.

"Maybe I should go with you this morning," Leslie said.

"I'm not a little boy, Leslie. This isn't the first day of school," Mark snapped.

Leslie recoiled. It's not the first day; it's the last. Where is the celebration?

"I really didn't mean to be *with* you. I would like to see the hospital."

"Sorry," he said with an edge. Then he asked more gently, "Why?"

"Well. I happen to know that there is going to be an *unexpected opening* in the cardiology fellowship program . . ."

"I thought you were going to Stanford."

"Maybe I need to get out of the Bay Area after all," Leslie said thoughtfully. *Maybe I need to get away from Eric and the memories.*

"You're serious, aren't you?" Mark asked.

"I just thought as long as I'm here—"

"OK, Dr. Adams. We leave in twenty minutes."

Leslie left to get ready.

"When do you think you'll be home?" Kathleen asked.

"By noon," Mark said decisively, but uneasily. They couldn't force him to stay no matter what they said. Could they?

"Is there anything I can do?" she asked hopefully. Anything other than pace and worry. She wished she had a reason like Leslie had to go with Mark, but she didn't. Except that she loved him.

"Just be here when I get home," he said, kissing her gently on the mouth.

"Give me a project, Mark. Anything."

"OK. You can put all my medical books in boxes. I'll take them to the medical school library next week."

"I wonder if the public library could use them," she mused. *I don't want you to have to go back next week.*

"Maybe. That would be fine if they could."

"You don't want any of them?"

"No."

All right, she thought, her tired violet eyes sparkling a little. At least he was letting her help.

Mark gave Leslie a quick tour of the Peter Bent Brigham Hospital. The tour ended at the cardiology research lab. Mark introduced her to two other fellows who were working in the lab.

"Leslie might want to apply for a position here," Mark explained.

"Great," they said in unison, smiling warmly at Mark's pretty blue-eyed friend.

"I have to go see Dr. Peters," Mark said when it was almost time for his appointment. "I'll leave Leslie here."

"We'll take care of her," one of the fellows said.

Leslie asked questions about the cardiology fellowship program, but after a while the conversation shifted to Mark.

"He was my resident when I was an intern," Leslie explained a little nostalgically.

"I bet he was a terrific resident."

"He was."

"He's about the best fellow anyone's ever known," one of them said without a trace of envy in his voice. They all respected Mark. Everyone always had.

The best. Of course, Leslie thought. Mark had been in with the director for thirty minutes. What if he convinces Mark to stay? Or what if he tells him he is making the biggest mistake of his life?

"Mark's a wonderful man," Leslie said. *Whether or not he's a doctor.*

Mark returned fifteen minutes later. He looked strained and pale, but he smiled at her. Then he retrieved several sheets of paper from his coat and handed them to one of the other fellows.

"This is a list of patients that I have seen in cardiology clinic or in consultation who need follow up."

Both fellows looked at the list. It was written in Mark's neat handwriting and described the patients' problems, medications and Mark's long-term plan for their care.

"Are you going somewhere, Mark?"

"I'm leaving," he said firmly, looking at Leslie. Her eyes glistened with support.

"Where are you going?"

"I'm, uh, quitting medicine. Right now I'm going home." Mark tried to sound pleasant. They were his friends, his colleagues, but they wouldn't understand.

He shook their hands quickly, warmly, capitalizing on their stunned silence to make his escape.

"It's been nice working with you," he said. "Good-bye."

Mark and Leslie walked briskly, without speaking, along the shiny corridors and down the concrete stairs until they reached the main entrance. The main *exit*. Leslie touched his arm lightly.

"How about your pager, Mark?"

"I gave it to the director's secretary. She said she'd take care of all the paperwork." Mark didn't slow his pace. He wanted to get out. To escape. Freedom was only a few feet away.

Then, only two paces from the front door, from escape, he stopped.

"I have to call Kathleen," he said firmly.

Mark retreated into a wood-framed phone booth in the hospital lobby. He emerged a few minutes later. There was life in his brown eyes again.

"We can't go home yet," he said smiling.

"No?"

"No," he said. His voice was soft, loving. "Kathleen is up to something. Besides, she's given us a shopping list that will keep us busy for at least an hour. She wants to cook a magnificent dinner."

Good for Kathleen, Leslie thought, admiring her. She is going to fight to make this work for Mark.

Between the liquor store and the fish market, Leslie finally asked Mark about his meeting with the director.

"In the end, he was very gracious. I don't know if he ever understood. He spent a lot of time talking about the brilliant career I was throwing away. Wasted potential—"

"You expected that," Leslie interjected.

"Yes. But it was hard to hear it from someone I respect so much," Mark said soberly. He sighed. "Anyway, in the end he shook my hand and wished me luck."

"That's nice," Leslie said. *I wonder if your father will be so gracious.*

Chapter 40

Kathleen greeted them at the door. Her cheeks were flushed with excitement, and her violet eyes sparkled.

She is so resilient, Leslie thought, admiring Kathleen again. And so courageous.

Somehow, despite her worry and fatigue, Kathleen managed to look fresh and eager. The apprehension, the knowledge that this was just the beginning, that they weren't home free, flickered in her eyes, but it was almost vanquished by the confidence and determination and vitality that, until recently, had been her trademark.

It must have taken great effort, Leslie thought, wondering where Kathleen found the energy and the strength. In her love for Mark, Leslie realized as she watched Kathleen look at him. Because she loves him so much.

"What are you up to?" Mark teased lightly, lovingly.

"Nothing. I just redecorated your study. Come and look," Kathleen said, pulling at his wrist.

"We have a car full of groceries. I guess nothing will melt, but some things could freeze."

"OK. The study can wait."

It became obvious to Leslie as they unloaded the groceries and put them away in the kitchen that Mark and Kathleen needed to be alone.

She needed to be alone, too.

"I'm going to take a walk," she said.

"It's zero degrees."

"If I could borrow some boots and a coat . . . I want to go walk around the campus at Radcliffe and Harvard." A sentimental journey.

"Would you like the car?"

"No. I'll take the subway. Thanks."

Kathleen gave Leslie boots, a down-filled coat, furlined gloves and a warm hat.

"When will you be back?" Kathleen asked.

"Before dark," Mark said firmly.

"I guess before dark," Leslie said, smiling. It was nice that he felt protective.

"That's perfect anyway. I think we all need an early evening tonight. I thought the champagne would start flowing at five," Kathleen said brightly.

"I'll be back by five."

After Leslie left, Kathleen led Mark to the study. Her heart pounded. Had she done too much? She didn't want to push him. She didn't care what he did. She only cared that he was happy.

The medical books were gone. The wooden shelves were filled with Mark's favorite books, the classic works of Shakespeare and Shaw and Joyce and Faulkner and Steinbeck. . . . Until that morning, most of the books had still been in boxes.

The framed documents that chronicled Mark's already distinguished career in medicine were gone. The Alpha Omega Alpha Honor Society diploma, the Doctor of Medicine degree—with highest honor—from the University of Nebraska, the Internal Medicine Residency certificate from the University of California and the California and Massachusetts licenses to practice medicine were gone, stored in a box in a remote corner of the attic.

Kathleen left his Bachelor of Arts degree—a degree in English—from the University of Nebraska on the wall, and in place of the medical documents, Kathleen had hung the picture of the Carlton Club.

"It's wonderful."

"I kept the diplomas. I gave the books to the public library."

"Already?"

"Is that all right?" she asked quickly, worried.

"Yes. Of course. How did you get them there?"

"By cab," Kathleen said simply.

"You are really amazing. I love you."

"Want to show me?"

"You bet." He began to kiss her. Then he whispered softly, "Kitzy."

Leslie stood in the middle of Harvard Square. The snow had begun to fall lightly, silently. Students trudged purposefully through the snow. She was the only tourist, the only one without a purpose.

But she had a purpose. She was retracing her steps. She was retracing the steps that had brought her here years ago, as a naive eighteen-year-old, wide-eyed and full of hope and energy. She loved the years she had spent here, and the next ones, the ones that trained her to be a doctor. Throughout that time, her steps had been sure, confident, buoyant, but somehow, the steps had led her astray, the footing had become false . . .

Because somehow the steps of her life had led her to Eric, to a wonderful limitless love that now—overnight—had turned into bitterness and hatred.

Leslie walked past the dormitory where she first made love and where she learned to recognize the smell of marijuana. She walked past the library where she had studied, eagerly, tirelessly pursuing her dream of becoming a doctor. She wandered by the lecture halls and the science labs and Harvard Square itself, where she had attended rallies and concerts and studied under the shady trees and laughed and kissed. . . .

As Leslie thought about her own memories—the happy memories of an innocent girl growing up—she began to feel the presence of other ghosts, other happy memories, other young, wide-eyed lovers.

This was the place of Charlie and Eric. They had loved each other here. And hurt each other here. This was where they had walked hand in hand talking of love and marriage . . . and where they had been when Victoria called to tell Eric about her pregnancy.

Had Charlie ever stood in this spot in Harvard Square—the spot where Leslie stood now—waiting impatiently for Eric to get out of class? In her mind's eye, Leslie saw Charlie, her cheeks rosy, her spun-gold hair tossed by the wind and her smile full of love as she waited, eager to throw her arms around Eric. To kiss him and tell him how much she missed him.

How much she missed him, Leslie thought. How much I miss him. But I don't even know him. The Eric I miss never existed, and I was never a part of the Eric Lansdale who does exist. Never as important as Charlie. Or Victoria. Or Bobby.

Never really important at all.

Leslie shivered. Was it from the bitter-cold winter day? Or the bitter-cold reality of her relationship with Eric?

At five o'clock Mark uncorked the bottle of champagne that had been chilling for the past thirty minutes. He filled the three crystal champagne glasses.

"A toast," Leslie said, lifting her glass of honey-colored bubbles.

"To what?" Kathleen asked, her eyes laughing, radiant. She and Mark had found each other and their love again. Maybe this time it was theirs to keep.

"To happiness," Leslie said. *To your happiness.*

Mark took a small sip then sighed.

"Wish me luck," he said soberly.

"Why?" Leslie asked.

"He's going to call his father."

Leslie and Kathleen more than sipped champagne as they waited anxiously for Mark to return. He was upstairs. They couldn't hear him.

Mark returned in twenty minutes. His face was white. His jaw muscles rippled.

Kathleen's violet eyes scowled with worry and anger as she waited for Mark to speak.

"Bad, huh?" Leslie asked, breaking the interminable silence.

"Bad," Mark said heavily. He took a deep breath. He had to tell them. He had to tell Kathleen. And Leslie was there. He had to say it now, to get it out. He said slowly, bitterly, "He said it would be better if I were dead."

Leslie gasped.

Kathleen's eyes darkened. Then she began to giggle.

"Kathleen!"

"My God, Mark! He's such a poor excuse for a father. He's a joke," she exclaimed. A pathetic, malignant horrible joke. He had already harmed Mark enough.

Slowly the color returned to Mark's face, and the jaw muscles stopped moving.

760 "He's also a bastard," Kathleen said hotly.

"Now you're talking," Mark said, smiling a little.

"Have some champagne, Mark," Kathleen said. *And forget about your father. Please. I know how hard this is, but we don't need him or his approval. We have each other.*

The phone rang.

Mark grimaced but didn't move. It was probably his father calling to deliver the final shot. But how could he improve on wishing his son were dead?

"I'd better not talk to him," Kathleen announced.

Leslie stood up.

"I guess it's my turn to deal with Papa Doc," she said. "You just left for the evening, right?"

"Or the weekend," Kathleen said. "Or forever."

Leslie answered the phone in the kitchen. Mark followed her.

"Leslie?"

"Eric."

Mark touched her lightly then left, pulling the door behind him, giving her privacy.

"I tried to call you last night at the hospital. The on call resident said that you were in Boston."

"I am." You know Boston well, Eric, she thought grimly. You and Charlie spent three years here together. Leslie was amazed by the flatness of her own voice and by the way her heart ached at the sound of his, gentle, caring.

But he hadn't cared. Not really.

"When are you coming home?"

Home? Never. Back to San Francisco . . .

"I'll fly back sometime this weekend," she answered vaguely. She would leave in the morning. Kathleen and Mark needed to be alone, and she needed to get on with her life.

"When can I see you?"

His voice sounded so hopeful. Leslie blinked back tears.

"Never, Eric. I . . . it's . . . over."

"*Over?*"

"I needed to know about that part of your life, Eric. It was so pertinent to us. To my career. To our future."

"I was going to tell you in Maui, but then I found out about you and James."

"I don't understand. . . ."

"It tore me apart. You know that. I couldn't tell you about Charlie then. I didn't want to do that to you."

"What about any time in the past two months?"

"I didn't want to hurt you."

"What about Bobby, Eric? Bobby. Victoria. Your revulsion for hospitals." Leslie's pain erupted into anger, forcing words from her lips that she didn't really believe. Or did she? She didn't really know Eric Lansdale. Anything was possible. She continued, her voice like ice, "Did you actually hate me, Eric? Because I was a doctor? Did you plan to punish me all along?"

"*Leslie*," Eric interjected, horrified. "Leslie, I love you. I love you more than anything in the world."

"I can't believe that, Eric. I can't believe anything you say because I know that you *don't* say the things that are the most important."

"Leslie, let me see you. Please."

"There is no point."

"Maybe it's just too soon."

"No." With each hour that passed Leslie forced the Eric that she loved out of her heart and replaced him with the real Eric, the man she had never known or loved. *That* Eric would be easier to forget.

"I would have told you, Leslie."

"When? The day I told you I wanted to have children?"

"You are so bitter."

"I trusted you, Eric," Leslie said heavily. "Did you want me to stop being a doctor? Was that going to be part of our future? Or was there ever really a plan for the future?"

"You were—are—my future, Leslie. I would never ask you to stop being a doctor."

I might have given it up for you, Eric. If you had told me. If you had given me a chance to understand. You were more important to me than anything. Ever.

"You just would have spent your life, our life, being uncomfortable every time I told you about my work? Every time we saw a little boy? What were we going to do about children, *our* children?"

"Before I met you, I never thought I would have a future with anyone. I never even considered having children . . . another child. I was going to tell you, Leslie. I was just putting it off because I knew it would be so painful. For both of us."

Tears spilled down her cheeks. *I miss you. I hate you. I can't go back to you. I can't live without you.*

"Leslie?" he asked gently.

"Good-bye, Eric." *Sayonara.*

"Leslie, wait! I love you darling, I tried not to hurt you and it backfired. It hurt you more. It was a *mistake*, Leslie. Because I love you so much."

"It hurt me too much, Eric. It was too big a mistake." Her voice was ice cold. Like her heart: cold and empty, except for the ache that wouldn't leave. "Good-bye."

At eleven Monday morning, Charlie walked into James's office. She didn't stop to knock.

"Come in," James said, arching an eyebrow.

"What's wrong with Eric?" she demanded.

"Nothing as far as I know."

"Have you seen him today?"

"I just spent an hour with him."

"And he seemed fine?"

"He seemed businesslike. As usual. Why?"

"I just spoke to him over the phone. I'm on my way to his office now. He sounded terrible," she said.

"Angry?"

"No. Upset." *Despondent. Like when Bobby died.*

"Let me know. If there's anything I can do—"

Charlie was gone. Moments later she walked into Eric's office without knocking. She saw it in his eyes. Sad, empty icebergs. His eyes reflected only the tip of the deep pain.

"Tell me," she said softly.

Eric told her, slowly, painfully, his voice full of loss and regret.

"Victoria is such a shrew!" Charlie exclaimed as Eric told her.

"No she isn't. She never was. This was all my fault. My own stupidity."

"Were you going to tell her?"

"Of course. Sometime. Sometime when she was rested and I was rested and we had some time together."

"That sounds like never."

"I was going to tell her, Charlie," Eric repeated firmly.

"Well, anyway, now she knows. Is she angry?" Charlie still hadn't learned anything that could explain the look on his face or the tone in his voice.

"She's hurt and angry. She won't see me. She says it's over."

"It doesn't make sense."

"It makes sense to Leslie. And she's the only one who counts."

"Why?"

"She says she can't trust me. She says that by not sharing something so important I made my relationship with her unimportant. She says that she doesn't know me."

Charlie thought about the blood-framed blue eyes that glowered at a prying television camera. Proud, astonished, indignant eyes. Leslie had her own standards, her own rules.

"What are you going to do?" Charlie asked carefully.

"There is absolutely nothing I can do," Eric said, his voice empty, defeated. "Except to hope that some day she changes her mind."

Charlie waited for three weeks before telling Robert. Charlie was waiting to see if Leslie came back. She didn't.

She isn't going to, Charlie thought. How do I feel about it?

When she knew the answer to that question she told Robert.

Charlie telephoned him at his home in Philadelphia on a Wednesday evening in February.

"What are you doing?" she asked as she always asked. She loved his answers. He usually said he was thinking about her. Or them. Together.

"I was wondering if I could pass the California Bar."

"Really?"

"Really. What are you doing?"

"Calling to tell you that I miss you. And to tell you about Eric and Leslie."

Robert knew from her tone that the news about Eric and Leslie wasn't good. He listened, without interrupting, until she had finished.

"How long ago did Victoria tell Leslie?"

"Four weeks," Charlie said. Then she added carefully, because he had to know, "I've known about it for about three weeks."

Charlie waited for him to ask the question: Why didn't you tell me, Charlie? There had been plenty of opportunities in the past three weeks for Charlie to tell Robert. They had spent all three weekends together and talked to each other almost daily.

The silence was so long that Charie finally answered the unspoken question.

"I didn't tell you right away because I didn't want to worry you. I thought Leslie might come back."

"I wouldn't have worried about Leslie and Eric," Robert said firmly. *Not nearly as much as I would have worried about you and Eric.* Would Charlie want to try one more time with Eric?

Charlie knew what Robert meant. And she knew that the fact that she hadn't told him right away meant that she was uncertain herself.

Charlie knew that she had to be certain before she told Robert, and she was telling him now.

"Do you know what I was wondering?" she asked softly, finally, after several moments of silence.

"No," he said sharply.

"I was wondering if I could pass the Pennsylvania Bar."

"You have to be very sure, Charlie," Robert said. *I will not compete with my son.*

"I am very sure. I love you, Robert. I love *you.*"

Chapter 41

"Where are you, Mrs. MacMillan?" Ross asked, relieved to hear Janet's voice. It was six-thirty in the evening on the last Saturday in March. He had been at the theater all day. She called fifteen minutes after he returned to their condominium on Sacramento Street.

"At the house," Janet said quietly.

"The *house?*" Two hours away. Why was she there? "Is Leslie with you?"

Ross knew that Janet had planned to spend part of the day with Leslie.

"No. I only saw her for a couple of hours."

"How is she?" Ross asked. *How are you? Why are you so far away?*

"She's terrible," Janet said with a sigh. "But she won't admit it. When the going gets tough, I guess Leslie turns into solid steel. She won't talk about it. She says she's fine—"

"But?" Ross asked gently. *Leslie's not fine. And neither are you. Why?*

"She's devastated. And so *restless*. She's like a hummingbird. She has to keep moving."

"She needs to talk to Eric."

"I know," Janet said. Then she added, "But I don't think she ever will."

Ross waited. There had to be more. There had to be something to explain why Janet had gone to the house by herself. The house, the green hills, the blue ocean . . . Janet's retreat. It was where she went when she needed to be alone.

"Janet?"

"Did you know about Mark?" she asked bluntly.

"Mark?" Ross hadn't spoken to Kathleen since October. "No. What?"

"He quit medicine," Janet said flatly.

"Oh," Ross said. Then he asked sharply, "Don't you think that if I knew I would have told you?"

"I wasn't sure."

"You should be."

I know I should be, Janet thought. But I'm not sure of anything right now. Too many changes.

"When did he quit?" Ross asked, feigning interest. He wasn't really interested. *Especially* if this was what had separated him from his wife.

"Over two months ago. Leslie has known, but she didn't want to tell me until—"

"Until what?"

"Until she was sure he was OK, I guess. Until she was certain he would make it," Janet said. Leslie had sounded certain.

"Why wouldn't he?"

"I don't know. Anyway, she says he's fine. Happy."

A long silence followed.

"What's wrong, Janet?" Ross asked finally.

He heard her sigh. A long heavy sigh.

"Life just feels so precarious to me at the moment. Too disrupted. Too many changes."

"Like—"

"Like Leslie and Eric. It seems so senseless that this has happened to them," she said. "And Mark. Even though he's finally done what will make him happy, I'm sure it's painful for him. Just thinking about those wasted years. Years of torment—"

"But *we're* happy, Janet," Ross interjected confidently. *There is nothing precarious about us, is there?*

"Yes," Janet said, her voice soft but distant. "Ross?"

"Yes?" *Tell me, Janet.*

"Do you think we'll ever have children?" she asked quietly.

"We've never talked about it, have we?" he asked gently.

"No. Do you want to have them?"

"Do you?"

"I think so."

"There's no hurry, is there?" Ross asked carefully. He sensed that this was an impulsive reaction to the precariousness Janet felt, a need to create something constant and lasting, but she had something constant and lasting already. She had his love.

"No. No hurry. I just wondered," she said softly. Then she repeated the question she had asked before. "Do you want children, Ross?"

"All I want is you," Ross said. "I want you now and you're two hours away. So I'm on my way—"

"No, Ross. I know that you have script rewrites to do, and I'm exhausted. I need a good night's sleep starting about now."

"Janet . . ."

"Really. I'll stay here tonight and drive down in the morning. I'll probably be there before you wake up."

"Are you OK?"

"*Yes*. Just a little sentimental or maudlin or something theatrical," she said, trying to sound amused at her own silliness. "I'll be fine in the morning."

"Well . . ."

"You're looking at the stack of script pages you brought home, aren't you?" she asked lightly.

"You know me so well."

"I'll see you in the morning," she whispered. "Good-night, Ross."

"Sleep well, darling," Ross said.

This isn't right, he thought. This isn't right at all.

* * *

Janet closed her eyes and thought about the events of the day. Seeing Leslie, watching Leslie suffer, made her sad. And hearing about Mark, even though the news was wonderful, made her nostalgic. But it was her own news that made her drive to the house in the country. To think.

At ten in the morning she had called the doctor's office to get the result of the blood test that had been drawn the afternoon before. It only confirmed what she already knew, what she had known for the past three months. She was pregnant.

How had she known? It wasn't because she felt ill or missed a period or noticed her breasts enlarging. There were no external signs at all. But she had known, almost immediately. She had known almost the moment the tiny being inside her had been conceived. She *felt* its presence, a new and wonderful part of her.

Janet wondered if most women felt the presence of the new life as early as she had. Or was it because this baby was so special?

Janet had come to the house in the country to think about the new life that was growing inside her. What would its life be like? Janet wanted her child to be happy, free of pain, always. But how could she guarantee that? Would all her love really protect her child against life's sadnesses?

What if her baby was like Leslie? A beautiful happy girl with sapphire-blue eyes and shiny dark hair and a loving heart? Loving and trusting until, one day, her dreams were destroyed and she was forced to suffer. Needlessly. Endlessly.

Or what if her baby was a little boy who, like Mark, believed that he had to be the best? A little boy whose father, Ross, believed in being the best, and whose mother was the best even though she didn't care. How could the child escape the pressure? What if his life was almost destroyed—as Mark's almost had been—by that pressure?

Janet sighed. Oh, little one, she thought, I will do everything I can to make your life happy. I will give you all my love, but you know that, don't you? You already feel it. Just as I feel you.

What about Ross? *All I want is you*, he had said. What if Ross didn't want the baby? Why hadn't she told him? When was she going to tell him?

I have to tell him, she thought. I have to tell him *now*.

Ross arrived at the house in the country at nine P.M. The house was dark. Janet's car was gone. He drove to the cottage, but she wasn't there, either. He returned to the house to wait.

Where is she? he wondered. The worry that had made him—within moments of ending their conversation—grab his car keys and drive, too fast, to their country home increased as he waited in the empty house. Where is she?

At nine-forty-five the telephone rang, startling him.

"Hello?" he answered quickly.

"Ross," she said. Her voice was soft, loving, distant.

"Where are you?" he asked as relief pulsed through him. Then he realized, the only way she can know that I'm here is if . . . "Are you at the condo?"

"It's sort of *Gift of the Magi*-esque, isn't it?" she asked. He could hear the smile in her voice.

"I think we're making progress," he said gently. He had known it was wrong for them to be apart, and he had gone to her. She had known it and gone to him. The signals weren't crossed; they were intertwined. The way they should be.

"I know we are," she said. "Except that you're there and I'm here."

"Because we love each other. Because even when something is wrong we need to be together," Ross said. He was so happy, elated, that Janet had decided to go to him.

"I love you," she said. Come to me so I can tell you about our baby, she thought.

"I love you, too. Now you stay put and I'll be there in two hours," he said amiably. He wasn't tired, just happy. He added carefully, it was only a guess,

"You both stay put."

"Both?" she asked weakly. "Ross, how—"

"Am I right?"

"Yes," she breathed. "Ross, is it all right?"

"Yes. Of course. I love you both," he said tenderly. "I love you both."

"Are you sure you don't mind?" Mark asked.

"You know I don't," Kathleen answered lovingly.

He *did* know that she didn't mind because he knew how much she loved him. Just as Kathleen knew how much Mark loved her.

It was Saturday, May seventh. Friday's mail had brought an acceptance letter for Mark from Harvard University into the graduate program in English. For the past three months, Mark had been auditing graduate seminars in English literature at Harvard. In that time, Kathleen had watched his wariness and uncertainty about quitting medicine transform into joy and enthusiasm for his new life.

Now he had been admitted into the program at Harvard, and he wondered if Kathleen minded if they stayed in Boston a little longer. . . .

Of course she didn't mind. Despite the lingering worries—despite the uneasy memory of the epilogue of Mark's short story—the past few months had been the happiest in Kathleen's life. She and Mark had fallen in love. Again. Better. More deeply. More securely, because Mark's life, his dreams, were more secure.

"You think you can stand three more years in Boston?" he asked as he kissed her neck. They were in bed. It was ten in the morning. It was something else that Kathleen loved about the past few months, the luxury of having him with her.

"I'll love it," she said enthusiastically. "This year I'm going to learn how to drive in the snow."

Kathleen's style—the energy and vitality that was her style—had blossomed again, nourished by Mark's love and his happiness.

"I'll teach you," he said.

"Do you think you could tell Harvard that you'll accept their offer *contingent* on an agreement that your earliest class of the day is noon?"

"What?" Mark asked, laughing. "I don't think Harvard sends negotiable offers. Why?"

"Tell them that your wife needs you *in bed* in the morning," Kathleen said. "Tell them you have to make love with your wife every day before you can even begin to think about Shakespeare."

"*Every* day?"

"Every day," Kathleen said dreamily. She was getting used to—*addicted* to—the long wonderful hours in bed with her sensual, romantic husband.

"I *will* tell them that you are my inspiration," Mark said seriously. *Because you are.*

"Do you know what I would like you to do?" Kathleen asked, suddenly turning to face him, her violet eyes thoughtful.

"Yes," he teased gently. "I thought I just did it, fifteen minutes ago."

Kathleen was silent, thinking. Maybe she shouldn't mention it. Everything had been so perfect.

"What, Kathleen?" he asked, concerned by the sudden seriousness in her eyes.

"I'd like you to learn how to swim," she said quickly, before she lost her courage. *So you can't ever fall off a boat and drown. By accident or . . .*

"Oh, Kathleen. I wish you had never read that damned epilogue," he said. He wasn't angry, just concerned. "I wrote that part for myself. I needed to. It was part of the process. I had to think about all the possibilities."

"I know," she said. But . . .

"I am so happy now. I have never been this happy. I never thought I could be this happy. Don't you know that?"

"Yes . . ."

"But you want me to learn how to swim," he said amiably, kissing the tip of her nose.

Kathleen nodded then smiled seductively.

"So when we vacation in Martinique next month you can make love to me in the turquoise-blue water."

"*That's* the reason?" he teased. He would take swimming lessons, starting Monday, because he didn't want her to worry ever again.

Kathleen started to nod, then slowly shook her head. They both knew the real reason.

"But it's a wonderful dividend, isn't it?"

Mark nodded. Then he frowned, wondering if he should tell her what *he* had been thinking about, worrying about.

He should, he decided. It was the way they were going to spend the rest of their lives. Together. *Including* each other in their dreams and sharing their worries. For better or worse.

"What, Mark?"

"I've been thinking about writing to my father," he said.

There had been no communication since the snowy night in January four months before when Mark's father told him it would be better if he were dead.

"Why?" Kathleen asked. But she knew the answer. It—Mark's unresolved relationship with his father—was a long, troublesome, loose thread.

"Because it still feels awful. It's probably worse for him than for me. I've made it. I've escaped and I'm happy."

"You've made your own happiness," Kathleen said. She did not have generous feelings about Mark's father. She added, "In *spite* of him."

"He never wanted me to be unhappy, Kathleen," Mark said, his voice gentle and sad. "He was just a man who wanted everything—the best—for his son. He thought that what he wanted for me *would* make me happy. That's not so bad, is it?"

"But he drove you," Kathleen said. Was Mark's father pushing Mark for Mark's sake? Or for his own?

"He was as much a victim of his hopes and dreams for me as I was," Mark said wistfully. "I actually feel sorry for him."

"So," Kathleen began, then paused. So Mark is an incredible, kind, generous man, she thought lovingly. But I know that.

"So I am going to write to him, explain it to him if I can."

"And?"

"And hope that now, or someday, he understands."

And all is forgiven.

Chapter 42

Toward the middle of May, Leslie realized that she needed to find an apartment in Palo Alto. She would be moving at the end of June. She set aside time on Saturday to drive to Palo Alto to look.

She needed to be nar Stanford Hospital. She would take calls from home but had to be available, close by, for emergency cardiac catheterizations and patients with acute myocardial infarctions and arrhythmias. The rentals near Stanford Hospital were almost exclusively large apartment complexes inhabited by young single adults.

You *are* a young single adult, she told herself. Even if you want nothing to do with other young single adults. Or anyone.

Joylessly Leslie signed a six month lease for a corner apartment in a beautifully landscaped complex complete with tennis courts and a swimming pool. It was walking distance to the hospital. Clean, neat and safe.

She should have been thrilled. But she wasn't.

The ache that reminded her constantly that she and Eric were no longer together, had lost their forever, only intensified as the days turned into weeks and months. She dreamed about him—terrible tormented dreams—and sometimes woke up with tears in her eyes.

At work she could focus her mind away from him, even though the aching emptiness was a constant companion. Leslie worked long hours, spending extra time with her patients and with the more junior residents, interns and students. She started to study for her Internal Medicine Board exam and spent hours in the library reading about cardiology so that she would be amply prepared for her fellowship at Stanford.

Time heals all wounds, she told herself, but she had no evidence that it was true. What if the wounds were too deep? too gaping? too raw? What if they healed with bulky, deformed scars? What if they never healed?

A hundred times, Leslie reached for the phone to call Eric, but she never dialed. She didn't know the man at the other end of the phone. He was, had always been, a stranger.

Leslie returned from her successful apartment-hunting trip to Palo Alto in the early evening. She had driven back to San Francisco along the coast highway. It was a flawless spring day. A warm gentle breeze carried the fragrance of lilacs and eucalyptus. The ocean beaches were crowded with swimmers, surfers, sunbathers, kite flyers and frisbee tossers. It was a day for Beach Boys' music, hot dogs, laughter and love. Leslie was a spectator, uninvolved with the humanity but still dazzled by the blue sky and yellow sun and azure sea.

Ten minutes after Leslie returned to her apartment, the doorbell rang.

"James," she breathed with a sigh.

"Hi. May I come in? I was just in the neighborhood—"

"Are you building a resort? Parnassus Palms?" Leslie asked sarcastically.

"*Hey,*" he said swiftly. "I'm not the enemy."

"Did he send you?"

"Leslie, I came to see you. I've come before. This is the first time you've been here."

"I spend as little time here as possible," she admitted. Her voice softened. It was nice to see James.

"Leslie," he said gently. Too gently. It reminded her of being loved.

Tears filled her large blue eyes.

"Oh Leslie," James said, wanting to hold her. She was so hurt. So vulnerable. So alone.

She had lost weight. Her shiny chestnut hair fell halfway down her back. Her huge blue eyes were tired, haunted and wary, as if on the lookout for someone who might hurt her again.

She was so beautiful.

"Sorry, James. I'm still a little emotional," she said as she wiped the tears that wouldn't stop.

He put his arms around her and held her tight. It felt so good. He felt so good. She needed to be held and loved. James used to love her. It could happen so easily again with James. . . .

Leslie stiffened.

"You're so tense," he whispered, his lips brushed against her hair.

You're strung so tight if I touched you you'd twang. The clever words of a fellow intern thundered in her mind. The intern had been referring to her inner tension. Her rigid critical standards. Her perfectionism. Was she too rigid? Did she expect too much from everyone? Did she expect too much from herself?

"James," she said finally. "It's too hard for me to have you touch me."

"Why?" he asked, releasing her but not moving away.

"I need—" *Something.*

"You need Eric," James said flatly.

"No."

"Leslie, look at yourself. This is tearing you apart," James said. Then he added softly, "Just like it's tearing Eric apart."

"I don't want to hear about him," Leslie said quickly.

"Well you just did. He looks about the way you look. He's pushing himself as hard as you are pushing yourself. The company has never been more successful," James said seriously.

"James, you know what he did!"

"I know what he *didn't* do. He didn't tell you about another woman because he knew it would hurt you. He didn't tell you about his experience with hospitals and medicine because he knew it would make you question your career. And he didn't tell you about a little boy who died because he knew it would make you sad," James said, his voice breaking slightly.

"Did you know?" Leslie asked.

"I knew there had been something with Charlie. I didn't know the rest until recently. Charlie told me, not Eric. Eric would never tell me about Bobby." *Because of Michael.*

"You didn't *need* to know, James. I did. It had such a direct impact on our life together."

"Maybe he didn't want it to. I know he would never have wanted you to give up medicine because of him."

"But I would have," Leslie said thoughtfully. "I wouldn't give up Radcliffe for Alan or my internship for whoever it was in medical school. But for Eric . . ."

All those years ago I would have given up going to Radcliffe to be with you, James. And now I would have given up everything to make a life with Eric.

"I don't think he wanted you to give up anything. Not your career. Not children. He must have been struggling with how to convince you of that once he told you. That may be why he put off telling you."

"Because he wasn't sure himself?"

"Until he met you, he never thought about having another child."

"He told you that?" Leslie asked weakly. Eric had told her that himself, the night he called her in Boston.

"He told Charlie."

"Charlie, Charlie, Charlie. Maybe now Charlie and Eric will get back together. It seems right somehow," Leslie said, remembering Victoria's words.

"Love doesn't work that way," James said. Not by *default*. "Eric loves you."

"I don't even *know* Eric," Leslie persisted. Why was James defending Eric? Why wasn't he helping *her?* "The most important part of his life was hidden from me—"

"Leslie, when a man loses his child that *is* part of his life, every minute of his life, for the rest of his life," James said emotionally. "Whether or not Eric told you the words, you knew that part of him. He couldn't hide it."

That was true, Leslie realized uneasily. Bobby had been there. In his eyes, in his gentleness, in the way he loved her.

Have I been wrong? Too rigid? Too unforgiving? I don't know. I don't know.

Leslie lapsed into silence.

"Leslie?" James asked finally as he watched new tears flood her eyes.

"This is your fault, you know," she sniffed bravely.

"My fault? Because of Maui? Because he would have told you then if—"

"No. Because a year and a half ago you became the gold standard," she said carefully. The gold standard for loving and for trusting.

"Even though it ended?" he asked gently. Then he said what they both knew. "It didn't end, did it? We just stopped seeing each other."

James looked at her for a long moment. He would always love her. That was why he was here now. Because he loved her. Because he knew she was suffering, and he wanted her to be happy.

"After it was," Leslie began, finally, awkwardly, unable to hold his gaze. "After we stopped seeing each other, I decided that the relationships that followed would be like the ones before: pleasant, comfortable, *safe* liaisons that didn't threaten my career or really intrude on my life or my privacy. Relationships that didn't consume me."

"In other words, relationships without love," James said.

"I had the memory of love." *The memory of you. And it wasn't bitter or sad.*

"And then you met Eric. And you realized that what we had . . ." James's voice trailed off. *What we had was—is—love, but it doesn't compare with what you found with Eric.*

"I knew that I could fall in love again. It wasn't a realization; it just happened, and now my memory of love isn't so lovely anymore. It's painful and angry and bitter. Now that it's over."

"It's not over, Leslie. No matter how much that smart, rational mind of yours tries to end it, your heart won't let it happen. Maybe Eric made a mistake. Maybe he broke some of your rules."

"James." She wanted him to stop. He was confusing her. He was telling her that she was too rigid. That when you loved someone the rules changed.

James didn't stop.

"You've broken some rules yourself, Leslie," James said quietly.

You had an affair with a married man. Because love changed the rules. Because it felt right despite the rules.

* * *

On the first Friday evening in June, three weeks after James's visit, Leslie dialed the unlisted number at Eric's penthouse. Until that moment, she hadn't thought specifically about calling him. But, she realized as her trembling fingers dialed the number she knew so well, for the past three weeks she hadn't thought about anything else.

The phone was answered on the second ring. But not by Eric.

"Hello! Hello!" the voice bubbled, a cascade of joy. "We're almost ready. Except Eric is pretending to have misplaced the wedding rings!"

Charlie. Leslie recognized the voice. *Wedding rings*.

Leslie stared at the receiver for a moment then returned it to its cradle. The ache in her heart made her want to scream.

"Who was it, Charlie?" Eric asked. He had overheard Charlie's words and watched her puzzled expression.

"I assumed it was Robert wondering what was keeping us. But it wasn't. Whoever it was hung up."

"Before you answered?"

"No. Five or ten seconds after I stopped talking. Maybe it was a wrong number," Charlie said. "You *have* the rings, don't you?"

"Of course," Eric murmured distantly. He had never gotten a wrong number call before. His number was unlisted so he didn't get calls for other Lansdales. It was possible that someone had misdialed, but it had never happened before.

What if it had been Leslie after all these months? Leslie would have heard Charlie's words, hesitated a moment, then hung up.

But Leslie wasn't going to call him. Not ever.

But what if she had?

Eric stood motionless in the living room, his mind bombarded with what ifs, his heart pumping with uncomfortable energy.

"Eric?" Charlie asked.

"I have to make a phone call," he said, surprised at his own words. He had made a decision. He couldn't lose more than he had already lost.

"*Now?*"

"Yes. Now," he said.

Eric left a stunned Charlie in the living room. He went to his bedroom and shut the door.

I can't answer it, Leslie thought, startled by the telephone ring. It was so loud, so intrusive. I can't talk to anyone right now.

Five rings.

Leave me alone, whoever you are.

Ten rings.

Please. Give me time to understand. To recover. To get back to hating him again. It should be so easy this time. . . .

Fifteen rings.

She answered it, finally, on the eighteenth ring. She answered it to make it stop ringing. The loud insistent noise made her ache even more.

"Hello?" she was surprised that she could make her voice sound almost normal.

"Leslie."

Eric. Leslie closed her eyes. *He's calling to explain to me about Charlie. I can't listen to it.*

"Leslie?"

"Yes."

"Did you just call me?" Eric held his breath.

"Yes." *I have to hang up.*

"Leslie, let me explain," Eric said quickly, sensing that she was withdrawing.

"There's nothing to explain. I understand." *I understand perfectly.*

"Leslie. Charlie and I are not getting married."

What did that mean?

Leslie waited.

"Charlie is marrying Father."

"Robert?"

"Yes. She thought it was Robert who called."

"Oh." *Oh.*

Eric waited. There was silence at the other end.

"Why did you call me, Leslie?" he asked carefully.

"I missed . . . miss . . . you." Was that why she had called? Just to tell him that? She didn't know. Except that now, hearing his voice, she knew there was more.

"I miss you, darling," he said gently. *Every minute of my life.*

He didn't sound like a stranger. He sounded like the man she loved. The father of a beloved little boy who died. Another woman's husband. Another woman's lover. They were all part of the loving voice that spoke to her. They always had been.

"That was it," she said weakly. "That was my whole prepared speech."

"Will you open the floor to questions?" he asked lightly, his confidence, his hope kindled by the warmth of her voice. And by the fact that she had called, finally, after almost five months.

"Sure," she said. Ask me the tough questions, Eric. I think I can answer them, she thought, her heart pounding. The emptiness and the aching were quickly retreating, and in their place was a familiar joy. A joy she had only known since Eric. Because of Eric.

"Can I see you?"

"Yes."

Can I kiss you and hold you and love you?

"When?"

"Now. Whenever." *Always.*

"The rehearsal dinner is this evening," Eric said. *I could miss it. They would understand.*

"You need to be there."

"I need to be with you more."

"I could . . ."

"Could you? Come with me?"

"Yes."

It meant that she knew what he knew. That they were already together. The love was there. Strong. Confident. They didn't have to search for it. They didn't have to spend long private hours trying to recapture what they had. They had to talk, to plan their life together, but they didn't have to find the love. It was there. It always had been.

"I love you, Leslie," he said, his eyes wet with happiness.

"I love you, Eric," she said as warm tears spilled onto her cheeks.

"I'll be over as soon as I drop Charlie at the Fairmont."

"Is that where the dinner is?"

"No. That's where Father is. The dinner is at a lovely place for weddings," he said softly, his voice full of love and happiness. *A lovely place for our wedding.* "A place with white lilacs and pink roses and canopied beds."

"Where," she breathed. She knew. And she knew he was talking about their wedding.

"You know."

"The Carlton Club."

About the Author

Before writing her bestselling novels *Roommates*, *The Carlton Club*, *Twins*, *Bel Air*, *Love Songs*, *Rainbows*, and *Promises*, Katherine Stone practiced medicine, specializing in internal medicine and infectious diseases. She lives with her husband in the Pacific Northwest and is currently at work on her next novel.